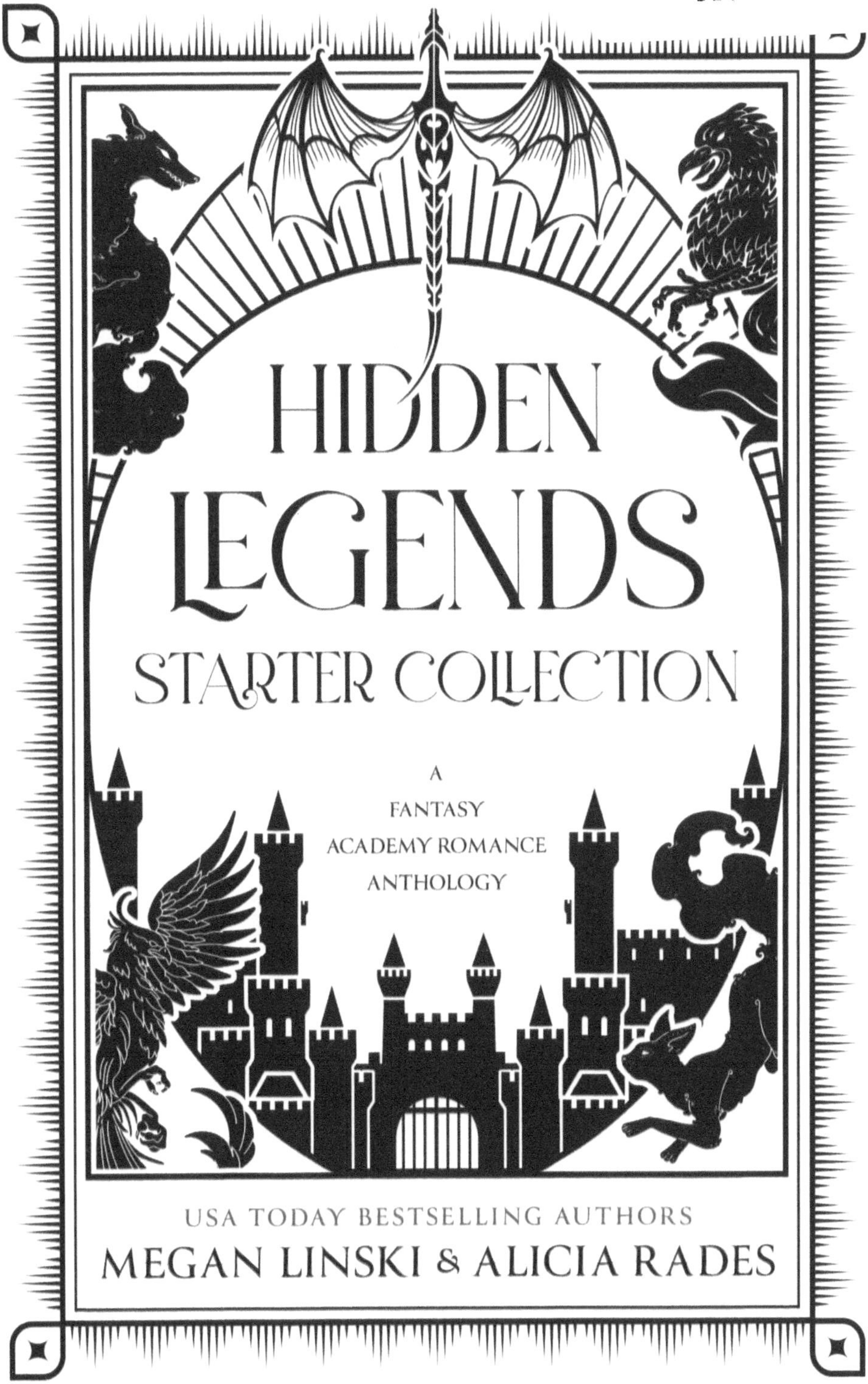

HIDDEN LEGENDS

STARTER COLLECTION

A
FANTASY
ACADEMY ROMANCE
ANTHOLOGY

USA TODAY BESTSELLING AUTHORS

MEGAN LINSKI & ALICIA RADES

HIDDEN
LEGENDS

Welcome to the Hidden Legends Universe! Contained within this special starter bundle are four novels:

- *The Fire Prophecy (Hidden Legends: Academy of Magical Creatures, Book One)*
- *The Wolven Mark (Hidden Legends: University of Sorcery, Book One)*
- *The Coven's Secret (Hidden Legends: College of Witchcraft, Book One)*
- *The Villain Institute (Hidden Legends: Prison for Supernatural Offenders, Book One)*

These stories are set in the same world, but in separate and unique magical societies. Every series stands on its own and can be read in any order. This omnibus is an introduction to the magical world of Hidden Legends, containing the first books in four different sagas within this universe.

To continue each series, visit us at hiddenlegendsbooks.com.

We the authors acknowledge that the United States of America is a country formed on stolen land. We respect and honor the indigenous peoples who have lived here for centuries, and we recognize there is still much work to do to make reparations and heal the damage caused to the many indigenous nations who were first here, both in the past and today.

May we remember the atrocities once committed, create a better world in the present, and look forward together for our future.

A special thank-you to our sensitivity reader Kris Riley of the Cherokee tribe for her invaluable feedback on indigenous life and culture, as well as her commentary on living with chronic illness.

This collection features characters with the following medical conditions. The information included is meant to educate readers on disabilities featured within the Hidden Legends Universe.

RARE DISEASE

In the United States, a rare disease is defined as an illness that affects fewer than 200,000 people. Although our character's disease is fictional, 25 to 30 million people in the US are currently living with a rare disease, many of which are not clearly diagnosed or have no cure.

COMMON VARIABLE IMMUNE DEFICIENCY DISORDER (CVID)

CVID is a rare and complex primary immune disorder that is estimated to affect 1 in 25,000 to 1 in 75,000 people worldwide, including the author of this work. It is categorized by low levels of immunoglobulins and antibodies, which makes the body prone to infection and other diseases. Patients are often treated with human plasma, which replaces the missing immunoglobulins people with CVID need to survive.

AMPUTATION

Amputation is the removal of a limb by trauma, medical illness, or surgery. Some 1.8 million Americans are living with amputations. Many amputees use prosthetics as a way of increasing quality of life after losing a limb.

AUTISM

Autism is a developmental disorder that impacts the nervous system and affects each individual differently, with a wide variety of symptoms. Challenges with social skills, repetitive behaviors, and speech are common. Autism can affect as many as 1 in 59 children.

LUPUS

Lupus is an autoimmune disease that affects approximately five million people world-wide. Symptoms may include chronic pain and fatigue, sun sensitivity, and rashes, among other complex symptoms. Lupus affects each patient differently, and symptoms can come and go throughout the course of the disease.

TYPE 1 DIABETES

Type 1 diabetes affects insulin-producing cells in the pancreas. Insulin is the hormone responsible for allowing sugar into the body's cells. Patients require insulin injections to regulate their blood sugar levels. Without treatment, symptoms may include fatigue, blurred vision, and—over time—life-threatening complications such as nerve damage, kidney damage, and eye damage.

DEPRESSION & SUICIDE

Depression is one of the most common mental disorders in America, and affects over 264 million people world-wide. Symptoms may include fatigue, insomnia, and suicidal thoughts or actions. Suicide is the tenth leading cause of death in the United States and affects people across race, age, and gender identity.

BIPOLAR DISORDER

Bipolar disorder is a mental illness that causes unusual shifts in mood, energy, activity levels, concentration, and the ability to carry out everyday tasks. Moods range from extremely elevated to extremely depressive, and can be intense. Psychosis, anxiety, eating disorders, and other conditions may develop. With proper treatment, people with bipolar disorder can lead full and productive lives.

BLINDNESS AND VISUAL IMPAIRMENT

Blindness is defined by an individual having severely impaired or absolutely no sense of sight. Total blindness is described as being unable to see anything with either eye. Vision loss typically affects an individual's ability to perform functions of daily living.

the fire prophecy

ACADEMY OF MAGICAL CREATURES BOOK ONE

MEGAN LINSKI & ALICIA RADES

Liam

ONE

ost of the world couldn't understand people like me.

I was never really normal— but I had never been *this different*. I came from a world where dragons exist and fairy tales are real, but it felt like all the magic had gone out of the world. Everyday, I saw mythical creatures glide across the skies with riders on their backs, witnessed people conjuring fire and controlling the earth and flying through the air.

Hell, even water obeyed my command. Waves rose and came crashing back down as I created them, and the ocean churned at my every whim. Rain poured from the clouds with just a blink of my eye, then froze into icy diamonds without me giving it a second thought.

But it wasn't the same anymore. It was no longer incredible or breathtaking. It just… was. I used to care about my powers.

I no longer cared about anything.

Except the rage. I was always angry or frustrated, sometimes for no reason, and it just never ended. I stopped having words to explain what happened to me long before I even comprehended what did.

I didn't know how to tell people. I just learned to deal with it.

I hated how people looked at me. I hated how I looked at myself.

They didn't understand what it was like to be on the brink of life and death constantly— fuck, I didn't even know. Not until after it happened. My entire life was turned upside down. I didn't even know who I was anymore. My life became nothing but questions. Was the man I was before just a lie? Or was the old Liam dead, and did this new, shitty one come to take his place?

I wished there was a way to make this better. And I wished he was here, so I could tell him I'm sorry, and that I wanted it to be me instead of him.

But he's not, and that's something I could never take back… something I could never fix.

Before, I hoped that someone could love me. For one incredible, amazing moment, I had someone that did. I actually believed for the rest of my life, I wouldn't have to be alone.

Now I knew that wasn't true. I was cursed to be an outsider, forever. And I deserved everything I got.

Grief is like being underwater, but never being allowed to come up to breathe.

sophia

TWO

"**S**ophia Henley, you're dead!"

It took everything I had not to bust a gut laughing. Amelia had threatened my murder enough times throughout my childhood that I knew her words were nothing more than an empty threat. Besides, all I did was admit to stealing a pair of jeans she'd left home while she was off at college. That was *hardly* a crime worthy of a death sentence.

I shot a smirk at my sister. "You'll have to catch me first."

I didn't give her a chance to respond. I sprinted forward, ignoring the burn in my legs as I raced up the mountain trail. The Salt Lake Valley was long behind us, with nothing but huge rocks and small shrubs covering the dry earth ahead of us. Pine trees dotted the surrounding mountain peaks. The higher I climbed, the narrower the dirt trail became, until I was running along a thin ledge. Sharp rocks jutted from the cliff to my right. It was easily a twenty-foot drop to the ground below.

Amelia would so regret saying that if I slipped and fell.

Good thing I was confident in my footing.

"Sophia!" Amelia shouted from down the trail. This time, it sounded like I was being sentenced for being faster than her. Because it'd be *so* unfair if I was actually better than her at something.

A high-pitched squawk filled the air above me. I glanced up to see Amelia's parrot circling my head. I wasn't sure what kind he was. When I asked Amelia after she brought him home from college, she just said he was "exotic." I didn't have the heart to tell her that "exotic" wasn't a species. I didn't even want to ask how much she paid for the rat gremlin. She took him every-where we went, though I wished he'd just stay in a cage. Amelia refused to buy one for him… said cages were inhumane.

He looked like some sort of parrot, but his beak was longer, and his feathers were a deep green, like the color of a luscious rain forest. I'd never seen anything like him before, especially not with his type of temperament.

The thing hated me, for whatever reason. Though I trusted my sister with my life, I didn't trust Kiwi.

I slowed. My chest heaved as I inhaled deep breaths.

"Sophia!" Amelia scolded once she caught up to me.

"What?" I asked innocently.

The path evened out, the sharp cliff behind us. Amelia plopped her butt into the dirt on the side of the trail, trying to catch her breath. The late afternoon sun beat down on us.

"When did you get so much faster than me?" she asked through heavy breaths.

"Right around the time I started walking." I shot her a teasing smile. I'd always been able to beat Amelia in a race— on land, at least. Amelia could totally school me in the water. Though, to be fair, I despised swimming.

She sighed and shook her head at me. "You're such a dweeb."

I scoffed and sat beside her. "I am not!"

She reached her sweaty arm around me and pulled me in close. "Of course you are. You're *my* little dweeb."

"Gross!" I protested, pushing away from her armpit.

"Come on, Sophia," she complained. "Give me a hug. I'm only home for a few days. I *miss* you."

I took a swig from my water bottle. "I'm not that gullible. You're just going to give me a wet willie or something."

Amelia laughed and wiped the sweat from her forehead. "We're not kids anymore."

I just rolled my eyes at her. It'd been four years since she moved out, but she was still my sister, which meant every time she visited I was subject to her teasing.

Kiwi landed in the dirt beside Amelia and immediately head butted a rock twice the size of his head. It rolled toward her hand. If I didn't know better, I'd say he was trying to offer the rock as a gift to her, but I was pretty sure he was just knocking his head against it for kicks. Despite what Amelia said, Kiwi wasn't exactly a bright bird.

Amelia sighed. "Forget about the pants. I just want to have fun with my little sister before I have to leave again for work."

Amelia had graduated college a few months ago and immediately got a job as a cruise ship attendant. She was only home for a week before she had to pack up and leave on her next cruise.

"I hate you, you know," I teased. "You have, like, the coolest job in the world."

Amelia shrugged, but she couldn't hide her smile.

"No, I'm serious," I said. "You get to travel the world on a cruise ship while I'm stuck at home for the next four years."

Amelia screwed the cap off her water bottle and held it to her lips. "Have you decided on a major yet?"

I shook my head as she threw her head back and chugged her water.

Honestly, I had no idea what I wanted to do. One day I was a kid, dreaming of becoming a wild land firefighter. The next my parents were telling me I had to get serious about a "real career." Before I knew it, I was filling out college applications and graduating high school without a clue of where I'd go next.

It seemed like everyone had their lives figured out but me. Amelia was going to travel the world on cruise ships, and my friends Emily and Leah were headed off to the same art school across the country. Even Kiwi— the idiot bird— seemed to know what he wanted in life. I didn't know what he was doing with that rock, but he sure looked determined.

Me? I was just hoping things would change once school started. I'd find my passion, and maybe a hot guy to share it with, and I'd make my mark on the world.

"It's okay," Amelia assured me, wiping water from the corner of her mouth. "You have plenty of time to choose a major."

"Yeah..." I grabbed a nearby rock and rolled it around in my hands, just so I wouldn't have to meet her gaze. I studied it intensely, taking note of the various shades of red woven together. It was cool enough to warrant a place in my rock collection. "It just feels like I'm going to spend four years exploring my options and still not know what I want to do."

Amelia rolled her eyes. "It's *normal* to feel that way, Sophia. You'll figure it out."

I glared at my sister. "Says the girl who's had her life figured out since she was five."

"That's not true," she countered. "I had no idea I wanted to work on a cruise ship."

"But you've always known what school you wanted to go to," I pointed out.

Amelia had gone to some school in Northern California that was so small it didn't even have a website. I was pretty sure the last four years of her life had been a scam, but she claimed she loved it there.

"The important thing about college is that you have fun—"

Amelia cut off when the sound of a twig snapping behind us reached our ears. Both of our heads snapped in the direction of the noise. My eyes darted between the bushes and shrubs on the mountainside, but I saw nothing. My shoulders relaxed, and I glanced to Amelia. Her eyes went wide in fear.

"Don't be such a wuss," I told her. "I hike this trail all the time by myself. I'm sure it was nothing."

Amelia kept her eyes on the landscape. "I just thought I saw..." She trailed off.

"Saw what?" I asked. Creeps didn't actually pop up out of the bushes, did they?

"Nothing." Amelia stood. "We should probably start heading back, though."

"But it's only half a mile to the top!" I countered.

"Which is, like, forever with this incline," she complained. "My legs hurt, and it's a long way back to the car. It'll be dark before we get back."

A half-mile was nothing, but it was my older sister I was arguing with. I'd never win.

"Fine," I relented. "But then you have to let me keep the jeans."

"No," she denied without hesitation, staring down at me and waiting for me to move.

I curled the rock I held into my fist and hopped to my feet. "You're a booger, you know that? You're a big, rotting clump of troll boogers."

"Wow," Amelia said flatly, like she wasn't at all impressed. "That's creative."

I smiled proudly, but my smile quickly faded when Amelia shot a nervous glance over her shoulder. The look in her eyes made my mouth go dry.

"You're okay, aren't you, Am?" All my teasing from earlier had disappeared from my tone. "You're not being stalked or something, are you?"

"What?" Amelia's voice rose at least three pitches above normal. The light laugh she threw in didn't sound the least bit genuine. "If I was being stalked, you'd know it."

I couldn't help but notice she hadn't exactly answered me. She started down the trail. Kiwi squawked and spread his wings to follow behind her. I remained quiet as we descended the mountain. Amelia didn't speak, either, but I noticed she had quickened her pace and kept glancing behind us.

It wasn't until night had fallen and we made it back to the parking lot that I finally spoke. I reached for Amelia's wrist before she could round Mom's crossover to the driver's side. "Are you going to tell me what's up, or not?"

Amelia's eyes scanned the dark, deserted parking lot. "Nothing's wrong. Just get in the car."

I planted my feet firmly on the pavement. "Not until you tell me—"

"Get in the car, Sophia!"

Amelia's tone hit me like a slap in the face. I rushed so fast to the passenger side door that she hadn't even unlocked it yet. Something was *definitely* up, and now that I had confirmation, I wasn't about to hang around to find out what it was.

The click of the lock hit my ears, and I swung the door open and scrambled inside. Kiwi flew in through Amelia's door, and she slammed it behind her.

"Amelia!" I demanded. "Talk to me!"

Amelia reached for her seatbelt and pulled it across her body. Her lips tightened as she turned the key in the ignition, but she didn't answer. The engine roared to life, and the headlights lit the bushes in front of us. My breath stopped when I caught sight of two small, shiny objects in the distance.

Eyes.

The creature was far enough away from the car that I couldn't see its body, but judging by how high its eyes seemed to hover above the ground, it was *huge*. Like, mountain lion huge.

"Am!" I cried. "There's something out there!"

Amelia gritted her teeth and spoke under her breath. "Yeah, I thought so…"

"Let's get out of here!" My heart slammed against my rib cage. In all the years I'd been hiking this trail, I hadn't seen anything larger than a big-horned sheep.

I racked my brain, trying to remember if sheep eyes glowed, but I was pretty sure they weren't nocturnal. Could it be some sort of canine? Maybe a deer? Yes! A deer. That wasn't so scary.

"No," Amelia said lowly, unclicking her seat belt and kicking her door open. "This ends now."

"What the— Amelia!"

"Stay here," she instructed. "Watch Kiwi."

Amelia slammed her door shut and headed straight for the bushes. What the hell was she thinking, going after a wild animal? If I didn't know better, I'd say *she* was the dweeb, but she wasn't this stupid.

I jumped out of the car behind her. "Amelia!" I hissed, keeping my voice as low as I could.

She turned back to me. The headlights of our car illuminated her. "I said to stay in the car."

"Are you insane?!" I wanted to rush over to her and drag her back to the car, but I still didn't know what kind of animal was out there. Fear stalled me, and I remained rooted in place next to the vehicle.

Amelia ignored me and stepped forward, disappearing into the darkness beyond the light of our headlights. She called out into the bushes, but I couldn't hear what she was saying.

Amelia's officially lost it.

The hairs on my arms stood. Kiwi let out a high-pitched shriek from inside the car and pecked against the windshield. Against my better judgement, I abandoned the safety of the vehicle and hurried forward behind Amelia.

"Come out, Naomi," I heard Amelia say. "Come and face me, you lousy piece of dirt."

"Amelia," I whisper-screamed.

Amelia had wandered so far into the darkness that I could only make out her silhouette.

"I told you to stay in the car!" her voice shot back.

She spoke with such authority that I almost considered turning back just so I wouldn't have to deal with her lecture later. Before I could make a decision, a shadow leapt from the bushes and slammed into her. My hands shot up to cover my mouth before a scream erupted from my lungs.

Amelia stumbled backward into the light, but tripped over a shrub and fell to the ground. She got to her elbows and scurried backward.

A low growl came from somewhere in the darkness. Every inch of my body shook, but I rushed forward and looped my arms under Amelia's to pull her to her feet.

"Am—" I broke off. I hadn't even helped her to her feet yet.

Up closer, I got a better look at the shadow in the darkness. It moved with finesse, as if every movement was calculated. The creature was stalking us, ready to pounce. It paced in front of us, its shoulder blades rising and falling with every step.

A cat.

But it wasn't the kind of cat you wanted to cuddle. This cat was bigger than me, with sharp claws and the kind of powerful teeth that could rip a human's throat out.

Amelia was right. I'm dead. We both are.

"Don't. Make. Any. Sudden. Movements." I whispered under my breath, completely frozen in place.

The cat in front of us was huge and covered in a coat of blonde fur. I'd never seen a cougar in real life before, but this seemed bigger, like some sort of African cat. Had it escaped from the zoo? I hoped that was the case and that it was used to humans… and that it wasn't hungry.

Against my instruction, Amelia jumped to her feet and dusted the dirt off her shorts, like she hadn't noticed the beast in front of us. Except… she stared right at it, almost like she knew the creature personally.

She turned from the cat and grabbed my arm. Her fingernails dug into my skin, but I couldn't bring myself to move for fear that it'd run after us. She tugged harder, and I had no choice but to stumble behind her.

"I told you to stay in the car!" Amelia scolded.

"I know, but—" A screech ripped out of my chest.

Amelia's hand fell from my arm as her body crashed to the ground again. The cat stood over her, baring its teeth. Before I could react, Amelia shoved her elbow up into the cat's nose. The cat immediately retaliated by swiping its claws at the arm she held protectively in front of her face.

Instinct overtook. I didn't even think about what I was doing when I drew my arm back and hurled the rock I still held at the cat. I didn't wait to see if I hit it. I bent and grabbed a thick stick in the dirt nearby and swung it upward to connect with the cat's jaw.

The dry stick snapped in half as it connected. The cat continued to stare down my sister, as if it hadn't felt a thing. I hurled the remaining half of my stick at its head. By sheer luck, I managed to hit it square in the eye.

The cat stumbled backward with a whimper, but before I could help Amelia to her feet, the cat turned its frightening gaze on me. I mean, it's one eye was winky, but that didn't make me feel any better. Sheer terror ripped through my gut, and my skin heated so much that sweat broke out across my brow.

A split second passed, then the cat lunged, launching itself through the air toward me.

My scream filled the air around us, and I threw my arms out in front of me. If I wasn't scared before, I was freaking *terrified* when a burst of red light shot across the space between us.

I didn't have the time to contemplate the strange phenomenon. I expected a blow to come, for sharp claws to rip into my skin and strong jaws to tear me apart, but instead, the cat twisted sideways and landed on the ground on its side.

I only let my shock last a split second. I rushed forward and grabbed Amelia's arm and dragged her to her feet. Together, we sprinted back to the car.

Amelia shifted into reverse before I even had my door closed. She tore out of the parking lot without looking back. Kiwi was going crazy, flying around the back seat.

"What were you thinking?!" I shrieked. "We could've been killed!"

"Forget about that!" Amelia cried. Her eyes darted between mine and the road. "Did I see you use *fire*, Sophia?"

"What?" Is that what that flash of red had been? Some sort of fireball?

"It was, wasn't it?" Amelia accused. "You're Koigni!"

"Koigni?" I practically yelled. "Have you gone insane?"

"No," Amelia bit back, obviously offended.

"You tried to pet a wild cat!"

Amelia's jaw tensed, but she softened her tone. "I wasn't trying to pet it."

"Then what *were* you doing?" I demanded.

"It doesn't matter," she said. "What matters is that Mom and Dad lied to me— to both of us."

I was momentarily struck silent. What did Mom and Dad have to do with this?

"They told me you were human— adopted." Amelia slowed the car to match the speed limit.

I swallowed hard. This had to be a dream, or maybe I'd been drugged. Apparently, an African cat attack in the middle of Salt Lake I could believe, but there was *no* way my parents had lied to me for eighteen years about being adopted. Sure, I was the black sheep of the family, with lighter hair and paler skin, but we told each other everything.

Yet that wasn't the most disturbing part of what Amelia had just said.

"*Human?*" My voice shook. "What else is there?"

Amelia pressed her lips together. "How do I put this?" She took a deep breath. "Sophia, you're magical… like me. You're an Elementai."

My brow furrowed. Maybe Amelia wasn't insane. Maybe she was just high. Maybe we *both* were high.

"Elementai?" I repeated the word. It felt strange on my tongue, like it shouldn't be there. "What are you talking about?"

Amelia hesitated. "I'm sorry you had to find out like this, Sophia, but there's no other explanation. You're Koigni, a Fire Elementai. Me, Mom, and Dad are Toaqua, Water Elementai."

"What do you mean?" I demanded. Amelia had better start making sense, or I was going to lose it.

Amelia swallowed, like she didn't know how to break the news. "It means you're one of us," she finally said. "It means you have magic."

THREE

A long time ago, this school felt like home. Now all it'd become was a painful reminder of everything I'd lost.

The halls of Orenda Academy seemed dark and intimidating, not warm and friendly. Only every other torch was lit, because of summer, and the clouds outside from the impending storm covered up the sun. I kept my head down and focused on counting the stones two by two, avoiding the eyes of the judgmental paintings and tapestries.

They were all of Elementai and Familiars. I wasn't a part of them anymore.

Orenda Academy was huge. It took me a half hour to navigate through the castle and find the Head Dean's tower. I knew every inch of this castle by heart, yet my steps were slow and hesitant. I didn't know what Alric wanted from me. Not yet.

I would say being summoned by him scared me, but I wasn't scared. After what had happened, I wasn't afraid of anything anymore.

Just living.

I entered the tower and climbed the dozens of steps that spiraled upward to Head Dean Alric's office. I grabbed the dragon's head knocker and knocked three times. The great iron doors opened of their own accord, and I stepped into the office.

The room was circular and large, packed with books from the floor to the ceiling in bookcases that expanded upward, the sunroof shining light into the middle of the marble floor. A fireplace burned, and Hawkei memorabilia was placed in an organized fashion in glass cabinets.

Head Dean Caspian Alric, the master Elementai that ran the place, stood in the middle of the room with his hands clasped behind his back. Each part of his suit was impeccably ironed and cleaned, his shoes shined. Though he was ancient, he moved with all the grace of a young man. His short white hair and sculpted beard were trimmed to neurotic perfection. Even the wrinkles on his tanned face appeared to fall exactly into place.

His dragon Familiar was circling above the school somewhere. I could hear the power of her wings through the walls outside as she buffeted them up and down, her dominating roar quivering the tower.

Good. I didn't want to cross Valda today.

The four other minor Deans were situated around the room in four chairs. Dean Alizeh from Yapluma, the Air House, stared at me like I was in a zoo, while Dean Hestian from Nivita, the Earth House, wouldn't look me in the eye.

Alizeh's Familiar was a large yellow thunderbird that hardly glanced at me. I didn't mind—I didn't feel like getting zapped today.

Hestian's Familiar was a white stag that had ivy leaves twisting up its legs and around its massive antlers, which were twelve-pronged on each side and six feet end-to-end. The stag clicked its hooves on the floor, but said nothing more.

They *pitied* me. It was a sickening feeling that I hated.

I noticed that Madame Eleanor Doya, Dean of Koigni, was missing her lioness Familiar. That was weird. Naomi was hardly absent from Madame Doya's side. Wherever she was, no doubt the lioness was stalking some poor soul on behalf of Doya's bidding.

Whoever had been stupid enough to cross Madame Doya would certainly regret it.

Madame Doya was dressed elaborately, as she always was, in a purple velvet dress and furs. She had multiple rings on her fingers. Her long red hair was curled, red lips puckered and tight. She had mastered resting bitch face better than anyone I knew.

My Dean from Toaqua, Professor Elliot Baine, was the only one who gave me an encouraging smile behind baggy and tired eyes. He had short cropped hair that was combed back, large square glasses, a thick and pointed nose, and a scraggly gray beard. He looked more or less thrown together, his suit sloppy with stains and shoes almost worn with holes, but despite his ragged appearance, I was glad he'd shown up.

His Familiar wasn't here, as she needed the ocean to survive. I was glad there was a fellow Water tribe member in here with me in case things got a little heated.

And I was already on my last nerve.

"What's this about?" I asked bluntly. It was more than a little rude.

Madame Doya raised an eyebrow, and the Nivita and Yapluma Deans shifted uncomfortably. Normally, a Third Year would get in trouble for mouthing off to their superiors... big trouble. A million punishments flew behind Madame Doya's eyes, but no one said anything.

I was testing them. I wanted to see how far I could push, how much I could get away with—just how *sorry they felt for me.*

Head Dean Alric didn't bat an eye at my attitude. By now, he was long used to it. "We've gotten notice of a missing child," he began. "Eighteen years ago, an infant was stolen from Koigni. We've recently located her in Utah, living with members of Toaqua."

"Toaqua stole a baby from the Fire tribe?" I asked in astonishment, before I shook my head. "No. It can't be true."

"It is true, *boy*," Madame Doya said in that condescending voice of hers, the one she reserved for literally everyone that wasn't from Koigni. "After all this time, we've discovered the missing child is alive and that she was stolen by none other than Robert and Susan Henley."

My stomach sank. I knew the family. Not very well, but well enough to know that yeah, they'd do something like this. There were multiple reasons that my tribe, Toaqua, would steal a Fire baby. Koigni and Toaqua were natural born enemies, and were always trying to one-up each other.

But what Alric said next floored me. "We believe the Henleys took the child to prevent a prophecy from coming true."

As if in unison, all the Deans spoke together:

*"The fated Koigni child, born in the Summer Solstice in the Year of the Dragon,
Shall bring glory to the greatest House."*

Hmph. I'd heard of the prophecy, but had always rubbed it off as F.A.S... that is, *fake as shit.*
Who believed in corny stuff like that?

Apparently, Madame Doya did, because she looked pissed. "This girl is critical to the elevation and status of my House. She needs to be returned to Koigni, where she belongs."

"And you, Liam, are the perfect person to bring her back," Alric finished.

Oh, great. Here we go.

"Okay... a lost Fire baby," I said flatly. "And you want me to go looking for her... why? Why not send someone from Koigni?"

"The Elders don't want a Koigni. They specifically requested someone from Toaqua to smooth over the delicate situation," Dean Alizeh spoke up.

Yeah, that made sense. Better to send someone from the Henleys' own Tribe to convince them to hand over the girl than a fiery, pissed off Koigni, I guess.

"Fine. But why me?" I stuck my hands in my pockets and stared at them. "I'm just a Third Year."

"We know well of your... troubles, Mister Mitoh," Alizeh said, with a wayward glance at Baine. "It was suggested that you should be the one from Toaqua to go, as it might help restore some credit to your name."

This was ridiculous. Why was this my problem, and why did I care? I didn't want to get involved in things that weren't my business. I just wanted to keep to myself. That's all I'd asked for in the past few months.

On the other hand... this was my chance. An opportunity to win my place back in society, after the horrible mess I'd created. Status meant everything to the Elementai. I didn't care about stuff like that, but my family sure did.

I couldn't bear disappointing my parents more than I already had.

"All right. I'll do it," I said.

"Hopefully you're capable," Doya clipped.

You ever had a teacher who completely hated you? Yeah, that was Madame Doya. I was lucky enough to avoid her most of the time, because she mostly taught Koigni classes, but I had gotten stuck with her after bonding with Nashoma. We were put into Predator Familiars together, a class Doya and Naomi ruled like dictators.

That class had been hell. I'd barely passed.

At Nashoma's funeral, Doya had the nerve to come up to me and say that her time teaching me had been a waste. If I thought I couldn't hate her any more than I already had, she'd surprised me once again.

"We have complete faith you'll bring Sophia back to us, Liam," Baine said. He nodded to me for encouragement.

"Sophia?" It caught my interest. "That's her name? Sophia Henley?"

"She's not a Henley. At least, she won't be for much longer." Doya's tone was cool.

"We don't know if this girl is indeed the prophesied child," Alric said. "But we do know that she belongs here, at Orenda Academy. It's time to bring her home."

I nodded grimly. "Fine. Then I guess I'm your man."

They gave me an address, along with a free pass aboard the *Hozho* cruise liner before they allowed me to leave.

I felt dizzy when I went back down the stairs, but I ignored it. By the time I reached the hallway, I was determined to continue on, but a sudden wave of pain bloomed at the bottom of my back and spread throughout my body, causing my muscles to involuntarily spasm. I let out a cry of pain and gritted my teeth.

This. Sucked. I put a hand against the wall to steady myself and took deep breaths to try and regain my composure.

Come on, just hurry up and die already, I moaned inwardly. I leaned against the wall and waited for the vertigo to pass. It was always like this: agony would come up suddenly and without warning. One moment I was completely fine, the next, the room would be spinning and I'd feel my legs turn to water. One too many times in the past few weeks, I'd passed out.

How embarrassing would it be if some stupid First Year came along and found me on the floor? Or anyone, for that matter.

My dad wanted me to keep moving forward in life. But he didn't know what it was like. Most people who lost their Familiars died off right away. The ones that stuck around were older, past my father's age, and they only stayed for a few months. Young people like me usually kicked the bucket a few days after their Familiar was gone. Elementai couldn't live without their Familiars.

Not me. For whatever reason, my useless body stubbornly hung on. After Nashoma died, I'd gone from completely fine to completely disabled in a few short months and *it fucking sucked.*

After a few minutes, my vertigo went away and I felt like I could walk again, though I was significantly weaker. To distract myself from the harsh throbbing radiating throughout my body, I thought of the task ahead.

I had to go clean up a mess a bunch of stupid old people had made. Typical. This Sophia girl was probably a spoiled brat. I knew her sister, Amelia. I didn't exactly *not* like her, but that girl's middle name should be *bossy.* She loved ordering people around. I bet her younger sister was worse.

I wasn't exactly shocked to find my father waiting for me at the entrance to the school. His Familiar, a grizzly named Tatum, was blocking the hallway so I couldn't get around.

Fat-ass bear.

My dad was wearing a suit, too, which meant he'd been called in for a council meeting. He rarely got dressed up unless he had to. Toaqua went with the flow.

Dad had a thick nose, and tanner skin than I did. His long black hair hung loose far past his shoulders. If anyone looked like an Elementai, he fit the bill. Something I no longer did.

He never came up to the school, not unless it was important. Somebody had probably told him about my summoning. Most likely one of my mouthy brothers or sisters.

Dad looked concerned, which I hated.

"How are things going, son?" he asked.

"You don't need to check up on me, Dad. I can handle things," I told him.

It was a lie, of course. I'd been such a mess over the summer, and he'd seen it all. I'm surprised he wasn't here trying to hold my hand.

"I wasn't checking up. Tatum and I were just passing through. Your sister wanted me to speak with Professor Lopez," he said.

Yeah. Right.

I resisted the urge to roll my eyes and said, "I'm guessing you know what this is about?"

Dad paused. His eyes narrowed as he said, "Yes. The missing Koigni girl has been found, I've heard."

There was an awkward pause. I pressed, "Dad, do you know anything about this?"

Dad cleared his throat. "There are some things, son, that are better left unsaid."

Tatum let out a growl of agreement, which just made me more suspicious. He was totally in on this somehow. I bet he'd helped the Henleys take her.

I didn't really care. My job was to drag her back, it wasn't in the details. Tribe politics bored me.

Dad changed the subject and said, "This is important, son. You must do everything in your power to convince this girl that Orenda Academy is the best place for her. Our family's reputation, and our House's, depends on it."

"I know, Dad." Being the firstborn son of the Water Chief had been fantastic, until I'd brought embarrassment upon the entire House a few months ago. After making sure I was okay, Dad's first priority had been coming up with ways to restore honor to Toaqua. As of yet, he hadn't managed to clean up the mess I'd made.

Dad was cautious with his next few words. "Liam, I know it hasn't been easy with Nashoma gone."

"Dad, I don't want to talk about it."

"I'm just saying, perhaps it is time to move on—"

"You ever try living without a soul?" I shot back at him, and he recoiled. "There's no *moving on* from that."

Dad stared at me, and I ran a hand through my hair. "I'm sorry, Dad. I'm just tired."

"I understand, son." He was letting me off too easy these days. "Go head home and relax. Your mother will help you pack for the trip."

I was twenty-one and didn't need Mom to pack my bags for me, but I bet she would anyway. She spoiled me. I listened to my father and headed out, blocking out the castle around me until I emerged into the evergreen forest that surrounded it.

But I didn't go to the ocean to head home. Not yet. Instead, I turned deeper into the woods, heading toward the burial ground.

Nobody was here, luckily. I moved around the burial mounds that were covered in flowers until I got to the newest plot, one that had only recently been constructed.

The hill was new, and was covered in dirt, not grass. A stone wolf's head totem stood before the gravesite. There were no other markings.

An empty plot was next to Nashoma's. We were supposed to be buried together. Not apart.

I kneeled on the ground and took out a few offerings from my pockets. His favorite food, beef jerky, some wildflowers from outside his den, and a couple of incense sticks.

I muttered a prayer in the ancient language of our tribe as I lit the incense and scattered the petals over the grave. I don't know what I expected. Some sign from the ancestors, some indication that Nashoma was here— but I felt nothing, and saw nothing.

I was totally alone. And fuck, it felt that way.

I hung my head. "I'm sorry, Nashoma," I whispered. "I don't know why I'm here anymore."

I couldn't help being bitter. My life meant nothing.

I'd lost everything.

sophia
FOUR

pparently, I *was* magic, but that was all Amelia had bothered telling me. It was an hour-long drive out of the Salt Lake Valley and back home to our cozy small town, but Amelia barely let me get a word in the whole time. By the time we got home the night of the lion attack, she'd worked herself up so much that I couldn't understand her ramblings. She threw around words like *Hawkei* and *Nivita*, as if she knew an entirely different language. I couldn't understand a word of it.

She blew up at Mom and Dad the second we walked through the door. "How could you lie to us?!" she demanded.

They acted deeply offended, like they couldn't believe Amelia would accuse them of such a thing.

Despite my desperate need to understand what was going on, Mom and Dad exiled me to my room to "deal with Amelia in private." I'd lain on my carpet with my ear pressed the vent in my floor and a blanket draped over my body, trying to hear everything downstairs. I couldn't hear most of what they were saying, and the bits and pieces I caught didn't make any sense.

"She can't go to Orenda," I heard Mom say. "She's a Koigni raised by Toaqua. The Elementai would have her killed."

I tried to tell myself that the events of that night hadn't actually happened, that I was drunk or something, but no matter how much I tried to convince myself otherwise, I couldn't get over how *real* it felt. How my heart pounded at the sight of the lion. How my skin heated when the fire shot out of my palm. How Amelia looked at me like I wasn't her real sister.

And who knew? Maybe I wasn't...

Sometime during the night, I drifted off. I woke to the morning light and peeled my face off the vent grate. A glance in the mirror showed evenly spaced white and red lines across my skin where the grate had dug into my skin. That was going to take a while to smooth out.

I was still dressed in my athletic shorts and t-shirt from the day before. I was in desperate need of a shower, but clean hair and a change of clothes could wait.

I tossed my blanket to my bed and left the room in haste. I nearly tripped over our cat in the hallway. The stupid feline jumped out of the way and hissed at me. He shot daggers my way, like I'd seriously offended him.

If I wasn't used to Oliver's constant need to avoid me, I might've been intimidated by the thirty-pound beast and his razor-sharp claws, but he just turned from me and continued down the hallway.

The house was eerily quiet this morning, which gave me chills because there was *never* a silent moment when Amelia was home. I padded softly down the stairs, listening for signs that anyone else was awake. I was usually the last one up, so it'd shock me if the rest of my family was still in bed.

I reached the bottom of the stairs and heard the cling of dishes in the kitchen. I crossed the hall and peered into the room. Mom, Dad, and Amelia all sat around the table, quietly scooping cereal into their mouths. They *looked* like my mom and dad. Mom, with her dark brown hair piled on top of her head and the first signs of age touching the corner of her eyes. And Dad, with his salt and pepper hair and a shadow of scruff along his jawline. They looked the same as every other day, but they moved like robots.

I hesitated in the doorway. What could I possibly say to them?

So, I'm adopted? You lied to me? Spill it, Mom and Dad. If those are, in fact, your real names.

Mom glanced up from her cereal bowl and caught my eye in the doorway.

"Sophia," she said with a wide smile.

She was acting far too cheerful. Another reason I knew last night wasn't just a dream.

She stood and pulled the chair out from beside her. "Sit down, honey. I'll grab you a bowl."

My initial reaction told me to do as I was told. I wasn't one to touch conflict with a ten foot pole if I could avoid it. But I knew I couldn't avoid it this morning. No matter what I did, I needed to tackle this issue.

Dad eyed me like he couldn't believe I hadn't accepted my mother's invitation to join them. Amelia looked half-surprised, too, but she mostly avoided everyone's gazes. Another red flag. How many were we up to now?

Mom turned from the cupboard. "Sophia? Aren't you going to join us for breakfast?"

I crossed my arms. "The only thing I'm hungry for is answers."

Mom's brow furrowed as she set my bowl on the counter. "What do you mean, honey?"

I glanced to Dad, hoping he would respond to my request, but he only dug into his cereal like he hadn't heard me.

I swallowed. "Amelia told me I'm adopted."

Mom let out a laugh so loud that it made the rest of us jump in unison. "Oh, honey, Amelia was only teasing. *Of course* you're not adopted."

Mom was a terrible liar— even worse than I was.

Amelia shot to her feet and slammed her hands against the table top. A loud *bang* filled the air. Bruno, who I hadn't realized was lounging under the table, jumped to his feet and scurried out of the room. The dog, who looked more like a coyote than anything, nearly ran me over on his way out.

"Can we cut the bullshit?" Amelia snapped.

Mom and Dad exchanged a glance, but they didn't back down.

"You can't keep this from her forever!" Amelia yelled, her eyes darting between the two of them.

Finally, Dad sighed and straightened in his chair. "She already knows, Susan. We might as well tell her what we can."

Mom's lips tightened. "I hoped it would never come to this..."

"We knew it would, eventually." Dad turned to me. "Amelia is right. We adopted you."

The confirmation was like a knife through my back. I didn't want to believe it was true. It wasn't just that this family wasn't my own. It was the fact that all three of them had lied to me my entire life. Even Amelia, who I'd grown up spilling every last deep, dark secret to, had lied to me. I trusted my family with everything, but now... a knot tightened in my chest until I could hardly breathe. My knees shuddered, and I held myself up against the door frame. I wanted to scream, to spew all the hateful words that were racing through my mind, but I was afraid that if I opened my mouth more than just words would escape.

Mom rushed to my side and took my arm. "Sophia, honey. Sit down, please."

I hardly noticed her leading me across the kitchen to the empty chair closest to the door. I sank into it, but my mind raced so fast that it hardly felt like I was in the same room as them.

They lied to me. Who lies about this kind of thing?

"Why?" I heard the word escape my lips, but it took me a moment to realize that I'd spoken it. "Why would you lie to me about something like this? If I'm not your daughter... where did I come from?"

Mom and Dad looked to each other again. Their stalling was getting on my nerves.

"Just tell her," Amelia demanded. "Tell her, or I will."

Dad frowned and scooted his chair closer to me. "Sophia, everything we've done has been to protect you."

I pulled my hand away from his when he reached out for me. He didn't get to comfort me. Not right now. "Protect me from what?"

"From the Elementai," Amelia answered.

Mom shot her a heavy glare, but her expression quickly softened when she turned back to me. "You were placed in our protection when you were a baby. In our world, it's forbidden for a Toaqua to raise a Koigni. We wanted to raise you as our own, and we knew that we would care for you well, but we couldn't do it in our society. That's why we left."

"Toaqua? Koigni?" I repeated. The words didn't sound real.

"We come from a group of people with the ability to manipulate elements," Dad explained. "There are four Houses of Elementai. Toaqua— that's us— are able to manipulate water. Koigni can manipulate fire, while Nivita control earth and Yapluma control air. You have the power of Fire, Sophia."

"No." I denied the truth immediately. If my family was running some sort of prank, they obviously hadn't thought it through very well. "I can't be from the Fire House. I'm scared of fire. Everyone knows that."

I can't be from the Fire House. My own words echoed in my mind. I said them like it was possible I'd come from another House. Was I actually entertaining the idea that I *could* be one of these Elementai?

Mom shook her head slowly… regretfully. "We only let you *believe* you were afraid of fire."

"What?" I asked in shock. *Another lie.* "But I fell into a fire pit when I was a kid. You wouldn't even let us have bonfires, or a fireplace, because you said I was too afraid of them."

"We only said that to keep you away from fire," Mom admitted.

"So that I wouldn't control it and freak people out?" I demanded. Is that what I was? A freak?

"No," Dad insisted. "Elementai don't get their powers until they're older. Yours are still very weak. We made up the story about the fire pit to curb your fascination with it. Fire can't hurt you."

Explains why I have no burn scars.

My blood boiled at the confession. What else had they lied to me about?

I lifted my gaze to meet Amelia's from across the table. "This is all true?"

Her eyes filled with apology. She nodded.

"Why didn't you tell me, Am?" I whispered.

"You think I didn't *want* to tell you I could control water?" Amelia replied. "In case you don't remember, Mom and Dad lied to me, too! I had no idea you were Koigni. I thought you were a normal human, until yesterday."

I got to my feet and paced across the room. How could I possibly accept what they'd just told me? Magic didn't exist.

I whirled back toward them. "What else should I know about the Elementai, about the Koigni? What did I need protection from?"

I stared at Amelia, but she didn't seem to have an answer for me. Mom and Dad had both gone pale.

Mom was the first to speak. "None of that matters. The fewer questions you ask, the safer you'll be."

"Safe from what?" I demanded.

Nobody answered me. My jaw clenched so hard I was afraid I might crack a tooth.

Finally, Mom stood. She pulled me into a hug. I wanted to push her away, but her hug was both a betrayal and a comfort. No matter what she lied about, she was still my mom, and nothing beat a mother's touch.

I still hated her right now.

"Sophia," Mom whispered into my ear. "I'm sorry we can't be more honest with you. You're just going to have to trust us."

The thing was, I wasn't sure I'd ever trust my parents again.

Three days had passed, and I was still avoiding my parents as often as I could. They didn't want to open up to me, so I refused to open up back. Amelia, at least, was sympathetic. She found me sitting on our old swing set in the backyard. We hadn't used the thing in years, but right now, it felt like the only thing that was normal.

It was pouring rain, and I was soaked.

I didn't want her sitting next to me. I wanted to be alone. But Amelia wasn't the type to give people space when they needed it. She took the swing beside me and opened her hands. The rain had stopped. I looked up and noticed that Amelia had made some sort of force field around us so that the rain slid off thin air and stopped pouring on me.

"That's kind of creepy," I said flatly.

"You'll be able to do creepy things, too." She smiled at me, but I didn't smile back. Instead, I scowled at Kiwi on her shoulder because I'd rather look at him than stare her in the eye.

"Come on, Sophia," Amelia encouraged. "You have to talk to me eventually."

"How can I talk to people who lie to me?" I bit back.

She frowned. "That's not fair."

"Really?" I said sarcastically. "Then why don't you tell me what really happened the other night?"

"It was a mountain lion attack," Amelia insisted, just like every other time I dared to bring it up.

"I've seen pictures of mountain lions," I said. "That thing was bigger."

"It just looked bigger because of all the adrenaline." She wouldn't budge on the topic, but I could still tell she was lying. If she really thought it was a mountain lion, she wouldn't have gone to investigate it.

"There are still other things you lied to me about," I pointed out.

"You're being unfair," Amelia said. "I knew you were adopted, but I didn't know you were one of us."

"Exactly," I emphasized. "You knew I was adopted, and you didn't say anything."

"It wasn't my secret to tell," Amelia said.

I bit my lower lip. "But we tell each other everything, Am."

"You don't understand," Amelia argued. "I couldn't tell you about the Elementai. Everything in our world has to be kept secret… for our survival."

I paused, considering this. "What's your world like?"

"It's *ah-mazing*," Amelia sighed with a dreamy look in her eyes. "It's incredible. It's everything you ever wanted. Imagine the best dream you've ever had, and then multiply that by a hundred. Orenda Academy was my home, and it'll be your home, too."

My home? "What do you mean?"

"You get to spend four years learning how to use your powers and how to take care of magical creatures," Amelia stated simply.

"Magical creatures?" I asked warily. My first thoughts flickered to the fat naked plant babies that came screaming out of the dirt in *Harry Potter*.

"Yes," Amelia said with a smile. "It's an Elementai's duty to take care of all animals that have magic. You'll learn more when you get to the academy. You'll bond with your Familiar, and—"

"My Familiar?" I asked. It was like she was speaking in riddles again.

"Your creature," Amelia clarified while stroked Kiwi's feathers. "Kiwi is mine. Bruno is Dad's, and Oliver is Mom's."

"Wait. Mom and Dad have Familiars?"

"Yes. Every Elementai has one."

"What is it?" I asked.

"A Familiar? It's your lifetime companion," Amelia explained. "The most important relationship you'll ever have."

I still didn't really understand Familiars, but if mine was anything like Kiwi, I'd take it back. The thought that creatures like dragons, unicorns, and griffins really existed made me feel worse. How had I gone my entire life knowing nothing about who I was? This was too much information at once.

"I'm probably going to bond with a plant," I said dully.

"Don't say that. Your Familiar is going to be so awesome. I just know it," Amelia said.

"So… what exactly did you learn at this school? Like, Water Math?" I asked.

Amelia laughed loudly. "No, Sophia. You learn how to use your powers, and how to use them to work together with your Familiar. You'll be in Fire classes, learning how to use your Fire magic."

I didn't know if I wanted to learn Fire magic. I would burn up my plant.

Amelia smacked herself in the head. "That's right! You're Koigni! You're going to have classes with Madame Doya."

"Madame Doya?" Her name sounded harsh, even when I said it. "The title sounds so formal."

"We only call her *madame* because she's on the Elder Council," Amelia explained. "She's really young to be an Elder, too. Like, Mom and Dad's age. Anyway, she's a total bitch. I had her for one class, and we never got along, mostly because she's so mean. She's probably going to hate you, too, because you're my sister. But maybe not, because she's the Dean of your House. She loves her little Koigni pets."

"Oh, great." I already had a strike against me. Madame Doya sounded horrible, like the kind of person who would find pleasure in whipping students if it were allowed.

Amelia was rambling now. "I loved Orenda Academy. There were so many hot guys from the other Houses, but I never got a chance to hook up with them because it was forbidden."

"Huh?" I really didn't want to hear about my sister hooking up, but the forbidden part sounded intriguing.

"People aren't allowed to mate between Houses. You can only date people within your own element class," Amelia explained. "You'll learn all about it once you get there."

Amelia made Orenda Academy sound perfect the more she talked about it. Yet there was so much I still didn't know. I wasn't good with the unknown. I was good with comfortable. *Nothing* about the Elementai made me feel comfortable.

There was still this voice in the back of my head telling me that Amelia was pulling my leg. But I knew that all of this… whatever it was… was real.

Eventually, I stood and headed inside. Amelia followed me in with Kiwi, and the force field around us trailed us to the front door. It shut off once we stepped inside, and the rain that had piled on top of it splashed down onto the porch steps.

"Do you really think I'll fit in at Orenda Academy?" I asked my sister as we entered the kitchen.

"No, because you're not going." Dad's sharp voice cut across the room before Amelia could answer. He had a coffee in his hand, but nothing else. He'd been watching us.

"How can you say that?" Amelia asked, disgusted. "She's an Elementai. It's where she belongs."

"She can't go. We'll find another way," Dad said, before he turned his back and left the room.

Whatever that meant.

"I guess that settles it," I said, defeated. "It doesn't matter what I know or don't know about Orenda Academy, because Mom and Dad won't let me go anyway."

Amelia just smiled… like she knew something I didn't.

My sister and I ate dinner in front of the TV every night since the lion attack. Mom and Dad didn't say anything about it, even though they had a strict no-food-in-the-living-room policy. They just let me avoid them. I wasn't sure if they were giving me my space or if they were avoiding me as well.

Amelia and I were curled up on the couch with our dinner when the doorbell rang the following night. Amelia didn't even blink and kept her eyes on the TV.

I stretched my foot across the couch and nudged her. "Get the door, Am. You're closer."

Amelia frowned. "*You* get it. I don't even live here anymore. I'm a *guest*."

I groaned, but set my dinner plate on the coffee table and rose to my feet anyway. I ran my fingers through my ponytail. I hadn't bothered with makeup today and was sure I looked like a slob. It was probably just a neighbor or something, so I guess I didn't really care what I looked like.

At least, I didn't until I opened the door. The guy standing in front of me looked nothing like one of my neighbors. He looked more like a security guard. A *hot* security guard, only without the uniform. He was tall, at least a half a foot taller than me, and made of muscle. His skin was a deep brown, and his straight black hair hung past his shoulders. His eyes were dark, and his jaw strong. He stood with his feet in a wide stance and his hands crossed in front of him, like he was here on some sort of official business.

He could officially business me. I mean, if I didn't faint into his arms like a crazy fangirl first. Did he have a fan club? Because I'd totally join.

"Sophia Henley?" he asked. Even his voice was hot.

Oh, God. He knows my name.

I stood in the doorway, my mouth agape. A million questions raced through my mind. Who are you? How do you know my name? Why didn't I put makeup on today? Did I even brush my hair? Why do you look like a god?

"Uhh…" That was all that came out of my mouth. I was officially an idiot.

"Who is it, Sophia?" Amelia called from the living room.

The guy's eyebrows rose at the confirmation of my name.

"I… uh…" *Good. You got one word out. Try another.* "Yeah, I'm Sophia. And you?"

"Liam," he said in a clipped tone, like he was in too much of a hurry to introduce himself properly. "I'm here to escort you to Orenda Academy of Magical Creatures."

What?!

"Amelia!" I shouted, never taking my eyes off Liam.

"What?" Amelia rushed into the hallway. Alarm settled on her face until her eyes fell upon Liam. Her expression immediately softened, but it held a hint of confusion. "They sent a student?"

"Yes," Liam said, though he didn't care to elaborate.

I stepped back from the doorway, suddenly feeling like I should be slamming the door in this guy's face. Mom and Dad *did* say they were trying to protect me from the Elementai, and here one was, standing on my front steps uninvited.

"Am, what's going on?" I asked in a shaky voice.

She didn't have a chance to answer before Mom and Dad entered the hall from the kitchen.

"Girls, what's—?" Mom's voice cut off when she caught sight of Liam in the doorway.

"Mr. and Mrs. Henley," Liam greeted with a nod of his head, like he already knew for certain who my parents were. The least he could do was say their names with some respect considering he was at their house, but he sounded more bored than anything, like he was forcing himself to be formal.

"Come inside," Amelia offered.

"Hold on," Dad objected before Liam had a chance to move. "What's this about?"

"I'm from Orenda Academy," Liam said. "I've been assigned to escort Sophia—"

"No," Mom cut him off. "Absolutely not. If you think we're going to let some Koigni come and take Sophia—"

"I'm not Koigni!" Liam spat, as if the word was poison on his tongue. "I'm Toaqua."

"Can we *not* have this conversation out in the open?" Amelia grabbed a handful of Liam's shirt and dragged him inside. She slammed the door behind him.

I whirled toward my parents. "I thought I wasn't going to Orenda Academy."

I still hadn't decided if it was something I *wanted* to do. Amelia kept saying it was where I was meant to be, but according to my parents, I'd be facing some unknown danger there. I wasn't exactly excited about throwing myself straight into harm's way without knowing what I'd be up against, no matter how much I wanted to spite my parents.

"You aren't," Mom said with certainty. She turned to Liam. "How did the school find out about Sophia?"

Liam's jaw tightened. "I don't know. They didn't tell me."

"I did." Amelia stepped forward. "I told them about Sophia."

Mom's hands clutched over her chest, horrified. "Amelia, what have you done?"

"I realize you're trying to protect our family from a lifetime of shame," Amelia said, "but Sophia has to go. She has to find her Familiar. If she doesn't—"

"You don't know what will happen if she goes to that school!" Dad roared.

Everyone's eyes went wide in stunned silence— except Liam, who still looked bored. My dad was always a gentle person, so to hear him yell… it was unusual, to say the least.

Dad's tone softened. "There's more going on here than you realize."

"Then tell us!" Amelia demanded.

Dad's gaze dropped. "It's... complicated."

"How can you say that?" Amelia cried. "Nothing's more important than your Familiar bond. You should both know that. How could you hide this from her? What were you planning to do when the day came for Sophia to bond and she didn't have a Familiar to bond with?"

Mom and Dad both dropped their heads. I steadied myself against the banister in the hallway, trying to keep my heart from racing a million miles per hour. I couldn't stand that they were fighting over me. If I knew what to do, I'd step in and end this argument right then and there, but the fact was, I had no clue if I was supposed to side with my parents or with Amelia.

"We knew it would happen eventually," Mom said in a near whisper. "We just... didn't know what to do about it. We were hoping we had more time."

"She's eighteen!" Amelia shouted, as if it was obvious their time was up.

Liam cleared his throat, and all eyes turned to him. "If I may... the Elders are aware of your crimes."

Crimes? Oh, crap. Were my parents criminals?

"They're willing to pardon you if you let Sophia come to Orenda Academy," Liam continued. "That being said, she *will* be attending one way or another. I suggest you take the deal the Elders are offering."

My head swam with the information Liam just revealed. They'd get me to that school *one way or another*. What were they going to do? Hold me prisoner? Take me by force?

This was all too much. My knees could no longer hold me up, and I sank onto the bottom stair next to the door.

"If you don't mind, I'd rather not get involved with your family affairs," Liam said. "I'll give Sophia time to pack her bags and say her goodbyes. I'll be waiting at the coffee shop three blocks from here. If she's not there in three hours, I'll be forced to contact the Elders. If you decide to run, they'll be shortly behind you."

Was he *threatening* us? Ugh, this guy was a total jackass. Cross me off the fan club list. I wasn't going anywhere with him.

Liam turned on his heel and swung the front door open. We all stared, dumbfounded, behind him. It wasn't until the sound of the door slamming stopped echoing in my ears that Amelia finally broke the silence.

"I can't believe you two," she snarled at my parents.

I didn't hear their reply, because I shot to my feet and raced up the stairs. I needed a moment alone to absorb what just happened.

In the safety of my own room, I finally had a chance to run everything over in my mind. I tugged my hair tie from my ponytail and paced back and forth across the room.

"I'm an Elementai. My parents are criminals. I'm being forced to go to Orenda Academy; otherwise, my parents will be punished," I whispered to myself. Saying it out loud didn't help ease my nerves.

How did my world change so much in just a matter of a few days?

A light knock came at my door. Before I could tell whoever it was to give me a moment of peace, Amelia poked her head into my room.

"Hey, Sophia," she said softly.

I fell onto my bed and buried my face in my hands. "What's happening, Amelia?"

I heard her cross the carpet and felt the weight of her body as she sat beside me on the bed. I expected her to hug me or something, but I wasn't sure I wanted her to. Though she'd been the most understanding about all of this, she was still a part of it. She didn't touch me, though.

"I know I don't have any clue on what you're going through," Amelia said. "But I really think you need to follow Liam to Orenda Academy."

"Why?" I asked, my voice muffled in my hands. I could just run away... somewhere the Elementai couldn't find me.

"Because you need to find your Familiar," Amelia pressed.

"I don't care about that," I said.

"I know you can't understand yet how important this is for you." Amelia's voice was soft, sad. "But if you can't do it for yourself, do it for Mom and Dad."

I finally lifted my gaze to meet hers. "What will they do to them if I don't go?"

Amelia swallowed. "My guess is they'd kill their Familiars. It's the worst thing that can happen to an Elementai, to lose your Familiar. Worse even than death."

This was so wrong. The Elders or whatever couldn't force me to go. Except... they could, and they were.

Bruno and Oliver would be killed, and Mom and Dad would never be the same. I couldn't do that to them, even though they had lied to me.

"Just keep your head down like you always have," Amelia advised. "Steer clear of Doya, and don't get yourself into any trouble. That should be easy for you."

True, considering I'd pretty much been invisible my whole life. I had every intention of staying invisible.

"Here." Amelia shoved a pair of folded jeans toward me. I hadn't even realized she'd been holding them.

The jeans we'd been fighting over.

"Am, I can't," I declined.

"Take them, Sophia," she demanded. "Take them, and think of me every time you wear them."

I couldn't believe this was happening. I didn't even realize I'd made a decision until I reached out and took the jeans.

"I should probably say goodbye to Mom and Dad," I whispered.

"No," Amelia insisted. "Even though they lied to you, they still love you. They'd risk their lives— and their Familiars— for you. You have to leave before they realize it."

My heart broke into a million pieces, but instead of feeling pain rip through my chest, I only felt numb. That numb sensation was probably the only thing that got me to rise from the bed and begin packing with Amelia.

Orenda Academy, I hope you're worth it.

Liam

FIVE

I hated coffee, but I needed it to keep me awake, because I'd been up for the past three days. I rubbed my face and stared at the stain on the table in the coffee shop. At this hour, no one was in here but me. I'd been waiting *forever*. I told Sophia to meet me here hours ago. What was taking so long?

Elders be damned. I wasn't going to waste my time waiting for some spoiled prep to figure out she wanted to grow up and join the real world. I was about to get up and get back on the ship to Orenda Academy when the door opened.

In stepped Sophia. She had a duffel bag full of clothes and a lost puppy-dog look.

She was hot, I guess. Long, chestnut brown hair, chocolate eyes, and a body that was totally bang-worthy. She caught my gaze. Ripples ricocheted in a shock wave through my stomach.

Then I remembered who I was, and everything inside me shut down. No girl wanted to be with someone like me— a crippled failure who'd lost their Familiar. Besides, she was Koigni, I was Toaqua. *Never going to happen.*

Amelia wasn't with her this time, thank the ancestors. Sophia sat down at my table and went to speak, but I got up and ordered her something. She looked like a chai latte kind of girl. I pressed it into her hands, and she looked down at it.

"Thanks." She looked up. "But I don't drink—"

"You're going to need it," I told her. "The walk to the ship is cold."

"Ship?" she echoed.

I resisted rolling my eyes. Never mind. I didn't think she was hot. She was annoying, and completely clueless. I couldn't stand people who weren't on top of things, and Sophia was about a hundred pages behind everyone else. I'd be babysitting a toddler until we got back to school.

She reminded me of a little kid. And that's exactly what I'd call her.

"Follow me, *pawee*." I stood up. She trailed me, sipping at her latte. I carried her duffel bag, though the weight of it instantly brought my fatigue surging back.

"Do you need help?" She caught me struggling.

"I got it," I told her as we exited the coffee shop and started down the street. I wasn't about to let her think I couldn't carry a duffel bag. Though it was getting *really hard* to keep faking it. A duffel bag full of clothes felt like a military backpack weighing me down.

Being disabled was a real pain in the ass.

We got out of the city limits and into the desert. Sophia hesitated when she reached the town sign. She touched it, then looked back at her old home.

"Well, come on," I said. I was trying not to gasp for breath, and trying to act normal, but it was hard. "I'm not going to abduct you."

Sophia snorted and shoved past me. "You couldn't abduct me if you tried."

Sadly, she was probably right.

We walked a mile into the desert, which might as well have been ten miles for me. I kept up a brave face so she didn't notice that my body was screaming. When the lights of the town had dissolved behind us, I dropped the duffel bag and struggled not to drop to my knees, looking up.

I took the golden pass out of my pocket and waved it in the air. Sophia looked at me like I was crazy.

We waited a few minutes. The desert was chilly at night. Sophia shivered. I told the cold to piss off.

"What… what are we waiting for?" she asked reluctantly.

"That," I told her. My eyes never left the sky as the clouds parted. Sophia jumped as the blaring horn of a ship coming into port echoed all around us.

Her mouth dropped open, and I grinned. From the sky descended a massive cruise liner, over a thousand feet in length, equally as tall and weighing two-hundred thousand tons. The ship was painted white, with elements of stark gold here and there. Sophia went to run, but I grabbed her arm and held her in place as the massive ship descended. It could fit over ten thousand passengers, along with two-thousand crew members, but there were rarely that many people on it. Elementai only used it when they wanted to go on vacations, mostly, and when the government insiders needed to get back home.

It wasn't meant to transport students, yet here we were.

The ship came to a slow park in front of us, the bottom suspended about a hundred feet in the air, before two Elementai on the ship's sides waved their hands. The earth jutted up above us and formed steps, a staircase made out of desert dirt, rock, and sand that met the cruise ship's platform. Two Familiars, a pegasus and a toucan, both landed on the ground beside the earth staircase and bowed to us.

"Welcome to the *Hozho*, the Elementai's premier cruise ship," I told her. "It's how we'll be getting to the Academy."

"It… it…" Her mouth bobbed up and down like a fish's.

"Yes, *pawee*, it can fly," I told her. "Hurry up."

Sophia grabbed her bag before I could (thank the ancestors) and ran after me. I began the climb up the long, torturous staircase, which was the last thing I needed after that walk.

"Why are you going so slow?" Sophia complained behind me.

"Shut up." I was already out of breath. We finally reached the top, and an Elementai reached out her hand.

"May I take that bag for you and deliver it to your cabin, miss?" she asked Sophia.

"Um," Sophia started.

"We'll be staying overnight. It's a long flight to the Academy," I told her. *Not to mention this big-ass ship doesn't move very fast.*

Sophia handed off her bag, and I gestured for her to follow me. The staircase was pushed back into the earth. The doors closed behind us and the *Hozho* rattled as it rose into the sky once more.

Sophia clung to the railing like a cat, shaking and terrified. I rolled my eyes this time.

"Come on." I grabbed her arm again and hauled her after me, from the deck and into the inside of the ship. Sophia's head went from this way to that as she tried to take in all of her surroundings and failed. The carpet was lush green with swirling designs, and the walls were wooden paneling with gold railings. We passed all sorts of shops, such as rare jewelers, clothing stores, and places that sold souvenirs and chocolates.

I think the Elementai with their Familiars is what impressed her the most. She had to be careful to avoid accidentally stepping on anyone in the crowded hallway. Elementai had birds on their shoulders, or small animals like rabbits or chinchillas in their arms. Dogs followed at the heels of their Elementai, while big cats like tigers and jaguars stuck together, yowling as if they were having some sort of conversation. Sophia had to press to the wall to let a moose with antlers that were as wide as the hallway pass by. Above us and imbedded in the ceiling was a huge inner tube filled with water. Water creatures, like manatees and otters, swam to where they needed to go.

Once, a unicorn shoved her out of the way. Sophia went to pet it, but I grabbed her hand.

"Don't touch another person's Familiar without permission," I told her sharply. "It's not allowed."

Yep, like watching a toddler. I dragged her out of the hallway and onto the deck, where it was more quiet. All around us was the murky grey of the clouds and a touch of condensation, a hint of the Toaqua on board doing their job.

She gasped when I led her to the main lobby. A crystal chandelier hung from the center, opening up to a massive ballroom with stained-glass windows and a shiny wooden dance floor. A classical band played soft music while attendants checked in guests. I gave our passes to the Elementai at the front desk, who handed us two key cards.

Sophia wasn't paying attention. She was twirling around on the dance floor like a princess in a fairy tale.

"It's gorgeous," Sophia said, looking around.

"It's something." I'd been riding the *Hozho* since I was a kid, but it still never failed to impress me. They were always adding more and more onto it. I was pretty sure there was a movie theater and an ice rink somewhere in here. Personally, I'd been fine with the waterpark. I'd been on this ship a million times over the years, and I still hadn't seen everything.

The ship bobbed up and down like a real cruise liner would, only it rode the air currents instead of the waves. I was a Toaqua, so I was immune to getting seasick, but Sophia looked a little green.

"Come on. Let's get something to eat," I told her.

"But I just had dinner," she protested.

"Yeah, well, good for you. I didn't." I led her to my favorite restaurant— known for native Hawkei food. It was late, so we didn't have to wait for a table. We sat on the deck outside the restaurant and watched the tiny hydras and dolphins playing in the pool below. Their Elementai swam and chatted in the water. They were Toaqua, so they manipulated the water to splash each other, causing mini-waves.

Their happy screams made me remember what I'd lost.

"You want anything?" I asked, looking up from my menu.

She shook her head. "No, I'm fine."

"Well, that's not happening," I muttered. She needed some food in her, to combat the sickness. Riding the *Hozho* on an empty stomach was a recipe for disaster, and I wasn't going to be holding the trash can all night for this girl. I'd seen her plate when I'd gotten to her house—she'd barely eaten her dinner. She had to be starving by now.

The waiter came back, and I said, "I would like the salted salmon with a side of buffalo stew. She'll have some acorn bread and ginger ale."

"Liam, I don't—"

I gave her a look, and she shut up.

I handed the waiter our menus. He came back with the acorn bread a moment later, and I nudged it toward Sophia. "Go on. It'll help."

She nibbled on it, and I noticed the green in her skin subsided. She ate half of the loaf, and I grinned. She'd lied about not being hungry.

When her ginger ale was half-gone, she put down the drink and sighed. "Thanks. I do feel a little better now."

I smiled. "Good."

By this time, my food was out. I was a gross eater, a true carnivore, but there was no shame in it. I really didn't care if people thought I was nasty. I inhaled the soup and started tearing into the salmon with my bare hands seconds after, chewing loudly. There was sauce smeared on the side of my cheek. Sophia stared at me with a disgusted look on her face, her nose wrinkled and lip curled.

I was starving. That was the only thing worth sticking around for anymore, the food.

I put the plates aside and wiped my face. Sophia was giggling.

"What?" I asked, throwing the napkin down.

"Nothing." The waiter took the plates away, and Sophia stared at me. "So, I've been meaning to ask you a few questions."

Oh, goody. "Like what?"

"Well, for starters… how the heck is this thing flying around, and why hasn't anyone noticed it yet? It's a huge cruise ship!" she belted.

"The Yapluma use the power of Air to keep the ship flying and afloat, while Toaqua move clouds in front of the liner so it isn't spotted by outsiders," I informed her. "The Koigni keep the boiler room running, so the rudder has control over where the ship is directed. The Nivita help it land and build the staircase. We all work together to make the ship possible."

"That's weird. Amelia made it sound like the different Houses hated each other," Sophia said.

She's not wrong. "Amelia was exaggerating. Yapluma and Nivita are opposites as Air and Earth, but they get along fine. Like I said, we all need to work together to stay alive and underground."

"I'm guessing Fire and Water don't mix?" Sophia asked.

There was a rolling in my stomach, and I shook my head. "No. To be honest, it would be weird for people at school to see you, a Koigni, talking to me, a Toaqua, outside of class."

She nodded glumly. "My House sounds terrible."

I wanted to high-five her, but I gave a diplomatic answer instead, because it's what my dad would expect me to do. "Our entire world is about unity. We need each other to keep our society running," I informed her. "That's why most of the Elementai live together, in the area around Orenda Academy."

"I thought Elementai would be all over the world." She sat upright.

"No. There are some Elementai spread around the earth and throughout the world governments. They're put there to keep our world secret. But most of the Elementai live together in Northern California, which is where we're going. It's… unheard of for an Elementai to be away from the tribe like your family is." I eyed her.

"Tribe?" she questioned.

"All Elementai come from one ancient tribe, the Hawkei. We still follow their customs and live in the same area they originated from long ago."

"Like Native Americans?" She stared at me blankly.

"There are many indigenous societies. All of them have their own traditions and are very different. The Hawkei are no exception," I said.

"I've never heard of the Hawkei before. They weren't in any history books I read," Sophia replied.

"We don't let in outsiders for a reason. Keeping our culture and stories secret is one of the only reasons our people are still alive." I crossed my arms.

"Amelia said something like that." She looked away from me. "But... I notice all the Elementai look different."

I sighed. "*We...* that includes you... have married and intermingled with many different cultures throughout the centuries."

"Oh." She sipped at her latte again. It was taking her forever to finish it. It was getting on my nerves. She didn't ask any more questions about the original tribe, which made it obvious she was the type of person that didn't care about history or tradition.

Oh, we were going to get along *splendidly*. And by splendidly, I meant not at all.

"Are there other... magic people in the world?" Sophia asked. "Or are there just Elementai?"

"There are a few groups who have magical powers. But none of them can bond with animals like Elementai can, and their magic is different. Only we control the elements. Our kind doesn't associate with them. We keep to ourselves."

"I feel like I'm so far behind." She dropped her eyes.

Tell me about it. "You'll catch up, *pawee*. I promise."

"Why do you keep calling me that?" Her eyebrows knitted together. "*Pawee*?"

"It means *little child*," I told her, smirking. "Because you act like such a kid."

"Thanks," Sophia said sourly. It made me smile more.

What I didn't tell her was there was another meaning behind the word, too. But that was a secret.

I stood. "It's nearly midnight. We should really get to bed. The ship will come into port early tomorrow."

Sophia followed me out of the restaurant. The traffic had started to die down, and many Elementai had returned to their cabins. We were basically alone out here.

I rounded a corner before Sophia did. I stopped in my tracks when I saw a large lioness prowling the deck, her eyes searching for something.

Naomi. I'd seen her, but she hadn't seen me... yet.

I didn't have anything to hide. I was bringing Sophia back, like Madame Doya wanted. There was no reason for her Familiar to bother me. Even so, just being around Naomi made me feel like a criminal— like I had something to hide.

Dad always said to follow my instincts. I wasn't about to question them now. Before Sophia knew what was happening I latched on to her, then dragged her behind a collection of lifeboats with parachutes, hugging her tightly to my body.

Sophia screamed. I slapped my hand over her mouth and whispered, "Be quiet! Someone's coming!"

Sophia's eyes widened when she saw the cat, then she went silent. Naomi stopped in front of the lifeboats, then raised her nose to sniff the air. Her lip curled, and she made a rumbling noise of discontentment before she moved on, her steps heavy with intent.

I didn't breathe until the lioness was gone. What was Naomi doing here? Madame Doya was at the school. Why were they separated?

Sophia kept quiet until I let her go. We stepped out from behind the lifeboats, and Sophia cried, "What the heck is that stupid cat doing here?"

"You know her?" My eyes widened.

"Yeah! That cat attacked me and my sister when we were hiking in the woods the other day," Sophia explained.

"Was anyone with her?" I asked quickly. "A woman?"

"Not that I know of," Sophia said slowly. "I just thought she was wild. She must be a Familiar. She seemed really focused on my sister."

My mind raced. What the hell had Amelia Henley been up to while she was at school?

"That cat is Madame Doya's Familiar," I told her. "I'm assuming you don't know her."

"No. But Amelia mentioned her." Sophia tapped her chin with a finger, thinking. "You mean to tell me that the lion who attacked me and Madame Doya are bonded?"

"Yes."

"But… Amelia told me it was just a mountain lion," she said quietly. "She should've known that was Madame Doya's Familiar. She took classes with her."

"Naomi is an African lioness, not a mountain. Amelia knows who she is. She lied to you." I had to be blunt. Sophia deserved to know the truth.

"She lied? Again?" Sophia deflated. Her face went into a pitiful, upset look.

"There has to be a reason for it." I struggled to recover, because even though I didn't like Amelia, I knew Sophia loved her and I really didn't want to get in the middle of family drama. "Maybe she was just trying to protect you."

"Maybe." Sophia chewed her lip. "But why not tell me the truth? What was she trying to protect me from?"

I hesitated. "Your guess is as good as mine."

This wasn't good. Madame Doya and Naomi couldn't be separated. If they were apart, it meant that they were looking into something important. Amelia had been poking her nose in places where it didn't belong, and I didn't like it.

Sophia crossed her arms. "Why would Madame Doya send her Familiar after us?"

I could think of a few good reasons, but I shrugged and said, "I don't know."

She didn't seem satisfied with my answer.

I led Sophia to her cabin. She used the keycard to get in. Inside, there were dozens of little Familiars making everything perfect. Hummingbirds plumped the pillows and straightened out the sheets, while monkeys and lemurs polished the mirrors and floors. They bowed to us as we came in before they scuttled away. I noticed that the Elders had spared no expense in Sophia's room. It was one of the nicest suites on the ship, with a King sized bed, a mini-bar, a living-room area collected around a fireplace, and a window that showed the clouds sailing by. She even got a kitchen, something my suite didn't have. Her duffel bag had been placed on the dresser. I noticed a pair of her pajamas had been neatly folded and set out for her immediate use.

She took a peek in the bathroom and squealed when she saw a Jacuzzi big enough to fit four people. There was also a vanity and a widescreen TV inside the room. I'm pretty sure her toilet was one of those weird ones that talks to you.

I myself was looking forward to getting into my own Jacuzzi tonight and not coming out for a really, really long time. My body was sore.

A raccoon wearing a sailor's hat and an apron pushed a little cart into the room. He handed Sophia a warm towel scented with lavender and a tiny box of chocolates.

"Thank you," she told him. The raccoon tottered out with his cart and shut the door behind him.

"Now that's what I call service," she said in a bright voice. She squealed happily before jumping on the bed.

By the ancestors, this girl was lame. And really cheesy. Why couldn't she just be cool?

"My room is right across the hall if you need anything," I told her. I really hoped she didn't come by. My duty was done, as far as I was concerned.

"I think I'm just going to hit the hay," she told me. I resisted snorting. She got off the bed and stood in front of me. "Thanks for showing me around, Liam. I really appreciate it. This ship is incredible."

Don't get used to it. "Like I said, I'm right across from you if you need anything."

She beamed at me, and I felt funny again, but it was probably just my nausea kicking in. I always felt sick after I ate these days. I headed across the room to my suite and filled up my tub, grabbing a beer out of the mini-fridge. I wasn't supposed to drink anymore, because it would probably make me feel worse, but screw it. Maybe the alcohol would help me sleep for the first time in days.

I laughed a little when I thought of Sophia. She was so naive. If she thought the ship was awesome, she hadn't seen anything yet.

Just wait till she got to the castle.

sophia
SIX

The cruise ship horn blared, sending a wave of disappointment over me. Liam and I stood on the deck as the ship descended into port the next day.

"What's wrong?" Liam asked with a heavy sigh.

"This ship is just so magical," I replied. "I'm not ready to leave."

He scoffed.

"What?" I asked. Had I said something wrong?

He just shook his head. "You've got a lot to learn, *pawee*."

Liam pointed over the railing. I peeked over the edge, and what I saw took my breath away.

"Welcome to Kinpago," Liam said.

Below, the clouds parted. Tall mountain peaks rose around us, but they were different from the mountains back home. These were covered with tall trees and lush greenery, and the caps were painted with snow. In the distance, a waterfall cascaded down the side of the mountain. To my other side, the ocean reached out to the horizon.

A city with winding streets stretched far across the valley. The buildings were short, no more than two or three stories high, and most were hidden beneath a thick layer of trees. There were all sorts of houses, but they were unlike any houses I'd ever seen. They were almost like elaborate huts, with stucco walls and thatch roofs. The streets were dirt, and there weren't any cars, just carriages pulled by an array of creatures like pegasi and unicorns. Thousands of people were down there, venturing in and out of little shops. It looked like a city straight out of a fairy tale.

"Get your bags," Liam said. "It's time to go."

Minutes later we descended a long flight of stairs made from earth. I couldn't take my eyes off the city in front of me. From this vantage point, there seemed to be a unique charm to it. I had the urge to explore the entire valley.

The air was chilly, in stark contrast to the dry desert air I was used to. I pulled my cardigan tighter around me as we made our way down the steps.

"You cold?" Liam asked.

"Yeah," I said. "It's a lot colder here than back home."

Liam shrugged. "You'll get used to it. Plus, you're Koigni, so it should be easy for you to stay warm."

I barely heard what he said, since the city once again stole my attention as we got up close. At the base of the staircase vendors lined the street, like we were walking straight into a magical farmer's market. I saw one group in a unicorn-drawn carriage. Another guy rode on the back of a huge beast that looked like a bear with horns. Large plants of all shapes and colors, bigger than even some houses, bloomed out of gorgeous painted pots. Streamers and banners, along with little stringed lights, criss-crossed over our heads and connected to various buildings. Every shop looked different, some with hand-painted signs, and others with ones that looked like they were made of metal. It was like everywhere I looked there was a different color, or something else going on. There were so many different smells, like bread cooking, and cinnamon and other spices. I heard music coming from all directions, along with laughter and conversation. It was so loud I had trouble hearing myself think.

"You're in the center of the city, where you'll find most of the stores, restaurants, and shops. All your magical needs can be supplied here," Liam said, like he wanted to get this over with. "Behind us near the cruise port are offices and shopping centers. Each part of Kinpago is split into various cultural districts, though the Hawkei district, the one we're now in, is the largest. For example, the Latin district is directly on the left, three blocks down, and on the other side is the Gay Quarter. About a mile down Main Street is Chinatown. You can find Little Bavaria on the other side."

Liam rattled on and on about all the areas of Kinpago, so quickly that it was tough for me to keep up with him. It seemed like every country from around the world was packed into the crooked streets and small spaces. People of all colors and nationalities crowded the streets, dressed in everything from casual daywear to traditional clothes from various places around the world.

Were they really all descended from the Hawkei tribe? Everyone looked so different. I'd never been in a place so culturally diverse…

"I didn't realize Kinpago would be so big," I said, glancing around in wonder.

Liam shrugged. "There are maybe ten, fifteen thousand people per tribe."

"Tribe?" I asked. "There are more than just the Hawkei here?"

"No. We're all Hawkei," Liam answered, sounding irritated. "I'm referring to the four Houses. Earth, Water, Fire and Air."

"Oh," I said, but I was quickly distracted.

The only things more beautiful than the people were the Familiars. They came in all shapes and sizes, their fur purple and blue and sometimes multi-colored. Elephants with rainbow manes and purple skin walked beside cats that had scales. A four-legged mammal the size of a horse, but that looked like a weasel with a large furry white mane and feathers, blinked at me before its Elementai called her, and she vanished before my very eyes.

I was pretty sure there weren't even names for some of these gorgeous creatures. They were things I hadn't even imagined seeing in story books.

In the middle of the street, a man in a beautiful outfit that was embroidered with beads and decorated with feathers danced to a couple of street musicians playing on flutes and drums. I wanted to stop to watch, but Liam grabbed my wrist and dragged me behind him.

I resisted his hold, my pace slowing to take it all in. A nearby booth buzzed with small critters. They were the color of emerald tiger beetles with wings like dragonflies. They glowed a soft yellow, blinking on and off like fireflies.

"Fortune Fairies!" the guy behind the booth shouted. "Get your Fortune Fairies! Said to bring you good luck and change your future."

I took a step toward them, but I didn't make it far before Liam tugged on my arm.

"Hey!" I protested. I just wanted to see what they looked like up close.

"Don't waste your money," Liam said. "Fortune Fairies are easy enough to catch on your own. Besides, they don't bring fortune to everyone."

While he spoke, my eyes fell upon white winged stallion ahead of us. My breath left my chest, and I stopped right there in the middle of the street. Children swarmed the pegasus and petted its soft white fur. The sign in front of its stall advertised pegasus rides. Nearby, a kid cried because his mom wouldn't let him "ride the pony."

I turned to Liam, who didn't look happy that I'd stopped again. "I thought you weren't supposed to touch someone else's Familiar."

"You aren't," he confirmed. "That pegasus isn't bonded yet."

I wanted to ask if it would ever bond, but before I could, a voice cut through the crowd.

"Mr. Mitoh!" a male voice called.

"Not interested, Jones," Liam replied.

I turned to see who he was talking to, and another wave of amazement overcame me. At this point, I was probably going to pass out from sheer overwhelm before we made it to the school.

An older guy with a lot of muscle stood on the other side of the street, holding the reins on two massive beasts. The front half of the beast looked like a stag, with a long nose and pointed antlers. The back half resembled a bird, with strong legs, sharp talons, and massive feathered wings. It even had a beautiful plumed tail spanning out behind it.

"What *is* it?" I whispered in wonder.

"They're peryton," Liam said, like they weren't interesting in the slightest. "Half-deer, half-bird."

What was this guy's problem? Was he so used to this place that he could no longer appreciate the magic in it?

"Mr. Mitoh," Jones repeated in a whining voice.

"We don't have the money," Liam told Jones before he could get another word in, though it sounded like a lie.

"Not to worry," Jones responded, taking no notice to Liam's rude tone. "These peryton have already been reserved, courtesy of Elliot Baine. They're to take you up to Orenda."

"Baine. Thank the ancestors," Liam mumbled under his breath.

His shoulders relaxed. He led me closer to Jones until we were close enough to touch the peryton. The one closest to me stared down with his big dark eyes. He was a large beast, but there was a gentle quality in his eyes. I was just about to reach out and touch him when a set of hands wrapped around my waist and swept me off my feet.

I let out a yelp on instinct.

"Up you go," Jones' voice said in my ear.

Before I knew what was happening, I was straddling the peryton with my knees tucked under his wings. Jones placed the reins in my hands, then adjusted the strap on my duffel bag so that it draped securely across my body.

"You're in good hands with Bud here." Jones patted the peryton's neck. "Just hang on tight, and don't startle him."

"But wait—" I started to say.

Jones smacked Bud's behind, and the creature lurched forward. My stomach dropped, and a shot of adrenaline rushed through my chest as we launched into the air. A scream tore out of my lungs. Within seconds, the market was far below us, and the people looked like nothing more than ants.

"Relax!" Liam shouted over the sound of the air whipping past my ears. He looked more comfortable on the other peryton's back than I'd ever seen him in the short time I'd known him. I think even a slight smile graced his expression.

I quieted, and the fear in my body slowly eased. Even with the flapping of the peryton's wings, I felt strangely secure on his back. Laughter bubbled up from my chest.

I think I can get used to this.

We flew over the city and toward the ocean, but we didn't reach it before the peryton shifted course, soaring parallel to the mountain range. As the town disappeared behind us, a large clearing came into view.

A castle bigger than the state capitol back home stood at the center. Pointed stone towers stretched into the air above the trees. The walls were long, sturdy, and thick. Hundreds of ornate, stained glass windows were placed here and there. Within the castle walls there were keeps that stretched high above the towers, while gargoyles of various Familiars sat perched along the castle's walls. The castle itself was surrounded by a series of narrow rivers and tall waterfalls. The sunlight glistened off the water droplets at the base of the tallest waterfall, creating a rainbow. A large, open patch of grass stretched out in front of the school's main doors, filled with flowers and elaborate fountains. There were hundreds of kids and Familiars down there, chatting excitedly with each other as they entered the school.

A roar caught my attention. My stomach lurched as I saw dragons— *actual dragons*— soaring in a circle around the castle. They weren't alone. Other flying magical creatures, like griffins and manticores, flew above the castle and played with each other, pretending to fight or making loud noises like they were chatting.

Holy crap. Amelia made Orenda Academy sound magical, but she didn't tell me I'd be attending something this spectacular.

Our peryton circled around a courtyard near the tallest tower. Birds of all different sizes and colors soared above the courtyard, while creatures followed behind their Elementai as they crossed the lawn. I caught sight of another pegasus, and I saw what I swore was a huge feathered serpent slither behind someone and into the open doors at the front of the school.

Bud swooped down so fast that I was afraid we'd crash straight into the ground, but he pulled back at the last second and landed gracefully at the center of the courtyard. Liam's peryton landed behind Bud, and he slipped off its back with ease. Meanwhile, I was acutely aware of all the eyes on me.

Liam reached up to help me off the peryton's back. I placed my hands on his shoulders to steady myself, shivering slightly as his hands touched my hips to lift me off. As soon as I landed, the perytons took off again and went back the way we came. Once I was on the ground, Liam let go of me like I was a hot potato.

Liam started for the grand double doors, but I remained rooted in place. The whole courtyard had gone quiet. At least a hundred pairs of eyes locked on me.

"Is that her?" someone whispered.

Liam hurried back to my side. "Are you coming?"

I still couldn't move. It didn't seem right when I was being oggled at like a zoo animal. "Why's everyone staring?" I asked under my breath.

"We don't often get outsiders," Liam explained.

Great. I'd already been pegged an outcast.

"You know, they'd stop staring if you followed me to your dorm," Liam said.

I was just about to take him up on that offer when a girl with long black hair and manicured eyebrows stepped forward. She wore skin-tight black pants that showed off her curves, and a orange top that accented her chest. Her liquid eyeliner and perfect contouring made it look like she spent hours every morning painting on her face. A group of five stood behind her— two girls and three guys. They all had the same tan skin and I'm-hot-and-I-know-it look. A large, beautiful red bird landed on the girl's shoulder. Her tail feathers were so long they trailed on the ground, and she had a feathery plume on her head, which accented black eyes.

"You must be Sophia Henley," the girl said with a smile. "I'm Haley. I'm from your House, Koigni."

Despite the look of disgust on Liam's face, I shook her outstretched hand. It was only polite.

"So, is it true?" Haley asked in a tone that had *gossip* written all over it.

I glanced to Liam warily. "Is what true?"

"For the ancestors' sake, she just got here," Liam snapped at Haley. "Could you let her get settled in before you start interrogating her?"

Haley narrowed her eyes at him. "I wasn't asking *you*. I think Sophia can speak for herself."

"Yeah, I can," I agreed.

Liam growled.

"But I have no idea what you're talking about," I added.

Haley crossed her arms. "Rumor has it *you're* the one the prophecy talks about. If the prophecy is to be believed, that is."

She had to be kidding. I mean, prophecies weren't a real thing. Then again... I had no idea what was real anymore after what I'd seen recently.

"Like you said, it's just a rumor," Liam reminded her. "No one even believes the prophecy. Someone made it up just to scare the Houses."

"Maybe Sophia can confirm it for us," Haley argued. She looked to me for a response.

"Look..." I didn't know what to say. This girl was talking crazy. "No one mentioned a prophecy to me."

"See?" Liam said. "Now, would you let her rest? She's had a long journey."

Haley's lips tightened. "I don't take orders from people like you."

Liam's nostrils flared. He opened his mouth, but I cut in before things could escalate any further.

"Actually," I said, "I'd just like to get checked into my dorm. But maybe later you can tell me more about this prophecy."

I wasn't betting on it. Haley didn't seem like the kind of girl I'd hang out with. She held her nose so high that she'd drown in a rainstorm. Liam left without saying another word. I hurried to follow.

"What does she mean by *people like you*?" I asked once we were out of earshot.

Liam hesitated, but answered anyway. "In our society, the stronger your Familiar is, the higher you stand on the social ladder. She's Koigni *and* her Familiar is a phoenix. She outranks just about everyone at this school."

"That seems unfair," I said. "Shouldn't social status depend on your intelligence and accomplishments?"

Liam didn't get a chance to answer. A fluffy red critter darted between his legs. He stumbled and cursed under his breath. The creature stopped several feet away and sat, curling its bushy tail around itself. *A fox.* It looked up at Liam with bright eyes.

"Sassy!"

A curvy girl in the strangest outfit I'd ever seen approached us. She wore a bright green tutu, with striped pink tights and blue sneakers. Her shirt was black with purple polka dots. At least five thick bangle bracelets hung from each wrist. She wore her hair in pigtails, a giant sunflower pinned to her head between them. Her hair was strawberry blonde. She stood out, even when you stripped away the quirky Dr. Seuss look.

"Leave the poor guy alone, Sassy!" the girl scolded the fox. She bent to scoop up her Familiar, but the fox leapt from her arms and made a break for it.

The courtyard buzzed with conversation again, but there were still a lot of eyes on us.

Quirky Girl didn't seem to notice— or didn't seem to care— as she chased Sassy between a group of nearby people. She dove forward to catch her Familiar, but it dodged out of the way. She sprang to her feet and didn't seem to notice she was covered in dirt. Haley's group pointed and laughed.

"Sassy, if you don't get back here, you're sleeping in the woods tonight," Quirky Girl threatened. "You know what are in the woods, don't you? Big dragons!"

Sassy darted between the legs of a tall, muscular guy. He stood on the outer edge of a small huddle of students who were no longer paying attention. Quirky Girl dropped to the ground and stuck her head *right between the guy's knees.*

Liam tried to stifle his laughter next to me. I just watched in horror. *How embarrassing.*

"What the—?" The guy glanced beneath him.

Quirky Girl dragged her fox out of the crowd and rose, as if totally forgetting anyone else was there. The top of her head smacked right into the center of the guy's crotch. Like, full sunflower pressed firmly onto dick.

I cringed. It was like watching a trainwreck. I couldn't take my eyes off it.

"What the hell?" the guy cried. He jumped away from her and grabbed one of his friends to use as a human shield.

Quirky Girl's eyes widened. "Oh, my ancestors! I am *so* sorry. I was just— my Familiar is—"

"You need to put that thing on a leash, *Imogen.*" Haley clipped each syllable in the girl's name as she made her way over. Her cronies followed behind her.

Imogen got to her feet. "That's cruel, and you know it."

"That thing is a hazard!" Haley snapped. "People who can't control their Familiars shouldn't have them."

"She is not!" Imogen pulled the fox closer to her chest. "She's just playful."

"Come on," Liam said from beside me. "Let's go."

"Hold on," I objected.

I dropped my bag at my feet and bent to my knees beside it. I dug inside for an extra tote bag I'd brought with me. I thought it would come in handy if I wanted to haul stuff with me to the beach or something. It was light blue, with bright pink flowers all over it. It would suit Imogen perfectly.

Liam groaned when he saw me pull it out. I ignored him and walked across the courtyard, abandoning him with my stuff.

"That *thing* needs someone to actually train it," Haley was saying when I approached.

I cleared my throat. "Um… Imogen?"

The whole crowd turned to look at me. Whereas everyone else's expression hardened when they saw me, Imogen's softened.

"Would this work?" I held the tote bag out to her. "You can keep Sassy by your side, but she can still jump out and run around when she wants to."

Imogen's face brightened. "That's brilliant. Thank you so much."

I opened the bag, and Imogen gently placed Sassy inside. She swung the bag over her shoulder and twisted from side to side, as if she was modeling it. Sassy peeked out of the top of the bag, looking positively content.

Haley looked me up and down. She was *not* pleased with my solution.

"Better?" Imogen asked her mockingly, like it didn't matter to her at all what Haley thought.

Haley pursed her lips. "I hope it suffocates."

The crowd drew a collective breath, but the following laughter told me more people agreed with her than were shocked by her heartlessness.

"And *you*," Haley pointed at me. "Be careful about who you stick up for. It could reflect badly on our House. I'll let it pass this time, because you don't know any better."

"Your House has enough of a reputation," Liam said from behind me. I hadn't realized he'd followed me. "I don't think the friends Sophia makes is going to change anything."

Haley stared him down but turned to me instead. "Just know that you've been warned. Blood is thicker than water around here."

Haley turned on her heel, and the crowd dispersed.

Liam handed me my duffel bag. "Can we *finally* go?"

I glanced to Imogen, who was petting Sassy and looked thrilled with her bag.

"Yeah," I said, slinging the strap over my body.

"Wait!" Imogen called when we were several paces away. "Thank you!"

"No problem," I told her, waving back to her and Sassy.

Imogen grabbed Sassy's paw and helped her wave to me. I turned away and followed Liam across the lawn, finally entering the castle.

He led me up the big stone staircase to a pair of doors three times my height. If I thought this world couldn't get any more magical, I was wrong. The doors opened up to a huge white foyer that stretched five stories high with a big gold chandelier hanging in the center. Balconies on every level wrapped around the foyer. The marble floor was dotted with large area rugs and big comfy chairs. Ahead of us, a huge grand staircase led to the second level. Tapestries and elaborate paintings hung from every inch of the wall, and a fireplace big enough to hold a dragon burned in the center. Suits of armor stood at attention around the doors and the fireplace.

"What... how...?" I couldn't manage to find the words as I tried to take in the splendor of it all.

Liam didn't slow his pace. How could he not just stop and stare? I hurried to keep up with him.

"It's a castle," I managed to get out. Because apparently I was really good at stating the obvious.

"Yeah," Liam said with a shrug.

"But— but how?" I stammered. "Did you magic it here?"

Liam looked thoroughly unamused. "No, we didn't *magic it here*. It was gifted to the Hawkei long ago."

"Oh," I said flatly. I wished he'd explain more, but Liam kept silent.

Liam led me down a long, wide hall on the second level. Tall arched windows outlined in elaborately carved stone lined one side of the hallway. Between them stood more statues of Familiars, except this time, they were accompanied by statues of Elementai as well. On the opposite wall hung large dreamcatchers, woven blankets, and feathered headdresses. It seemed like the castle was a mix of old medieval architecture and Native American historical pieces. Everywhere I looked, there was something more beautiful to stare at.

Liam's pace slowed the farther we walked. He stayed silent the whole time.

"Thanks for sticking up for me back there, by the way," I said to break the silence.

"Yeah, well, don't get used to it," he growled.

What the hell?

"A simple *you're welcome* would suffice," I responded.

"You're welcome," he said flatly.

Moments later, Liam stopped in front of a set of large doors. The handles were golden and were crafted in the shape of flames. They were intricate and nearly looked like the real thing.

"Look," he said, "we're from different Houses. I shouldn't be sticking up for you, and you shouldn't be sticking up for Imogen. We only work together when we have to. Haley is right. You'll alienate yourself from your House if you keep acting this way. My advice is to find yourself a Koigni friend and stick close to them."

Any ounce of happiness I'd found in the magic of this place instantly disappeared. I knew Amelia said you couldn't date outside your House, but you couldn't be *friends*, either? What kind of society was this? I thought Liam said these people were all about unity. They seemed full of bullcrap to me.

"This is your dorm." Liam gestured to the doors beside him. "It's where I leave you. Good luck." That was all he said before he started down the hall the way we came.

"Wait, Liam!"

He turned back to me, his brow furrowed. "If you have any questions, ask a member of your House."

The unspoken words in his tone were clear. I wasn't his problem anymore.

Liam turned his back on me. Nerves twisted in my gut. How could he just leave me alone?

I took a breath and stepped toward the doors. I glanced down the hall one last time to watch him go. My heart broke a little. Liam hadn't exactly been friendly since we met, but at least with him, I hadn't been alone. Now the one person here who'd helped me make any sense of this place was abandoning me.

Jerk.

I gripped the door handle and pushed. I half expected that Liam had lead me to the dungeons, but I stepped into a common room. Sunlight spilled in through a tall window, and through a sunroof that opened up in the ceiling. There were four fireplaces, each with plush red chairs surrounding them, and two rows of study tables in the center of the room. A flat screen TV hung on the wall. Two long hallways split off in either direction, which I guessed led to the dorms. The room was swathed in colors of deep red, orange, and yellow. It seemed cozy and warm.

At least thirty people were inside. All eyes turned to me, and the whole room quieted.

Was it going to be like this every time I entered a room?

I swallowed. I must've looked like a deer in the headlights. No one bothered to step up and tell me what to do. Was I supposed to claim a room, or just hang out in here until my advisor showed up?

The doors banged open behind me. I jumped.

"You can all relax," Haley said in a bored tone as she entered, followed in toe by her posse. "She's not the one. She's just a bastard."

Wait… what? I was *so* not interested in indulging in any drama. I was planning on keeping my head down like Amelia told me to. But I had to say *something*. I mean… what the hell?

"*Excuse* me?" I snapped.

Haley crossed the room to the closest fireplace, and her phoenix fluttered behind. The two boys sitting there immediately got up, and Haley's group took their place.

Haley tossed her dark hair over her shoulder and looked at me with a shocked expression. "Oh, I didn't mean it in a bad way."

Since when was that word *not* meant in a bad way?

"I just meant… your mom was Toaqua, wasn't she?" Haley asked. "You're Koigni, so she must've whored around with some Koigni guy or something."

I was too stunned to move, even though every fiber of my being told me to punch the girl in the face.

"You don't even know my mother," I snarled.

Haley shrugged and turned away. A part of me wanted to reach out and pull a chunk of her hair out, but the rational part told me to walk away.

"At least *my* mom raised me right. I'm not sure you can say the same."

It wasn't until everyone in the room inhaled a collective gasp that I realized I'd said it out loud. *Mortified* didn't even begin to describe how I felt. I wasn't the kind of girl who said things like that.

Haley just gaped at me, so shocked she couldn't even respond. I wasn't about to stick around to hear whatever she came up with. I whirled around and rushed through the doors I'd just entered.

The problem was, I didn't know where to go from there. Even if I missed orientation, I would've thought *someone* would greet me with a welcome packet or a quick tour. This place wasn't very welcoming, to say the least.

I slumped down the hall and dropped my bag on the floor. My whole body shook as I leaned my shoulder up against the stone wall. The events of the last few minutes repeated over and over in my mind. It was like high school all over again. I thought I was done with that.

I stared down the hall, my eyes passing over each magnificent statue and tapestry. I couldn't believe I was here. I already missed my parents. I wondered how they took the news the night I left. I hoped they were safe and that Amelia had convinced them not to come after me.

Speaking of Amelia… I reached into my bag and grabbed my phone. I found Amelia's number in my contacts and hit the call button. I just wanted to hear her voice. Maybe she could answer some of my questions, like where to pick up my class schedule. We hadn't had much time to talk about that kind of stuff once I stopped acting like a turd and actually listened to her.

"Hello?" Amelia's voice was like music to my ears.

"Hey, Am—" I cut off when my phone flew upward out of my hand. "What the hell?"

I whirled around, expecting it to be some sort of hazing ritual led by Haley. Instead, I came face to face with an older woman. She had curly red hair, long lashes, and high cheekbones. Her green velvet dress hung to the floor, and she wore a ton of jewelry. The fumed expression in her eyes gave her away immediately.

Madame Doya.

She looked just as mean and ornery as Amelia described her.

And I just swore at her. *Woops.*

"Sophia?" I heard Amelia's faint voice on the other end of the line. "Why are you calling me? Didn't I tell you—?"

I didn't get a chance to hear the rest of what she said, because Madame Doya hit a button on the screen, and the call went dead.

"We do not allow students to have communication with the outside world," she stated sternly.

I gaped at her. "But… you have TVs?"

She pursed her lips. "Students are allowed access to streaming services and local channels. Once you graduate, you may access telephones and the Internet, but not until you are trained in proper communication channels. We can't take any risks. This phone should've never been allowed on campus."

"I was only calling—"

"It doesn't matter who you were calling," she cut me off. "The rules are in place to keep our society safe."

Of course. This wasn't a school. It was a prison.

So, basically high school…

I dropped my gaze, because I was a goody-two-shoes who never talked back. Yes, I admit it. Despite the anger coursing through my body, I fell victim to her authority.

"Yes, ma'am," I whispered.

"Here." Madame Doya shoved a folder in my direction. "You'll find your class schedule in here, along with your dorm key and a map of the school."

I took the folder. That was it? That was my entire welcome?

Madame Doya stared down at me past her nose, like she didn't know what else to say. She cleared her throat. "Welcome home, Sophia."

I stared after her as she breezed down the hall toward the main stairs, all the while trying to force down the lump in my throat. What she'd said bothered me to the core. This place was the furthest thing from home. I'd momentarily let myself become distracted by the magic of this world, but the truth was, I would never belong here. My own House didn't even want me here.

I was completely and utterly alone.

I tried to tell myself that I didn't feel bad when I left Sophia in front of the Koigni dorms, but I kind of did. She seemed so lost and helpless when I abandoned her at the doors and turned away.

But I couldn't go in there with her. She was from the Fire House. Time to stop holding her hand.

The Water dorms were swathed with sapphire and silver, Toaqua House colors. Pools were embedded everywhere in the floors, and Water Familiars dove in and out of them, along with Elementai. The lighting in here was bright and fluorescent, until you went down the right corridor, which was darker and more relaxing, like a spa. Unlike most of the cushy furniture throughout the rest of the castle, the furniture in here was made of wicker and waterproof. Everything got wet. It was like a constant summer party in here. Toaqua could never stay dry for long.

"Hey, Liam, jump in with us!" Wyatt waved to me in the water. He was hanging on to his walrus Familiar, who was tugging him around. Wyatt had been one of my best friends, before. I hadn't seen him all summer.

I wasn't in the mood. "No thanks." I turned my back on them and headed to my dorm. I heard mutters behind me, but I ignored them. I wasn't a part of them anymore.

My room was clean, which I was sure was going to last about a week. By next Friday it'd have clothes and shit all over it. There'd be so much clutter it'd be difficult to walk. I wasn't really an organized guy.

I found my schedule sitting on my bed. Baine must've dropped it off. I picked it up and opened the letter. Usually, students above First Year level got to pick their classes. But I'd been so depressed over the summer that I told the school they could pick for me. I glanced at my schedule. They were a bunch of random classes. Medical Care of Familiars, Advanced Toaqua Magic III, Magical Herbs and Plants, Survival Instincts, and Basket Weaving.

Fricking *Basket Weaving*.

There was nothing that specified any course of study. It was so obvious they didn't know where to put me. But I really couldn't blame them. I didn't know where to put me, either.

Last year I'd been *so looking* forward to signing up for Hunters and Gatherers. But that was out of the question. For that kind of class, you needed a predator familiar to hunt with.

Which I no longer had. I knew what my schedule would've looked like if Nashoma were still here. Interhouse Diplomacy, Ceremonial Tradition, Communing with the Ancestors, War and Negotiation.

Classes to prepare the Son of the Chief to one day take over.

But I knew my chances of becoming Chief of Toaqua were long done. That was my brother Ezra's job now. Dad would never let a Familiar-less Elementai take the role of chief after he stepped down, even if I was his first-born.

Most of the students were staying in their dorms tonight, but I still had a few things to get from home. I left the Toaqua dorms and headed back to the main entrance.

On the way through the courtyard I saw that Haley was outside again, gabbing with two of her clones. Her phoenix, Anwara, was sitting on her shoulder. A jaguar and a winged python, Familiars that had to belong to Haley's friends, were playing on the grass. Haley's Familiar was watching the other animals with interest. Her eyes gleamed longingly as she watched the winged snake and the jaguar wrestle. She seemed a bit lonely.

Anwara nudged Haley with her head, then bounced a little on her shoulder, fluffing her feathers. She clearly wanted to play.

"Anwara! Cut it out!" Haley snapped, and Anwara shrunk on her shoulder. "Why do you want to go and make a fool of yourself? Sit still and behave!"

Anwara hung her head lowly. She didn't coo. Haley went on bragging loudly about the advanced classes her mother had gotten her into while Anwara watched the other Familiars play with a bit of a tear in her eye. Haley's friends pretended like nothing had happened.

I felt a wall of rage rise in my chest. I *hated* people who mistreated their Familiars. I would do anything, anything at all, to have just five more minutes with Nashoma, and here Haley was treating her poor phoenix like it was some designer purse to show off, one that was born simply to do her bidding.

I gritted my teeth but didn't say anything. I'd already caused enough trouble with Haley when I stuck up for Sophia.

The last thing I wanted was another lecture from Dad. Even worse, if I kept messing with House lines, the Elders would get involved. I knew I was already in their line of sight.

If I didn't want to mess things up more than I already had, I needed to keep my head down.

Orenda Academy was run like any other college. I had classes scattered throughout the week on different days and times. Mondays and Wednesdays were loaded, with three different classes, while I only had two classes on Tuesdays and Thursdays. I liked night classes, but the stupid school had signed me up for mostly mornings and afternoons. I hated myself for not picking my own schedule as I dragged my ass out of bed Monday morning and stumbled into the shower.

I showed up late to Advanced Toaqua Magic III. It was held right on the beach. Baine was already lecturing when I showed up. His Familiar was swimming far beneath the surface somewhere out at sea. Everyone else was gathered in a circle around him with their Familiars. As a Third Year, I was the only one without one. I hung back and tried not to be seen.

Which Professor Baine was insistent on screwing up. "Liam!" he announced the moment he saw me. "You're just in time. Come on. We're practicing shields today. Amy, you can be his partner."

Amy wrinkled her nose, but quickly rearranged her face when she saw me looking. We moved toward the ocean until our ankles were deep in water.

I barely had time to get my shield up before Amy clenched her hand, causing a jet of water to rise up from the ocean. She sent it hurtling toward me at a high speed, directed toward my face. I raised up my hand in a sharp manner and a wall of water came up, stopping Amy's jet midstream.

I knew the tribe had resentment toward me for what had happened over the summer, but damn. This was a bit much.

Amy snarled. She started tossing bits of water at me faster, one right after the other in fast succession. They nearly looked like bullets with how fast they were going. They got larger, stronger. Yet my wall held. It didn't break, or waver, and I smirked. I still had it.

Amy couldn't break my shield, and she was getting pissed. Whatever. Even though I was now weaker than almost everyone in my tribe, I was still really good.

I just couldn't keep it up as long. Amy's hits kept getting harder and harder, and I was starting to sweat with the effort of keeping the wall steady. I couldn't spar like the rest of them anymore, and I hated myself for it.

"That's enough, Liam," Baine said sharply when he saw me leaning over my knees, trying to catch my breath. "Take a break."

People were staring. He was coddling me and embarrassing me in front of everyone. I wanted to kill him.

I let the wall drop spontaneously, and it splashed Amy. She jumped back and glared at me, but I didn't say another word.

"Amy, you can take turns sparring with Jack and Lira," Baine told her, like I wasn't even there. Amy gladly left me behind, and Baine walked over to me.

"You know better than to push yourself. I've told you this before," he said.

"I can keep up with everyone else, and do even better," I growled through gritted teeth. "I'm more talented than anyone here."

"But I don't have to remind you what you lack." Baine shook his head. "One day, you're going to have to face the truth, Liam. Your greatest weakness is your biggest strength, and you need to learn how to implement it to your advantage."

"Advantage." I snorted.

"You think you're better despite your illness. I know you are. But prove it," Baine said, with force. "You're smart enough to find a way around it. But if you keep trying to be like you were before, just like everyone else… well, you and I both know it's not going to work."

Baine turned his back on me to help the rest of the class. I was breathing hard, but it wasn't from exhaustion.

It was from rage.

Forget this. I wouldn't be looked down upon because I was different. I was ditching. I grabbed my backpack and headed out of there without another word. My next class wasn't for another hour, but I didn't care. I wouldn't be seen as the *weak one*.

I was thinking about ditching Basket Weaving too, but I really couldn't afford to get into anymore trouble. If I skipped too much, I'd get kicked out. I hardly cared, but I knew what my tribe would think, so I forced myself into Professor Amber's classroom at eleven.

Her classroom was one giant wicker basket perched on top of a tower. Inside, tons of blankets and rugs were scattered all over the floor, alongside giant pillows. Incense holders hung from the ceiling and created a smoky atmosphere. I had to resist gagging when I saw Amber's Familiar, an orangutan, actually playing a wooden flute for ambiance.

This class was full of gossiping girls. Not one single male soul in here but me. I sat on a pillow before a loom and let myself be engulfed by the estrogen.

What a hippie class. At least it was an easy credit. And I got to sit down.

Professor Amber waltzed in. She was wearing a long skirt, covered with a draping shawl and actual feathers weaved into her curly hair. She danced… literally danced… into the room with bare feet while she twirled her arms above her head like some sort of witch.

"Greetings, fair children," she sang. "I am Professor Amber. Welcome to Basket Weaving." She bowed to us, and her Familiar mimicked the movement.

"Today, you will be learning the art of storytelling through the magical art that is weaving. In this class, you will understand how to intricately bind together the forces of thread and straw into a unison of sensual and delightful purpose."

Professor Amber made making a basket sound sexual. She sat down at her loom.

"Pay attention, everyone," she said while taking out a collection of threads. "This technique is to be used for your blissful understanding and pleasure."

Yep. Definitely sexual.

She demonstrated the technique. The girls watched in interest and I tried not to fall asleep. She then handed out thread to all of us in baskets, and stood at the head of the room.

"I will be playing the drums and the gong for sound healing while you work. Feel your soul heal through the vibrations that are played," Amber soothed.

I was ridiculously spiritual, but this was even pushing it for me. I winced as she struck the heavy gong again, then got to work. I had nothing else to do for these two hours.

After a while, I fell into a kind of stupor. Weaving the blanket wasn't difficult on my body, and it didn't require that much concentration. It was repetitive work, one that required me to focus, but not think overly hard. It was sort of nice… like being there, but your body is just existing, doing the same movements over and over, and the rest of you is floating.

Kind of like being high. Maybe.

"Liam, your weaving is so perfect!" Professor Amber praised. She snapped me out of my concentration. I found that everyone was staring at me jealously as Amber displayed the loom, and my blanket, to the class. "Never have I seen a beginner make such a beautiful beginning of a piece!"

I looked around the room and saw that while the thread on everyone else's looms looked choppy and loose, my stitches were tight and uniform. I blushed so hard everyone could probably see it through my dark skin. I had to resist punching my loom.

Professor Amber continued to brag loudly about me to the rest of the class until it was over. I shot out of there as quickly as I could when we were finally released. I was definitely switching this class the minute I could. *Stupid-ass Basket Weaving.*

I wolfed down lunch and headed to my last class of the day. Magical Herbs and Plants was held beside the greenhouse, off a small connecting room called the Alchemist's Lair. Inside were circular stone tables with small wooden bowls, pestles, and vials. Each desk had an alchemy brewing station. Professor Perot strutted around with his peacock Familiar, teaching everyone what the different plants in the greenhouse meant and how to use them.

I scowled. This class was for Elementai who wanted to be medicine men and women, healers. Something I definitely wasn't interested in.

Yet I didn't know my place in society anymore… which Baine had made clear this morning… so I figured I could at least try it. Professor Perot taught us that plants like burdock, clovers, chickweed and dandelions could be consumed in a food shortage emergency, something that was in high stock around here. The lecture was long, but interesting. I was happy when I successfully made a poultice for stopping bleeding wounds out of clay and cayenne pepper.

Magical Herbs and Plants wasn't going to be so bad. It might even help. Alchemy was going to be something I needed after I graduated. Familiars and Elementai got hurt all the time, mostly by magical afflictions. If some sort of potion or plant could help them feel better, or create some sort of spell that could save them in a pinch, I wanted to know.

If I couldn't help myself anymore, maybe I could at least still help my tribe.

I left Magical Herbs and Plants feeling more positive than I had in months. This semester was going to be easy. I turned to head back to the Toaqua dorm to, you know, brood and be alone.

And maybe work on my basket weaving in private. But I'd die before I told anyone that.

I halted in place when my eye caught Sophia in the middle of the hallway. She was looking at her folder, shuffling through her papers like mad and turning on the spot. It was obvious she was lost and trying to find her way around. No one stopped to help her, not even anyone from her own House. That was typical of Koignis. You had to keep up, or they'd literally throw you to the flames. They didn't take well to weak members. The Koigni House valued strength and power above everything. Something Sophia *did not* emulate.

Sophia looked really upset. Tears were welling up in her eyes, and her bottom lip was trembling. She was two seconds away from a breakdown.

Oh, by the ancestors. I needed to go save this girl, before she embarrassed herself in front of everyone yet again. People didn't let things slide around here. They'd remember it forever if she broke down in the middle of school.

But before I could, I hesitated. How far had I actually gotten in life by being *nice*? Being nice was only for two things. One: making hurting people feel better. And two: using it to get what you wanted. Nobody ever got anywhere by being *nice*. If being polite didn't work, you had to take what you wanted by force.

Sophia had to learn that, or she'd get eaten alive out here.

I stood there watching her, wrestling with a decision. She wasn't my problem anymore. Yet, she was.

People were funeral pyres. Every single one of them was scrambling to light the nearest match as quickly as possible, and then, once they were on fire, they complained that the fire burned.

I was no exception to this rule.

Nope. If I had learned anything about people, it was that you could give them a hundred options, and every time, they'd always pick the worst decision they possibly could.

Sophia was a bad decision. But she was one I couldn't help but make.

I rolled my eyes and stomped over there. Her expression cleared as I came into view. Without a word, I yanked the folder out of her hands, opened it, and scrolled through her schedule. Typical First Year stuff. Except...

We had Medical Care of Familiars together tomorrow. *Fuck.*

"Your first class is Beginner Koigni Magic I. It's down the hall, to the left. The door is by the statue of the dancing sprite. If you hit the cafeteria, you've gone too far." I threw the folder back at her. She scrambled to catch it, and papers got jumbled in her arms.

"Th— thank you," she stuttered.

"Don't mention it," I told her sharply. "Like, ever again."

I shoved my hands in my pockets, turned around, and stormed off. Which I was getting exceptionally good at doing lately.

I glanced behind my shoulder, just to double-check on her. Well, she seemed a bit more organized, at least. She had a clearer direction of where she was going.

I sighed. Sophia was sweet, but she needed to learn how things ran around here. She couldn't keep being lost and confused. She had to find her place at Orenda Academy, fast.

And I needed to learn how to stay away from her.

I was grateful for Liam's help in finding my first class, but it would've been more helpful if he'd told me what a *sprite* actually was. I wandered down the hall, my folder shaking in my hands. I gave myself an hour to explore the castle and find my first class, but it looked like that wasn't going to be enough time, even with the map in front of me.

I was starting to think Liam gave me the wrong directions just to get in a good laugh. It wasn't hard to doubt the guy when he acted like a total ass.

What was with him, anyway? He always had a stone-cold look on his face and often breathed heavily, like he had no concept of simple relaxation. He acted like just being alive was difficult. Weird.

Eventually, I hit the cafeteria Liam had mentioned. I turned around and headed back the way I came, looking for any signs of a dancing statue. I ran my hand across the fabric of my jeans— Amelia's jeans— hoping they would bring me luck. So far, I felt so out of my element that I wasn't sure they weren't cursed.

I need you, Am. I wish I didn't have to do this without you.

My eyes finally fell upon a statue of a woman wrapped in flowing fabric. She rose on one bare foot, the other off the ground and her hands in the air.

This must be it.

I glanced into the open door beside the statue. The room was one of the biggest I'd seen so far in the castle, with a high ceiling and a massive fireplace along the far wall. The area in front of the fireplace was empty, and there were scorch marks along the hardwood floor. Several large couches faced the empty area. I guessed the space was for training and the couches were for observing. Tables and chairs were set up in front of a chalkboard in the opposite corner of the room. Tall bookshelves lined the classroom area, and candles burned all around the room.

A red-headed woman sat behind a large desk near the chalkboard, shuffling through papers. Besides that, the room was quiet. I was the first one here.

Madame Doya looked up from her desk. She had that same hard look on her face as the first time I met her. I was starting to think it was a permanent expression.

"Can I help you?" she asked, like she had no intention of actually helping me.

I glanced down at my schedule, as if one more glance might help me make sense of everything I'd been trying to understand since yesterday. "Um… yeah. Is this Beginner Koigni Magic I?"

"It is," she answered. "But you're early."

Since when did teachers chastise you for being *early*?

"I— uh— wanted to make sure I was on time," I said lamely.

Madame Doya looked up at me with tight lips, but simply nodded and gazed back down at her papers. "You may take a seat and practice conjuring a flame in your palm until the rest of the class arrives."

Practice conjuring fire? I thought that was what this class was for. To teach me how to do it.

"What are you just standing there for?" she snapped without looking up from her desk.

I sank into the closest chair two rows back. "I don't know how to conjure fire yet."

Madame Doya's head snapped upward. "Excuse me?"

I fiddled with a corner of my folder. "I mean, I used my fire once, but it was an accident. I didn't know I was supposed to know how to use it before class started."

Great. I was going to be light years behind my classmates.

Madame Doya frowned deeper— if that were possible considering the ever-present downturn of her lips. "You should know how to conjure a basic flame by your age."

"My dad said my powers would be weak until—"

"Your dad?" Madame Doya interrupted. "It was my understanding that you'd never met your father."

What? Who would tell her a lie like that?

Realization dawned. She was talking about my biological father.

"I meant my adoptive father," I said. It felt so wrong to call my dad that.

"Robert Henley is *not* your father," she stated in a tone that stung.

"Oh, I, um…" What was I supposed to do? Agree with her?

Madame Doya stood from her desk. That was the first time I noticed the creature lounging at her feet. My blood ran cold as a huge African cat with blonde fur stood and followed Madame Doya over to one of the nearby bookcases. I swore the cat *scowled* at me, like it knew something.

It does, I told myself. I licked my dry lips, but my tongue felt like sandpaper. This was the cat that had attacked Amelia and me just days ago. Naomi. I knew it. I urged to demand an answer from Doya about what her Familiar was doing hundreds of miles away, stalking my sister and me in the Salt Lake Valley, but fear blocked my words. I didn't want to draw any more attention to myself than I had to, and I had a feeling that the more I dug into that, the more danger I'd put my family in.

Madame Doya didn't seem to notice I'd gone completely tense at the sight of her Familiar. She pulled down one of the thickest books I'd ever seen and flipped it open. She walked over to me and dropped the book so hard onto my desk that I jumped back a few inches.

"Your father's name was Anthony Greyson, and your mother's name was Lucy Greyson. They were both highly respected members of the Koigni House."

Madame Doya pointed at the page in front of me. I glanced down at it, but continued to watch the lioness out of the corner of my eye. She stood still but stared back.

Names and birthdates lined the page. It was a genealogy chart, and sure enough, the names Anthony and Lucy were written beside each other, with a line connecting them to the name Sophia Greyson. My birthdate was written below the name. It wasn't exactly a shock considering my parents admitted I was adopted, but it still didn't feel right to see my name written that way, connected to a man and woman I'd never met.

"Your *adoptive father* was nothing more than a thief," Madame Doya accused in disgust. "He stole you away from this world when you were only a baby. You must learn to accept that fact."

I sat there dumbstruck. She couldn't actually believe my parents *stole* me, could she? I mean, apart from the whole lying-about-being-adopted thing, my parents were the best. I was sure that whatever happened when I was a baby, the Greysons wanted my parents to have me. And I didn't care what anyone else said. Robert and Susan Henley were the people who raised me. They were— and would always be— my real parents.

God, I missed them. And thanks to Doya, I couldn't even call them to tell them that.

I forced down the lump in my throat, but my voice still came out small. "Do they— Anthony and Lucy— know I'm here?"

"They don't know anything," Madame Doya said coldly, "considering they're dead."

"What?" I asked breathlessly. I wasn't sure I'd heard her right.

"Your parents died shortly after you were born." Madame Doya spoke without emotion, as if she wasn't delivering earth-shattering news.

I sat still for several beats, absorbing the information. "What does this mean? Am I the prophesied one?"

Whatever it meant to be the prophesied one. With all that talk the day before, no one cared to tell me what the prophecy actually said.

Madame Doya's nostrils flared as she inhaled a deep breath. "I believed you could be, but anyone capable of fulfilling the prophecy should actually be able to *do* magic."

What was it with this woman? She knew how to deliver a blow with the most minimal of words. Talking to her felt like being thrown into a lion's den without a weapon. At this rate, this lady was going to chew me up and spit me out by the end of next week. She petrified me.

Voices from down the hall met my ears, and a group of students entered the room. I turned to see Haley at the front of the group, her phoenix on her shoulder. I noticed she was the only first-year Koigni in the group with a Familiar. She stopped talking the moment she laid eyes on me.

Madame Doya slammed the book on my desk shut, stealing my attention from Haley. She scooped the book up in her arms and began her way back to her desk. The lioness followed.

"Everyone please take a seat," Doya said in a bored tone. "We'll get started shortly."

To say I was behind my classmates was an understatement. These people could light a fire in the palm of their hand with a snap of their finger. Literally. I didn't even have the snapping-my-fingers part down.

Haley showed off by lighting up the wood in the fireplace from halfway across the room and sending it whirling up the chimney like a fire tornado. If that was the kind of thing Koigni could do on their first day, I wasn't sure I wanted to see what they were capable of after four years of training.

Maybe by then I'd be good enough to burn Haley's perfect eyebrows off, if I was lucky.

"Come on, people!" Madame Doya yelled across the training area. Apparently, my classmates weren't doing as well as I thought. "This isn't Nivita magic. We're not moving mountains here. All I'm asking is to see you sustain a flame for ten seconds. It'd be nice if some of you could conjure a flame at all."

She shot a glare my way. It didn't go unnoticed. Haley followed Madame Doya's gaze and smirked.

Maybe if Madame Doya actually tried *teaching* us something instead of just yelling like a drill sergeant, we'd have made some progress since the beginning of class. I didn't dare ask her how it was actually done. I probably wouldn't get a direct answer, anyway.

"I want to move on to fireballs by next week," Madame Doya said. "At this rate, it'll take us a month, and everyone but Haley will be repeating this class next semester. Sophia!"

I immediately froze from where I stood near the fireplace, my fingers pinched together in preparation to snap them. I knew it wouldn't work since I'd already tried a hundred times since class started.

"What are you doing?" she demanded.

I blinked a few times, unsure how to answer. "I'm trying to conjure fire…"

"Yes," Madame Doya emphasized with raised eyebrows. "Which you have yet to do."

I swallowed hard. "I… I'm not sure how. I didn't have Koigni parents to teach me." Surely everyone could understand that.

"Everyone back to their desks," she instructed.

The class hesitated.

"Now!" she boomed.

Everyone scurried back to their seats. Madame Doya walked so lightly that she seemed to float across the room. She stopped at her desk, where her Familiar lay on the floor, and grabbed one of the candles burning there. She brought it to her face and blew the flame out. Everyone watched with interest as she turned and started her way down the aisle of desks. My heart pounded with every step of her feet. She headed straight toward me.

I prayed she would pass me by, but she stopped beside me. My mouth went dry as she set the candle in the middle of my desk.

"Light it," she commanded.

What?

I just sat there, glancing between her and the candle. Was she serious?

"You should be able to conjure a flame for a simple candle," Madame Doya insisted. "Perhaps you need a little pressure to push you in the right direction."

Everyone's eyes were on me. I could feel it even without having to look up. Haley snickered from across the room.

"What are you waiting for?" Madame Doya asked. "Light the candle."

I stared at the charred wick. Anything not to look her in the eyes. A slew of emotions surfaced— anger, embarrassment, fear. The list went on. It made my blood boil. I thought for a moment the candle might actually light from the power of my emotions. But the seconds ticked by, and all that happened was a tension headache formed in my head.

Whispers spread across the room.

Why won't she just light it?

She's not going to get it.

Is she even Koigni?

Hot breath passed by my upper lip, and my eyes burned. I focused every inch of attention I had on that candle wick, and nothing happened. Why wasn't the damn thing lighting? Why wouldn't Doya tell me how to actually do it?

Because she finds pleasure in tormenting you, for whatever reason.

I must've reminded her too much of someone she hated.

"Enough!" Madame Doya's voice cut off the whispers and snapped me out of my concentration.

But I couldn't take it another second. When I looked up, all eyes were on me. It felt like the walls in the room were getting smaller and smaller, and they would crush me if I didn't make it out *now.*

And so I did the only thing I could do.

I ran.

I wasn't sure what came over me. I'd never ditched class before, and certainly not when I'd already attended the first half of it. I mean, who *does* that?

Me, apparently.

"We've got a runner," someone teased as I rushed out the door. I couldn't even think straight enough to tell if it was Haley.

I was already winded by the time I reached the end of the hall. To be fair, it was a long hall, and I was sprinting pretty fast, but I continued forward. I had to get as far away from that room as I could.

I raced out the first doors I found, down a long flight of concrete steps and onto a worn path carved through the forest. I only slowed when I was far enough into the trees that I felt safe from other students or staff spotting me.

I needed to get into nature. It was the only place I felt safe, felt normal.

The sound of running water traveled through the forest. The farther I walked, the louder it became. Finally, I reached the water I'd been hearing for the last five minutes. A tall waterfall rushed down the side of a cliff and followed a narrow river over rocks and down the mountainside. White water sprayed into the air, sprinkling the trees hanging above the river. A narrow footbridge with rails crossed over the water, but I abandoned the trail and sat on one of the rocks closest to the bank.

I curled my knees to my chest and rested my chin on them. My mind raced, and fury coursed through my veins. Madame Doya should've been fired for how she treated students. And Haley shouldn't have even been in Beginner Koigni Magic if she was that good. They singled me out because I was new, because I was an easy target. I didn't want to be here. It was—

The sound of a creature trilling in the trees above me distracted me. I looked upward and spotted a small, fluffy white creature the size of a fat squirrel jumping from branch to branch. It moved so fast I couldn't catch a good glimpse of it. All I saw was that it had white fur and a fluffy tail almost as big as its body.

I shot to my feet on the rock, completely alert and captivated by the critter. It trilled again. Its voice was melodic and exotic. Whatever the creature was, it wasn't like anything I'd ever seen before.

I followed the critter with my eyes. The way it stretched out its arms and swung from branch to branch was effortless and adorable. I had the strangest urge to climb up the tree and swing from the branches with it. I actually cracked a smile.

The creature reached the end of a branch hanging over the river. I caught enough of a glance to see it was male. He stretched forward to grab a branch on the next tree, but it was a few inches out of his grasp. The animal glanced behind himself, as if calculating what he had to do to make the leap. He scurried back along the branch and stopped. He set his eyes forward, then sprinted away from the trunk of the tree.

The creature kicked off from the end of his branch and soared through the air. He grabbed ahold of the leaves on the tree he'd been aiming for. The whole branch bowed, and then the leaves he held snapped off the tree.

My stomach lurched as the critter flipped through the air and landed in the water with a hard splash. The water rushed so fast that when he came up for air a second later, he was already several yards down river from where he fell in.

I couldn't explain why I did what I did. I didn't even give it a second thought. I just jumped. One second I was standing on a boulder along the bank, and the next I was in the middle of the river, with shoes on and everything.

The current caught me as soon as I jumped in. I was *so* not a water person, but my parents had forced me into swimming lessons as a kid, so I wasn't completely useless. But I'd underestimated how fast the current flowed. The water rushed over my head and pushed me over rocks that cut into my skin. I tried to dig my feet into the river bottom to slow myself, but each time I manage to gain a hold on a rock, the current swept me off my feet again.

Finally, my head broke the surface long enough for me to inhale a deep breath. The current slowed, and the river grew wider and deeper. Up ahead, tiny white hands shot out of the water, and then they were gone again.

I kicked my legs and pushed myself forward. Not far ahead, the river turned back into rapids. Huge boulders stuck out of the water, threatening death to anyone who came too close. If I didn't reach the critter soon, I was going to die. *He* was going to die. And I couldn't let that happen. I couldn't explain the overwhelming sensation that told me that if I somehow survived without him, it just might kill me anyway.

A high-pitched cry filled the air and echoed off the mountains. The creature resurfaced and tried to swim upstream without making any headway. Dread filled my entire body.

I stretched my arm forward and stroked as fast as I could toward him. Relief washed over me when I finally reached him. The critter grabbed on to my arm and climbed onto my back, leaving both of my arms free to swim to shore.

It took all the strength I had to get us to dry land before the rapids hit, but I crawled to shore in one piece. I fell onto my stomach, heaving in heavy breaths as my heart pounded against my rib cage. I wasn't sure I'd ever been closer to death. And all for…

What was it?

Whatever it was, it was worth it, I decided.

I rolled over, and the creature jumped off my back. I expected him to run away now that he was safe, but when I twisted my head, he was still there, so close that all I saw was a coat of white fur. He shook his fur out, covering my face in another layer of water droplets.

I sat up to wipe the water off my face with the back of my hand, then looked down at him. Oh, my heart. It was the cutest thing I'd ever seen. I thought my heart might explode.

He had big, fur-covered ears like a fennec fox, with a fluffy tail, chubby cheeks, and a small black nose. Two tiny, rounded horns protruded from the top of his head. His paws were miniature and adorable. The thing that got me, though, were his eyes. I'd only ever seen eyes that big and round in cartoons and on stuffed animals. But here he was in real life, staring up at me with sparkling blue eyes that took up half his face. The creature's expression softened, and I swear he *smiled* at me.

I was so entranced by his stare that it didn't even register how strange it was that he reached out for me. I extended my arm back. His tiny paws grabbed my fingers, and he hopped forward to rub his face into my hand. His eyes never left mine.

Around us, time seemed to slow to a stop. My entire body froze. I was certain even my heart had stopped beating, and I knew for sure I wasn't breathing. Something in that moment changed everything. It was like I'd been missing something my whole life, and when the tiny critter's gaze locked on mine, a piece of my heart had been returned to me. It was like I'd lived my whole life going through the motions just to lead me to this moment.

Time started to move forward again, but neither me nor the creature moved. My senses ignited, rooting me in place. A light, warm breeze brushed across my skin and through my hair. I felt a heartbeat pulse through my skin, but it didn't feel like my own. The sound of the birds chirping met my ears. They sang a tune that sounded a lot like the lullaby my mom used to hum to me as a kid. The birds' voices came together as a choir, singing in perfect harmony. As I stared down at the creature, the taste of my father's homemade cherry pie washed across my taste buds, and the smell of Amelia's apple-scented shampoo filled my nose. It didn't make sense what these reminders of my family were doing here out in the woods hundreds of miles from home, but one thing was certain. I'd never felt more at home in my life. My entire body tingled with glee, and tears rose to my eyes from sheer overwhelm.

The creature's eyes glistened, mirroring my own. He never looked away, as if he too was captivated by the magic in the air.

I forgot all about what happened in Madame Doya's class earlier. I forgot about wanting to leave this place. I forgot about *everything*. It was like nothing but me and the little creature clinging to my finger mattered. For the first time in… forever, I felt truly at peace.

The critter trilled again, pulling me from my daze. The warm wind died down, chilling me to the bone, and the sound of the birds I'd heard no longer reached us.

The critter nudged me again. I laughed and scratched behind its ears. He let out a low rumble, like a cat's purr. I was pretty sure he liked it. The more I petted him, the more I laughed, but inside, my mind was fixed on the strange moment that just occurred between us. Had I imagined it, or was there something bigger going on?

"What's your name, little guy?" I asked out loud.

He made a small noise that sounded a lot like *Esis.*

"Esis?" I asked, as if he could actually communicate with me. "That's your name?"

Obviously, he didn't answer, but he let me pet him like he was happy with whatever name I gave him.

"Okay, Esis." I scooped his tiny, fragile body into my arms, cradling him into my chest. He clung on to my shirt in a surprisingly comfortable position. I giggled and stood. "You're not going to let me go, are you?"

Of course not. Why would he? The mere suggestion didn't make any logical sense.

He let out another noise that sounded like he was rolling his tongue. I loved the little noises he made. They were the cutest sounds in the world. I wanted to keep him.

Screw whatever rules their might be. I *would* keep him. He was mine now, and I was his.

I stared down at the small fur baby in my arms. He had his foot in his hands and was chewing on his toes. How had my heart not exploded yet?

"I'm going to take you up to the school and find someone who can check you over," I told him. "I want to make sure you're all right."

I glanced around the forest, wondering how I was going to find my way back to the castle. I started upstream, hoping to meet up with the trail I'd come down.

Water squished through my sneakers, and goosebumps broke out on my arms. It seemed to take forever to walk through the brush upstream. I was starting to think maybe I was following the wrong river or something when the bridge I'd seen earlier came into view. I hurried along the trail and back up to the castle.

I wasn't sure where I was headed, but I knew I wasn't going back to Madame Doya's room. I'd find another professor to send me in the right direction. The hall was empty when I entered, but it wasn't long before a familiar voice met my ears.

"What happened to *you*?" Haley sneered when I passed a hall on my left. She and her group of five were hanging out around a serpent statue, gossiping. I hoped it wasn't about me, but it probably was. "Did you get into a fight with a Toaqua?"

I gritted my teeth. "No, actually, I jumped in to save—"

"*That?*" Haley turned her nose up when she spotted Esis in my arms. "You saved a dust bunny?"

Her cronies echoed her laughter. I was officially royally pissed off. Esis made a noise that sounded a lot like a comeback. Good. At least *he* knew how to stand up to her.

"I—"

"What's going on?" A woman's voice cut me off.

I whirled around to find Madame Doya standing behind me. She looked me up and down, clearly displeased by my soaking appearance. Her Familiar stood beside her. Naomi's lips curled back over its teeth as she glared at me. I pulled Esis closer to me, just in case the lioness thought she was hungry for a snack.

I spoke before Haley could. "This little guy fell in the river. I wanted to get him to a vet— or whatever you have around here— to make sure he's okay."

Madame Doya eyed Esis. "You can take him to Professor Fawn, but it's hardly worth it."

"What do you mean?" I asked.

"No one knows what that creature is, so even if he could be treated, we wouldn't know how to treat him," Madame Doya explained, like Esis' life was about as important as the dirt on her pointed heels.

"Thank you," I said, just to end the conversation. "I'll go find Professor Fawn." Not like I had any idea where to find him— or her— but I'd do anything to get out of this hallway.

"I bet she bonded with it," Haley muttered under her breath before I could even take a step.

I paused, wondering what exactly that would feel like. *Had* I bonded with Esis?

"What's it like to bond with Familiar?" I asked Doya, expecting a disapproving glance and curt answer, which is exactly what I got.

"It's different for everyone," she replied.

Even without a clear explanation, somehow I knew… the moment we'd shared in the woods left no doubt. Esis and I had bonded. Which meant I was never letting him go.

The lioness stepped forward and let out a low growl. I instantly took two paces back.

"Calm down, Naomi," Madame Doya scolded, placing her hand on the lioness' back.

Naomi glanced back at her and dropped her head. Madame Doya raised an eyebrow, but her lips turned down.

"It seems that you *have* bonded," she said, eyeing Esis with disgust. "I expected better from a member of my House."

What the hell did *that* mean?

"Now it makes sense why she can't produce a flame," one of the girls in Haley's group said to the other. She spoke under her breath, but I heard every word.

My jaw tightened. I knew I couldn't snap back, not in front of Doya.

"If you bonded, I guess that means you'll be competing in this year's tournament," Haley said with a smirk.

"Tournament?" My voice shook. She was only saying it to scare me, right?

Madame Doya sighed, like she couldn't believe how uninformed I was. I blamed her for that, considering she was the head of my House.

"Yes, the tournament," she bit, like it was obvious. "Each student who has bonded by the end of September every year will be entered into the Elemental Cup to prove their bond with their Familiar and their place in our society."

That didn't sound too bad.

Madame Doya scowled at me. "I suggest you don't make skipping class a habit. You'll need all the help you can get preparing for this tournament considering your current… circumstances. Your competition will be fierce."

Madame Doya glanced to Haley, who had a smug expression fixed on her face. I knew instantly she meant that Haley would be in this year's competition with me.

I bit back the string of nasty words that danced on the tip of my tongue. "I'm not too worried about the competition."

Haley's face fell. "You *should* be worried. You'll never survive with *that* Familiar."

The blood drained from my face when no one countered her. Haley wasn't just insulting me. She was serious. I realized… this was a *deadly* competition.

It was clear that if I didn't learn how to use my fire, this tournament would kill me.

Liam

NINE

I wasn't looking forward to Medical Care of Familiars. But it wasn't like I had a choice whether or not to go.

The class was held in a large medical room tied on to the medical wing. Medical equipment hung on the walls, and long desks with sinks were placed among the room in uniform manner. The room was stark white, and the fluorescent lighting in here was so bright it was enough to make you go blind. It looked like the literal inside of a hospital. I'd spent enough time in one over the summer, so it churned my stomach to look at.

I was late again (a bad habit that I was developing, but fine with), and most of the class was already here. I saw that Haley and her morons were in this class, too. But my attention only lingered on them for a moment, because my eyes went directly to Sophia.

There was a tiny animal sitting on Sophia's shoulder. It was white and looked like nothing but a big fur ball rolling around her torso. Sophia giggled as she played with it, and the little puffer let out tiny mews as she tickled it.

It made her happy. Which made me happy, I guess.

"You've bonded!" I said as I walked up to her. She saw me coming and grinned. My heart skipped a beat, but I ignored it. Feelings were for losers.

"Yep." Sophia was stroking the little critter on her shoulder, who had calmed as I'd approached. "Isn't he just so cute and fluffy?"

He was, even though I didn't know *what* he was. "What's his name?"

"Esis," she responded cheerfully. "I just got him yesterday. I found him in the woods."

Like I'd found Nashoma. "Is that a ball of lint?" I asked, smirking.

"Stop it!" She recoiled away from me, holding Esis. "Don't pick on him!"

"I'm just teasing. He's cute." I reached out to scratch Esis under the chin. His eyes rolled back and he grinned, thumping his foot.

I looked at Sophia. "How did Fire class go yesterday?" I didn't even know why I was asking.

Her smile fell. "Terrible, actually. Everyone else can make fire snap from their fingers. I tried, but it didn't happen."

"You can't even make a flame?" I asked, surprised.

Sophia looked down in shame. "No. I can't even light a candle."

Hoo boy. She was gonna have one hell of a time during the tournament with Esis. His survival skills seemed nonexistent. She'd better hurry up and master Fire quick, before she became one of the casualties.

Thinking of Sophia dying made me really sad. So I didn't. I was just glad I wasn't required to join the tournament because I'd lost Nashoma. Competing against Sophia wouldn't be fun, but being on a team with her would be a nightmare.

"Don't worry. This class will be easier," I told her. I was reassuring her. Why, I didn't know.

"Liam!" someone said behind me. I turned to see Jonah next to me, his hippogriff Familiar following behind him.

Jonah was huge. And I mean *huge*. He was easily six-foot-five, and towered over everyone else at Orenda. His brown hair was up in a man-bun, and a thick beard grew halfway down his chest. He wore a red plaid shirt with loose dark-wash jeans, and boots I'm pretty sure a dragon could fit into. His arms were as big around as tree trunks, for crying out fricken loud.

Jonah had bonded over the summer. Jonah's hippogriff, Squeaks, was dancing around and knocking stuff over behind him. I'm pretty sure she had ADHD, because no matter what the class was Squeaks couldn't stand still. She was as big as a draft horse and brown in color, with ginger feathers that gleamed in the light. Her eyes were yellow, her beak pitch-black. I had to step out of the way to avoid getting my foot stomped as she continued her frantic dance, hooves tapping a beat.

Jonah and I hadn't really talked since what had happened with Nashoma, though he and Squeaks had come to the funeral a few weeks later. I shook his hand and bumped my shoulder against his.

"Hey, man. What's up with you?" Jonah asked.

"Not much." I shrugged. "Same old shit."

"I was worried you wouldn't come back this year," Jonah said. "I'm glad to see you didn't give it up."

Sophia was eyeing me curiously. I forced a laugh and said, "I stayed to annoy you."

"Always, buddy." Jonah's eyes followed Renar (a tall, thin guy who I always thought had a face that looked like a rat's) as he entered the classroom and sat at one of the desks in the front row.

"You preoccupied? Because, you know, I can always leave you two alone," I poked.

Jonah's attention was still on Renar. "Yeah, yeah, you're hilarious. Hang out later?"

He didn't wait for me to answer before he crossed the room and slid into the seat beside Renar, talking lowly and nudging him with his shoulder. Squeaks muscled her way in beside him and sat down next to the desk.

I rolled my eyes. That was Jonah. He was always after the D.

"I thought people from different Houses couldn't be friends?" Sophia asked me in a low tone, a small smile on her face.

"Shut up," I mumbled to her as the professor entered. Sophia didn't get it. A Toaqua guy being friends with a Yapluma dude was no big deal. Not like Sophia's and my friendship would be. Water and Air could mix. Water and Fire... no go.

"Gather 'round, everyone!" Professor Costas said, and eventually, the chatter quieted down.

I focused on Costas. I'd had her before. She wore a long white coat, with a stethoscope hanging around her neck. She was short and looked cute, but she'd seen her fair share of blood and gore.

"Welcome to my class," Costas started. "Now, I know many of you are wondering why this class is necessary, as for most of you, you will be staying within the ranks of the Elementai, and will be near enough to emergency medical care."

Professor Costas paused to gaze around the class. "However, some of you will be taking positions within the tribe that will require you to be away from home and away from other Elementai. When you're out in the field, you won't be able to get to medical care quickly. In a majority of cases, you will be alone and must rely on yourself to save your Familiar's life. Which is why the majority of this class will be held outside, away from the equipment you undoubtedly won't have while exploring the wild. Follow me!"

Professor Costas led us outside, to where a collection of really creepy life size Familiar dolls were lying around. They were in various shapes and sizes of animals, and were meant to practice on.

I was feeling a little glum. Maybe if I had taken this class last year, I could've saved Nashoma.

Also waiting outside was Costas' Familiar, Hera. She was a hydra, a large reptile with nine heads, green in color and very intimidating. She walked on four legs with large, rounded claws, and was about as big as a small house. Venomous fangs protruded from the mouth of each head, along with a collection of poisonous spines along the creature's back all the way down to her long, whip-like tail. From what I'd heard from other people, Hera was a real sweetheart.

I'd believe that *after* I'd spend enough time with her to know one of her nine heads wasn't going to eat me.

"Pair up, everyone!" Costas yelled loudly. "For this, I'll need you to work in teams!"

The best people were gone in seconds. Jonah immediately paired up with Renar, which I saw coming. Everyone else already had a partner, which meant I was stuck with Sophia.

She immediately gravitated toward me, and of course, I took in the sorry orphan, because I was a sorry orphan too. We sat next to a doll that looked like a tiger, and Costas held up a bandage with splints.

"Listen up, and pay close attention. I will be instructing you on how to create a splint for broken bones," Costas started. She demonstrated on Hera, and I tried to watch. but I noticed Sophia was nodding off, her eyes following Hera around the gardens instead of listening to Costas' instruction.

Learning to set bones was useful, but it was tough work for the first day of class. Sophia couldn't wrap the bindings tight enough, and I think she ended up breaking the doll's leg worse than what it originally was. I face-palmed at least five times.

Esis didn't make things any easier. He kept on running around over the doll, squeaking and tumbling like he didn't see the point in wrapping up a broken limb. At one point he sank his little teeth into the wrappings and started tugging at it, trying to play. Sophia laughed, but it wasn't funny to me.

At least we weren't the only ones struggling. Haley got frustrated and ended up throwing her doll, which made me chuckle under my breath. Jonah was sitting around and letting Renar do all the work. While Renar was binding up the doll's leg, I caught Jonah looking at his ass. I got Jonah's attention, pointed to Renar when his back was turned, and made humping movements with my hips.

Jonah went red and flipped me off. I laughed.

"What's with you guys?" Sophia questioned, raising an eyebrow.

"Jonah's been crushing on Renar forever, but he hasn't made a move," I explained.

"Hm." Sophia nodded, then went back to wrapping the mangled doll's leg. Esis stared at me, his eyes getting bigger... and bigger... and bigger.

By the time I ripped my gaze away, I'm pretty sure his giant pupils were covering the rest of his face. That thing was an alien or something.

By the end of the class, bandages were everywhere. A couple of girls were crying in frustration, and Haley was bitching. Most everyone had given up.

Costas' face was thin and brittle. She obviously wasn't impressed. "The majority of you will need to study up. This is not an easy class. If you perform like you have today, you are going to fail. Tomorrow, we'll be learning how to perform CPR on your Familiar, and next week we'll get into poisons. Class dismissed."

People scattered out of there. Professor Costas was a hard-ass, but at least she was fair. She was far from Madame Doya. I looked down at our doll. We'd managed to fix the leg back to normal, and the bandages were wrapped tightly now, but I'm pretty sure if it had been a real tiger Sophia and I would've killed it.

Sophia looked happy, though. "We actually make a pretty good team, don't we?"

Esis let out a *mew*, and I told Sophia, "Don't get your hopes up."

We stood up to leave. We didn't mean to walk together, that's just what happened.

Near the entry to the gardens, Haley was taking out her frustration on another Koigni First Year. "You know Costas was talking about you, Taylor," she said. "You're never going to pass."

Taylor was in tears. I think she was Levi's little sister, which would make sense— Haley and Levi dated over the summer before he realized what a bitch she was and thankfully dumped her. But that meant his little sis had to spend a whole semester of enduring Haley's torments. Poor girl.

"Leave her alone, Haley," Jonah bit at her, laying a hand on Taylor's shoulder. "Yours looked worse."

Haley's eyes narrowed, and she sneered. "Aren't people from Yapluma supposed to be thin and small? How do you expect your hippogriff to lift your fat ass, Goliath?" Haley goaded, and her friends roared at the insult.

"He's another abomination, like Sophia," Kelsey, Haley's second-in-command, added. "His mom probably slept around with some Nivita guy. This is why Houses shouldn't mix. You get all these freaks running around."

"Right? Sophia's so inbred she can't even light a candle. Her magic's useless, just like her stupid Familiar," Haley said, shooting Sophia a nasty grin.

Haley and her friends roared. Esis puffed up into a little ball of fury, hopping up and down on Sophia's shoulder and stomping his tiny feet. Sophia tried to comfort him— his tiny cheeks swelled up as he made a quick *whoosh* sound. Sophia looked troubled, like she didn't know what to do.

Jonah moved closer to Taylor and whispered, "Are you okay?"

Taylor slapped his hand away. She backed up, wiping away more tears. "Stay away from me." She took off as fast as she could, and Haley grinned. She knew she'd won.

Haley then looked at me. She dug around in her bag for something, and then threw it at me. "Here. I thought you might need this, Liam. Finish the job, since you're no good to the tribe anymore."

It hit me. My insides cringed as my hands caught what she'd tossed. A rope.

Sophia's face was red with rage. Sophia didn't understand what Haley's comment meant, not really, but it still pissed her off. She opened her mouth to say something.

But I wasn't dealing with this. Haley's actions didn't deserve a reaction. I stuffed the rope inside my pocket, then grabbed Sophia's wrist to pull her away before a bigger scene was made. Jonah turned his back on Haley to look for Renar, but he was already gone.

"I'm getting really tired of people picking on me," Sophia grumbled as we walked away.

There was a large stone fountain with a statue of a thunderbird taking flight on top of it. Nobody was around, and Sophia paused to catch her breath. She was furious.

"So then do something about it," I told her. "Fight back."

"Fight back?" She gave me a condescending look. "You just dragged me away before I could say anything."

"Because you've got to fight in the right way. You can't just say whatever you want. Haley's mean, but she's also super smart," I told her. "Not to mention she'll go running to Madame Doya the minute you open your mouth. You've got to fight with actions, not words."

Sophia sighed. "I guess you're right."

She sat on the edge of the fountain. "This sucks. I was so happy when I found Esis. It was like everything was going to be okay," she started.

I nodded. I knew the feeling. "And?"

"And... then Madam Doya ruined it." She made a face.

"Typical of her."

"I'm supposed to be some prophesied child, but I can't even make a tiny flame. Everyone talks about unity, but it's just crap. No one wants to help me. And now there's this tournament, and..."

She sighed in defeat. "I don't know, Liam. I don't know how to do this."

The thought crossed my mind to help her. I wasn't supposed to be teaching a Koigni how to use a flame. I didn't even know how to do it myself. But the thought of Madame Doya's bitchy face as she gazed down in Sophia in disappointment was enough to make me act. "You'll show her. Come on, follow me."

I started walking toward the forest, where we wouldn't be seen. She followed. When we were deep enough into the trees, I motioned for her to put down Esis. She put him up on a tree branch. He looked down at us in interest, large ears forward.

"If you want to beat Haley, you have to show her you're better than her at magic," I started. "Nothing she could say will trump that. It'll eat away at her."

"How? She's the best in my class, and I'm the worst." Sophia's shoulders slumped. "She's had years of practice."

"You need someone willing to teach you. Not just yell at you," I started, before I paused. "And I guess that sad sack is me."

"You?" She raised an eyebrow. "But you're Toaqua. How do you know how to conjure fire?"

"I don't. I'm just guessing. But it's all elemental magic, right? Can't be too difficult."

I showed her. I hovered my hand over the ground, and dew droplets rose from the dirt, leaves and grass to form a ball of water in my hand. I moved it back and forth, weaving my hands like a wave as the water swished in the air from this side to that.

"Let your magic flow through you. It's an extension of your body. You are connected to the earth and everyone in it. Everything is a living thing, and is willing to help you. Use that connection to summon your power."

Sophia tried. She raised her hands and tried to conjure magic, but all that resulted was a look that made her seem like she had to shit.

"I don't get it," she said. "Can you explain another way?"

I thought for a moment. Harnessing water was all about self-control. You had to let peace and harmony flow through you steadily before you gathered it into a powerful force. Water sustained life, but it could also take it.

Fire was different. Fire was raging and angry and was fueled by strong emotions unbound by any force. Koigni were strong and ill-tempered. They burned off of pride. It was one of the reasons Haley was so good.

No wonder Sophia couldn't create a flame. She was too meek, too gentle. She had to get pissed. I literally was going to have to light a fire under her ass.

"Think about Madame Doya. How she humiliated you in front of everyone, and how badly you want to prove her wrong," I said. "Meditate on how that feels."

Sophia scrunched up her face. Moments passed, and became minutes. I wondered if we'd be out here for hours.

Suddenly, a ball of flame appeared brightly in her palm. She opened her eyes, mouth falling open in delight, but the flame only lasted a few seconds before vanishing.

"Did you see that?" she screeched happily, bouncing. "I did it!"

"You did. You see? It's not that hard." I shrugged. "Madame Doya's just a terrible teacher."

"Yeah." She grinned and looked up at me. "Thanks, Liam. I just hope I can do it again in Madame Doya's class."

"You've got it," I encouraged. "Just trust in yourself, and the ancestors will guide you."

"Ancestors? I don't believe in anything like that," Sophia said. "All that spiritual stuff is really silly. My parents didn't raise me like that. Believing in the afterlife is for people who can't stand on their own."

Esis looked at his Elementai like he couldn't believe what she'd just said, ears back and little lips trembling. I went to bite back something sharp before I held my tongue. Here I was helping this girl, and she was blatantly disrespecting our religion, our culture. She just didn't understand what it meant to be part of the Hawkei.

No good deed goes unpunished, I suppose. *Now* she was acting like a superior Koigni. Great fricking timing. This was why the Elders didn't allow outsiders.

Esis came down from the trees. But instead of going to Sophia, the squirrel reject went for me. He landed on top of my head and screamed in what seemed like a victory as he perched on top of my skull.

"Dude, get down." I tried yanking him off, but it didn't work. Esis was set on riding on top of my head. He'd made a nest in my hair and was clinging on to the strands to hold on, making loud cooing noises like he was the captain of this ship.

"He likes you." Sophia grinned.

"Yeah, well, I don't like him." I gave up and let him sit there. It wasn't like he weighed anything. We started back to the castle, where hopefully I would find a vice grip to pry the little bugger off.

But then there was more than the sound of our footsteps crunching the earth. Someone was giving an audible shout.

A cry for help.

"Did you hear that?" Sophia looked at me.

I paused to listen for a second, then nodded when I heard the voice again. "Yeah. Someone's in trouble."

Esis took off. He leapt off my head and started jumping from tree to tree toward the screaming.

"Esis, wait!" Sophia cried. We broke into a run to keep up with him. He became a little white dot in the leaves, zig-zagging this way and that.

Sophia was ahead of me. She didn't look where she was going, and someone stepped onto the path, who Sophia slammed into.

"Oof!" the figure cried. Imogen again.

"What are you doing here?" I asked her as she untangled herself from Sophia. I helped both girls up and stared at Imogen. She was wearing these large bunny ears that looked like antennas poking out of her hair. Sassy was nearby, rising on her hind legs curiously.

"I had some free time and was out looking for wolpertingers. Sassy loves to play with them," Imogen said. "We were adventuring until we heard screaming, and we came this way."

I was pretty sure whatever Imogen said didn't exist, but I went along with it. Another voice broke through the woods.

"Oy! There you guys are!"

From behind us and with a bunch of twigs in his hair came Jonah, grinning like a wildcat.

"Jonah? What the fuck?" I asked. Squeaks was having a hard time getting through the trees. The hippogriff crushed bushes and knocked over saplings on her struggle to get to Jonah, squawking her irritation at him.

"I saw you and Sophia go into the woods together, and I got curious." Jonah waggled his eyebrows. "But then… I got lost."

"Typical." I rolled my eyes. Jonah wasn't very good with directions.

Esis was hopping up and down in the tree ahead of us, peeping and wanting us to keep up. There was another scream.

"Let's go," Sophia said, and she led the way.

"Isn't it so interesting how we're all going on such an adventure? I think we're going to be very good friends," Imogen said pleasantly amongst the backdrop of the horrified wailing.

"Yeah. We're a fucking group, all right," I mumbled. The Kogini girl who couldn't conjure fire, the gay Yapluma guy who was too big to be from Yapluma, the weird Nivita girl who creeped everyone out, and me, the Familiar-less cripple. This joke was too damn perfect. If anyone saw me together with all these people at the same time, I'd be a laughingstock.

The trees eventually ended and cleared. Below us was a large cliff about fifteen feet tall, and at the bottom was a thick black tar pit, sticky and deep.

Tar pits weren't unusual around here. There were quite a few dotted throughout the woods. Most people knew to stay away from them, but apparently not this time.

The yelling was coming from Professor Perot. He was submerged in the middle of the pit up to his neck, the only thing being free his arms and his head. His peacock Familiar, Baxtor, was fluttering around the pit trying to get Perot out. But he had changed. Baxtor's body had morphed into a bird representing a cloud. His body, feathers and plumage were transparent and white, and he fluttered over Professor Perot frantically. With each beat of his wing, he tried to summon the winds to get them to lift Perot out of the muck, but his magic just wasn't strong enough. All the rampaging air managed to do was buffet the trees around and knock a few limbs down. The lower Perot sank, the weaker Baxtor got. He was sinking too, struggling to keep himself aloft as Perot gasped for air.

Perot's eyes caught us on the cliff. "Children!" he shouted. "Go away from here! This isn't something you can see!"

"We'll get you out!" I yelled back.

"It's too late! Leave!" Perot coughed, the thick tar rising up to his chin.

He already considered himself a goner. Not on my watch.

"We need to find a teacher," Jonah said. He went to run back the way he came, but I snagged him by the arm to hold him back.

"There's no time. He'll be dead by the time we get help. We're going to have to work together," I said.

I raised my hands. My power searched the tar pit below for some sort of liquid. It was in there, but it wasn't much. I gritted my teeth and tried to make the liquid beneath Perot move upward. I managed to budge him up for a moment, but once I let go, he sank right back down.

"There isn't enough water in there for me to manipulate. Tar is earth. Do you think you could try, Imogen?" I asked.

"I can." She took a deep breath and stepped forward. She raised a hand toward the tar pit.

We stood around her in a circle, waiting for something to happen. The tar pit bubbled and rumbled, but nothing else happened. Imogen gasped and dropped her hand.

"I can't." Imogen wiped a bit of sweat from her brow. "I'm sorry, Liam, but I'm just a First Year. If I had a bit more experience, I could."

"Fire won't help. If I try to burn it, he'll be killed in seconds," Sophia said.

"Air is already useless," Jonah said grimly, staring at Baxtor.

"We're going to have to figure out another way." I put my hand to my mouth and thought. We had ten minutes, maybe, before Perot went under. But if our powers didn't work to get him out, what would?

"There!" Sophia interrupted my train of thought by pointing to a loosely hanging tree branch Baxtor had blown free. She walked up to the branch and ripped it off, handing it to Jonah.

"Jonah, can you get your Familiar to dangle this over the professor? Maybe she can yank him out," Sophia said.

"Worth a shot," Jonah replied. He handed the branch to Squeaks, who took it with her beak. She flew over Perot and dangled the branch over him.

"Professor! Grab the branch, and she'll pull you out!" Sophia cried.

Professor Perot reached up to grab the branch. Once he had ahold of it with two hands, Squeaks pulled. His upper body rose out of the tar, but from the waist down, he was still stuck. No matter how hard Squeaks pulled, she couldn't yank him free.

"It's not working," Jonah said. He appeared tired at Squeaks' struggle. "She's not strong enough."

Sophia looked desperately at me. I got an idea. "Here." I pulled the rope Haley had thrown at me out of my pocket. It was just long enough. I tied a loop, then handed the end of it to Sophia, Imogen and Jonah. "We'll slide down the embankment, then get this around him. With all of us, we should be able to pull him out."

Sophia nodded. "Right."

This was way dangerous. We had an equal chance of falling in and getting trapped ourselves. But there wasn't really any other plan. I slid down the embankment first, on my back, then Sophia followed, trailed by Imogen and Jonah. At the bottom was a thin strip of dirt we could stand on. Perot saw what we were doing, and his eyes widened.

"Don't risk your own lives, children! I'm not worth it!" he yelled.

"Yes you are," I said firmly. "Let go of the stick for a moment. We'll lasso you and pull you to shore."

Meekly, Perot did as he was told. I concentrated, focusing my eyes on him. We only had one rope. If I missed, it was game over.

I tossed the rope, and thankfully, it looped around Perot. He adjusted it so it was around his waist, then reached up to grab the branch Squeaks was dangling again.

"All together!" Sophia shouted. "Pull!"

We yanked on the rope. It wasn't an easy task. Perot really was stuck. Even with all of us pulling, he remained trapped.

"Harder!" Sophia shouted. "I know we can do this!"

Her confidence wasn't helping me, but it obviously did something for Jonah and Imogen, because Perot began to move through the tar toward us. Baxter flew forward and latched his talons under the branch Squeaks was holding, helping her pull up. Sassy lunged forward and sank her teeth into the rope to help Imogen pull. Esis hopped up and down on the cliff above and cheered us on.

"It's working!" I shouted. Perot was getting closer and closer to shore. "Keep pulling! He's almost there!"

With a monumental effort that was gonna pull out my back, all of us yanked at once. Perot came free of the tar pit and landed onshore, heaving. Squeaks dropped the branch and Baxter flew forward, landing on the shore and pecking at Perot's head.

"I'm fine, Baxtor," Perot breathed. "I'm fine."

"Professor, are you all right?" I asked him. "What were you even doing out here?"

"I was looking for magical mushrooms for our class next week, before I tripped and stumbled down the embankment," Perot said. "I didn't see the pit, and fell in. I would've died if you and your Familiars hadn't come along."

Perot was obviously very weak, and his clothes were stuck to his body. Sophia moved forward and said, "Come on. We've got to get him back to the castle."

Shadows loomed overhead. We looked up and saw that Madame Doya was there with Naomi, as well as Head Dean Alric. Valda landed by his side, staring down the pit. She was an amethyst dragon, with brilliant gemstone eyes that stared down in concern at Perot. Her large leathery wings blocked out a portion of the sun as she stared down at us.

"Perfect timing. Thanks for all the help," I grumbled.

"Perot! Can you stand?" Alric called down.

"I… I am strong enough to make it up the embankment, but not to walk much after," Perot said.

We helped Perot up the hill before we climbed it ourselves. By this time, I was exhausted. I still had a long walk back to the castle before I sank into my nice, warm bed. With help from Alric, Perot climbed onto Valda's back, and she spread her wings to take him to the medical wing.

Now that Perot was out of the pit and safe, Baxtor changed back into a regular peacock. He cooed as he followed behind Valda to safety.

"You children are remarkable. Thank you for risking your lives to save Perot's," Alric said to us. "I'm afraid the situation would've ended quite differently, if you weren't involved. Madame Doya and I were just on our evening walk before we heard the shouting. I daresay we wouldn't have reached him in time."

The guy was practically astounded that we'd stuck out our necks to rescue a teacher. People had morals every now and then, didn't they?

Madame Doya didn't look happy. In fact, it looked like she was almost displeased we'd saved Perot's life.

"It's nothing. Don't mention it," Sophia said, smiling.

Don't mention it? Are you kidding? I wanted to scream at her. Wasn't there some sort of award we'd get for this? Really?

"Yes. Well." Alric forced a grimace at her. "I think it'd be best if you returned to your dormitories. I also think it best if we keep this between us, and prevent gossip from spreading."

Jonah nodded like a brainless doll, and I took the first opportunity I could to get the hell out of there.

Great. We weren't even going to get any credit for this. All because of Sophia.

Sophia, Imogen and Jonah followed me back to the castle. I expected us to split up at the door, but they kept trailing me, along with their quirky Familiars. Esis was sitting on Sophia's shoulder again, and was singing some sort of peppy tune.

Ancestors, it was like the soundtrack to a sitcom or something, and I was living it.

"You guys want to eat together?" Sophia gestured toward the dining hall. Her cheeks were a bit pink. "I… well, I usually eat alone, but it'd be nice if you'd like to join."

"I'm in." Jonah rubbed his stomach and threw an arm around Squeaks. "Me and Squeaks are always down for some grub."

Imogen's smile spread wide at Sophia's invite. "Sure! Liam, you want to come?"

I was starving, but I wouldn't be seen with them. I wanted some alone time. "I'm not hungry. I'm heading back to my dorm."

I turned my back before they said anything else. Sophia's face was crestfallen. I felt bad about being a dick, but still. I knew that I'd messed up.

It was one thing to be polite and be acquaintances. Maybe even friends. But being in a life-or-death situation was an entirely different story. I didn't want to be that close to anyone. I was supposed to be the lone wolf.

I'd formed a bond with these people, which was a critical mistake.

The next day, Sophia was still following me around like a puppy dog, which was irritating. She couldn't stop talking about how amazing it was that we'd saved Perot. Since I wasn't getting some type of reward, I just wanted to forget about it.

"You were pretty cool yesterday," she commented after she'd caught me coming in from Water class, and I groaned. "You're a good leader."

"Don't say that. I don't like helping people," I growled.

"You helped me earlier." She leaned against a window in the hallway. Esis was in her arms, and he did that weird staring thing with his eyes again when he looked at me, his little mouth forming a tiny grin. That fluff ball was gonna give me nightmares.

"Totally different."

"Uh-huh. Sure it was." Sophia's tone was so smug I no longer doubted she was a stolen Koigni child.

"You were the one who came up with the plan," I said. "I just helped."

"What I said earlier is true. We make a good team."

"Oh, yeah. Fire and Water. Great mix." I rolled my eyes. "Think whatever you want, Soph."

I didn't mean to call her that, but I did. She brightened like a lightbulb, and I wanted to hit myself. By the ancestors, it was so hard not to let her in.

"Out of the way!" a teacher's loud shout caught my attention. Baine was clearing a path through the hallway, shoving students aside and directing them to get to the wall. A massive group of professors were behind them. Their faces were drawn and grim, not worried but accepting a dark fate. Students froze like statues, clinging to their Familiars as they saw what was behind the teachers.

Some creature was in the back of a wagon pulled by a black chimera. I couldn't tell what it was, because the animal was covered in a black, velvet shroud. It was utterly still, and didn't move.

The sight of the black shroud caused my body to convulse. I gagged, and almost threw up. Pangs of agony shot through my spine and spread throughout my back, and the room turned wavy. I got lightheaded. My body shuddered violently, and I turned away from Sophia so she wouldn't see, pressing my head against the cool rock and shaking.

"Liam?" I felt Sophia's soft hand on my back. "Are you okay?"

I took a few deep breaths and blinked back tears. "I'm… fine." I forced myself to regain my composure and turned back, forced myself to watch the gruesome scene, where I already knew what had happened.

Behind the cart was a boy. Carter. He was from Yapluma. A guy was on either side of him, helping him walk. Carter's face was ashen, and his steps were staggering. The guys more or less carried him as he dragged his feet, his eyes dull and lifeless. All the color had gone out of him. It looked like someone had sucked everything out of him that made him… himself. He said nothing, eyes staring straight ahead, dried tears on his expressionless, void face. Saying he looked half-alive would be a compliment. Carter was more or less a walking corpse. It was the scariest thing to witness.

He was nothing. A shell. There wasn't anything left.

I'd looked the same way when they brought me in. I *felt* the same way. I was the only one in this hallway who knew what Carter was feeling, because not so long ago I had been the one trailing behind that cart, staring at the lifeless form that had been Nashoma, buried under that black shroud.

I jumped when I felt someone coming up behind me. It was Imogen. She snuck between the two of us and kept her voice low.

"You guys hear the news?" she said.

"What's going on?" Sophia asked, confused. I kept quiet and let Imogen explain. This was too painful for me.

"It's Carter. He and Tiara had an accident in Flight class," Imogen whispered.

My stomach sunk. "What happened?"

"Carter misdirected her. They hit a tree, and Tiara spun out into the target they were supposed to fly through. It impaled her through the heart," Imogen hushed. "She died while they were trying to get her back to the medical wing."

Imogen sighed. "Poor kid. He did so much, too. Volunteered for the community, captain of the sports teams and everything. All that's done now. But at least he accomplished something while he was here."

I felt like I was going to throw up again. Sophia was really pale. Horrified screams began echoing down the hallway. The girls turned their heads, but I just closed my eyes and wished it was over.

When the wailing got louder, I was forced to look. I knew him. James, from Nivita. He was beside himself. A couple of girls tried to comfort him as he sobbed. His screams shook the walls as tears streamed down his red face. He was cradling his small dragon Familiar in his arms tightly. He couldn't fly on him yet, but I think that they were in Flight class with Carter and Tiara, too. I bet they'd watched the whole thing.

"Poor James," Imogen said softly. "It's just so sad."

"Are James and Carter really close?" Sophia asked.

"They're best friends," Imogen said lowly. "Or they were. James knows he's gonna have to say goodbye soon. Carter's a goner."

"What do you mean?" Sophia asked, and my heartbeat quickened. "He's okay, isn't he?"

Imogen shook her head. "No. He's not. Elementai can't live without their Familiars, and vice versa. Carter's as good as dead."

"You mean… if you lose your Familiar, you die?" Sophia hushed her voice as the procession passed us by.

Imogen waited until the group was gone before she nodded solemnly. "Yep. It's how it works. You can't survive without your soul."

There was a lump in my throat that was hard to swallow. *Yeah. Except for me.*

"How… how long can you survive without your Familiar?" Sophia said, pulling Esis closer to her.

Imogen shrugged. "If you're older, a few weeks. Months, maybe. But students rarely last a few days. I'll be surprised if Carter makes it through the night. The bond is still too fresh. Nobody outlives their Familiar for long." Imogen shot a look at me. "Well, except for Liam."

"*What?!*" Sophia physically jumped into the air, and I cringed. "Liam's Familiar is dead?"

"Thanks for reminding me," I said sourly. That comment hurt. It felt like she'd slapped me or something.

Her jaw fell slack. "Liam, I…"

"You mean you didn't know?" Imogen's eyes went wide, and she gave an apologetic look toward me. "I'm sorry, Liam. I didn't mean—"

"It's okay, Imogen," I told her quietly.

"You lost your Familiar? I didn't know you'd bonded." Sophia's face is shocked, and in pain. "How?"

"I don't want to talk about it," I said immediately. I didn't want her to press. But she was Sophia, so she did anyway.

"But I—"

"I don't want to talk about it, Sophia." My tone was so harsh she physically recoiled away. I took a walk before she could ask more questions, and before I said something I would regret.

Carter died sometime in the night, as I knew he would. He wasn't strong enough to survive for long after Tiara died.

Lucky bastard.

The school was a little somber the next morning, but mostly normal. It wasn't unusual for students or Familiars to cork off around here. People died every year in the Elemental Cup, after all. Students were given resources on what to do if they were struggling, Carter and Tiara's funeral date was announced, and that was it.

I avoided Sophia. I couldn't face her now that she knew what was wrong with me. I caught her chasing after me a couple of times to apologize, but I managed to duck out and get away from her every time.

I knew the moment was coming where she'd be creeping outside the Toaqua dorm, waiting for me to come out. So I more or less held myself hostage in my room so she wouldn't be able to find me. I knew I could only run from her for so long. We had class together, after all.

That didn't mean I wanted to see her a moment before I was forced to. It hurt too much to face her.

When Ezra told me that Baine wanted to see me, I knew I had to leave my room. I hoped Sophia didn't bump into me on the way. But my brother looked worried. He wouldn't tell me what it was about when I pressed him. I strolled down to Baine's office, thinking that this was finally the moment where I'd be expelled and they were making my House Head tell me.

Baine was hunched over his desk, papers and books scattered everywhere. Little fairies, glowing bright with white light, zoomed around him and made chirping noises. He ignored them, face grim, as I weaved my way around the various trinkets and objects scattered around the room. A carved staff, a few totems, lots and lots of artifacts from his travels around the world were placed in every open spot available. Statues, paintings and scrolls were literally stacked against the walls in piles. Baine had been an explorer for the Hawkei before he became a teacher, venturing through ancient crypts and tombs for the Elders.

I had no idea why he gave up such a cool position just to grade papers for lazy college kids. Maybe, after all those years, he just gave up on whatever he was looking for.

By the ancestors, it was such a mess in here. Baine was a disgusting slob. No wonder he hadn't found a woman to put up with him.

"You wanted to see me?" I asked as I came to a stop at his desk. My shoe crunched a papyrus map and kicked a small golden sculpture. I hoped they weren't important.

"I wanted to warn you before your summons came," Baine started.

"Summons?"

"For the Elemental Cup."

My entire body turned cold. I think I literally shivered— even the fairy lights in the room seemed to dim. "Why would they be summoning me? I'm not competing."

"Yes, you are." I hoped this was some sort of sick joke, but Baine was completely serious. "The Elders have decided that despite your loss, you will be competing in the Cup anyway. It's the only way for you to prove your worth to the tribe. If you don't participate, you'll be exiled. You know what that means, Liam."

I was going to be sick. *This* was sick. I got that the Cup was some sort of coming-of-age ceremony for every Elementai, and that the Elders wanted everyone to compete.

But without Nashoma, I'd *die* out there. And probably get my teammates killed, too.

"I can't enter the Cup! I don't have a Familiar anymore! Nashoma's *gone*," I argued.

"I'm sorry, Liam. But the rules are absolute," Baine said firmly. "It doesn't matter that you lost Nashoma. All Elementai who've bonded with a Familiar over the previous year are required to enter the tournament in order to continue their education at Orenda Academy. That includes you. I'm sorry. You don't have a choice."

A pit of horror formed in my gut, growing larger with each passing second. It didn't matter that my Familiar was dead.

I was being forced to enter the tournament anyway.

sophia

TEN

Life at Orenda Academy was lonely, especially now that Liam was avoiding me, but Esis made everything better. He was my constant companion everywhere I went and cheered me up every time I felt like I was missing home. It was like he could feel my emotions and knew exactly how to make me happy. Usually, he just snuggled into my hair, but one night he actually fanned my hair out on my pillow and gave me the most amazing scalp massage. I didn't care what anyone said about my furry little bundle of joy; he was one of the most amazing, intelligent creatures I'd ever met.

But even Esis couldn't ease my anxiety when it came to dinner time. I stepped into the cafeteria with Esis on my shoulder, knowing I had nowhere to sit. The room was vast, with hundreds of tables situated in rows throughout the room and modern-day booths lining the outer wall. Near the main entrance sat a buffet line piled with some of the most delicious food I'd ever tasted. On the opposite side of the main doors were heating trays with foil-wrapped burgers and wraps that people could take back to their dorms.

The cafeteria was bathed in natural brown tones, with soft lighting that made it look like a fancy restaurant. Along the far wall, a huge mural depicted each House's element from left to right. The orange Koigni fire faded into green trees for Nivita, which swirled into purple wisps for Yapluma and finally blue waves for Toaqua. I'd noticed that there seemed to be an unwritten rule about sitting closest to your element in the mural, with Koigni always sitting toward the left of the room, Toaqua on the right, and Nivita and Yapluma in the middle.

As I stepped into the buffet line I eyed the Koigni section, knowing that if I was going to stay in the cafeteria for dinner, I'd probably have to sit over there. The room was packed with people and their Familiars and buzzed with conversation. I didn't notice a single empty table in the Koigni section. I contemplated whether I should introduce myself to someone or just claim one of the empty tables in another section. It was like I was in middle school all over again.

I made it through the buffet line and stared out at the crowd. I decided to take the easy route and just sit at an empty table when a guy passed by me and his elbow knocked into my shoulder. My tray jumped in my hands, and my plate went flying. The ceramic clattered to the floor, and my potatoes and gravy went everywhere.

"Watch where you're going," the guy snarled before continuing on his way to the Koigni section.

Of course he's Koigni, I thought as I bent to clean up the mess.

Esis jumped down from my shoulder and began licking at the mashed potatoes on the floor.

"Ew, Esis. Don't do that," I scolded, pulling him away from the potatoes. He already had most of them cleaned up.

"Here you go." A pair of hands shot out in front of my face, offering me a pile of napkins.

I glanced up to see Imogen dressed in a floral dress that suited her figure but had *way* too many ruffles on it. Her hoop earrings nearly touched her shoulders, and her hair had been twisted into three separate braids. Her heels were shiny blue like metallic nail polish, with four-inch heels whose points split into three different directions in the shape of bird talons. They looked like something from one of those runway shows where the models wear the most ridiculous things but the outfits never hit the market.

"Thanks," I said shyly, taking the napkins from her.

Imogen gestured to Sassy in the tote bag that hung from her shoulder. "Sassy and I were just going to sit down. Do you want to join us?"

"Sure," I answered far too quickly while I mopped up my spilled food.

"Excellent." Imogen clapped her hands together. "We sit over there, in that booth."

She pointed to a large booth in the corner of the room. Toaqua occupied the tables surrounding it, but Imogen didn't seem to notice.

I stood with my pile of dirty napkins piled atop my tray. "I'll join you in the buffet line. I need a new plate, anyway."

Several minutes later, we slid into our booth in the corner. I sat across from Imogen and faced the wall. I felt more comfortable not being able to see the eyes I knew were on me. Esis jumped down from my shoulder and sat beside me. He placed his little hands on the edge of the table, but he could barely see over the top of it. I was going to need to get this little guy a booster seat.

"How are you liking Orenda Academy so far?" Imogen asked.

"Oh…" I glanced down, completely taken off guard by the question. "It's, um, okay."

"Oh, right," she said wrinkling her nose. "You're Koigni. You probably have Doya. The professors make all the difference. I'm really bummed I didn't get the guy I wanted for my cultures studies class. He's a total dreamboat… I mean, for an old guy."

I just nodded along.

"How many classes are you taking?" she asked.

"Not many," I answered. "I'm only taking the minimum amount of credits, which I guess is good because I'm going to need the extra time to practice my Fire."

"I know what you mean," she agreed. "Beginner Nivita Magic is already kicking my butt. And I have it almost every day of the week."

"Me, too," I said. "Beginner Koigni Magic takes up most of my schedule, then I'm in Medical Care of Familiars a few days a week. I have my first Dragonology class tomorrow."

"Ooh!" Imogen said in excitement. "I'm in Dragonology, too!"

I smiled. It'd be nice to know someone in each of my classes.

"So, what's the dealio?" Imogen asked, discretely dropping a piece of meat to the floor, which Sassy promptly followed and scarfed up. "Is that all you're going to eat?"

I glanced down at my meat and potatoes. "Are you kidding? This looks delicious."

"Sure, if you're bored of traditional Hawkei food," she agreed. "But you aren't even taste-testing half of what they have at the buffet. Are you going to get adventurous, or what?"

I tucked a strand of hair behind my ear. "I tend to play things safe."

"Ah," Imogen said in understanding as she took a bite of food. "Well, not today, girlie. Here, try a bean."

Imogen pushed a long purple bean pod onto my plate. It was slathered in some sort of oil and spices and didn't look appetizing in the slightest.

"What is it?" I asked, unable to keep the skepticism out of my voice.

Imogen shrugged. "We call them magic beans. The ancestors blessed them ages ago, and they prospered in this area. They're like a green bean."

I poked the bean with my fork and held it up to examine it. "But it's purple."

"So? Purple vegetables are delicious," Imogen said. "Beets, eggplant, carrots…"

"Um… carrots are orange."

Imogen shook her head. "Carrots weren't orange until the 17th century. Now, eat up."

Trusting her judgement, I put the bean to my mouth and bit into it. To my surprise, it was juicy and delicious, like the best green bean I'd ever tasted.

"Good, right?" Imogen asked with raised eyebrows as she dropped another piece of meat on the floor for Sassy.

"Delicious," I agreed. "But… are you supposed to be doing that?"

I glanced around the dining hall and couldn't help but notice that Imogen was the only person feeding her Familiar regular food. Other Familiars just sat there watching people eat.

Imogen lowered her voice. "Not really, but you won't tell, will you? Sassy's a fussy eater."

I shook my head. "I won't tell."

"What about him?" She cocked her head toward Esis. "What does he eat?"

"I don't know," I admitted. "I talked to this guy at the Familiar nutrition center, but he didn't know anything about Esis' diet. He suggested he might like bugs, but when I tried to go digging for worms, Esis turned up his nose at them. The only thing I've gotten him to eat so far is burgers from the takeout line."

Esis was barely the size of my head, but I swore he ate more than I did. I was pretty sure there was a black hole in the pit of his stomach somewhere. The trashcan full of wrappers in my dorm room was proof of his appetite. I wasn't sure where all the food went. I was just grateful I didn't have to pay for it and that all our food was sponsored by the school.

"As long as he doesn't starve, that's all that counts, right?" Imogen said.

I smiled. I could really get used to Imogen's positive attitude.

After that night dining with Imogen, I didn't have to sit alone in the dining hall anymore. Imogen was there every night, and she always stood and waved me over as soon as I filled my tray. At first I thought it was strange, like she was trying to draw attention to herself, but I'd come to realize that was just part of Imogen's over-the-top personality. She honestly didn't even notice the attention.

Strangely, I felt comfortable in her presence. It was easier to ignore the eyes on us with her around.

Three weeks passed, and Liam had managed to avoid me the entire time. He'd skipped out on our Medical Care class the first week following the tar pit incident. When he returned the next week and Professor Costas instructed us to pair up, he didn't even look at me. He headed straight for his lumberjack friend, Jonah. I got stuck with a first-year Toaqua who wouldn't even look me in the eye.

But, thanks to Liam, I was actually making progress with my Fire. I sat on the rocks next to the river almost every night practicing conjuring and manipulating flames. Esis perched on a rock beside me. He clapped and trilled as if he were my own personal cheerleader. I hoped that with enough practice, Madame Doya would stop looking down her nose at me in Fire class. So far, no such luck.

"It's just a piece of wood!" Doya shouted in class one day. "I'm not asking you to set the entire forest on fire!"

The class stood in a line facing the room's massive fireplace. A small log atop a cast-iron firewood grate five feet in front of each person. We were each to light our log on fire from a distance. Madame Doya paced down the line of students, analyzing each of us as she went. Naomi prowled behind the logs, watching for any signs of flame.

I laser-focused my attention on the log in front of me. I did as Liam had instructed and focused on pulling my anger to the surface. I didn't like that I was angry all the time these days. I'd grown up learning how to control my emotions, but I had to throw all that out the window if I was to survive at this school.

"It's embarrassing you're trying so hard, Hudson," Doya scolded the guy next to me. "This should be simple for you."

I couldn't help it when my gaze flickered from my log. Hudson looked like he was suffering from a hernia. Poor guy.

"Stand straight, Tabitha," Doya yelled to a girl at the other end of the room. "Conjuring fire takes confidence."

Just as she said it, Haley's log burst into flame. Haley squealed in excitement and high-fived Kelsey beside her. The phoenix on her shoulder ruffled its feathers in delight. Haley's eyes caught mine on hers, and her face instantly fell. She glanced to my log and smirked.

Tiny little hands grabbed my ear. Esis tugged on me until I finally tore my gaze off Haley. He made three quick noises and pointed to my log. He settled back into his spot on my shoulder and wrapped my hair around his body. It was hard to find my anger when he was a constant comfort.

The smell of burning wood filled the air as two other logs lit up in flames. Beside me, the bark on Miranda's log was slowly shriveling as embers burnt the delicate outer layer.

"Sophia!" Madame Doya's harsh voice called.

There it was, that noise that was sure to get my blood boiling. I could already feel my skin heating.

"Yes?" I asked, trying to sound cool and collected. I didn't want to give her anything else to yell at me about.

Madame Doya held her nose high as she made her way over to me. "We don't have all day. You're bonded now, which means your powers should be easier to access. I expected your log to light long before any of your classmates'."

"Yes, Madame Doya," I said through gritted teeth. "I'm doing my best."

"Then why, dare I ask, is your log not on fire yet?"

My teeth gritted as I focused on my log. I *was* going to light this bitch on fire if she didn't stop pestering me. Nothing was ever good enough for her. Madame Doya stood there, observing. I could feel her eyes on me as all the tiny little hairs on the back of my neck stood up. Naomi stopped behind my log. She gave it a good sniff before turning her face down in dissatisfaction. She was almost as bad as Doya.

I felt my magic rise within me, but I didn't know how to direct it across the space between me and my log. Still, I tried. I pictured my magic flowing through the hardwood floor, because I thought it'd be easier than air to go through.

The smell of burning hair filled my nose. A second later, Naomi leapt backward. I just barely caught sight of the patch of singed fur on her paw before she burst into flame. Literally.

Esis buried his face in my hair, and I stumbled backward, completely shocked. The back of my knees hit into one of the couches, and I fell onto it. My eyes widened. Every inch of Naomi's fur lit up with orange flames. I could still make out the shape of her face through the fire, but the blonde fur was nowhere to be seen, as if the fire had replaced it all.

Holy guacamole! Had I lit Naomi on fire? I didn't mean to!

Except… Naomi didn't scream. She didn't back away in pain. It was like the flame engulfing her body didn't hurt her at all. Instead, she stood rigid, her flaming eyes fixed on me.

"I'm sorry!" I cried. "I— I didn't mean to."

The whole class watched as Madame Doya stepped forward and placed a calm hand on Naomi's flaming body. "Calm down, Naomi."

Naomi's ragged breathing slowed, and the flames died down. Her blonde fur returned, untouched, but she never took her eyes off me. I was frozen in shock, though my heart hammered. What had just happened?

Madame Doya whirled toward me, her lips tight. "We do not harm other people's Familiars, Sophia."

Except that Doya looked like she was two seconds from ripping Esis off my shoulder and snapping his neck in revenge. I held him closer to me, just in case she decided to try anything.

"I'm sorry," I repeated, stumbling over my words. "I don't know what happened."

"I think it's obvious," Madame Doya raged. "You burnt Naomi's paw."

I did what?

"So… those flames… I didn't do that?" I asked slowly.

Madame Doya furrowed her brow. Then, realization dawned. "You can't even light a simple piece of wood on fire. Naomi is a fire lion. It takes much more power than you're capable of to engulf a creature like her."

I stared at Naomi just so I wouldn't have to look Doya in the eye. Naomi's gaze was almost as equally terrifying. When my eyes jumped to the other side of the room, I saw that Haley was standing with her arms folded over her chest, a look of amusement on her face. I should've burnt her instead.

Madame Doya turned to the other students. "We'll pick up here later this week. I expect everyone to be able to accomplish this task by the end of class on Thursday. Class dismissed."

Everyone scrambled across the room to grab their things and hurry out the door. I was still shaking in shock, though Esis tried to comfort me by rubbing his fluffy belly against the skin on my neck. It helped a bit, but I wasn't about to waste any more time. I wouldn't be left alone in this room with Doya.

I hurried to my feet and grabbed my bag at my desk. I filed out of the room with everyone else. In the wide hallway, I felt like I could finally breathe. Students broke off in both directions. Some headed to the cafeteria, others to their next class, and some back to the Koigni dorms.

I tried to stay away from the dorms as often as I could. The Koigni common room wasn't a welcoming place, and when I tried to find some peace and quiet in my own room, there was usually someone giggling in the hall while the scent of smoke wafted from under the crack in my door. They thought they were hilarious. I thought they were idiots.

I quickened my pace toward the doors at the end of the hall, but I stopped dead in my tracks when I caught sight of a man with dark hair and a strong build.

Liam.

He leaned against the big stone lip that outlined one of the tall castle windows. He was surrounded by a group of five other people. A large, multi-colored bird that fluttered around like a hummingbird hovered above one girl's head. A guy almost as big as Jonah was petting the ears of a stag that appeared like it crawled straight from Mother Earth's lair. It had forest green fur, with twisted antlers that looked like bark-covered tree branches sticking out of its head. I wasn't great at spotting the differences between Houses yet, but judging by the guy's size and his Familiar, he was definitely Nivita.

Liam faced away from me, but I could tell by the way his shoulders shook that he was laughing at something the Nivita guy said. Of course. Because he only acted like he had a stick up his ass when he was around me.

He didn't notice me. Now would be a perfect time to finally catch him and apologize. My feet started moving in his direction before I even decided to approach him.

I cleared my throat. "Liam?"

No way was he escaping on me this time. I totally had him cornered.

Liam turned around... only it wasn't Liam. I mean, he *looked* like Liam. He had the same muscular build, same long black hair and dark skin. He even had the same eyes. But the shape of his nose and his jawline were off by just a hair.

Liam Clone smiled at me. Inside, I was screaming in embarrassment. Instinct told me to flee, but before I could, Liam Clone spoke.

"Sorry to disappoint you." He smirked.

I took a step back. "I'm *so* sorry."

He shrugged. "Hey, it's okay. I can pretend to be Liam if you'd like." Liam Clone stood straighter. His eyebrows tightened, and the corners of his lips turned down as he deepened his voice. "I'm Liam Mitoh. I swear by the ancestors that I will sulk around until the day I die."

I totally lost it. His voice was spot-on, and he looked *exactly* like Liam when he scrunched his face up like that. I could almost believe I was looking right at him. Liam Clone's face relaxed, and he laughed along with me.

"That was a *really* good impression," I said, giggling.

"I would hope so," he replied. "I've had a lot of practice imitating my brother. It gets on his nerves."

"You're Liam's brother?" I shouldn't have been shocked. I mean, the guys were practically identical twins.

"Yep. Ezra," he introduced, sticking his hand out.

I shook it. "Sophia."

"Ah." He nodded his head in recognition. "*You're* the pain in his ass."

Esis drew in a breath of surprise. He didn't take well to crude language.

My shoulders slumped involuntarily. "He calls me that?"

"Not directly," Ezra said with a roll of his eyes, like it was just a joke.

Still, the statement bothered me. What if Liam hated me? I mean, it explained why he'd been avoiding me. I wasn't sure what I'd done wrong besides mention his Familiar, and I'd been trying for three weeks to apologize for it. Was it really that bad?

"Hey," Ezra said softly. The laughter in his voice had vanished. "I didn't mean it like that. I just—"

"Ezra," the Nivita guy interrupted. Ezra looked at him. "We've got to head to class, but we'll catch you later, okay?"

"Yeah, no problem." Ezra waved as his friends headed down the hall.

He turned back to me, but I knew he was just going to say something about his brother. I didn't want to talk about Liam, so I spoke before Ezra could.

"That guy with the stag is Nivita, isn't he?" I asked.

"Yeah," Ezra confirmed with a shrug.

"I thought people from different Houses weren't supposed to be friends." I'd been sure that was one of the reasons people stared at Imogen and me so much at dinner.

"Where'd you hear that?" he asked. "My brother?"

I nodded, though Haley had mentioned it, too.

"Don't listen to him," Ezra said. "He takes things like that way too seriously. He makes a bigger deal out of most things than they are."

"Oh," I said flatly. Liam sure sounded serious about… everything.

Ezra's gaze traveled past me, and his eyes lit up. "Speak of the devil…"

I turned around to see Liam— the real Liam— headed down the hall toward us. He took one look at me and whirled around in the opposite direction. He wasn't even sneaky about it. It was obvious he saw me.

"What's up with him?" Ezra thought aloud.

"He's mad at me," I admitted in a small voice. "He avoids me every chance he gets."

Ezra looked amused. "My brother can be a real… *eh-hem*… sometimes. Come on. He's not getting away this time."

Ezra jogged forward, calling out Liam's name. Liam quickened his pace but didn't look back, pretending as if he hadn't heard him. I followed quickly behind. Ezra reached Liam and draped an arm around his shoulder.

"Hey, brother," Ezra said casually just as I caught up with them.

"Hey," Liam replied without emotion.

"Sophia tells me you've been acting like a dick lately."

"I did not!" I objected.

"Yeah, well, it's true, isn't it?" Ezra glanced between both of us, grinning.

Liam stopped walking and stood rigid. He still hadn't looked at me. "Maybe you should mind your own business, Ezra."

"Maybe *you* should learn some manners," his brother bit back. "Sophia said she's been trying to apologize, and you've been avoiding her. The least you can do is let her say what she wants to say, and then the two of you can go your separate ways."

Liam's nostrils flared. He and Ezra stood eye-to-eye, staring at each other. "Fine."

Liam looked down at me expectantly. It suddenly occurred to me that I had no idea what I wanted to say to him. I just knew I had to say *something* or I'd never get the chance.

I swallowed. "I'm sorry."

"Is that it?" Liam asked with raised eyebrows. He turned to leave.

"No," I said quickly, stopping him. "I'm sorry I freaked out about your Familiar. I know it really has to hurt, and I get why you're upset. My reaction was uncalled for. I hope we can still be friends… if you're okay with that."

Liam's features hardened when I said the word *friends*. I wasn't sure if he'd ever considered us friends. The realization broke my heart. I waited for him to actually admit it out loud, but before he could say anything, a voice cut through the silence.

"Liam. Sophia. Just the two people I was looking for."

A man with messy gray hair and salt-and-pepper stubble approached us. His eyes were young and free of wrinkles, though they looked tired. I guessed he was around my parents' age, despite the premature graying of his hair. The man wore khakis and a baby blue button-down shirt tucked into his slacks. He had one of the sweetest, caring smiles I'd ever seen. He seemed like the kind of person who was always under constant stress but told the best dad jokes.

I immediately noticed Imogen and Jonah following behind him. Jonah's hippogriff glanced up at a small dragon statue and almost tripped over her own feet.

"What is it, Baine?" Liam suddenly seemed less annoyed.

Baine. Where had I heard that name before? I quickly recalled that he was the one who sent the peryton for Liam and me to get to school.

"We were headed to lunch," Baine said, gesturing to Jonah and Imogen beside him. "Would you like to join us?"

"He says he has great news!" Imogen bounced on her toes. Sassy peeked out from the bag hanging from Imogen's shoulder.

"What kind of news?" I asked curiously.

"We can talk about that once we get our food," Baine said kindly.

"I'm not hungry," Liam declined.

Baine shot him a look I didn't quite understand. "You should come along anyway. How about you, Ezra? Are you hungry?"

"Nah," Ezra replied. "Thanks for the invite, but I'm actually going to be late for History of the Hawkei as it is. I'll catch up with you later."

Ezra strolled away casually, walking in a cocky manner with his head thrown back. As he walked down the hallway, about ten different people from all Houses waved or acknowledged him in some way. It was clear Ezra was the golden boy— the Academy's most popular student. He had this air around him that was hard to resist. It didn't matter what House you were from, it was obvious people loved him and wanted to be around him.

Unlike his brother. He and Liam were totally different.

He said he was going to History. Why wasn't I enrolled in that class? I was sure it'd be helpful. The library didn't exactly have many published books on the Hawkei. I'd tried looking for them and didn't find any.

"Shall we go?" Baine suggested, like he wasn't giving Liam a choice. We followed behind him.

"So, what do you think of Baine?" Imogen whispered to me from several paces back.

I shrugged. "I don't know."

"He's hot, right?" She wiggled her eyebrows.

My eyes darted to the back of Baine's head. "*He's* the professor you think is hot?"

Imogen blushed.

"Ew, Imogen. He's like… fifty."

Imogen grinned. "Yeah, fifty shades of sexy."

I almost gagged. "If you're into the disheveled look…"

"He's not disheveled," Imogen argued. "He's… sophisticated."

"When you said an older guy, I thought you meant in his thirties. Not old enough to be *your father!*"

Imogen smirked. "All I'm saying is that if I needed to sleep with someone to boost my grade, I would—"

"Dear Lord," I cut her off as we reached the cafeteria. "Please don't finish that sentence."

Imogen just shrugged and hurried into the line.

Baine suggested we eat outside, so we all grabbed premade wraps from the takeout line. These weren't like the usual wraps I ate back home. They were made with a fried flatbread and filled with beef, beans, corn, and a delicious seasoning that was the perfect blend of sweet and spicy. I wasn't sure if the cooks at Orenda used magic in the food here, but sometimes, I wondered. It even beat my dad's cooking, and he was the best cook I knew.

I pushed the thought away. I couldn't bear to think about my parents. I missed them too much.

"What's wrong?" Imogen asked. "You don't like the wraps?"

"They're great," I replied, glancing down at the wraps in my hand, one for me and one for Esis.

Baine led us outside to a grassy hill with a clear view of the ocean through the trees. A pleasant breeze passed through my hair as I sat. I handed Esis his wrap, and he jumped down from my shoulder. He pulled the plastic wrap off and gobbled his food down before I'd even bitten into mine. I giggled at him as he snuggled into my lap.

"So, what's the news?" Imogen asked eagerly as she plopped down in the grass beside me.

Sassy rolled around in front of her. Imogen pulled a plastic container from her bag, and I nearly gagged when she opened it. The thing was stuffed to the brim with fluffy white carcasses. She pulled out a dead mouse by the tail and tossed it into the air. Sassy caught it in her mouth before it hit the ground. On the other side of Baine, where Jonah and Liam sat, Squeaks gave a jealous squawk.

"I'm sorry," Imogen said gently to the hippogriff. She turned to Jonah. "Do you mind?"

Jonah answered with a full mouth. "Go ahead."

Imogen tossed another mouse into the air. Squeaks swallowed it in one gulp.

"Ew, Jonah," I complained. "Can you not chew with your mouth open?"

"Sophia hates it," Imogen said with a teasing smile. She knew I couldn't stand the guy who usually sat two tables away from us and always chewed like his parents had never taught him proper table manners.

Jonah took another huge bite and chewed loudly, taking extra care to keep his mouth open as much as possible, like he didn't care in the slightest. A smirk touched the corner of his lips.

Liam scowled at Jonah's gross display. Imogen just giggled.

Baine leaned back on one hand. "It's nice spending time with friends, isn't it?"

"Get to the point, Baine," Liam groaned. He hadn't taken a single bite.

Baine sighed. "I was getting there. You do consider each other friends, don't you?"

"Of course!" Imogen said, before Liam could deny it.

He would've. I just knew it.

"Good," Baine said with a nod of his head. "Because the four of you will be spending a lot of time together. I've requested you be placed on the same team for the Elemental Cup. I will serve as your mentor."

"What?" Liam exploded, shooting to his feet. "This is bullshit! First I'm forced to participate. Now I'm placed on the reject team?"

Esis' ears perked up. He didn't like that comment. Neither did I.

Jonah rose to his feet beside Liam. "Calm down, dude. I understand that you're feeling—"

"You don't understand shit," Liam snapped. "At least you have Squeaks. You might actually survive out there with her. For me, this is a death sentence."

"There's a reason I put you four on a team together," Baine said calmly. "I'm aware of what happened at the tar pit. Based on what I heard, you four worked together well. No one's going to let you die in the tournament, Liam."

"Yeah," Imogen agreed. "We won't leave you behind."

"That doesn't matter," Liam growled. "I still don't have a chance."

"You do," Baine countered. "Do you know what the leading cause of injury during the tournament is?"

Liam's jaw tightened, but he didn't answer.

"Death and injury occur when teams don't work together," Baine explained. "Accidents occur when there are disagreements, when a team member runs off thinking they can get through an obstacle alone, or when someone tries to show off their strength instead of working together. If you let your team members help you, they won't let you down."

Liam's hands clenched into fists. "I'm not sure I can believe that."

The look Liam shot me was like a knife through the heart. My chest compressed. He had to know I would do everything I could to help one of my teammates.

The thing was, I didn't think it was that he didn't trust me. He didn't think I was capable.

"Liam's right." My voice barely broke through the lump in my throat. "This isn't a good team. We'll never work together."

It killed me to say those words. I didn't even realize how true they were until they came out of my mouth.

"I'm sorry," Baine said regretfully. "I didn't realize you felt that way about each other. But there's no changing teams now. You're stuck with this team until the Elemental Ball."

"There's a *ball*?" I asked. Lovely. Because a dance was *just* what I needed when the one guy I might've said yes to hated my guts.

"Yes," Baine replied. "It takes place following the tournament. It's a celebration to present the participants as full members of the tribe."

"Please," Liam scoffed. "It's a party to celebrate the winners. We all know that."

Jonah frowned. "We have no chance of winning with that kind of attitude."

"Who said I wanted to win?" Liam asked.

I couldn't help but feel that Liam had a point. I just wanted to survive. My jaw clenched as my anger once again surfaced.

"You're all capable of winning," Baine assured him. "But you'll have to set your differences aside. You must choose to work together."

"Why? What's the point?" Liam snapped.

"I agree." I couldn't believe I'd said the words until they escaped my mouth. As soon as I started, I couldn't shut them off. "I was *forced* to come here. I left my family and my entire life behind. Now I'm told I have to team up with the guy who dragged me here if I want to live?"

This was bull. All of it. I just wanted to go home. I wanted to see my family again. I didn't even care about Amelia's teasing or Dad's stinky socks. I missed Mom's hugs and Dad's deep belly laugh. I missed driving into the city to shop at the mall all day with my friends. I missed my own bed and all the memories I left behind.

The only good thing about Orenda was Esis… and maybe Imogen. I'd thought there was more to Liam, too, but now I wasn't sure.

Baine looked completely dumbstruck. I'd surprised everyone with my outburst.

"The Elemental Cup tests and secures your bond with your Familiar," Baine said slowly. "It also tests your ability to work with other Elementai and determines your place in society. It's my understanding that you're here for a reason, Sophia. That reason being the very thing you left behind."

My parents.

I knew exactly what he was saying. If I didn't play my part, I'd no longer be able to protect my family. I recalled how Amelia said my parents' Familiars could be killed for my parents' crimes. If what Imogen told me was true, that Elementai didn't live long without their Familiars, my parents were as good as dead. I'd never let that happen.

I had only one choice. Suck it up, work with Liam, and make sure he doesn't quit on us.

Liam whirled around and started back toward the castle. I scooped up Esis in my arms and instantly chased after him. I didn't look back to see if anyone else was following.

"Liam, wait!" I called.

Liam stopped abruptly and spun to face me. "I just want to be alone right now."

He pierced me with his dark eyes. Though his eyebrows were tight, there was a softness in his eyes when he looked at me. My gaze flickered to his lips. I had the sudden urge to brush my lips against his, to take away his pain and make everything better.

What am I thinking? Liam would never kiss me. He hates me.

"You want to survive, don't you?" I blurted.

Liam hesitated. "Yeah, I guess so."

"So do I. Whether we like it or not, we need each other. Can't we just try to get along?"

When he didn't say anything, I added. "For Imogen and Jonah's sake."

Liam's features softened. "If we have any chance of making it through that tournament, there's something we need to do first."

My curiosity piqued. "What's that?"

Liam sighed and glanced around, like he didn't want to talk about it out in the open. "Meet me by the fountain next to the greenhouses tomorrow at dusk. We can talk then."

Liam

ELEVEN

I headed down to the fountain the minute the sun was starting to cast the earth in a warm autumn glow. Ezra cried out something when I left the Toaqua dorms, but I ignored him. This was important. I couldn't be distracted right now from what I was trying to tell Sophia.

She was about to get a huge wake-up call.

When I saw her, I paused for a moment to observe. She was working on homework, crouched over a pile of papers that was sitting on an open textbook on her lap. She sat on the ground with a muddled expression I couldn't decipher, the fountain towering over her and looking like it was about to attack. Esis was on her shoulder, peering at her homework like he was reading it, too.

I noticed something strange. Sophia kept switching her pen from one hand to another, writing with both, chewing on her bottom lip like she couldn't grasp what the book was trying to tell her.

"Can't decide which hand to write with?" I asked as I approached. She looked up and grimaced a bit when she saw me. She obviously was in a mood. Esis, though, peeped and grinned like he'd never been more ecstatic to see me. Weirdo.

"I'm ambidextrous," Sophia said. "I play with my hands when I get agitated."

Hm. She could use both hands equally. Dad once told me that was a sign of a strong Elementai. Maybe she *was* someone I needed to watch out for, and not someone who was weak. "Why are you anxious?"

"It's just… this work. I don't get it." Sophia huffed a stray strand that had fallen out of her ponytail away from her eyes. "The Elementai world is confusing, but Koigni magic is the most frustrating of all. There's no rhyme or reason to it."

"What do you mean?"

"For me, everything has to be even. Symmetrical," Sophia explained. "I don't like when things are out of order, and Koigni magic, it's all feeling. Chaos isn't my thing. I can't handle it."

I didn't say anything. Even after my help, Sophia was still struggling. She wanted perfection and organization. But fire was rampage and chaos. Sophia kept suppressing the part of herself that she was most— probably on account of being taught to suppress it by Toaqua parents, whether she knew it or not.

She'd been raised like a Water child, and she clearly wasn't. You couldn't put a square peg in a round hole. At some point or another, she was going to have to embrace who she was.

Maybe she would, after today.

"Come with me," I said. I jerked my head in the direction of the forest. Sophia slammed her book and threw it in her bag. She went to fling it over her shoulders, but I shook my head.

"Leave it," I told her. "It'll be here when you get back."

"You've still got your bag," she countered.

"It's got things we need," I insisted. "Just do as I ask."

She did. I turned into the forest with my hands in my pockets, and she followed, Esis wrapped tightly in her arms.

We walked for about ten minutes before we came to the base of a mountain. It towered above us like a proud warrior who refused to move in spite of outstanding odds against it. A range of smaller mountains dotted the area around it and spanned along the seashore, but the one in front of us was the most prominent. It was craggy and spiked, and a thin dirt path wound its way up to the summit. The very top had snow dotted upon it, but we wouldn't go that far.

She looked at me. "Up?"

"Up," I responded. "It's a mile climb. There's a well-worn path. You can make it," I told her.

"Shut up. I go hiking all the time. I know I can make it," she muttered under her breath.

I laughed under my breath before I took the lead. I was feeling well today, so I'd picked tonight to make this hike. There was no guarantee that I'd be able to tomorrow, and this couldn't wait. Sophia needed to know.

I was out of breath pretty quickly, but I continued to put one foot in front of the other as we ascended the rocky slope. It was slow going, and we were silent. Sophia kept looking at me like she was concerned, and I hated it.

I stumbled for a moment. She reached out to catch me with the hand that wasn't holding Esis, but I shoved it away.

"I've done this a million times. I don't need your help," I grumbled.

She scowled. "You're sick, aren't you?"

"Define *sick*." God, she made it sound like I needed to be on bedrest. The nerve of this woman.

She tilted her head. "What's wrong with you?"

A part of me jerked inside, and I said, "No one knows."

She was looking at me in a way that physically hurt. I didn't want her stupid pity. I was just as normal as she was. Just had a broken body.

I wanted her to see me that way, too. But I felt like that was wishing for the moon.

When we finally reached the top, an inner peace washed over me and I was able to breathe normally again. This was my favorite view, hands down. The mountaintop looked down upon the entire forest and all of Orenda Academy. The castle was far below. From here you could see the masses of magical creatures flying around it. The summit we'd reached was a relatively flat space, a decently sized area of a few hundred feet that was encapsulated in a circle. The ground was nothing but dirt and rock, with a few remnants of wooden bowls filled with incense people had brought up here. The sky had turned to a burning orange now, streaked with lines of red and purple. It cast the mountainside in a bright glow of warm, muddled colors mixed with elongating shadows.

At the center of the circle was a large totem pole. It had the symbols of each of the Houses,

Fire, Air, Water, and Earth stacked upon each other, with Nivita on the bottom as a growing leaf, Toaqua depicted as a rushing wave within a water droplet, Yapluma as a gust of wind, and Koigni symbolized by a singular flame.

Koigni was only topped by one other totem. Anichi… the Soul House. Anichi was commemorated with a complicated swirling design, meant to symbolize the spirit.

Sophia stared at the Anichi symbol like she didn't know what it meant. She was going to hear the whole sad story today. Esis hopped out of her arms and skittered around the totem pole, looking up at the Anichi totem with an unhappy expression.

It was lonely up here. And quiet. I put my bag on the ground and turned to face her.

"What is this? Why did you bring me here?" she asked.

"Sit down, Sophia." I gestured to the dirt below the totem.

"What, on the ground?" She gave me a skeptical look.

"Yes, Sophia." I gave her a hard look. "Today would be nice."

She sat. I took out a tiny placemat that I made in Basket Weaving (yes, I was proud of it, thank you) and set it on the ground before I placed another group of items upon it. A stick of sage, a leather pouch mixed with various incenses, a small leather drum, and silver bells on a wristlet. Lastly was a wooden smudging wand, with eagle feathers splayed out in a fan across the top and small designs carved into the wood. The wand was old, and had been made with the feathers of my grandfather's Familiar. It'd been a present from my dad when I turned eighteen.

Usually this type of thing would require more people. There'd be dances, multiple chanters, and songs that would go on for days. Elementai would be wearing ceremonial outfits, not jeans and t-shirts. People didn't just up and summon the ancestors on a whim— and definitely not on a Tuesday.

I could get in trouble for this. But this was my birthright. It was something that I wasn't going to let be taken away from me.

Sophia stared at me. Esis had left the totem to crawl into her lap. I sat on the ground and let my wrists hang off my knees.

"The first thing you need to understand is that there weren't four original Houses," I said. "There used to be five."

"What?" Sophia reeled back. "How? What happened to the fifth House?"

"Let me start from the beginning." I cleared my throat. "Hundreds of years ago, the Hawkei had no power. They were just normal human beings, a tribe of people who sought to live in peace like anyone else. And, for a long time, they did."

My tone turned dark. "Then the colonizers came. They brought all kinds of diseases our bodies couldn't fight off. They hunted down our food and stole our land. They hated us for our brown skin and customs that they considered strange. At first, we thought coexistence was possible, but more and more settlers kept coming, and they didn't want peace. They wanted us gone. There weren't enough of us to fight back. A war meant certain extermination. We were dying."

Sophia looked down at the ground. Her expression was sad, and a little muddled.

"Our shamans pleaded with the ancestors to save us from our fate. Suddenly, the skies opened, and from them flooded a dazzling array of magical creatures, hundreds of them in number. When they reached the ground our spirits fled out of our bodies and attached themselves to the creatures. Once the bond was set, we found we could control the elements— Earth, Water, Air, Fire, and Soul."

Sophia's eyes were as wide as Esis' now. The little guy perched on Sophia's arm, his ears up and listening intently.

"Though we had our creatures to defend us now, and our magic, we still knew we needed to hide. So we walked until we found a special place of seclusion, a world that was so far removed the colonizers didn't dare venture through it. The forests and mountains surrounding it were filled with deadly animals, thick tar pits, and treacherous mountains. The weather was harsh and changed constantly. There was no gold and little room for farming. The strangers didn't want it. The land was dangerous, but we would make it work. We had our magic now, and we had our Familiars."

"Then what happened?" Sophia was immersed in the story. Esis' little tail waggled, and I smiled slightly.

"We knew we had to diversify to survive. You've noticed that there are a variety of races within the school. The Elders believed the more footholds we had in cultures around the globe, the better chance we had if the colonizers found us again. Nivita and Yapluma went to places like Africa, South America and Asia to find partners and bring them back here. At first, it was for diplomatic reasons, but then people started falling in love. Koigni worked on mating with influential and rich Europeans to gain power. Toaqua is the most traditional House, so we stayed behind to manage the tribe… which is why I look like me and you look like you." I grinned at her.

"I always wondered about that." She cuddled Esis. "Sometimes I don't think I've got any Hawkei in me, because I can't see any traits."

"Don't believe that. You've got Hawkei blood in your veins just as much as I do," I told her. "If you didn't, you wouldn't be able to summon fire. You wouldn't have been able to bond with Esis."

Sophia stroked Esis' head, and I continued. "Arthur Cedrick was a settler from Europe, but he wasn't like the others. He was a friend to the Hawkei. He'd been outcasted from his family and from his town because he preached that the Hawkei and the settlers needed to live in peace. When he had nowhere else to go, the tribe took him in. He used his large family fortune to build a castle here, to remind him of those that he missed growing up in Scotland. He had no known heirs and offered the castle as a gift to the Hawkei before he passed away. The Elders used it to create Orenda Academy, a place where Elementai could come to learn how to use their magic. The castle had been specially designed by Arthur's daughter, Anna, who wanted the estate to go to the Hawkei and crafted it specifically for use of our powers."

"I thought you said Arthur had no known heirs? How could he have a daughter?" Sophia asked.

"Anna died before Arthur. She had some sort of disease. Her illness was so strong not even the Anichi could heal her, only prolong her life for a time," I explained. "Arthur was so grateful for extending her life that he left us everything he had."

"So Anichi could heal?" Sophia asked.

"Anichi was the strongest House. They had control of the spirit, of healing," I told her. "They ruled each of the five Houses equally. They had the power to heal Anna, at least for a time."

"If they were the strongest House, how come they aren't here anymore?" Her eyebrows knitted together in confusion.

"Something horrible happened. Koigni… destroyed them." I closed my eyes and shook my head. "Koigni was jealous of the power that Anichi had and wanted it for themselves."

"That's awful." Sophia frowned.

I nodded. "Koigni was looking for something, some sort of object that only the Anichi had and that gave them the power to rule. Whatever it was became lost to legend, but the stories say that whoever had possession of this item could control the fate of the Hawkei— even control the ancestors."

Sophia held her breath, and I continued. "A great war broke out between the Anichi and the

Koigni. The other Houses tried not to get involved, which ended up to be a grave mistake. Toaqua's, Nivita's, and Yapluma's inaction led to the demise of Anichi House. Koigni completely destroyed them. Healing magic was gone with the Anichi. So was whatever the Koigni were looking for."

I paused. This part was hard to explain. "The Koigni felt like they were in charge now, but the destruction of Anichi brought upon the Elementai a terrible curse. Without the healing House, we could no longer heal ourselves or our creatures if disease or terrible injury came to one of the tribe. Neither could we communicate with the ancestors as easily as we once could, because with Anichi remained that gift. We no longer had a ruling House, so each of the Houses became divided. We began to fight amongst ourselves, which led to more death and slaughter. We were killing each other faster than the settlers ever had, and worse yet, we were at risk of exposing ourselves to the outside world."

The wind blew, casting a few strands of hair in front of my eyes. I swept them away and said, "It became clear that after Anichi was destroyed that if we didn't stick together, the Elementai would die out. So we became forced to rely on each other for survival. We stopped mating with outsiders, and the Elders ruled that people could only marry within their own Houses. We stayed within the confines of the village instead of venturing outside, except for rare occasions. Once Anichi was gone, everything changed. Elementai could no longer survive without their Familiars as they could before. Our world had become different."

I stopped speaking. I stooped down to slip the bell wristlet over my wrist and to pick up the drum.

"What are you doing?" Sophia asked, totally confused.

"You need to see that this is more than just a story," I told her.

I started playing a steady beat on the drum. Every time I brought my hand down, the bells on my wrist jingled, until the drum and the bells were creating a harmonious rhythm.

Sophia didn't know the Hawkei language, but I did. I made low chants in my throat, repeating a song that my father had drilled into my head from the moment I could understand language. I made the words mingle in time with the drum. Sophia watched curiously, mesmerized as I continued to cry out to the ancestors.

Calling them down.

After a few minutes, I put down the drum and stopped chanting, but still, the music continued. Other voices were there to replace mine now, humming a far-away song that was getting closer and closer with every second.

"What's that music?" Sophia looked around, scared. "Where's it coming from?"

I didn't answer her. Somewhere in the distance, an eagle cried, and I thought I heard a howl drifting on the wind. The sounds mingled with the dancing bells and the beating of the drum. The whispering got louder, approaching us from every angle. Sophia squeezed Esis and scrunched up into a tiny ball.

I needed a piece from every House. Air was already all around us. I scooped up a bit of dirt and threw it into the wooden bowl for Nivita, then summoned what water I could from the ground. It formed in my hand, and I kept it tightly within my concealed fist before I threw the incense bag inside the bowl. I looked at Sophia.

"Fire, Sophia," I told her. "I need fire."

Despite her fear, she focused her intention on the incense bag in the bowl and lit it up. Her flames burned the bag quickly, sending smoke into the air and the smell of the incense floating around the mountain. The herbs burned quickly, turning to embers within moments. Before the embers could die out completely, I lashed out my hand to grab them, and Sophia gasped.

Ignoring the burning in my palm, I clenched the smoldering embers tightly before I flung them upward into the setting sky.

From the embers burst all colors, every shade possible known to creation. These colors flooded outward and upward, encircling the area and creating a spinning whirlwind around us that felt like the inside of a tornado, a column that spun up as far as the eye could see and into the sun. The entire mountaintop lit up with its glory. Sophia's hair whipped around her face as she jumped to her feet in alarm. Esis leapt out of her arms and onto the ground, squeaking and wiggling in delight.

I too rose as the colors spread. From them emerged shapes and figures. Magical creatures. Dragons spiraled above, gigantic winged beasts like chimeras and large birds at their sides. An enormous firebird with ruby feathers and a orange beak cawed triumphantly, and a jet of flame shot across the sky. Within the whirlwind of color, other creatures spanned, running upon thin air like it was the ground. There were feathered serpents, perytons, alicorns, and species that had long since gone extinct. Aquatic creatures like leviathans and megalodons swam around Fire animals such as manticores and blazing pegasi. Among them were creatures such as big cats, like lions, panthers and lynxes, woodland creatures such as deer, bear, and raccoons, reptiles and fish transforming into their elemental forms as they ran by— Fire and Water.

Some of these creatures I didn't even know the names of. There were hundreds, so many that they made a swirling wall on all sides that blocked out everything except the colors that painted the wind. It was hard to distinguish them all. One creature with a thin neck, a small face and long limbs that was entirely made of water swam by me. Its companion, a twin to it in everything except that it was made of fire, blazed by and intertwined itself with the Water creature. They danced in unison as they returned to the stampede of charging animals.

A group of white stags circled Sophia, jumping around her before bounding off into the air. She gasped, pressing a hand to her mouth when a humpback whale swam by. Sophia gaped at the performance of the ancestors, tears streaming down her cheeks. She reached out to touch them, but their spirit essence floated through her fingers without any sense of actually being there.

I laughed as a pack of wolves ran through me, ruffling my hair. They transformed into Water canines and became a singular wave, sweeping throughout the area like it was the ocean.

A wyvern spiraled down from the sky and landed in front of Sophia. As he did, he changed shape to resemble a muscular warrior wearing a feathered headdress. Another creature, the firebird, landed in front of Sophia to become a red-headed woman wearing a ballgown with a corset. A blazing hound made of flame came to a stop in front of her to morph into a man with a cowboy hat, and a white griffin landed beside him to transform into a beautiful woman with long black hair that reached her ankles. They bowed to Sophia. She took a few steps backward, unsure of what she was experiencing.

My ancestors came down and started landing in front of me, too. They were wearing all types of clothing from various time periods, changing from animals like kelpies, krakens, and gigantic sea monsters. A pale-faced girl, her dark hair in two braids, stood near me and gave me a gentle smile. They bowed to me, too, and I nodded my head in return. Once I acknowledged them, they changed back into their animal forms and took off into the dazzling array, joining again with the crowd that was ever enclosing around us, the sound of their song welling in our ears.

I thought I saw an eagle soaring far above, out of my reach, and I wondered if it was my grandfather. The song was swelling louder and louder, and I knew it was time to bring this to a close. With a singular movement, I swung my arm over my head and downward. I opened my palm and allowed the water residing in my hand to splash upon the burning incense that was still inside the bowl. The smoke went out, and in a few seconds the ancestors retreated into a slit in the sky, taking the colors and the song with them.

When the ancestors were gone, Sophia and I were left in complete darkness. There was nothing above us except the littered array of bright stars against a dark sky. Night had come. Silence thickened the air between us, and it was harsh and ringing now that the loud chanting and drum beats were gone.

Sophia was shaking. I didn't know what to say to her, but she spoke.

"That was… beautiful." Her voice cracked. Esis waddled over to her to put a paw on her shoe, and she looked down at him.

"That's our destiny," I told her. "I don't pretend to have all the answers to life, or to even know where the rest of the human race goes after death. I don't even know where the ancestors go. But they're here with us, and that's our meaning. You don't die until your purpose in this life is done. Once it's accomplished, you move on to be with the rest of our kind. Elements, Elementai, and Familiars, all united as one in perfect harmony."

Her face was still pretty white. "Who were those people that bowed to me?"

"They were your guides. Those particular ancestors that came down to greet you agreed to watch over you and specifically be involved in your life before you were born," I said. "Every Elementai has their own ancestor guides."

"They changed. From human to animal," she said.

"Our Familiars fuse with us and our magic when we die. We truly become one," I explained.

Sophia sniffled. She wiped her nose and looked at me.

"Do you understand now? Our people were almost *exterminated*. Everything that meant anything to us was taken and destroyed. Our culture and religion is all we have," I told her. "That's why the Houses need each other to survive. I know you think this is all stupid political bullshit, and everyone's trying to one-up each other all the time."

I sighed. "And, yeah, a lot of it is that. But underneath it all is a pact for survival. To be frank, if we all don't work together, we're still facing extinction. And all of us agree that our creatures deserve better than that. If we're gone, there's no one left to take care of them. And you know as well as I do they wouldn't survive in this modern world. Not without someone to protect them."

Sophia nodded. She wiped away remnants of the tears that were still drying on her face and picked up Esis. "Yeah. I… I get it, Liam. I understand why you brought me up here. It took something like this to make me realize who I really am."

Esis purred happily. She kissed him on the top of the head, and I gathered my things.

"Ready to head down?" I asked.

"Yeah." She chuckled. "I'm starving, actually. I haven't eaten much all day."

"I'll sit with you," I blurted before I could stop myself. "It's no big deal. I haven't eaten, either."

Sophia grinned. *Stupid, stupid.* Just a few weeks ago I was refusing to be seen in the cafeteria with her, and here I was changing my mind.

We started heading down the mountain. I noticed that Sophia was unusually silent, even more so than when we'd started heading up here. "Something bothering you?" I asked.

"Nothing. It was just…" She hesitated. "There was a wolf standing there, staring at you. He was sitting by your side the entire time we were on the mountain."

Talk about a punch to the gut. It was nearly enough to knock me off my feet. My eyes burned, and I struggled to catch my breath. All the air had just gone out of me.

"He was your Familiar, wasn't he?" Sophia said softly.

There was a lump in my throat. "Yes."

"You can't see him?" She sounded sad.

"No." My reply was heavy.

"Oh." She looked down. "I'm sorry."

"It's okay."

She brought her beautiful face back up to look at me. "What was his name?"

"Nashoma. His name was Nashoma."

She was quiet for a moment. "Do you mind telling me what happened?"

The words were hard to get out. "He died for me."

Sophia didn't press any further. She just clung tighter to Esis.

"And yes, before you ask," I added, "I'm the only one of my kind. No one else in our history has ever survived their Familiar's death, not since Anichi was destroyed. Not even one."

Sophia didn't answer right away. For days afterward, I couldn't figure out why Nashoma had sacrificed himself for me, as his death would cause my own, too. He knew that. Every Familiar did.

But I hadn't died— I'd survived, and managed to go on without him. Though how he could've known that, I didn't understand.

Maybe he'd known something I didn't.

While I was still lost in my thoughts, Sophia added, "Well… for what it's worth, I'm glad you're still here, Liam. You've been a good friend to me. I like having you around."

A small part of my spirits lifted, and I gave her a tiny grin. "Thanks, Soph."

We continued our descent, but we were closer together this time, walking so our bodies almost touched. I felt fine right now, but a part of me knew I'd be paying for this walk the next morning. I only had so much energy to give these days, and I'd spent a lot of it climbing up and down this mountain.

Sophia, though. She was worth it.

I almost wanted to reach out and hold her hand, because, you know, I'm a masochist who loves torturing myself. My fingers reached out for hers, but I brought them back before she noticed. I called myself a wuss and reminded myself that we had rules.

"Can any Elementai do that?" Sophia asked abruptly, snapping me out of my stupid internal debate. "Like, if I learned how to do it, could I summon the ancestors, too?"

"There are only a few Hawkei who can summon the ancestors. The Elders, chieftains, and firstborns of chieftains," I explained. "My dad is Chief of the Toaqua tribe, so I have the ability to call them."

"Do you know anyone else who can?"

"Haley can. She's the firstborn of a chief," I said. "Her mother is Chieftess of Koigni."

"Of course she is." Sophia made a bitchy face. "What else has she got that I don't have?"

"Well, for starters, her tournament team is probably phenomenal. Madame Doya already chose her for her front runner, and Doya doesn't take losers. Most likely, she has the best pick from every House."

"You're not helping me feel better, Liam. You called us the reject team," she said sourly.

"Because we are. We're the kids that nobody wanted, so we got stuck together," I said.

"Baine wanted us. He specifically chose us for his team," Sophia argued.

"Baine's being sympathetic. Or stupid. He's about three fries short of a Happy Meal. It's not a compliment that he's our coach. People complain about getting him every year." I crossed my arms. "I just want to get this thing over with and come out on the other end with all my limbs intact."

"That's not good enough. I want to win, and rub it in Haley's stupid face," Sophia snapped.

"That's Koigni thinking. You need to get it out of your head that we have a chance of winning this thing," I shot her down immediately. "The only thing I'm concerned about is making it out alive, because people do *die* in this tournament, Sophia."

"What if we just refused to do the tournament?" Sophia asked me. "What then?"

"No one is truly forced into the Elemental Cup. People have walked before," I tell her. "But if you walk, you become an outcast. You're banished from the tribe and never allowed to speak with any Elementai ever again. Even worse, your Familiar will be taken away from you. You won't die, because your Familiar is still alive, but you'll be separated forever. An Elementai that is too cowardly to enter the tournament is considered unworthy to have a Familiar."

"How did this whole thing get started, anyway?" Sophia asked. "Did the Elders just decide to throw a contest where people die for fun?"

I smirked. "No. Before the Familiars came, the Hawkei had a coming-of-age ceremony for every person in the tribe. They were expected to survive in the wilderness for three days alone. After Anichi fell, that ceremony turned into the Elemental Cup. This tournament is every Elementai's way of proving they belong here. That they're valuable to the tribe."

"Well, I think it's sick that we should have to prove we deserve to live." Sophia's face was scrunched up in a snarl.

"You don't understand. Back then, weak people would bring the tribe down. They'd take up resources and harm everyone's way of life. It was considered honorable to give your life for the tribe's," I argued.

"Things aren't like that anymore," Sophia said harshly. "We have more resources now. We should change."

I took a deep breath. "Look. I get that you don't like it. And I can understand it's barbaric and dated. But this is your way of proving that you and Esis can contribute to our society, and that you're strong enough to help raise magical creatures."

"What about you?" She raised an eyebrow, challenging me. "What do you think of all of this, especially considering your situation?"

My situation. It didn't take her long to make me blissfully happy and piss me off again all in the same hour, did it? "I get that people like me would've died out there, a long time ago. But I'm not turning my back on my tribe."

"Not even to save your life?"

"No. If I'm being forced to do this, I'm going to show everyone that I still belong here. That I'm not useless," I growled. "And since you're doing it, too, you should use it as your opportunity to show that you're really one of us— a true Elementai, not an outsider. Don't do it for Haley. Do it for yourself."

Sophia's expression cleared. She glanced at Esis and stroked his fluffy fur. "Yeah. I get what you're saying. I'm no coward. And after everything you've shown me today, I want to prove that this is where I belong. And I'm definitely not giving up Esis. Anyone who tries to make me can go straight to hell."

"Good," I responded sourly. My face went back to that shriveled-up pout that I hated and that I only realized that I did now. It'd been set like that for months, and I hadn't even realized.

Sophia had shattered that statue today, and bringing it back now was terribly uncomfortable. But I didn't want to smile right now, because she'd poked the bear. Irritating.

"What, now that we're heading into school you're going back to being emo?" Sophia asked, laughing as we reached the bottom of the mountain.

"I'm not emo," I grumbled, and we headed back into the forest. "You're pushing your luck."

"Oh, really? What are you gonna do?" She punched me in the shoulder and drew herself up. "Give me one of your salty comments, Water boy?"

"Shut up." I laughed under my breath. I nudged her with my shoulder, and she nudged back.

It was by accident, but when Sophia leaned against me, I didn't pull away this time. We were leaning on each other the entire way back to the castle. Esis happily cheered and left Sophia's shoulder to hop on my head again.

When we saw the spires of the castle coming into view, it was like we were electrically jolted apart. Both of us retreated from one another until we were at least a few feet away, like it was a crime to be seen together.

I guess it kind of was.

Esis, though, didn't come off my head until Sophia pried him away. He took a good chunk of my hair with him, too, the little shit.

"So… dinner?" Sophia asked reluctantly, as if she was scared I was gonna bow out on my promise now.

"Dinner," I confirmed. I followed her into the cafeteria. It crossed my mind that people might talk if they saw us eating together, but I pushed it out of my head. They could look. We were tournament partners now, after all. We had to talk to each other to strategize. People wouldn't think too much of it. We had an excuse.

Far too convenient of an excuse. Don't get too close, I reminded myself.

It was too late for that. I really liked Sophia.

Which meant that I was totally screwed.

sophia
TWELVE

Orenda Academy was starting to feel more and more like home with each passing day following our trip up the mountain. If it wasn't for Madame Doya's class and the fact that I still worried about and missed my parents, I might actually feel like I could stay here forever.

"Sophia!" Madame Doya snapped one Thursday during class— just like almost every day. She had led us outside to a clearing in the forest. Dry pine needles and leaves littered the ground. We hadn't even started the lesson and she was already yelling at me.

The sound of my name snapped me out of my thoughts. I'd been focused on how things had changed since Liam took me to meet my ancestors. He had returned to being my partner in our Medical Care of Familiars class, and I'd even caught him smiling a time or two over the past several weeks. For the most part, Haley had left me alone, and the other Koigni in my dorm had grown bored of playing pranks outside my door.

Imogen and I continued to hang out when we weren't in class. We spent most of our time outside the castle, either walking the mountain trails or scouring the beach for cool rocks. As a Nivita, Imogen could sense the minerals in the rocks and knew where to find the pretty ones before I could even see them. Esis had a blast digging through the rocks to help. He always managed to find the shiniest rocks on the beach. The ledge of my dorm window was filling up with rocks far too quickly.

I was making progress with my Fire, but it was easier in class, where Madame Doya made my blood boil. Still, that didn't seem good enough for her, despite the fact that I was outper-forming all my classmates besides Haley. Two other girls and a guy had since bonded with their Familiars, and their skills were catching up. But until they did, I was maintaining the notion that Doya had absolutely nothing to yell at me about. She, apparently, didn't get the memo.

I forced myself to hold her gaze. "Yes?"

"I want you and Haley up here in the front," she instructed with tight lips, as if I was wasting her time. A low growl bubbled up from Naomi's throat beside her, warning me to hurry up.

The crowd of students parted. I stepped forward. Esis sat cradled in the hood of my sweatshirt but tugged on my ponytail to get a better look. Haley crossed her arms and smirked from beside me. The phoenix on her shoulder held her head high, mirroring Haley's attitude. Above us, the October sky was overcast, and it looked like it might rain.

Doya projected her voice across the clearing. "In today's exercise, we will be extinguishing fire rather than conjuring it. You will each be paired up, and each pair will take a turn putting out their fires. You must work together quickly and efficiently. We don't want to start any forest fires."

Doya shot a narrowed gaze my way, as if she believed I was most prone to letting things get out of hand. Naomi mimicked her. Anger settled in my gut like a bag of rocks. How much more could I possibly prove myself to her? I'd already shot flames from my palms, generated heat without a flame, and shaped my Fire into a sphere, all before ninety-nine percent of my classmates did. Plus, I was the only one who managed to set my hair on fire without singeing a single strand. Miranda had ended up needing a pixie cut to get rid of the damage, and I was pretty sure Haley had cut at least two inches off her hair.

Granted, I lost one of my good ponytail elastics that day, but that was a small price to pay for the victory. Doya had just looked down her nose at me but didn't say anything. I considered it a compliment.

"Haley and Sophia, you're up first." That was all Madame Doya said before she stepped aside.

In the blink of an eye, a band of fire lit a mere two feet in front of us. Pine needles cracked as the flames licked several feet into the air. The needles burned so quickly that the flames were already spreading across the clearing at an alarming rate before I had a chance to react.

I'd already resigned myself to the fact that Madame Doya would never give us any clear instruction. She used a "throw-them-into-the-lion's-pit-and-watch-them-fend-for-themselves" type of teaching style. I didn't bother asking how she expected us to complete this task.

I turned to Haley. "Any ideas?"

Haley's gaze was already narrowed at the fire, and her brows constricted as if she was thinking hard. "Yeah," she snapped. "You could help me."

The more Haley concentrated, the bigger the flames grew. I took several steps back, but I could still feel the heat radiating across my face.

"We don't have all day," Madame Doya chastised. "If you let the whole clearing burn, no one else will get a chance."

I listened to her words, but only to drive my anger at her. It always seemed to help me do better in her class. Behind me, Esis kneaded the back of my neck. I brushed his small paws from my skin.

"Not now, Esis," I whispered, but he ignored me and continued to press his paws into my muscles. It was surprisingly relaxing, which was *totally* not what I needed right now. Like Liam had said, Koigni magic took strong emotions, and I needed to channel everything I had right now.

I concentrated on the fire. Its warmth didn't just touch my skin— its energy permeated down through my muscles and into my bones. My body buzzed to its frequency, but it was different than controlling my own Fire. Doya had conjured this fire, and though it felt similar to my own, there was something slightly off about it. It seemed angrier and more brutal, as if I could feel Doya's emotions pulsing through the flames.

The fire continued to spread, roaring and crackling. Dark smoke rose into the air.

"What are you doing, Sophia?" Haley snapped. "Help me!"

I blinked to clear my vision and focused on the fire. My mind raced with possible solutions, but so far, we'd only learned how to *conjure* fire, not extinguish it. We'd been using traditional means until now.

I imagined the flames dying down, burning to nothing but embers, but they didn't. I tried to pull the flames together, to create a fireball that would keep them from spreading, but that only separated a fireball from the other flames that continued to rage through the clearing.

"Stop it, Sophia!" Haley yelled as she took another step back, as if it was entirely my fault the fire was growing.

The flames burst higher, like they were exploding with Haley's anger.

That's it! I realized.

Fire was made of rage and fury. It thrived off untamed emotions. Extinguishing it would require just the opposite.

I took a deep breath and focused on the soothing massage Esis was giving me. I ignored Haley's remarks and Doya's hard gaze, letting everything around me fade until it felt like I was alone in the forest with Esis and the fire.

I willed the energy sizzling through my bones to calm, but it pushed against me.

Haley.

"You have to calm down," I told her. "Anger and frustration will only make it worse."

"Yeah, because that's so easy," Haley said with an eye roll.

I forced my annoyance down. Haley didn't deserve any of my energy anyway.

Just stay calm, I told myself. *Nothing good will come out of anger today. You can do this. You can control it.*

Images flashed through my mind as I tried to focus on the things that would calm me most. I pictured Amelia's smiling face, which only made me smile since I was wearing her jeans today. I thought of my parents. A pang entered my chest, the same one that hit every time they crossed my mind.

Not working, I told myself.

I quickly switched focus. Instead of focusing on the things I'd lost, I focused on those I'd gained. I thought about Esis, about his soft paws on the back of my neck, the way he purred when I held him in my arms, and the way he looked at me with his big blue eyes as if I were the only person in the world he could ever love. My heart swelled at the thought of him.

My thoughts flickered back to last week when I was sitting in one of the big comfy chairs in the castle foyer waiting to meet up with Imogen for lunch. Esis was jumping from armrest to armrest, tagging my fingers that I wiggled in the air above him. I giggled until my gaze lifted and I spotted Liam passing through the hall at the top of the grand staircase. Our eyes met for a moment, and my heart flipped in my chest when I witnessed a ghost of a smile touch his lips.

The flames in front of me shrank from several feet high to mere inches. I held the fire back, keeping it from eating away at any more dry debris. It fought against me, the energy pressing against my chest like a snowplow. I threw my walls up, blocking the pressure out and funneling my calm energy into it. The fire eased more and more until there was nothing left but embers. I forced the final bit of Fire energy off my chest with a calming breath, and the remaining embers sizzled away to nothing. A large circle of black, charred debris at least ten feet across stood as a reminder of our exercise.

Haley breathed a sigh of relief. "Whew. I did it!"

She glanced to the other students proudly. Kelsey gave her a thumbs up, but Hudson and Tabitha both looked at me like they knew I'd been the one to extinguish the flames by myself. I looked to Doya, expecting some sort of praise, but she just pursed her lips and looked away from me. Beside her, Naomi shot daggers my way.

"Ben. Kelsey. You're next," Doya barked.

She ignited another fire as soon as they made it to the front of the group. I turned in complete shock and found my way to the back. My mind raced as I watched group after group struggle with the task. Doya had to put most of the flames out herself, save for one group toward the end who'd I'd seen whispering and strategizing beforehand. Clearly, I was outperforming most of my other classmates. What about that wasn't good enough for Doya?

The calmness I'd felt during the exercise quickly washed away. My frustrations grew the more I thought about it. Doya hated me since the first day I showed up in her class. It was more than just her normal distaste for students, too. Did she hate Amelia so much that she had to take it out on me? What had Amelia done to her? Or was there something else going on here?

I had the entire class period to mull it over in my mind. By the end of class, I was bound and determined to figure out what the reason was. That disappointed look she liked to give me had punched one too many holes through my gut.

I hung back by the edge of the trail we'd come as soon as she dismissed the class. She'd just put out the last group's fire and didn't see me standing in the trees until she spun around. Her face immediately fell.

I was going to say her name, but that look sent the words right back down my throat. *Maybe I shouldn't do this.* Esis tugged on my ponytail, snapping me back to attention. I was *totally* doing this, whether it risked her tossing me out of her class or not.

"Class dismissed, Sophia," Doya said with a sharp edge to her tone.

I forced my voice to remain even. "I know, but I'd like to talk with you." I purposely didn't ask her permission. She'd probably deny me the opportunity and tell me to find her during office hours.

Doya sighed and started down the trail with Naomi at her side. "Fine, but make it snappy."

I hurried along behind her. I only took a second to gather my courage. Anything more than that and she'd for sure yell at me again. Honestly, it was impossible to please this woman.

"Why do you hate me?" I spit out the words before I had a chance to second guess myself.

Madame Doya whirled around, her velvety dress and red hair swirling around her. She spun so fast that I nearly rammed into her. I took a step back, my heart thumping like a bass drum against my chest. I couldn't believe I'd actually worked up the courage to say it.

"Excuse me?" she bit. Naomi growled protectively.

I swallowed hard, though my pulse continued to pound through my ears. There was no backing down now. "It's pretty obvious that you hate me. I just don't know why."

Madame Doya scoffed and turned her back to me to head down the trail. "Do you honestly think I treat you differently than any of my other students, Sophia?"

I thought about the way she praised Haley whenever she executed a task with precision. She didn't exactly praise many other students, but most of them weren't as good as Haley, either. I was *certain* there was no one else in class she yelled or snapped at more than she did to me.

"Yes," I stated confidently.

"I'm hard on you because I want to push you to be better, Sophia," Doya said from in front of me. "I expect much more from you than the others."

She was lying. I completed most of the tasks she required from us. I had a sure shot at passing this class. What more could she expect? Why would she even care?

"Why?" I pressed. "Is it because I'm bonded? Other people have bonded, and—"

"No," she said in a clipped tone. "It's because..."

She trailed off, like she didn't want to answer. "It's because you show more promise."

I couldn't see her expression as we walked along the trail, but I could hear the lie in her voice. There was something she wasn't telling me.

"I know that's not true," I said, my heart finally slowing. "I came into your class knowing nothing. I had about as much promise as a slug."

We emerged from the trees and reached one of the staircases at the edge of the castle's lawn.

I took two steps at a time until I was beside Doya. Naomi climbed the stairs on her other side, giving Esis the stink eye as he chewed on the string of my hoodie.

Doya kept her gaze fixed forward on the castle. "That may be true, but look how far you've come."

I wasn't sure if that was meant to be some backhanded insult or a compliment. I guess it made sense why she thought I had promise. It also made sense why my Koigni classmates weren't fond of me. I came in with less potential in my entire body than they had in their pinky fingers, bonded with the cutest, most harmless Familiar around, and I still showed them up. I bet they were starting to think there was some truth to that prophecy after all.

Which reminded me…

No one had actually told me yet what the prophecy said or what I had to do with it. Every time I asked Imogen, she just said she didn't know *exactly* how it was worded and didn't want to give me false information. Which was quickly followed up by *"Besides, it's just an urban legend."*

Which, coming from Imogen, sounded like a complete lie. If anyone believed in the prophecy, Imogen would. She believed there were freaking *wolpertingers* in the forest, which Jonah kindly explained to me didn't exist. Urban legends were kind of her thing.

I'd resigned myself to believing that meant the prophecy was bad news for me and that maybe I didn't *want* to know what it said. But I was feeling bold today. The question slipped out before I could stop myself.

"What does the prophecy say about me?"

Madame Doya stopped dead at the top of the stairs. I took another step toward the castle before realizing she and Naomi had both frozen up. I turned to her.

Esis dropped my hoodie string and straightened.

"That's why you're hard on me, isn't it?" I asked. "You want me to be better than everyone else— even Haley— so I can fulfill the prophecy?"

Doya folded her hands like she often did, but the muscles in her forearm bulged beneath her sleeves as her fingers tightened together. "That may be part of it," she admitted, though she kept her emotional walls up as she spoke.

Of course it was.

"It's going to be kind of hard for me to fulfill this prophecy if I don't know what it says, won't it?"

Honestly, I didn't know where my confidence came from. Usually, I'd avoid Doya at all costs. I half expected her to snap back at me, scolding me for my attitude.

Instead, she glanced toward the sky. "It's going to rain soon, Sophia. I can't stand out here all day talking about this. I have another class soon."

I side-stepped to block her path. "Why are you keeping this from me?" I demanded. Koigni magic tingled through my skin as my anger surfaced. *Oh, that's where the confidence is coming from.* "Do the Koigni *want* me to fail?"

Madame Doya blinked rapidly, as if I'd just slapped her in the face. "No. Of course not."

Naomi snorted, like I'd offended her.

"Then why aren't you helping me?" I demanded.

"I *am* helping you!" Doya all but roared. "I'm doing what I was assigned to do. I'm teaching you how to use your magic."

Well, damn. I wasn't expecting that answer. Yet it wasn't enough.

I crossed my arms. "Whose job is it to tell me about the prophecy? Because whoever was supposed to do that screwed up and forgot."

A muscle fluttered in Doya's jaw, and she glanced around. The closest people were way across the lawn near the courtyard. They couldn't hear us from here.

Madame Doya caved with a sigh and lowered her voice. "The prophecy says that you will be the one to bring our House, the Koigni, to glory. *The fated Koigni child, born in the Summer Solstice in the Year of the Dragon, shall bring glory to the greatest House.*"

Wait. That was a good thing? Weren't the Hawkei better off with a democracy where *all* the Houses had a say in things, not one where the Koigni controlled everything?

"That's it?" I asked. It seemed so simple.

"Isn't that enough?" Doya snapped.

"I don't know," I replied in uncertainty. "I thought the prophecy would be more... dangerous."

"Of course it's dangerous," Doya barked like I was an idiot. "The other Houses don't want this prophecy to come true. They're watching you, Sophia. If you value your life, you will push yourself harder in my class— in all your classes. And take pride in the House you were born into. It's the only one you have."

My hands shook at her words, and Esis' fingers tightened in my hair. That sounded *bad*.

My voice quickly lost its confident tone. "Does the prophecy say anything about how I'm supposed to do this?"

Doya glanced around again to make sure no one was within earshot. She spoke firmly. "There is more, but I expect you will not repeat this part to anyone, as it is for Koigni ears only."

Naomi glared at me. I swore she raised an eyebrow in my direction. After a beat, I realized Doya was waiting for my response. Honestly, I didn't know if I could keep the information quiet. Depending on what it was, I would be tempted to tell Imogen.

But something told me I wasn't prying the information from Doya's lips without complete and utter honesty. I was playing by her rules.

"I won't tell anyone," I promised.

Doya took a breath. "You will have to find a powerful item that will serve to fulfill the prophecy."

"A specific item? Where am I supposed to find it? What does it look like?" So many questions raced through my head. Chief among them... was the prophecy even worth fulfilling?

"I don't know." Madame Doya's features hardened, quickly turning her back into her usual unhelpful self. "I'm not the one who will fulfill this prophecy. You are. But for the ancestors' sake, Sophia, tread carefully. The other Houses have not yet confirmed you are the one, but as soon as they do, you better be ready. They would rather see you dead than see the Koigni in their rightful place of power."

With that, Madame Doya turned and hurried across the lawn toward the back of the castle. Her dress billowed out behind her, and Naomi prowled in her wake.

I stood at the top of the steps, completely stunned. A shiver crawled down my spine as my eyes traveled toward the courtyard. People from all Houses swarmed the lawn. It suddenly occurred to me that any one of them might want me dead. And I hadn't even done anything wrong yet.

Yet. Key word. Did that mean I *would* fulfill this prophecy? Would *I* be responsible for the downfall of the other three Houses?

It didn't seem possible, but I couldn't shake the feeling that the ancestors wouldn't have delivered this prophecy if it weren't true.

"Girl, where have you been?" Imogen demanded with a smile when I met up with her in Dragonology later that day.

I'd spent the last three hours poring over books with Esis in the library, searching for any further information about the prophecy. But as I'd already come to find, the library was useless when it came to Hawkei history. I'd learned they much preferred passing down stories orally rather than writing them down. Who knew how much the prophecy had been twisted since it was first foretold?

"Sorry I'm late," I said vaguely as I joined her in the back of the class.

The sky above us had darkened since earlier, but it hadn't started raining yet. I'd asked Imogen once why the Elementai didn't just control the weather around here, and she told me they didn't like to mess with it because it could damage the ecosystem. Plus, you never knew if another Elementai was messing with the weather a few miles away. It was strictly forbidden, except in controlled cases like the cruise ship and during the tournament.

Dragonology took place in a clearing along a ledge between the castle and the ocean. It made for a perfect view of the beach. We'd spent the first half of the semester in the classroom studying dragon anatomy and taking care of Aisha, a baby dragon whose mother had abandoned her because she was born with a limp wing. She reminded me a lot of Squeaks. Today was our first class outside, and it was our first chance to meet a full-grown dragon up close and personal. As excited as I was about this opportunity, my mind was elsewhere.

I stared down the mountain toward the beach. Students prowled the rocky shore near the pier, but it wasn't the crowd that caught my eye. A quarter mile down the beach from them, a guy with long black hair sat alone on a big rock. He stared out across the vast water and twisted something beige around in his hands, almost like he was knitting a sweater. I'd recognize those broad shoulders and silky black hair anywhere.

Liam.

A whistle sounded from beside me, pulling me out of my daze. I turned to Imogen.

She wiggled her eyebrows and sang, "Somebody's got the hots for *Liam.*"

"Shut up." I swatted at her. "I do not. Besides, I'm not allowed to date anyone who isn't Koigni."

Which meant my love life was going nowhere. Koigni guys were all assholes.

"Says who?" Imogen challenged. She placed her hands on hips, on top of the floral skirt she wore over skinny jeans.

"Um… everyone?" I pointed out.

Imogen rolled her eyes. "So you can't marry him. That doesn't mean you can't have fun."

I suppressed a smile. "You're naughty."

Imogen smiled proudly. "Live a little."

An involuntary frown crossed my face. I wasn't the kind of girl who broke the rules, not even for a guy like Liam.

"Seriously, come here." Imogen grabbed my shoulders and shook me. "Just relax. Let all that tension go."

Esis cooed from my shoulder, but his voice vibrated. I didn't feel much like smiling, but I couldn't help it.

"Okay, okay," I said through suppressed giggles. "I'm relaxed."

"Good, now—"

"Everyone." The sound of Professor Curt's voice cut Imogen off. "Meet Kalina."

He gestured to the trees and stepped aside. Aisha, who he'd taken a fondness to, sat on a rock near him and scratched the back of her blue ear with her hind leg.

From out of the thick forest stepped a beautiful dragon coated in shiny red scales. Long horns protruded from her head, and short spikes traveled the length of her spine and down her tail. She only took a few steps out of the trees before lowering herself to the ground and folding her bat-like wings across her back. She held her head high and looked positively comfortable despite the thirty pairs of eyes staring back at her.

"She's magnificent," I whispered in wonder.

Esis huffed like he was offended.

I'd seen plenty of dragons since arriving at Orenda Academy, but I'd never been this close to one before. None except Aisha. Aisha was the size of a medium dog, while Kalina was bigger than a pickup truck. She held herself in a way Aisha never would. She was basically a work of art.

"Don't be shy," Professor Curt encouraged. "Kalina is my Familiar. She will not harm you—unless I tell her to, of course." He let out a light laugh. "But I assure you I won't. It's perfectly safe."

Imogen bent and scooped up Sassy in her arms, who'd been playing with her shoelace the whole time. "Let's go meet a dragon!"

Imogen pushed through the group and was the first to approach Kalina. I followed closely behind her with Esis on my shoulder. Kalina sat as still as a stone when Imogen approached. She held Sassy up to Kalina's face, as if introducing them. Sassy promptly let out a loud sneeze, her whole body tightening under the pressure. Kalina drew her head back in surprise, but she quickly stretched forward to give Sassy a good sniff.

Imogen cradled Sassy in her arms. "Oh, sweetheart, are you allergic to dragons?"

Whispers broke out behind us, but I was so used to it now that it barely registered.

Sassy reached out a paw to touch Kalina's nose. If she wasn't careful, her paw would fit straight up Kalina's nostril.

I giggled at the thought, which drew Kalina's eyes to me. She stared at me with a look in her eyes I couldn't quite place. Admiration, maybe? Whatever it was, it was inviting.

"Come on," Professor Curt said, motioning for me to step forward. "She likes you."

I wanted to pet Kalina, but she was so large and confident, it was intimidating. She could literally bite my arm off. I stepped forward anyway and gently reached out my hand. Kalina bowed her head, allowing me to pet the space between her eyes. Her scales were soft and warm.

"Good, good," Professor Curt said. "Anyone else?"

Several other students rushed forward to marvel at his beautiful Familiar. Imogen and I were pushed aside.

"You're fine, Sassy," Imogen said, bouncing her in her arms. "You've never had any problems with Aisha, have you?"

Imogen held Sassy up to Aisha's face. The baby dragon immediately stuck her tongue out and dragged it across Sassy's cheek. We both laughed.

"I think they like each other," I giggled.

"Of course they do," Imogen agreed. "Who wouldn't love this little red fur ball?"

From my shoulder, Esis stretched out a hand, as if he wanted to touch Aisha. I bent to Aisha's rock until they were close enough to touch. Esis grabbed her small horn and climbed onto her head. She spun in a circle, nipping playfully at him as he slid down her back. Sassy squirmed in Imogen's arms as if she wanted to play with them.

"Oh, my gosh!" I exclaimed. "They're too cute."

Behind us, a guy scoffed. I threw a glance over my shoulder to see Brandon, a Koigni senior, and his Familiar, an orange cat the size of a lynx, staring at us.

"Is there a problem, Brandon?" Imogen snapped at him.

He shot her an unamused expression. "That dragon's not *cute*. There's a reason its mother abandoned it."

My gut twisted at his blatant disregard for another being's life. What did Aisha ever do to him?

"Screw you, Brandon," Imogen shot back at him. "You wouldn't know cute if it bit you in the ass."

I stifled a laugh. Sometimes Imogen's bold personality was a blessing.

"Yeah, well—" Brandon started to retort, but Imogen turned away, ignoring him. He huffed but apparently couldn't come up with a strong enough comeback, because he let it drop.

Esis reached the point behind Aisha's shoulder blades, right between her wings. He stretched out to her limp wing like he was about to climb out onto it.

"Hey, there, buddy," I said, scooping him up off the dragon's back. "We don't want to hurt her."

Esis' small claws dug into the fabric of my sweatshirt as he tried to pry himself away from me.

"Whoa." I held on to him tighter. "What's up? Where are you going?"

Esis struggled harder until his hands were clamped around the exposed skin on my hands, digging in so deeply that I thought he might draw blood. Instinctively, I yelped and dropped him in the dirt.

I rubbed my hands while Esis scurried up the rock and returned to Aisha's back. "Ow, Esis. What's gotten into you?"

Esis grabbed Aisha's wing again and pumped it, as if encouraging her to take flight.

"Esis, she can't fly," I told him, as if he could understand. I noticed for the first time that Aisha's wing looked straighter and stronger than normal. Maybe she'd eventually grow out of her deformity.

"Relax," Imogen insisted. "They're just having fun."

Except I could tell something was wrong. Esis had never jumped out of my hands like that before.

Esis trilled and continued the flapping motion. Aisha stood high on her rock and began flapping her good wing.

"See?" Imogen said. "Just having—"

The words died on her lips as Aisha's body lifted into the air. Esis cheered in victory the same moment my stomach dropped to the ground. I should've been happy for Aisha, considering none of us ever thought she would ever fly, but I wasn't. I was terrified for Esis as I watched them climb higher. Aisha dropped several feet between each flap of her wings, as if she was simply limping along. Sheer terror filled me as a slew of possibilities rushed through my mind. Esis could fall and get hurt! I couldn't let that happen.

Behind me, all infatuation with Kalina died as everyone's attention turned to Esis and Aisha as they rose above the trees.

"Esis!" I ran after them. If he fell, I'd be right there to catch him.

Professor Curt didn't seem at all concerned with my Familiar's well-being. He just laughed in disbelief and said, "That's my girl, Aisha. You're flying!"

I rushed into the trees to stay under them. I tried to keep an eye on them, but I only caught glimpses of blue scales through the canopy. The top of a tree moved as Aisha's toes grazed it.

"Esis!" I cried.

Oh, God. Ancestors. Whoever. Don't let my little guy die! He means the world to me.

His trill of excitement echoed through the trees.

"Esis! You get down here *this* instant!" I screamed.

To my horror Aisha caught the top of another tree and her body slammed into the next one. It pulled her from the air like a giant monster reaching for its prey, and she and Esis went tumbling to the ground. Twigs snapped on their way down, and pine needles rained to the forest floor. They both landed in the dirt with a sickening *thud*.

My gut immediately tightened like I'd been punched. I quickly rushed forward to where

Aisha and Esis lay sprawled. Aisha's bad wing was even more twisted than before, and blood trickled out of a wound on her face. The red liquid was in stark contrast to her blue scales. Her eyes were closed, and I wasn't sure she was breathing.

Beside her, Esis lay still. My heart hammered ferociously against my rib cage. I skidded onto my knees beside them. My hands shot out to cradle Esis, but before I touched him, his eyes popped open and he sprang up to his feet. Dirt coated his white fur. Though he normally dusted off, he ignored it this time. He ignored me, too, pushing my hands away when I reached for him. His eyes locked on the cut on Aisha's face.

I froze as Esis stood beside her. He was barely the size of her head, but he bent over her like he was the stronger, wiser of the two. He placed his tiny little paws on either side of her wound and then closed his eyes.

My eyes widened as Aisha's cut began to knit itself together right in front of my eyes.

"Esis," I whispered. *What kind of magical creature are you?*

I didn't have a chance to finish my thought aloud before someone cleared their throat from behind me. I whirled around to see that Imogen had followed me. She held Sassy in her arms.

"Imogen, I— I—" I glanced between her and Aisha, who was starting to wake. The cut had completely vanished, and her scales were perfectly intact, as if nothing had happened at all.

I didn't know what to say. This changed everything. It meant that Esis wasn't just a helpless Familiar after all. He was *powerful*. So powerful that if anyone got wind of this, they might take him from me.

Like Doya had said, I needed to tread lightly. This kind of thing just might get us killed.

I could barely think straight, but there was no denying Imogen's expression. Her usual smile had vanished, and her mouth hung open slightly. She didn't even blink.

"Imogen, please—" I couldn't finish my sentence before Professor Curt and the rest of our class rushed up behind her.

Professor Curt knelt beside me to inspect Aisha's injuries, but I never tore my gaze from Imogen's eyes. Before I could rise from the ground and drag her away to talk about what had just happened, she'd whirled around and bolted past our classmates and out of the trees.

It was in that moment that the skies decided to open. Rain fell to the ground in large, heavy drops, soaking my clothing and Esis' fur within seconds. Students scattered but I remained frozen, staring through the trees where Imogen had just ditched me.

A chilling fear traveled down my spine. *Imogen saw.* She saw Esis heal Aisha. She knew as well as I did that Esis wasn't all he appeared to be. The only question was, would she honor our friendship, or would she turn us in to the Nivita Elders?

I wasn't sure how long Esis and I had before another House confirmed the prophecy and decided to kill us for it.

THIRTEEN

Survival Instincts had been held in the woods almost every time I went to it, but since it was pouring out today, it'd been moved into Professor McCauley's main classroom, located in the dungeons.

Professor McCauley wasn't one to be afraid of "a little rain," but when there had been a tornado sighted nearby, Head Dean Alric put his foot down and forced us to relocate inside.

McCauley had ranted that young people today were coddled before she started her lesson. Made me laugh.

Good thing, too. I could keep the rain off of me, but I didn't want to hear the rest of the class whine that it was too wet. I guess the Yapluma would get their kicks when the rest of us were carried off by a twister, though.

Although… I would almost rather be outside in these dangerous conditions than inside McCauley's creepy classroom. There were no windows down here, and besides the wooden desks, the only decor she had were multiple arrays of skeletons, both human and Familiar. They were mounted throughout the room in various poses before dark tapestries that depicted gruesome scenes. Every day was Halloween when McCauley was concerned.

"When you are in a survival situation, the first thing you need to do is stop and assess your surroundings," Professor McCauley boomed. "It is better to create a plan and execute it than to hesitate too long and lose precious seconds. If you panic, you will most certainly end up dead."

McCauley's Familiar, Bram, was lurking around the room and making people shiver. I ignored him and tried to focus. Professor McCauley's Familiar was a wendigo, and it was creeping out the majority of the people in this class. It was easy to tell why. The wendigo had the skeletal body of a horse, with wolf's paws and a reptilian tail. The head was merely the skull of a deer, the antlers intact. Its black skin was drawn tightly over its skeletal form, and its bones clicked together as it wandered around the room.

Bram hissed and gnashed his sharp teeth near a student who'd fallen asleep. The guy woke up screaming, and the class laughed. I was pretty sure the dude pissed himself.

Bram chuckled like he was pleased before he moved on. The thing looked like it could survive in the wilds alone without a problem. In fact, Bram looked like he could survive, kill, and maim everything within a hundred miles of wherever he'd been abandoned.

McCauley was pretty creepy herself, and had to be close to a hundred by now. She matched her Familiar in looks, taut skin stretched over thin bones. The two of them appeared to be walking skeletons. McCauley dressed in all black, only increasing her frightening appearance.

They should've retired from teaching to become crypt keepers years ago. I was pretty sure McCauley was gonna outlive me.

This wasn't McCauley's class— Professor Devante usually taught Survival Instincts— but he and his wife had just had a baby, so McCauley was filling in for this semester.

Not that I minded. Professor McCauley had sneered at everything that had tried to kill her off so far, so obviously she knew a thing or two about staying alive.

"Water is more important to find than food in a survival situation. Depending on the situation, you will either need to find a source or have a Toaqua draw it up for you," McCauley preached.

Water was easy. I could supply it if we ran into a pinch, and Sophia had fire.

Unless one of us died, and the rest of us were screwed.

"If there is adequate access to water, the human body can survive around twenty days or so without food. Keep in mind, however, that by this time you will be very weak, and it will only take a matter of days without food before you become useless and unable to harvest or hunt." McCauley scanned the room with piercing crow eyes. "Therefore, daily nutrition becomes very important, for both you and your Familiar."

McCauley took a tray and began passing it around the room. "These types of plants are local to the region, and edible. You can find them in many places on earth. Memorize their appearances and names."

When the tray passed to me, I focused on it. Cattails, the inside of conifer bark, acorns, wild blueberries. Not exactly the most delicious, but when you were hungry, anything looked good.

I passed the tray behind me, and McCauley said, "There will be a quiz next time you come in. Anyone who doesn't pass I don't expect to last long. Class dismissed."

People gathered their things and headed out. McCauley's comment was obviously directed toward the tournament. Besides me, there were at least four other people in here who were going to be competing. I knew she was watching us and expecting us to do well.

I passed a bunch of squealing girls in the hallway complimenting one of the girls on her brand-new Familiar. I wasn't sure what it was, but it looked like a pink pom-pom. At least she had a year to bulk the thing up before she was forced to compete.

I winced as the girls squealed again and continued on. I thought Survival Instincts was going to be a blow-off class, but now that I was forced to be in the tournament, I made myself pay attention. And it was a good thing, too. I'd already learned how to make a quick shelter.

I no longer skipped class. I'd need every piece of information available to keep me and my team alive out there.

I heard someone else giggling— and I knew that voice. Around the corner was Sophia. She was leaning against the wall with a bunch of books in her hands. Esis was perched on top of them. Ezra was with her, grinning coyly. They hadn't seen me.

I was about to turn around and go the opposite way before Sophia said to Ezra, "Seriously, your Liam impressions are the best."

"Aren't they?" Ezra snorted. "It took months of perfection to get just the right scowl."

I slunk against the wall at Ezra's comment, hiding. Ezra and Sophia were *talking about me.*

The little bastards.

I was about to round the corner and confront them before a question from Sophia stopped me in my tracks. "So… what was Liam like? Before he lost Nashoma?"

What was I like? What made her think she had the right to ask that question?

I decided to hold back and listen in. Eavesdropping wasn't right, but hey, it was way better than playing the fool.

Ezra laughed. I imagined him looking up, because any time someone asked him a question the idiot always had to glance skyward, like the answer was on the ceiling. "What was he like before Nashoma? Well, let's see. His favorite thing was swearing. Still is. I think he started saying the F-Bomb when he was like, ten."

Sophia laughed, and I smiled. Yeah, that pretty much described me.

"He laughed a lot. He was always up for an adventure, whatever it was. He loved exploring. He wasn't a big sports guy, but he enjoyed being active. Hiking was one of his favorite things."

"I love hiking, too," Sophia said quietly.

"And he loved helping people," Ezra added. "He'd jump in any time to lend a hand. He had the biggest heart."

"Seriously?" Sophia's tone was doubtful. "None of that sounds like Liam."

"Is it really that hard to believe?" Ezra sounded amused. "Word around school is that he's the reason your Fire started emerging, and pretty strong, too."

Dammit. Should've known that would get out somehow. The damn trees had ears around here.

"It's just…" Sophia paused. "He was pretty blunt about it when he told me he hated helping people."

"Don't believe him. He's just being a jerk. It's like his default setting is grumpy nowadays."

Sophia and Ezra laughed together, and I scowled. *Thanks, assholes.*

"Nashoma just amplified those traits," Ezra said. "He became super brave. He was never afraid of anything. And he was a really good leader. Better than I ever could be."

Doubt that, Ez. People adored my brother. They rotated around him like he was the sun. I'd never been like that— popular.

"And now he's not the same," Sophia said.

"Now…" Ezra sighed. "He's secluded. He doesn't like being around anyone, not even me. He goes to class and then locks himself up in his dorm. I can't talk to him without being insulted."

Ouch. That was kind of true, but it hurt. I had been a dick to Ezra lately, along with everyone else.

"He seems very spiritual," Sophia commented. I think she was trying to direct the conversation into a more positive light.

"He is. He's super religious. Not that it isn't true, or anything, but I think Liam was more into our culture than any of us because he took the responsibility of being firstborn so seriously. It really hurt him when our dad told him he wasn't going to be chief anymore."

Fuck yeah it did. Second most painful day of my life was when Dad brought me in to tell me he was passing on the chief hood to Ezra. Fricken sucked.

"You said he was a good leader, but that he likes seclusion," Sophia mulled. "What does that mean?"

"He's always kind of been a lone wolf, pun intended," Ezra said. "Even before he lost Nashoma, he found it hard to let people in. He'd shoulder other people's problems but never share his own. It's just how he is."

"I bet he would've made a really great chief," Sophia said.

That small bit of praise made me want to fly. It was nice Sophia believed in me.

Until she said, "How do you feel about being chief?"

I imagined Ezra shrugging. "I don't know. It is what it is."

I knew he wasn't into it. But it wasn't like he had a choice now. My one bad decision had cost me Nashoma, but it had also cost my tribe its leader, and my brother his future.

"Do you… do you think he wants to make it through this tournament?" Sophia asked. "He said he didn't want to die, but…"

Sophia made a good point. Yeah, I didn't want to die. But I didn't really want to live, either. I was caught in the middle.

Ezra's voice became heavy. "I don't know. We were super close before Nashoma died. Then once it happened, it's like he couldn't see me anymore. He just… forgot about me."

A surge of guilt rampaged throughout my insides. Ezra and I had been close. We'd practically hung out every day, even after I started at Orenda. That had changed pretty quickly over the past few months.

I made a mental note to hang out with Ezra more often. I didn't realize it until now, but I missed him.

"Are you excited to find your Familiar?" Sophia asked him, trying to change the subject. "I wasn't sure, but once I found Esis, it's like my entire life changed. I'm so happy now."

"I don't know." Ezra's tone was guarded. "Not really."

Not really? What the hell was that supposed to mean?

"I get scared, you know," Ezra said, quietly now. "After seeing Liam go through what he did, if having a Familiar can cause you that much pain, I'm not sure I want one."

Double whammy. If I was guilty before, I felt like melting into the floor now.

This was my fault. My grief over losing Nashoma had pushed my brother into thinking having a Familiar was a terrible thing. But though my time with Nashoma had been so short and the pain afterward so intense, I wouldn't have changed a thing.

Not for anything.

Ezra paused. "Why are you asking about Liam, anyway?"

Yeah, pawee. Why are you trying to dig up dirt on me?

She hesitated. "We're tournament partners. It's my job to know as much as possible about him. I depend on him for my survival out there."

It was a great excuse, but I didn't buy it. Neither did Ezra. I could hear it in his voice. "Well, if the rest of us can't get him to open up, maybe you can. He really likes you."

"You think?" Sophia's voice sounded hopeful.

"Oh, yeah. I know my brother. He's really mean to the ones he likes the most. It keeps them from getting too close." I heard footsteps. "I've got to get to class. Catch you later."

"Yeah." Sophia went the opposite way, I assumed. I turned the corner and saw them going in different directions.

Sophia's hair was bouncing up and down on her shoulders behind her. I longed to explain to her that I really wasn't as big of a prick as she'd been told.

But I couldn't, you know, because I was.

I took a step forward to go after her, but then thought better of it. I needed to spend my free hour alone.

BANG, BANG, BANG.

I was jolted out of my dreams at the loud noise and wrenched awake. Somebody was trying to bang down my door at eight o'clock on a Friday morning.

I moaned and rolled over in bed. I was going to kill whoever was out there. Fridays were my days to sleep in, and my body fricken ached all over. Twelve hours of sleep hadn't done anything to dull the pain that'd been coursing through me last night.

"Liam!" I heard Jonah's voice outside the door. "Let me in, man!"

People from other Houses weren't usually allowed in dorms that didn't belong to them, but people made an exception for Jonah— mostly because he was friends with my family, and also, because the female RA's from my dorm loved having a gay best friend around. As long as no teachers found out, it wasn't a big deal.

He was going to bust the door off its hinges. I staggered out of bed and wrenched the door open.

"I swear to the ancestors, Jonah, you're gonna die," I snapped immediately.

Jonah looked down once at me in my boxers. "Good morning, sexy."

"Are you checking me out? Because I'm seriously not in the mood," I growled.

"Baine called us in for a training session for the tournament," Jonah said. "We gotta go. It starts at nine, beachside."

"Oh." It was like Baine to ruin a perfectly good Friday. "Fine."

I slammed the door in his face, threw on some clothes, and staggered outside without combing my hair.

Jonah offered me a doughnut. "Breakfast?"

The sight of it made me feel like puking and devouring it at the same time. Chronic illness was fucking stupid. "Yes." I grabbed it and shoved it down my throat.

"You've got jelly on your face," Jonah sang out. He was way too chipper in the morning.

I waved my hand as we walked by the pools. A huge wave welled up out of them and crashed down on Jonah, soaking him from head to toe.

"What the hell?!" Jonah yelled at me as Toaqua people laughed. "Was that really necessary?"

"Was it necessary to ram on my door to wake me up, Paul Bunyan?" I snapped.

"You wouldn't have woken up any other way," Jonah said back.

I rolled my eyes, because I knew he was right. I raised my hand and the water soaking him was drawn out of his clothes and hair, leaving him completely dry again. I opened my palm, and it splashed on the floor over his boots.

"What'd you do that for? Maybe I *liked* looking soaked and seductive," Jonah said.

By the ancestors, I couldn't deal with him this early in the morning.

"Why are you even studying to be an Elementai, Jonah? Why don't you just become a model for some sex toy catalogue instead?" I asked.

"If only." Jonah sighed dreamily. I slapped myself in the forehead. It'd been a joke, but seriously, I could see Jonah leaving school for such an opportunity.

Squeaks was waiting for us outside of the Toaqua dorms. She squealed happily when she saw Jonah, and followed us outside. She stumbled over her big feet a few times and knocked over a couple of statues on our way out. I shook my head. If I ever met a more clumsy hippogriff than Squeaks in my life, I'd protest for the species to continue.

It was still cloudy outside, but the storms had passed late last night. When we got to the beach, Squeaks tripped and went head over heels into the sand. While Jonah helped her up, I looked around for Sophia. She was there, sitting on a large rock by the shore.

Imogen wasn't with her, which was odd. Those two girls were hardly apart lately.

"Hey," I said as I approached her. Sophia looked up, and I asked, "Where's Imogen? It's almost nine."

"She isn't coming," Sophia said. "She has a cold."

"You heard from her?" Jonah asked.

Sophia went slightly pink. "Uh… no. I haven't talked to Imogen since yesterday. A Nivita girl from her dorm hall told me that this morning, before I left."

This was irritating. Our first training session, and Imogen was skipping. Usually I wouldn't care if someone didn't show up because they got sick. Like, stay in bed, because I don't want that shit. I hated when classmates showed up with a cold or the flu. All you were doing was making people miserable and spreading it around.

But this was survival, and we only got so many chances to get this right before we were literally tossed into the threshold of hell. She'd better be puking out her guts right now, because having a cold wasn't a good enough excuse for, you know, learning how to avoid death.

"That's okay," I forced myself to say. "She needs to take care of herself and get strong for what's coming."

"You don't seem to think that way when it comes to yourself," Sophia said.

"I have different standards for myself. If I stayed in bed every time I felt ill, I'd never leave my room," I told her.

Jonah and Squeaks nodded solemnly behind me, in unison. It was a little weird.

"What about Sassy?" I asked. "Is she gonna show?"

"I don't think so." Sophia shook her head.

She couldn't even send Sassy? This was getting interesting. I was starting to think that Imogen not showing up was because of something that happened between her and Sophia and not this imaginary cold.

Drama was the last thing we needed right now. These girls needed to get it together.

"Imogen should be here. There are only two more sessions after this," Jonah said.

"What?" Sophia's expression became surprised.

"We only get three training sessions with Baine," I told her. "More than that is considered cheating."

"Great." She wrinkled her nose. "I guess we should make the most of it."

We waited on the beach for Baine to show up. But nine o'clock came, and then nine thirty, and Baine was nowhere to be seen.

Okay, this was majorly annoying. First Imogen wasn't coming, and now Baine was late to his own damn training session. We were so going to lose.

"I'm about ready to head back to my dorm," I said. It'd been annoying before, but now it was seriously pissing me off. Did Baine even care if we survived?

"Let's just wait a few minutes longer." Sophia looked around. She was getting nervous.

"Hold on a minute, guys…" Jonah looked around, and Squeaks' head swiveled on her neck. "Do you hear something?"

I paused and listened closely. There was… the rushing of water— the approach of an oncoming wave.

"Jonah, get Sophia up in the air!" I screamed.

I ran toward the forest and paused at the edge while Jonah took Sophia's hand tightly. He pushed his free palm toward the ground and the two of them rose into the sky, hovering far above the beach. Sophia clung tightly to Esis as she was sent soaring into the skies. Squeaks followed them, beating her wings so she could match their height.

Then it came. Trees bowed over as a massive wave came rushing out from the forest. I immediately threw my hands up in front of me, fingers wide, to prevent the wave from knocking me over. The water swelled around me and rushed back into the ocean, but it was hard. I struggled to keep my balance, and my strength, as the force of the powerful wave threatened to bowl me over.

Jonah saw that I needed help and curled his fingers into his palm. Immediately I felt the wind pick up around me and it spun quickly in a circle, protecting me from the water. Sophia was looking around above me, unsure of what to do.

The wave was getting stronger, harder for me to fend off. Eventually, the water broke through Jonah's shield and crushed my magic. I was dragged underneath the wave and rushed out to sea. I heard Sophia screaming.

I couldn't tell which way was up. But I knew I needed to breathe. Summoning what magic was left within me, I pushed my hands downward and the water around me shot me up like a rocket. I broke onto the surface. I felt Jonah's Air magic around me as I was lifted to the clouds, where he, Sophia, and Squeaks were levitating.

The wave below us had vanished, returning to the ocean. The beach was soaking wet, and a few trees had been knocked over. As far as we could tell, everything was safe. Jonah drifted us downward. We landed and looked around, not sure what had just happened.

Without warning Jonah was knocked down to the sand by a jet of water that slapped him in the back of the head. He groaned, and as Squeaks raced to check on him the pools of water she stood in turned to ice. Her feet were caught. Squeaks squawked and tried to pull free, but as hard as she tried to escape she just couldn't break the hold the ice had on her.

The ice was spreading. It was growing over Jonah and Squeaks' legs, their bodies. I tried to use my own Water magic to stop it, but it was far too strong. Whoever was controlling the element had more experience than I did. No matter how much I willed the ice to turn to water again, it just wouldn't obey my command.

Sophia raised her hand to shoot a jet of fire at the ice so it would melt and set Jonah free. But as she was doing so, I saw several small streams of water right from behind her. They formed into snow, then changed into daggers of ice, spinning in the air and shooting directly for Sophia's back.

"Look out!" I shouted, and I ran toward her. I was too far away, so I would never get to her before the knives did. But Sophia had good instincts, and she was able to spin around and duck before the daggers implanted themselves in her form.

I was already on my way, so I ended up tripping and knocking her down before she could free Jonah. Esis flew from her arm, landing a few feet away.

"Liam!" Sophia shouted in frustration. "I had it handled!"

"I just wanted to make sure you were safe," I shot back, but this was no time for arguing. Before our horrified gazes, Jonah and Squeaks were slowly being taken over by the ice. We rushed over. Sophia used her power to try and melt the ice, while I did my best to try and break it apart. Esis scratched at Squeaks with his little nails, but it was no use. Sophia's Fire wasn't powerful enough now. The ice had spread too far, had been given too much time.

I tapped on the ice with my knuckles. I could see Jonah inside, but he didn't move.

Oh, shit. He was dead.

I had helped to kill my best friend, now I knew. I was definitely cursed. Everyone who came around me met an untimely end. Maybe Haley was right and I was a burden to the tribe…

Suddenly, the ice turned to water and Jonah broke free, gasping for air. Squeaks crashed out of her icy prison and tumbled onto the ground. Esis made chattering sounds, looking her over and making sure she was all right.

"Jonah! Are you okay?" Sophia worried. He was coughing and gasping for breath.

"I used the pockets of air within the ice to survive, but there wasn't much in there," Jonah said. His skin was blue. Sophia lit a fire in her palms to warm him up, and he huddled close to it, shivering. Squeaks came up behind him and wrapped herself around his form, using her wings as a blanket.

"Well, I can hardly say I'm impressed," a voice behind us said. Baine was standing there, looking thoroughly disappointed and even more glum than usual.

"You did this?" I asked furiously. This was total bullshit.

"Yes, I did, Liam. And it's far from the worst you're going to experience out there during the tournament," Baine quipped back immediately. "If that was your best effort, none of you will make it past the first task."

"It wasn't our best," Sophia protested. "We were just unprepared."

"Do you think you're going to be prepared for what's coming?" Baine raised an eyebrow. "No one is going to hand you a list of what you're going to be put through, Sophia."

"Can't you just tell us what the tasks are?" Jonah whined, shivering under Squeaks' wings.

"Even if I would, I couldn't. The tasks change every year. This makes it so no one has an unfair advantage," Baine said.

Jonah groaned. Baine turned toward me with his hands in his pockets. "I'm surprised, Liam. I thought you trusted Sophia, but the way you acted made it seem like you don't think she has the ability to back you up."

"That's not true!" I snapped. "She's strong enough. Her magic's nothing to downplay."

Sophia's face was red. "No. You were too busy trying to *protect me*. If this had been real, Jonah would've died!" Sophia shouted.

I cringed. Yeah, that had been my fault. My first instinct had been to protect Sophia before anyone else. I told Jonah to get her out of the way of the wave before we made a cohesive plan to combat it together, and I messed her up when she was trying to save our friend. She saw the knives coming.

So why did I feel the need to interfere?

"The tribe as a unit is more important than any one person. You have to learn this, Liam," Baine said sharply. "There are no heroes or martyrs in the Elemental Cup. Only survivors and casualties."

My cheeks burned. Our first test as a group, and we'd horribly failed.

"Did you really have to put us through all that?" Jonah asked. He'd stopped shivering now and looked pissed.

"That's why I sprang on you. You need to learn to expect the unexpected," Baine said. "The tournament only gets harder each year. I will put you three through whatever I have to in order to make sure you survive."

You three? Baine didn't even notice one of our teammates was missing. I was going to start hitting my head against a tree in about two seconds.

"Get up," Baine told all of us roughly. "We've already wasted precious time."

Who's fault is that, since they showed up late? I thought bitterly. This guy was too much.

Jonah stumbled to his feet with the help of Squeaks. The rest of the morning was spent with Baine drilling us on our powers, doing so many summoning reps that it made my arms hurt. I sparred with Jonah and Sophia both, but none of us managed to get a hit on the other. I could've, seeing as how I was a Third Year and had sparring experience, but I already felt bad enough I'd hurt Jonah, so I left him alone, and Sophia…

I couldn't fight her, not even for practice. It just wasn't in me. She noticed, because her Fire kept getting more and more intense with every fireball she tossed at me. Fury burned in her eyes, but the angrier she got, the gentler I became. I just fizzled her fireballs out with my Water and tried not to look her in the eye. Esis watched us closely, his eyes darting back and forth with every bit of magic we flung at each other.

When it was time to break for lunch, Baine appeared even more disappointed than he was before. We headed back to the castle without him. Jonah mumbled that he had a headache and was going to lie down.

When we could no longer hear Squeaks tripping over things, I knew they were gone. I was going to head back to the Toaqua dorms, but I followed Sophia to the Koigni hall instead.

Before we got to the doors, she rounded on me. "You think I'm so weak I need to be escorted?"

"No. I just…" I hesitated. "I just wanted to hang out with you."

Her face softened a little, but my response wasn't enough to calm her down. "I already know that I'm the outcast here. But I thought you were the one person who believed I was capable of being your teammate. Now I know you just think I'm weak."

Damn Baine for putting words in my mouth. "It's not about being weak," I told her. My voice was calm and steady. "I just reacted today. That's all."

"If you react and don't think, we're all dead out there," she said harshly. Esis was at her feet, looking between us with droopy ears. He didn't like it when we fought.

"I just wanted to protect you." I leaned against the wall. "Is that so wrong?"

Sophia chewed her lip. "No. But you know how things go in the Elementai world. You have to be the strongest. Otherwise, people won't respect you. I may be new here, but I've learned that much. You can't protect me everywhere, Liam."

I was regretting so much of everything I'd told her when she got here. I wanted to take it all back and convince her things were different, but that would be a lie, because they weren't. "I think you're strong," I told her. "This was just the first training session. It's okay we made mistakes. We still have two more chances."

Sophia nodded. "I guess you're right." She put her hand on the Koigni door. "I would love to hang out, but I have to practice. See you later, Liam."

When she shut the door in my face, the sound of the door clicking was like a gunshot to my heart. I backed away from the door slowly, unsure of what I would do with myself. I'd been secretly hoping Sophia would come with me to town. Get some food, see stuff.

Not like a date, you know. Just friends.

I realized I really didn't want to spend another weekend hiding in my dorm like I had been. I decided to go look for Ez. Maybe he had nothing going on. I thought about hitting up Jonah, but he was in a rough way. He probably wouldn't get out of bed now until Monday.

I wracked my brain for other people to hit up, but I hadn't talked to most of them in… months.

Had I really pushed everyone in my life so far away?

As I walked back to the Toaqua dorms, Baine's words resonated in my head. I had to trust that Sophia was strong enough to stand on her own. It's not that I didn't believe in her or her powers.

I just didn't trust whatever the Elders had created to take us down.

I'd already lost Nashoma. I didn't want to lose her, too.

Exhaustion settled into my bones on Saturday morning. I lay in bed staring up at the ornate carvings in the shape of flames on the ceiling, thinking about yesterday. Baine's training session should've motivated me to train harder, but I couldn't seem to summon the energy to get out of bed. I just kept playing scenarios in my head of what obstacles we might face in the tournament and all the possible ways Liam would manage to screw it up— or save me. One of the two.

Thinking about Liam was always dangerous. Every time he crossed my mind, I thought about the pain he was in without Nashoma. I contemplated telling him about Esis so that Esis could heal him, but I also didn't want anyone knowing about Esis' power. It was the only way to protect him. And if I had to choose between a guy I might possibly be falling for and my Familiar— my literal soul— my Familiar would win out. Every. Single. Time.

I only wished I could find a way to protect them both.

Esis stretched from where he slept beside my head on the pillow. His weight shifted, and suddenly his big blue eyes were hovering over me. He placed a small palm on my cheek and made a chipper sound like a songbird.

I sighed. "I know it's time to get up, buddy, but I'm just not feeling it today."

I'd spent every weekend since I'd been summoned training with my magic so I wouldn't die in this stupid tournament, but all I really wanted was a break. And I didn't mean another study session in the library, either. Reading over the stats of previous years' tournaments was just depressing. There'd been more deaths in the tournament in the past few years than in the last century, and sometimes they didn't even find the bodies. The Elders were seriously stepping up their game so our generation had to work harder than any before to prove our place. I'd hoped the records would teach me something about what was to come, but I was starting to think that it didn't matter how much I trained or how much studying I did... I'd never be ready for this.

The only thing that would keep me alive was making sure my team was willing to work together. But I still hadn't heard from Imogen, and I wasn't sure Liam wanted to talk to me after the way I blew him off last night.

Which totally sucked because for some reason, all I wanted to do was hang out with him.

Esis patted my face again. When I turned my eyes to him, he stuck a thumb in his mouth and started sucking on it.

I couldn't help but smile. "Are you hungry, buddy?"

He nodded.

I forced myself to get up and stroked my hand through his fur. "Fine. We'll go grab breakfast after I take a quick shower."

Esis immediately jumped down from the bed and scurried across the room. My dorm was bigger than my room back home, with fancy decor that went beyond anything I could ever imagine. Deep red velvety sheets hung over the sides of my queen-sized bed. The bed frame was made from metal rods painted in gold, with a bed knob in the shape of a flame at the end of each post. The bed sat upon a large, ornate area rug, but the rest of the room had hardwood flooring. The walls were red to match my sheets. The long curtains in front of my window had various shades intertwining to create complicated patterns. Across the room stood a small brick fireplace with a plush red chair in front of it like the ones in the common room. Various other pieces of furniture were scattered around the room, including a vanity by the bathroom, a dresser near the walk-in closet, and a nightstand next to the bed. A candelabra chandelier hung from the high ceiling. The room was beautiful— I couldn't argue with that. But it seemed more like a place you'd spend the weekend than a place you'd call home.

Esis hurried into the open bathroom door. He jumped toward the towel rack, his tiny little fingers stretching high into the air. He chirped in victory when the towel came sliding down. It draped over top of him, but he burrowed his way out and dragged the towel into the bedroom behind him.

I stood, laughing. "Thank you, Esis. You're so helpful." I bent to pick up the towel and gave him a pat on the head.

He cooed in response.

Esis sat outside the bathroom while I showered and changed. At my dresser, he handed me my hairbrush and hair tie. He made sure to choose a green hair tie to match my shirt since he knew I didn't like to mix colors.

Esis perched atop my shoulder as we made our way to the dining hall for breakfast. The bright morning sunlight shone through the tall windows, casting rays across the red carpet in the Koigni hall. Like most Saturday mornings, the castle was quiet. When we reached the cafeteria it buzzed lightly with conversation, but most of the tables remained empty.

I grabbed two breakfast sandwiches from the takeout line and turned back to the main doors to head outside when I heard the sound of someone calling my name. I spun around and my eyes scanned the cafeteria. They landed upon Imogen in the corner, who was waving me over.

Relief flooded through me to see a familiar face, but it was quickly replaced with sickening doubt when I reminded myself what had recently happened between us. Then again, no Nivita Elders had shown up at my door to drag Esis away, so maybe there was still hope that Imogen hadn't abandoned me after what she saw.

I sighed and approached her, knowing I was going to have to face her sooner or later. Today she wore brightly-colored rainbow leggings with a rhinestone t-shirt. Her strawberry blonde hair was tied into a high ponytail with multi-colored strings mixed into the strands. Sassy's fluffy red tail poked out from beneath the table.

"I was starting to think I'd never see you again," I said lightheartedly as I slid into the seat across from Imogen. My heart felt anything but light.

She furrowed her brow. "Why wouldn't you see me again? I was sick, not dead."

I unwrapped the foil from one of the breakfast sandwiches and handed it to Esis. Suddenly, I didn't feel like eating. "Why'd you run away from us the other day? You weren't sick then, were you?"

"No… oh, my ancestors!" Imogen smacked her palm to her forehead. "You must've thought the worst of me! I'm so sorry. I should've got in touch with you sooner. It was just that inspiration struck, and I *had* to get home. Then my little brother got me sick, and it was just this whole thing." She waved her hands like it didn't really matter.

"So, we're still friends?" I asked cautiously.

"By the ancestors, of course we are!" Imogen placed a hand over her heart as if she was having a heart attack. "What did you *think* happened?"

I glanced around the cafeteria, but no one was close enough to hear us. I lowered my voice anyway. "I thought after what you saw, you might turn me and Esis in to the Nivita Elders." I dropped my gaze and bit my lower lip.

"What?" Imogen asked in disbelief. "I would never do that to you, Sophia."

I pulled Esis down from my shoulder and cradled him in my arms. "I'm just scared that if anyone knew what he could do, they might try to take him away from me. This kind of power isn't normal, right?"

Imogen took a bite of pancake and shook her head. "No, it's not. And it's probably best if you don't tell anyone else about it."

I gazed up at her, hopeful. "So, you'll keep our secret?"

"Girl, I'll take it to the grave." A moment later Imogen's eyes lit up, and she leaned forward to rest her elbows on the table. "Do you want to know what I've been doing the past few days?"

"Yes," I said, intrigued.

A smile spread across her face. "I've been researching Esis' origin. Do you want to come over to my house and see what I found?"

I couldn't contain my eagerness. "Absolutely!"

After we finished breakfast, Imogen led me outside and through the gardens.

"My neighborhood is pretty far from the school," Imogen explained, "so we'll have to borrow a ride."

"Ooh," I said in excitement. My mood had drastically improved now that I knew Imogen and I were cool. "What kind of ride are we talking about? A peryton? A pegasus? A dragon?"

"No, no," she said, shaking her head. The strings in her hair swung from side to side. "I prefer to keep my feet on the ground. You know how to ride horseback, don't you?"

"Um… is it complicated?" My only experience riding a horse was at a petting zoo when I was six, but I wasn't sure that counted, considering the trainer held on to the reins the whole time and I only rode the horse for maybe five minutes.

Imogen shrugged, sending Sassy bouncing in her tote bag. "That's okay, the unicorns are very well trained and do most of the work anyway."

"I get to ride a unicorn?!" I exclaimed in excitement.

"Yeah," Imogen said, like it was no big deal. "Come on. We're almost there."

The trees opened to a large clearing with two huge red stables sitting side-by-side. Each of them had large sliding doors. I peered inside the first building to see a row of stalls on either side of the barn. I caught sight of several different creatures, including two perytons and a pegasus. Several guys milled around, tending to the animals.

"This way," Imogen said, gesturing me over to the second building.

A cool breeze rushed through the stables when we stepped inside. I didn't know why I was expecting to inhale a floral scent, as if the unicorns farted rainbows and pooped butterflies, but all that hit my nose was the scent of a barn— hay, wood shavings, leather and dust.

My eyes fell upon each unicorn as we passed. They had the body of a horse, with the same long nose, pointed ears, and large frame, but everything else about them looked as if they'd just stepped out of a fantasy painting. The first unicorn was completely white, with a mane that took the shape of cool blue water. It was as if a waterfall was flowing right out of its head, the water droplets disappearing into the air like magic. A shiny silver horn stretched a foot in length and twisted to a sharp point.

The next unicorn had brown fur, with hooves the texture of tree bark and a mane the color of grass. Its horn was like an expertly-carved branch growing out of its forehead with intricate carvings etched into it. I couldn't tell if the designs were natural or placed there deliberately, but given the magical beauty of these creatures, I guessed they were born that way.

In the next stall stood a black unicorn whose mane and tail flickered red and orange— like real flames. It was a wonder the stables hadn't burned down. Its horn looked as if it had been forged from a black matte metal, with subtle but elegant ridges traveling the length of it.

"Hey, Cade," Imogen greeted cheerfully as she strolled up to one of the guys scooping out an empty stall.

Cade shoveled a pile of used shavings into his wheelbarrow, then looked up at us. He wore a skin-tight cotton t-shirt that stretched across his broad shoulders and toned chest. His skin was naturally tan, but most of his Hawkei genes had been traded for Latin American features. He had short dark hair, and his brown eyes were soft and friendly.

Cade definitely had a sexy vibe going on, but looking at him in that way made me feel like I was cheating on Liam. Which was so totally weird, because we weren't together. I immediately pushed the thought from my mind.

Imogen, on the other hand, was eyeing Cade up and down like he was a god. I guessed he was Nivita, but he didn't have a Familiar at his side, so it was hard to tell.

"What can I do for you today?" he asked in a friendly tone as he wiped sweat from his brow.

"Is anyone up for a ride?" Imogen walked over to the nearest stall, the one with the Water unicorn inside, and patted her hand on the top of the door. "What do you say, Kiki? You wanna go for a ride today?"

"Kiki just got back from a ride last night," Cade said. "How about Daisy and Jack?" He gestured to the two unicorns in the stalls beside Kiki.

Imogen's eyes lit up, and she stepped toward the Earth unicorn. "I love Jack!"

Cade opened the door and coaxed Jack out of his stall. "You're not going to braid ribbons in his tail again, are you?"

Imogen swatted at him, and her cheeks grew bright red. "Shut up. He looked gorgeous."

Cade smirked playfully. "If I'm going to sign Jack out to you, you have to *promise* not to bring him back dyed purple or some crazy shit like that."

Imogen giggled like a little school girl. It was so unlike her. Esis threw his hands over his eyes and then slowly peeked out between them. He clearly couldn't watch their obvious flirting.

"I won't. I swear," Imogen promised.

Cade moved to the next stall to get the Fire unicorn. "Good."

"I'll bring him back blue," Imogen deadpanned.

"Imogen," he complained, but he didn't sound truly bothered.

"Fine," she relented. "I won't do anything weird. He's beautiful just the way he is. Aren't you, Jackie boy?"

Imogen rubbed Jack's head. He nuzzled into her arm, as if searching for treats.

"And here's Daisy," Cade said, patting her back.

Daisy stepped out of her stall until she was just a foot away from me. I reached up to stroke her soft black fur. It felt like velvet. Warily, I reached out for her fiery mane and was surprised when my fingers passed straight through it without feeling a thing. I glanced down at my hand, like I expected it to be blistered or something.

"She won't hurt you," Imogen said. "She's magical. Remember?"

Daisy pivoted on the spot until her middle was facing me.

"She likes you," Cade said. "She's inviting you to climb on her back."

I stroked her fur again, but hesitated. "Don't I need a saddle and reins?"

Cade laughed. "Not with unicorns. Would you like a boost?"

Before I could answer, Cade was helping me onto Daisy's back. I gave an involuntary yelp, and Imogen giggled. She didn't need any help hopping onto Jack's back. She jumped and swung her leg onto him, then sat there comfortably with Sassy secured safely in her bag. Sassy poked her head out and glanced around, looking positively at peace atop the unicorn's back.

I, on the other hand, clamped my hands around Daisy's neck, hoping I wouldn't topple off her back and be trampled. Esis chirped and hopped off my shoulder. He climbed up Daisy's head and wrapped a small hand around her horn. He stood there proudly, like a captain holding on to the mast of his ship. Daisy didn't seem to mind.

"Make sure to keep them both hydrated. Imogen knows the drill." Cade winked at her, and she went beet red.

"Thanks, Cade," Imogen said as Jack started leading her toward the open door.

Daisy followed. My hold on her tightened as I swayed from side to side with each step.

"Wait!" Cade called just as both of our unicorns stepped outside. "You forgot something."

Cade stopped beside Imogen and wiggled his fingers. Next to him, a green plant rose from the ground. Its thin stem twisted and grew until it stopped in front of Imogen's nose. A small purple flower bloomed at the end of it, confirming that Cade was Nivita.

Imogen smiled and plucked the flower from the long stem. She placed it in her hair behind her ear. "Thank you, Cade. You're the best. We'll see you later."

She waved. Cade returned to the stables while Imogen and I started down a nearby path. It wasn't as wide as the roads back home, but since no one used cars around here, I figured it must've been the main drag into town. Daisy and Jack walked beside each other at a brisk pace.

"So...?" I wiggled my eyebrows.

Imogen looked at me innocently. "Yeah?"

"Why haven't you ever mentioned him before?"

"Who? Cade?" Imogen's voice rose at least three pitches when she said his name. "He's just a guy I grew up with. He was my older brother's best friend. What's there to say about him?"

"How about the fact that you're totally crushing on him and never *once* mentioned it?"

"What?" Imogen squeaked. "I am not! Cade is just... Cade."

"Yes, sweet and handsome Cade," I agreed. "Who you have the hots for."

Imogen rolled her eyes and then stared straight down the road. "Girl, are you high or something?"

I laughed. "Okay, so you don't like him. But you *have* to know he likes you."

"Well, that answers that question. *Clearly* you're on drugs. No guy ever pays attention to me. I'm fat and weird."

"You're not fat," I countered. "And maybe he likes you *because* you're weird. I like your quirks."

Imogen pressed her lips together. She didn't look convinced.

I was starting to feel comfortable enough on Daisy's back that I loosened my grip on her mane. "He made sure you didn't leave without giving you a flower."

"So? He always does that."

I stared at her with raised eyebrows.

Imogen inhaled a deep breath. "Oh, my ancestors! I never knew. I totally friend-zoned him!" She threw her hands over her face and nearly fell off her unicorn in the process.

"Tell me about him," I said.

"I don't know what to say. We've known each other my whole life… we used to play in my treehouse when we were kids."

"So you're close?"

Imogen shrugged. "I guess you could say that. He was there when I bonded with Sassy almost a year ago." She dropped her head and bit her lip. "Anyway, that's not important. Cade and I can go weeks without talking, but we always pick right back up where we left off."

We reached town while she was recounting a story about how Cade and her brother had convinced her the forest was haunted. I listened to her story, but my eyes roamed the city. The only other time I'd seen it was when Liam and I had arrived, but that was only the smallest part of town. There was so much to see in the heart of the Hawkei village that I couldn't seem to take it all in.

We rode along the narrow streets of the Chinatown district. Paper lanterns hung above our heads, and the scent of fried rice and noodles filled my nose. From there, we passed into the Hawkei district. People milled along the streets and stopped at carts that sold things like potions and Hawkei food, such as corn roasted with butter and spices. I'd seen this part of town before, but it was like seeing it for the first time all over again. I barely had time to take it all in before Daisy turned and led us down a secluded street.

We left the buildings behind and traveled into the forest, where some of the largest trees I'd ever seen grew. They rose at least three-hundred feet into the sky. We hadn't made it far before my eyes fell on a large structure hanging high in the trees. I squinted, trying to make out its shape. Soon, more and more structures of similar size came into view.

Treehouses.

"Oh, my gosh!" I exclaimed. "When you said treehouses, I thought you meant a playhouse in your backyard. I didn't think you literally lived in a treehouse!"

Imogen laughed. "I'm Nivita. Where else would I live?"

I gazed upward in wonder. The treehouses were huge and suspended at least forty feet in the air. Each one was supported by at least three different trees. They all had wooden exteriors like log cabins, with wrap-around balconies, big windows, and slanted roofs, but each had its own unique charm. A network of bridges passed from house to house.

Daisy and Jack stopped below one of the bigger treehouses. I barely noticed we'd stopped. I was still trying to take in the sheer size of this neighborhood suspended in the trees. It went on farther than I could see.

Imogen slid off Jack's back and adjusted Sassy in her bag. Then she reached out to pat Jack's head. "You did so well, Jack! You deserve some carrots later. We'll be back soon, okay?"

I swung my leg over Daisy's back and landed softly on the ground. Esis chirped and scurried off Daisy's head and onto my shoulder. I glanced around, looking for any sign of steps or ladders to get up to the house.

"You look worried," Imogen said.

I turned back to her. "No. I was just wondering how we get up there. Are there stairs or something?"

"Yeah, but we're not going that way."

"Um… okay. How do we get up, then?"

"Oh, it's easy." She giggled. "Well, not for you."

"What does that mean?" I asked curiously. I wasn't going to have to learn how to climb the tree without footholds, was I?

Imogen smiled. "It means you'd burn this whole forest down if you tried my method. Here, stand over there."

Imogen took me by the shoulders and guided me away from the unicorns and to the base of the nearest tree.

"Don't try this at home," she warned. "Here we go."

Before I knew what was happening, something tickled my leg. I lifted my foot in surprise, but it grabbed ahold of me and wouldn't let me go. I looked down to see a thick tree root snaking up out of the ground and curling around my leg like the tentacles of an octopus. Several more roots crept out of the dirt and secured themselves around my legs, all the way up to my hips.

"Relax," Imogen said as another root wrapped itself around her. "I'm not going to hurt you."

I relaxed as she instructed and held tightly on to Esis so he wouldn't fall. The tree roots grew more and more until they were lifting us up into the sky. Although it should've freaked me out, I felt secure in the roots' hold, as if they were a safety harness keeping me from plummeting to the ground. We ascended skyward like an elevator. The roots arched over the railing and set us down on the bridge. Their hold on me loosened and they shrank away. I glanced over the top of the railing to see them retreating into the ground until they were completely gone. The dirt shifted to cover them, as if they'd never seen the light of day.

"That was really cool, Imogen," I said.

"Yeah, it's cool now," she replied. "Living in a treehouse wasn't so cool when you were a kid who had to walk *all* the way down fifteen houses to get to the stairs. You wouldn't believe it, but I could barely keep a weed alive. I didn't learn the shortcut until recently. Anyway, you wanna meet my parents?"

Imogen started down the bridge toward the nearest house, which rose two stories high and was supported by five massive trees. I hesitated as nerves settled in my gut. I knew Imogen didn't care that I was Koigni, but I wasn't sure her parents would like me. Like she said, I could literally burn this whole forest down. There was probably a reason they didn't have many entrances that other Elementai could enter through.

"What's wrong?" Imogen asked when she reached the front door.

I swallowed down the lump in my throat. "Will your parents be fine with having… a Koigni in their house?"

Imogen smiled. "Of course. Don't worry about it. My parents are a lot more… progressive than most. They think all the Houses should mix and that we should do away with most of our traditions."

My shoulders relaxed. "That's good to know."

Imogen turned and swung the door open. "Mom! Dad! I'm home! And I brought a friend!"

Two young boys raced in from the living room and body-slammed her with a group hug.

"I thought you were going back to school," the taller of them said, gazing up at her with a twinkle in his eye. He looked like he might be six, while the other boy looked around four. They both had Imogen's strawberry blonde hair, but they didn't have her sense of style. They dressed normally, both wearing jeans and a t-shirt.

Imogen bent to her knee. "I had to come back because Sassy missed you!"

On cue, Sassy leapt from her bag. She jumped playfully at the younger boy, who let out a gleeful laugh. Imogen stood, giggling as she watched her brothers tickle Sassy. Sassy rolled over like a dog and they scratched her belly.

I glanced around to take in the home. Everything was bathed in natural wood tones, from the hardwood floor and walls to the cupboards and the furniture. It was like something you'd see out of a travel magazine if you were looking for a quaint cabin getaway. A long wooden table with eight chairs around it sat to our left beside a pair of double glass doors that led onto the balcony. Beyond that sat a full kitchen. To our right was a living room with two long couches and a TV above a cute metal fireplace. A hallway behind the stairs stretched back into the house. The pile of dishes in the sink and toys scattered around the living room gave the home an obvious lived-in vibe.

"How old are your brothers?" I asked, trying to remember if she'd told me before.

"Oh, gosh," Imogen said with a sigh. "Levi is four, and Quentin is seven, then Roland is ten and Soren is fifteen."

"So, you're the oldest?" I asked.

"No. Well… yeah." Imogen dropped her head.

I laughed. "Well, which is it?"

"It's, um, complicated." Imogen didn't meet my gaze. "My older brother— the one who was friends with Cade— he's, uh, not around anymore."

My heart immediately sank. "Imogen, I'm so sorry. I shouldn't have asked."

"No, it's okay," she said, finally meeting my gaze. "You didn't know."

I bit my lower lip, wishing I had words for her. "Why didn't you mention anything?"

"I didn't want to scare you."

"Scare me?"

Imogen nodded. "Yeah. Because of how he died."

"Are you talking about Trace?" Quentin asked while still petting Sassy.

Levi stuck his bottom lip out. "I miss Trace."

"It's almost been a year, you know," Quentin told Levi.

"I know," Levi said, "but I can still remember him from when I was three. I can even remember from when I was two. Trace was the best brother ever… until he died in the tournament."

The breath left my chest. I suppose I couldn't blame Imogen for never mentioning him to me.

The conversation came to an abrupt halt as a blonde woman descended the stairs. She wore a pink polka-dotted scarf around her head and a blue dress that looked like it came straight out of the fifties. A pair of black cat-eye glasses famed her face. I could see where Imogen got her quirky fashion inspiration from.

The woman was followed by a type of canine I'd never seen before. It looked like a Pomeranian, but with longer ears. Its fur was completely white except for the rings of blue outlining its silver eyes and the matching tufts of blue on its ears. It wore a pink scarf around its neck that matched the one in the woman's hair.

"Hey, Mom," Imogen greeted. "Where's Dad and the boys? It's strangely quiet in here without them."

"Mushroom hunting," her mom answered.

"Yum… mushrooms." Imogen gestured to me. "This is Sophia, by the way. The girl I was telling you about."

Her mom's face lit up. "Oh, hello, Sophia!" She held her arms out as she made her way over to me. She drew me into a hug.

I squeezed her back awkwardly.

"I'm Gracie," she said, pulling away from me. "Imogen's told me all about you. Oh, who's this little guy?"

She smiled at Esis but didn't try to pet him. I was grateful for her respect of my Familiar.

"This is Esis," I introduced, scratching behind his ears. He responded with a purr and nuzzled into my fingers.

"He's so adorable!" Gracie clapped her hands together.

Gracie's dog barked once at Esis and then let his tongue hang from his mouth cheerfully. Esis jumped down from my shoulder and circled the dog. Gracie's Familiar nipped at Esis playfully as they chased each other around. Across the room, Sassy perked her ears up and quickly joined in on the game.

Imogen's brothers burst into a fit of laughter. I couldn't contain my own giggles. There was just too much cuteness in one room to handle all at once.

Gracie tore her eyes off our Familiars and turned her attention back to Imogen and me. "So, what are you girls up to?"

Imogen's eyes darted toward me but quickly returned to her mother. "Um... we're working on something for Dragonology. We need to use the library."

Gracie's brows drew together. "You've already spent so much time in there the last few days. Your teachers are pushing you too hard. When I attended Orenda, we didn't have homework. And don't even get me started on the Elemental Cup. It's ludicrous how times have changed. Your father and I both—"

"Mom," Imogen cut her off. "Can we not do this again?"

Gracie looked at me, then back to Imogen. "You're right. Now's not the time. I'm sorry. You two go have fun. Can I bring you anything?"

"No, but thanks, Mom," Imogen answered before gesturing for me to follow her down the hall.

Sassy and Esis scurried behind us. We passed by two bedrooms and a bathroom before reaching the door at the end.

Imogen paused with her hand on the doorknob. "You like books, right?"

"Of course." I bounced on my toes, eager to see her family's library.

Imogen smiled. "Then you're going to love this."

The door swung open, and my jaw promptly dropped to the floor. When she hinted at a library in her home, I pictured a few shelves of books and a couch or something. This was much, much more than that.

The room was twice the size of the living room, with a vaulted ceiling and tall bookcases that covered every inch of the walls on my left and my right. There was even a short wooden ladder leaning against one of the bookcases so that you could reach the top shelf. The wall opposite the door was made entirely of glass and overlooked the beautiful green forest. Beneath the window, a plush couch stretched from wall to wall, providing the perfect reading nook. It was long enough that Imogen and I could easily stretch out on either side at the same time. A round table with two chairs sat in the middle of the room with several thick books stacked atop it. The same natural wood tones that covered the rest of the house were present in the library as well.

"Holy crap," I whispered breathlessly as I stepped into the room, taking it all in. "Your family really loves books."

Imogen just shrugged, as if it was normal for families to have their own home libraries. She pulled out a chair at the table and flipped open the book at the top of the stack. "Yeah, I guess you could call us bookworms. Most people just call us crazy."

"What?" I squeaked, sliding into the chair across from her. "Why would they say that?"

The truth was, I kind of understood. Imogen and her mom were a little... out there.

Esis hopped past me and jumped onto the couch. He fluffed one of the throw pillows before curling up on top of it. Sassy lay beside him. It was one of the first times I'd ever seen her sit still.

An unamused expression crossed Imogen's face. "Have you *met* my family? Anyway, no big deal. We might seem a little crazy, but being crazy has its perks."

"Like?" I prodded.

"Like the fact that our family is the only one brave enough to speak the truth."

I leaned my elbows on the table, intrigued. "The truth about what?"

"I don't know. Just things that no one else believes in. It's funny that we live with creatures of legend— unicorns and dragons and things like that— but none of the Hawkei actually believe in things they can't see with their own eyes. We have our own myths, you know. Gallyswanks, womgrombits, lillybats, you name it. They were all real once, yet most of the Hawkei refuse to believe it."

"Why wouldn't they believe it?" I asked.

Imogen shrugged. "After the war that killed the Anichi, certain species started dying off. I guess none of the Houses want to admit they were responsible for the mass extinction."

"How can you be sure these creatures existed?"

Imogen sat up straighter and pushed her open book toward me. "My ancestors made sure we wouldn't forget. Kimoko Kahnee was one of my great-great-great-grandfathers. Or something like that. Anyway, a lot of greats. In our native language, his name loosely translates to *brother of the beloved animals*. And he lived up to that name. He was very close with the magical creatures that roamed our valley. He recorded everything he saw. He discovered several new species, actually."

"That must be really cool," I said. "To be related to him, I mean."

"It is," Imogen agreed. "But he wasn't very well-known. My family has been pushing for years to get his journal published, but the Elders claim they can't authenticate it and don't want to be putting misinformation out to the masses."

My lips turned down. "That's unfair."

Imogen rolled her eyes. "Tell me about it. Anyway, the good news for you is that Kimoko wrote about the kurbles in his journal."

"Kurbles?" I asked with raised eyebrows.

"Yeah, that's what Esis is," Imogen said, in a dead serious tone.

I couldn't help it when I burst out laughing. "You're kidding."

"No." Imogen didn't even twitch.

"I'm sorry. I just don't think it fits Esis. It just sounds so..."

So what? Cute and cuddly? I glanced to Esis. His eyes were closed, and his chest rose and fell slowly. My heart filled with all kinds of positive vibes.

I turned back to Imogen. "Who am I kidding? Kurble totally fits him."

"Agreed. Anyway, I totally forgot I'd ever read about kurbles, until I saw Esis heal. There aren't many creatures who can do that, so when I saw it, I instantly knew I had to check out Kimoko's journal for confirmation. And it's right here." Imogen turned the book toward me and pointed to the left-hand page. "See? Kurbles."

The entry was entirely handwritten. At the top of the page was a surprisingly good sketch of a kurble, though it had black spots like a cow, unlike Esis' flawless white fur. Below the sketch was a list of words in a language I didn't recognize. Underneath that was the English translation in a different handwriting.

Size: Up to six pounds
Temperament: Good-natured and playful, but protective and territorial. Fights when threatened.
Abilities: Healing
Notes: Eats a high-calorie diet, buries feces, and cleans self. Enjoys climbing and collecting shiny objects.

"That's it?" I asked in disbelief. There was nothing here I didn't already know, except the part about kurbles fighting. Though now the horns on Esis' head made sense. Somehow, I couldn't imagine Esis fighting anyone or anything.

"Unfortunately, yes, that's it," Imogen replied. "What else do you want to know?"

I turned the page, as if expecting more information on the next page, but it just led to another entry on something called wilmoths. "I don't know… maybe what he eats."

"He eats hamburgers," Imogen said simply. "Obviously."

I couldn't tell if she was being serious or trying to make me laugh. "Yeah, but they can't be healthy for him."

"Look at him." Imogen gestured to Esis on the pillow. "He's fine."

I chewed my lower lip while I watched Esis. His ear twitched while he slept. "Yeah, I suppose. I just… I wish I knew more about him."

Imogen sighed. "Maybe it's a good thing no one does, you know?"

"Yeah," I agreed after a brief silence. "No one else does know, do they? I mean, what about your parents or other relatives?" Worry filled my chest as I considered the possibility. What if someone recognized him for what he was? They could take him for his powers.

Imogen shook her head. "I don't think so. I searched through all of our books that might mention kurbles, and this was the only one it was in. I read these books cover-to-cover hundreds of times as a kid, and I barely remembered kurbles existed. I don't think anyone else knows. And I didn't tell my parents the truth of what I was researching, either."

Relief washed over me. "Good. So we can keep this between us, then?"

"Of course," Imogen agreed. "I wouldn't want anyone knowing if Sassy had unique magical powers like this, either. Your secret's safe with me, Sophia."

My shoulders completely relaxed. "Thank you, Imogen. You're a really great friend."

We spent the rest of the morning combing through the books in Imogen's family library. We didn't expect to find more on kurbles, but I couldn't let go of the hope that we would. I wanted to know all I could about them. What if Esis was allergic to something? How would I medicate him if he got sick? What if he had weird anatomy, like four stomachs or two hearts? How long did kurbles survive? And how old was Esis, anyway?

All of these questions assaulted me, but by mid-afternoon, I didn't have an answer to any of them. Esis had woken up and lay curled in my lap on the sofa while Sassy batted at him from the floor. Piles of books sat beside me on the adjacent cushion.

I rubbed behind his ears. "I'm sorry I couldn't learn more about you, buddy."

Esis snuggled into my belly, as if letting me know it wasn't my fault and that he forgave me.

"We should probably call it a day," Imogen suggested. "We need to get Daisy and Jack back to the stables, anyway."

Imogen had ducked out of the library earlier to give them a snack and water, but they needed a more substantial meal.

"Okay," I agreed. "You ready, Esis?"

He jumped out of my lap, trilling. Sassy chased after him toward the door.

"Whoa, girl," Imogen said with a laugh, following behind them. "Not so fast."

We made it down from the treehouse the same way we came and started the long journey back to the school.

"Hey!" Cade called cheerfully when we returned to the stables. He wore a clean blue shirt, so I figured he hadn't been in the stables all day. The way he looked at Imogen— and how she responded with flushed cheeks— I guessed that he came back just for the chance to see her again. "I was starting to think you got lost."

"Nah," Imogen said, patting her unicorn's back. "Jack would never lead me astray."

"Of course not," Cade said. He stepped up to Daisy and handed her a carrot, which she promptly gobbled out of his hand. "What are you girls up to tonight?"

"Oh, uh…" Imogen looked to me, as if begging me to say something. I'd never seen her look so flustered.

"Imogen's free," I blurted. "But I'm busy. She could use some company at dinner."

Imogen's eyes went wide, as if she didn't think I was doing her a favor. She'd thank me later. "Sophia, weren't you just saying—?"

"That I was going to grab takeout and meet up with Liam?" I cut in. "Yep."

What the heck, stupid mouth? Why was meeting up with Liam the first excuse I came up with?

"Ah, well, if you have plans, I'll let you get to them," Cade said while helping me down from Daisy's back.

Imogen just blinked at me, completely shocked. "I— I guess I'll help Cade with the unicorns and then… then we'll get dinner together?" She said it like a question, like she couldn't believe this was actually happening.

"It's a date," Cade said before turning a light shade of pink himself. "Well, not a date, but…"

"Oh, no," Imogen agreed immediately. "Not a date."

Imogen hopped down from Jack with ease and readjusted Sassy in her bag before leading Jack into his stall.

"Have fun on your *not-a-date*," I whispered to Imogen under my breath before raising my voice and waving to both of them. Esis waved from my shoulder. "See you later!"

Imogen shot me a huge, excited grin that Cade couldn't see. I turned away with a sense of victory filling me. I had successfully managed to get my best friend to go out with her very-obvious crush. Pride followed me all the way back to the castle and down the deserted hallway on my way to the cafeteria… until I heard the sound of my name.

I ducked behind the sprite statue next to Madame Doya's classroom when I realized the voices I'd heard were hers and Haley's. What the hell were those bitches saying about me?

"Yeah, I know," Haley said in a bored tone. "I've been following her, but honestly, the girl is a total bore. She's either sitting in her dorm or hanging out with her weird Nivita friend."

"She's started asking questions," Doya said, with almost no emotion. "It won't be long before she finds it. And when she does—"

"*I know*," Haley cut in. "I'll be right there to report back to you. Honestly, I don't know why you worry. Sophia's probably going to die in the the tournament anyway, especially with that useless fur ball of hers. I saw their first training session, and it was… laughable at best."

Anger pulsed through my veins. What the hell did Haley know? I urged to singe the sleek black hair off her head just to teach her some manners.

"Yes," Madame Doya responded coolly. "I'm well aware, but as I recall, your first session didn't go well either, did it, Haley?"

Oh, burn.

Haley went dead silent.

"That's it for now," Doya said. "I'll see you tomorrow after class for training. Let your team know."

"But we've already used up our allotted training sessions." Haley sounded confused.

"And?" I pictured Doya raising an eyebrow. "Who's counting? You let me worry about the rules. You just worry about your training, and keeping an eye on Sophia. Understand?"

My breath froze in my chest. I should've known Doya would cheat! But sending someone after me, to spy on me? That was crossing a line. Esis nearly jumped off my shoulder— to give Doya a piece of his mind, I presumed— but I held him back.

Haley's voice fell. "I understand."

The sound of footsteps met my ears, sending a wave of panic through me. I pressed myself to the wall, diving behind the statue so I wouldn't be seen.

Haley breezed out of the room and headed in the opposite direction of where I stood. Anwara flew behind her. My entire body remained tense until she was out of sight, and for at least another minute afterward.

When I was satisfied that Doya wasn't going to exit her room and that Haley was long gone, I stepped out of my hiding spot and bolted.

I raced toward the castle's main entrance, knowing there would be enough people there or in the courtyard that I could duck into the safety of the crowd. I didn't feel safe going back to my dorm, not when I knew there was a target on my back. In the deserted hallway, nerves rushed up and down my arms, making my whole body shake. It felt as if someone was watching me, even though I knew Haley and Doya hadn't known I was there. Still, I glanced behind myself just to make sure I wasn't being followed.

Just as I turned my eyes forward to round the corner, I smacked into something hard. I stumbled backward and caught Esis before he could tumble off my shoulder.

Whomever I'd run into cursed under their breath. When I gazed up, I saw the most beautiful pair of dark eyes staring back at me.

"Liam," I breathed. "Thank the ancestors!"

"What's wrong, Sophia?" he asked, immediate concern laced in his tone. He held on to both my arms. His eyes darted between mine as if searching for an answer in them.

"I— I heard Doya and Haley…" I swallowed deeply, still trying to catch my breath. "Liam, I need help."

Liam sighed and ran a hand over his face. He took a deep breath to collect himself. "What are you talking about, Sophia?"

"I overheard Madame Doya and Haley talking about me," I tried again, this time in a calmer tone. "Apparently, Haley's been following me. Liam, I'm literally being stalked."

Liam just stood there with worry in his expression, but he didn't say anything.

"Liam?" I prodded.

"I don't know what to say, Sophia," he replied. "You *just* told me you didn't want me to protect you. Now you're asking me to? You come to me all the time asking for help, then you push me away. Make up your mind."

"I—" I stared up at him, completely speechless. I mean, I couldn't say he was wrong.

Tears welled in my eyes. I tried to blink them away, but it only made them rise higher until the floodgates opened and a tear ran down my cheek.

"Shit," Liam muttered. "Please don't cry, Sophia."

"It's just— I'm just—" *A bawling mess.*

Slowly, Liam reached out and ran his thumb over my cheek, wiping away the tears. I sniffled and looked up at him. The most intense look of care filled his eyes. Without thinking, I threw myself forward into his arms. My hands flew around his neck, and my head rested just beneath his shoulder. Tears soaked into his t-shirt.

He tensed momentarily before relaxing and pulling his arms around me, squeezing me tight. Warmth tingled across my torso where he touched me. He smelled like a warm jacket and the rain-kissed needles of an ancient pine forest. I'd never felt as safe and protected as I did in Liam's arms. That only made me want to cry more, as if it was an invitation to let my emotions flow.

"It's okay, Sophia," he whispered, rubbing my back. "Haley's not worth it. Forget about her."

"How can I forget about her when she's stalking me?" I asked, burying my face deeper into his shoulder.

Liam sighed, like he didn't know what to say. He probably hated me right now. He didn't seem like the kind of guy who could handle crying girls. But I also couldn't bring myself to pull away. He was like a protective blanket hiding me from the monsters that lurked in the corners of the castle.

"How can I help, Sophia?" he asked softly.

I drew away from him and wiped my tears. "I don't know. I just... I guess I just needed to tell someone."

Liam nodded like he understood, then reached out and grabbed my hand. My breath caught, and my stomach did this whole flip-in-my-abdomen thing.

"I know what you need," Liam said as a light smile touched his lips. "Let's go have some fun."

Liam
FIFTEEN

Yeah, I knew what it looked like. Sophia Henley and Liam Mitoh, holding hands in the hall. Big whoop. Luckily, everyone was at dinner, so nobody saw us together. But I knew if they did, it would be a huge deal.

I knew what most guys in my situation would do. They'd take her back to the Toaqua dorms for a quickie in the pool.

But Sophia didn't need a quick bang. She needed to feel normal. And I really needed that, too. It'd been a long time since I'd felt any sense of normalcy.

We left the school grounds and headed into Kinpago. The village was pretty crowded this time of day, with everyone going home. I made sure to drop Sophia's hand the moment I sighted any people. She frowned, but the look in her eyes told me she got it. Esis chittered from her shoulder like he disapproved, but he could bug off.

"I'm starving," Sophia told me as the variety of delicious smells wafting through the square filled our noses. "What's good around here?"

"You pick. Any place you want, except that one, that one, and that one." I pointed out over half the restaurants in the square.

"You're picky." She giggled.

"I prefer traditional Hawkei dishes," I told her. "But I chose last time we ate, so I'm nice enough to let you choose this time."

"Such a gentleman." She scanned the square before her gaze settled on a tiny Italian place in the corner. "I want pizza."

"Of course you do." I smiled at her, because she was so utterly predictable.

"You don't? Who doesn't like pizza?" she said, astonished as we headed into the restaurant. I held the door open for her as we went in. It was empty in here, except for the waiter perched by the host station.

Sophia was still gaping at me and my hatred of pizza when we slid into a booth. Esis had an equally shocked expression, which didn't surprise me, because he was a garbage disposal. Anything you gave the little fur ball he sucked down in a manner of seconds.

"I really hate Americanized food. Like, buffalo burgers are fricken amazing, but it has to be not processed. I can literally taste the chemicals." I made a disgusted face. "Good thing the tribe grows and prepares most of our own food, because otherwise, I'd starve the way our food system in the US is."

"So you're not a fan of fast food?" Sophia asked. Esis jumped down from her shoulder and onto the table.

"Ew, don't even mention it. You're gonna make me puke."

She laughed. "I love drive-through chicken nuggets."

"Stop."

The waiter stopped at our table. I didn't know his name, but I knew he was from school, because I recognized him from my Survival Instincts class. He gave us a bit of a look— the Koigni girl and the Toaqua guy together— but I guessed he wanted a tip more, because he just dropped off the menus and said, "What can I get you to drink?"

"Water," both of us said at once, and we looked at each other.

The waiter walked off, and Sophia opened the menu. "What do you want?"

"Like I said, your choice." I crossed my arms and didn't even look at the menu. "This little outing is to make you feel better."

"Like you couldn't use it, too," she grumbled under her breath. Esis bared his little teeth at me, and guess what? I bared mine right back.

"How about we just share a pizza? Half and half?" she asked.

"Fine by me."

The waiter came back and placed the waters on our table. "What would you like to order?" he asked us, like this was the last place he wanted to be.

"We're going to share a medium— uh, I mean, large," Sophia stuttered as Esis screeched loudly. "On my half, I would like pepperoni, sausage, bacon, green pepper, onion, mushrooms, tomatoes, and pineapple."

By the ancestors, that sounded so gross. Esis clapped his hands happily and jumped down onto the table.

Sophia looked at me. I opened my mouth and said, "Just the crust, thanks. No cheese, no pepperoni, no sauce, nothing."

"Are you crazy? You can't just get the crust," Sophia said, shocked.

"Watch me." I stared back at her with a smirk on my face.

The waiter gave me a look like I was nuts, but wrote it down. "Anything else?"

"I think we're good," Sophia said. The waiter walked off, and Sophia laughed. "That's going to be one lopsided pizza. I don't even know how they're going to cook it right."

"Hopefully the little Fire critters in the back will figure it out." I shrugged.

She gave me a scathing look, one that I found quite adorable. "Is it your purpose to make life as difficult as you possibly can for everyone else?"

"Just the ones I find annoying."

"So… everyone," she said flatly.

I grinned. "Maybe."

This was ridiculous. The stupid grin hadn't left my face since we'd come here. I probably looked like one happy idiot. I hadn't smiled so much in months. It actually made my face hurt a bit. It was like my mouth had forgotten how to do it.

The sweet look fell from her face as something crossed her mind— I saw it in her eyes. "You never answered me earlier. About Haley. Do you think it's something I should be worried about, her spying on me?"

This again? I had hoped she wouldn't bring it up. The memory of her tears from earlier caused the grin to slide from my face. I didn't want her to start crying again. I hadn't known what to do, and I felt like shit, like it'd been my fault she'd started crying. It'd been terrible.

"Don't worry about Haley. She might be stalking you, but so what? Everyone is watching us now. The tournament is only a few weeks away," I told her. "Doya probably told her to spy on you to get ahead in the tournament."

"I don't know," Sophia said slowly. "It sounded like whatever Haley was supposed to be watching me for, it was pretty specific."

"Doya could be sending Haley after you to get into your head," I said. "You can't let that happen."

"That could be true," Sophia mused. "Doya's team is cheating, by the way. They've had more than three practices."

"That's a big shock," I replied sarcastically. "What else is news, the sky is blue?"

"Shut up." Her cheeks turned pink, but she laughed. "I thought I should tell you, I finally got together with Imogen. She's been doing some research, and she found out that Esis is actually a rare animal called a kurble."

"A kurble," I repeated. "Sounds like something Imogen made up."

Esis let out a little growl. He put his head down and charged at me. He head-butted my arm with his stubby little horns, but I pushed him away.

Sophia didn't confirm or deny my claim, which made me think that whatever Imogen had found most likely had come from her head. But I was curious and felt like playing along, so I asked, "So, do kurbles have any special magic?"

"Uh…" Sophia glanced to Esis before shaking her head quickly. "Nope. No. None that we found."

"That's disappointing," I said. "We could've used some in the tournament."

Sophia nodded slowly. Sophia went on and on about kurbles, but most of everything she said was stuff we already knew about Esis just from being around him. I was hardly paying attention to what she was saying. I got that it was disrespectful, but I kept on getting sucked into her eyes.

While Sophia was gabbing, Esis did something weird. He waddled in front of me, puffed up his chest and fluffed his tail, expanding his ears and screaming.

"What the hell is he doing?" I asked, thinking he was gonna self-destruct.

"Oh, it's nothing," Sophia said, petting him. "It's just something kurbles do. I think it's a mating call, though I don't know why he'd be doing it now."

I swear to the ancestors Esis was wiggling his eyebrows at me at a very suggestive way. I was gonna kill this little shit. Next thing I knew, he was gonna start tossing roses and singing a serenade.

The server emerged from the kitchen and placed the pizza on our table, giving us a weird look. "Enjoy your uh… meal."

Our pizza looked so stupid. One half was literally nothing but bread, and the other half was loaded with every disgusting thing Sophia could bear to pile on it, including, ugh… pineapple.

But it was us, kind of. Sophia kept talking throughout the meal, but I stayed quiet. I wasn't much of a talker, and it was nice to hear her voice instead of the one inside my head.

By the end of the meal, I was pretty sure Esis had eaten more slices than either of us had. The server came back to an empty tray. He poorly hid his disgust as Esis burped happily and put down the bill.

Sophia reached out, but I snagged it before she could. "I got it," I told her. "I offered."

Her eyes glittered. We left the restaurant and looked around. By this time, it was dark. The crowds had thinned, and most of the adults had gone home. There were more students out this time of night, looking for places to hang out and something to do. We needed to go somewhere more private, before we ran into someone we knew.

"Come on," I told her. "I know a great place. Follow me."

Her eyebrow raised as we headed out of town. Usually by this point I'd be exhausted, but I was having a good day today. My body was actually cooperating for once, and I wanted to take full advantage of it… before I paid the price tomorrow.

I took her into the woods, but it was away from the castle instead of towards. Eventually, we reached a part of the forest that was so overgrown we had to stomp on the brush to clear a way through.

"Nashoma led me here a long time ago," I told her. "I didn't know why, or what for, but I'm pretty sure we were the only ones who knew about it."

I parted the foliage in front of us and let her step through. Her face brightened in wonder as she looked around, a wide smile spreading across her face.

Behind the overgrowth was a clearing, a small meadow of blooming white flowers called fairy lanterns spreading throughout the emerald grass. A stone beach nestled up against a deep pool, sapphire-colored and so clear you could see the bottom. A large waterfall poured down on the other side of the pool, the top cascading down from a mountain stream somewhere above us. Fall was mild here, so the trees didn't have a lot of color, but they made up for it by having magical butterflies as large as my face nesting in the trees, their wings glowing a crystalline blue. Grapevines twisted up the trees, and the moon shone through a hole in the top of the forest canopy, casting everything in a silver glow. The only sounds were the rushing of the water and the symphony of crickets in the bush.

Sophia looked brilliant. If I could make her smile like that every day, I'd never have to do anything for the rest of my life. That much would be enough.

"Liam, this is incredible," Sophia said. She put Esis down and spun in a circle around the clearing. "It's like a fairy tale."

I said nothing. I gently lifted my hand and turned it to the side. A wall of water rose from the pool, but it was soft and quiet. Within the water was a bunch of beautiful, colorful fish. They had broad and silky tails like betas, but had patterns on their bodies and heads like koi. They were neon and glowed in the dark underneath the color of the moon. I wrapped the wave around Sophia to give her an aquarium. Sophia laughed and reached out with her fingers, touching the wave.

When her fingers ran through the water, I gasped audibly, though she didn't hear it. To touch an Elementai's element was like touching their spirit— and she went right through whatever I still had. Despite her being across the clearing, her skimming the water felt like she was caressing my face.

Esis became alarmed and started batting at the water with his paws to try and reach the fish, but only ended up splashing himself. His touch was like an itch.

The fish in the water nibbled at Sophia's hand. She giggled, and I slowly brought the wave back. I returned the water and the fish to the pond and looked at her.

"Your element is so beautiful, Liam," Sophia said in a breathless way. "I wish I could do something like that."

"You'll be able to, one day." I walked over to a tree with large, twisting branches. I held my hand out and helped her climb it. We scaled upward until I pointed out a thick branch that I liked to sit on, one that would support our weight. As we climbed, the butterflies scattered and began dancing all around us, giving an elaborate show. Esis followed, climbing the limbs easily and squeaking.

I hadn't counted on the branch being so small. I'd only sat up here by myself, but it definitely wasn't big enough to hold two people. The end result was that Sophia was pretty much sitting on my lap.

"Oof. I'm sorry," Sophia said as her ass plopped down against my leg, and she blushed. "There really isn't a lot of room up here."

"Yeah." She was like, literally leaning against me and everything. I had nowhere to put my arms. They were above me, holding on to some branches when she sat down, but I couldn't hold them like that forever. I gave up and just put my arms around her, because, you know, it was more comfortable.

Yeah, sure. Whatever you say.

Sophia didn't seem to mind, but her magic gave her away. Her shoulder was pushing up against a tree branch, and it was starting to crackle.

"You're gonna burn the tree down," I told her.

"Sorry." I felt her temperature decline by a few degrees, and the tree stopped smoking. But that hardly helped, because now *I* was hot, and it definitely wasn't from her magic.

"Oh, wow," Sophia breathed, and I looked up. The butterflies had flown up against the sky and had changed their colors, their deep blue morphing to become the background of the starry night. You could see them as their wings beat against the darkness, making the constellations look like they were moving.

"They take on the background of whatever they're around, when they're threatened," I told Sophia. "It's a special sort of camouflage."

She nodded. Esis had totally disappeared. I had no idea where he went.

All around, tiny little yellow lights with wings of dragonflies started appearing. They buzzed around us, hovering up and down in a circle where they sat. I could hear their little melodic voices as they swarmed around our little spot.

Sophia gave an inquisitive look.

"Fortune Fairies. I told you about them earlier." I reached out and snatched one from the air. Carefully, I gave it to Sophia. She cupped it in her palms and moved her face close.

"They're like fireflies," Sophia whispered. The glow from the fairy lit up her face, and she looked up.

"Supposedly they only come to people with good luck. If they don't come near you, you're cursed." I snorted. "Someone didn't give them the memo about me."

She laughed before she opened her hand and let the fairy go. It floated away slowly, humming a pleasant tune. She leaned back and nestled against me, sinking her shoulders into my chest.

Alarm buzzers were going off in my head, but I took that alarm and smashed it against the wall, because, hell, I never liked being woken up anyway, and this was one damn good dream.

This was college. What was the big deal about a little bit of cuddling, anyhow?

My mind wandered. Surely there were people who screwed outside of House boundaries. Dating or marriage, no way, but hook-ups between Houses had to happen. One-night stands. Casual sex.

Bullshit. Your "casual sex" with Sophia would last a lifetime.

Hell yeah, it would. Sleep with her once, I'd never get over her.

I couldn't get over her now.

"Liam?" she asked, looking at me.

"Hm?"

"What are you thinking about?"

Inappropriate things that I shouldn't be. Things that are forbidden. "Nothing."

She seemed to sense that something was on my mind, because she said, "I know you wouldn't want anyone to see us like this."

"We aren't doing anything," I told her, which was a lie, because we'd already crossed so many boundaries.

"Right," she said, like she was trying to reassure herself. "We're just friends."

That was like a punch to the gut. It was almost a test, to see how quickly we could go to *just friends* to *something more.*

I wanted to say something that would confirm, but all that came out of my mouth was, "You ever had a boyfriend?"

What the hell was wrong with me right now?

She made a face like she didn't like to talk about it. "A few, but nothing serious."

"That sounds intriguing." And it did. She made the entire sentence seem ominous.

"I'm happy high school is over." She bounced her heel against the tree trunk. "It was nothing but a lot of drama. I had a bad falling out with a lot of my friends. By the time senior year hit, I was pretty much alone. I mean, I hung out with a few people, but I always felt like a third wheel."

"Oh. I'm sorry." High school had been okay for me. Just fine, nothing memorable. But Sophia made her four years sound awful.

"It wasn't your fault. I just went along with what was expected of me," she said. "It's one of the reasons I avoid conflict so much. There was always so much of it at school growing up. I had a tight-knit group for a while, but I couldn't really connect with them. They were all interested in the arts, and I loved being outdoors. There wasn't anyone I could share that with."

"It was the Elementai in you. All of us love being in nature," I told her.

"I guess." She shrugged. "I always thought it was because I was a weirdo. That I was different."

That made me really sad. "I don't think you're weird."

"Thanks. Life was just… so boring." She sighed. "I miss my parents, but even after how hard it's been my first semester, I don't think I could go back now. This world is just so full of wonder and amazing things to see. I'd die if I went back there and did the same thing day in and day out."

"You never really answered me about the boyfriend thing." By the ancestors, why was I being so nosy?

"You first," she said. "Have you had any girlfriends?"

My stomach churned just thinking about it. "A couple, but there was one girl I really liked. She was a Toaqua girl named Mia. We got together because it was expected of us. Our parents basically hooked us up from the moment we were born. I was supposed to be chief, so I had my bride hand-picked for me."

"What happened?" Sophia asked.

My throat got kind of tight. "It just didn't work out, I guess."

"Liam," Sophia said, in a tone that suggested she wasn't buying my crap.

I sighed and said, "The truth is, I was into her way more than she was into me. She wanted to marry a chief, someone who could give her a good life, and I promised that. But then Nashoma died, and she told me she didn't want to be with me anymore. My dad let her out of the marriage contract, you know, because I didn't have a Familiar and I wasn't considered fit to marry."

"That's awful." She gave me a sad face. "Does that mean you can't marry ever?"

This was a tough conversation to talk about. It made my chest feel like there was a giant weight on it I couldn't lift off. "Not ever, but you'd have a hard time convincing a girl to marry someone like me."

I wasn't sure if I meant the Familiar-less part of me, the sick part, or both. Sophia didn't say anything, but looked thoughtful.

"I still see Mia around school from time to time, but we don't talk anymore," I said. "She's got another boyfriend now."

We really didn't talk, either. Mia always turned away whenever she saw me. I didn't blame her for breaking up with me, because it was what everyone thought she was going to do after Nashoma died, but I didn't think she would abandon me completely and act like I didn't even exist. At first, it really stung.

The funny thing was, I'd ceased to have any sort of feelings for Mia at all now that Sophia was around.

"That sucks. I'm sorry that happened to you," Sophia said kindly.

"Yeah, well. That's what you get for being stupid and wasting your virginity on someone who doesn't love you," I said, and I leaned back against the tree trunk.

"You had sex with her?" Sophia seemed shocked.

"Yeah. I guess I thought it would make her love me more. Or love me at all, really." I put an arm behind my head and looked up. "The shitty thing was, I found out she'd been screwing the guy she got with after me while we were still together."

"That really is terrible. I can see why you didn't want to talk about it," Sophia said.

"It's over with now," I said quickly. "Nashoma never really liked her. He always had a face whenever she came around."

Sophia laughed loudly. "I hope Nashoma would've liked me."

"I think he would've liked you very much." In fact, I didn't have to think about it. Deep down in my core, I just *knew* he would've loved her.

Sophia shivered, but I don't think it was because of the cold. "Okay. You told me yours, so I can tell you mine. I was friends with this guy in high school, and I really liked him, you know?"

I could see where this was going. "So, he turned you down, or…"

"It was prom night," she started. "I felt like I was so in love, and I wanted to try going all the way. We went together as friends, and I tried hitting on him, and he started flirting back. He was a complete gentleman until we got in the limo together. We started making out. We got to second base, but halfway through, I changed my mind."

This story was taking a way worse turn than I thought. The bones in my hands cracked. "And?"

"He reached up under my dress. I told him to stop but he got really mad. He told me I needed to finish what I started. He wouldn't stop groping me," she said. "I yelled for the driver to stop, then I got out of the car and walked the rest of the way home. When I got back to school the next week, he'd told everyone in my class I was a tease."

I was really far away from the pool, but the water down there was churning furiously. "Are you serious?"

"Yes. It kind of sucked." Her voice was choked up, but she cleared her throat. "It's over now. I'm over it."

She wasn't. I could tell by her voice. "I'm sorry I wasn't there. I would've beat that guy's ass."

She laughed again, and her expression cleared. "I bet you would've."

"I'm not kidding." If I could figure out who this guy was, I'd go looking for him and hunt his ass down.

Sophia seemed to notice I was serious. She turned around and touched my face. "Hey. It's all right."

I calmed down a little bit, but the possessiveness raging through me wasn't helping. Who the fuck did this guy think he was, assaulting Sophia like that? What gave him the right?

"Anyway, looks like we've both had really bad luck when it comes to love," she said, and her tone seemed lighter. "Hopefully the future will be better."

"Hopefully," I responded, though the answer came out more like a growl. I didn't like the thought of Sophia being with anyone who treated her like that. She was mine. *Mine.* My saucy little virgin.

Aw, fuck. I needed to take things down a notch. Fast.

There was a crackling noise by my ear, like little twigs snapping. I turned my head and saw that Esis had reappeared, dangling down from the trees. Sophia hadn't noticed him there. He had a small flower in his hands with a thin, twisty stem, and was holding it out to me.

He literally wanted me to give it to Sophia. This little shit was trying to play matchmaker! It was bad enough even the tree was trying to hook us up. That was *not* taking things down a notch.

"No," I told him softly. "That's not allowed."

His ears went back, and he hissed at me. Esis shoved the flower at me more insistently, this time poking me in the eye.

"Ow! All right!" I took the flower from him and he went scampering upward again. He was probably watching the whole thing from above, like it was his own personal daytime soap opera.

I was so nervous, but I handed the flower to her. My hand almost shook. "For you."

"Really? Thank you." She took it graciously. "Where'd you get it?"

"I don't know," I told her flatly. "It appeared like magic."

I heard humored chattering from the trees. If I got my hands on that little guy, he was going into the pool.

"That's so sweet." Sophia took the flower and wrapped it around one of the fingers on her left hand, tying a knot. She held it out happily. "It looks adorable. Thank you."

I felt a little more cheery. Okay, so the little guy had some moves. Maybe he was big with the kurble ladies.

Without warning, rain started pouring down from the sky. And I mean *pouring.* It was coming down in buckets. Sophia yelped and slid downward, off my lap and shimmying down the tree. I followed her, though not as fast.

"Hold on, I got it," I said when I reached the ground. I raised my hand. The raindrops falling down suspended in mid-air, frozen all around us. I thought of my intention, and the raindrops turned to crystal ice, resembling diamonds. I turned my wrist in a circular motion. The diamonds floated toward Sophia, nestling in her hair and giving her a shining headpiece, an ornate necklace and a shimmering dress.

Sophia's mouth opened wide and she gave a delighted sound of joy. Right then, she looked so beautiful, like a crystal princess. Nobody on earth had any idea how badly I wanted to kiss her. I hadn't kissed anyone in months, but Sophia made me want to again. I took a step toward her, because I wasn't a coward and I was going to do it.

But I was a coward, because I noticed some of the diamonds were sizzling against her skin. And I was reminded she was Koigni.

Almost as soon as the downpour started, it stopped. When I let the diamonds drop off of her and fall onto the grass, melting into the earth, the spell was broken, and it was like she woke up.

"Weird, huh?" Sophia said, looking skyward. "I've never seen a storm come and go so quickly before."

I said nothing. She didn't need to know it wasn't a storm at all, but how I felt.

"Do you…?" She started, then she waited a moment. "Do you think we could spend the night out here, just talking? I like being with you, Liam. It makes me feel better."

Talking with her was so easy. And it made me feel better, too. "Sure. Whatever you want, *pawee.*"

We sat next to each other in the grass. Sophia talked about a lot of things— her old friends, her parents, Amelia, and especially Esis. He was up in the trees somewhere, cooing a song. Me, I just listened.

It was too late. There was no turning back now. I'd made my feelings for Sophia clear.

I just hoped that she felt the same.

I woke up the next morning curled against someone in the grass. At first, I thought it was Nashoma, and I was so happy that he was back. But then I realized my hand was tangled up in hair, not fur, and that Nashoma *didn't have boobs*.

I jolted awake with a start and skidded backward. Sophia had been curled up against me for ancestors knew how long. She was still asleep, breathing lightly with a smile on her face.

My body was pretty warm instead of the cool, usual Toaqua temperature it rested at, which meant I'd had my arms around her for quite some time now— possibly hours.

We'd literally picked opposite ends of the clearing to sleep on! How did we end up spooning randomly in our sleep? I looked around and saw Esis bathing in the pool, washing his fur with the water. He gave me a devious smile as he cleaned his fat cheeks.

He probably rolled us together in our sleep or something. He didn't look strong enough to do that, but I wouldn't put it past him.

I skirted away from her before she woke up. My movements didn't wake her, and I didn't want to touch her again to shake her awake, so I threw a twig, and when that still didn't wake her up, a small rock.

It bounced against her leg, and her eyes flew open. "Ow!" She sat up and rubbed her calf. "Did you really have to do that?"

"Yes. Now get up," I snapped. "We haven't got all day."

"Great. Mean Liam is back," she grumbled, pushing her hair out of her face. It'd fallen out of her ponytail and gotten all wild, which wasn't helping my *morning situation*.

"Mean Liam never left. Hurry up. I want breakfast," I told her.

"Breakfast is probably over." She yawned, and pointed at the sun. "It's almost noon."

Dammit. She was right. We'd way overslept. Hopefully nobody noticed that both of us had been gone from our dorms last night. "We need to get back," I told her, and I got to my feet. "Come on."

I went to head out of the clearing, but before I could, Sophia cried, "Wait!"

I turned around. She ran to the tree we'd climbed on last night and raised her hand. A small bit of fire appeared in her palm, and she moved it slowly over the tree trunk, burning an inscription into the wood.

"There." She stepped back, proud of her work. I looked at it. With her magic, she'd carved our initials into the tree: *S* and *L*.

"This is our place now," she said. "We've claimed it."

I couldn't decide if that was really cute or really annoying. "Come on, dork. Let's go."

Esis ran after Sophia, trilling and hopping on her back. We headed back to town, but this time, we didn't hold hands. We were acting like friends again now, instead of… whatever we'd been last night.

We were passing by Professor Baine's house. Baine lived closer to castle in Kinpago, instead of within the Water tribe's borders underwater, because it was a quicker walk to the school. He had a house on the beach, which I'm guessing he liked to be at whenever he wasn't bothering me.

I hoped Baine wasn't around, because he'd probably talk to us about the tournament and I wanted to keep thinking about Sophia's perfect everything. But whatever romantic daydreams I had for Sophia were completely smacked out of me by the sight that was waiting around the corner.

The air left my lungs, and Sophia gasped. It was November and chilly as fuck, but Baine was outside his damn house in a tight yellow Speedo, spread out on a lawn chair and sunbathing like it was the middle of July. As if anyone living wanted to see that much of him.

Today confirmed it. I had seen too much in my short life.

We tried to run away, but Baine heard our footsteps and lifted his head, waving. "Ah, Liam. Sophia! How are you this morning?"

He was talking to us and acting like this was completely normal. Ancestors have mercy. Even Esis was covering his eyes. He made no attempt to be shy about it.

"Um… we're good, thanks!" Sophia called back. "You?"

Of course Sophia would play along. Baine shrugged and said, "I have nothing to complain about. You all right, Liam?"

I grimaced and nodded, because I knew the minute I opened my mouth I'd be yelling at Baine to put some pants on.

"You have another training session tomorrow, by the way, seven o'clock in the evening," he told us. "Don't be late."

"We'll be there!" Sophia shouted back, and she grabbed on my arm to tug me away. I felt like screaming my head off, until Baine's house was out of sight and we were safely within the village limits.

Sophia was laughing. I'm pretty sure my skin had turned a nauseated green.

"I'm going to be scarred for life," I moaned, rubbing my face. Why did our tournament instructor, and my head of House, have to be so weird? Even worse, I had to claim him.

"Does Baine have a Familiar? I've never seen one," Sophia said.

"He does," I said. "She lives in the ocean."

"What is she?"

I smiled. "That would spoil the surprise, wouldn't it? I'm sure you'll see her during one of our sessions. She's incredible. It's bizarre something as beautiful and powerful as her would pick *Baine* to be her Elementai."

We passed by a little food cart selling one of my favorite things. My stomach rumbled and I pulled Sophia to a stop.

"What is it?" she asked as the vendor handed me three fluffy, fried pieces of heaven, round in shape and flat.

"Fry bread," I told her. "It's amazing. You'll love it."

I put venison, lettuce, tomatoes, sour cream and salsa on top of mine. I made a replica for Sophia before we started walking around again and eating. Esis had already sucked down his and was patting his stomach happily.

"Hey, Liam!" I heard Jonah cry out. He was walking ahead of us, Imogen by his side. Jonah was wearing a heavy flannel jacket, while Imogen was wearing overalls with bright pink galoshes and a magenta fuzzy jacket that looked like it'd once been a carpet. Her hair was up in pigtails, bows tying them together, and she was carrying a wicker basket. Sassy had an equally large bow tied into her tail. She rode on Squeaks' rear, who was making loud squeaking noises. Esis peeped as he saw them coming and jumped off Sophia's shoulder, chattering at Squeaks' hooves. The hippogriff lowered her head and clacked her beak at Esis like they were having a conversation.

"Hey, Imogen," Sophia said in a teasing way as they joined us. "How was your date with Cade?"

Imogen turned pink and said, "It wasn't a date."

I rolled my eyes. I don't know who Imogen was trying to fool. She was totally into Cade, and vice versa. They needed to stop avoiding their feelings and just get on with it.

That's the pot calling the kettle black.

"Anyway, how was your *date* with Liam?" Imogen jabbed, and she put her hand on her hip. She gave a smirk as she and Jonah made eye contact.

Sophia gaped like a fish, unsure of what to say. She'd told Imogen we were hanging out last night, before I even knew she was looking for me?

Sophia went to answer, but I subbed in for her, "It went great, thanks. What are you guys doing here?"

Sophia glanced at me. She was surprised I hadn't denied that we'd been on an actual date— even though, really, that wasn't what it was. It wasn't what it had started as, anyway.

"I met up with Imogen coming out of the gym. Somebody's gotta take care of these babies." Jonah flexed his muscles, kissing his biceps. Behind him, Squeaks did a similar pose, sticking out her butt and trying to show off. Esis flexed his tiny arms and copied her.

"And I met up with Jonah while Sassy and I were looking for treats to catch burlangers," Imogen said cheerfully. "We decided to do some grocery shopping together." She lifted her basket.

"Yeah. Needed protein shakes. Gotta keep the machine well oiled," Jonah said in a very obnoxious way. "What were you guys doing? You look like you spent a night in the woods."

"We were, um…" How did I tell them we'd done just that?

"We just got lunch," Sophia finished. "We were heading back to school. We're going to hang out in the Commons and just chill."

The Commons was the only place in Orenda Academy where students from all Houses could hang out. Sophia had just read my mind.

"We'll come with you," Jonah offered. "We should probably get to talking about strategies for the tournament."

My stomach sank. Right. The tournament. I'd forgotten all about that.

We headed up the long pathway back to school, avoiding the crowds and maneuvering around the carts. The sun was starting to come out from behind the clouds, and Imogen sighed happily. "Oh, I've had such a nice morning."

"Lucky you. We just saw Baine in nothing but spandex," I mumbled.

"What?" Jonah laughed loudly. "How'd you manage that?"

"He was tanning outside his house in his swimsuit." Sophia giggled. "I thought Liam was going to have a heart attack when he saw."

"I wish. It would've ended my suffering." Now she had me thinking about it again, dammit.

"There are a lot of girls who think Baine is super hot, not just me," Imogen quipped. "People gossip about how sexy he is all the time."

"Not me." Sophia shuddered. "I always thought he looked like a dad. He's not hot at all."

"He's got a dad bod. Trust me, it's nothing to behold," I told them. "Those girls are nuts."

"My ancestors, Liam, you ruin everything," Imogen said.

"Yeah, you're such a sour grape," Jonah added. "Lighten up."

"I'm not a lamp," I grumbled. Of course, the entire conversation the way back to school was about if Baine was or was not hot. Sophia and I were on one side, while Imogen argued that she could see why some people would want to go out with him.

"I'd probably give it a chance, if I had the opportunity," Jonah said. "I'm not into old guys, but I'll try anything once, and I bet he has experience."

"Jonah, you'll fuck anything that walks," I told him. "Can we seriously stop talking about this? He's our tournament mentor. It's creeping me out."

Jonah went to argue back, but we were stopped by someone in the hallway. It was Professor Perot, and his peacock Familiar, Baxtor.

Perot had been really nice to me in class ever since I'd helped saved him. I skipped a few times and he still gave me credit, not to mention I know the last few tests I'd failed miserably and I'd still gotten top marks. He'd been acting weird, though, not talking to me much, just smiling a lot.

"Oh, Professor," I said. He stood in front of us awkwardly, wringing his hands. "You need something?"

Perot seemed to swallow, then gave a nervous smile. "I just wanted to thank the four of you again for saving my life. Baxtor and I are very grateful."

"It was really no problem." *Except I threw out my back dragging you out.*

"Well, yes." He flushed. "The thing is, I have been thinking on how to repay all of you for your bravery. And while I can't think of what I could do for you three"— he eyed Sophia, Jonah, and Imogen—, "I think there *is* something I can do for you, Liam."

"Oh," I started. "Okay."

There was an awkward moment of silence, and Perot gestured to us. "Follow me."

We hurried after him. He led us to his classroom, and then to his desk, where I noticed an assortment of papers and vials were scattered. Squeaks knocked over a couple of glasses on our way in, but Perot paid her no mind.

He sat down at his desk and said, "I've been looking into your case, Liam. I've heard about your illness, and think that with enough research and time, I'll be able to discover what ails you... maybe even cure it."

"You're serious?" My mouth dropped open. I felt like I was suffocating. My heart was practically beating out of my chest. This was too good to be true. Just a name would be a miracle, but a cure... that was unthinkable.

Then came the doubt. I shook my head. "No. No, I've been to the best medicine women and men in the tribe. Nobody knows what's wrong with me, or how to help me."

"I can't promise anything," Perot started, and Baxtor bobbed his head. "But I am a researcher, not a doctor, so I can look at your case from a different perspective. I think that a life for a life is the best way to repay my debt."

"Did you hear that, Liam?" Sophia said excitedly. "There might be a cure!"

Her expression was hopeful, but at the same time, I didn't want to believe it. I'd been through so much in the past few months. Hoping for anything, even just a diagnosis, seemed like a setup. It was easier to go on being miserable than to be let down again. That would really suck.

"Hold on," Jonah said. "I thought Liam was sick because Nashoma died."

I wanted to punch Jonah. He needed to mind his own business.

"It might be," Perot said. "But I have reason to believe that maybe Liam's condition isn't linked to Nashoma's death at all, but perhaps something that was dormant until that point. Grief can be a powerful trigger for chronic illnesses. We won't know for sure unless we do some testing."

"You are the only person who's ever survived the death of their Familiar, Liam," Imogen added. "Maybe this would be how to find out why."

"Some of the processes for investigating your illness would be... invasive," Perot said slowly. "It wouldn't be a quick or easy process. But it'll be worth it in the end if we can determine exactly what's going on with you. Of course, it's your choice, Liam."

Everyone in the room looked at me, perched on my answer. I wasn't sure. I really didn't want to be put through anything else, being poked, prodded and questioned about something that was already deeply personal, not to mention a really sensitive subject. Half of me didn't care if I was suffering from something that was worsening, or even terminal. I just wanted to be left alone and enjoy the time that I had left, however much that was.

But then I saw the look on Sophia's face, and I knew what she wanted me to do. She didn't want me to give up. She wanted me to keep fighting.

Fine. If I had to be a guinea pig to get some answers, I'd be a guinea pig. "I guess I'm for it," I said. "What do you want me to do?"

"First, I'll need a sample of your blood, among other things," Perot said. He took out a few syringes with needles, and I swallowed. "I wouldn't need you back in until I'm done analyzing the results."

"I'm ready," I said. I wanted to get this over with. Hurry up and stick me like a pincushion.

I thought Perot would take me to a back room or something, you know, somewhere with a bit of seclusion, but he began sanitizing my arm and sticking me right in front of everybody. I didn't like needles, but I wasn't about to look like a wimp in front of my team. I expected the gang to turn their backs or something, but instead they kept on talking while Perot took his samples and set several vials of my blood aside. Imogen was blabbering about burlangers, while Jonah and Sophia happily subbed in.

Everyone was acting really natural, while here I was, looking like I belonged in a hospital. "Um," I started as they all kept gabbing on. This was awkward. A little privacy, please?

But then I realized something. They weren't staring at me like I was in a zoo. They kept carrying on like it was okay I was getting treated and experimented on. They were acting like me being sick was okay.

Yet they weren't acting at all. It was genuine. I didn't feel different.

I just… felt like everyone else.

"Oh, sorry." Sophia straightened up and looked down at the tons of needles shoved into my arms, as if she suddenly just realized they were there. "We can go."

I had to laugh. Sophia was totally clueless, and I loved it. "You're here now. Just stay."

A few minutes later, I was a little lightheaded. Perot had made it sound like he only needed a tiny bit of blood, but it'd felt like he took a gallon. Looking at all the vials on his desk made me want to throw up.

"You'll want to watch him," Perot said as he eyed me getting up from the chair woozily. "He's a little pale. He should be better by tomorrow."

"Lean on me, bro," Jonah said, and he flung an arm around my shoulders. "I got you."

Jonah was practically carrying me out the door. Sophia thanked Professor Perot and waved goodbye as she and Imogen followed us.

"Where to?" Imogen asked cheerfully. Squeaks snuck her head under my other arm and lifted me up so my toes were dragging on the ground, but I pushed her away. I didn't need to be carried like some wounded war hero, for ancestors' sake.

Sophia said nothing. She was watching me carefully out of the corner of her eye.

"The Commons sounds pretty good right now," I said. My voice was kind of slurred. "Those couches are like… so plushy."

Plushy? I was really out of it.

"Cookies, man," Jonah said wisely. "Just a shitload of cookies."

Jonah threw me on the couch when we got there. We got the good seats, the ones by the fireplace with the big TV. Imogen sat on the rug against Squeaks with Sassy in her arms, while Jonah took the big armchair. Sophia sat on the other side of the couch and flung her legs over mine. Jonah left for a while and came back with literally three bags of cookies, which we all polished off while watching a movie. I'm pretty sure I slipped off one or two times, but I can't remember. Sophia kept looking at me, and when she wasn't, Esis was, his eyes wide and unsure as he curled up on Sophia's lap.

He seemed… guilty. Though I'm not sure why.

That afternoon was pretty perfect. To people passing by, I'm sure we looked like a bunch of friends just hanging out.

But we were so much more than that. For the first time since Nashoma died, I felt like I wasn't a freak, and it was nice.

Maybe I could get used to these people.

sophia

SIXTEEN

"What's the deal with you and Liam?" Imogen asked.

We sat on the beach, staring out at the ocean. The November air was chilly, and the sky overcast. In the distance, snow was falling, covering the peaks of the mountains around us. I pulled the sleeves of my hoodie over my hands and wrapped my arms around me. I'd become used to the colder weather of Northern California these past few months, but I was starting to regret not packing a heavier coat. I called upon my Fire, raising it just to the surface of my skin to ward off the chill.

I shrugged, keeping my eyes on Esis. He was digging in the rocks and placing the shiniest ones into a pile at my feet. "Do we have to have this conversation again?"

It'd been a week since Liam took me to see the waterfall, and I still didn't know how to answer the question.

"Again?" Imogen repeated. She petted Sassy in her lap, who was batting at the lime green bows at the ends of Imogen's braids. "Sophia, you blow me off every time I ask about it. I think I deserve to know what's going on between my teammates. The tournament is only a few weeks away. Should I be concerned?"

"About me and Liam?" I laughed. "No. I'd be more concerned about Jonah's raging hormones."

Imogen covered her mouth with her hand to stifle her giggles. Our second training session went better than the first, but the moment Jonah spotted Renar passing by our obstacle course with a couple of friends, he lost all focus. He stumbled off the root bridge Imogen had built to get us over a pit of quicksand. Squeaks nearly got stuck trying to rescue him. All Jonah could talk about afterward was how appalled he was that Renar didn't even notice and try to help. Liam was furious with Jonah and totally erupted on him, though I thought he overreacted.

Imogen rolled her eyes. "Men. But that still doesn't answer my question. You and Liam? What's going on?"

"I don't know." I absentmindedly rolled one of Esis' rocks around in my hand while I contemplated the question. What *was* going on between us? I liked Liam a lot— I knew that much for certain. After he told me the story about Mia, the girl who broke his heart, all I wanted to do was show him how much I cared about him. I sensed that after Mia, he didn't feel like he deserved to be loved.

And he was so, *so* wrong. I just wished my heart was enough to heal him. But I knew Liam would never accept it… though I hoped he would, one day.

"I told you about that magical night we had together," I said. "But we haven't really talked about what's happening between us."

"Oh, I see the problem," Imogen said. "You need to *define your relationship.*"

I frowned at her. "Like you and Cade have?"

"This isn't about me and Cade. Besides, we're just friends."

I nodded slowly. "Sure you are."

"Why don't you just tell Liam how you feel?" she asked.

Nerves ignited in my chest just thinking about it. "I can't. What if he doesn't feel the same way? Things would be weird between us, and we can't have that before the tournament."

"So you'll tell him after the tournament?"

I dropped my gaze. "I don't know. I can't just come out and tell Liam that I'm falling head over heels for him."

"Why not?" Imogen asked. "I mean, if he feels the same way, what's the harm?"

I resisted the urge to bust out laughing. "We're just friends, Imogen. Like you and Cade. Liam doesn't feel that way about me."

It broke my heart and made it feel as if rocks had settled in my stomach. I wanted Liam to like me back. I'd run the scenario so many times through my head, what it would be like to tell him I liked him, for him to say it back. He'd reach down and brush the hair out of my eyes while I ran my fingers across his chest. I'd go breathless just being in his presence. Then he'd kiss me—a mind-blowing, passionate kiss I'd only ever dreamed about. He'd sweep me into his arms and carry me into the sunset, and we'd live happily ever after.

And then he opened his mouth in real life, shattering any hope of that fairytale coming true. I lived for the moments his fingers accidentally grazed across mine when we walked beside each other in the hall, the way his eyes lit up when we were together, and the smile that crept across his face every so often when I saw him staring out toward the ocean.

But that's all they would ever be. Moments. I couldn't have forever with Liam, even if I wanted to.

"Girl, you're blind," Imogen said, pulling me from my thoughts. "There's some serious sexual tension going on between you two. Can't you feel it?"

My eyebrows shot up. "Sexual tension? Oh, my God, Imogen. I must've missed the romance section in your library. You've been reading too much. I highly doubt Liam feels *anything* sexual toward me. I'm always in this baggy hoodie and jeans, with my hair tied into a ponytail and almost no makeup on. *No way* he finds that attractive. That one day I wore my hair down and that low-cut shirt like you told me to, he barely stole a glance at me."

Imogen rolled her eyes. "That's because he was trying to be subtle about it. Trust me, from my perspective, he was drooling."

Butterflies fluttered in my stomach at the possibility.

"Next time, wear a push-up bra," Imogen advised. "He'll have his face down your shirt in one-point-five seconds."

It sounded gross, but I wouldn't mind it. Liam could do whatever he wanted to my cleavage and more.

"Ugh, Imogen, can we—?"

"Oh, my ancestors!" Imogen hopped up to her knees and flapped her hands excitedly. Sassy rolled onto the ground, looking shocked. Esis paused with a rock in his hand and alarm in his eyes. "I know what you need!"

I leaned away a few inches as her hands nearly assaulted my face. "Um… what do I need?"

"You need a dress," she stated, like it was obvious.

"I don't wear dresses."

"For the *ball*," she emphasized. "You need to buy a smoking hot dress so Liam can't keep his eyes off you."

I bit my lower lip, considering her idea. At least it would be after the tournament. And it was a good excuse to dress up for him.

I sighed. "Okay. I might even wear a push-up bra."

Imogen jumped to her feet and bounced on her toes. "Yay! We can do your makeup and your hair and everything. You're going to look so hot he'll want to get nasty with you on the dance floor."

"Oh, my ancestors, Imogen." I turned beet-red as I stood. "Don't say stuff like that."

"What?" she asked innocently. "Nasty?"

I rolled my eyes. "Yes. That."

"Nasty, nasty, nasty," she teased. "It's not a bad word."

If possible, I flushed even redder. "No, but you're talking about me and Liam. If we… did it, it wouldn't be nasty."

Imogen wiggled her eyebrows. "What *would* it be like?"

"Imogen!" I shoved at her playfully while Esis scurried up my pant leg to crawl onto my shoulder.

Imogen only laughed. "Okay, fine. I'll stop. Let's go get you a dress that'll make Liam crazy."

"No. Absolutely not." Imogen sat in a plush chair outside the dressing room of a little boutique shop in Kinpago called *Delilah's*, giving feedback on each dress I tried on.

I spun around to admire the dress in the mirror beside the dressing rooms. It was black, with a silk skirt that fell to the floor and a lacy top with three-quarter-length sleeves. "Why not? I think it's beautiful."

Esis clapped from the armrest of Imogen's chair.

"See?" I said. "Even Esis likes it."

Imogen frowned. "We're going for *kiss me now*, not *kiss me when I'm fifty*."

She'd had a similar response to the last three dresses I'd tried on.

"If you're such a fashion expert, what do you suggest?" I challenged.

"I'll be right back." Imogen smirked and rose from her chair. Sassy followed behind her.

I sighed and glanced around, my hands on my hips. The shop was packed with row upon row of colorful dresses, each one unique. A big window at the front gave a wide view of the street beyond, where people and their Familiars passed by. My eyes caught a creature that looked like a skunk, but had long tail feathers instead of fur.

I turned back to Esis. "She's going to come back with lingerie, isn't she?"

Esis just looked at me with his big eyes and shrugged.

"Here we go," Imogen said as she returned. She held up a long red dress with skinny straps and a neckline I already knew I was going to hate. She didn't miss the frown on my face. "It's for Liam, remember?"

I sighed and took the dress from her hands. "I'll try it on."

Imogen smiled. "Good. I'll go grab a few more for backup."

I returned to the dressing room, holding the door open a moment to let Esis jump inside behind me. Inside, I slipped off the black dress. My heart sank as I placed it back on its hanger. I loved it, but Imogen was right. It wasn't the type of dress that would stop Liam in his tracks. I stared at the red dress in uncertainty. It might do the trick, but it also might give him the wrong idea. Then again, Liam wasn't the *wham bam thank you ma'am* type of guy, was he?

"This dressing room is open," a woman said outside, making me jump. I'd been staring at the dress for far too long. "You let me know if you need anything." I heard the dressing room door beside mine close.

Shaking off my nervous jitters, I pulled the dress up over my hips, slipped my arms under the straps, and zipped the back. When my eyes fell on myself in the mirror, my insides did a weird summersault that was a mixture of both *hot damn* and *no thank you.*

Esis' brows shot up, and he whistled at me.

The hem of the dress touched the floor, but there was a slit that traveled all the way up to my hip. The front plunged to reveal more than I cared to ever show in public. If I did my hair up real nice, I'd be a knockout. But honestly, I'd spend more time worrying about a nipple slip than anything else.

"Come on," Imogen called when she returned. "Let's see it."

"I'd rather not," I replied.

"Please just indulge me, Sophia," Imogen begged.

"Fine," I agreed, "but I'm not buying it."

I quickly checked the price tag and nearly passed out. Unless it rained hundred-dollar bills from the sky, there was no way I was buying this dress. I'd barely brought that much money with me to Orenda in the first place. I wasn't about to blow all my cash on an outfit I'd wear for only a few hours— even if it did earn Liam's attention.

I took a deep breath and opened the door. Esis scurried out in front of me and sang a three-note tune as if he was announcing the arrival of a queen. Imogen's eyebrows shot up, while I crossed my arms over my chest.

"You look hot!" she sang with a wide smile.

I turned to the mirror, feeling incredibly self-conscious. "Do I?"

Imogen placed the dresses in her arms down on her chair and stepped forward to peer into the mirror behind me. "Maybe if you dropped your arms I could see the full dress."

Nervously, I let my arms fall to my side.

"Woop woop!" Imogen cat-called.

I quickly glanced over at two other patrons browsing the aisles, a mother and a daughter. They both looked up and caught my eye, but then continued flipping through dresses. Imogen didn't even notice.

"By the ancestors, Sophia Henley has boobs!"

"Shut up!" I swatted at Imogen with one hand and covered my cleavage with the other. "If you like it so much, you can wear it."

Disgust crossed Imogen's face. "Me in that? Can you imagine? I'm not buying a dress. I've been working on a homemade dress for the past year. It's going to be epic."

I heard the dressing room door beside mine click open, but I didn't think anything of it. "Maybe I'll have to make my own, too, because I'm not buying this one."

Someone scoffed from behind us. "Why would you?"

I whirled around to see Haley step out of the dressing room with her phoenix Familiar behind her. She wore a strapless black evening dress that was even more revealing than the one I had on. It was accented with golden beads that twisted around the bust in an elegant pattern. And damn it, she looked freaking perfect in it. *Bitch.*

"You'll never get a chance to wear it," Haley snarled. "You'll die in the tournament anyway."

My blood boiled, and my fists tightened. I held back my anger, only to keep the dress I was wearing from bursting into flames. Beside me, Esis bared his teeth and growled.

"What the hell's your problem?" The words slipped out before I could stop myself. It was better than losing control of my Fire and burning *Delilah's* down.

Haley just shrugged. "No problem. I'm just stating a fact."

"Well, you can shove your facts right up your pretty little ass. I'll see you at the ball."

My heart slammed against my rib cage. Holy crap. Had I just said that? Where the heck did those words come from?

Haley just stood there glaring at me. I held my breath, waiting for her to throw a fireball at my head or something. Instead, she just rolled her eyes and whirled around, slamming her dressing room door behind her.

My jaw dropped in disbelief as I turned to Imogen. I didn't make a sound, but my face said it all. I couldn't believe what I'd just done. Imogen let out a light squeal and threw her arms around me, squeezing me tightly.

"I'm so proud of you!" she whispered in my ear.

Just as we drew apart, Haley's door swung open again. She was dressed back in her normal clothes— tight black pants and a low-cut shirt that her boobs were spilling out of. The dress she'd been wearing hung over her arm. Her lips were tight. She didn't meet either of our eyes as she passed by, but she made it a point to step on the hem of my dress and slam her shoulder into mine. I rubbed my shoulder as Haley continued on her way, her Familiar in her wake. Then she turned back to me.

"Oh, Sophia?" she said, like she forgot to tell me something.

"What?" I snapped.

Haley held her head high and glanced down at my feet. "You might want to put that out."

I looked down to see flames singeing the corner of my dress. Imogen and I both immediately started stomping on it. By the time the flames were out and I glanced up, Haley had already left the store.

I gritted my teeth and turned to Imogen. "That wasn't me, you know. That was Haley. Now I have to buy the dress."

"Nah, it's fine," Imogen said. "We'll slip it into her dressing room and let her take the blame. It was her fault anyway."

I sighed. "Yeah, but—"

"Hot. Dayum." A female voice cut me off.

When I turned toward the voice, I couldn't believe my eyes. A woman with dark hair and a parrot sitting on her shoulder stared back at me. I must've been hallucinating or something.

"Amelia?!" I squeaked. I forgot all about Haley and rushed forward to throw my arms around my sister. Kiwi squawked. I squeezed her as tight as I could, letting all of my overwhelmed emotions flow into the embrace. "What are you doing here?" I cried as I drew away from her, still unable to believe it.

"I was headed to Orenda to see you, but then I saw you through the window and came in to say hi," Amelia explained.

"No, I mean, what are you doing here in Kinpago?" I was so excited that I pulled her into another hug.

Amelia laughed and squeezed me back. "That's what I was headed to Orenda to tell you about. I'm moving to town!"

"What?" I squealed, unable to contain my excitement. I missed her so much. "Why are you moving? Tell me all about it!"

I pulled her over to the sitting area, and we sank down next to each other. "This is Imogen, by the way, and her Familiar, Sassy."

Imogen smiled and reached out a hand to shake Amelia's before sitting down. Esis hopped onto Amelia's armrest and nuzzled his head into her hand, inviting her to pet him.

"And this is my Familiar, Esis," I said.

Amelia's expression softened, and she stared down at Esis with wide eyes. "Oh, my ancestors. He's adorable! Can I keep him?"

"Sorry, he's not for sale," I said with a laugh.

Amelia cradled him in her arms, and Kiwi squawked again. Apparently, he didn't like that.

"What are you doing here, Am?" I asked again. I wanted to hear all about her journey and how long she was going to stay.

Amelia took a deep breath. "Well, you know my job on the cruise ship?"

I nodded eagerly. "You could've told me it was a flying cruise ship, by the way."

Amelia laughed. "Yeah, well, you wouldn't have believed me, would you?"

I shook my head. "Probably not."

"Anyway, I got a promotion, which means I get more vacation days. I have a friend who's offered for me to crash in his guest room whenever I'm in town, until I find an apartment of my own. I'll be here for a few days before I leave again. Then I should be back at the end of December just in time for the Elemental Cup. I guess this means you'll be competing?" She glanced down at Esis.

"Yes. Oh, my gosh, Amelia. There's so much to tell you. Life has completely changed since I've been here. I wish I could've talked to you sooner. How are Mom and Dad?"

Amelia didn't look at me when she answered. "They were really upset at first, but they've come around. I visited them a few weeks ago and let them know I'd be coming into town soon to check on you. They won't be happy to hear you'll be in the tournament your first semester, but they'll be happy you've bonded."

"I wish they could come watch," I said sadly.

Amelia's expression fell. "They would if they could. Here. They asked me to give you this." Amelia pulled a thick envelope out of her purse and handed it to me.

"What is it?" I asked, taking it.

Amelia shrugged. "I didn't open it."

I peeled back the flap and peeked inside. My heart nearly stopped when I saw the wad of cash. With that kind of money, I'd actually be able to afford this dress— plus a new coat. A piece of paper was folded up inside. I pulled it out and began reading.

Sophia,

We miss you so much. We wish we could come to see you, but we fear it would cause more harm than good to visit you in Kinpago. We would not be welcome. We wish we could tell you all about it, but it's not something we can explain in a letter. We just wanted to tell you that we're sorry for how we acted. We never meant to push you away. We only wanted you to be safe. We wish we would've taken the chance to tell you goodbye before you left. We hope that everything is going well at Orenda Academy.

With Love,
Mom & Dad

P.S. We know the school takes care of everything for you, but we've enclosed some money in case you need anything in town.

Tears welled in my eyes. I could practically hear my parents' voices in my head saying the words directly to me. I didn't like that they were being distant, but right now, I hardly cared. My heart ached for home, to see them again. I quickly dashed the tears away.

Amelia leaned forward and placed a hand on my knee. "It's going to be okay." She eyed me up and down. "Is this the dress you're wearing to the ball?"

I shook my head and forced a smile. "No. I just tried it on for fun."

"Good," Amelia said. "It's awful and so *not* you."

"What?" Imogen asked in disbelief. "It's gorgeous."

"Yeah, if you're an escort," Amelia deadpanned.

Imogen threw her head back and laughed. "Fair enough. What *should* Sophia wear?"

A smile crept across Amelia's face. "I know just the one."

Curious, I stood and followed behind Amelia as she led us down an aisle and to the other end of the shop. She pointed to a mannequin in the window. My heart lifted when I saw the dress. It was an A-line sky blue dress with a tulle skirt, flowery lace petals above the waist, and a corset back. The neckline was cut just below the collarbone, with cap sleeves that looked modest and elegant. It had an antique style to it that I knew would suit me perfectly.

"I can't wear that," I said immediately, despite every muscle in my body itching to try it on.

"Why not?" Amelia asked.

"She's right," Imogen agreed, stepping forward. "It's not sexy enough. We're trying to impress a guy."

Amelia's gaze shot to mine, her eyebrows raised. "Ooh, a guy! Why didn't you say so?"

She beamed at me excitedly. Would her reaction be different if she knew the guy I was crushing on wasn't Koigni?

"No," I sighed. "It's not that. The dress is too… Toaqua. Everyone's going to expect me to arrive dressed in something like this." I gestured down to the red dress I wore.

Amelia pressed her lips together. "Maybe that's exactly why you *should* wear the blue dress."

My shoulders fell. I wanted *so* badly to wear it, but it would only draw attention. Everyone would think I was trying to cross House boundaries or something. I had no intention of drawing anyone's eye except for Liam's.

"I know you don't have Toaqua blood in you, Sophia," Amelia said, "but you have a Toaqua heart. You were, after all, raised by Mom and Dad."

"If that's the dress you want, then get it," Imogen encouraged. "Don't worry about what anyone will think. Go against the grain for once."

A shy smile spread across my face. Why was I so worried? I ignored the stares that followed every time I was with Imogen, and her dress was bound to be wild enough to keep the eyes off of me. It was just a blue dress. It wasn't like I was publicly disavowing my Koigni heritage.

"Fine," I said. "I'll try it on."

After talking to the lady at the front desk, she helped us strip it off the mannequin. I returned to the dressing room and slipped it on.

Oh, my ancestors. It was perfect. Esis quickly picked his jaw up from the floor and chippered in approval.

"You like it, buddy?" I asked.

He nodded.

"Can you help?" I turned my back to him and sat on the dressing room bench. Esis' little hands tugged at the ribbon in the corset back, tightening it for me. "Thanks."

I stood and looked at myself in the mirror. It fit like a glove. I absolutely loved it.

"Hurry up," Imogen called. "Sassy's getting antsy. She wants to see it."

I took a deep breath and opened the door. Amelia and Imogen both went speechless, their eyes wide.

"It's gorgeous on you, Sophia," Amelia said once she found her voice. "He's going to love it."

I twirled around for them, mostly to hide the blush rising in my cheeks. "You think so?"

"Absolutely," Imogen said. "All you need now is to ask him to the ball."

I immediately stopped twirling. "I'm not asking him."

"Why not?" Amelia asked.

I didn't know the answer. "Um... isn't that his job?"

Imogen scoffed. "This isn't the Dark Ages, Sophia. Girls can ask guys to dances. If you want to go with him, you should ask him."

"Maybe..." I shrugged, enthralled by the idea but not sure I could go through with it. "I'll think about it."

"So, that's the one?" Amelia asked.

My heart fluttered. "It's the one."

"Cool. So, what are your plans for the rest of the day? I was hoping we could go out for lunch and catch up," Amelia said.

"That sounds like fun," I agreed. "Are you coming, Imogen?"

"Nah," she said with a wave of her hand. "I'll go find Cade and we'll hang out."

"In that case, have lots of fun," I told her. "Don't go too crazy."

Imogen rolled her eyes. "Girl, I'm way past crazy. But you already knew that. I'll see you later."

Imogen left the shop while I headed into the dressing room and put my normal clothes back on. Amelia, Esis, and Kiwi followed me up to the register, where I pulled out a few of the bills my parents had given me and handed them to the cashier. Luckily, the dress was far cheaper than the red one— and twenty-five percent off. I *loved* a good deal. I usually only bought things when they were on clearance, anyhow. The lady behind the counter placed the dress on a hanger and in a long plastic bag for me. I draped it over my arm as we left *Delilah's*.

"So, tell me what you've been up to," Amelia encouraged as we headed down the street toward the square.

"I don't know," I said with a sigh. "Mostly going to class, studying, training for the tournament. But we have more important things to talk about, don't we?"

Amelia plastered a look of innocence on her face. "No. I don't think so."

"Am..." I frowned. "You obviously know more about this prophecy and what happened with Mom and Dad than you're saying."

Amelia didn't meet my gaze. "What do *you* know about it?"

"Not much," I admitted. "The prophecy may or may not be a myth. If it's true, it apparently has something to do with me. According to Doya, Mom and Dad stole me as a baby. Oh, and I'm supposed to be looking for some magical object I know nothing about?"

Crap. I wasn't supposed to mention that... but this was Amelia. I could trust her.

Amelia whirled toward me, stopping in her tracks. "Listen to me, Sophia. You're wrong. About everything. Mom and Dad didn't kidnap you. They adopted you. Whatever it is you think you're looking for, you need to stop."

I gaped at her. "Am..."

"Doya's just trying to get in your head," she insisted. "Really. Just ignore this prophecy thing, and you'll be okay."

Amelia started down the street again, obviously unwilling to say more, but I couldn't bring my feet to move beneath me. I knew I could trust Amelia with my life, but something told me she wasn't being entirely honest with me.

Liam

SEVENTEEN

I felt like I was being a wimp, but the day of our last training session, I was nervous. We *had* to get this one right. If we messed up today, it would mean our performance in the tournament would be a disaster. Baine had already told us that students who failed the final evaluation before the Elemental Cup always lost at least one to three people in the tournament.

I didn't want to lose anybody. Which meant we had to do good today.

I stopped at the Koigni dorms an hour early to pick up Sophia. Usually I'd still be in bed, but I couldn't sleep last night. I kept having messed up dreams about Sophia. They started out good… really good… but then they always ended with her being crushed under a pile of rocks.

Obviously, I wasn't about that life, so I'd stayed up most of the night weaving baskets trying to calm myself down, and trying to talk myself out of sneaking into the Koigni dorms just to see if she was really okay.

"Esis wouldn't let anything happen to her," I muttered to myself. I didn't know what the little fur ball would do, or could do if Sophia got into trouble, but he cared about Sophia just as much and probably even more than I did, so it comforted me a little.

Finally, she walked out of the Koigni dorms in an oversized knitted sweater and thick jeans with hiking boots. Esis was bundled up in her arms, wearing a tiny wool hat and gloves. The sight of her safe and well killed my anxiety attack instantly.

I noticed she was wearing a bit of makeup today, which was weird. It was only going to run in the water. She'd never worn makeup a few months ago, but lately, it was everyday. I wondered why that was.

She bypassed a good morning and said, "I brought a wetsuit, like you said. I'm wearing it underneath my clothes." She paused. "Though why we're going swimming in early December, I have no idea."

"You'll be okay," I told her. "You have your Fire to keep you warm. But Jonah and Imogen don't, so it'll be up to you to regulate their temperature while we're out there."

"What about you?"

"Water doesn't bother me, no matter how cold it is. My body can withstand ice."

She looked doubtful. "Why do we have to go out into the ocean, anyway?"

"Baine," I answered simply. "He's going to be using his Familiar, and she has trouble walking on land, so we have to go to a platform on the ocean. You shouldn't be complaining. It'll be much harder for Haley to spy on us."

She nodded thoughtfully. "How are the others going to get there?"

"Imogen will make an earth bridge out of the bottom of the ocean, and Jonah will fly there using air. Your element is the only one that's useless for travel."

"Ha ha," Sophia said bluntly. "So, how are *we* going to get there? You'll take us by water?"

I smiled. "That would be too easy."

I led her outside the school, and we started strolling through the gardens. Secretly I'd been keeping something in the bushes near the greenhouses for ages, and today I was going to show Sophia.

"Cars aren't allowed, you know. And I'm betting bikes aren't, either." Sophia seemed to be reading my mind. "But you look like the type of guy who'd have one anyway."

"Bikes are for guys who have big egos and desperately want to impress people," I told her. "They're a huge sign of being insecure."

"So… guys like you?"

I smirked and didn't answer. I turned the corner, where I weaved my way through a bunch of brambles and hauled out an old motorbike. It was a bit rusty, but it ran good. I hadn't driven it in a while. I hoped it still worked.

"I should have guessed." She crossed her arms. "You're so cliche, Liam."

"It was my dad's," I told her. "It'll be faster than taking perytons."

"How the hell is a bike going to get us into the middle of the sea?" she asked.

I rolled my eyes. "Just trust me, all right? Quit asking questions."

She sighed. "Well, what do you want me to do with Esis?" She held him up.

"Put him in this bag." I showed her a saddlebag attached to the side of the bike. "As long as he stays inside, he won't fall out."

"Do as you're told, Esis," she said to him as she slipped him inside the bag. She buttoned up the sides, leaving enough room for air. He peeked his little head up so his big eyes could see through the slit on the side of the bag.

"Once it starts, we have to get on, fast," I told her, and I slung my leg over the bike. "It's really loud."

I started it up. It was cold, so it took a few tries, but finally the engine roared to life. I looked expectantly at Sophia to get on. She stared at the bike like it was a bomb about to go off.

"Well, come on," I snapped. "I don't have cooties."

My tone snapped her out of it, and she sneered at me. "You're always so aggravated," she complained as she hopped on behind me.

"Well, maybe if you weren't so *aggravating*, I'd be in a better mood," I told her.

"Yeah, right. You've got a stick up your ass whether I'm around or not."

Couldn't argue with that. Sophia slipped on behind me, and her warm, soft body pressed against my back. It wasn't doing wonders for my vow of chastity.

Her arms were dangling downward. "You do have to hold on to me, you know," I told her. "Unless your pretty ass wants to go flying off."

She blushed before she stuck out her tongue at me. "Don't get too excited about it," she snapped. She wrapped her arms around my middle and squeezed tightly. Something in me stirred, and I told it to shut up. I revved the bike so that we took off flying.

Immediately, it felt like a vice was squeezing my middle. I gasped. Sophia was holding me so tight that it would cause bruising, her face pressed into my back in fright. I was sore enough on a daily basis. I tried to suck it up and pushed the bike faster, but it only made her crush me more.

Ancestors, she was choking me. I couldn't even expand my lungs. She was strong. I slowed down and stopped the bike on the side of the path. She let go, and I let in a thankful gasp. I turned around and looked at her. She seemed positively frazzled.

"Look," I said, "you don't need to hang on to me like it's life or death."

"I've never rode a bike, so sue me," Sophia shot back. "I know you don't like me touching you."

"That's not what I meant, Sophia."

Her comment bit into me. We were getting on each other's nerves this morning, and it was more than usual. For the past few weeks we'd been hanging out more often, but it was always with Jonah and Imogen around. We hadn't really been alone since we'd woken up in the clearing, but it was obvious something was different.

Nothing had progressed since that night by the waterfall, and it was bothering both of us. The tension was so bad I thought we were both about to burst.

I think Sophia wanted an answer on what we were. And I wasn't ready to give that yet, because I didn't know myself.

"I'm fine with you touching me anywhere— you know what I mean," I said when Sophia smirked. I could hear Esis' little chatters of delight from inside the bag. "What I mean to say is, it doesn't bother me. But I can't drive this thing if you make me pass out."

Sophia turned a little paler than before. "I'm just scared to fall off."

I gave her a look and lowered my voice. "Do you honestly think I would ever let you fall?"

Her expression cleared. She shook her head, and a few strands of hair fell into her face. "No."

"Good." I turned back around, and her arms encompassed me once again. "Then stop being a baby, and just trust me."

Sophia reluctantly put her arms back around my middle. This time she was holding on a little less tightly. I started off at a slow speed, then pushed the accelerator until the trees were racing by in a blur.

"Hold on," I yelled. "I'm going to speed up."

She didn't respond, so I kicked it into high gear. The bike's speed became faster and faster, until I really had to focus on where I was going in order to keep it steady. I took sharp turns and curves at a high speed, leaning into them. Sophia followed my movements easily instead of resisting against them, and for a moment, it was like we were one body.

There was a large hill that ended in a drop-off into the sea. The trees parted and disappeared as we raced up the hill. Sophia looked ahead and noticed there was nothing below but the ocean.

"Liam!" she screamed. I laughed and launched the bike off the hill and up into the air.

The bike was suspended for several moments. It was like everything was in slow motion. Sophia was screaming, and I felt more alive than I had in weeks.

We crashed down on the ocean, but instead of sinking into the water, we started riding on top of it. I barely had to think about it as the water rushed upward to support the bike. Sophia gasped in amazement, and I grinned wildly as I pushed the bike to its limit.

We had to be going a hundred and fifty miles an hour on the water. Water splayed out on both sides of the bike as I drove upon the ocean, and Sophia's screams turned to whoops of happiness. I could feel her racing heartbeat pounding through my back. Esis let out a exhilarated cheer from within the bag. I went breathless for a moment, loving riding my bike on the sea. Ancestors, I loved the water.

Dolphins jumped up beside the bike, and a whale in the distance smacked its tail down to say hello. I performed a few fancy maneuvers and did a wheelie to impress Sophia. The water was there to support the bike each time, putting it back in balance if I made a mismove. Sophia's fear had turned to joy. By the time the platform came into view, I actually heard her let out a little sound of disappointment.

The platform was nothing more than a wooden surface suspended in the middle of the ocean, almost a hundred yards long. I slowed down, and the water rose to make a ramp up to it for the bike to ride. I parked the bike, and we got off. Sophia's hair was a mess, and so was Esis'. He looked puffier than usual when she took him out of the bag.

"Wow, Liam. That was… it was incredible," she said, and her words were a little stuttered.

"Glad I pushed you now?" I asked. We walked toward the center, where Baine, Imogen, Jonah, Squeaks and Sassy were already waiting. I nudged her shoulder, and she nudged mine.

"It's nice of the two of you to show up," Baine started. He seemed in a sour mood, but I couldn't imagine why. It was killing my vibe. I was the only one allowed to be an asshole, after all.

"Sorry we're late, Professor," Sophia started. "It was my fault. I had something I needed to do before I came."

My curiosity peaked. What was Sophia doing before she met up with me?

"Miss Henley, I understand that you have a life, but from this moment on nothing is more important than this tournament," Baine said. "I hope you can understand that."

Sophia nodded meekly. Baine waved his hand and said, "Start practicing drills. We'll begin in a moment."

We separated. Sophia began practice by tossing fireballs around, while Imogen and Jonah started casting with both Earth and Air. I was more or less bored, just weaving water around. How was this going to help us survive, exactly? Baine needed to start teaching us what to do, instead of just barking at us. I felt completely unprepared for this.

"Hey, Liam, can I talk to you?" Jonah asked after a few minutes. He approached me like he had something important to say.

"Uh… sure, buddy," I started. What was this about? Jonah led me to the other side of the platform, away from everyone's earshot.

"I wanted to address the elephant in the room." Jonah seemed somber. What could this possibly mean?

"Uh, okay," I said. I shrugged. "What's up?"

He sighed very dramatically. "I'm sorry, but I feel like I have to tell you this. You've been acting… different, lately, and I think I know why."

I couldn't breathe. This was an emergency. Did he figure out my secret? Had he put together that there was more between me and Sophia than I was willing to admit? My heart thudded against my ribcage. "Jonah, listen. It's not what it looks like."

"Don't try to deny it, Liam. I'm not blind," Jonah started. "You've been acting like a love-struck puppy, and while it's cute, it's really desperate and kind of sad."

This was it. He was going to guess, and I couldn't deny it. If it was that obvious to him, how many other people had put it together?

"You can't tell anyone," I started. "People would freak out if they knew."

"Liam, baby, trust me. I'm not going to tell a soul," he said. "It would be *so embarrassing* if people knew you had a crush on me."

Had a crush on… then it hit me.

Oh. My. Ancestors. The buffoon actually thought that I was acting weird lately because I liked *him*, but in all reality, I'd been weird because I liked…

"That's not what it is." I shook my head. "Jonah, I'm not gay, I like—"

"Don't try to deny it, Liam. I know I'm hard to resist, even for a straight guy like you," Jonah said.

"Jonah, it's not—"

"Look, Liam, we've been friends since we were like, six. It's just gross," Jonah said. "You know I like Renar, and to be honest, you're too scrawny to be part of *this* package." He gestured to himself. "I'm just not that into you. I hope you understand."

My mouth dropped open. Jonah patted me on the shoulder and said, "There, there. I know I'm not easy to get over, but you'll find someone else."

I was too shocked to do anything. Jonah put his arms around me and gave me a really tight hug. "It's okay, bro. I know you're broken hearted, but we can still be friends."

He gave me a fucking *kiss on the cheek* before he ambled off to talk to Imogen. I was left standing on the platform with an open mouth.

What. The. Fuck? Was everyone going crazy around here?

Jonah should know I wasn't into him. I liked girls! It was clear I was into—

I stopped myself dead in my tracks. I wasn't going there. I promised myself weeks ago I'd stop.

Not that it was working, anyhow.

Sophia had made her way over, curious. "That looked really intense."

I shut my gaping mouth. I went to the other side of the platform to be by myself and, apparently, quit giving Jonah the wrong idea. Baine reached out and grabbed me by the arm.

"Liam, a moment please," he said, turning me around.

Oh, by the ancestors. Did he think I was in love with him, too? "What?" I snapped, in a tone more vicious than I intended.

Baine raised an eyebrow, and inwardly, I recoiled. Baine was still my head of House, and an Elder on the council, too. I needed to show him respect.

"Sorry," I said quickly. "What is it?"

Baine let go of my arm and stepped back. "It's the last training session before the tournament. It's only a few days away. There isn't any time left for me to deliberate. We need a Captain."

Inwardly, I groaned. I already knew where this was heading. "I don't want to be responsible for anybody. I'm no Captain."

"I don't think you have much of a choice. Imogen and Jonah aren't leaders; they're followers. You already know that."

"Why not choose Sophia?" I asked. "She's Koigni. They're born to do that type of shit."

"I *was* going to choose Sophia, but she isn't ready. The potential is there, but she's not in a place where she can back up a team, Liam. That means it's up to you. They need a Captain."

"I'm not a leader," I said, shaking my head and backing away.

"On the contrary. Nashoma wasn't any mere wolf. He was an Alpha. And he wouldn't have chosen anyone who wasn't his equal," Baine said firmly.

Did he really have to bring my Familiar into this? "Nashoma isn't here."

"But you are. And there has to be someone who leads the pack," Baine said. "Listen, Liam. I know you don't want it to be all up to you, but if there's no chain of command and no one for them to follow, it's going to lead to disorganization. Then you're all going to die out there."

He really knew how to sell it to a guy. "Fine," I said, rather salty. "I'll be the damn Captain. Just don't expect them to listen to me."

Baine ignored me. He led me back to the center of the platform where the rest of the group was waiting.

"Liam's the boss," Baine announced to the group. "He'll be serving as your Captain. You'll be taking orders from him during the Elemental Cup."

"What?" The gust of wind Jonah had been blowing around died instantly. "But Sophia—"

"Needs more time. Time we don't have," Baine said strictly. "Does anyone have a problem with it?"

Jonah opened his mouth, but before he could say anything, Baine answered, "Good. Then let's move on."

Jonah shut his trap and gave me a look that obviously said he thought we were all going to die. Imogen seemed nervous. Did these people really think I was that incompetent?

I couldn't blame them, really. I didn't believe in myself either.

Sophia didn't seem bothered she wasn't Captain. In fact, she looked relieved.

"Gather around," Baine announced. We stood in a circle around him, and he said, "The first thing we should do is test your weaknesses and see where you stand."

He snapped his fingers and pointed at Imogen. "You. You're the shortest. I've noticed you've had trouble summoning your element."

"Yes, sir," Imogen said. She looked around, unsure of where this was going.

"Earth Elementai are supposed to be strong— the strongest of all the elements. We need to know you can carry your weight… and be able to move mountains."

Baine fixed his glasses, thinking. He pointed to Jonah. "Your teammates might get injured during the tournament, and it'll be critical that you can get them to safety. I want you to try and carry Jonah for me, please."

I nearly choked. He had to be kidding. I'm pretty sure Jonah's one arm weighed more than Imogen's entire body. She was barely five feet. She hardly came up to his waist.

Jonah, of course, was more than willing for an opportunity to play actor. Jonah laid down on the platform and pretended to be dead, squinting through one eye to peer at her.

"Well, come on," Jonah said. "I'm bleeding out, here."

Imogen gulped. We were in the middle of the ocean, so unless she shifted the ocean floor, which was already wet and unstable, she wouldn't be able to move Jonah. She instead tried the old-fashioned way and swung his limp arm over her shoulder before wiggling under his back to carry him on her back.

Imogen tried to lift Jonah, but all it resulted in was Imogen falling over.

"Come on, Imogen. You can do this," Baine encouraged.

This guy was asking for the moon. Imogen eventually managed to get Jonah onto her back, before she huffed and puffed for a few moments and tumbled over sideways again. Sassy tried to help her by putting Jonah's leg on her back, but it flattened the poor fox to the ground.

"I've seen what I needed to," Baine said, waving his hand. "Please stop."

Imogen was breathing like she had just lost a marathon. Jonah gave her a look and said, "You've killed me. Way to go."

"Jonah," Baine said abruptly. "It's your turn. I want you to cross the platform— without making a sound. Sneaking around and staying silent will be crucial for your success during the tournament, and your size already puts you at a disadvantage."

Jonah straightened up. He swallowed nervously before nodding. He crunched into a sneaking position. His crouch was still about the height of an average person.

I had the immediate thought that Jonah should take off his gigantic boots, but Jonah was dumb, and I couldn't help him. Every step he took across the platform sounded like it was coming from a giant.

Squeaks didn't help. Her hooves tip-toeing across the wooden platform resembled a tap dance. Before they reached the end, she tripped, and she sprawled into Jonah head over hooves. The two of them made a crashing sound as they rolled off the platform and into the water.

Baine seethed as Squeaks and Jonah pulled themselves out of the ocean. He was getting agitated. "Very well."

He turned around and looked at me. "Liam, we already know your weakness is going to be endurance. But there's no way to test that with the amount of time we have, and there will be little rest during the tournament, so you're going to have to find a way," Baine said simply.

"Gee, thanks," I grumbled, and I crossed my arms. He didn't need to remind me that I'd already be slowing the team down out there. But coming in last place was better than not making it there at all.

"Sophia!" Baine said abruptly, and she started. "I want you to create fire-rain and shelter the rest of us from it."

"Like… right now?" she asked meekly.

"You have to be able to control and sustain fire at a moment's notice, without thinking about it. By now it should be second nature to you," Baine said. "There's no telling what kind of fire-power you'll have to fight against during the tournament. You need to learn to expect what's coming."

Baine looked at her expectantly, and so did everyone else. I glanced away to try and take the pressure off her, but I think she took it as a sign I didn't believe in her, because her face became more panicked.

She raised her hands, palms facing the open sky. Her arms shook as she tried to make fire-balls rain down from the heavens, but all she managed to do was make a few embers trickle down through the air.

I didn't like fire, obviously. Hated it, in fact. But I still felt bad for Sophia for being unable to control her element. This was advanced Koigni stuff— things that older students would know, not freshmen.

But it didn't matter. There were people of all ages in the Elemental Cup. She had to be just as good as the others if we were going to make it through this.

"Come on, Sophia," Baine growled. He pushed her, bunching his hand into a fist to shake it at her encouragingly. "You can do this! You have the potential!"

"I'm sorry!" she yelled. Her face scrunched intensely. "Just… give me a few moments to get angry!"

Sophia, you haven't learned anything. She thought firepower was about being pissed off all the time, and that wasn't it at all.

Course, that was probably my fault. I'd been the one how to teach her to access her element, after all.

Sophia gave a gasp and doubled over. A few fireballs came down from the sky, but they were small and sizzled out quickly in the ocean. All that was left was a few lingering flames flickering around her fingers.

When she looked at me again, the fire in her hands blazed out of control. Baine had to bring up water out of the ocean to put it out.

"Boo!" Jonah shouted, giving a thumbs down. Squeaks copied him and gave a hiss. Sophia blushed and quickly put her Fire away.

I felt so bad for her. She'd just been introduced to this world, and already, she was trying to do magic that I wouldn't expect seniors to be able to do on a whim.

"This isn't getting anywhere." Baine sighed and rubbed his eyebrows. "All right. I've had enough. I'm just going to throw you into it."

Baine walked toward the edge of the platform. He knelt down by the water and whispered something to it before he stood. He was watching the waves closely, eyes narrowed.

I could feel her beneath us, moving through the water. The ripples she created washed over my skin, even though I was standing here dry on the platform. She wasn't but a few feet below us. A long shadow loomed underneath the platform, and the water trembled as a low croon emitted from the ocean.

"What's that?" Sophia said in fear. She backed up a few steps, looking around. Esis was doing the same, glancing this way and that from Squeaks' back. Sassy danced nervously, waiting.

I smiled. "Thalassa's coming."

"Who?"

It soon grew too loud to answer. The swelling of waves crashed upon the sea, and the clouds parted as the shadow grew closer to the surface, the sun blazing down on a magnificent creature that crashed out of the water.

She was bigger than any Familiar I'd ever seen— even bigger than Alric's Familiar, Valda, or Costas' Familiar, Hera. Her scales were a dark cerulean blue, and they shone as she broke through the water and leapt over the platform, performing an elaborate jump. Sophia's jaw dropped as she watched Thalassa soar over us and dive back down on the other side, causing a huge wave to rise up and come crashing back down. Thalassa broke the surface again, splashing her beautifully fanned tail behind her.

The sea serpent had kind eyes that glimmered like sapphires, long lashes in the designs of coral donning her eyelids. She held her massive webbed paws in front of her body and looked down at us from high above. Thalassa was so big, she nearly blocked out the sun. What little light that did burst through hit her blue scales and bounced off in a million different directions, creating rainbows. There were wings on her back, enabling her to glide if needed, but they functioned more as fins than for flight. Thin spines lined along her back, and two pointed horns accented the top of her head, thin whiskers drooping down from her lips. She smiled slightly, revealing sharp and pointed teeth.

Baine's face brightened in joy, and he laughed, spreading his arms out wide. Thalassa lowered her head so that it was at Baine's level, and he wrapped his arms around it (what he could, anyway). Her skull was larger than Baine's entire body. Her eyes closed in happiness, and she let out a contented note that was high-pitched and shook the platform.

"*That's* Baine's Familiar?" Sophia squeaked.

"Not what you were expecting, is she?" I asked smugly.

"She's so beautiful," Imogen whispered in awe, and she held tighter on to Sassy.

Baine let go of Thalassa and motioned her downward. She lay her head on the platform. He climbed on and sat in the nook where her head ended and her neck began. He held on to her horns as he rose back up.

"Your task for the day will be to subdue Thalassa and me," Baine called from above. "If you can get us to submit, you'll have passed the final session and be ready for the tournament."

"But… she's a Water creature. What about my Fire?" Sophia asked reluctantly.

"You won't hurt her. Trust me," Baine said. "Not even your Fire will be enough to damage her— not at Year One level. What I'm asking is for you to get her to surrender."

"Believe me, Sophia. All your Fire could do to her is tickle," I told her.

"I'll give you five minutes to strategize before I make my attack." Baine hung on as Thalassa dove downward and swam away.

I turned to the group and tried to think. This was going to be a challenge. Thalassa was practically a mile long, and she was a goddess of the water. Pinning her down was going to be near impossible.

"First things first," I told the group. "We need to get changed."

"I'm always down to strip," Jonah said. Thankfully, everybody was wearing their wetsuits underneath their clothes, so I wasn't subjected to that. I paced by the waterway and tried to come up with a solution.

"Well?" Jonah asked me. "What's the plan, big guy? We've got like, two minutes left."

"Give me a minute," I muttered. I had to play to Thalassa's weaknesses, but as far as I knew, she didn't have any.

"Sophia, Imogen, get onto Squeaks," Jonah told them. "She's not big enough to carry me, but she can handle you two."

Imogen and Sophia did just that, and Esis joined Sassy on the platform. Who was leader, here? "Jonah will be able to fly around. I'll handle being on the water," I told them. "We'll take Thalassa and Baine on from all sides."

"What's our strategy?" Imogen asked me.

I didn't know. Taking on Baine alone during the first training session had been hard enough. I didn't know how we were going to beat him and Thalassa.

"I might be able to pin her down in the ocean. Make the currents strong enough so she can't move. If you guys distract her, I'll make it so she won't know what's coming."

"Will it work?" Imogen asked.

I shrugged. "It's a long shot."

Jonah looked up, and his face paled. "Well, it's what we got, because she's coming this way!"

Thalassa was sailing toward us full speed, carrying Baine, who had summoned a large wave behind him. Squeaks took off with Sophia and Imogen, and I leapt into the water. It swelled around my middle and carried me throughout the ocean, safely out of the way. Jonah jumped off the platform. The air carried him upward so that he was floating far above Thalassa. Esis and Sassy stayed on the platform and ducked, getting soaked by Baine's wave.

"Now, guys!" I shouted. I summoned deep waters from below and surged them over Thalassa's body, trying to make her stay still, but controlling her fins was like holding back a propeller on the *Hozho*. She was strong.

Our attack was disorganized. Instead of working together as a unit, we all seemed to be doing our own thing. Jonah, Sophia and Imogen all focused on a different place on her body to attack instead of one spot, shooting their elements at her with everything they had. Thalassa shook as if brushing off flies and yawned.

Sassy and Esis were still on the platform. They ran back and forth, throwing little pebbles and coral that had washed up on the wood at Thalassa to get her attention. Obviously, she gave them none.

Esis got tired of being ignored. He jumped off the platform and onto Thalassa's tail, running up her back and avoiding the little spines. He wove this way and that, avoiding Baine as he reached her head and beat his tiny little fists into Thalassa's temple.

"Esis!" Sophia shouted. "Get back here!"

He didn't listen to her and kept ramming her on the forehead. Thalassa's eyes crossed to look at him, as if he was an annoyance.

The brave little fucker. I was honestly impressed. "Sophia, get Esis back to you!" I shouted. "This is it!"

Squeaks flew close to Thalassa, and Esis leapt from Thalassa's head and into Sophia's arms. They soared out of the way just as Thalassa clamped her jaws over the air they'd been soaring through a moment before.

There was no coddling at Orenda Academy, obviously. Baine didn't mind breaking our bodies if it meant we'd be prepared for the competition.

Esis had given me an idea, though I wasn't quite sure what it was yet. I broke my concentration and scanned over my teammates. Despite Sophia shooting out fireballs, Imogen tossing large sections of sand over Thalassa's back to weigh her down, and Jonah doing his best to create a windstorm that kept her in place, Thalassa acted like she was out for a morning swim.

She paddled around, almost bored and opened her mouth to roar at us. It sent Squeaks into a spiral she only recovered from last minute.

Baine wasn't bothered, either. He was easily holding on to Thalassa with one hand and keeping my magic at bay with the other. I was at war with Baine, and though I found I could keep up with him, which was encouraging, I couldn't surpass him.

The plan wasn't working. Thalassa was too big to control, and Baine had too much power over the water. We couldn't beat them in a show of brute strength. We were going to have to improvise.

My mind worked furiously. This session was all about weaknesses, but it seemed like neither one of them had any.

One of Sophia's fireballs went rogue and went ricocheting toward Baine. It was already fizzling out, but Thalassa turned quickly and brought her tail fin up to block Baine from the hailing embers.

I was confused. The fireball wouldn't have even hurt Baine if it did hit him, but Thalassa protected him anyway.

Then it clicked. Thalassa *did* have a weakness. It was Baine.

"Guys!" I shouted. "Get in front of Thalassa! Keep her eyes ahead!"

"Are you crazy?" Jonah screeched. "That's right in the line of fire!"

"It's only for a few moments!" My tone seemed to convince them, because Sophia steered Squeaks in front of Thalassa and started shooting. Her fireballs smacked at Thalassa's snout, while Imogen's mud-pies splattered in the serpent's eyes. Jonah blasted an assault of wind at Thalassa, causing her to be unable to go forward. Sassy stood on the platform, yipping as loud as she could.

Thalassa shook her head and closed her eyes, trying to stop the assault so she could see again. Baine was forced to grab on with both hands in order to keep himself balanced, and his magic instantly halted.

"There's the opening," I whispered. But instead of trying to subdue Thalassa, I went for Baine. I lashed out a hand and a stream of water raced upward and wrapped itself around Baine's torso, pinning his arms so he couldn't use his element. I yanked it downward, and Baine was dragged underneath the ocean on a trip to the bottom.

Thalassa screeched. She splashed around, kicking her large flippers in search of Baine, and causing a tidal wave.

When she didn't find him, she twirled around and looked at me.

"Give up, Thalassa," I told her calmly. "It's over."

Thalassa lowered her head calmly and bowed to me. Only then did I bring Baine splashing to the surface. The four of us returned to the platform. Thalassa brought Baine back up to us with her tail, placing him gently beside us.

"Well done!" Baine coughed and wiped water away from his eyes. "Well done, children!"

"Did we pass?" Imogen asked, squeezing Sassy.

"With flying colors. I daresay you're ready for the Elemental Cup to begin." Baine swept his hair out of his eyes.

What a relief. I felt a little better, before I realized that this was it— there were no more training sessions. Next time, it'd be the real deal.

"I applaud your innovation, Liam," Baine congratulated me. "Sometimes you've got to outsmart what's in front of you instead of beating it down."

I nodded. I felt a little bad we'd won by manipulation, but hey, this was life or death. "Thanks, Professor."

"I suggest all of you rest up as much as you can before the tournament, and train sparingly, as to not reach your peak before its time," Baine said. "You'll do well. All of you."

His opinion of us had drastically changed in a short time. Taking that as a dismissal, I headed toward my bike, which was now waterlogged, by the way. I motioned for Sophia. She slid off of Squeaks and joined me.

I successfully drained all the water out of my bike and was able to get it started again, but it ran like shit. Like, shittier than before. Despite being Toaqua-proof, this thing was seeing the end of its days. I got back on and Sophia slid behind me. Esis scurried across the platform and jumped into the saddlebag. We took off before Baine could hold us back.

I drove slow on the way back to Orenda. I hid the bike back in the bushes before I leaned against the stone wall, looking at Sophia. She seemed like she… disapproved of something. Esis sat at her feet, looking up at her.

"Shouldn't we have stuck around to talk more about the tournament?" she asked.

My stomach clenched nervously. "I didn't want to stand around and talk about the inevitable," I told her. "I hate discussing variables and what-ifs. I'll just take life as it happens."

"It's not just about you," she said. "Jonah and Imogen are nervous, too. Especially Imogen." Sophia sighed. "She's worried she's going to end up like… well."

Yeah, I'd heard what had happened to Imogen's brother last year. It'd been brutal.

"It's just going to make us more anxious," I said. "We need to focus on the now."

"You mean enjoying the time we have left."

Her tone was so direct. I put my hands in my pockets. "Yes."

Her expression didn't change. I knew what she was thinking. She thought I was running—like I wanted to run from my sickness, from a possible diagnosis, from everything.

So what if I was? I wanted to keep running. Just a little while longer.

"Why would you do that to Professor Baine, drag him under like that?" Sophia asked. "He could've died."

"It's pretty hard to drown a Toaqua," I told her. "We can hold our breath longer than others. Baine was never in any danger."

She pushed her hair away from her eyes. "It seemed cruel."

"We did what we had to do. Like we'll have to do out there," I insisted. "We don't have a choice."

"What if we do?"

"Sophia, we've been over this," I said firmly. "Elementai society doesn't work that way."

She huffed before she changed the subject. "I can see why Baine keeps Thalassa in the ocean instead of with him," Sophia said. Her tone was lighter, and she was trying to smile.

"Right. Can you imagine fitting her in the castle? Insane." I gave her a weak grimace back. Fuck, I was tired. I didn't realize it until now, but my entire body was aching. Fighting Baine today had wreaked havoc on me, and he wasn't even the worst we'd face out there. To make things worse, I could feel a cold coming on. My chest was congested and my head throbbing. It'd come out of nowhere, no warning.

We were in trouble. I had to get better before the tournament, otherwise, Imogen would be dragging *me* around instead of Jonah. Right now, all I wanted to do was crawl back to my dorm, take a long bath, and go to sleep.

"Hey, Sophia," I said, and I pushed off the wall. "I don't really feel well. Talk to you later?"

"Okay." She frowned, seemingly sad to see me go. I went to walk off, but before I could, she called out, "Liam?"

My heart throbbed. I turned back around. "Yes?"

She hesitated before she cautiously said, "I was thinking… about the Elemental Ball… would you like to go with me?"

My cold was temporarily forgotten. It felt like I was rushing through the ocean a million miles an hour. Sophia was asking *me* to the dance?

I knew what the rules were, that I should say no, but I wanted to say yes. Really badly. I opened my mouth, torn between the two answers, but the only stupid thing that came out was, "But… aren't I supposed to ask you?"

She gaped at me for a moment, unsure of what to say before her face turned red. "How dare you!" She stomped forward, and Esis covered his eyes. "These… these aren't the *Dark Ages*, you know! Independent, strong women can ask men out to dances whenever they like!"

"Um," I started, having no idea what she was talking about.

Her expression changed. It went from really pissed to really, really depressed.

"Never mind," Sophia said. "It was a stupid idea. I just thought—"

"No." I caught her wrist as she turned away, and she looked back up at me. "No, Sophia, I— I would really like that. I'd love to go to the ball with you."

Her eyes brightened. "Are you serious?"

"Yeah." I let go of her wrist and nodded. "It'd be cool."

It'd be cool. Really fucking smooth, Liam. I'm pretty sure at our feet, Esis did another facepalm.

"Oh." It wasn't the reaction she'd been looking for, but what did she expect? For me to grab her and sweep her off into the sunset? Did girls still want those types of things? Hell, I didn't know.

"Is that okay?" I asked. By the ancestors, I was going to puke. She was going to take it back, because I couldn't even say yes the right way.

"Of course." She smiled. "I guess it's a date."

She slayed me. A fucking date. "Awesome." I backed away. "I can't wait to go to the ball with you."

"Me either." She held her breath. "That is, if we make it through the tournament."

"We'll make it," I said instantly. "No problem."

"Your attitude sure has changed." She grinned.

"I want to go to that ball, and I want you there with me," I said. "Trust me. We'll be partying as full Elementai by the end of the tournament."

Her expression brightened like the fire she cast. She waved goodbye, and Esis copied her movement. I raised a hand in farewell before I headed into the castle. I was practically skipping up the steps.

Shit, a dance. I needed a suit. And better shoes. I hated dances. What was wrong with me?

My mind whirled with questions of why Sophia would pick me to be her date for the ball. Maybe it was a way for Sophia to redo her prom and have a better one with me.

Me. She asked *me.* Who was acting like the girl now?

As I walked up the steps to the dorms, the cold came rampaging back, and I felt awful, but I hardly cared. I was going on an official date with Sophia Henley. *To the Elemental Ball.*

Things had changed now. I was determined to survive this fucking tournament, come hell or high water. All to put on a monkey suit and dance with the girl of my dreams.

Some women were just worth walking through firestorms for.

It was finally here. The day of the tournament.

And I was freaking. The eff. Out.

"We haven't practiced enough. We should've trained longer. What are we going to do without Baine out there with us?" I paced back and forth in mine and Imogen's changing room, my hands shaking. My Fire raged just on the surface, begging to escape. "Oh God, Imogen! What if someone gets hurt and Esis has to heal them? Liam will kill me when he finds out I never told him—"

Imogen's palm cracked against the side of my face. "Pull yourself together, woman!"

I froze in place, completely shocked. Did Imogen just *slap* me? What the hell?

"Seriously, Sophia. You can't go out there like this." Imogen acted tough, but I could see the worry in her eyes. She crossed the room and sank into one of the chairs in front of the big mirrors lined with bright lights.

Our morning had started with a big celebratory breakfast for the contestants, followed by a speech from Head Dean Alric. It was supposed to prep us for the tournament and get us motivated, but afterward, I only felt more clueless and hopeless than ever.

After Alric's big speech, our teams had been ushered into carriages pulled by unicorns and led away from the castle. Liam gave us a pep talk in the carriage, but it sounded forced and nervous, like he was only doing it because he was team Captain.

When the carriages stopped, we entered a huge stone building at least five stories tall. The arena. Through the trees, I couldn't even see either end of it. The exterior looked a lot like a mini version of the castle, but the inside was more modern. We followed everyone else down a long hall with doors that had our names on them. The rooms were the size of my dorm, with two sets of uniforms hanging from the hooks on the wall to our right and loads of makeup sitting on the counter in front of the dressing mirrors on our left. There were chocolates set out for us, but I didn't have the appetite to eat them. As soon as Imogen and I were safely inside our shared room, I promptly started to freak out.

"Let's just take it one step at a time," Imogen suggested, taking a deep breath.

"Okay," I agreed, but I couldn't keep the worry from my tone. "First step?"

"First step is to get dressed before our makeup artist arrives."

"Makeup artist?" I asked, glancing to all the hair and makeup supplies in front of us. "Isn't that kind of… pointless?"

"We have to look nice for the opening ceremony," Imogen said, like it was obvious. She grabbed a blush brush and began tickling the end of Sassy's nose with it. Esis jumped out of my arms and joined Sassy on the counter, waiting patiently for his makeover.

"Why does anyone care?" I asked. "Our makeup will be a mess after the first trial."

Imogen shrugged. "I don't know. They just want us to make a good impression. We want to look good on TV, and it'll help us win bets."

I gaped at her. "This thing is *televised*?!"

She nodded. "On our local station."

"And no one bothered to tell me?" I started pacing again.

"I didn't realize you didn't know," she said innocently.

"And what's this about bets?" I demanded.

"Oh," she said, like it was no big deal. "It's mostly to raise money for the school, since they get a portion. But it gets everyone in Kinpago involved and excited."

My eyes went wide. "They're excited to watch their own children die?"

Imogen's face fell, and she turned away from me. Shit. I'd gone a step too far. I really did need to pull myself together, or I was going to tear my team apart.

"I'm sorry, Imogen," I said softly, taking a step toward her. "I didn't mean—"

"No, you're right," she cut me off. "It's sick. Really, it is. I never said I agreed with it. Let's just get ready, okay?"

I nodded and turned to the uniform marked *Sophia* on the wall. The shirt was a form-fitting, sweat-wicking t-shirt. It was completely black, except for the white cap sleeves. On the back was a red emblem in the shape of a flame. I slipped off my lucky jeans and pulled the uniform pants on. They were made of a soft black fabric and hung loose and comfortable on my hips. They had tons of pockets on them. Finally, I put on a pair of high-top hiking boots, also black. Everything fit perfectly. Imogen's uniform was the same as mine, except with a green leaf on her back for Nivita.

It wasn't long before our makeup artist showed up with a tiny chameleon-like Familiar at her side. The woman's name was Coco, a shortened version of a Hawkei name I couldn't pronounce. She was thin and tall, with legs that went on for miles and sleek black hair that fell to her waist. She had long eyelashes that were probably fake and perfectly manicured eyebrows. Her eyeliner was flawless.

"Hello, ladies," Coco greeted with a smile. "Are you ready to get beautified?"

Coco was nice enough, but I got the sense that she didn't like me and Imogen. At first, I declined makeup at all. I wasn't trying to impress anyone. But Imogen insisted I go with at least a subtle amount of makeup for the cameras.

"Okay, but I'm not coloring in my brows or using lipstick," I compromised.

"Please," Coco begged. "You'll look beautiful. I promise." Clearly she was hoping to showcase her best skills for us.

"I'd rather not," I said, actually proud of myself for not caving in. "But I'll let you curl my hair."

Coco looked pleased with that, but frowned when I promptly pulled my fresh curls into a high ponytail. Imogen let her go all-out on the makeup, but when Coco insisted on taking the green bows out of her high pigtails, Imogen protested.

"Sorry, but no can do," Imogen said. "The bows and the pigtails are here to stay."

"If that's what you want." Coco tried to hide her disappointment, but I could hear it in her voice.

"Are you ready?" Imogen asked as soon as Coco left. She took a long, nervous breath.

"I guess so," I answered, glancing at my bag in front of me on the counter. "I just wish I would've had a chance this morning to talk to Amelia."

A knock came at the door, and someone stuck their head inside. "What about me?"

I leapt up from my chair and threw my arms around Amelia's neck. "Am! I'm so glad you're here."

Amelia slipped inside the room, followed by Kiwi. "I had to sneak in, but it was worth it. I wanted to wish you good luck out there."

"Thank you," I said. "So… how bad is it? The tournament."

Amelia frowned. "I'm not going to lie. It's tough, but if you stick with your team and work together, there's no reason you shouldn't make it."

I could think of about a thousand reasons.

"I placed a bet on you, so you better make it," Amelia said with a laugh.

"I will," I promised, even though I knew now wasn't the time to be making promises I couldn't keep. "We all will."

I sniffled involuntarily and turned to my bag to pull out a small envelope.

"I wanted to give this to you, Am… to give to Mom and Dad." I handed her the envelope and wiped my eyes. "It's not much, just stupid stuff like how much I love them and that no matter what happened when I was a baby, I still love them and—"

Amelia's body crashed into mine, halting my babbling in its tracks. She squeezed me tightly, which only made me more emotional. A tear slid down my cheek.

"It'll be okay, Sophia," she said, her voice cracking.

"Great," Imogen said lightly. "Now I'm going to cry."

I gestured to her, and she joined us in a group hug. Esis hopped off the counter and onto Imogen's shoulder, wrapping his tiny arms around my neck. Sassy rubbed her fur against our ankles.

Amelia drew away when a whistle sounded from down the hall. "That's your five-minute warning. I better leave before they line you up. I'll be in the stands cheering you on, okay?"

I nodded.

"Here." Imogen shoved a tissue in my face, and I gladly took it. I had already ruined my makeup. I knew it was stupid to put it on.

"Bye." Amelia waved as she left the room. It felt like my insides were caving as I watched her go.

I cradled Esis in my arms, and we waved back. Before the door swung shut, Jonah stuck his head inside.

"You two beauty queens ready?" he asked. "It's time to line up."

Imogen scooped up Sassy, and we followed Jonah out into the hall. It was crowded with contestants, all wearing the same uniform except with different colored sleeves and symbols for their Houses. Jonah and Liam both had white sleeves to match mine and Imogen's uniforms. Baine stood there with his hands crossed in front of him, looking proud. Squeaks followed beside them. I tried to catch Liam's gaze, but he just stared ahead down the hall with a hard look on his face.

Hiding his emotions once again, I see.

A guy with a goatee who didn't look much older than me held a clipboard in his hand and was directing everyone to where they needed to go. "This way and to the right," he called. "Make way for Familiars. Line up in this order: white, purple, pink, blue, yellow…"

Nobody really paid attention beyond his first instructions. We all started down the hall and to the right.

"Of course we're first," Liam mumbled.

I glanced between Imogen and Jonah. "Is that a bad thing?"

I mean, I didn't want to go first, but Liam made it sound like it had some sort of hidden meaning.

Imogen leaned over and whispered to me. "They save the best for last."

"Oh," I said flatly. Which meant everyone expected the least from us. We really were the reject team. "They must've placed us in the wrong spot." I only said it to uplift my team, but I could see it on their faces that they all knew I was bluffing.

We entered a large corridor wider than the Koigni common room, with a high ceiling fit for a dragon to pass through. I wasn't surprised when I saw a red dragon at the end of the hall. TVs lined the wall opposite us. They all played the same thing, but it was too loud in the corridor to hear what was happening on the TV.

"White Team, you're first," the guy with the goatee repeated. It was difficult to hear him over all the chatter.

"Come on," Jonah said glumly, gesturing to the front of the line. "Wouldn't want someone taking our spot."

"Don't let this get you down," Baine said. "You're ready for this."

"Losers!" a Koigni guy called as we passed him.

Liam whirled around, but Jonah caught him. "Save your energy for the course," Jonah warned, pushing him along.

Reluctantly, Liam gave in. We stopped at the end of the hall beside a pair of huge doors that looked like they belonged in an aircraft hangar.

"Let's come up with a motto," Imogen suggested. "We're seriously lacking some team spirit."

"How about *Let's not fucking die*?" Liam offered, crossing his arms.

I was preoccupied, my attention locked down the hall. I was trying to get a good look at which team they were saving for last. My eyes caught Haley's at the back of the line. She smirked, sending my blood pressure skyrocketing. She stood next to Doya, but thank God Doya didn't notice my eyes on them. Beside them was a Koigni guy with tree trunks for arms, who was petting the dragon I'd seen earlier. Haley and him weren't on the same team, as evidenced by their mismatched sleeve colors— hers red and his metallic silver— but they were definitely both top picks.

I glanced around for other members of the Red Team. I spotted a huge Nivita guy who had to be half-giant. He stood beside a creature that looked like a lion carved from marble, though it moved with ease.

The Yapluma member of their team was a girl with short black hair spiked in the front. She had at least three piercings, two in her lip and one in her nose. Her eyes were ringed in thick black eyeliner. She looked like the kind of girl who thought she was a vampire and would suck your blood just to prove it. Beside her sat a huge black cat similar to a jaguar, but with leathery wings attached to its back and sharp teeth that curled over its lip as if in warning.

The Toaqua girl beside them didn't have a Familiar, which I could only guess meant it was an insanely powerful sea creature like Thalassa.

I looked between Esis, Squeaks, and Sassy, then to Liam's empty side. It was pretty clear why we were going first. And damn it, I didn't want Liam to be right.

I guess we're just going to have to prove everyone wrong.

Baine stood at the front of our group and adjusted his glasses. "You have nothing to fear. The contestant pool is small this year, so the other teams shouldn't get in your way. You're prepared for whatever else you might find out there. Just trust each other, and I will see you soon."

Liam rolled his eyes and muttered, "Great pep talk."

Baine shot him a pointed expression. "Did I perhaps make a mistake in choosing the team Captain?"

Liam hesitated, then stood up straight. "No, sir."

Baine nodded approvingly. "Good. I wish you all the best of luck."

Goatee Guy rushed in front of us. "White Team, you're up in less than thirty seconds."

"Smile," Baine encouraged. "You're on TV."

Esis slapped his cheeks three times and then grinned. Nerves knotted in my gut, but I forced a smile to my face as the massive doors slid open. The intense sound of thousands of hands clapping spilled into the wide corridor. Sunlight assaulted my eyes, and I had to cover them to see properly.

"First up, we have the White Team!" an announcer's voice boomed through the speakers.

I blinked a few times before I could finally make out the scene beyond the doors. A huge stage spanned out in front of us, bigger than the concert stage at the huge music festival Amelia took me to when I was in high school. Rows upon rows of seating stretched far beyond the stage, rising high in the back of the stadium. There must've been at least ten thousand people here, if not more. It looked like most of Kinpago had come to celebrate the Elemental Cup. My heart pounded so hard that I didn't hear what Goatee Guy said. I only saw him waving us forward.

Liam led us out onto the stage, where Alric stood in front of a microphone. We stepped out into pleasant air and clear skies. I assumed this was one of those times when Elementai were allowed to control the weather. The roar of applause quickly turned to sounds of criticism. People booed us and yelled obscenities at our team. I caught a guy in the front row yelling, "Get off the stage!"

"Well, folks," the invisible announcer said with a light laugh. "It appears the White Team is *not* a fan favorite, though that's not a shocker if you've been paying attention to the board."

Liam walked across the stage rigidly, but Jonah and Imogen didn't let the comments bother them. They smiled and waved, looking excited like they were supposed to.

All I wanted to do was run back the way I came and find a place to hide in the woods or something. The tournament couldn't be any worse than what it felt like to walk across that stage. I thought I might puke right there in front of everyone.

My eyes scanned the stadium walls, keeping my gaze above everyone's head so I wouldn't have to look at the faces of my fellow Hawkei who were basically cheering for my death. My gaze fell upon a pair of huge screens. The first was an image of my team walking across the stage, reflecting this exact moment. I saw the surprise cross my expression when the camera angle switched to a close-up of my face.

Uncomfortable didn't even begin to cut it.

Beside that screen was another that showed the team colors in rows, with stats alongside them. Underneath the bets column, I saw that only three bets had been placed for our team.

Probably Amelia, Baine, and Imogen's parents. The Red Team was up to over six thousand bets.

"I think I'm going to be sick," I whispered to Imogen, but she didn't hear me over the roar of the crowd.

We stopped next to Alric at centerstage. He guided us to stand on small stickers stuck to the stage floor while the announcer continued his spiel.

"First up, we have Imogen Ahnild, Nivita, with her Familiar Sassy, a red fox!" The announcer made it all sound exciting, but the crowd didn't look pleased in the slightest. Still, Imogen beamed and waved to them despite the booing.

"Next up, Jonah Chanee, Yapluma, with his Familiar Squeaks, a hippogriff!" a second announcer said.

My heart raced, and my mouth went dry. I knew they were coming to me next, and I feared what they might say about me... about Esis.

"Beside Chanee, Sophia Henley, Koigni, with her Familiar... oh dear ancestors, what is that thing?" The first announcer let out a deep belly laugh as the cameras zoomed in on Esis.

I pulled him close to my chest. The entire stadium broke out into laughter, but he didn't notice. Esis just waved at them as if he was the star of the tournament.

"I think that may be a rabbit of sorts, Louis," the second announcer cut in.

"You think so, Eli?" the first announcer said.

"Maybe a chinchilla?" Eli guessed.

"That is certainly what it looks like," Louis said with a laugh. "Either way, I don't think it's going to help them in the tournament."

"I think you're right, Louis." Eli chuckled. "Let's move on to our final contestant on the White Team. Ladies and gentlemen, put your hands together for Liam Mitoh, Toaqua, with his Familiar—"

Eli cut off mid-sentence, and my blood ran cold. The camera's focused on Liam's face. His jaw was tense, and his skin had gone pale. One by one, the audience members began to fall silent until only whispers passed over the stadium. It was agonizing.

Eli cleared his throat into the microphone. "Liam Mitoh, Toaqua. Familiar deceased."

A gasp spread across the audience, but I had the feeling they weren't surprised at all about Nashoma's death. It was more like they were shocked Liam was showing his face and still going through with this.

Liam rolled his eyes straight at the camera and turned to Alric. "Can we get this over with or what?"

Alric's blank expression turned into a forced grin, and he leaned into his microphone. "Ladies and gentlemen, I present to you, the White Team!"

Nobody clapped for us except Imogen, Jonah, and Esis.

"Before we welcome our next team, is there anything your team would like to say?" Worry touched the corners of Alric's eyes.

Liam stepped forward, but Imogen slipped in front of the microphone before he could reach it.

"I think I speak for my entire team when I say we're really excited to be here," Imogen said in an excited voice I could tell was fake. "I won't let you down, Mom and Dad." She blew a kiss to the crowd before turning on her heel and gesturing for us to follow her to the other side of the stage where rows of chairs were set up for the contestants.

"What was that for?" Liam growled when we took our seats.

Imogen shrugged as they called the next team on stage. "I didn't trust you. You'd probably flip off the whole tribe on TV."

Liam looked momentarily shocked, but it quickly turned into a smirk.

"Translation," Jonah leaned over and whispered to me, "he was totally planning it."

Liam frowned. "I was not. Shut up and watch the ceremony."

It felt like hours before all the teams made it across the stage. Any hope I had of making it through this tournament gradually waned as they presented more and more powerful Familiars.

By the time Haley's group made it on stage, I was feeling completely hopeless.

"Red Team," Alric said. "Is there anything you'd like to say?"

Haley was the first at the microphone. Anwara fluffed her feathers, looking proud on camera. "We're so grateful for everyone's support," she said in a sickly sweet tone.

Ugh. Gag. She was so fake.

"We can't imagine how we'd *ever* make it through this tournament if you didn't believe in us." Haley shot a smirking glance my way.

I didn't let my emotions show since we were on camera, but inside, I was fuming. She was using her speech to insult us! *Bitch, our three people believe in us more than your six thousand put together!*

"You can rest assured that the Red Team will make it back to the finish line first," Haley concluded. "May the ancestors bless you!" Haley waved at the cameras, a big fake smile plastered on her face.

Alric stepped to the microphone as Haley's team headed for their seats. "As you all know, it is now time to send the contestants on their way. We will be coming to you live as soon as they hit the course. Ladies and gentlemen, one last round of applause for the contestants of this year's Elemental Cup!"

The crowd went wild. All around us, the contestants stood and cheered. I quickly got to my feet to join them, but I merely clapped for show.

Soon we were ushered backstage and outside, where the covered carriages we rode in were waiting for us. This time, however, they weren't being pulled by anything.

"Everybody in," Goatee Guy shouted. "Larger Familiars will follow behind you. All you need to remember is to head for the flag. Good luck!"

Our team climbed into our carriage. Squeaks got in last, squeezing herself between the facing benches so that her feathers brushed our legs. It was a tight fit.

"What do you think our first task will be?" Imogen asked.

"I don't know," Liam replied flatly. "That's kind of the idea, isn't it? To surprise us. That's what Baine's been training us for."

I sighed and stared out the window. "I hate surprises."

Jonah smirked. "Sweetheart, you'd better get used to them."

Just as he said it, the carriage lurched into the air like an elevator. I immediately went tense and gripped the side of my seat.

"It's just Yapluma," Jonah said lightheartedly. "Same way they move the cruise ship around."

I breathed a sigh. "Oh."

"Okay, so our team motto?" Imogen said as our carriage rose into the sky. "What was your suggestion, Liam? *Let's not fucking die?*"

Liam's expression was a strange cross between amusement and anger. "You betcha."

Imogen nodded. "Okay. I like it. No matter what, I've got your back."

"Me, too," I agreed.

"Me, three," Jonah said.

Liam sighed. "If I have to..."

"Yes," Imogen insisted, sticking her hand in the middle of the carriage above Squeaks' back. *"Let's not fucking die* on one, two, three?"

I stuck my hand on top of hers, and Jonah followed. Liam didn't do anything, until Jonah punched him in the arm. Liam sighed and stuck his hand out.

"One... two... three..." Imogen said.

We cheered the team motto, but it was anything but in unison. Everyone said it at a different time. Imogen and I laughed. Even Liam cracked a nervous smile. I glanced back out the window to see we were high above the ground now and headed out over the ocean.

"Is everyone feeling all right?" I asked.

"As good as I'll ever be," Liam answered.

"Good," I said, pointing. "Because I think our first task is Water."

Everyone glanced out the windows to the vast ocean below us. Sassy peeked out the window beside Imogen.

"There's an island!" Imogen shouted, pointing.

Jonah groaned. "And the flag for the finish line is way over there on the mainland."

I glanced to where he pointed and saw a huge orange flag flapping above the trees near the horizon. There were miles upon miles between us and the finish line. We had to make it across the ocean, over a mountain and through a large part of the woods before even coming close. I couldn't even see Kinpago or the castle from here.

"Crossing the ocean shouldn't be hard," I said. "I mean, Liam can control the water. Squeaks can take me and Imogen over, and Jonah can fly."

Jonah's eyebrows shot up. "You've really never watched one of these things before."

I shook my head. I mean, that much was obvious.

"You're delusional if you think the only thing we have to do is cross the ocean," Jonah said. "Princess, there's going to be a thousand things that will knock you on your ass before you make it back to the mainland."

I held my breath. How bad could it be?

"We don't have any more time to strategize," Imogen said as our carriage descended.

We landed softly on the sandy beach of a small island miles off the coast. The other teams began piling out of their carriages, glancing around and keeping an eye out for the first obstacle — whatever it was. I reached for the carriage door.

"Wait," Imogen said, placing her hand on mine to stop me. "Whatever happens out there, I want you guys to know I love you."

Imogen had no idea how comforting that was.

"I love you guys, too," I said, glancing between each of them. My cheeks went beet-red when my eyes connected with Liam's. I quickly averted my gaze and climbed over Squeaks to duck out of the carriage just as Jonah was professing his love for us, "but not in that way."

Once all contestants were on solid ground, the line of carriages rose into the air and headed back toward the mainland. Two dragons and a pegasus circled above us, each with a person on their back. They didn't wear the contestant uniforms, so I had to guess they were the camera crew.

I glanced to the other teams, but everyone looked just as clueless as we were. The Pink Team was already working on an earth bridge, while the guy with the dragon was ushering his team onto his Familiar's back. Haley just stood there with her hands on her hips, staring out into the ocean. She looked positively relaxed, like she knew what was coming and already had a plan of attack.

"Who wants to bet Doya was cheating beyond holding extra practices?" I muttered.

"There's a reason Doya's team is always one of the top picks," Imogen sneered.

"Team motto, guys," Liam snapped. "We're not here to beat the other teams. Let's just focus on getting to the finish line in one piece."

"Agreed—" I started to say, but a high-pitched scream across the beach cut me off. Several people gasped around us as the sky turned an almost immediate dark gray.

"Incoming!" Jonah yelled.

I followed his gaze, and terror spiked through my body. We didn't have time to discuss our plan.

A tidal wave was headed straight for us.

Liam

NINETEEN

Sophia and the rest of the group were looking at the massive wave coming toward us like it was their doom.

I knew better. I could feel the water moving the moment we were put on this island. There wasn't just one giant tidal wave coming toward us.

There were *four*.

On all sides. And I could feel the people controlling them. They were Elders. I couldn't stop them, not even if I tried. I turned on the spot. Sure enough, three other waves equal in size to the first were barreling toward us. Such a thing shouldn't be possible— most Toaqua would find something like that impossible to pull off, as it went against the rules of nature— but apparently the tribe was pulling out all the stops for this tournament.

Everyone else on my team had realized what I'd known minutes before. They started screaming as the waves rushed toward us at a high speed.

I had to get us off this island. If I didn't, I'd hopefully survive, but the rest of my team would certainly drown.

The majority of the other teams were already off the island. The Pink Team was running down the earth bridge they'd made while their Toaqua member made a shield around them with water to push back the tidal wave. The wave simply moved around the blockade and kept going. The Silver Team was flying over the ocean on a dragon, safe far above the waves, and the Green Team had created a boat out of water. They sailed over the tidal waves a little less successfully, though no one fell out as far as I could see. The Orange Toaqua member had taken her team underwater and was trying to pull them through the inside of the wave by a bubble she'd created, but that was risky. Even from this distance, I could tell she was at risk of losing control.

Purple had decided to tag-team the challenge, with their Yapluma member flying two people above the ocean and the Toaqua teammate skirting himself and another partner overtop of the waves.

The Blue Team had created a chamber of ice and was skating across the water, though it wasn't working very well. The water pressed down on the ice tunnel, making it crack under the pressure of the wave, and people were slipping inside trying to get away from the raging water.

Yellow wasn't doing much better. They'd gotten off the island, but their Toaqua was a First Year. It was all he could do to keep his team's heads above water as the ocean battered them this way and that. Their Familiars, a unicorn, a chimera, a gargoyle and a manatee, pushed their Elementai onto their backs and tried to paddle through the violent waves, though the approaching tidal wave soon swallowed them all.

Haley, as always, was prepared. She and her team were calmly riding on the back of a liopleurodon, who assassinated the waves. The giant marine reptile handled the waves like they were nothing while Dina, the Toaqua team member I knew, kept the rest of them dry as her Familiar did all the work of getting them to the mainland.

"Liam!" Sophia screamed at me. "What do we do?"

I realized we were still the only team left without a game-plan, and froze. My mind calculated our options. We didn't have many.

"Put the Familiars on Squeak's back, and send them away," I ordered. "They won't be any use out here. Jonah, send Squeaks to shore to wait for us."

"Do what he says!" Jonah shouted at Squeaks, waving his hand. She hesitated and stomped her hooves, looking scared at the prospect of leaving Jonah.

Sophia was crying as she put Esis onto Squeaks' back. Esis grabbed hold of Squeaks' feathers and tilted his head, like he didn't understand. Imogen was upset, but she at least seemed somber as she put Sassy onto Squeaks' haunches.

"Sophia, we'll see them soon, I promise," I told her, and she nodded.

The waves were growing closer. I pointedly looked at Jonah, and he smacked Squeaks on the hindquarters, shouting, "Squeaks, go!"

Squeaks took off. She soared into the sky, taking Esis and Sassy away to safety. The three of them looked at me, seeming even more lost now that their Familiars were gone.

"What now?" Imogen asked weakly.

I knew this was my task, but ancestors, did I have to do *everything*? "Hold on!" I told them. I created a spinning waterspout that reached out and grabbed the three of them by the waists. They screamed, and I concentrated on making the waterspout larger, growing it above the approaching tidal waves. Soon, they were high above me, appearing like tiny dots in the sky, though I could still hear them screaming their heads off. I trusted Jonah to regulate the air for the girls so they'd be able to breathe as I increased the height of the waterspout.

Any time I had left to get myself off the island was wasted. Sound was drowned out by the roar of the waves. They blocked out all light, darkening the island and creating shadows. Each wave had to be fifteen-hundred feet tall. They'd crush me when they came down.

I barely got my teammates above the approaching tsunami before it crashed down upon me. I managed to create a small shield of water around my form that took most of the blow and made it so the water wouldn't break my bones, but that singular act of pushing back the waves completely shattered my magic and made me weak. My shield broke, and I was caught up in the undercurrent. I held my breath just before the waves dragged me under.

The average person could hold their breath for up to two minutes underwater. I could go for six. People like Baine could withstand ten, but I wasn't going to push my luck. I tried figuring out which way was up, but the waves spun me around so much I lost all sense of direction. I was quickly pulled a hundred feet below the surface. I couldn't swim. I couldn't do anything but let the ocean do as it wanted with me.

My poor mother was probably watching the TV right now and wailing in grief. It would be really embarrassing for my tribe that the Toaqua chief's son had been killed by his own element, but with how my year was going, I really shouldn't have expected anything else. I bet when

Haley won, she'd go back home and rewind the moment of my death over and over, laughing harder and harder each time she saw it. A Toaqua drowning. Hilarious.

Even so, in the back of my mind, I made sure that Jonah, Imogen and Sophia were safe and far out of the tsunami's reach.

The waves spun me around. I was at the mercy of them— until I realized that I was born to be in water, that it was time to act and stop being stupid. If I died, my magic would stop working and my team would end up just like me.

I wasn't about to let that happen. I was the firstborn son of the Water Chief, dammit. I could die in this tournament, but later. Not now.

It took everything, but I used my powers to put myself upright in the churning ocean and stop the spinning. I was running out of air, fast. I couldn't tell how long I'd been under, but I was starting to see stars, and my vision was growing dark.

I put what I had left into pushing myself upward. I worked with the wave instead of against it, summoning my magic so the upwelling surrounded me and rushed me back to the surface. My head broke, and I took a deep gasp of air.

My waterspout was still spinning, but it was smaller now. The island was gone, engulfed by water. The tsunami was no longer there, yet the ocean was churned in its place.

Where there once had been light, now there was only darkness. Huge black clouds covered the sky, and rain was falling down torrentially. The wind picked up. The sky looked like glass as dozens of lightning bolts shot across it.

They were using Yapluma Elders to create storms and Koigni to make lightning, as if we didn't have enough to worry about. I looked upward to where the waterspout still was. My team was dangerously close to the storm.

Sophia was a First Year. She couldn't handle lightning.

With my right hand held up out of the water, I started to bring them back down. But before I could, a colossal roar got my attention.

The Green Team's water boat had a large tentacle wrapped around it. The team members scattered as the tentacle cracked down on the boat, and a giant squid rose up out of the water.

A fucking kraken. To make things worse, the Elders were sending their damn Familiars after us!

The Pink Team was running on their earth bridge from a megalodon that swam beside it. The oversized shark chased after them and blocked the way, preventing them from creating another bridge and forcing them to reevaluate.

Out of the corner of my eye I saw that a few other teams, though I couldn't be sure which ones, were trying to defend themselves against a gargantuan blue crab and a killer whale.

Haley's team was fighting off a leviathan from the back of the liopleurodon, and though they'd been making fast progress, I could tell the creature was giving them a hard time and blocking the way to the beach.

Nothing had gone after us yet, which meant we were lucky. We needed to move.

I lost track of who was on whose team as bodies started flying around. People were thrown out of the air and tossed into the ocean, either by the storm or whatever creatures they were fighting. Somehow, the red dragon from the Silver Team was knocked out of the sky and sent crashing into the sea. I lowered my team back to the ocean's surface while directing the rest of my power downward. The churning ocean split, and we were carried downward until our feet hit the ocean floor and I was holding up two separate walls of water on either side of us.

The shore was at least another mile off. My arms were starting to wobble under the effort of holding the ocean apart.

"Liam?" Sophia turned and looked at me.

"Don't dick around," I gasped. "This is hard."

I had to keep the ocean parted so we could get back to shore. My team started to run. They raced toward the beach while I walked forward steadily, my arms held out in front of me.

It felt like I was bench pressing the Pacific. My entire body screamed. It was incredibly painful, but I was used to pain, and I was fucking stubborn. The whole damn ocean was going to have to kick my ass before I'd let my team die.

Then a spasm wracked through my back, and I let out a gasp of agony. I fell to my knees, unable to control my body's reaction to the sheer effort of holding up my magic. The walls still held, but water was starting to splash over the sides and onto the sand.

I could do this if Nashoma was here. But he was gone. I couldn't pull from his strength. Just another reminder that I was doing this alone.

"Guys, Liam needs help!" Sophia shouted. She'd noticed I'd fallen. She, Imogen and Jonah came rushing back, instead of pressing ahead like I wanted them to.

No, don't come back for me, I wanted to scream, but even talking took too much effort. I gritted my teeth as my upper body started to go numb. Water was pouring in over the sides of the walls now.

"We're not going to abandon you!" Sophia said. She and the others stood around me, their faces pale with fear, but also set in a determined way that told me they wouldn't leave me behind no matter what.

I couldn't do it. The two walls came hurtling back down, and as the water started rushing in I screamed, "Everyone grab on to me!"

They didn't fucking hesitate. Jonah, Imogen and Sophia latched on to my arms, and as we were submerged underwater I used my magic to propel us forward like a bullet.

I rocketed us toward shore. And damn, it wasn't easy, the fatasses. We were easily going hundreds of miles an hour. We'd reach the beach in less than a minute, but already, I could feel Sophia's grip on my arm start to loosen. I glanced to the left and saw that her eyes were half-closed. She was Koigni. She couldn't last as long in water as Imogen and Jonah. I had to go faster.

It hurt, but I urged my element to give me just a little bit more. The beach was in sight— but then I ran out. There was just no more magic left.

We started to slow down. I tossed Sophia upward, and Imogen and Jonah let go. We broke the surface. The two of them started paddling to shore.

Sophia was sinking. She was about to pass out. I swam up behind her and put my arms under hers, grabbing her shoulders so both of us were tilted upward. I swam backward until I was able to pull her onto the beach. She came to, coughing up water once we hit the sand. I let her go and rolled onto my back as the earth rocked like the waves.

Everything hurt. I'd pushed my limits far past what I knew I had the ability to do, and I was paying for it. Little needles were pricking me all over my body, while a steamroller mashed my insides. It was so painful I really wanted to cry.

But we were probably still on TV, so I sucked it up and forced myself into an upward position, even though it made my eyes water.

I took a shuddering breath. We were safe. For now.

Squeaks raced up the beach with Esis and Sassy on her back, giving a happy squawk as she head-butted Jonah.

Well, at least someone was having a good time.

"Esis!" Sophia scrambled up and got Esis from off of Squeaks' back, while Imogen held Sassy. I was too weak to dry everyone, so we stayed wet.

I looked back at the ocean. What about the people who had been behind us? What was their fate?

The Yellow Team had to be gone. There was no way. They were in the water when the tsunami had crashed onto shore, and the Toaqua freshman had been struggling before then. I'd barely made it out alive, and I was a Third Year.

The rest of them had no chance.

A deep cavern of dread started eating my insides. That had only been the *first* challenge. What kind of hell did we have still waiting for us?

"What do we do now, Liam?" Imogen asked weakly. The team looked at me, expecting an answer.

Shit. What *did* we do now? I wasn't sure. I was supposed to be Captain. What did Baine say?

Protect the pack. Protect the pack. Right. "We have to get a sense of direction," I told them. "Then we can start heading toward the flag. We're sure to run into the other tasks along the way."

We couldn't see the sun. Clouds blocked them out, no doubt an effort from the Elders to prevent us from figuring out which way was north.

"I can do that," Imogen suggested, kneeling down to the ground. "I can feel the earth's magnetic poles."

"Me too," Jonah said. "I can sense which way the wind is blowing and use the currents to judge where we are."

"Fantastic." I lay back down on the shore and closed my eyes. I needed to rest. Just for a minute.

Sophia walked over to me, then knelt on the ground. Esis chattered in her arms. "Liam? You okay?"

"Peachy, *pawee*." *It hurts to literally exist right now.*

Esis made a mewling sound and put a tiny paw on my arm. For some reason, once the little guy touched me, I felt a little bit stronger. Everything went from being unbearably agonizing to mildly tolerable. I was able to sit up easier this time.

"The flag's this way," Imogen said, walking toward us with Jonah by her side, pointing north. "Though it's really, really far away."

I got to my feet. "Good. Let's get moving. We'll walk until nightfall." I tried not to wince, but it was hard, and I was pretty sure the team noticed.

"Liam, get on Squeaks," Jonah suggested.

"No way." A rolling, sharp pain went through my gut. I involuntary clutched at it, bending over. This sucked.

"Liam." Sophia stared at me. "You have to."

"You'll slow us down," Imogen said gently. I know she meant it to be kind, but it stung.

"There's no way I'm hitching a ride when the rest of the team is walking," I told them sharply.

"Liam, just do it," Jonah said. "You saved our asses back there. Quit nursing your pride, or I'm carrying your ass. And I'll make sure it looks as gay as possible for the cameras."

I figured we'd all have to take turns riding on Squeaks sooner or later, so I just gave up. "Fine." I climbed on Squeaks, though it was no easy effort, and held on to her feathers as we headed into the forest.

Sassy and Esis led the way, chattering. I think I fell asleep on Squeaks' back, because I closed my eyes and everything went numb.

By the time I opened them again, it'd gotten dark and we were in a clearing. I felt a little better, but where the pain once was, now there was soreness.

"We just stopped," Sophia told me quietly. "We haven't run into anything so far."

"Glad I didn't miss any action." I slid off of Squeaks' back. Imogen and Jonah both looked exhausted. Esis' eyes were drooping.

"We have to find drinking water," I told the team. Right then, I couldn't draw up a droplet out of the ground if I wanted to.

"There's a freshwater spring nearby that we passed," Jonah said. "We can drink from that."

"Okay, good," I said. "We also need shelter."

"Imogen can do that," Sophia offered before Imogen said anything. "She's good with roots and things."

I looked expectantly at Imogen. She blinked, then nodded. She raised her hands. A few roots popped out of the ground, but it was nothing monumental. Sassy played with them before looking at Imogen and giving a bark.

"Come on, Imogen," I said in frustration. "This should be easy for you." I'd seen her do harder things at home.

Imogen grimaced, then a large collection of roots rose up out of the earth. I stepped forward and started weaving them together. The rest of the team followed suit, bending the roots into something that would shield us from the elements, creating a dome that would encompass the four of us fully.

Imogen looked embarrassed. I wasn't sure what was coming tomorrow, but I was pretty sure Earth was next. I worried Imogen wouldn't be up to the task.

"You're not weaving it tight enough. It looks sloppy," I said to them. Imogen and Jonah glanced up at me, but didn't say anything.

"Liam, it doesn't need to be perfect," Sophia shot back. I went to open my mouth, but found myself too tired to argue.

Sophia moved her way over to me on the other side of the shelter. "Liam, you're being hypercritical," she whispered to me. "You have to stop."

I noticed that both Jonah and Imogen looked a little down. "I just… I want everyone to make it out of here," I told her. Some Captain I was, demoralizing the team.

"I get it, but you don't have to be that hard on them," Sophia said. "They're doing the best they can."

Sophia brushed my hand before going back to twisting the roots. Esis gave me a little pat on my leg.

About an hour later we had a shelter made, but it was obvious we were all starving. Squeaks' stomach was making rumbling noises, while Sassy had her nose to the ground, sniffing. Esis rubbed his belly and stuck out his lip.

"I'm going to look for something edible," I said. "You guys stay here."

It took another hour, but I managed to scrounge up a few cattails, conifer bark, and acorns for us to eat. It wasn't much, but we had to consume something. I passed it around. Jonah took it with a wrinkled nose, but the girls didn't complain. We sat in a circle outside the makeshift shelter and ate in silence around a campfire Sophia had made.

Squeaks ate a majority of the acorns. Esis sniffed at the conifer bark I offered him and turned his nose up at it.

Jonah sighed as he chewed on his bark. "This blows," he complained. "What I'd do for a burger right now."

"If you talk about food, I'm going to kill you," Imogen said. Sassy put her ears back and hissed at Jonah.

"Come on, people. Our ancestors lived like this every day for thousands of years. We can suck it up for a few nights," I told them.

"Uh, wrong," Jonah said. "Our ancestors lived like this, but they didn't have giant monsters chasing after them, or other Elementai out there literally trying to kill them."

I flipped Jonah off, because he ruined everything.

"That guy with the dragon is probably at the finish line by now," Sophia said glumly as she munched on a cattail.

"There are rules against flying," I told them. "You can fly through one of the challenges, but for the rest, you have to walk, to make it fair. Otherwise people with flying Familiars would just race to the ending, fly over all the challenges and win easily."

I shivered. I suddenly realized it had gotten very cold. Small white flakes began descending from the sky. It was snowing, and we didn't have much in terms of clothing.

"Snow," Jonah said, looking upward.

"It doesn't snow in this part of California, except for the mountains," Imogen protested.

"During the Elemental Cup it does," I replied. "Everyone, get inside."

We huddled inside the shelter, but it was still fricking cold. The light snowfall outside was quickly turning into a blizzard.

"Sophia, we need warmth. Before we freeze to death." I told her.

She nodded. She reached outside to gather the firewood we'd harvested while I poked a hole in the roof through the roots. She lit a fire and we gathered around it, arms wrapped around our forms.

Even with the roaring fire inside, it was still really cold, and we didn't have blankets or coats. It looked like the Water part of the challenge wasn't over yet.

"Can you regulate the temperature any more, Sophia?" I asked. My teeth were almost chattering. I was pretty sure I was turning blue. The cold couldn't hurt me in Water form, at least, but the temperature certainly could.

"I'm trying. I've never been met with this much… resistance before." Sophia shivered. "It's almost like someone's blocking my powers."

Damn Elders again. On the ground, Esis waddled up to Squeaks. He nestled against her feathers like a pillow before pulling Sassy to him, using her tail as a blanket. Esis sighed happily, totally cozy. The rest of the Familiars huddled up together, unbothered by the chill.

"Hey, Esis has the right idea," Jonah started. "Let's cuddle."

"No," I said flatly. Ancestors, this tournament was pushing every button I had.

"We're supposed to survive, and that means not becoming an icicle," Jonah shot back. "But if you're opposed to the cuddling part, there are other ways to keep warm." Jonah winked.

"I'm gonna hit you," I growled.

"Jonah's just playing around," Sophia said. "Besides, it's not like these outfits are exactly sexy." Sophia pulled at her suit.

"Baby, unisex still has the word *sex* in it," Jonah said.

I was getting real tired of Jonah's shit.

"Jonah's right," Imogen said. "Not about the orgy thing, but we *will* stay warm if we share body heat."

"Nothing shares body heat like a big love-pile," Jonah added. "What do you say, Liam?"

I shivered again, and Imogen said, "Well, I'm not waiting around for *your* approval."

She lay on the ground next to Squeaks, and Jonah followed her. He reached out and grabbed Imogen, crushing her to his giant chest. She giggled. Sophia was usually shy, but it must've been so freaking cold she didn't care, because she lay next to Imogen and scooted against her.

"Come on, Liam." Sophia raised her eyebrows. "Your turn."

"Uh-uh." I shook my head. "Nowhere in the rulebook did it say in order to make it through this, I have to spoon my teammates."

"You can be little spoon." Jonah wiggled his eyebrows.

"Hell to the no." I really was cold. My body was giving in.

Sophia looked really concerned about me. She and Esis were mirrors, both big eyes that were adorable and sucked me in.

Fine. If I was cuddling with anyone, it was going to be Sophia. Because we'd already done it once, and to be honest, I kind of liked it. Though having Imogen and Jonah here was really killing the mood.

I got down on the ground and slid my body against Sophia's, so that my head was resting on one of Squeaks' legs. I shivered when she put her arm around me, though it wasn't because of the chill.

"This doesn't leave the hut. *Ever*," I said. I was glad the cameras couldn't see us inside the hut, because this was taking things a step too far.

"This is like a porn I watched once," Jonah spoke up.

Ancestors help me. I was going to murder these people.

"Relax, Liam." Imogen spoke up. "We're all friends here."

"Reluctantly."

Sophia giggled against my back. I smiled. It was warmer, at least. And I was glad Jonah was on the other side of the hut, because I didn't trust him not to make it weirder than it already was.

"Goodnight, everyone," Imogen said pleasantly. "I hope we all have sweet dreams."

Never mind. Imogen made it weird, anyway.

"Goodnight, my lovelies," Jonah said. I immediately heard a large snore afterward. The bastard had already slipped off.

"Goodnight," Sophia said, and she sighed, sinking her head between my shoulder blades. That little touch sent fireworks skyrocketing through my skin.

Squeaks, Esis, and Sassy all sounded off with their own farewells. There was silence, and Imogen said, "Liam… you didn't say goodnight."

I sighed. "Goodnight. Now everyone shut the hell up!"

The next morning, the fire had burnt out, but I noticed that when I woke up it wasn't cold anymore. The snow outside was gone, which meant the weather was back to normal— for now.

I wondered if anything was waiting for us out there. It didn't occur to me that we should've posted someone to keep watch, but we were all so tired last night I doubt that it would've done much good anyway.

I closed my eyes again, wanting to rest for just a few more minutes. I got woken up when something furry and bloody got shoved in my face.

"Ugh!" I shouted. I sat up. In my lap fell a dead rabbit, its throat ripped out. Sassy looked up at me proudly, swishing her tail.

"What is it?" Jonah replied sleepily. The others sat up, woken by my yell.

I rubbed my eyes. At Sassy's feet was a collection of six rabbits, freshly hunted. I could hardly believe my eyes. Her snout was bloody and she grinned with pride.

"Sassy!" Imogen squealed. She hugged her fox enthusiastically. "Good girl!"

"Finally, something substantial to eat," Jonah said.

Sophia looked at me. "Do we have time? Or should we hit the road?"

I hesitated. Cooking the rabbits would slow us down, but we weren't trying to win. It was more important to stay alive. We needed energy.

"I can skin and butcher them," I said. "You guys can cook them up."

"All right, *Mom*," Jonah said. I sneered at him.

Sophia stayed on the other side of camp while I did the dirty work. This kind of stuff didn't bother me, because I grew up doing it with my dad, but Sophia turned green when she saw me sharpen a rock to a point to use as a knife. She was fine with cooking them, though. Soon we were gathered around the fire with full stomachs again, though I knew what little protein the rabbits had wouldn't last long. I hoped Sassy would keep hunting.

Squeaks consumed two rabbits herself, raw. Sassy didn't eat, so I supposed she'd already fed herself. I noticed that Esis ate a few bites of the rabbit, but not much. Still, he didn't seem to be fatigued. Was Esis a kind of animal that could go a few days without a meal, and live off fat stores? It would explain why he ate so much when there was food to go around.

We were on the road again before late morning. We'd been walking for two hours and hadn't run into anything. I'd gotten nervous.

The mountains were looming in the distance. Imogen pointed to them. "We need to get over those. That's the biggest hurdle to getting to the flag."

Sophia stopped in her tracks. "I don't know, guys," she started. "I think we should go the other way." She pointed deep into the forest.

"But that's in the other direction, and it's overgrown," Jonah said. "Why would you want to go there?"

Sophia shrugged. She seemed anxious. "I don't know. I just… have a feeling."

I raised an eyebrow. "We need more than feelings, Soph."

Sophia chewed on her lip. She didn't want to speak up. "Well… a straight shot to the flag is the obvious way to go, which means everyone will be going that way, and through there, we'll meet the biggest obstacles. Going around might take longer, but it reduces our chances of getting hurt."

She had a good point, but Jonah shook his head and stepped in. "No way. It doesn't matter which way we go, there will be obstacles everywhere. The hike up the mountains won't be easy, but it'll be quick. We should go that way."

"I agree," Imogen said. "Do we want to get this over with, or not?"

"You're Captain," Jonah said, poking me. "You decide."

Way to put me on the spot. I looked between my friends. For some reason, I had a feeling that climbing up the mountains was a bad idea, too. I wanted to do what Sophia said.

But on the other hand, Jonah and Imogen had an actual plan. If we went any deeper into the forest, there was a chance we'd get lost. It was pointless to aimlessly wander around when we only had so much energy to spare.

"Let's just try the mountains, for now," I said, and Sophia's face fell. "If it doesn't work, we can turn around."

Sophia didn't say anything when we left the forest. I didn't want her to be mad at me, but I was just trying to save everyone's life.

The closer we got to the mountains, the more we saw signs of the other teams. We found footprints, remnants of food, and abandoned campsites. By my estimate, all the other teams… the ones that were still around, anyway… were way ahead of us.

Who cared? We still had everyone. Couldn't say the same for—

My blood ran cold as I saw a body lying on the ground with red sleeves. It was the Toaqua from Haley's team, the one with the liopleurodon. She was lying in front of a stone house that looked like a Nivita had constructed. Sophia gasped, and the other two halted in their tracks. I walked up to the body and knelt to the ground to inspect it.

Her eyes were still spread open. She'd frozen to death last night in the cold. Her fingernails were bloody, and there were marks on the door— like she'd been trying to claw her way in.

I couldn't believe it. Haley used her to get off the island, then just… disposed of her. And her teammates had let her do it.

Sick bitch.

I got up. "She's gone, guys. Been dead for hours."

"Shouldn't we bury the body?" Sophia asked.

I shook my head. "The officials will come to get her shortly. We need to keep moving." I hated leaving a fellow Toaqua there like that, but what could I do? She was dead. There was no bringing her back.

I heard sniffling behind me. Sophia was crying. She put a hand on her mouth, trying to suppress the sobs that were coming out.

"Hey," I said. I reached out and pulled Sophia into a hug. "There's nothing we could do."

Sophia sniffed. When I let her go, Esis jumped onto her shoulder and gave her a kiss on the cheek.

Imogen and Jonah were stone-faced. They'd grown up in this society. They knew that not everyone made it out of the tournament alive, though it was different seeing it in real life instead of on screen.

"Let's go." I gestured to my teammates, and they followed. The Toaqua girl's blue eyes were burrowed into my conscience as we continued onward. Haley wouldn't be blamed for murder. The Elders would say that the girl should've been smart enough to survive on her own. That's what this tournament was all about, anyway.

About a mile up ahead, we ran into the mountainside— and more bodies. I assessed the situation. Two Elementai, one from the Silver Team and one from the Blue. Their Familiars lay beside them, expressions gaping and legs positioned like they were still running.

"Looks like they were crushed," I mused. I was distracted, thinking about where the other teams were. Maybe if we could figure out what they ran into, we could avoid it ourselves.

Esis was acting crazy. He was running in a circle around us, making loud screeches at the top of his lungs and trying to get our attention.

"Esis, what's wrong?" Sophia said. She tried to pick him up, but he wouldn't let her. He pushed her away and kept dancing around, pointing at the mountains.

"Esis, what—?"

Sophia got my attention when she cut her sentence off. Imogen and Jonah both had large, gaping mouths. I slowly turned to stare at what they were looking at. The reason why the Elders had made it snow so much last night socked me in the gut. Large boulders barreled down the side of the mountain, picking up speed, along with a torrent of snow.

I figured out what the other teams had met. It'd been a landslide, and another one was coming our way.

sophia
TWENTY

"Liam!" I cried as I stared up at the landslide barreling toward us, my heart slamming against my chest. I scooped Esis into my arms and held him tightly. "What do we do?"

He froze, eyes locked on the incoming landslide. It was like he was someplace else entirely.

"Liam!" I shouted to get his attention.

He hesitated for a second before shouting, "Run!"

The four of us took off sprinting in different directions. Sassy was cradled in Imogen's arms as she started in the opposite direction of Liam and me. Squeaks ran alongside Jonah directly away from the landslide, as if they could outrun it. It was total chaos.

"This way!" Liam shouted, catching their attention.

Imogen and Jonah quickly joined us as we raced parallel to the mountain. I glanced up, and fear rocked my body. The landslide must've been half a mile across, and it was coming in fast. There was no way we could outrun it. We had to think of something. Quick.

"Can't you… stop it… Imogen?" I asked through labored breaths.

"Could you stop a freaking *fire tornado*?" she shot back in a distressed tone.

I'll take that as a no.

"Jonah!" I called as I ran. "Can Squeaks get us above it?"

"Not all of us. We have to stick together," he answered.

"Imogen," Liam snapped. "We need shelter, *now*. As strong as you can."

"Do you have any idea what you're asking me to do?" Imogen fired back.

"Yes!" Liam roared. "It's do or die out here! You have less than thirty seconds to decide what you want it to be!"

Imogen skidded to an abrupt halt and bent to the ground to bury her fingers in the earth. The landslide must've been two hundred yards from us now. It'd land on us any second and squash us. I hadn't been counting on dying in this tournament, but now it seemed like a reality.

Imogen shot to her feet and pointed. "Straight ahead and around that boulder!"

Nobody questioned her. There wasn't time. We raced around a boulder jutting out from the mountainside and found ourselves in front of a tall rock face. I noticed a small opening that sank far back into the rock, but it was only big enough to fit an arm in.

Imogen shoved Sassy into Liam's arms. "There's a small cavern here. I just…"

She raised her hands and pointed them at the rock. Her eyebrows constricted, and her jaw tightened.

I stole another glance at the incoming rock and squeezed Esis tighter. *Come on, Imogen!*

The rock surrounding the hole tumbled to the ground, widening the hole until it was three feet across. It stretched back at least fifteen feet. Liam rushed forward and tossed Sassy inside.

"Everyone in!" he shouted. I could barely hear him over the roar of tumbling rock above us.

Imogen scurried into the tunnel behind Sassy, and Esis and I quickly climbed in after her.

"No way!" Jonah protested, eyeing the small tunnel with a knitted brow.

Liam stomped forward and shoved a fist into Jonah's shirt. "Get in there now, or so help the ancestors. I'm not going to watch you die! Squeaks, get in!"

Squeaks dove in behind me. Her body was so large that she barely fit and blocked all the light behind us. The earth rumbled above us, but I pushed forward despite my trembling limbs.

The shaking of the earth intensified. Somewhere beyond the deafening sound of tumbling boulders above our heads, a shriek echoed throughout the tunnel.

"What happened?" Imogen shouted, but I barely heard her.

I tried to glance back to see what was wrong, but Squeaks' beak poked my butt, and she nudged me forward. Worst case scenarios ran through my head. Had Liam been crushed? Did Jonah make it into the tunnel?

The rumbling passed over us, and I held my breath, waiting to hear if everyone was okay.

"Sophia!" Liam called. Jonah sobbed beside him.

Relief flooded through me.

"We need some light!" Liam demanded.

I was so relieved I could cry. My voice cracked. "I— I can't. Squeaks is in the way."

"Come this way," Imogen said in front of me. It sounded like her voice was bouncing off the walls of a cavern much bigger than the the tunnel I was crawling through.

I heard Esis scurry forward and followed behind him. I produced a small flame in my palm to see that the cavern was twice the size of my dorm room, with a ceiling tall enough to stand in. Small tunnels broke off in various directions, but nothing that was wide enough to fit through, unless we sent Sassy or Esis. My light cast shadows across Imogen's face, which was etched in worry.

"We need that light sooner than later!" Liam yelled.

"Squeaks!" I cried. I ducked back inside the tunnel and pulled at her front leg. She wouldn't budge.

Jonah groaned in pain, and I felt Squeaks tense in response. "My leg!" Jonah cried. "I'm hurt!"

"I know you want to help, Squeaks," I said, "but none of us can help Jonah if you don't move."

That got her attention. She crawled forward and pulled herself out of the tunnel, nearly getting her butt stuck in the process. I relit my flame and held it into the tunnel opening.

"What happened?" I asked in a rushed breath.

"I don't know," Liam shot back. "Jonah, can you crawl?"

Jonah was just a lump in the tunnel. All I saw was his bun wiggle as he shifted his head, but I wasn't sure if it was supposed to be an answer. Beyond him was nothing but blackness. The layers of earth from the landslide had buried the entrance.

I tried not to think about running out of oxygen or starving to death. All I cared about right now was whether or not Jonah was okay.

Esis jumped into the tunnel and hopped over Liam. He grabbed Jonah's arm and started tugging, as if he could help drag him.

Jonah groaned and rolled over. His face was bright red, and he was breathing hard. "I'll make it. Just give me a minute."

Liam waited until Jonah pushed himself to his elbows and began dragging himself along army-style before crawling forward. I took Liam's hand in mine— the one that wasn't flaming— to help him out of the tunnel.

Imogen and Liam helped Jonah out of the tunnel, with Squeaks right beside them keeping a close watch. Jonah stood on one foot but held his other up, taking in long, deep breaths.

"Sit down," Liam instructed, guiding Jonah to the ground.

Squeaks dropped to her belly behind Jonah, allowing him to lean against her for comfort. We all hovered around him. Imogen rubbed his shoulder, and I held my flame close so everyone could see.

"A falling rock hit my foot while I was climbing into the tunnel," Jonah explained.

"Let me look." Liam reached for the hem of Jonah's pants, but Jonah swatted him away.

"Dude," Jonah snapped. "Don't touch it."

"Do you think it's broken?" Imogen asked in a shaky voice.

Jonah stared at her with a pointed expression. "Do I look like a doctor to you? All I know is that it hurts like a mofo."

Liam stood. "You're alive, and that's what matters."

Esis inched forward and reached his tiny paws for Jonah's shoe. My hand instinctively shot out for him, holding him back as worry ran through me. I couldn't let him show his power now. Liam would hate me. I knew I had to tell him… eventually. But during the middle of the tournament was not the time. This kind of secret could tear our entire group apart, which could get us all killed. As much as my gut twisted watching Jonah huff in pain, I'd rather we deal with a broken ankle than with a teammate's death.

Imogen caught my eye when I pulled Esis away. I shook my head at her. I couldn't tell them yet. Imogen turned away, but didn't say anything. She looked visibly paler than normal, and her pigtails were in disarray. Her arms shook as she cradled Sassy.

"Okay, Imogen," Liam said. "You're up."

Imogen glanced up at him with a blank expression. "What?"

"The landslide is over," Liam said, like it was obvious. "You can unblock the entrance."

Imogen's eyes nearly bulged out of her skull. "Are you serious? Liam, you know that—"

"What other choice do we have?" Liam cut her off. "Do you want to send Esis down one of these tunnels to see if there's a way out? It would take him ten years to dig us out with those little paws."

Esis crossed his arms, offended.

"Are you even going to try?" Liam challenged.

Imogen hesitated, then set Sassy down. She sighed and walked over to the wall of the cave and placed a flat palm to the rock. She closed her eyes and took a deep breath.

When she opened them, her face fell. "The smaller tunnels go on forever. And there's almost fifteen feet of dirt the way we came. That's more than what my brother had—"

"I don't care what trial he faced," Liam said, his hands tightening into fists. "He's not here right now. Right now, we have you, and you're our only way out of here."

Liam was growing visibly distressed by the second. Jonah was starting to rock back and forth, muttering something under his breath like a prayer. Imogen's eyes brimmed with tears. I was feeling exhausted, hungry, and useless. Had our team already reached its breaking point?

"My Water and Jonah's Air is useless down here," Liam said. "And all Sophia's power is good for is sucking up oxygen."

My eyes widened, and I instantly reduced my flame. Jonah gasped through the darkness.

After a moment of silence, Imogen spoke. "I— I can try…"

"Good," Liam said flatly. "Let's get on it."

Imogen's hands ran across the rock as she lowered herself back into the tunnel.

"Liam," I said.

"What?" he snapped in a harsh tone. As soon as the word left his mouth, he took a breath and spoke softly. "Shit. Sophia…"

"You need to calm down," I told him. I tried to keep my voice steady, but inside, my heart was racing. "If Imogen is going to get us out of here, she needs to concentrate. Sometimes you can be a bit harsh."

Liam scoffed. "Yeah, well, I'm team Captain. If we want to survive, I have to push you guys."

"No, Liam," I insisted. "You don't have to be like that all the time."

He just shrugged.

"The landslide is past," I said. "Why are you still freaking out?"

Liam took a long breath, then let it out in a *whoosh*. "Because I'm an asshole."

I couldn't help but giggle. "That's not true. You always have a reason."

Liam dropped his gaze, his expression suddenly shifting. There was a sad look in his eyes when they met mine again. He spoke softly. "This is… this is a lot like how Nashoma died."

My heart fell. He wasn't just scared for us… there was something darker in his eyes, like he was reliving Nashoma's death and trying to keep it all together at the same time.

I reached out a hand. My fingers grazed against the skin on his arm, sending electric tingles up my hand. My fingers trailed down to his, and I felt his hand tremble beneath my touch.

"I'm sorry," I whispered.

A stretch of silence passed between us. Time seemed to slow as I stared at the shadows flickering across his face. I only snapped out of it when I heard Imogen shift in the tunnel next to us. I didn't know why I was still touching him, so I pulled away.

Liam cleared his throat. "How's it coming, Imogen?"

Imogen sniffled. "I… I can't do it. It's too much at once."

"Take it layer by layer," Liam suggested, irritation entering his tone.

"It doesn't work like that," Imogen called back down the tunnel. "There's a limit to my powers— a range. Any earth between me and the end of that range acts as a barrier. I'd have to move it from the inside out, or all at once."

"Come on back, Imogen," he said.

As soon as she emerged from the tunnel, Liam ducked inside.

"What does he think he's doing?" Imogen asked under her breath.

"Just let him go," I said. "He needs something to do."

"He's wasting his energy," Imogen said, her voice cracking. "There's no way out. We're going to die down here."

Imogen broke into quiet sobs and stomped over to the other side of the tunnel. My light barely reached her. She curled up in a ball beside Sassy in the corner, while Jonah had his eyes squeezed tightly shut and was chewing fiercely on his lower lip.

I turned to Imogen, but as I approached her, she buried her head into her knees and turned away from me.

"Go away," she mumbled.

My stomach sank, and tension formed in my head. "I just want to help," I whispered, squatting down next to her.

"You can't help me," she sobbed without looking up. "Go help Jonah."

I backed away from her slowly, feeling like the worst member of the team right now. I was useless.

"Hey, Jonah," I said softly as I approached him.

His eyes were still closed, and his breathing was ragged. Guilt consumed me. I wanted to offer Esis to heal him, but I couldn't bring myself to do it. Not yet, anyway.

I sat beside Jonah, holding Esis in my lap with one hand and a flame in my other. "How bad is it? Your foot?"

He shook his head without looking at me. "That's not what's bothering me."

I breathed a sigh of relief.

"It's this damn cave," he muttered. "I don't do small spaces. I'm totally claustrophobic. There's hardly any air down here. I can't use my element."

"Oh," I said flatly. How was I supposed to help with *that*? "Would you rather I put my flame out? Then you wouldn't know the difference."

Jonah slowly peeled his eyes open, but quickly shut them again. He nodded.

I closed my hand, and the cave went dark. I could still hear Imogen in the corner and Liam shuffling around in the tunnel. Jonah reached out in the darkness to take my hand. He squeezed it so hard that I thought he might crush my fingers, but I bit my lower lip to keep from crying out. As long as I was helping *someone*, that was all that mattered.

"You know, Jonah," I said. "When I'm scared, I like to sing a song."

"I'm not scared," he said, though I could hear the fear in his voice. "I'm just… uncomfortable is all. But… you can sing me a song anyway."

I hesitated. I was in choir in high school, but only so I could goof off with my friends. I'd never considered myself a good singer. But I opened my mouth to sing anyway. The truth was, I was a little scared myself, and I knew it would help. I went with the first thing that came to mind, a lullaby my mom used to sing to me when I was a kid, one I'd nearly forgotten until now.

> *"Earth, Water, Fire, and Air*
> *Gifted to us by the breath of a prayer*
> *Separated these powers shall be*
> *Until reunited in sweet harmony."*

My voice drifted away on the last note. I'd never really paid attention to the words until now. Maybe my parents hadn't hidden *everything* from me…

"What are you doing, Sophia?" Jonah asked.

"Huh? Um… singing?"

"You're butchering the song," he accused.

I laughed lightly. "I never said I was a good singer."

"Your voice is fine," Jonah said. "But the lyrics are all wrong."

"What? No, they're not. My mom used to sing it to me all the time when I was a kid."

"Yeah, well, your mom must've changed the lyrics," Jonah said with amusement in his tone. At least I was cheering him up.

"Okay, so how does it really go?" I challenged. I only did it to indulge him, even though I knew I was singing it right— *my* version, at least.

Jonah began singing, taking on the same tune I'd used, though he sang horribly off key.

> *"Earth, Water, Fire, and Air*
> *Powers almighty for children to share*
> *Those in the clouds will forever be*

The perfect balance of harmony."

I raised my eyebrows, though he couldn't see me. *"Those in the clouds*? It sounds like you think very highly of yourself, Yapluma," I teased.

"You're *both* singing it wrong," Imogen said from her corner, though she was being anything but playful. "The original song didn't have any lyrics. It's the tune the ancestors played when they gifted us our powers. Each House took the tune and turned it into something else. So if you want to be accurate, you wouldn't use lyrics."

It sounded like something she must've read in one of her books. She didn't sound interested in it. It was more like she was stating fact.

"Let's hum it, then," I suggested.

Jonah and I began humming the tune, though the last line was a little shaky, since we couldn't quite agree on the rhythm. Eventually, we compromised until Jonah began drifting off. He slumped against Squeaks like she was a pillow and began snoring.

I sat there for another hour in the dark, trying to not make any noise so that Jonah could rest. But I couldn't take the sounds of Liam clinking rocks together in the tunnel. It didn't matter how determined he was. He wasn't going to dig his way out of here. I could hear his breathing becoming more and more labored with each passing minute. He needed a serious reality check.

"Liam," I whispered, bending down to the tunnel opening with a flame in my hand. All I could see were the soles of his shoes, since rocks and dirt were piled up around the rest of his body. When he didn't acknowledge me, I repeated his name.

"What?" he snapped, turning his head back to me. His forehead was covered in sweat, so much that long strands of hair stuck to the sides of his face.

"You need to rest," I said.

"No," he protested. "I need to get us out of here."

"We'll get out," I assured him, though I couldn't know that for sure. "But maybe we can take turns. You're working yourself too hard, and you need a break."

"I'm fine," he lied. "You can save the lecture for when we get out of here."

"Liam," I said firmly. "You need to stop."

He glanced back at me. "I'm making progress."

"You're making yourself sick," I countered, taking note of the faraway look in his eyes.

"Trust me," he said, "I've handled worse."

"Yeah, well, I haven't," I snapped back. "What am I supposed to do when you pass out? We have no resources down here. You're no use to us unconscious. Please, just take a break."

Liam clenched his teeth before letting out a sigh. "Sophia, I—"

"No excuses, Liam. Lie down and rest."

I wasn't going to put up with this. He didn't get a choice. I climbed into the cave and reached for his ankle.

"Ancestors, *pawee*." He jerked away. "Fine. I'll take a short break."

"Good," I said, satisfied.

I backed up to let him out. Liam stood straight and wiped the back of his hand across his forehead. His knees visibly shook, and he looked two minutes from passing out.

I pointed to a level spot near the edge of the cave. "Lie down. I'll start digging."

"You don't have to do that, Sophia."

"Why not?" I raised an eyebrow at him. "Because I'm a girl?"

Liam shook his head. "No, but..."

"But what?" I asked. I knew digging would be useless, but Liam didn't seem like the kind of guy who could rest if nothing was being done. Only one person could dig at a time, so at least he wouldn't feel the need to jump right back into it.

Liam shrugged. "I don't know. It's... it's cold down here, don't you think?"

It sounded like he was just making small talk, but I wasn't really in the mood for that. Instead, I stomped up to him and grabbed his arm, dragging him over to where I'd pointed. He seemed curious and didn't speak.

I sat down and patted the spot next to me. "Come on."

Liam did as he was told, though it seemed to take him forever to lower himself to the ground, as if he had the body of an eighty-year-old. Which I could tell through his skin-tight shirt was *definitely* not the case.

I lay on my side facing him, and my arms curled in front of me and pressed against his chest. His breath rushed across my face, and I caught the scent of a pine forest after a fresh rain. He hesitated a moment before draping an arm across my body. Esis scurried up next to me and snuggled into the small space between us. I called upon my Fire just enough to warm the surface of my skin. Liam's body felt so cold on mine, like the chill from the ocean, but I barely noticed.

Instead, I was focusing on the nervous pounding of my heart and the voice in my head screaming. *When the hell did you grow a pair of balls, Sophia?* Seriously, where did the courage to yell at and then cuddle a guy I wasn't even dating come from?

My body trembled against his. I only hoped he didn't notice. Fantasies of what I'd like to do with Liam— *to* Liam— here in the dark ran through my mind. I couldn't control it. I should *not* be thinking things like that at a time like this. Besides, it wasn't like anything was going to happen between us.

Which might've been a lie. *Something* was definitely going on. I could feel it. Liam shifted his hips until I could no longer feel *him* against me.

"Better?" I asked, my voice shaking.

Liam's shoulders relaxed. "Better," he whispered.

It felt like hours had passed when I finally woke. I didn't have the sun to judge by, but I guessed it was already morning. Jonah and Liam were still asleep, but Imogen sat staring at the tunnel with a blank expression on her face. I wiggled out from under Liam's arm. Esis stirred but didn't wake. He shifted just enough so that his head curled down by Liam's chest and his butt stuck up in his face.

"Hey, Imogen," I said softly as I made my way over to her. A small flame in my hand lit up her face. Sassy lay curled up in her lap. I took a deep breath, but it didn't feel like I was getting enough air.

"Hey," she said flatly without meeting my eyes.

I sat beside her and spoke in a whisper so I wouldn't wake anyone. "Are you ready to talk about it?"

Imogen shook her head.

I bit my lower lip, unsure of what to say to her. I settled for the truth. "We need you, Imogen. Liam may think he can dig his way out of here, but he's just being stubborn. We need a Nivita. We need *you*."

"I'm sure that's what Trace's team said to him, too," Imogen mumbled.

"Is this... is this how your brother died?" I asked. I wished there was a way to tiptoe around the subject, but there wasn't. We had to face this head-on if we hoped to make it out of here.

Imogen nodded. "Trace failed his trial. His team wanted to take a shortcut through the mountain. They thought that by going through a cave they could bypass the trials and make it to the finish line first. But you can't outrun the trials in these mountains. The cave collapsed, separating their team. The Koigni girl and Yapluma guy on their team said Trace and the Toaqua girl were far enough ahead that the cave-in wouldn't have crushed them. Which can only mean one thing… Trace failed. He couldn't get them out. The half of his team that survived had to backtrack to the cave entrance and face the rest of the trials alone. They were the last team to make it back."

"Imogen," I whispered. "I'm so sorry."

"Can you imagine?" she asked rhetorically, like she hadn't heard me. "I found out about my brother's death while watching TV in my living room. His teammates walked out of that cave without him, and I just…"

She broke into sobs again, her shoulders shaking. I wrapped an arm around her but didn't say anything. It took Imogen a few minutes to compose herself again.

"It's funny," she said. "The day I lost my brother, I found my soul." She stroked Sassy's fur.

"That's when you bonded?" I asked.

She nodded sheepishly. "As soon as I saw Trace didn't make it, I ran out of the house and into the forest. Cade was there because his family was watching the tournament with us. I didn't want him to see me cry, so I ran. He followed, calling my name. I kept going until I tripped over a rock. I remember just lying there with my face in the dirt, letting my tears soak into the earth while I thought about how I'd never see my big brother again. I heard Cade's footsteps behind me. He bent down and ran his hand through my hair and down my back. He told me it was going to be okay, that I'd see Trace again one day. I told him I didn't want to wait until death to see him, that he should've made it out of the tournament alive. Trace had promised me he would.

"And then— I remember it so vividly— Cade went rigid, and the whole forest went silent. It was like time had stopped. He whispered my name and told me to look. When I lifted my head, there Sassy was, staring at me through the underbrush. I still remember every detail of our bonding. The color of the trees seemed brighter, and I heard the sounds of a flute in the distance. It smelled like the pages of an old book and tasted like honey. It was enough to give me a sliver of hope. Sassy walked toward me until her whiskers were tickling my face… and then she licked me."

Imogen let out a light laugh, but her face quickly fell again. "It just doesn't seem fair."

"No," I replied sadly. "It doesn't. But Imogen, this isn't the same thing."

"It's exactly the same," she argued.

"No, it's not. That rock out there? Those aren't the same rocks your brother had to move. And you? You're Imogen, not Trace. You have different strengths."

Imogen sighed. "If we have any chance of making it out of here, I have to move more rock than I ever have before. I know I'm Nivita, but I'm not good with dirt and rocks. I'm better with plants."

"Okay… well, that's a strength."

Imogen glared at me. "It's not exactly going to help us, is it?"

My mind raced a million miles per hour. What could I possibly say to her to convince her to give it another shot? An idea suddenly struck me.

"Yes!" I cried. "Maybe it will."

Imogen's eyebrows drew together.

"I saw this documentary once," I explained. "It showed a time-lapse video of roots growing through concrete until the concrete broke. Imogen, your power is *strong*. What if you used the roots to get through the dirt and rocks?"

Imogen's eyes lit up, and I could see the gears turning in her head. "You think that will work?"

I honestly didn't know. "All I know is that we can't give up yet. I believe in you, Imogen."

Imogen visibly blushed. "I guess it's worth a shot."

Yes!

"But Sophia," Imogen said in warning, "if this doesn't work, I'm sorry."

I refused to accept her apology. "It will work, Imogen. Trust me."

A hint of a smile touched the corner of her lips. "I do."

"Then let's get going," I encouraged.

Jonah stirred. "Hey, what's going on?"

"We're strategizing," I said vaguely as Imogen and I stood. I didn't want to tell him and put too much pressure on Imogen.

"Oh, okay," Jonah said in a groggy voice. "Let me know when we're out of the woods."

Imogen scoffed. "Sweetheart, if this works, I'll carry you out of the woods myself."

"Deal," Jonah agreed.

Imogen just rolled her eyes and started for the tunnel. Sassy climbed in behind her. I squatted at the entrance to offer my light. Imogen crawled over the loose rocks Liam had left behind and to the end of the tunnel where a pile of dirt blocked the path. She placed her palms flat to the rock and took a deep breath.

I waited. And waited.

Finally, she dropped her hands and twisted back to me. "There are roots all around me. I can get to them, but I'm going to need some time to figure out exactly what I'm doing. I don't want to risk caving in the tunnel."

"That's all right," I told her. "Take all the time you need."

"We don't have forever."

My head snapped in Liam's direction. He'd woken up. He pushed himself to a sitting position, disturbing Esis. When Esis realized I was all the way across the cave, he quickly rushed to my side.

"We'll eventually run out of air," Liam said.

"Stop it, Liam," I groaned. I glanced into the tunnel to make sure Imogen hadn't heard him. She was in her own little world, focusing on the earth.

He shrugged. "I'm only stating fact."

"You're being a pessimist," I told him. "We won't get anywhere with that kind of attitude. Just let Imogen do her thing."

Liam held up his hands in surrender. "You know, for a girl who didn't want to be team Captain, you're doing an awful lot of lecturing."

I shrugged. "Yeah, well, someone has to keep you in line."

Amusement touched the corner of his lips. "Of course that'd be your job, *pawee*."

"And I take that job seriously," I said. "Sit back and relax while Imogen works her magic."

It took another fifteen minutes until I saw the ends of the first roots snake through the dirt.

"Don't get too excited just yet," Imogen warned. "Plants can be kind of touchy. It might take a while."

Slowly, the roots began to carve out the dirt until the sunlight peeked through and touched our little cave. I let out a sigh of relief.

"Almost there!" Imogen yelled back.

The path she'd created widened more and more, until the sunlight flooded through the long dirt tunnel and onto the rocks Imogen lay on. Thick layers of root outlined the dirt, pushing back against the hard earth and providing structure to the new length of tunnel.

"Imogen, you did it!" I cried.

She shot me back a shy smile, then raised her voice to yell, "Time to go!"

Sassy and Imogen crawled forward, while I turned back to Jonah. He was struggling to get to his feet and stumbled when he tried to put weight on his bad ankle.

"Do you need help?" I asked.

"Nah," he said with a wave of his hand. "I've got this."

He tried another step, but his ankle twisted under him. Squeaks was there in under a second to steady him. Liam rushed to his other side and grabbed Jonah's arm to drape it over his shoulder.

"Can you crawl?" Liam asked him.

Jonah nodded. "I think so."

"Good," Liam replied before turning to me. "Go ahead, Sophia. I've got him."

I hesitated. Liam's knees shook under Jonah's weight. He didn't look like he was doing well. I wanted to go last to make sure they both made it out all right.

"He may need help at the end," Liam said. "Imogen can't pull him out on her own."

He had a point.

"Okay," I agreed. "I'm right in front of you if you need anything, Jonah."

I turned and crawled through the tunnel behind Esis. The sunlight was blinding when I emerged, but it felt good on my skin. I barely recognized the landscape around me. Where there was greenery yesterday was only mounds of dirt and rock today. Trees had been plowed over, and I couldn't even see the boulder we'd run around the day before.

Imogen took in the devastation, her eyes traveling far down the mountain through the path of the landslide. "It's a shame the Elders had to kill so many trees. I hope they restore this area when the tournament is finished."

"Hopefully they will," I agreed.

Jonah moved slowly through the tunnel, but eventually, he reached the end. His hands searched the opening for something to grab on to and pull himself out. Imogen and I each offered a hand to help. It was like trying to drag out a full-sized tree. It took all my strength. The guy was huge. Squeaks pushed from the other side of him, and we managed to yank Jonah out. He lay in the dirt to catch his breath.

As soon as Squeaks squeezed out of the tunnel, I turned back to it to offer my hand to Liam. His palm was clammy and slipped in mine, but he took it anyway.

"Good job, Imogen," Liam said through heavy breaths. He sat beside Jonah and wiped at the sweat on his brow. Dark circles had formed under his eyes.

"Are you going to be okay, Liam?" I asked.

He nodded. "I'm more worried about Jonah. Should we take a look at that ankle?"

Jonah sighed. "I guess we're going to have to."

Liam reached for Jonah's shoe and began untying the laces. Gently, he pulled Jonah's shoe off and then peeled back his sock. Everyone leaned in to take a look. Honestly, it didn't look that bad. There was only a slight bruise and swelling on the back of his foot.

Liam scoffed. "Seriously, Jonah? This is it?"

"You think I'm lying?" Jonah shot back. "It's in a *very sensitive* area. Besides, broken bones don't always look bad from the surface."

Liam's eyebrows shot up. "You think you broke something?"

"Well, um…" Jonah hesitated. "I don't know. I might've…"

Liam sighed, then glanced up to the peak of the mountain. We had a long trek ahead of us. As my gaze followed Liam's, I noticed a creature circling above us. It was smaller than a dragon but bigger than a bird, and looked as if someone was flying on its back. I squinted at it and realized it was a winged lion. Another member of the camera crew, I was sure. Everyone in Kinpago was probably laughing at us. We had to be at least half a day behind the other teams.

Liam's jaw tensed. "Can you at least *try* walking?"

"I don't know," Jonah snapped. "Can you *try* showing a little compassion?"

"We can try wrapping it," I suggested quickly, before they bit each other's heads off. "Like in our Medical Care of Familiars class."

"We don't have a first-aid kit," Liam pointed out.

"I'm sure we can find something," I said. "Like some sort of vine."

"Forget about it," Jonah insisted. "Squeaks can carry me."

"You up for it, girl?" Imogen asked as she stroked Squeaks' feathers.

Squeaks nodded and straightened her back, eagerly waiting for Jonah to climb on. Imogen and I each took one of Jonah's arms and helped him up.

As soon as he was on Squeaks' back and she started forward, her front foot caught on a rock, and she stumbled. Jonah's hands flew out to catch himself, but he landed on his bad ankle. He let out of a cry of pain as his leg crumpled beneath him. He rolled down the mountainside a good fifteen feet until coming to a stop.

"Oh my God!" I screamed the same time Imogen and Liam cursed the ancestors.

The three of us raced over to him. From up the mountain, Squeaks hung her head in shame. Jonah slammed his fist against the dirt to keep from screaming. My gut twisted. I couldn't watch this.

"Esis, come here." I gestured to him.

Imogen's eyes met mine, and then she glanced to Liam, though he didn't notice. "I have an idea," she blurted.

Esis hopped into my lap. I pulled him close but paused to listen to her.

"I can... I can carry Jonah," Imogen said.

Liam scoffed. "We all know how that worked out last time."

"That's because I wasn't thinking about it like an Elementai," Imogen pointed out. "I'll use the trees to carry him. Just watch."

I held my breath. Nothing happened for several seconds, but then the ends of tree roots rose up from the ground.

Jonah drew in a surprised breath when the roots lifted him. His body hovered just inches above the ground and glided along from one group of roots to the next, as if riding a conveyor belt. Imogen was careful with his foot, making sure to keep it elevated without letting the roots touch the tender spot.

Jonah glanced around to see he was off the ground. "Well, this is... kinda cool. It's like a little massage."

Liam stood and crossed his arms. "Do you think you can keep that up, Imogen?"

She nodded. "Once we reach those trees, I'll use the branches to hold him up."

Liam looked skeptical, but Jonah just raised his arms into the air and made a rock-and-roll sign with his hands.

"Crowd surfing, baby!" Jonah teased.

Liam just shook his head and frowned. "Fine. Whatever works. Let's get going."

Hours passed as we climbed the mountain. Though we'd stopped for lunch to cook up the two chipmunks and a squirrel Squeaks had caught for us, we were all starting to slow down. It wasn't a very substantial meal, and the incline was killing my legs. I was certain everyone else felt the same. The higher we climbed, the thinner the trees became. The clouds darkened, blocking the sun, and the air cooled. I could see it in Imogen's tired eyes that she was straining to stretch her magic by moving Jonah from tree branch to tree branch.

Jonah had passed out, snoring as the trees grew around his form, cradling him and passing him from one tree to the next like a bucket brigade.

Liam looked the worst of all. His hands shook, and his hair was in disarray around his face. His lips were dry and cracked, and his face paler than normal. His eyes glazed over, but he kept them locked on the mountain peak— like that was the only thing pushing him forward. He shivered, but when I'd offered to share some of my warmth, he declined.

"I think we need to take a break," I suggested.

"We're almost to the top," Liam said without slowing his step.

"The trees are thinning, and we need to figure out something else for Jonah," I pointed out. "Maybe he can try riding Squeaks again."

Liam whirled around, almost stumbling over the rocks at his feet. "Or maybe he can try walking like the rest of us."

"Liam, he's hurt—" I started, but he promptly cut me off.

"Please," he scoffed, gesturing to Jonah hanging in the trees. "He's living in luxury there. The dude's taking a fucking *nap* while the rest of us are climbing Mount Fucking Everest."

I stopped in my tracks, completely taken off guard by Liam's tone. Imogen came to a halt behind me. Jonah's snoring and the sound of heavy winds were all I heard.

I blinked several times, trying to find the words. But what was I supposed to say to *that*? Liam obviously wasn't looking for comfort.

Imogen stepped in for me, though her tone was anything but comforting. She was beyond irritated. "I'm sorry, Liam," she snapped. "Were you looking for a free ride to the top? I mean, did you want to break an ankle? At least you can *walk*!"

"Yeah," Liam bit back sarcastically. "I have so much to be thankful for. Thanks for the reminder. Never mind the fact that—"

He cut off abruptly.

"What?" Imogen demanded.

Liam turned away from her and fixed his eyes on the mountain peak again. "Nothing," he mumbled.

"No." Imogen stomped up to him and stood on her toes so he couldn't avoid her gaze. "I want to know. What were you going to say?"

A muscle popped in Liam's jaw. "It doesn't matter."

Imogen crossed her arms. "It does. If you have something to say, say it."

He spoke through clenched teeth. "Sophia's right. We need a break. Besides, I know a plant in this area that might help relieve some of the lumberjack's pain."

Liam shoved Jonah's shoe he still held into Imogen's hands. Then he whirled around and started down the mountain.

"Liam!" I called, but he ignored me. I turned to Imogen. "He's being ridiculous."

"I know," she agreed. "But it's Liam. He needs to cool off."

I nodded. "Thank you, by the way. For carrying Jonah to keep our secret."

Imogen shrugged like it wasn't a big deal. "We don't need to piss Liam off more than he already is."

"Agreed," I said. "I plan on telling him… but after the tournament. We don't need him abandoning us in the middle of it. He's coming back, right?"

Imogen glanced to his retreating form. "Yeah. He's coming back."

Imogen lowered Jonah to the ground beside us. He stirred, and his whole body shivered.

"I don't know how we're going to get him over the peak of the mountain," Imogen said.

I bit my lower lip, staring down at him. "I think we need to heal him."

"Liam will know something's up," Imogen protested.

"He already thinks Jonah's faking it," I argued. "Right now, Jonah is worse off than Liam. We need to help him."

Imogen hesitated. "Fine. But Jonah can't tell Liam. Not until we make it out of here. Liam will freak."

"I know. Esis, come on buddy."

Esis hopped down from Squeaks' back and scurried over to where Jonah lay.

I knelt down beside them. "Do you think you can help him? The same way you helped Aisha?"

Esis nodded eagerly, then placed his tiny little hands on Jonah's skin just above his sock. I didn't get to witness his miraculous recovery since the injury was internal, but watching Jonah's energy return was magical enough on its own. Slowly, color returned to his face, and his eyes fluttered open as the bruise faded.

"How are you feeling?" Imogen asked.

Confusion settled over his face, and he wiggled his foot. "Surprisingly well. How long was I—?"

Jonah cut off when he saw Esis at his feet, his tiny hands on him and his eyes closed. Realization crossed Jonah's face.

"Holy shit!" Jonah cursed as he shot upright to a sitting position. "Esis can *heal*?!"

"Yes," I confirmed in a nervous tone. "But it's a secret."

"Why didn't you say anything sooner?" Jonah demanded. "He could heal Liam!"

"Shh," I cried, slapping a hand over his mouth. He promptly stuck his tongue out to lick me. "Ew! Jonah, really?"

"Don't put your hand on my mouth," Jonah snapped back. "But... seriously, Sophia? How could you not tell Liam? He could finally get better!"

"I know. And I want him to. But can you imagine his reaction?" I pleaded.

Jonah contemplated it for a moment. "He still has a right to know. If Esis healed him, we could make it back faster."

"I know, I know," I insisted. "But what if it tears our group apart? If Liam feels betrayed... if he feels like he can't trust us..."

"We can't deal with that right now," Imogen finished for me.

Jonah still looked skeptical. "How long have you known?"

"A few weeks," I said, dropping my gaze. "We kept it secret to protect Esis. I don't want anyone taking him from me."

"You could've trusted us," he said.

"What would you do if Squeaks had unique magical abilities?" I asked. "You'd do whatever you had to in order to protect her, wouldn't you?"

Jonah glanced to Squeaks, who was nipping playfully at Sassy on her back. "Yeah. I guess I would."

"Please don't tell Liam," I begged. "I need to protect Esis. We need to protect our team."

"Liam's my *best friend*," Jonah said harshly. "You want me to keep it a secret that the cure for whatever he's suffering from is right there in front of him?"

"Yes. Because we have no choice," I said firmly.

Jonah hesitated. "Fine. But you better tell him after we make it out of here. Not telling him... it's cruel."

I flinched. "I will," I promised.

"I'll let him ride Squeaks to the top," Jonah said. "He's lighter than me, so she should be able to take it."

"If she doesn't trip over her own feet," Imogen mumbled.

Squeaks shot her a death glare.

"Sorry, Squeaks." Imogen shrugged. "You're kind of a klutz."

Liam's loud footsteps and mumbling reached my ears. He was already on his way back. I could see him trudging through the thin trees.

"This forest is fucking useless!" he shouted.

"Ancestors," Imogen muttered. "He's like an emotional hurricane. I thought Toaqua were supposed to be gentle."

Jonah just rolled his eyes. "Can I have my shoe?"

Liam stomped out of the trees and toward us. "Excellent. You're up. Looks like you don't need that painkiller after all."

Jonah forced a painfully fake yawn. "Nah, dude. That nap really helped. My ankle's feeling better. I think I can walk from here."

Liam huffed and started back up the mountain. He muttered under his breath loud enough for us to hear. "Unbelievable. Yet no one listened when I said you were being a baby."

"Hey," Jonah called as Liam distanced himself from us. "You wanna ride Squeaks?"

"And fall down the mountain when she trips?" Liam yelled back. "No thanks. My own two feet are pretty reliable."

Which I could tell was a total lie, because he was struggling to walk. Why was he so stubborn?

"Are you coming or not?" Liam asked.

We all hurried behind him. Nobody spoke as we continued our trek, finally cresting the mountain and starting down the other side. Hours passed until the sky began to darken into evening.

"We need to stop," Jonah finally broke the silence.

"We still have some daylight left," Liam replied. "It won't take long to make a shelter now that we know what we're doing."

"I don't mean stopping for the night," Jonah said. "The pressure in the air just shifted. I think a storm is going to reach us soon."

Liam glanced to the darkening sky above us. The clouds rushed by, swirling into indistinct shapes that warned of danger. The wind around us picked up almost instantly, and thunder rumbled in the distance.

"How soon?" Liam asked.

"Um, now!" Imogen shouted, pointing above us.

I followed her gaze, only for my stomach to instantly bottom out. A funnel cloud was forming in the clouds above.

And it was going to land right on top of us.

Liam

TWENTY-ONE

As if we didn't have enough to deal with. We'd just gotten over being buried alive, and we hadn't even gotten a good night's rest before a fucking twister decided to fuck up the party.

This monster was no joke. It hadn't reached the ground yet, but I could see that the funnel cloud was a quarter of a mile across and had huge power. The roar of it was so loud that it was hurting my ears. Once it reached earth, it would send us flying all the way across the country.

I quickly analyzed the area. There were no ditches to lay down in, and outrunning the twister wouldn't work.

"Imogen, can you get us underground?" I asked at the top of my lungs as the tornado drew closer. I could barely hear myself. I didn't know how the others would.

"I don't have enough time!" Imogen shouted. "It would take a few minutes, at least!"

That was it, then. We only had one option.

"Jonah, you're up!" I shouted. "This is your task!"

Unlike Imogen yesterday, Jonah looked completely determined. His face was completely calm as he shouted, "Imogen, use the tree roots to hold everyone down! I'm gonna end this big bastard!"

Imogen did as she was told. She wrapped the surrounding trees roots around our legs and ankles, securing me, Sophia, Sassy, Esis, and herself down. For extra precaution, I drew up water from the ground and froze it around our feet and between the roots so that we were firmly held in place. The ice crept up Esis' body until only his head was sticking out. He gave me a scathing look I ignored.

Jonah didn't need to be held down. He forced the air around him and Squeaks to calm, making an invisible shield that the tornado couldn't penetrate. But he could only protect himself, not us.

Squeaks remained outside with Jonah, taking a wide stance and screeching at the tornado, like it was a challenger that had encroached on her territory. Jonah wasted no time and threw his hands out in front of him, shooting out a strong gust of wind that was meant to break the twister's rotation.

The twister seemed to slow, but it didn't stop its descent. The moment the twister touched down about fifty feet away, things really started going to hell. Rocks and debris were picked up and thrown around as projectiles, and smaller trees began getting uprooted.

"Look out!" I shouted. Imogen and Sophia ducked as a sapling was hurtled toward us full-speed. It was hard to move around against the strength of the storm.

Jonah kept increasing his power, trying to break the funnel of the twister, but it wasn't working. No matter how hard he tried to get the tornado to break and the winds to go in a different direction, it only seemed like the twister gained intensity. Squeaks kept her wings pinned to her sides and concentrated, giving what power she could to Jonah.

Even from a distance, I could tell Jonah was working really hard. The twister was more powerful than he was. A majority of his magic went to keeping himself anchored. But he couldn't be tangled up in the roots like us, because he still needed to move around in order to use his element. He was stuck.

I heard large breaking noises as trunks behind us were shattered by the force of wind. The larger trees were coming up, too. There had to be four or five Elementai behind this twister, controlling it. I couldn't imagine how the Elders expected us to survive this. I could feel the ice starting to crack around our heels, and the roots were starting to break, too. It wouldn't be long before the twister pulled us up.

"Squeaks, I need help!" Jonah screamed.

Squeaks ruffled her feathers and shook her head. There was a fierce glint in her eye. She drew a deep breath and then opened her mouth, screaming at the top of her lungs at the twister.

The very ground shook, and it wasn't because of the twister. Squeaks' shout caused the twister to waver, rocketing back and forth at the force of her cry. Jonah's Air gathered around her and pushed the tornado backward. Squeaks walked forward, still braying, and the tornado started to head in the other direction. It was backing off!

Holy shit! Squeaks is powerful.

I thought that Squeaks was going to have it handled, but then she coughed and staggered to her knees. She got back up, but when she shouted again her scream wasn't as strong as it had been before.

The twister buckled at her shout, but remained, then started spinning toward us again. Squeaks' scream had weakened the tornado, but it hadn't broken it.

"I can't control it!" Jonah yelled. "But I have an idea. Everyone, let go!"

"*What?*" the three of us shouted in unison.

"Are you crazy?" Sophia yelled.

"Just trust me!" he cried back. "Imogen, let go of the roots! Everyone make a chain!"

There wasn't time to argue. I melted the ice around Sassy and Esis first. Esis dragged himself toward Sophia and held on to her leg while Sassy launched herself at Imogen, clinging to the front of her shirt. We all held hands, me grabbing on to Sophia's and Imogen's as the last of the ice melted. Imogen began to release the roots, and we started to lift into the air.

"I hope you know what you're doing!" I yelled at Jonah as he grabbed Imogen's hand. Squeaks unfurled her wings. She was immediately carried off, swirling around the edge of the twister.

I realized Jonah's plan the second before it happened.

"Everybody hold on!" Jonah screamed, and the roots broke loose.

We were instantly carried off into the air. The twister sucked us up, and all sound drowned out as we entered into the eye of the storm. The tornado spiraled us around violently. I felt like my arms were going to be ripped off as I held on to Imogen and Sophia's hands. My stomach churned as we were sent spiraling around. I was going to throw up.

Though I couldn't hear anything, I could see the horrified looks on everyone's faces and I knew they were yelling. Imogen was crying, Sophia had her eyes closed, and Esis' chubby cheeks were getting blown back by the wind. Sassy dug her nails into Imogen's chest, holding on for dear life.

The only one who wasn't screaming his head off was Jonah. Though we were in the middle of the tornado, his eyes were narrowed in concentration. He was completely calm, like he was born to be up here.

Using his element, Jonah ricocheted us away from the tornado. We went flying hundreds of feet above ground at a high speed, but it was away from the twister.

Once we were out of the reach of the vortex, we started falling. Fast. While we were all screaming our heads off, Jonah shut his eyes. Calm air gently came up beneath us to support our weight like a parachute. We drifted toward ground at a leisurely speed until our feet hit the grass softly.

Squeaks was already there waiting for us, peeping happily. The mountains were far in the distance now. We had landed in a valley on the edge of the forest.

I collapsed when my feet hit the ground, and so did Sophia and Imogen. Jonah was the only one still walking. He had his hands on his hips and was looking very full of himself. "There. Safe and sound."

I gagged. Sophia held her head like she had a headache. Imogen lay spread out on the ground with Sassy, who had all four feet above her so it looked like she was dead. Esis rubbed Sophia's temple until she rose to a sitting position.

Jonah raised an eyebrow. "Hey, you guys okay?"

"Are we fucking okay." I closed my eyes and tried to make the earth stop moving.

"I hate heights." Imogen shivered. She sat up, and Jonah helped her to stand. "I like keeping my feet on the ground."

"Well, let's hope that we never have to do that again." Jonah clapped Imogen on the shoulder.

After a few moments, I managed to push myself to my feet. The ground was still moving, but it wasn't like that hadn't been happening for me for the past two days now, anyway, so I forced myself to rise. I needed to tough it out. "Let's hope so. That was some pretty spectacular stuff, Jonah."

"Wasn't it?" Jonah threw an arm over Squeaks. "But it was nothing me and my girl couldn't handle."

Squeaks chortled and nipped at Jonah's hair. His bun had come loose in the chaos, and now his hair was down around his face. It was a mess.

Imogen's lips quivered. "You know, Jonah, with your hair down like that you look like a sexy Viking."

"Yeah." Sophia giggled nervously. "Like Thor."

"More like Tarzan." He brushed back his messy hair with one hand. "Though if you ladies want to play Jane, I'm sorry to disappoint. I'm looking for a wild man myself."

Imogen and Sophia burst out laughing. It was the kind of laugh people made when they were on the edge and just needed to loosen the tension. Jonah joined in, and I shook my head. This tournament was making us lose it.

We walked for a while, until we reached the trees again. "We should rest," I said. "We barely slept in that cave."

The group nodded in agreement. Imogen began building her root house again, and Sophia and Esis started looking for firewood. Jonah dragged over two large logs for us to sit on. I sat down, and Sophia put her kindling in the middle before starting a fire.

I wanted to help the group, but I just couldn't. I didn't have anything left. I managed to draw up a small well of water we could use to drink before I put my head in my hands and sank it between my knees. I. Felt. Awful.

Sometime, I started coughing. Hard. Jonah kept looking at me, but I ignored him. I struggled to take deep breaths and concentrated on just breathing.

I didn't know how long I sat there, but after a while, I could smell rabbit cooking. Sophia offered me a leg, but I shook my head. Just looking at it made me queasy.

"Liam, you have to eat," she said, shoving it toward me again. I took it and forced down a few bites, though my stomach churned and cramped with each swallow.

After a couple of minutes, I stood up. "Hey, guys, I'm going to scout ahead really quick," I told them. "See where we should go in the morning."

Nobody questioned me. I took off into the woods, far enough away so nobody would hear, and threw up the few bits of rabbit Sophia had forced me to take.

I felt clammy. I pressed a hand to my forehead and flinched at how hot it was. I was running a fever.

I coughed again, and quickly covered my mouth with my hand. I slowly drew it away. When I did, I noticed my fingers were covered in blood.

The grim reality set in. I was dying. I knew that already. I'd been hiding that from my team since we'd gotten buried in that mountain. It'd taken everything I had to get us this far.

I knew I wasn't going to make it through this tournament. I'd never see my family again, that much I was sure of. My only goal now was to get my team as far as I could, before the end. They didn't realize why I was pushing them so hard, because they thought we had no time limit.

Oh, we had a time limit, all right. It was me. And my clock was ticking, fast. It wouldn't be long now before my time would be up.

I knew I'd been a bigger asshole than usual during this tournament. I didn't mean to. I'd been trying to control my temper, but I wasn't a superhero.

They didn't realize how hard this was. They all had their Familiars to lean on for support. I had no one. When I fell, I had to catch myself. Doing this tournament with a Familiar was difficult, but without one… it was fucking impossible.

I wiped the blood off my face and hand before I headed back to the fire.

"That was quick," Jonah remarked suspiciously. His eyes followed me as I sat down.

He was on to me. Whatever. I shrugged, and Imogen commented, "Hey, guys… do you realize that there's only one more task left?"

"Yeah," Jonah said, clarity dawning on his face. "We're almost done. We might get to go home tomorrow."

I thought about it. We *did* only have one more task. This awful tournament wasn't going to go on forever. There was just one more trial we needed to pass. Maybe I'd last that long.

I coughed violently again, and didn't let myself get my hopes up. I had a day left, if that.

Sophia didn't say anything. She stared into the fire with Esis curled up in her lap, looking haunted.

Fire was the only thing left. That meant it was up to Sophia. I didn't know if she believed in herself enough to do it.

That frightened me. We didn't come all this way just to die tomorrow, did we?

Well, I did. I just didn't want that to happen to everyone else.

"Hey, Imogen," I said, and she looked up. "I'm sorry I was such an ass back there in the cave. I didn't want to hurt your feelings. I just knew you could do it."

Imogen didn't say anything, but Sassy climbed up on my lap and licked my cheek a few times. Her tail swished back and forth happily, and I knew Imogen had forgiven me.

"That goes for all of you," I said, looking at Jonah and Sophia. "I know I've been kinda rough on you guys so far. But I know you can make it through this thing. If I push you, it's because I want you to succeed. Sorry if it comes off in a shitty way. I can be over the top sometimes."

"Sometimes?" Jonah asked, and Sophia smirked. Everyone laughed— including me.

I cleared my throat. "Anyway, what I'm trying to say is… I believe in you guys. And I'm sorry for constantly freaking out on you."

"Aw," Imogen said, and Sassy let out a happy bark. Esis clapped, and Sophia smiled.

"Group hug!" Jonah announced, and he got off his seat.

"No, this isn't that kind of—"

Nobody heard me. Imogen, Jonah, and Sophia rushed toward me and gave me the biggest, most sappy hug that has ever happened in all of existence. Sassy twirled herself around my legs, and Squeaks threw out her wings to encompass us fully. I could even feel Esis on the top of my head, squeezing me tight.

"All right, all right," I said, and I pushed everyone off of me. "That's enough of that. This isn't the Bleeding Hearts Club."

I yanked Esis off of my head and handed him back to Sophia. Her eyes… they were sparkling.

"We're totally going to do this, guys," Jonah said. "We're going to get through the tournament, and it's going to be together!"

Imogen and Sophia cheered, but I only plastered on a fake smile. I knew they'd have to make it to the finish line without me.

Imogen and Jonah went to bed before Sophia and I did. They took Sassy and Squeaks inside the root hut, and soon it was just the three of us gathered around the fire. Esis sat by the flames and rubbed his little paws together to keep warm.

Sophia crossed her arms and held them tightly against her body. "I'm worried, Liam. What if I can't do it?"

"You can," I told her. I was starting to shake, but it wasn't because of the cold. I tried to force myself to stay steady so she wouldn't notice.

"I don't know." She threw a stick into the fire. "We don't know what's coming. I'm not prepared. I'm not ready. I'm—"

She dropped her head, and Esis put a paw on her calf for comfort.

I'd go over to her, but I was having trouble moving at all at the moment. "Come here," I said. I opened up an arm, and Sophia got up. She left her log to sit next to me. I pulled her close and laid my head on top of hers as we stared at the fire. Her just pressing against me was enough to make me feel a tiny bit better.

My pants were practically doing the happy dance. Despite the fact that my body was shutting down, my dick was working just fine. I couldn't seem to help the fact that I got a boner every time I got within three feet of Sophia. Though we were in a life-or-death situation, all I wanted to do was lie down for another long cuddle and… something else.

Last wish, maybe?

She sighed. "I don't think I can do this."

"You don't have a choice," I told her softly.

"You don't understand, Liam. I'm not strong enough. I'm going to fail."

"No, Sophia." I grabbed her shoulders and shook them. "You have to pass that task tomorrow and get Jonah and Imogen through this, you hear me? *Whatever it takes.*"

She stared at me. "I notice you didn't mention yourself."

I stayed silent, and she added, "It seems like you're saying if something happens, to go on without you."

My heartbeat sped up. "I didn't say that."

"Sounds like it."

She pressed further into my chest. "That was really sweet, apologizing to Imogen and Jonah," Sophia said quietly.

"I'm not above apologizing," I told her. "Ancestors know I'm the biggest fuck-up on this team. I know how to ask for forgiveness."

"You're not a fuck-up, Liam. You're the best person I know," Sophia said.

"You've met a lot of shitty people, then." I laughed under my breath, but secretly, I felt like flying. I can't believe she thought so highly of me. I didn't deserve that.

"I really do mean it." Her voice became heavy. "But I can't help but wonder if that was really an apology, or a goodbye."

My insides rolled, and I shuddered. "What do you think, Sophia?"

"I think you're the one who cares the most, but you don't like people getting too close, so you push them all away," Sophia said. "This isn't goodbye, Liam. We cross that finish line together, or not at all."

It was awesome she didn't want to give up on me, but I was a lost cause. "Sure. I promise, *pawee*."

She seemed a little less nervous now. "I'm glad you're here, Liam. I want you to be there with me when we finally reach the end."

I just wrapped my arms tighter around her for an answer. I wanted to be there more than anything. But the truth was, I wouldn't be able to. My body wouldn't let me.

The hardest part of this tournament wasn't going to be losing my life. It was going to be leaving Sophia.

"Well, well, well, what do we have here?"

A huge figure blocked out the sun. It was Jonah, looking down on us with a smug smile on his face. Squeaks was nearby, her head tilted in curiosity.

Sophia untangled herself from my limbs and stretched. I slowly pieced together what was going on.

Aw, fuck. We'd fallen asleep by the fire, while Imogen and Jonah had spent the night inside the hut. I damn well hope the cameras hadn't caught that.

Imogen was nearby, and she had the most satisfactory smile on her face. "Ha. I knew it."

"Shut up, Im." Sophia sat up and yawned. She rubbed her eyes and brushed her hair out of her face.

Though my body felt like it'd been pummeled by a ton of bricks, I rolled onto my stomach and forced myself onto my feet. I was sweating all over, and though it was cool out, I felt like it was a hundred degrees. My fever had gotten worse overnight. My throat was dry, and it hurt to speak, but I knew my team needed a final pep talk. It'd probably be the last one they'd get from me.

"Okay, team. We're tired, gross, and hungry, but we're almost there," I said. "Let's finish this."

It felt like I had concrete on my feet. But we only had a few miles left to go, maybe a little less. I forced myself forward, and my team followed.

As we walked through the forest, I noticed the team separated. The girls were up ahead, talking lowly. I'd bet money Imogen was interrogating Sophia about us. Nothing got the team moving quite like gossip.

"Hey, what's up between you and Sophia?" Jonah asked me without so much as a *good morning*. "Are you two together?"

Like I said. Screw food and a shower. The latest on my sex life was enough to sustain Jonah for days. "Enough, Jonah." I sighed.

"Did you guys *do it*?" Jonah whispered. "I want all the deets."

Squeaks widened her eyes and squawked.

"No, Jonah," I said in irritation. "Besides, there's not exactly a convenience store around here to swing by and pick up condoms."

"Hey, when nature calls," Jonah offered.

"If you really think Sophia and I are gonna bone when we're in the middle of—"

I stopped mid-way through my sentence to take several short, quick gasps. I literally couldn't breathe. It felt like there was an elephant sitting on my chest. I tried gasping for air again, but hardly any came through. My mind whirled, and the earth started spinning. It felt like I was underwater and there was no way up. Jonah's playful expression changed to concern.

"Liam," Jonah said, and he stepped in front of me. He grabbed my shoulders and looked me in the eye. "You need to breathe, brother. There's hardly any air getting through your windpipe. I can feel it."

My gasping had gotten the attention of the girls up ahead. They turned to look at me while Jonah took one hand off my shoulder and started making back-and-forth motions with it.

He was literally pushing air through my lungs. Imogen held her breath, while Sophia squeezed Esis. Esis had little tears welling up in his eyes, but I couldn't be sure why. Why was the little bugger so upset?

"I'm… fine," I said as I got my breath back. My throat was open now, and I could feel air filling up my lungs. I didn't have to struggle. Things righted themselves for a minute before I coughed, hard.

This time there was no hiding it from the team. A huge globule of blood came out of my mouth and nose, and I struggled to catch it. I stumbled forward before Jonah caught me. The girls gasped when they noticed the blood, and Jonah's eyes narrowed.

Jonah put a hand on my forehead before I could push him away. "He's running a fever," Jonah said viciously. He was pissed.

"You didn't notice how hot he was?" Imogen turned toward Sophia, surprised.

"I… I thought it was just because I'm naturally warm," Sophia said. "I couldn't tell."

I coughed again, and more blood came up. I wiped it away with my sleeve, but that didn't stop the looks my team was giving me. Even Sassy and Squeaks' mouths were open.

"Liam…" Sophia spoke softly, like she couldn't believe it. Like this was her worst nightmare, happening right in front of her.

"Liam, this is bullshit. Why didn't you tell us you were this sick?" Jonah asked. His hands were bunched into fists.

I opened my mouth, unsure of what to say. How could I tell them this was it for me?

But I didn't get a chance to answer, because right then a fireball whizzed by my head.

I jumped backward. The fireball whirled by my face and smashed against a nearby tree, singeing it.

At first I thought it was the trial, but then I noticed we weren't alone. Haley was standing across the clearing from us, along with Anwara, her two teammates and their Familiars.

At the start of the competition, Haley had looked confident. Now she was a mess. Her outfit was stained and torn, and her hair was in tangles around her face. She and her teammates were sporting various scrapes and bruises. Anwara was missing feathers, while the stone-lion had chunks of it that were gone and the winged jaguar was carrying a hurt paw. They looked like they hadn't rested in days.

"Haley," Sophia started, and she put herself in front of me. "What are you doing here?"

Haley didn't answer. Her face contorted into a snarl, and she yelled, "Attack!"

Fire, Air and Earth started coming at us from all sides. We had no choice but to react. Imogen immediately brought up a wall of dirt that we ducked behind. Sophia started tossing fireballs back at Haley, while Jonah blew a gust of air at his fellow Yapluma, trying to push her back. Imogen was in a battle with the Nivita guy. Her plants acted like whips, breaking apart the stone boulders that he tried to chuck at us.

This crazy bitch was literally trying to kill us! All for a damn trophy. Had she lost her mind?

I heard loud squeaks and snarls, and I dared to look over the wall. Squeaks was in a tussle with the stone-lion, while Esis and Sassy both were taking on the winged jaguar. The jaguar was bigger and more threatening, but Sassy and Esis were small and quick. The cat couldn't get a firm grip on them. They bit and scratched at the jaguar, taking turns distracting it. The stone-lion was too heavy for Squeaks to move, but Squeaks wasn't exactly tiny herself, so she used her bulk to throw the other Familiar around while her hooves chipped at the lion's rock-hard skin.

Anwara was flying above us. She opened her mouth to breathe a jet of flame, but I summoned my element and water came splashing upward into her mouth. I used what power I had to keep the phoenix subdued, dousing her in as much water as I could summon from the ground. Anwara was soaking wet, but she continued to try and light us up, all with desperate glances back at Haley. Haley grew more furious with her Familiar every time she failed to hurt one of us.

Teams sometimes tried to sabotage each other on their way to win during the Cup, but a full-on war between two teams had never happened before. This was absolutely ridiculous. I bet the fans back home were loving this drama.

"Haley, we're outnumbered!" the Nivita guy shouted. "We should go!"

"No! We're not going to lose to a bunch of freaks!" Haley screamed. She increased her fire-power, but she was the only one who did. The Yapluma girl was starting to back off Jonah, and the Nivita guy hesitated in throwing more boulders, unsure of what he should do.

But the Yapluma girl had made up her mind. She dropped her hands and stopped summoning her element, causing Jonah to halt his attack. Her winged jaguar batted Sassy and Esis away, returning to his Elementai's side.

"I don't want to do this anymore, Haley!" she screamed. The Yapluma girl backed away against a tree. "We shouldn't be attacking our own people, even if they are our competition! It's fucked up!"

"Shut up!" Haley screeched.

"It's just a stupid Cup! I'm leaving!" The Yapluma girl turned her back on Haley and stomped away. Her Familiar followed her, trotting to his Elementai loyally.

Haley gritted her teeth. "Nobody turns their back on me."

Haley screamed, and the sound that came from her mouth was so primal… it was almost evil. At her command, the trees around her Yapluma teammate lit up in flames. Branches crashed to the ground, and a large one cracked and fell downward, landing on the Yapluma girl and her Familiar. I could hear their agonized screams as they started burning to death.

"Haley! Stop!" Sophia screamed in horror, but Haley only increased the size and heat of the flames.

Haley grinned widely as her teammate cried for help, and her right eye twitched. The Yapluma girl tried to escape by pushing outward with her element, but the Air she provided only fueled Haley's Fire.

"Stop it!" Sophia had enough. She ran forward and pushed Haley down. Sophia used the power of her element to suppress Haley's and make the fire smaller. I snapped out of it and brought water coursing up from the ground.

I tried to put it out as quickly as I could, but it was no use. The Yapluma girl and her Familiar were already dead. There was nothing left but their blackened corpses.

Haley laughed. It was twisted and sick. It wasn't even human. Sophia's entire body was shaking as she backed away from the charred bodies.

Haley only had herself and her Nivita teammate left. She had to make sure both of them survived in order to pass the tournament.

The Nivita boy was pale. He reached out to steady himself on his stone-lion, staring at the blackened husk of the person that had been there just moments before.

Haley took off running. It was only a few seconds before the Nivita boy and his stone-lion followed. Anwara soared after, but her sharp eyes lingered on the fallen tree and the ashes that remained.

Sophia heaved for air next to me. Her face was red, eyes absolutely burning. Her expression was furious, and her whole body shook in rage.

"*Haley!*" Sophia screamed. She started forward and chased after her housemate. Esis tried to stop her by yanking on her pant leg, but she shook him off and continued to pursue Haley.

"Sophia, don't!" I yelled, but it was too late. Sophia had already taken off. Imogen, Jonah and I raced after her, trying to catch up. Haley was drawing us to the one place we didn't want to go.

The final task.

sophia
TWENTY-TWO

Evil! She's pure evil!

Rage rocketed through me as I raced through the woods behind Haley. Flames begged to escape through my closed fists. My hands burned until I couldn't take it anymore and fire shot between my fingers. I didn't know what I was going to do to Haley when I reached her. All I knew was that somebody needed to teach her a lesson.

Haley and her teammate dodged around thick trees and jumped over fallen logs, their Familiars close on their heels. She shot a glance back over her shoulder. A satisfied smirk touched her lips when she saw how far behind I was. Her laughter echoed through the forest.

My legs burned as they moved beneath me, and my head spun. I hadn't eaten much the last few days, and it was starting to show. The way Haley moved so quickly and agile, she'd probably shoved some energy bars in her pockets before the opening ceremony.

"Sophia!"

I heard someone's voice behind me, but I barely registered it. All my attention was focused on Haley. She was headed straight for a sharp decline in the forest, an area that looked as if a river had once flowed through it. In a last-ditch effort, I drew my arm back and hurled a fireball at the back of her head.

She jumped before my fireball made it to her. Her body dropped out of view as she slid down the ravine.

I pushed past the heat climbing up my legs and raced faster. I reached the ravine and braced myself. My feet dug into the dirt to slow my fall down the hill, but I managed to keep my footing. My eyes darted from one side to the other, but Haley was nowhere in sight. She was gone.

Sassy jumped into the ravine behind me, Squeaks and Esis closely following. Squeaks tripped over a rock on the hillside and tumbled the rest of the way down. She landed with her wings spread out beneath her and her legs straight up in the air. She quickly righted herself and shook her head. Esis scurried up my pant leg and onto my shoulder.

Imogen almost lost her footing as she raced after me, but a loose rock jumped upward on her way down the hill. She stepped on it to steady herself before stopping beside me. Jonah and

Liam made it to us a few seconds later. Liam gritted his teeth and breathed heavier than I'd ever seen him breathe before.

"Sophia, stop!" Imogen demanded.

I barely heard her. "I think she went this way."

I took a step to my right, but Liam's hand shot out and grabbed mine. He instantly pulled away as if my skin had burned him.

"Sophia," he said, concern etched in his features. "We can't waste our energy fighting against other teams."

"She *killed* her teammate," I growled, unable to control the anger coursing through me. I couldn't remember the last time I'd felt so out of control— probably never. "She *murdered* someone."

"I know," Liam said with a sigh. "But we can worry about Haley later. We're almost to the final trial, and—"

Jonah's scream cut through the air. He ducked just as a fireball at least a foot across whizzed by his head. It landed in a pile of dead leaves that instantly burst into flames.

My eyes darted in the direction it came from, only to see that another dozen fireballs were headed our way, each one bigger than the last.

We all took off running in the same direction down the length of the ravine. Beside me, Liam tripped, but I caught him before he could face-plant. His body slumped against mine. He was so weak now that he could barely walk.

"Duck!" I shouted as another incoming fireball headed our way. I couldn't even tell where they were coming from.

Above us, trees lit up in flames. Jonah and Imogen, along with their Familiars, hesitated ahead of us to make sure we were coming.

"We have to get out of here!" I cried.

Jonah climbed the steep side of the ravine. He reached out a hand and helped Imogen up in a single swift motion.

I supported Liam's weight and helped him over to Jonah. Jonah grabbed Liam's hand and heaved him upward. Liam tried to stand, but by now, his legs were pretty much useless. Squeaks pushed on Liam's butt with her head to help him up. Esis tugged on my hair just in time for me to see another fireball flying in my direction. It flew so close to me that it singed the hair on my left arm and ignited the leaves on the ground only a foot away from me. Heart hammering, I reached out for Jonah and hurried to my feet beside them.

Sheer hopelessness slammed into my gut when I finally got a good view of the landscape above the ravine. Ahead of us, the entire forest was engulfed in flames as far as the eye could see. A sharp pain assaulted my nostrils as I inhaled thick smoke. It felt as if a cinder block had been dropped on my chest as heavy air settled in my lungs. The heat radiating off the nearby flames was almost unbearable.

This was *bad*. My team couldn't take as much heat as I could. I had to get them out of here now.

"This way!" I shouted. I guided them through a maze of flames, following the path of fresh underbrush. Fire was closing in on the greenery quickly, narrowing our way out.

Flames completely overtook the path ahead of us. I whirled around, searching for an alternate route, but I couldn't see one... couldn't *feel* one. I stopped in my tracks in a small circle of untouched earth. It was barely ten feet across and shrinking by the second.

Imogen's eyes darted around the forest as if calculating our options. "It's your trial!" Imogen cried to me over the crackling sounds of burning wood. "What do we do, Sophia?"

I didn't really have time to think about it, but I also didn't know the answer. When I tried to access the fire to test its power, it was too much. Rage and prejudice hung thick in the magical flames. I could literally feel the hatred of the Elders as they pressed their Fire toward us. They *wanted* us to die, the misfits we were. We didn't belong in this society, and they wanted to make sure we knew it— or they were testing me, seeing if I was the prophesied child they'd been waiting for. But prophecy or not, there was no way I could calm the Elders' Fire on my own.

Instinct told me to do the exact opposite.

"I have to make them bigger." I aimed my hands at the closest flames that were creeping across the forest floor toward us.

"No!" Liam wheezed. His body was half-draped over Squeaks' back. He barely got the words out. "You have to calm the flames."

"Agreed," Imogen said, looking worried. "You need to clear a path."

I hesitated. The Fire inside of me begged to escape, as if it was trying to tell me something. But my teammates were right. Calming the flames made the most sense. They were more experienced at this Elementai stuff than I was, so I was just going to have to trust them.

It wasn't going to be easy. Putting out Doya's flames in class was hard enough. I didn't know how I was going to calm *myself* first, not while I was still fuming over Haley— and while my teammates were dangerously close to cooking to death.

I stared at the flames in front of me, willing them to shrink. They were almost as tall as I was, and growing.

From beside me, Jonah started humming the melody to the tune we sang in the cave. Imogen joined in. My anger and worry slowly began to wane at the comforting sound of their voices. I did my best to ignore the heat and the heavy smoke.

Slowly, the flames in front of us shrank enough that we could trample over the embers. I started forward, attacking the next flames as I went. Sweat dripped from my brow, and my knees shook. I could feel my energy draining with each passing second.

I glanced ahead of us and saw nothing but burning forest. Behind us, I could see where the fire ended at a clearing only fifty yards away. My gut twisted at the thought of turning back, but I'd rather keep my team alive than rush to the finish line.

"I don't know how long I can keep this up!" I told my team. "We should turn back."

Nobody had a chance to agree or disagree. Just as I said it, a wall of fire surged in front of us. It was at least twenty feet tall and so unexpected that I leapt backward, nearly tripping over Sassy. Esis teetered on my shoulder but quickly righted himself.

The flames' power surged through me. I had less than a split second to decide my next move. Against my better judgement, I acted on instinct. I took hold of that power and threw my anger back at the wall of flames.

The flames shot high into the air, touching the tree tops and burning the leaves above our heads. When they calmed a second later, they were barely higher than my knee. It was better, but not enough to walk through.

"Soph—" Liam tried to speak but started coughing uncontrollably instead. Blood shot from his mouth and sprayed on the ground below him.

Guilt shook my body. How had I not noticed how sick he was getting before? Liam could barely hold himself up. There was no way we were making it to the end of this fire labyrinth with him conscious.

I rushed forward and guided his arm over my shoulder. "We're going back. We'll find another way once Liam's feeling better."

He'll feel better soon, I told myself with each step I took. *Once we make it to the clearing, Esis will heal him. Liam's temper be damned. I can't keep it a secret any longer.*

"Let me"— Jonah coughed through the smoke— "help."

He reached out for Liam's other arm, but before he could grab it, a fireball flew down from the sky and whizzed between them. Jonah jumped back next to Imogen and both of their Familiars.

"Let's get out of here!" I shouted.

My words were drowned out by the wind picking up around us. Air rushed by my face, throwing my ponytail in every direction. The flames died down for a moment in the wind, but quickly came back in full force as soon as the energy pulled back. Flames rose high above our heads, and sweat dripped down my skin. I willed the flames to shrink just long enough that we could make it out of the wildfire and into the clearing up ahead.

I started forward, but Imogen's scream caught my attention. I whirled around just in time to see a swirl of fire cutting through the space between us. Sassy jumped backward and *yipped*, letting me know she'd been burned.

Esis gasped and jumped off my shoulder. He leapt through the underbrush, straight for the wall of flames separating us from the rest of the group.

"Esis!" I cried.

He disappeared into the flames, sending my stomach plummeting downward.

"Imogen! Jonah!" I screamed. The flames were so high that I couldn't see them.

"Go ahead of us!" Imogen called back. I could barely hear her over the angry roar of the fire.

"No!" I yelled. "I'll get you out!"

"I'll manage it!" Jonah screamed back. "Save Liam!"

I hesitated, but I didn't have the luxury of thinking it through. Liam coughed and doubled over, stumbling out of my grasp. He caught himself by landing directly on a flame burning a sapling beneath him. He jerked his hand away, but the damage had already been done. His palm was red and blistered. He stared down at it with a blank expression, like he barely knew what was going on. If I didn't get him out of here *now*, the thick smoke was going to kill him. But...

"Esis!" I cried. I held my hand up in front of my face, shielding my eyes from the burn of the flames. I didn't hear if anyone replied.

My Familiar was gone. I had no idea where he went, or if he was even still alive.

Liam sputtered again and rolled onto his side. I didn't want to leave everyone else behind, but I had to help Liam. Jonah and Imogen at least had a fighting chance. Liam only had me.

My hands shook as I reached for Liam, to help him to his feet. His arm draped limply around my shoulder while mine wrapped around his waist. He was seriously heavy and was dragging his feet, but I forced myself to hold on to him and put one foot in front of the other.

"Earth, Water, Fire, and Air..." I began singing, knowing that the distraction was the only thing that would get us through the flames. My voice cracked, and tears began to slide down my cheeks. I could barely see the clearing anymore, but every few seconds, it revealed itself through the flickering flames.

Almost there...

"Gifted to us by the breath of a prayer..." I continued.

Sobs broke out in my chest as Liam's head lolled to the side, resting against mine. "Please, Liam," I whispered. "Stay with me."

He coughed again, but it sounded more like wheezing.

The flames ahead of us were dying down, but they weren't going away completely. Behind us the flames grew higher and higher, licking into the sky like a beacon to the ancestors. The underbrush around us had almost been completely consumed. I didn't have a choice but to head forward into the smaller flames.

My boots stomped out most of the flames as I dragged Liam forward, but there was a wall of fire beside us that made it increasingly harder to breathe. Liam's arm was starting to slip from my grasp as sweat coated our skin, drenching us both.

"Not that much farther," I said, though I had no idea if he was still conscious. "We can do this!"

My knees wobbled beneath me. I could barely hold Liam up. I thought I might collapse right there for the wildfire to consume us. At least it'd be a quick death…

And then, just like that, we broke through the flames. Cool air rushed around us, and I inhaled a deep breath. I dragged Liam farther away from the flaming trees until the heat was barely a tingle across my skin. When I glanced back I saw that the flames were no longer advancing on us. They stopped abruptly at the edge of what looked like an invisible wall, as if the Elders were keeping them contained for a purpose. Above us, dark clouds swirled, as though a thunderstorm was rolling in to make the last task even worse.

I dropped to my knees and gently laid Liam down on the earth beside me. His eyes were closed, and his face expressionless. His arm flopped to the ground when it slid off my neck.

"Liam! Liam!" I pressed my hands to the sides of his face, smacking him lightly in hopes of startling him awake. "Open your eyes! Please, ancestors! Liam!"

Tears streamed down my face and fell onto his shirt. I inhaled a deep breath to steady my trembling fingers, then dipped my head down to his. I intended to give him mouth-to-mouth to breathe some clean air into his lungs, but before my lips connected with his a noise bubbled up from his throat.

I pulled back and stared down at him. "Liam?"

He cleared his throat and forced his eyes open. It looked like he was trying to lift bricks with his eyelids. "I'm fine, *pawee*."

I sniffled. "You're not fine. Not in the slightest."

"Leave me," he said in a dry, scratchy tone.

"No." I shook my head.

Liam coughed so hard that it took him a good ten seconds to get over it. When he could finally speak again, he asked, "Where's Esis?"

Concern knotted in my gut. "He— he went after Sassy."

"Go," Liam begged. His eyes finally opened enough that he met my gaze. "Believe me, you don't want to lose him. You don't want to live like this." It sounded like it took all his strength to tell me that.

"I can't just leave you!" I protested, wiping my runny nose.

"You have to, *pawee*," he insisted. "I'm dead weight… literally."

"Don't say that," I sobbed. "You—"

Liam reached out to me. His rough fingers ran over the skin on the back of my hand. His bottom lip trembled, and his eyes glistened as he gazed up at me. "I was never going to make it back alive, Sophia. We all knew it from the start. I got you all this far, but you're going to have to get everyone else to the end."

"Liam, please…" Tears flowed from my eyes like a river.

"Stop acting like you have a choice, Sophia," he said softly. "You can't save me."

"I could have. I still can." My head dipped so low in guilt that I rested the side of my face on him.

The rise and fall of his chest was so comforting. I couldn't let him go. I knew it was selfish, but I would miss him too much. He was the first thing at Orenda Academy that made it feel like home. I'd never truly thought we wouldn't make it to the finish line together.

Liam raised his hand and laid it on my head, brushing away my flyaway hairs. "Sophia, please go. The team needs you. Esis needs you. There isn't time."

I lifted my head and blinked away the tears. He was right. I didn't have the luxury of lying to myself, of convincing myself he would make it. It was a miracle he'd made it this far. It tore my insides into a million tiny little pieces that could never be put back together, but I had no choice.

Liam's heavy eyelids fell shut. "It's okay, Sophia. I've had my extra time. I'm ready to go."

"Liam," I squeaked in a small voice.

"What, *pawee*?" he asked in a labored tone.

"I— I—" I couldn't bring myself to tell him how I felt about him. I would never be able to leave his side if I did.

Instead, I brushed the hair out of his face and bent to press my lips to his forehead. "Please tell Nashoma about me."

He sighed heavily. "I will," he whispered.

That was the last thing either of us said before I rose to my feet and raced back into the flaming forest.

The smoke was thicker than ever. I coughed uncontrollably and squinted my eyes. I could hardly see anything as I walked back through the flames.

"Esis!" I shrieked. "Imogen! Jonah!"

No answer.

A terrifying thought occurred. What if the rest of my teammates were gone? What if I was the only one left?

"Ancestors, no!" I cried aloud. "Please, please, please…"

In front of me, four figures swooped down from the sky. I took a step back, startled. I didn't recognize the Familiars at first… not until they shifted, their coloring washing across the landscape like a watercolor painting. Two men and two women stood in front of me, gazing at me with proud looks upon their faces. It was like the fire didn't bother them one bit. Why would it? They were only spirits… my ancestors.

I remembered them from the night Liam took me up to the mountain to meet them. It was the same four: the warrior in a headdress, the guy in a cowboy hat, the redhead in a ballgown, and the woman with long black hair.

They'd been watching over me, and they'd come to answer my prayers.

I cleared my throat. "Please, ancestors. I've lost my Familiar. I need to get to him."

None of them spoke. They simply turned in unison and pointed to my right.

"Thank you!" I exclaimed. I wished I could stay around and get to know them more, but now, there wasn't time.

They each offered a sweet smile and took a bow. I bowed back. When I lifted my head, they were gone.

Without hesitation, I sprinted in the direction they'd pointed. I ran maybe thirty yards before my eyes fell upon a small white figure moving through the trees. Relief and panic swept through me all at once.

Esis scurried around on the surface of a large rock. Flames engulfed the earth on all sides of him. He glanced upward, as if calculating whether or not he could reach the branches above him, but those too were on fire. Fear glistened in his big blue eyes, and he let out a tiny scream of horror. He was searching for a way out that he was never going to find.

"Esis!" I screamed across the space between us.

His ears perked up at the sound of my voice, and his eyes scanned the forest until they landed on me. He stood on his toes and reached his tiny little arms upward for me.

"I'm coming!" I called.

I concentrated on the flames between us, forcing them to die down. My concentration broke when a tree branch snapped from behind me and slammed to the ground. It landed with a thundering *thump*. The crackling sound of burning trees surrounded us. I was completely out of time. If I waited for my power to control this fire any longer, we'd both be pinned beneath falling branches.

So I did the only thing I could. I raced into the flames.

I managed to keep the ones around me lower than my hips, but they licked up from the ground and seared the skin on my legs. My pants caught fire just as I reached the rock and lifted myself up onto it. I immediately grabbed Esis and wrapped him in my arms.

But I barely had a second to enjoy the relief flooding through me. The fire covering my pants burned my skin. I knew I was Koigni and could hold fire in the palm of my hand, but facing someone else's Fire was unbearable. If it was normal fire, I'd be fine, but this was magical, powerful. Pain radiated up my leg as I tried to smother it by clapping my hands against my pant leg. The slapping motion made it even worse.

What was I doing? I couldn't fight a Koigni's power with this *stop, drop, and roll* shit. As Esis snuggled into my shoulder I held my hand just above the flames scalding my skin. I pulled against their power, fighting to kill the flames.

To my relief, they disappeared before my eyes, and all the Fire in the immediate area died down, leaving nothing but blackened trees and ashes. There was a huge hole in my pants, and my skin was blistered, but I was still conscious. I could still find the others.

Esis hopped down from my shoulder and onto the rock, then placed his tiny little hands on my leg. *Of course! Why didn't I think of that to begin with?* The burning pain crawling up my leg eased. Right in front of my eyes, the blisters shrank, and the red burns faded until there was nothing left but smooth, untouched skin.

I scooped Esis up in my arms and hugged him close. "Thank you! I'm so glad you're okay."

Esis chippered and glanced around nervously.

"Right." I rose to my feet, glancing around our rock in search of an exit. Truth be told, one way wasn't any better than the other. "Which way did the rest of them go, buddy?"

Esis' eyes widened at the question. He lifted a hand to point one way, but hesitated and pointed in another before pulling his hand back and shaking his head.

He doesn't know.

Unease swept through me. Imogen and Jonah could be anywhere… they could be dead. I had three-hundred-and-sixty degrees of burning forest to search through. I'd never find them. The best I could hope for was that Jonah had been able to get them out.

Esis jumped out of my arms and looked around. His little nose twitched as he rose up on his hind legs and his ears perked up. He gave a long, lonely call, but nobody answered.

He glanced back at me, unsure. In the pit of my stomach, I knew.

Esis was looking for Liam.

"He's gone, Esis," I said. I forced the words past the lump in my throat. "I had to leave him behind."

Esis' blue eyes swam. He couldn't speak, but I knew what he was saying. *But you love him.*

I forced back a sob. "It doesn't matter. He's already dead. He told me to go. He's not going to make it. He was never going to."

Esis stared at me like what I said was a lie. I tried wiping my face, but the tears kept on coming. I didn't want to live a life without Liam. It was impossible to think about. Everything I knew about being an Elementai, about this world, he taught me.

Everything I wanted, he was.

I put my head in my hands and cried. "I don't know what to do." I didn't know what direction my friends were in, or how I could help them if I did find them. I'd left the man I loved to suffer a painful death. I wasn't an Elementai. I was just a stupid girl from Utah. I didn't feel like I could do anything.

I heard the sound of chimes on the wind, and a low drum accompanied by a slight breeze. I looked up. My ancestors had returned. They gathered around Esis and me in a circle. Three of them— the warrior, the cowboy, and the woman with black hair— started to dance, twirling and circling to the beat of the drum.

The red-headed woman in the ballgown approached me slowly and reached out.

My hand was shaking, but I allowed her to touch me. I couldn't feel her skin against mine, but I could see it. The red-haired woman took my hand and smiled at me gently. She didn't speak, but when she squeezed my hand, powerful emotion flooded through me. It was small and warm, spreading throughout my body slowly and making me feel happy and safe all over. It was love, and the love my ancestors gave me swept away any doubts or insecurities I had about not being good enough to finish this tournament, not being good enough to be an Elementai... not being good enough to save Liam. That kind of love stopped my tears and made everything seem like it was right again.

It was the same thing I felt every time I thought of Liam.

In that moment, I knew what I had to do. Liam Mitoh might be ready to leave me, but I sure as hell wasn't ready to leave him. I was going to save his life, then we'd go and find Imogen and Jonah together.

Even if I failed, I was going to be there with him as he died. So he wouldn't be alone— and so I could finally tell him what I felt for him was real.

"Thank you," I whispered to the red-haired woman. She smiled at me again, then slowly vanished as the breeze swept by.

My ancestors gradually faded away, their colors bleeding into the wind. But I knew they weren't truly gone. Though I could no longer see them, I knew that they'd always be by my side to guide me.

Esis chittered at my feet. He tilted his head to the side and looked up.

"How good is your healing ability, Esis?" I asked.

He gazed up at me with those big blue eyes and shrugged.

"Well, we're about to find out. We're going back for Liam."

This was the last way I wanted to die.

I lay flat on my back on the ground and looked up at the sky. It took all my energy just to breathe, and every breath got harder. The pain had mostly gone away, and my body had gone numb. Though parts of me were burned, I could feel myself growing cold as each breath grew more and more shallow. For a second I thought my heartbeat had stopped, until I realized just the sound was growing fainter in my ears, beating lighter against my chest.

To make things worse, it'd started raining. And it wasn't a little drizzle, either. The rain was coming down so hard and in such big droplets that it made it hard to move my limbs. The wind was whipping against my face, and the fires raging in the distance still filled the air with smoke, so it was even harder for me to breathe. Dark clouds gathered above, and lightning crackled throughout the sky while thunder shook the earth. I was absolutely soaked in a matter of seconds. The dirt quickly became thick mud underneath me, and my clothes absorbed the mess. I tried to make the rain stop, but my element was like the rest of my body. It just wasn't working.

Have you ever felt yourself actively dying? It's like, the worst thing ever. You can feel your organs shutting down and everything getting weaker. The smallest task takes a tremendous amount of effort. It's like your entire body's giving up, but at the same time, you've never wanted to live more than in that very moment. Your intention is to cling to life, but the vessel you're riding in says no.

I hoped that during the tournament I would get taken out quickly by one of the tasks, but my luck wasn't that good. I was dying, but it was slowly. This could take hours.

I didn't know how I was going to say goodbye to this world. I wouldn't get a goodbye with my family. Sophia had been all I had, and fuck, that nearly did me in. I didn't want her to leave me. More than anything, I wanted her to stay by my side so I wouldn't have to be alone.

But at the same time, I didn't want her to see me die, and I knew Jonah and Imogen needed her more. So I let her go.

But that's what you did for people you loved. You sacrificed your life so they could go on.

That's what love *was*. Anyone who didn't agree, who said that love was just chemicals in your brain or selfish fulfillment or whatever, was just fucking stupid.

And ancestors, I loved her. My heart was so full for her it was about ready to break.

Being on my back was putting a lot of pressure on my lungs, so I forced myself to roll over onto my stomach. I didn't know where I harnessed the energy, but I somehow managed to force my weak limbs into doing what I asked. I ended up flat on my face in the mud. The dirt actually felt like a pillow against my head. I wanted to close my eyes, but I knew the minute I did, that would be it, so I forced them to stay open.

I had wished to die for months, but now that the time was here, I wanted to stay. I had been so foolish. I'd wasted so much time longing for the end I didn't realize what a gift I had when I had it. I wished I could go back and see Sophia smile one last time, or make Jonah laugh again, or just hang out with my brother. Instead, I'd squandered away my time hiding away in my room and being too scared to face the world.

I let out another breath. They were getting really shallow now. Maybe it wouldn't be as long as I thought. It sucked it had to be on TV.

A pair of black paws appeared in front of me. Yep, definitely not as long as I thought, if Nashoma was already here.

"Hey, buddy," I rasped. "You here to take me home?"

I couldn't see anything but his paws and the end of his tail. I was too weak to lift my head up. Nashoma didn't bend his head down to lick me or anything, just stood there. *Get up.*

I would've died of shock if I wasn't already there. "What?"

Get up.

"Are you fucking serious?" I had to struggle to get the words out. "Nashoma, it's over. It's time to go home."

Get up. He was stubborn. His paws didn't move.

"Didn't you hear me?" My mouth twisted in a snarl that was half-agony, half-rage. "I'm ready to die!"

GET UP.

Apparently, he didn't think I was. "This is crap," I muttered, but it was more of a wheezing gasp. I tried to push myself upwards, but my arms shook, and I failed. I only ended up face-planting in the mud again.

Get up, Liam. Get up! His paws started to dance in front of my face. At his insistence, I reached out with both hands and pulled myself through the mud. He moved out of the way, walking beside me and shouting, *Get up, get up!*

Other people's Familiars probably greeted them with hugs and kisses on the other side. My jackass Familiar had to make me prove I was worthy. Crawling on my hands and knees would've been faster, but I couldn't manage that, so I more or less slid my body along the mud. Nashoma started to bark, and I managed to move a little faster. My hand that was burnt all to hell was throbbing, but I ignored the sharp pain jolting through it and continued on to ancestors knew what.

A cave came into view, only about ten or so steps away. I realized Nashoma's plan. In the cave, the cameras wouldn't be able to see me and I could die in peace. It wouldn't be televised for the entire tribe to see.

I wanted to die with whatever dignity I had left. So I forced myself to crawl on my stomach toward the cave. I could hear Nashoma's steps beside me as the mud turned to solid rock.

I reached the cave wall. Somehow, I forced myself upright and into a sitting position. It was easier to breathe that way. I lay back against the rock and heaved for air. At least I was out of the rain.

"Out of the sight of the cameras," I breathed, and I reached out a hand to graze Nashoma's fur. "Good idea, buddy."

My hand brushed nothing but air. He was already gone.

I tried to roll my eyes. Even that was too much effort. Whatever. I'd see him again in a minute, anyway.

Colors were starting to muddle together and become fuzzy shapes. I think I saw a group of people gathering around me, though honestly, I was so delirious I couldn't be sure. In a tree outside the cave an eagle looked down and cocked his head, giving a sharp cry.

"Grandpa?" I gasped. It was the last thing I had the strength to say. My head lolled to the side. I saw someone running toward me, a fuzzy white shape at their feet, before I slipped away.

I came to slowly. I wondered if I had melded with Nashoma yet and what that would feel like, but then I realized that I was very much still in my own body and still hurting, though not as bad as before.

And I was *still in this fucking cave.*

But it was all right, because Sophia was there. She kneeled next to me on her knees, her beautiful face studying me carefully. Her thin eyebrows were scrunched together as if she was watching something take place.

"Sophia?" I whispered. I pushed myself upward off the wall, before I realized I shouldn't have the energy to do that. I started, and Esis gurgled unpleasantly. He was on my lap and looking pleased with himself.

"Liam!" Sophia flung her arms around me and squeezed me tight. I hugged her back, but I was still kind of in shock. What was going on here?

"Sophia, let go. I can't breathe," I gasped. She was crushing me. Poor Esis was getting squished between our chests.

"Oh, sorry." She backed away nervously, and Esis plopped out between us. Esis massaged his head and grumbled at her.

"You always give the tightest hugs," I said, and I rubbed my ribs. "Not a bad thing," I added when she opened her mouth.

"Liam," Sophia said, and she pointed. "Look."

I did. My hand… it was okay. The blisters and burn wounds were gone. It was like the skin was brand-new. I brought it in front of my face and turned it around. Not a mark on it. In fact, all the scratches and bruises I'd sustained from the tournament were also gone. I was no longer sore, and my lungs felt clear instead of full of blood. The only thing that still remained was the constant inflammation pulsating through my muscles that I usually felt on a daily basis. I hardly even registered it. I even felt hungry… starving, in fact. That was a miracle in itself.

"I'm… I'm not fucking dead," I said, stunned.

"No, you're not," Sophia said. She looked even more relieved than I felt.

"What the hell happened to me?" I asked. "I was pretty much dead, and now I feel fine. Well, not fine." I shifted uncomfortably. "I still hurt. But it's like I was at the start of the tournament. I can breathe fine and everything now."

Sophia hesitated. "I… I don't know what happened," Sophia stuttered. "I just came back to find you, and when you weren't where I left you… oh, God, Liam."

She put a hand over her mouth and tried not to cry. "I thought you were already dead and that the officials had come and got you, but Esis made me follow him, and I found you here. You were all healed up when I arrived."

"This cave must be super magical," I said, looking around. "It's the only way to explain why I healed so fast. Maybe it's one of the original sites of the tribe, or a place where the ancestors commune."

Sophia made an *em-hm* noise and said, "Yeah, that must be it."

Esis let out a trilling noise. Inside, I was hollow. Nashoma hadn't come to take me to the ancestors. His only job had been to get me to the cave, to heal me.

I felt tremendously grateful and horribly bereaved all at once.

"Liam, I was wondering. How… how do you feel?" she asked cautiously.

I rolled my shoulders back. "I don't know. Not one-hundred percent, but I can walk and stuff."

"Oh." She seemed disappointed.

"Yeah, I guess it would be too much to hope that the cave would cure me completely, right?" I asked cheerfully. But I sure as hell wasn't complaining. Being disabled was a big step up from being dead, so I was going to take it and be grateful. "Did you find Imogen and Jonah?"

She shook her head. "I just found Esis. He pretty much convinced me I had to come back for you."

"Did he really?" I scratched Esis between the ears. "You miss me, little guy?"

Esis gave me a sneaky grin and wagged his tail.

I looked at his Elementai. "Sophia, why did you come back?" I asked lowly. "I didn't want you to stay. I wanted you to be safe."

Her brown eyes were heavy with all sorts of unsaid things. "Liam, I think you know why," she whispered back quietly.

She leaned forward. I didn't realize it was to kiss me until she had done it.

You ever just stand in the ocean and let a wave crash over you, but it's a lot more powerful than you thought and it ends up knocking you off your feet? That's what it felt like when Sophia kissed me, except ten times stronger. If her existing was the wave, kissing her was like the whole damn ocean. Her lips were warm against my cold ones and felt really soft. She smelled like crushed autumn leaves, and smoke, and even like the ocean at midnight. She put so much emotion into the kiss I could feel it, and I allowed the strength of her feelings to wash over me as she brushed my face.

Without thinking, I reached upward and caressed her hair back, running my fingers through her hair until my fingers were entwined in her locks and holding the back of her neck. Sophia moved forward. Her lips didn't part from mine as she sat on my lap and hooked her legs around my hips. I wrapped my free arm around her waist and held her tightly to me as she deepened the kiss even more, drinking from me as if I was her life.

She parted her mouth a little, and I let my tongue slip in. Sophia moaned and moved against me, biting sharply on my bottom lip before pushing her tongue into my mouth in response. Ancestors, this was fucking amazing. Like, the best kiss of my life. I squeezed her even tighter and gave an involuntary thrust up. She responded by rolling against me and I. Nearly. Died.

"Liam," she groaned.

I took her mouth against mine again before she could say more. I had to keep kissing her, because if she said my name like that again, I'd lose all self control.

It got to me how incredible we were together. Months of repressed emotion and want came boiling over as her hands ravaged my hair, her fingertips rippling down my chest. My eyes were closed, but the way she made me feel took away any need I had to see. It was almost too much to handle. My entire body felt like it was riding a huge wave that could see over the entire world, only to come spiraling back down before it rose to the top again.

I thought that she'd stop kissing me, that she'd get tired of it, but she didn't. She kept loving me like she didn't realize I was just broken parts. I always thought that when you kissed someone new, you had to get used to the way they did it, but not us— we kissed each other like we'd been doing it for ages.

We didn't even have to think about it. We just let it be. It was like we were made to exist together.

I knew right then. She could kiss me forever and it wouldn't be enough.

Why did Sophia come back for me? I knew why. It was because she loved me.

When she finally pulled back, I'm pretty sure it was only because both of us had to breathe. Esis gave a low whistle. Sophia blushed. I grinned and pushed him over. Ancestors, I was literally seeing stars. That had made me lightheaded. How long had we been making out? Was it just minutes? Because it felt like days.

That kiss had been everything I'd secretly dreamed of and hoped for since I walked into her living room back in Utah. I only wish I'd been the one to kiss her first.

Sophia stared back at me. She was slightly panting. "Liam… what are we?"

I didn't know what to say. How could she ask me something like that when my hormones were raging and all I wanted to do was tackle her and make love to her on this cave floor, even with Esis watching?

But then something registered in my brain, and the question made me run cold. What *were* we? Obviously more than friends. Were we boyfriend and girlfriend? I hated the word *lovers* because it creeped me out and made it seem like what we were doing was dirty and wrong.

We were in love with each other. Obviously. Neither of us could deny it anymore. But what did that mean? There were still rules we had to follow. Toaquas and Koignis couldn't be together. Our world wouldn't allow it.

I wanted to say, *I love you and let's run away together,* but what came out was, "We should probably talk about that when our lives aren't in danger and when we know our friends are okay."

She nodded. "Right." She clambered off my lap and nearly fell over. It made me laugh under my breath. I got up and reached out a hand to pull her to her feet. When her hand was in mine, I didn't want to let go. Sophia gave my fingers a reassuring squeeze before she finally pulled away. It was hard to look at each other, because we'd just acknowledged the elephant in the room that we'd been avoiding for months.

And damn, it was taking up the whole cave.

"Where should we go?" I asked, just to break the tension and move on from that bomb kiss that I desperately wanted to go back to.

Sophia put a hand to her chin and said, "I have a feeling we should see where this cave leads. Back there is just a bunch of smoke and fire. Maybe Imogen and Jonah are already ahead of us."

"I'm following you."

Esis led the way, his little nails clicking on the stone as Sophia moved forward. I stayed behind and tried (and kinda failed) to not watch her ass.

I was alive, dammit. I was making the most of it.

Unlike the cave we'd gotten stuck in the other day, this one was well-lit, with multiple holes in the top and walls that were made of black stone with small silver flecks. It was more like a cavern. It looked like the rain had cleared up and the sun was out again, from the sunlight that was bursting through the top of the cave. From what I could tell, it was around dusk, from the orange light gleaming in through the crevices in the ceiling.

My steps were really bouncy. I felt like I was on top of the world.

"You seem like you're in a good mood," Sophia said, and she smiled.

"Fucking giddy." And I meant it. That'd been a close call back there. Not to mention my not-dying prize had been kissing Sophia Henley, because that had been pretty rad.

"I bet that kiss had something to do with it," Sophia said coyly. "Something else is pretty happy, too."

"You mind your business, *pawee*," I told her. "There's still some things I have to teach you, and believe me, I'm gonna have fun doing it."

Sophia blushed. The pink in her cheeks got me excited. I couldn't wait until I could put my lips all over those cheeks, and her hair, and about a million other things...

I needed to stop. We were still at risk out here. All that fun stuff would come later.

Sophia and I went quiet, both lost in our own heads. Eventually, we came to a place where the cave split. Esis went to the right side and started hopping up and down, pointing down the long pathway.

"I think he wants us to follow him," Sophia said, turning to me.

"That little guy has good instincts, and so do you, Sophia," I said, pointing at her. "I think if we had listened to you all along we wouldn't have gotten so turned around in this tournament."

Sophia had a determined look on her face. "I don't know. But I am sure that I'm never going to make the mistake of second-guessing myself ever again."

I was happy about that. Sophia had come to school so unconfident and unsure. She'd even been too scared to confront Haley. Now she had faith in herself. It was enough to make me proud.

The tunnel ended and widened into a huge opening, where the cave opened up to the great sky. Here, I could see that the sun really was setting. It bathed the entire cavern in a blood-red glow. A tiny waterfall trickled down from an unknown source into a silver pool that was only about as deep as our ankles. But that wasn't the strangest thing about the cave.

It was a totem— at least, that's what I could describe it as. It looked as if it was carved from white bone, and had all five House symbols on it— Koigni, Toaqua, Nivita, Yapluma, and Anichi at the very top. It was only about as big as my palm, and could fit in my hand. It was floating— literally floating— over the middle of the silver pool, and was bathed in a soft ray of white light that seemed to emit from the totem itself.

A soft music hummed in the background. Chimes, drums, and the whispering of the wind. I'm certain I heard the ancestors' voices in there somewhere.

My element wavered within me, signaling something was up. The closer I got to the totem, the more my Water wanted to freak out. Whatever that totem was, it was insanely magical.

Esis stood by the edge of the pool and looked intently at Sophia. It was like he was asking her to grab it.

Sophia was transfixed by the totem. Her face glowed, and she had a strange expression on her face, like all she could look at was the floating talisman. She started walking toward it slowly, her feet entering the pool as she approached.

"Sophia, don't touch it," I said, wary. "We don't know what it is, or what it does."

"It won't hurt me, Liam," she said. Her voice was far-away, enchanted… it was like she was under a spell. "I just… I know it's meant for me."

Like that made a whole lot of fucking sense. I opened my mouth to say something, but found myself absent of words as Sophia reached out and grasped the totem in her hands.

I had to duck as a blast of air shot backward from the totem. It blew Sophia's hair back and created a whirlwind as the sun was swept out. The room was bathed in colors of silver, blue, and white shadows. Dark figures of creatures I didn't know the names of ran along the stone walls, creating an ancient dance that had long been forgotten. Sophia held the totem tighter in her hand and blue fire lit up her form, creating a raging inferno that she was completely immersed in. But the blue fire didn't hurt her— it just made her more beautiful. It grew and intensified, shooting up to the ceiling in a spectacular show. Sophia looked up at the dazzling display, stunned by the show of magic she was creating. Esis' blue eyes widened and he cheered loudly, like his Elementai had finally accomplished what she'd been destined for.

I about fell to my knees. I had to force myself to stay standing as I watched Sophia bring the totem close to her heart. She was like a goddess, invincible and unreachable. When I saw her like that, holding the totem with that blue fire blazing all around her, I didn't need to ask if she was the one the prophecy was talking about.

I knew she was.

The prophecy was real. Sophia was the one who was to bring glory to Koigni. Everything… *everything* the Fire House had talked about for hundreds of years… had been about her.

The rumors were true. The end times for the Hawkei were here. Koigni House was going to take over and rule over everyone.

And Sophia would be the one to end all things for the Elementai.

The blue fire eventually died down. The shadows fled, along with the dark creatures. The sunlight came back to the room again. Sophia looked over her shoulder at me, her chestnut hair settling around her shoulders.

This was crazy. Sophia was strong, stronger than I ever imagined. She was only a First Year, but give her enough time and her magic would make fools out of us all. She was so powerful she could rule the entire tribe. I bet she could even take it over by herself, if she wanted.

And I was in love with her. If I thought things couldn't get more complicated, I was a damn liar.

Sophia moved toward me. I took a few steps back, and she paused.

"Liam, what's wrong? You look like you've seen a ghost." She seemed puzzled.

I had a hard time responding. It hit me. I was afraid of her.

I snapped myself out of it and said, "Hey. Are you okay?"

"I think so." She made a face. "What was all that?"

Poor *pawee*. She was always so behind. Guess that was a good thing in this circumstance, though. "I'm not sure," I lied. "But I think you should put that totem back."

"Put it back? No!" she said, and Esis hissed loudly. "I'm not doing that. Besides, where do you want me to put it? It was floating in mid-air!"

Good point. I was really glad the cameras hadn't caught what had happened, because I didn't know if Sophia was ready to face all of that.

I wasn't sure if I was, either.

She opened her hand and looked at the totem. Beneath each House were various inscriptions. It was ancient Hawkei, but it was some sort of code I couldn't read. "What do you think it means?"

"I have no clue." I tried to study it, but I was spooked. All looking at that totem did was make me nervous, but I no longer thought it was the totem that was all-powerful. That was Sophia herself. Whatever that thing was, it was just a tool that she used to channel her power. She didn't realize that.

"Should we tell Imogen and Jonah about this?" She held the totem out for me to take.

I shook my head and folded her fingers over the totem, gently pushing it back toward her. "No. I think this should stay between us."

Sophia nodded and pocketed the totem in one of her pant pockets, securing it with a button. "Okay. Our little secret."

We sure were coming out of this cave with a lot of secrets. This was like the Tunnel of Love slash Tunnel of Stuff-I-Didn't-Want-To-Get-Involved-In.

I grabbed her hand and tugged on it. I was almost scared to touch her, like I would get shocked, but that was stupid and I told myself to stop being a dumbass. "Come on, Sophia. Let's get out of here."

Sophia lingered a moment longer in the cave, like she didn't want to leave it, before she finally relented to me tugging on her arm. We walked out of the cavern and into the cool forest air just as the sun was going down over the horizon. Sophia lit up a tiny fire so we could see as we hiked through the woods, looking for Imogen and Jonah.

After a few minutes, Sophia spoke. "Liam," Sophia said cautiously. "You're acting different."

I shook my head. "I'm fine, *pawee*. This tournament has just been really something."

Esis chattered in agreement, and Sophia nodded. I felt guilty. I didn't want to treat her different. She was still my sweet Sophia, wasn't she? I couldn't imagine her hurting a fly. She was too nice and innocent. She was still a virgin, for crying out loud. I didn't think she could kill anyone, or be a dictator over an entire tribe.

But that's not what the prophecy said. And judging by what I just saw, Sophia could slaughter anyone with her powers in the blink of an eye.

Maybe I was getting ahead of myself. The prophecy only said that she would bring Koigni glory. Maybe it wasn't as doom-and-gloom as the Toaquas made it sound. What if instead of taking over the tribe, Sophia helped the Koignis learn how to get along with the rest of us?

Doubtful, Liam. You know how Koignis are.

No. Not Sophia. She wasn't that way. Not all Koignis were like that.

Sophia was incredible. She was a wonderful person... and her element was soon going to be unchallenged.

If the wrong Koignis got their hands on her... they could turn her bad. They would try, anyway. I didn't think Sophia would turn— not unless something awful happened to make her that way.

My eyes wandered toward Esis. There were Koignis alive who would hurt him to get Sophia to do what they wanted, I was sure.

It was all the more reason for me to stay close to her.

You can't protect her forever, Liam.

I could fucking try. I'd give my fucking life to defend her now, I knew that. I'd do everything I could to keep the Koigni Elders from getting their filthy hands on her. Anyway, if Sophia did end up going crazy and taking over the tribe, she probably wouldn't kill me if I was her sugar baby. And I'd still be in love with her anyway, so it was a win-win.

I heard branches snapping in the trees ahead of us. I held out an arm to hold Sophia back. "Wait," I said lowly.

She paused. We proceeded with caution toward the noise, peeking out through the branches.

Thank the ancestors, it was Jonah and Imogen! They were alive, huddled up against Squeaks for warmth, Sassy in Imogen's lap. They didn't look hurt or injured. They were awake, but on the verge of nodding off.

I went to go say hi, but Sophia held me back, a mischievous smile on her face. She crept through the bushes until she was right in front of them.

"Boo!" Sophia yelled loudly. Jonah and Imogen both screamed. They toppled over as Squeaks got up and ran for cover. Sassy nearly jumped out of her fur.

Sophia laughed. "Surprise!" she cried. "It's us!"

Jonah's eyes widened in shock, and Imogen's face spread into a wide grin. Sassy gave a happy *yip* as she rushed to greet Esis. Squeaks was so excited to see us, she started doing a dance.

"You assholes!" Jonah roared. "Do you realize how glad we are to see you?!"

Jonah stormed forward and picked both Sophia and me up at the same time, raising us off the ground and hugging us tight. When he dropped us, Imogen latched on to Sophia and clung to her best friend like she was all she had in the world.

"You guys stuck around? Why didn't you go forward?" I asked, baffled.

"We couldn't move on without you guys," Imogen insisted. "We weren't gonna leave you behind until we were sure we had no other choice."

My cold, dead heart was about full of all the affection I could take today, but Imogen's words made it melt a little faster. "Thanks, Imogen."

Jonah pumped his fist in the air. "You have no idea— wait." Jonah paused. His eyes widened as he looked me over. "What happened to you? You look... better."

"It's a long story," I started. "I went into this cave, and I passed out. When I woke up, I was completely fine." I shrugged. "Weird, huh? It must've been magic."

Jonah and Imogen looked at each other. "Yeah. Weird," Jonah said.

"We're almost at the finish line," I continued. "We still have each other. We can still do this. Sophia?"

I looked at her. She seemed so much more sure of herself than she did last night. She stepped forward and said, "I wasn't ready before, but I am now. I can handle my task, guys. It was really rough before, but I have an idea on how we can get through the flames."

Her hand fell over the pocket that held the totem.

"You've got this, Soph," I said finitely. "I trust that you can handle this alone."

"But she doesn't have to," Imogen said, realization dawning on her face.

"We'll work together," Jonah suggested, and his words sped up as he got excited. "I'll send away the smoke so we can breathe, Liam and Imogen can use their elements to try and douse the flames, and Sophia can control it. If we all lend a hand, we can get through the final task together."

Sophia's face glimmered. "You guys mean that?"

"Of course!" Imogen flung her arms around Sophia's and Jonah's shoulders. "What are friends for?"

Squeaks squawked in approval. From her back, Sassy and Esis cuddled up against each other and gave noises of agreement.

"All right," I said, satisfied I didn't have to come up with the plan for once. "If we feel like we can take this, let's get this over with."

The team cheered, and we started walking toward the finish line again. The final task was only a short walk away, but I didn't feel terrified of it anymore. We'd already been through hell and back. We'd seen the worst and come out stronger. Nothing could break our team now. I was sure of it.

"So, Liam..." Jonah said as a really bad way to start off a conversation, and I suppressed a groan of irritation. He held me back, away from the girls as we headed forward. "I can't help but notice something's changed between you and Sophia."

"And how'd you gather that, Jonah?" I asked tiredly. I hadn't even touched her since we got back.

"I sense the sexual tension in the air," Jonah said, and he waggled his eyebrows. "What exactly happened when you guys were separated from us?"

I decided to cut out all the sad stuff and get straight to the point. "We might have kissed."

Jonah gave a girly squeal. "You guys *kissed*? No way."

"Keep your voice down! Yeah, so we kissed, big deal," I snapped back under my breath. "It's not like we banged or anything."

Up ahead, the girls had their heads together and were giggling. I bet anything Sophia was up there telling Imogen every minuscule detail of our make-out session.

I hoped I was impressive. She'd impressed me. I prayed Sophia didn't think I drooled or anything, or worse, that I sucked at kissing. How embarrassing would *that* be? I thought I was pretty good.

"This is just the start," Jonah said, rambling on. "Before you know it, you guys will be making *the cutest* babies. I'll get to be Uncle Jonah."

Jonah's stupid words brought up all sorts of emotions. Part of me was like, *Hell yeah! I hope she lets me put a baby in her!*

But a bigger part was like, *Yeah, never gonna happen.*

"It was just a kiss, dude. Let it go." I sighed.

"Oh, my ancestors. Liam, are you in love?" Jonah's jaw dropped.

"Shut up," I growled.

"You are!" Jonah jumped up and down and clapped his hands. "I'd never thought I'd see the day! My little boy, all grown up!"

"I'm older than you, jackass."

"Aw." Jonah reached out to pinch my cheeks, and I slapped his hand away. He craned his head around. "Hey, girls! Liam's got a crush!"

"Okay, that's it. Team meeting!" I shouted loudly, and everyone turned to look at me. I slashed my hand through the air to get their attention and said, "Newsflash, and as *I'm sure everyone has heard*"— I shot a look at Imogen, and she giggled— "me and Sophia made out in the cave. So what? Can we please move forward and end this thing? I really want to go home."

Jonah smiled like it was his birthday. Imogen was giggling, and Sophia was beet red. I caught her eyes, and we both grinned and looked away.

"Like Liam said, it was *just a kiss*," Jonah said, mocking me. "And... a lot more than that." He scrambled the words together quickly. "But, he's right. We need to get home. We have a ball to get to!"

Imogen *whooped* happily. She jumped on Jonah's back and he piggy-backed her ahead, letting out a victory cry.

Sophia and I stole a glance at each other. She was still pretty red. "Liam Mitoh's got a crush, huh?"

"Yeah I do," I whispered, and I dared to reach out and brush my fingers through hers for a few seconds. I was really fucking glad the cameras only caught visuals and couldn't record audio from so high up, because what we were saying was so incriminating. There'd been talk of hooking the contestants up with microphones a few years ago until the tribe decided it was too expensive. Thank the ancestors they didn't go through with that plan.

The mood got somber as we approached the site of the final task. All jokes fell to the wayside as everyone got serious. We really screwed up last time. It wasn't just Sophia's fault. And we needed to rely on each other to reach the end.

We finally reached it. We stood in a line, watching as flames sprang up out of nowhere before us. They didn't approach, but they didn't move, either. The flag was on top of the mountain just on the other side of them. They were even hotter and angrier than they were before. I could feel the heat from here.

Sophia swallowed. She stepped forward and said, "Let's do this, guys. Together."

Sophia led the way. Her powers pushed against the flames, protecting us as we headed back into the inferno. The rest of us got right to it. Jonah redirected the smoke away from us and manipulated the oxygen so it didn't empower the flames any more than it already was. Imogen piled dirt on top of the fire. The Familiars walked behind, calling encouragement as we continued at a steady pace.

I summoned as much water as I could from the earth and used it to put out as many of the flames as I could, though they basically sprang back up the minute I got rid of them. But with our combined efforts, it was easier than before. It was still hot, but we slowly made progress. The flames were pressing inward and getting closer, but none of us panicked. We just continued calmly as a unit.

We didn't have to say anything, but it was decided between all of us that if one of us didn't get out, none of us got out. We were in this together or not at all. We'd survive as one or die as one. There was no other option.

Mid-way through the flames, Sophia turned and locked eyes with me. Passion ignited between us, hotter than the flames closing in, and it was like I could see the change in her. Something behind her gaze clicked, and I saw her face clear. She knew what to do.

"Guys!" Sophia said. "Pull back your elements! I can do this!"

"Are you sure?" Jonah cried back. "We're doing pretty good as it is!"

Sophia gave a broad smile. "I can handle this. I know I can."

Imogen and Jonah seemed nervous, but I wasn't. I had complete faith in my girl. "She's got it, guys!" I shouted. "Trust her!"

At the same time Jonah, Imogen and I stopped casting, the fires roared to life beside us and rushed in to devour us alive.

But instead of making the flames smaller, Sophia made them bigger.

Imogen, Jonah and I ducked. But we shouldn't have. The flames ricocheted backward and rocketed toward the sky. Yet we didn't feel the heat. The air around us was cool, the temperature regulated. Although there were twenty-foot walls of fire raging around us, it felt like we were walking through a freezer. The flames were so close I could reach out and touch them, but even so, I didn't think they would burn me even if my hand was stuck in the middle of them. Sophia had them under her command.

The sight of Sophia's magic, what she could do… it was nothing less than fucking incredible.

"Stay close to me," Sophia instructed. Her face blazed like the flames she controlled. "We're going home."

Sophia proceeded forward. Esis jumped off of Squeaks and ran to be on Sophia's shoulder, where he belonged. I looked up at the massive fire walls, hardly able to believe what was happening. Was this really real?

Everything felt like it was in slow motion. We must've looked like total badasses for the cameras, walking through the flames with Sophia in the lead like they were nothing to handle. Even I could feel the rage of the Elders as they tried to break through Sophia's magic. But it didn't work. She sustained her protective shield around us with no more than a bat of an eyelash.

This was impossible. A Koigni couldn't do this.

An *Elder* couldn't do this.

But Sophia could. I worried her secret about being the prophesied child wouldn't stay secret for long.

We finally reached the end. Sophia shut her eyes, and as she did, the fires behind her went out completely. My. Jaw. Dropped.

When she opened her eyes again, she smiled. "That's it. The final task is done."

I felt so relieved. I wanted to fall on my ass and cry. Imogen and Jonah jumped up and down, holding on to each other. "We did it, we did it!" they cheered.

I could see the orange flag. It was literally right up there, only thirty feet or so above us. All we had to do was climb. "There's the finish line, guys!" I shouted. "Let's go!"

Squeaks trotted up the mountain like it was nothing. Sassy nipped at Imogen's heels cheerfully, while Imogen and Jonah sang the elements song, off-key and loudly. I started up the mountain at Sophia's side. My body screamed in protest at the hint of climbing one more mountain, but I blew it off and told it to behave, just this once. Nothing could ruin this moment. Not today.

"Sophia, you did great back there," I said as she hiked beside me. "I knew you had it in you all along."

She cleared her throat. "I realized something, Liam," Sophia said. "All this time, I thought anger was the key to Fire. But it's not. When I saw all you guys helping me, I felt such strong emotion for you all, and the ability to handle the flames just came on its own. Passion and love is the key to sustaining a flame. What I feel for you helped me gain control of my powers."

When she said that, I wanted to kiss her again. But we were back on camera, so I just said, "I'm glad, Soph. Really."

The last bit was kind of hard. The rocks were so jagged and craggy that it was almost impossible for anyone to climb them alone.

But we didn't have to do it alone. We helped each other climb, giving a boost and taking turns pulling each other up the mountain. The Familiars helped where they could, giving an extra push or lift when we needed it. It was like we were one long chain, and we got the system down, each of us doing our part to make sure everyone made it to the end. When we got to the summit, Imogen and Jonah reached down and grabbed me by the arms, yanking me to the embankment.

I reached down for Sophia's hand. She wrapped her fingers around my forearm, and I pulled her to the top. The flag waved in front of us in the wind.

We were here. All of us had made it. I gave everyone a look, and said, "On the count of three. One, two, three!"

All four of us grabbed on to the flagpole. From far away, I could hear the drums being played in the arena as a signal that a team had made it to the finish line. A floating carriage instantly came down from the sky, and I felt myself shaking in relief.

Food. A shower. A bed. It was only a short ride away.

We scrambled to get inside the carriage as soon as possible. I didn't even care that I was crushed against Squeaks' ass. Everyone was smiling. I wasn't sure if it was from delirium or happiness, but I didn't care.

You did good, Liam, I told myself, and I realized with a start that I'd done it. I'd kept my team alive for the entire tournament, even myself. Sure, I kinda cheated a little with the magic cave, but specifics.

The carriage floated down into the arena and landed on stage. I looked out the window and noticed that the arena was completely sold out again, full of people looking to welcome the teams home. As the doors opened, we all tumbled out of the carriage and landed on our faces. A graceful exit, as what we were known for.

We clumsily got to our feet. Squeaks shook her feathers, and we could hear it. The entire arena was completely silent. A single raindrop could've fallen and we would've heard it. Every face in the stadium stared back at us with an open mouth, like they couldn't believe it.

Aw, shit. Had we arrived so far behind the other teams that the whole tribe was stunned about how slow we were? When had the other teams showed up? Days ago?

Head Dean Alric hurried onstage. At least he'd stuck around to welcome us. I felt sorry for wasting his time. He was a nice guy.

Alric cleared his throat and spoke into the microphone. "Please welcome this year's winners of the Elemental Cup, the White Team!"

The stadium absolutely erupted. It sounded like the walls were about to come down, the crowd was so loud. The stage shook with the weight of the applause. My legs wavered beneath me, but I don't think it was from the cheering.

"Looks like the White Team went from being the least-favorite team to being adored by the fans." The announcer's voice, Eli, echoed over the stadium. You could barely hear him over the crowd.

"Everyone loves an underdog, Eli," Louis replied. "And this team definitely came from behind to win."

Wait. Winners?!

It took me a minute to realize what was going on. Jonah and Imogen were freaking out. Jonah was blowing kisses to the crowd, Squeaks copying him. Imogen was holding on to Sassy and crying tears of joy. I bet she hoped her brother could see her now.

Sophia had a smug look on her face. She turned to look at me and said, "Told you."

This was too good to be true. We'd won the Cup? I didn't know how we'd beaten the other teams back, but I didn't care. We'd gotten every member of our team through the tournament alive, and we'd *won*. That was practically unheard of.

Baine was hurrying onstage. He was wearing this really outrageous pinstripe suit that was bright turquoise with a blue carnation pinned to the front. He looked like a proud dad. He was carrying a golden trophy that was as big as my torso and had the symbols of all four Houses engraved on it.

"Congratulations," he said as he passed it to me and Sophia. Each of us took a handle. "I told you there was something special about this team."

Sophia and I looked at each other. Simultaneously, we lifted the Cup up to the crowd in victory. The stadium exploded again. I'm pretty sure the sound could be heard from here to San Francisco.

I caught sight of my family in the stands. My brothers and sisters were high-fiving each other, and my mother was weeping. Dad puffed out his chest and nodded to me, giving a thumbs up.

"We won," I said. It was almost like we were in a dream. "We really fucking won."

The reality of everything I'd been through in the past couple of days hit me like a tidal wave, and I wasn't ready for it. I had turned to smile at Sophia, but the Cup had already slipped out of my grasp, and my eyes were rolling in the back of my head. My knees buckled beneath me. I didn't realize I had collapsed until I hit the ground.

I heard Sophia calling my name, and the crowd screaming.

And then, nothing.

sophia
TWENTY-FOUR

Liam Mitoh was perfection in every sense of the word. I didn't care that he could barely walk a half mile most days and breathed as if an elephant was sitting on his chest. He'd just been dealt a bad hand in life. It was what was in his mind and heart that mattered. It was the way he called me *pawee*, as if it meant something more. It was the night he took me up to the mountain to meet my ancestors and dance with them. It was the red-hot passion in the cave when I kissed him. Those were the things that truly mattered.

Which was why when I watched him collapse on that stage, my heart shattered into a million pieces.

I'm so sorry, Liam. I'm sorry I couldn't save you.

I'd cradled him in my arms as Esis placed a tender paw on his forehead. Tears rolled down my cheeks. I didn't even worry that the cameras were watching. Even a week later, guilt settled into my stomach like a heavy rock.

"I can't do this, Imogen," I said nervously, turning away from the mirror.

Imogen's dorm room was smaller than mine, and the decor was almost the complete opposite. Whereas my room assaulted you with shades of red, her room was bathed in lighter, natural tones that had a more welcoming feel. The walls were a wooden texture like the hardwood floors, and her twin bed sat low to the ground, as if to keep her closer to the earth. Various plants were scattered throughout the room, including ivy that framed the window. Late December sunlight spilled into the room, bouncing off the bright white furniture. I wasn't really supposed to be in the Nivita dorms, but Imogen wanted to get ready for the ball together. And now I wasn't even sure I wanted to go— not if Liam wouldn't be there.

"Yes, you can, Sophia." She dusted blush across her cheeks in the bathroom.

Across the room, Esis and Sassy played together, chasing a piece of yarn Imogen had tied phoenix feathers to.

I plopped down on Imogen's bed, taking in shallow breaths, and not just because she tied my dress too tight. "It doesn't feel right without Liam."

"He'll be fine," she said with a wave of her hand. "He'll be out of the hospital in a few days."

Ugh. I didn't need the reminder about how long it'd be before I got to talk to him again. I wasn't allowed to visit him since I wasn't family, so I hadn't seen him since the medics carried him off stage.

"Everyone's going to want to congratulate us for winning," I pointed out. "It doesn't seem fair that he won't be there. He's the one who got us through."

Imogen peered through the bathroom door and frowned at me. "It was a team effort. You know we couldn't have done it without you."

"I know." I sighed. "But I never could've gotten us through the last task if it wasn't for Liam."

"What do you mean?" Imogen asked, turning back to the mirror to apply her makeup. "Was it the kiss?"

My heart lifted in my chest at the thought. That kiss with Liam was everything a first kiss was supposed to be, and more. If I thought Orenda Academy was magical when I arrived, it was nothing compared to Liam's kiss in the cave. That was beyond the realms of magic.

I knotted my hands in my lap. "I... I don't know. I guess something just happened in the cave that helped me realize how to control the fire."

Imogen raised an eyebrow toward the mirror. "What all happened? I thought you guys just kissed." She drew in a sharp breath. "Should I be expecting little Toaqua babies running around here soon? Oh, ancestors. I hope they have Liam's eyes!"

"Imogen!"

She laughed.

The truth was, I hadn't told her about the totem Liam and I had found, though I didn't think that had anything to do with making it through the last task. Still, I didn't feel like I should mention it. It was like the ancestors *wanted* me to find it, but they didn't want me telling anyone I had it. I'd secured a string around it and usually wore it around my neck, tucked under my shirt, but I'd left it in my room for the ball.

"I already told you what happened," I said. "We kissed. That was it."

My stomach sank. Was that really it? Was that all it would ever be? I wanted so much more with Liam, but even if we officially got together, we'd always have to keep it a secret. *Koignis and Toaquas couldn't be together.* It totally sucked.

"What about when Esis healed him?" Imogen asked. "You never really told me about that."

I shrugged. "What's there to tell? Liam was almost dying. Now he's back to normal. Well... almost. Once he gets out of the hospital."

"And when he does, will you finally tell him about Esis?"

My mouth went dry. I wasn't ready to think about that yet. "I... I don't know. I was ready to tell him all about it in the cave, after Esis had healed him. But when he told me he was still in pain, I couldn't bring myself to do it. I don't want him to resent us... because Esis can't cure him completely."

"You have to tell him," Imogen insisted.

I glanced over to Esis, who was tugging at Sassy's tail. "I know. But I want to test it more first and see what Esis' limits are. I don't want Liam to get his hopes up."

"Okay..." She sounded uncertain, but she set her makeup down and stepped out of the bathroom wearing a plush robe. "We can worry about that later. Are you ready to see my dress?"

I sat up straighter. "I'd love to!"

"Okay, but you have to close your eyes."

I placed my hands in front of my face, careful to not mess up my makeup Imogen had spent the last hour applying for me. I heard Imogen's closet door open and the sound of fabric rustling.

She spoke while she changed. "You probably already know this, but everyone likes to represent their House when they go to the ball. Usually, people just dress in their House colors: red, orange, or black for Koigni, green or brown for Nivita, blue or silver for Toaqua, and purple for Yapluma. Well, I wanted to do a little more to represent my House… and the others. So… what do you think?"

I pulled my hands away from my eyes and opened them. My jaw dropped when Imogen twirled. The top half of her dress was made from twigs, as if it were a whicker corset. The skirt was layered in fern leaves so thick that it bulged out at least three feet in all directions. Flowers of all different colors were woven between the leaves, creating intricate colorful patterns. It reminded me of the mural on the wall in the dining hall, with red flowers for Koigni swirling into blue for Toaqua and purple for Yapluma.

"Oh, Imogen," I said breathlessly. "It's beautiful."

"Oh, wait." She turned to her dresser and pulled open the top drawer. When she turned around, she lifted a flower crown to her strawberry-blonde hair. "What do you think?"

I stood and walked over to her. I couldn't take my eyes off her dress. "I love it!"

Even Esis stared up at her in awe.

"Really?" she asked nervously, twirling around for me again. "It's been really hard keeping everything alive."

"Yes, really," I said. "I adore it."

Imogen smiled. "Thanks. So… um… since neither of us have dates, I kind of invited Jonah to escort us to the ball. I hope that's okay."

Just another reminder that Liam wouldn't be there, but if I had to go with anyone, I was glad it was these two.

I forced a smile. "Yeah, it'll be fun."

"Good," Imogen said. "Because he'll be here like… now."

On cue, a knock sounded at the door.

I drew in a mock breath of disapproval. "Imogen. A guy in your dorm room? Such a rebel!"

She swatted a hand at me before crossing the room to open the door. Jonah stood in the hallway with a proud smile on his face. He wore a black suit with a purple tie and a matching calla lily on his lapel. His hair was down from his usual bun, and it hung loose around his shoulders. His beard had been trimmed up nicely. Hot damn. He looked like Aquaman or something. I didn't know why other dudes weren't lining up to take *him* to the ball.

"Ladies, your ride is here." He stepped aside and gestured to Squeaks, who was wearing a purple vest that matched his tie. She was attached to the cutest little pony carriage. I absolutely adored it, but there was no way both Imogen and I would fit, especially with Imogen's dress.

"Just a second," Imogen said. She hurried over to her closet and pulled out a pair of high heels that looked like they'd been carved from wood. She slipped them on. "Okay, ready."

Jonah extended a hand and helped Imogen and me into the carriage. Imogen's dress draped over my legs, but I was surprised to find that we both fit.

"Esis, come on." I gestured to him.

He smoothed down his fur and straightened his blue bowtie, taking one last glance in the mirror before bounding over to me and hopping on my lap. Sassy wore a flowery collar and jumped on Squeaks' back for the ride.

Jonah shut Imogen's door and then turned to us. He folded his hands formally. "Ladies, as winners of the Elemental Cup and now the owners of a *very large* sum of money, which regrettably, I had to split between you, I would like to inform you that you are now officially Elementai Princesses… at least for tonight, that is."

Imogen leaned over to me and whispered, "He talks like we're rich. Does he realize how much my parents and your sister got from betting on us? Talk about *money!*"

Jonah continued like he hadn't heard her. "Fortunately for you, you have breasts." He gestured to Imogen's generous cleavage and wiggled his eyebrows. "Which means guys will be fawning over you two all night long. But unfortunately for you"— he adjusted his tie and held his head up high— "I call dibs."

I burst into a fit of laughter while Imogen plucked a petal from her dress and tossed it at him. He used his Air power to blow it away.

"Oh, shut up," Imogen laughed. "Take us to the ball before I turn into a pumpkin!"

Jonah cleared his throat and turned to Squeaks. "As you wish."

Squeaks pulled us down the hall of the Nivita dorms and past the common room, where a thick tree big enough to have reading nooks cut out in it grew up through the ceiling. The wheels on our little cart squeaked down the hall and filled the quiet air. The castle was pretty much deserted by now, since everyone was attending the ball and we were running a little late. Jonah led us down three different hallways before we reached the third-floor balcony that looked over the grand entrance. I held on tight to the side of the cart and pulled Esis close to my belly when we reached the stairs, half expecting us to tumble down them. But Jonah used his Air power to keep our cart floating while Squeaks trotted down the steps. We took a second flight all the way to the first level, and our wheels touched ground again.

The main entrance buzzed with conversation that spilled out from the ballroom. A few people milled around beneath the elaborate chandelier, and others were looking down on us from high up in the fourth and fifth floor balconies. A couple of people noticed us pull up in our little cart and were staring, but it didn't really bother me. They were probably just looking at Imogen's dress. Or maybe we drew eyes because we were the winners. Whatever. I was used to it by now.

Jonah led Squeaks to the ballroom doors before pulling on the reins. Inside, the sound of soft music played, and I could see a large crowd of people and their Familiars spinning around the dance floor.

"Ladies," Jonah said formally. "Thank you for riding the Hippogriff Express. We do take tips, but we unfortunately cannot provide services at the end of the night if you are feeling a little tipsy, seeing as your host himself will be too drunk to drive." He gestured to himself before extending a hand to help me out of the cart.

Imogen hopped out by herself and snorted at him. "Apparently if we need anything, we know exactly where to find him."

Jonah smirked. "I'll be at the bar, chatting up hot guys and making Renar jealous."

Imogen scanned the dance floor like she hadn't heard him. The ballroom was gorgeous and bigger than any banquet hall I'd ever seen. At least twenty huge golden chandeliers hung from the high ceiling. Various shades of velvety curtains framed long windows, some of which were open to different patios. A string quartet played at one end of the room next to an empty DJ stand, while a bar ran the length of the other. Tables were set up near the bar, where people sipped their drinks and chatted amongst themselves. The setting sun cast a dull glow across the room but reflected off glittering surfaces, from the polished marble floor to the jewelry hanging from girls' necks, bringing the whole room to life.

"Looking for Cade?" I asked.

Imogen twisted her hands together. "Yeah. He never asked me to the ball, but I was hoping he'd at least want to dance with me."

"I'm sure he will. And I think I see him over there." I pointed to a guy in a green tie talking to a girl with a unicorn Familiar beside her.

Imogen's eyes lit up. "Oh, good. I'm going to say hi to him."

She hurried off with Sassy at her heels, and I turned to Jonah. He was struggling with the pony cart, trying to unhook it from Squeaks' hips.

"Um… do you need help?" I asked.

"Nah," Jonah replied. "I've got this. You go ahead."

I hesitated. I didn't really want to interrupt Imogen and Cade, and I had no one else to talk to. But Jonah seemed a little embarrassed that he got the cart stuck, so I turned into the ballroom to give him space.

My eyes scanned the thick crowd. I saw a few people I recognized from my classes. I even noticed Haley sulking near one of the patio entrances. She was wearing the revealing dress I'd seen her in at *Delilah's,* but had her arms crossed and a tight look on her face. Anwara sat on her shoulders, swaying back and forth slightly to the music until Haley swatted at her to stop.

I turned my gaze from Haley and looked to the other side of the ballroom. I knew it was useless, but I was hoping to spot Liam in the crowd. For obvious reasons, I didn't.

My eyes fell upon at least one friendly face, though. *Baine.* He was actually put together today, with his hair slicked back and his stubble freshly shaven. He wore a light blue vest beneath his black suit. I guess when he cleaned up I could kind of see where Imogen crushed on him a little, but he was so *old.*

I was just about to make my way over to him, just so I had someone to talk to, when the sound of my name caught me off guard. I turned to see Madame Doya coming my way. She wore a long, silky dress that matched her fiery red hair. Her makeup was immaculate, and her nails freshly done. She held a glass of champagne that was nearly gone.

I forced a friendly smile, only because I didn't think anyone would appreciate me singeing the ends of her curls. I was so glad I was done with her class, though I had no idea if I would have her again. I hoped not.

"Madame Doya," I greeted pleasantly.

Esis growled from my arms, but I squeezed him lightly until he stopped. I glanced around for Naomi and saw her prowling around by the entrance with a golden headpiece, looking my way every so often with that heavy gaze that reminded me so much of Doya.

"Sophia," Mádame Doya said coolly. "Congratulations."

My whole body tensed. There was no way I heard her correctly. "Um… thanks?"

"I must speak to you about something." Doya grabbed my elbow and started leading me to the corner of the ballroom before I could protest.

I followed, only because I was curious about what she had to say. Would she finally apologize for the way she treated me in her class?

Doya glanced around the room and lowered her voice. "You need to know what winning the Elemental Cup means."

"Uh… okay." I had no idea where she was going with this.

"The Elders weren't sure before if you were truly the prophesied one. Now that you've won the Cup, they will be keeping a very close eye on you. Don't screw it up." Her eyes narrowed.

My jaw went slack. It almost sounded like she expected me to fail.

I fixed her with a challenging gaze. "Screw up how? What does the prophecy mean, exactly? What am I supposed to do?"

Doya sighed and pulled me tighter into the corner. "I, along with the other Koigni Elders, believe there is a war coming between the Houses. Koigni House has more… political sense than the others. But the other Houses are unwilling to work with us. If we had full power, we could bring order to all of Kinpago, but the other Houses won't allow it. If a war breaks out, our numbers could be cut in half. Thousands of Koigni could die, and our House would be shamed to the highest degree. It's up to you, Sophia, to save us."

Oh, shit. Doya wasn't playing around. The thought of thousands of people dying because of me churned my stomach. My House was truly counting on me.

I swallowed, but my throat felt like sandpaper. "What do I have to do?"

Madame Doya's expression hardened. "The prophecy is unclear. I once believed all would be revealed when you arrived, but that's clearly not the case. I now believe that the prophecy is longer than expected, and the Houses are hiding pieces of it from one another. The magical arti-fact you will have to find… that's something Koigni never shared with anyone. The other Houses have been keeping secrets as well. You, Sophia, will need to uncover those secrets to discover how to fulfill the prophecy and prevent total Elementai annihilation."

Her words echoed through my head. *Total Elementai annihilation.* My knees shook. I nearly forgot I was standing in a room full of people. She couldn't truly believe that if I failed, this entire magical society would fall, could she?

My eyes met hers, and I witnessed a fire behind them that told me everything I needed to know. She totally and thoroughly believed every word she said. Sure, this place had its issues, but there were thousands of people living in Kinpago, not to mention the magical creatures. I couldn't let this magical place be destroyed, the place that Liam, Imogen, and Jonah called home… and the place I thought was home as well.

But… Doya was jumping from one impossible task to another. There was no way I could do what she was asking of me.

"I'm not really cut out for this," I said. "I barely know anything about Hawkei history. I'm only a First Year."

Doya held her head high. "I will train you."

Wait… what? This lady was talking crazy talk.

My brow furrowed. "Um… okay. Why didn't you offer earlier?"

Doya pursed her lips. "You had yet to prove yourself on your own. I was trying to protect you."

The crease between my eyebrows deepened. "Protect me from what?" I demanded. I couldn't help it when the words burst out of me. Doya made no sense, and it was enough to make my Fire rise to the surface. I pushed it down before we both lit up in flames. "You spent the entire semester pushing me away and making me feel like a failure. Now you claim it was for my own protection?"

Doya cleared her throat and glanced around, as if making sure I hadn't caught anyone's attention. I didn't care if I did. I just wanted Doya to tell me the truth.

She returned her gaze to mine and lifted her chin. "I can't reveal everything at this time. Just remember, Sophia, the Elders are watching. You must be cautious. And you must not tell anyone what I've just told you. Do you understand?"

The pointed expression she gave me was almost enough to burn a hole straight through me — and it may have, if I weren't Koigni. It was clear that I didn't have a choice. I had to find the missing pieces of the prophecy and fulfill it. Either she or the Elders would make sure I would.

"I'll be careful." I purposely didn't answer her question directly.

"Good," she said in a clipped tone. "Enjoy your night. It may be one of the last you have before everything changes."

Doya turned from me and started toward Naomi by the doors, leaving me completely frozen in place and shocked by her words. Esis growled at her, pulling me back to attention.

"Relax, buddy," I told him while I stroked the fur around his nubby horns. "She doesn't mean it. She's just got a stick up her ass, and she has to say stuff like that to make herself feel better."

I was a liar, and there was no doubt in my mind that Esis knew it. Doya didn't joke around… ever.

My gaze scanned the ballroom nervously. I worried that everyone could see my arms shaking and the sweat breaking out across my brow. Then my eyes fell upon a champagne glass in a Toaqua girl's hand.

Alcohol. I needed some.

Pulling Esis closer to my chest, I navigated through the crowd and to the bar. I'd never had alcohol before, unless you counted that sip of beer I had at my friend Emily's when we were sixteen. I didn't even swallow it because it tasted like piss. But maybe champagne would taste better. At least it would take the edge off.

"Hey, Sophia!" Jonah called from where he sat at the bar.

I squeezed between a group of people and stopped next to him. "I need a drink."

Jonah eyed me curiously and raised his glass to his lips. "What's wrong?"

"What?" I asked innocently, brushing hair out of my eyes. "Nothing's wrong? Why would you think that?"

Esis poked my arm, as if calling me out as a liar. *Yeah, yeah.*

"I didn't take you as a drinker is all," Jonah replied with a shrug.

"Yeah, well, it's to celebrate," I told him. "We won. I think I deserve a drink."

Jonah nodded his approval. "What can I get you?"

I thought about it for a moment, but Jonah was right. I wasn't a drinker and didn't have the faintest clue of what to get. "Um… something that doesn't taste like piss?"

Jonah let out a deep-belly laugh. "That doesn't leave many options."

I swore my face went pale, which only made him laugh harder.

"I'm kidding. How about I surprise you?" he asked.

"Okay," I agreed.

While Jonah waved down the bartender, somebody reached past me to place a tip on the counter. The bar was so crowded that his body pressed against mine. Heat radiated across my skin as his shirt brushed across my shoulder and his breath ran across the side of my cheek. Somehow, without even looking, I *knew* it was him. It was like my body was in tune to his. It had to be, considering the way my heart fluttered and my head spun just from the close proximity.

I whirled around, beaming. "Liam!"

Esis leapt from my arms onto Liam's shoulder. I flung my arms around his neck, squeezing them both tightly. His pine forest scent filled my nose. Liam gasped, and I quickly pulled away. Esis stayed put on his shoulder, pulling at strands of his long black hair.

Liam's eyes were bright, and a smile stretched wide across his face. He looked so amazing that I could almost believe he wasn't sick anymore. Liam looked me up and down, and desire flickered across his eyes. He totally loved my dress.

I liked his outfit, too. He wore black slacks and a white collared shirt, with the sleeves rolled up to his elbows. Hot damn. Why were forearms so sexy? A red tie hung around his neck. I'd never seen him wear the color before. Dare I say it actually looked really good on him?

"I thought you weren't coming," I said, still trying to get over the initial shock of seeing him here. It was like a dream.

Liam shrugged and pulled his hair out of Esis' grasp. "I snuck out."

My heart sank. "Oh. So they didn't discharge you? How are you feeling?"

Liam wrinkled his nose, but that radiance about him never faded. "I'm fine."

I rolled my eyes. "Which is code for, *I feel terrible and don't want anyone knowing.*"

Liam hesitated, then dropped his shoulders. "Maybe. I'm the same as always, I guess. I'll survive."

Jonah stood and held out a hand toward Liam. He took it, and they did that weird guy handshake-hug thing.

"We're so glad you made it, man," Jonah said before sitting back down at his stool. "And you wore the tie."

Liam smoothed out the red fabric and avoided my gaze. "Yeah… I, uh, it was all I could find on short notice."

"Obviously," Jonah said. I didn't miss the wink he shot Liam's way, as if they shared some secret I wasn't a part of.

"I'm so glad you're here to celebrate with us." I resisted the urge to throw my arms around his neck again. With Liam here, I didn't need the alcohol to take the edge off. Just his very presence made me forget all about the bad in the world. "I still can't believe we won."

Liam scoffed. "Yeah, well, it's easier when you're not trying to kill off your teammates."

Jonah took another sip of his drink. "Thanks, by the way, guys. You know, for not killing me."

I swatted at him playfully. "Stop it! We would never do that." I lowered my voice and hissed, "We're not Haley."

"I need to tell you something about that." Liam glanced around to make sure no one was listening and leaned in. Even if someone was eavesdropping, there was no way they could hear over the chatter around us. "All of Haley's teammates are dead."

I drew in a sharp breath. "But that Nivita guy—"

"Didn't make it," Liam interrupted. "Haley only passed because she got him to the finish line alive. But only barely. He was in the hospital with me. He passed away a few days after the tournament."

My hand shot over my mouth. "That's horrible."

Liam and Jonah nodded in unison. Meanwhile, my eyes scanned the crowd for Haley. She was no longer standing by the patio, and I didn't see her anywhere else.

"Sophia." Liam pulled my attention to him. "Don't go looking for trouble. Second place is still a highly honorable position. Haley has proven herself to the tribe and will become Chieftess of Koigni after her mother steps down. It wouldn't look good for you to pick a fight with her."

I gaped at him. "I wasn't going to…"

Okay, yeah. Maybe I was. I just wanted to see her show some remorse.

But Haley could wait for another time. I wasn't going to let her ruin the magic of this night.

I reached for Liam's hand and started toward the dance floor, but he remained firmly rooted in place. "Come on." I tugged at him. "Let's dance."

Liam stumbled a step but quickly righted himself. "No, Sophia. We can't."

My bottom lip jutted out. "Why not?"

Liam lowered his voice. "Don't you notice something about the couples?"

I looked toward the dance floor and didn't see anything out of the ordinary at first… until I realized it was all color coordinated. "So they're all dancing with members of their own House. Who cares? We were on the same team. We deserve to celebrate together."

Liam bit the inside of his lower lip.

I crossed my arms. "Well, if you're not going to dance with me, I want to dance with Esis. And seeing as he's not going to leave your shoulder, you'll have to dance with me, too."

Esis peeked out from a curtain of Liam's hair.

Liam sighed, and smiled a little. "I guess I can't really say no to that."

I pulled Liam out onto the dance floor. His left hand came up to meet my right, and his other hand settled high on my back. Electric tingles spread up and down my spine. Oh, ancestors. How was I supposed to dance with my heart going haywire? Seriously. The damn thing was trying to beat its way out of my chest. Surely Liam could feel my blood raging through my veins. He was Toaqua and sensitive to all the water in my body. He had to feel the shift in energy.

His hand dropped further down my back as we started to spin, and I gasped. Oh, what I wouldn't give to let those hands roam over me.

Liam gazed down at me with soft eyes, and I stared back into his. The whole ballroom seemed to fade away around us. It felt like I was in a fairytale, floating across the room like a princess who'd found her prince. If I could just lean in and kiss him again, the way we did in the cave—

"Ow!" I cried as Liam's feet stumbled over my toes.

He hopped backward. "Sorry. I'm so sorry."

I giggled as Esis leaned over Liam's shoulder to get a good look at my feet. "It's okay. I'll be fine."

Except my toe was throbbing. It seemed as if *I'm fine* was starting to become a code word between us.

"Good," Liam said, "because people are staring."

As much as I didn't want to take my eyes off him, I did. People were, indeed, staring. I even saw one Koigni girl pointing our way.

"Seriously?" I asked with an eye roll. "You barely stepped on me. We can't be dancing *that* bad."

Liam's lips tightened. "It's not that. What we're doing, Sophia… it's kind of an act of rebellion."

"An act of rebellion?" I asked. "By dancing together?"

Liam shrugged but continued twirling me around the dance floor. "We're wearing each other's House colors *and* dancing together. It kind of looks like… something."

"Well, it is something, isn't it?" I asked. "I mean, *shouldn't* we challenge House boundaries? How else are we going to be together?"

Liam's entire body tensed, but he didn't stop dancing. "Do you… uh… want to get out of here for a second? Away from all these prying eyes?"

What was he suggesting? Every instinct told me to answer with a *hell, yes!*

Instead, I just said, "I guess so." All the while, my heart was beating ferociously. *Liam Mitoh wants to get me alone!*

Liam led me off the dance floor. We passed through the patio doors and out into the gardens. It was cold outside, but not chilly enough to cover up. Either I was too hot from my Fire rising to the surface under Liam's touch, or the Elders had allowed a small weather change for the event. Either way, I found the evening air peaceful.

There weren't many people out in the gardens. The farther we walked from the doors, the fewer people there were.

"Where are you taking me, Liam?" I was partially worried and partially excited. He was walking too fast for a leisurely night stroll, so he either wanted to break some bad news or break some more rules.

Liam stopped me behind a big bush sculpture of a pegasus. The wide wings and the darkening sky helped conceal us from the people back in the ballroom. Esis jumped off Liam's shoulder and climbed up the pegasus sculpture's wings, then hopped from the end of it to the next sculpture of a horned bear.

Liam took my hands in his. "Sophia, what you just said about us being together… I don't think you understand."

My brow furrowed. "What's there to understand, Liam? It's against the rules. So we'll change the rules. No big deal."

"*No big deal?*" Liam hissed. "Sophia, this is the way it's been for hundreds of years. These rules aren't just about controlling us. It's to keep our powers stronger so that no other House dies out after Anichi."

I shrugged. "So we just don't have kids. Simple."

Holy crap. Were we seriously talking about having kids? We'd only kissed once! But damn it, that was all we needed. It didn't matter what Liam said about the House rules. There was no turning back from the line we'd already crossed.

Liam raked his fingers through his hair. God, he looked sexy when he did that. I wanted to run *my* hands through his hair… and down his forearms… and in other places I probably shouldn't be thinking about. Which could definitely lead to kids someday.

"It's not that simple, though," Liam said. "The Elders would never allow it. This isn't just about us, Sophia. If we started dating, then so would other people."

"So what? Is there actually any evidence that children from two Houses are weaker?"

Liam opened his mouth, but hesitated.

I raised an eyebrow. "Liam, I don't care about the rules. I want to be with you."

"Ancestors, Sophia. You can't talk like that."

"Why not? It's the truth."

"Because…" Liam sighed and glanced toward the castle. No one was close enough to hear. "Because if you say things like that, it just might come true."

"I know. I wouldn't say it if I didn't want it to happen, Liam."

He stared down at me, his expression hard to read. He looked conflicted— like he wanted to agree with me but argue at the same time.

A thought suddenly occurred, and I drew away from him. "Do you… do you not want to be with me?"

Liam looked hurt by the question. "Of course I do. But we don't have a choice."

I relaxed slightly. "You always have a choice, Liam."

His hands balled into fists, and his lips tightened until he couldn't hold it in any longer. "Aw, fuck, Sophia."

Liam growled. He honest to God growled. And then like a wolf trapping his prey, he pounced on me. One second he was standing a few feet away from me, and the next he'd swept me into his arms and claimed my lips for his own.

The world spun around me so quickly that I could no longer feel the stone path beneath my feet. Liam held me tightly to his chest. One hand tangled in the hair at the base of my neck while the other settled on my hip. His lips parted, and I took the invitation to deepen the kiss. My hands ran up his back until they climbed so high they reached the side of his face. I pulled him in even closer until every possible inch of our bodies were touching. My hands moved to his hair, tangling into the strands like he did with mine. He inhaled a sharp breath in response.

Heat exploded through my chest like fireworks. I didn't even care if my Fire surfaced and burned my dress off of me. Liam would like that, I was sure. And damn it, so would I. But my Fire didn't escape. It hung out just below the surface, just enough to feel amazing and to warm Liam's cool skin.

Kissing Liam was like witnessing a fire tornado colliding with a hurricane. We stood in the calm eye of the storm while the elements combined and raged around us. The fire stood no chance against the rain, but the rain couldn't put out the fire. It burned brighter when the rain touched it until the two elements matched each other's rhythm and swirled together to become one. The way Liam made me feel was breathtaking and… impossible. Yet here we were, Fire and Water. We shouldn't mix, but we did. We *so* did.

Liam's tongue grazed my bottom lip, and I moaned. Which only made him wrap his arms tighter around me. His hand hesitated on my hip, as if he wanted to touch me in other places but wasn't sure he was allowed. I didn't know what I was doing until I did it. I untangled my fingers from his hair and guided his hand to my backside. It surprised me considering I didn't know until that very moment how comfortable I'd become with him. I knew Liam would never hurt me, and there was so much I wanted to share with him. My heart... my soul... my body. He just sort of rested his hand there, like he didn't know how far to take this.

Read my signals, Liam! I want more!

I wrapped my hand around the collar of his shirt until I had a fistful of tie, and I tugged him even closer— if that were possible. Liam gasped.

Squeeze my ass, damn it!

Message received. Liam's hand tightened on my butt as my tongue slid deeper into his mouth. Heat traveled down my chest and settled between my thighs. Being with Liam like this was unlike anything else. It was so overwhelmingly amazing that I thought I might cry. Feeling this way should be illegal—

No sooner did the thought cross my mind did it hit me that that was exactly what this *was*. It was illegal. Liam and I were breaking the law by kissing like this... by kissing at all.

Elders be damned. Breaking the law was great. If I knew it'd feel like this, I would've rebelled sooner.

Esis chittered, pulling me out of the spell Liam had put on me. We both jumped away from each other. Esis was sitting on the bear statue's head, staring at us with interest.

After a moment, Esis put his hands together and began a slow clap, then rose to his feet and cheered for us. My face went beet red, as did Liam's.

"Esis," I scolded. "Calm down. It's not a big deal."

I apparently lied a lot.

Esis hopped down from the bear bush and scurried over to me. I bent and scooped him into my arms.

"We should... probably get back..." Liam sounded out of breath.

"Yeah," I agreed in the same shaky tone. "We probably should."

Liam gestured to my hair. "You should probably..."

I smoothed down the strands. "Yeah. You too."

Liam ran his fingers through his hair and started toward the ballroom. If he thought that was the end of this, he had another thing coming.

"So... what was that, Liam? Was it a farewell kiss?"

He didn't meet my gaze. "I— I don't know."

"Well, will it happen again?"

Shut up, Sophia. You're ruining it.

Liam stopped and turned toward me. He gazed down at my hands, but we were where people could see us again, so he didn't take them. "It's up to you, Sophia. I'll never be able to resist you."

My heart swooned at his words. "I guess you'll just have to wait and see what happens, then." I smirked. "Let's get back inside before Imogen and Jonah start accusing us of things."

Liam laughed. "They wouldn't exactly be wrong, would they?"

"No. Definitely not."

We walked past a group of Koigni in the gardens. The guy from the Silver Team, the one with the big dragon familiar, shot us a look of disgust. I'd heard he came in third place and lost one of his teammates. I bet he wasn't too happy we won.

I entwined my fingers in Liam's hand and breezed right by him. Liam squeezed my fingers back, but dropped them as soon as we entered the ballroom. I spotted Imogen and Jonah by the bar, Sassy and Squeaks nearby. We started making our way over to them.

Before we reached them, Haley stepped in front of us. Anwara ruffled her feathers, and Haley crossed her arms.

"Congratulations, *White Team*." Haley didn't sound the least bit genuine, but I'd already made it a point not to let her ruin my night.

"Thank you," I said kindly.

Haley blinked a few times, like she didn't think she'd heard me right. "I wasn't actually complimenting you, you wolpertinger. Do you know how embarrassing it's been to lose to a bunch of misfits?"

"Haley, do we have to do this?" Liam protested.

I shrugged, but inside, my Fire raged. "That must be the worst. You know, right after killing all your teammates."

Haley's face twisted in anger. "Anything's fair game out there. I did what I had to do to win."

"And you still didn't," I snapped.

Haley's eyebrows shot up, and a fireball formed in her hand. She was going to use it.

Liam quickly pulled water from six champagne glasses in people's hands around us and doused the flames. Water splashed up on Haley's dress, and she shrieked. All around us, people were starting to stare. A few took in sharp breaths, but the ballroom was big enough and plenty was going on that our little confrontation barely stirred the crowd.

Haley held out her other hand, but before she could conjure flame my hand shot out and clamped around hers. I pushed back against her heat, stopping her Fire in its tracks. To anyone else, it looked like a mere handshake, as if I were apologizing for the mishap, but I made sure to put as much strength and hostility into my grip as I could. I even added a bit of my own heat for good measure— only as a warning. Then I leaned in close enough for only Haley and Liam to hear.

"This isn't the Elemental Cup anymore," I hissed. "You can't just do whatever you want. But should you decide to, I will be there to extinguish your flame. Every. Single. Time. I know you're watching me, Haley, and I'm not afraid of you. Be careful, or you just might get burned."

And then I swept past her with Liam at my heels, leaving her standing there wet and dumb-struck. Esis clapped from where he was cradled in the crook of my elbow.

"Holy ancestors, Sophia," Liam whispered. "That was hot."

I smirked. There was surprisingly a lot more where that came from.

Imogen rushed away from Jonah and squealed when she reached us. "Tell me I just saw what I think I saw!"

Jonah was close behind her. "Did you just tell Haley off?"

I beamed, still riding the high of Liam's kiss and standing up to Haley. "Yeah… I think I did."

"That's my girl," Jonah said, clapping me on the back.

"Just as long as, you know, you don't start shooting fireballs at each other across the dance floor," Imogen teased.

"I won't be throwing anything at Haley," I promised, "but I can't say I won't be setting the dance floor on fire. It looks like the DJ is about to take over." I pointed toward the guy tinkering with a computer behind a pair of huge speakers.

"Yes!" Imogen gushed. "We should've choreographed something."

"Aw, man," I said. "That would've been fun."

"If you're all going to dance, I'm going to need a drink," Liam announced before turning to me. "Can I get you anything, *pawee*?"

Imogen's eyes went wide beside him.

"Yeah… uh, surprise me?" I suggested.

"Sure." Liam headed toward the bar.

Imogen and Jonah watched him go, then whirled back toward me in unison.

"Oh, my ancestors, Sophia," Imogen raved. "He called you *pawee*. That is so sweet!"

I glanced between the two of them, feeling like I was missing something. "Yeah, so? He calls me that because I'm so inexperienced— like a child, he said."

"But that's not the only meaning," Jonah pointed out.

"It isn't?" I asked, uncertain. Whatever the second meaning was was probably horrible. They seemed too shocked for it to be anything else. "What's the other meaning?"

Imogen exchanged a glance with Jonah before she finally spoke. "*Cherished one.*"

"He's basically calling you his soulmate," Jonah whispered. "It's like, the most beloved word a Hawkei can use to describe someone."

My heart tumbled around in my chest as I stared at Liam, who was leaning against the bar. No way did he mean it like that. *No way.*

But then he lifted his gaze and smiled at me, and I knew. Whether Liam admitted it or not, he was in love with me.

Come hell or high water, we would be together. This society couldn't stop us. Even the prophecy couldn't stand in our way. Sure, my knees buckled just thinking about what was to come— about the prophecy, and the people who might die because of it. But more than anything, I didn't want to see Liam hurt. We were in this together, now until the end.

No matter what the Elders did to keep us apart, I would watch this society burn before I ever found myself separated from Liam Mitoh. It didn't matter if we were *allowed* to be together.

I would forever be his *pawee*.

Liam

TWENTY-FIVE

I was tired. My muscles were sore, and it took a lot of effort just to move around. Every now and again the room would spin a little.

Yeah, I felt like shit. But I felt like shit everyday, so that wasn't new. This was one of the most amazing nights of my life, and I wasn't about to miss this. Not for the world.

My doctors were gonna flip when they found out I'd not only snuck out, but also had been drinking, but I won the damn Elemental Cup for crying out loud. I deserved a beer.

I snuck another glance at Sophia out of the corner of my eye. I'd been staring at her all night, but I couldn't keep my eyes off her. Her chestnut hair was in large curls, and she wore sparkling eyeshadow that brought out her chocolate eyes.

Her dress was phenomenal. I was *so* into the fact she was wearing blue. Turned me on. And I think she liked that I was wearing red, too. I was really glad Jonah had told me to wear a red tie, though I didn't get why at the time. He and Imogen must've set this up. Wearing Koigni red when I was Toaqua was huge— just like Sophia wearing blue wouldn't go missed.

Not to mention we couldn't seem to part from each other for a second. We were basically wearing signs that screamed we were together.

I took a shot for courage. Whatever. I didn't want to think about that right now. I just wanted to enjoy the rest of the night.

I took the beer and the mixed drink the bartender handed me and walked back to Sophia. I noticed there was something different about her. She was looking at me... a bit weird. Like she'd just found out some big secret or something. Were those *tears*?

Fuck, I must've done something wrong. I held out the drink for her to take. I was so nervous I ended up spilling part of her drink on her dress.

"Oh, shit, sorry," I said hastily. I grabbed a napkin off a table and started dotting her midriff, trying to clean up the mess. I hoped it didn't stain.

Sophia actually laughed instead of yelling at me for ruining her gown. "Don't worry about it." She took a small taste of her drink, and her face lit up. Her earlier weirdness was forgotten.

"I hope you like it," I said. Ancestors, I was embarrassed. I threw the soaked napkin on the table.

"What is it?" she asked, taking a sip.

"Sex on the Beach," I rattled off mindlessly, and Sophia gave me a grin. I reddened a bit and said, "Don't take it like that. It's fruity and girly. Something I thought you'd like."

"It's something I'd like, all right," she said coyly, chewing on her straw. She was eyeing me provocatively.

"Down, virgin," I told her. "You don't even know what you're asking for."

She blushed a little, but then added, "I thought virgins were supposed to be hot to guys."

It was *totally* hot, but I didn't need to encourage us. We were already bad enough. "Come on, *pawee*." I laughed and took her arm, guiding her to the table where Imogen and Jonah were.

Her smile got even broader when I called her my little pet name. Had someone told her something?

Imogen and Jonah were at the table, drinking and chatting. Sassy and Esis were both on top of the table, and it looked like they were having a drinking contest.

"Chug, chug, chug," Jonah chanted, pounding the table. Sassy gurgled and fell over, spilling her mug of ale, but Esis managed to finish his and let out a loud burp, patting his stomach happily.

Cade had joined them at the table, along with my brother. Ezra had a girl on either side of him, both of whom I was pretty sure were his dates. Player.

Cade had his arm around Imogen's waist at the table. She leaned against him, looking super happy. Were they a thing yet, or…?

A Nivita girl in a green gown came up to the table and put her hand on Cade's shoulder. "Hi, Cade," she said, batting her eyelashes. She totally ignored that Imogen was all over him. "Would you like to dance?"

"He's kind of busy at the moment," Jonah snapped at her. The girl's eyes narrowed at him.

"No, it's okay." Imogen pulled away from Cade and looked down. "You can go if you want, Cade."

Cade seemed puzzled— like he didn't know what to do. If I could read his mind, I would've sworn he thought Imogen was sending him away. "Oh… okay." He got up and walked away with the girl, and Imogen frowned sadly.

Ugh, Imogen, get it together. You practically just let him walk away!

"You look really beautiful tonight, Im," I said, to try and bolster her confidence. "Your dress is great."

"Oh, thanks." Imogen smoothed out a flower on it bashfully. "I guess. Maybe I should've worn something more traditional."

"Bitch, please," Jonah said, and he flipped his hair over his shoulder. "You're the prettiest slut in this room."

Imogen forced a smile for him, but I couldn't help but notice her eyes followed Cade as he half-heartedly danced with the Nivita girl. If I didn't know any better, I would figure Cade wanted to ask Imogen to dance… he was just scared that she was so shy, she'd say no.

I looked at Sophia, and she shrugged sadly, in a way that said we couldn't help Imogen if she wasn't ready.

Ezra gave me a sly grin as I pulled my chair closer to Sophia. "How *you* two doing?"

"We're fine, Ezra," I said, putting emphasis on the words so he wouldn't ask questions.

But Ezra was a pain in my ass, so he kept prodding. "You two were gone for a while."

"Yep, just slipped out for a minute," I told him sharply, and he snickered. Sophia gave me side-eye, asking questions with her gaze.

I'd told Ezra about the kiss Sophia and I shared during the tournament. I didn't mean to, it'd just slipped out when I was still kind of out of it and doped up in the hospital. I was lucky he was the only family member around at the time, though he hadn't stopped teasing me about it since.

Still, I trusted him to keep his mouth shut. So that brought the total number of people who knew to… three.

That was a dangerous number. Luckily, the two Toaqua girls were too busy fawning over my brother to read too much into what we were saying.

Ezra stood up. "Ladies." He offered an arm to each girl, and they took it as they swaggered toward the dance floor. Three more Toaqua girls materialized around my brother, and I swear all of them were fine taking turns dancing with him.

Jonah leaned in once Ezra was gone. "Dude, does he know?" he asked, thumbing at Ezra.

"Yes," I said lowly, before I grimaced and glanced at my girlfrie— I mean, Sophia. "Sorry, Soph."

"I don't care," she said, and she waved her hand. "I'm fine with your brother knowing."

Of course she didn't mind, because she didn't know what that meant. "The more people who know about… us… the more we're at risk," I told her.

"Is there an *us*?" Imogen asked curiously, her happiness back. She and Jonah leaned forward like they couldn't wait to hear all the juicy details.

"Who are you guys, the Hawkei tabloid reporters?" I asked. "You two know because there was no keeping it from you during the tournament, but now that we're back home you need to mind your own business."

Thankfully, that was the moment the music changed from classical to modern, and the lights darkened, giving the ballroom a club-like atmosphere. Jonah jumped up from his seat like he'd been electrocuted, gossip about my love life forgotten.

"This is my song!" he squealed, and ran onto the dance floor. Squeaks followed, racing after her Elementai almost deliriously.

Imogen jumped up from the table and grabbed Sophia's hand. "Come on!" The two girls raced off after Jonah. Esis and Sassy scampered to follow. I got up to lean against a pillar and watch them from afar.

Imogen and Sophia didn't hold back at all. The girls bounced up and down to the music, grinding against each other like we were at a strip club. They pounded their fists into the air, did a waltz, and then the tango. At one point Imogen got down and did the worm, rising up on all fours to shake her butt. Sophia slapped it, and they almost fell over laughing. They were fun to watch. It's like they didn't care about what people thought of them, only having fun.

Jonah was worse than the both of them. He was twerking in the middle of the dance floor, shaking his ass so hard I'm surprised it didn't fall off. Squeaks copied him, wiggling her hindquarters until the music increased in tempo and she did her best moonwalk.

It didn't help that Jonah was requesting the filthiest songs he could think of. The DJ made faces, but since Jonah was a Cup Champion, he couldn't protest. Some other gay dude in a purple suit, with eye glitter and false eyelashes, sauntered onto the floor with his griffin Familiar. He did some crazy sick moves, gliding along the floor like he had choreographed steps for each song. Jonah copied him until half the dance floor stood back to watch them in complete awe.

I was pretty sure Jonah had spent the last few months practicing his moves more than preparing for the cup. It pissed me off a little, but the tournament was over now, so whatever. He could have his fun.

People were watching on the sidelines, whispering to each other and laughing under their breath at my team's ridiculous dance moves. But fuck them. They were having the time of their lives out there.

"Hey, you were on their team. Do you think Sophia Henley and Imogen Ahnild are lesbians?" a dude I didn't even know leaned over and asked me when Sophia and Imogen started doing some sort of sexy dance against each other. His friend was next to him, watching me carefully for a response.

"Um, no fucking way," I said, irritated. "They're just friends."

"I swear that Sophia girl is bisexual," the other bro said, nodding his head as if that sealed the deal.

Couldn't confirm that for sure, but at least I knew she liked dick. I mean... I *couldn't* say for certain, because I hadn't shown that part of me to her yet and didn't know that she wouldn't run off screaming, but I was pretty sure she was into dudes. The way she was dirty dancing with Imogen, though, even made me wonder.

Imogen knelt down on the floor. She pulled a small box from her dress and presented it to Sophia, opening it like it contained a wedding ring. There was a small bracelet inside, one it looked like Imogen had made, with Koigni and Nivita charms attached. Sophia squealed and pretended to accept the fake proposal tearfully. It made me chuckle how close they were.

"See. Total lesbians," the bro added.

Great. The way this school was, half the student body would be utterly convinced the girls were engaged and getting married next summer. People were so stupid. They were just girls being girls.

Though if the Elders did suspect they were engaged lesbians from different Houses (which, if it did happen, I was leaving this whole society) at least it wouldn't be as severe... because they couldn't reproduce together. They'd probably just end up with some jail time and a fine.

It was different with us. I could get her pregnant. And that's what the Elders feared the most.

"Sophia *is* cute, though," the bro said, interrupting my thoughts. "Too bad she's from Koigni."

"For sure. What I'd give to get my hands on that body. Sucks she's not Nivita," the other dude groaned.

"Hey, back off," I growled. The guys stared at me with open mouths, and I stomped off before my big mouth could get me into more trouble. I couldn't be protective or jealous. Not in public.

And it sucked. I had noticed that half the guys in here were eyeing Sophia, especially the Koigni guys who knew they actually had a chance.

But maybe they didn't have a chance, because her heart belonged to me.

Watching her out there, enjoying herself with Imogen and Jonah, made me think back to our second kiss in the garden and how perfect it'd been. In the moment, I couldn't control myself. After a week of not feeling those lips against mine, I just had to kiss her. When she'd practically forced me to grab her ass, I nearly came right then and there. Sophia had the *most perfect* ass. It was better than even my dreams had been. I was scared to touch her, because I worried she'd get triggered because of what that creep had done to her on prom night.

But she didn't. She wanted me just as badly as I wanted her. Which boggled my mind. How could someone as incredible as her love me?

Sophia gestured for me to join her and Imogen. I shook my head, and she frowned. She seemed hurt.

Sophia didn't understand. She thought I didn't want to be with her. That wasn't it at all. She wasn't taking this seriously. If people found out about us, we could be banished or imprisoned. Worse, we could be executed.

She would be separated from Esis. I didn't have anything to lose in this game, but I wouldn't do that to her.

Still… her words gave me hope. Maybe there was a way we could change the rules. Maybe the tribe would make an exception for us.

It was doubtful.

Sophia kept glancing at me. It made me feel bad. She really wanted me out there with her.

Fuck it. I went to the bar, ordered another shot, and took it before I strolled onto the dance floor.

At this point, Sophia and Imogen did some sort of coordinated dance— though I was pretty sure Imogen had made it up off the top of her head and that Sophia was just following along. Esis and Sassy copied them, trying to duplicate the moves their Elementai were making. Jonah had joined in, and with Squeaks as backup, they looked like a horribly uncoordinated boy band.

Sophia saw me coming. She reached out and grabbed my hand, pulling me in.

I was a terrible dancer. I couldn't keep up with the rest of them, but I still tried to follow Imogen's movements, trying to play along. People moved off the dance floor and gave us room as we started tripping over each other, then getting down the rhythm of the dance. At the end of the song, we pretty much fell against each other laughing. I was breathless, and Sophia gasped for air. Her eyes sparkled, like she wished this night would never end.

If I was a sap, I'd say something nauseating, like I believed in that moment the four of us would be friends forever.

The lights came up again. Dinner was ready. We staggered off the dance floor and returned to our table. Baine was sitting there waiting for us. As our tournament mentor, he was supposed to eat with us.

"People were staring at Imogen and me when we were dancing," Sophia said before we sat down. "Like we were freaks."

"They're just jealous they don't have the courage to dance like that," I told her gently. "Don't let them bother you. Their opinions don't matter."

We sat down, and Baine grinned at us. "Enjoying the ball?"

"Yes," we all responded in unison. Servers started bringing us plates of roast corn, ground cake, buffalo steak, a sweet berry mixture, and a bowl of mutton stew.

Oh, thank the ancestors. I hadn't had such a good meal in like, weeks. The hospital food wasn't bad, but it was nothing like the school's cooking.

Baine immediately dug in. He wasn't as bad of an eater as I was, but he ate loudly and had to constantly use his napkin to smear away the juices on his face. I couldn't understand this obsession women had over him.

"By the way… how did we win, Professor? I thought for sure we'd come in last," I asked before taking a bite. I tried to eat more politely this time, seeing as we were at a ball after all.

"You mean you didn't watch the recaps?" Baine's eyes widened.

I glanced at my teammates, and we all shared the same expression. I didn't have to ask. None of us wanted to watch the replay of our Cup win. We probably would, someday. Right now, it was just too fresh.

"Well, let's see." Baine raised his fingers and started ticking off names. "The Yellow Team failed at the first task. None of them made it out of the ocean alive."

A pit sank in my stomach. That's what I'd been afraid of.

Baine continued, as if he wasn't talking about college kids dying and just making polite dinner conversation.

"The Silver Team came in third, but lost one of its members in the avalanche. The Blue Team was fourth, but only had two members left by the time they made it to the end. Two died, one from the avalanche and and one from dehydration," Baine noted. "Purple and Orange were both next, but they decided to unify their teams instead of fighting, and they made it to the end together, although there were only six of them left by that point."

Baine cleared his throat and eyed Sophia. I could tell he was thinking about how our team and Haley's had fought against each other. Nobody had brought it up, because it wasn't polite and anything was legal during the Elemental Cup. But it was still shocking, because it hadn't been done before. As far as I knew, no one in the history of the Cup had ever *murdered* their teammates.

"What about the rest?" Jonah asked, clearly to steer the conversation away from Haley's insanity.

Baine shrugged. "The Green Team tried to avoid the mountains, but got lost in the woods and had to backtrack, which cost them a few days. And, well, the Red Team... I'm sure you've heard what happened with them."

Baine made a unfortunate expression. Out of the corner of the room, Madame Doya came into view, Naomi prowling proudly at her side.

Every move that she made was elegant and poised. She was a gorgeous lady, and beautiful to watch, even if she was the most evil woman in the world... though I was pretty sure Haley had booted her to second place in the past few weeks.

It had to be an embarrassment for Doya to only have Haley survive, even if she did get second place. Her behavior... or rather, her murders... had been filmed on live TV for all to see.

Those families weren't going to be happy with the Koigni tribe. They'd blame every Fire person alive for their kids' deaths, not just Doya and Haley. Despite nearly winning the Cup, Haley had shamed her tribe. And I was sure Sophia's incredible display during the Fire challenge didn't do much for any of the other tribes but make them all nervous.

It seemed like we *were* heading toward a war. And since I was pretty sure Sophia would be at the center of it, that scared the hell out of me.

"The Pink Team came in last, but they took their time and made sure they were prepared before they went into any challenges." Baine slurped the last of his soup. "Besides the Pink Team, you were the only other team that had all four members survive."

That was a humbling statement. "It sounded like we just got lucky," I said.

"Way to ruin everything," Sophia said, and she elbowed me.

"You won because you paced yourself well and worked together. None of the other teams took care of each other like you four did," Baine said. "Not to mention that instead of doing things the conventional way, all of you did things in a way that worked best for you."

We all looked at each other with soft smiles. Baine was right. We had each other's backs. Now and always.

Baine rambled on and on about the rest of the teams and how they had performed during the tournament, which was fine, because it gave the rest of us time to eat. I had my meal down in seconds, though Imogen and Sophia took forever. I'm pretty sure Jonah drank more than he ate.

As Baine went on about how the other contestants had died... falls, cave-ins, or lost within the region... I got a little confused. As far as I could remember, there were deaths every year, but the death toll had been steadily going up every year since I'd attended Orenda. Were the Elders making the contest harder or something?

I'd noticed Baine's eyes had hardly left Madame Doya's form the minute she strolled into the room. He rose to his feet and bowed to us.

"Well, at any rate, I'm glad you four did so well," he said, rather hurriedly. "I hope you enjoy the rest of your night."

Baine went to the center of the room and held out a hand to Madame Doya. Naomi growled, but after a moment, Doya took it, and soon they were turning on the dance floor. Baine's awkward and stiff dad-moves looked very strange next to Doya's intricate twirling.

Baine and Doya danced in a very proper way together. It more or less looked polite. I figured it was expected of them to dance together, since they were both the top two mentors this year.

"I wish the Hawkei didn't celebrate death," Sophia said, and she whooshed out a breath. "I don't understand how they can watch their children die and be happy about it. This Cup is so cruel. I wish there was a different way."

"Well, no one's really happy," Jonah explained. "It's just what's done."

Imogen pursed her lips like she didn't agree, but didn't say anything. Sophia looked sad.

"This is how our society is, Sophia," I told her quietly. "People don't really consider it barbaric. Just how things are."

She bounced her foot. "Well, maybe someday the rules will be changed, and the Cup won't require sacrifices."

There she went again with changing the rules. She didn't get it. No one could change anything, not even if they wanted to.

The servers brought out peach crumble for dessert, and the invitation of sugar was at least enough to get Sophia talking about more pleasant things.

"Are you sticking around during the break?" Sophia asked me. She fed Esis a bit of peach crumble off her fork, and he nearly fell over with how delicious it was.

"I, uh, won't be around much," I said regrettably. "After Christmas I usually travel with my Dad on the *Hozho* to Europe. Water tribe stuff."

"Aw." She seemed disappointed. "But isn't Ezra supposed to handle that stuff from now on?"

I shrugged. "Yeah, but Dad still wants my help, I guess."

Which was hopeful. Maybe if I couldn't be chief, Dad could still give me a place in the tribe. Not something as entitled as Elder, but at least some position where I could be useful.

"Hm. Well, I'll miss you," she said.

"I'll miss you too, *pawee.*"

Imogen and Jonah gave each other another cutesy glance when I called Sophia that, and I sent them a death glare. Imogen and Jonah totally knew what I was calling her, and I bet they'd told her, the little shits.

"What are you doing over break, Jonah?" Sophia asked. She gave her fork to Esis, and he used it to suck down the rest of her dessert.

"I'm going to every rave this side of California!" Jonah practically yelled. "Squeaks and I are going to hit all the Hawkei nightclubs, won't we, girl?"

Squeaks squeaked excitedly, thrilled at the prospect of partying with Jonah over New Year's.

I made an obnoxious sound. Jonah was going to come back next semester with a month-long hangover— Squeaks, too.

"Are you spending Christmas with your fam—?" Sophia started, but I quickly shook my head *no* at her. She went quiet. Luckily, Jonah hadn't heard her.

"Jonah's spending Christmas with my family," I told Sophia quickly. "He usually does."

"Oh." Sophia said quietly. "Are his parents here to celebrate our Cup win?"

Unfortunately, Jonah had heard that. "They couldn't be here. They were, uh, busy," Jonah said quickly. Then, after a few seconds, he hurriedly added, "But I'm sure they're proud of me."

Sophia had the good sense not to ask any more questions. Personally, I was glad Jonah's asshole parents weren't here, along with his snobby older sister and her stuck-up girlfriend. Jonah's family was awful. Though it looked like he still wasn't over sticking up for them, which broke my heart. I'd hoped he'd finally seen the light, but I guess not yet.

Imogen changed the subject, thank the ancestors. "We're spending a quiet Christmas at home before we go exploring the Mayan ruins in Guatemala."

"I don't know where I'm going to go," Sophia said glumly. "I'm sure Doya won't let me go back home."

"You can stay with me," Imogen offered cheerfully. "Mom would love to have you. We always need extra help exploring."

"Thanks, Im." The girls smiled brightly at each other.

"Will Cade be there?" I teased. I knew his family usually vacationed in South America this time every year.

Imogen blushed. "I don't know."

Jonah and Sophia teased Imogen about Cade for a few minutes while we finished our desserts. Esis was practically rolling by now, and Sassy had peach crumble smeared all over her whiskers. We went back to the dance floor, because as I'd learned in the past hour, Sophia couldn't be contained if there was good music on.

"Hey, losers," a dude called out as we passed. "Congratulations on getting lucky!"

I knew him. He was Kent, from the Blue Team. I noticed that he was wearing sunglasses at night, which was a totally douchey thing to do. His friends, people from Silver and Green, snickered.

I'd noticed that since we'd been crowned Champions, some people had been trying to suck up to us, to increase their status in society. Not everyone was like that, though. It didn't matter that we'd won the Cup. To some people, we would always be outsiders.

I went to say something back, but Jonah beat me to it. He threw his shoulders back and swaggered toward Kent like he had something to say.

"Uh, no," Jonah said in a very sassy way. He moved forward, swaying his hips with attitude. He snatched the sunglasses off the guy's face and put them on his own. "We're not losers. That's not our name. For your information, we're the Reject Team, *bitch.*"

Jonah strolled out of there in style, his hands waving above his head. Sassy strutted after him like a peacock. Sophia laughed, and Esis gave Kent the finger on both hands. Imogen scuttled off to the bar with Sassy, giggling. I couldn't stop grinning as we joined Jonah on the dance floor, who was currently dropping it so low I'm surprised he didn't fall over.

"Reject Team, huh?" I asked as Jonah bumped against me.

"Don't blame me, you came up with the name," Jonah replied.

"I think it's perfect for us," Sophia said. She was absolutely glowing.

Imogen had come back. She was carrying four glasses of champagne, which she distributed to each of us. "Here's one for the Reject Team!" Imogen cheered, and she raised her glass.

Sophia and Jonah raised their glasses to meet hers. I wasn't about to be the asshole who ruined the moment, so I raised my glass too and clinked it against the group's. I downed it in one go.

I felt like I was gonna ride the high of this night for the rest of my life. We were tournament winners, and we were freaking awesome. Fuck everyone else.

Jonah and the two girls resumed their crazy dancing. I more or less did that fist-bump thing guys do when they don't know how to dance, because, well, I didn't, and I didn't want to stand there looking like a jackass.

I noticed Professor Perot was there at one of the tables, Baxtor hopping on his lap. He winked when he saw me. He'd visited me a few times in the hospital. I'd had to sign a waiver so the doctors could give him my medical results for his research. As far as I knew, he hadn't made any progress on what was wrong with me. It was a bit frustrating, but since I'd squeaked by death more than once in the past week, I decided to let it go.

As the night wore on, Jonah got less and less in control of himself, and more and more drunk. He slammed drinks like they were going out of style, and impressed the girls with his flexibility.

"Jonah's… out of control," Sophia said, though I wasn't sure that was the right word for it as we watched him tumble, doing a breakdance.

"Nobody can quite drop it to the floor like Jonah," I said, rolling my eyes. He had every gay dude at Orenda's eye on him. Even some straight dudes in here were checking him out.

Except for one. I noticed Renar had hardly glanced his way all night. Jonah was too drunk to notice.

Oh— shit. Maybe that *was* the reason he'd been drinking so much. I shook my head. Jonah deserved so much better than that piece of shit.

The crazy music became slow, changing into a song I hadn't heard since high school. Jonah grabbed the gay Yapluma guy and was turning drunkenly around the room with him, casting desperate glances at Renar. Squeaks' eyes seemed to frown, and she turned away from her Elementai.

I noticed Imogen had disappeared. Where had she gone off to? Sassy was still here, on her hind legs and swaying back and forth while Esis held her up in his version of a slow dance. He seemed refined and cool, like he'd done this before. Show-off.

Sophia stared at me expectantly. This was different than the dance we had earlier to the string quartet. It was more intimate. I knew we shouldn't, but I didn't want to tell her no.

She raised an eyebrow. "Aren't you supposed to ask me to dance?"

There was that Koigni attitude. I chuckled and took her into my arms, wrapping my arm around her waist and taking her free hand while she put the other one on my shoulder.

It became very obvious very quickly that she wanted to do this dance her way. She pulled me around like this was her job and not mine.

"I'm the man, I'm supposed to lead," I protested as she dragged me in the other direction. We were totally uncoordinated.

"Then act like it," she leaned forward and whispered in my ear, giving me a smirk.

Oh, *that* was a challenge. She wasn't just talking about dancing, either.

"Maybe you need to learn to *listen* to me," I hissed sharply. I pressed my hand onto her lower back, yanking her to my body.

She gasped, and I made sure that *I* led this time as we continued to waltz around the room. As the song went on, we pressed together even closer, until we hardly moved at all and were more or less just swaying against each other. She let her head rest on my shoulder, and I allowed mine to fall so that it lay against her head. I wrapped her tightly in my arms and squeezed her, hoping I would never let her go. Snowflakes began to fall from the ceiling, something extra the Toaqua teachers added for ambiance. People were watching, but I didn't care.

I wanted to be this close to her all the time. It wasn't fair that couldn't happen.

Change the rules.

I wanted to. So badly.

The song ended. I hated prying myself away from her, so I didn't let go, more or less just pulled away a little.

"You should kiss me right now," Sophia said lowly. Her tone made me want to do it, but I knew what would happen if I dared.

I wrinkled my nose. "*You* need to behave."

I pinched her ass, quickly so nobody else saw. She jumped and made an adorable squealing noise.

People were staring at us, whispering to each other behind their hands. Screw them. To them, we were just teammates celebrating our Cup win.

I finally untangled myself from her. We headed off the dance floor without even holding hands. Sassy and Esis followed us, dizzy from their slow dance. I noticed Sophia was pouting.

"This sucks," she complained. "A dance like that and I didn't even get a little kiss at the end."

"If you're a good girl, you'll get it later," I said, under my breath so only she heard.

I sent her a smoldering look that told her to do as I said. Sophia turned pink and went quiet, and I felt a grim note of satisfaction.

Oh, she was going to be fun to tame. My mate.

Agh! I had to stop doing that! There were consequences to this shit!

Now that the slow stuff was over, Imogen was back. Her eyes were kinda red. She looked like she'd been crying.

It was probably over Cade. But I didn't want to ask and make her more upset.

Jonah stumbled toward us, and I grabbed on to him so he didn't fall onto the floor. "Let's take a picture, guys!" he slurred. "So we can remember this night forever!"

He fished in his pocket. I nearly fell over when I saw that he had a smartphone in his hand.

"How'd you sneak a phone in here, Jonah?" I marveled.

"I have ways," he said wisely. "Quick, let's take one before the teachers see. Ready?"

He turned the phone around to take a selfie, focusing in on all of us. "One, two, three!"

Sophia gave a squeal and jumped into my arms. I caught her and managed to smile just as Jonah took the photo.

We looked at the picture. Jonah was front and center. Imogen was on the right side, beaming a bright smile, Sassy squirming out of her arms. I held on to Sophia on the left, and Esis was on top of my head, cheering. Squeaks was in the back, giving the camera a sultry look. Jonah hastily shoved the phone back in his pocket.

I told the others I had to piss, and went to the bathroom. When I came back Jonah, Imogen and Sophia were huddled together. Their expressions looked serious, like they were talking about something important. I only got the last fringes of the conversation as I approached.

"I just need more time. He's not ready," Sophia said anxiously, and she squeezed Esis to her.

Jonah gave her a look I couldn't read. "That's not fair, Sophia. You need to tell him."

"Tell me what?" I asked as I sauntered up to the group. Everyone's faces went kind of pale, especially Sophia's. She wore a panicked expression.

Were they talking about me?

"Uh… nothing important," Sophia said quickly. "It doesn't matter."

Imogen fiddled with her dress. Jonah had a disapproving look on his face, but I chalked it up to his drink being gone. Sophia stuttered to explain, but I pulled her to my side before she could answer.

"Hey, you don't have to tell me everything. I trust you," I told her.

Sophia turned a little pink, and Esis crossed his arms. I was curious and wanted to ask more, but at the same time, I figured it wasn't anything major. As much as I doubted the team at the start of the semester, I fully trusted each of them now. They were my friends, and Sophia was amazing. We'd all survived the tournament together.

My friends wouldn't hide anything from me.

Imogen left the ball shortly after that with Sassy, saying she was tired… but I figured it was more to look for Cade. Sophia, Esis and I danced to a few more songs, though none of them were slow and Sophia and I didn't get intimate again— which was a good and bad thing.

Jonah. Was. Drunk. He was on top of the bar, singing shrilly and shaking his chest like he had boobs. Squeaks was just about as plastered as he was, and was knocking over stools as her eyelids lolled. The three crates of beer bottles she'd gone through were scattered all over the floor.

"Get off!" The bartender started slapping Jonah with a towel. Jonah slowly clambered down from the bar and ended up falling on his face.

Everyone else had more or less gone home. There were a few stragglers on the dance floor, but for the most part, the ballroom was empty.

"All right, bud, here you go," I said as I pulled Jonah to his feet. He hung on to me, barely able to keep his balance. "I think it's time we took you to bed."

"I'd say," Jonah drawled. "Somebody has to."

"Not like that." I started guiding him toward the door, and Sophia followed. His hippogriff moaned on the floor.

"Sorry, Squeaks," I told her. "You'll have to walk. Can't carry you."

Esis patted her head, and Squeaks was able to stand. Incredibly, she walked in a straight line. How was Squeaks less clumsy when she was drunk versus being sober?

As we dragged Jonah into the hallway I noticed Ezra was leaning against the wall, kissing the girls we saw from earlier. Yes, both of them. He would make out with one girl for a few seconds before he'd turn his head and make out with the other. The girls watched with wide and adoring eyes, as if they loved watching him kiss another girl just as much as they liked being kissed by him.

Ez was really milking the college life. What exactly was this magical effect he had on people, especially women? He got away with everything.

Ezra opened his eyes and pulled his mouth away from the one girl as we dragged Jonah by. "Hey, Liam," he said. "Dad's walking around. He's looking for you. You'd better be careful."

"Thanks, Ez," I told him, giving him a nod. We took Jonah around the corner. Fuck, he was so heavy, but luckily the Yapluma dorms weren't far from here.

"What does your dad want?" Sophia asked. Jonah gagged, and I tried not to recoil from him. If Jonah threw up on me, I was going to lose it.

"Ancestors only know. Probably to yell at me for sneaking out of the hospital," I told her. That was all I needed, my dad following me around to babysit.

We finally got to the Yapluma dorms. I let go of Jonah, and he leaned on Squeaks. He was able to walk on his own a little better now, so I hoped he made it to his bed. Or, at least, a couch.

"Why'd you guys make me leave?" Jonah asked. I doubted he would remember this in the morning. "I was having so much fun!"

"You're wasted, Jonah. You need to get some sleep," Sophia said kindly.

"Yeah, sure," Jonah slurred. "You guys just want to get rid of me so you can do this."

Jonah turned his back, put his arms around himself and made movements like he was making out. I pushed him, and he fell over again. He barely managed to pull himself up by Squeaks' legs.

"Take care of yourself, brother," I said as I pushed the door open for him. Jonah and Squeaks stumbled inside, and I heard the sound of him puking just as the door closed.

Poor guy. He was gonna wish he was dead in the morning.

Sophia turned toward me. "So... now what?" Her face was slightly worried, but also, anticipatory.

"What do you mean? It's time for bed," I said blankly.

Sophia stared at me before she burst out laughing. Esis put his head in his hand and sighed.

"No, I mean..." Her expression cleared up, and the humor left. "Are we going somewhere?"

I had no clue what she was talking about, until Esis did that mating-call thing again he'd done when we'd gone out for pizza. She was talking about... wow. I felt like an idiot.

"I don't think we're ready for that," I said. I reached out and put my arm around her waist as we walked back to the Koigni dorms. This time of night, no one was in the hallways, so I wasn't worried about being seen too much. Plus, right now, I just wanted to touch her, because I knew I wouldn't be able to for the entire break.

If ever again.

"I just thought you would expect something, you know. Because it's the night of the ball, and this is college, after all." She talked quickly, like she was trying to explain herself.

"I don't expect anything," I said, amazed. How many shitty guys had Sophia met in her lifetime?

"You're such a gentleman." She smiled softly. Esis skittered up her dress and sat on her shoulder. He was eyeing me, as if expecting me to respond a certain way.

"I just… think it's too early to talk about sex," I said quickly. "Especially when we don't know what we are."

Esis glanced back to Sophia's face, which had fallen. "Right," she said.

I was pretty sure that was the best answer. I didn't think Sophia wanted to sleep with me tonight, anyway. She seemed like she wanted more from me before that happened… if it ever did… though I wasn't sure what that would be.

We stopped in front of the Koigni dorms, and Esis slid down the front of her dress and to her feet. We had to make this quick, as her dorms were the most restrictive and there was no telling when we could be found out. Saying goodbye in front of them was dangerous, but I didn't feel safe letting her wander back to them alone at night, even if we were at Orenda Academy, the safest place in the world.

"So what about my reward for behaving?" Sophia asked, putting her hands on her hips.

"Reward? I didn't say you'd get a reward," I teased.

"That's not fair." She pouted her bottom lip out like a little kid, like the *pawee* I'd come to love so much and want to claim as my own. Seeing her like that, it was hard to come to terms with the fact that she was far more powerful than I was… more powerful than all of us.

And one day, she was going to determine the fate of this tribe. Thinking about it made my legs want to become water.

I laughed lowly and forced myself to calm down. "Well, I suppose you *have* been good, haven't you?"

Her face brightened, before she paused to ask something. "About… what you call me. *Pawee.* Jonah and Imogen said you were calling me your soulmate," she whispered. "Is that true?"

I knew they had told her. But that was okay. I raised my hand and brushed back the curls from her face. "You shouldn't have to ask, *pawee.*"

Then we were kissing again. Fuck, it's like everytime we got even a second alone we couldn't keep our hands off each other. Her mouth ravaged over mine like she couldn't get enough, and I squeezed her to me as I tasted her, wishing this would never end and I would get to kiss Sophia Henley every day for the rest of my existence. Even if I did, it wouldn't be enough.

When she pulled away, her breasts heaved against my chest. "When did you know?" she asked quietly.

I took a deep breath and said, "I don't know. From the first moment I saw you. Always."

The way she looked at me… I'd never had anyone look at me like that before. Not any of my other girlfriends. Not Mia. Just Sophia.

I was okay with living in secret and hiding our love forever. I never thought I'd get a second chance at love. Sophia was all I ever wanted. This unbreakable connection between us would be enough for me.

But I didn't want that for her. I didn't want her to be married to a cripple. I didn't want her to suffer through never letting anyone know we were together, and never having kids. I didn't want her to lose her Familiar. I couldn't do that to her.

It didn't change the fact that I felt like I'd been waiting for her all my life, and in her, I thought I found the only person who matched me. Sophia was the one girl who could love a man without a soul.

Sophia trailed out of my arms. "Will I see you when we get back to school?" She swallowed. "Like this?"

I knew what she meant. "Yes. That's a promise." I gave her a quick peck on the lips again before she turned to open the door. Her fingers trailed away from mine. Esis gave me a salute and a wink, like I'd done good, before he vanished into the dorms.

"Bye, Liam," Sophia said quietly, and she closed the door. I waited for a moment.

"Goodnight, Sophia," I whispered long after she was gone. "I love you."

I wish I had the balls to say it to her face. But that was scary, and I had a lot to think about over break first before I ever went that far.

Sophia wanted a relationship. So did I. But I needed time to figure out if that was something that was worth the risk.

And... I had to go back to the hospital. Which sucked. Time for another IV in my arm and machines beeping all night. Yay me.

I hurried to the medical wing, because I'd been gone long enough. I shouldn't have been surprised when I saw Dad sitting on a bench outside, Tatum sleeping beside him. The bear's shoulders shook with loud snores as he dreamed.

Dad rose to his feet, but Tatum still slept. I felt pretty guilty as my father stomped toward me. He didn't look happy.

"How'd you know how to find me?" I asked.

Dad bluntly said, "I knew you had to come back eventually."

Well, he was right about that. No matter what I did, I'd always end up *back here* it seemed... in a hospital.

"You're supposed to be in bed." Dad's tone was heavy. He'd hardly left my bedside all week, which had been annoying as much as it had been endearing.

"I wanted to celebrate my Cup win," I said. "I took care of myself. I was fine."

I hoped he couldn't smell the booze on my breath, because if he did, he'd totally flip out. He'd taken it really hard that I almost died in the tournament, harder than even my mom had.

Dad gave a disapproving glance at my tie. "You're wearing red. I noticed Sophia had on blue."

Shit. I had hoped he hadn't seen her dress. Wearing the wrong *colors* was a big deal around here. How would people react if they knew Sophia and I had kissed, and were considering a relationship?

"It was just..." I shrugged. I didn't have a good answer. Dad sighed, and shook his head.

"Liam, about you and Sophia..." Dad started.

"It's not what it looks like." I quickly went to explain. "We're just friends, we're not—"

"That's not it." Dad cut me off. "The Water Elders *want* you to get close to Sophia."

It felt like a brick wall had smashed into my face. "What?" All the air rushed out of me. "Why?"

"Liam, listen." Dad put his hands on my shoulders firmly, to steady me. "I have to tell you something. Son, there might be a way to bring Nashoma back. The Water Elders have found a way, that, maybe... he can still be alive."

The sentence winded me. I was glad Dad steadied me, because I was weak on my feet. Tears sprang to my eyes. I couldn't control them. Pure desperation at the thought of getting Nashoma back, to make up for what I did, was screaming in my chest. A way to bring my Familiar back? A chance to restore my soul? It wasn't possible.

"Are you saying the Water Elders can bring Nashoma back to life?" The words sounded fake, even though I was sure that's what my dad was telling me. My hearing went all fuzzy and I got a little dizzy. This couldn't be real. I had to be dreaming.

"Yes. But, Liam, you don't understand. If you want Nashoma back, you're going to have to do something for the Water Council," he said, slowly so I could comprehend him.

"I don't care. What is it? I'll do anything," I said in a rush.

Dad's face sobered. His expression became grim as he said, "Liam, if you want Nashoma back, you're going to have to kill Sophia Henley."

END OF BOOK ONE

Continue Liam and Sophia's story in The Water Legacy (Hidden Legends: Academy of Magical Creatures, Book Two).

the wolven mark

UNIVERSITY OF SORCERY BOOK ONE

MEGAN LINSKI

ONE

T he world was wide and open, and I couldn't wait to spend the rest of my life exploring every inch of it… savoring every slip through reality.

My powerful legs propelled me forward, though the tall pine trees that towered hundreds of feet above me. My paws landed on the lush, rich ground, thudding a pagan war sound that signaled to the world we were hunting. My tail flew out from behind me as my white fur blended into the thick ferns that coated the area. My sharp ears could pick out the sound of waterfalls in the distance, birds chirping, lake churning with fish. My nose caught onto the scent of the mountains… fresh rain… and I enjoyed the blissful sun rays as they beamed onto my back.

This forest was old… very old. Probably as ancient as the world itself. The original founders had come here millennia ago to form the country of Malovia in Eastern Europe, and had left the wilderness mostly untouched. They took only what they needed to survive and build the community. That was the way of the Arcanea. Our world was one from medieval times, a living, breathing monument in the modern, digital age, passed down from our fae ancestors. We stuck to the old ways, as was our tradition.

My name was Prince Ethan, and one day, I would be King of the Arcanea. I wanted to follow in the footsteps of my fore rulers. I wished to protect nature and my people equally. Arcanea, magic, and the land, living together in perfect harmony. It was my dream.

I ran for a mile more before I came to an open clearing. I paused to catch my breath. I wanted to give an experimental howl, to see if any other wolvens were nearby, but that might scare the monster off. I stayed put, trying to figure out where to go next. I'd run all around the nature preserve, but it went on for hundreds of miles. Even working together, my father's entire hunting brigade probably hadn't covered a tenth of what was out here.

I heard the roar of a dragon above, along with a long shadow. I searched the skies, and changed into my human form. Fur became clothes, and I went from standing on four legs to two. I sat on a nearby boulder to wait.

There was a loud sound nearby like a creature was landing, and the ground shook. I heard a rustle in the trees, and the scent of scales and smoke. A few moments later, a man stepped out of the trees and stood beside me, smirking.

"Miss me, white wolf?"

I tossed a rock at the dragon shifter. "I just saw you this morning. Far too soon, in my opinion."

Stefan dodged the rock, and it hit a nearby tree. It made a blasting sound and shattered off a chunk of the trunk, sending bark and splinters everywhere. I suppose I must've thrown it too hard.

Stefan gave a sarcastic noise. "Your temper's getting worse than mine. You could've killed me."

"It would've bounced off your thick skull. Nothing can penetrate that boulder you call a head."

"That's not the only part of me rumored to be harder than stone," Stefan boasted.

I would've laughed if I knew that wouldn't encourage him, so I forced the grin off my face. I didn't want to spend the rest of my time out here listening to crude jokes from my buddy. We had a job to do.

Stefan was the same age as I was, twenty now, and was taller and broader than me. He had black hair, black eyes, and a look that dared someone to try and piss him off. And oh, how he enjoyed himself when they did. He liked toying with his prey, human or animal. We were in the same grade at Arcanea University, both about to head into our Third Year.

"Did you see any trace of it?" I asked him, specifically referencing the monster in question.

Stefan shook his head before he drew out his cell phone. He sent a quick text, probably to his commander, before shoving it back in his pocket.

Although our race made use of modern technology alongside our ancient customs, we kept our society hidden from humans to ensure our survival. After all, if the human world found out there were sorceresses mated to men who could change into dragons, wolves, alicorns and griffins, they'd surely kill us all. There were a lot more of them than there were of us. Our sorceresses kept our city hidden from humans with their magical illusions and wards, to prevent such a chaotic event.

But sometimes, there were mistakes. And if whatever we were hunting got out into the human world, it could expose us. Which meant we needed to kill it. Fast.

"I lost whatever we're trailing somewhere over the falls," Stefan said. "It just up and vanished."

"Dammit." This was concerning. The monster had already slain three people, and we had yet to discover what it was. This forest was huge— one of the largest in modern Europe. It could be anywhere.

"Sure you're not losing your touch, High Prince of the Arcanea?" Stefan asked in a scathing tease.

I smiled. Stefan was a prick. But it was always good to have a dragon as a best friend, so I kept him around. No one liked to argue when you had muscle to back you up, and in the land of the Arcanea, violence was the only language people knew.

"I'm quite bored. Want to race?" Stefan asked.

I laughed. "Not much of a contest, with me stuck on the ground and you using your wings."

"Better run fast, then." Stefan pounced, and rose into the air. His body shifted mid-jump to become a large black dragon, nearly twenty-five feet in length. He tore down trees as he ascended, spreading his leathery and spiny wings to their full span. His scales were the color of obsidian rock, and sunlight bounced off his scales, as if light couldn't bear to touch the inky-blackness. Long, curved horns grew out of his head, and white, sharp fangs hung over the lips of his mouth. Spines grew along his back, ending in a sharp barb at the end of his tail that he'd threatened to stick me with one too many times. He gave a roar that sounded like an insult. I gave him a rude gesture in response. He was already several lengths ahead of me.

We were supposed to be working, but we'd been trailing the mysterious monster for three days now, and we were exhausted. So what was the harm in having a little fun?

I bounded back into my shifter-skin and chased after him. I increased my strides in order to catch up, and found that I had to push myself to retain speed. Stefan was more or less gliding effortlessly over the trees. I was no small wolf by any means— nearly twelve feet in length myself and half that in height— but I had yet to gain my wings as an Arcanea, and therefore had to run everywhere I went. Asshole.

Stefan was having a delightful time up there. I could hear his barrel-laughs as I struggled to catch up. He lit the trees on fire up ahead, and I had to dodge around flames as the forest ignited around me. I nearly burned my paw on a falling branch, and I could smell the fur on my tail singeing.

"You dick!" I shouted. Stefan only laughed harder. In our shifted forms, we could still speak using telepathy, and I wanted Stefan to know just how much of a jerk he was.

Time to show him who was boss. I bounded off my back legs until they were burning, trying to catch up, and victoriously felt the shadow of Stefan pass me as I came out ahead. Stefan noticed that I was getting the upper hand and increased the beat of his wings to match my pace. We were neck and neck now.

The trees were getting thicker here. We had to slow down. I attempted to use my magic to call out to him. *"Stefan, watch out for that—"*

Too late. Stefan ended up losing control and careened into a section of trees. They uprooted, and the sound of wood cracking rang out through the forest. I moved like hell to get out of the way as Stefan went barreling through the trees at high-speed, wrecking everything his body came in contact with. Finally, his mass reached a structure that would not be moved, a large stone wall that had worn away from part of the mountain. He slammed into it, and debris from the stone wall went crumbling as the dragon came to a complete stop.

"... Tree." I watched as the dragon went slinking down to the ground. I nearly died laughing as the dragon shook his head, dazed. He changed back into Stefan, sitting on the ground and holding his head. A huge chunk of forest had been torn down by his crash-landing.

"Oy." Stefan shook his head again. "You win this round, mate. Must've been weighed down by my big—"

"What are you two boys doing?"

A pleasant voice broke our banter. The King of the Arcanea broke through the trees to join us. He wore a wide smile, and paid no attention to the destruction that Stefan had caused on his way down.

Father's stance was wide and commanding. His long hair was gray, broad shoulders covered by a long cape of bear's fur. People said he was a mountain of a man, though I was nearly as tall as he was. His large hands were covered by rabbit skin gloves, one of which grasped a tight dagger in his belt, set with ruby gemstones.

"Aw, Da, just goofing off," I said. The royal guard wasn't with him, which I was thankful for. Dad had a tendency to be less of himself and more of a king when people were watching him.

Father's eyes slightly narrowed. "This isn't a game, boys. There's a monster on the loose."

I knew he wasn't mad. A chuckle was playing at the corners of his mouth.

"I'm convinced it flew off. It shouldn't be taking this long to locate a wild beast," Stefan said. He sneezed, and a bit of smoke came out of his nostrils.

"You have a right to be concerned. Something's… different about this one." Father rubbed his beard. "I can't quite put my finger on what it is."

I slung my arm around his shoulder. "What do we have to worry about? After all, we've got the best monster slayer this side of the country on our side."

Like the rest of my kind, I was attending Arcanea University to become a monster hunter. I'd had no better teacher growing up than my dear old dad. He could behead a monster in less time than it took most Arcanea to assess the situation.

Father shook his head. "Experience is no substitute for information. I don't believe I've ever hunted a creature this elusive."

He made a face. "Perhaps I should send you boys back to town. This monster could be out of your skill level."

Stefan made an obnoxious noise. "Unkillable by *us*? I don't think such a monster exists."

I scoffed and rolled my eyes. Stefan had the mind that he could destroy anything. If the Seven Gods themselves challenged him to a duel, he'd accept.

Father still seemed troubled. I spoke up. "I've killed my share of monsters. Why would this one be any different?"

Father frowned. "I'm not sure, son. Monsters usually leave clues behind. This one… it's too clean. There's no scent, no tracks, no indication that it's been in the area at all, although it must've been to kill those people. Something's not right."

I didn't like how he spoke. When we'd found the bodies of the slain Arcanea, they'd been just outside of town, bodies ran through with twisting roots that rose up from the earth. Blood and entrails everywhere, though there was no indication the monster that had killed them desired to feed. The bodies hadn't been touched after they were killed. This creature seemed to murder for sport.

Father waved his hand, as an indication for us to follow. He pointed upward. "Search the skies, Stefan. Perhaps there's something we're missing. Maybe the creature can fly."

Stefan became his dragon form, and took off. The black dragon quickly became a spot in the sky as he soared through the clouds, on a hunt for something none of us were even sure existed.

My father transformed, from his brusque human body to his wolven form. The old wolf's gray fur seemed to be getting whiter and whiter by the day. On his back two large, feathery wings rested. He kept them tucked in close to his side as he prowled through the brush.

I followed his lead, and changed myself. Father towered beside me as we stalked the woods, keeping close to the ground.

Father's feathers brushed me as we walked, and I had to suppress a sharp feeling of jealousy. Within the four Factions, dragons, griffins, and alicorns were the only Arcanea born with wings. Wolvens like myself and sorceresses had to earn them. I had yet to prove to the Seven Gods my worthiness, and therefore, remained wingless. I wasn't sure what I had to do in order to earn my wings— it was different for everyone.

For some Arcanea, their wings never came at all. It was a nightmare that haunted me daily as I continued to age. It wasn't exactly *expected* for a wolven to have wings… a lot of my kind lived and died without them… but the Circle would never accept an ascender to the throne who couldn't fly.

"Where's the rest of the hunting party?" I asked Father, using my wolven magic to communicate telepathically with him.

"Scattered throughout the area. They're close-by." Father's amber eyes focused forward. *"Have you given any thought to the King's Contest?"*

The King's Contest. It was due to be held this year. Father was aging, and soon, it would be expected for a newcomer to take his place. Twenty years had passed since he'd taken the throne, and now, the Seven Gods demanded that another be chosen. But the crown wouldn't just be handed to me by birthright… I'd have to fight for it, against a handful of other greedy competitors who wanted the throne for themselves. It was the only way to prove I was strong enough to lead the Arcanea.

"It's all that's been on my mind." So much was true. I'd been practicing for the King's Contest since I'd learned what it was, shortly after I could walk.

"I know you are ready with strength and skill. Your magic is strong, as are your chances of winning the Contest." Father paused to look at me. *"But you can't do it alone."*

I suppressed an inward groan. I already knew where this was going.

"Don't give me that look. I won't be around forever, Ethan. I need you to find a mate, so that you can carry on in my place and make sure Malovia is protected."

I wasn't sure why having a Marked to stand by my side as queen was so damn important. And I'd told him so, many times. *"Perhaps I'll never find a mate. I haven't yet. Maybe the time's already passed,"* I said.

"Don't speak of such things." Father's tone was gruff. *"Do you wish for the Seven Gods to curse you?"*

"I am not cursed." I spoke sharply. I knew others whispered such things about me, going unbonded for this long. Most people found their mates within their freshman year at Arcanea University. As much as I wanted to prove the rumors wrong... I didn't feel ready yet to find a bride.

"Your queen is your greatest ally. She is your fiercest warrior, your most loyal protector, and your most faithful friend. A king cannot run his kingdom properly unless he has a sorceress to stand by his side." Father sighed. *"And I am worried you may never find yours."*

"I'll find someone." If I wanted to participate in the King's Contest at the end of the year, I had to have a mate first. The rules said I needed to be engaged first in order to compete. Yuck.

"I don't want you to find just any girl. This is the most important decision of your life. Time is running short," Father scolded. *"You don't want to end up like me."*

I made a non-committal sound. I knew my mother was not my father's Marked. My father's true mate had run off a long time ago, though he never said why. He always vowed he could've accomplished ten times more than what he already did if his real Marked had become his queen, although he never spoke this openly in the presence of my mother. He loved her, too, and Mother was an accomplished sorceress herself... but having a wife wasn't the same as having a mate, something he'd drilled into my head from the moment I'd come out of the womb. There would always be a part of him that was missing, and he didn't want the same to happen to me.

Myself, I didn't get it. I was never one for romance. Didn't interest me. Girls were pretty, and they were nice, but I had bigger concerns on my mind than dating them. Mostly snowboarding and hockey, and learning as much as I could from my dad about ruling Malovia, so I could do the same one day.

Father seemed to notice I was getting melancholy, so he pressed his shoulder into mine. *"I have faith that within the year, you will find your true mate. But whatever may come, know that I will always be proud of you. You will be a great king."*

The statement humbled me. I'd spent most of my life fearing that I would screw up. That I'd fail to win the King's Contest, or even worse, somehow ruin the kingdom.

My Da had faith in me. And that meant everything.

I went to say something back, but words failed me. As I finally came up with something, there was a cracking sound somewhere up ahead—— the sound of saplings breaking in half.

"Shh. Something's here." Father paused. I kept my mouth shut and pricked my ears up, listening.

I heard something moving before us, tearing up roots. A strange scent filled my nose. It wasn't like anything I'd ever smelled before. It was equal parts sweet and woodsy, as well as slightly rotten. It screamed at me to keep away.

"*It's there. In the glen,*" I whispered. There was a part up ahead where the trees broke and the wilderness became a long, sloping valley. That's where our monster was.

Father crouched. "*Perhaps we can sneak up on it, before it determines we are here.*"

This would be an easy kill. Sneak up, jump, and give a fatal bite to the monster's neck before it even saw us coming. We'd barely see any action.

I followed his lead. "*I'm right behind you.*"

"*Stay low.*" Father advanced. I remained behind him, though it was hard to see where I was going with his big wings in the way, blocking my view.

The trees ended. Father crouched, then sprung, spreading his wings wide. I copied him, raising my lips in a snarl as I leapt into the air, planning to tackle whatever he had spotted into the ground.

But then Father faltered, and his wings drew back. He weaved in the air and hovered over the ground, avoiding whatever he'd initially tried to attack. I had no such way to prevent myself from halting my charge, so instead, I shifted my weight in mid-air to turn away. I hit the ground and rolled, wondering why the hell my father had drawn back.

When I lifted my eyes to witness the creature, I understood why. We had made a critical mistake.

The creature was like something out of a storybook. It was twelve feet tall, with tree roots for feet and long, dangling arms that dragged along the ground and ended in black claws, connected to a masculine form. Its head was that of a deer's, with large antlers growing out of either side of its head. The deer's head had sharp, ravenous teeth, and a skeletal body that had grey skin dangling loosely off bone. Plants grew out of every orifice. It was hard to tell what was bone and what was branch.

It was much worse than we feared. A *leszy*… a leshane. A demonic deer spirit of the forest, rumored to be given black powers by the Seven Gods themselves. We couldn't fight this.

Father knew it. "*Ethan, run!*" he shouted. I didn't need to be told twice. I tried heading to the safety of the trees, but the leshane raised his clawed hand, and roots sprung up along the edge of the forest, preventing my escape. I had to dodge as roots sprung up from the ground in a brutal attack. They barely missed my torso as they stabbed upward through the dirt.

Father had changed back into his human form. He was blowing on a twisted ram's horn, signaling to the other hunters that we needed help. As he continued calling the others, I did my best to outrun the leshane as its magic followed me through the valley. The ground shook underneath my feet like an earthquake as roots went shooting up from the ground moments where I'd been before. One false step, and I'd be impaled.

Father snarled, and he erupted into his wolven form. He took to the skies and charged at the leshane, trying to distract it. He attempted to get close, but every time he tried the monster swung his large claws, preventing him from landing a secure bite.

Now that the leshane was distracted, I went to help. I ran forward and sank my teeth into its leg. It was like biting through a tree. The leshane gave no indication that it hurt, merely kicked me off. The blow sent me sailing into the root wall. I heard something crack, most likely my ribs. I moaned in pain, struggling to get up as I watched my father war with the leshane.

The leshane's claws came too close, and they cut across my father's chest. He snarled, and blood went everywhere. The cut was deep. I gasped. Despite the agonizing pain in my ribs, I forced myself to stand and return to the fight. My father needed me.

I pleaded with the Seven Gods to send help as I launched myself onto the leshane's back. I dug my claws in and refused to let go, pinpointing where was best to sink my fangs in. But I wasn't sure where to bite. We'd never studied leshanes in class, as it was assumed anyone who was unlucky enough to find one in the woods would be dead within minutes anyway. There was nowhere to rip out a jugular or pierce a vein. Every part of the leshane was wooden and bone. I didn't think I could break its neck. This truly was a creature sent by evil.

In response to me clinging on, the leshane grew wooden spines out of its back, sharp and dangerous. One of them went through my paw. I howled in pain and let go, dropping to the ground and rolling away. My father remained in the air, blood pouring from his wounds as the leshane continued to advance.

The leshane threw back its head and let out a wicked cry. There was thundering in the trees, and a sleuth of bears stampeded through the root wall and into the valley. There were dozens of them— the leshane had used dark magic to call them to his aid.

This was bad. This was really, really bad.

Father paid no attention to the bears, just kept focusing on the leshane. One bear tried to whip him out of the air, until Father turned on him and pinned him to the ground, tearing out his throat before returning to his original task. The leshane battled cooly, as if certain that this was a battle it would win.

Finally, I heard the sound of help coming. Griffins and alicorns came flooding out of the trees to defend the king. They leapt over the root wall that the leshane had caged us in and charged forward. Eagle-lion hybrids battled alongside unicorns with massive wings, struggling against the bears that the leshane commanded.

I searched the skies for dragons, but they'd been sent farther away than the other groups, and it would take them longer to arrive. Where was Stefan? We needed him!

With the arrival of the griffins and the alicorns, the leshane changed. It mutated from his horrifying form to become a monster that ran on four legs, a skeleton poking through skin, dripping thick blood. It looked more animal than human now. The leshane moved with incredible speed, appearing a blur as it ran through the valley. He passed griffins and alicorns alike, slaying them both. Roots came up to suffocate or spear through the Arcanea gathered all around the woods. I watched the scene in horror, paralyzed. I wasn't sure what to do. People were dying. Our warriors were falling to the leshane. We were all going to die.

Father hadn't given up. His grey pelt was soaked with blood, but he was determined to bring down the leshane at whatever cost. He ran at the creature with teeth bared. My father and the leshane met, rearing up on their hind legs to strike out at each other with antler and fang.

I was limping now, and could only move but stiffly for the pain in my ribs, but I wasn't content to die unless it was on my feet and defending my country. I charged forward, and took my father's side as the two of us tag-teamed taking the leshane down. I got a mouth full of splinters each time a bite managed to hit its target, but I didn't care. This was life or death.

There was a roar from above, and a black shape blocked out the sun. My heart lifted.

Stefan had finally arrived! He hovered above the scene, pumping his massive black wings, and let out a stream of fire that billowed around the leshane and set it aflame.

The leshane made a high-pitched, screaming sound and went for the closest thing it could take its anger out on— me.

Things happened so slowly that I felt the moment would replay for the rest of my life. The leshane, still on fire, lunged forward with its jagged mouth wide open— my father went to push me out of the way. The leshane got its sharp fangs around my leg, slightly above the knee. There was a tearing sound below, like bone and flesh breaking.

The pain was incredible, white-hot and blinding. But I couldn't focus on it with the sight of my father's body limply dangling from the root that had sprung up out of the ground, a thick knot of wood speared clean through his chest.

I was briefly aware of the feeling of the monster biting clean through, and my father's dying screams, before the world went dark.

emma

TWO

"Your immune levels didn't change during testing. The diagnosis is positive, Emma."

It felt like all the breath had been beaten out of my lungs. I nearly had to gasp my next word. "What?"

"You have it," Dr. Luticifo repeated. His words had a bit of sadness, but there was more of a formality there— like I was just another number in a sad statistic... not a human being.

A hollow feeling grew inside me and settled there. I was certain I'd carry around that emptiness for the rest of my life. I was different now.

Then a bit of denial surged through me. This wasn't real. I couldn't be sick. No way.

But I was. Now I knew. I had a disease that no one knew of and that I could hardly pronounce. I hardly knew what any of this meant.

Common Variable Immune Deficiency disorder. It was a rare disease that hardly anyone knew about. It basically meant that my immune system didn't create enough antibodies for me to fight infections. I was one out of sixty-thousand— or more.

I could die. A bacteria or virus could come along, I could catch it, and that would be my end. It was a terrifying reality that I didn't want to deal with. Because I couldn't handle it.

I swallowed the lump in my throat. "So what do we do now?"

"We start treatment," the doctor said. "You'll need to take infusions of human plasma to replace the missing antibodies, monthly or weekly, your choice. You have the option of intravenous or subcutaneous."

Sub-what? "I don't need infusions," I argued. "I'm fine."

Dr. Luticifo gave me a disapproving look. "I know you believe you can keep yourself healthy just by being stubborn, but that's not the case. You'll *need* these infusions to survive, for the rest of your life."

It seemed so dire. Dr. Luticifo rattled on and on about all the different options I had. His voice sounded like it was muddled and full of static. I was too trapped inside my own head to listen.

"That sounds good," I said in a far-off tone. I wasn't even sure of what I was agreeing to. All I could think of was that I had known all along I was sick. I'd felt it in my bones the first time Dr. Luticifo had suggested we do testing. I'd just been waiting to hear the confirmation.

Dr. Luticifo again repeated subcutaneous or intravenous. I chose subcutaneous… sub-q, I called it, because I hated long fucking words… because he said I could do it myself and didn't have to bother with going to a stupid hospital. He set things up as I checked out at the front desk. I proceeded out into the parking lot of the hospital, feeling like a zombie and probably moving like one, too.

I got into my beater of a car and slammed the door shut. I looked at the papers they'd given me at the front desk before I angrily threw them to the floor. I slammed my hand against the steering wheel and got a headache for my trouble.

"This is bullshit," I said. I was eighteen fucking years old. I was too young to have a chronic illness. It'd get in the way of my skating. It'd get in the way of *everything*.

But that was my life. Mom always said she had bad luck. I had the worst.

I started up my engine. Tears beaded at the corners of my eyes, but I wiped them away and told them to fuck off. I didn't cry. I was tough.

I knew where I had to go. I left the hospital and floored my car in the direction of the ice rink. I ended up cutting someone off and they beeped their horn at me, but I flipped them off. Screw them. I was definitely having a worse day than they were.

I didn't feel relief until I pulled into the parking lot of the ice arena. I grabbed my bag and headed into the rink, hoping I wouldn't run into anyone I knew. I didn't like people in general, and I liked talking less. I didn't think I could handle making small talk after the news I got.

The ice was empty today. Thank God. No one was hanging around the rink in the middle of a weekday. I avoided making my way to the front desk, as I didn't need to pay. I worked part-time at the rink in order to get ice time for free, whenever I wasn't pulling long hours at my mom's diner as a waitress.

Dr. Luticifo had told me that I'd have to quit working eventually. That I'd be too weak to hold down a job as time went on. I was better off on welfare— you know, for my health.

This thing was sounding more and more like a death sentence and less like a diagnosis.

If I couldn't hold down a job, my hope of being a pro athlete was long gone, too. Not that it had been much of a possibility in the first place. But thinking about that only made me more depressed.

At least I hadn't gone to college. That would've been a waste of money.

I pulled on my tights, a black practice skirt, and slipped on a fleece practice jacket before throwing my red hair up into a bun. I went onto the ice and a gust of cold wind hit my face. *Freedom.* No matter what happened, nothing could touch me here.

I warmed up by practicing all my spins before I moved onto jumps. I did all my doubles with ease, then practiced my triples. The triple toe loop, triple loop, and triple flip was easy. I messed up my triple-triple combination a few times and stepped out of my triple lutz before trying it again and landing it perfectly.

This was it. The big moment. I focused all my intention on my goal. I built up speed, then took a flying leap forward.

It was wild and undisciplined. I corrected myself and was able to get myself into the correct jumping position. I felt myself going around once, two times. I felt excited. I was going to do it this time!

Then the bad news from earlier broke into my head, and I faltered. I ended up landing on my ass in a very painful way as I lost control of the jump and went crashing back down to the ice.

Dammit. No matter how hard I'd practiced over the past few months, I still couldn't land a triple axel. It was really frustrating. I tried again and again, but the result was always the same. I either popped it or fell.

This wasn't getting me anywhere. I was here to try and feel better, not beat myself up over what I couldn't do. I skated to the box, where a music player system was set up. It connected to the speakers that were over the ice. I put in a CD, pressed play, and skated out to my starting position on the ice.

My long program was set to the music of Swan Lake. I tried to put as much passion and emotion into my program as possible, though it felt like I was going through the motions. I did all my jumps and spins with ease, skipping over where the triple axel was supposed to be and doing a triple loop instead. As the program continued, I noticed my legs were shaking.

This is what I loved to do. I wasn't going to let any shitty diagnosis take it from me. I slowed down and focused more on the choreography instead of the technical elements. I came to a halt at the end of my program, chest heaving.

I felt dizzy. The world blacked out for a moment as the ice spun around me. My lungs felt like they were on fire, or were being ripped in half— or both.

It had gotten harder and harder lately to perform that program like I'd used to. Now I knew why.

I grabbed a bottle of water at the boards and chugged it, to recover my strength. As I drank, I noticed someone standing in the corner of the rink near the stands.

He was around my age. He was pale and tall, with dark hair and dark eyes. He had a prominent nose and sharp facial features. Not to mention he was really fucking ugly. He wore a long black trench coat and was staring at me with a very intense look. His hooded eyelids didn't give any perception of warmth. He reminded me of one of those predator dudes they tell you about on crime shows.

He'd been watching me perform my program. Weird.

Something in my gut told me this guy was no good. I was about to skate over there and confront him before he turned his back and vanished. He walked through the double doors that led to the rink and out of sight.

Remembering his gaze made shivers run down my spine. It had been creepy. No— worse than creepy. The guy had acted like he knew who I was. Like he had come here for a reason. Had a competitor sent her fugly-ass boyfriend here to spy on me?

Whatever. He was gone, so I didn't need to worry about it. I wrapped up my practice session before I went back to the locker room to take my skates off and change. Once I stepped off the ice, a dark cloud settled over me, and the hollowness settled in my gut again.

I really wanted to go to the gym and do some yoga, distract myself further, but my body felt sore and I didn't want to push it.

I got a phone call in the locker room. I answered it, feeling like I was about to drop a bomb on the world.

"Hey, Emmaline," Mom said. "Are you out of the doctor's yet?" Her voice was dripping with sweetness. She'd been nagging me to tell her the news the moment I heard. I didn't call her right away, because I didn't want to face the truth.

"I have it, Mom." It hurt to say to her. More than it had hurt to hear the words myself.

"Oh, honey. I'm so sorry." Mom sounded genuinely upset. I hoped she didn't cry about it. I hated when Mom cried.

"It's okay. I'll pull through it." I didn't want Mom to worry. This was just one more hurdle in my life I had to get over. No biggie. I could conquer this, too. I had everything else.

"Tell you what. How about we go to the Detroit Zoo tomorrow? Would that help?" Mom asked.

I loved the zoo. I'd wanted to study zoology before I'd lost my scholarship. I went there so often that I had a membership. "Sure," I said.

"I have to get back to work. I just wanted to check up on you," Mom said. I heard the busy clatter of the diner in the background. "How about I take you out to dinner after my shift? *Antolli's* tonight?"

Spaghetti was my favorite. "That sounds good, too. Thanks, Mom."

I hung up. My hands were shaking. At least it was over with, and she knew. There was no one else in my life to break the news to. I didn't have a father. Mom had told me I was the result of a one-night stand a long time ago, and she didn't even know the guy's name. There were no other relatives or grandparents to tell. It was just me and her.

I didn't have anywhere else to go, so I went home. I considered going to the bookstore and grabbing a book, but I didn't have the extra money, and it was too hot out today to frequent the coffee shop I usually hung out at. I was quickly running out of distractions. It felt like the world was forcing me to confront my diagnosis, something I couldn't handle.

I felt a sense of peace as I traveled up the gravel road. My house was pretty big, made of stone and set in the woods far back from the main road. My mom had money from running the diner, but despite putting her whole heart into the restaurant, the building she had bought was a money pit. She made enough to keep the doors open, pay the bills, and pay for ice skating and horse riding lessons for me growing up, but it certainly didn't return enough income for a college fund.

I threw my bag on the couch and fell onto it. I channel-surfed for a minute, but nothing caught my attention.

I looked out the big window in the living room, to the trees outside. I couldn't sit still. It was like I needed to move my body, just for something to do. If I didn't, I felt like I was going to go insane. I just had to get rid of all this nervous energy. I was tired from practice, but I needed to go for a walk in the woods. To clear my head.

The woods were the one place that would calm me down. Whenever I was angry or upset, I'd go for a walk out here, and it was like all the bad stuff just slipped away. I felt nature's soothing effect as the smell of pine trees wafted through my nostrils. My feet crunched upon the thin dirt path. My anxiety slowly ebbed, and I began to think more clearly. As I wandered through the forest, I tried giving myself a pep talk. I needed to buck up. I wasn't dying… not yet, anyway. I was just… dying faster than the normal population.

It might be a painful existence, but still one worth living. My ancestors had dealt with stuff like this for thousands of years. It wasn't that long ago that most people died young. Modern medicine and technology had saved us. We had it good in the modern era.

If I just kept thinking positively, it wouldn't be so devastating—

I heard a *crack* in the woods behind me. I thought it was a deer, and barely glanced over my shoulder. But my eye caught sight of something terrifying… black fur.

My heart started beating rapidly. Could it be coyotes? But coyotes didn't come out in the daytime to hunt, and whatever I had glimpsed had been huge. Was it a bear? I really hoped not. The last thing I needed was to face off with a bear after an already terrible day.

I quickened my steps. As I walked down the forest path, I heard footsteps behind me. Okay, I was *definitely* being followed by something. Or hunted.

Then the most unbelievable thing happened. The air cooled, and the sunlight faded as clouds began gathering overhead. I saw small white snowflakes trail to the ground, dancing all around me in a precarious display.

It was the middle of the damn summer. No way would it snow, not even in Michigan.

This was just too freaky. I turned around and faced whatever the hell was following me, but the footsteps stopped. I wasn't fooled.

"All right. I know you're there. Come out and show yourself!" I shouted.

I knew my voice would scare off any animal that followed. But what emerged from the trees wasn't an animal. It was a man… the same one from the ice rink earlier.

I was officially terrified. This dude was a stalker. He was going to kill me. But I knew I couldn't show any fear… that would only increase my chances I'd end up dead from the situation.

"Get the hell away from me," I said. I took a step backward, looking for something I could use to defend myself… but there wasn't anything in sight, not even a branch.

The stranger didn't obey my command. He took another step toward me, smiling.

"A woman shouldn't be walking these woods alone. Where are your friends?" the stranger asked. He approached me in a twitching way— like a spider killing a dying insect caught in its web.

I let out a vacant laugh. He was a poor stalker. "You obviously don't know me very well. I don't have friends."

"Oh, really?" his grin widened. "Well then, this will be far too easy. Why don't you play with me?"

"No thanks. I don't play well with others," I said. I went to turn away, but the stranger lunged in front of me.

"Don't try to run," he said coolly. "You have something I want."

That was it. I punched him in the nose. Blood went squirting everywhere, and the stranger let out a strangled noise, clutching his face as he fell to the ground. I took off in a run, darting down the path the way I came. I had powerful leg muscles from skating. I could outrun him.

The stranger did something insane as he rose up to his full height. He growled. He honest-to-God *growled*. Just like a creature would. It sounded like something an animal would make.

I dared to look behind me. Disbelief rippled through my core as I watched the stranger transform, erupting into a powerful black wolf.

My jaw dropped open. This was no average wolf. It was practically as big as a horse. It could fit half my body in its mouth, for crying out loud.

But like hell if I'd stop running. There was no freaking way. I increased my strides and kicked it into high-gear. I heard the heavy footsteps of paws behind me as the creature caught up. I could practically feel his hot breath on my heels. I was going to be dinner.

When the wolf's teeth grazed my ankles, I knew I had to stop running and fight back. I spun around and ducked out of the way, off the path. The wolf went past me before it spun around on all fours, baring its fangs.

The wolf pounced. Fear went spreading through my body at an alarming rate. It was paralyzing, gluing me to the spot as the wolf came closer and closer. It was only a few seconds, but it felt like hours. My life flashed before my eyes as the wolf aimed his mouth toward my neck, intending to rip out my throat.

Aw, hell no. I ain't dying today!

That steely resolve of rebellion caused me to do something fucking crazy. I raised my right hand and closed my eyes shut.

There was a warm sensation spreading throughout my hand, and it was as if a flood of power exploded from my fingers. I heard a loud yelp. I opened my eyes and my mouth dropped open as I saw a great blue light exploding from my fingertips. The light had smashed into the wolf like a laser beam and slammed him against a nearby tree. The beam went straight through the tree, leaving a gaping hole that smoked and left burning cinders.

The tree wasn't the only thing that looked like Swiss cheese. The wolf had a massive hole gutting its chest, leaving a cauterized, gaping wound where muscle and blood should've been. I could see clear through it to the other side— like a window in his torso.

I would've thrown up if what I'd done hadn't been so fucking cool.

"Oh my God." I advanced on the wolf, though I kept my distance. Before my very eyes, I watched as the wolf changed back into a man. The hole remained in his chest, leaving the stranger vacant of a heart, his hooded gaze staring upward at the sky like he was still shocked.

Oh shit. *Oh shit.* I killed him. Like D.E.A.D. dead.

I forced myself not to panic. I'd slain a freaking werewolf. I didn't even know they existed until a few moments ago!

The thought came to me that wolves ran in packs. He probably had friends running around, and I bet if they saw me standing here, they'd put two and two together and get pretty pissed I'd murdered their buddy.

I took off. My breaths were sharp and stabbing by the time I got back to my house. I went and locked all the doors, shut all the windows and drew the curtains. I kept the lights off and crawled onto the couch, wrapping my arms around my knees and shivering.

I just killed somebody. Holy shit. But was that person really a *person*, or was it an animal? Was I hallucinating or something? None of this could be real. I remained on the couch and didn't move, jumping at every sound the house made.

A few hours later, I got curious if the body was still there. Remus Lupin and the American Werewolf gang hadn't come around to eat me yet, so I figured there had to be no more wolves left in the area. They would've been able to track my scent back to the house, right? If there were any nearby, I would've been found by now.

I weighed the pros and cons of returning back to bury the body for hours. I worried someone would find it and somehow trace it back to me. It was a paranoid thought, and it wasn't like I'd left a weapon behind— but still. I'd committed a murder. I needed to hide the evidence, before someone… either the police or the wolf's friends… discovered the remains and came after me.

Criminals always return to the scene of the crime, I guess. It was dark by this time, but that didn't deter me. I headed into the woods with ovaries made of steel, along with a shovel, and decided that if there were any more wolves, hopefully my hand would do that freaky shit again and I'd be fine.

While I was walking, I got the notion that I couldn't see. At the thought, my fingertips started glowing again… like they had when I'd killed the wolf. They served as a flashlight as I continued forward, lighting the path with a shining light.

I held my hand in front of my face with a pounding heartbeat. "Holy crap."

Was I an alien or something? None of this shit had ever happened to me in my life!

I held my breath as I returned to the clearing where I'd been attacked. I knew this was the one, because the tree I'd hit with my blast still had a hole in it.

But there was no body, only traces of blood left behind— like someone had been dragging a body along in the dirt.

The man had disappeared. Okay, maybe I hadn't killed him. Which was even worse, because that meant he was out there looking for me.

If the body was gone, either he was still walking around with a hole in his chest, or somebody had moved it. I didn't care which. Either meant that I was still in trouble. I needed to get the heck out of here.

I headed back to my house. As I did, I felt a strange sensation spread over my palm. It was an uncomfortable itching, like I'd had an allergic reaction or something.

I raised my palm in front of my face to observe it. I watched, transfixed, as a black mark in the resemblance of a paw print took shape on my right hand— the same hand I'd used to kill the wolf.

THREE

That cursed day in the forest changed my life forever. The leshane was killed, but his slaying came at a terrible price. I lost my right leg in the process of killing him.

Even worse, I lost my father.

I couldn't bear that the King of the Arcanea was dead. My dad was gone. I wouldn't see him again until the Father Stag of the Hunt came to take me onward to the Great Hunting Fields, where my dad and I would finally be reunited.

I'd been lost in grief for weeks. Worse still, my mother was inconsolable. The Queen of the Arcanea had locked herself in her room and refused to come out since she'd been told the news. When they'd said the king had sacrificed himself for me, the wailing began.

She hadn't been able to look me in the eye since. I knew I'd never be able to fix what I did. I'd put myself in a vulnerable position, and my father had paid the price.

Three months passed in a blur. I wasn't ready to face what I knew had to be done. I wanted to curl up in a ball somewhere and hide.

But the throne was on the line. Now that my father was dead, my place in the King's Contest was being questioned. People were wondering if they should deny me my right to compete for the monarchy. Since I was born, I'd always been expected to win the King's Contest, and take over ruling Malovia in my father's footsteps.

Now I was a cripple who wasn't considered worthy. A boy who'd caused the death of one of the greatest kings in Malovia's history. A son that had killed his own father due to a silly mistake. People were whispering that the kinghood belonged to someone else.

I refused to let my crown fall to anyone who wasn't me. So I was attending the Gathering of the Arcanea tonight, to make my intent to compete in the King's Contest, and make sure the royal court knew where I stood.

Around midnight, I started getting ready. It took me fifteen minutes to put on my prosthetic leg. I still wasn't used to it. Lord Lucien wanted me to work on my timing, as there would probably come a day when I would need to get it on in an emergency, to be ready to fight.

The things regular people took for granted.

When my leg was taken from me, I'd been made a prosthetic from the best medical companies that money could buy. It was high-tech, and expensive. I had to learn to walk again. I had to learn to do *everything* again.

The prosthetic didn't transfer when I shifted into my wolven form. My back right leg was missing when I became the wolf— an empty gap showing where a limb once stood.

I'd become known among the Arcanea as the three-legged White Wolf. It was humiliating.

I put on the black pants and black hussar's jacket, fitted with gold trimmings, before I looped the black velvet cloak around my shoulders. I was still in the required mourning period, so I donned the black clothes without complaint, though I much preferred navy… the wolven Faction colors. I slipped on my boots and looked in the mirror. I very much looked like a prince.

Good. Perhaps it would remind the Circle to know their place.

I left my room in the royal quarters and journeyed through the Palace of the Arcanea. The castle was forged out of white stone. Elaborate portraits of the former Kings of the Arcanea and their queens were placed all over the walls, next to statues of armor decorated with elaborate white wings— the traditional suits of the warring Arcanea. Monster pelts and mounted heads of evil creatures hung beside banners that displayed the golden Arcanea coat-of-arms on every wall— four sections each, showing a wolven, griffin, alicorn and draken in symbolic unity, displayed against a royal purple background.

Guards decked in silver armor saluted as I walked by, and I nodded to them, though secretly I tired of this special treatment. I couldn't wait to get back to Arcanea University, where law dictated I be treated as a regular student. I would never be *truly* normal, obviously, but the setting would be far less formal than it was here.

The guards had to shout to open the gates as I wandered past the courtyard and into the dark forest beyond. From here, I could hear the beating of leather drums and pagan wails from afar, signifying the royal council meeting was about to begin.

I shifted into wolven form and ran toward the sound, clothes becoming fur once more. My prosthetic leg vanished. Anything material that Companions wore or carried, like jewelry, wallets, or other things, was changed by their magic and became a part of their spirit, waiting to be used again once the shifter form was done with. My prosthetic would reappear when I became human again. My paws made heavy beats in the ground as they ran in time to the music that was growing closer and closer.

As I ran, I pondered what I was going to say to them. I needed to make my intent clear, but no explanation seemed good enough. I supposed I'd have to wing it.

I smelled the burning of torches as I came close. The King's Circle was the official royal court of the Arcanea. Every Faction— the wolvens, the griffins, the dragons, and the alicorns— elected two officials each to serve on the council, along with their mates. The males were given the title of Lord, and the females the title of Lady. I'd have to show all of them I still deserved a chance— but at least I had one ally.

I came to a halt and shifted back into my human form when I saw a battalion of guards standing alert in a circle around a closed-off section of the woods. A man stood amongst the darkness, waiting for me.

Lord Lucien's brown hair was long and fell around his shoulders. He was in his fifties, and had a rugged and trim face that was slightly scarred, as he had seen a lot of battles with monsters. His form was lithe and muscular.

I knew many women were in love with him, and the men respected him. He was smart and clever in a way most people could only wish for. He was one of the best warriors the Arcanea had and the most popular teacher at Arcanea University. I felt honored he'd spent his time over the summer mentoring me when I certainly knew he had more important things to do.

He was a wolven, like me. For some reason, he still wanted me on the throne. And he'd committed himself to it.

Lord Lucien shook my hand as I came near. "Ethan. I'm glad you decided to come."

"There was no decision about it." I kept my tone clear. "It's the least I can do, to repay you for what you've done."

Lord Lucien was the only one who'd made sure I still stood a fighting chance at winning the Contest. He'd re-taught me how to hunt and fight with a prosthetic as a man, and using only three legs as a wolven. We'd trained every day, from sun-up to sunset, until I was exhausted and could stand no more.

During those first few weeks, I wanted to give up. I was angry. I didn't want to fight anymore. But Lucien wouldn't let me. He forced me to keep going until I collapsed, allowing me to rest for a while before demanding I get back up again. As a result, I became better than I ever was before— stronger, even, than I had been with both of my legs.

The relentless training kept my mind off of what had happened. I was too busy learning how to fight again to wallow in endless grief. I thought I'd lost everything, but Lucien gave me a purpose— to win the King's Contest at all costs.

If it weren't for him, I wouldn't be here. Most likely would've taken my own life out of shame and guilt. That man made sure I retained a fighting chance.

I was a more powerful warrior than I ever had been. Now all I needed to do was prove it to the Circle.

"Don't thank me. I've done nothing worthy of repayment," Lord Lucien said. "I merely did my duty to the crown."

Lord Lucien clapped a hand on my back and guided me toward the guards. "Now let's hope you can pull this off."

The guards remained stiff as we came near, their hands on their axes. Their eyes were weary as we approached.

"The Prince of the Arcanea wishes to speak with the King's Circle," Lord Lucien announced to them. "He uses his birthright to demand you let him pass."

The guards glanced at each other, as if unsure what to do, before they meekly stepped aside. I wondered if someone in the Circle had told them not to let me in. I would remedy that.

As we entered, both Lucien and I changed. He became a large brown wolven with giant wings and yellow eyes as we moved forward.

The trees parted, creating a circular area that was surrounded by blazing torches. In the middle of the space was a large flat cauldron, hanging from three chains and suspended over a bonfire. In the cauldron burned a variety of herbs and incense, making the area smell sweet.

The Sacred Gathering. It was named so because it was a place of power. Magical energy was drawn from there. Our ancestors had used it for thousands of years prior to perform spells and healings. Miracles and wonders had been performed at the Gathering, but it had been many years since the site had deemed anyone worthy enough to use it. The Gathering was a living, breathing soul, and it determined who its power went to depending on the plea of whoever came to use it.

Not just anyone was allowed into the Sacred Gathering. You had to be a member of the Circle… or of the royal family. It was a concern that an untrustworthy soul could use the power of the Gathering for unholy purposes and their own personal gain, convincing the spirits that lived in the earth there to work for evil instead of good. As such, the Gathering was only allowed to be visited by members of the hierarchy, for meetings only, and never alone. It was protected at all times, our most precious law. Penalty for a peasant wandering into the Gathering was death.

Members of the Circle were spread out in an oval around the Gathering, each of them with their mates. The drums and chanting grew silent as I approached. On the silver throne directly across from me sat the current leader of the Arcanea.

Now that my father was gone, a steward had taken his place. Bartok Solomon had been a hurried replacement by my father after the last Steward had unfortunately died, and his position was supposed to be temporary. He'd only been chosen to become the Steward a few months ago, and only then because there were few willing to take his place. Offspring of the Steward could never compete in the King's Contest for up to three generations, as it was supposed that such temptation would make the Steward disloyal to the king and partake in assassination attempts, to get their own children that much closer to the throne.

Steward Solomon had no children, so he'd been an easy option. But he was never meant to be permanent. Steward Solomon would run things until the King's Contest was over and a new monarch had been chosen. He was part of the griffin Faction, and as far as I knew, had a good heart.

I almost felt sorry for him, being shoved into this. He was close to retirement and had taken up the position as a favor. Never had he imagined that he'd have to hold the throne temporarily.

As I approached the Circle, the sorceresses exposed their palms to me. Each of them had dark marks on their right hand, indicating which Faction of the Arcanea they belonged to. There were paws for wolvens, a dragon's foot for dragons, a hoof print for alicorns, and a bird's foot for griffins.

I went to the Marked that belonged to Steward Solomon and licked her hand. Ursula Solomon barely hid a sneer as my tongue touched her palm. Lord Lucien likewise licked her palm, and we fell back to an empty section of the Circle before we transformed.

I looked around. I knew my mother should be here, but she wouldn't be. She was too caught up in her grief.

Though something *was* curious. Lady Magdalina, Headmistress of Arcanea University, wasn't here either. What was so important that she'd dare to miss a Circle meeting?

Steward Solomon cleared his throat. He looked extremely uncomfortable. "Prince Ethan, why are you here? You are not permitted to interrupt our sacred council meeting."

I dared to step forward. "I am permitted by birthright. I am here to announce that I fully intend to participate in the King's Contest this December. I henceforth put forward my desire to compete."

Whispers, among with a few outraged cries, echoed around the Circle. Steward Solomon tried to quiet the crowd and failed. Lady Ursula raised her hand with a sneer, and at her cruel gaze, the rest of them fell silent.

"Why would we nominate *you*?" Lady Iris asked. She stood beside her alicorn mate and threw back a harsh laugh that had no humor in it. "You killed our king."

Her words were like a dagger in my chest, but I ripped the dagger out and threw it aside as I said, "My father intended that I be the one to take the throne. That doesn't change now."

"You must have the backing of one of the Circle to participate. No one will nominate you after what you did," Lord Morgane snarled. He was a dragon, and close to my father. I knew he blamed me for what had happened.

Lord Lucien stepped forward. "I have already chosen to nominate him. He has my backing for the King's Contest."

The rage was louder this time. For all the objections I'd believe the court would have, I didn't think it would be this bad.

My father was popular, well-beloved. It didn't matter that I was his son. People considered me his murderer.

Lord Morgane gave Lord Lucien a smoldering stare. He was minutes from transforming any instant. "You only wish to back the wolvens, Lucien, to keep the crown within your Faction's power. Give another Faction a chance. One that didn't cause the death of our leader."

"The leshane killed Lycus Nowak, none other," Lucien announced, and he turned in place to gaze at all of the Arcanea standing near. "He died in battle, and is certainly roaming the Great Hunting Grounds with Tomir by his side in the Eternal Hunt. We should not punish his son for Lycus receiving an honorable death."

The rageful protests turned to mumbles. "Aye," Lord Boris said, one of the griffins. "He's with his sister now, Tomir be praised."

The heads of the Circle bowed in respect. It was a horrible thing for an Arcanea to die old in his bed and not with his sword on the battlefield. At least Da had been given a death that those in the afterlife would find honorable.

Lady Iris shifted uncomfortably. "Merely being in the King's Contest doesn't mean that he'll win. Though it would be… *questionable* if the boy who had been unsuccessful to save the former king succeeded in winning the throne."

"I fail to see how he could do that, without having all four legs."

A low and surly voice came out of the darkness. A man my age was illuminated by the fire as he came forward. He had short black hair, hooded eyelids, and even darker eyes. His form was thin and lithe as he proceeded into the Gathering. He smirked over the shadows flickering across his face.

My cousin; Elijah Zlodia. We used to be close. Like brothers, even. Not anymore. I didn't even know that he was here. Too busy hiding in the shadows waiting to spring on me, no doubt. What was he doing here? As a member of the royal family, he had the right to attend Circle meetings, but what interest did he have being here on this night?

A fellow wolven came forward. My great uncle and Elijah's father, Lord Zlodia, spoke up. "My son wishes to make his intention known. He also will be competing in this year's King's Contest, with my backing and nomination."

Elijah's mother, Lady Korva, beamed with sickening pride at her mate's side.

Elijah's grin grew bigger, and I felt sick. Of course. Elijah was here to make his King's Contest declaration, just like I was. He couldn't even wait until the mourning period was past and my father was cold in his grave.

Elijah threw back his shoulders. "It's time the Arcanea had a real king around here. One who isn't so weak as to fall to leshanes and leave behind a crippled son."

I couldn't hold my temper. I attacked. I exploded into my wolven form and charged at Elijah, leaping into the air with exposed, snarling jaws.

He was waiting for me. Elijah changed into a black wolf the moment I came near, and met me with an open mouth. Both of us sank our fangs in at the exact moment. He bit harshly into my shoulder, missing my neck. It should've hurt, but I barely felt it. We fell into a growling, writhing mess on the ground, scratching each other with our claws and sinking our teeth into flesh. I saw red, and the rest of the world fell away. We were equal fighters, and Elijah had yet to earn his wings, like me. This was a fight I could win.

There were enraged shouts and screams echoing throughout the Circle, and I heard shifters stampeding forward. A griffin pulled me off Elijah, while a dragon yanked him away from me. We transformed, and fought to get back to each other as we were dragged apart.

"That is *enough*! How dare you defile the Sacred Gathering!" Lady Iris screeched as Elijah and I were separated. Her alicorn mate, Lord Radcliffe, herded me away with his horn, while Lord Morgane kept Elijah away by baring his fangs. When I got back to Lucien, he put his hands on my shoulders, though I felt it was more an act of keeping me in place than a sign of comfort. The shifters went back to their places and transformed back to their human selves, though everyone looked on edge.

Elijah baited me. He'd know I'd lose my temper and provoked me to attack him, so that I'd piss off the council and he'd look like the victim.

A momentary thrill of fear went through me. Elijah had I had broken the law. We'd drawn blood and fought in the Sacred Gathering. Would I be prevented from entering the King's Contest for such an act?

Steward Solomon glanced around, looking nervous. His eyes locked with Lord Zlodia's, who was giving him a penetrating stare.

The steward cleared his throat. "Ethan, Elijah, if you two wish to have a Companion's duel, now is not the time to do so. Another infraction will cause severe penalties for the both of you."

Relief ran through me. It was a miracle that the Circle had let that pass. Lord Zlodia had to be pulling strings. He really wanted his son on that throne.

"This type of thing cannot be allowed. It's been chaos ever since Lycus died. The Circle is in shambles," Lord Tremaine announced.

"Our world will be back to normal once we have a proper king," Lord Morgane insisted, and he raised a fist. "We must remain unified. The Contest will weed out the weak and determine who is our rightful king."

"By the Seven Gods, it'll be me," I announced boldly. Lucien's grip tightened on my shoulders, telling me to calm down.

Steward Soloman raised an eyebrow. "If you wish to take the crown, you need a mate. Companions aren't allowed to take part in the King's Contest unless they've bonded with a sorceress. You know this."

He had me beat there. At my age, I was one of the few shifters at Arcanea University who hadn't bonded yet. I knew I needed a mate… a sorceress… one called *Marked*… to be my queen. I wouldn't be able to compete in the Contest otherwise. It had been my father's last worry that I'd never bond.

I didn't want to before. But I'd changed my mind. Not for myself, but for my sense of duty and honor to the country. I'd promised my Da before he died I'd find a Marked to share the throne with, and I wouldn't break that vow to him.

Elijah had a cocky grin on his face, and the steward noticed. "That goes for you too, young master. You are also unbonded. I suggest the pair of you spend your time searching for mates instead of bickering with each other on who's going to earn the throne, for if you are both single by the time the Contest arrives, neither of you will be allowed to compete."

The grin fell from his face. I couldn't keep glee from running through my veins. I had Elijah beat in that department. What woman would want to be with a sniveling, sneaky coward like him?

"I'll find a mate before the King's Contest begins," I announced. "At the Choosing ceremony before the trials, I'll be bonded. You have my word."

"I suggest you hurry, young prince. You have four months before the King's Contest begins," Lady Iris spoke. "Then we shall see how serious you are."

It was clear that my declaration was over and that the council intended to return to other matters. I turned to leave. Lucien stayed behind, to conduct business with the rest of the Circle. Elijah followed me on the way out.

"You know, you're a grown man now. You can stop being my shadow," I told him under my breath. "It's rather pathetic you keep trying to copy everything I do."

"That crown is mine," Elijah snarled. "I'll spill blood before you get your hands on it."

He slammed into my shoulder as he left the Circle. I avoided rolling my eyes. He could be so dramatic.

I passed the section of guards, then shifted. I ran on the way back to the castle, looking skyward at the stars and wondering what it would be like to fly… wondering what it'd feel like to finally gain my wings… if I ever did.

Four months to find a mate, the supposed love of my life. That wasn't enough time. I didn't even know where to start.

But I'd make it work. I had to. My kingdom, my country, depended on it.

FOUR

N early a month passed, and though I stayed on high-alert, nothing happened after the mysterious wolf attack. I went to work, went to the rink, and went home without being attacked or followed. Nothing suspicious or weird happened. It was quite boring. I was starting to think I'd somehow made the whole thing up in my head.

Except for the mark on my hand. It wouldn't go away. I'd tried everything I could think of to get rid of it, but it never faded. If anything, it became more prominent, growing darker and darker with every day that passed. It looked like I'd gone to a tattoo shop and gotten an inky wolf print permanently embedded on my hand. I kind of hated it. It was messed up that a random-ass mark had appeared on my hand out of nowhere like magic. If the judges saw it during competitions, they'd mark me down for it, so I covered up the mark with makeup as much as I could and attempted to ignore it.

I also tried to do the light-thingy with my hand again. No go. It wouldn't work. I felt really stupid walking around the woods with my hand raised, trying to summon some sort of blue light I wasn't sure I had fabricated or not.

I tried not to think about it, but when I was working at the diner, the strange mark was all that was on my mind. It was either busy or boring at the diner, and that gave me far too much time to wonder about what the mark meant and why it had appeared. I was trying to figure out how many shifts I'd have to work to get this thing removed when I accidentally spilled a man's drink all over him— for the second time.

"Dammit girl, can't you watch what you're doing?" he yelped as he jumped back. Brown pop dripped all over his white button-up and his pinstripe pants.

"Sorry, sorry." I blotted his shirt with a napkin, but he shoved my hand away and sneered. I already knew I wasn't getting a tip.

"If you'd focus more on your work instead of getting tattoos, maybe you'd be a better waitress," he remarked, with a snobby glance down at the paw print. I cringed.

"Geez, Emma, can't you handle *anything*?" Delilah, one of the other waitresses, rolled her eyes as she went to fetch the mop— *again*. During my employment here, we'd gone through at least three of them. I was pretty clumsy off-ice, so I didn't know why my mom had chosen me to be a waitress. It was like asking for trouble. The other waitresses hated getting me on their shift, because a lot of their time was spent cleaning up my messes.

I'd never fit into this world. I didn't belong here— though I wasn't sure I belonged much of anywhere. I couldn't even handle a minimum wage job. I longed to get out of Detroit, but it wasn't like things would better anywhere else. I'd probably still be spilling things on businessmen. I spent the rest of my shift hiding from Delilah and pretending to do dishes, while really scrubbing the heck out of the mark on my hand. It didn't fade a bit.

I had to figure out what this freaking thing meant. But who was I gonna ask? Gandalf?

When I got off my shift that night, I surfed through the mail to see if anything had arrived for me while Mom lit a fire in the living room. I'd ordered new skating gear online and needed it for practice.

But I didn't see a box. Instead, there was a letter in the mail, addressed to me. A long envelope made of parchment paper had my name on it, written in black ink and fancy cursive on the front.

There was no return address. On the front of the letter was inscribed, *Notification of Your Acceptance.*

My fingers itched to open it. Was this some kind of college acceptance letter? I hadn't applied anywhere. I went to open the letter, but before I could, Mom snatched it out of my hands. She'd silently come up behind me without me noticing.

"Hey! What the hell!" I exclaimed. I chased after my mom as she stalked into the living room. "That's mine!"

"You don't need to read it. It's not important." Mom threw the letter into the fireplace, and I watched it burn with a sinking feeling. Mom had never done something like that to me before. What was in that letter that she didn't want me to read? Things were getting weirder and weirder around here. I wanted to argue with her that what she did was wrong, but the look she gave me was so serious, I was put off confronting her. I went up to my room and made sure to slam the door. Loudly.

On the last Monday of August, there was a knock on my door. I was washing dishes. I dried my hands and went to open it quickly, as my mom had a headache and went to lie down. I didn't want whoever was banging on the door to wake her. She often had migraines, and I did whatever I could to help her with them.

I opened my mouth to tell whoever it was to fuck off and go away, but the words fell flat when I came face to face with what I immediately knew was an extraordinary person. A woman stood outside my door. She wore a light blue pantsuit, had deep blue eyes, and a pixie cut that styled her white hair in a fashionable way. She wore heels, light makeup, and was carrying a designer purse that she clasped with elegant hands. Her shoulders were thrown back in a poised way.

"Are you Emmaline Sosna?" the woman asked, politely, but with a brisk sharpness to her voice.

"Uh… yeah," I said slowly. "Who's asking?"

She didn't introduce herself. The lady strutted into my house like she owned the place. She put her designer purse on the closest armchair and sank onto the couch in a delicate way, sighing in a slightly dramatic fashion.

"Would you mind making me some tea? I've had a very long journey, and your local airport is… dismal, to say the least." She gave a pleasant smile. "Biscuits would also be nice. You refer to them as cookies here. I do love my sweets."

Who da fuck? Who was this bitch, coming into my house and ordering me around like she was the Queen of England?

But she had a quality to her voice and a light in her stare that made me feel compelled to obey her. It was clear she wasn't messing around. She *expected* me to do what she asked.

I had the thought this lady might have some idea about the wolf that had chased me the other day. I decided the best way to get information out of her was to give her what she wanted.

Still, I wasn't going to show her I'd be that easy of a pushover. "Can I at least get a name?"

"In time." The woman gave another polite smile. "Although, I suggest you do get a move-on with that tea. Tea and I are as close as coffee and Americans, if I'm right with the comparison. I hope I'm not being rude."

She was, but it was rude in a way that I was kind of… used to. I couldn't really describe it. She had this warm and welcoming atmosphere about her that was comforting, even though I had no idea who the hell she was. I turned into the kitchen and put on a pot of hot water. Out in the living room, I could hear the woman whistling and talking to my mom's pet cockatoo, like it was a person or something.

Weirdo.

When the tea boiled, I poured it into a fancy china cup. I figured that this lady wouldn't find a normal mug acceptable. I handed the cup to her on a saucer. "I'm afraid we only have green."

"It's perfectly fine, thank you." The woman took a sip and made a face. "Though what accounts for tea in this country would be equivalent to fish water in mine, I'm afraid."

Everything that came out of this lady's mouth was off-putting. It was offensive and funny at the same time. I hated how much I liked her, even as she was insulting me.

"I hope you do forgive me for barging in like this," she began. "But you see, I simply *had* to come by, as we never received an answer from your letter."

My letter. I thought back to the letter my mom had destroyed. This lady was here because of *that?*

It was at that moment my mother decided to come downstairs. My mom had red hair, like me, though her eyes were blue and not green. Her skin was pale, but despite being in her early forties, her skin showed little signs of age. Most people mistook me for her sister and not her daughter. Though years had passed, she looked the same as I'd remembered her being when I was a little girl.

Mom paused at the bottom of the stairs, placing a hand on the railing when she saw the stranger. Mom *hated* company, and she hated unexpected visitors even more. She had a weird thing about talking to people outside of the diner— almost in a paranoid sort of way. She'd never had any friends, as far as I knew of. Most of the time growing up, it was just me and her. I expected her to go loony at this crazy lady's arrival, and throw her out.

"Hello, Evonna," the woman said cheerfully at my mother's arrival. "I haven't seen you in quite some time. How have you been faring?"

My jaw dropped open as Mom's face became unreadable, and she responded, "I'm quite well, Bianka. Thank you for asking."

Holy flying fucks, my mom and this lady *knew each other?* This was just getting better and better.

Mom walked forward. She poured herself some of the tea in the kitchen before she went to the liquor cabinet and tipped some whiskey inside of it. She handed the bottle to the old lady, who took it gratefully and poured a significant amount into her own cup. Mom sat down on the armchair next to the woman's purse and threw a hand over her eyes, as if she was extremely tired.

"Sit down, Emma," Mom said. "It's finally time to tell you."

Tell me? Tell me what? My movements felt robotic as I slowly sank to the other end of the couch, opposite the old lady. The mysterious woman put her tea down and turned to me, keeping her knees closed and her upper body tilted slightly forward.

"Now. Down to business," she said, like we were in a meeting. "I'm pleased to introduce myself. I am Bianka Magdalina, though you may call me Lady Magdalina. I am Headmistress at the prestigious Arcanea University in Malovia."

Mal-what-now? What was this lady talking about?

"Show me the mark on your hand, dear." Lady Magdalina's tone was pleasant, but firm. She gazed at my right hand like she knew what I was hiding.

I was aware that I was gaping like a fish. That had to look appropriate. "I have no idea what you're talking about."

Lady Magdalina made a skeptical noise. "Come now, Emmaline. Let's not lie to each other. Show me your hand."

It was clear that the best liar in the world wouldn't be able to pull the wool over her eyes. I extended my right hand, and Lady Magdalina grasped my wrist. She pulled it up to her eyes to observe the mark. Mom watched, looking at the mark on my palm like it was her worst nightmare.

"Ah. A wolven. As I expected," Lady Magdalina said fairly, placing my hand back on my knee. "Like your mother, although a griffin would've also been unsurprising."

She might as well been speaking a foreign language. "I don't know what you mean."

Mom took a deep breath. "The truth is, Emma, you're not human. You're an Arcanea."

Reality crashed into me so hard it sucked the air out of my lungs and almost knocked me off the couch. Inside, I'd always known I'd been different. There was something about me that other kids could sense, and I knew it, too. I'd always been a loner, because I didn't feel like I belonged. Mom always seemed like the only person who could truly get me.

But I didn't expect to be *this* different. I wasn't even human? Where did I come from, Mars?

"What the fuck is that?" I belted out. Lady Magdalina made a face at my language, and I cringed. Even now, I wanted to earn her approval, and that I had offended her made me self-conscious.

Mom remained unmoved. "The Arcanea are a magical race. There are many supernatural cultures spread throughout the world, Emma, but you're part of one of the oldest. Other magical peoples call us the Arcane. Our ancestors came from another realm, another dimension that isn't part of this world, and settled in Malovia halfway across the world. You're one of us… a fae."

"Fae?"

"The correct term for fairy." Magdalina spoke lightly. "Or *faery*, as some call it. The legends about us are true, Emmaline. We do exist."

I already had so many questions. I didn't know where to start, so I asked the easiest one first. "Where's Malovia?"

"In Eastern Europe," Lady Magdalina answered. "The country is run by a monarchy that is formed completely of the Arcanea. No one, save for our own kind and the magical races scattered throughout the globe, knows we exist. We're a hidden, secret society, and we mean to keep it that way."

I swallowed down a large lump in my throat. "Magic? Magic is real?"

Mom nodded. "Yes, Emma. I have it. You have it. We all do. The Arcanea specialize in spells and illusions. Female Arcanea become sorceresses— they're known as the Marked. Male Arcanea are known as Companions, and change into shifters."

"Huh? What's a shifter?" I felt really dumb.

"A shifter is a person that can transform into an animal," Lady Magdalina said. She cast a disapproving glance at my mother, obviously displeased she'd failed to teach me anything about this world for eighteen years. "Our Companions have four different Factions— wolvens, which are winged wolves, dragons, griffins, and alicorns. Each Companion belongs to one Faction and can only change into their born animal. Unlike Marked, Companions belong to their birth Faction for life."

"You can switch Factions?" There were so many rules to this thing already. I had to be on my toes if I wanted to keep up.

Mom nodded. "Females can. I came from a griffin father. Your uncle, my brother, was a griffin, but when I came of age, the mark on my hand showed I belonged to the wolvens. A sorceress of any blood can bond with any shifter Companion, no matter where they've come from. The mark on their hand designates who they truly align with."

I tried to process the information. But my mind wouldn't let me. It rebelled against the idea that this was real, that any of this was real. I was just a kid from Michigan. Fricking Detroit, even. Fairy tales didn't happen around here.

"I don't believe you," I said harshly. My mom wouldn't lie to me about something this important my entire life. It had to be some kind of a cruel prank. "Prove this is real. Do magic right now."

Mom blinked at me. She slowly extended her right hand. With her left, she made a swirling motion above her skin. As if she was removing makeup, a smudge of tan liquid, nearly paint-like, rose into the air and dissolved. There on her palm was an identical wolf print, just like mine. She'd used magic for years to hide it from me.

"A simple illusion," Mom confessed quietly. "But one that did the trick."

I was speechless. Lady Magdalina added, "And, just in case that doesn't convince you…"

She waved her hand carelessly, and I gasped as the living room disappeared around us. Gone was the TV, the rug, the coffee table. Instead, giant tropical trees rose around us, and I heard the chatter of monkeys as the air became thick and humid. The temperature rose, and sweat beaded on my brow. I saw toucans sitting in the trees, and an anaconda wrapped around a tree. Macaws chatted by sloths. I swear I saw a jaguar slinking through the heavy vegetation next to colorful butterflies.

Instead of couches and chairs, Mom, Lady Magdalina and I sat on large rocks next to a rushing stream, where droplets sprang out of the water and splashed against my legs. We were in the middle of the Amazon rainforest. I reached down and ran my hand through the cold water. When I brought it back up, it was completely wet.

Then Lady Magdalina snapped her fingers, and the rainforest vanished. We were back in my living room. I was struggling to catch my breath.

"How's that for an illusion, Miss Emmaline?" Lady Magdalina asked, proud of herself.

"Show-off," Mom muttered under her breath. Lady Magdalina had a grin like a cat who ate the canary.

My whole body shook with anticipation and want. That'd been one of the coolest things that had ever happened to me. It'd been incredible. I wanted to be able to do that— to use magic.

Then something replaced the wonder as I caught Mom's eye. Absolute rage.

"Why wouldn't you tell me?" I asked Mom. I was beyond pissed. "I never belonged here. America isn't anywhere close to Malovia! Why would you take me away from a place where I belonged, and never tell me about it?"

Mom sighed. "Emma, there are things you don't understand."

"Yes, Evonna. I myself would like to know the truth of what happened all those years ago," Lady Magdalina said, and she crossed her arms as she raised her eyebrow.

"It doesn't matter. It wasn't important," Mom deflected quickly.

Lady Magdalina let out a haughty huff before taking another sip of her tea. "Surely."

Mom remained tight-lipped. It was obvious that whatever Mom was hiding *was* important, but she wasn't going to tell Lady Magdalina… at least, not with me around.

More freaking secrets. Why hadn't she told me anything? Was I that untrustworthy?

I opened my mouth to say something else, but Mom cut me off and said, "I had my reasons, Emma. Please, don't ask anymore about it."

My blood boiled underneath my skin, but there was nothing I could do to change her mind. She obviously didn't trust me with whatever she was hiding.

I ignored Mom and turned to face Lady Magdalina. Now that I knew this was real, my brain was starting to piece this thing together. "So… the mark on my hand shows I belong to the wolf Faction?"

"Yes." Lady Magdalina nodded. "It shows that one day, you are destined to mate with one of the wolven kind, and become their bride."

"Ew. Gross." I wrinkled my nose. I didn't want to be engaged to some slobbering dog-man — though it might be better than a slimy reptile.

"It is not *gross*." Lady Magdalina sniffed at my improper language. "The bond between a Marked and her Companion is the most powerful connection the Arcanea have. It is something true and sacred."

Something horrible hit me. "There was someone here a month ago. A man that could change into a wolf. He tried to attack me. Was he my mate?" Were all Arcanea like this, taking their chosen mates by force?

"Oh, by the Seven Gods, no," Lady Magdalina seemed deeply bothered, and shuddered. "Mating doesn't work like that. That was a rogue."

"A rogue? Here?" Mom seemed concerned. She didn't appear bothered that I'd said I'd been attacked by a wolf. I bet she already knew.

Lady Magdalina's face darkened. "The Arcanea do have enemies, Emma, some within our own kind. The Black Claw is a fanatic group that seeks to gain power within Malovia and over-turn the monarchy, our governing body. Killing Marked makes Companions weak, as they'll never bond, and a Companion is significantly less powerful without a mate by their side. Most likely, they discovered you were here and sent an assassin to take your life."

"No." Mom's tone was full of denial. "They couldn't have found us. I've hidden us too well."

"My dear, I managed to find you after all these years," Lady Magdalina reminded her patiently. "If you slipped up even once, and the Black Claw found out, they'd be after Emma to prevent her from bonding with someone who wasn't in their group— especially if they had a speculation about who she may bond with."

"Do you?" I asked her. "A headmistress coming all this way for one student is a bit suspi-cious. You could've sent someone less important. You didn't have to come all this way your-self… unless you had a theory about my…" It made me sick to say the word.

Lady Magdalina smiled. "You're a clever one. I do have an inkling of who your mate may be — and he is very important. That is why I'm here. Though I will refuse to say anything more about it. These things work best when the individuals work the details out themselves."

A bad taste filled my mouth. This lady flew across the ocean to set me up on a date. I'd always had really bad luck with guys, and had sworn them off awhile ago. I'd intended to become a lonely cat lady. Now I felt like my future had already been chosen for me— like I'd been sold off to some guy I'd never even met.

I remembered what I'd done to the wolf, and a rotten feeling grew in my gut. I might as well come clean now. "The wolf who attacked me… I killed him."

Lady Magdalina nodded. "Yes. I know. The Arcanea have already investigated the case and have informed me of what happened. The magic you used was a powerful light illusion."

"But if it was an illusion, how did that—"

"If the illusion is strong enough, and cast by a powerful-enough Arcanea, that illusion may become reality," Lady Magdalina said. "My suspicion is that your survival instincts kicked in, and triggered your magic in a way that made it so powerful it eliminated the threat."

My mouth went dry. "Am I in trouble?"

"You? No." Lady Magdalina shook her head. "The Companion you killed was an active participant in the Black Claw. He was certainly here to kill you. If anything, you'll be regarded as a hero."

That was a relief… even though guilt still resonated with me for killing the guy in the first place, no matter what the reason.

"The body was gone when I went back to see it," I said.

"I took care of the body," Mom said.

Heaviness coated me like a blanket. "You… hid a body for me?"

Mom gave a sad laugh. "You're my saving grace, Emma. I'd do anything for the child I love, including hide a hundred bodies."

Some of my anger at my mom dissipated. She'd covered up a murder that I'd committed to protect me. That was crazy love. Yeah, she'd lied to me for ages about who I was, but the more I found out about the Arcanea, the more dangerous they sounded. She probably had a good reason for covering everything up.

"The Black Claw is getting bolder and bolder with the throne being empty," Lady Magdalina announced. "Since the passing of the King of the Arcanea, they've stepped up their efforts to throw the country into chaos. It doesn't surprise me that they're going after more unbonded Marked than ever before."

Mom froze on her chair. Every part of her tensed up as her eyes were shadowed by pain. "The King of the Arcanea is dead?" Mom's face went stark white. Her fingernails gripped the armrests.

Lady Magdalina's tone became gentle. "I'm afraid so."

Mom's lip trembled, and a few tears streamed down her face. I leaned forward and wiped them away. "Mom, don't cry."

She didn't listen. More tears came out of her eyes. Lady Magdalina took a handkerchief out of her pocket and handed it to Mom. "There now, Evonna. I know you and Lycus were close friends. But you needn't worry. He died in battle fighting a leshane a few months ago. He is in the Great Hunting Fields now."

Mom dabbed at her eyelids with the handkerchief before she let out a few sobs. It was hard to watch. Mom was a tough woman who never cried. I realized that this was a world that had really hurt her. Lady Magdalina let her cry without giving complaint.

Eventually, Mom cleared her throat and pulled herself together. Her grief turned to stubbornness. "Well, there's nothing we can do about it now. But the fact remains that Emma is *not* going to that school."

"Emmaline *will* attend Arcanea University," Lady Magdalina said. "She will learn how to control her magic, she will bond with her mate, and she will finally be among her people in a place where she belongs."

"You will not take her!" Mom shouted. For as friendly as she'd been, now her anger was unbound. She *really* didn't want me going to this place.

"Excuse me? It's my decision," I said sharply. I caught Lady Magdalina's stern look, and I asked, "What happens if I refuse?"

"I don't think you understand the gravity of the situation, Emmaline. This is a very exclusive opportunity that won't happen again. The Arcanea don't often allow outsiders. They threaten our way of life," Lady Magdalina said. "If you turn down this one chance, you won't be given another, and the Black Claw won't stop hunting you. We cannot protect you unless you're within the realm of the Arcanea. Malovia is where you belong."

Talk about ominous. Mom stood with clenched fists. "I can protect her," she said harshly.

"And what about when you are gone? You won't live forever, Evonna," Lady Magdalina responded.

Mom's knuckles cracked. Lady Magdalina frowned and said, "I hope you don't find me overstepping my place, and I apologize in advance, but I did look at your medical files before I came here, Emmaline. I have connections."

She'd looked into my medical files? That was totally invasive! This lady had no boundaries!

But I hardly cared about that. Another idea had broken into my mind. "Can the Arcanea cure my disease with magic?" I asked.

Lady Magdalina frowned. "I'm afraid not. Healing magic is exceptionally rare in the supernatural world, and doesn't always work. It is not a capability that the Arcanea have. I know your health isn't in the most optimal condition. It will get worse, if you refuse to attend Arcanea University and learn your magic."

"What does she mean, Mom?" I asked, looking at her.

Mom's face was red with rage. "When an Arcanea comes of age, they come into their powers. Any Arcanea that doesn't use their powers experiences physical consequences," she admitted through clenched teeth.

"Is that the reason why I'm sick?" I asked. Hell, I hoped not.

Lady Magdalina shook her head. "Your condition is genetic, Emmaline. It comes from the human side of your DNA. It has nothing to do with the Arcanea. What your mother is talking about are side-effects from allowing your magic to build up in your body without any release. It won't kill you, but it'll cause significant pain. Your condition will get worse because of it."

"That's why I have migraines, Emma. If I don't use my powers, the magic builds up in my body and becomes unbearable," Mom explained. "I try not to use my magic, so I don't draw attention. Arcaneas are attracted to other Arcaneas. They'd sense we were here if I used my powers."

"Precisely," Lady Magdalina said. "I've been in America for days, searching for you. When you killed the rouge, Emmaline, I sensed such a burst of power from you that I knew a strong Arcanea had to be in the area. It only took a bit of investigating to find you."

I looked at Mom. "So… all those vacations we couldn't afford…" I filled in the blanks. We'd taken them every year, whether the extra funds were there or not, and never been to the same place twice.

Mom nodded. "Yes. I went away to use my powers, in locations far enough away and scattered throughout the U.S. so that the Arcanea wouldn't be able to find us. I haven't been able to leave recently, because of finances. That's why the migraines have gotten worse."

"But… why did you feel the need to hide us, anyway?" This magical society sounded weird, but cool. I was instantly drawn to it. Why wouldn't Mom want to raise me in a world where spells and illusions really worked and sorceresses were real? I wanted to be a badass, too. Normal was boring.

"The world of the Arcanea isn't something I wanted for you. It's painful and brutal. The life of a monster hunter isn't easy. You have to be strong to survive," Mom insisted.

"But there is beauty in the pain," Lady Magdalina interrupted. "Arcanea University is where she belongs. You know it, Evonna. It's cruel to keep her away from that any longer."

The anger flooded away from her expression. Mom hung her head, like she knew what Lady Magdalina said was true.

Though secretly I agreed with Lady Magdalina, my mom was still my mom. I wanted to side with her.

"Um… I don't know if I want to go to a college that teaches you how to turn people into frogs or whatever," I said.

Lady Magdalina laughed. "What do you think we are? Some coven for witches that has no place in the civilized world?" She laughed again before she shook her head. "We have museums, shopping centers, cultural areas and theaters that are the best in the world. Most prestigious of all, Malovia is famous for winter sports. Our hockey teams, ski resorts, and bobsledding arenas have produced many champions."

"I'm a figure skater," I said bluntly. "I do have a career to consider, and my training is here in Detroit." Not that it was much of a career. That'd pretty much been ruined after my diagnosis.

"We have plenty of facilities for you to practice your sport. The ice arena at Malovia hosts some of the best trainers in the world, including myself," Lady Magdalina stated. "I've taught many Olympic athletes, and would be agreeable to take you on as my student if you enrolled at the University."

This place kept sounding better and better. But what was the catch?

"I don't think we can afford this," I started. "I'm an American. I'd have to go through an immigration process, and find housing, and—"

"Darling, you don't understand," Lady Magdalina said kindly. "You have *Arcanea blood*. That automatically makes you a Malovian citizen. There's no immigration process required. You'll be given the benefits all of our countrymen receive— including free education and healthcare. Your housing will be in the dormitories at the university. All your expenses are already paid for."

That made one hell of a difference in my decision. It moved me from thinking leaving Detroit was impossible to very critical. Healthcare in Malovia was free. Healthcare in America was not. I'd seen the estimates on my medicine the insurance company had delivered, and they weren't anything to sneeze at. Treatment for my illness could literally bankrupt my Mom. I hadn't started the infusions yet, because I was worried about the cost. I'd been putting them off because they were so expensive.

Still, it was obvious I needed them. My fatigue was killing me, draining any energy I had to even do simple tasks, and I'd gotten a ridiculous amount of colds in the past few weeks alone. In. The. *Summer.* I couldn't get better from one virus without catching another infection the next day. Much longer without these infusions, and I wouldn't be able to skate. I wouldn't be able to do much of anything besides sit on the couch and wait to die.

It seemed like I didn't have much of an option *but* to go to Malovia. If I stayed here, I'd break my family financially and end up going nowhere with my life. But if I went on ahead to this weird school, things would be taken care of. I could get my medicine. I wouldn't have to worry about paying for being sick, just worry about getting better. Besides— I'd always wanted to see Europe, just never had the opportunity to go. And I was being given a chance to go to college for free… something I'd always dreamed of… even though the school probably wasn't accredited and definitely a rip-off. Like, a school for magical sorceresses and men who could turn into animals? I'd seen it was real with my own two eyes, and still didn't believe it.

But that was the thing. I didn't have a choice whether to believe it or not. These weirdo Black Claw fuckheads were after me now, and would most likely kill me and my mom if I didn't end up going to a place where I'd be protected. The only place on earth where I would be safe from them would be Malovia.

Going to Arcanea University would be scary. But it would also be an adventure. And I was really tired of living a boring life. I couldn't *stand* being bored. To me, it was worse than being sad. This magical society sounded dangerous, but interesting. Besides skating, nothing else kept me going. I'd prayed for something exciting to happen ever since I'd left high school, and nothing ever did. This was what I'd been asking for, and it'd showed up on my doorstep. Could I really turn it down?

I knew I couldn't. I didn't care how unsafe it was. I'd just gotten diagnosed with a disease that could end my life at any time. I craved some sort of meaning to my existence ever since. Now wasn't the time to play it safe. If I was short on time, I wanted to make every minute count.

I put on a brave smile. "I think I want to kill some monsters."

"That's the spirit!" Lady Magdalina praised, while Mom's expression dropped. "I already have a flight booked for you. Pack your things, and we'll be off."

What, so soon? I didn't even have any time to *process* all of this?

By the eager expression on Lady Magdalina's face, clearly not. Mom's eyes were heartbroken. It nearly killed me to see her like that.

Mom extended a hand to me. "Come, Emma. I'll help you pack."

I took it, and she led me upstairs to my room. I got out a suitcase and started packing things in silence with Mom beside me. I looked around my room. Would be the last time I'd ever step foot in this house? Would I ever come back home to Michigan again?

Would I ever see my *mom* again?

Mom put a bunch of sweaters in the suitcase. "It's cold in Malovia. You'll need to keep warm."

My throat got hot, and tears dotted my eyes at the thought of leaving my mom to go to a place where I had no friends, no family, and no idea of the culture there.

"Emma…" Mom straightened up after she put a few wool socks in my suitcase. "Lady Magdalina means well. She's a wonderful woman, the best of the Arcanea. I admire her very much. She's a dear friend to me."

Mom took a breath. "But she'll ask you to do things that will be extremely difficult, and she expects success every time," Mom pleaded. "Think about that before you agree to go."

I searched her face and found only honesty. She both looked up to and feared Lady Magdalina. I wasn't sure why.

Despite what Mom said, I trusted Lady Magdalina. She was an iron lady, the type you wanted to lead you into war, because you knew she'd win. She was the kind of woman that intimidated men and demanded what she wanted out of life. I liked that about her, and she had picked me. I knew she'd push me, but I was a figure skater. I could handle it.

I didn't want to hide from life like my mom, regardless of whatever reasons she'd chosen to do so.

"This is my decision, Mom. I want to go," I said. "You can't stop me."

She looked away from me. "No. I suppose I can't."

That didn't mean I wanted to abandon her. "Mom, come with me," I begged. "Sell the diner. We can start over in Malovia. I don't want to do this without you."

Mom smiled slightly. "I'm afraid that's not possible, Emmaline. At least, not at the moment."

She had so many secrets. Secrets I was afraid I'd never learn. I reached up and wrapped my arms around her. "I'll miss you so much."

Mom hugged me even tighter. "I'll miss you as well, saving grace. But Lady Magdalina is right. Malovia is where you belong. Arcanea University is the most wonderful place in the world. I promise that you'll love it there, just like I did."

I hardly cared if I did or I didn't. I was mainly going there to keep my Mom safe from the Black Claw freaks. They wouldn't hurt her if I was gone. They'd follow me back to Malovia.

I forced my tears back. Crying wouldn't do any good. I was going on an adventure, to learn how to do magic at a college for sorceresses while Lady Magdalina tried to play undercover matchmaker between me and some werewolf dude. I hoped to God he was hot.

I was giving up my mom and everything I'd ever known for this. *This slobbering dog better be one hell of a catch.*

FIVE

I knew I was in trouble when my mother, Queen Antonia, summoned me the day before I moved my things into my dormitory at Arcanea University.

It was supposed to be my last day in the palace until next semester. I had hoped to slip out without being noticed. But nothing ever got past my mother. This was harder than facing the Circle. I sighed and dutifully proceeded after the servant who had informed me of such matters, cursing my luck.

Mother sat in the tearoom, in a large armchair by a ceiling-length window that looked down on the city from above. The armchair was high-backed, and sat on a bearskin rug that my father had killed himself. The room was full of decorations, paintings and treasures from around the world. Mother was a world-traveler who liked comfort and nice things. Father made sure she had them.

It was unusual to see her not at my father's side as I entered the parlor. Now that he was gone, it seemed she had lost her place in this world.

"Sit down, Ethan." She stirred her tea slowly. She liked it black. Today she'd forgone the mourning clothes and was wearing an oversized red dress. It was one of the last gifts my Da had given to her. Her face was done perfectly with makeup, and her black hair was fashioned into an updo. Grief was no excuse for looking like a mess, in the land of the Arcanea.

I lounged on the couch and threw a leg up. Her nose wrinkled, but she didn't complain. She didn't like when I didn't sit properly. I was a pretty casual prince, as far as they went.

"I heard you declared your intent to enter the Contest," Mother said. Her black eyes looked to me. I said nothing.

Mother didn't want me to enter the King's Contest. She wanted to keep me safe. People died in the Contest every time it was held. It was a deadly competition not everyone survived.

I knew what her true thoughts were. She didn't want me to win. If I became King, it put me at risk for assassinations. I would have to risk my life to lead the Arcanea every day. She didn't want to lose the one thing she had left.

"I don't approve," she said immediately, and pursed her lips. "There's too much at risk. What if something happens to you? Do you want to leave me here alone?"

"Nothing will happen to me. I'll be fine," I insisted. "Father was preparing me for this. He had been since the day I was born. It's my rightful throne."

"Your father was going to be here when you declared. He was going to stand by your side when you became king." Mother's voice is sharp. "He is no longer here, and so now things have changed."

"Do you think me incapable?" My voice rose.

"I think you care too much," Mother snapped. "A king cannot go around trying to solve every problem his country has, and I know you, Ethan. You will try."

I sneered, but I knew she was right. Mother loved me, but she wasn't good for loving anyone else. Her list of people she cared about included me and Da, and he was gone. Besides taking care of me, her only purpose in life had left her. She'd let every last Arcanea on earth die if it meant saving her son.

Peasants were even lower on the list of things she found important. Commoners might as well be cockroaches to her.

And she knew I'd put my people first, before myself. Which scared her.

"There's no need to talk of this right now," I said. "Steward Solomon will take care of things while—"

"Steward Solomon is a fool. We both know it." Mother put down her tea with a snap. "He couldn't rule over a molehill. Look at what's happened since your father's been gone."

She was right. The Arcanea were more than uneasy. There'd been near panic after my father's death was announced. Monsters were getting braver. Hunters were having to go out every night to hunt them down to prevent them from entering the city. Sorceresses were working full-time to cast spells to protect themselves and their houses. The only place that seemed safe anymore was Arcanea University, and that was because it was protected by the strongest Marked and Companions in the world. The Circle was barely keeping control. Worse still, Solomon had made it obvious he couldn't handle the job. He'd locked himself up in his quarters of the palace and refused to come out more days than not. Without a strong leader, the Arcanea wouldn't listen. They'd look after themselves and their own, and to hell with everyone else.

"Whoever takes over after Solomon steps down is going to have his hands full," Mother said. "It's going to be madness regaining the trust of the people. The Factions will be fighting for power, and these are desperate times."

I knew she was right. The four Factions usually got along, as patriotism and our country came before any individual race. We weren't like the Houses of the Elementai in America, who couldn't unify if you forced them to. But every twenty years when the King's Contest came around, the allure of power took over, and each Faction would work their hardest to make sure one of their own kind was put on the throne.

The division never usually lasted more than a year or so. Arcanea were undyingly loyal.

Once the new king proved himself, each of the Factions would die for him. But before then? There would be assassination attempts, undercover plots, espionage. Only once the new king survived all of that would he be deemed worthy to become a true ruler.

Yes. Becoming the new king would be dangerous. But allow someone to do that in my place? Never. I knew what I was getting into.

"To back down now would look cowardly. I won't do it," I told my mother.

"Would you rather look like a coward or lose your life? No, I know the answer. You don't have to say it, you stubborn boy." Mother took another sip of her tea, looking cross.

I drummed my fingers against the armrest. "If you really think I'm about to quit and let Elijah have a shot at the crown that is mine, you don't know me that well."

"Elijah is another one. Pasty-faced fool. And stop that," she added, glaring at my drumming fingers. "It's painfully annoying."

I stopped. She sighed and said, "I shouldn't have to tell you that the Factions aren't our only worries. The Black Claw is rumored to be regaining power."

I sat back in surprise. "The Black Claw?"

"Yes," Mother hissed. "Listen more closely the first time."

The Black Claw was a fanatic cult, one that believed in dark magic. They'd caused quite a few problems in past years, including starting an uprising that had nearly led to a war. But my father had practically wiped them out during his reign. There were so few of the Black Claw left that I didn't even think they were still around. I didn't consider them a real threat.

I mulled in thought. "You really think the Black Claw stand a chance of coming into power?"

"They're already coming into power. You're not paying attention."

"You're just being paranoid." I barely listened. The Black Claw was nothing to worry about. Sure, some Arcanea still feared them, but I wasn't one of them.

Mother shook her head. "There's been talk of human sacrifices increasing in the highlands. Deep in the woods, where no one can find the bodies. The Black Claw is attempting to please the Dark Stag of Wrath, and gain his favor. With your father gone, they stand a chance of gaining more followers. Weak-minded people who are too afraid to stand on their own, or those who seek power."

"People are disappearing?"

Mother nodded. "In the villages. And it isn't due to monsters."

That was concerning. "Are you certain it's the Black Claw?"

"Who else could it be?" she insisted. "Your father was concerned about them before he died. He was working on a plan to draw them out and eliminate the rest of them. Unfortunately, his time drew too short to carry out this plan. Don't inform anyone of this. He was to keep it between us."

This was news to me. "Why didn't he tell me?"

"I don't know, Ethan. Yet it makes sense. When was the last time a leshane was in Malovia? Long ago. What kind of dark magic was used to summon such a creature out of Droga's underworld?"

Her lip trembled. "And now your father is gone." She didn't cry this time, but she looked like she might.

I got off the couch and leaned forward to embrace her. "I'm sorry, Mother." I didn't know what else to say. I still felt like all of this was my fault— that all of the Arcanea were left vulnerable due to the mistake I'd made. I was responsible for every one of my people, and I'd let them down.

Mother sniffed. "The Seven Gods help me. If you go through with this, Ethan, I'll never forgive you."

I stood up. "Then I guess I'll have to beg for your mercy, because I don't intend to withdraw my declaration."

I walked away before she could say anything more. She knew where I stood, and I wouldn't change my mind.

I thought about what she'd said as I packed the last of my things into my suitcase. If my father had been right, and the Black Claw was coming back into power, I'd hunt down every last one of them.

He'd died before his mission to end the Black Claw was realized. So I'd end them for him.

I waited until nightfall to embark on the streets of Dolinska, just past the hour of midnight. I donned a black cloak, throwing the hood over my eyes, along with black breeches and boots. I fitted a wooden wolf's mask over my eyes, white in color, before I locked my bedroom door and fastened a hook to my window. I quickly rappelled down the side of the palace tower. It was a hundred feet down, a straight shot, but it didn't bother me. I'd done this hundreds of times.

When I hit the ground, I yanked the hook so that it came off the window, then rolled the rope up and tucked it into my secret spot behind a barrel before taking the servant's door into the city. It would be much more difficult to sneak out once I attended the university, but I'd make do. I wasn't about to give this up.

The streets were mostly empty. A self-imposed curfew had fallen upon the city since my father had died. No one seemed much in the mood to celebrate the end of the warm summer days. Everyone was nervous.

The streets of Dolinska were cobblestone. Gothic buildings rose up five stories in height around me, enclosing in the area. Renaissance mansions and Baroque churches of massive structure were built here and there among the massive spread of food carts, coffee shops open to the air, and vendors selling potions and magical items. All were closed for the night. The streetlights were dim, and the elaborate fountains sculpted in shapes of Companions and Marked were turned off. There were only a few shops open— shady bars, strip clubs, and establishments of a magical nature no Arcanea frequented unless they were dabbling in things they shouldn't be.

I had no fear of being spotted, so I shifted into a wolf and ran throughout the city streets, sure of where I was headed. There were regular humans in Malovia, and they were afraid of us. Even though this was the modern age, fairy tales and folklore still ruled the country. They spoke with hatred of sorceresses and their trained monster hunters. They didn't know we truly existed, but rumor and myth had been passed down generation to generation of unfeeling Arcanea and their love for blood and coin.

Anyone not Arcanea wasn't permitted to live in Dolinska— the government found excuses to avoid allowing humans into the city, and the city was surrounded by such thick forest that nobody but the Arcanea bothered to come here, anyway. The nearest human settlement was a tiny farming town, and it was at least thirty miles away.

Many humans still didn't go out at night. A good thing, too. Centuries past had done nothing to curb the amount of monsters still lurking in the country. They avoided humans now more than in the past, because technology scared them and was unfamiliar, but every now and then one got brave enough to step out of line and go hunting.

That's when people started disappearing. More often than not, they went after tourists who didn't know the area and didn't respect the culture. Malovia was mostly Christian, but the local folks still participated in pagan ceremonies and followed traditions that had been carried out by their ancestors long ago.

Mother was sure those disappearances weren't monsters, but the Black Claw. Monsters usually left traces. The Black Claw did not. They came and vanished like a thief in the night.

Salt was sprinkled across many doorsteps. On some doorways hung crosses. Others, antlers. On a few mantles was the smearing of dark blood— deer's blood, an offering to the Seven Gods for protection.

Monsters usually couldn't cross these paths, if the magic had been done right. Didn't mean the Black Claw couldn't. It usually took a powerful Marked to keep them out.

After fifteen minutes of running, I came to a stop at my destination. It was a narrow alleyway that led to a few apartment buildings that had a statue of two snarling wolves in the middle. Rumor had it that there was a group murder in this alleyway a few nights ago. Three Arcanea dead. I was determined to investigate. Black Claw, or monsters. Which was it?

Lord Lucien wouldn't approve of what I was doing. But I didn't care. Something had to be done, and I'd been at it for months.

I investigated. The scene had long been cleaned up, but I was a Companion, and I could use my magic to see what had been done in the past. I cast a spell to intensify my sight and senses. I saw a glowing on the ground where blood had once been— it'd been a massacre. I witnessed outlines of bodies lying on the ground, and deep scratches in the cobblestone. The spells that had been cast left dark residue on the ground, like gunpowder. Something had come at them from behind and prevented them from defending themselves properly.

From what I'd read in the paper, the people killed hadn't been taken from the scene. I didn't see any signs of a struggle. That ruled out the possibility of the Black Claw. They usually took people alive, to sacrifice in dark rituals later. That meant it was a monster.

I tried using my magical sight to judge what spells had been used, but no good. I didn't see any signs. I recalled the article in the paper. One griffin and two Marked. Throats ripped out. The authorities hadn't caught whoever… or whatever… was responsible yet.

If their throats were ripped out, that usually meant either wraiths or ghouls. Couldn't be sure of which yet. Ghouls liked to eat their victims, but the paper didn't specify if the victims had been consumed. I put my nose to the ground and tried to get a smell.

No scent. That definitely meant wraiths. They were vengeful spirits who wreaked havoc in the afterlife. Usually victims of horrific ceremonies, whose souls sought revenge.

Maybe Mother was right. Wraiths in the area could mean that the Black Claw was committing more vile ceremonies. I stomped my paw in frustration. Wraiths were difficult to catch. I was sure this was outside my skill level, and I was fighting alone.

But I reminded myself I was hunting the wraith. It wasn't hunting me. I had the advantage. I wasn't going to crawl back home with my tail between my legs when there was a possibility that the wraith could kill someone else.

I changed back into my human form. I needed to get a bird's eye view, and since I didn't have wings, I was going to have to do it the old-fashioned way. I started scaling buildings. I swiftly climbed the apartment complex I was standing next to, and once I got on the roof, began surveying my surroundings.

The wraith wasn't up here. I perched on a gargoyle, scanning the streets below for the wraith. They were invisible to humans and Marked, but a Companion could see them clear as day.

Finally, I spotted it. A black shadow hovering over one of the buildings. The wraith looked like a skeletal figure in black cloth, a shroud covered in swaths of dark blood. I couldn't see its face, or any other features. It was as large as a human male, but I remained cautious. I knew it could kill me.

And it had seen me. There went the element of surprise. Instead of attacking, the wraith let out a terrifying screech and made a run for it.

I wasn't about to let it get away. My footsteps fell hard against the clay shingles of the rooftops as I gave chase. I had to jump from building to building in my pursuit of the wraith. It glided soundlessly above the ground. I made a lot of noise as I darted to keep up with it. I was forced to parkour off of buildings, ledges, and balconies while the wraith merely flew over them. Damn not having any wings.

I managed to catch up. I changed into a wolven mid-jump as I tackled the wraith. It squealed, and scratched at my eye as we tumbled off one of the buildings and to the ground. We fell into valances and canopies that ripped and slowed our descent as the cobblestone streets loomed closer and closer.

Finally, we hit the ground. The wraith broke my fall, and I ended up uninjured as I rolled off the top of it. The wraith hissed and stood to its full height, unbothered by the rough landing. Ghosts couldn't be injured in such a way.

Wraiths could only be killed once you freed the trapped spirit. But you had to make it weak enough to do that. I changed back and ripped my father's jeweled dagger out of the hilt on my belt. It was ceremonially blessed by sorceresses, and so, could hurt ghostly forms.

I charged at the wraith. It glided out of the way, but not before I sank the dagger into its middle. It was like slicing through air. I met no resistance, but I knew I had harmed the beast when it howled in rage. Dark magic flickered off its form and flung at me, but I managed to roll out of the way and only caught the edges of the spell.

The magic stung, like accidentally putting your hand on a hot stove. If the spell had actually hit me, I would've been consumed with pain, and the wraith would've easily finished the job.

I barely got to my feet before the wraith lifted a hand and I was blasted back. It screamed, and the windows in the buildings around us shattered. I wanted to cover my ears and block out the sound, but instead I gritted my teeth and rolled out of the way of the falling glass.

The wraith came at me several times, each time extending bony fingers toward my throat from under its black covering. It intended to rip my jugular out. I jumped out of the way and pierced its cloak three more times before it finally backed off. It tried to get away, but I stepped on the edge of its cloak and pinned it down before sinking the dagger into where I presumed the heart would be, if it had one.

The wraith squealed in pain. I waved my hand over the wraith and purple magic exploded from my palm, passing through the wraith and releasing the trapped spirit.

The wraith let out one last squeal before it exploded into a cloud of dust. I coughed, then wiped off the dagger on my cloak.

I wasn't sure if the wraith would be gone for good. Usually, to banish them completely, you had to undo whatever crime had been committed against them. Resolve unfinished business. But the protective spell would at least keep it out of the city for a few days.

I noticed something. Where the wraith had once been was a small doll— a child's plaything.

I picked up the doll and observed it before tucking it into my pocket. The wraith had left it behind for me. I had to return it somewhere— it was important to the spirit. Otherwise, it would come back. I would have to do some investigating to see where it came from.

Lights came on above me, and I heard voices. I looked up to see Arcanea poking their heads out of their broken windows, wondering what the hell had happened and what was causing all the noise. *Shit.*

"The Phantom!" I heard a boy cry out from above. Then there were more voices joining it. *The Phantom, the Phantom.*

I hated that cursed name. I couldn't change into my wolven form. They'd see three legs and know it was me. I kept my mask on and my hood up as I high-tailed it out of there. Cheers and applause followed me as I fled the scene.

Not everyone in Dolinska thought I was a hero. It wasn't long before the authorities arrived to give chase. I could hear the cries of the authorities as they came after me. Griffins and dragons took flight, while wolvens and alicorns stayed on the ground in pursuit. I had to pin to the walls and avoid the lights Marked cast with their hands in their search. I stayed low to the ground and hid behind various objects as I outran the authorities. The Arcanea Alliance— the local police— didn't like the Phantom coming in and doing their job for them. Made them look bad. I knew they'd love to catch me. But I'd be damned if I ever let them.

I needed to get to the palace, and back in bed before I was discovered. I took a risk and bolted. A few Marked saw me and cried out to their Companions that I was getting away, but I knew these city streets better than anyone else. I was able to zig-zag down a couple of unknown alleyways and lose them before they even knew what happened.

When I got back to the palace, the whole thing was lit up with the announcement that the Phantom had been seen again. *Dammit. More complications.*

The servant's door was now locked. I'd have to scale the wall. I chose a lightly guarded part of the wall surrounding the palace to get back inside. Once I'd scaled it and landed in the palace courtyard, I planned to make my way back to my grappling hook, so I could pull myself up to my bedroom and inside without another thought.

But when I rounded the corner to do just that, I saw a plethora of guards around the barrel where I'd hid the hook. I couldn't get to it. I either had to find my way around the guards, or risk falling to my death climbing up the tower without assistance.

I chose risking the fall. There were too many guards to sneak past, and if I was caught as the Phantom, there went my chances of participating in the King's Contest— not to mention guaranteed prison time. Vigilantes were outlawed in Dolinska. I wasted no time and started climbing. I had to stick to the wall and stay still a few times as searchlights from the Marked passed me by, but with luck, no one saw me. *Thank Luka.* The thief god was on my side tonight.

I nearly slipped a few times on my way up. Damn prosthetic. Once, a stone on the side of the tower crumbled beneath my feet, and I was left hanging by one arm.

I wasn't about to quit and forced myself to haul my body higher. At this point, my arms were shaking. My energy had nearly given out. I was nearly going to let myself fall until the memory of Lucien's determined words kept me going. I forced myself to climb until I had reached my bedroom window, and pulled myself in. A Marked's searchlight passed by the window just as I slid safely inside.

I laid on the rug in my room, spread out on the floor and panting for breath. Not having wings was really getting in the way of my life. I hoped I'd be blessed with them soon.

I remained on the floor, too nervous to even breathe. Eventually, an hour passed and the search was called off. I let out a sigh of relief. My identity was safe. The true name of the vigilante the city called the Phantom would remain a mystery.

My back cracked as I got off the hard floor, and I groaned. I removed the mask and cloak, shoved them into a drawer, and fell on my bed face-first. Dawn was in a few hours. I only had a little time to get some sleep before I'd have to report to Arcanea University in the morning.

But a bit of lost sleep was well worth the city's safety. If I couldn't be king right at this moment, I'd do what I could to protect the Arcanea in the meantime. This was the only way I could restore my honor, and fix what I'd done by killing the king. While the city slept and the throne was still uncertain, the Phantom would guard the streets, and keep the people free from danger until the King's Contest was done.

I just hoped I could keep my identity safe until then.

SIX

If I expected Lady Magdalina to escort me to Arcanea University, I was sorely mistaken. She rode with me and my mom in the car to Detroit Metropolitan Airport before handing me my flight ticket and wishing me farewell, saying she had more business to do in America before the semester at the university began.

I'd never ridden in a plane by myself before, but I had no choice, and Lady Magdalina made it obvious she expected me to handle it. I said a tearful goodbye to my mom at airport security, then proceeded forward, dragging my suitcase behind me and feeling like all the world was ahead of me.

My heartbeat was pounding in my chest. I felt like I was walking on air. Even though I was leaving everything I knew behind, it was to experience a brand-new world. Who knew what waited for me on the other side?

When the airplane came in, I found myself staring slack-jawed at the biggest and fanciest jetliner I'd ever seen. The side of it read *Malovian Airlines*. When I stepped inside the plane, I was greeted with velvet red carpet and private drink coolers for every reclining seat. The plane even had a bar. It was very different from the rickety planes me and Mom usually took on vacation.

I was shocked when the airline hostess led me to a very cushy seat right up front in First Class, one that extended to become a bed. I was given a sparkling water and a fancy dinner of slow-braised steak and asparagus. Hot towels were distributed at my request. The seat came with a TV that had unlimited movies. Apparently, Lady Magdalina only flew in style. Hell, if all Arcanea lived like this, I could get used to it. Lady Magdalina had hinted they only liked the best of the best.

The red-eye from Detroit to Malovia was pretty quiet, and due to the swanky seats in First Class, I slept through most of the twelve-hour flight. I woke up well-rested when the plane landed at eight in the morning. Longing for a bath, I grabbed my suitcase and made my way off the plane, thankful I'd managed to avoid baggage claim.

The airport was directly connected to the train station that would take me the rest of the way to the school. I momentarily panicked for a moment when I closed my passport and made my way out of international arrivals— I was in a foreign country, by myself, with no knowledge of the language or people. Arrivals and departures were announced heavily over the loudspeakers in words I didn't understand. I was way out of my element.

Dozens of well-dressed people passed me by, but no one stopped to offer me directions. They mostly moved around me like I wasn't even there. I wanted to ask for help, but I didn't know if anyone in Malovia knew English.

I felt like my red hair put me out of place. Most people around here had either brunette or black hair, and dark eyes, not green ones. I took a look at all the women dressed in long wool coats, mink hats, and high-heeled fall boots. I wished I had worn something a little more formal than designer sweats, fur boots, leg warmers, and a grey parka.

I was totally out of place here. Magdalina had told me that Malovia would be my home. How could it be? This was a nice place to vacation, but not to stay. I didn't belong here.

I told myself to snap out of it. Magdalina said I was an Arcanea. I was one of them. I belonged here just as much as any of them did. Time to buck up.

Thankfully, most of the boards that showed directions to the different trains were written in Malovian and English. I read my directions to my train, Railway 5, and felt relieved when I approached the boarding site and saw a sign stating that the train was headed to Arcanea University.

I waited on the platform anxiously. I expected some official to come out of nowhere and say that I wasn't supposed to be here— that I was an American and I needed to go back home— but no one did.

After ten minutes or so, I heard a loud train whistle. I turned, and my mouth dropped open as I watched a massive modern train proceed toward me. The train was made of glass, and edged with gold trim. It blew back my hair as it came rushing into the station and made an abrupt stop. On the side of the train were the words, *The Malovian Railway.*

I took a look at the map. The Malovian Railway had multiple tracks running all around Europe, but only one took you to Arcanea University. I gave them my pass and was directed to the back of the train, where the students usually sat.

Damn. This train was swanky. The walls were made of dark hardwood, the floors a carpet that was an intricate pattern of red and gold. Paintings hung on the hallway walls in silver frames, and miniature chandeliers lit the way down the long hallway to my cabin. Beautiful women with curled hair and painted faces carried trays of champagne and caviar up and down the aisles.

I was handed another glass of champagne by a smiling assistant. I didn't know what else to do, so I sipped at it politely. Growing up in figure skating, I'd grown used to being around people who had a lot of money, but this was a bit over the top, even for me.

I sighed with relief when I collapsed into my cabin and shut the glass door behind me. I sat on the velvet seats and opened the Malovian travel guide that Magdalina had given me. I shuffled through the pages. My destination was a little over an hour away. The train would eventually stop in a city called Dolinska, Malovia's capital. From there, it was only a short walk to the university.

Thank God. I really didn't want to drag my bag all the way there.

I looked out the window, watching Malovia's green hills and white mountains roll by. The landscape here was certainly breathtaking— the trees a mixture of dark green coniferous pines and deciduous trees that were already showing off a vibrant display of orange, yellow, and red leaves. Everywhere I looked there were beautiful, cascading waterfalls and crystal streams that glistened like sapphires as the water rolled down over the sharp rocks that coated the valleys. The skies were mostly gray overhead, coated in clouds, though shimmering yellow sunlight broke through patches every now and then and lit up the landscape in a beautiful halo, like a blessing straight from the heavens. It was the kind of place that seemed like it was always dawn, or always sunset. Eventually, the valleys changed into tall mountains with icy caps that spread in both directions as far as the eye could see.

Malovia looked like a fairy-tale land. Even though I lived here now, it still seemed like my arrival here was a dream.

I was surprised it wasn't snowing. It was only early September, but there was already a chill that permeated the air. Bits of frost were starting to fog around my train window, creating intricate patterns that I brushed my finger over. I was glad I'd packed an extra jacket. Malovia was the kind of place where it stayed cold all year round.

After awhile, I got a little hungry. I left my bag in my cabin and went looking for something to eat.

The train was massive. I totally got lost in a matter of seconds. I found a golden door that I thought led to the cafe— but when I opened it, my jaw dropped open.

People were walking around in freaking *swimsuits*. Pools of hot water were built into the floor, and a cascading waterfall fell from thirty feet above. Tropical plants bloomed everywhere, and the air around me felt muggy and hot— ninety degrees or more. It was nothing like the chilly Malovian atmosphere I'd only experienced seconds before. People swam in the steamy pools underneath blazing sunlight, and I heard the singing of tropical birds in the background. It was like I'd walked straight into South America.

How could you have an entire *hot spring* in the middle of a train? With a glance down, I saw with a jolt that my normal clothes had vanished, replaced by a bikini that showed *way* too much skin.

It must be illusion magic, right? That was the only explanation I could think of. This stuff wasn't real— it just tricked your brain into thinking it was.

Feeling off, I left the room and returned back to the main hall. Once I closed the door behind me, the swim suit disappeared and my clothes returned.

I really had to get used to this place. I resumed my mission of looking for the cafe, though I was careful not to open any more doors that I passed.

Finally, I found the cafe, sitting at the front of the train. This time of day, they were selling pastries. The glass case encompassed a variety of delicious cupcakes and cookies, each one looking more perfect and savory than the last.

"What can I get you?" the attendant asked from behind the counter. She had a thick Slavic accent, and my God, she was gorgeous. Her sleek dark hair and blue eyes were perfectly accented by the railway uniform she wore. She could be a freaking model.

"You speak English?" I asked in surprise.

She bobbed her head. "Yes. American, aren't you?"

"Yeah," I confessed nervously. "It's my first time out of the country. I worried I wouldn't be able to communicate with anyone."

The attendant smiled kindly. "Everyone in Malovia has to study English in high school. It's the language classes at the university are taught in. I'm assuming you're a student?"

I bobbed my head. It was a relief to know that I wouldn't have to learn an entirely new language overnight while attending Arcanea University.

"Most Arcanea speak Malovian only in their own homes. I'm certain you'll be fine," she stated. She tilted her head, then added, "You seem a little pale."

"I just walked into some sort of hot springs room. I'm new to illusion magic, so it was a little unexpected." I gave a nervous laugh.

"The Malovian Railway has several enchanted illusion rooms for our guests to enjoy," she replied. "Besides the room with the hot springs, there's also a ski resort room, a water park, and a mini shopping center, as well as sleeping cabins for guests taking longer journeys. The illusions help to pass the time while traveling."

"Thanks for explaining all this to me." I felt way behind. I hoped I could catch up, but at the same time, I was relieved that everyone spoke English and I wouldn't be totally lost here.

I bought a cherry pastry, then headed back to my cabin. I thought the pastry was another illusion, until I licked the sugar off the top and decided it definitely had to be real.

In the hallway, I noticed a girl walking by. She had sleek brunette hair, and makeup done to perfection. She was wearing a crisp outfit that looked like it'd come from the pages of a magazine, and high heels.

Two girls followed behind her, identical twins. They were dressed similarly to the other girl, who I worked out was the head bitch, and were very tall. They had hooded eyes and square faces.

I was so busy looking at them that I didn't realize where I was going. The train jerked to the side unexpectedly, and I slammed right into the leader. My cherry pastry smeared all over the front of her outfit.

The girl gave a gasp and jumped backward, shaking her hands. Shit. I'd just ruined her designer tee. My mouth opened to apologize. "I'm sorry. I didn't mean to bump into you."

The girl glared at me. In a thick accent, she said, "Are you serious? Can't you watch where you're going?"

The girl waved a hand. The jelly on her shirt vanished instantly, and I had to blink twice. Did I just see that?

I realized that I was in a place where magic was real, and people probably did this all the time. I bet I looked really stupid in that moment.

The girl was giving me a stare at my astounded look. I quickly rearranged my face and said, "Sorry. Didn't mean to bump into you."

"It doesn't matter if you didn't mean it, it happened anyway," the girl bit back. "You're lucky I'm in a good mood, otherwise, you'd be paying me for my shirt."

Wow, okay. She didn't want to play nice. That was fine. I was good at that, too. "I apologize. But to make up for it, do you mind if I buy you some manners, or common decency? You're obviously in need of some."

The girl's mouth dropped open again, and the twins gasped behind her. I gave her a smirk. Yeah, I knew how to play this game. Very well, in fact.

"You look like a student," the girl started. "But I've never seen you before."

"Yeah, I'm not from around here." I gave a casual shrug.

"Obviously." The girl raised a sneer. "I'm Gabriella Ciar. Gabby for short. This is my first year at Arcanea University. Yours as well?"

"Yes." I didn't give her specifics, but my accent gave me away.

"You're an American." Gabby narrowed her eyes. "I just got back from vacationing in Ibiza. Italy's *amazing*. I expect you've never been out of the country. You've got a lost puppy-dog look about you."

One of the twins barked behind her hand. The other laughed. My, they had this down to a system, didn't they? I wasn't impressed.

"Morgan, don't embarrass me," Gabby snapped. She rolled her eyes. "Your taunts are like a child's. Get some class."

Morgan cringed. The other twin reached out to touch her sister's arm, but Morgan yanked it away.

"I'm fine, Melissa," she mumbled. Melissa frowned and stared at the carpet. Gabby smiled slightly.

I was able to tell them apart now, because I noticed Morgan had a tiny scar around her eyebrow that Melissa didn't have. It had also taken me two minutes of conversation to see that Gabby often pitted them against each other. What a great friend.

Gabby crossed her arms. "Since you don't know, let me give you the rundown of how things *work* around here," she snarled. "My family has power. Since I don't know who you are and have never heard of you, I'm guessing you're a nobody. That makes you not worth my time. So stay out of my way, or I'll *make* you."

"She'll probably bond with a weak Companion," Melissa suggested. Morgan giggled.

"As long as she doesn't bond with any one *decent*," Gabby added. "I'll let you know right now, the top picks of the men are mine. You can have the scraps once I'm done choosing. My family's been waiting for me to make my match for years, and you can be sure *I'll* have the best mate."

I drew myself up straight. No way was I going to let this go down without a fight. My bite was worse than my bark. "Those are a lot of tough words. Sure you can back them up?"

Gabby scoffed. "Please. Can you even *do* magic?" Gabby raised an eyebrow. Her two clones did the same behind her. Holy hell, did she program these girls to follow her around and copy her every move?

"Not yet," I said. "But it's probably best you have a head start, because it won't be long before I embarrass you with what I can do."

Gabby's mouth opened slightly. Yeah, I said it. Didn't regret it, either. Girls at the rink back home knew better than to mess with me. She'd learn, too. I didn't have any idea how to do magic— wasn't even sure if I'd be good at it. But I wasn't about to let this girl push me around.

Gabby quickly rearranged her face and sneered. "You're overconfident. Let's see how long it lasts. The new meat doesn't last long around here."

She shoved past me. Her friends followed, their noses turned up so high that if it was raining they'd drown.

Great. Gabby was the first person I'd managed to meet in this place who went to my school, and she was a total bitch. I hoped not all Arcanea were like that, but I didn't count on anyone being friendly. I was an outsider, after all.

Calm down, Emma. Day one, and I was already making enemies. It was so like me. My presence was usually enough by itself to piss people off. I couldn't lie when I said I liked starting trouble. I had a problem keeping a handle on my big mouth. It liked to open before my brain usually caught up with it. Oops. Sorry, not sorry. I'd learned a long time ago that if you wanted to survive, you had to fend for yourself or get eaten alive.

I wondered what she'd said about Companions. Gabby acted like she was going to waltz into school and handpick the best guy to be her mate, but according to Lady Magdalina, that's not how it worked. You didn't choose your mate; the magic chose for you. It was supposed to be some deep, everlasting bond that transcended the laws of nature or some shit like that.

I thought everything Lady Magdalina said was woo-woo nonsense, but after I met Gabby, I hoped I didn't end up getting left out. I was worried that no one would pick me and I'd be the loser cat lady for the rest of my life.

Still, I felt bad for the poor guy that got stuck with Gabby's ass for the rest of his life.

I still ate my smushed pastry, because fuck Gabriella Ciar. And it tasted pretty good. When the train finally stopped, I got my bag and disembarked. I was left standing on the edge of a platform made of cobblestone, in a bustling station of tan brink and tall pillars, a glass ceiling hundreds of feet above my head.

I turned in place, unsure of where to go next. The signs were in Malovian, and I had no idea what direction the school was in. I glanced at my map again, but it didn't help. I wasn't very good at reading maps in high-stress situations, and this was one of them.

Without being conscious of it, I looked for someone to help me. My sight fell on a young girl around my age. She looked like a student. She was wearing an expression that seemed... I don't know... confused. Her form was lithe, skinny and athletic. She was wearing an oversized, light-pink sweater that had fuzzy wisps coming off of it, along with pale skinny jeans and fur boots. Her blonde hair was almost pale-white, and she had these giant glasses on her face that extended from her cheeks to her forehead. They looked a little ridiculous and cute at the same time. Her makeup was done lightly, but professionally. She carried a duffel bag that was just as fluffy as her sweater.

The girl's face lit up when she saw me. She ran toward me, hauling her fluffy bag. "You're just the person I was looking for!"

"I was?" I asked, completely caught off guard.

"Yes!" she exclaimed excitedly. "I had a feeling I was waiting for something, or *someone*, but I didn't know who or why, yet here you are and here I am!"

The girl let out a cheer and threw her arms around me, giving me a tight hug. I was shocked, but didn't want to push away and be rude. The embrace was warm and friendly. I was frozen, and didn't hug back.

"Sorry, I'm a hugger," she said as she pulled away, giggling. "I just *love* meeting new people."

"Have we… met before?" I asked. Otherwise, the hug would be weird— but this girl looked like she knew all about weird.

"Nope!" she sang. She stuck her hand out, grabbed mine, and shook it so frantically it yanked my body around. "I'm Odette Oksana. I'm a First Year at Arcanea University. Alicorn Faction."

She showed me her palm. I briefly saw the mark of a hoof on her palm before she drew it away and started talking again. "I've never seen you around, so I assume you're a freshman, too."

Odette talked so fast I had trouble keeping up. It was like this girl was on a permanent sugar-rush.

"I'm Emma," I managed to blurt out.

"Great!" I barely had time to get my name out before Odette started pulling on my arm. "Let's go up to the school together! I know the way. I'm sure we'll have lots to talk about! How did your summer go? Mine went *fantastic*."

I hesitated. I was afraid of trusting Odette. After all, Gabby hadn't exactly rolled out the welcome wagon.

But Odette seemed so nice and sincere— and a bit naive. It was like looking at a human version of a *My Little Pony*. I figured following her around would be better than making a fool of myself trying to navigate this city alone.

"Sure," I said. "Lead the way."

I wasn't sure I had much of a choice, anyway, because Odette had already pulled me halfway across the station by this time. She practically skipped as she moved, and walked on her toes.

"Do you dance professionally or something?" I asked, noticing the way she moved. She walked upright and poised at all times, like she was in constant awareness of how her body moved. I knew the feeling, because figure skating required that, too.

"Oh, yes. Ballet," Odette said. "I've been traveling with the Russians for awhile, but I gave that up to come to the University. Do you do arts or sports?"

That made my ears prick up. Dancing with the Russian ballet was insanely impressive. Odette had to be amazing. People trained for their entire lives and didn't get in, and she had stopped that for Arcanea University. This had to be one special place.

Odette was peering at me, waiting for an answer to her former question. "Figure skating," I belted out.

Odette squealed. "Oh, we're so close, then! I like skating, but I was better at ballet, so I stuck with that instead. I bet you're *so* beautiful on the ice!"

The minute we stepped outside the train station, my mouth dropped open. My entire world opened up to a brand-new universe.

The first thing I saw was some sort of half-bird, half-lion thing standing right in front of me. It had golden feathers, a large beak, and the back legs of a large cat, with two massive wings on its back.

I was walking too fast, and I ended up slamming into the creature. I was thrown backwards — the creature was nothing but muscle.

A griffin, I realized. They really did exist.

It was bigger than an actual lion. I was sure the thing was going to break my neck in two. A shiver of fear passed over me as the griffin turned its massive head at me. I was dinner, most likely.

The griffin I'd bumped into was eyeing me with piercing yellow eyes. I realized that I was looking at a person, not an animal, and swallowed. "I'm sorry. Excuse me. I didn't mean to run into you."

The griffin gave me a weird look and slunk out of the way. He probably thought I was some crazy person, looking at him like that. After all, this wasn't a zoo.

I realized there were more of them standing outside the train station— a whole flock. The griffins were mostly white, brown, black and gray, although I did see an unusual mix of colors, like green or red. Some had the back legs of tigers, cheetahs, leopards or panthers instead of lions. It was hard not to gawk at them in amazement. I pardoned myself again and wove my way around the griffins as I ran after Odette, who was still gabbing.

I heard a massive roar that shook the cobblestones beneath my feet and looked up. There were dragons— *literal dragons*— flying through the skies. They were all different colors, scales glimmering like gemstones, some as small as a car and others as large as a building. The sun reflected off of their scales and shone in all different directions. They had horns, some straight and some curled, and spines along their backs with tails that ended in arrowheads. Each of the toes on their feet ended in knife-like claws. When they opened their mouths, I observed fangs that were as big as me.

Farther above, two dragons breathed *literal fire* at each other. I wasn't sure if they were playing or having an argument. The fire-breathers descended, and once they approached the ground, changed back into flesh-and-bone men. It seemed like they *were* having an argument, because their voices grew louder as they passed. They yelled Malovian at each other and shook their fists.

"Well, come on, silly!" Odette said, yanking on me. "It's like you've never seen a dragon before!"

I didn't want to say that I hadn't, so I put on a straight face and followed her through the crowd of people coming out of the train station. Most of them were students, like us— the semester started tomorrow, so I shouldn't have been surprised.

I wasn't quite sure what an alicorn was before I got here, but now that I saw them face to face, the best way I could describe them was unicorns with wings. Their coats were all the colors horses could be— gray, chestnut, bay, roan, dun, black, palomino, and about a million others. I think I saw a zebra one somewhere in the crowd. But their horns were curved slightly, not straight, and instead of horse tails they had oxen ones, and feathers around their hooves. Their horns seemed to be made of rare stones like diamonds, or some sort of precious metal. The alicorns glimmered as I walked by. I wasn't sure what to be more impressed by— the beautiful horns or their wings. The alicorns ruffled their feathery appendages, snorting with impatience and stomping their hooves as they waited for guests to arrive.

I shot Odette a smug glance. She said she was part of the alicorn Faction. Pretty winged horses fit her personality perfectly. I wondered who her special guy would be. Someone who had no problem dealing with sparkles and sunshine, I hoped.

Then I noticed them. The wolvens. There were so many. They stalked throughout the city with rolling shoulders and heads held high. Their coats were various shades of red, gray, black, silver, and white. Most of them were only as big as horses, though a few rivaled the size of the dragons above. Their coats were thick, lush and beautiful. I wanted to reach out and stroke my hands through their fur, though I was sure I wasn't allowed.

On the backs of some of the wolvens were large, feathery wings that matched the colors of their pelts. A couple of wolvens gave a running start before they leapt into the skies, spreading their wings to take flight among the griffins, dragons, and alicorns.

I'd never seen wolves with wings before. I supposed that's why they went by a different name. I realized that I was going to bond with one of them. I wasn't a chicken shit by any means, but these wolves were huge... one bite could easily end my life.

Whatever. I'd already killed one of them, and thought nothing of it. If I had any problems with guys, I'd just blast a hole in them. Problem solved.

Some of the Companions had women on their backs. I could only presume they were mates. The Marked that rode the shifters flew through the air and walked through the city bravely, with determined faces or bright smiles.

They seemed so proud and carefree. I wanted to be like them, but doubted I could be.

Suddenly, the world Lady Magdalina told me about didn't seem like a fairytale anymore. It was real. This wasn't a dream.

We finally left the area outside the crowded station and entered the streets of Dolinska. Odette went on and on about ballet as I took in the sights around me. The beauty of Dolinska rivaled the streets of Paris, or Krakow. I hadn't been to either, but I'd seen pictures, and this place was just as incredible. It was like walking into a movie. I wasn't sure what was more amazing— the city, the shifters, or all the sorceresses casting incredible spells around me. The Marked made pretty butterflies appear, or doubled themselves so they had identical clones, or changed their hair and eye color with a wave of their hand. There was an explosion, and I looked over my shoulder to see that one Marked was making fireworks come out of her hand to the delight of the children around her feet.

I realized that someday, I was going to be able to do that, and my heart lifted. This was way bigger than anything I'd ever imagined. I was so glad that I'd made the choice to come here.

The city was packed with vendors and carts. Marked boasted about love potions, claiming they'd be able to find your mate within a week of consuming. Dragons sold scales for jewelry, while alicorns waved their horns and made new dresses appear on the Marked in front of them. Wolvens fought in a makeshift arena in the middle of the square, then shifted back to human form and started boxing as people made bets and cheered them on.

Nearby, someone had placed a stereo on the ground, and polka music blasted out of it, Marked danced with their Companions, who were both in human and animal form. Incredible smells met my nose, and my eyes widened as we passed a bakery that had the most delicious looking cakes and pastries I'd ever seen. We passed churches with jaw-dropping stained glass windows that had the designs of shifters held within. We walked by tiny street cafes that were packed with people, human and animal, looking to get a sip of espresso, or, as I noticed, colorful, sparkling drinks I'd never seen before.

"Spells," Odette said, catching my look. She went to a cafe to purchase one. She brought back a purple drink in a tiny paper cup and sipped it. Odette giggled, and her feet elevated off the ground for five seconds or so. She floated toward me, coming back down with a hiccup.

"Bottoms up!" she said. She handed it to me.

I took a sip. My stomach went light for a moment before I fluttered a few inches off the ground and came back down. My stomach flipped. It was the weirdest experience of my life. My mood felt significantly elevated, and I felt more energized. The Arcanea had the best energy drinks ever created.

There was so much in this new world to explore. I wanted to soak in every moment of it.

"You must've not been in Dolinska for some time. You sure are walking slow," Odette said pleasantly. "I don't mind. It's such a nice day, and you're such a nice person. Isn't it great to enjoy a walk with friends?"

I was still trying to figure out why she'd taken such a liking to me. I didn't do much of anything except exist, breathe, and look interested when Odette talked to me.

There were a few cars on the street, but they were all designer sports cars. It looked like most of the people around here drove carriages pulled by Companions, or sometimes just regular horses. Odette stood at the edge of the street and looked for one.

"We could walk, but I'd prefer to take a carriage," she said. "My bag's getting rather heavy, and—"

There were loud screams. My head jerked to the side, and I screamed as a carriage came roaring into view. The horses pulling it seemed to have gone mad. They barreled through vendors and destroyed carts on their way through. Marked and Companions both scattered to get out of the way. The carriage was headed right this way!

I grabbed Odette and pulled her to safety as the covered carriage skidded to a stop on the curb where we'd been standing just moments before. The horses danced on the spot as someone yanked on the reins. I scrambled to get off the ground, helping Odette to her feet.

I looked up to see who'd nearly ran us over. It was another girl. She had pale skin, and straight black hair that was down to her waist, with a bright red streak going down the right side. Her outfit was the most unusual thing about her. She wore a black lace corset and long skirt, high-heeled, lace-up boots, long sleeves, fishnet stockings, and rings that looked like spider webs. She wore black nail polish, black lipstick, black eyeshadow. A black lace choker was tied around her neck.

She was a goth. I don't think I had seen a goth since I was fourteen years old. I was still recovering from my mild heart attack when the girl spoke to me.

"Hey." She tossed her long hair out of her eyes. "You need a ride?" she asked. She was breathless.

"Yes!" Odette said before I could say anything. She threw her duffel inside and climbed abroad. "Come on, Emma!"

I hesitated. This could end badly. I was pretty sure this girl wasn't a real taxi driver. "I—"

"Bitch, get on!" the goth girl screamed, and she grabbed hold of my wrist and pulled me into the carriage as she laughed. She snapped the reins, and the horses took off running. I fell against the seat, onto another suitcase that wasn't mine or Odette's. Another student, like us. My own suitcase fell on top of me as the carriage jostled around. I heard more screams behind us, and the sound of hoofbeats and wings.

"Oh, no," Odette said, frowning as she looked behind us. "It's the Arcanea Alliance. Bother."

I didn't need an explanation to know they had to be the local law enforcement. "Can you explain to me why we're running from the cops?" I shouted.

"Bobby Kowalski," Goth Girl said, like the name was the only explanation we needed. "That dragon hasn't left me alone all summer. I swear to the Seven Gods he wants to bond with me."

She pointed to her mouth and made a gagging sound. "He still doesn't realize that it's not gonna happen. I stole his carriage and ended up crashing into another one trying to get away from him. Simple hit and run, my bad. They'll probably add reckless driving too, if I get caught."

"Who are you, exactly?" I asked. People on the streets jumped out of the way to avoid getting run over. The police behind us had to slow down in order to avoid hitting anyone. We were losing them.

"Irena Delmare," she said quickly. "But I hate my first name, so you'd better call me Delmare."

"Point taken," I said. "And you're a…?"

"Dragon Faction," Delmare breathed. "I like bad boys."

She showed me her right hand quickly before returning it to the reins. On her palm, I saw the mark of a reptile footprint, with long claws.

I wasn't surprised. Dragons seemed like they'd go hand in hand with her personality. She was destructive and loud. Didn't mean that in a bad way— it meant she was fun.

"Dragons are so big and scary," Odette said, and she shuddered. "Are you sure you can handle being bonded to one?"

Delmare snorted. "Dragons should be afraid of me."

I smiled. I liked her.

"What about you?" Delmare asked. Odette looked at me in interest. I didn't realize I hadn't yet told them.

"Wolven." I said the word like it was mine— like it was something I belonged to. With a start, I realized that it was. I *belonged* to the wolven Faction. They were mine, and I was theirs. If the mark on my hand was right, I was going to bond with a wolf. My future husband, my soulmate, was probably somewhere nearby, milling amongst the students at the University.

He could be anyone. Knowing that the person I was meant to be with was within the vicinity of the city made my palms sweat. I could meet him *today*. I wasn't sure I was ready for this. I wasn't even sure what bonding would be like. Would I lose my entire world, my sense of self, once I formed a bond with a complete stranger I'd never met? I wasn't ready to sacrifice who I was for some guy. I never would be.

"Ah," Delmare said. "Noted. Makes sense, with the standoffish personality."

"I'm not standoffish!" I shouted.

"Temper, too. Goes with your red hair," Delmare said. "Don't worry. Doesn't bother me much. Dragons are famous for that, too."

She had me pegged. "Why don't you just pull over?" I asked.

Delmare laughed. "And turn myself in? Never. This is too much fun." She slapped the reins again. I glanced behind us as Delmare took a turn onto a side street that nearly made the carriage tip over. Odette and I clung to the seats like cats before the carriage righted itself and came slamming back down on two wheels again. Delmare took a few more crazy turns, zigzagging around the multiple alleyways that Dolinska seemed to provide. I was getting dizzy.

Finally, the cries of the police were far in the distance. We must've lost them. "Whoa there," Delmare said, and she pulled on the reins. The horses came to a slow walk, snorting. "Easy now."

She turned around to look at us as the horses pulled forward. "So, Arcanea University, huh?"

"Yeah. First Year!" Odette peeped.

"Me too," Delmare said. "Got any hobbies?"

"Ballet!" Odette said.

"Ice skating," I rattled off.

"This is a school for jocks," Delmare mumbled irritably under her breath. "Does anyone do *art* anymore?"

I shook my head. "I can't draw worth a crap."

"I crochet," Odette added. "Does that count?"

Delmare let out a sigh. "Oh, well. I guess it's only me."

We left the alleyway and ended up on a wide road that led up a hill. There were a lot of carriages on this road, and it was packed with kids lugging their bags. This had to be the way to the university. "Why did you pick us up in the first place?" I asked.

"I don't know." Delmare shrugged. "Seemed like fun."

Delmare was definitely the impulsive type. Odette smiled and said, "You've certainly made my day. Maybe we can do this again sometime."

What, run from the cops? No thanks, I thought. But Delmare laughed.

"I'll drop you off at the gate. I should probably return the carriage." Delmare grinned wickedly. "Bobby still needs a ride."

My mouth dropped as we rounded the top of the hill. An enormous palace came into view. It was orthodox in style, with large domes, spiraling towers and warm, yellow stone. The estate was huge, several stories tall, with ornate windows and decorative statues of winged soldiers lining the outer edge, rooftops made of copper that had turned green over the years. A huge, fancy gold fountain was placed in front of the giant entryway into the palace. The courtyard was a collection of cobblestone and flora, bigger than my local state park back home. In the distance, a couple of students swam in a large lake that a dragon paddled around happily.

It looked like the Winter Palace in Russia, or even Versailles in France. It was that freaking big. This was a massive estate, a place for kings and queens. There had to be thousands of students that came here.

Odette leaned over and nudged me. "Welcome to Arcanea University. Aren't you *so* excited?"

I was more excited than I'd ever been in years. A momentary bit of fear ran through me. The place was so big! How was I supposed to find my way around it for classes?

We came to the large gate, and Delmare pulled the carriage to a stop. Odette and I disembarked and got our bags. She gave us a salute as we waved goodbye.

"See you girls around," Delmare said, and she trotted the carriage off. The way she said farewell was like we'd been friends forever. It was nice.

But it was also strange to me, so I tried to shake it off. I turned to face the university. There were hundreds of students mulling in the courtyard in front of the palace. Could I really do this?

Odette was giving me an expectant look. I decided I had to. I followed her through the thick crowd of people and past the gate. When we got inside, the garden was more beautiful than I'd imagined. The grass and paths were sculpted to make curling formations. Golden fountains and flowers were everywhere. Hedges had been trimmed in the shapes of wolvens, dragons, griffins, and alicorns. Parts of the garden had mazes to wander through, or shaded areas where students lounged and talked. Whoever the gardener was, he deserved a major raise.

"The university used to be the old palace for the monarchy," Odette explained. "That's why it's so big."

There were guys everywhere. They were acting especially boorish, punching each other and wrestling, calling out to the girls who passed by and looking desperate. They shifted into their animal forms, playing games and contests with each other to show off their strength. Some girls paid them attention, but most of the females who walked by simply ignored them.

"It's just the boys," Odette told me, rolling her eyes and waving a hand. "All unmated Companions go nuts when their mates show up, and at the start of every new school year, they get even stupider than normal trying to impress the new freshman who aren't bonded. It's rather sad, really."

I felt like it was mating season and I was some kind of animal. It was bizarre. But when in Malovia, do as the Arcanea do. I copied Odette and kept my eyes forward as we passed the huge crowd of guys performing their Dumbass Olympics in the yard.

I didn't feel scared or intimidated by the guys begging for my attention— more or less amused. It was kind of funny, watching them fall all over themselves trying to get a girl. The guys back home weren't like this. Too many of them that I knew kept three or more girls on the side and didn't commit to any of them.

"You need to get your uniform," Odette told me with a bright smile. "Trust me, you'll love them. They're so fabulous."

Uniforms sounded terrible. But I doubted this school would let you walk around in a tee-shirt and jeans. Everything looked so fancy. Odette led me to a covered table in the garden, where a group of students were handing out white boxes. They looked older than us by a few years.

There was a guy handing out boxes at the edge of the table. He was tall and lengthy, with blue eyes and blonde hair. He was wearing a polo shirt and khakis that I thought seemed too formal for summer. He blushed pink as we approached.

"Hello, Theo. How was your summer?" Odette asked pleasantly.

Theo seemed lost for words, before he cleared his throat and said, "Fine, Odette. And yours?"

"It was amazingly delightful!" she squeaked. "May we have our uniforms, please?"

Theo nodded. "I'm glad you're finally here at the university, Odette. Last year was lonely without you."

He was dropping hints, but they went over Odette's head. "Thank you." She batted her eyelashes, and Theo gulped.

"So what do alicorns *do*?" I asked him out of curiosity. "Do they practice magic like the Marked, or do they fight monsters like the other Companions?"

Theo let out a *hmph*. "Alicorns are fierce and respected warriors. We often don't get the respect from the other Factions we deserve, though our horns and hooves are often bathed in blood."

...O-kaay… somebody had issues about being a pony. I wasn't trying to be rude, just genuinely interested. Odette reached up and ruffled his hair. "Oh, Theo. Don't be that way. Emma's new. She doesn't understand."

She kissed him on the cheek, and he stilled. He looked positively afraid of her. Some warrior.

Theo backed away and scanned the clipboard on the table before sorting through the group of boxes behind him. He hesitantly handed us two. "Here you go. Don't get into any mischief, now."

"Wouldn't dream of it!" Odette exclaimed. She gave a little twirl.

Theo gave a grim nod. As we walked away, I jerked my thumb at him and asked, "What's his deal?"

Odette giggled again. "Theo's always been a little shy. Don't know why, though."

I glanced backward and caught Theo staring at Odette's butt as she walked away. He turned red when he noticed that I saw him and hurriedly went back to what he was doing.

Shy, huh? More like a major crush. It seemed like Odette was oblivious about it. "Do you think you'll bond with him?"

"*Me*? Oh, gods no," Odette said in an alarmed way. "Theo and I have known each other since we were children. We were in ballet class together. He's a wonderful dancer. But we're just friends. It's not like that. He's basically my brother."

Odette sighed. "Someday, I'll meet my alicorn prince, and we'll be dancing away into the sunset. It'll happen this year, I just know it."

Theo was glancing Odette's way again. The stare was longing and desperate. Seemed to me that Odette's alicorn prince was right in front of her, and she didn't even see it. "Yeah. I'm sure you will."

"Come on. Our dorms are upstairs. They're separated by Marked and Companions. I hope you're by me," she peeped.

When we stepped inside the castle, I became even more impressed. Paintings of Marked and Companions lined the walls. Expensive and elaborate drapes hung over huge windows, and matched the plush carpet underfoot. The windows themselves were huge and large, letting in copious amounts of light as we passed fancy sculptures, priceless vases, and royal artifacts of the monarchy in glass cases. The university was more like an art or history museum than a school. I wanted to stop and look, but Odette was hauling ass, so I told myself I'd be back later.

We finally reached the girl's dorms. When I got my room assignment, it nearly knocked me on my ass. My room was decorated in navy blue and silver, and had a four-poster bed next to a large fireplace, a comfy armchair, and a large rug. A beautiful armoire stood next to my open window, which looked down upon the gardens.

Luckily, Odette's room was right next to mine. At least I'd have someone friendly nearby. I didn't have a roommate, so she'd have to do.

"The uniforms are assorted by Faction. You're a wolven, so all your outfits will be blue and silver," Odette informed me. "I'm an alicorn, so all my outfits are white and purple. Dragons are red and black, and griffins are green and gold. Aren't they just lovely?"

I took out the pieces of my uniform and laid them on the bed. There were two different versions of the outfit. One was a button-up white shirt with a blue blazer that had a silver wolf's paw embroidered into the collar. It came with a blue tie, blue tights, and the choice of a knee-length blue skirt, or thick pants for the cold months.

The second uniform was a hunter's coat, wool, long-sleeved and blue in color, with silver embroidery of flowers weaving throughout the jacket. The jacket was knee-length, and fitted to my body. I figured it was meant for use in the winter. The outfit came with Mary Jane shoes and knee high black boots.

The uniform also came with a heavy, hooded navy cloak, which I assumed kept out the cold when Malovia got super chilly. I put it on as an experiment, and I absolutely loved how glamorous it made me look. It was like… modern-day fairytale style.

Okay, I admit, I liked it. The Arcanea were pretty fashionable. They could certainly dress me better than I could myself.

Odette had already changed into her outfit. She was in no way shy about showing off her matching unicorn bra and panties. It was like we were sisters and she did this every day. Her uniform was identical to mine, except the colors were white and purple, and she had an alicorn hoof embroidered into her blazer collar instead of a wolf print. She put her hair up into a messy bun on top of her head and kept it in place with a pencil.

"You wanna walk around some? It's lunchtime, and I'm starving. We could get lunch in the cafeteria," she said.

"Sure," I said. My stomach was growling. All this walking around had made me ravenous. We left our bags, and Odette led the way once more.

"I know my way around because my aunt teaches here. I'm lucky that way," Odette said. "The cafeteria isn't far. We just have to get through the grand ballroom."

The grand ballroom turned out to be my own personal nightmare. The walls were lined with mirrors, and large chandeliers hung from the ceiling, lighting up the room. It was absolutely packed with students, more than what were hanging out in the gardens outside.

I wasn't sure if I didn't get along with people and that was what caused my social anxiety, or if my social anxiety made me not get along with people. Either way, the sight of a group of students my age in an enclosed space was enough to make me break out in hives. I stood frozen before the grand ballroom, not sure whether to walk into it or run away screaming.

"What's wrong?" Odette asked as I stared at the crowded entryway.

I swallowed. "I don't do well with crowds," I said. "I'm… I'm not very good at making friends."

Odette put her arm around my shoulder and gestured to all the people around us. "Look! Friends! And they're all waiting to meet you!"

Odette sure had an optimistic view on life. I was certain that most of the people in here didn't want to be my friend, but fuck if that deterred her. She guided me through the ballroom like this wasn't my personal nightmare. At first, I wanted to freak out, but as I felt Odette's warm hand on my shoulder, I began to calm down. She was right. There was nothing to fear about this. It was fine.

Then I saw him, and my entire life changed.

He stood no more than a few yards away from me. Even from such a distance, it was like I could hear his heartbeat— hear him breathe.

He was already wearing his school uniform. Blue and silver— a wolven, like me. He was only wearing the shirt, though, the white sleeves rolled up halfway past his elbows, and his tie was loose around his neck. His hands were shoved into his pockets, and his dark hair was really messy.

He looked tired— there were bags under his amber eyes, like he hadn't gotten enough sleep the night before. Still, he seemed cheerful. There was a beautiful grin on his face. I loved his smile. It was crisp and white. It lifted me up and made me feel everything good about the world. He was the most gorgeous guy I'd ever seen.

I really wanted to see him change— see what he looked like as a wolf. I bet he was gorgeous to observe. I wondered what color his coat would be.

The guy laughed, and lifted his hand to wave his fingers. Purple sparks and smoke flashed out of his hand. It was incredible to witness. I briefly noticed something change in his gaze.

That's so weird. He did magic… and his amber eyes flashed violet. Just like the color of the spell.

He was talking to a curly-headed girl. When he cast the spell, she laughed, and a flash of intense jealousy rose up in me. It was hard to keep down. I wanted to walk over and punch that girl in the face for looking at him, though I didn't have any reason.

As fast as it came, it was gone. I was left standing there, shocked. Why was I jealous of that girl talking to some rando guy? I didn't know him. I didn't even know his name.

Odette caught me staring. "I'd suggest looking the other way," she hushed under her breath. "He's taken."

"I wasn't looking," I said, feigning ignorance.

She laughed. "Liar. *That's* Ethan Nowak," she told me.

My heart dropped. "He bonded with *her?*" I stared at the girl. Ethan told another joke, and she laughed again. I had no good reason, but I already hated her.

"No." Odette shook her head. "He hasn't bonded with anyone."

A bit of hope rose in my chest, but I pushed it down. I was here to get an education, not find a man. "How can he be taken if he hasn't bonded?" I said, confused.

"Well," Odette said, flustered. "He's been here for three years, almost, and he hasn't found his mate yet. It's assumed he's never going to. He's supposed to find a bride before he participates in the King's Contest this December, and since he can't find a mate, Chastity is probably going to be his first choice. They've been on and off forever, and she's a wolven, like him. She's the girl he's talking to."

Ethan's eyes connected with mine. When they did, time seemed to stop. Everyone— and I mean *everyone*— in the square disappeared. Odette was no longer by my side. It was just me and him. My breath hitched in my throat and caught, and my heart literally ceased beating. A deep shiver started at the top of my head and flowed throughout my entire body. The way he was looking at me, so intensely… I felt as if I could sink into those amber eyes and fall forever.

Ethan seemed confused. He stared at me with a blank look, his mouth slightly hanging open.

Then he did the most awful thing. He turned away. The effect was equal to feeling a knife slide into my chest. It hurt. Badly. I never wanted him to turn his back on me ever again.

In response, I faced away from him and headed the other way, in the direction of the entrance to the school.

"What's the King's Contest?" I asked, as a way to get my mind off of Ethan. For some reason, when he looked at me… I don't know. Everything about Arcanea University changed.

"It's the way the Arcanea determine who's going to be king," Odette explained. "Whoever wins gets the crown, but participants have to be bonded or engaged to enter. Prince Ethan just declared his intent to enter."

"He's a *freaking prince*, too?" Could this guy get anymore perfect?

"Yes. He's part of the Malovian monarchy. If Ethan wants to participate in the Contest this December, he'll have to hurry up and find a girl."

"Oh." The word came out in a tiny rush of breath. It sounded small and quiet.

"Well, even if you did want to be with him, you'd have to get in line. Every wolven girl this side of Malovia is desperately in love with him. The ones who aren't are still after him, because they want to be queen," Odette said.

I put the prince out of my mind. He was out of bounds. Off-limits. I was new here. I didn't know anything about the monarchy. He was way out of my league. Ethan was a walking target, and I was no queen.

Odette was right. Best to stay away.

We finally left the ballroom, and Odette hooked her arm in mine. "Now, who wants crab legs? I'm starved!"

SEVEN

My mate had arrived at the school. I could feel it. She was here somewhere, among the new arrivals.

It was driving me crazy. I was sure I'd go mad with the want. I didn't know what having a mate would feel like before, but now that she was close, everything was different. My entire life, my whole existence— it all centered around her.

For the first time, I knew exactly what my Da had been talking about.

The thing was, I was *sure* I'd seen her among the students— felt her somehow. I'd made eye contact with her, that was for certain, but there was so much going on and so many new people coming into the school it was hard to tell who she was. There were so many new scents and auras resonating throughout the area. I couldn't tell which one belonged to her.

I knew I had to seek her through the wolven freshman girls. But I had a busy semester ahead of me. I was taking a mess of tough classes, not to mention I had my duties as a vigilante, and preparing for the King's Contest ahead. I didn't know how I'd find time to locate my mate.

But finding her was the most important task of all. I needed her for the Contest, but more than that, *I needed her.*

I wracked my brain, trying to remember her face, but there were so many faces that were brand new. I hoped to the Seven Gods that she'd show herself during class today and that my search would be over. I'd lose my mind in the meantime.

I couldn't keep my mind on breakfast. I barely ate. It felt like my entire body had been consumed by a vicious fever, and the cure wouldn't come until she was by my side.

It was wholly unbearable.

Around eleven a.m., I headed to the forest outside the school for my first class. It was taught by Lord Lucien— Monster Hunting 101. It was a freshman class, but I'd retaken it on account that I'd failed it my first year, and the year after that. I already knew how to hunt monsters from birth, so I considered the class a useless recap of the basics, and never bothered to go to class.

Still, it was a requirement for graduation, so it'd be in my favor to not to blow it off. I still felt like I needed a bigger reason to actually show up.

When I turned the corner to see a gathering of freshmen around a large oak tree near the school greenhouses, I got my reason.

302

I saw her red hair first. It was long and flowing down her back, and it rippled in the sunlight, casting off a golden glow. I was staring at her back— she was tall and thin, with legs that went on for miles but a round ass that Arcanea women were famous for.

When she turned around, my breath caught. Her eyes were green as emeralds. Her skin was so pale it nearly glistened, and she had pink lips that were barely open in a slight gasp. As she brought her hand up to tuck a lock of hair behind her ear, I noticed a black paw print on her palm. A wolven, like me.

It felt like she was the only thing that mattered. The only thing that made sense in a world that didn't make much sense to begin with.

I found her. My mate. What a stroke of luck!

She caught my gaze. I realized that I'd seen her in the entrance hall yesterday as I was showing off my magic to Chastity. Why hadn't I realized it then? I was so stupid.

She noticed I was staring. Her eyes glanced down and chewed on her lip nervously. A jolt of fear went through me as I realized that sorceresses could reject their mates. This first meeting was everything. If I came off as an ass, I could lose her… and I'd never be the same.

When you met your mate, you didn't just barge in and declare it to them. You had to win over their heart first. You had to court them, to avoid messing up the mating process. And that's exactly what I intended to do.

I had to play it cool. I strode toward her with my hands in my pockets. "You look a little lost."

Why was that the first thing out of my mouth? Her cheeks turned pink, and she said, "Kind of. It's my first class here. I have no idea what I'm doing."

"Don't worry. You'll get along fine." I bumped her shoulder against mine. "If you don't, they'll just feed you to the dragons."

She paled. I nudged her— gods, even barely touching her felt incredible. I laughed. "I'm kidding," I said. "You'll be fine. Lord Lucien doesn't leave those in his class behind."

She still seemed worried. "Aren't you Prince Ethan?" she asked.

So she already knew who I was. I wasn't surprised. "That's me. Though I prefer not to be called *Your Majesty* while at school. It's rather annoying."

"So what should I call you?" she asked.

"My friend Stefan calls me Prince of the Assholes," I said. "Though you can call me Ethan."

She laughed. It was a light, tinkling sound, like the music of the fairies. "I'm Emma."

Emma. What a pretty name. My mother had a favorite novel of the same name.

I didn't get to say much more, because Lord Lucien decided to show up at that very moment. He was in his wolven form, and pulling a cart that was full of bronze weapons. When the cart was before the class, he pulled off the harness using his teeth and transformed back into human form.

Emma's mouth dropped open when she saw Lucien change, but she looked around and quickly snapped it shut. She realized she was the only one here shocked by his transformation.

Something was different about her… she had an accent that wasn't from here. American, maybe? How much did she know about the Arcanea, exactly?

Lord Lucien's eyes sought out Emma's, and he smiled kindly at her. She seemed to relax under his friendly gaze.

"First things first," Lucien announced. "This will not be an easy course for most of you. Weak-minded Arcanea do not survive the battlefield. There is no such thing as fighting fair when battling a monster. You will be expected to play dirty, and keep up with the most brutal of creatures if you wish to preserve your life."

Lucien took a long sabre off the cart and demonstrated, swooping the sword in long movements. "A warrior must be tough and disciplined. They must stay calm in the most chaotic of situations. And they must be convinced that they will win any battle."

Lucien threw his cloak over the cart. "Pick a weapon and follow me. We'll start with drills."

He headed into the trees. Students ran to the cart to get the best weapons. Emma hung back in hesitation. By the time we got to the cart, there were only a few options left, though Emma seemed overwhelmed by it all.

"There are so many weapons here. I don't even know what to pick," Emma said, looking confused at all the different options before her.

"Well, if you're a beginner, I suggest you don't pick a spear or a mace." I rifled through the weapons until I found something sturdier— a *karabela*. It was a long, curved blade, a thin sabre that was usually used by sorceresses riding their Companions into battle.

I handed it to her, and her arm instantly dropped. The blade sank into the earth. "It's so heavy," she said. "My arm's gonna kill by the time we're done."

"Well, yeah, it's not going to be light." I smiled at her. "You can handle it."

She still looked doubtful as we followed the rest of the class to the woods. Lucien led us to a large, flat area and ordered us to spread out. I picked a spot with Emma in the back.

"I thought we'd be studying theory or something, not how to handle swords on the first freaking day," Emma whispered, flustered as Lucien began to bark instructions.

"It's sink or swim at Arcanea University," I told her. "Don't doubt yourself. You're stronger than you think."

"Yeah, right." Her tone was bland. Lucien started swinging his weapon, demanding that we follow his movements and keep up with them. As he instructed, he yelled at us to keep a wide stance, to stand tall, to be light on our feet and keep our balance all at once.

This was so boring to me. I knew all this. My time was preoccupied with watching Emma.

She was sweating with the effort to keep up. Her first few times swinging the sword, she lost control and fell over.

"You're going to hurt yourself," I told her. I ignored Lucien and corrected her stance, my hands burning at the touch of her skin. "You don't need to put so much force into it. Precision and remaining in control is more important than butchering your opponent. What if you swing too hard and you can't pull your sword out? Then you'll be left without a weapon. Practice a bunch of light strikes in quick succession, instead of one big blow."

"Am I really going to have to kill things while I'm here?" Emma huffed. She struggled to catch her breath.

My expression was utterly serious as I said, "You won't want to. But someday, you'll have to."

She seemed bewildered. I didn't get why.

Well, I had a good motivator to come to class, at least. Emma was woefully behind on learning weapon play. She'd need more than just Lucien to teach her. I'd have to be here to help her keep up with the rest of the class. The rest of them probably had a blade in their hands the moment they could walk.

"You want to stagger your opponent!" Lucien called over the crowd. "Get them off their feet, and knock them off balance! Imagine your strikes as a star pattern, where you slash your weapon downward or upward diagonally to cause the most damage. Strike vertically from top to bottom to cause devastating hits. Only parry a blow as a last line of defense! When dealing with monsters, always use offense as your first choice, and limit their opportunity to have more time to kill you!"

"They should've given us a textbook or something," Emma panted. I chuckled.

"Textbooks aren't very good out in the field. Unless you want to bludgeon your enemy to death," I said.

"Well, it'd be nice if someone gave me the rundown," she gasped. She swung her sword, and it was a totally sloppy strike. "I pretty much learned about this world last week."

Wait. She knew *nothing?* Was she really that far behind?

"What do you mean? You didn't know about the Arcanea?" My heartbeat picked up.

"My mom kept this world from me. She ran away from the Arcanea when I was born, and never told me about any of it," she explained to me. "So excuse me for struggling to keep up."

I couldn't believe this. She didn't know *anything?* She was an outsider and she was *here,* learning how to be an Arcanea?

A whiff of her scent passed me by. It was delicious— the smell of freshly fallen snow, a clean smell like ice, and something soft, like mittens. I caught a warm, sweet scent— similar to amber, or chocolate. Her scent drove me mad with want and desire.

But underneath that heavenly scent was something else. It was an intense smell, something heavy. A different combination of chemicals and hormones. The human nose couldn't detect it, but a Companion could.

She was sick. Something chronic. I couldn't tell what it was— it was unique. I'd never smelled anything like it before. All I could derive was that it was permanent, and it was serious enough that it had changed her life forever.

A cold wave of devastation flowed through me. How could my mate be sick? I didn't want her to suffer. This couldn't be real. It wasn't happening. And yet, it was. My mate was a girl who didn't know anything about the Arcanea, a mate who was going to struggle to keep up not only because she was behind, but because her body would challenge her in every way it could.

I felt like crying for her, but that would only freak her out. Gods, my emotions were overwhelming right now. People had told me how the bonding experience was intense and hard to endure, but I'd never believed them. I held it in as best I could and tried to focus on her movements again.

"Why are you looking at me like that?" Emma had caught my stricken expression. Did she even know?

I wiped the heartbreak off my face and said, "Nothing. Just… don't thrust like that. The stab is weak. Your hand is too loose. You'll never break through flesh in that way."

She smiled weakly. "I've never been told my thrusts are weak before."

The joke broke through some of the sadness, and I laughed lowly. "Bet you haven't."

Lucien had stopped teaching the group now and was breaking off to give individual pointers to students. I turned toward Emma and gave her more instructions. "Use your environment to your advantage. Don't let the sun hit you in the eyes— there, you see? You can't attack if you're blinded. Slashing is always better than stabbing, most of the time— only jab the blade forward if you've got an opening. You're getting better."

I turned to her and held up my sword. "Here. Try and attack me." We'd get in trouble with Lucien if he caught us, as we weren't supposed to start on sparring yet, but he looked pretty busy with a freshman boy who was handling his sword like a flopping fish.

"Attack you? With an actual sword? I'll cut you open," she objected. "We should do this with sticks or something first."

I laughed. "You aren't going to hurt me. Just try."

She seemed wary about it, but shrugged. "Okay, you asked for it."

Emma charged forward, sword over her head. I was easily able to kick her away and said, "Don't raise your sword so high. It leaves you open to attack and defenseless. Being aggressive is always the better way, but there's a smart way to do it."

She came at me again. This time, I countered her strikes, and we fell into a rhythm. "Try to use body leverage against me. The key is to counter my attacks and be strategic about where you're placing your blade. Don't just bludgeon me with it."

I was impressed that she was able to keep up, but judging by her athletic figure, she had to work out or play sports. That probably helped to keep the illness at bay. "Good!" I said as she was able to effectively feint away a hit. She was getting better.

"Why are we learning this? Are all Arcanea good for is monster hunting?" Emma questioned aloud as we broke apart. She needed a break.

"No," I told her. "In fact, most of the Arcanea have other jobs. But every one of us needs to learn how to hunt monsters, to protect the country."

"What do you mean?" She'd stabbed her sword into the ground and bent over her knees to take a breather.

I leaned back. "Malovia is one country, but our borders are very important," I told her. "Around it are magical walls that the Marked have put in place to keep the monsters in. They're strong, but if too many monsters attack the border walls, they become vulnerable. That's why it becomes important to keep them contained, and slay them if they try to get over the border. We Arcanea are the only thing standing in the way of monsters escaping into the world and slaughtering millions of people."

"Can't the other magical races handle it?" Emma asked.

I laughed. "I wouldn't trust them with it. We're the best butchers. There are a few races who might try to make them pets."

Her expression was thoughtful. "But where do all these monsters come from? Do they just pop out of the ground?"

"Kind of, actually," I admitted. "Monsters come from a portal in Malovia— a passageway that leads to the underworld."

"The underworld is real?" Her eyes widened. "But if that's true… why don't the Arcanea just seal it up, so no more monsters get through?"

I shook my head. "Many sorceresses have tried and failed. But you cannot seal off a portal that's been made by a god, especially a dark god of black magic. No one has that kind of power."

"Gods?" She raised an eyebrow.

I sighed, "Ah, *onawilke*, you've got a lot to learn."

She gave me a resentful look. "I know I'm behind. I'm just trying to keep up."

"Give it a few weeks. You've got Arcanea in your blood. Soon it'll be second nature." I squared her shoulders so we could spar again. She wrenched her sword out of the ground and raised it, but before we could practice once more, there was a scream on the other side of the practice area. We spun around to witness something slink down from the trees above.

A giant snake, forty feet in length, slithered around the training arena. It was dark green, with a black diamond pattern on its back and a rattler that it shook as it weaved around the trees. It's fangs dripped purple venom, and its glittering eyes scanned the students as if choosing which one to have for a snack.

It was a *meluza*— a serpent-woman. Lucien quickly ushered students back against the trees, away from the monster. "Everyone stay calm! I have this handled!"

Lucien charged forward with his sword in hand. His arm moved so fast that it appeared to be a blur. I heard the clash of the sword against the snake's fangs as the two struck together. The snake tried to strike out several times, but Lucien was too quick. He opened up several wounds on the snake's middle and one on its head. The snake hadn't yet put a single mark on him.

Many people didn't look too afraid— if anything, they were impressed by how well Lucien was handling the snake. Emma, however, was terrified. She froze in place as she observed Lucien and the snake dance, her face shocked by the brutality of battle.

Then something unexpected happened, as it often did with monsters. The snake brought the tip of its tail lashing upward, and it knocked Lucien off his feet. The snake slithered away from

Lucien as quickly as it could, to get away from the threat. It was looking for victims that were easier to kill.

The closest people to it were me and Emma.

I put myself in front of Emma as the snake rampaged closer. By instinct, I exploded out of my human form and into my wolven skin. I snarled, lifting my upper lip as the snake came closer.

The snake saw me in its way and tried to divert its path, but I charged. I ran toward it and sank my teeth into one of the wounds Lucien had caused, opening it up further. I ignored the tangy, awful taste of snake flesh. The snake hissed and whirled its head around to bite me, but I let go and rolled so it sank its own fangs into its body. The snake pulled out its fangs and curled up in pain. It was immune to its own venom, but that didn't mean it wasn't painful.

The *meluza* struck out several more times, but I was light on my feet. I managed to slide out of the way wherever the snake's head went. Several times, it sank its fangs into the dirt instead of into me. The snake was becoming furious— the eyes shone with malice and hatred as I continued to outsmart its moves.

But I miscalculated. I went to deliver a blow at the wrong time, and the snake plunged. It missed sinking its fangs into me, but it still knocked me over. I struggled to roll onto my belly and watched the snake slither away.

No! It was going after Emma! I pushed myself onto my paws, but the world was dizzy and I had trouble finding my feet.

Emma had her sword in hand and held it in front of the snake— when it came too close, Emma managed to cut her sword along the snake's jaw. It was barely a scrape, but the snake skimmed backward in surprise, not expecting a reaction from such an easy target.

Good girl! I internally cheered. I just had to reach her in time…

But Emma was doing perfectly well on her own. She had a precise angle to dive her sword into the snake's head, right in the area where the neck and skull connected. It'd be a killing blow, if Emma managed to deliver it.

When Emma raised her sword to shove it into the *meluza's* skull, the monster noticed. In a flash, it changed— where there once was a monstrous, giant snake was now a naked young woman, shaking and frightened, her long black hair tangled and falling down to her knees. The woman curled up into a ball at Emma's feet and looked up at her pitifully. Emma held back her strike.

No, Emma, don't fall for it! I raged inside. I was still so far away. My paws pounded against the dirt to get to my mate.

"Please don't hurt me," the woman begged. "I mean no harm. I just wish to be left alone."

Emma stared at the *meluza,* her hands shaking so hard that the sword quivered in her grasp. Emma did the worst thing an Arcanea can do in that situation. She hesitated.

Those few seconds of mercy were all the monster needed to take advantage. The woman's innocent smile changed into a vile sneer that was soon replaced with fangs. In seconds, so fast you'd miss it if you blinked, the woman was gone and the snake was back in her place. The snake crouched and lunged forward, fangs exposed as she sailed toward my mate.

It was like the entire world flashed before my eyes. I moved without thinking, without knowing what my body was doing. All that mattered was that I put my body between the *meluza* and Emma. As the *meluza* lunged for Emma, I leapt forward with a wild snarl, and sank my jaws into its throat.

The snake hissed violently. I tore my jaws away so that blood streamed out of its open wound. In one clean movement, I changed back into a man and grabbed Emma's sword, performing an up strike so that the *meluza's* head was cut clean off.

I heard the sound of the snake's head hitting the grass, and its body was still. A few people were clapping and cheering behind me, though I barely heard it. They'd been impressed by the fight. The bloody sword fell out of my hand, landing next to the severed head.

Lucien strode toward me. "Well done, Ethan. As you all can see, technique is very important when fighting a monster of this size. Some of you should hope to be half as proficient as Ethan is by the time this course is over."

I was heaving for breath. When I turned back around to face Emma, she seemed confused. Her eyes looked to me— then glanced downward.

I felt gutted. She saw me for what I really was, in my wolven form. She'd seen I had no leg.

My temper exploded. "Why the *hell* would you do that?" I demanded, rounding on her. I took her by the shoulders and shook her. "Why wouldn't you kill it when you had the chance?"

Emma gaped up at me. "I—"

I let her go. I stomped away, pacing in circles. I was covered in blood and murderous, looking savage. She seemed terrified of me.

"You don't ask questions! You don't hesitate! You cut their head off and live to see another day, before they kill you first!" I made a slashing motion across my neck, and Emma cringed. "Anything less will get you killed out there!"

"Ethan! That is more than enough," Lord Lucien snapped. "You are right that Emma made a mistake, but she is a freshman, and new here. Your reaction is uncalled for. Now leave my class."

His eyes were narrow and stern. I made a sharp noise, rolled my eyes, and walked off. "Whatever." I didn't want to do this. I couldn't be near this right now, this, this… *insanity*. I heard whispers as I left. Good gossip about how Prince Ethan had killed a *meluza* and lost his shit in class would travel fast around the school.

"Ethan!" Emma yelled after me. "I'm sorry!"

I didn't acknowledge that I heard her. Instead, I changed into a wolven and ran into the woods, away from the school. I was looking for a monster to kill, something to take my rage out on. I found nothing but my own vacant terror.

I didn't mean to yell at her, or lose my temper. She just didn't realize that she'd scared me— she didn't realize what I'd been through. If I had met her and lost her, all in the same day… if that *meluza* had managed to get its fangs in her… it'd be like losing my father all over again. I felt weak and desolate at the thought.

I replayed the moment her eyes looked at my leg over and over. Then the cold reality hit me. Emma wouldn't want someone like me— a cripple without a leg, with a scarred past and a bad reputation that preceded him. She didn't understand this world. She'd been thrust into a new reality with no sense of direction, and it showed today in the way she'd failed to kill the snake. An Arcanea wouldn't have hesitated.

She couldn't be queen. It wouldn't work. She wouldn't be able to handle the responsibility of it. She couldn't take a fight with one monster. How could she stand up against an army of them, again and again and again? Being queen was an unforgiving job. It'd nearly killed my own mother several times.

Emma hardly understood what an Arcanea *was*. I wanted to protect her. I didn't want to put her at risk. But she wasn't a warrior. She was just a girl. And what kind of match would we be for the kingdom, with not just one of us disabled, but *two* of us? How could we manage to win the support of the people? Were we even fit for the job?

For the first time in my life, I hesitated when I thought about becoming king. I considered backing out of the King's Contest and turning down the throne… all because of this one girl who I barely knew.

But I couldn't do that, could I? My people depended on me. They needed a strong king, someone to lead them when times got too miserable to endure, and my father's legacy was on the line. Either I could have the crown, or I could live a life with Emma. I couldn't have both.

It seemed like I had a choice to make. The monarchy… or my mate.

EIGHT

'd seen the look in Ethan's eyes as he ran away from me. It cut me so deeply that it felt like a blade was still sawing out a cavern in my soul.

I thought his wolven form was beautiful. He looked so strong and proud. I wanted to run my fingers through his thick white fur and bury my face into his shoulder. The animal he became was muscular and gorgeous. It took my breath away.

Then he'd noticed me staring at his lost leg. The pain in his expression was obvious and agonizing. I hardly cared if he was missing a limb— but to Ethan, he acted like he'd lost the world. He didn't want me to see, and I had. Stupid eyes.

He'd yelled at me for hesitating to kill a monster. I knew I'd made a mistake, but he expected me to murder a begging woman without batting an eye. I wasn't at that point yet. I wasn't sure if I ever would be.

I couldn't handle this place. It was too brutal, too savage. I'd thought I was tough, but the tough I knew was nothing compared to the Arcanea.

I went to get a quick lunch in the cafeteria. Every meal here was like a four-course feast served at a fine dining restaurant. Though I'd only wanted something small, I ended up ordering a watercress salad and a pasta with scallops. I was gonna be six hundred pounds by the time I graduated.

On my way to my next class, I passed Odette. She was talking to Delmare— they were sitting on a stone bench in the courtyard near a giant sculpture of an alicorn, chatting away. Both of them were wearing their uniforms.

Odette noticed my frown as I approached. "What is it?" Odette asked. "You seem upset."

"Yeah, who pissed in your cereal?" Delmare added. Odette smacked her playfully.

I waited before I dared to ask the question. "I had class with Ethan Nowak. He took his wolven form, and one leg was missing… but in his human form, he still has all four limbs?"

"Oh, it's a prosthetic," Odette said. "Ethan lost his right leg while fighting a leshane a few months ago on the hunt. It killed his father and everything. A lot of people still blame Ethan for the king's death."

"You mean his father was slain right in front of him, and he lost his leg in the process?" How absolutely horrible. I couldn't even imagine. I wasn't an emotional person, but tears sparked at the corner of my eyes thinking about how awful it must've been. No wonder he'd freaked out on me.

"Yep. Very tragic. But his wolven form doesn't have a prosthetic, so..." Odette shrugged.

"Are injuries like that common among the Arcanea?" I asked.

Odette made a noise. "Emm... not really. If you lose a limb or an eye, you're considered one of the lucky ones. Typically, people don't walk away if a monster gets their claws in them. But no good Arcanea dies of old age."

"A horrid death," Delmare added, and she shivered.

"You mean... you'd rather be killed by a monster than die warm and old in your bed?" I asked.

"Of course!" Odette exclaimed. "How else do you expect to get into the Great Hunting Grounds that lie beyond? The best warriors with the best deaths get to join the Eternal Hunt. It's a great honor."

"If you live to be ancient and don't have any scars, people think that you're lazy and not doing your job," Delmare informed me.

The Eternal Hunt sounded a lot like Valhalla to me, but I didn't tell Odette that. I didn't know the rules here, and didn't want to offend anyone. "I keep hearing about the Seven Gods," I said. "What are they?"

"Are you serious?" Delmare let out a deep laugh. "You must be joking."

"I just found out about the Arcanea a week or so ago. My mom hid this world from me," I explained.

"Whoa," Delmare said. "So you have mommy issues. Me too."

"Well..." I wouldn't say that, but Delmare pointed out the obvious. My mom and I obviously weren't as close as I thought we were if she kept things from me, especially something on this scale.

"Pop a seat!" Odette patted the spot next to her, and I squeezed in between her and Delmare. Odette crossed her ankles and said, "Okay, so the first thing you have to understand is that the Arcanea don't come from Earth. We actually are descended from fae that come from another dimension called *Edinmyre*."

"Faeries, right?" I asked.

"Yep." Odette nodded twice. "Our ancestors were fae who mated with humans, and they produced the Arcanea."

"Can you still get to Edinmyre?" I asked.

"Nah." Delmare shook her head. "The portal to Edinmyre was closed off long ago, and no one has been able to find a way back since. No one knows who shut it, either."

"Why did we leave?" This was all so confusing to me.

"It was a very long time ago. But as the lore goes, we had to leave, or we wouldn't survive the war between the Seven Gods," Delmare added.

"The Seven Gods..."

"Right," Odette said. "There are Seven Gods total who were the ultimate authority in Edinmyre. First is Tomir, King of the Seven Gods, also known as the Father Stag of the Hunt. He's the god of virtue. He's the leader of the Eternal Hunt in the Great Hunting Grounds. Only the greatest and bravest Arcanea are allowed into the Eternal Hunt, though most Arcanea make it into the Great Hunting Grounds. It's our version of the afterlife."

"So... what happens if you don't get into the Great Hunting Grounds?" I asked.

"Then you go down," Delmare said, and she chuckled.

"Getting to that," Odette said. "Next is Droga, the Black Stag of Wrath. He's the god of agony and suffering, the god of poor death. He's basically the grim reaper among the Seven Gods. Those who serve him value power, and try to please him through sacrifice. He's the only god that doesn't live in the Great Hunting Grounds. He exists in the underworld instead. Arcanea that serve dark magic go there— like the Black Claw."

A chill crept over my skin. "What about the others?"

"Well, let's see." Odette tapped her chin. "There's Vesna, the Blue Doe of Knowledge. She's the goddess of wisdom, and is usually worshipped by sorceresses. Then there's Radek, the Red Stag of War— the god of bravery. Warrior Arcanea follow him. Then there's Neva, the Specter Doe of Shadow... she's the goddess of time. Last is Luka— the Ghost Stag of Chaos. He's a thief god, the god of vigilantes and peasants."

"You're forgetting one," Delmare said. "Milonna, the White Doe of Peace."

I felt a shiver when she said Milonna's name. I don't know what it was— when she uttered the moniker, my stomach did flip-flops and a great warmth spread over my body, stronger than anything I'd ever felt. I longed to feel it again.

"Oh, yeah!" Odette popped up in her seat. "Milonna, too. She's the goddess of love, fertility, and romance. She's Tomir's wife. She leads an all-female brigade of the Eternal Hunt called the *Brygada.*"

"So we fled Edinmyre because the gods were fighting," I clarified.

"Tomir and Droga, to be exact," Delmare stated. "One fought for light magic, the other for dark. Droga ended up losing. It was this whole ordeal. The legends are truly epic."

"But since we left Edinmyre, we can't go back," Odette said sadly. "Not that we haven't tried, anyway."

I nodded. "So do the Arcanea worship *all* the gods, or..."

"Not really. In December, there's a yearly event called the Choosing," Delmare said. "It's a big pagan celebration, with a ball at the end of the ceremonies. There, you pledge yourself to your mate if you've found them, and pick a god or goddess to worship. All Arcanea devote their lives and service to one of the Seven."

Panic rode through me. Not only did I have to devote myself to a mate, I had to pick a god to align myself with as well? This was too much. I didn't think I could handle it. Which one of the Seven was I possibly going to pick?

"You have time to figure it out," Delmare said, catching my expression. "You won't be called to participate in the Choosing until you find your mate, and either accept or deny their bond."

I was already feeling overwhelmed. But I didn't want to show it and look like the girl who was always behind. I checked my watch. "I've gotta go," I told them. "I've got Illusion 101 in fifteen minutes."

"Have fun!" Odette said cheerfully.

I waved goodbye and tried to shove the thought of being forced to choose a mate out of my head. I proceeded toward the center of the courtyard, where a round stone pillar was set. According to my campus map, Illusion 101 was at the top of that tower. I entered and began climbing steps, taking them slow. I was in pretty good shape, but I felt weaker than normal.

It was obvious my disease was advancing. I was looking forward to starting treatments this week. Shoving needles in my stomach didn't sound fun, until you literally needed them to keep existing.

When I reached the top of the tower, I paused for a few moments to catch my breath before I went inside. Mahogany desks formed a half-circle around a professor's desk. The floor was emerald carpet, while the walls were white stone. Skeletons of dragons and griffins hung from the ceiling, and on the shelves lining the walls were a variety of interesting objects in jars— preserved butterflies, shimmering crystals, and live fish swimming in liquids that were purple instead of blue. One jar even had a swirling formation inside of it that looked like an actual storm. Lanterns holding burning candles levitated over the desks by themselves, and a green fire blazed in the hearth, giving the room an eerie glow.

Most students were already here, all female. I'd gotten the impression that many of the classes at the university were separated by gender, as Marked and Companions learned different things.

I caught Gabby sitting up front with Melissa and Morgan. Ew. I didn't want to sit anywhere near them.

The only seat left was next to a girl in the back. I headed toward it and dumped my stuff onto the desk. It went scattering everywhere. I went to clean it up.

"Sorry," I told my partner. "I'm kind of messy."

The girl had a mane of black hair over her face so I couldn't see it, and didn't comment. She kept her head bowed and remained still.

She was anti-social. Great. So was I. We'd get along great.

The door slammed shut, and I jumped. I heard the thumping of heels on the carpet. "Enough foolish gabbing, ladies," a cool voice behind me said. "Let's see if we can get those pretty little heads to do something else besides exchange gossip."

My eyes gravitated toward my teacher. She was a tall woman, thin, with a pinched face and eyes that said she'd have no problem throwing you out of her classroom if you crossed her. She wore a long, dark dress, and had her hair up in a tight bun that looked like it pulled her entire face back. Her lipsticked mouth gave an unwavering sneer.

She seemed… pleasant.

"I am Lady Korva, and this is Illusion 101," she began. "I expect anyone who is a student of mine to *keep up*. You will not be coddled in this classroom. Illusion is the bread and butter of a sorceress's magic. If you cannot do this, you cannot be a Marked. It is as simple as that."

No one dared to speak. Lady Korva clasped her hands together. "Sorceresses are the bond that hold the Arcanea together. Without us, our Companions would certainly be lost, and our race would die out. I cannot stress enough how important your duty is as a mate and future wife to whosoever you bond with. You need to be prepared to defend your Companion at all costs, for as the saying goes here in Malovia, the queen protects her king."

Korva prowled the room like one of the monsters she was warning us against… cunning and calculating, as if waiting for someone to make a mistake, so she could pounce on us. "Illusion is *intention*. The magic is created by summoning our will within us, and forcing that reality upon another's mind. There are limits— for example, you may disguise a building so that it appears not to be there at all, but those experiencing the illusion will still run into a brick wall if they attempt to walk forward, whether their mind sees it or not. You can make someone believe that they've been run through with a sword, and still kill them— though their body may remain undamaged, the perception that they've been fatally wounded will convince the brain, the heart, and all affected organs to begin shutting down, thus ending your enemy's life. The mind is the most powerful thing in the world. Trick it, and you will be able to bend anyone you wish to your will."

Lady Korva crossed her arms. "Imagination is key to an illusionist's arsenal. Whatever you can think, you can create. That is, if you're strong enough."

Lady Korva straightened up. "Let's see how many of you are prepared to harness your magic, should the need arise. Each of you, take an empty jar from the wall."

She snapped her fingers. Girls hustled out of their seats to grab empty jars lining the shelves. I rushed to get one before they were all gone, but I found that the girl I'd sat by had already grabbed one for me.

"Thanks," I told her. She said nothing. Damn, she was shyer than I was.

Lady Korva grabbed the jar with the storm inside of it from earlier and lifted it up high to show it to the class. "This is an example of a minor illusion. As you all know, Arcanea cannot manipulate the elements— that magic lies only with the Elementai. But we can, however, produce the *illusion* of a storm, and on a much minor scale. It is critical that every Marked knows how to generate these kind of illusions, to produce a distraction for enemies should their Companions be put in danger. I want each of you to produce an illusion that mimics weather inside your jar before the class is over. Begin now."

There was the sound of scraping chairs and scuffling jars. Lady Korva began sweeping the room to observe. My mouth was left hanging open. She hadn't even given us instruction. I didn't know how to do this.

I tried to remember what I'd done when I'd burst an illusion out of my hands to kill the wolf, but my mind went blank. I hadn't thought about it, it'd just been instinct. I did my best to try and force some sort of… I don't know, *something* inside of my jar, but nothing happened. I was just staring at blank air.

At least I wasn't the only one struggling. Melissa had busted open her jar trying to trap tiny lightning, and Morgan wasn't able to conjure more than a cloud inside of hers. Gabby could create a torrent of rain inside her jar, but it vanished the moment she looked away from it, and she was swearing under her breath with frustration.

My head turned to the right to look at my partner, and my mouth nearly dropped open. She'd already created a mini-typhoon within her jar, and was watching it closely as the waves crashed within underneath a collection of black, churning clouds.

"How did you do that?" I asked. It'd taken her mere seconds.

"Oh, it's easy," the girl said behind her hair. "I've been doing it for years."

"Can you help me?" I asked.

The girl paused. She turned in her seat toward me and slowly parted the curtain of hair from her face.

The girl's face was unlike any I'd ever seen. Her skin was mostly dark, though there were white splotches over her eyes and mouth, with freckles dotted over both. She was totally unique, and beautiful to look at. I wasn't sure if she had some sort of pigmentation variation or if it was a birthmark, but I had the thought that she looked incredible.

Bet she didn't feel that way, though. She was probably self-conscious about it.

"I'm Kiara," she said quietly. Her uniform tie was gold. A griffin.

"Emma," I said back. "Now can you tell me how to do this thing, before Lady Dominatrix comes over here and beats my ass?"

Kiara gave a tiny smile. "Picture a storm," Kiara whispered. "Visualize whatever you want to create in your head, then direct that intention to the jar. If you believe it'll come, it'll happen."

Sounded hoky to me, but I'd try it. I tried to imagine the type of storm I wanted to create. I pictured it in my head— ice, surrounded by fireballs.

It wasn't real, but as soon as I thought about placing that thought in the jar, they appeared. Tiny pieces of hail, surrounded by mini-fires, started falling inside the jaw and tinking against the side of the glass. I nearly fell out of my seat.

"How did I do that?" I gaped at the storm inside the jar, feeling both shocked and elated.

"What we're creating isn't real. That's why it's easy," Kiara said. "Bringing illusions to life is much harder. We have to get ourselves to believe, and others will see it, too."

A shadow fell over our desk. Kiara went quiet as Lady Korva loomed overhead. She picked up my jar, and sneered when she brought it to her face to look at the ice and fire raging within.

"That isn't a real storm. It doesn't exist," Lady Korva said. She slammed the jar back down on my desk. The storm disappeared, the ice melting and fire fizzling. "Try again."

What, was creativity not honored here at Arcanea University? I thought I'd get extra points for thinking outside the box.

Clearly not. Lady Korva was the type of woman who obviously ran things like the military. Step out of line and you'd face her wrath.

"Fine," I said. I picked the jar up again, made a show of shaking it, then placed it back on the desk, empty. "There. I did it."

"There's nothing in there," Lady Korva snapped.

"It's an *invisible* storm," I said.

Lady Korva's face went red. A couple of girls put their hands over their mouths, and Kiara cringed in her seat. "Miss Sosna, if you think you're going to come into my class and disrespect me, you are sorely mistaken."

"You asked me to create an illusion, and I did. Why does it matter what it is? It's made up anyway," I said.

People gasped. Lady Korva's eyes flashed. "I assure you that what we do here is not *made up*. It's the difference between life and death," she snarled. "With that kind of attitude, I expect your Companion to be slain within a year of bonding with you. Figments of the imagination are not enough to fool advanced monsters, especially childish notions such as yours."

A coldness went through me. I'd only been here a day or so, but even I knew you didn't speak of a Marked's Companion that way. She'd made it sound like I couldn't protect him if I had to— whoever he was.

Even though I had yet to meet my mate, I still felt fiercely protective of him. Lady Korva had crossed a line.

Her eyes went to Kiara. Kiara's typhoon had died to little more than a bit of sloshing water inside her jar. Lady Korva sniffed. "A pathetic attempt."

Lady Korva opened the jar and dumped the water all over the desk before placing the jar back before Kiara. "Try again."

Kiara focused her attention on the jar, but with everyone in the class looking at her, she lost her ability, and began to shake. Kiara couldn't recreate her magic under pressure.

Lady Korva made a scoffing sound. "What I expected from a griffin."

Kiara stared at the wooden desk. Lady Korva turned away from Kiara and said, "I didn't expect much from you because of who your parents are, Miss Mazurski, but even this is disappointing. Perhaps if you study hard enough, you can learn to cast a powerful-enough illusion to get rid of the hideous mark on your face."

Kiara's lip trembled. Gabby and her clones laughed under their breath. As Lady Korva walked away, Kiara quietly gathered her things.

"Don't go," I pleaded, but too late. Kiara hurried to rearrange her hair in front of her face and ducked her head behind her books as she ran out of the room crying. When she was gone, a couple more girls dared to laugh.

I felt rage well inside of me until it boiled over. This was bullshit. What kind of teacher was Lady Korva, making Kiara cry on her first day?

My mouth spoke before I could rein it in. "I'd rather have a face like Kiara's than one that looked like it just got done sucking on a lemon."

Lady Korva whirled around so fast I was surprised she didn't get whiplash. "Miss Sosna, out of my classroom!" she barked. "You may not come back until you learn to hold your tongue!"

"Gladly." I didn't care how things landed as I threw them into my bag. I was hauling ass out of there before she decided to cut my throat.

When I got to the bottom of the tower, I saw Kiara running across the courtyard. "Kiara, wait!" I shouted, but she didn't listen. She disappeared into a crowd of sophomores before I could catch up with her.

I stood at the bottom of the tower and felt terribly sorry. Yep. The world of the Arcanea could be more brutal than I ever predicted.

"Eyes up! Arms straight. Come now, Emmaline, is that really the best you can do?"

My breaths came in quick puffs as I stroked around the ice, working on my speed. I had my first practice with Lady Magdalina as my coach that afternoon, and hell, she was *tough*. She pushed me harder than anyone else ever had, even my mom. We'd only been on the ice for an hour, and already, I felt like I'd been there at least two.

The ice rink on campus was huge, and state of the art. It had three Olympic-size rinks, and leather stadium seats instead of stands. On the upper level was a gym, and a couple of dance studios where Odette was currently practicing. This rink was exclusive to figure skaters, while the other two were dedicated for hockey. I heard the sound of boys yelling and smashing each other into the boards through the thick walls. Companions played hard when it came to ice sports.

I switched to skating backwards and did some crossovers before I went into a triple loop. I leaned too far out of the jump and went down. I slid into the boards.

Lady Magdalina made a *tsk-tsk* sound. "Again, Emmaline. Perform a tighter rotation this time. Your arms are too loose."

Delmare, who'd followed us along just for the hell of it, was currently eating nachos she'd gotten from the vendor in one of the seats that surrounded the ice. She gave me a thumbs-up as I struggled to get off my ass. I groaned. I was gonna be hurting tonight. I returned to Lady Magdalina, dusting snow off my tights.

My eyes caught someone as they came onto the ice. Shit, it was Gabby. Motherfucker. She was an ice skater, too? What *didn't* this bitch do?

Lady Magdalina looked at her as she approached. "Try the jump one more time, Emmaline, then our session is over. Gabby's lesson is up."

Gabby wrinkled her nose when she saw me. "Ew. You're here."

"Yeah," I told her. "Turns out you don't own the rink, so."

"Just stay out of my way and don't mess up my jumps." Gabby's eyes narrowed.

"Girls, play nice," Lady Magdalina scolded. "Save it for the competition."

Gabby sneered. I went to do my triple loop again. This time, I landed it flawlessly. Lady Magdalina clapped lightly. Gabby rolled her eyes.

"Cool down, Emmaline, and call it a session. You've done well today," Lady Magdalina said. "Gabby, warm up, then I want to see your program."

My body was tired and sore, but it was so worth it. I was going to excel under Magdalene's teaching. I bet once I started infusions my energy would come back and I'd blow Gabby out of the water.

I stroked around the rink and pretended to drink my water, while really, I was observing Gabby perform her program. She was skating to Swan Lake, too, just like I did, but she played the part of the Black Swan, while I always skated to the part of the White.

It was really fucking ironic.

She knew I was watching her, too, and landed every jump. Not one spin wobbled, and her footwork was flawless. Gabby's eyes were totally directed at me as she finished her program with a smirking smile of victory.

I was gonna wipe that smirk off her face. I resolved I'd train harder, and get better before the competitive season in Malovia began in January. Like hell I'd lose to her. I'd be fine with second-to-last place as long as she was under me.

When I came out of the locker room, Odette and Delmare were waiting for me in the rink lobby. Odette had her ballet bag over her shoulder and was wearing a big smile on her face. Since school was over, all of us were back in our normal clothes. I had on skinny jeans, a white racerback top, and leg warmers over sneakers. Odette wore a cute pink dress that had purple horses on them. Delmare sported combat boots and ripped fishnets with a leather skirt. The best part of her outfit was the spiky black bra she wore over a see-through, long-sleeved black shirt.

I had to give it to Delmare. She was one brave ass bitch.

"That was the best lesson ever!" Odette beamed. "Even better than the last one."

"I'm sure you say that every time," I said. I noticed Theo walking out the glass double doors ahead of us. "Is Theo in your class with you?"

"Oh, yes. He's been my dance partner since we were little kids," Odette said cheerfully. "We work well together."

Oh, geez. I could only imagine. That had to make things awkward… for him, anyway.

There was nothing quite like the feeling of the warm sun on your body after you left an ice-cold rink. It sent pleasant pinpricks running up and down my skin. It wasn't a long walk back to campus from the rink— it only took us five minutes to walk up the cobblestone path through the gardens back to the university. On our way, we passed Chastity— the girl that everyone said Ethan was going to marry.

"Please don't tell me she ice skates," I moaned when she was out of earshot. I don't think I could take anymore competition, even though I really didn't have a problem with Chastity… just her attachment to Ethan.

"No. Chastity skis and snowboards," Odette informed me. "She goes to the gym to condition in the off-months."

Snowboarding was totally cool. I bet Ethan found that really attractive.

What the hell? Why was I thinking of him? He'd yelled at me. He obviously didn't feel that way toward me.

When we got back to school, Delmare, Odette and I helped ourselves to a dinner of beef tenderloin in the dining hall. By the time we were done, Delmare had suggested a horror movie marathon back in her dorm. Odette didn't like scary movies, but I was a fan of gore, so we managed to talk her into watching at least one. She was practically shaking in her skirt as we walked back to the girls' dorms.

"Can't we watch a cartoon? I love cartoons," Odette protested.

"Violence makes things interesting. Aren't you an Arcanea?" Delmare asked.

"An *alicorn* Arcanea," Odette protested.

"The way Theo was talking made them sound like the bloodiest of all." I laughed.

Odette peeped. "Theo doesn't know what he's talking about."

Both the boys and girls dorms connected to a big, open space that people called the Rec Room. There were couches, TVs, and games inside, including air-hockey and foosball tables, along with a separate area set up for video game tournaments. It was the only area of the college that was decorated in a modern fashion, with posters of bands and celebrities on the wall and giant, body-sized bean bags on the floor. The far wall was completely made of glass, and gave a view of the entire gardens. Basically, it was a place where everyone could hang out without getting in trouble. For a college, this place had strict rules on boys and girls being alone together. They really did hold the Companion-Marked bond sacred.

When we got to the Rec Room, it was humming with excitement. Everyone was on their phones and showing them to each other while gossip buzzed. At Arcanea University, people were allowed to have cell phones, though I'd been informed this morning that any use of them to expose the Arcanea's secret on social media or otherwise would result in immediate expulsion— something, so far, no one wanted to chance.

"What's everyone talking about?" I asked. Delmare took out her phone and started scrolling.

"The Phantom!" a boy shouted near us. "He's been spotted!"

"Who?" I asked. Delmare showed me her phone. She was on the website of *The Annual*

Arcanea; Dolinska's local newspaper. At the top of the site was a photo of a tall, hooded man, wearing a wolf mask over his face. He was cloaked in shadow. The photo had been taken from far away— the person snapping the shot had gotten it just before the figure ran off-screen.

I felt… attracted to the photo. Didn't know why. Something about it just resonated with me. It was something about the eyes.

"The Phantom is a vigilante," Delmare told me. "He solves crimes that the Arcanea Alliance can't, and fights criminals that they can't touch. He showed up a few months ago out of nowhere. They've been trying to catch him ever since."

Holy crap, this place had *superheroes*, too? It was like I was living in a comic book or something.

"If he's doing good, why do they want to catch him?" I asked.

Delmare huffed. "The po-po don't like people stepping on their turf. He's a hero, but he's still breaking the law. There's no due process with this guy. He leaves messes behind. But it'd be so juicy to figure out who he is."

I stared at the photograph and felt just as curious as everyone else did. Who was the Phantom, and why did I feel like I knew him?

ethan

NINE

I'd been careless. Someone had taken a gods-cursed photograph of the Phantom, and now it was making the rounds around Dolinska like wildfire.

The picture wasn't great, which was my only blessing. Any closer and the police would've been able to make out facial features. Not good. I couldn't make such a mistake again.

I knew I should be lying low, but I was close to busting open a set of slayings that had been committed in nearby warehouses. I planned to go out tonight to resume my investigation after class was over.

Wolf Pack Theory was a class only open to wolven Companions, and was held in the late hours of midnight to 2 a.m on Tuesdays and Thursdays. I often reserved times after these night classes to do vigilante work. Tonight was no exception. As the new moon rose, I proceeded into the cover of the woods. I was glad I could see in the dark, for the light being cast above was a mere sliver.

I smelled the other wolvens before I saw them. A group of about ten or so was up ahead of me, all in their wolven forms. Some of them had wings, though most others didn't.

Elijah was in this class. He lifted his lip and displayed his fangs to me as I passed. I snarled back. He was such a joy to have around.

Professor Lucien was at the center of the circle, and in his wolven form. He rustled his feathers as a brisk, chilly wind passed by.

I caught the smell of a woman passing, and everyone's head lifted. The level of testosterone in here was legendary. Each time a female walked by, every man's head craned to look at her—not that many females walked by this time of night, anyway.

"*Boys, pay attention,*" Lucien began. "*We'll be running rounds tonight. Each of you needs a refresher after the summer break.*"

Several people moaned. Nobody liked doing rounds, including me, but they were important. Wolvens could produce formations to hunt down monsters that other shifters couldn't. It was easier for us to work in groups.

"*I'll be giving chase. If you let me come close enough to touch you, you'll fail for the day,*" Lucien said. "*I'll give you a fifteen second head start, no less. Arrowhead formation, beginning now!*"

The wolves scrambled to get into formation as class broke into a run. Elijah, being the ass he was, took the spot at the front reserved for the alpha. I wasn't as much as a dick and took the back right corner, so that the ten of us made an inverted triangle. It wasn't long before I could hear Lucien's heavy foot beats behind. His hot breath was practically on my heels. If I failed because of Elijah today, he'd have to deal with me.

The pack moved as one through the trees, keeping formation even though there were obstacles in the way and Lucien was hot on our tail. *"Good form! Those of you with wings, circle formation. The rest of you on the ground, jagged dancer."*

Three wolvens spread their wings and took to the sky, creating a circle that they flew in like vultures from above, waiting to strike down on their prey. Me and the other wolvens still on the ground took a zig-zag pattern, and used it to weave in and out of trees. Lucien managed to jump on the back of the last wolven in line, and he whined as he went down. We picked up the pace, not wanting to join him in receiving no credit.

"If I can catch you, a monster will have no trouble!" Lucien warned. *"Use the environment to your advantage! Snake formation!"*

The line changed, and our zig-zag became more of a weaving line. Of course, I ended right next to Elijah. He was behind me, trying to shove his way up front, but I wouldn't let him.

"Get out of my way, peg leg," Elijah growled. He stepped on my tail, and I wasn't stupid enough to assume it was an accident.

I tried to ignore him, but that ended up being the wrong decision. He reached out and knocked my back leg out from under me, causing me to lose my balance. I toppled forward into the wolven in front of me, and the whole line went down. We went tumbling headfirst down a hill, and the world spun for a moment as various bruises and scrapes littered my sides.

When we finally came to the bottom of the embankment, many people were groaning in discomfort, or dizzy. Elijah, one of the few to remain upright, came running down the hill with a smug smile on his face.

I leapt to my feet and bared my fangs. As soon as he came within distance, I lashed out with my paw. He jumped backward and landed in a crouch, ready to spring forward onto me so we could fight.

Lucien was between us before either could act. *"We are working on rounds today, not dueling,"* he said sharply. *"If both of you wish to fail, I'll be more than happy to have you sit out for the rest of the class."*

Elijah gave me a hateful glare, but said nothing else. Lucien gave a low growl and said, *"Let's try again. If anyone pulls another stunt like that, I'll see to it that they will not graduate. Rock formation!"*

Lucien made sure to separate us for the rest of the class. We ran more rounds and drills until two hours had passed and many wolvens were lying on the ground, struggling to catch their breath.

Not me. I still had a long night ahead of me.

Lucien shook his head. *"So many could not keep up. The summer's made you soft. I plan to beat that out of you by the time the first snow comes. Class dismissed."*

Elijah looked fine. He was one of the few that hadn't passed out during rounds. He was in top shape. It was clear he'd been training for the Contest all summer. I kept my eye on him and didn't turn my back until he was well out of sight.

I became my human form once I entered the palace. The halls were dead and quiet at this time of night. I avoided the dormitories and instead went to a different part of the castle— the dungeons.

They hadn't been used in years, and were supposedly blocked off to students, but I'd found a way in through a hidden doorway that posed as a bookcase in the library. The hidden halls were a secret to anyone who wasn't in the royal family— special passageways had been built behind the walls of the palace for the king and his kin to use in case of emergencies when the palace was built in 1700, but had been forgotten about long ago. I only remembered they were there due to something my father had said in passing shortly before he died.

I emitted a purple light from my hand, to guide the way through the dark passageways and long tunnels that weaved like a maze. Finally, I came to the end of my destination. It was an underground bunker that had a door leading to the streets of Dolinska. I sparked a fire in the fireplace, then used it to ignite the torches scattered around the room. The flames illuminated the room. My cloak and mask were tucked into a locked trunk near the door. A scattered maps and clues splayed over an old wooden table. Bunks were placed alongside the walls, but I never used them.

It was the perfect hideout for the Phantom. I highly doubted the Arcanea Alliance expected the vigilante to be a student.

I changed into my outfit then quickly scanned the maps, where I'd outlined a trail. There'd been ten murders at Arcanea warehouses in the area, where we shipped out our famous Malovian wine. The wine was enchanted by sorceresses, and was of high value in the magical marketplace. Production had been slowed due to bodies showing up around the area. A few more people who worked for the wineries had gone missing entirely.

The people that were found killed had been consumed, so I knew we were dealing with a monster and not a person. The only question was what kind.

I stood before the warehouses shortly after, on a rooftop that overlooked where the bodies had been found. My nose could smell the protective charms that the sorceresses had put over the warehouses for security purposes. I couldn't break them— a Marked needed to do that. So I'd need to go around.

There were sewers leading into the warehouses, I was sure. I dropped down, then searched the ground for a manhole. When I found one, I popped the lid and slid inside. I fitted the cover over the hole as I proceeded through the large pipeline beneath. When I was certain I was inside the warehouse campuses, I found another manhole and came out the other side.

My guess was successful. I was inside the magical ward now. I tried the first door I came to, and found it unlocked— Arcanea didn't typically lock doors when they had magic to protect whatever was inside.

The contents of the warehouse didn't arouse any immediate suspicion. All that was inside were hundreds of wooden barrels full of wine, stacked up to the ceiling.

Then I smelled it. The body. It was freshly killed, within the last hour or so, and still warm. Metallic blood was seeping all over the concrete floor.

My eyes quickly caught other small details through the darkness. Spilled barrels, claw marks— the signs of a fight, or struggle. The blood showed signs of someone else being dragged along the floor. There'd been two people here, both attacked at the same time.

I heard sucking noises. Something was feeding on the corpse. The dead eyes of a Marked stared out at me as I approached. As I drew closer, my sight illuminated green scales.

The monster was long and thin, reptilian, with four legs and a long, snake-like neck that ended in a pointed head with venomous jaws. It wasn't much bigger than a large dog, but that didn't make it any less dangerous. Its vicious red eyes caught me as I approached, and it hissed, lashing a whip-like tail.

Momentary shock went through me. A *beithir*? What was it doing here?

The *beithir* went to run. I chased after it. The creature scattered between barrels of wine, and I slipped on the blood trying to catch up. It spit venom at me, which I quickly dodged. Sizzling green liquid landed on the floor next to me and ate up the concrete. I got within reaching distance and extended my arm for the tail, but it lashed me in the face and left a small mark. My hand instinctively went up to my face. Before I could do anything else, the creature left through the door I'd come out of and hurried away into the night.

I groaned. Who knew where the monster had went?

Something wasn't right here. *Beithir* weren't native to Malovia. They could hardly be classified as monsters, and didn't come from the underworld. They originated in Scotland. They were more of a magical creature than anything else. Dangerous, yes, but not specifically out to harm human beings in service of Droga.

Yet this *beithir* had. He'd killed two people before getting away the last time. Yet there was no easy entrance for the creature, as far as I could see. I'd had a hard enough time finding a way inside, and it couldn't come in or out through the wards that defended the warehouses.

The evidence was clear. The monster couldn't have gotten in unless someone had let it.

I examined the body. There was a large, gaping hole in her middle— the *beithir* had shot his venom at her, and it'd ate away at her body. Claw marks, like those from a griffin, were deeply embedded in the floor— I even found a missing talon that had been ripped off, and a few feathers the griffin had lost while trying to get away. Next to them were bloody footprints that looked human, and a few scraps of frayed black cloth.

Her Companion had been taken by force. It was the only thing I could conclude from the situation.

I searched the warehouses extensively, but I didn't see any other sign of the *beithir*, or clues as to where the captured Companion had been taken. I'd scared the reptile into hiding. I found pieces of where the monster had been— a nest, even, made of old, oily rags— but nothing else. I destroyed the nest before a thought came to me.

Someone had let the monster loose inside the warehouses in order for it to hunt down and wound fellow Arcanea. If the *beithir* didn't kill it, they'd kidnap whoever was left alive, now that their monster had made the job easier. What they did with them, I didn't know.

This went way deeper than a few monster slayings. If I truly wanted to figure out what was going on, I'd have to leave the monster alive, and come back tomorrow to see who was following it around.

Puzzled, I went back the way I came through the sewers and resumed my walk to campus. I wouldn't figure this out tonight.

I took the rooftops on the way back home. Less conspicuous. I was nearly back to Arcanea University when I heard screams— they were coming from a female.

Instinctively, I knew they were coming from Emma before my brain registered the fact. I increased my strides along the rooftops to get to her. What was she doing out so late at night? Didn't she know these streets held danger?

I came to a stop on the edge of a rooftop that hovered over an alleyway below. There, Emma had her back pressed against a dead end, while two hooded figures approached her. They wore cloaks of all black, with grotesque masks of skulls painted in red blood covering their faces. They advanced slowly on her, saying nothing, appearing as horrid ghosts from hell about to take the life of a frightened mortal.

"Don't come any closer, or I'll fry your ass! I've done it before!" Emma shouted. Her voice was tight with fear. She raised her hand and attempted to make light come out of her palms, but it was weak, and her magic failed her. Her power got dimmer and dimmer with every steady step the strangers used to approach, arms extending to grab her. Her whole form quivered as they continued their slow advancement, remaining silent and stoic.

Rage blinded me and made adrenaline pound through my system. They had the nerve to threaten my mate? How *dare* they!

I fell from the rooftops and landed in front of Emma. She gasped— the figures stopped their advancement toward her as they stared upward at my form.

"I suggest you walk away," I said lowly. "Or the consequences for remaining here will be your lives."

The masked figures didn't listen. They lunged forward, one of them exploding into a grey alicorn to deal with me, the other reaching out toward Emma.

I reacted in mere seconds. I grabbed my dagger and shoved my shoulder into the charging alicorn, knocking it over. Then I whirled around and grabbed the one who was trying to hurt Emma. I shoved the dagger into its stomach— a fatal blow. I heard the person gasp. The alicorn on the ground— who I assumed had to be her Companion— let out a high pitched scream.

I shoved the masked figure backward, ripping out the dagger. She clutched at her stomach, attempting to hold in her innards. The alicorn scrambled to get up and used his neck to lift his Marked onto his back. Hoof steps clattered into the night as the shadowed figures fled, the one I'd stabbed leaving a blood trail behind.

Normally, I'd follow to finish the job, but I wouldn't leave Emma's side. You'd have to take my other leg before I'd leave my mate alone after what had just happened.

I turned around, and my cloak swooped behind me. Emma was still shaking. I longed to put my arms around her and hold her, calm her down— but she'd already been terrified enough by masked men tonight. "Are you all right?"

She gaped at me. I think she was speechless, or going into shock. Her expression was frightened. She didn't know who I was.

"It's fine," I said gently. "I'm not going to harm you. Now I ask again— are you hurt?"

She finally found her voice. "I... I don't think so." She pried herself slowly off the wall. "Who were those people?"

"Servants of the Black Claw," I told her. "Most likely, they were here to take you as a human sacrifice."

"Sacrifice?" Her eyes grew wide, and she swallowed. "Well, thank you for saving me."

"Don't thank me. It was foolish for you to be wandering these streets after dark. You should know better," I told her gruffly.

Her cheeks turned red with anger. "I just wanted to go for a walk. I'm a student at the university. I couldn't sleep, and the city's beautiful at night," she protested.

"It doesn't matter. You could've been killed. What on earth are you doing out at three in the morning?" I couldn't keep the harshness out of my tone. I wanted to shout and rage at her. What she didn't understand about this world... it almost resulted in me losing her tonight.

Emma raised an eyebrow. "Your voice sounds familiar. Who are you?" She took a step closer.

I ignored her. "You shouldn't be walking around at night by yourself. It's dangerous to be on your own, even in a city like Dolinska. Monsters still prowl here."

"Well, escort me back to the school yourself," she snapped, and she crossed her arms. "Or I won't go."

I rolled my eyes. "You're a stubborn woman. Very well."

I extended my hand to her. Slowly, she took it. When our hands touched, I felt a powerful warmth surge through me. It went up my arm and traveled through every pore of my body, settling in my gut and creating a home there. It was emotional and powerful, and flowed through me like my very blood. It felt like holding lightning in my hand.

Emma had felt it, too. Her eyes widened and her lips parted a bit, color flashing in her emerald eyes.

I tugged on her hand and said, "Come on. I don't have all night."

She narrowed her gaze at me. "I'd be fooled, seeing as how you're walking around looking for trouble."

"You're a mouthy one." We proceeded through the streets of Dolinska, holding hands... I was so intently aware of every movement her body made next to mine that it made my form feel like it was on fire. What was this unexplainable, undeniable connection between us, and how could anyone on this earth live without it? How could I, after so many years?

There were nightly wards around Arcanea University as well, but you could pass through them if you were a student or part of the staff. I hoped Emma didn't know about them, because if she did, she'd have one more clue to piece together who I really was. But as we passed through the wards to enter the school grounds, she said nothing. I breathed a sigh of relief.

Emma went to go through the front gate of the school, but I tugged her back. "Not that way."

We went around, through a backdoor in the gardens that few people knew about, hidden behind a square hedge. This part of the gardens led directly to the dormitories.

"Which one?" I asked as I looked up at the rows and rows of windows above us. Emma pointed.

"It's three stories up. The only one with a balcony. I got lucky," she said.

"I'll say." I reached into my cloak and grabbed my grappling hook gun. I shot it at the balcony, and it hooked over the side. I grabbed Emma around the waist and said, "Hold on tight."

I pressed the button on the gun, and the line pulled us upward. Emma clung her arms around me as we rose. Gods, the feeling of her body pressed into mine was making my instincts go mad. It was like a million sensors were firing off in my head all at once. My head clouded over so that it was hard to think. The only thing I could conjure in my imagination was the sight of Emma beside me— Emma in my bed.

I'd never been like this before. It was too much to handle.

When we got to the balcony, I lifted her over the side before I climbed over the railing. I unfastened my grappling hook, sliding it back in my cloak.

"You got something else impressive under there?" Emma asked. She smirked.

"If you're trying to make a crude joke, it's not funny," I told her.

"It's funny to me." She snickered. I rolled my eyes.

"You need to stay inside the school at night. Don't go walking around on your own," I told her.

"Excuse me? Who are you to boss me around?" she shot out quickly.

My temper raged. I wanted to respond back that I was her mate and that she needed to listen to me as much as I would her, but instead, I said, "The Phantom commands you."

"Ooh, scary." She waved her hands. "Some weird guy in a mask tells me what to do, and I'm supposed to listen?"

"I *did* save your life. I'm not expecting to take time out of my day to rescue your pretty little ass again, so if you want to repay the favor, you'll do as you're told," I snapped.

She huffed. "Fine. I'd say that was a fair deal." She tapped her fingers against the balcony.

I kept my gaze fixed on her. "I'll hold you to your word, Miss Sosna."

I hesitated. Shit. I'd never meant to say her name. Her eyes widened, but before she could say another word, I started scaling the wall. In less than a minute, I was on top of the roof and out of Emma's eyesight.

My heart felt like it was in my throat, making it hard to breathe. That was a close call. I'd nearly slipped up and given myself away.

I wasn't so sure I hadn't.

TEN

I'd met the love of my life. He was the Phantom.

It was a big jump to make, but when our hands touched and he interlocked his fingers in mine, there was no doubt in my mind. I felt the magic there, binding our lives and fates together. It was an undeniable attraction that nature itself couldn't ignore.

The Phantom was my mate. I only needed to discover who he was, so that we could be together.

I was certain that I'd run into him before. He knew my name. He had to be in one of my classes. And Odette had told me about the wards around the school that were placed at night. You couldn't pass in or out of them unless you went to school here, which meant that the Phantom was somewhere among the male students at Arcanea University.

But there were thousands of guys here. I couldn't tell you how many I'd met in the past few days. The Phantom could be any one of them. Narrowing it down wouldn't exactly be easy, but I did have hope… he'd bonded with me, which meant he was a wolven. Besides, nobody but a wolven would run around with a *wolf mask* as a disguise. The guy really needed to up his game when it came to the secret identity department.

I'd have never met him if I didn't make a spur of the moment decision to take a nighttime stroll through town. I missed my mom. I wanted to know more about the world she came from. Okay, maybe a midnight walk through town *wasn't* the safest way to do it, but I'd tossed and turned all night. I couldn't sleep while picturing her at my age, roaming magical alleyways and performing magic like she was born to do so all her life.

I'd wondered why the streets were so empty, and I found out— the Black Claw cornered me long before I'd even realized they were following my trail. It had been scary learning about them in the first place, but actually seeing them in person, coming toward me with those freaky skull masks, had made them horribly real.

Then the Phantom had saved me. Even better, he'd *bonded* with me. Now all I needed to do was solve the mystery.

A couple of weeks had gone by, but I still wasn't used to things at Arcanea University. If I was useless at illusion, I was even worse at Intro to Enchanting. The enchanting classroom was in the shape of a crescent moon, with a wall of windows that looked out over campus. There

325

were a variety of round tables covered in purple velvet cloths, surrounded by an assortment of large armchairs where we did the enchanting. Professor Calliope strode around the room, observing as we attempted to infuse swords with magical energy.

Professor Calliope was a dragon Marked who had long black hair and a robe that appeared as if it was made of starlight. She was old, dignified, and strict, but I liked her. She treated everyone the same, and if anyone had the nerve to get cocky, she'd take them down a peg.

"Clear your mind," Professor Calliope spoke strongly over the girls struggling to enchant their weapons. "Focus your intention on the blade, then visualize the color of the spell— the color of the enchantment of protection is *blue*. Guide your hands over the blade, hovering slightly by an inch or two. If done properly, the blade will glow with a similar hue to the magic, and the sword will provide an added defense while taking down monsters."

Calliope demonstrated again, and a sparkling blue magic floated from her fingertips and landed on the broadsword displayed on the desk in front of the table. "Enchanting is the magical art of infusing objects with a certain intention, similar to illusion," she spoke. For example, if you enchant a teacup with the intention of happiness, whosoever drinks from that cup will immediately experience an elevated mood. Likewise, if you wanted to enchant a sword for better defense during battle, you would cast an enchantment of protection, like we're attempting to do today. Alicorns in particular should experience ease while casting enchantment charms, as their magic is best suited for shield magic, but all Marked should be able to cast some sort of protective enchantment, should the need arise."

Not me, apparently. We were supposed to use these swords in our next Monster Hunting class with Lord Lucien, so I wanted to get this right. I didn't want to be the only loser without a working enchanted blade on Monday. Everything at Arcanea University connected together, and if you failed in one class, it would affect your performance in the others.

I held my hands over the sword and tried to focus, but I couldn't see the blue light, nor could I picture my intention. I didn't feel safe, not even within these stone walls. The Black Claw were out there, and they'd nearly killed me twice now. Who's to say they wouldn't try again? I didn't feel protected at all. I felt scared.

The blade glowed red, and Professor Calliope stopped at my table. "That's wrong, Emma. That's the enchantment for fear. Which works well if you're attempting to get the monster to flee, but is not the purpose of this class."

She waved her hand, and the red color from the sword faded, drifting into air like smoke. "Take a moment to realign yourself."

She walked off. I glanced around the room. Many girls had already gotten the spell. The room was lit up with blue. I was one of only three who hadn't nailed it yet.

I sank low in my seat. I'd never get this.

"It'd be easier if you tried to relax," Kiara said beside me. "I know it's difficult."

I was surprised at the sound of Kiara's voice. She'd sat next to me in all my classes, and was my partner for most of them, but hadn't said a word since Lady Korva had spoken nasty things to her face.

I huffed. "Is there an easier way to do this?"

Kiara shrugged. "You can add certain crystals to create a circle around the object for easier enchanting, but those are only to be used with advanced spells where the magic doesn't want to take."

"But what if I'm not strong enough?" I asked.

"The magic is inside of you. That's what makes the spells work. You have it, you just need to learn to access it," Kiara said. "Picture it as a well you're drawing from. It'll come easier."

Kiara's words gave me inspiration. I decided to try again. This time, I closed my eyes and placed my hands slightly over the sword. I pictured my powers as a huge waterfall, hundreds of feet high. I saw myself standing at the bottom of it with a wooden bucket, ready to draw from its endless supply without worrying if there was enough.

I needed to feel protected. I thought of the Phantom, and how he'd come from out of nowhere to save me. I'd never have to worry about being in danger or being hurt again as long as he was around. He'd protect me from anything. I remembered the cool and comforting look he'd given me when he'd left me on the balcony beneath the stars. It was unlike anything I'd experienced in the world.

I felt a tingling warmth spread from my palms, and I opened my eyes. The sword now gleamed blue.

"See? You can do it, Emma," Kiara encouraged. "You merely need to have faith."

Professor Calliope stopped by our table again. "Looks like Miss Sosna works better with her eyes closed than open to direct the magic. That's the sign of an advanced Marked," she praised. "You're an excellent sorceress. You merely need to get out of your own head."

I was beaming when I left class. Kiara fell in-step beside me. She hid a tiny smile behind the many books she carried.

"I finally did it! I'm such a badass," I said. "Thanks for all your help, Kiara. I couldn't have done it without you."

"Yes you could've. You did the work, not me." She shuffled the books in her arms as we wandered through the crowded hallways, keeping her head down. "Where are you off to now? Another class?"

"I'm actually meeting up with my friends. Want to come?" I asked her. I stopped in front of a stained glass window that had a bench in front of it.

Kiara bit her lip. "Um… I don't know." She scuffed the ground with her shoe. "I don't really do well with new people."

"I didn't either, before I came here," I told her. "I promise you'll like them. Odette and Delmare are awesome."

She looked down. "It's not that."

I sat on the window seat. "Why don't you tell me about it?"

Kiara hesitated. The look in her eyes was fearful— like she worried that if she said what was really on her mind, I'd use it against her later.

She slowly took a seat across from me. "I'm surprised you want to be seen with me. Seeing how I look like… well, this."

"Your face is beautiful. Fuck anyone who tells you otherwise," I stated.

"It's the mark of an outsider," she said quietly. "My mother was a Marked who mated with a human. I came out with a mark on my face, and all over my body."

"But why does that matter? It just makes you unique," I said.

"You don't understand. It was a huge scandal when my mother mated with someone who wasn't our kind, that she never found a Companion to guard. She didn't do her duty to our people," Kiara explained. "When others found out she was pregnant with me, they tried to stop the pregnancy. They called me a halfling baby. That's why Lady Korva told me to fix my face. So people wouldn't know I was half-human."

"Oh my gosh." I put a hand over my mouth. "That's horrible."

She nodded. "We were allowed to live in Dolinska, but on the outskirts, as outcasts. I have more human blood than faerie. People say it makes me weak."

"That's bullshit. You're more talented with magic than anyone in our class, probably the whole school, even," I said. "If anything, your human blood makes you stronger."

"I don't know." She nuzzled her head into her books, so that her nose was hidden behind it. "I just don't want to be picked on anymore. This is embarrassing, but to be honest, I've never had a real friend."

I placed my hand over hers. "I'm an outsider, too. I didn't know anything about this world until recently. I didn't even know Arcanea existed."

"Really?" Her eyes widened.

"Yes," I told her. "And you shouldn't be worried about being bullied by my friends. They're pretty weird themselves. I wouldn't hang out with them if they were jerks."

Her eyes nervously darted away from mine. "Okay. If you say so…"

"I know so. Come on." I hooked Kiara's arm in mine, and stood up. "Odette is going to love you, I just know it. She never sees the bad in anyone. And as long as you laugh at Delmare's shitty jokes, you should be fine."

Kiara looked nervous as hell. "I hope they like me, too. I've been having trouble talking to people of my own Faction. Griffins aren't very approachable. I want to talk to the boys, but they're intimidating. Not scary so much as all-business."

She sighed. "Sometimes I wonder if I'll ever bond, or if I'm destined to mate with a human just like my mother."

"You'll find an amazing griffin to bond with someday," I told her. "I bet he's looking for you right now. And if you pick a human, that's fine, too. What matters is that he makes you happy."

"I hope so." She

sighed. "Have you found your mate yet?"

My pulse quickened. "Yes. But I don't think he even knows I'm alive."

"That's too bad." She frowned. "I hope you two get together soon."

A bitter loneliness crept into my throat. "So do I."

Odette and Delmare took pretty quickly to Kiara. It wasn't two minutes into the conversation before Odette was making Kiara swear to come over for a makeover later while Delmare was asking if she wanted to go get tattoos.

Kiara as pretty uncomfortable, at first, but she got used to the two extroverts throwing themselves at her within the hour. By Monday, she'd officially been inducted by Odette into our little group.

The first week of fall in Malovia was bitterly cold. The leaves were turning a burning orange and bright red, and tiny snowflakes were beginning to fall on the golden evenings that quickly summoned winter. At Kiara's request, I kept my head down in my classes, and did my best not to piss Lady Korva off— I was getting better at enchanting, though illusion still eluded me, and I still was having trouble keeping up with the drills in Monster Hunting 101. My other two classes—Intro to the Monarchy and Intro to Flight—were all history and theory, but I worried about my Flight class the most. I didn't have my wings yet, as some sorceresses did, and I feared the day would soon come that I'd be asked to use them.

I was practicing illusion by myself near a fountain of a Marked with beautiful butterfly wings that afternoon. I was trying to make the statue come alive and flutter its wings, but all I'd managed to do was change the stone from gray to red, and I was stuck trying to figure out how to put it back.

I gave an angry sigh. "How the hell." I waved my hands and tried again, focusing on my intention, but all the statue did was get redder.

"Having trouble with that?"

I heard a voice behind me. It was Ethan. His hands were in his pockets again. He was giving me an amusing look, like it was so funny I was busting my ass trying to make the statue come alive.

"If you're going to tease me, go away," I told him. I waved my hands again, and the statue gave Ethan the finger. I smiled. Not the result I wanted, but I'd take it.

Ethan laughed. "You can't be that bad if you're using objects to insult me."

"I'm horrible. Don't even go there." I dropped my hands to my sides with a *smack*. "How do you guys do it? I'm way behind everyone else."

"Marked are far better than Companions at magic. It's you guys who hold the most power," Ethan said.

"Could've fooled me." I made a face. "Great. Now the thing's stuck like that."

"No it's not." Ethan waved his hand. A purple hue settled over the statue, and the red color I'd put into it drained away, until the statue appeared to be its normal self again. Once again, Ethan's eyes flashed violet when he performed magic.

I crossed my arms. "Show-off."

"The Arcanea who struggle the most with illusion find themselves incapable of being fake," Ethan told me. "It's a compliment, Emma, not a weakness. Being unable to conjure an illusion simply means you're too honest."

That made sense. Gabby was an exceptional illusionist, because she was the fakest bitch in school. "So how do I become a better illusionist?"

Ethan leaned in and whispered, "Be a better liar."

He walked away, his broad shoulders strolling with a casual amble. His words caught my attention. What exactly did Ethan have to hide?

I thought about what I knew about the best illusionists. I knew Delmare wrote poetry and short stories in her free time. She'd even composed a novel that she'd self-published online. I read it, and thought it was really good. A bit dark, but that was Delmare. She was good at illusion casting. She had experience creating other worlds other people could hardly dream up.

Me, I was too rooted in reality. I struggled to use my imagination for anything my eyes couldn't see, and it was killing me out here. I didn't know why I still had trouble being inventive in a world where anything was possible.

Maybe it was because my mom had kept it from me for so long. I knew she wasn't ready to tell me why, but someday, I needed to know.

"Saw you talking to Ethan," Odette teased as I met up with her in the hallway to head back to the girls' dorms. "He seems to like you."

My cheeks blushed, but I said, "You told me he was taken."

"He was, but now I'm not so sure," Odette said cheerfully. "He sure does seem to have eyes for you lately."

I brushed it off. Ethan could look at me all he wanted. I only had eyes for the Phantom.

"Emma!"

Kiara came jogging down the hallway. "I wanted to ask you. We needed to pick up that new book for illusion class. Would you like to come with me?"

"Sure, I'll go along," I told Kiara. "Do you want to come, Odette?"

"No, thank you. I have to meet up with Theo," she told us pleasantly. "Have fun!"

She trotted off, and Kiara and I looked at each other. "Do you think she'll ever realize she has a thing for Theo?" I asked Kiara.

Kiara shook her head. "Probably not. But you think she would. They hang out practically every day."

That was an understatement. *Every hour* was more like it. If I was with Odette, it wasn't unusual for Theo to be too far away.

We decided to walk, as it wasn't that far. The streets were crowded in the late afternoon, and we had to press close together to avoid being lost in the crowd. Kiara took me to this tiny bookshop in an alleyway that twisted and turned. A stone gargoyle in the shape of a griffin blocked the door.

"Watch this," Kiara told me. She waved her hand above her head. "The password is… *password.*"

White magic fluttered down from her hands, landing on the stone gargoyle's head. The gargoyle came alive, and moved out of the way so we could enter inside.

"Keeps monsters out," she told me pleasantly. "And those who don't know the secret code."

"Why would a bookstore need to be guarded?" I asked as we stepped inside.

Kiara's lips turned upward. "Siona has some… *items* in here that are strictly contraband."

Enchanting Whispers was unlike any bookstore I'd ever been into. It had a coffee shop set up in the corner, tables clustered next to the windows that looked out into Dolinska's streets. There were shelves upon shelves of not just spell books, but fiction and poetry of all genres. Glass jars with tiny pixies hovered on their own over the bookshelves and illuminated the space. It smelled like coffee and pumpkin inside, and a bit of white sage and incense.

There were a bunch of people in here— they read the newspaper at tables or browsed the shelves while sipping on tea. Along the back wall, I understood what Kiara was getting at when she said the store was stocked with contraband items— there were twisted black wands that looked like they'd been made of roots, staffs set with glass globes, and crystals hanging from long chains.

Arcanea were forbidden to use wands, staffs or crystals to channel their magic. They were considered tools of the Black Claw. It was a scandal if a sorceress drew from any power that wasn't her own… Lady Korva had drilled that into our heads since the moment I showed up in her class. It was seen as weak to rely on tools to use magic.

"I've got one," Kiara whispered to me as we passed, and she showed me a small white crystal embedded on a gold chain, hanging underneath her shirt. "Not everything they say up at the school is right. Crystals can be used for white magic."

"Is that how you've been able to catch on so quickly?" I asked.

She nodded. "I have a natural talent for it, but the crystal helps me focus and center my powers. You should pick one out."

My eye lingered on an amethyst crystal dangling on a chain, but I shook my head. "Maybe later."

"Kiara!" A loud voice caught our attention. A dark-skinned woman, only a few years older than us, gave us a bright smile.

Kiara grinned. "Sis!"

The woman and Kiara hugged. As they drew apart, Kiara turned to me. "Emma, this is my big sister, Siona. She runs the shop."

"Pleased to meet you," I said. I noticed there was a green stone hanging around Siona's neck, similar to Kiara's. I had a bad feeling her mixed heritage wasn't the only reason people chose to judge Kiara.

Siona slid a hand through Kiara's hair. "What brings you girls in today?"

"We need a book for illusion class. Lady Korva requested it," Kiara said.

"I think I have the one," Siona said. "Though you're lucky. There's only two copies left."

Siona and Kiara went down another aisle. I went to follow, but something caught my eye.

It was an old book— covered in so much dust I couldn't read the spine. It was purple velvet, and had rusting golden clasps. I took it down off the shelf and dusted it off, coughing as I did so.

The title was written in a language I didn't know, though it wasn't Malovian. It wasn't like any language I'd ever seen— scrawling letters in a pretty, ornate cursive font. I opened the book, and the sound of crinkling, antique parchment with worn edges hit my ear. This book was super old. It could've come from the Middle Ages. I turned the crinkling pages and saw paragraphs of the same strange language, although there were ornate drawings of winged Marked and Companions within.

The book looked like it'd been handwritten, not printed, the drawings done by a skilled artist with a quill. They were so beautiful. I pressed the book to my chest. I didn't know why, but I had to have it. The sketches inside were so pretty.

Siona was ringing Kiara up at the cash register. "Hey, how much for this?" I asked, putting the book on the shelf. Kiara sneezed as dust from it rose into the air.

"That old thing? You can have it." Siona wrinkled her nose. "It's been sitting on the shelf for ages, and nobody's bought it. I don't even remember purchasing it for the shop."

"Wow, really? Thanks," I said, pressing the book to my chest.

She laughed. "Don't thank me. I should be thanking you for taking that old tome off my hands. Now I can put something in its place that'll actually sell."

Siona put the old book and our two new textbooks into an eco-friendly bag and handed them to Kiara. "So, how's old battle-ax Korva treating you girls?"

Kiara's face fell. I knew she didn't want to tell her sister what Korva had said to her. "Just about as well as an old battle-ax would."

"I thought so." Siona's expression was grim. "I wasn't fond of her either when I was in school. I've enchanted the stone griffin outside to vomit on her if she tries to come near my shop."

Kiara and I laughed. We waved farewell to Siona, and began the walk back up to the university.

As the city turned into heavy woodland, Kiara gave a shiver. "Something doesn't feel right."

"What do you mean?" I asked. What was it with Arcanea and *feelings*?

"I don't know." She bit her lip and looked down. "I can't put my finger on it. But my stomach's churning. Like something bad is going to happen."

Just that very moment, the two of us heard screaming. It sounded like it was coming from a bird in distress— a very large one.

"Someone's in trouble," Kiara said. Her face had gone pale. "Come on."

She ran into the woods, following the sound of the voice. "Kiara!" I shouted. I had to rush to keep up. My breath soon came in labored gasps. Shit, she was fast, and my energy wasn't what it used to be. "Slow down, will you?"

She didn't listen. She stopped far up ahead of me, where it looked like things dropped off over a cliff. I skidded beside her and looked down. Below us was a ravine, a nearly-vertical twenty-foot drop that ended in a canyon that was circular in formation.

A griffin had fallen down the ravine. His feathers were gold, and he was in a curled-up position on the ground, his right wing bent at the wrong angle as if broken. He tried to flap his wings to fly, but it only resulted in blood gushing from the gaping wound. He couldn't go anywhere, nor could he climb the ravine. He was trapped. Kiara observed him in stark terror.

I cupped my hands around my mouth. "Hey! Are you okay?"

The griffin's eyes widened when he saw us. I realized he was the same one I'd accidentally bumped into outside the train station weeks ago. *"Don't come down here!"* he shouted. *"It's not safe!"*

We saw what he meant when a large, hairy spider ventured out of the cave at the bottom of the ravine. It was huge, with large pinchers and dozens of beady red eyes. Venom dripped from the pinchers as it approached the griffin. The spider drew near. The griffin swung his talons at the spider, hissing at it to back off. The spider retreated, but only a short distance away. It was biding its time to attack until the griffin passed out from blood loss.

"Hold on down there! We're going to get you help!" I shouted. "What's your name?"

"Alexei! And hurry!" he called back. *"I don't think I can hold out much longer!"*

The spider attacked again. Alexei lashed out with his beak and struck at it, causing a wound. The spider backed away again, but the effort to wound the insect had made Alexei weak. He transformed into a man, though he remained on all fours and struggled to breathe.

I worried if we went back together and left Alexei alone, he'd be dead when we returned. I didn't know what to do. But no mind, because Kiara made up my mind for me.

"He'll be eaten alive!" Kiara shouted. She dropped the bag of books. "You go back, Emma. I have to do something."

Before I could grab her, Kiara slid down the ravine. She landed on the ground and ran to Alexei, putting a hand on his shoulder. "You need to stay conscious. If you pass out, it'll be the end for you."

Alexei's eyes grew huge at the sight of her, and he nodded feebly. Kiara turned to face the spider. "All right. Let's see if you like *this!*"

Kiara sent a bolt of blazing yellow light out of her palm. It hit the spider in the face, and the monster squealed, rubbing its eyes frantically. Kiara didn't stop. She threw bolt after bolt of light at the creature. My mouth dropped open. Kiara couldn't tell Lady Korva off, but she could face a man-eating spider to save a stranger. This girl needed priorities.

Welp, I couldn't just leave the two of them there, so I figured I might as well join them. I copied Kiara and slid down the ravine, taking my place at her side.

"What are we facing?" I asked.

"It's a *taranticula*. One bite of its venom will kill you," Kiara told me quickly. "They don't like extreme temperatures."

"Well, let's see if we can turn it down, then." I imagined a blue substance between us and the spider— something that would hurt when you touched it, like dry ice. I was shocked when it appeared before us. The spider put its foot into the substance as an experiment. It screeched and violently drew its limb back immediately. The limb looked frostbitten.

I smiled. Looks like I performed well under pressure.

I figured that would be enough to get it to leave us alone, but guess not, because the spider drew back and fired a large ball of green goo at us from its pinchers. I dove to the side, and Kiara grabbed Alexei, dragging him away from the goo ball before it could touch us. The liquid sputtered and smoldered on the ground, eating away at the stone beneath our feet like some type of acid.

Right. Don't let *that* touch you, either.

Kiara and I had no time to make another plan of defense, because the spider started firing off venom balls like a machine gun. I dodged, and Kiara did her best to yank Alexei out of the way at every possibility.

The spider paused for a moment, as if to refill his venom. Alexei's head was lolling on his shoulders. "Leave me. You'll die, too," he begged weakly.

"We aren't leaving you behind," Kiara said firmly. She had him propped up against her, one of his arms thrown over her shoulder. She looked at me. "What do we do?" she whispered.

"I don't know," I said. I was still new at this monster-hunting bullshit, and Kiara couldn't help me when she was busy protecting Alexei. We couldn't climb up the ravine, either, because we'd jumped in without thinking and were stuck down here. We only had a few seconds before the spider recovered and we'd have to dodge venom bullets again.

"Emma! What are you doing?!" I heard a voice from above. I looked up. Ethan stood at the edge of the ravine, alongside a dark-haired boy I didn't know.

"I think it's pretty fucking obvious we're trying not to get eaten by a giant spider!" I shouted. "So if you wanna help, it'd be greatly appreciated!"

I heard the sound of Ethan swearing, and he said, "Stefan, get them out. I'll deal with the spider."

"It's a *taranticula*," Kiara corrected. I rolled my eyes.

There was a rushing sound— the noise of transformation. The dark-haired boy had transformed into an enormous black dragon, who spread his wings so he could drift down the ravine. He landed in front of us, blocking us off from the spider.

Stefan roared, and the spider cowered at the sight of him. There were perks to having a dragon around, I guess. Stefan opened his mouth, and flames came furling out from it, making the temperature in the area rise by ten degrees and causing the spider to flee for its life.

While the spider was attempting to get away from the flames, Ethan jumped off the ravine. He changed into a wolven mid-fall and landed on top of the spider, crushing it to the ground. Ethan raised an open mouth full of fangs before he sank them into the spider's head, causing black blood to gush out of the monster's skull.

The spider gave a few involuntary twitches as it died. Ethan stepped off of it once it was dead.

Totally bad-ass.

Ethan advanced toward us, changing back into a human as he did so and wiping his mouth of blood. He looked… really pissed. I couldn't imagine why.

"The beast is dead. He won't be trapping Arcanea down here any longer," Ethan snapped. He shot me a harsh look. Really? What did I do to deserve that?

"What about the venom?" I asked him. "Won't it kill you?"

"My fangs sank into its brain. I didn't get any of the venom on me," Ethan said.

Ew. The taste of brain was probably very unpleasant.

But we still had a problem. Alexei was fading, fast. The cut on his wing had changed as he did, and turned into a large gash that started on his left arm and went all the way down his back. It was pouring blood. Alexei faltered, and Kiara went to catch him.

"On Stefan's back," Ethan instructed. He lifted Alexei onto Stefan like it was no problem. By this time, Alexei had passed out. Ethan helped Kiara up. She sat between Stefan's spikes, holding onto Alexei's body securely.

Then I felt hands boosting me up. My entire body got warm as I felt Ethan lift me upward and set me on Stefan's back. He got on behind me and put an arm around my form, holding me tightly while grasping one of the spikes for support.

Stefan started forward before I was even ready. He sank his giant claws into the ravine walls and began scaling them like a gecko. I clung to Ethan, because I was worried if I tried to grab onto the spikes like the rest of them, I'd accidentally slice my hand open. They looked sharp.

When we got to the top of the ravine, Stefan stopped. "We'll get off here. Stefan will fly faster with just two," Ethan said, and he slid off.

Stefan looked at him with glittering, red eyes. *"Back off on the snacks and it wouldn't be an issue."*

"Ha ha," Ethan said dryly. Stefan rumbled with laughter.

As I dismounted I ended up losing my balance. I would've fallen forward on my face if Ethan hadn't been there to catch me. I collided into his chest. I looked up, and for a moment caught his eyes. My heart skipped a beat. My breaths became faster as we shared a glance between us. It was so brief, I barely noticed it.

Back off, Emma. You belong to the Phantom, not this dude.

I pulled away. Ethan seemed regretful to let me go. I stooped down to grab my backpack and our bag of books from the ground. "I've got these, Kiara. Meet you back at the dorms."

"Okay." Kiara was barely paying attention to me. Her eyes were too fixated on the boy in front of her, studying his face like he was some sort of puzzle.

"Kiara, he's a griffin," I teased.

She blushed. "I know."

"Oh gods, don't start this shit," Stefan complained. *"At least not with me around."*

Stefan spread his wings. The black dragon lifted into the sky and carried the two of them off to school, in the direction of the medical chamber.

The moment he was gone, Ethan whirled on me. "Why are you always getting into trouble?"

My mouth dropped open in outrage. "Me? Yeah, because I go *looking* for things to kill me. It's a pastime of mine."

"It sure as hell seems that way," he growled under his breath.

"Look, if you didn't want to save me, you didn't have to. You could've walked away and let the spider eat me. At least you wouldn't be bothered to take time out of your day." I crossed my arms.

"You're impossible," he grumbled. "Come on. We need to get back to the school."

"Nah, I think I'll just stay out here and look for something else to attack me. After all, I'm good at that, right?" I asked sarcastically.

"Now, Emma."

I knew better than to resist the command in his tone. I shook my head and followed after him. Ethan remained close by my side as we got back on the path to Arcanea University, our shoulders nearly touching. I'd figure he'd put his arm around me if he wasn't so pissed.

"This isn't my fault. Bad things just happen to me," I argued.

"Apparently. I'm in half a mind to lock you up in your room and never let you out." He gave me a half-smile that was rugged and intense.

"A princess in a tower, eh? Funny. Usually the wolves who come to play want to keep her out, not in." I gave him a harsh stare. "You know, so they can keep reminding her of her mistakes."

"Look. I'm sorry for the way I treated you in Monster Hunting on your first day. It was uncalled for," Ethan said. He took a big sigh, as if this was a hard thing for him to do— admit he was wrong. "But I… lost someone. And I don't think I could handle it if I saw the same thing happen to you."

My anger softened. "Your father."

He nodded. "Yes. So please don't take it personally. Being an Arcanea is serious business, and I don't want to see anyone else get hurt."

My stomach sank. I wasn't anything special to him. Just an Arcanea he didn't want to become another statistic, like all the others.

I crossed my arms around my torso and held myself. "Well, believe it or not, you're not the only one who's saved me. I went for a walk the other night and was cornered by the Black Claw. The Phantom chased them off. He saved me. So maybe you're right when you say I go looking for trouble, even though I say trouble finds me."

A thoughtful look crossed his face. "So you've met the Phantom. I wouldn't consider yourself lucky. People who get tangled up with him often end up hurt."

"I beg your pardon?" I asked. Anger boiled beneath my skin. How *dare* Ethan talk about my mate that way? It wasn't right. He had no fucking clue.

"The Phantom is a menace. It'd be best for everyone if he was caught. He impedes the justice system in this city," Ethan rattled off. "The sooner he's put behind bars, the better."

"He saved my life!" I shouted.

"So have I— twice now. It's really not anything special," Ethan said. "The whole school will probably get a chance before you graduate."

I felt my face turn red. "It doesn't matter. The Phantom and I— we have a connection."

Ethan paused. "What do you mean?"

The words were coming out of my mouth before I could stop them. "I felt the bond. He and I are mates."

A horrified expression crossed Ethan's face. That was before he suddenly broke out into an insulting laugh. "Mates? You can't be serious. Dream on, Emma."

"I am serious."

Ethan stopped laughing and shook his head. "Okay, this isn't funny. The Phantom is mixed up in some really shady business. If you go looking for him, you could get hurt."

"Well, apparently I'm good at that, right?" I snapped back.

He frowned. "That's not what I meant. I'm just saying… I know the Phantom. Not personally, but I know *what* he is. And there's a darkness in him that you don't want to mess with."

"You don't know a damn thing." He could fuck right off. The spires of the school were coming into view now. Ethan and I crossed through the west gate. The moment we did, I made sure to separate myself from him further.

Ethan took a steadying breath. "All I'm saying is, don't go chasing after fairy tales when reality is right in front of you."

Oh, this guy was rich. Was he *jealous* of the Phantom? It was sad.

I tried to contain my fury before I said, "Whatever happens between the Phantom and I is none of your damn business."

I ran off before he could say anything more, and shoved my shoulder into the double doors so I could get away from him. The guy was a judgmental jerk.

Ethan was wrong. I wasn't going to stay away from the Phantom. If anything, I was going to run toward him.

And nothing anyone could do or say would stop me from seeing him again.

ELEVEN

Emma thought she was in love with the Phantom. She didn't realize that she was truly in love with *me*.

When we'd touched as I was in disguise as the Phantom, the mating bond fell in place— and it couldn't have come at a worse time. We'd brushed each other before, in Monster Hunting 101, but this was different. Holding hands after we'd been in a life-or-death situation together was intimate. It provoked the magic to come out and seal our souls together forever.

But how could we truly be in love? We barely knew each other. She'd only been in my life for a few weeks. She didn't know me yet— who I truly was. I wanted more between us than just primal instinct.

If we were going to be together, I wanted her to like me for me. I wanted us to be real. I didn't want us to be together because some magical bond told us we had to be. And I had to get to know her better, too.

I'd made the Phantom out to be a villain when she brought him up. I had to disapprove of the Phantom in public as much as possible, to lead away any suspicion that it was me, but with Emma I was over the top about it. I told her those things because I wanted her to stay away from me. The Phantom and Prince Ethan were two totally different beings. They lived in different worlds, one light and the other dark.

Of course, it had to be the tortured side of me that she fell for. And not the man underneath the mask.

I was walking a very thin line here. If Emma tried getting in contact with the Phantom again… it would lead to consequences for her. I had enemies. The Black Claw knew I was onto them, and if anyone guessed that the Phantom had someone in his personal life he was close to…

She'd become a target. For both the Black Claw, and the police. If she found out who I was and kept my identity a secret for me, she'd risk getting accused of charges herself for conspiring with me. That is, if I ever got caught.

Then there was the matter of the King's Contest. I still didn't know what I was going to do about that. The Contest was quickly approaching, but I didn't know if I should make my bond with Emma clear, or protect her by choosing another girl as my queen— someone stronger and more likely to survive, someone who didn't mind risking their lives for a chance to be in the monarchy. It wasn't uncommon for Marked or Companions to perish in the Contest. And I wasn't sure I could sign Emma up for that, especially if she didn't want what I was offering.

Everything I was doing was putting Emma in danger. And that's why I needed to keep pushing her away— so she could be safe. It would be far better for me to pine for her for the rest of my days than it would be to grieve her death.

I was coming back from hockey practice one Friday afternoon when I saw her again. She'd been avoiding me since the last incident with the giant spider. She was sitting on the lawn of the school, surrounded by textbooks and looking puzzled.

Despite myself, I gravitated toward her. She wrinkled her nose in disgust as I dropped my hockey gear and sat down beside her. I noticed she was wearing a big-knit sweater, along with black leggings and light pink leg warmers.

I was really into leg warmers. And socks. I *loved* knee-length socks on girls. Couldn't tell you why. Yeah, I had a sock-fetish. Wasn't afraid to admit it, either.

"I didn't say I was ready to talk to you," Emma said. She turned a page idly and tried to ignore me.

"I didn't think you were, but here I am anyway." I leaned back and smirked. "You looked like you needed some help."

"Not from you." She gave me the finger. I laughed.

"Come on. What's troubling you?" I asked.

She made a face. "I've been here for nearly a month now, but I still don't understand this world. Nobody's told me the basics. I'm expected to know everything about the Arcanea, but I barely know why spells work in the first place."

"Well, there's your problem. You can't master magic if you don't know what it is," I said.

She gave me a sour look. "I suppose *you* could teach me?"

"Of course." I put my elbows on my crossed legs. "There are multiple branches of Arcanean magic," I explained to her. "Illusion is obviously the first, and the most important. Sorceresses are gifted at illusion. Companions are as well, but they aren't half as powerful as Marked. The second is shifting— only Companions can change into animals. The third is enchanting— infusing objects with special charms that change its composition for a certain purpose. The fourth is alchemy, which almost every magical race can do, so it's nothing special."

I rolled my shoulders, to stretch them. "The fifth skill depends on your Faction as an Arcanea. Alicorns have shield magic, which means they're better at protection spells and can cast shields to defend themselves and each other. Dragons have battle magic— they can create magical bombs, or use their powers much like weapons."

"Wow," Emma said. "That's intense."

"Isn't it? But I think griffins have the worst of it." I kicked my leg out. "They're empaths. They can feel the emotions of others. Which is useful in battle, because you can predict what your enemy is going to do, or if someone is being dishonest with you, but they can never turn their magic off. They're constantly feeling multiple emotions all the time. Their own, and others."

"Is that why Kiara is so quiet? Because she's trying to handle everyone's emotions?" Emma asked.

"Probably," I said. "Griffins are easily upset. They just can't help it. They process everyone's feelings in the room all at once, if they don't learn how to block it out. They have to be specially trained so they don't go insane with experiencing everyone's feelings."

"What can we do?" Emma asked.

"Telepathy," I responded. "All wolvens, male and female, can cast their thoughts extremely far to mentally speak to each other. Although all Companions can speak mentally, only wolvens can speak to other Arcanea over long distances. We're talking up to fifty miles, sometimes more. The female wolven have extra abilities, though. They can levitate objects with their mind. Someday you'll be able to do that, too."

"Lady Korva talked about that briefly in my illusion class, but didn't go into it much, so I didn't understand what it was," Emma said.

"That's because they want to start you with the basics. You're just a First Year. They won't get into the magic of different Factions until your second semester," I told her.

She nodded. "Makes sense. But I still feel like there's more to it. Something the school doesn't teach. I've heard people... I don't know, whispering about it in the hallways. Like it's something forbidden."

"If you want to get technical, there's a sixth branch," I said. "Dark magic. It's what the Black Claw uses. Its drawing power from living creatures, or from the dead, to make yourself stronger. If you called it by a specific name, it'd be known as *shadow manipulation.* The Black Claw can make themselves appear as shadows, and usually, you don't see them coming until it's too late."

"Holy shit. That's horrible." Emma cupped a hand over her mouth.

"It's pretty bad," I confessed. "I've stumbled upon... ceremony sites where the Black Claw have performed their sacrifices, and they never look good."

Emma seemed conflicted. "In class, we were told that wands and crystals were objects of dark magic, and we should never use them. But I've seen someone I know wear one around their neck."

Emma didn't trust me with that information. She was protecting someone. But who? "Wands and crystals aren't necessarily bad. They've just been used as tools by members of the Black Claw for so long, people see them that way," I explained. "They've been used before to store life energy from sacrifices, but they can hold good magic, too. But I'd tell your friend to keep that crystal pretty close, unless she wants to cause trouble for herself."

"She's pretty careful. Plus she's got me. I'll kick anyone's ass who tries to mess with her," Emma vowed.

I smiled. She was brave, and she defended her friends. I liked that about her.

She tapped a pencil against her chin. "One thing I don't get is how we're able to do all of this. I know we're descended from faeries from a different world, but there has to be a scientific explanation behind it all."

"The faeries we're descended from had extraordinary power, rumored to be gifted to them to the gods themselves," I said. "If you look at our cells under a microscope, they can shift and influence the environment to create hallucinations on the mind, so that we can perform illusions."

"But what power enables us to do this? Stuff doesn't just happen," she argued.

I shrugged in a carefree way. "What's the power that keeps your heart beating? What's the power that wakes you up every morning and makes conception possible so life can go on? Sometimes there just isn't an explanation, *onawilke.*"

"Is that a Malovian word or something?" she asked in a sassy way.

"Yes. It means *little wolf.*" I gave her an affectionate grin, and she turned slightly pink.

"I am not a little wolf," she grumbled. She seemed irritated by the name, and it only became more endearing to me.

An idea came to me. "You know... I don't have class until tonight," I started. "And there's something I want to show you."

Her one eyebrow raised. "Then show me."

I got to my feet and extended a hand. She took it, and as I pulled her to her feet I swear I felt the mating connection spark between us.

We returned to our dorm block and left my hockey gear and her book bag behind. I changed out of my jersey into my school uniform, as I had class later and didn't want to waste time once we returned.

"Where are we going?" Emma asked as I led her off campus and into the twisting woods of the Malovian landscape, keeping my eyes open for any monsters that lurked.

"Somewhere secret." Twilight was lighting up the landscape. The shadows and colors loomed against the twisting trees, and I kept Emma close to my side... just in case something was to spring out from behind.

Eventually, the trees opened up to a clearing. Stone ruins formed a circular structure that resembled what was left of an ancient tower. Ivy and other plants had overtaken the ruins, and dead leaves clustered against the crumbling stone.

Within the ruins of the old castle was a giant willow tree. It was an unusual size, over a hundred feet tall, its growth blessed by magic. The trunk of the tree was beautiful. In the bark were the designs of faeries with gorgeous wings, their shifters morphing into the wood with them. The carvings stuck out of the bark, and were delicately designed. There were hundreds of carvings within the bark, and the fronds of the willow tree shifted and moved on their own, as if the very tree had come to life.

"You can relax," I said to Emma as we walked into the clearing. "This land is sacred ground, blessed by the priestesses. Monsters can't set foot here."

Her shoulders slumped. "Why are we here?"

"I wanted to explain to you something of our heritage," I explained. "The ruins are a faery fort— a place of supernatural fae activity. Our powers are strengthened here."

"What is this place?" she asked. She nearly tripped over a rock before I caught her last minute. I helped her over a ruin carefully as we made a path to the tree.

"There used to be a chateau here. It was called the *Zamek Marzenia*; the Castle of Dreams. It was where the fae kings used to rule," I explained.

"What happened?

"The castle was destroyed after the split of the Seelie and Unseelie courts. No fae king has lived in this place since."

"Seelie? Unseelie?" Her eyebrows knitted together.

"I'll explain in a moment." We sat at the base of the tree. I reached out and took her wrist— when I placed her hand against the bark, she jumped.

"It's okay. It's not going to hurt you," I said.

"The tree is warm. I can feel it pulsing— like it has a heartbeat," she said.

"Because it does," I said. "This is the Willow Maiden. She's been here for many years."

"Are you going to tell me what happened here?" Emma pressed both of her hands to the tree in wonder, her eyes widening as she felt the energy coursing through the willow.

"The first thing you should know is that there used to be two types of fae; two very different courts," I began. "The first was the Seelie, the day court— they are the court that uses white magic, the court modern-day Arcanea are descended from. The other was the Unseelie— the court of night. They used dark magic. They no longer exist."

She sent me a puzzled expression. "Why not?"

"There was a great war many years ago, between the Seelie and the Unseelie. It happened after we left Edinmyre. The two sides fought for who would have control of Malovia, and more importantly, what they would do with humans. The Seelie wanted to integrate, while the Unseelie wanted to use humans to grow their power," I explained. "The Seelie won, and outlawed dark magic. The Unseelie died out because of it."

"So there are other types of fae besides us?" she asked.

"There used to be. There were sidhe— fairies of the underground. There were also water fae, who lived in pools and rivers, and brownies— household fairies who used their powers to help humans. If I had to list all the fae that ever lived we'd be here a long time, I expect."

"Do they no longer exist?"

"No one knows." I shrugged. "They haven't been seen for hundreds of years. The only fae on record that we know are still alive are the Seelie."

"Can you tell me more about the night court?" Emma asked. She crossed her legs and held her ankles.

"The Unseelie were known as tricksters. And according to the stories, they were ruthless." I felt a shiver creep up my spine. "They were quite malevolent, and their dark magic was rumored to be so powerful that even the gods feared them. They worshipped Droga, and had other shifter forms than us— dark creatures that could manipulate shadow."

"Do the Black Claw worship the Unseelie or something? They sound very similar," Emma questioned.

"The Black Claw actually claim to be the last living descendants of the Unseelie that died out long ago. They see it as a sort of genocide that the Unseelie were wiped out, and wish to restore what's left of the bloodline back to power."

"Well, they're going about it in the wrong way," Emma mumbled.

I laughed lowly. "You could say that."

I waved my hand around. "This was the place where the Unseelie were finally defeated, but before they fell, they cursed Malovia to a cruel end, and used their dark magic to seal the curse. The priestesses bless this area every year to keep the Unseelie curse from spreading further than this valley, though the Willow Maiden absorbs most of the dark energy and turns it into white magic."

"So what's the deal with the tree?" Emma looked up. "It's definitely not ordinary."

"A very old story." I leaned in closer. "There was a priestess called Jadwiga Waldemar who swore to keep the Unseelie magic bound within the valley. A shifter fell in love with her, and tried to steal her away." I shrugged. "When she left the valley with him, she succumbed to a terrible affliction and died. The shifter could not take from the valley what was never meant to leave, and Jadwiga was committed to keeping her vow, even if it meant her death."

"That's horrible." The color drained from Emma's cheeks.

"When he returned her body to the valley, it took root, and grew into the willow." I ran my fingers through a few fronds. "Jadwiga kept her promise and is protecting the valley even to this day."

"It's a beautiful story, but a little creepy. No way I could be a tree forever." Emma shook her head. "Only the Arcanea have tales this weird."

"There are other magical cultures where women have become trees. It's quite common, actually," I said.

"I swear if I become a tree in any way, shape, or form, I will wait for you to come by so I can beat your ass with my branches, because it was probably your fault," she grumped.

I laughed again. "I doubt that's going to happen. As far as I know, Jadwiga is the only Arcanea who ever changed in such a way."

"Thank the gods." She ran her fingers over the bark again. "Can you tell me more about ancient fae? How are they different from us?"

"Not much has changed. Though we've integrated with the humans so much, some of our customs have been forgotten." I put my back against the Willow Maid. "Fae used to be extremely tricky. Our favorite thing to do was mess with humans. The reason we have illusion magic is to fool humans. We'd make fae circles out of mushrooms and create portals to Edinmyre they'd get lost in, or give them bad contracts that were worded in such a way it ended up turning out awful for the person that asked for help. We also used to take their babies for our own, so they could mate with our kind and leave changelings in their place."

"That's fucking horrible!" Emma burst in disgust.

"Nobody ever said fae were nice," I pointed out. "We have a bit of a bad rep in the magical community."

"I can see why." Emma huffed. "Are there any other ridiculous fae customs?"

"This tradition has died out, but the fae didn't like saying *thank you*. If a deed was done, the fae wanted you to remember it, instead of expressing gratitude. In the ways of the old magic, nothing was ever given without something in return. Gifts were never truly gifts, as nothing was ever given for free. It was once our greatest law. Then we left Edinmyre, and if we wanted to assimilate among the humans, we needed to change."

"Why would you want to? The fae had tremendous power. I don't see why they needed to blend in with humans if they had all this magic to use against them." Emma wrinkled her nose.

"They did have one thing against us. They had iron."

"What's that got to do with anything?" Her eyes narrowed.

"Iron is poisonous to fae. We can't touch it without being burned," I said. "I still have a scar on my hand from accidentally scraping it once as a child." I lifted my palm and pointed to it—just before my thumb was a blotchy red scar that would never quite go away.

"But we use steel swords, and that comes from iron," she pointed out.

"With fae, specific words mean specific things. That's how illusion magic works. It's how fae were able to trick humans into bad contracts for thousands of years," I explained. "When iron is tempered into steel, it becomes something different. The quality of the metal and its compounds are broken down, making it safe for us to use. But iron in its purest form is highly deadly to fae. That's why we use other metals to make our weapons, like bronze and copper, and avoid using it to construct our buildings as much as possible."

"Is there anything else fae are vulnerable to?" She glanced around the valley, probably expecting me to start making a whole list.

"Fae are pretty indestructible. But besides iron, we're allergic to yarrow, and St. John's Wort," I said. "I don't suggest getting anywhere near either."

"I took St. John's Wort once. A girl at school gave me some herbal pills to calm me down before a test, and I got *so* sick," she said with clarity, as if a realization was dawning. "Mom freaked out when I told her I'd taken them, and I didn't get why. I was ill for a week afterward."

"Well, now you know," I said.

Emma shifted closer to me. She was so close that I could smell her perfume. Her red hair drifted across my cheek when the wind blew.

If it wasn't that small incident that made me completely fall for her once more. I was already so far gone.

"Do you really think all Unseelie magic is bad?" she asked. "That *all* dark magic is evil?"

"I've been raised all my life to believe so."

"That's hardly an answer."

I sighed. "I don't know if it was right that all the Unseelie were killed. But I do know that Seelie shouldn't tamper with dark magic. That includes you, Emma. Seelie blood runs in your veins. You're a fae of the day court. You'd do well to remember that."

Emma said nothing more about it. Only got a grim expression on her face. She rose slowly to her feet. "Thanks for the lesson, Ethan, but I have to get going. I've got practice at the rink in an hour."

"Yeah. I've got class, too." Not that I was looking forward to it. Professor Waldron was hardly my favorite teacher.

As we left the Willow Maid, Emma's red hair bounced on her shoulders. I tried not to stare too long. She seemed lost in contemplative thought— it only felt right to pry.

"What are you thinking about?" I questioned as we walked through Arcanea University's gates.

Emma hesitated. "I'm not certain. I just have a gut feeling there's more to the story than we know. Something about the Unseelie just doesn't add up."

"You could be right." The fae liked their secrets— even now, parts of our history remained hidden from us. And I wasn't sure how far our ancestors had gone to completely conceal... or perhaps twist... the truth.

Emma and I separated once we got back to the castle. On my way to my evening class, I noticed a headline blaring across one of the TVs in the dining hall.

The *beithir* I'd been hunting had been captured and killed. The Arcanea Alliance had somehow cornered it yesterday night and destroyed it.

Damn. I'd missed my chance to figure out who'd set it loose. The suspect was still at large, and there was no way to find them now.

The officer they were interviewing said that they expected the slaughters and disappearances at the warehouses to stop, but I was doubtful. The monster hadn't been the sole reason people were vanishing. That was the responsibility of the Black Claw.

I'd hit a dead end investigating the case. I needed to find out where these cultists were hiding. Maybe then I could put a stop to the murders plaguing the city.

Interspecies Cooperation was one of the few Companion classes I had indoors. Companions of all grades were in here, talking and goofing off before class. I took a seat in the back and tried to imagine where the Black Claw could be.

"Gods, I can't wait until this semester is over," Stefan complained in front of me. "Professor Waldron is *so boring*. He needs to fucking retire."

Agreed. He was a griffin that was older than Malovia itself, I bet. The only thing we did in this class was listen to him lecture for an hour about how important interspecies collaboration was. It was enough to put you to sleep.

The sound of thuggish laughter caught my attention. That Alexei guy we'd saved the other day from the *taranticula* was in this class. He sat up front and mostly ignored everyone else, keeping his eyes straight, though someone had set their sights on him.

It was Elijah. He and his goons were throwing wads of paper at him. When Alexei didn't respond, Elijah and his boys took turns shoving Alexei and smacking the back of his head.

I rolled my eyes. This was fucking college. Couldn't these clowns grow up? We were beyond grade school bullying.

Alexei stared forward and tried to ignore them, but it was obvious he was getting pissed. His hands were bunched together into fists, and his face was glowing red. I expected him to explode into a pile of feathers at any moment.

I wasn't the only one who noticed. An alicorn kid, Theo, was watching the situation from the other side of the room cooly, his arms crossed. He wasn't impressed with Elijah's stupidity.

Time passed. Fifteen minutes went by, then half an hour. Professor Waldron never showed up. Where was he? It was weird for him to be late.

Elijah and his friends were still tormenting Alexei. Most of the class had tuned in to watch the spectacle, though nobody stepped in to interfere.

I wanted to stick up for Alexei, but I knew if I did, his reputation as a Companion would be ruined. As a male Arcanea, you were supposed to be able to stand up for yourself at all times. If someone else had to intercede on your behalf, you'd be seen as a coward, and weak. People would never let you forget it. It would be worse than the bullying. I didn't want Alexei branded with that kind of label, although I longed to do something about it.

Alexei was going to explode any minute. I tapped Stefan on the shoulder and gestured to Alexei. "Looks like Eli's about to get a talon in the face."

Stefan gave a stony expression. "Right." Stefan stood up. "Hey guys, let's fucking blow. It's obvious Waldron's not coming."

There were mumbles of agreement, and chairs were scraped backwards as people got up to leave the room. I felt like my time had been wasted.

I thought Elijah would get bored and go somewhere else, but that didn't happen. Three of his thugs trailed behind as Elijah continued to shout insults at Alexei.

"Hey, chicken boy," Elijah shouted. "Why don't you come back and polish my boots? They need cleaning."

"Fuck off, Eli," Alexei called behind him, but he didn't stop walking. That was smart. He wouldn't be able to take four on one, and he knew it.

I caught another figure lingering behind. Theo was following them. He kept a decent distance, although the gaze he gave the situation was calculating.

Couldn't let him have all the fun, right? "Hey, let's go," I said, dragging on Stefan's arm. "There's trouble."

Stefan's eyes sparked. "Trouble? I'm in."

Thought so. Stefan was always ready for a fight. We came to a broad hallway in the west wing. Elijah and his group were still far ahead of us, though Theo was closing the gap.

"Hey, chicken boy, I'm talking to you!" Elijah called again. He went to grab Alexei's shoulder to turn him around, and that's when it happened. Alexei lost his patience. He changed into a griffin and lunged at Elijah with his beak exposed.

Elijah didn't even flinch. He grinned as he transformed into a wolf and pounced. Two Companions at his side morphed alongside him. Both of them were alicorns; one gray, and the other black.

Elijah held Alexei down while the alicorns took turns kicking him with their hooves. Alexei struggled to get Elijah off of him, but he was powerless to do so while he was getting kicked in the face.

I meant to stop the fight before it happened, but now that it had turned into an all-out brawl, there was no stopping it. I changed into a wolf and knocked Elijah off of Alexei, while Theo, who had gotten there before I did, galloped with his horn down at the other two alicorns. He drove them away and started fighting the black alicorn, the one I knew as Zander.

Alexei staggered to his feet and was able to start battling the gray alicorn, Oren, lashing out with his beak and talons.

Now that it was a fair fight, Oren looked scared. He backed away and shook his head as Alexei's attacks pressed him into the wall.

Stefan wasted no time at all and changed into a dragon, his massive form swelling so that it took up the hallway. His back hit the ceiling, causing stones to crumble from above onto the floor below. Elijah's dragon friend, Andrik, changed as well, his red scales contrasting sharply against Stefan's black coat. The two dragons lunged at each other. Windows shattered and walls crushed as they wrestled, slamming their bodies against the stone.

We were causing a ruckus. Any moment now people would come running. I put my teeth to Elijah's throat and growled. "*Not so big when it's a fair fight, are you?*"

Elijah snarled. He made a go at my jugular, but I swiped his muzzle away. He kicked me away, then called to his friends, "*Let's get the fuck out of here!*"

You didn't need to ask Oren twice. He was already fleeing down the hall, his hooves making a clatter on the stone. Alexei was bleeding, but he stood victorious, his head held high as he watched Oren make a break for it.

Zander gnashed his teeth as he waved his sharp horn in the air in Theo's direction. *"I'll be seeing you later."*

"I count on it," Theo said darkly. Zander turned and ran after Oren, though I'd say it was far from a cowardly flight. If anything, the look in his eyes that he gave Theo before he left posed a threat.

Stefan and Andrik were still tangled up in each other, though they were human now, and throwing punches. A particularly rough punch from Stefan knocked Andrik to the ground. He hastily got up and gave in, turning to go after Elijah.

"Sure you don't wanna go again, An-*dick*?" Stefan called scathingly after his opponent. Andrik flipped him off before the four of them disappeared behind a pillar.

The hallway was completely destroyed. Stefan and Andrik had done most of the damage. They'd even put a hole in the roof. But the rest of us had done our part, too. There was blood from Alexei, and maybe a few others. Place looked like a freaking crime scene.

I heard excited voices coming from around the corner saying there was a fight. That wasn't good.

"We gotta go," Theo started, looking around in a panic. It was like he suddenly realized what he'd just done and was paranoid he'd get caught for it. Alicorns were stingy with the rules like that. Didn't want to be seen as anything but goody-goody.

"Yeah. Let's leave, before teachers show up," Stefan said breathlessly.

I was in agreement. Didn't want to be around when people noticed that the west wing had basically collapsed.

We made a run for it. I didn't know if anyone saw us or not. We didn't look back, or stop until we were outside and far away from the west wing, on the other side of the school. We halted by a portrait of a fae woman and leaned over our knees to catch our breath, trying not to gag.

"You guys didn't need to step in. I had it handled," Alexei breathed. He was sporting a black eye where one of the alicorns had kicked him.

"Yeah, for sure, since you clearly weren't getting your ass beat before we showed up," Stefan shot at him. "But next time, I'll back off. Sure you've got it covered."

Alexei went to start toward Stefan, but I got in the way and put a hand on his chest. "Hey, don't be pissed at him," I started. "We were just trying to help. Next time, we'll let you eat dirt."

Alexei took a deep breath to cool off. "Yeah. I guess you're right. Thanks for having my back."

Stefan put his arms around Alexei and Theo's shoulders. "I'd say we had a good fight, gentlemen. Let's go down to *The Drunken Dragon* and have a beer to celebrate."

Theo wrinkled his nose. "Beer is distasteful."

"Wow. All right, have a wine then, sissy," Stefan said. "But as far as I'm concerned, we should all have a celebratory drink for a brawl well-won."

Alexei hesitated before visibly relaxing, the tension in his body draining. "To be honest, I'd love a drink right now."

Alexei remained quiet as we gathered around a circular table in the pub. He stared at his mug and kept his shoulders hunched, even as Stefan was picking on Theo for ordering chardonnay instead of ale.

"You're pretty quiet," I told Alexei before I took a swig. He jumped in his seat like he was frightened, before staring at me.

"Sorry," he said. "It's just weird. I don't usually hang out with... people."

"Too much to deal with?" I asked.

Alexei sighed. "Yeah. Emotions are a lot."

He was reclusive, even for a griffin. I knew that all griffins were empaths, but their families usually taught them a bit about handling their powers before they got to the university, so they weren't complete social rejects. Alexei acted like he didn't have any control over his abilities at all.

"Didn't your parents teach you how to handle empathy?" I asked.

He shook his head. "Don't have any. Grew up alone."

That would explain it. No wonder he couldn't control his temper and constantly got into trouble. I didn't want to make him feel worse by asking about his childhood, which I suspected had to be shit, and said, "You should probably work on that. Eli isn't going to back off if he thinks he can get a rise out of you."

He gripped his mug. "It's just… I could *feel* their hatred. They didn't have a reason for going after me. They just thought it was funny," he said. "Most people when they pick on you, there's a tiny bit of remorse, you know? They know they're doing wrong. Eli, though… he just didn't care."

Alexei took a deep breath. "It's nice hanging out with you, though. You seem pretty flatline."

Little did he know. I just kept my emotions so well under wraps, he couldn't feel them. "Can't say the same for those two."

I gestured at Stefan and Theo. They were ignoring the conversation all together. Stefan had gotten Theo into a headlock, and Theo was trying to get out of it. It was obvious they were just playing around, so I didn't interfere. Stefan was amused, though I could tell Theo was vastly annoyed. He kept commenting how this was improper behavior for a public place and that Stefan needed to unhand him immediately.

Alexei gave the slightest of smiles. "Yeah, well, your dragon friend's got about three emotions, as far as I can tell— happy, horny, or pissed off. And the alicorn is just exceptionally irritated."

"You've got us pegged." I clapped him on the back. "Tell you what. I'll buy you another drink, on me."

Alexei paused. Then he relaxed under my arm, and said, "Well, if you're buying…"

Another drink turned into more than just *a drink*, if you get what I'm saying. Three hours later the four of us stumbled out of *The Drunken Dragon* more pissed than sober. Alexei was smiling pleasantly, his head obviously in a buzz.

Theo, who had lectured about the improprieties about being intoxicated in public, was drunker than all of us. He had his arm around Stefan, and the two of them were singing Malovian folk songs. They'd warmed up to each other quickly.

I had a clearer head than the rest of them, but not by much. I led the way back up to school and tried not to trip over my own feet as we stumbled up the stairs leading to the dormitories. Alexei fell over, and Theo giggled behind him. Gods, we were so drunk.

Then I smelled it. The blood. It was metallic and tangy, stinging my nose. I threw my arm out to stop the boys behind me. "Wait," I told them. "Something's not right. Can you smell that?"

They sniffed the air, and immediately sobered. It wasn't that late in the evening, just past dinnertime. I bet everyone was still in the cafeteria. The blood was fresh, warm. The smell only got stronger as we came closer to it.

We rounded the corner to the main hallway that led to the dorms. There, in a place where someone would want a body to be found, was Professor Waldron.

But he wasn't alive. His corpse had been attached to the wall several feet above the ground. A large spear was embedded in his chest, pinning the body in place on the wall. Blood dripped down from the corpse and onto the floor below, creating a thick pool that spread throughout the carpet. His gut had been cut open, and entrails spilled out of it, hanging in a grotesque display.

There beside him on the wall was a message written in his own blood. *The Black Claw has found its master. Hail to the dark god Droga. Hail to the Hidden King.*

TWELVE

"**B**ut who's the Hidden King?" I asked.

Ethan gave a long sigh. "I don't *know* who the Hidden King is. Nobody does. That's why everyone is freaking out."

I put eggs benedict and bacon on my plate, my favorite breakfast of all time. The usually-bustling cafeteria was quiet and somber today... as it had been since Professor Waldron had been murdered a week ago, and that hideous message had appeared on the wall.

Ethan seemed irritated and on edge. I couldn't blame him. He'd been one of the people to find Professor Waldron's body, along with Stefan, Alexei, and Theo. It had to be traumatic for all of them.

"But you must have *some* idea," I insisted as we sat down at one of the nearest dining tables. Ethan had a plate piled high with bacon, eggs, sausage, ham, and about a million other meats.

Perfect for a wolf, I guessed. I don't think I'd seen him eat a vegetable since I'd met him.

Ethan shook his head and bit into a strip of bacon with a sullen look. "I don't. The Black Claw has never had a leader, let alone a king. It's like they just made it up to scare people."

"Leaving a body hanging from a spear in the middle of Arcanea University is more than a scare tactic. It's a clear threat," I pointed out.

Ethan rubbed his face. "I know, Emma. It's just weird. A few months ago, people... including me... thought the Black Claw was gone for good. Now since my dad's been gone, it's like they're out in full force all over again."

A permanent frown was embedded on his face— as if Ethan thought he was the reason for the Black Claw's return, and blamed himself for Professor Waldron's death.

I reached out and grabbed his hand, squeezing it lightly. "Hey. It isn't your fault."

He gave me a slight grimace. "You'd have a hard time convincing me of that."

I bumped my foot against his underneath the table. "Maybe I'll kick it out of you."

His grin faltered. "It's just... there've never been *two* kings in Malovia. This... Hidden King has got to be some sort of challenge to the throne," Ethan said. "They see an opening now that my father's gone, and want to take it."

"They can't overthrow the Malovian monarchy, can they? They'll never have enough support from the people to back them up," I said.

347

He shook his head. "All I know is, the King's Contest can't get here quick enough. We need someone to hold the crown. Things are getting darker every day."

I munched on my eggs. "Are you still thinking of entering that thing?"

He nodded. "Yes. It's my duty."

"But is it what you want?" I asked.

"Does it matter? Malovia needs me." Ethan finished wolfing down the rest of his meal, then stood up. "I've got class. There's a sub now for Interspecies Cooperation. Let's see if he's worth his weight."

"I hope things go all right," I told him. "But don't go blaming yourself for what happened to Waldron. There was nothing you could do. Even if you guys got to the hallway earlier, there's no guarantee those Black Claw freaks wouldn't have killed you, too."

He let out a huff. "Just… be careful, okay?" Ethan warned. "Arcanea University is supposed to be safe, but somehow, the Black Claw broke in and managed to kill Waldron without being seen. Don't go anywhere unless you have someone with you."

Usually, I'd protest, because I was a loner who liked my private time, but true worry shone in Ethan's eyes. He had a good point, too. There were murderers walking around the school. I could be next.

"Okay. I'll be careful." I waved a hand in farewell. I watched the rolling of his shoulders as he strode away, until he was out of my sight. An uncomfortable weight settled in my stomach once he vanished from my view… like it always did these days. Whenever Ethan was around, I was at ease, carefree. The second he left me alone again, anxiety rose in my gut. It was like I knew he'd protect me if more shit went down, like it had with the *meluza*.

As much as Ethan and I argued, he was my friend. I liked him, despite the fact that he could be a total jackass. He was always helping me in Monster Hunting 101. Thanks to him, I was somewhat competent with a weapon that wasn't my mouth.

And I worried about him, too. The Black Claw was after the throne, and he still wanted to enter the King's Contest. I bet the local terrorists would love to eliminate a prince from the running for the crown.

I finished off my breakfast and booked it to Introduction to Flight, my mind still on the murder.

I'd gone out several nights looking for the Phantom, but hadn't seen any sign of him since our last encounter. If anyone could solve this mystery, it was him. I bet he was already on the case.

I pined for him in a way that was embarrassing. I saw him in my dreams almost every night. I approached him slowly, raising my hands to lift the wolf mask off his face so he would reveal himself to me for good. But before I could glimpse his face, the dream ended.

Every. Freaking. Time.

It was maddening. Enough to drive a girl crazy. I knew the Phantom felt a pull to me as I did him. Sooner or later, he had to show up in my life again… and I'd yell at him for staying away for so long. I wanted to get to know him, the true him. The real person behind the mask, instead of the superhero everyone said he was.

I knew he had a dark side and was no saint. He couldn't fool me. And I had fallen for the dark side of him just as easily as I'd fallen for the hero. I obsessively read every article I could find about the Phantom and all the speculations about who he could be. It was all gossip and hearsay— nothing substantial to go on.

I hoped to the Seven Gods he wasn't eighty or something. Shit, that'd be my luck. I could deal with ugly, but I didn't do age gaps well.

I walked into Flight class right on time, which was surprising, because being late was my specialty. Flight class was held in a giant glass bubble in the inner courtyard of the palace grounds, one that was circular shaped and at least a hundred feet tall. It was called the Conservatory, and it was one of the most beautiful places in the school. The temperature in here was controlled at a warm seventy degrees, and inside, a variety of magical plants grew that Marked used in potions. Palm trees that were purple in color and had long, purple fronds that moved like arms sat placed next to ferns that had tentacles for leaves. Signs were put next to Venus flytraps, which were the size of small dragons, warning people not to get too close or risk being swallowed whole. The greenhouse caretakers fed them steaks daily to keep them happy, and prevent them from actively seeking out students to feast on. Large puff mushrooms got up and hopped around, while toadstools played leapfrog and swam in the green pond. Lily pads whose roots took the shape of women rose out of the water, dancing as we walked by.

Professor Mara was at the center of the Conservatory, surrounded by Marked and Companions alike. This was one of the few classes where boys and girls were put together, as everyone needed to learn how to fly. In the middle of the bubble was a stone fountain with the sculpture of a dragon, alicorn, griffin and wolven woven together. Each of their bodies had wings that melded into one another. It was a gorgeous fountain, at least twenty feet tall, and at the base were all kinds of swirling circular designs, with a Malovian mantra carved into the bottom I couldn't yet read.

Arcanea were obsessed with circles for some reason. Hell if I could tell you why.

"Line up, class," Professor Mara said. "Today, I'll be demonstrating the basics of flight, as well as techniques you can use to bring out your own wings. I know many of you are freshmen, and that some wolvens and Marked among you do not yet have their wings."

Her face remained impassive. "However, if I deem that by the end of this semester you have not made significant progress in at least *finding* your wings, rest assured that you will be back in this class next semester. I do not award points to people who do not try."

I felt a paralyzing fear flood through me. We'd been mostly studying flight in the classroom. I didn't know we'd actually have to *fly* to pass this class. I was still doubting I had wings at all. Okay, sure, I could do magic, big whoop. This lady was going to have to do a lot of convincing to make me believe I had giant hidden wings on my back.

I joined the long line that surrounded the stone fountain. Professor Mara stood in front of us. "Watch closely."

She spread her arms. Yellow wings, like those of dragonflies, appeared behind Mara's back. The class *oohed* in appreciation. She raised her arms higher, and her wings fluttered, lifting her upward until she was flying easy circles around the fountain.

"The trick is to treat your wings like any other limb," Mara called down to us from above. "Trust that they know what to do and how to carry you, and you will not fall. It takes practice using your wings, like building up a muscle. Imagine yourself light as a feather, able to be carried away by the slightest breeze. But if you doubt yourself in any way, know that you will never get off the ground."

Professor Mara landed. "One last note. Be sure not to look down— it's the most certain way to fall. To fly, you must always look up. I don't wish to be scraping anyone off the ground today."

A couple of people chuckled, but I felt nauseous. She was kinda serious.

Professor Mara clapped her hands. "Right. Those of you who can fly, I'd like to see what you can do. Up, up! The ones left on the ground, I'd like you to try summoning your wings. It isn't as hard as you think it is, girls— and boys, for those who are wolvens. You just have to believe, for whatever you truly believe in will become your reality. Everyone's wings are different. They take on different appearances due to your personality, and are truly unique to you. Once you have a clear understanding of who you are, they will emerge beautifully."

Believe, believe. It was like a mantra here at Arcanea University. I never used to think that you could believe yourself into a new reality until I got here. I should've believed I'd win the lottery back home and I'd be a gazillionaire right now.

In minutes, dragons, griffins, and alicorns were flying around the Conservatory like this was just a blow-off class to them. If it was any consolation, most of the Marked were still left on the ground, though a couple of them had managed to bring their wings out. Companions came down and flew by their side, coaching them as they rose higher.

I closed my eyes and tried to concentrate. I tried to make big-ass, badass wings come out of my back so I could show everyone I was cool, too, but when I was sure I felt fluttering, I reached behind me and brushed nothing. I jumped into the air a couple of times to experiment, but it felt more like warming up for the ice. This was getting nowhere. My wings just wouldn't come.

Gabby was smirking at me from the other side of the room. She could tell I was having trouble. When I finally got tired of her obvious staring and went to send a sneer her way, she took it as an opportunity to show off. Great, translucent wings like those of a bat's, blood-red in color, emerged from her back. She rose into the air with a smile so huge I longed to slap it off her face.

The only small joy I got from watching Gabby buzz around the room was that she was pretty shaky, and she couldn't go very high. I bet she'd just gotten her wings yesterday. Beside her, Morgan sprouted wings that looked like a Monarch butterfly's, and rose to flutter beside Gabby. She shot me a smug look and spread her wings wider, like she thought that would impress me. Melissa stayed on the ground and made faces as she struggled to conjure her own wings.

I forced myself to turn away from her and the twins and try again. My concentration was broken by a couple of wolven boys who were wrestling and laughing nearby. It was clear they didn't give a shit about flying. They wouldn't pass this class.

It was disheartening to watch more and more people get their wings as the class went on. Marked grew beautiful wings of gossamer, wings that sparkled and shone rainbow colors. They seemed to come in every shade and shape.

I tried and tried, but still struggled to get the hang of this class. I shouldn't have felt left out — half the class was still wingless, like I was— but I did. I felt like a loser.

After an hour of practicing, Professor Mara clapped her hands. "That's enough. It was a valiant effort for today. *Most* of you—" she glanced at the wolven boys, "—did well. We'll resume again next week."

I was fuming as I left the Conservatory. *What gives?* I flew every day on the ice. I performed death-defying jumps during practice that most people would be terrified to attempt. I soared through the air on a daily basis, just on blades instead of wings. How was that any different? If anything, this should be easy for me.

Gabby glided by me, hitting me on the shoulder as she passed. I had the urge to pluck a stink-bomb from one of the magical plants that grew them nearby and fling it at her head, but she had flown away before I could do so.

Why was she so threatened by me? It was really kind of pathetic. There were a million other people in this school she could pick on, yet her targets were set on me.

I guess it was kind of a compliment. As the outcast, I should've been the weakest threat. But I'd only been here a month and a half, and I was making Gabby shake in her skates. I was already showing her up at practice. She might have an edge on me in magic, but I matched her on the ice. It wouldn't be long before I caught up in the Arcanea world, too. Then I'd show her what was up.

If I ever got my wings, that was.

Ugh. I was glad the week was over. I went back to my dorm, threw my bag on the floor and changed out of my uniform as quickly as possible.

I was mentally and physically exhausted. And it wasn't just from class. My body felt weak and tired— like I was totally drained, and was in need of a battery charge. My limbs shook, and a wave of nausea hit. I felt like I was going to collapse any moment.

Knew what that meant. Time for a treatment. I went to my mini-fridge and got out a glass bottle of refrigerated human plasma. I had four bottles in there, a month's supply, along with a new box of medical supplies sitting in the corner of my dorm room. All my medication was being shipped to the school's medical ward by the Malovian government, which I could pick up every month so I'd always have a steady supply.

I changed into a baggy shirt and loose yoga pants, then took two pain relievers and an allergy pill before I got to work.

I drew the clear plasma out of the glass bottle with two plastic syringes, then screwed four strands of long, thin and clear tubing onto the syringes. The tubing ended in tiny needles smaller than the tip of my finger. I pushed the syringe so that the plasma flowed through the tubing, until it was primed through the needles at the end.

This was the hard part. I tied my shirt around my middle using a scrunchie, then wiped my stomach clean with alcohol pads. I began inserting the needles, one by one in various places around my stomach.

I nearly fainted the first time I did this. I'd never poked myself with a needle before, but it was either that, or deal with going to the hospital every week to have someone do it for me, and no way was that going to happen. I could take this.

Three of the needles went in easily and painlessly, and I secured them with transparent, square dressings that would stick to my skin and ensure the needles didn't slip.

I pushed in the last needle. It was blunt, and caught on my skin. I couldn't bring the needle back out and try again due to risk of infection, so I was forced to stab it on through. I hissed. Black dots swarmed my vision, and I gritted my teeth. I pounded my fist against the desk. Who knew a little needle could hurt so much?

But whatever. They were in. I secured the last needle with the tape, then put the first syringe into a small machine— an infusion pump. It was plastic, smaller than my forearm, and easily transportable. I turned the pump on, and it started pushing the plasma into my system.

I put the infusion pump into a small tote bag that had gray foxes on it, and slung it over my shoulder so I could walk around. I grabbed the TV remote and a blanket as I settled on my bed to watch some movies.

The plasma itched as it went in, causing a red rash to spread across my stomach. The doctors said that was normal, but I wasn't supposed to scratch at it. It killed me. I put on a heating pad to get some relief, and focused my attention on the show in front of me.

But it was hard. My body felt achy and worn out as the plasma continued to do its work. I struggled to keep my eyes open as my favorite show kept playing. It was like my brain was out there floating, and my body was full of rocks, still stuck on the ground.

The doctors told me the first twelve months of the infusions would be awful, as the medicine was still working on getting all the junk and germs out of my system. I couldn't imagine feeling like this for twelve months straight. But once the year was over, I'd feel a lot better. I'd crave the infusions instead of hating them, and the side effects would stop. My body would get used to the medicine and would eventually feel off without them, like I was being charged like a battery.

Next year couldn't come fast enough. Not to mention this shit was making me gain weight. I needed to retain a figure for the ice, but the medication was ruining it. Didn't have a choice, though.

I couldn't imagine doing this every week for the rest of my life. It was hard to think of, in that moment. I wondered if I'd ever grow used to it.

There was a knock on the door. I wanted whoever it was to go the hell away, but they kept on knocking. I sighed and got up. No easy feat, either. My feet felt like bricks. I dragged myself to the door and opened up just a crack, so I could peek my head out but the rest of my body was hidden. I didn't want everyone in the dorm halls to walk past and see me.

"Hey, Emma," Odette peeped. "I was wondering, do you wanna go for a walk? It's beautiful out today."

I was allowed to go places with my infusion pump in. I could just throw it in the bag it came in and walk around with the pump on my back, allowing the treatment to work its magic while I roamed where I pleased. I could go with Odette today. It wouldn't be a big deal.

But I wasn't ready yet. I didn't want people to see me like this— walking around school with a bunch of tubes coming out from under my shirt. They'd ask questions, and they wouldn't understand when I explained. They'd think I was different. Like some kind of freak. *What's wrong with you?* I didn't want to say.

"Maybe tomorrow," I said. "I'm kinda feeling tired."

"That's okay, I just have some free time, so I figured I'd offer," Odette said. "Theo wanted to go to a recital later tonight. So let's hang out at noon tomorrow, kay?"

I nodded and shut the door quietly, feeling queasy. I gently lowered myself back onto the bed and resumed frying my brain with more TV.

Two hours later, and I. Felt. Like. Shit. The medicine had finally finished infusing, and my stomach was swollen from all the plasma it absorbed. I took the needles out and placed four bandages over the insertion sites. I glanced at the mirror and had a thought I looked like a little kid.

I threw the needles into a plastic medical box before rushing to the bathroom. I spent fifteen minutes over the toilet gagging, but no food came up, even though I'd been munching for awhile. I'd eaten through all the food in my dorm. The infusions made you like that— inhale everything in sight.

The brain fog was major right now. I could barely string two sentences together... barely remember my name. It was like everything was one major *duh*. I felt like little birds were tweeting in a circle around my head. I didn't even turn the TV off before I curled into a ball on my bed and pulled the blanket over me, closing my eyes.

I woke up from my nap about an hour later. I felt a little better— more energized, though still kind of groggy. Maybe those infusions really were working.

That was one thing to be grateful for. I did some research on magical races that could heal. Healing magic was rare, and the few races that had healing magic at all didn't have infinite power. There was only so much they could do. They weren't miracle workers, and couldn't tackle the kind of illness I had. Magic wouldn't heal my body, so I'd have to rely on the powers of modern medicine.

I was only a month into these infusions and I was already tired of them. I needed comfort. I wanted to go to the rink, but right now, there was just no way.

The scariest thing about my disease right now, at least to me, was my struggle to continue being active. I had to leave the ice early the other day because my body just couldn't keep up. The look on Gabby's face was so smug.

I'd been an athlete all my life. I didn't know who I was without skating. I wouldn't let my disease take that away from me, too.

I needed some fresh air, to clear my head. I wished I'd taken up Odette on that walk earlier, but at the same time, I just couldn't. I wasn't ready.

Ethan had told me not to go wandering off on my own, and I'd promised him not to. But I couldn't sit around here. It felt like the four walls were closing in on me. So I resolved to stay inside school grounds where it was... mostly... safe.

It was around three o'clock. I forced myself to roll out of bed and get a shower. I put on a white sweater with an oversized flannel scarf, dark-wash skinny jeans, and knee-high boots. I left my purse, as I didn't think I would go anywhere I'd need it, and left the dormitories.

I shuddered as I passed the place where Professor Waldron's body had been found. It'd been long since cleaned up, but if you looked closely, you could still see where the spear had been embedded in the wall. It was really messed up. I'd barely been at this school for a month and a half, and already, murders were taking place on campus.

Well, I guess that was one good thing about Arcanea University. You'd never be short on gossip, and there was no possibility you'd be bored.

I passed through the gardens. I noticed Ethan playing frisbee with his dragon friend, Stefan. Ethan changed from a wolven and back again as he and Stefan tossed the frisbee back and forth.

I smiled. It was nice to see him enjoying himself. He seemed really pent up after what had happened.

"Hey, *onawilke*," Ethan called as I passed. He jogged over. "Where you off to in such a hurry?"

I didn't know I was hurrying. "Just out. Is it any of your business?" I teased.

Ethan blinked before giving a wide smile. "Perhaps I'll *make* it my business."

He changed into a wolven and bared his teeth. "*You better run, onawilke.*"

I gave a yelp and made a run for it. People laughed as Ethan gave chase throughout the school grounds. Stefan cried out for us to get a room as we ran past him.

Usually, I didn't like the attention, but with Ethan it was different. I liked messing around with him. It made me feel better when he wasn't taking life so seriously. It made me feel like I should be that way, too.

I left the main gardens and went to a part of the school that was more secluded— the outer grounds. They were still surrounded by the school's fencing, but it was such a long walk to the palace that practically no one came out here. I laughed and ducked behind a hedge as Ethan spun out while trying to catch me. As he launched himself upward, I took the opportunity to hide next to a wolven statue.

I had to hold my hand over my mouth to keep from laughing. If he heard me, he'd catch me.

I heard the sound of Ethan's giant footsteps before I felt his large shadow looming. I squealed and tried to bolt, but I felt huge paws on my back and I went face-first into the grass.

I turned over. Ethan was on top of me, back in his human form and laughing. I punched him in the shoulder and pushed him away. He rolled off, still snickering as he stared up at the sky.

"So I can't outrun a wolf. Big deal," I said, though a large smile had spread across my face.

"You could if you had wings," Ethan said. He sat up, brushing leaves off his jacket. "I'm sorry to say I'm stuck on the ground."

That wiped my good mood away. My smile fell off my face, and I said, "You're not the only one. Flight class is currently sucking ass right now."

Ethan gave me a quizzical expression. "Having trouble finding your wings?"

"Yeah. And Gabby is making sure to rub it in my face at every opportunity." I sighed as I pushed myself to a sitting position.

"We could take you to a cliff and throw you off of it. Fly or fall," Ethan teased.

"Ha, ha," I said dryly. "Sure I'll fall."

"You wouldn't have to worry. I'd be at the bottom to catch you." He winked.

What was up with him? He was being so sweet lately. I hoped he didn't ask me to be his chosen so he could participate in the King's Contest. I didn't want any part in that crap. I was no queen. And Ethan was *definitely* not my prince charming.

I preferred the Robin Hood types.

Ethan got to his feet. He held out a hand to pull me up, and I took it. He almost threw me into the next century with the force of his pull. I shook my arm out and said, "I just want to get my wings. I need to pass this class."

"You will," Ethan promised. "Give it some time."

We started on the way back to the main campus. The skies had turned in seemingly moments… it'd been sunny and cool only moments before, but now the winds had developed a strange chill to them, and grey clouds that were nearly black in color blotted out the sun. It looked like it was going to rain.

"Strange," I said. I held up my hand as I felt raindrops hit my head. "Do you think it's going to storm?"

Ethan was looking upward. His gaze had changed from carefree to concerned. "I don't know. Something's not right."

The minute he said that, a haunting figure emerged from the trees. Her feet floated several inches above the ground, and a haggard old hand extended out of a tattered and ragged brown robe. From beneath her cloak's hood I could see a large, crooked nose, decaying flesh, and warts that spread all over her ancient body. She was hunched over, and had a wizened face with so many wrinkles that you couldn't count them all. She looked to be hundreds of years old.

I knew what she was— a hag. Lord Lucien had taught us about them in our Monster Hunting 101 class. They were witch-like monsters created by users of dark magic. What was one doing on campus?

"Emma, get away from her." Ethan planted himself in front of me. He changed into a wolven and snarled, snapping his jaws in warning.

The hag didn't seem bothered by Ethan's threatening stance. Instead, her old eyes sought me out. She pointed at me, and spoke in a wheezing voice. "*You. It is you the one the gods have sent.*"

"Me?" I squeaked. Ethan curled around me protectively, but the hag made no move to advance. She kept on speaking in that strange, unearthly voice.

"*And there shall be a sorceress who is above all Marked,*" the hag chanted. "*She will be written as destined and cursed, for there is not one who is as strong as she, nor one who is so damned. Realms shall bow to her will, but never shall she escape her cruel fate. She will be known as the Worldweaver. She who holds the power of the Arcanea will be their final end, for when the wolf howls, the Worldweaver who rules over reality itself will surrender her magic… and die.*"

"When will this happen?" I asked. I felt the blood leave my face as a chill ran over my spine.

The hag bobbed her head. "*Before the first of the snow melts away at the end of the fourth winter, you shall meet your death.*"

I put a hand out to grasp Ethan's fur, so I could remain standing. Four years? That's all I had before I died?

"You sure you've got the right girl?" I asked weakly. Ethan's growl remained low in his throat.

"*I bear a warning, Worldweaver. Hags are the keepers of foretelling and future, and we will be your guides as you approach the coming end,*" she spoke. "*Beware of the one they call the Hidden King, for he will bring your death.*"

"Go now! Be gone!" Ethan shouted. He leapt forward, jaws wide, to sink his teeth into the hag. She vanished in a flash of light and black smoke. The moment she disappeared, the grey clouds cleared and sunlight came back into the area.

I was left shaking. Ethan turned back into a human. He tried to hide it, but worry and concern devastated his features.

"I'm gonna die?" I peeped. Shit. Maybe it wasn't such a good idea to come to this school after all.

"Don't listen to her, Em. Hags can't be trusted," Ethan said firmly. He brought his arm around me, and held me tightly to him. "They're monsters, and we're Arcanea. We can't take anything she says as the truth. It was probably some kind of trick."

"Well, she seemed to know exactly what she was talking about," I protested.

Ethan frowned, and said, "What I heard was a lot of gibberish. Worldweaver? I've never heard of such a thing. And Emma, I don't mean to hurt your feelings, but…"

He took a deep breath. "The hag said that this woman could harness extreme magical power, and *onawilke*, you haven't even gotten your wings yet. It doesn't sound very much like you."

The statement didn't sting at all. I didn't care about being the weakest Arcanea alive if it meant I got to keep my life. "But why would she come to me at all? It doesn't make any sense. Plus she mentioned the Hidden King. That's kind of a big deal."

Ethan shook his head. "Why do monsters do anything? It was probably just to scare you, get you off your guard. Who knew what might've happened if I hadn't been here? She was trying to distract you, so she could get a quick meal. That was all."

I nodded, but I was more or less agreeing with him because I wanted some validation that what the hag said wasn't true… even though I was terrified that it might be.

He nudged me. "Come on. Let's go back to school and get some dinner in you. You look as pale as a ghost."

I wanted to shoot back that he didn't have a lot of color in his cheeks, either, but I was too shaken up for playful banter at the moment. Ethan kept on reassuring me on the way back to the palace, but to be honest, it felt like he was just giving me excuses.

"Before the first of the snow melts away at the end of the fourth winter, you shall meet your death."

I had a rotten feeling in my stomach that Ethan Nowak wasn't telling me the truth.

If there was ever a time to be worried, it was now.

Hags were monsters, sure. They were known as the bringers of misfortune and woe. But despite their horrid appearance, they were subjects of the gods. In many Arcanean legends, the god king Tomir often sent hags to his heroes, usually before they were whisked off on some incredible deed or quest.

Many of whom never returned.

The fact that the hag hadn't harmed us, either, also wasn't a good sign. If she was hunting, she would've attacked first and spoken later, if at all. But she'd appeared suddenly, spoken her warning and left, as if she'd been sent to deliver this prophecy specifically to us.

I made excuses for Emma because I didn't want to scare her. Yet I knew what the hag had spoken would come true. Within four winters, Emma would die.

Unless I did something to stop it.

I wasn't sure how to prevent the future, or even if I could, but I had to do something. I couldn't let my mate perish due to some strange oracle. It didn't make any sense. Perhaps if I got some more information, I could change what was to come.

The hag had spoken about the Worldweaver. I didn't know what that was. I'd never heard of the term before. I was sure anyone I could consult on the topic would think I was talking nonsense. I'd gone to the library and scanned for books on the subject, but nothing came up. It was a dead end.

Two names. The Worldweaver and the Hidden King. The hag said that he'd bring her death. So I'd have to find out who he was, and kill him first.

The Hidden King was associated with the Black Claw, according to the note left behind by Professor Waldron's murderer. That made things simple. I'd have to find a member of the Black Claw and interrogate them until I found out who the Hidden King was.

The idea of torture sickened me. But I would do it, if it meant protecting Emma.

For several nights, I searched the city and the woods for Black Craw tributes, but didn't find any. The fuckers had been everywhere only a few nights ago, but now, they'd all but vanished. I couldn't locate them anywhere. Similarly, the disappearances in the city had stopped. It was as if the group was pulling back— waiting for something.

The end of October neared, and I hadn't gotten my teeth into a single Black Claw tribute. I wasn't giving up, but I had the feeling that I needed to change my strategy. I was going about this wrong, but at the same time, I had no idea on how to proceed.

The Friday before Halloween, Professor Victor stood at the front of the Interspecies Cooperation class and made an announcement.

"We're going to be trying something a little different today," he said. "Now, as you know, most freshman Marked aren't introduced to their Faction powers until their second semester, but Professor Lunesta and I think that this year's recruits could use a formal introduction."

His smile widened. "So, we'll be mentoring them today. Everyone, follow me to the training arena."

Some people groaned, but most guys were excited. It was nice when you got to spend class time with some girls for a change.

I didn't get why we were doing this. Professor Lunesta taught Introducing the Monarchy, which had nothing to do with Interspecies Cooperation— or Faction magic, for that matter. Was this some new thing the school was introducing?

The training arena was outside, in the woods. It was more or less a large, circular patch of grass surrounded by trees. When I got there, I saw a long line of freshman girls waiting in the arena.

My heart immediately jumped when I saw red hair. I didn't know Emma was in this class. That was a bonus.

Professor Victor shouted over the noise, "Partner up, everyone! Pick someone of your own Faction, please!"

I immediately made a beeline for Emma. She scowled as I poked her in the side and said, "Picked you."

"Of course you did. Can't let me meet anyone new, can you?" she asked.

"Why do you need to meet anyone new? I'm the best there is," I said. She rolled her eyes.

Elijah gravitated toward Gabby like they were magnets. They gave slight smiles and looked each other up and down, like they were about to do it right there on the lawn. Total sex eyes.

Ugh. They deserved each other. They were both rotten.

I craned my neck to see who everyone else had gotten. Theo had grabbed onto Odette, obviously, who was currently chatting his ear off. Alexei had paired up with Kiara, the girl that was really shy and had helped us rescue Alexei from the *taranticula*.

Although, right now, Alexei was acting like the shy one. He was blushing beet red.

Alexei gave Kiara a sheepish look. "I'm sorry," he said. "I get that I'm supposed to be helping you, but I don't know how to control my powers. I'm kind of a crappy empath."

"It's okay," Kiara said brightly. "We'll work it the other way around. I can teach you."

Alexei blushed even harder. I shook my head. He had a total crush on her. It was obvious.

Loud shouting pulled my attention to the side. Stefan had slid up to a goth girl and was wearing a sly grin. Her expression was red with rage.

"*Babycakes*? You sexist ass!" she shouted. She slapped Stefan on the chest and said, "I can't *believe* you'd call me something so derogatory!"

I think I knew her. Emma hung out with her a lot— her name was Delmare.

Stefan grinned wider and said, "The words only get dirtier from here, babycakes. You can call me something naughty, too. Promise I won't mind. The filthier, the better."

"Ugh! You pig!" Delmare searched the class for another dragon Companion to pair up with, but too late. They were already taken. She narrowed her eyes in disgust at Stefan. He wiggled his eyebrows suggestively.

"Companions, shift into your animal form!" Professor Lunesta instructed. "Use your magic to demonstrate to your partner how to use Faction magic!"

I changed into a wolven, and the rest of the Companions followed. Theo stomped his hoof and spoke gently, like a father talking to his child. *"Listen, Odette. Shield magic is very simple. All you have to do is focus on creating a defense around something you want to protect, then expand that intention outward to create a large force field nothing can cross. Like so, see?"*

A blooming light emerged from Theo's horn. It wrapped itself around Odette protectively, like a large bubble. Theo prodded at the bubble with his horn, but the shield wouldn't break. It'd bounce off any attack that came at it.

Odette giggled maniacally and said, "Let me try, let me!"

The large bubble burst as Theo drew his magic away. From the tips of her fingers, Odette created tiny shield bubbles that were miniature versions of Theo's. But instead of expanding them, she started shooting them in bubble beams at Theo. They burst at his side and knocked him over. He scrambled to get back on his hooves.

"No, Odette, not like that! Ouch, that hurts!" Theo cried. Theo galloped away, and Odette laughed as she chased him around the training arena with her bubble beams.

Alexei was lying on the ground as a griffin, with Kiara leaning against his side. Her legs were crossed, and she stroked his feathers calmly as she said, "You just have to work on blocking the emotion out. Imagine creating a wall between you and everyone else."

"I… I'm not sure how," Alexei confessed. His eyes were squeezed so tightly it was almost like he was in pain. I bet that he could feel every emotion running through the arena in that moment.

"You have to pick out your own feelings from everyone else's. You'll know which ones are yours, because they'll be stronger," Kiara said calmly. "Everything that isn't yours, try pushing outward. Or simply turning down the volume."

Alexei's features visibly relaxed. Kiara smiled and said, "See? You're getting it."

Nearby, Stefan and Delmare were creating a scene.

"Come on, shoot me, babycakes!" Stefan danced around, creating minor earthquakes as he jumped back and forth. Other teams glared at him as he shook the ground. *"You know you wanna knock me on my ass!"*

Delmare bared her teeth. She attempted to conjure a small ball of what looked like red electricity, but she couldn't hold onto it. The ball flickered out before she could harness it to throw.

"Don't tell me you're just a pretty face," Stefan chided. *"Hit me with all you've got, honey!"*

Delmare lost it. She screamed, and the red ball swelled to an enormous size within her hands. She cranked her hand back, and tossed it as if throwing a grenade.

People dove out of the way. Stefan's eyes grew wide as the red ball approached. It socked him in the chest, and on impact, the trees blew backward with the force of the blow.

Stefan went flying. When he landed, shockwaves rippled across the earth. I had to cling to the ground with my claws to keep my balance. Emma fell over.

Delmare cheered with victory, raising her fists to the sky. Stefan remained on his back, four legs in the air, and didn't get up. A couple of people sent them harsh glares and rude gestures before they returned to the exercise.

Emma got off the ground. She wrenched her eyes away from the disaster that was Stefan and Delmare and looked at me. She raised an eyebrow. "So… how are you supposed to teach me how to levitate stuff if you can't do it yourself, since you're not a Marked?"

"It's all theory. It's not much different than communicating across long distances," I said. *"The same techniques are used."*

I turned to face a large rock on the ground, about the size of my paw. *"Try to lift that."*

"That?" Emma scoffed in disbelief. "It's kinda big for my first time."

"That's what they all say," I commented. Emma face-palmed, and I couldn't resist a chuckle.

"Are you done laughing at your own jokes?" she asked. "I don't want to be behind in this class, too."

I cleared my throat and said, *"Yes. Anyway. It's the same as if you picked it up with your hand. It just takes mental energy instead of physical. Imagine lifting the rock into the air, but don't move your arm. The intention is simple."*

"Well, if you can understand it, I'm sure it is," she said. I laughed again.

Emma focused her eyes on the rock. A few moments passed, and nothing happened. But she didn't break her concentration. The rock wiggled, and her mouth dropped open in shock. "I'm doing it!"

"Almost," I said. *"Now try lifting it."*

The sound of applause drew away our attention. Gabby had uprooted an entire oak tree and was levitating it three feet above the ground. Her face was strained, but the tree remained suspended in mid-air.

How the fuck was she doing that? She was a freaking *First Year*. She shouldn't have that kind of power.

Elijah held his head up proudly, like he was doing it himself. If he wasn't a Companion, I'd suspect he was. But Gabby was doing it all on her own. What was going on?

Professor Victor and Professor Lunesta looked similarly confused. Something was up here.

Emma seemed downcast. "Why does she has to beat me in everything?"

"Forget Gabby. That's not normal," I told her. *"Why do you give a shit what she does, anyway? Focus on what you can do."*

"Which is practically nothing," Emma said in discouragement. "I'm tired of always being the weakest one in the class."

She glanced at me. "You know I am. I know what people say about me. That whoever bonds with me is getting the short end of the stick."

Fury rose up in me and made me feel like I was going to snap. I'd heard the rumors, too, but so what? They didn't know anything about what was between me and my mate. *"Screw those people. I believe in you,"* I told her. *"That should be enough."*

"You think I'm being stupid, but I *know* I'm bound to the Phantom," she protested. "How can someone like me ever be worthy of him? He's an amazing shifter, and I'm nothing. I don't know if I can survive in this world without him."

Oh, Emma. If only you knew it was the other way around. *"If the Phantom truly loves you, he'll accept you however you are,"* I said firmly. *"But I know you can do this. If he were here, he'd be telling you the same thing. Don't prove him wrong."*

Emma sighed. She sent a last glance toward Gabby, who'd let the tree fall back on the ground, and steeled her expression. "Okay. I'll try again."

She fixed her eyes on the stone. This time, it wiggled immediately, rocking back and forth. Slowly, it rose into the air, turning slightly as if on a rotating axis. Emma's expression brightened as she rose the stone in front of her face and kept it levitated.

"Way to go!" I cheered. Emma let the rock drop back down to the ground. She wavered on her feet.

"That took a lot more effort than I expected," she said. "It was actually kind of... hard."

"It's not easy," I confessed. *"But with time, you'll become more... Emma? Emma!"*

Her eyes rolled back in her head as she collapsed. I changed back into a human immediately and caught her before her head hit the ground.

"Emma!" Odette called. She'd stopped chasing Theo around as she noticed her friend faint. She, Delmare, and Kiara came racing over. I cradled Emma in my arms, lifting her as I stood. She was so light and tiny. I never noticed before.

"See? Told you she was weak," Gabby called. "She can't even lift a little rock."

"Miss Ciar, that is enough," Professor Lunesta snapped. Gabby kept her mouth shut after that, though both her and Elijah were wearing giddy looks.

"I think she's okay," I told her friends. "She's breathing fine. Just wiped out."

They still looked worried. I held Emma closer to me and looked to Professor Victor. "I think she needs to rest. I'll take her back to her dormitory."

"Yes, that's all very well, Mister Nowak. Make sure to tend to her carefully. You are excused," Professor Victor said, waving me off.

The activity resumed, and I walked toward the school. As I entered, everyone's eyes gravitated to me, then to Emma hanging limply in my arms.

Emma blearily came round as we passed the cafeteria. "What… happened?"

"You fainted," I told her. "I'm taking you to bed."

That sounded wrong. I stuttered as I said, "I mean, uh— I'm taking you to lie down." Fuck, that wasn't right, either. And now it was provoking images that were about to give me a hard-on.

Great. Emma needed me, and all I could think of was getting her naked. Not the right time, Nowak.

She blinked a few times, trying to comprehend what I was saying, before the meaning suddenly hit her. "What? No!" Emma weakly pushed against me. "Put me down. I can't be seen like this."

"Too late," I told her. "Everyone's already noticed."

She groaned. Her head hit my chest, though she didn't try to get away. She was still too tired.

When we got to her dorm, I put her down on the bed and covered her up with a blanket. She stared straight ahead at the wall and said, "How am I ever going to be a sorceress if I faint every time I do advanced magic?"

I sat on the edge of her bed. "You can get stronger," I told her. "It's like ice skating, right? A little at a time. You don't do jumps before you learn how to glide. If you work yourself up to it, I'm sure you can handle it."

A bit of hope came into her gaze before it quickly faded. "I guess so."

"You need water," I said. I got up and headed to the mini-fridge and yanked it open.

"Ethan, don't," she protested.

I didn't listen. Inside, I found water, along with a shit ton of snacks— damn, Emma loved junk food— along with several strange glass bottles that were filled with a clear liquid. They looked medical.

I took out a glass bottle and turned it in my head. Human plasma? "What are these for?" I asked.

"Nothing. Just leave it," she said.

She wasn't ready to tell me. I bet it had to do with her condition. I still didn't know what it was. Had it been the reason she'd passed out today? It was so severe that she needed plasma to survive?

I put the bottle back and instead grabbed a water bottle. I wouldn't pry if she wasn't ready. I handed the water to her, and she took a few sips.

"I think I should stop by the rink and tell Lady Magdalina you won't be coming to practice," I said slowly. "You have lessons on Fridays, right? You should probably skip."

"Fuck all if I will," she said violently.

"Emma."

I stared at her, and she let out a resentful sigh. "Fine."

She closed her eyes and snuggled into her pillow. I made way for the door. "My classes are done for the day. I'll be in my dorm if you need anything."

"Not like I'll be able to get up anyway, let alone make it down the hall."

Her tone was resentful. I decided saying anything else would probably be a mistake, so I left quietly.

I isolated myself in my room and tried focusing my attention on the hockey game that was playing on my TV. It was a big one, a game I'd been looking forward to all week— Malovia versus Russia.

But I couldn't think straight. My mind kept wandering back to what I'd found in Emma's dorm, how she'd fainted— how she didn't want to tell me what was wrong with her.

What was Emma trying to hide from me?

I hardly saw Emma at all the following week. She was avoiding me. She kept her distance in Monster Hunting 101 and didn't sit with me at breakfast like usual. I didn't even spot her at the rink after hockey practice, which was unusual. She was always there. Had she been so tired from last Friday she'd taken the rest of the week off from skating?

Whenever she saw me coming, she'd blush and turn the other way. It was like she was embarrassed or something. I didn't get why. Yeah, fainting in class was kind of humiliating, but I didn't care that she did. It wasn't a big deal to me. Did she think I actually thought less of her? I must've come off as a major jerk or something.

On Halloween, I was able to corner Emma before she emerged from her dorm that afternoon. She jumped as I silently came around the corner.

"Holy shit, Ethan." She glared at me. "You scared the crap out of me."

"Well, I thought I'd have to sneak up on you at some point, since you've ran away every time you've seen me coming."

Her mouth gaped. "I've… I've been busy."

"Uh-huh. Busy running away from me." I put two arms on either side of her, locking her in. Her back braced up against the wall as she stared up at me. "Can't run now," I whispered.

Emma swallowed. "You need to get out of my way. I have to study."

"Studying would be a sin today" I told her. "It's *Heimskanun.*"

"What?"

"It's an Arcanean festival, celebrating the transition from harvest to winter. It's one of our biggest holidays," I told her. "And don't tell me you have to go to class, because there aren't any today. They've all been canceled in favor of the holiday."

She bit her lip. "I think Odette and Delmare said something about it, but I hardly listened. They invited me to come with them, but I turned them down."

"Now why would you do that?" I asked.

She shrugged. "I'm not big into social gatherings."

"Well, that's no good. There's a pagan celebration taking place in town. I dropped by to see if you'd like to come with me. And unlike your friends, I won't take no for an answer."

"Me?" Emma gave a skeptical look. "I'm surprised you want to be seen with me, after what happened in class."

"Come on, Emma. It wasn't a big deal." I rolled my eyes.

"You're not the one that fainted." She went to move past me, but my arms locked her in. I grinned.

"I won't let you by until you say yes," I teased.

She huffed a lock of red hair out of her eyes. "Fine. Just so you'll stop tormenting me."

I gave a low chuckle and leaned down to whisper in her ear. "I don't plan on ending your torment for a *very* long time."

I was teasing myself. But I hadn't promised myself I'd *stay away* from Emma— just that I wouldn't make any romantic advancements toward her. Didn't mean we couldn't be friends, right? *Just* friends.

She shivered and pushed me away. "So, where are we going?"

"The festival is taking place in the middle of Dolinska right now, but the most important part of it is visiting the *Katedra da du Boyina*— the Cathedral of the Goddess," I said. "You'll see what I mean when you step inside."

"Okay…" Emma said, reluctant to follow. She deposited her things back into her dorm. I grabbed her shoulder.

"Hold on," I said. "You need to be properly dressed. You can't go in your uniform."

I took her hand and dragged her to my dorm. There, I pulled out of a shopping bag a long, ankle-length dress with long sleeves. It was white and flowing, made of cotton, with embroidery of tiny red, green, pink and black flowers on the bodice and skirt. She gasped as she observed the dress, her green eyes widening.

I handed it to her before pulling out another item, a floral headband with red and white flowers, along with tiny leather sandals.

"Women wear their hair long and flowing for the festival, with floral crowns," I said. "I thought these would look beautiful on you."

"These are gorgeous, Ethan." Emma stared at the dress, unable to take her eyes off of it. "You got them for me?"

"Well, I knew you wouldn't have anything for the festival, so I thought I'd surprise you," I said." I wanted to make the festival as amazing as possible for her.

She could barely contain her excitement. "Hold on. I'll get ready." She headed into my bathroom to change. When she came out, it nearly took my breath away. Her red hair fell in soft waves under the floral headband, and the dress fit her perfectly, tucking in at her small waist and flowing around the curves of her body.

"Is everyone going to be dressed this way?" she asked. I noticed a bit of self-consciousness in her tone.

"Mostly," I told her. "Come on. I don't want you to miss a thing."

Dolinska was bustling with activity when we arrived. The streets were packed with Marked and Companions, dressed in true Malovian fashion. The Marked wore dresses similar to Emma's, while the Companions wore knee-high black leather boots, red embroidered shirts, and navy jackets with matching pants. Streamers and ribbons flowed through the air, along with confetti, and the smells of incense rose into the air. There was folk music everywhere— it sounded like the songs of the faeries as musicians played wooden flutes, goatskin bagpipes, fiddles, and large string instruments.

People were dancing to the sound in the streets, in their shifter and human forms. Companions that had opted to remain as animals wore harnesses made of woven flowers. Stages had been set up for dancing or band competitions, or even demonstrations. One Marked performed illusions for children with puppets, while a group of sorceresses nearby put on an air show with owls and hawks. Companions had a drinking contest nearby, while Marked awed the crowd by spinning wheels of fire and swallowing flaming torches. Acrobats, both Marked and Companion, did flips and tricks throughout the streets to an applauding crowd, while a heavy lifting contest took place near the vendors. Companions lifted huge logs and threw giant stones as high and far as they could, to massive cheers of the crowd. It looked like a very muscular dragon had won the contest, and he raised a fist in victory.

In the center of town, there was a jousting contest. Marked rode their Companions at each other with lances in full armor and tried to knock each other off. Once both were on the ground, the Marked and Companions both did battle, and fought each other with ancient swords.

There'd be something similar during the King's Contest in December, but that would be an actual tournament, not for fun and show. People would get hurt.

I pushed the thought out of my mind. The King's Contest was still months away. I didn't want to bother myself with such worries today.

Emma was awed. She observed the archery contest near the jousting tournament with bright eyes and a wide smile. "Okay, you didn't tell me it'd be *this* awesome. This is incredible. It's like stepping back in time to the Middle Ages."

"Told you it was cool." My eyes caught some familiar faces dancing in the town square near the music.

Odette had gone all out for the festival. She was wearing a headband made of different colored fall leaves, her white dress embroidered with orange and brown thread. She was laughing and spinning around with Theo in the middle of the square, who was dressed in a traditional way similar to Odette's.

They had *matching outfits*. This was getting bad. Out of all people, why couldn't Odette see that Theo's heart was set on her?

Delmare wasn't too far. It wasn't any surprise that her dress was pure black. Even her headband had black roses on it. She looked like the queen of death. She was sitting cross-legged on a barrel and looking very cross, holding onto a mug of ale with an irritated expression. Stefan was right next to her, leaning on a brick wall and obviously flirting hardcore.

Odette caught Emma's eye and squealed. She left Theo's arms and hurried over to Emma, throwing her arms around her before clinging to me.

I leaned into the embrace. I'd learned that with Odette, you just accepted hugs.

"Emma! I'm so glad you could make it!" Odette sang. She eyed me up and down, and a huge grin split her face. "So *this* is the reason you didn't want to come with us. You could've told us you had a date. I wouldn't have minded."

"No, it's not like that," Emma rushed to explain.

"Oh, hush, silly." Odette giggled. "It's no big thing. I hope you two enjoy the festival!"

Odette skipped off to rejoin the dancing circle. She fell into Theo's arms, and raised up onto her tiptoes to kiss him on the cheek. He blushed so red it would make tomatoes jealous.

Stefan had moved onto flexing his muscles to try and show off. Delmare was ignoring him and staring at us. She cupped her hands around her lips and mouthed, *Save me.*

Emma laughed under her breath and said, "We should probably go and help her."

"That's all you," I said. "Stefan doesn't quit when he's on the hunt."

As we approached, I heard Stefan boasting loudly, "Yeah, I'd say the average dragon my age has killed around... I'd say... *ten* monsters by now? But I've killed around thirty. They just see me and run, you know?"

He was totally bluffing. He'd killed five, three with my help. I wasn't sure what happened with the other two. Probably got lucky, or sat on them or something.

"Anyway, I'm at the top of my class." Stefan made an arrogant noise and cleared his throat. "Best at fighting, and all that."

"Oh, *gods*, would you please just shut up?" Delmare complained. In one fluid motion, she tossed her ale onto him. It splashed Stefan in the face and soaked his clothes.

He gasped and jumped backward. Delmare tossed the wooden tankard down at his feet before stomping off. The thinnest of smiles shone on her face.

Stefan was shocked for a moment. The ale dripped onto the cobblestone. He was completely soaked.

Then a delighted smile lit up his expression, and he used his hand to wipe the dripping ale from his eyes. "Aye. She's a feisty one. I love the chase. She only gets more and more exciting."

Stefan hurried after Delmare. I held in a laugh. Emma watched them go with a confused expression. Stefan caught up to Delmare. He tried to put his arm around her, but she pushed him into a nearby fountain. Water went everywhere. She laughed along with the rest of the crowd as he floundered to pull himself out of it. Despite being made a fool of, Stefan was grinning.

"I don't get it," Emma said. "Why doesn't Stefan leave her alone? It's obvious Delmare's not interested."

"I wouldn't say that. He'd back off if she told him to go away. He understands no means no," I pointed out. "But she hasn't yet refused him, has she?"

Emma thought about it for a moment. "No. I suppose she hasn't."

"People romance in different ways, *onawilke*," I told her, and we began our walk away from the square. "It is not up to us to decide what makes sense, especially in the realm of love."

She rolled her eyes. "You talk so fancy."

"I am a prince. I suppose it's strange, for an American," I said.

"Americans can be fancy!" Emma protested.

I snorted. "If you say so."

She shook her head. "You Europeans think Americans are all southern accents, big guns, and cowboys."

"Aren't you?"

"You'd better stop while you're ahead." She scowled. "Sometimes I feel like I have a big sign on my forehead that screams I'm from the U.S."

"Well, you show some pretty tell tale signs," I said.

"And what are those?" she asked.

I glanced skyward. "Let's see. You're loud, outspoken, and insanely curious. You walk with a confidence and optimism only Americans have. But Malovians are opinionated and arrogant, anyhow, so that doesn't matter much." I shrugged, before I smiled. "People say they can tell when someone's an American because they're too nice and polite, or they smile too much, but no one ever mistook that with you, Emma."

"Yep. I'm a real asshole," she said, and I laughed.

We came to a stop near a river that ran through the middle of town. A large stone bridge led to an island in the middle of the river, where an enormous cathedral rose. It was made of stone, built with gothic architecture, four tall towers and elaborate statues adorning the outside. Each of the statues surrounding the walls depicted one of the seven gods and goddesses, and underneath them were sculptures of prominent Arcanean historical figures— mostly kings, queens, and warriors. A cobblestone court surrounded the cathedral, and people milled around it respectively.

"Whoa," Emma said, peering up at it. "It has to be, like, two hundred feet tall."

"And twice as long. It's one of our most sacred ceremony sites," I said. I took out a red head-scarf and handed it to her. "Here. It's considered disrespectful if you don't cover your hair."

Emma wrapped the red head scarf over her hair and flower headband, and we went inside.

As we entered, the sound of an organ and bells chimed throughout the hollow space. Emma turned in place, her mouth dropping open. The vaulted ceilings towered next to circular stained glass windows with millions of colors. They cast rainbows onto the floor as we passed different sections and vestibules, one for each god and several for different Arcanean saints. Candles and incense were in front of the section statues, so people could bring offerings or pray. This time of year during the festival, it was heavily crowded.

I dropped my voice to a whisper— we were supposed to be quiet inside. "This cathedral was built in honor of the goddess Milonna. People often come here to pray for healing, or ask to find love. It is not unusual for unbonded Marked to venture here to ask for Milonna's help in finding a Companion."

We walked up the long hallway between the pews. A statue of the goddess Milonna stood at the head of the altar. Many young sorceresses were on their knees before it, giving offerings of flowers, fruits and vegetables, praying for a mate.

Emma stared at the statue as if she was called to it. A multicolored light from one of the stained glass windows shone down on her, creating a halo effect as she observed the statue of the goddess with wonder.

One old woman struggled to get up the aisles. She was having trouble walking. Emma noticed and hurried to help her. She grabbed the woman's arm and aided her up the aisle.

"You look like you could use a hand," Emma said as she guided the woman into a nearby pew in front of the Milonna statue.

"Thank you, my dear," the wizened old woman spoke. "An old sorceress like me needs help to get around these days."

"Have you come to pray to the goddess?" Emma asked kindly.

"Oh, yes," she said. She sighed as she sat down into a pew. "For love, as all Marked do this time of year. My mate has long since went on to the Great Hunting Fields. I hope this winter to join him."

Emma frowned slightly. "But then… you will die."

"Death is nothing to fear, my child. I have lived a good life. I long to be young again in the realm of the gods," the woman said. She smiled at me and said, "But your journey has just now begun. You have a good mate there— I can see it in him. Enjoy the time you have together, for it doesn't last. Before you know it, seventy years will seem like seven, and he'll be gone."

Emma didn't move to correct her. She patted the old woman on her back, and the woman bowed her head to pray. As Emma moved beside me, she seemed bothered.

"She thought we were together," Emma whispered as we left the old woman behind us.

"Let her think that. What's the harm, anyhow?" I said.

"I guess nothing," Emma said, and she spoke no more about it.

I knew what the harm was— for me, anyway. I couldn't possibly allow myself to hope that Emma and I would be together one day, truly. It was too risky for her.

"This place reminds me of some elaborate Christian churches," Emma said. "I don't understand the style."

"Many Malovians are simultaneously pagan and Christian," I told her. "It sounds strange, but in our country, we follow the old ways and traditions of our ancestors, as well as Catholicism and other branches," I said. "It's a blending of the two religions for the new world. As such, you get things like cathedrals being built for gods, and ceremonies being held for Jesus— and so on and so forth."

We stopped when we reached the end of the cathedral. A long casket was set out, made of gold and precious gems. The casket was surrounded by hundreds of burning candles on tall silver stands. Behind it was a large statue of a bearded man, adorned in Arcanean regalia with a tall crown. He lifted a sword to the sky and looked triumphant. A plaque was set onto the casket. *Lycus Nowak, King of the Arcanea.*

My father would've hated it. He despised pomp and circumstance, but this was our way.

"Is this your dad?" Emma asked as we approached.

"Yes," I said. "The monument was built shortly after his death. All kings and queens of Malovia are interred here at the cathedral. A year after his death, he'll be moved to the crypt underneath the building, to lie with the rest of our royal ancestors."

Emma picked up an incense stick out of one of the holders. "May I?"

I nodded. I picked up an incense stick, too, and we lit them both. Emma and I put our incense holders together as we simultaneously lit the biggest candle.

Emma glanced at me as we stuck the incense holders into a sandbox to fizzle out. "You know, I think your dad would've been proud of you. You're kind of a cool dude."

Wasn't sure of that, but I smiled back anyway. "Thanks."

We left the cathedral. Emma removed the headscarf and said, "I think this is my new favorite place in the city. It's so beautiful."

"It is," I said. "Eight hundred years of history, all in one place. I just hope it keeps standing."

"What do you mean?" Emma asked.

"The Black Claw often targets the cathedral. It's one of the city's greatest treasures. If they managed to topple it, it would destabilize the region and demoralize the people," I said. "They'd have a much easier time taking over things if the city was in despair."

"Do these assholes regard anything as sacred?" Emma asked in disgust.

I shook my head. "No. Nothing that regards to anything except power, maybe."

I bumped her with my shoulder. "Anyway. Let's not talk about the Black Claw today. There are other parts of the festival I want to show you."

We spent the day watching the different entertainers and participating in the events. There was so much food— Malovians liked to eat. There was kielbasa, cabbage rolls, dill pickle soup, and lots and lots of ale.

And pierogi. Sweet pierogi. I loved pierogi. You didn't mess with my pierogi. I was shocked to find out that Emma didn't know what it was. Growing up in Detroit, with a large Slavic population, she should've known. But I knew when I watched her take the first bite of that fried potato dumpling, she was in love.

Around dusk, I took Emma's hand. "The ceremonies are starting. Would you like to watch?"

"Ceremonies? Sure," Emma said, baffled. She stared at our joined hands, but made no move to pull away.

It was just holding hands. Friends held hands, right? "Come on. Follow me."

There was a large crowd of people on the path that led outside of town and into the forest. The setting sun cast an orange glow and long shadows upon the woodland.

We came to a very large, open area. The seats were wooden stools that were more or less stumps of old trees that had been cut down. They made a circle around a circular space lit with wooden torches.

A large black cauldron sat in the middle. Many people sitting nearby had brought at least one piece of firewood with them, or baskets of vegetables fresh from the harvest.

Emma and I shared one of the largest stumps. Odette and Theo resurfaced, along with Delmare and Stefan. Odette waved from across the way, sitting on Theo's lap. Delmare and Stefan sat cross-legged on the ground in front of them. Stefan seemed to be telling a story. Miracle upon miracles, Delmare actually looked slightly interested.

I wondered where Kiara was, along with Alexei. I'd seen them together over the past week, but they hadn't appeared all day at the festival. Where could they be?

"What's the ceremony for? And what's with all the firewood and vegetables?" Emma asked. The area had grown quiet. People knew something was about to happen.

I leaned over and dropped my voice to a whisper. "During *Heimskanun*, the veil between the death world and our world is thin. Winter has arrived, literally taking the life of the land with it. It is believed that the spirits of our loved ones cross over from the Great Hunting Grounds to be near us until tomorrow ends. So our priestesses help the spirits cross over by portraying the journey from life to death and wearing grotesque costumes to scare off evil spirits sent by the dark god, Droga. As for the wood and food, you'll see."

Just then, the torches dimmed. The area was barely lit by the light of the flames. Voices quieted as the sound of drums gathered. The nature of the festival immediately turned somber. Laughter and smiles died to be replaced with solemn faces.

From within the trees, figures emerged. Seven sorceresses wearing deerskin dresses, their braided hair adorned with feathers, came into the area. They walked with bare feet and had crowns of deer antlers, to portray the Seven Gods. Their faces were smudged with ashes and black makeup. Long robes made of fur hung from their shoulders and trailed along the ground. Smoke rose from incense bowls they carried, which they placed around the cauldron. All of the women were middle-aged, or older. The eldest, the High Priestess, was certainly at least seventy— but she walked with a grace that women a quarter of her age couldn't accomplish. She carried a staff that was wrapped with dying flowers, set with the skull of a stag.

Their Companions protectively surrounded the sorceresses in a circle. They were in their shifter forms. Their fur, scales, or feathers were also painted black— dirt from the graves of those gone on, mixed with ashes.

Younger sorceresses, in their twenties or so, stood at the edge of the circle, beating leather drums, clicking bones and antlers together for the ceremony's music.

As the incense was placed around the cauldron, the sorceresses held out open arms to the crowd. The onlookers deposited fruits and vegetables into their hands as gifts, and the sorceresses threw it all into the cauldron.

The High Priestess reached into a leather bag at her hip and pulled out a bouquet of fresh flowers— the last of the season. She used a match to ignite them, and tossed them into the cauldron. The whole thing went up in a blaze, creating a huge fire that illuminated the faces of everyone in the area.

The High Priestess threw her hands into the air. "I call upon the Seven Gods to accept this offering— to guide us as we reflect upon the past year and all its blessings that the harvest has brung. Let our old harmful beliefs die, and painful pasts be released as we move forward into a new beginning. Allow us to look back on the previous season, discover where our weaknesses lie, and change us from the inside out as we renew to become better followers of the Old Way."

The young sorceresses playing music began to yip and howl. The priestesses pulled from their leather bags wooden masks, grotesque and monstrous. They danced around the flames as the High Priestess lifted her hands higher.

"We ask Tomir for his protection against evil monsters, and that this ritual shall scare away all that is dark and harmful. We ask he protect us against his dark brother, Droga. We pray this winter shall pass quickly, bringing life to our land when spring comes again."

The dancers picked up the pace. Their Companions joined them now, spinning around their Marked in ghostly shadows. I knew this dance well. The sorceresses were to be the warrior Arcanea, fighting against shadow, and the shifters were the monsters… ever on the hunt, looking to destroy the Arcanea for good in an endless battle that waged throughout time.

The High Priestess raised her voice. "We ask Milonna, Tomir's wife, for love and fair death. We ask the thief God, Luka, for justice, and his sister Vesna for wisdom. We ask Radek for truth and honesty, and beg the phantom Neva for more time— time that is never enough, and that is always cut short."

The cauldron's fire blazed higher and higher. The High Priestess turned to the crowd. "Anyone who wishes to call upon the favor of a loved one beyond the veil is now allowed to come forward, and place an object of theirs into the Eternal Flame."

Many people rose from their seats. Young and old formed a line to the cauldron, all holding a different item. Two young parents threw a tiny wooden rattle into the cauldron before an old man kissed a photograph and tossed it within the flame. A little girl sitting on her father's shoulders dropped a woman's flute, and then a little boy's toy car, into the fire. A group of teenage girls were crying as they slowly fed a prom dress into the burning flames. An Arcanean warrior did a salute as he placed a Malovian army uniform on top of the crumbling logs.

When the line had died down, I got up and reached into my pocket. I could feel everyone's eyes on me as I withdrew my father's dagger. I tossed it into the fire, and the metal hissed as it began to overheat and dissolve onto the ashen wood. Normally, you wouldn't be able to melt metal with an average flame, but this was no ordinary fire. The Eternal Flame was blessed by the gods, the wood enchanted to burn brighter and hotter than any average flame.

I returned to my seat. Emma's gaze flashed to me before she put a hand on my knee. I gave her a soft smile.

After the offerings were placed, the High Priestess called out, "May we remember those who have passed on to the Great Hunting Grounds before us, and know that one day, we too shall join them, for the greatest blessing of the gods is a good death."

The High Priestess threw back her head and let out a primal cry. She began to chant and sing as she left the area. The other priestesses followed her, and the younger sorceresses stepped forward to keep watch over the Eternal Flame.

People got up and began to follow. I prodded Emma and said, "Come on. Now it's time to be part of the processional."

The High Priestess led the way through the woods as hundreds of people followed. The priestesses passed out candles, and we shared our wicks to light them as we proceeded through the forest. Emma and I stayed at the back and watched the dozens of flickering flames dance. By this time, darkness had fallen, and the forest was completely pitch black under the thin light of the nearly-vanished moon. It was a very powerful time for magic.

I noticed Emma faltered on the winding walk up the mountain path. I put my arm around her hips to steady her.

"You okay?" I asked.

"Yeah." She was breathing a little hard. "Thursdays aren't great days for me."

"We're almost there," I told her.

She nodded before she said, "Distract me. What happens next?"

"Tomorrow is the *Dyzen da du Merte.* The Day of the Dead," I said. "I'll be at my father's monument in the cathedral, keeping vigil. The rest of the city will also be at grave sites, lighting candles. Altars placed with photos and treasured items of our deceased loved ones will be laid out at our homes, with a burning candle to signify the presence of the absent, until midnight when it is blown out. It's one of our most honored traditions."

Emma breathed and said, "I think I'm gonna need your help making it up this mountain."

"Here. Lean into me." I pulled her closer. Emma pushed her weight into me until I was more or less lifting her with one arm as we climbed. Again, I was astonished with how light she was. No wonder she was able to do jumps on the ice with ease.

Emma shivered, and I said, "You cold?"

"Yes. It got chilly fast. Though the cold doesn't usually bother me," she said.

"Here. Take my jacket." I slipped it off and put it around her shoulders. They seemed to sag under its weight. She seemed a little bit more comfortable, and my chest glowed.

I was doing a very poor job at keeping Emma at a distance. I didn't know how much longer I could keep this up, honestly. It was breaking me.

When we reached the mountain's summit, the crowd gathered around the High Priestess in a half circle. The music stopped, and all was silent. We stood respectfully to take in the sound of the wind whistling, the owls calling, and the leaves rustling in the trees.

The High Priestess raised her staff, and the Arcanea around us took a collective breath to blow the candles out.

FOURTEEN

The festival was absolutely beautiful. The ceremony afterward had been one of the most incredible moments of my life. And I'd experienced it all with Ethan by my side.

After it was over, I felt inspired. While most of the citizens of Malovia were praying at grave sites on the Day of the Dead, I went to the bookstore and purchased a leather journal. I started writing down all the things in my past that I wanted to let go, and the goals I wanted to focus on in the future.

The theme of renewal and rebirth around this time of year motivated me. I didn't have anyone to mourn— no one I was close to in my life had died— but I still wanted to take part in the holiday.

By the time I was done writing, my list was pretty long. I had a lot of things on it— like forgiving my mom for lying to me, and to change my perspective on my diagnosis— to learn what my new body would teach me, instead of mourning what I never really had in the first place.

Ethan would be so excited. He'd be thrilled that I was getting into my heritage.

After a few moments, I tapped my chin with my quill and added another note.

Discover the identity of the Phantom.

What the old woman had said in the cathedral spoke to me. You could never have enough time with the one you loved. If the hag was right, I only had four years or less left to live, and I didn't even know my mate's name. I needed to spend every moment I could with him, before the end— if the end was coming soon, that was.

My illness had changed me, that was for sure. Although it wasn't exactly terminal, it was, more than likely, life-limiting. Unlike most people, I had a pretty good idea how I was going to die… if my disease got to me, anyhow. I'd catch a virus I couldn't get over, or my lungs or liver would fail, or I'd get a cancer that wasn't curable. Those were the most likely ways.

Or I could die in a random accident or something. Who knew? It was weird, but all this talk of death hadn't depressed me— it just made me want to go out and live more. It was kind of morbid, but it made me… excited.

I'd seen my illness as a curse, but it was literally more of a blessing. It was teaching me how to live every moment. I needed to do more than just meaninglessly exist. And honestly, that was so much worse… to be fine physically, but to live a life that had no purpose. That was a slow death that nobody wanted, but that most people experienced.

I couldn't live like that anymore. I didn't have the time to waste. I had to make every moment count, and cherish each second like it was a gift. I wanted to be *alive*.

I wanted to show Ethan what I'd come up with, but I knew he was at his father's tomb today and wouldn't be back until later that evening. I spent my night alone (all my friends were out celebrating with their families) but on Sunday morning, I fully expected Ethan to show up to school.

He wasn't there. I figured he must've gone back to the palace or something to see his mom. He was a prince, after all, and class didn't resume until Monday. I bet he had better things to do than be here.

I was kinda bummed. At this point, I was reconsidering showing Ethan my list at all. Maybe he'd think it was dumb.

I ditzed around all day in Dolinska by visiting the different shops and cafes. It was near dinnertime when I headed back to school, my leather journal tucked tightly against my side. By this point I'd decided not to show Ethan my new resolutions at all. It'd become something private and sacred. I wasn't sure I wanted to share that with him. I didn't know how he'd react, and I didn't want him to think less of me. It was better to keep things like this to myself.

I came down a hallway that had arches opening to the gardens and saw a peculiar sight. Lord Lucien was kneeling beside a round pool in one of the inner courtyards, staring down into its depths. He was in his human form, gazing at something at the bottom of the pool below, although what I couldn't be sure. Was he looking at his reflection, or something deeper?

I liked Lord Lucien. He was always fair, and he was a good teacher. He looked really… sad. It felt wrong to just walk by.

"Hello, Professor," I said. He rose to his feet when he saw me. "Are you all right?"

Lucien forced a grin. "Yes. I am quite fine, Emma. All Arcanea are melancholy this time of year, after all."

"Have you lost someone that you had to honor on the Day of the Dead?" I asked.

He gave me a sad smile. "All the people I grieve are still alive, I'm sorry to say."

He gestured to a stone bench near the pond. I sat down on it, and he followed my lead, swooping his cloak behind him. The birds were chirping in a pine tree above us, and I caught a whiff of the last dying flowers of fall lying on the edge of the pond. That golden sunlight that was always so characteristic of Malovia reflected off the pool, making the water look yellow. The first snow had fallen last night, and it had stuck, coating the ground with patches of white.

"You mean…" I thought for a moment. "You don't speak to your loved ones anymore?"

"In a way. I am not a very popular or beloved man, even within my own family," he admitted.

This made me wonder why. Lord Lucien was a badass, and he was really nice. Ethan highly respected him, and I did, too. What would make his family abandon him?

"What about your parents? Are they still alive?" I asked. I hoped I wasn't being invasive.

But Lucien didn't seem to mind. "My parents are still alive. We are… how do you say it… estranged," he said. "I have not spoken to them for many years."

"What about your mate?" I blurted, before I hurried to apologize. "You don't have to answer that. I'm being nosy. Sorry."

Lucien let out a laugh. "It's all right. You're merely curious. And sometimes, it's nice to talk about these things. I haven't spoken of what has happened in years."

"So… what did happen?" I dared to pry.

"My mate rejected me long ago, when I was young," Lucien said. "We were together for a few years before she decided she wanted nothing to do with me."

"Oh my gosh. I'm so sorry." I was gutted by the statement. I couldn't imagine rejecting your mate— worse, being rejected by them. It was the worst fate that could ever be dealt to an Arcanea— worse even than death, to be cursed to wander the earth with a part of you missing forever.

"It's all right. It was her decision," Lucien said. His voice had taken on a heavy tone that pained me to hear. "But I never did move on. Sometimes I wonder what she's doing now. If she's found anyone else."

Lucien clapped his hands on his knees. "Enough talk from an old fool. What have you got there?"

"Oh?" His eyes were on my leather journal. I blushed. "Oh, it's nothing."

"Must be something. You seem keen on hiding it," he teased.

I made a face. "It's… kind of my new resolution list. I don't have anyone to grieve on the Day of the Dead, so I decided to use the holiday for reflection instead. It's kind of stupid, huh?"

"Not stupid at all," Lucien said. "In fact, I think it very wise. Not enough of us are focused on self-improvement."

"I could use some self-improving," I grumbled as I propped my elbow upon my knee. I leaned forward and put my chin in my hand. "I'm further behind than anyone at this school. I can't use magic very well, and I can't fly. I can't even find my wings. I'm the worst sorceress ever."

"You're far from the worst. I've had many students come through my classroom that don't put in half as much effort. You're quite the exception. I can tell you're a hard worker."

"I passed out when trying to use telepathy. I'm the laughing stock of the school."

"That's not unusual. Many students pass out when summoning Faction magic for the first time. I did," Lucien said.

"Really?" My eyes widened as I turned to look at him.

He nodded. "Whacked my head on a desk when trying to communicate with another wolven a mile away. Still got the scar."

He parted his hair back and showed me. There was a thin pink line on the top of his temple. I started to feel a tiny bit better.

I played with my journal. "I don't know. I wish I could keep up with everyone else. I'm falling behind. I bet I don't even have any fae blood. I'm some kind of fluke or something."

"Heads up." I barely had time to raise my eyes before a large snowball hit me smack in the face.

I squealed and leapt up. My leather journal fell to the ground. Chunks of snow fell off my cheeks as I wiped my eyes. Lucien had gotten to his feet. He had a snowball in hand, and was tossing it up and down playfully.

"Well, come on." Lucien raised his eyebrows. "Aren't you going to retaliate?"

I stood there, open-mouthed. Was I really about to get in a snowball fight with my teacher?

Lucien chucked the snowball he had at me, and I leapt to dodge it. Okay, that was it. This meant war.

I stooped to the ground and scooped up a bunch of snow. I formed a ball before I chucked it at Lucien's head. He ducked and sent another snowball sailing back, yelling, "You can do better than that!"

I made two more snowballs and threw them. One missed, but another smacked him square in the chest. "Ha!" I shouted. "Caught you!"

It didn't deter him. Lucien grabbed a gigantic clump of snow in his large hands, hurried over and dropped it on my head. It slipped inside my clothes and ran down my back. I screamed at the cold, and Lucien laughed.

"I'm gonna make you pay for that!" I took a handful of snow and tossed it in his face. Lucien blew snowflakes off his lips and shook his head free of the snow chunks. Before long, we were both running around the courtyard, tossing snowballs back and forth at each other and laughing.

Lucien had cheated and had taken refuge behind a stone wall. I hurled snowballs at him as fast as I could make them, and they splattered in the places where he poked his head out to see. It should've been weird that I was having a snowball fight with my middle-aged teacher, but it wasn't. It just felt like fun.

Lucien came out from behind the wall. Now was my chance. "That's it. You're toast!"

Without thinking about it, I raised my hand. Of their own accord, three snowballs formed on the ground, rising quickly into the air. I laughed as I pointed them at Lucien and prepared to fire.

He gave a broad grin.

"See," Lucien said. "What did I tell you?"

I stopped what I was doing. I realized with shock that I was levitating three snowballs off the ground, my arm whirled backward as if I was a pitcher, ready to toss them at Lucien in great succession.

The minute I realized that I was actually *using telepathy*, the snowballs dropped out of the air and crushed on the ground. I tried again to form the snowballs and make them rise, but now that I realized I was doing magic, it was like my powers wouldn't work. I scrunched up my face and concentrated, but nothing happened. It was as if my magic had decided to get up and walk away.

"What the hell? I just did it!" I said.

"You get in your own head, Emma," Lucien said. "What you can do comes naturally, if you don't think yourself out of it. You have the ability to do what *any* sorceress can, and so much more. Let it come when it will."

I took a deep breath. Lucien was right. "I guess I have a confidence problem," I admitted.

"As we all do." Lucien strode forward and placed his hand on my shoulder. "I've been watching you for awhile, and I know you have the ability. Once you become more self-confident, the magic will be easy. Give yourself some time. No accomplished sorceress was created in a day."

My shoulder was warm underneath his hand. I glowed with the praise. "Well… good to know someone here believes in me."

"I always will. I am your teacher— my job is to make sure you are ready to take on this world, whatever it may bring." He shook my shoulder before letting his hand drop. "No matter how discouraged you may get, you must not give up. Just say the word, and I will be here to help you. With anything."

"Thanks, Professor." I felt so much better than I did this morning. There was actually hope for me. Lucien thought that I could do this— survive as an Arcanea. And I'd prove to him I could. I didn't want to let him down.

No matter what, I wanted to make Lucien proud.

I waited until after midnight to sneak out of my dorm and down to the main grounds. I knew I shouldn't be up late, as I had ice practice tomorrow, but dammit, I wanted some answers. An alert had come up on my phone about an hour ago that the Phantom had been sighted in Dolinska, so I knew he was running around. If he was a student, and tomorrow was Monday, he'd have to come back to campus tonight to avoid raising suspicion about who he was. So I'd lie in wait and catch him in the act, tonight.

The Phantom would have to come through one of these damn doors. There were only three entrances to the school— the main gate, the right-side gate, and the left-side gate. Unless he scaled the walls of the school, he'd have to come through one of those entrances. I had no doubt that he could climb walls, especially with that fancy grappling hook thingy, but that attracted attention, and I bet he wanted to remain as inconspicuous as possible now that the sighting report was live.

He probably wouldn't come through the main gate, as it was fairly secure and open. Anyone who was looking for him would spot him coming a mile away. The left side gate was closest to the city, while the right-side gate led through the woods.

The woods would be the most secretive option, but it was a long walk to that entrance and it'd take time, not to mention he'd likely encounter monsters lurking in the shadows. However, I was pretty sure there were Alliance forces walking around the Dolinska city gate, so he couldn't go through there.

I decided to wait by the forest entrance. I picked a rather large blackberry bush to hide behind, then sat down and waited.

By two in the morning, I was cold, tired, and exhausted. I could barely keep my eyes open. Snow was falling again, and I was caught in a weird rotation of shivering and yawning every three seconds. The Phantom had better hurry his ass up, or I was leaving.

Footsteps snapped me out of it. I glanced over the leaves of the blackberry bush and saw a man was approaching, cloaked in shadow.

He was coming. Now was my chance. I shrank lower in the bushes and waited for my opportunity to pounce.

When the figure got closer, I sprung. I jumped out of the blackberry bush with a wild yell and landed on the man's back. I wrapped my arms around his shoulders and my knees around his legs, trying to get him to collapse beneath me.

It didn't work. The figure grabbed my arms and sent me flying ten feet forward off his back. I screamed as I went sailing. I hit the ground hard and ended up rolling. Ouch.

"Oh, gods, Emma!" A familiar voice sounded panicked. My cheeks burned red as I realized the person I'd jumped on was most certainly *not* the Phantom.

Ethan grabbed both of my arms and hauled me up off the ground like I was some sort of rag doll. He put me down and started brushing the dirt off my clothes. My jeans were totally ruined with grass stains.

"What are you doing, *onawilke*? Trying to get yourself killed?" Ethan said roughly. "There are more than just monsters who'd rip you apart for pulling a stunt like that around here, and they wouldn't ask questions first."

I was totally embarrassed. It seemed like every time I went out looking for the Phantom, Ethan got in the way. "It's none of your business," I grumbled.

Ethan's mouth fell open. "None of my... it bloody well *is* my business, seeing as how you tried to yank my head off my shoulders!"

I let out a huff. "I was waiting for the Phantom to come by, all right? I know he was sighted tonight, and I've figured out he's a student. I put together that this was the most likely place he'd come through, to get back to Arcanea University."

Ethan stared at me in a moment of disbelief. "And... you'd thought you'd just jump a dangerous vigilante, and he wouldn't retaliate?"

"He's my mate. He wouldn't hurt me," I said.

"Not on purpose! You're lucky as hell that it was me," Ethan spat. "What if it'd been some harmless pedestrian, minding their own business? You'd be facing assault charges. Or worse, an Arcanea that would gut you as soon as you'd laid a hand on them." Ethan was shaking, he was so mad. But I didn't care.

"Oh yeah, *some Arcanea* is just walking around at two a.m., in the woods in Malovia when the Black Claw is on the loose. That doesn't sound suspicious." I rolled my eyes.

I put my hands on my hips and raised my eyebrow. "Hey. What were *you* doing out this late, anyway?"

"I just got back from the palace. My mother needed my help with some things," he rattled off.

"You don't have a royal escort or anything, to make sure you get back here safe and sound, princey poo?" I asked.

He bunched his hands into fists. "I told you. I don't like being treated different while I'm here."

I went to open my mouth, but he raised a hand to stop me. "No. Why are you questioning me? You have no right. I'm the one who should be asking the questions, here. This obsession with the Phantom is a little nuts. You're like a crazy ex-girlfriend who's turned full stalker. It's insane."

I felt like I was going to explode with rage. "Don't talk to me about crazy! You haven't found a mate yet. You don't know how it feels."

"Oh, fuck off, Emma." Ethan shook his head.

I was silent for a moment. Ethan had never spoken to me like that. I'd obviously touched a nerve.

He jerked his head. "Come on. Let's go. It's not safe out here for either of us."

"I'm not going anywhere with you. I'm staying right here and waiting for the Phantom." I crossed my arms.

"If you don't follow me right now, I'm tossing you over my shoulder and carrying you back," Ethan snapped.

There was the undertone of a growl to his voice that sounded wolfish and demanding. It scared me a little… and, okay, maybe turned me on. Like, a lot.

Wait. No, no, I wasn't supposed to get turned on by Ethan. I was taken. That would be wrong.

I raised my chin and said, "If you want me to move an inch from this spot, then you're going to have to make me."

"Wish granted." Ethan started forward. I yelped and went to run, but Ethan grabbed me around the waist and tossed me over his shoulder as if I was a bag of grain. I screamed and beat my fists into his back as he started walking.

"I can do this all day, so you might as well stop," Ethan said as he hiked me back to school. "Your punches feel like a back rub."

It was useless. I gave up and let myself sag there like a sack of potatoes. I watched the outline of Ethan's ass move through his jeans as he walked.My eyes glued to the waistband of his boxers, which had risen upward as his pants sagged past his hip bones.

Okay, I was mated, but that didn't mean I couldn't look at other guys, right? Ethan had a nice… view.

"Are you going to behave now?" Ethan asked as we passed through the threshold of the castle. He began the long walk down the hallway that led to the dorms.

"Probably not," I said back. "Would you expect otherwise?"

Ethan grumbled a few swear words under his breath and said, "At the very least, can I put you down now be sure you aren't going to run away?"

"Nah. I like being carried. Saves me from having to walk."

Ethan smacked my ass, *hard*. I yelped, and he said, "There's more to come if you don't start acting like a lady."

"I am no lady."

"We all know that by now, Miss Emmaline."

Ethan slid me off his shoulder when we got to the staircase that led up to the dorm rooms. Our gazes connected. The look that Ethan gave me was so warm and full. As mad as he'd been a few minutes ago, he suddenly looked... really happy.

I had a sudden thought that came out of nowhere. What if I took Ethan back to my dorm, and what if we—

Guilt overtook me. Flirting with Ethan was harmless, but I was pretty much cheating on my mate by allowing my mind to wander. How could I even think of messing around with Ethan? Shit, I felt bad. I needed to stop.

I wrenched my eyes away from his and started climbing the staircase. "Well, this was fun, but I can take it from here. I know where my room is."

"I don't think so. I'll accompany you," he said, taking the stairs two at a time.

"What are you going to do? Sleep outside my door all night to make sure I stay inside?" I challenged.

"If you keep it up, sure."

"Maybe I'll build a rope of pillowcases and sheets and scale down the window," I suggested. "I never liked being a trapped little princess."

"I won't have any trouble coming after you."

When we got to the top of the staircase, Ethan suddenly paused. He flung out an arm to stop me.

"I smell blood," he said. He put an arm around my shoulders. "Something's not right here. We should go get a teacher."

I noticed that, down the hall, my dorm room door was propped open. A thin red trail was leaking out from within. "It's coming from my room."

"Emma!"

I didn't listen. I shoved past Ethan and ducked away as he tried to catch me. I ran full-speed toward my room. When I got there, I had to press a hand over my mouth to prevent a horrified scream from leaking out.

Morgan was on the floor. She had large gashes across her chest and neck— gashes that were weeping blood and that had torn her clothes. A huge pool of blood spread around her lifeless body. Her face was pale, and her form was unmoving. I was sure she was dead.

"We need to get her to the medical ward." Ethan was immediately beside me. He stooped down and picked up Morgan. Her blood soaked his shirt, and her head rolled lifelessly on her shoulders.

My mouth gaped. "But... but..."

"She's still alive. I can hear her breathing," he told me. "We need to hurry."

Ethan started to move. I followed him at a quick pace as Morgan's blood dripped on the carpet, creating a trail.

People started to stir as we ran through the hall. They came out of their rooms with sleepy gazes. A crowd began to grow around the entrance to my room.

"No one woke up when this happened? I can't believe no one heard the attack," I asked Ethan as we ran.

"Not if she was attacked from behind and didn't have time to scream," Ethan said.

We reached the medical ward in what seemed like minutes. The doctors and nurses wasted no time in getting Morgan onto a gurney and wheeling her into emergency. After she was taken back to surgery, we were escorted into the waiting room by one of the nurses. I stared at the blood drying on Ethan's shirt and tried not to be sick.

I didn't like Morgan. She'd been a bitch to me ever since I'd arrived. But that didn't mean I wanted her to die.

"Breathe, Emma." Ethan poured water out of a plastic white jug and into a paper cup. He forced me to drink it and take deep breaths, rubbing my shoulders in tiny circles. How the hell could he be so calm at a time like this?

A short time later, Lady Magdalina came storming into the waiting room like she was leading a warrior's brigade. She had Lady Korva flanking her, as well as Lord Lucien.

Lucien seemed pale and bothered. Korva's face was red with rage. Magdalina turned toward me with a calm expression and asked, "What happened?"

Ethan rushed to explain before I could. "Emma and I returned to her dorm around a half an hour ago. When we got there, we found Morgan inside. She'd obviously been attacked, though we weren't sure by what."

"Why were you not in your dorm this time of night, Miss Sosna?" Lady Korva's tone was firm and demanding. She was acting like I'd been the one to hurt Morgan.

"She was with me," Ethan said immediately, before I could answer. "We were exploring the grounds together and lost track of time."

I did my best to hide my surprise. Ethan was covering up for me?

Lady Korva's nostrils flared. "Students should not be outside their rooms after midnight."

"That is beside the point now," Lady Magdalina said quickly. "I am more concerned about how and why Miss Bianca was injured in the first place."

Lord Lucien hadn't said a thing since he arrived. He looked like a ghost. His eyes kept fluttering back and forth, to me and then to the floor. It was weird.

"What was Morgan doing in my room anyway?" I asked.

Lady Korva narrowed her eyes. "You are not in a position to ask questions, Miss Sosna. You've been a troublemaker since you've arrived at this school. I personally am regarding you as a key suspect."

"Be reasonable," Magdalina snapped. "Morgan's injuries were caused by magic, power that is beyond Emmaline's current abilities."

Lady Korva kept her lips tightly pinned together, but the look she gave me clearly said she still thought I was responsible.

Lucien broke his silence and reached into his pocket. "This was in Morgan's pocket. It seems she snuck into your dorm to pull a prank on you."

He handed me a small jar of silly string. I really had to resist rolling my eyes. Really? Morgan was so immature.

Then I realized she was paying for it. She wanted to prank me, sure, but now she was fighting for her life. A knot rose up in my throat.

"You two are dismissed," Lady Magdalina said. "We will do what we must to find the perpetrator of this heinous crime. The rest of you, with me."

Lady Magdalina swept away. Korva gave me a hated stare before she left with a sniff.

Lord Lucien seemed apologetic. He gave a quick nod of his head and bounded after the sorceresses.

I sank slowly into a chair. "I just don't get it. Why would anyone want to attack Morgan? She's mean, but she's harmless."

Ethan's face was dark as he said, "Morgan wasn't the target, Emma."

The meaning of his words sank in slowly. As they did, a cold terror overtook my body. Ethan was right. The attacker didn't mean to go after Morgan. They wanted me. That's why they'd been hiding in my dorm. Someone had been waiting in my room, to do to me what they'd done to her. She'd just gotten in the way.

I'd become a target. Here at Arcanea University, there was someone who wanted me dead.

The only question was... who? And why did they consider me a threat?

FIFTEEN

It'd been a week since Morgan had been attacked, and nobody knew who did it. An investigation was underway to find out what exactly had happened, but like the murder of Professor Waldron, it only turned up dead ends. No evidence had been left behind, and there were no clues indicating who had performed such a deadly assault.

Morgan survived the attack with minimal injuries. She'd lost a lot of blood, but she hadn't been seriously hurt, and had minimal scarring. Morgan couldn't remember who had attacked her. She'd never seen their face, and had fainted once she was attacked. She couldn't even recall what spell had been used.

But regardless of who'd tried to murder her, Morgan blamed Emma. She'd loudly told anyone who would listen that she thought Emma was behind the attack and that this was a way of getting back at her, because she had wings and Emma didn't.

She wasn't the only one. There were many students at the school who said we never should've allowed Emma in, and that this was what we got for letting an outsider attend Arcanea University. A lot of people kept their distance from her, as if they too were afraid she'd suddenly snap and turn on them.

An assault and a murder, all in the span of a few weeks. And at Arcanea University, no less. This was a huge problem. I had a feeling both crimes were connected. The Black Claw was inside the school somehow, watching. And for some reason, Emma had become their target.

My urge to find out exactly what was going on had increased tenfold. My mate was directly in danger. If the Phantom couldn't find out what the Black Claw was doing, then Prince Ethan would. I had power. I'd ordered spies to be placed around the palace in the guise of employees, to report back to me periodically if they noticed anything unusual. Still, they found nothing.

My mind was still preoccupied with the attack during my Forging Master Weapons class on Thursday. Myself, along with the rest of the class, had been tasked with learning how to make swords for the majority of the semester. We were working with enchanted steel, which was easier to forge and safe for fae to use, but broke far more easily. I heard swear words often as people created cracks in the weapons they worked. Each student had been given their own forge, along with a hammer and common tools. The blacksmithing classroom was outside, in one of the inner courtyards next to the Conservatory.

Professor Desmona was a warrior of epic proportions. A griffin Marked, she'd killed more monsters than anyone else I knew and was a master blacksmith. She could forge any weapon out of any metal but iron, and her swords could kill a monster in one swing. She was a towering woman, over six feet tall, and had muscles that would put most Companions to shame. Her blonde hair was cropped short around her ears. Instead of wearing sorceress robes or dresses like the rest of the female teachers, she donned long breeches, woolen tunics, and leather aprons.

I'd often seen her in full chain mail and armor, participating in the various tournaments that were held throughout the year. She was one of the few Marked that had been knighted, an honor usually reserved for Companions. My father was the one who had given her that honor. Because of that, I think she liked me, but it certainly gave me no favoritism. She was tough on everybody.

"If your sword is of shabby quality, I *will* have you start over next semester, and you will fail this class," Professor Desmona said loudly as she passed me. "You cannot kill a monster with a blade that won't cut butter."

Several people groaned, but I kept my head down. If you complained, Desmona was more likely to take off points. I didn't think she was mated, which was odd for a Marked of her age— early thirties or so. I wasn't sure if she'd found her mate yet or if he had died, and I didn't have the balls to ask.

I had been working all semester on hammering away at my sword after it emerged heated from the forge so that it obtained a proper shape. Today, I was sharpening the sword using a grindstone. Professor Desmona didn't believe in using modern tools for weapon-making— said they created poor weapons.

After I was done with the sharpening, I'd harden the sword by heating it to a very high temperature, then place it into a quenching tank. I'd repeat the process at a lower temperature to temper the sword. I was just now getting to the part where I'd be able to add a hilt.

This was nothing like working on the daggers and tiny weapons I'd made in my Simple Weapons courses the past two years. This was taking all my craftsmanship. These swords were supposed to be for our careers as monster hunters after we graduated, but I didn't need one— I had my father's. I wasn't sure what I was going to use this one for once I was done crafting it. A backup, maybe?

I was behind everyone else, but I believed in taking my time with this. I'd wanted to make the sword special and wanted to spend a considerable amount of time carving an intricate design into the metal— a wolf pack running through the woods, on both sides.

Most of the other students hadn't bothered inscribing anything special on their weapons. They'd go out and purchase professional ones after graduation, and leave these at home. But me? I don't know... for some reason, I felt that creating this sword was of grave importance, and it needed to be perfect.

Professor Desmona walked by and observed my work. She put a hand out, and I gave the blade to her. She took in the weapon with an approving nod. "Very good, my prince. This will be a weapon that will stand the test of time."

Professor Desmona was the only teacher on campus who still used my royal title when referring to me— and no way in hell would I challenge her on it like all the others. She'd kick my ass. "Thank you."

I took the sword back and resumed my work. A Marked girl whose sword was curved and bent after she forged it wrong gave me a sour look.

Class ended at five, but I stayed at the forge long past that, until six o'clock. I wasn't satisfied with my work until I knew I was ready to move onto the next step. Professor Desmona was working on forging armor when I passed, but still, her eyes glinted with an approving glaze.

She liked that I put in more time than all the others, but I liked the forge. My blacksmithing skills had proved useful in creating a variety of items, such as my grappling hook that I used when surveying the city as the Phantom.

Also, it took my mind off of things I couldn't control— like the fact that I couldn't protect Emma.

After I was done, I took a shower, then headed downstairs to get some dinner. Emma was in the cafeteria with Delmare, Odette, and Kiara. They were sitting at a table in the corner. All the tables around them were empty, and people avoided being near them like they had the plague.

I got three cabbage rolls and slid into the seat next to Emma. "Rough crowd?"

She glumly played with her pasta. "Everyone thinks I attempted murder."

"Not everyone," Odette piped up. "We're still here with you."

"I'd still hang out with you even if you *did* do it," Delmare added through a full mouth. "Morgan's a jackass."

Emma put her face in her hands. Kiara, who was on her other side of her, put a hand on her shoulder. "Don't worry, Emma. They'll figure out who's really behind this, and everyone will owe you an apology."

"If you think these stuck up pricks are going to apologize, you're in for a rough go of it," Delmare said.

Emma groaned. "I keep getting into trouble. I thought the attacks would stop once I left home."

"You were attacked before you came to Arcanea University?" I asked, shocked.

Emma nodded. "Yes. It was a huge black wolven, no wings. It found me in the woods outside my house, back in Detroit. I managed to kill it with my illusion magic. Lady Magdalina said he was sent by the Black Claw. She promised me I'd be safe here, but I guess not."

This was turning my dinner. Emma had almost been killed once before. But she was all the way in America when the attack happened. Why would someone from the Black Claw want to hurt her? She was an innocent girl that had no ties to any of this. She didn't even know about our world until it was forced on her.

Emma shrugged. "I don't know. Lady Magdalina said that the Black Claw sends out assassins to kill unbonded Marked, so that they'll never mate with their Companions and Malovia will become weaker, and easier to take over."

That sounded like a bunch of bullshit. It would take far too many resources and too much effort for the Black Claw to be interested in taking out unbonded Marked one by one. They had bigger issues to face here. They wanted her for other reasons.

But I didn't want to worry Emma, so I said, "Yeah, maybe."

"Lady Magdalina said you'd bond with someone important," Odette sang. Emma waved at her to try and get her to shut up.

"Did she?" I leaned in closer, curious. How would Lady Magdalina have any idea of that?

Emma nodded. "She did. Lady Magdalina must know the Phantom personally."

I suppressed a groan, but Emma caught my look of disgust. "I see that. I don't care if you don't believe he's my mate. We've been over this."

"One thing I don't get," Kiara said, interrupting me before I could say anything to Emma, "is how this could be happening at Arcanea University. Security is insane here. It has to be, to prevent monsters from getting in. Lady Magdalina is extremely gifted. Her magic is stronger than anyone else's in Malovia."

"Is it?" Emma asked.

"Lady Magdalina is the most powerful sorceress alive," Delmare said. "The Black Claw is rumored to be terrified of her retaliation. Whoever is committing these crimes is either not afraid of her— which is crazy, because that's basically suicide— or they're cocky enough to think that they can get away with it."

"Which probably means that they're right under her nose," Kiara said. "There's no other way they could get away with all of this, unless they were a student or a teacher. Someone Magdalina trusts."

Emma sat in silence for a few moments before she said quietly, "I think it's Lady Korva."

I nearly choked on my food. "Lady Korva?" I asked in disbelief. "What does she have to do with any of this?"

"It's clear she doesn't like me. She accused me of hurting Morgan the moment she got a chance to," Emma pointed out.

"Yes, but what reason would she have for targeting you?" I asked.

The aura around the table became awkward. Odette looked the other way, while Kiara blushed. Emma didn't say anything— just stared at me like it was obvious.

Delmare threw her hands up and blurted out, "Oh gods, Ethan. Lady Korva thinks you're going to pick Emma as your mate for the King's Contest. Fucking duh."

"What?" I stuttered. "That… that's impossible. We could never—"

Emma took my bad cover up as disgust and snapped, "That's okay, I know you'd never pick me, anyway. Lady Korva sees us hang out a lot, so in her twisted mind, she probably figures that you like me."

"Yeah, and if you don't have a mate before the Contest, you can't compete," Odette pointed out. "Lady Korva wants her son to win. So if she takes Emma out, her chances of Elijah obtaining the crown get a whole lot better."

I tried to think quickly as Emma stared me down. To be honest, I still wasn't sure what I was going to do about the King's Contest. Yes, I'd found my mate— but she didn't know, and I wasn't going to reveal that information to her and put her in more danger than she was already in. She wouldn't believe me, anyway. She was so wrapped up in the Phantom fantasy that the only way I could prove to her that we were bonded was to blow my secret identity— and I wasn't about to do that.

At the same time, the Contest was less than two months away. I didn't have time to keep dawdling around with this decision. Either I had to tell Emma we were bonded, or I had to find another girl to take her place.

The thought made me feel like my guts were being ripped out. Another girl couldn't take Emma's place. Not ever. And I didn't want to live my life with any other queen by my side but her.

I was silent for too long, and Emma sneered, "We all know you're going to pick Chastity. Why don't you hurry up and do it?"

"Chastity? My ex?" I said, confused. "I haven't talked to her in weeks."

"She's not going to be your ex for much longer, is she? She's going to be your *queen*," Emma snarled.

"Whoa there, everybody calm down." Delmare extended her arm between me and Emma from across the table. "Just chill."

Emma huffed, and I rolled my eyes. "Okay, fine. Maybe Lady Korva is going after you, because she's worried about the King's Contest and thinks I'm going to choose you, so she wants to make sure I can't compete by taking you out. But that doesn't explain why she'd go after Professor Waldron, or align herself with the Black Claw."

"I don't know. But it's the best explanation I've got." Emma crossed her arms and sank back in her chair. "But I've got no proof. And if Lady Magdalina trusts Lady Korva, then it'd be all too easy for her to sneak around the headmistress's back and commit murder."

"Well… let's find some proof, then," I suggested.

Emma's eyes widened, and she uncrossed her arms. "What do you mean?"

"If you think Korva's hiding something, then she's a threat to all of us. We can't just sit here and allow more people to be mutilated or murdered. She needs to be exposed," I said.

"You mean… you could order a search through Korva's stuff?" Emma asked.

"I could. I am a prince, and I have the authority," I said, before I hesitated. "But if I ordered a search, it'd go public. And if nothing was found that was incriminating, it'd be a huge scandal. It would affect my entry into the King's Contest. I'd prefer we do this a bit more… quietly."

"You guys aren't talking about sneaking into Lady Korva's office!" Kiara squeaked. "That's strictly forbidden!"

"Not her office. She wouldn't keep anything here at school. Too risky," I said. "She'd hide evidence at her house."

"Breaking and entering? I'm in," Delmare said, and a wide grin spread across her face.

"Guys, this is really dangerous," Odette said nervously. "Are you sure you want to go through with this?"

"Of course I do," Emma said, without a moment's hesitation. "Ethan's right. We have to stop this before anyone else gets killed. You guys don't have to follow, but I'm going."

"We're *obviously* going to help," Delmare said, and she wrapped her arms around Kiara and Odette. "Just tell us what you want us to do."

Odette and Kiara both seemed anxious, but neither one of them backed out. I leaned forward, and their heads came inward toward as I began to whisper. "Lady Korva lives on a huge estate on the royal grounds," I said. "It's staffed by guards and servants twenty-four seven, not to mention her husband rarely leaves the estate."

"So how do we get in without being seen?" Emma asked.

"We wait until nightfall, when everyone's asleep. She has an office on the third floor. We can scale the walls and sneak in," I said.

"Or we get the boys to *fly* us up," Odette said, and her eyes glittered.

"Odette, no. The more people we involve, the riskier it is we'll get caught. We can't trust anyone," Delmare said.

"I'm guessing by *the boys* you mean Theo, Stefan, and Alexei?" I asked.

Odette bobbed her head enthusiastically, while Delmare mouthed *no.* I gave it some thought.

"Backup would be nice to have," I admitted. "Just in case we get into trouble. I don't want to drag them into this, but at the same time, I trust them. They can create a distraction that'll make it easier for us to break in."

"Okay, so let's go." Emma got up from the table and started walking. I wolfed down my last cabbage roll and headed after her, while the girls followed.

I wasn't so sure if Lady Korva actually had anything to do with the attacks, but I did know my aunt— she'd do anything to make sure Elijah got that crown. If she hadn't committed the attacks herself, I was at least certain she was involved. Something strange was going on around here.

And tonight, I intended to find out what.

"Are you guys ready for this?" Alexei asked.

We were waiting in the bushes outside of the Zlodia estate. I'd managed to sneak everyone onto royal grounds due to my clearance, but we didn't have long. There were eight of us here. Eventually, someone would notice we were gone from the university and would sound the alarm. Nearly a dozen students missing from their beds on a Thursday night would cause a panic, with how on edge everything was lately. We had to move quickly.

"Ready or not, we've gotta do this," Emma said. "Is everyone good with the plan?"

There were murmurs of agreement around us. I focused on the house. The Zlodia mansion was massive. It was five stories and built in the Baroque style. It boasted elegance and money.

I could see Lady Korva's office from here. It was high in the air, and had dozens of windows. They were locked from the inside. We wouldn't be getting in that way, not unless we broke them.

"So let me get this straight," Theo said. "You want us to create a distraction, while you and the girls walk right into the Zlodia mansion and find… whatever it is you're looking for?"

"That's the plan," I said. I was shocked we'd managed to rope goody-two-shoes Theo into helping us. But all it took was a little begging from Odette, and he'd caved like a house of cards.

"I am very good at creating distractions," Stefan said, and his grin widened. He playfully elbowed Delmare.

"Shut up," she growled. "Can we get moving? I'm freezing my tits off out here."

"Right. Let's go." Me and the girls went one way, while Theo, Alexei and Stefan went the other. When we were directly planted behind the back entrance of the house, we huddled together and waited.

There was a loud *boom*, followed by the sound of an explosion. Glass went flying everywhere as the greenhouse on the other side of the estate exploded into flames. I could barely see the outline of a dragon hovering above, black scales blending in with pitch night.

I rolled my eyes. Stefan certainly couldn't be trusted to be subtle.

Servants and guards came running out of the estate in droves. Theo and Alexei, who were both in their animal forms, hovered at the edge of the burning greenhouse. The guards went to give chase, and the two of them flew off into the forest. The servants massed around the greenhouse and quickly got to work on trying to put the fire out.

"Move." I ran out of the bushes and to the back door. It was locked, but when I rammed myself against it, the door gave way. The girls followed me inside, and we pressed ourselves to the walls as we crept through the shadows, ascending the stairs.

There were giggles behind us from Odette, as well as loud swear words from Delmare every time she accidentally ran into or broke something. So much for not leaving any traces behind that we were here. I should've just done this myself. In, out, done. It would've taken me no more than a few minutes. The girls were quickly proving to me they had no experience doing special-ops. Even worse, I had to leave most of my gear in the hideout so I didn't incriminate myself, so we were doing a lot of this the old-fashioned way.

A sudden light came on in front of us as we were climbing the staircase to the third floor, and I flung out my arm to stop the girls from going forward. "What's this?" I heard Lord Zlodia's sleepy voice ringing throughout the hall above.

"A fire, sir, in the greenhouse," a servant replied. "It's been taken care of. Everything is under control. Go back to sleep."

Lord Zlodia mumbled, but the light turned off and we heard no more from him. The servant above blazed past us— we all held our breath as he passed on the other side of the staircase. I was sure we'd been seen, but it was dark, and the servant was in such a hurry he didn't even notice us glued to the wall. We all breathed a sigh of relief as soon as he was gone.

"Hey, Ethan? What's the penalty for breaking and entering in Malovia?" Emma whispered.

"Into a lord's house, on royal grounds? You don't want to know," I told her.

We reached the third floor. There were so many doors— I wasn't sure which one led to

Korva's office, until Emma strode down the hallway and guessed by peeking her head inside the first door she opened.

"It's clear," she called. We picked up the pace. Emma opened the door and revealed Korva's office. We hurried inside, and I locked the door behind us.

Korva's office was huge and expansive. Dozens of bookcases lined the walls, packed with hundreds of books. A large oak desk with a high-backed chair sat in the middle. The floor was crowded with alchemist vials and various objects useful for enchanting. Cauldrons, jars of ingredients, and strange artifacts littered the ornate rugs. A stuffed raven sat on a perch in the corner. It seemed to watch us with a creepy stare.

It looked more like a library than an office. By the Seven Gods, there was a lot of crap in here. It could take hours to go through. We didn't have that kind of time. I was glad we'd brought five people to search.

"Start looking," I said. We scrambled to comb through the stuff. I gently sorted through the items, starting with the books that looked like they'd been read recently. "Try not to make it look like anything's been—"

There was the crashing sound of a vial behind me. Odette stood above a smashed collection of glass, raising her hands in an apology.

I sucked in an irritated breath. "Touched."

Fifteen minutes passed. We went through as much as we could, but everything we came across was either mundane or unimportant. Maybe we'd been wrong and Lady Korva had nothing to do with the attacks. If that was true, we needed to get out of here. Before we got caught.

"Hey, guys. Look at this." Emma stood behind the oak desk. "I found it in a secret compartment underneath the drawer."

In her hands was a necklace. The chain was made of black lace, an obsidian medallion in an oval shape dangling from it. She held it out to us, and I took a step back.

That medallion seemed like it was sucking me in. A rotten feeling emanated from it, twisting my innards and siphoning all the air out of the room. It was like I could hear an eerie chant humming from the object— something grotesque and foreboding. Emma took a step forward, and I cringed. I wanted her to get that necklace the hell away from me.

Kiara put a hand to her throat. "That's Unseelie magic," she whispered.

"Put it back," Odette hissed, clinging to Delmare.

Emma ignored her. She held it up to me to see. "Will this be enough to prove Korva's a murderer?"

I shook my head. "No. And if it was, you've just put your fingerprints all over it."

Emma scowled. "Well, I'm not leaving here empty-handed."

She pocketed the necklace. There was a tap on the glass outside, and we jumped.

Alexei and Theo had lost the guards. They were hovering by one of the large picture windows. We unlocked it, and pushed it open. Theo asked, *"What did you find?"*

"Tell you in a minute," I said. I opened the window wider. I helped Kiara onto Alexei's back, and Odette onto Theo's.

Stefan was sitting on the roof. He curled his neck over and poked his head into the room. *"Hop on, babycakes. I'll give you a ride,"* he said to Delmare.

"As if." She pushed his head away and got onto Theo's back, behind Odette. I helped Emma clamber onto Stefan's head, then pulled myself onto the dragon behind her. I made sure to close the window behind me before we took off.

Theo, Alexei and Stefan flew us above the royal grounds so there'd be a better chance we wouldn't be spotted. After we'd touched down in the woods outside Arcanea University, the five of us put our feet back on the ground while Theo, Alexei and Stefan changed back.

"So? Did you guys find *anything* in there?" Stefan asked.

The girls glumly shook their heads, and I added, "Not anything that proves Lady Korva has something to do with the attacks."

"Great." Theo sighed. "I risked getting arrested for no good reason."

"Oh, it was an adventure, anyway!" Odette said optimistically. "And so fun, too."

We began the long walk back to the university. "Well, that was for nothing," Delmare said in defeat. "Looks like Lady Korva can continue her killing spree in peace."

"Not for nothing. We found this." Emma showed her the obsidian necklace. "Kiara's right. It's definitely dark magic. I can feel it."

"Yeah, but not enough to prove Korva's got any sinister motives. Possessing an object from the Unseelie isn't even a felony. It's a minor offense," Kiara stated.

"Depends on how powerful it is," I said. "But Lady Korva could just buy her way out of a sentence like that, anyway."

"Doesn't matter. I don't think something like this should be in Korva's hands," Emma finished. She placed it back inside her pocket.

There were muted murmurs of agreement. I kept quiet, but secretly, I had a bad feeling that necklace shouldn't be in Emma's hands, either.

SIXTEEN

"Pick up the pace, ladies! This is basic magic!" Lady Korva barked at the head of the classroom.

Illusion was still proving to be my least favorite class. Today, we were learning how to transfigure our appearance. Beside me, Kiara scrunched up her nose. She turned her hair pink, then blue, then back to black again.

I tried to make my hair purple, but only the roots changed. I checked the mirror on my desk again to see if I'd managed to make my freckles disappear, but no go.

Lady Korva stalked around the room in a mood more sour than usual, which was entirely impressive— even for her. She'd been in a bad way for days. She obviously hated that her necklace had turned up missing, but no reports of a break-in at the Zlodia mansion had been reported, nor had there been any gossip on the grapevine that a thief had taken something from Lady Korva. It confirmed my suspicions that the necklace was something she wanted to hide.

I didn't want to get rid of the necklace. Ethan had already assured me something powerful like that couldn't be destroyed by students at our level, and I didn't know or trust any other sorceress to ask them to destroy it for me. Lady Magdalina could, I was sure, but then she'd question where I got it, and I wasn't sure if I'd be in trouble when I revealed that I'd stolen it from Lady Korva.

I worried if I tried to get rid of that someone else would find it, and we'd end up in a worse situation later on. So I threw it into a dresser in my dorm and tried to forget about it, though the necklace was still at the back of my mind.

Across the room, Gabby was working on shrinking her nose. She'd accomplished making it a smaller size. Beside her, Morgan worked on making her boobs larger. They were so ridiculously big that they seemed comical on her small frame. Beside her, Melissa attempted shrinking a few pounds off her figure. It didn't work, and she frowned as she looked into the mirror.

"Changing your appearance is vital when blending into a crowd," Korva announced. "The illusion won't last forever, but a skilled sorceress will be able to keep up a disguise for at least the span of a few hours— if not days."

Morgan waggled her huge boobs at Gabby. Gabby rolled her eyes and leaned closer to the mirror, continuing to change her nose to find one she liked.

"Plastic surgery is way cheaper when you're an Arcanea," I said to Kiara.

"Wouldn't you change yourself if you could?" she asked. Kiara changed her skin so that it was one even dark color instead of differently-toned.

"No," I said. "I like the way I am." What I wanted to change about myself, magic couldn't fix. There was no spell alive that could cure my disease.

"I think I look better this way." Kiara turned to me. She was searching for approval, but I wouldn't give it. She was beautiful the way she was. She didn't need to go changing herself.

"I don't like it," I said. "You don't look like you."

"No. I look normal." Kiara lifted the spell, and the patches on her face reappeared. She sighed. "Too bad it doesn't last forever."

I successfully managed to turn a streak of my hair purple by the time class ended, but that was as far as I could go. I left it in as I walked down the hallway to my Monarchy class, passing by the Observatory as I went.

Odette came bouncing to my side. "Did you hear?" she squealed, appearing like an excited, frantic puppy.

"What is it?" I asked, wondering what could possibly provoke Odette into this kind of excitement— besides literally everything.

"Gabby just bonded yesterday. With *Eli*," Odette whispered.

"What the fuck?" I looked ahead. Gabby had left class before me and was cuddling up to a brawny dude at the end of the hall. He had hooded eyes and was kissing Gabby for the entire hall to see, as if bragging that he'd found a mate.

I knew him. Elijah Zlodia. He wasn't in any of my classes, but it was no secret he and Ethan didn't get along. He was Lady Korva's son.

"Oh, that's not good." Kiara narrowed her eyes. "He's definitely going to compete in the King's Contest now."

My eyes caught Ethan's form stomping down the hallway. He had a book at his side, his knuckles white as he crushed the spine between his fingers.

I went to speak. "Ethan, did you—"

"I heard." Ethan's tone was dark, and his face was shadowed. He was obviously pissed that Elijah had bonded. He refused to look at either of them as they continued making out along the wall.

His eyes briefly scanned me as he passed. The look in them… it was as if he was trying to make up his mind on an impossible decision.

Once Ethan was out of earshot, Kiara said, "Ethan better hurry up. Time's running short. If he doesn't pick a mate soon, they won't let him into the Contest."

"Yes, but how can you possibly pick a mate if you're not bonded? How do you know you're making the right decision?" I said.

"He doesn't have time to dawdle. If he wants to be king, he has to make up his mind," Kiara pointed out. "The ball's only a few weeks away."

"Ball?" I asked.

"The King's Ball. It's a party before the King's Contest begins," Odette clarified. "Everyone who's anyone will be there. Each competitor has to announce their mating bond to the entire city, as well as declare their allegiance to a certain god or goddess at the Choosing before the party begins. It's there that all potential queens are presented."

"Thank the gods I'm not participating." I'd go to the dance, but no way would I want to be shown off to all the Arcanea like some sort of trophy.

"Well, Gabby is," Kiara said with a sigh. "Here's betting she'll do nothing but go on and on for the next few weeks on how *she's* going to have the best dress."

"Yeah, well, maybe she'll decide on a nose by then." I checked my watch. "We'd better hurry, guys. Class is starting in a few minutes."

The three of us had to jog to make it to class on time. Introducing the Monarchy was held in a large classroom that had high ceilings about fifty feet tall, and arched windows along the stone walls. Most of the class was here already, and was a mixture of both Marked and Companions.

"What took you guys so long?" Delmare asked as we slid into our seats near her desk.

"Busy talking about Gabby and her prince charming," I said scathingly.

"Oh, yeah. Zlodia's a real prick." Delmare pointed to her mouth and pretended to gag before a sly smile lit up her face. "Good thing you'll give Gabby a run for her money, huh Em?"

"What?" I let my textbook fall open with a *flop*. "Hell no. You're not suggesting what I think you are."

"That Ethan's going to pick you as his mate for the Contest? Obviously," Kiara said.

I made a skeptical sound. "In your dreams."

"Or in yours," Odette piped up, and Kiara giggled.

"Oh, don't bullshit us, Emma. That boy has the total hots for you," Delmare said. "Ethan's definitely got some nasty sex fantasies when it comes to you and him."

"Don't make me barf." I shook my head. "Really, you guys are hilarious. Ethan and I are *just friends*. If we were anything more, we would've bonded by now, and nothing's happened."

"Doesn't matter. Bonded or not, Ethan has to pick *someone*, and you're the only girl he likes," Odette sang.

"Bonding doesn't work that way, anyway. It takes time, and is permanently forged by a decision. He has to ask, and you have to accept," Kiara said. "Who's to say he *won't* pick you?"

"Don't you want to be a princess?" Odette squealed.

I went to bite back, but Lord Lucien walked to the head of the classroom, and the conversation died down. As he gathered his papers, Delmare showed me a quick stick-figure drawing she'd done. It was obviously supposed to be me and Ethan in a very sexual position.

"Fuck off," I whispered, and I threw my pencil at her.

"You guys are totally gonna *do it*," she hushed back, before Lord Lucien started writing on the chalkboard. All fell silent as he turned around.

"Modern Malovian history," he began. "For the majority of this semester, we've been focusing on studying great kings and queens of the past— those who have led Malovia to become the great country it is today. However, today we're going to focus on something a little different. In light of our nation's recent loss, I believe that this class would be best spent focusing on the accomplishments of King Lycus Nowak."

A few hushed whispers broke out. I immediately became interested. Nobody talked about Ethan's dad. It wasn't exactly forbidden, but everyone seemed more or less scared to bring him up— as if they'd raise a ghost.

Lucien raised his hand. A spell sprung forth from it. Fog filtered out of his fingertips and created a circular sphere. Within the sphere came the likeness of a man— early fifties or so, a gray beard and long gray hair disguising soft wrinkles.

He looked ridiculously noble, like a king should. I didn't find many traits in him that were Ethan's except his amber eyes. Ethan must look like his mother.

"King Lycus took the throne nearly thirty years ago, during very dark times for our country," Lucien began. "Ten years after his reign began, there was an uprising in Dolinska like none had ever seen before. The Black Claw extremist group had gotten out of hand. Their numbers ranked in the thousands. It was a very real fear among the Arcanea that they would take over the city— even the monarchy, and eventually, the country."

Lucien waved his hand, and the fog changed to reveal an image of Dolinska burning. Black Claw tributes moved throughout the streets, killing any who got in their way. Some Arcanea ran— some chose to fight. Bodies began piling up on the streets, and blood poured down the cobblestone from all the fallen Marked and Companions. The skies darkened with clouds of black smoke that rose from the burning buildings. It was like watching an incredibly gory movie, except a knot formed in my throat when I realized that this wasn't fiction. What was happening before us had been real.

"The scene you see is from my own memory," Lucien said. "Eighteen years ago, there was a crisis in Dolinska unlike any other. We called this day *Palennoc*, otherwise known as the Night of Burning Skies. Thousands of Arcanea perished on this night. The Black Claw swarmed into the city and began slaughtering thousands in a sacrifice to the dark god Droga. It is only due to the work of King Lycus that the Black Claw are no longer here today."

My eyebrows scrunched together, confused. Lucien was talking like King Lycus had eliminated the Black Claw altogether. That might've been true, for a time, but they were back now. Certainly not in as great of numbers as before, but they were still lurking around.

"King Lycus gathered the greatest of the Arcanea warriors and led an attack on the Black Claw," Lucien said. "There was a great battle in the city square. Both sides suffered heavy losses, but in the end, King Lycus was able to kill or otherwise eliminate those within the Black Claw's ranks. Those who fled the country were found later and executed."

Images of Lycus' funeral popped up within the fog. I immediately spotted Ethan among the crowd, sitting in a wheelchair. Ethan must've not had his prosthetic yet. A woman stood behind him, her hands on his shoulders. I took her as the queen.

Ethan's face looked so hollow. It was clear he blamed himself. I wanted to reach through the fog and touch him— bring him some sort of comfort. It was horrible seeing him like that. It carved a pit in me that I didn't know existed. That pit went far down, to a place where it was so dark I was sure the sorrow never ended.

"King Lycus was one of our country's greatest protectors. He eliminated a huge threat to our kind and ensured our race would have a future in the world we inhabit," Lucien said. "Whosoever succeeds him by winning the throne in this year's King's Contest will have high expectations placed on their shoulders."

The funeral scenes changed, and the fog dissipated. Delmare raised a hand. Lucien pointed at her. "Yes, Miss Delmare?"

She leaned forward. "I heard that there's more to the story. That the Black Claw was looking for someone that night."

Lucien seemed slightly uncomfortable. "There is an old legend. A rumor. But it's never been confirmed, and this is a history class. I prefer to tell facts over fiction."

"Myths and legends can be history. They're part of our lore," Odette said. There were murmurs of agreement around the room, and everyone gave the professor a curious stare.

Lucien sighed. "Very well. If you insist."

He put his hands behind his back and began walking around the room slowly. "As you all know, the Black Claw worship Droga. There is a very old story among them that Tomir, the King of the Gods, and Droga, his brother, waged war for possession of our home world, Edinmyre, and that is why the fae came to live on Earth amongst humans. During the war, Tomir ended Droga, and brought him to Earth, imprisoning him in a stone grave somewhere in Malovia."

Lucien paused, as if considering how much to reveal. "Prophecy is considered a dark art by

Arcanea, gifted by evil forces to Black Claw tributes wishing to foretell the future. The… *prophecy* goes that there is one whose blood can bring Droga back to life, and release him from his tomb prison. There is no other explanation of who this person may be, except that they will be known as the Worldweaver."

I felt the color drain from my face immediately. The entire room turned cold, and my hands started to shake. I pulled them underneath my desk and bunched them in my skirt to hide it.

"Whosoever kills the Worldweaver and brings their blood to Droga's throne will receive great power from Droga, after he is resurrected," Lucien explained. "From then on, the Dark God will rule over this world. He will gather an army to challenge his brother Tomir once again in Edinmyre's lands. It is said that the Black Claw were looking for the Worldweaver on *Palennoc*, to find them and sacrifice them to the Dark God."

I had to take deep breaths to prevent myself from throwing up. Delmare raised her hand and said, "That means that the Worldweaver is still alive, right?"

Lucien shrugged. "It is merely a story, fabricated by fanatics. If someone with extraordinary magical power beyond normal Arcanean capabilities existed within our ranks, they certainly would've been found out years ago."

The class uttered mumbles of agreement. I popped right up from my desk. "Lord Lucien, may I be excused? I'm not feeling well."

Lucien's mouth hung open for a moment. "You… are looking a little green, Miss Sosna."

"Thank you." I gathered my things and ran out of the room. Everyone turned in their seats to look at me as I hurried past.

I spent five minutes in the bathroom, heaving. Nothing came up, but I still felt sick.

The Black Claw was after me. Somehow, someway, they knew I was the Worldweaver— or at least, they suspected. That's why someone was waiting in my dorm room that night. They wanted my blood so they could resurrect the Dark God and be bestowed with magic beyond imagining.

I brushed my hair back and leaned against the stall wall. I needed someone to talk to about this. I couldn't carry this on my own.

But the only other person who knew that I was the Worldweaver besides myself (and the Black Claw, obviously) was Ethan.

I got up and headed back to my dorm. I couldn't talk to Ethan right now. He was in Master Forging Class, and that didn't end until at least five. I'd have to wait.

I wasn't able to do anything but curl up on my bed and stare at the wall for the next hour and a half. When it was five, I headed down to the forges outside the school. They were empty — the only person still working there was Ethan.

He looked pretty hot, all dirty and covered in black soot, but now wasn't the time for all of that. I had bigger issues than getting my rocks off. Mostly, staying alive.

"Ethan!" I cried out as I jogged toward his forge. "I need to talk to you!"

Ethan jumped when he heard me coming. He quickly went to cover something up. His movements were hasty and suspicious. It was like he was trying to hide something from me.

"What are you working on?" I asked curiously as I approached.

"It's nothing," Ethan said quickly. He threw a leather blanket over whatever he'd been forging and said, "What did you need to talk about?"

I took a deep breath, but no words came out. Ethan put a hand on my elbow. "Emma, you're shaking. Let's go sit down."

He guided me to a stone bench nearby. I took a few gulps of air before I blurted out, "They're after me."

"Who's after you?" Ethan's eyebrows knitted together in confusion.

"The Black Claw. Lucien told me. I mean, he didn't *know* that he told me, but I figured it out," I scrambled to say.

"Whoa, slow down. Explain everything," he said slowly. He took my hands in his. Somehow, the touch of his rough skin against mine made me calm down.

"I was in history class, and Lucien told us this story. A prophecy, really. During the Night of Burning Skies eighteen years ago, the Black Claw was looking for someone whose blood can raise the Dark God from the dead. He said that the Worldweaver is the only one who can resurrect Droga. That's me."

Ethan's expression paled a little, but otherwise, he didn't react. "I know of the story, but never heard that the Worldweaver is the one who can raise Droga from the dead. I hadn't heard that name since the hag told it to us. Emma, are you sure Lucien didn't get his facts mixed up or something?"

My mouth dropped open. "You don't believe me."

"No, I didn't say that," Ethan said. "But I don't want you to jump to conclusions. How does Lucien know what the Worldweaver is, anyway? Isn't this all a little weird to you?"

I wanted to hit him. How could he be so naive? This explained so much about what was happening lately. How could Ethan sit there and try to be optimistic about something that was so obviously true? I needed his help! I needed him to help me come up with a plan. I didn't want to ignore the truth and pretend like everything was okay, when really, I was in danger of losing my life.

Then I realized that this went beyond what I'd learned today. I realized that I was mad at Ethan. And had been ever since I saw Gabby kiss Eli this morning. It didn't make sense— I just was. And his denial about me being the Worldweaver was pushing me over the edge.

I popped up from the bench so quickly I was surprised I didn't get whiplash. "When are you going to get it through your head that all of this is *real*?" I snapped. "The Black Claw wants my blood, and they'll kill me to get it. I'm the Worldweaver, whatever that means, and I need you to help me deal with it!"

"I don't *want* to think that way, Emma. I want you to be safe," Ethan said firmly.

"It doesn't matter what you want! Facts are facts!" I shouted. "Living in denial isn't going to help when the wolves come knocking at your door! They're after me. You just can't admit it."

"Emma, calm down. We can work something out," Ethan said as he rose to his feet beside me.

I shoved him back, hard. "Screw you! If you're not going to help me figure out a way to stay alive when these psychos are clearly looking for a way to kill me, then I don't need you."

I whirled around and headed for the tree line on the border of the academy grounds. Ethan took a step after me. "Emma, wait—"

"Leave me alone! I need a break." I headed into the woods as twilight fell. Thankfully, Ethan kept his distance and didn't follow.

I knew not to head too far into the woods. There were monsters out here, though I wondered if getting eaten by one of them would be a better option than allowing the Black Claw to use my blood to bring an evil god back from the dead.

I walked until I hit a stream. Then I kicked a tree and let out an angry yell. This was impossible. Ethan was being such a douche. Why couldn't he just face reality?

I sat by the edge of the stream and put my head in my hands for a moment. I felt exhausted. All this stress was only making my condition worse. The little amount of energy that I had each day was being sucked up by all this fear. I didn't know if I could make the walk back to the school without passing out. Shit, maybe I *should've* let Ethan follow me.

I sighed. I stared down at the rushing water and wondered if there was a way out of this.

The thing was, I wasn't even that scared of the Black Claw. Or dying, really. I'd come to terms with that when I got my diagnosis.

I was afraid of living in fear. Of constantly having to be on guard and looking over my shoulder. That was far worse than anything the Black Claw could do to me. I didn't want to be afraid to live.

"I just want to be brave," I whispered.

Slowly, I stood up. The world wavered a little, and the ground beneath me shook, though it had everything to do with me and not the earth. I put a hand on the same trunk I'd kicked to steady myself, took a few deep breaths, and turned around to head back.

My jaw dropped open as I witnessed an incredible sight before me. A deer stood directly ahead, in the middle of the woods. Intuitively, I knew it was a female. She had white fur that was purer than freshly fallen snow, and winding golden antlers that sprouted out of her head like tree branches. The antlers grew tiny emerald leaves, and there were dozens of points, twisting together to make a complicated mess of root-like art. The doe had a small, dished face, and a golden mane around her ears and head. Her cloven hooves were made of pure silver, and the air shimmered around her, as if sparkling. Butterflies and birds hovered around her form, landing upon the collection of antlers. She was huge— nearly the size of a small elephant. Though the sun had set by now and it was supposed to be dark, the entire forest was lit up with golden light. The dead trees and grass grew new green shoots, like we were in the middle of spring and not late fall.

Great, now I was hallucinating. But this seemed entirely real. When I breathed, the air felt cleaner, more new. The doe took a step toward me, and I stumbled backward into the stream.

Do not be afraid. Do you know who I am? the doe asked. Her voice was like silk gliding across skin, or the taste of warm honey on a cold winter's night. It was motherly and friendly and home. I wanted to sink into it.

I shook my head quickly. I'd lost the ability to speak.

I am Milonna, the goddess of your foremothers. I am the White Doe of Peace, good death, fertility, romance, and love, she spoke gently. *I am here to guide you on your quest, Worldweaver. It was I who sent the hag to you, to foretell the prophecy.*

I slowly came out of the water. "Why… why are you here, goddess?"

To tell you that I have chosen you as my champion. She blinked her eyes, and her long eyelashes fluttered.

"Me?" I gaped. "Why would you want me? I'm sick. I can barely do magic. You should choose someone else."

Do not question why. The Dark God is coming, to ravage souls and destroy the world of the Arcanea. Only you can stop this, Milonna said firmly.

"What do you want me to do?" I asked in a stuttering voice. Finally, some direction.

The answers will come in time. But more important is the journey, she replied. *Know that when you are at your greatest need, I shall be there to show the way.*

I swallowed. "The Black Claw wants to kill me. I'm afraid."

It is they who should be afraid of you, for I have bestowed in you a power even the gods fear, Milonna spoke.

She took a few steps toward me. I did not dare to move. Milonna stretched out her muzzle, and the tip of her velvet nose brushed against my fingers. A white light glowed from my hand as she drew away. As it dimmed I felt a powerful and strong warmth hum throughout my soul.

Go, now. Those who seek your life shall not claim it until the proper time, Milonna said. *And do not be afraid, for I walk beside you, Worldweaver. Now until the ending dawn.*

Milonna faded away before my very eyes. With it, she took the daylight and the spring, until I was left shivering in the cold darkness once again.

Something inside me had changed. I could feel it. I wasn't as afraid as I once was.

Courage was building up inside me and growing stronger with every passing second. I had Milonna to protect me. She had chosen me as her champion. I didn't know why, but it had to be for a reason. She was the goddess of my foremothers, and had chosen *me*, an outsider, over all other Arcanea to save the country. She wouldn't have come to me unless whatever she had planned for me was of vital importance.

And whatever she'd ask of me, I'd follow. No matter the consequences.

SEVENTEEN

It was the end of November. The King's Contest was two weeks away, and I still hadn't declared a mate.

I didn't know what to do. I was stuck. The crown, or Emma? An unbearable decision.

Elijah hadn't stopped gloating since he'd bonded with Gabby. Every day in class he smirked at me, like he'd already won. I'd had enough of his ridiculous behavior and wanted to smack the smug look off his face. Couldn't wait for my chance during the King's Contest.

If I ever got there. I didn't have any more time. It was now or never. Time to make a decision.

I stood outside Emma's enchanting class and waited for her to emerge. She'd ignored me in Monster Hunting class the day before and was obviously still mad about our argument.

It wasn't that I didn't *believe* her about being the Worldweaver. That wasn't it at all. If anything, I believed her wholeheartedly. If her blood could bring back the Dark God, then she was in a lot more danger than I thought. I just didn't want to accept that she could be at risk. It was painful to consider that she might be the one thing the Black Claw needed to regain power.

When Emma came out of class, she immediately went to go the other way. But I hurried to catch up with her. "Emma! Emma, I need to talk to you!"

She rolled her eyes. "Not now, Ethan."

"Would you slow down and let me speak?" I grabbed her arm, forcing her to a halt. She turned around and narrowed her eyes, giving me a fierce glare that shook me to my core.

Damn, it turned me on when she looked at me that way. I pushed aside the fantasies in my head and got straight to the point. "I'm sorry about the other day. You're right, I wasn't listening to you. And maybe I am living in denial."

"You didn't even want to hear it," she snapped.

"I know. And that's wrong, but did you ever stop to think it's because I care about you?" I asked.

Emma tilted her head. She seemed… surprised. "If you care so much, why don't you help me figure out a plan instead of running away from the obvious?"

"How are we supposed to *plan* this, Emma? We don't even know what we're up against." I leaned inward and dropped the level of my voice. "Look, it's pretty clear that you *are* the

Worldweaver. I get that. And the Black Claw may be after your blood. But if we don't have information, there's nothing we can do except keep you safe and try to investigate as we go."

She gave an impatient huff. "I know you're right."

"Always am." I elbowed her playfully, and she shoved me away.

"I'm still mad at you," she said. "You've been acting weird ever since Eli bonded, and I hate it."

"I know I've been a grumpy asshole. Can I make it up to you?" I asked. "We could go out tonight."

She raised her eyebrow. "Are you asking me on a date?"

My stomach flip-flopped. "Do you want it to be a date?"

She peered at me suspiciously, and said, "Let's go. Where are you taking me?"

I put my arm around her shoulders. "Wherever your heart desires, my lady."

She stared out the window. Outside, the snow was falling in thick, heavy chunks. In the gardens, the pond had completely frozen over. I smiled slightly. "I think I have an idea."

We headed back to our dorms and changed out of our uniforms. I grabbed my skates, and she grabbed hers. She came out of her dorm wearing a thick woolen sweater, skinny jeans, a knitted hat... and Gods, leg warmers. Leg warmers were *so* sexy.

"You're just going to wear your hockey jersey? Aren't you going to be cold?" she asked.

I shook my head. "Companions run pretty hot even in the most frigid of conditions."

"Hm." She cocked a slight grin. "The better to keep me warm, then."

I liked that. I took her gloved hand in mine and said, "We should hurry up. Before it gets dark."

She squeezed her hand in mine. I liked how it felt— like there was no other person I'd rather have by my side right now than her.

When we got to the pond, we sat on a fallen log and slipped on our skates. My one skate was specially made to fit my prosthetic. It wasn't much more than a blade that fastened onto the prosthetic, in the area where the foot would be. I could interchange the foot and the blade so I didn't need to remove the whole prosthetic in order to skate. It'd had a nice price tag, that was for sure. I thanked the gods I was a prince and could afford it. I couldn't imagine if I was poor and didn't have the money to pay for a specialized prosthetic so I could skate again. If I couldn't play hockey, I think I'd wither up inside.

As I fastened on the blade, Emma glanced over in interest before she ducked her head. She wanted to see how it worked, yet desired to give me privacy.

I wanted to show her. But at the same time, I wasn't ready. So I just fastened the skate onto the prosthetic and tested out the pond before I skated onto it. I gestured for her that it was safe to follow.

Emma carefully stepped out onto the pond. Once her blades hit the ice, she grinned. She instantly took off, though not as fast as she did on a clean surface. The pond was rough, unlike the rink's even edge. Still, she did jumps and spins like it was absolutely no effort for her whatsoever.

She was so beautiful on the ice. I loved watching her. It was so clear that skating was where she was meant to be.

I skated toward her and extended my arms. She didn't see me coming as I wrapped my arms around her waist, picking her off the ice and spinning her around. Emma laughed as I lifted her upwards, carrying her around the pond in my arms.

"Put me down, asshole." She slapped my chest and laughed again.

"Not so fast." I spun a few circles before I let her back down. I took her hand, and she twirled in a circle underneath it, like some kind of fairy tale princess.

The snow was so dense. It made a veil in Emma's red hair and coated her eyelashes as it came down. She leaned back and caught them with her open mouth, giggling.

"Watch this." I lifted my hand. My magic began to form an illusion. The snowflakes falling in the air formed together into figures. All around us, hundreds of ice dancers made of snow took form on the pond's surface. Snow men and women danced in each other's arms, performed lifts and twists on blades that were made of ice just like the pond's surface. Emma's mouth opened in wonder as the skating couples twirled and leapt around us in a dazzling display.

I took Emma in my arms and began to copy them. We spun together, my arm wrapped around her waist, her hand in mine as we made our way around the pond, whirling with the snow dancers.

"You know how to ice dance?" Emma asked in surprise.

"A bit. I took a few figure skating classes. In Malovia, it's required for all hockey players. Teaches you to have better balance and to skate faster," I told her.

"The hockey players back home think figure skating's for girls," Emma remarked.

"That's because they're wimps. Figure skating is a very difficult sport. Why do you think I chose hockey?" I laughed.

"Probably because you like hitting people," she suggested.

"You got me there." I let her go and changed into a wolven. I backed up several feet, then ran at her full-speed and pushed my head into the small of her back. I picked up the pace, my nails digging into the ice, and Emma squealed as she glided ahead of me. I ran until we were going circles around the pond, the trees flying by in a blur. We blasted through the ice dancers sending them exploding into nothing more than snow dust.

As I slowed to a walk, Emma turned in place. She took my face in her hands and said, "I'm so glad I've finally found someone who likes being on the ice as much as I do."

I stared up at her. She appeared radiant. This was her element. Nothing bad could touch her here, it seemed. Nothing bad could touch *us*. It was like we were in our own little world when were were on ice.

I changed back into a human, and we skated around for an hour or so before Emma started to get tired. I noticed she was almost panting as she performed spins and jumps. We held hands as we lapped the pond a few times, but at this point, I was pretty much pulling her along instead of her doing the gliding. What was wrong with her?

"We should get off," I said. Emma's efforts to stroke around the pond had gotten considerably weaker in the last fifteen minutes or so.

"Get yourself off, then. I'm not horny," she said between gasps. Her joke fell flat amongst my concern.

"Emma, that's not what I meant. You look exhausted," I said.

I thought I was going to have to drag her off the ice, but Emma obliged me and skated toward the edge of the pond. We sat on the log and took off our skates. The wind had picked up, and the snow was falling faster than before.

"Do you mind if I ask a question?" Emma asked tentatively as we unlaced our skates. I unfastened the blade on my prosthetic and reattached the foot in its place.

"Go ahead. I'm an open book," I said.

Emma hesitated, before she asked, "When you lost your leg, was it hard to learn to skate again? Or did it come easy to you?"

I thought about it for a moment. No one had ever asked me that question before. "I don't know," I said honestly. "There were so many things I had to relearn when I lost my leg. Walking. Running. Fighting. Even regaining my balance. It was hard stepping back out on the ice, at first. I didn't think I'd ever play hockey again."

I looked up at the sky. "But honestly, I think hockey helped me to learn *how* to walk again, instead of making it harder. Being on the ice has always made me feel so secure. Skating with my prosthetic was like learning a new skill— like shooting pucks, or running defense. I don't remember learning to walk, but I remember my first time on the ice with a hockey stick. I was able to relate to it far easier."

She nodded. "That makes sense."

Emma was quiet for a moment. I wondered what was on her mind before a chilly wind swept by and caused her to shiver. What had turned into a heavy snowfall was now becoming a full-on snowstorm. Emma shielded her eyes from the torrent of snow as I got to my feet. I couldn't even see the school through the thick snowfall that was enveloping the school gardens.

"There's a cottage on campus that's not too far from here. It's closer than the main campus. We should go there and wait the storm out," I said.

"Fine by me." Emma put her skates and mine into my hockey bag, then flung it on her back. I transformed into a wolven.

"*Hop on. We'll get there faster,*" I said.

Emma paused, and I added, "*Unless you want to freeze.*"

Slowly, she grabbed my scruff. I knelt down so she could hoist herself onto my back. She sat comfortably behind my shoulder blades. Emma rubbed her gloved hands up and down my fur, and I resisted quivering. That felt really good.

"*Hold on tight, so you don't fall off,*" I said. I crouched down in the snow and bounded forward. Emma startled on my back, then I felt her hands dig into my fur as I started racing through the snow. She flattened herself onto my form, her legs clinging to my sides. I felt her body move with mine as I raced across the gardens.

I didn't have to adjust my strides, or slow down, or worry she would fall. She sat upon my back easily and rode upon my form like she'd been meant to do it her entire life.

And it made me feel lonely. This was how Marked and Companions should be. Always together, as one. Yet Emma and I could never be.

The snow was getting in my eyes and making it hard to see. Thankfully, the outline of the cottage came into view. I skidded to a stop in front of the door, and Emma swung off my back. I changed into a human and opened up the door. Once we were inside, Emma let the skate bag fall to the floor, and I immediately worked on getting a fire going in the fireplace. It sprung to life. A warm glow overtook the entire room. The cottage was small, no more than a kitchenette, a couch, a few armchairs and a double bed, but it was cozy— and far better than getting caught out in the cold.

"What's this cottage even here for?" Emma asked.

"The groundskeeper used to live here, but he died a few years back. The new one lives in Dolinska, so this place has been sitting empty for awhile. The school keeps the electricity and water running to it, in case one of the staff needs a place to stay," I explained.

I walked across the room and reached inside the refrigerator to pull out champagne and seafood. I grabbed a couple of boxes of pasta from the cupboards. "Surprise. I'm making you dinner. Scallop puttanesca."

She gave me a sly grin. "Ethan Nowak, you planned to bring me here."

"Maybe I did. Is that a crime?" I asked.

"I bet that snowstorm outside isn't even real. It's probably an illusion." Emma crossed her arms.

"Actually, it's not. I couldn't conjure up something like that, anyway. Just a well-timed act of fate." I smiled at her.

I filled up a pot with water to boil and worked on preparing the scallops. I got two glasses down from the cupboard and popped the champagne, pouring a glass. I handed one to her. She took it and looked around. "So… how many people come to fuck in this cottage?"

I chuckled. "About as many as you'd expect. It *is* an empty cottage on a college campus, after all."

"Uh-huh. And how many girls have *you* brought in here?"

"None," I said honestly. "I haven't screwed around with anyone."

She came into the kitchen as I mixed olive oil and lemon juice together. "Seriously? I thought you'd have been with hundreds of girls by now."

I shook my head. "Arcanea are supposed to save themselves for their mates. But not everyone does. I wasn't very interested in girls growing up, I suppose." I began chopping cherry tomatoes and black olives in half.

"What about you and Chastity?" Emma challenged.

I put the knife down in thought. "Chastity was a formality."

"That sounds romantic." Emma snorted.

"You don't understand. Growing up, people expected me to be with *someone*. I was a prince. I was expected to find a mate so I could succeed the throne when the time came. Then years passed, and I never did." I shrugged as I cooked. "Chastity was who my mother wanted. She was an easy choice."

"But you never loved her."

"I *cared* about her. But I never felt anything for her." I put the scallops on to simmer. "I was guilty about it forever, because I knew she was in love with me. But I knew I could never give her what she really wanted. She was the one who broke it off with me. She got tired of waiting, I think."

"Well, being in a relationship with someone who doesn't love you back can't be easy," she said.

"It's better to be single than to be with the wrong person. Arcanea know that," I said.

As the water boiled, I added the pasta. Emma was being quiet. She stared into the fireplace. I could see her mind was working overtime. I longed to know what was going through her head.

"What about you?" I asked. "Was there anyone you liked growing up?"

She shook her head. "No. Like you, I had no interest. Skating was everything to me. I knew I needed to focus on that and have my career come first."

She scoffed. "Not like anyone wanted me, anyway."

"What do you mean?" I leaned against the counter. Emma's eyes roamed up and down my body. Was she checking me out?

"I never really fit in, at school or anywhere else. I was too abrasive," she admitted. "People thought I was weird, so I kept to myself. And I liked it that way. Mostly. It was hard when I was a kid, being without friends, but by the time I got to high school I stopped caring. It was easier to be alone than it was to try and make friends. People were scared of me."

"But you can't tell me no guys were interested in you. You're too pretty," I objected.

She gave a small smile. "Thanks. If they were, I never knew it. Guys are intimidated by women who speak their mind, and, well… you know I can't keep my mouth shut."

I chuckled. "Yeah, I know all too well. So you didn't do anything social growing up?"

She shook her head. "No. I never went to prom, or any of that. I was too busy on the ice. Skating was my life."

"That's a shame." I stirred the pasta. "I never had problems making friends, but that didn't have anything to do with me. People wanted to suck up to me because my dad was king. I don't think too many actually cared about me as a person. Everyone was always worried about offending me. It got old fast."

"Stefan doesn't seem to mind telling you off," Emma said.

"He doesn't. That's why we're still friends," I said. "I got rid of everyone who I thought was just trying to use me to get what they wanted. That ended up being a lot of people, in the end."

A few minutes later, the pasta was done. I combined all the ingredients, and Emma and I sat down to eat.

"Oh my God. This is like, amazing." Emma let out a moan as she popped another scallop into her mouth. "You're such an amazing cook."

"You look like you're going to have an orgasm." I laughed.

"This is way better than an orgasm." She took another bite and asked, "How did you learn to make such awesome food?"

"I have many talents." I was barely eating, myself. I was too nervous. I didn't get why. We were just two friends having a meal together and talking. It wasn't a big deal. It was like hanging out with Stefan.

Except when I was hanging out with Stefan, my mind didn't constantly assault me with inappropriate images of screwing him on the table. Gods help me.

Emma was done with her drink. "More champagne?" I asked.

She eyed the bottle, then shook her head. "No thanks. I don't need any more."

That was weird. It was clear she wanted some. Did she think I had dastardly intentions with her? Had I put off that bad of an impression? I was trying to be a proper gentleman.

"As you wish, madame." I poured another glass for myself. Maybe drinking the entire bottle could calm my nerves. I should've brought more champagne.

She giggled. "There you go, talking fancy again."

"It's a bad habit. I was raised to have proper manners and etiquette at all times. Part of being a prince," I told her. "Except it didn't come in handy with speaking to people my own age instead of with diplomats at dinner parties. I had to learn how to act like… how you say… a commoner."

"None of that here. I'm an American," Emma proclaimed proudly. "We don't believe in any of that class-system bullshit. You are what you make yourself to be."

"It's honorable. I always admired the attitude Americans have toward bettering themselves."

I sighed. "Here in Malovia, that's not possible. A person can't rise higher than their designated station. Whatever you're born as, you remain for life. Even if you become a king, if your mother was a maid, you'll always be known as the son of a peasant and not as a true monarch."

"That's horrible." Emma's brows knitted together.

"It's the way things are. People have a very strange way of looking at things around here." I played with my fork. "I was lucky to be born with royal blood. It opened up more privileges for me that other people don't have. Even in today's modern area, mating outside your class is considered scandalous. Commoners must stick with commoners, and high-class with others of their station."

Emma scowled at her empty plate. "I bet I'm considered the lowest of the low."

"You're an outsider. You don't have a designated class, which is good for you, because you can rise to be anything." I frowned apologetically before I added, "Although many people will still consider you an outsider forever. No matter what you accomplish."

She scoffed. "Like that bothers me. I've been a misfit all my life."

"Because you're a rarity." I reached across the table and took her hand. "Not many people can aspire to be like you. And people are jealous of what they cannot become."

I rubbed the back of her hand with my thumb for a moment before I stood up. "Well, these dishes aren't going to clean themselves."

"I'll wash, you dry?" Emma suggested. I smiled and nodded.

As I began putting away plates, Emma snorted. "What's so funny?" I asked.

"It's weird. A prince doing dishes," she said.

"I can do dishes," I said indignantly. "Along with a host of other things."

"I would figure you'd think yourself above menial chores," Emma teased.

"Of course not. What a silly notion." I reached into the fridge. "Hot chocolate and cheesecake for dessert?"

"Oooh. Of course, yes."

We sat on the couch in front of the fire and shared a blanket that draped over our shoulders. The storm sieged outside, and our empty dessert plates and mugs sat abandoned on the coffee table. Emma had her legs curled under her and was leaning against my chest. I had my arm around her as we watched the logs crackle beneath the flames.

My mind screamed at me. What was I doing? I was *cuddling* with Emma. I wasn't even sure how it had happened. We'd just finished eating, sat back and... bam. We didn't even think about it. I hadn't noticed we were pressed against each other until it'd actually happened, and by then, I didn't want to pull apart.

Damn mating instincts. They naturally drew us to each other without us having to consider it. I needed to remedy this, and soon.

"What do you want to do when you become king?" Emma asked. Her voice broke the silence. She looked up at me, her chin sitting on my shoulder.

I shifted. "Abolish the class system. Make things fairer for the people in Malovia. A lot of things are regulated here by big business. Names and titles. Money and power. I don't want it to be that way any more. People should be free to break out of whatever constraints society has put on them."

"That's honorable."

"I suppose." My voice trembled as I said, "I just want to live up to what my father did. He was a great king."

"I've heard your dad was an awesome king, but I have a feeling that you're going to be even greater." She leaned her head against my shoulder. "I know you'll win the Contest."

"I need a mate first. Can't compete without one."

"You'll find one in time. You'll be a good king."

"There are other competitors. It's far from a sure thing," I said.

"None of them can compare to you. They aren't worthy," Emma objected. "If anyone deserves that crown, it's you."

I dared to say, "You'd be a good queen."

"No, I wouldn't." The mood had grown melancholy. Emma stared at the flames with a certain type of vacancy in her that I couldn't express, but that I wanted to fill.

"Why not?" I asked.

She took a deep breath. "I haven't told anyone at school about this. But... I'm sick."

It wasn't something I didn't know. But I pretended. "How sick?"

"Sick enough." Her eyes were void of emotion as she said, "It's called Common Variable Immune Deficiency Disorder. It's a rare genetic disease. There is no cure. My immune system basically doesn't work. My system doesn't make enough antibodies to fight against infections. When your immune system shuts down, the rest of your body doesn't work, either. A simple cold or flu could kill me— that's why I have that plasma in my fridge. I have to infuse it every week in order to stay alive."

My whole body went numb. It was hard to process this information— that my mate could be in so much pain. "You haven't seemed sick often this semester, at least."

"I've been lucky. And I've been hiding it. I've caught something pretty much every other weekend. Turns out college campuses are a great place to exchange germs," she said in defeat.

That explained why she'd been hiding out in her dorm so much. She was isolating herself to prevent herself from getting sicker. "Is there anything I can do to help?"

"What can you do, Ethan? There's nothing *I* can do." Her eyes were glistening as she turned toward me. "This is forever. It's never going away, and it's only going to get worse the older I get. I have to learn to deal with it."

She quickly wiped away a few tears. "That's why I wouldn't be a good queen. I don't even think I'd be a good mate. Who could want me, broken like this?"

I took her face in my hands gently and said, "Any Companion in their right mind would be *honored* to have you as their mate."

The way she looked at me in that moment— it was like time itself stilled and we were the only two people alive.

We moved forward instinctively, like moths drawn to a flame. Her lips were only inches from me now, and gods, they were intoxicating. I longed to move my mouth over hers and make her mine.

Having a mate was dangerous. They'd take your whole heart, and you were powerless to do anything in return. You'd do anything for them just to gain their favor. I was a dog worshipping at Emma's feet right now, and that's how I wanted it.

I was moments away from connecting with her lips. This was it. I was really going to do it. I was going to break through the useless things that separated us, and unite us as mates.

Our perfect moment was shattered when the window broke. Both of us jumped, and I grabbed Emma to pull her away from whatever threat had arrived. I pushed her behind me as I got up from the couch and went to observe the broken glass.

It was nothing. Just the storm. The wind had smashed a tree branch outside against the window and shattered it to pieces.

I turned around and looked at Emma. She was giving me a sheepish look, cheeks pink with embarrassment. It was clear that we'd gathered our senses and there was no going back to the moment we'd just shared. It was hot in here, and it wasn't from the fireplace.

"We should get back," I suggested. "It doesn't look like it's safe here."

She nodded without another response, and picked up the empty mugs and saucers to put them in the sink. I killed the flames and left the ashes to smolder as we left the tiny cabin— the place where everything had changed, and there was no going back.

The snowstorm had died down. We could see our way back to the school now. I transformed into a wolven to shelter Emma from the harsh wind as we began our walk to the main campus. Emma kept her arms folded and head down, her eyebrows knitted together as if thinking as she clutched my hockey bag to her chest.

I couldn't reverse my actions. What had happened had happened, and there was no going back. But it had helped me make a choice. I made my final decision. I loved Emma, and I wanted to protect her, but I couldn't become king without her by my side. Choosing another mate would be torture after what we'd just shared. It would hurt her just as much as it would hurt me to stay away. Eventually, it would ruin us both. I couldn't do that to her. Denying the connection we held was like denying the laws of nature itself. No matter what, I couldn't stay away from her, and she couldn't stay away from me. I was sure of that. Instinct itself would keep pushing us together.

More than that. It was love.

I had no other choice. Before the week was out, I'd ask Emma to be my mate.

And I hoped she'd say yes.

EIGHTEEN

I didn't know how to explain it. I was the Phantom's mate. But I had feelings for Ethan Nowak, too.

I didn't know that was possible. I figured that once you found your mate, all other possibilities of hookups with other people became obsolete. Apparently, mating wasn't that simple.

Unless there was another answer. Maybe I wasn't in love with two different people. Maybe they were the same person.

Could Ethan be the Phantom? He had to be. There was no other explanation. I knew the Phantom was a wolven, and that he had to be a student. Ethan fit that description. But how did you confront someone with information like that? How could I expect him not to laugh in my face? Even if he was the Phantom, he'd probably deny it, and it wasn't like I had any proof.

The question ate away at me. I had to know. On the first day of December I headed to the Rec Room. Ethan had asked me to meet him there early in the morning so we could study for our exams together. He was sitting on a couch in front of one of the giant TVs, working on homework.

Kinda. His papers were spread out on the coffee table in front of him, and the TV was on, but he wasn't paying attention. He was staring out the window overlooking Dolinska, his chin resting on his fist. He was kinda pale.

I gathered my nerves and strode across the Rec Room. At this time of day, most people were either outside, playing in the snow, or they were enjoying the Christmas festivities in Dolinska. Nobody else was here. Ethan couldn't use other people as an excuse for not telling me the truth.

I sat directly across from him. "We need to talk." I didn't give any other greeting.

"Hey, Em." Ethan winced and shifted in his seat, like he was uncomfortable. "What is it?"

I took a deep breath and tried coming up with ways to phrase it. *Look, buddy. I know you're the Phantom. We nearly kissed the other day. I probably would've screwed you in that cabin if that broken window hadn't stopped me. I am one-hundred percent sure at this point you're a superhero. So just admit it, so we can become mates and I can get some of that big dick energy you've got going on.*

It was a bad idea to say all of that. I resolved to get to the point. *Ethan, you're the Phantom. I won't tell anybody. Just spit it out already.*

But as I opened my mouth, a flashing alert came across the TV screen and halted the program that was on. "We interrupt this broadcast to bring you a special news bulletin." A newscaster came on screen, looking deadly serious. "We currently have live footage of the vigilante known as the Phantom as he terrorizes the city. The Arcanea Alliance is now in pursuit."

What the fuck? No way. The screen changed to show a man in a cape and a white wolf mask leaping from building to building as the police gave chase. Dragons, griffins, and alicorns flew after the Phantom and cast magic at him while wolvens circled in on the ground, but they missed their target every time. Even when they got close, the Phantom managed to slip away.

Confusion hurtled through me like a hurricane. It was early morning. The Phantom had never been seen before in the daytime. He always came out at night.

I watched the figure jump from rooftop to rooftop as the camera panned after him. Eventually, he slipped out of sight as he dove into an alleyway. Police pursued him and vanished from sight as well.

Ethan's eyes were pinned to the screen, just like mine. The police swarmed the area, but their expressions became clueless. It was like the Phantom had vanished out of thin air.

"It seems like the Arcanea Alliance has lost the trail yet again." The newscaster sounded disappointed. "The identity of the Phantom will continue to remain a mystery."

My thoughts became a puzzle that I had no hope of solving. I was pretty sure Ethan was the Phantom— but Ethan was right here with me, as I was watching live footage of the vigilante being chased through town.

There was only one explanation. Ethan couldn't be the Phantom. There was just no way— not unless he had the ability to be in two places at once.

"What was it you wanted to ask me?" Ethan said as the alert ended.

"Um… I just need help with my paper for Lucien's class," I lied. I'd already finished the paper, but I had to tell Ethan something, right?

"We can work on it tomorrow. I haven't started mine yet." Ethan got to his feet. I jumped right up, too, though it was weird and I didn't know why.

Suddenly, Ethan staggered forward. He probably would've dropped to his knees if I hadn't been there at the last minute to hold him up. He looked like he was gonna puke.

"Oh my gosh! Ethan, are you okay?" I asked.

"I think I'm getting sick," Ethan mumbled. He pushed me away and began shuffling forward. "I'm sorry, I don't think I can study today. I'd better go lie down."

"I'll get your stuff for you." I collected Ethan's things as he stumbled into his dorm. When I got there, he was already lying in bed, face-down on the pillows. I put his papers on his desk. If Ethan was getting sick, it was dangerous for me to be around him. I couldn't catch what he had and risk my health. But I didn't care. I just wanted to make sure he was okay.

"Do you need anything?" I asked, but I didn't get a response. He was already sleeping. I figured it was best not to disturb him and turned off the light, shutting the door behind me.

There were so many emotions raging through me I didn't know what to do with them. Ethan and the Phantom were two different people, which meant that I had to make a choice. Ethan, or the Phantom. I couldn't have both.

The Phantom was supposed to be my mate, so he should've been the obvious choice. But I felt such a strong connection between Ethan and I. It was so powerful. Not something I could easily deny. I didn't think I could give that up for a man that I shared a bond with, yet didn't know personally.

When I left Ethan's room I saw Odette, Kiara, and Delmare in the hallway. All of them were bundled up for the outdoors, snow melting on their shoulders.

"Oh my goodness!" Odette covered her mouth as she watched me close the door. "*Emma*! You're *sleeping* with the prince?"

"Hey, can't say we didn't see it coming," Delmare said, and she laughed.

"What? No. Ethan's just sick," I said. "I was lending a hand."

"Oh, you were lending a hand, all right," Delmare snickered. She made a motion like she was jerking someone off, and Odette giggled.

I rolled my eyes. "Calm down, guys. I've never seen Ethan's dick."

"Not like you don't want to," Delmare shot back.

I couldn't help turning pink. Kiara said, "Lay off, guys. They're not even mates. Emma, do you want to come with us?"

"Where?" I asked. I got a sinking feeling when Kiara said that Ethan and I weren't mated, but it was the truth— I belonged to someone else.

"My sister's having a sale today at *Enchanting Whispers*," Kiara said. "We should go and see what kind of cool things we can find."

"Sure." I wasn't doing anything else today. I got my coat, hat and gloves and we headed out. I felt bad for leaving Ethan behind, but he needed rest— not me bothering him.

The skies dropped a light snowfall. The streets of Dolinska were filled with kids tossing snowballs and making forts. The town was decorated with garlands, red ribbons, strings of cranberries and white lights. Christmas trees adorned with dozens of ornaments were on every corner, along with carolers and elaborate light displays. The Arcanea really got into the winter holidays. It was like a competition to them to have the best decorations.

"So tell me how Christmas works around here," I said. We passed a sleigh being pulled by an alicorn with a wreath around his neck. Santa… or, as people around here called him, *Father Christmas*… sat in the sleigh and waved as the alicorn pulled him through the snow. Children screamed and laughed as they ran after the sleigh.

"One rule. Don't let Krampus catch you." Kiara snickered.

"Our main holiday is the Winter Hunt, which is on the same day as the King's Ball, then we celebrate Christmas after," Odette explained. "Many Christmas traditions began as pagan Yuletide festivities, so we tie them into our holiday. Normally, most of Arcanea would participate in the Yule ceremonies for the Winter Hunt, but that's being put off this year because of the Contest."

"What's the story on the Winter Hunt?" I asked.

"It's an old legend," Kiara began. "Droga, the Dark God, chased away the sun during the Autumn Equinox, but Tomir and his Eternal Hunt chase it back and bring light to the earth during the Winter Festival."

Speaking of the gods… "Guys, I have something to tell you," I began.

"Don't tell us you're expecting," Delmare said.

"Not exactly." I hesitated before I said, "I think I saw one of the gods. Her name was Milonna."

All three of them screeched to a halt. Kiara reached out and grabbed my arm, whirling me around. "You what?"

I swallowed. "A couple of weeks ago, I was in the forest by myself and a doe came out of the woods, but she wasn't just any deer. She told me she was a goddess."

"Emma, you need to tell us everything," Kiara said. She and Odette wore twin expressions of concern. Even Delmare had turned deathly serious.

I launched into the story of what had happened at the river with Milonna. As I continued, their faces got more and more scared. I was pretty sure Odette started to sweat.

"Then she told me I'd be her champion and she'd be with me always," I finished. "What does that mean?"

"Emma, are you *sure* you saw her?" Kiara asked. She'd asked the question a million times.

"Yes, I saw her! I'm pretty sure I didn't imagine a giant talking deer in the middle of the woods," I replied sourly.

"No, you don't get it. This is really important. Are you *absolutely sure*?" Delmare asked. She squeezed my arm so tight I felt like it was gonna fall off.

I hesitated before I said, "Yes. I wasn't drunk or anything. She was definitely there. She touched me."

Odette's eyes began to water. She started to cry. Little sniffles came out of her. Kiara put an arm around the alicorn girl, looking grim.

"Odette, don't cry. It's nothing to be sad about," I said, totally confused.

"It is!" Odette wailed. "It's so horrible!"

"That I was contacted by a goddess?" I was totally bewildered. What were these girls getting at?

Delmare frowned. "Milonna… well, Emma, she only shows herself to Arcanea who are destined to die young."

I think my heart stopped beating. "What?"

"She chooses her champions to go on great quests for her, but they never make it out alive," Delmare explained quietly. "The quests are great and important, but her champions always die at the end. There are no exceptions."

The statement made my blood run cold. It confirmed what the hag had prophesied about me. I had four years or less. I was starting to think my disease wouldn't have a chance to get to me. Whatever Milonna wanted me to do would knock me off first.

"Have you told Ethan about this?" Kiara asked. Her eyebrows knitted together.

"No," I said. "Why would I? The only people I've told are you guys."

"Don't," Kiara said firmly. "This would break his heart."

The mention of Ethan stirred something in me. I didn't want to die, I wanted to live. Who were the gods to dictate how my life was gonna go? I wasn't going to kick the bucket unless I had a say in it. I was going out on *my* terms.

"Well, I don't care. The stories are wrong," I said. "Everyone *else* might die on Milonna's quests, but I won't. I'll be the first to survive."

Kiara and Delmare glanced at each other, but Odette hiccuped and squeaked out, "You think so?"

"Of course." I took her hand and squeezed it. "I'm not dying until I'm good and ready. The gods aren't ready for me and the underworld doesn't want to take me. I cause too much trouble."

Odette hiccuped again and giggled, but Kiara and Delmare didn't lift a smile. I'd failed to convince them.

When we got to *Enchanting Whispers*, Odette skipped to observe the crystals. Delmare and Kiara remained at the coffee bar and talked in low voices, shooting glances at me. I ignored them and scoured the books. What effect did myths and legends have on my life, anyway? Not a damn bit.

In one of the rows of shelves, I caught a long mane of fiery-red hair out of the corner of my eye, and my mouth dropped open in disbelief. What the hell? She was here! "Mom!" I shouted.

The woman turned around, and my spirits lifted as I recognized her green eyes and kindly stare. It really was her!

Mom's smile widened. "Emma. I'm so glad to see you."

I rushed into her arms and held her tightly. She still smelled the same— her hugs were still warm and soft. I pulled away slightly to gaze up at her in amazement. I couldn't believe she was right in front of me.

"You look amazing." I'd never seen my mom look so healthy. Her skin was glowing, and she'd put on weight. Her hair and makeup were done, and her nails shone with red polish. She was dressed like an Arcane would be, in a designer dress and coat, with high-heeled boots.

"I can use my magic now. The migraines have stopped completely." Mom ran a hand through my hair. "I closed down the diner and moved to Dolinska. I just purchased a cottage outside the city. I'm thinking about opening up a restaurant in town soon. I wanted to come see you sooner, but I didn't want to distract you during your semester exams."

"Mom, that's wonderful. So does that mean you're here to stay?" I asked.

She nodded. "You were right. Malovia is where I belong. This is our home. I wanted to be here to watch you go through school."

"I'm so happy you're finally here." I didn't have to be separated from my mom anymore. This was like a dream come true. "Do you want to meet my friends?"

"I'd love to." We rounded the corner, and Odette, Delmare, and Kiara glanced up as they saw me coming near.

"Guys, this is my mom," I said. "She's here to stay."

"Wow, you guys look so much alike," Delmare said. "It's like looking at twins."

"It's a pleasure to meet you, Ms. Sosna," Kiara said. She reached out to shake Mom's hand, and she took it.

"Your mommy has such pretty eyes!" Odette exclaimed. "I always thought wolvens had the most expressive eyes. Like windows to the soul."

Mom smiled warmly at Odette. "You're an Oksana, aren't you? I was very close with your mother growing up. She's a beautiful dancer."

"Oh yes, she is." Odette nodded. "Though she had to give it up. Bad ankles."

"I'm sorry to hear that." Mom frowned. "It's really too bad."

"Yes. I think she's mentioned you before, though I can't remember what about." Odette gave a quizzical look.

Mom laughed, but it sounded a little... forced. "I bet she has."

That sounded ominous. There was no telling what sort of hijinks my Mom got mixed in when she was in school. Or if her relationship with Odette's mom was still good.

"You have lovely friends, Emma. I'm glad to see you're getting along so well at the university," Mom said. But her eyebrows were pinched together, and thin lines had formed around her mouth. Something was on her mind.

"Mom, what's wrong?" I asked.

"There's some things we need to talk about," Mom said slowly. "If your friends don't mind. I don't want to drag you away."

The three of them shook their heads, and I said, "We can talk, Mom."

Mom took my hand. She led me across the cafe to a small table on a secluded side of the store behind a bookshelf, obscuring us from view.

She lowered her voice. "I've thought about it, and I think it's time you knew about my past. People will talk now that I'm back, you see, and I want you to get the story straight from me."

"Talk about what?" This was coming out of nowhere.

Mom took a deep breath. "I've heard you've been talking to Prince Ethan."

"Yes." What did this have to do with her past?

"Well you see, long ago, I had a close relationship with his father. King Lycus."

"What kind of relationship?" I could see where this was heading, and I didn't like it.

"Emma, I ended up bonding to *two* shifters," Mom explained. "Ethan's father and... someone else."

"You bonded to two different people? Like, two mates? Is that even possible?" My mouth dropped open.

"It's exceptionally rare," Mom said. "But yes. It can happen."

My thoughts were going a million miles a minute. Did the same thing that happened to my mom happen to me, too? After all, I had feelings for both the Phantom and Ethan. It was the only thing that made sense.

Then I thought something really gross. Did that mean my dad was actually Ethan's dad, too? Holy crap, I hoped that wasn't true. We'd almost kissed, and I'd had some... *inappropriate dreams* about him lately. I didn't want to be involved in some freaky incest shit.

"Mom, please don't tell me Ethan's my half-brother." I was totally going to puke.

Mom shook her head. "No, Emma. I never slept with the king. You're not related to the prince at all. But your father... he's the *other* shifter I bonded with. His name was Anastazy Ignacy. He's your biological father."

I was floored. It was like Mom took a hammer and hit me over the head with it. My thoughts were slow and sluggish. "But... I thought you told me you didn't know my father. That it was a one-night stand."

"It was a lie, meant to protect you," Mom said. "I thought you were better off not knowing."

An emotion I didn't understand took root and grew inside my heart. Hope. There were hundreds of possibilities. I could finally meet the father I never knew, and gain a missing piece of myself I thought I never had.

"Does he still live in Dolinska? Does he know who I am? Can you introduce me to him?" My words got jumbled up, they came out so fast. I wanted to leave. I wanted to leave right now and go see him.

"I'm afraid that's not possible," Mom said. Her voice was tight. "He's no longer alive."

Crushing disappointment flattened me from above. Years of hopes and dreams shattered into a million fragments inside my soul. I didn't know something like this could still hurt. Or that I had so many hopes about one day meeting the man who'd made me.

I stuffed down the tears that threatened to spill over and forced words out from a strangled throat. "What happened to him?"

Tears beaded Mom's eyes. I couldn't imagine the pain she was going through— losing her mate like that. It had to be hell. "He was murdered by the Black Claw."

I was so shocked I couldn't even speak. I didn't want to believe her. It was too horrible.

Mom cleared her throat, though a tear dripped down her cheek. "Long ago, when I was only a few years older than you, I was engaged to King Lycus. Our wedding was set to take place upon our graduation from Arcanea University. I loved Lycus. He was my closest friend. We went through the King's Contest together, and won. I *put him* on that throne. But I betrayed him, because I was having an affair in secret."

Mom wiped the tear away. "Anastazy and I weren't supposed to happen. I was promised to the king, but we shared a bond I couldn't deny, no matter how hard I tried. I'd bonded with both of them, but I chose Anastazy. After Lycus and I won the King's Contest, I couldn't handle the pressures of becoming the new queen. I didn't want to make a public declaration of the mating bond refusal, and I didn't want to break Lycus's heart and humiliate him in front of his people, so I rejected Lycus' mating bond in private. Lycus was devastated, but he chose another queen, as was his duty, and married Antonia. Ethan was conceived soon after."

Mom sniffed. "Sometime after the prince was born, Anastazy and I ended up getting pregnant with you, and by then, I knew there was no turning back. Anastazy decided we should run away together, and leave the country."

Mom put her face in her hands and rubbed her eyes. "But the night we were to leave, the Black Claw came for me. They had received a prophecy of a girl who would resurrect the Dark God Droga, a baby I carried in my womb. They wanted to kidnap me, and hold me prisoner until you were born, then sacrifice you in order to bring the prophecy full circle. Anastazy wouldn't let that happen. He died protecting the both of us."

Mom was full out sobbing now. I reached out and wiped her tears away. I was crying now, too. This was all so awful. But at least I knew now that my father loved me, wanted me. He wouldn't have died for me if he hadn't.

"I got to safety that night, but I knew the Black Claw wouldn't stop hunting me, not even if I was queen. I needed to get you far away, so the Black Claw wouldn't find us," Mom stuttered. "I ran away to Detroit with you. And I did what I had to, to keep you safe."

"Did the king ever know?" I whispered.

"No," Mom whispered. "I never told him. He never knew about Anastazy or the pregnancy. He died thinking I rejected him because I didn't love him, but that wasn't true."

I put the pieces together. "So… you think people are going to figure out you cheated on Lycus?"

"Yes. I'm sure people have already been discussing it. Gossip runs thick in the Arcanean circles. I'm sure they think you're some sort of bastard. They don't realize you were conceived within the legal confines of a mating relationship." She took a tissue out of her purse and dotted her eyes.

"Does that matter?"

"To the Arcanea? Yes. Bloodlines are everything. To have a child with someone who isn't your proclaimed mate… it's basically sacrilege. People think I'm damned to the underworld."

"You aren't going to hell, Mom. You had to make a lot of tough decisions." I pondered for a moment. "But couldn't you tell people about Anastazy now?"

"And admit that I was fooling around behind the king's back? No. That would only bring humiliation upon you, and Lycus' memory. It's better if people just speculate your parentage rather than know the truth. Then they can't use it against you. And people would never believe me if I told them I bonded with two shifters. They wouldn't consider it possible. The only thing that protects your reputation now is that people don't know the truth."

"This is some medieval sexist shit, Mom."

"I know. But it's how our world works. Adultery is the worst sin the Arcanea know. No one will forgive you if they find out you cheated on your mate. It goes that way for boys, too."

Mom bunched up her tissue. "I just wanted you to know the truth. Though I suggest you don't tell anyone about this. If word gets out what really happened, you'll be outcasted from society forever. And I don't want that for you. You seem different, Emma. You're so happy here."

"I am." I reached out to grab her hand. "I just want to make sure you're happy, too."

"I will be. There are a lot of memories here. But in time, I'll learn to heal." She took a ragged breath.

I felt so bad for her. Both of her mates had died, and she was alone in the world. But she wasn't completely alone, because she had me.

"Mom? Do you think you could take me around town and show me all the places you and my dad went? I want to learn more about him," I asked. It was crazy to hear the words come out of my mouth, but if my father wasn't alive, I at least wanted to hear about him and find out what kind of man he was. Maybe we shared more in common than I knew.

Mom took a small mirror out of her purse. She fixed her runny makeup before forcing a watery smile. "I think that's just what we both need."

Mom and I hung out for the rest of the day. We walked around campus and explored her favorite spots, as well as my dad's. One in particular was a small lake within the school grounds in one of the inner gardens. We laughed and talked about what Anastazy was like. I learned that he'd liked pasta, like me, and didn't take creamer in his coffee, and that his wolven fur was a deep, rich brown. It was so little to go on, but already, I felt like I knew him personally. These little details made him a real person instead of a phantom in my mind. It almost felt like he was still here with me.

When darkness fell, Mom went back to her cottage and I returned to the dormitory. When I got to the top of the steps, Ethan was waiting there for me. He appeared much better than earlier— like he hadn't been sick at all. It was kind of weird looking at him knowing that my mom had an old fling with his dad, but at least she hadn't had sex with him.

Something I couldn't promise I didn't want to do with his son. Damn this double-mating thing.

"You look like you're feeling better," I said.

"I am," Ethan said. "It was some passing thing. I just needed to sleep."

"That's a relief to hear." I leaned against the wall. I was tired from walking around all day. I wanted to rest. He needed to hurry this up, so I could climb into bed and pass out.

Ethan bounced on the spot. He seemed... nervous. "Emma, can we talk?"

Oh, gods. "Depending on what it's about."

"It's serious."

Wasn't it always? "Okay. Shoot."

"Let's go somewhere more private." Ethan turned on his heel, and I suppressed a groan. My legs felt like they were gonna fall off. I was gonna get old walking around this school.

Ethan led me to a balcony that overlooked the forest beyond. The moon shone overhead while large snowflakes trickled down, coating his shoulders in white. The stars glimmered in the blackness around him.

Ethan looked gorgeous. I wondered if he was casting some sort of illusion over my heart. Choosing between him and the Phantom was impossible.

"What's this about?" I asked.

Ethan stood in silence. The only sound that could be heard was that of the falling snow. Then he uttered something unbelievable.

"I was wondering if you would be my partner for the King's Contest."

My mouth dropped open in shock. My friends were right. Holy shit, this was actually happening. My heart thudded out of my chest as my lungs struggled to breathe. I gaped like some stupid fish for a moment, eyes wide like saucers, before I pulled myself together and said, "You have to be joking."

He flinched. Did I offend him? Oops.

"Does this seem like a joke to you?" Ethan said. "I'm serious."

"When you say partner... it's more like mate," I said.

"Yes. It *is* mate. I'm asking you to be my mate, compete in the Contest with me, and become my queen if we win," Ethan said.

"You realize this is basically a marriage proposal," I stuttered. I didn't know how many surprises I could take today.

"Yes. And I'm sorry that this isn't exactly elaborate, but I didn't have much time to plan this out," he stuttered.

"When did you decide to do this? Yesterday?" I asked sarcastically. "Was I your back-up choice?"

"Gods, Emma, no." His brow furrowed. "You were the *only* choice."

He probably meant it to be romantic, but it came out as insulting. I scoffed. "You had other options. Chastity being the first."

"I don't want Chastity," Ethan said. "She resents me. It would be a long and horrible marriage."

"But you're giving her what she wants."

"No. I wouldn't be." He shook his head. "She wants to be queen, but more than that, she wants me to love her. That's something I could never do."

"You think you could love me?" I dared to ask.

Ethan hesitated for a long moment, as if calculating his response. "I could try."

Not a very convincing answer. His guard was up. I didn't know why.

"Then let me ask you another question," I said slowly. "Do you think *we* could be mates?"

Ethan's eyes widened. He nearly staggered with the effort of keeping himself upright. It's like I'd punched him in the gut or something. "I... I thought you believed you were mated to the Phantom."

"I am," I said. "But don't you think it's possible I'm bonded to two people?"

"I didn't know such a thing was possible."

"You're avoiding the question."

"Do you *think* you're bonded to me?"

I shrugged. "I'm not entirely sure. I feel *something* for you, but it's not anything like what I feel for the Phantom. That's something much deeper. A bond I can't explain. With you it just feels... normal."

He frowned. "Then there's your answer."

"Not from you."

He took in a deep breath. "I think we have a natural connection. But don't you think if I knew you were my mate, I would've told you months ago? That's not something a shifter can easily deny. What reason would I have to hold back my true feelings?"

Disappointment flowed through my veins. I didn't think he was lying. Why would he? Ethan spoke the truth. There was no mating bond between us.

...Yet I wasn't entirely convinced. There was *some* kind of bond there, though I didn't know what it was. Attraction, at the very least. We had some chemistry. Maybe Ethan and I could be mates, just that our connection was weaker than the one shared between the Phantom and I?

But that wasn't enough for a lifetime of commitment. I balled my hands into fists at my sides.

"I don't want to be Queen of the Arcanea."

"Forgive me, but I don't think it matters what you want," Ethan said gently. "My life is about service. I'm here to give myself up to the people of Malovia. That's my purpose. It's about sacrifice. I don't *want* to ask you to become queen in order to protect the Arcanea. But Emma, I'm asking."

"You're asking me to give up my life."

"Yes. Because it's what has to be done. People are depending on us."

He was right. The right thing to do was clear. The main contenders to the throne were Ethan and Elijah. If Ethan didn't have a mate, he couldn't compete. And then Elijah would probably win.

The thought of Elijah on the throne with Gabby's smug, bitchy smile beside him made me want to hurl. Neither one of them cared about the Arcanea. They only cared about themselves. They'd run the county into the ground and ruin the Arcanea for their own selfish purposes.

Ethan wasn't like that. He was good, and just, and kind. He was the king the Arcanea needed.

But he needed me. And if I refused… there'd be no one else to turn to. He'd waited too long to find a mate. I had to wonder if it was on purpose. Sure, he was a prince and could pick any random girl, but whoever he picked had to stay at his side… forever. There was no such thing as divorce among the Arcanea. That kind of thing was forbidden in our culture. You'd be shunned forever if you took wedding vows and then decided to abandon your mate. If you had to refuse them, it was supposed to be done *before* you legally wed. Ethan would be removed from the throne if he ever broke his mating vows.

We were friends. He knew he could deal with me for the rest of his life. With any other girl, he'd be taking a chance.

I mean, I had to admit, the thought of being queen was kinda badass. I'd be taken care of for the rest of my life. And I'd get to order people around. The only person above me on the Arcanea pecking order would be Ethan. I wouldn't be an outcast anymore. People would be forced to respect me. It would be good to be the queen.

Yet it came with a lot of duties. I'd be responsible for an entire nation of people. Wars, famines, disasters… I'd be expected to handle it all. It was a lot to ask of a girl from Detroit.

Ethan thought I could handle it, which was endearing. Maybe I could. He wouldn't ask me to be his queen if he thought I'd be a bad one. He cared about his people too much.

But if I said yes… I'd lose the chance to be with my one true mate forever. I'd lose the Phantom.

With a sinking feeling, I realized I had to face facts. The Phantom wasn't coming for me. I'd waited for weeks and weeks, and he never showed. I didn't think he cared about me at all.

I loved the Phantom, but he wasn't here. Ethan was. Ethan was standing right in front of me, begging me to take his hand and become his queen.

It would be an arranged marriage. Probably a loveless one. I don't think I could love another person like I loved the Phantom. It just wasn't possible. He'd taken up a place in my heart that I could never let go.

I was facing the same decision my mom had long ago. But what if my mom had made a mistake? Her choice to follow her heart had brought her nothing but misery. I didn't want to end up like that.

"Why did you pick me? Give me one good reason," I said.

"Because we're friends. Because we get along. Because we work well together. It's a smart decision," Ethan listed off.

Parts of me seethed. He could've said I was pretty. Maybe even lied that he had a crush on me, at least. Would it kill him to fake a little bit of romance? Not set this up like it was a business transaction.

"So you think you can put up with me for the rest of your life. Big deal. That's really profound," I shot at him.

"Emma, not everything in life is a fairytale romance," Ethan snapped. "I know you want flowers and feelings and to be swept off your feet, but this is a practical arrangement. It's what's best."

"For you, maybe." This was insulting. I had feelings for Ethan, but it was clear he had none for me. Which really fucking hurt.

"Em, I want more than just the magic." Ethan's expression hardened. "This is a vow to stick with me through thick and thin, a commitment you can never take back. If you don't think you can do that, walk away."

"I don't even have time to think about it! The King's Contest is *two weeks* away!" I shouted. "You haven't even given me time to consider."

"I wasn't sure of it myself until recently. I'm sorry I didn't give you enough time, but Emma, I need your answer now. There's not enough time to give it any thought."

"That's your own fault, Captain Procrastinator."

Ethan huffed impatiently. He held the bridge between his nose and his eyes with two fingers. "Dammit, you're so frustrating."

"This is your own fault for springing a marriage proposal on me at the last minute."

"What's holding you back?" He dropped his hand, and our eyes connected. "Tell me."

What was holding me back? A million things. I was eighteen years old, and Ethan wanted me to make a lifelong commitment to him when I barely knew him. I was mated to the Phantom. I didn't know if I'd be a good queen. Hell, I didn't even know if I could help Ethan win the Contest.

But beneath all of that was fear, and it was the real reason I didn't want to say yes. I was afraid Ethan would always love his people more than he'd love me. If he ever learned to love me at all. I'd be giving up my soulmate for a loveless marriage.

But that wasn't important. We were talking about the welfare of thousands of people, here. If I was queen, I could make things different for people like my mom.

And it would be a hell of a lot easier to get revenge on those Black Claw bastards for killing my dad. I'd have unlimited power. Power that would come in handy, that I could use.

I cocked out a hip and said, "Convince me."

"What?" His eyebrow raised.

"Convince me to be your mate!" My arms floundered. "Prove that you deserve me. Or at least want me."

"I mean... I'm a prince. There are benefits to marrying me," Ethan stammered.

It was like no one had ever asked him to prove himself before. Did he just expect women to fall at his feet?

"I couldn't give a damn you're a prince. I was never impressed by guys with money," I said. "What are you bringing to the table? You need me. It's not the other way around. Prove you want me."

Ethan looked completely lost. Prince or not, men were still men, and they were clueless creatures. "I don't get what you mean."

"Gods, Ethan!" I threw my hands up. "You're about as romantic as a stick up the ass!"

"I take offense to that." His eyes narrowed.

"You haven't done anything to show me otherwise."

He paused for a moment before he said, "I... thought it was obvious I wanted you."

Heat flooded through me and settled right in my panties. Holy hell, he actually said something that turned me on and made me feel like I was more than an easy option. Was he admitting that he actually liked me? Or that he thought I'd be fun in bed?

Did he *love* me?

Maybe my friends were right again, and there was more between Ethan and I than I wanted to admit.

This idea actually had some merit. But I was about to blow it out of the water with my next statement. "Ethan, before you decide to make me your queen, there's something you should know."

"What is it?" He tilted his head. "I know you said before you never dated anyone, but if you've slept with other people casually, I don't care. You didn't grow up in this world. You couldn't have been expected to abide by our laws."

"What? No." I cringed. "I haven't slept with anybody."

Ethan's eyebrows rose in surprise. "Oh."

"Don't act so freaking shocked," I spat at him.

He scratched his head. "Well... you're a beautiful woman, Emma. So excuse me for not expecting you to be a virgin."

Well, that was a nice and unexpected compliment. I felt another jolt between my thighs before I shook my head and said, "Anyway… it's something else."

I took a deep breath. "My disease is going to complicate things when it comes to giving you heirs," I said. "People with CVID get pregnant and have babies all the time, but it's high-risk, and there's a chance I could pass my condition down to a child. If you marry me, you have to know that I may never be able to give you children."

Ethan's face was hard to read. He didn't say anything for a long moment. I couldn't even read the emotions behind his eyes. It was like they were completely closed off to me. I had no idea what was going through his head right now.

Then he made a careless gesture. "It's fine. We'll figure that part out later down the line. Heirs aren't important at the moment. We have to win the Contest first. But Emma, I need your answer *now.*"

I was shocked to hear that answer. Even though he knew I might not be able to give him a prince or princess— something crucial to the security of the monarchy— he still wanted me anyway.

That was a huge sacrifice for him to make. And it was one that sealed my fate.

I made my decision. If Ethan was willing to give up the chance to have blood-related heirs, then he truly did deserve to rule. He cared more about the Arcanea than he did himself, and he was certain I was the right choice for his queen.

The Phantom wasn't coming for me, and I was tired of waiting around for him— tired of waiting around for true love. I wasn't like my mom. I'd choose duty and practicality over romance, unlike what she'd done. Maybe things would work out better that way. A marriage of convenience.

If I had to settle, at least it'd be for a prince.

"What if I say yes? You realize if we lose the Contest, you still don't get to be king, and you're stuck with me," I said. "You can't go back on mating decisions once they're publicly announced."

"Yes. It's a risk I'm willing to take," Ethan said.

Of course it was. Because he couldn't give me an easy out. This was all riding on me. A million images flashed through my mind— Gabby's shocked face when I stole the crown away from her. My dad being murdered by the Black Claw. Me gaining my revenge on the cult as queen…

… And perhaps the sight of a very naked and very muscular shifter boy with a missing leg lying in my bed. If we ever got that far.

It was the last thought that convinced me. "Fine. I accept your proposal. I'll become your mate."

Ethan's shoulders sagged, and he smiled in obvious ease. "Thank you, Emma." He took my hands in his and squeezed them. "You don't know how happy this makes me."

"No problem." It'd be nice if we kissed or something, but I wasn't about to expect that from the Prince of Abstinence. He'd had an opportunity to kiss me before, and he hadn't gone through with it. Now that he knew we probably wouldn't have kids, he'd have an excuse to never fuck me. We'd work our way up to a peck on the lips by the time we were fifty.

"It's getting late," Ethan said. He rubbed his thumb over the backs of my hands, and damn if it didn't feel good. "You should probably get some sleep. We have a lot to do to prepare for the Contest."

"When do you want to announce our bond?" I asked. Gabby and Elijah had wasted no time telling everyone they were mates.

"At the Choosing," Ethan said. "It'll give us an advantage. No one will see it coming. They'll have expected me to drop out by then."

Was Ethan really that ashamed to be with me? "Fine. I guess we can use the element of surprise." Gods, our marriage was already like a chess game.

But this is what I'd decided. And in my gut was a feeling of firm satisfaction. My intuition told me I'd made the right choice. Duty over love.

I needed to get a dress for the King's Ball. No future Queen of the Arcanea could show up wearing jeans.

NINETEEN

The illusion took all my energy and made me weak for days. It was powerful sorcery— stuff I shouldn't be messing with. Duplicating yourself and powering the illusion with enough magic to become a solid form was extremely difficult. Arcanea had died from it. The spell itself had made me sick. I could only sustain it for a short period of time. I'd cast the duplication spell the night before, and made sure that the clone would be seen on live TV so Emma would witness the broadcast as we studied the next morning.

The spell had completely drained me. But I had no other choice. I was certain that Emma was onto me. If I hadn't done something, she'd have discovered my secret identity, and then there'd be a whole list of things to explain alongside asking her to join me for the King's Contest.

I already had to convince her to marry me against her will— while lying to her about the fact we shared a mating bond. I didn't want to admit I was a vigilante on top of it. I debated back and forth for days about confessing to Emma that we were fated mates, but if I did that, I'd have to tell her the truth about the Phantom. Knowing the man behind the mask would only put Emma at risk, and now that we were contestants for the Contest, she would be in enough danger as the bride of Prince Ethan.

I needed her to be focused on winning the King's Contest. If she knew I'd been lying to her about being the Phantom, she'd be beyond furious— along with distracted.

And if she *ever* found out I lied to her about her being my one true mate… she'd never trust me again.

Trust was the one thing we needed in order to win the Contest. We had to get that throne. One way or the other.

The night of the King's Ball had arrived. But first, Emma and I had to go through our Choosing ceremony, declare ourselves to our gods, and announce that we were mated.

The ceremony was to be held in Dolinska's square. Every Arcanea had to go through their Choosing ceremony once they'd found their mate at the end of that particular year, but the King's Contest participants were going first.

At seven o'clock, I waited at the bottom of the winding staircase that led up to the dorms. I was worried about how tonight was going to go, but there was no turning back now.

I heard a door open from above, and I turned. I hardly recognized the woman standing there until I realized she was my mate.

Emma had white flowers woven into her red hair, which was tied back into an intricate formal braid that ran down her back. She wore a ball gown that was made out of multiple different fabrics. White silk brocade made up most of the large skirt, with silver flowers embroidered into the navy fabric. On top of the silk skirt was blue tulle in a variety of different shades, bunched up around her hips in a triangular fashion. Silver tulle flowers, handmade and stitched with diamonds, were placed on top of the tulle. The diamonds embellished the corset top, which hugged her curves and pushed her breasts upward. Around her neck was a thick and glimmering aquamarine necklace, with dangling earrings to match. White gloves covered her hands all the way up to her elbows.

She was fit to be a queen. As I tried to comprehend the flood of powerful emotions that were coursing through my veins at the sight of how gorgeous she was, I knew she was mine. Completely and wholly. The gods had chosen well for me.

I only hoped I'd meet her expectations.

When she came near, I reached out a hand to take hers. She lifted her skirt and proceeded down the rest of the stairs with an elegance most girls could only dream of achieving. It had to be the figure skater in her.

"You look handsome." Her eyes met mine before they roved my body up and down, taking me in.

"Thank you." I was wearing the traditional wolven court uniform for my status; a navy blue coat with silver buttons, a silver sash across my chest, long black pants, and a white fur cloak off my shoulder. A few medallions hung off the left side of my coat to show my royal status. "But I'm sure no one will notice me, standing next to you. You're radiant."

She flashed a dazzling smile and said, "Shall we go?"

"Of course." We walked together down the hallway. She linked her arm in mine, and I was certain that we *looked* the part— unsure if we could pull it off, though.

"Where are the others?" Emma asked curiously.

"They'll be meeting us at the ball." As contestants, both of us were required to keep a court — knights for me, and ladies in waiting for her. We had to have six people beside us, one from every Faction. We'd picked the obvious choices. Stefan, Alexei, and Theo for me, and Delmare, Kiara, and Odette for her.

The skies were dark when we ventured outside, and a heavy snowfall was trickling down from the skies. A carriage was waiting for us, pulled by a white horse. The driver opened the door for us, and I helped Emma inside. It was a struggle to get her giant skirt past the door.

As the carriage started down the cobblestone streets, I rummaged inside a trunk that had been placed inside. "You'll want this." I handed Emma a white fur shawl, one to match my cloak. "It's cold in the square. I didn't want you getting sick."

"Thank you." She wrapped the shawl around her shoulders and stared out the carriage window. "So how does this work? Do I get a title?"

"Each of the Contest participants are called contestants. Whoever wins the Contest will be given the title of Prince, and his Marked, Princess. Once they're crowned, they're bestowed the title of King and Queen, but the coronation won't happen until one year after the Contest's passing."

"What happens to your rank if we don't win?" Emma asked.

"I'll still keep the title of Regent Prince even if I lose, but I'll cease to have any true power." I balled my fists. "That's something we cannot permit to happen."

Emma nodded. An intensity burned in her eyes. She wanted this as badly as I did. She believed she was making a huge sacrifice by marrying me. If we didn't win, it'd all be for nothing.

However much I wanted to… I couldn't bring myself to tell her we were fated mates. I didn't want the distraction. Even if all I wanted was her in my arms tonight.

The square was crowded with thousands of people who'd come to see the contestants be pledged. When the carriage stopped, I exited and helped Emma step down. The loud conversation in the crowd died, and everyone turned to look our way.

There was complete silence. Emma took my arm, and people cleared a wide path for us as we walked toward the contestant stage. The mouths of Marked and shifters alike dropped open in disbelief. We'd arrived late, and on purpose. I wanted the other contestants to think I was backing out before showing up to intimidate them at the last second.

Lord Lucien was waiting by the stage. He nodded kindly to us as we began climbing the wooden stairs upward.

"Nervous?" I asked my mate as we neared the top.

"Of course not," Emma said. "This isn't the first time I've performed for an audience."

Wouldn't be the last time, either.

Elijah, I was pleased to see, was furious. He was certain I was going to drop out. He had a difficult time keeping a straight face as he observed Emma and I. I swore he'd burst out of his skin and change into a wolven that instant if diplomacy didn't demand that he behave.

Gabby didn't look too happy, either. She was practically shaking with fury as her dagger-like gaze pierced into Emma's skin. My mate wasn't the slightest bit intimidated by her. Emma held her nose high up in the air like Gabby was beneath her as we took our place onstage alongside the other contestants.

"Congratulations, cripple. You've found a wife," Elijah snarled as I passed.

Emma lifted her eyebrow, but that was her only reaction.

"The proper way to refer to me is *your highness*," I replied back coolly. "Don't forget your station."

"For now," Elijah said. I didn't allow him to say anything further, because I led Emma to the opposite side of the stage. There were sixteen contestants total, four from each Faction. Eight potential kings and eight potential queens, ready to take their shot at glory.

In the center of the stage was a giant wooden arch, twisted with gnarled branches and pine needles. The same priestess that had led the Day of the Dead ceremonies came forward. Today, she was wearing a thick fur cloak that draped down her shoulders, with a deerskin dress and an antlered headpiece.

The High Priestess raised her hands, and the crowd quieted. Her magic amplified her voice so the entire square could hear. "People of Malovia!" she cried. "We commence a celebration of great meaning! Tonight is the official opening of the King's Contest, and the beginning of our quest for a new king!"

The crowd of thousands cheered. Their noise was so loud it shook the mountains. I'd appeared before an audience many times before, but this was different. My authority as alpha was being questioned.

That would cease after the Contest was over.

The High Priestess extended her hand to the alicorn couple near the center of the stage. "We shall begin the opening ceremonies with the declaration of Choosing. The contestants will announce their chosen mates, and declare which god or goddess they are devoted to. Albin Eryk and Krystyna Manfred, please step forward."

Albin and Krystyna came underneath the arch. The High Priestess told them to join hands, and the square became deadly silent. Her voice took on a serious tone as she asked, "Do you, Albin Eryk, join yourself to this sorceress in mind, body, and spirit, proclaim her to be your mate, vow to one day be married with her in sacred union, defending her at all costs?"

Albin cleared his throat. He seemed nervous. His voice stuttered when he spoke, "I proclaim that Krystyna Manfred is my mate, for now and forever, until my watch is over and until the end of time."

The High Priestess turned from him and to Krystyna. "Do you, Krystyna Manfred, vow to join yourself to this shifter in mind, body, and spirit, proclaim him to be your mate, vow to one day be married with him in sacred union, loving him despite whatever cost?"

Krystyna hiccuped. It was such an odd thing to do that most people were taken aback. Her eyes widened, and she rushed to say, "I proclaim that Albin Eryk is my mate, for now and forever, until my watch on the hunt is over and until the end of time."

Rapturous applause and cheering rose from the audience. Cannons went off somewhere, as was tradition, and music struck up to be played. Huge smiles lit up the faces of both Albin and Krystyna. It was obvious that they were actually fated mates and not just together for the sake of the Contest. As Albin and Krystyna took their place back in line, the noise quieted, and the High Priestess called up the second alicorn couple.

Each of the other three Factions was introduced until finally, it was time for the wolvens. Emma and I would go first. The High Priestess gestured to us, and Emma and I came forward underneath the arch.

"Join hands," the High Priestess said, and I took Emma's hands in mine. They were colder than I thought they were. I rubbed them with my thumbs to try and warm them, and she smiled slightly.

The High Priestess looked at me. Do you, Ethan Nowak, join yourself to this sorceress in mind, body, and spirit, proclaim her to be your mate, vow to one day be married with her in sacred union, defending her at all costs?"

"I proclaim that Emmaline Sosna is my mate, for now and forever, until my watch on the hunt is over and until the end of time," I recited, the words sending a thrill through my body.

Emma didn't know I meant every word of it. Her eyes were fixed clearly on me— like I was the only person she could see.

There were whispers at Emma's name. It was strange. It was like the crowd was in shock. I didn't understand it.

"Do you, Emmaline Sosna, vow to join yourself to this shifter in mind, body, and spirit, proclaim him to be your mate, vow to one day be married with him in sacred union, loving him despite whatever cost?" the High Priestess asked Emma.

Emma hesitated. She didn't respond right away. Long minutes passed… the seconds became torturous and agonizing.

Oh, shit. She was going to back out. She was going to change her mind in front of all these people, and completely break my heart.

She couldn't do this to me. Not here, not now. I'd lose it. I'd lose everything if I lost her.

Then Emma swallowed and said, "I proclaim that Ethan Nowak is my mate, for now and forever, until my watch on the hunt is over and until the end of time."

Relief flooded through my veins and made my shoulders sag. She'd accepted my mating offer. It was done. She was mine. Now and forever.

A warmth spread through me at the thought. Emma belonged to me, and I belonged to her. That's what mating was. It was how it should be.

Nobody applauded or cheered when Emma took her vow. All there was to be heard was stunned silence… until someone from within the crowd broke the quiet.

"This is preposterous! Her mother denied King Lycus his mating bond!" a sorceress screamed.

"She's a bastard queen! Her mother conceived her outside the mating bed!" another yelled.

I stepped forward, ready to jump off the stage and find whoever was saying this blasphemous nonsense. Emma, a bastard? How dare they accuse her mother of such crimes?

Something struck me. I knew my father's mate had denied his bond, and that's why he ended up marrying my mother, but he'd never told me who his *true* mate was. What did Emma have to do with any of it?

Was Emma's mother the one who'd turned away my father's love?

The crowd's voices began to raise. It looked like a riot was forming. The High Priestess raised her hands. "Ladies and gentlemen, please," she cried. "Save your accusations until after the King's Contest is over."

The crowd settled, though resentful eyes turned our way. "Emma, what's going on?" I whispered under my breath as we left the arch.

"Tell you later." Emma's face was hard as stone. She knew exactly what the crowd was talking about. I figured it was best to trust her and ask questions after the ceremony was over.

Gabby and Elijah were after us. The way they proclaimed themselves to be mates was boastful and over the top, instead of sensitive and authentic like Emma and I. It made me feel sick. They were clearly loving all the attention.

After all the contestants had made their mating declarations, the High Priestess came forward and said, "Now each contestant will announce to which of the Seven Gods they pledge their loyalty. Albin, please come forward."

Albin pledged himself to Vesna, the goddess of wisdom, while Krystyna chose Radek, the god of truth. The High Priestess worked her way down the line until it was once again Emma and I's turn.

My knees shook as I approached the arch and kneeled before the priestess. Mine would be a controversial choice, but I'd made my decision long ago. This was what was right in my heart.

"Ethan Nowak, to which god do you align?" the priestess asked.

I proclaimed loudly, "I pledge myself to Luka. The Thief God."

More shocked exclamations ran through the crowd, but I did my best to ignore them. No king had ever pledged themselves to Luka, the god of peasants, before. Most picked Tomir, the King of the Seven Gods. Emma and I were certainly causing a stir tonight. When I looked back at Emma, her eyes were narrowed, as if she was trying to figure something out.

The crowd booed as Emma made her way to the arch, but she kept her eyes fixed ahead as if their hatred didn't bother her. She kneeled gracefully before the High Priestess and bowed her head.

"Tell me, my child," the High Priestess said. "Which god do you pledge your life to?"

"I pledge myself to Milonna," Emma said. "The goddess of love."

That was a typical queen's choice. It was probably the least controversial thing we'd done all night. Emma got up and made her way back to me. When she stood at my side, her body pressed against mine.

"Don't let me fall," she whispered. Her knees were wobbling from nervousness.

"Never." I looped my arm around her waist and supported her weight. Her shaking ended as I tightened my grip around her.

I wanted to punch Elijah in the face as I watched him swagger up to the arch like he'd already been crowned king. He kneeled before the High Priestess, but only took one knee, not two.

A sign of disrespect if I ever saw one. He constantly spit in the face of our customs. Some king he'd make.

"Elijah, who do you swear your allegiance to?" the High Priestess asked.

"I swear myself to Droga," Elijah said. "The Dark God."

A unanimous gasp rose up among the crowd, and a bottomless pit formed in my stomach. I shouldn't be surprised, but I was. Elijah had sworn himself to evil.

The crowd had backed away several paces from the stage, staring up at Elijah like he was some kind of curse. Never mind about Emma and I causing a ruckus. Elijah had totally stolen our spotlight and put it entirely on him. The King's Contest was very interesting this year. Elijah rose to his feet, pleased at all the pale faces in the crowd.

The High Priestess gaped. "Are… are you quite sure?"

"Very," Elijah replied. "Droga is the god I choose to serve."

The High Priestess closed her mouth. "Very well," she replied. "May the Seven Gods honor your decision."

Elijah swept back to his spot on the stage. Several contestants moved away from him, as if they didn't want to get too close. The only people who'd ever served Droga were users of dark magic. But it wasn't illegal to pledge yourself to any god, and Elijah was well within his right to declare Droga his master.

At least Emma and I had a better chance now with the support of the people. The majority of them wouldn't back up Elijah, with the choice of god he'd just made.

Gabby made the same choice. She pledged herself to Droga with a wide smile and giggles, like she was swearing her soul to a paradise instead of an evil being. Gabby sneered at Emma as she passed by, but Emma did her part of acting regal and kept a polite expression, though her hands bunched in her dress. I could tell she wanted to claw Gabby's eyes out.

The High Priestess came forward and lifted her hands. "The contestants have made their declarations! Let us celebrate by beginning the festivities of the King's Ball!"

The crowd cheered, though the applause was subdued and hesitant. A path was cleared as the contestants left the stage and made their way back to the carriages. I relaxed as the carriage doors closed behind Emma and I and began moving in the way of the palace.

Emma's lip was trembling. She looked like she was going to cry. "I'm so sorry, Ethan. I should've told you before we got here."

"Should've told me what? Don't cry." I reached over and wiped away a singular tear off her cheek. "I'm proud you kept it together in front of all those people."

"Like I have a choice. Dammit, I'm ruining my makeup. Odette's going to have a cow." Emma fished in her clutch for a tissue and dotted at her eyes before she said, "I knew word would get out about me."

"What do you mean? We don't have a lot of time, so tell me quickly," I said.

She took a deep breath. "I just found out recently, but my mother told me she was mated to your dad, the king. But she broke that mating bond, because she bonded with another shifter."

"So that's why you brought it up the other day. I didn't know that could happen," I said.

Emma's voice was tight. "I didn't either, but my mom swore it could. His name was Anastazy Ignacy. The Black Claw killed him. He was trying to protect me from being taken by them, so they could use my blood to raise Droga. They knew about me, even back then. Mom took me to America, to protect me."

Emma shook her head. "But people don't know all that. They probably think my mom screwed around with a human or something."

"If you say that your mother bonded with two shifters, I believe you," I said. "But you have to know this. I don't care about anything they're saying, Emma. We're in this together, you and me."

"But not everyone believes me. They don't know my true bloodline. They consider me unfit to rule by your side. I've caused a scandal and embarrassed you," she protested.

"There are always scandals in the royal court. It's nothing new." I rolled my eyes. "If anything, you've only made us more interesting."

Emma let out a skeptical noise. "Yeah, well, people love drama."

"That I agree with." The palace came into view outside the window. "Look, Emma. We're passing through the gates now."

I parted the curtains in the carriage window, and Emma gasped. The palace came into view, lit up by spotlights made from illusions. She left her cloak behind on the seat as the carriage began to slow.

The carriage stopped before the grand staircase that led to the main entrance, and Emma held my hand tightly as we climbed them. The double doors were made of gold and over a hundred feet tall. They opened by magic as the contestants approached. The palace had been decorated for the King's Ball, adorned in garlands, wreaths, and colored lights. Candles hovered in the air over the long hallway, and guests wearing their finest attire drank champagne as servants hurried this way and that.

"This is your house?" Emma gaped.

"Well, I live here, so yes," I replied. "It'll be your house too, once we win the Contest."

"You know what? Marrying you will be worth it, just to live in a palace." She grinned.

I laughed. The long hallway ended and opened up into the Imperial Ballroom. There was a fifty-foot tall Christmas tree in the center, decorated with silver and gold ornaments. Our reflections shone off the polished marble floor, and paintings of former kings and queens lined the embellished walls. A string quartet, accompanied by a pianist, played soft music in the corner. Tables with floor-length tablecloths and chairs adorned with ribbons made a circle around the room. An illusion made snowflakes fall from the ceiling, though they vanished before they reached the floor.

My mother, the queen, sat on a throne that was placed on a raised platform so she could observe the party. She caught my gaze, then her eyes flickered to Emma. She raised an eyebrow and turned her eyes away.

She hadn't approved of my mating choice, but that was on her. It was too late to go back now.

"Is that your mom?" Emma hushed. She stared at the queen with wide eyes.

"Yes," I replied. "We'll meet her later. Right now, it's time for the feast."

Odette, Delmare, Kiara, Theo, Stefan, and Alexei were already at a table near the head of the room, waiting for us. Our friends had barely followed the dress code. Odette was wearing a ballgown that had a jeweled white top and a pastel rainbow skirt, along with a diamond headpiece that made it look like she had an alicorn horn nestled in her curls. Delmare looked like some sort of queen of spiders, with a long-sleeved black evening gown made entirely of lace. Her wore heavy eyeshadow and black lipstick, along with a ribbon choker. Kiara's dress was— by the gods— low cut in the... erm, chest area... and *cheetah print.*

Theo had opted for a regular black tuxedo, though Odette had pressured him into wearing a rainbow tie. Stefan's tux was wrinkled, and burned at the edges. Alexei had opted for a tan suit instead of a black tuxedo, and was totally out of place among all the other men here.

It was like none of them had gotten the attire requirements. We'd certainly attract attention. I helped Emma into her chair before taking a seat. I was trying to get over how odd it was to see Stefan in a tux.

"Thank the gods you showed up," Stefan moaned. "I'm fucking starving."

"Don't swear here," I snapped. "People will overhear you."

"Let them!" Stefan smirked. "Bring on the ale! I want to be unable to walk before the night is over. You'll have to carry me out, babe."

Stefan prodded Delmare's side, and she rolled her eyes at him.

"You're so uncouth." Theo sniffed before taking a sip of champagne. "That's just what Ethan needs, a drunk knight in his court making things harder for him."

"Like they're not difficult enough," Alexei subbed in. "We overheard your Choosing didn't exactly go as planned. People are starting to talk."

"I hope some of you tried to dispel the rumors about us," I said bluntly.

"Oh, certainly," Theo said. "If you consider Stefan making dick jokes helpful to the cause."

"*Severed* dick jokes," Alexei added.

Theo's mouth was a thin line. "Yes. I'm certain he offended a diplomat before we even walked in the door."

I groaned and put my face in my hand. "I hate you all."

"Hey, the monarchy needs a little livening up," Stefan said. "Once you're king, Ethan, there are gonna be some *big* changes around here."

I should've picked better knights. At least Emma's ladies in waiting were behaving. Somewhat.

"Ooh," Odette said, eyeing a brawny alicorn shifter on the other side of the room. "He's quite attractive. Do you think he's noticed me?"

"Odette, you already have a date. It's Theo," Kiara hissed. "You can't be seen flirting with another alicorn when you're part of Emma's court. It'll make people talk."

"No one will *see* us. We'll go behind one of the tapestries and make love," Odette crooned.

Theo abruptly stood up from the table. The chair made a loud *screech* as it was sent hurtling backward, causing several people to look our way. "I need more champagne." He briskly walked away and took two flutes off a servant's tray, downing them both.

Soon after, servants brought our plates. They were full of sausage, pierogi, paprikash, buttered noodles, cucumber salad, golabki, and angel wings for dessert.

I tried to focus on my food, because no one was behaving. Odette kept sighing over the other alicorn, and Theo drank more than he ate. Alexei was having a hard time keeping his eyes on Kiara's face and not her bosom as she talked on and on about various topics, though I don't think she noticed.

Emma picked at her food. I reached under the table and grabbed her free hand. I gave it a squeeze. "Hey," I whispered. "You need to eat to keep your strength up. It's going to be a long night."

"I know," she whispered back. She grimaced and put a hand on her stomach. "I'm just nervous."

"Are you going to be sick?" I whispered.

"I won't be. I promise." Emma pushed her food around her plate listlessly. "I don't want to mess this up."

I picked up my fork and cut into a pierogi for her. I held it upward and said, "Here, just focus on me. Eat."

Her eyes connected with mine. She opened her mouth slightly, and I slipped the pierogi inside. She chewed and swallowed. I continued cutting up her food for her and feeding her as her gaze remained connected with mine. My whole body was growing hot. Gods, this was kind of sexy.

"Does it help if I feed you?" I asked lowly.

"Kind of," she admitted. She was starting to relax. My eyes drifted downward to sneak a glance at her breasts rising and falling in the corset.

People were staring at us— including my mother— but damn all if I cared. You were supposed to show that you loved your mate in public. I wanted people to think I was with Emma because we shared a mating bond, not that she was a last minute choice for the Contest.

Even if Emma didn't know the depths of my affection herself.

As I watched her lips form around the last bite, I had the idea I wanted her pretty mouth on other things. But that wasn't proper to think about at royal parties.

"What the hell are you guys doing over there?" Stefan asked as he watched us. "Some sort of foreplay?"

"Stefan, shut up," Theo slurred. He sloppily raised a hand to push Stefan over, but ended up knocking into Alexei instead. The glass of champagne Alexei was holding flung out of his hand and splattered all over the front of Kiara's dress. Kiara gasped as her front was soaked.

"Oh, gods, I'm so sorry." Alexei grabbed a napkin and tried to pat the champagne away, though his face grew red when he realized that his hand was close to Kiara's almost-exposed breasts.

"It's fine." Kiara waved her hand, and the champagne cleared away, leaving her dress clean. "Common cleaning illusion. No one will notice."

Alexei shrunk in his seat. Kiara acted like it wasn't a big deal, but the griffin himself was red with embarrassment.

Delmare literally snarled as Stefan stuck a noodle in his mouth and let it dangle off the other end. "Hey. Irena. I take one end of the noodle, you take the other, and we'll eat until we see where this leads?" he mumbled.

"If you touch me, I'm going to hit you," Delmare snapped, though a blush had started to creep over her cheeks. She was eyeing the other end of the noodle like she was actually considering his request.

"Please do. Hard," he pleaded. Delmare only held back because Emma kicked her under the table.

This was a mess. As our plates were cleared away, I immediately stood up. As entertaining as this was, Emma and I needed to get away from the circus.

"Would you like to dance, my lady?" I bowed to her before extending a hand.

Emma took it lightly and rose to her feet. "I'd love to."

As we proceeded toward the dance floor, the music started up into a light waltz. Emma grinned as she said, "Let's show all these asshats who the next King and Queen of the Arcanea are."

TWENTY

I was in *my* element now. I could dance better than any fucker at this party. Time to show everyone up.

As we crossed to the dance floor, Ethan put a hand on my hip. I placed my free hand on his shoulder and noticed how strong it felt. I ran my fingers over the muscles there, enjoying the feel of his broad stance. I wanted to run my hand in other places… down his chest, and his arms, and the front of his pants, but I denied myself the pleasure. Reputation was everything around here, and I couldn't be seen feeling up Ethan in the middle of a ball, even though we were proclaimed to be mated.

Ethan looked every part a prince. I'd never seen a man look so attractive as he did in his court uniform. His eyes gleamed, and his mouth was set in a slight smirk that was… for lack of a better term… really fucking hot.

He was incredibly handsome. It was almost enough to make me fall for him.

Almost.

It was nice having a dance partner who actually knew how to *dance* for a change. Most of the other goons back home couldn't do much of anything besides fist-pump. As Ethan swept me around the dance floor, I resisted the urge to press my body against his.

I wanted to take in all of him. I didn't care about his missing leg. I just wanted to see *him*.

I hadn't overlooked the fact that he'd chosen to serve Luka, the Thief God. Luka was the god of peasants. Ethan did have a commitment to serve the people. It was honorable. It stirred something in me I didn't know was there before.

Things were different between us now. Ever since he'd asked me to be his partner for the Contest, we'd gone from *just friends* to *something more*.

Yes. Everything had changed.

"You have the nicest dress at the party," Ethan whispered in my ear. His lips brushed against my neck as he said it, and I shivered. Right now, all I could think about was how badly I wanted Ethan to rip this dress off.

My heart ached when I remembered the Phantom. But that couldn't be helped. I'd chosen to let him go. I was Ethan's now.

And dammit if I didn't want him to fuck me on this dance floor in front of all these snobs.

"I *hope* I have the nicest dress," I managed to joke. "It certainly wasn't cheap."

"Of course not. You deserve only the best." Ethan spun me around before he put his hand on the small of my back and drew me closer.

I gulped. Uh-oh. This was getting a little intense.

"You remind me of an ice princess," Ethan whispered. "Like a queen out of a fairy tale."

He was really laying on the flattery. Bonus points for him trying to stir up the romance when he knew I'd given up my one chance at true love for him.

Oh, well. Like I said before, I could've done worse than a prince.

The other couples began to join us on the dance floor. Many of the other contestants were dancing respectfully, but Elijah and Gabby were clearly making the whole thing about themselves. They waltzed around in an elaborate way that took up most of the room and drew unneeded attention.

Gabby had chosen to wear a red dress that had a high-neck collar with black lace around the corset, along with a red cape that swept off her shoulders and trailed behind her. She looked like a fucking evil queen, and played the part all too well. Elijah wore a tuxedo of all black to match his dark heart.

Gabby sneered at me as Ethan and I spun past. It took everything in me to hold myself back and not rip her hair out.

Screw Gabby. My gown was prettier, and probably more expensive. My mother had spent over a grand on it. Mom told me she'd taken part in the King's Contest, too, alongside Ethan's dad. She'd helped him win.

But after she'd made sure he was crowned king, she picked Anastazy. Could I do the same? Could I break the vow I made to Ethan after I put him on the throne, and resume my search for the Phantom?

With one look at Ethan's face, I knew I couldn't. He looked so happy. I couldn't break his heart. Not even for love.

As the dance ended, there was applause. Lord Lucien had shown up. He put a hand on Ethan's arm and said, "I beg your pardon, but Steward Soloman and some other members of the Circle request your presence." Lord Lucien took a glance at me. "You look very lovely, Emma."

"Thank you," I replied. Lord Lucien appeared very charming himself, his long hair slicked back. He was very attractive for an older man.

Ethan turned to me. "Will you be all right while I deal with dreadful matters of state? I don't want to drag you into the boredom."

"I'll be fine. Go," I told him. Ethan walked off with Lucien, and I took the opportunity to go look for the girls. I found them gossiping by the statue of an alicorn. The boys were nowhere to be seen.

"Where did everyone go?" I asked as I broke into the circle.

"Well, in Stefan's words, he went to *go find some ale that doesn't taste like horse piss*," Delmare said.

"What about Alexei?" I asked.

"He's hiding from Kiara," Delmare whispered. Kiara smacked her on the arm, and Delmare snickered wickedly.

"He has no reason to hide from me," Kiara said. "I've done nothing."

"Except give him a hard-on!" Odette peeped, and she covered her mouth with her hands. Delmare held her gut as she bent over laughing.

Kiara scowled. "Everything is about dicks with you girls."

"Is there anything else to talk about?" Delmare glanced at me. "Where's princey-pie?"

"Talking to some boring old people, most likely," I said. A couple of people were watching me. I turned my back to them and asked, "How's the public reception going?"

"You're not very well liked, I can tell you that much," Kiara said. "The gossip going around is… to be desired."

"Like I give a shit what a bunch of stuffed shirts say about me," I hissed. They didn't know a thing about me.

"Either way, you and Ethan have fallen to last place for favorites," Kiara said. "Well, almost last. Elijah and Gabby sunk to the bottom once they announced their allegiance to Droga."

I glanced at the demonic couple themselves, but if they had fallen out of favor with the public, it didn't seem like it bothered them. They laughed and beamed at diplomats as if they were the public's first choice.

"Why are you even here, anyway?" Delmare broke in. "A few weeks ago, you acted like you and Ethan being together was impossible."

"We're not together. This is an arrangement out of mutual benefit," I said under my breath.

"That sounds romantic." Delmare snorted.

"It doesn't have to be. It's practical." I sounded like Ethan. Gods, he was already getting to me.

"But we thought that you'd already found your mate?" Kiara asked.

"Yeah. You said that you were mated to the Phantom?" Odette said, placing a hand on her hip.

I sighed, and played with the end of my braid. "I am. But I don't think he's ever going to come for me. I got tired of waiting."

"Ah. So you chose to become a gold digger instead. I approve," Delmare said, raising her glass in a toast.

"It's not like that!" I burst. My voice came out louder than I intended. Several people looked our way, and I dropped my tone a few octaves. "Ethan and I… there's something there, but I don't know what it is. Maybe I just want him in my pants, I don't know."

"At least you finally admit it," Delmare said.

"I think it's more than that," Kiara said. "You two… you look at each other in a way I've never seen before."

When Kiara said that, a glow bloomed in my chest and radiated throughout my entire being. It passed through my stomach and limbs, gleamed from the top of my head to the tips of my toes. It made me feel warm, as if being encompassed in a loving embrace. It was… unexpected to say the least.

"Do you really think that's true?" I whispered.

"Well, how do you feel about him?" Odette asked. The girls' inquisitive eyes bore into me.

I tapped my chin for a moment. "I've never thought about it before. But if I guess I had to put it into words… I wake up every morning thinking of him. And he's the last thing I think about when I go to sleep. I feel like he replaces something in me I didn't even know was missing. When he's there, I'm happy, and when it's not, it feels like… like nothing matters."

Kiara and Delmare's gazes were wide. Odette made a *pshing* sound and waved her hand. "That's nothing," she piped up. "I feel that way about Theo!"

Awkward. Kiara, Delmare and I knew what Odette was admitting, but I don't think Odette realized it herself.

It was at that moment the classical music changed, and modern dance music began flooding out of enchanted speakers that hovered over the dance floor.

"Ooh, I love this song!" Odette piped. She skipped away, presumably to dance by herself in a very twirling, ballerina manner.

As Odette left, I turned to the other girls. "How long do you think it's going to take before Odette realizes that Theo is her mate?"

"That girl? Never." Delmare snorted.

"Poor Theo." I searched the room for the alicorn himself. For as much lecturing as Theo had given Stefan on keeping sober, the alicorn shifter was swaying on his feet, continuing to down glasses of champagne.

"Why doesn't he just tell her?" I asked. "He certainly knows they've bonded, even if she hasn't figured it out."

"Don't get involved in another mated pair's business, Emma," Delmare said wisely. "It only leads to trouble. Besides, you need to focus on making a good impression tonight."

"Putting on a performance, you mean." Ethan had been parading me around like a show poodle since the Choosing began. Not that I didn't *like* being on his very brawny arm. It was nice to be showed off and made to feel like I was someone to envy.

"Yes! It's all an act. It can't be that different from ice skating," Delmare said.

"It's really not."

A shadow fell over me from behind. I figured it was Gabby, and took in a breath so I could give her a piece of my mind.

Kiara and Delmare gasped at the same time, ducking into low curtsies. "My queen!" Kiara exclaimed. I whirled around— my mouth fell open at the sight of the woman in front of me.

It was Ethan's mother, Queen Antonia. She was wearing a dark navy gown, her dark hair fashioned into an elaborate updo that was woven around a silver crown at least ten inches in height. I didn't know how she kept upright with that gigantor thing on her head. It looked like if she nodded, she'd fall over.

"Emmaline. So wonderful to meet you," Queen Antonia said, though she didn't make it sound wonderful at all. More like water torture.

"My queen." I forced myself to get a grip and curtseyed as well, though not as low as the others. It was probably clumsy and American, because the queen sniffed as I rose to my full height.

"So this is your court," she said. Her gaze roamed over my ladies in waiting. I could tell she disapproved of their outfits, though I wasn't sure what she thought about mine. "Charming."

I gulped. The queen turned slightly and said, "I request a moment with you, Emmaline. Privately."

Like I could refuse. I clasped my hands in front of me to stop them from shaking as Queen Antonia led me out of the ballroom and into the hall. We entered into a parlor, where the very walls looked like they were made of gold.

It hit me just how much money Ethan had. Just how powerful his family was. How powerful *he* was.

I'd failed to see him like that at school, because he didn't act like a prince there. He just seemed like my friend. Like any other average guy.

Now I realized he was so much more. What the hell was I doing here? I didn't belong here. I didn't belong at Ethan's side. I could never fit into a royal lifestyle like this. The most I could do was pretend.

Queen Antonia shut the door behind her and faced me. "Forgive me for taking my son away from you. There was no other way."

It took seconds to piece something together very quickly. Steward Soloman hadn't requested Ethan's presence at all. That was just a distraction so the queen could get me alone.

The Circle might be the ruling body in Malovia, but it was clear who really ran the show.

"Let me be frank," Queen Antonia said. She took a slow step toward me, and gods, it freaked me out more than any monster I'd ever seen. "You were not my first choice for my son's wife. You weren't the second. In fact, you weren't even on the list."

Queen Antonia curled her lip. "An outsider as heir to the throne. The daughter of the woman who broke my husband's heart, no less. An American, with no proper breeding. Not even a full-born Arcanea. You're not fit to be queen."

I wanted to tell her she was wrong, but I kept silent. If I wanted Ethan to be king— and I did, for him, because he deserved it— I had to get along with the in-laws.

She shook her head. "I was hoping he'd pick Chastity. But for some reason, he chose you, and it's too late to go back. What I want to find out is why."

I had to steady my voice so it didn't shake. "Why don't you ask him yourself?"

"Careful, girl." The queen's eyes flared. "You haven't won the Contest yet."

I bit the inside of my mouth and said, "I couldn't tell you why Ethan—"

"Prince Ethan. Remember you have no title."

I took a deep breath. "Why *Prince Ethan* chose me. He barely told me himself. All he said was that I could help him."

"And are you going to?" Queen Antonia raised an eyebrow.

I didn't know what was proper to say, so I forced out, "I'm well prepared to win the Contest. I'll do whatever it takes."

"I hope you are," Queen Antonia said coldly. "Because if you lose, and cost my son his kingdom, there will be consequences for you. Whether it is your fault or not."

Fear constricted me. What would the queen do? Would she compromise my medical supply somehow? Would she go after my friends?

Would she hurt my mother?

"Your embarrassing display at the ball tonight has made a mockery out of my son, and that cannot be allowed to continue," Queen Antonia went on. "Your behavior might be permissible in the United States, but in Malovia, you'll find things are different. You have quite the audacity to show up here with that humiliating court."

Rage flared up inside of me, cold and bitter as a snowstorm. Queen Antonia might be head bitch around here, but nobody insulted my friends.

The most powerful woman in all of Malovia was threatening me, and the only way I could put a stop to it is if I took her place. Which I fully intended to do.

"Allow me to make something very clear, *my queen*," I said, in the rudest tone I dared to use. "I *do* know why your son chose me. Because he knew I'd make damn well sure to get the job done."

The corners of her mouth lifted. Queen Antonia got so close to me I could smell the perfume dotted around her ears. "Oh, you're a wolven, all right," she said. "You've got the blood of the hunt on you. Maybe you're good for something yet."

It was then the doors flew open. They slammed against the walls as an elderly woman in a glittering evening dress glided into our presence, heels clicking sharply against the marble floors. I sagged in relief as she approached.

"Lady Magdalina," Queen Antonia breathed. "I wasn't expecting you tonight."

"Yes, I'm certain you weren't," Lady Magdalina said sharply. "Now if you don't mind, I'd like Emmaline to return to the ball. I am her sponsor for the Contest, after all, and it's better if she doesn't hide away in here with you."

I didn't know she was my sponsor. Queen Antonia stepped away from me and said, "As you wish, Headmistress."

I hurried my ass out of there as quickly as I could. Lady Magdalina strode beside me, though it was almost more of a march.

"Thank you for saving me," I told her. "I didn't know if I could stand it a moment longer."

"You mustn't allow her to threaten you, Emmaline," Magdalina told me. "Queen Antonia doesn't deal kindly with her rivals, and you're threatening her place on the throne. If you don't show her you're an equal, she'll use you as her plaything."

"But I'm not her equal. I have no title yet," I told her.

"She respects strong magic. And she respects power," Lady Magdalina said. "Make sure to show her you have both during the Contest."

When we got back to the ballroom, Lady Magdalina left me to go speak in hushed tones with Lord Lucien. He seemed concerned, but didn't move to do anything, merely fixed his eyes on me from across the room.

What Lady Magdalina said was eating away at me. I was a threat to the queen. She didn't want me coming on her turf and messing up her business. Was Queen Antonia reluctant to give up her rule? Even if her own son took her place? What a selfish bitch.

Kiara, Delmare, and Odette were at my side within minutes. "What happened?" Kiara breathed.

I felt like I was going to faint. "Bathroom. Now," I squeaked.

We ran to the nearest powder room. I collapsed in a chair. The girls hovered around me. Kiara locked the door behind us. Odette fanned my face, while Delmare got me a glass of water from the cups placed out in a golden cart near the sink.

"Snap out of it," Delmare spat. "You've gotta pull yourself together."

My voice was hoarse. "Guys, the queen's totally after me. If I don't win this Contest, there's no telling what she'll do to me. Or any of us." I chugged the glass of water and tried not to throw it back up.

"You're not going to lose," Kiara said calmly. "You've got this under control."

"Yeah, if I don't frickin die first." I'd checked stats, and at least a quarter of the contestants always perished in the Contest. It was a deadly competition that not everyone walked away from. I was sure I'd come out of it alive when I'd agreed to be Ethan's partner, but now I wasn't so certain— especially with the queen watching my every move.

"Like Ethan would ever let anything happen to you." Delmare rolled her eyes. "He'd give up the Contest first before he'd let you die."

My heart rate began to slow. A hated emotion festered in my chest. Hope. "You think so?"

"Yeah," Odette piped up. "He needs you to win! Both contestants have to survive in order to take the crown."

A glum cloud settled over me. "You're right. He wouldn't let me die." If only for the fact that he needed me to win.

"I don't think that's what she meant," Kiara said, with a quick glance at Delmare. But I was barely listening. I rose to my feet.

"Come on, girls." I was still a little unsteady, but I was starting to get my bearings back. "I've gotta get back out there."

Delmare was right. I had to pull myself together. Right now, I looked weak, and if I continued to behave that way the other contestants would eat me alive tomorrow. I couldn't afford to look incapable. If I was going to be a queen, I needed to act like it.

I intended to head back to the ballroom, find Ethan, and stick to him like glue the rest of the night. He would protect me, and it'd look better if we gave a united front. This might be a dance, but it was more like a battlefield. People intended to divide us tonight, so they could get in our heads. It would be much harder to do that if we were together.

Except there was one problem. We ended up getting lost. The palace was massive, and I'd been in such a hurry to get to a restroom that I hadn't looked where I was going, and neither had anyone else. I remember the powder room being right off the main hallway, but we'd obviously taken a wrong turn coming out, because we were nowhere near the ballroom now. The music kept getting quieter and quieter as we continued to roam the castle's dark halls.

"Shouldn't there be a servant or something, to tell us where to go?" Delmare complained. "We've been walking forever."

I went to respond, but I heard harsh and hushed voices ahead of me. One of them sounded like Gabby.

I put a finger to my lips to tell the other girls to be quiet, and we pressed against the wall. Gabby's voice, along with Elijah's, rang out in a sharp whisper from around the corner.

"Waldron's death was supposed to deter the other contestants. It didn't do a damn thing!" Gabby hissed.

My eyes widened. They were talking about Professor Waldron's murder. I pressed myself even closer to the wall, and the girls huddled around me.

"I wouldn't say it didn't have benefits. Cibor was a notable opponent for the alicorns, and he dropped interest in the Contest after I took care of Waldron. Albin and Krystyna are laughable replacements," Elijah replied.

My blood ran cold. Elijah *took care* of Waldron? Did that mean… he killed him?

"You should've done a better job," Gabby spat. "It wasn't enough."

"I tore his organs out and put him on a spike. I'm not sure how graphic you want me to go," Elijah replied coolly.

Odette made a small sound, but Delmare wrapped her hand around Odette's mouth so she'd be quiet. My heartbeat quickened when there was a pause— but then the two resumed their conversation.

"I get that it made a few people drop out. The competition is much easier to conquer, but we needed *Ethan* to quit. He's our biggest challenger," Gabby hissed.

"Do you honestly think he and his welp bitch are a threat to us?" Elijah sneered.

"She's Magdalina's favorite. That's a problem for us. She needed to be taken out."

"That was your task, and you failed. It was your fault Morgan got the bad end of your spell instead of Sosna."

Kiara grabbed my arm. I grabbed her back and held on tight.

"I didn't intend to hurt Morgan," Gabby said slowly. "You know that was an accident."

"You should've checked before you cast the curse!" Elijah said, voice rising.

"I would've revealed my position!" Gabby burst. "The plan was to hide in her dorm until Sosna showed up, and kill her so Ethan wouldn't pick her for the Contest. If I had known Morgan was going to pull that prank, I would've waited another night."

"Well, your poor execution got us into this situation now," Elijah said. "Your efforts to take Sosna down should've became more desperate after you failed the first time!"

"Magdalina is *always watching her*," Gabby insisted. "It's not as easy as you think. I barely got away with hurting Morgan! The headmistress has her eye on me. Why couldn't you just take care of the situation altogether, and eliminate Nowak?"

"You know why I couldn't do that. The prince is too powerful. If I had tried anything against him, and failed, Queen Antonia would've suspected me first, as I'd be the obvious choice. Then she'd have my head." Elijah's tone was thick with disgust.

"It doesn't matter." Gabby's tone was nervous. "We can eliminate them during the Contest. It's a dangerous competition. People die every time."

"Forgive me, but I think we'll be too busy worrying about saving our own necks to be preoccupied about slitting theirs," Elijah said sarcastically.

"We still need Sosna's blood," Gabby said. "Even after this is all over. Otherwise, our deal with the Black Claw is null and void."

I was so stunned I couldn't move. Elijah and Gabby knew about the Black Claw's plan to use my blood to raise the Dark God? How?

"I'm well aware." Elijah's voice had grown cold. "It's something to worry about after the Contest is over."

"We need to worry about it *now*. If she dies during the Contest, we have to gather a large enough vial to perform the ceremony."

"We'll make it work. The Black Claw wouldn't have declared me the Hidden King if they didn't believe I'd fulfill their dark prophecy. They claim I'm the one they've been waiting for."

"And are you?"

"Is there any doubt?"

There was silence for a moment, and Elijah said, "Come. We need to get back to the party, before we're missed."

The four of us along the wall started, but their footsteps faded in the opposite direction. We didn't move away from the wall until it was clear both of them were out of earshot.

Holy shit. Elijah was in with the Black Claw. The cult had him in their pocket. They'd proclaimed him the Hidden King.

I don't know why I was so surprised. This should've been obvious from the beginning. By the gods, how could I have been so *stupid*? The signs were right in front of me all along. Guess I should've spent more time solving murders instead of chasing after the Phantom.

If Elijah won the Contest and was put on the throne, Malovia's worst nightmare would come true. The Black Claw would have total control of the monarchy, the country, and everyone in it.

"What the hell was all that? Did Elijah just confess to murder?" Delmare asked.

"And Gabby, too. She tried to kill Emma!" Odette peeped.

"We need to tell the authorities about this," Kiara said. "Elijah and Gabby will be kicked out of the Contest for such crimes."

"No," I said slowly. "They won't be."

The girls gaped at me. "What are you talking about, Emma?" Delmare asked.

"We don't have any proof," I said. "What's it going to look like if I accuse them of murder on the night of the King's Ball? People will think I'm trying to get them kicked out, so Ethan and I have a better shot at winning."

"But... we heard them with our own ears," Odette said.

"We didn't record it," I said. "Without evidence, it's our word against theirs. We don't have any proof."

Delmare frowned. Kiara and Odette both dropped their gazes in defeat. They knew I was right.

"Should we tell Ethan?" Delmare asked.

I hesitated. Ethan had the right to know about this. But at the same time, the King's Contest started tomorrow. This would be a huge distraction. He'd be so busy trying to get justice for Waldron that he wouldn't focus on winning the Contest, and there'd be a bigger chance we'd lose.

Everything rode on us getting that crown. This would have to wait.

"We need to keep this a secret, for now," I told the girls. "I'll tell Ethan what Elijah did after the Contest is over. Then he might be able to do something about it."

Kiara nodded. "Right. None of us will say a word."

"Not to any of the boys, either. They'll tell Ethan," I said sharply when Odette opened her mouth. "This stays between us girls."

"Ooh, a secret." Odette's eyes widened. "Don't worry, Emma, we'll keep this on the down-low."

"But Gabby said they would try to kill you during the Contest. Shouldn't we be worried?" Kiara asked.

"They can damn well try." I narrowed my eyes. "All I can say is, they'd better watch their backs."

"Agreed," Kiara said firmly, and she nodded. "It's the job of the ladies in waiting, and the knights, to protect their contestants and make sure they make it through to each task safely. Don't worry, Emma. The rest of us will make sure Gabby and Elijah don't tamper with your stuff. You and Ethan just focus on winning that Contest."

We were still lost, but when we headed in the direction Gabby and Elijah had gone, we found our way back to the ballroom. I didn't see either of them mingling with the crowd. The only person I recognized was Theo, who was sitting at a table by himself and looking rather forlorn.

The four of us dispersed— Kiara went off to go find Gabby and Elijah. Her idea was to tail them for the rest of the night at a distance, just in case the two of them decided to try to come up with a plan to off me and Ethan. We gave Odette the job of acting natural, so at least one of us didn't look suspicious. Delmare headed off on her own, to look for Stefan and Alexei.

Before I found Ethan, I wanted to talk to Theo first. He just looked so freaking pitiful. I slunk into the seat beside him and adjusted my skirt. He barely glanced at me. His eyes trailed Odette as she weaved her way around the ballroom.

"You want to tell me what's going on?" I asked. I flung a leg over my knee and bobbed my foot to the music.

Theo barely glanced at me before finishing his drink. "I have no idea what you're talking about."

"Bull," I spat at him. "You've been eyeing Odette all night. You're wearing a fucking rainbow tie because she wanted you to. Something's up between you two, and it's more than a little crush."

Theo sighed and set down his drink. "You've caught me, Emma. As has everyone else. What do you need to know?"

"When did you bond with Odette?" I asked. "And why is it taking you so long to tell her the truth?"

Theo paused for a moment, his fingers roaming over the champagne glass, before he said, "I bonded with Odette when we were kids. It's really rare for that to happen. I was only seven, she six. We were chosen as the lead dancers for the children's ballet, and, well… when I held her in my arms, I knew."

"Didn't she feel the mating bond connect, too?" I asked.

Theo shook his head. "It's not as obvious for sorceresses. The connection isn't as strong, not until they accept it. Sometimes it's easy for a Marked to overlook a bond, or be confused by it. You can feel something, but it might not be what you think."

Theo scratched his head. "The thing is, it was such a long time ago I don't think Odette remembers. You know how she forgets… things."

I nodded my head. Oh, I knew. "You have a polite way of putting how bubble-headed Odette can be."

He grimaced. "Well… she has a quirky personality, but there's more to it than she lets on."

"What do you mean?"

"Odette is on the autism spectrum."

"Really?" My eyes widened. "I didn't know that."

Theo nodded slowly. "Autism isn't as commonly diagnosed in girls, because they hide their symptoms more than boys do. But Odette had a lot of meltdowns when she was younger, so she was quickly diagnosed. She has trouble when her routine is changed, you know?"

Thinking over Odette's behavior in the past… yeah, I could see that she had autism. She struggled with social cues, and burst out words when it wasn't her turn to speak in order to be heard. Her emotions could be over-the-top, and she could get obsessive with her interests—ballet, for example.

"But she seems so outgoing," I said.

"She's friendly and loving, yes, but she never had a lot of friends. She was always too shy and had difficulty fitting in," Theo said. "She must've felt safe with you the first time she saw you at the train station. She usually doesn't latch onto people like that. It takes her time."

I felt a strong wave of affection for Odette. I think I loved her more than I ever did before in that moment. "I can see why you want to do this the right way."

"Odette thinks in a different way from most people. She sees the world in an incredible perspective, and I think that's beautiful. I'd never want to change anything about her," he said softly. "She's perfect the way she is. In every possible way."

Theo's tone oozed pure admiration and love for Odette. It was touching to hear. "She is perfect. A perfect friend. I hope she can be more than that to you… someday."

"I don't want to push her into anything," Theo rushed to explain. "I never told her I bonded with her, I just waited for her to come around on her own. But watching her be obsessed about finding a mate, when I'm right in front of her…"

Theo's face twisted. "It's really hard. It feels like my heart is breaking. But no matter how hard I try, I can't make her see me as anything more than a friend. And I'm worried it's going to be that way forever. Or worse, that she'll get desperate and throw herself at another alicorn—one who doesn't love her back. Not all Arcanea follow our laws, Emma. Some shifters use people."

I was sorry for him. Theo really loved Odette. But he wanted her to come to him, not the other way around. With Odette, the only thing that worked was giant neon signs.

"Odette needs something obvious," I told him. "She won't get the message any other way."

"But Emma—"

"You're not forcing her to be with you. Just… show her your true feelings. I don't think she has any clue you want to be more than friends."

Theo smacked his mouth a few times. "I think I'd rather be run through with a blade."

I rolled my eyes. "Don't be overdramatic."

"It's not dramatic. This is my mate," he insisted. "If she rejects me, I'll be alone forever. I don't think I could look for someone else. I would prefer to be alone if I'm not with Odette."

"Odette isn't going to reject you. Deep down, I know she loves you. She just hasn't realized it yet."

Theo stared at the champagne glass, watching the colors of the ball swirl in the light. "I understand. But I'm not willing to take the chance that I'll lose her for good."

I felt defeated. This conversation was going nowhere. Theo wasn't willing to put his heart on the line. And until he did, Odette would never know the truth.

I was relieved when I saw Ethan standing at the head of the ballroom, near the thrones. Luckily, his mother wasn't there. I hardly cared if I looked dignified as I hurtled myself across the room to his side.

"Hey," he said. He wrapped an arm around my waist, and I grew warm where he touched me. "You've been gone awhile. Anything interesting happen?"

I was almost bursting with the need to tell him everything. There were so many secrets that I was keeping from him… so many things he deserved to know.

But he couldn't. Not yet. I'd tell him the truth when it was the right time. For now, lying to him was the only way to keep him alive.

"No," I said. "Nothing."

"Me either." Ethan sighed. "This party's rather boring. I think it's time we take our leave. We've stayed as long as required to be polite."

Thank the gods. I don't think I could stand being here a moment longer. Not only was I tired of being watched and hounded by people, I was starting to get tired. My body was exhausted. I was already worried about how it'd hold up tomorrow. I needed to get as much rest as I could.

I took Ethan's arm, and we weaved around the crowd so we could get back to the main hallway. On our way out, I saw that Odette was finally paying attention to Theo. She was dancing with him, much like a five year old would dance with their father. Her feet were on his, her arms wrapped around his neck as he walked her back and forth. She laughed, and Theo lit up with the biggest smile in the world.

A couple of snooty old ladies were glaring at them and whispering but that their behavior was improper, but I sent a harsh glare their way, and they quickly scuttled off.

That's right. I was gonna be the new queen, bitch. The rules were changing around here.

We stepped outside the castle and into the falling snow. I heard raised voices. Delmare had found Stefan. They were having a fight, but I wasn't sure what it was about. They were screaming at the top of their lungs. The argument seemed like a serious one— not the annoyed bickering they usually had on a daily basis.

Alexei had backed off at a distance, his hands over his ears as he tried to block out the argument. It looked like his empathy powers were going into overdrive now that emotions were running high.

"I can't take this," Alexei said, and he pushed past us into the castle to get away from the fight. The argument only increased in volume. The carriage drivers watched the fight in a combination of interest and disgust.

"Irena, would you just *calm down*?" Stefan said. All playfulness about him was gone, replaced by a stern demeanor. I'd never seen him act that way before.

"Don't call me that!" Delmare shouted. She got right in his face. "*Delmare* is my name!"

"Irena is your name, too! It's your *first* name!" Stefan took another step forward until they were inches apart. "Why can't I call you that?"

"Because I don't like it," she hissed.

"Why not? It's a pretty name," he countered.

"Because *I'm not pretty,* okay?!" Delmare shouted, almost at the top of her lungs.

With a start, I realized that Delmare had meant it. She really did believe she was ugly.

There was way more to her pushing Stefan away then I ever thought there was.

Stefan's gaze softened. He took his hands and gently cupped them around her face. He lowered his voice as he whispered, "Yes you are."

Delmare's lip trembled. "I don't deserve this. I don't deserve *you.*"

Delmare pushed Stefan away and ran from the carriages, into the palace gardens. I went to follow, but Stefan noticed us and raised a hand.

"Don't. I'll talk to her." Stefan rushed after Delmare. The two figures became dark shadows as they vanished into the black night beyond.

Ethan's brow furrowed. He appeared troubled. "Do you think they'll be all right?"

"I hope so." I shook my head. You'd think living in a society where magic picked out your soulmate for you, dating would be easier. But from what I'd seen, the bond only made love ten times harder.

I shivered, and Ethan said, "We need to get you back to school, before you get a cold. Come on."

The way he tucked me under his arm as we walked to our carriage made me feel like I was the only girl in the world— the only woman that he could ever love.

I wished more than anything that were true.

Once we arrived at the university, Ethan cloaked my fur cape over my shoulders. The carriage rode off. Ethan and I were left standing underneath the stone archway.

Neither one of us wanted to part, it seemed. He looked like a painting, the backdrop of the campus around him and the falling snow coating his dark hair and eyelashes.

The fact that I was going to be married to him, but would never actually, completely be able to have *him*… have his heart and soul… was a hard pill to swallow. It tore me up inside.

"The Contest will begin at noon tomorrow. We're expected to be there by eight, to begin preparations," Ethan said. "I will be at your door by seven, so we can travel together."

"Swell." If there was one thing I hated, it was getting up early. Ethan owed me big time.

Ethan sighed. "It's going to be a long day."

"Right," I said sourly. "Let's just get this over with. So you can get what you want."

"What do you mean?" Ethan took a step closer to me.

I took a deep breath. "I get that you're just doing your duty. And yeah, I know that the country needs you and all. But I hope you understand what kind of sacrifice I'm making by joining you in this. What kind of a risk I'm putting myself through. It's not because Malovia needs us. I'm doing this for *you*… because I want you to be happy. I know you don't feel the same way, but I—"

The bell tolled midnight, and Ethan did something crazy. He leaned in to kiss me.

I don't know if he meant to, or if it just happened. One moment I was looking into those perfect eyes, and the next, his hands had reached out to yank me against him. His mouth ravenously pressed against mine.

The kiss was soft, and warm, and deliriously heated. It was better than anything I could've imagined. An empty part of me began to fill up as his gorgeous lips moved over mine, and a radiating buzzing spread throughout my body, beginning at my core and flowing all the way to the ends of my being.

I didn't know how to react to this. I'd never kissed anyone before. Never cared to. Men were too much work. But by the gods, *Ethan*. I wanted to fall inside of him and soar forever. This kiss felt like a flawless jump performed on the ice. It was better than a gold medal being placed around my neck after the perfect program. The kiss had every bit of the feeling of flying that skating gave me, but there was so much more behind it. I was surprised I didn't grow wings. I couldn't believe Ethan's lips were against mine. His touch was fueled by so much passion… and unspoken words that were brought to light without ever being said.

As if by instinct, I relaxed, and my eyes closed. I leaned into the kiss and moved my hands over his chest as the affection deepened. Ethan dared to drift his hands downward so they settled on my hips, but gods, I wanted more. Like, take-my-panties-off-*now* more.

I decided to take things up a notch. I lightly bit his lower lip before I glided the tip of my tongue against his. Ethan let out a moan, as if that one little motion drove him insane. He came closer and pressed his hips against mine.

I felt something brush up against my leg, and I realized… he had a freaking hard-on. Like, bad. It was so intense that I could feel it through the layers of my skirt. I'd never felt a guy's dick against me before, but just the sensation of Ethan rocking against my pelvis as we made out made me love it. All I wanted was for him to be in me, right then, right now.

But hell if it stopped there. My cloak slipped off as Ethan's hands roamed over my bare shoulders. He deepened the kiss and pushed his tongue further inside of my mouth. I accepted his offering and groaned. It seemed involuntary when I fisted my hands inside his hair and yanked his head back. I kissed him like this would be the last time. If all I had was this kiss forever, it wouldn't be enough. I needed to drink from this river of pleasure every day. Our chemistry was like some kind of drug, taking control of my mind and intoxicating every part of me until I could hardly stand to breathe.

Oh, gods. Please, touch my boobs.

I grabbed Ethan's hands and tried to put them over my breasts. But the moment I did that, it was like the spell ended. He broke the kiss and jumped back, taking a few quick breaths. His hair was wild, due to me messing it up, and the look in his eyes were panicked… like he couldn't believe he'd just done what he did.

Well, at least the question if he found me attractive was solved. I thought I didn't float his boat at all, but I turned out to be completely wrong.

I'd believed we'd never have sex. Now I was thinking my virginity wouldn't last till morning.

Ethan cleared his throat. "You… we should get to bed."

"What are you referring to?" I dared to ask. Ethan reddened a deep scarlet.

He managed to choke out, "We need sleep for tomorrow. It's already late."

Ethan took my hand. Our fingers intertwined as we entered the school and climbed the staircase back to the dormitories. My head was freaking spinning, and I needed to change my underwear. I could barely breathe. That kiss had been the most incredible thing I'd ever experienced. All I was thinking about was when we'd get to make out again.

Ethan stood at the entrance to my dorm and gave my hand a squeeze before letting go. His eyes locked on my face. "Goodnight, Emma."

Like the wolf he was, Ethan silently swept away and vanished. I was left paralyzed, the feeling of his roaming hands all over my body still caressing me like a phantom.

I didn't understand how I could fall for two people. But I did know one thing.

Prince Ethan was officially crazy. And I was officially in love with him.

TWENTY-ONE

The day of the Contest was finally here, and I hadn't gotten a lick of sleep the night before. I'd been too busy tossing and turning as I recalled what it felt like to have Emma's lips on mine.

I'd never kissed anyone like that before. The experience wasn't something I could put into words. It was all feelings and instinct. When my mouth was on hers, I felt like an animal. A powerful beast who wanted nothing more than to stake my claim and take her with an eager thirst.

And make her enjoy every second of the process.

It was improper, it was crude, and I *loved it*. That kiss was all wolf. It was a longing need. Enough to make my instincts go crazy. I hated to admit I'd done some not-so-mentionable things well after turning in for the night. Several times. Yet it wasn't enough to satisfy the need. When she'd put my hands on her breasts— so cruel. It was enough to make a grown man fall to his knees.

My body craved Emma's. But I couldn't have her. Not yet. There was business to attend to— and if I didn't pay attention, Emma and I would never get our chance to be together before our lives were taken by the Contest. Sex, unfortunately, would have to wait.

Early that morning Emma and I had been escorted to the tourney area. There was a wooden arena outside of the city where the Contest would be held. Beyond that were multiple tents for the contestants and Contest officials.

We didn't speak on the way to the tourney. Neither of us dared to mention the kiss last night. Both of us were acting like nothing ever happened— which was absolutely suffocating. I wanted to address things, but now wasn't the time. Our minds had to be focused on survival.

As contestants, Emma and I had gotten our own tent. There was a bed for rest, a table, chairs and pillows, along with trunks for our things and carpets lining the ground. A changing screen lined the back of the tent. When we arrived, we saw two hunks of metal sitting on the table, along with clothes in navy and black. Embroidered on the clothes was a wolf's head emblem against a checkered background. Our tourney flag and colors.

"What's this?" Emma asked.

"Armor for the Contest," I told her. "You're going to need it."

Emma glanced at me. I was certain we were both thinking the same thing. I had no problem stripping in front of Emma whatsoever... except for one small caveat. I didn't want her to see my missing leg. Or my prosthetic.

Emma sensed that I didn't want her to see me change, and I was pretty sure she didn't want my eyes all over her naked body... not at the moment, anyway. Cumbersomely, she picked up her armor and tourney colors and went behind the screen. I busied myself with putting on my own gear and tried not to imagine what her breasts looked like, which was pretty much impossible.

When she emerged from the screen, both of us were fully armored and ready to begin the tourney. She'd tied her red hair back in a complicated braid that would remain secure during the contest. A few feathers had been woven into the strands, as was Arcanean tradition.

I opened a wooden chest and pulled out a small jar. I opened it to reveal a black substance, and began smudging it upon her skin. I made a pattern so that it looked like wings had created a mask around her eyes.

"What is it?" Emma asked.

"War paint," I said. I stepped back with a smile, then led her to a mirror. "Now you look like a real Arcanea."

"I look like a pagan hooligan," she replied sourly.

"That's the idea."

Emma turned her face a few times in observance, then smiled. "I like it. It makes me seem fierce."

I stood beside her, and both of us gazed into the mirror. The two of us appeared like we'd stepped back in time.

"So how is this thing gonna go?" Emma asked. "Please tell me it only takes one day."

"There are four tasks total, four rounds," I said. "Out of the sixteen contestants, eight are eliminated in the first round. In the second round, two more are eliminated, and in the third one, two more after that. Only four contestants— two pairs— are left for the last round."

"What are the tasks?"

"The first one is the joust— yes, exactly what you're thinking of," I said as she blinked. "You'll ride on my back and try to knock the other sorceress off her shifter. It's the best of three. Once you get them down twice, the objective is to make them tap out during a duel."

"Or?"

"Or finish them off. If the other pair kills their opponent, even if they lost the two out of three, they'll still technically win. If we lose the joust, we're immediately out of the competition," I said.

"Okay..." Emma said slowly. "How about round two?"

"Round Two is a race. It's an obstacle course of sorts, where you gain points by hitting targets while trying not to get killed," I said. "Whoever has the most points *and* finishes in a decent placing gets to go on. If you're in the last two placings, you're eliminated."

"And Round Three?" Emma asked.

"Three is always kept secret," I said. "The judges don't want the contestants to know what the trial is. But it almost always involves some sort of monster."

Emma chewed her lip as she thought. "What's the last round?" she asked.

"It's a challenge by combat. A duel between the last four contestants. We'll fight until the other pair is killed, or surrenders," I said. *If we make it that far.*

"I'm guessing whoever wins the duel is crowned winner?"

"Correct."

Emma's expression hardened. "Okay. Let's do this thing."

"Are you sure you're ready to risk your life?" I asked. Because I wasn't willing to risk hers.

The other contestants were going to have to kill me before I'd submit, but if Emma's life was threatened, it wouldn't be that easy for me to fight back. I'd probably give in.

"I wouldn't have said yes just to back out now," Emma replied. "Time to show them what we've got."

That was the spirit. "One last thing." I ventured to the other side of the room, where a long rectangular chest had been laid out. I opened it and unleashed a sword from inside. The blade was double-edged, with a silver hilt that had one of the royal sapphires set into it. Designs of running wolves had been tediously etched into both sides of the blade's surface. It was very light, as I knew Emma grew fatigued easily, so I wanted her to have no trouble carrying it. The entire length was no more than three feet long, and simple to handle. It was the kind of sword I'd seen her use during class and learn how to brandish easily.

"What's that?" Emma's eyes grew wide as I approached. I held the sword out at arm's length, offering it up to her.

"It's a sword. You'll need it for the tourney. I forged it for you during class." I was glad I'd found a good use for my project.

Her mouth opened slightly. "You made this... for me?"

"Of course I did. You're my mate. It's customary for a potential king to present his sorceress a weapon before the tourney begins."

Emma's hand raised. She paused, and said, "You started making this for me long before I said yes."

I felt blood rush to my cheeks, and admitted, "Yes. Perhaps I did."

I extended the blade to her. She took the hilt from my gloved hand. She did a few experimental swings with it before her face brightened. "I like this. It fits perfectly."

I gave her a smile. "You'll need to christen it with a name before we begin. It's good luck."

"What are the Malovian words for *ice* and *storm*?" she asked.

"Ice and storm? Hm. That'd be *lod* and *burzan*, respectively."

"Okay then. *Lodburzan* it is," she replied. "Icestorm."

She glanced at me. "Did I do that right?"

I laughed. "You did fine. It doesn't need to be complicated."

I grabbed the sheath. My arms wrapped around her waist as I buckled it around her hips. Emma's breath hitched. I could smell her blood as it pumped faster through her bloodstream. In response, my dick tightened in my pants.

With all the work we did getting this armor on, no way it was coming off... no matter how badly I wanted it to.

Emma slid *Lozburzan* into its sheath and turned to me. "I'm ready. Let's get this thing over with."

I was more than happy to oblige. The sunlight hit our faces as we left the tent. The temperature was mild, though a light snow was falling delicately from the clouds above. Our friends were waiting for us in the stands— they'd been assigned special seating as our court.

Emma and I walked through the tents and to the Field. It was a gigantic wooden structure over three hundred feet tall and seven hundred feet long, and open to the elements. Twenty thousand people were sitting in the stands today. The rest of Dolinska was sitting in their homes, watching the broadcast live.

The other competitors were gathered outside the Field, waiting to go inside. Everyone was wearing armor, like us, and stood speaking with the officials and their sponsors for the tournament. Lord Lucien was waiting for us at the gate.

"There you two are," he said in a relieved tone. "You were the last to show up. I was afraid you weren't coming."

"Shouldn't have worried," Emma said. She was ridiculously pale. I was afraid she was going to pass out.

Lucien gave her a grim smile, and said, "Courage, *dzika*. You'll do well. I'm sure of it."

He walked off to talk to an official. Emma leaned in. "What exactly did he call me?"

"He called you *my child*. It's a common blessing in Malovian, for protection," I informed her. Emma swallowed and squeaked, "Great."

Elijah and Gabby were sending us harsh sneers, as normal. Both of them were dressed in black armor, and had used so much war paint over their eyes I was shocked they could see.

At the sight of Gabby, Emma's lip curled and she seemed to buck up a bit. The color returned to her face, and a sharpness like steel came into her eyes as she turned her back on them.

"Someone's tense this morning," I remarked under my breath as Elijah shot me the finger behind an official's back.

"I'd rather die than see that snobby bitch get the crown," Emma hissed. "Even if we don't win, we make sure they don't, either."

"Agreed."

Just then, Steward Soloman came forward. He raised his hands, and all conversation fell silent. "We'll be drawing the order for the competition, as well as the match-ups for the joust. Gentlemen, please come forward and take a number."

An official held out a velvet bag for us to draw from. Elijah shoved his way to the front and went first. I got in line and ended up taking the last number from the bag.

The numbers were etched onto antler fragments from deer. I turned the fragment over in my hand and read the number on the front. Number eight. Emma and I were going last. Splendid, as usual.

I looked around for who our opponent was, which would be number seven. My stomach sank when I saw it sat in the palm of a giant shifter. He was a dragon, and a senior. His mate was an advanced sorceress. She hadn't even brought a sword because she was so confident in the power of her magic. What tough luck.

"Who'd we get?" Emma asked curiously. I pointed. Emma let out a gagging sound when she saw the dragon mark on the girl's hand.

"*Those* are our competitors?" Emma yelped.

"Yes," I said glumly. "They are."

"How do you expect us to joust against a *dragon*?" Emma hissed.

"We have no choice." At this point I was doubting we'd make it past the joust, but too late to go back now.

The doors to the Field opened. Steward Soloman raised his voice and said, "The first four competitors, hold back for the beginning of the joust. The rest of you, proceed up to the competitor booth and wait your turn for the joust."

Emma shivered next to me. The thousands of people in the crowd reflected in her gaze. "Ethan, I don't think I can do this."

"Just keep your eyes on me," I told her. We strode forward, and a wave of nerves washed through my stomach as loud cheers shook the stands. Trumpets sounded, and confetti fell to the ground as applause swallowed up every other sound. Emma floundered for my hand. I took it tightly and squeezed it as we followed the other competitors up the stairs and to our designated box.

A long wooden barrier that looked like a fence divided two sides of the jousting field. The first team was a griffin and his Marked. He'd already changed into his shifter form. His sorceress sat on his back holding a long golden lance in one arm and a shield in the other.

On the opposite side of the arena was a dragon couple. The dragon was on the smaller end, twelve feet tall or so, but still had an obvious advantage of height over the griffin. The Marked that sat on his back held a red lance and a shield she could barely lift.

The two riders squared off on opposing sides of the fence. A bell rang, and the shifters stampeded forward.

The dragon lowered its head as it charged toward the griffin with its teeth bared. I was sure that the dragon had the advantage as they approached, but the griffin Marked leapt into the air as it came near the dragon.

The griffin Marked aimed true. The dragon sorceress lowered her lance a second too late, and the opposing rider's lance knocked right into her. She barely managed to hang on as her shifter ran toward the other end of the field.

The griffin Marked won that round. The two riders rounded the fence on the end of the field and turned around to go at it again. Lances lowered, the competitors raced onward. The griffin rider was preparing to strike the dragon Marked just as she had before.

But the dragon Marked was waiting this time, and slammed her lance into the shield of the griffin rider before she could raise her lance in attack.

A point for the dragon. They were neck and neck.

I was on the edge of my seat the third time they charged at each other, not sure who would win. The dragon rider carried her lance clumsily, as if it bothered her to hold. I was certain the griffin rider, who looked more experienced, was going to knock her off.

The two opponents met in the middle of the field. But instead of using her lance to force the enemy rider off, the dragon Marked tossed herself off of her dragon's back and tackled the griffin rider to the ground. The crowd groaned, and the two sorceresses wrestled upon the earth. Emma gasped in surprise.

The dragon and the griffin both turned on each other. The griffin took to the skies just as the dragon shot out a jet of flame. The griffin's feathers barely got singed as he turned around and lashed out with his talons. His blow caught the dragon's eye. The dragon stumbled backward, blood dripping from the wound. Before the griffin could fly away, the dragon brought his tail up and smacked it into the griffin. He went tumbling through the air and slammed into the boards with a horrible crunching sound. The crowd *ooed*, and the griffin changed back into a man. His shoulders trembled as he attempted to force himself to get up, and failed.

Satisfied, the dragon transformed back into his human form and turned to observe the sorceress fight. Per rules of the tournament, he couldn't interfere at this stage, but he could watch.

The two sorceresses had drawn swords and were dueling fiercely. Loud shouts and yells from them rang through the arena, along with the sound of clashing steel. Both of the Marked were skilled swords women, but the dragon Marked was obviously better. The griffin sorceress struggled to keep up as she dodged slashes and jabs from her opponent.

The griffin Marked searched for her mate frantically. When she saw him lying helplessly at the other end of the field, she let out a cry and dropped her sword, leaving an opening. The dragon Marked saw her advantage and kicked the other girl's feet out from under her, pointing a sword at her throat.

The griffin Marked raised her hands in surrender. The Field erupted into thunderous applause, and the two dragons raised their hands in victory. The griffin Marked got up and ran to the other side of the arena. She pulled her mate to his feet before putting his arm around her shoulder and helping him limp off the field.

Personally, I thought he had it lucky. A hit like that was enough to break a shifter's back. The two winners strode to the competitor's box and sat on the stand below us with huge smiles. An official called names, and four more people left the stands.

The joust went on. Every single one ended in a bloody duel, though nobody had died yet.

There were a few broken bones and many grievous injuries, but none significant enough to cause death. A griffin couple and an alicorn couple won the next two rounds.

Eventually, it was Elijah and Gabby's turn. They were up against the other alicorn couple, Albin and Krystyna. The two squared off before charging at each other full speed. Albin lowered his horn, and Elijah bared his fangs as the opponents drew closer and closer.

Krystyna dropped her shield too far in an attempt to lean forward and jab her lance into Gabby's. That was her mistake. Seeing an opening, Gabby raised her lance. As if she was stabbing with a sword, she thrust it forward. I caught her lips moving as Gabby mouthed a spell.

Gabby's lance slipped right past Krystyna's shield and kept going. The lance embedded itself through armor, into Krystyna's chest and clear through to the other side of her body.

Everyone in the stands gave an audible gasp. As Elijah ran past, Gabby held onto her lance and ripped it out. Krystyna went spinning off of Albin's back and landed on her back in the dirt. Even from here, the large, gaping wound in her torso was clear to see. The whole thing had happened in seconds.

Albin let out a high-pitched whinny as Krystyna fell from his back, though it sounded more like a scream. He skidded to a stop. The alicorn's eyes rolled back in his head, and he reared up, flashing out his hooves as he continued to cry out.

When Albin came back down on all fours, he changed into a man again, and crawled to Krystyna's side. At this point, she was already dead. Her eyes stared out lifelessly, mouth hanging open, as Albin reached out and pulled her onto his lap. Tears streamed down the shifter's face as he began to sob. Albin wailed, clinging Krystyna's lifeless body to his chest. Blood pouring from her wound soaked his armor and clothes, creating a puddle around his legs.

Gabby and Elijah stopped at the end of the arena. Both of them were grinning with a sickening satisfaction.

Nobody in the arena cheered or moved. Nobody made a sound.

After a few long moments, alicorn officials hustled onto the field. I recognized a lord and lady from the alicorn Faction with them, probably sponsors. They leaned down and spoke to Albin while others tried to pry Krystyna's body away, but he wouldn't let go.

An official from the dragon Faction muscled his way into the circle and managed to yank Albin and Krystyna apart. An alicorn carried her body off the field while others had to drag Albin past the gated doors. A large circle of red stained the ground where Krystyna's body had been.

Gabby and Elijah returned to the competitor stands as if they'd done nothing. They brushed dust off their armor and stared at the field, bored already they had to wait this long to get on with it. The other competitors in the stands inched away from them, giving them their own space.

A chill ran up my spine. Gabby and Elijah weren't here to lose. They were going to play dirty. And by the gods, if they had to kill every contestant in their way of getting that crown, so be it.

My own dazed stupor ended at the sound of Emma's heavy breathing. Tears ran down her face, and her whole body was trembling. She was having a panic attack.

"Emma. Emma, look at me, you have to focus." I took her face in my hands and stroked her cheeks with my thumbs gently. Emma took deep breaths as she tried to breathe, but she was more or less gulping down air.

"That can't happen to me. It can't," she forced out. Across the way, Gabby was giving a snotty smirk of triumph, but I ignored her.

"That's not going to be you. I'd die first." I wiped the tears away from her eyes. "I vow on my life I'll never let anything happen to you."

I wrapped my arms around her and hugged her tightly to me. People eyed me, yet I ignored them. We were showing weakness in front of the other opponents, but I didn't care. The only thing I cared about was making Emma feel safe and secure.

And right now, I didn't feel like I could, because in a few minutes I'd be putting her at risk out there.

"I don't like this, Ethan. That wasn't right," she forced out. Her trembles ceased as I held her against my body. Her frantically beating heart began to steady as its rhythm synchronized to mine. It was an exhilarating feeling unlike any in the world.

"Em, if you're not okay with this, we can go home," I said. "I'll forfeit."

"You'll do that?" An edge of disbelief entered her tone.

"Of course I will. Just say the word." It was a crazy notion, but I'd give up the crown so she wouldn't be afraid. It wasn't even something I had to consider. Just something I naturally *did*. This was what mates were supposed to do. Be ready to sacrifice it all for love.

Emma paused, as if considering it. The thickness in her voice thinned as she cleared her throat and said, "No. No. I want to be here. I want to do this. I'm sure."

"Okay," I said gently. I pulled away, though it was agonizingly painful for me to do so. "What can I do to help you in this moment?"

She grabbed onto my hand again. "Just keep me the fuck away from that dragon when it's our turn. And don't let me fall off. Or get impaled."

Nausea churned in my gut, because I couldn't promise anything. "Done."

I had Emma calmed down by the time we were called to the joust. Her demeanor had completely changed. The panic had dulled from her eyes and been replaced by a strong determination. Not a sliver of fear was recognizable in her expression. It was almost as if she'd become emotionless.

"Are you ready?" I asked.

"I've been visualizing. It's something I do before each competition," she said. "This is just another show. Nothing more."

When we got down to the arena, I changed into a wolven. Emma swung herself onto my back, and Lord Lucien handed her a broad blue shield and silver-colored lance.

"Keep your eyes up," Lucien told Emma. "Aim for your target, and it'll hit true. Ethan— be agile. The dragon is intimidating, but he isn't fast. You have the advantage of being swift."

I growled to let him know I heard him, then approached the fence line. Muttered conversation enveloped the area. No one pointed, but everyone looked to the same place.

This was the first time I'd presented myself in public with my missing leg. School didn't count— this was being broadcasted live to thousands of people.

I couldn't imagine what people were saying about a three-legged wolven attempting to win the King's Contest. I was so embarrassed I wanted to skulk home with my tail between my legs.

Then Emma stirred on my back, and I no longer felt afraid. I felt brave. What did I have to be ashamed of? The most beautiful sorceress in Malovia was my chosen queen. We were the underdogs, certainly, but we had just as much a chance of winning as anyone else. Time to prove that I belonged on that throne.

We squared off against the other competitors on the opposite side of the jousting field. The dragon was green in color. Smoke furled out of his nostrils as he faced me. The sorceress riding him gave a challenging smirk as she lowered the lance.

I leapt forward into a charge. Emma's legs tightened around my belly in an attempt to hold on. I could feel her movements as she raised the lance.

The dragon was several feet taller than I. The opposite sorceress had the advantage. We drew closer and closer, and the ground shook as the dragon charged past. I heard a loud crunching sound, then felt Emma careen backward with the rough force of the other rider's lance as it smashed against her shield.

Dammit. We lost a point. Emma gasped in pain— I slowed my steps as we neared the end of the field.

"My arm," Emma moaned. "Fuck, it hurts."

"*Are you all right?*" I asked. Broken arms were common during jousts. I didn't want Emma getting hurt.

"It's just bruised," she gasped as we rounded the corner. "That bitch packs a mean punch."

"*Give it right back to her.*" I charged again, picking up speed. The dragon and I faced off. He had a glittering menace in his black eyes, flames flickering from his mouth as I drew near.

Emma was prepared this time. She had her lance aimed before the other sorceress decided on her target, and her body weight shifted forward as she rammed the lance into the shield of the other rider. It knocked the dragon sorceress sideways and nearly tossed her off her mount.

"*Well done, onawilke!*" I cheered. We rounded the corner for the last time. We were both tied up. This would determine who won.

The dragon and I catapulted at full speed. The crowd was roaring— the sound made my ears ring. Emma and the dragon sorceress lowered their lances at the same time and aimed. It would be close.

I heard the shattering of a lance as I ran past the dragon, and looked back. Emma had broken her lance as she rammed it against the opposite rider's shield, but she hadn't gotten hit herself. We'd won the joust.

But the dragon and his rider weren't willing to give up yet. The sorceress turned around and shot a spell at Emma, knocking her off my back. She went rolling to the ground, and I jerked to a halt. The other Marked slid down her dragon's back and began running at us with raised hands.

"*Emma!*" I shouted, but it was all I had time to say, because the earthquake beneath my paws told me a dragon was coming. I spun out of the way as a blast of flame ignited the ground where I'd just stood. The dragon roared and extended his jaws, but I jumped out of the way of his snapping fangs and instead ran to the wings, where I grabbed a good chunk in my teeth. I jerked my head to the side, ripping a hole in the dragon's sensitive membranes. The shifter roared in pain.

He moved his tail overhead to crush me, but I let go of the wing and rolled out of the way. The tail came crashing down, and the spikes got stuck in the earth. As the dragon unsuccessfully tried to lift it from the earth, I jumped into the air and rammed him in the shoulder.

My blow was so powerful it sent the dragon crashing onto his side. He roared in frustration, emitting a barrel of fire from his insides as I jumped onto his sensitive stomach. I sank my claws in to get a good hold. Before the dragon knew what was going on, I put my fangs to his throat.

"*Stay down, or I'll kill you,*" I warned. The dragon froze, and didn't move again.

Out of the corner of my eye, I watched as Emma and the other sorceress waged war. The Marked opposite Emma sent illusion spell after illusion spell in the direction of my mate. Emma had to dive and roll in order to avoid being hit by the other sorceress's complicated magic. Glittering purple balls of electricity rocketed at Emma from the hands of the other Marked, exploding once they hit the earth. Her teeth were bared in concentration. She knew if she didn't win this, it was all over.

But Emma's whole life had been about training to be on her toes, and she could maintain her balance and outmaneuver the other sorceress with ease. The other Marked's eyes grew large when Emma got close. Emma unleashed her sword, then kicked the sorceress's legs out from under her. Emma aimed the sword at the Marked's heart, breathing intensely with a deadly look in her eyes.

Slowly, the other sorceress raised her hands in surrender, and the crowd went wild.

I got off the dragon, and changed back. Across the way, Lord Lucien was applauding loudly, a large smile on his face. It hit me that we'd managed to make it past the first round, and I smiled in relief.

"That was a good fight." The dragon had changed back and was looking at me in approval. He extended a hand for me to shake, and I took it. "I've never had anyone beat me in a duel before."

"My best friend is a dragon. I know their weak points," I said with a shrug. "What's your name again? I didn't catch it during the ceremony."

"Philip. My mate is Margot," he replied. "I don't have to ask who you are. Everyone knows. Though I'm not sure about your mate. I haven't seen her around before."

"Emma. She's new here," I said. "If you don't know her, you will soon enough. She has a bit of a temper. I don't think she'll go down easy."

Philip laughed. "I'd better go talk to my mate. She's probably hopping mad right now, though she doesn't want to show it."

Opposite the field, Emma was shaking hands with Margot. Margot seemed similarly genuine, although more disappointment shone behind her gaze than Philip's. If anything, he seemed relieved.

"I hope you win the Contest. If you can beat me, you deserve it." Philip let out a sigh. "Now I can get my father off my back. Pesky dragon families, you know?"

As Philip walked off, Emma ran at me. She jumped into my arms and flung her own around me. "Ethan! We won the joust!"

"That we did." I spun her around and held her close. I swore I'd gotten my wings right then as she clung me tightly to her. This had to be what flying felt like.

I put her back down on the ground. Her hands rested on my shoulders as she said, "I'm glad you're not hurt. Though my arm really freaking hurts."

"We can have Lord Lucien look at it back at the tent," I said. "For now, let's get some food in you. You need to keep up your strength."

I put my arm around her as we left the Field. Only three more rounds to go.

Yet each round after this would only get more difficult. This was just the beginning.

emma
TWENTY-TWO

We'd gotten past the first round, but I'd almost gotten killed out there. Miss Dragon Lady had nearly smoked me with one of her bombs. Lord Lucien said my arm was fine, but I wouldn't be able to move it much tomorrow. He cast an illusion spell to trick my brain into thinking it was okay, so I could use it like normal during the competition without feeling any pain. It would last until the Contest was over, then I'd pay for it the next day.

Ethan had told me I'd made fighting Margot look easy, but I hardly believed him. A couple of those magical balls had fried my hair as they whizzed past. If Margot was the easiest thing to get past in this competition, then we were in trouble.

I was embarrassed about my breakdown earlier. I had to pull myself together. I had completely lost my shit while watching the joust.

I couldn't do that again. I needed to be strong. For the rest of the tournament, I wasn't going to show one bit of fear, no matter what happened. I was here. Time to stop crying about it and win.

Though I was afraid we couldn't win. Not without a little bit of help.

Ethan had ducked out of the tent for a moment to talk to Lucien. I kneeled before the trunk and opened it. I ruffled through the clothes inside and pulled out a small black box that I'd snuck in under my cloak. I checked over my shoulder to make sure no one was watching, then opened it.

The dark necklace— the one I'd stolen from Lady Korva. I'd snuck it out of my dorm this morning and into the tourney tent before anyone noticed. I'd only brought it just in case, and left it behind during the first round, but now it was clear we needed an edge.

I didn't want to cheat, but this competition was way harder than I thought it would be. There was too much at stake here. Our lives were on the line— not to mention the fate of the country. Ethan and I had to use every advantage we could get.

Queen Antonia told me there'd be big problems if I didn't make sure Ethan won. She'd make me pay if we didn't get that crown. She'd go after my mom, my friends... everyone I loved.

Not to mention there was the problem of Elijah and Gabby. They'd run Krystyna through without flinching during the joust. They'd even seemed *happy* about it. It was so sick and twisted. If they could do something so horrible to her, just to get past the first round of the Contest, there was no telling how they'd ruin the country if they got in control of it.

They didn't care about people. All they cared about was power.

And people would die if Gabby and Elijah won. Which I wasn't willing to risk.

I had no choice. My magic wasn't strong enough to work on its own. I was only a First Year, for crying out loud.

Then came the worst consequence of all. Ethan. I needed to keep him alive. I would do anything— *anything*— to get him through this Contest in one piece. Whether we won or not, this was a deadly competition. If there were personal consequences to me for saving his life, so be it.

Was Unseelie magic really all that bad? I wasn't convinced that it was. All my professors had beat it into my head that Unseelie magic couldn't be trusted, but maybe they were close-minded. Still... Ethan had warned me there were harsh consequences for Seelie fae using dark magic. Was this Contest worth the risk?

Milonna, help me, I pleaded. *Tell me what to do.*

I got no response from the goddess herself. This was a hopeless decision. Just as I was about to put the necklace back, I turned toward the head of the tent, and my heart leapt into my throat.

It was the hag... the one who had told me I was the Worldweaver. She still appeared as formidable and harrowing as ever— I felt a shiver run up my skin as I took in her frightening appearance. How had she gotten in here? She'd come instantly, silent, appearing in my tent with no forewarning.

My prayer. Milonna must've sent her. I extended my hand, revealing to her the dark necklace.

"What should I do? What are Milonna's instructions?" I asked the hag. "Should I use Unseelie magic, or not?"

The hag didn't respond, just stared at me with hollowed eyes. I tried another way. "If I don't use this, what will happen?" I questioned hoarsely. "Will we survive?"

It was then the hag moved her pale lips. *"If you do not seek the power of the dark necklace, the prince will die."*

I felt my mouth go dry. Bile rose in my mouth at the thought. Ethan, dead... I'd do everything I could to prevent that. "Will we win the Contest?"

"He will be king," the hag responded. *"But only if you do what you must."*

That settled it. I remembered that the fae of old didn't like to be thanked, so instead, I replied, "I'll remember this."

The hag bowed her head to me before, in a wisp of wind, she vanished.

A thick weight had settled in my gut. I had to use the necklace, whether it was black magic or not. There was too much at stake.

I put the necklace on underneath my armor, and covered it up with the fur cloak. Ethan didn't need to know about this. He was too much of a goody-two shoes. He wasn't willing to bend the rules and compromise his morals in order to keep the nation, and its people, safe.

Good thing he had a queen that had no such reservations.

I'd just closed the trunk when Ethan came into the tent. Kiara and Odette joined him. None of them seemed happy— not even Odette.

"What's going on?" I asked, intuitively knowing something was wrong.

"Albin's dead," Odette said. She sniffed, as if something so horrible was hard for her to say out loud.

"What? The alicorn shifter whose mate died in the joust?" I asked. I wanted to add, *who Gabby killed*, but didn't, because I didn't know who was listening outside our tent.

"Yes," Kiara said sadly. "It's awful."

"How did he die?" I asked.

Ethan's mouth was thin. "A member of his court went to check up on him after the joust. They found him in his tent with a note saying he wouldn't go on without his mate. He took his own life."

A hand went over my mouth. "By the gods."

Something awful crossed my mind. "Are... are they sure it was a suicide?" My eyes went to Ethan's, and we were both thinking the same thing. I wouldn't put it past Elijah and Gabby to finish the job.

Kiara nodded. "There were members of his court standing watch outside their tent. Nobody went in or out during or after the joust except Albin, and people were with him up until the point he was alone. Not to mention the knife used was clearly his— and the note his hand-writing."

My stomach churned. In my opinion, Albin might've ended his life, but Elijah and Gabby that had killed him, too. There was no reason for Gabby to do what she did. She could've won the joust without murdering Krystyna. She just did it because she gained pleasure from the act.

Gabby might be a princess of flame, but I was one of ice. And I was going to freeze her out of this fucking competition.

"So what are we going to do about *us*?" I asked Ethan. "Albin killed himself, but Krystyna didn't. And I think I'm pointing out the obvious when I say we need to watch our backs."

"I've already talked to Stefan. He and Theo are going to guard the tent during the competition," Ethan said. "With two people already dead, we can't take any chances with people tampering with our things."

"I'll taste all your food!" Odette vouched. "I want to make sure there's no poison!"

"That's very kind of you, Odette, but I'm sure we'll be fine," I said. Ethan had forced some food into me after the joust, but I didn't think I could take another bite the rest of the day. I was too nauseous.

The trumpets sounded again to summon us to the next round. Ethan and I headed back to the Field, where the contestants were gathered around the gate.

I looked around at the contestants who were left. So many had been eliminated by the joust. There were still participants from every Faction, but I bet they'd be gone after the race was over.

Shifters were transforming for the race. Ethan changed, and I climbed onto his back. I was damn well lucky I'd had horse riding lessons growing up. I loved riding, but never got why Mom let me continue with lessons, as we couldn't afford it. Little did I know she was teaching me how to ride a shifter.

I'd never told Ethan this, but secretly, I loved being on top of him. He felt so strong and powerful. He could run faster than any horse I'd ever been on. His strides were long and lengthy, and they moved fluidly with my body. I never worried about falling off with him. Being with him in this way just felt... natural.

The crowd roared once again as we entered the Field. It'd been completely changed since the joust. Now the Field was set up like a giant, winding racetrack. Various targets were placed around multiple obstacles. There was a large black pit of bubbling goo, a couple of jumps, and several barricades that the contestants all had to pass in order to reach the finish line on the other side. They were so large not even a dragon could cross over them easily.

Whoever reached the finish line first was important, but hitting targets along the way with the crossbow was even more critical. The winner of the race received ten points, but there were many more targets scattered around the arena. You could win the race by hitting targets instead of coming in first. I planned to shoot down as many as I could while Ethan dealt with the obstacles.

Lady Magdalina strolled to our side as we came to the starting line. I hadn't seen my sponsor since the tournament had begun. I didn't know where she'd been until now. She was wearing a glittering, gossamer dress that seemed so light and airy. I didn't know how she wasn't floating above the ground. She was carrying a small, one-handed crossbow, which she pressed into my hand, along with two dozen tiny arrows in a small quiver.

"Stay vigilant, Emmaline," she said. "Not everything in this race is what it seems."

She wandered away and took a seat by Queen Antonia, who was in the royal box on the ground level of the arena. Antonia's cold eyes surveyed me in a clear message— *don't mess this up.*

I tied the quiver to my sword sheath, then put an arrow into the crossbow as Ethan lined up with the other shifters. The other sorceresses already had their crossbows at the ready. Gabby pointed hers at me and pretended to shoot, giving a harsh laugh. I rolled my eyes and set my gaze forward.

The shifters anxiously danced on the starting line, eager to break free. I gathered a chunk of Ethan's fur in my left hand and held on tight. A shudder quivered through his form at my touch. I looked ahead to the jumps. All of them were significantly high, and what was worse, they were all on fire.

Because this wasn't hard enough. I prayed that Ethan's fur wouldn't ignite like a candle when we passed over them.

A gunshot went off, and Ethan sprang forward. The contestants slammed into each other and pushed each other out of the way in order to gain the lead.

Wind blew back my braid, and the snow picked up, becoming thick chunks careening through the air. I clung on tightly with my thighs as Ethan sailed over the first jump. The flames licked at my boots, and I felt heat press all around me. When we landed, Ethan continued running toward the next jump. We hadn't been burned.

The first target neared; I closed one eye, took shot, and missed.

As Ethan leapt over two jumps in a row, I reloaded and fired twice more. Again, my arrows sailed on past their target. Fuck. I swore, and reloaded the crossbow.

This time, the target was on my left side. I decided to experiment and switched the weapon to my left hand. This time when I shot, the arrow hit right on the bullseye.

I was a better shot with my non-dominant hand. Strange, but whatever. I lifted my left hand again and pulled the trigger. The arrow hit its intended target. I quickly reloaded and shot again. I hit yet another target, and the crowd cheered.

That was the last of the jumps. Ethan was running neck and neck with an alicorn and a dragon. Elijah had taken the lead. Gabby was hitting every target they passed. I picked up the pace, reloading arrows as quickly as I could and gathering points.

The jumps ended and we made it to the next obstacle— the barricades. They were long spikes that jutted out of the ground next to spears that sat at an angle. It looked like some sort of medieval death wall used in battle.

Flying had been banned for this round of the contest, so it was against the rules to soar over the barricades. The task was to find another way around, to show your intelligence. Most of the contestants skidded to a stop as they approached the barricade, eyes flashing as they considered how to get around it.

An alicorn ahead of us tried to jump over the barricades and speared himself in the shoulder. His sorceress had to take a knife and cut him free while he screamed in pain.

Ethan paced at the barricades, taking deep breaths. His tone was thick with frustration. *"These damn things! How the hell are we supposed to get through?"*

"Calm down. We'll find a way around it." I felt insanely pressured to do something. Next to us, Elijah and Gabby were slowly working their way around the spikes. Elijah had changed back to a human, and although it was slow going, the two of them managed to slither on through the barricade like the snakes they were… although Gabby ended up tearing her calf in the process. She cried out in pain, blood spurting through the wound. Elijah transformed into a wolven and hefted her onto his back as they pressed on to the next part of the race.

What Elijah and Gabby had done worked, but I didn't want to chance Ethan and me getting stabbed with one of those spikes. Other contestants were trying it the same way, and they weren't getting very far. Especially the dragon couple. They'd almost tripped, and the guy was so big that a spear had stabbed his shoulder. His mate grabbed him and saved him from getting impaled at the last second.

"I have an idea." I drew my sword and began hacking at the spears. I didn't expect them to break so easily, but was shocked when the blade cut through the wood like butter. The barricade didn't react like I expected it to, but I wasn't asking questions. I just hacked away at the spikes and spears like no tomorrow, until I'd cleared enough of a path that Ethan could jump over and safely to the other side.

The pit was next. A bubbling black pit of tar was the only thing that remained between us and the finish line. A couple of contestants had caught up to us and jumped right into the pit in an attempt to swim across, but they sank instantly. The dragon couple was drowning in the goop. They gasped for air as the goo pulled them downward like glue, preventing an escape.

Elijah snarled as he paced back and forth at the pit's edge, unsure of what to do. Gabby was barking orders at him, but it didn't appear that she had any idea what to do.

It was another test of our creativity. There had to be a way across the pit. We needed to use magic. Lady Magdalina told me if illusions were powerful enough, they could become reality. I needed to create an illusion that was strong enough to become real.

I lifted my hands and closed my eyes. I tried to envision something that would help us cross, and ended up thinking of a bridge.

I felt the metal of the dark necklace hiding beneath my cloak glow and become warm. It became hot against my skin, stinging, almost unbearable, but I refused to acknowledge the pain. We had to get across somehow.

I wasn't using my own abilities to create the spell. I was drawing Unseelie magic from the necklace itself. The snow that was falling from above swirled to create a bridge of ice that crossed over the black pit, connecting from this side of the obstacle to the other.

Ethan didn't hesitate. He raced over the bridge as I sagged forward onto his back, trying to catch my breath. The spell took so much energy. My body felt loose and watery. I was so weak.

"Emma. Can you hear me?" Ethan said softly.

I stirred on his back, feeling like I was going to pass out. My vision was darkening. I forced myself to remain conscious and said, "Yes, Ethan. I'm with you."

Once the other sorceresses saw what I did, they all copied me and created bridges of their own to climb over the barricades with, though not all of their spells worked. Some illusions weren't powerful enough to hold their weight— others got halfway up the bridge before the illusions failed and caused them to go tumbling down into the pool. A griffin couple wailed in pain behind us, but I turned my head forward and didn't look back. I didn't want to know their fate.

Once we got over the pit, the snow around us got worse. It turned into hail, and the skies darkened as the storm turned into a full-out blizzard. It became difficult to see what was ahead. The weather couldn't cooperate for five more minutes, could it?

Yet the finish line was in sight, and Ethan and I were in the lead. We were going to win this thing!

Then everything changed in a moment. The blizzard increased its intensity, until all that was around us was a blank whiteness that enveloped everything. The snow was so fierce, I couldn't see anything. Not the arena, not the other contestants, not the race track. I could barely see the hand in front of my own face. Ethan's white fur became one with the blizzard.

A crackling sound met my ears as the ground below us turned to ice. A deadly cold settled on my body and deep within my bones. It was an unnatural cold. Something I'd never experienced in my life and had nothing to compare to. We'd had bad winters in Michigan growing up, but this was beyond anything I'd ever experienced. I'd never been so cold. I could be dunked naked in a freezing lake in the middle of the Arctic and it would've seemed like summer. This… it was unbearable.

Ethan had halted completely. His fangs were bared as he moaned with obvious agony. *"I… can't move,"* he forced out. *"I'm frozen."*

I was freezing, too. My body was slowly becoming a statue, from my feet upward. I tried to move my legs, and found them stuck. We were literally becoming blocks of ice!

"Emma," Ethan gasped, but said nothing more. I squeezed my chilled fingers into his fur and tried to work out a way out of this.

Something about this didn't feel right. I shouldn't have been able to manipulate the snow I'd used to create an ice bridge earlier, even with the necklace helping me. I wasn't an elemental. The weather didn't obey my command.

Unless the snow wasn't really snow.

It's not real, I realized. The snowstorm was an illusion. The whole race was. The targets, the obstacles, even the storm… all it had ever been was a grand illusion. I wouldn't have been able to make that snow bridge earlier if the snow had been *real* in the first place.

"It's not real," I gasped. Ethan's eyes widened with realization.

"An illusion," he whispered. *"But a powerful one."*

Indeed. It was strong enough to hold on past the realization that it was fake. I knew what we were experiencing wasn't really there. It was a spell cast on our minds by sorceresses, but damn if it didn't still hurt regardless.

"I can't break this myself. I don't have enough magical energy," Ethan argued. *"No one does."*

I did. But I couldn't tell him how. "Ethan, just leave it to me."

"What are you going to do?"

I didn't answer. Instead, I focused my energy inward on the necklace. I imagined the cold lifting… the storm breaking… warmth returning to the earth again.

It didn't happen right away. But once again, the dark necklace burned my skin, and I felt its power channel into me. I forced it outward with my palms, and the blizzard was blasted back, displaying a clear path from here to the finish.

I'd destroyed the illusion. Not just for me. For everyone.

"You did it! The illusion broke!" Ethan cried. *"I can see the finish!"*

A jet black shock of pain ricocheted up my spine as the spell left my body, causing my eyes to roll backward. The insane cold melted away to be replaced by warmth and sunlight. This time, I did pass out, but Ethan was there to catch me. I fell forward onto his back, darkness enveloping me as the sound of his steady paws beat onward toward what I hoped was the end.

"Ethan, is she all right? It's been awhile."

"All of you, give her some air. She needs the rest."

"What she did out there wasn't natural. I've never seen such power in my—"

"Back. Off."

That was Ethan. He sounded… really protective. And intense. There was a wet washcloth dotting sweat away from my face. My eyes fluttered open. I was back in the tent, lying on the bed. Ethan was hovering over me. He was the one holding the washcloth. His eyebrows were knitted together in concern. I noticed that my armor, as well as Ethan's, had been removed, and we were only wearing our tourney colors.

Odette, Delmare and Kiara were close by. They'd gathered around the bed and seemed as worried as Ethan was.

"What's going on?" I hated how faint my voice sounded. My stomach churned, and a pounding headache expanded across my temple. Man, this sucked.

"We won the race," Ethan said. "But only by a hair. Elijah and Gabby came in second."

He paused for a moment, then added, "But we wouldn't have won at all if you hadn't cast that spell."

There was a beat of silence, before Kiara spoke. "Emma… how did you do that?" Kiara whispered. "How you broke that illusion… it shouldn't have been within the power of a high priestess."

Ethan's gaze landed on mine inquisitively. I licked my lips and said, "I don't know. I just… did what I had to, I guess."

Kiara's lips pressed together. She knew I wasn't telling the truth.

"What about the other contestants?" I pressed a hand to my mouth. I felt like I was going to puke.

"Nearly everyone made it to the end, but only a few are going on to the next round. The griffin couple froze to death," Ethan said.

"How could they have froze to death? The snowstorm wasn't real," I said in confusion.

"Powerful illusions can trick the mind into believing that they're experiencing whatever the eyes see," Ethan said. "In bitter cold, the organs slowly shut down. That's what happened to the griffin couple. They convinced themselves the whole thing was real."

Never mind. I *was* going to puke. I gagged— Ethan lunged for a bucket. He handed it to me seconds before I tossed up the remnants of my earlier meal.

The room spun again. Ethan was at my side again with a glass of water. I sipped it slowly, trying not to throw up that, too.

Delmare sat on the bed and rubbed my back. "You're one tough bitch, lady. I would've lost by now."

"Yeah. You've made it halfway through!" Odette piped optimistically. "Just two more rounds to go!"

I groaned. I put the bucket on the other side of the bed and lay back. Delmare took the glass of water. Ethan brushed his fingers against my cheek lightly.

"Take some time to recover. We've got a few hours before the next round," Ethan whispered. "You probably need a nap."

"Fucking probably." My eyes were already drifting shut. I heard footsteps as Delmare, Kiara and Odette left the tent.

But not Ethan. I felt the mattress dip as he slid next to me. He pulled me against his chest. I counted the beats of his heart as he wrapped his arms around me before I shivered. It felt like that harsh cold from earlier had settled in among my insides, and wouldn't move. I was grateful for the shifter warmth that Ethan provided. It settled over me like a blanket, and soothed my fears.

"Hey." He rubbed my arms up and down, creating friction there. Hot damn, if only we didn't have two more rounds to go and I didn't feel like shit. I'd be busy trying to get those pants off of him and seeing what he had under there. I mean, the guy was missing a leg, but not the leg that mattered.

"Hey." I coughed a few times and snuggled into his chest. Never cuddled with a guy before, but this was nice. Wish it wasn't right after I'd just hacked up breakfast.

"Are you sure you're okay to continue?" If I heard him right, his voice sounded a little choked up. "I'm... really worried about you. You scared me back there."

He was being so sweet. I smiled slightly and inhaled his woodsy scent. It sent a thrill from my nostrils right down to my panties. "It was just a tough round. I'll be fine after a break."

Ethan didn't answer. His fingers were lightly stroking my braid. It was putting me to sleep.

"I'll warn you, I'm a loud snorer." I yawned.

He chuckled. "Maybe I think that's cute."

"You won't when it keeps you awake."

"Trust me, Em. I could sleep through the next war. Noise doesn't bother me."

I scoffed. "Whatever you say."

Ethan leaned down. I wasn't sure what he was doing, until my entire form melted as his lips pressed against my forehead.

He'd kissed me on the head. Oh my gosh. I felt like I was glowing or something. My insides fluttered with joy. It was crazy how such a small gesture could have so much meaning behind it. And I felt every bit of it.

Ethan Nowak actually cared about me. Did I dare to believe he loved me?

Because gods, did I love him. Now more than ever. This Contest was bonding me to him like nothing else could.

I moved my legs to make myself more comfortable. One of them ended up lying over Ethan's. I felt the cold metal of his prosthetic press against my calf through his clothing.

His entire body stiffened with shock. It was like he wanted to cringe away— like he wasn't ready for me to acknowledge that it was there.

"It's okay," I breathed. I tangled my legs with his, and Ethan relaxed. His arms drew me tighter to his form. My body ached as my thoughts weaved in and out of dreamland.

The King's Contest didn't have accommodations for disabled people. I needed to suck it up. Ethan had problems, too. I wasn't the only one who had issues to work around. He was getting by just fine.

Ethan's disability is a bit different. He's missing a leg. You're missing an immune system, functioning organs, and just about everything fucking else.

I was exhausted. And we were only two rounds into this thing. If we were going to win, we had two more to go— and the last one would be a literal fight to the death.

I didn't think I'd make it that far. I was ready to collapse with the end of the second round. My body wasn't going to let me go through yet another part of this competition. I needed rest. I needed a shower and a bed. I needed to go home and pretend this was all a bad dream.

But I loved Ethan. I was doing this for him. I'd used black magic for him without blinking an eye, and I'd do it again. I didn't care about the cost. He needed me to hold on and make it through this thing.

So I would. I'd put that crown on his head even if it killed me.

TWENTY-THREE

I was terribly concerned about Emma. She didn't look good.

Forget that. It was an understatement. She didn't look *well*. In fact, if I had to put it into words, she looked like the epitome of walking death.

I hated myself for doing this to her. I'd put her in this situation. I wished I'd abandoned the throne and not gone through with the Contest at all.

And yet we were so close. We were halfway through. Our chances of succeeding had increased drastically. There were only a few more couples we had to beat. The crown was literally within our grasp.

We'd fallen asleep together in the tourney tent. She slept for far longer than I did. I wanted to remain in bed forever and listen to the sound of her steady breaths as they rose in and out of her gorgeous body. It was an enchanting rhythm that sounded sweeter than any music in the world.

I hoped that she didn't care about my leg. Maybe she didn't care there were parts of me missing. But I was too afraid to ask.

I shook her awake a half an hour before the third round began. She didn't want to eat, but I begged and pleaded with her until I was able to force some bread and soup down her throat. It was late afternoon at this point, and she needed to keep her strength up.

Emma seemed a little better after the nap. Her eyes shone brighter, and clear. Emma stood tall and fastened the sword hilt around her, which I had taken off after the second round. We got our armor back on just before we were called to go.

Kiara entered the tent. "It's time." She glanced at Emma, then sent me a disapproving look that made me uneasy.

She didn't need to drop hints. Kiara obviously thought that Emma was lying about the second round. Everyone in the audience had been stunned. The officials, too. An illusion like that had never been broken before during the Contest. It had taken several sorceresses to cast, and was exceptionally strong. Emma was a First Year Marked who barely knew her way around a spell. How she'd managed to break that illusion and end the blizzard was beyond me.

Yes, I knew Emma was lying, too. But I didn't know what about, or why. She had help breaking that illusion. She had to. But for now, I didn't think it wise to ask. The past was behind us now, and we had to keep moving forward.

Maybe I just didn't want to know the truth.

Emma put a hand to her forehead and grabbed onto the table to keep herself steady. I immediately rushed to her side, my hands on her hips to keep her upright. "Emma. Steady now." I hoped she wouldn't faint again.

She grimaced. "Cast an illusion spell."

"What?"

"Make me look pretty! I can't go out looking like this. It'll make me seem weak," she said.

She was right. Her face appeared taunt, and dark circles had formed under her eyes. The officials wouldn't consider her strong enough to go on.

I waved my hand, and violet sparks flashed out of my fingers. The dark circles faded, and color popped into her cheeks as her red hair brightened and skin smoothed. It looked like she'd just walked into a salon and gotten a complete makeover.

She gave a heavy sigh as she glanced at the mirror. "There. Much better."

I held a vacant expression. Emma might look better, but she didn't have me fooled. I bet she still felt awful.

"Why do your eyes do that?" she asked. Her gaze narrowed. "Turn purple when you cast?"

"Oh, that? I'm not sure," I said, shrugging my shoulders. "It's just something that happens."

"Hmph. Odd."

Kiara handed a glass bottle to Emma, one that had a sparkling blue substance inside. "Here, drink this. It's one of my sister's potions. It'll give you energy for the task ahead."

Emma popped the cork and started chugging. The potion was gone in mere seconds. A smile brightened her face. "Thanks, Kiara. I can actually feel it working."

"Don't thank me. You need it." Kiara led the way back to the Field. The doors were closed to the arena this time. Steward Soloman stood outside of it while contestants and sponsors chattered in low voices outside.

An earth-shattering roar silenced the contestants and caused the crowd to cheer. That didn't sound like it came from a dragon. Several contestants blanched— Steward Soloman proceeded forward.

"For this task, contestants shall enter the Field one by one, with their chosen mates," he began. "Inside are several monsters, each hand-picked by officials. All mated pairs will have to fight a different monster, one that the officials believe challenge you and your mate's weaknesses. Slay the creature, and you shall move on to the next task. Surrender, or lose your life... and you shall not proceed beyond this point."

There were three other mated pairs beside Emma and I. Gabby and Elijah were one of them. The only other people who'd made it this far were a dragon couple and an alicorn. Everyone else had been eliminated.

"Order shall be determined by your placing in the last round," Soloman finished. "Prince Ethan, Miss Sosna, you're up first."

Hell of a lot better than going last. Lord Lucien strode beside us. His expression was pale and grim. I was shocked when he drew both of us into a tight embrace.

"Stay safe out there," he said gruffly. "You can beat this thing. Use what I taught you."

When he let us go, I could tell by the look on his face he was worried. That wasn't a good sign at all. Lucien rarely lost his courage unless there was something to be concerned about.

Emma drew her sword. I drew my own as the gates opened to let us through. They shut behind us with a resonating *thud*.

The Field was completely empty, save for a cage that had been placed at the opposite end.

The cage was made up of thick walls of steel, so we couldn't see what was inside. The box wavered violently on its place on the ground, as if whatever was inside was trying to break out.

My heart jumped up to my throat. What kind of a monster had the officials picked for us to battle? What creature inside could possibly challenge the weaknesses between Emma and I?

The door to the cage was yanked upward by the magic of sorceresses, and from within the darkness sprang a monster I'd prayed we wouldn't get.

The monster stood nearly twenty feet tall. It walked on four reptilian legs that ended in sharp claws, grey, matted fur all over its body. Its tail was long and feathered, and around its shoulders was a black mane of fur. The face was goat like, with large nostrils and pointed ears. The creature had four yellow eyes, two on each side of its head, and large antlers that were red with dried blood. There was something oddly humanistic about its features that only added to its bothersome form.

It was a *biez*— a type of demon. They were commonly referred to as minions of Droga, and originated from the underworld. How had the Circle managed to get their hands on one?

The *biez* opened its mouth and bellowed, revealing three rows of jagged sharp teeth. It pointed its antlers down and charged at us full-speed.

Emma and I both scattered in different directions. It took the *biez* seconds to cross the arena. When it missed both of us, the monster rose up on its hind legs and screeched again, crashing down to the earth.

The ground quivered beneath us. I lost my balance and went down, although Emma managed to stay on her feet. The monster turned and faced me. Staring into its vicious eyes was like looking directly into the pit of hell.

Emma gave a wild scream and charged at the *biez*. She jumped onto its back with her sword raised, and stabbed it near the base of the spine. Her blade connected, and dug in. The *biez* screeched and kicked her off. She went flying several feet, her sword rolling away from her.

When I saw that the monster had hurt her, white-hot rage flooded my system. I didn't care that this was a monster I'd never fought and didn't think I could kill. All I wanted was to destroy it, and teach it to never touch my mate again.

I brought my sword up and hurtled myself at the *biez* head-on. I aimed for cutting the tendons in its legs, but the monster lashed out with its front claws. I had to jump and duck to avoid getting sliced open as the *biez* attacked. I felt its hot breath swarm around me as I rolled out of the way of its sharp teeth. My cloak got caught in the monster's fangs, but it ripped so I could get free. Any closer and the monster would've had me in its jaws.

The *biez* gave out another great scream. I dove out of the way as it spun completely around, so I wouldn't get crushed by the monster's giant feet.

I noticed on the other side of the arena a long blood trail, along with the feathery remnants of a limb. Emma stood smiling about the pile of feathers. She'd cut off the monster's tail.

Now it was pissed. The *biez* completely forgot about me and charged after Emma. It lowered its antlers and picked up speed, shaking the ground in a thunderous charge.

"Emma! Get out of there!" I screamed. I gave chase, though I couldn't catch up with the *biez* while hauling my sword around.

The sound of the crowd drowned out and became mute as my sights focused on my mate. The smile slid off of Emma's face. A visage of complete horror took over as she turned tail and ran in a zig-zag pattern, to try and get the *biez* off her tail.

For as big as it was, it was also agile. It had no trouble following after Emma until eventually, it caught up with her. Its jaws snapped forward, and Emma screamed and tripped. She grabbed her sword and swung it upright just as the *biez* was going to sink his teeth in her.

The sword ended up stabbing the creature in one of its giant eyeballs. The demon screeched, and rubbed a paw over the eye that was currently gushing blood as Emma scampered away.

I caught up with the *biez*. I stabbed my blade into its side, but barely broke the skin before it turned around. The monster lowered its head and hooked one of its antlers around my body. The *biez* threw its head back, and sent me flying. I hurtled ten feet and dropped my sword somewhere along the way before I came to a rolling stop on the grass. I groaned, feeling the hit my back had taken as I'd slammed against the ground. That wasn't an easy fall.

I got on all fours and bared my teeth. Screw the sword. Time to do things the old-fashioned way; with teeth and claws. I transformed. A snarl emitted in my throat as I jumped skyward and landed on the monster's back.

I sank my teeth into its shoulder, and immediately, a vile taste filled my mouth. The *biez* rolled— I barely managed to avoid getting crushed under its weight. I ripped my mouth away and aimed for the jugular, but the monster reached backward and wrapped its long fingers around my form before it slammed me into the ground. Its sour breath filled my nostrils as it bent downward, fangs dripping saliva.

I was certain I was done for until I heard Emma give a heathen cry behind me. There was the sound of blade slicing though sinew, and the *biez* loosened its hold on me. I wriggled free. Emma had stabbed the monster in the neck, but she'd missed the artery, and now her sword was stuck. She struggled to yank it out, eyes growing wide with fear as the monster hissed and reared back.

"Leave it!" I charged. I managed to snatch Emma up with my teeth, tossing her upon my back and getting her out of the way before one of the *biez's* claws sliced her in half. Emma's sword continued to stick out of the monster's neck, but it didn't do any damage. The beast merely scratched at it, like it was a minor annoyance. Emma clung to my scruff as I raced to the other end of the arena, so we could get a second to breathe and come up with a plan.

"How are we supposed to kill this thing? It's immune to everything we've tried!" Emma shouted. She slid off my back, and I changed. Not even my wolven form was any use against this monster. It was like no matter what Emma and I did, the creature just shook it off.

"Got any ideas?" Emma asked as the monster turned. It proceeded toward us in slow and deliberate movements. As it grew nearer, it began to crouch… like it was planning to deliver the final blow.

This wasn't any good. To hunt a *biez*, you needed to stay far away and chuck things at them, like bombs. We didn't have any of those, and now, neither of us had our swords. It was dangerous getting close range with these things. We'd gotten lucky so far. One hit, and we were done for.

But what we did have was magic.

"Ethan!" Emma screamed as the *biez* went to spring. "What do I do?"

"Use your magic!" I screamed.

"How?"

"Get creative!" I brought my hand backward before swinging it forward again, like I was pitching a ball. A jagged purple fragment, like the end of a spear, sailed through the air like a throwing knife. The magical weapon hit the front of the *biez's* chest and sank in, making blood squirt everywhere. The monster groaned in response.

I threw several more, and all of them hit their target. Although they slowed the *biez* down, they didn't kill him. Blood covered his chest where my magical throwing knives had hit him, but it wasn't enough to destroy him.

Emma had her eyes closed. Her hands had formed a circle before her chest, and in the middle of them was a large blue ball of light— one that was growing larger and larger by the second and was swirling with a magic I'd never seen before. My mouth dropped open in wonder. The ball of light crackled with intensity and power. How was she doing this?

Emma's eyes opened, and the green of them flashed a bright blue before she shouted, "Ethan, stay back!"

I didn't ask any questions. I just got the hell out of the way. Emma tossed the vibrant blue ball in her hands as the *biez* leapt to attack. The monster screamed, opening its mouth to devour us both. Its shadow loomed overhead— waiting to swallow us whole.

Emma's ball of light sailed past the *biez's* mouth and down its throat. It was then she grabbed my arm and pulled me out of the way. We tumbled forward together as the *biez* sailed past us and crashed on the ground. Instinctively, I put my arms around her so I'd take the brunt of the fall. She landed on top of me, and I cried out as I smashed onto my hurt back again.

I expected the *biez* to get up, but it didn't. It lay perfectly still, its body smoking. Emma and I slowly rose to our feet and approached the beast. Its eyes were blank, mouth dangling open. There was a large hole in its gut that Emma's magic had made, and organs were leaking out. The insides were black and smoldering, as if they'd been burned... or frostbitten.

By the gods. It was dead. Emma had done it.

The roar of the crowd returned again, and it was deafening. We'd really given them a show. We'd certainly proved we deserved the monarchy with a performance like that.

Roses and other flowers were tossed from the stands and onto the field as sorceresses came forward. They levitated the body of the beast out of the arena before another steel cage was brought in for the next contestants. As we left the arena, Steward Soloman's mouth was dangling open in shock. He quickly shut it before he ushered the next couple through. No more than a few feet away, a couple of lords had their heads together, flashing Emma looks of disbelief as we passed.

"Emma, that was incredible." I couldn't believe this was the same girl who'd struggled to lift a rock a few weeks ago during class. What had changed?

"It was the same way I'd killed the Black Claw recruit back in Detroit when he tried to murder me," Emma said. "Just a lot bigger."

When we got back to the tent, our entire court was waiting for us. "Emma! Holy shit!" Delmare threw herself around Emma and squeezed her tight. "That magic was incredible!"

"Well done, man." Stefan clapped me on the back and handed me a beer. "Though I would've gotten it done in half the time."

"Of course you would." I handed the beer off to Alexei, because I didn't need to drink before this was all over. "But it was really Emma's doing."

"Sure was!" Odette cheered. She was on Theo's back, and raised a fist in victory. "We need to start planning things for the coronation party!"

"Hold on, guys. Don't celebrate just yet," Emma said. "There's still one more round to go."

"Yeah, and you'll totally crush it," Delmare said. "You've only got to kick the last couple standing out of the competition. It should be easy compared to all the other challenges."

I forced a grimace. I certainly hoped so.

Kiara was standing near the entrance of the tent. She barely smiled as we passed. "Well done, both of you."

"Thanks," I said. I nodded to her, and turned to the group. "Can you guys give us a bit of space? Emma and I need to strategize."

There were a few more claps and cheers as Emma and I ducked into the tent. Kiara eyed me before she swept away. Kiara wasn't dumb. She knew what was really on my mind.

Once I was certain we were alone, I faced my mate. "Emma, what's going on?" I crossed my arms. "A couple of weeks ago you were struggling to do minor magic. Now you're flinging spells around like some master sorceress."

Emma's expression hardened. "Hey, maybe I do well under pressure," she said. "Back off, all right?"

I raised an eyebrow. I didn't like that tone. "I'm your mate, and your partner for the Contest. I deserve to know. If something's going on, and you're using magic to manipulate our placings, you'd better tell me now." I made sure my voice sounded stern.

Emma stared at me blankly. Then she sighed and removed her cloak, reaching inside her armor. "It's this."

I didn't recognize what she brought out— not at first. But when I caught sight of the black lace, and the dark stone dangling from it, I put the pieces together. The necklace. The one we stole from Lady Korva. I'd forgotten all about it. And Emma was wearing it in the *Contest*?!

My temper broke. I stormed forward and yanked the necklace off her neck. The lace snapped easily. The stone itself was blazing hot— I could feel it leaving blisters on my palm.

"Hey!" Emma shouted. "Give that back!"

"Like hell! Do you realize what's going to happen if this necklace is found on you? We'll be forced out of the Contest!" I hissed. I tossed it to the other side of the tent. I was furious. I didn't care where it went.

"Kiara gave me a potion before the last round started. How is that any different?" she asked.

"It was an *energy potion*! Those are allowed!" I shouted. "Unseelie magic isn't!"

"Keep your voice down!" she hissed. "So I cheated. So what?"

"*So what*? Do you think this is a joke?"

Emma stormed forward, her hands balled into fists. "Can you honestly say that if I hadn't had that necklace with me, that we would've survived that race, or the fight with the monster? Because if I didn't, I'm pretty sure we'd be dead right now. I used dark magic to save *your life*."

That shut me up. I knew she was right. We wouldn't have gotten this far without that necklace. One or both of us would have perished.

Yet that wasn't the only thing I was concerned about. "Did you honestly make this decision of your own accord without even bothering to consult me? I thought we were a team!"

"You don't understand. The hag came to me. She said this was the only way," Emma stated.

"You saw the hag *again* and you didn't tell me?" By the gods, I just wanted to keep that thing *away* from her!

"I prayed to Milonna and asked for her help. She sent me the hag. She told me we wouldn't win unless we used the necklace," she insisted.

"I don't want to win this way!" I hissed.

"I don't care what you want, Ethan. There's more we're risking than your honor if we lose," she snapped back.

"You don't know what that necklace is doing to you. Stuff like this always comes with a price," I said.

"And I'm willing to accept it in order to help us win!" Emma's hand moved to her neck. She rubbed it, as if it was bothering her.

I knew what she wasn't saying. She was willing to accept the pain that came with dark magic... in order to give me my dream.

Such a thought gutted me.

I had to take a few deep breaths in order to prevent myself from erupting. I came closer. "Show me your neck."

"Fuck off." She cringed away from me.

"Emma. I'm not giving you a choice."

She hesitated for a moment before, slowly, she removed her hand. Underneath her armor and the tourney colors were harsh burn marks, set into the skin where the necklace rested. The burns were bloody and discolored. The veins around the area were black, spiderwebs lacing over her porcelain skin.

I felt sick to my stomach. "By the gods, Emma." Seeing the way that necklace had burned her… it brought tears to my eyes. I could barely speak past the lump in my throat. The anger drained right out of me to be replaced with agony.

"I did it for *you*," Emma forced out through a strained force. Tears rose up in her eyes, and a few broke free down her cheeks. "All of it was for you."

Her words broke me. I was ready to pack up and go home. This was too much. My ambition was too much. If she was willing to use Unseelie magic so I could become king… no. I wouldn't let that happen. I refused to allow my mate to sacrifice her good health so I could achieve my goals. I'd be no kind of mate if I allowed this to continue. I didn't deserve to marry Emma if my dreams required her suffering.

I stepped away from her. "I'm going to the officials. We're withdrawing from the Contest."

Emma's mouth dropped open. "We can't drop out! We're in the last round!" she protested.

"Because we swindled the system! We shouldn't even be here," I hissed.

"And if Gabby and Elijah get through to the last round, and no one else does? You're just going to hand them the monarchy on a silver platter?" she spat.

That got me to pause. "Didn't think about that, did you?" she asked quietly. "I've been watching them this whole tournament, and they're willing to do whatever it takes to win, Ethan. Which means so do we."

"I won't stoop to their level," I said firmly. "And I'm disappointed you thought you had to."

Her eyes watered again. "I don't think you understand how this world works. You have to play dirty if you're going to get anywhere."

"No. *You* don't get how this world works. You're new to everything here, Emma!" I shouted. "I know you haven't had an easy life, but I lost my leg! My *father died*. I know better than anyone how terrible this world can be, but no matter how far I'm pushed, I won't bend my morals."

Emma gave a soft, skeptical noise and whispered, "You just haven't been pushed far enough."

A heat of anger flared through me again, but it was there and gone in an instant. Being mad at Emma… gods, it was so hard. And it was even harder to be upset with her when she'd been willing to hurt herself for my benefit.

Yet she was right. We couldn't stop. We'd come too far. And there was too much at stake if we backed out.

I lowered my voice and made it gentle. "All right. I understand why you did what you did. But we can't do it again. Just… please promise me that you'll never use dark magic after this. And you won't use the necklace to get us through the last round of the Contest. We play fair."

Emma's resolve broke. "Fine," she said. "I won't use it in the last round. It's just a duel, anyway. We can beat whoever's out there."

I sure hoped so. Things fell quiet between us. We sat on opposite sides of the tent and didn't speak to each other.

I hated the tension that was between us. But at the same time, I didn't know what to do about it. I felt guilty that we'd gotten this far at all. Yet Emma had a point. We couldn't let Elijah and Gabby win. No matter what.

Hours passed, and night fell. Eventually, Lord Lucien entered to deliver the news.

The other two couples had died in their battles against the monsters. Elijah and Gabby were the only other couple to pass the last test.

In the last round, we'd go head to head in a duel for the crown.

emma
TWENTY-FOUR

I knew Ethan was disappointed in me, and it was the shittiest feeling in the world. He acted like I *wanted* to cheat. I desired to rip that necklace off my neck as we were fighting the *biez* last round. Having that thing on fucking *hurt*. It burned— not just my skin, but also my insides. I was starting to realize why our professors warned us about using Unseelie magic.

But we needed it, and badly. That monster would've killed us both if I hadn't used the necklace to save our asses. The monster would've killed *Ethan*... and dark magic or not, I'd do whatever it took to rescue him from a painful death. There was nothing on this earth, good or evil, I wouldn't do to save that man.

Yet I promised Ethan I wouldn't wear it in the last round. We'd play fair in order to win. I thought that was a good compromise.

Besides. I didn't need dark magic to kick Gabby's ass. I could do that all on my own.

As we were getting ready to leave, I faced Ethan. "I'm sorry," I said. I grabbed his arm lightly and gave it a squeeze. "I didn't mean to upset you. I should've consulted you about using the necklace."

Ethan's expression was hard to read. "What's past is past," he said. "We need to focus on what's ahead."

He raised his hands and stroked a few fingers across my cheek. "I forgive you. And whatever happens next... know that I'm still proud of you."

The small movement was enough to make my knees go weak. Ethan was such a god. He had this freaking power over me I couldn't explain. Before he'd chosen me as his partner for the Contest, we'd merely been friends, but ever since that kiss... it was like the connection that drew me to him was getting stronger and stronger. The Phantom remained in the back of my mind, but at the forefront was Ethan— and everything that he could do to me.

And I wasn't talking sexually. The man had a connection to my soul that I couldn't describe. He could break me so easily with just his words. Or a displeased look.

I never wanted to let him down again.

A cold winter wind blew by as we left the tent, and I shivered. It was nightfall by this point, the stars shining above like twinkling lights over the city. I was still tired, but the energy potion had given me enough strength to make it through this thing— along with pure spite. I wanted nothing more than to wipe the sneer off of Gabby's face, and make her pay for killing Krystyna.

Lord Lucien and Lady Magdalina were waiting outside of the Field main gates. Gabby and Elijah were at the gates on the other side of the arena. We'd enter at the same time, bow to each other, and then the match would begin.

Lucien appeared as stoic as ever. "The Seven Gods are here. They are making their presence known at the crowning of the next king. You can feel them in the air."

I couldn't feel anything, but Ethan nodded in agreement beside me. Lucien's eyes locked with mine and said, "Keep your wits about you, Emma. Ethan, come with me. We must strategize."

Lucien beckoned Ethan to follow him with a jerk of his head. Lady Magdalina placed a hand on my arm. She gently led me away from Ethan so we could talk alone. "Lord Zlodia and Lady Korva have prepared their son for this moment all their lives. You need to be on your guard, Emmaline," she whispered. "This is no ordinary match."

"What do you mean?" I asked. My heartbeat quickened in my chest.

"Elijah and his mate do not wish to leave any question as to who deserves the crown. They will seek to take your lives. Keep in mind that there are no rules," Lady Magdalina told me harshly. "Gabriella is a student of mine. She's ruthless on the ice, and even more so out here. She won't hesitate to kill you. Save her life, if you can. But whatever it takes, don't let her win."

My mouth was dry. "What if I can't do this alone?"

"Call upon Milonna for help," Magdalina said. "Gabriella has sworn herself to the Dark Lord, but you have chosen to follow the queen of the gods. She will appear to you today if you call on her name."

I didn't know if that was true. Right now, I couldn't sense anything magical or spiritual about this. All I felt... as much as I hated it... was fear.

And it wasn't that I was afraid of Elijah or Gabby, or even of dying. I was terrified of watching Ethan lose his dream. I thought death would be preferable to that.

"Promise me, Emmaline." Magdalina's fingers whitened on my arms. "Promise me you won't walk out of that arena without a win."

Mom had told me Lady Magdalina would ask me to do impossible things. I felt like this was only the start. "I promise."

She grimaced. "Good. Let's get you ready."

A half an hour later Ethan and I stood side by side, waiting for the gates to open. We'd sharpened both our swords, and were now merely waiting for the moment when we'd be allowed to enter.

Ethan looked nervous. His face was blanched, and he bounced next to me nervously. I wondered if he was cold or if he was just trying to burn off some anxiety.

"Emma," he started, and I looked toward him. "We'll do this together."

I reached out and threaded my fingers through his. "Always."

Ethan gave a forced smile. The doors opened, and I let go of his hand. As we entered, Gabby and Elijah proceeded toward us. We met in the middle of the arena. Elijah, as always, looked far too confident. He gave an obnoxious sneer, flashing his teeth as he laid a hand on the sword at his side.

Gabby was mere inches from me. She let out a snarky laugh under her breath before she whispered, "Sure you don't want to back out?"

"You're the one who should be scared," I growled back.

"If only. You have no idea what's coming."

Gabby said nothing more. Trumpets sounded again. Ethan sank into a bow, and I copied him, giving a proper curtsey.

Elijah barely dipped his head before he sprang forward, unleashing his weapon. But Ethan had been expecting it, and was waiting for him. Ethan drew his sword and battered Elijah's away before the blade managed to knick his armor.

Just like her mate, Gabby didn't finish her curtsey. She'd hardly bent her knees before I saw a flash of red magic zoom by my face. I ducked quickly to the side and let it whizz past.

Those shitheads had attacked before the bows were even over! What dicks. Elijah and Ethan began an assault of swords that was both impressive and deadly. Their blades became a blur, and the sound of clashing steel rang out in the arena as their two weapons engaged again and again.

I hardly had time to glance at them before I noticed Gabby charging at me, her weapon drawn. I drew my sword and brandished it in a wide arc as a last-minute line of defense. It ended up working, and knocked Gabby off balance. She fell to the side, and I slashed forward, but she rolled out of the way and my blade hit nothing but air.

Gabby's sword was lighter and smaller than mine, but she definitely knew how to use it. Her movements were agile and fierce. She came at me, again and again. I didn't have time to plan my own offense while dealing with her sharp jabs and precise movements.

Yet as I fought off her sword, I realized that I knew all her tricks. Ethan and I had practiced these maneuvers during Lord Lucien's class. They were nothing new to me. Gabby's eyes grew wide with surprise as she realized that I was able to anticipate her every move.

But anticipation wouldn't be enough to win this fight. Gabby was a skater, like me, so I knew getting her to lose her balance was probably impossible. Instead, I counted her blows, and paid attention to her style. This was all stuff Ethan had taught me how to do. Learn how your enemy fights, then use it against them.

I learned Gabby's weakness within a short time of sparring with her. She was too impatient. She wanted to kill me now. I got used to her timing, and when I thought I had the rhythm down, thrust forward. My sword scraped against her armor, and she gasped. She lashed out a kick to knock me off my feet, but I sprang away to a safe distance. A few seconds longer and my sword would've sliced her artery.

That made her mad. I kept a cool head as Gabby ran at me full speed, her sword raised, a wild scream escaping her mouth. Our swords flashed as we dueled and came within arm's length. She raised a fist to punch me in the face. I swung aside to avoid it, and purposefully smashed my forehead against hers.

She fell backward, dazed. My head hurt, but a smile of rage spread across my mouth. I charged forward. Gabby rolled out of the way before my blade sank into the grass where her torso had been.

As she sprang to her feet, Gabby's teeth were clenched with rage. A thrill of exhilaration went through me. She might've grown up in this society, but I was a better swordswoman. I had a natural talent for it, and I'd been taught to fight by Ethan Nowak, a prince of the Arcanea. She couldn't best me this way.

And she knew it. Instead of approaching me again, Gabby hung back, her eyes calculating as she tried to decide the next best way to get me down.

A vicious snarling tore away my attention from her. Across the arena, Ethan and Elijah had abandoned their swords. They'd changed into wolvens, and were rolling on the ground attempting to tear each other's throats out.

Ethan whipped out his paw. His claws caught Elijah in the face and tore. Elijah gave a howl as a long gash ripped across his eye, spurting blood. The injury was so deep that I knew it would scar.

In retaliation, Elijah lunged forward. He sank his teeth into Ethan's neck and pulled. Ethan yelped. I gasped, but as Elijah pulled his fangs away I saw that he'd bitten into the shoulder more than Ethan's neck.

It didn't look like Elijah had damaged anything major, but the blow had done heavy damage to Ethan. He moved slower, and resisted putting weight on the shoulder Elijah had injured. Even worse, Ethan had sustained several injuries already and was bleeding. Red liquid poured heavily from his wounds and stained the ground. He breathed heavily, shaking his head as he backed up from Elijah.

I wanted to run to him, make him safe and put my sword through Elijah's skull, but I knew that getting in the way of two alphas vying for dominance was a sure way to get myself killed. I hesitated, not knowing what I could do.

Gabby saw that I was distracted and took her shot. She threw her sword to the side. As I jerked my head back toward her I saw that a ball of red magic had formed in her right hand.

She tossed it my way before I could move. Her blast hit me in the chest, sending shockwaves throughout my system. I went flying backward. My sword was knocked out of my hand, and I landed on my back twelve feet away from where I'd been standing.

As I struggled to catch my breath, a horrible truth overcame me. I was a better warrior, but Gabby was a more proficient sorceress. Her magic could easily best mine any day.

Gabby grinned wickedly as she approached. "You'd better run."

I scrambled to my feet. Another one of Gabby's magic bombs blasted near my feet. It tripped me up. I fell on my face again. I was hardly able to stand before I had to roll out of the way from another blast.

I couldn't let myself get hit with another one of those spells again. Her magic had zapped my strength. I sent back a few bolts of blue magic back at her, but without the necklace, they were weak and underpowered. I heard the crowd around me shout in confusion. I'd shown incredible magic in the last two rounds. They were probably wondering why I wasn't kicking Gabby's ass right now.

As another one of her spells nicked my heel, I turned around. All right. I was done running. I faced Gabby and began chucking sapphire balls of light her way. They were the size of baseballs, and most fizzled out before they even made their way to her. One of the balls of light hit her, but it hardly left her winded before she shot another spell back at me.

Her magic was stronger than ever. It smacked me in the face and smashed me into the ground. I saw stars, and fought off the urge to pass out as I pushed myself onto my knees.

I tried to gather the magic for another spell. But it didn't work this time. The ball of blue light in my hand sputtered and crackled before it disappeared completely— before I could even throw it Gabby's way. She proceeded toward me with hands glowing red, a cackle of malice growing in her throat.

Shit. I was fucked. I was *so fucked*.

I did the only thing I could. I abandoned the fight and ran to Ethan. By this time, Elijah had gained the upper hand. He grabbed Ethan by the scruff and tossed him a good ten feet. Ethan went tumbling to the side and came sliding to a stop. The ground where he'd rolled was stained with blood. His legs shook as he attempted to get up. They refused to hold his weight, and he collapsed.

"Ethan!" Tears beaded my eyes. No, no, this couldn't be happening. Ethan was down. I couldn't take on Elijah and Gabby by myself. I needed him to rise up and fight!

But he couldn't anymore. The duel with Elijah had taken too much out of him. I fell to my knees at his side, and my hands fisted in his white fur.

Ethan shuddered. "*I couldn't do it*, onawilke. *I'm so sorry*."

"It's not your fault," I whispered. A tear ran down my cheek. After everything we'd done, everything we'd sacrificed… it was all for nothing.

Gabby had rejoined Elijah. The black wolf stalked toward us with a raised lip, head down, his fangs streaked red with Ethan's blood.

"I'll tear off your remaining leg," Elijah growled. *"Along with all your other limbs."*

Ethan whimpered in pain. He couldn't fight back. Elijah had bested him. A shiver of terror ran up my spine.

This was all over. We were going to lose.

Gabby raised her hand. A red ball of magic, one equal to the spell I'd created in the last match, shone in her open palm. "Say goodbye, losers."

I threw my arms around Ethan and held on tight. I closed my eyes and prayed that it would be quick. I didn't want to feel any pain, but more than that, I didn't want Ethan to suffer.

Lady Magdalina's words forced their way into my mind. *Call upon Milonna for help.*

I didn't think it would help this late in the match. I didn't see how. But I was out of options, and I wanted to stand a good chance at getting into the Great Hunting Grounds if I was really going to die today.

Goddess, help me, I pleaded. *Show me the way.*

When I spoke those words from my heart, it was like the match paused. A soft feeling entered my chest, and my eyes fluttered open. Elijah and Gabby faded away. So did the arena. Even Ethan vanished from my side. Everything dissolved as I rose to my feet. The world around me became silent and steady.

I was standing in a beautiful forest in the middle of springtime, golden light enveloping me in a warm, sunny embrace. I heard the sound of birds, and the leaves whispering, and the rushing sound of a brook as water trickled against the rocks. I even think I heard the voices of women far in the distance, laughing and singing against a new dawn.

Milonna was there. She looked the same as she had last time— a beautiful white doe, with twisting tree branches for antlers, a halo of light surrounding her form. The weakness and fear left my body as she proceeded toward me with graceful steps. As I stood in her light, peace came over me, giving me the feeling of coming home.

You cannot give up, Worldweaver, Milonna said gently. Her voice sounded musical and soft… like that of a mother. *Your time has not yet come.*

"Goddess, I can't beat them," I said. My head hung in defeat. "I've tried everything, and I've failed. Ethan and I can't win this. We don't have the power."

The power to become queen is inside of you, Milonna whispered. *You need only to bring it to life, and face the sun.*

Milonna reached out and closed the space between us. Her soft muzzle met the place where my heart beat against my chest, and a radiating light burst from her touch.

When her nose caressed my heart, something incredible happened. The forest around me vanished. Milonna was gone, and the arena came rushing back.

Ethan was still on the ground, and Elijah was still in his wolven form. Gabby was at his side, the spell still burning in her fingers.

But I was looking down on them this time, not up at them. I was hovering above the ground, my feet dangling upon thin air. Both Gabby and Elijah were gazing at me with open mouths— I suddenly realized I was at least twenty feet above them.

I had *wings.* They were in the shape of snowflakes, different shades of shimmering sapphire sparkling like diamonds across the length of their span. The edges of them were fringed with white, like frost, and the moonlight bounced off of their reflection, creating small rainbows that dazzled throughout the arena. They were the largest wings I'd ever seen on any sorceress— twelve feet on either side— and glowed with a silver light that moved fluidly. They beat of their own free will, keeping me suspended over the challengers below.

Ethan weakly raised his eyes. A brightness illuminated his gaze as he took in the sight of me hovering above him, like a noble protector.

He was proud of me. That was enough to make me want to fly. I no longer felt tired or weak. Now, I felt strong.

Elijah bared his teeth and growled. *"Well, what are you waiting for?"* he barked at Gabby. *"Go get her!"*

Gabby snapped her mouth shut. She brought out her wings, and beat them furiously as she rose to my height. Magic burned in both of her hands now. She fired both shots at me, but instinctively, I rolled to the side. My wings kept me aloft, and steadied me in the air as her missiles flew by and exploded behind me.

She immediately sent several more shots, but I looped in the air and dived, avoiding each one. I didn't know how to fly, but it was like the feeling came naturally to me— like skating did. I'd paid attention in Flight class, even though I hadn't gained my wings yet, and I applied the information I'd been taught as I spun out of the way of Gabby's spells. She screamed in rage as each of her blasts missed me, her magic failing her.

I smirked. "My turn." I searched inside me for my light— the power Milonna had given me. From within, I was able to draw out a flickering ball of sapphire.

I gave a laugh that sounded half-mad. "Better run," I sang, repeating her taunt from earlier.

Gabby's eyes widened. She turned and fled. Her wings beat like mad as she flew in a jagged pattern to outmaneuver me.

But, as I'd learned, my left hand was a great shot, and with it I barely missed. I flung the ball of magic in her direction. It slammed into Gabby's back and she spun out. Her wings failed to support her as she crashed against the earth, *hard*, and the crowd let out a moan.

Her eyes fluttered shut, and she didn't stir. Gabby had been knocked out by the force of my blow. She wasn't getting up again for some time.

Now I had to deal with Elijah. I turned in mid-air and flew his way. The glint of my sword shone at me from the ground. I picked it up as I flew past, aiming my sights for Elijah.

He saw me coming. Elijah's eyes fixated on Ethan, who was still lying helpless on the ground. He surged forward, jaws extended, to finish the job and end Ethan's life forever.

But my wings were faster, and I got to him first. I kicked out my foot as he dove for Ethan's neck, and it collided right with Elijah's stupid face. He was knocked over backward. I landed as Elijah struggled to his feet.

I thrust my sword out and pressed it against his neck. Elijah gasped, eyes red and bloodshot as they locked with mine.

"Emma," Ethan rasped. *"Don't kill him."*

A moment's worth of hesitation crossed through me. Don't kill him? Why not? He'd caused us nothing but trouble. He'd murdered someone. He would've killed Ethan if I hadn't gotten here first. I should do away with him, and Gabby, too.

Yet Ethan was my mate. He was my alpha, and I loved him. I didn't have to do as he commanded. But I chose to.

I dug the point of my blade into Elijah's neck and drew blood. "Surrender," I breathed. "Or I'll run you through."

Elijah raised a lip and growled. Then he transformed back into a man and raised his hands in defeat, bitter hatred emanating from his every feature.

The crowd exploded. Thunderous applause, along with shouts of victory, rang out in the stands around us. My wings faded away as I landed. I lowered my sword and turned on the spot, my mouth dropping open in awe.

"All hail the King! All hail the Queen!" the crowd was chanting.

Elijah had dragged himself away and was sitting at Gabby's side. Ethan had changed back—he was lying on the ground on his back, still bleeding and wincing in pain.

"We did it, Emma," he whispered. "You did it."

"Ethan." I knelt down. "Is it bad?"

"I'll survive." He gasped as he pushed himself to a sitting position. "I'll need your help getting up, though."

"Of course." I pulled Ethan to his feet and put his arm around my shoulder. The audience cheered even louder as he stood. I helped him limp to the gates while flowers were tossed into the arena.

Now that the fight was over, it felt like the strength Milonna had given me was fading. I was exhausted. It was hard dragging Ethan around— he was a big guy— but it wasn't long before Lord Lucien ran onto the field. He took Ethan from me, and a huge weight was removed from my shoulders as my mate leaned against him instead. Lady Magdalina had followed, and she gave me a nod of approval as we met near the gates.

"Well done." Lord Lucien's smile was broader than I'd ever seen. "Well done, you two."

"Thanks." Ethan's head lolled on his shoulders. He was almost out of it.

"Ethan, do you realize what we've done? We've won!" I said. "You're going to be king!"

"King. I can hardly believe it." Ethan's voice was faint. It was like he could barely process what was going on. I worried about him.

"We need to get him patched up. To the medical tent it is," Lady Magdalina said. Ethan grumbled something incoherent.

"You should visit the medical tent as well, Miss Sosna," Lucien said. "That was a hard fight."

"I'll be all right," I told him. "What I really need is to change out of these clothes." My armor, along with my tourney colors, were filthy. I looked around. "Where's our court?" It'd be nice to see my friends right now.

"They're waiting in the winners circle, where you'll be presented after Ethan gets his bearings," Lucien replied. "I suggest you get cleaned up before joining them."

Lady Magdalina put a soft hand on my back. "That was excellent work, Emmaline. I knew you wouldn't let me down."

Small praise, but I was used to it from a figure skating instructor. "Thanks, Coach."

When we got to the medical tent, Lucien ducked inside with Ethan. I went to follow, but Magdalina blocked my way.

"I know you want to be with him, but trust he's in good hands," Magdalina said firmly. "It's time for you to be concerned with yourself. A queen must put on her best appearances to the public."

I hated to leave Ethan's side. But I felt like I'd get in the way at the medical tent, and I wanted everyone's focus to be on helping him.

Then I realized… Lady Magdalina had called me a queen.

Holy shit. I was Ethan's bride. That made me a…

It hadn't seemed real before. During the ball, the Contest, it'd all seemed like a game. A slim chance at something I'd never have. Now it was in my grasp.

I was the next queen of the Arcanea. Ethan and I… we'd rule over them all.

Lady Magdalina escorted me to my tent. She put a hand on the small of my back and said, "We'll send Ethan along to escort you to the celebration once his injuries have been tended to. I eagerly await your arrival at the winners circle."

She gave me a smile that seemed to hide so much more before she strolled away in that careless, elegant way of hers.

Lady Magdalina had plans for me as queen. I was certain of it.

The emptiness of my tent was a welcome refuge. It was quiet in here, and far away from people. I didn't feel suffocated. I could recharge.

As I gazed into the mirror, I wondered what I would look like with a crown on top of my head. I was an outcast back home. Everyone avoided me and hated me there. Now I'd become the most popular woman in Malovia overnight. How was I going to handle the change? It was all too much to handle.

I'd put Ethan on the throne, yet I didn't consider the consequences of becoming royal. Probably because before, I never thought we'd win.

Yet we had. And it was going to change everything.

I needed some space. I needed something simple and average, something comforting. I struggled out of my armor and threw my tourney colors on the floor. Once I was naked, I used the water basin and a washcloth to wipe off all the dirt and grime that had accumulated on my skin during the Contest, all the while wondering what I'd gotten myself into. I washed away the war paint, and brushed out my braid so that my red hair became soft and wavy over my shoulders.

A simple cotton dress, navy in color with long, billowing sleeves had been lain out on the bed, along with fur boots and a cloak. Gods, how I missed jeans. Or even pajama pants. Couldn't I show up in those?

The dress felt more like a nightgown as I slipped it over my skin. It was comfortable, and soft. I thought that I could fall asleep in it. I didn't know how I was going to stay awake during this party. My eyes were already closing shut. I sat on the bed, to try and make the room stop spinning.

So many had died today in the attempt to gain what I had. I didn't even think I wanted it. I wondered if I was being ungrateful. Or selfish.

The tent flap fluttered open. My heart rose in hope, wanting it to be Ethan.

But it wasn't. It was fucking Gabby. She was still wearing her tournament armor. In her hand she carried a cell phone.

I gave her a scathing look. "It's a little late to try and kill me, don't you think?"

Her nose wrinkled. "I'm not here to kill you, Sosna. Unfortunately, I lost my shot at that a few moments ago. I'm here to make a deal."

I cruelly laughed as I rose from the bed. "You want to make a deal with *me?* I'm going to be queen, bitch. I'm in a pretty good fucking position. What could you possibly offer that I'd be interested in?"

Gabby strolled toward me. Once she was at my side, she unlocked the cell phone and went to her camera application. "How about this?"

A video played on her screen. It was surveillance of some back alleyway in Dolinska. There was a man there, facing the camera. I didn't know who it was, until I looked closer. My stomach dipped as I recognized the face onscreen. Ethan.

But it wasn't *just* Ethan. He was wearing the clothes of someone I knew— a dark cloak I recognized. Ethan fitted a mask onto his face… one of a white wolf.

Ethan waved his hand as he cast a spell. A duplicate of the Phantom, of *himself,* appeared before him.

Ethan doubled over in pain just as the clone took off. Then he turned and drew a grappling hook from the belt around his waist. He shot it in the other direction, and the line pulled him off view of the camera as he rose to the rooftops.

The truth of it all slammed into me so hard that it almost knocked me off my feet.

Ethan was the Phantom.

Ethan was my true mate. The one my soul had bonded with. My one and only love.

Gabby caught the astounded look on my face and let out a barking laugh. "You've *got* to be kidding me! You didn't know about this, either? Does he tell you *nothing*?"

Apparently, he didn't. Ethan didn't trust me. The revelation hollowed me and created a black pit of despair within my soul. Ethan had all this time to tell me he was the Phantom… knew that I was desperately searching for him… and he'd kept his mouth shut.

He'd cast some kind of illusion spell, to duplicate himself and trick me into thinking the Phantom was someone else. It'd all been an elaborate ruse. But why?

I couldn't let my feelings show. Gabby was here. I reorganized my features and gave her a cold glare. "What do you want?"

"The only thing I've ever wanted," Gabby replied bluntly. "Power."

"Why didn't you tell the authorities about the Phantom before the Contest if you wanted to get rid of Ethan so bad?" I snarled. "This would've knocked him right out of the running."

"News just came in a moment ago, sweetheart. The Black Claw delivered this to my tent personally. Seems like I'm the one person in Dolinska who knows." She grinned. "Besides you and the Black Claw, anyway."

"So turn him in now. He'll lose the crown," I snapped.

She made a tittering sound. "Now why would I do that when I can just force the new leaders of the Arcanea to do whatever I want?"

Gabby turned off the cell phone. She moved around the tent in a gloating way as she continued. "If I tell the authorities who Ethan is now, they'll remove him from the throne, and the Contest will have to start all over again. Elijah and I aren't taking our chances and going through with a new competition. Not when we could have the both of you working for us."

"I'll never work for you," I growled through my teeth.

"Then your fiancé goes to jail." She shrugged. "I could really care less either way. I'd get a thrill seeing Nowak behind bars."

I seethed. "I've got dirt on you, too. I know you and Elijah killed Waldron."

She rolled her eyes. "Big deal. Got any proof?"

When I didn't respond, she smirked again. "Of course you don't. But the dirt on you I can actually back up. Video evidence doesn't lie. Human technology can't be manipulated by illusion magic. And I'd be willing to bet there's a ton of circumstantial evidence that'll fall right into place once Nowak's name comes into the picture. The police have been watching the Phantom for a while now. They only need the last piece of the puzzle to put everything together."

"I hate you," I snapped.

"Hate me all you want, Sosna. It's just business." Gabby flipped her hair over her shoulder. "This is how the monarchy works. It's all threats and back door deals and dirty politics. Better get used to it."

I crossed my arms. "What's your deal?"

"It's simple. You do what I tell you to, and convince Ethan of the same thing. But there's a caveat. I don't want Ethan getting any idea we know he's the Phantom. You can never tell him that you know the truth," Gabby said. "It compromises things. He's free to do his vigilante side gig, and you can be his little queen… *if* you both do as you're told."

I swear a vein in my forehead twitched. I could feel it. "That's not good enough, is it?"

"No. There's a second part to the deal," Gabby added sharply. "You don't tell anyone about Waldron. Or anything else Elijah and I decide to do. We've got the Black Claw in our hands. And we'll use them as we see fit, without any interference from you or the authorities."

"You expect me to just sit back and do nothing while you go on a murder spree?" I hissed. "Fat chance."

"If you say a word to the Arcanea Alliance about *anything* Elijah and I are involved in, you can kiss your mate goodbye." Gabby's eyes narrowed. "Eli and I have big plans for this city. And we don't plan on letting anyone get in our way."

I gave a low, guttural laugh. "When Ethan's king, he'll take care of you. Once he's been coronated, your asses are fried. I'll tell him everything."

"You breathe a word of this to Ethan, now or in the future, and he'll be locked up before either of you know it. Our deal remains a secret. The Circle will never allow a vigilante to keep the throne." Gabby raised an eyebrow. "It's your choice."

My insides seethed with rage. I hated the thought of becoming Gabby's puppet. I didn't want to sing and dance to her tune for the rest of my life.

But if I didn't... she'd make sure I'd pay for it. By losing my mate for good.

"Fine," I snapped. "It's a deal. But you'd better hold up your end of the bargain."

"As long as you hold up yours," she breathed cooly. "If this goes right, all of us will be able to live happily ever after."

My temper snapped. "Leave now," I said. "Or I'll have you thrown out."

It was the first order I'd given as queen, and gods, I meant it. Gabby said nothing in response. She merely turned, and strode away with her shoulders thrown back.

Gabby had lost the King's Contest, but I had a bitter feeling in my heart that made me feel like she'd won.

My legs weren't able to keep me upright once she left the tent. I fell upon the bed. My knees curled inward, and my hands ran through my hair as the earth-shattering reality rushed through my veins.

I was Ethan's true mate. The Phantom and the prince were the same man. We were meant to be together, forever.

And Ethan had known that from the beginning.

He'd *lied* to me. After all this time... months, even... he had never told me the truth. And I didn't know why.

But I couldn't even tell him that I knew. Because if I did, Gabby would expose his true identity, and he'd go to prison. I'd lose him forever. If I got too close... cared about him too much... fell for him harder than I already had... it would be too difficult to keep the secret. The closer Ethan and I became, the more I put him at risk. Keeping him at a distance was the only way to save his life.

Ethan could never know that I loved the true man behind the mask. All thanks to fucking Gabby.

And yet... I knew the secrets Ethan kept, too. He cared for me. He truly and deeply did. He'd tried to deny it, even to my face, but it was *so* obvious to see. He had so much adoration for me built up within him, which, for some reason, he felt the need to hide.

Ethan Nowak *loved me*. The fact of it was enough to bring tears to my eyes.

I turned on my back and stared up at the ceiling of the tent. I could forgive Ethan. Whatever reasons he had for concealing the Phantom, they had to be good ones. He wouldn't have withheld the truth from me if he had any other choice. He was too honorable.

But I couldn't forgive Gabby. And by the gods, I wanted to make her pay. She couldn't torture Ethan and I like this. Not forever.

Eventually, the truth would come out. And when it did... there'd be a war.

I was the new ruler of the Arcanea. But more than that, I was Ethan's. I belonged to him, and he belonged to me. We shared a primal connection that flowed through our blood, a bond that was solidified by the magic of our fae ancestors. That man was my heart and soul. No matter what was to come, I'd do anything to defend him. I'd live for him. I'd die for him.

Whatever the consequences, I'd stand by his side. Now and always.
The monarchy was a game of chess. And in chess, the queen only had one goal.
To protect her king.

TWENTY-FIVE

I couldn't describe the range of emotions that were coursing through me. I'd finally accomplished my task. I'd won the Contest, and the right as king. I'd followed in the footsteps of my father and hopefully made him proud. I was going to be ruler of the Arcanea.

And it had been Emma's doing. Elijah had bested me during the duel. He'd injured me so badly I couldn't fight back. I'd thought we'd lost for sure, until I looked up and saw the most beautiful wings above me. Emma's wings.

She didn't need the necklace. She was powerful all on her own. I owed everything to her. I had truly chosen well.

At the medical tent they bandaged up my injured shoulder, as well as all my other wounds. I was given an energy potion, and a potion of herbs to help me heal. Shifters healed faster than most other supernaturals, and after I was patched up, I was already feeling better. I still walked with a limp, but I was sure it'd be gone by morning. My body was bruised all over, yet I hardly felt the pain. I was too elated. I'd won the Contest and was on top of the world. Nothing could ruin my triumph this day.

As soon as the healers let me go, I left the medical tent and hobbled back to my own. Emma. I wanted to see her. I needed to thank her for everything that she'd done. I didn't know how I was going to repay her for our victory, but I wanted to start right now.

I entered our tent. Emma was sitting on the bed. One hand was on her head. She was looking down at the ground. A glass of half-finished red wine sat on the bedside table nearby.

She looked devastated. I didn't understand. We had won! What was so upsetting about that?

"Emma." A broad smile crossed my face. I was smiling so hard it nearly hurt.

When she looked up, a visage of relief came across her pretty features, as well as other emotions. I thought I saw a flash of resentment— strange— before it faded away to be replaced by something more passionate. She stood from the bed and rushed toward me.

I hurried to her as fast as I could. With my good arm, I picked her up and crushed her against my chest in a wholesome embrace. She hugged me back. She cast her arms around my shoulders and buried her face in my neck, as if she was trying to hide herself from the world.

When I set her down, she looked at me in a way she never had. Her eyes narrowed, and she tilted her head to the side in curiosity.

It was… unsettling. Like she knew something about me now that she hadn't before. Or she was trying to picture someone else in my place.

"I can't believe it." The grin wouldn't melt off my face. "We made it. We're going to be king and queen, Em."

The corners of her mouth tilted upward slightly. "Yeah. I guess we are, aren't we?"

A bit of my enthusiasm dampened. I thought she'd be more excited. I stroked her hair back and cupped her face in my hand. "What is it you want, Emma? You're queen now. Whatever you ask for, you'll have. I want to give you the world."

"I don't want anything," Emma replied honestly. "I just want you."

That went like an arrow straight to my heart. It melted away my tough wolven exterior and exposed a soft shifter. One who wanted to crawl onto my mate's lap and beg for her attention.

I pulled myself together and said, "Well… I suppose I should get out of these filthy clothes. We have a celebration to get to." They'd removed my armor at the medical tent to take care of my wounds.

"Let me help you." Emma went to the water basin. She dipped in a clean cloth as I stripped away my shirt. She began wiping the dirt off of me.

I shivered as she lightly caressed the cloth over my chest and abdomen. Every nerve of my body fired off when the tips of her fingers pressed against my skin. Her eyes surveyed me hungrily and intensely as she watched the water trickle slowly down my muscles. She was definitely checking me out.

By the gods. This was some kind of torture. My senses were overpowering.

Emma put her hands on the button at the top of my trousers. It was a gesture that both thrilled me and frightened me. I wanted her to take my pants off— badly— but then she'd see my prosthetic, and my missing leg.

I shied away from her hands. It was involuntary, but it still happened. Emma frowned, like my reaction bothered her.

I wasn't ready to be that vulnerable. Not yet.

She stepped away and put the cloth back in the basin. While her back was turned, I ducked behind the screen. A new set of clothes had been placed there for me. I stripped quickly and tried to slip the clean pants on as fast as possible. As a result, I tripped, and fell against a tent wall. I righted myself and finished buttoning with trembling hands.

"Do you need help?" Her voice sounded hopeful.

"No, I'm fine," I told her. I could still dress myself.

"Okay." Disappointment rang throughout her tone. I hated to tell her no, but still… I didn't want her to see that part of me. Ever.

I knew it would have to happen eventually, though my heart pleaded it never would. She'd probably think I was less of a man. It was better to keep the illusion.

When I stepped out from behind the screen, Emma didn't hesitate. She flung herself at me. I didn't know what to do. Her body crashed into mine, and our lips met as one. Shock and surprise came over me at the unexpected kiss. My rigid form was put at ease as her soft mouth melded with my own. She placed her arms around my neck and trailed her fingers through my hair, giving tender kisses that landed delicately against my mouth.

It was like I couldn't control myself. My hands went to her hips, but they didn't stay there. As her mouth opened to accept my tongue, my hands started to wander. My fingers grazed against her breasts before wandering downward to squeeze her ass. She gasped, and the noise only increased my desire.

That one little noise spurred my longing and made me crave her body. The wolf inside of me was going nuts. It scratched and pawed at my insides, demanding that I hurry up and take her as my own. I needed Emma at my side. I needed her as my mate.

Emma pushed me backwards, and I fell against the bed. My body extended as Emma climbed on top of me and began kissing me harder as her figure moved over mine. Emma straddled my hips, then took one of my hands and placed it on her right breast.

Gods, it felt more than amazing. It sent a rush through my body. She sank her hips firmly against my dick, which was hard and begging for attention. The pressure sent a shiver through my body that I couldn't control. Emma pressed down even harder, and I was unable to control letting a moan escape from my mouth. She gasped in response and moved over me faster. I was aware that the bulge in my pants was growing. She rocked back and forth over my hardened cock, and I swear I felt moisture coating her panties through my trousers.

We were basically having sex with clothes on. This was way too much. I don't think my body could take it. The effect she had on me was overpowering. She could ask me anything right now and I'd give it to her. I was a helpless dog begging for a treat. Emma was my master, and I'd do whatever she told me. I'd play fetch as long as I received the reward.

Emma slipped out of the sleeves of her dress and pushed the shoulders off her body, so that the top of the gown bunched around her middle. Underneath, she was wearing a strapless push-up bra, blue in color. It was the only thing that kept her breasts concealed. The burn marks from the necklace were still visible, but at the moment, all I could focus on was the curves of her body.

Yes! That's exactly what I wanted. I wanted to see her exposed body, perfect and moving above me. My eyes wandered over the curves over her bosom, and her perfect navel. I couldn't resist touching her. My fingers wandered across her skin. I dared to slip a finger inside one of the cups of her bra and found that her nipple was hard as diamond.

Emma hissed with pleasure. I slipped my hand underneath the bra cup and fondled her breast within my hand. My thumb and my forefinger rubbed her nipple.

I desperately ached to be inside her. I didn't know what it would feel like, only that it would be the fulfillment of my needs as an Arcanea. Emma threw her head back and moaned again as I continued to play with her breasts delicately, treating them like they were the most precious treasure in the world.

I wanted to see what they looked like. I fiddled with the clasp on the bra. When I took too long, Emma growled in frustration and hooked her arms behind her back, to help me take the bra off.

Just as I had unfastened the hooks, the tent flap rustled and an alarmed scream made both of us jump.

"Odette!" Emma screeched. She had an arm across her chest, to pin her bra there.

Odette had her hands over her eyes. "I didn't see anything! Honest!"

Emma and I looked at each other. Both of us were blushing red. A nervous laugh escaped Emma's mouth, and I joined her. It would be just like Odette to walk in during such a moment.

Odette kept her hands firmly on her face. "I just came in to say everyone's waiting for you. But if you want to have sex first, I'm sure no one will mind."

"Nooo," Emma said. She hopped off me so quickly it made my dick cry. "Don't tell anyone we're having sex. We'll be right out."

Odette turned on her heel and immediately stalked out of the tent without uncovering her eyes. I slid to a sitting position on the bed, and Emma turned her back to me. "Hook me back up?"

If I thought her sliding off me was torture, this was the real thing. I fastened Emma's bra, and she pulled her dress back on, concealing everything from view. "Odette's going to think we're some kind of sex hounds. We didn't even get that far," I told Emma.

She wasn't looking at me. "I know. But I want to keep what's between us, between us."

I could understand that. I mean, people *expected* us to have sex, because we had proclaimed each other as mates. That didn't mean we wanted Odette singing it for the entire kingdom to hear.

"Anyway." Emma shook her hair around her shoulders, and I nearly died. "Should we get going?"

The wolf in me growled with displeasure, and demanded that I rip Emma's dress off right now and get back to what we were doing.

But diplomacy had another way, so I extended my arm to Emma and said, "Very well. Let us leave."

We walked in silence among the tents on our way to the celebration. It was like the two of us only knew one way or the other— distance, or incredible closeness. We were always bouncing between them. I wanted to find a happy medium that would satisfy us both. Emma was acting like I was a complete stranger again, and I didn't know why.

"Is there something on your mind?" I asked her. "You seem troubled."

Emma didn't answer for a long moment. "I'm not ready for sex, Ethan," she began. "I don't know if I'm ready for any of this."

My heart dropped. That wasn't something I wanted to hear. I didn't care about the sex part — I cared she was telling me this was moving too fast for her. It was hard to understand why she was pushing me away.

I wanted to dive right into a relationship with Emma, and everything that came with it. I wanted the kissing, the touching, the being there for everything and the bad stuff that came along with it, too.

But we'd only become engaged a few weeks ago. Prior to that, our relationship had been purely platonic. We'd been thrown into this without any kind of lead-up. We'd only kissed twice. And I had asked the world from her beforehand.

I brought her to a stop. She faced me. "Emma, I will never force you into anything," I vowed. "What's between us is purely your choice. No matter what we do."

She bit her lip anxiously. "I enjoyed fooling around with you. It felt good. It felt right."

She shook her head. "I just... I'm worried about getting too close."

I knew how she felt. To be too close was dangerous. It made you vulnerable. And love was enough to make an Arcanea lose their minds.

Look what had happened to Albin.

Emma didn't want to lose herself in me. Because she wasn't ready to go that far. The passion between mates could save you. But it could just as often destroy you.

"I was just following your lead. But if you had asked to stop, I would've," I said.

"I don't know what came over me back there," she confessed. "I care about you, Ethan, but in that moment... it was like I lost control."

"You shouldn't blame yourself. The mating bond can be a powerful thing."

Shit. I had slipped up, and she caught it. Emma raised an eyebrow. "I thought you said you didn't believe we were bonded?"

I hastened to cover my tracks. "I merely meant we had chosen each other."

Her eyes dampened with sorrow. "Of course."

She hadn't brought up the Phantom once during this tournament, and she didn't bring him up again now. I found it odd. Had she forgotten about him completely? Gods, I hoped so. I wanted her to love me, not him. He was a part of me I wished to hide from her forever.

But mating didn't work that way. There weren't supposed to be secrets between spouses. Especially not ones this big. But what other choice did I have?

Emma took a breath. "Right now... I want us to be more than friends, and see where it goes. Is that okay with you?"

Sadness stirred within my chest. We had made a commitment, yes, but she didn't need to follow through with anything more than what the royal engagement demanded of her. She didn't have to kiss me, or sleep with me, or even *love me* to rule as queen. At this point, we just had to work together.

If I truly wanted Emma, I was going to have to pursue her, and win over her heart. Just like a wolf on the hunt, I became excited by the challenge.

"That's perfectly fine," I said. "I for one am excited to see where this goes."

A soft smile came across her lips. "Me, too, Ethan. Me too."

I loved it when she said my name. It sounded like a song. I was being flowery, but so many emotions were coursing through me. It was like trying to hold back floodgates when all I wanted to do was let the doors open and have the water rush over me.

But if Emma wanted to start with a small glass... I'd stand back willingly and savor every drop.

The celebration tent was huge. It was more than a hundred feet long, and packed with guests. Lord Lucien and Lady Magdalina greeted us at the entrance. When we arrived, hundreds of Arcanea broke into loud cheers and claps. The tent was alight with warmth, decorations, and the smells of a gourmet feast.

Our court was waiting for us at the end of the tent. They sat at a long table covered with food and ale. Stefan was already half-drunk, and was composing awful ballads that he'd made up on the spot about me and Emma's victory. Theo was pointedly attempting to ignore him. Delmare and Odette sent both of us feisty, pointed looks as we drew near, giggling like small girls.

Delmare smirked as we inched past. "You two need any condoms? I've got a box." She snickered.

"Only if you and Stefan are done using them," Emma said back fairly.

Delmare flushed pink. I'm pretty sure she'd have given us the finger if we weren't surrounded by diplomats. Stefan was so buzzed he didn't notice.

Emma and I took seats at the middle of the table. I noticed two members were missing as I counted heads. "Where's Alexei?" I asked.

"He's sick, unfortunately. Kiara's tending to him," Delmare said. "Emotions around the Contest were too high. He couldn't handle it. But he and Kiara send you their congratulations."

"We'll have to celebrate together later!" Odette peeped. "All of us!"

I didn't comment. I was sure Alexei was sick, but I had a feeling Kiara held back on coming for another reason. She probably didn't think we deserved to win.

As the feast began, I noticed Lady Korva eyeing Emma and I with pure, undisguised hatred. It was clear how much she despised us for stealing the crown away from her son. If there was an assassination attempt, I'd pick her to be the first suspect.

"So how does this thing work?" Emma asked. "We won the Contest, so what next?"

"There's a five month period after the King's Contest has ended, for the Circle to give trials of competence to the newly elected king and queen," I told her. "We'll be coronated at the end of next semester."

"You mean we have to go through more tests?" Emma turned green.

"They're not hard. Mostly questions of intelligence and political matters. They merely want to ensure they're not putting an idiot on the throne," I told her. "The tests won't be difficult to pass."

Emma didn't look convinced. It was then that a shadow fell over our table. It was Elijah. A heated darkness had come over his expression, smoldering with contempt. He was so jealous it was laughable. Glee flooded my veins as I observed his pouting exterior. He was such a child. The scar that I'd given him during the duel was slowly healing, but it'd be permanent.

"Congratulations," he seethed. "You won the crown."

"It was a good fight," I said. "You should be proud of how you placed."

Elijah rolled his eyes and made a disgusted noise. He couldn't stand to be bothered with common decency. Second place wasn't good enough for him.

Elijah's beady eyes landed on Emma. His lip curled. "That was quite the performance. Seems you aren't a helpless whelp after all."

I nearly rose from the table. Elijah caught that he'd gotten to me, and Emma's hand wrapped around mine. She gave my fingers a squeeze, to tell me to calm down. She responded cooly, "You should be thankful I didn't finish the job. Because I wanted to."

Elijah's teeth flashed as he gritted them together. His fists bunched up, and he ground out, "I suggest you watch what you say, little bitch. As you saw with Nowak's father, kings can die fairly quickly. And it's not uncommon for the new leader to force the previous alpha female to submit. Maybe you'll even like it."

The wolf inside me snapped. When Elijah made that threat against Emma, I completely lost it. Red hot rage consumed me and took away everything except a primal instinct I had to protect my mate.

The table upended as I transformed on the spot. Screams shattered the night. I flew over the table, and my paws landed on Elijah's shoulders. I pinned him to the ground, bearing my canines. Elijah was so shocked that he froze beneath me, and with my weight pressed against him, he couldn't move. My breath was hot on his face as I dove in to end his life for good.

"Ethan, stop!" Lord Lucien was there at an instant. He threw his arms around my shoulders in an attempt to hold me back. Several other men came forward, to drag me off of Elijah. I was distinctly aware of Stefan and Theo.

It took multiple people to drag me away. I finally changed back as the all-consuming fury began to die out, and Elijah scampered to his feet, the blood drained from his cheeks.

Fear. I could smell it on him. Even now, I still wanted to end him. I'd asked Emma to spare his life during the Contest because he was my cousin, nothing more. That appeared to be a mistake.

"Stop the feast!"

Gabby's voice broke through the commotion. My eyes flashed upward; Emma rose from her seat. Gabby came blazing in through the entrance of the tent, officials behind her. Their old faces seemed stern and condemning. Steward Soloman was with them. He, too, seemed solemn and strict. Lady Magdalina met them in the middle of the room.

"What is the meaning of this?" she burst. "How dare you interrupt the feast of the king!"

"He doesn't deserve a feast, and neither does she!" Gabby pointed at Emma. "She cheated!"

Astonished gasps scattered throughout the tent. My stomach bottomed out. *Oh, no.* This couldn't be happening.

Steward Soloman came forward. "I'm afraid there's been a mistake," Steward Soloman announced. "We must alter the results of the Contest."

"For what reason?" Magdalina snapped.

Steward Soloman fished in his robes. "Because of this."

He opened his palm to show the dark necklace. Whispers ran throughout the room. "This item was found in Prince Ethan and Miss Sosna's tent, after being searched. Miss Ciar brought it to our attention that the two of them were influencing the competition unfairly. This evidence has sealed the charges against them."

Lady Korva immediately stepped forward. "She used dark magic to win!" Lady Korva gestured her hand wildly at Emma. "Is the Circle going to allow this blatant insult against them?"

"Prove it," Lady Magdalina snapped. "Prove that this wasn't planted in their tent!"

Heads turned in Emma's direction. No one spoke a word, or dared to breathe. Emma appeared like a terrified girl before a pack of wolves.

"Go on," Lady Magdalina said confidently. "Unseelie magic leaves traces. Remove your cloak. Prove them wrong."

With a trembling hand, Emma was forced to withdraw her cloak. Sounds of distress and disbelief echoed around the tent as the scars around her neck from wearing the necklace were clear for all to see.

Lady Magdalina was at a cross between horror and disbelief. Lucien, I was ashamed to see, appeared wholly disappointed.

"This proves it!" Lady Korva burst. "The magic she used weren't from the abilities of her own talent! She drew them from a dark source!"

Steward Soloman shook his head. "A terrible illusion, I see. It seems there is only one thing to do, in this case."

He turned toward the crowd and raised his voice. "As Prince Ethan and Emmaline Sosna altered their results of the Contest through unholy means, the crown must pass to the second place winners; Elijah Zlodia and Gabriella Ciar."

"*No!*" Emma and I both shouted at the same time. No one listened. Scattered applause rang out like death bells within the tent. Elijah beamed proudly, with a fond look at his mate. Gabby only had eyes for Emma, and she raised her head in a gloating matter.

"Restart the Contest! Put on another tournament, to choose a different king!" Emma blurted.

Steward Soloman frowned. "I'm afraid that's not possible. Although what you and Prince Ethan did is a crime, it's not a significant enough charge to hold an entirely new competition. You merely cheated. And although it costs you your placing, it does not throw out the results of the other contestants. We cannot wait another year to perform the ceremonies and ask for the blessing of the gods once more. The crown must go to the runner-up."

"Don't be so upset. You cheated," Elijah taunted. "Don't break the rules of the Contest and maybe you would've been able to keep your placing."

Emma made a sarcastic noise. "Looks like being offended can even win you a throne these days," Emma spat back.

"That's enough of this," Steward Soloman said firmly. "Miss Sosna, Prince Ethan, please remove yourselves and your court from the winner's table."

I was in such shock, I couldn't believe this was happening. Emma and I had the throne in our grasp. And it'd been cruelly taken away.

"Remember our deal, Sosna," Gabby purred as she strolled past, with a snarky glance at me. "Just because I'm going to be queen now doesn't mean anything's changed. Keep your wolf in line."

Emma hurtled a hated look her way. Elijah took my seat, and Gabby sat beside him. Emma, myself, and our court were forcibly escorted out of the tent. The sounds of the party resumed, and they were a painful reminder of everything we'd lost. Every laugh and delighted noise ached at my core.

Our worst nightmare had come true. Elijah had control of the crown. He'd become king. And who knew where Malovia would be after that.

"What deal was Gabby talking about, Emma?" I whirled on her. My anger was so overwhelming— I could hardly see straight.

Emma gave me a steely look. "Gabby came into our tent while you were getting fixed up. She threatened me. She told me that if I didn't do as she said while I was queen, she'd hurt you. I'm supposing she's turning the deal around now, so that if we try to stop her in any way from *being* queen, she'll take your life. And mine, possibly."

Her tone was guarded, and she wouldn't meet my eyes. Had her and Gabby made some sort of back-door deal? She was hiding something else... would these secrets ever end between us?

Hypocritical bastard, a bitter voice taunted, but I ignored it.

"I'm gonna kick that bitch's ass," Delmare snapped.

"What are you going to do, Irena?" Stefan had stepped in— he immediately sobered up as he rounded on her. "You can't touch her now without getting hurt. She's going to be queen. Once they crown her, it's all over."

"I'll crown her, all right," Delmare raged.

"Enough," I growled, and all fell silent. "We need to talk about this someplace else."

The others gathered my meaning. We left the tents— darkness enveloped us as the arena was left behind and lights faded. We drove further into the woods, until Emma had to light a spell so that we could see. Only when we were in a clearing devoid of the chance of being overheard did we stop to congregate in a circle.

Godsdammit! I punched a tree. My knuckles hurt, but I didn't care. Close. We were so fucking close. We had everything, and then Gabby tore it away.

I'd been focusing on Elijah the entire time. My mistake. It was his mate that was the real threat.

"This isn't right," Emma whispered. "The hag told me you'd be king. She said—"

"She *lied*, Emma!" I all but roared. "When are you going to understand that monsters don't tell the truth?"

Emma's eyes watered with tears. I hated hurting her like this, but by the gods, how could she be so naive?

"What hag?" Delmare looked utterly confused. The others wore similarly confused looks.

"It doesn't matter right now," I replied viciously. "What matters is we lost. We fucking lost."

There was silence for a moment, until Odette broke it. "Why would you do that, Emma?" Odette spoke weakly. "You shouldn't have cheated."

Emma's head hung low. "I know I shouldn't have." Her voice trembled. She barely held back tears as she said, "You just don't understand how hard it was to survive out there. What I would do to keep Ethan alive."

My heart clenched at the admission. Emma had been the one who'd cheated, yes.

But I was the one who'd failed. She still didn't know much about this world— I was her mate. It was my duty to lead and guide her, and I'd been utterly unsuccessful in doing so.

"I can't even imagine," Theo agreed. "But that doesn't make what you did right."

Emma's eyes turned on me. I could barely look at her right now. Her choices had cost us everything. They'd cost us our future. My legacy. The safety of the country and all of Malovia's people were now at risk, because of a dumb decision she'd made— and my inability to protect her from making that decision.

I was furious with her... yet angrier at myself for being so blind. Enraged that I hadn't been able to defend my title, and my mate.

But being mad wasn't going to change things. And rage wouldn't stop what was coming. I could be as angry with Emma as I wanted, but what good would it do?

"What's past is past," I snapped. "We lost the throne. Now what are we going to do about it?"

The quiet reigned, and an owl hooted somewhere in the distance. Stefan spoke. "Is there anything we *can* do?"

"There must be." Delmare's voice was firm. "I personally don't give a fuck that you guys cheated. I would've done the same thing to make sure Gabby and Elijah didn't win. Your only mistake was getting caught."

Theo shook his head. "I don't agree with what Emma did. But she was backed into a corner. And who we have now for Malovia's future is far, far worse."

"Exactly," I raged. "And it can't be allowed to happen."

"So we take care of them," Emma said. "Get rid of them before they pass the final tests, and take the monarchy back."

"We can't kill them now. What would that look like?" I angrily kicked a rock, and it went scattering into the darkness beyond. "We'd be the first suspects."

"We should've slain Elijah and Gabby in the arena," Emma whispered.

"We aren't murderers. It wouldn't have been the right way," I shot back at her.

"You think your father stayed on the throne without spilling a bit of blood?" Emma questioned. "Kings have to kill, Ethan. It's part of the job."

"I know that, Emma. But that doesn't mean I want to start my rule that way."

"Well, now that we didn't, it's not going to start at all." Furious tears fell from Emma's eyes. "We lost everything. Because of me."

"No. Because of me." My form shook. "If I hadn't attacked Elijah, everything would've been fine. I should've controlled my temper. I made us look like fools."

"He provoked you. He knew he could get to you through me," Emma said weakly. "He was merely a distraction, so Gabby could steal the necklace from our tent."

Stefan stepped in. "It's no use blaming yourselves. What's done is done." The dragon smoldered, and his eyes narrowed before he said, "But I think we need to make a pact. Right here, right now. Elijah and Gabby are going down. No matter what."

A bluster of wind shook the bare trees. "Stefan..." Theo said quietly. "You're suggesting treason."

"So what if I am?" Stefan said. "Do you want to live in a country where that bastard makes the rules?"

Theo fell silent. Stefan's eyes burned as he surveyed our faces. "I know we have to stop this in whatever way we can. Murder might be out, but there are other ways to get rid of a king. Are any of you with me?"

Delmare was the first to come forward. "I'm in," she said. "Whatever you guys are up to, I'll help in any way I can."

Odette hesitated. Then she took Theo's hand. She looked up at him, and he nodded in response.

"Theo and I will lend a hand," Odette said. "But guys... we need to be very careful."

Emma drew her head up high. "I made a huge mistake, one I wish I had never considered. But I'm going to do whatever I can to rectify it. I promised Ethan when I became his mate that I'd protect the people of Malovia. And in the name of Milonna, that's what I'm going to do."

All eyes looked to me. I stepped into the center of the circle. "I want to thank everyone for being there for Emma and I," I began. "I don't want to put anyone in any danger. Especially not my friends. But I think we can all agree that if we don't risk our lives, and do something about this, the very fate of the country is at stake."

I took a steadying breath. "No more games. No more contests. We fight from the shadows to bring Malovia into the light. We save our people, and our country. We do whatever it takes."

Elijah and Gabby were going to shatter this nation into a million pieces unless we stopped them. Emma, myself, and our friends were going to make this country whole again. I had lost my chance to be king, but we'd find another king to take Elijah's place— one who would bring the country into a rebirth, instead of torturing it with a slow death.

There was no time to waste. Our fight started now.

END OF BOOK ONE

Continue Emma and Ethan's story in The Dragon Oath (Hidden Legends: University of Sorcery, Book Two).

the
coven's
secret

COLLEGE OF WITCHCRAFT BOOK ONE

ALICIA RADES

Several Months Earlier

The coven claimed the town cemetery was haunted, which made it the perfect place to sneak into tonight. See, when I was a kid, I lost a bet to my buddy Grant. Loser had to go through with their Evoking Ceremony in the darkest, creepiest place we could find. Nothing beat the abandoned mausoleum on the far side of the cemetery.

"Let's speed it up, losers!" Chloe called from ahead of us. "The witching hour is approaching."

It was the end of November and freezing out. Snow dusted the ground, and the wind bit at my face. Tall trees rose up on either side of us, and the narrow dirt road ahead was so dark that I couldn't see the end of it. Above us, the moon was half full, and the stars didn't do much to illuminate the Connecticut landscape. The darkness didn't bother me, though. I was used to it.

Grant leaned over to me. He wore a thick dark winter coat that matched the color of his eyes. His black hair was gelled to stand on end in a trendy way that seemed like too much work. He looked a lot like his mom and had inherited most of her Latin American features.

Grant spoke in a low whisper. "Lucas, remind me again why we invited her."

I shrugged and glanced ahead at Chloe, who wore a dark jacket over a black dress and thick tights. She carried a black leather bag and walked with a skip in her step. I swore, that girl thrived off the energy of the moon or something.

The truth was, I didn't know why I'd invited Chloe. We weren't dating, and she could be kind of a bitch sometimes. But when she asked to come see what an Evoking Ceremony was like, I couldn't refuse. I'd watched my brother's and Grant's ceremonies, and they'd helped me prepare for tonight. She hadn't had a chance to take part in one yet, so I figured I could at least prepare her for her own.

"We're coming, princess," Grant called up to her.

She tossed her raven hair over her shoulder and stopped in the middle of the path to wait for us. "Get to know me a little more and you won't be calling me princess."

She winked at him, and he shot me a curious glance. The two didn't know each other well. Chloe and I met in high school. She still had a year left, while Grant and I were in our first year at Miriam College of Witchcraft. He'd moved away from Octavia Falls when we were kids after his parents split, and he'd only just moved back for school.

"What am I *supposed* to call you?" Grant asked.

"Wicked," I joked, cutting in.

Chloe cackled for show. "You know it. Now come *on*, Lucas."

She grabbed me by the arm when we reached her and started pulling me down the road. She squeezed so tight I thought I might lose feeling in my hand.

"Where's Eric, by the way?" Grant asked. "Is he meeting us there?"

"Dunno," I said.

I was staying home for the weekend and had checked his room before I left, but it was empty. It wasn't unusual. My older brother didn't sleep well and often went for midnight walks to clear his mind—to quiet the voices in his head. I shouldn't have taken it personally, but I really wanted him here with me tonight. I already knew my parents wouldn't be. Dad didn't care, and Mom was dealing with enough already.

"Forget Eric," Chloe said, clearly not reading my fallen expression. "We're here."

Where the thick forest ended, a towering iron gate began. On the other side stretched an endless graveyard, with headstones large and small reaching up toward the night sky.

"You're up," Chloe said, clapping Grant on the back.

Grant stepped forward and wrapped his hands around the lock that secured the gate shut. He'd gone through with his Evoking Ceremony last month and was the only one of us three who had magic. He was an Alchemist—and had the cauldron mark on the back of his arm to prove it.

Grant muttered an incantation under his breath. *"We seek to step upon this grass. Unlock this gate and let us pass."*

A green glow lit up his hands. Tendrils of magic swirled out of his palms and twisted around the gate. Then came a soft *click*, and the gate swung open.

Grant smiled proudly and stepped inside the cemetery, holding the gate open for Chloe and me. "Easy peasy."

Chloe snorted. "I don't know why they even bother locking this place up."

I shrugged. "To deter people, I guess?"

"Well, nothing's going to deter us," Chloe stated confidently.

"Come on." I cocked my head in the direction of the mausoleum. "It's this way."

They followed me through an endless maze of gravestones, until we reached a line of trees. We left the graveyard and stepped into an overgrown forest. Prickly berry brush, fallen logs, and sharp rocks lined the forest floor, but I walked right over them and continued on my way.

"Are you sure this is the right spot, Lucas?" Grant struggled through the brush as it caught on his clothes.

"For sure," I replied. "It's just up here."

Just as I said it, the mausoleum came into view. The bricks were covered in moss and had weathered over time, and the roof had long ago caved in. The building had to be as old as our town itself.

Apparently, the bodies had been removed and buried elsewhere, but rumors said some of the skeletons remained. According to legend, certain spirits wanted their bodies to stay in the mausoleum, so they hounded a group of Seers until they gave in and moved their corpses back to their proper resting place. The rumors had never been confirmed, of course, but Grant said he hoped to see a skeleton tonight. I told him he wouldn't be able to handle it, considering he'd screamed when he saw the plastic hand we'd put in the punch bowl at Halloween.

Chloe looked amazed. After a few moments, she picked her jaw up off the ground and said, "Well, what are we waiting for?"

She rushed ahead. I stepped over broken bricks and shattered beer bottles to follow her. It was kind of creepy inside, with a small bit of moonlight illuminating the shadows. The room wasn't very big, barely the size of my bedroom. Most of the grave markers had been smashed, leaving behind large holes in the walls that could fit a casket. Others were intact. I wondered about those, but I wasn't curious enough to investigate. The ground was flat concrete, but it was covered in dirt, dust, and broken bits of building.

Chloe kicked rocks and other debris aside, making room for the ceremony. She set her bag down and pulled out five candles—one to represent each of the five Casts within our coven. Tonight, our goddess, Mother Miriam, would awaken my magical powers and assign me to one of the Casts. I was pretty sure I'd get Mentalist like my parents—the Cast known for their telepathic and telekinetic abilities—but it was hard to say. We all thought Eric would be a Mentalist, and he'd been gifted the powers of a Seer.

Chloe placed the candles in a wide circle, then pointed to the center. "Lie down, loser."

Grant frowned at her choice of words, but I didn't care. Like I'd told him before, it was Chloe's term of endearment.

I sat on the cold ground, propping my elbows on my knees. "Well, Grant. Take it away."

"Okay, if you're ready." Grant plopped himself cross-legged in front of me on the other side of the candles.

Chloe used a lighter to light each of the five candles, then found a seat on a huge rock, watching intently. The light cast flickering shadows across the walls of the mausoleum. My heart started to pound heavily in my chest, but I didn't let it show.

"We're not to the witching hour yet, so allow me to say a few words before we begin." Grant snapped his fingers, and a small leather-bound book materialized out of nowhere. He opened it to the first page.

"Aw, man," I complained. "Do you have to?"

Knowing Grant, it was something stupid, like a collection of roasts to rile me up before the ceremony.

"Yes, I have to," he deadpanned. He cleared his throat before he began reading. "Evoking Ceremony… what is it?"

Chloe groaned. "We know all this."

Grant frowned up at her. "Humor me, would ya?"

Chloe didn't say another word as Grant returned his attention to the book.

"As I was saying…" He made a show of reading the passage like it was a scary story. "*On the eve of a witch or warlock's nineteenth birthday, at the witching hour, they become eligible to contact Mother Miriam through a sacred ritual called the Evoking Ceremony. This ritual can be performed only once, and only on the night of eligibility.*"

He broke character to add, "So don't screw it up, okay?"

"I'm not going to screw it up," I huffed.

Grant turned back to the book and continued. "*Through this ceremony, the witch or warlock will be tested by Mother Miriam. If she judges you a fit for the coven, your powers will be awakened, and you will bear the mark of one of the five Casts within the Miriamic Coven. Should you fail Mother Miriam's test, you shall be banished from the coven for all eternity.*"

His voice fell dramatically at the last three words.

I raised an eyebrow. "All eternity?"

Grant shrugged. "That's what it says here."

I rolled my eyes, but inside, I was quivering. I didn't know what would happen during the ceremony or how Mother Miriam would test me, since the trials were different for everyone.

But I knew one thing. I couldn't be banished from the coven. This was my home. These were my people.

Grant continued reading. *"The ceremony requires at least one witch or warlock who has already undergone their Evoking Ceremony. Place five candles in a circle"*—he gestured to the candles we'd already set up—*"and repeat the following incantation."*

He paused for a moment, and Chloe eagerly asked, "What's the incantation?"

"That's for me to know and you to find out," Grant said. "Lucas, you're going to need to lie on your back. Says so here."

"Okay." I did as I was told and stretched out across the cold floor. My gaze turned up through the gaping hole in the roof—if you could call it a roof anymore, since there was almost nothing of it left. I stared at the stars, trying to force my pulse to slow. I shouldn't be afraid of what was to come, so why was my body freaking out?

Grant checked his phone. "We have one minute until midnight. Are you ready, Lucas?"

I took a deep breath. "Ready as I'll ever be."

"Good," Grant said. "Let us know if there's anything we can do to help you feel more comfortable."

"Conjure a space heater?" I joked.

Grant nudged my foot with his. "Shut up and relax, smartass."

I gave him a salute, and he chuckled.

He stared down at his phone a few seconds longer. It felt like an eternity. Finally, he took a breath and set his phone aside. "The witching hour is upon us. We can begin."

I heard Chloe shift on her rock, but she stayed silent, which was actually kind of shocking. The girl never shut her mouth.

Grant began to mutter the spell beneath his breath. *"The clock has struck the witching hour. It's time to wake this warlock's power. We call our goddess down to earth. To bear witness to this new rebirth. A series of tests he shall partake. And join the coven before day breaks."*

My body began to rise from the concrete as Grant repeated the incantation. I knew this would happen, as I'd seen it in ceremonies before, but the sensation was stranger than I imagined. I felt as if I could fall at any moment, but I tried to push the fear from my mind. I trusted Mother Miriam and the rituals she'd put in place for the coven. She wouldn't have us do this if it could hurt us. So I closed my eyes and relaxed.

Grant's voice continued as he repeated the incantation over and over again. The words started to fade together as I let the magical feeling of floating in mid-air overtake me. Warmth entered my bones, which was weird because of how cold it was outside. A little warmth was all I needed to know that this was working, that I could take whatever Mother Miriam threw at me. I belonged in the coven, and no trial was going to change that.

Suddenly, the sensation of falling jolted throughout my body. My eyes shot open as my body slammed into the ground, knocking the wind out of me. I sprang upright to a sitting position, my heart pounding against the walls of my chest. Shit. Something had gone wrong.

As my pulse slowed, I glanced around. It was so dark that all I saw were shadows. For a second, I forgot where I was. It took me a moment to make sense of my surroundings. The crumbled bricks of the abandoned mausoleum were scattered all around me, and the candles Chloe had set up were still there, but they'd been blown out. My friends were nowhere to be seen.

Concern whipped through me. I reached into my jacket pocket to pull out my phone to use as a light, but it wasn't there. I checked the other pocket, then my pants, but it was gone.

Fucking Chloe. I should've known she'd pull some stunt like this. I was fuming.

I got to my feet and called out into the forest. "Really, guys?"

There was no reply, except for the sound of the wind whistling through a hole in the wall. A chill traveled down my spine, and my breath turned to ice in the air.

"It's not funny!" I shouted. "This isn't the time for some stupid prank."

All that met me was silence—until I heard the sound of a stick breaking in the distance. I stepped out of the mausoleum and started making my way through the brush toward the noise. Thick fog blanketed the forest floor, so much that I could barely see the underbrush beneath my feet. The moon was all I had to light my way.

"Grant?" I yelled into the trees. I couldn't believe he'd agreed to go along with this!

By now, he was probably crouched somewhere with his hand over his mouth, trying not to give his location away. Any second now, he'd burst into laughter he couldn't hold back.

Except the laughter never came.

I slowed my step and listened closely. It was eerily silent—so much that the hair on the back of my neck stood. That was never a good sign.

"Guys, you need to come out right now!" I demanded sternly. I wasn't screwing around. This whole thing was starting to freak me out.

I opened my mouth to shout again, but before I could get anything out, a groan met my ears. It was a pained groan that sent my stomach plummeting to my toes—the kind you couldn't fake. I immediately started racing in the direction it came from as worry slammed into me. The groan came again, louder this time. I only ran faster, dodging around thick tree trunks and jumping over thick brush.

And then I saw him. A figure lay on the ground in the fog, curled up in the fetal position and shivering.

I came to an immediate halt, but I couldn't make out what was happening in the darkness. I took a cautious step forward, my heart racing. "Grant?"

If this was all an elaborate plan of Chloe's, I was going to curse the bitch the second I got my magic.

The figure let out another pained cry, and I nearly shit myself. The voice was familiar, but it wasn't Grant's. All the blood drained from my face—though it felt as if it was being sucked out of my entire body. My knees went weak, and my hands shook at my sides.

"Eric?" I stepped closer, until I could make out his features in the shadows.

Eric lay in the middle of the forest next to a thick oak tree, clutching his stomach. A dark substance coated his hands—

Holy shit! It was blood! And it was everywhere. It was so thick that it dripped out of his hands and soaked into the forest floor. It looked like he was trying to hold his guts inside himself.

I dropped to my brother's side in an instant. "Eric! What are you doing here!?"

Eric's face had paled until it was entirely void of color. A thick sheen of sweat coated his skin—even though it was ice cold out and all he wore was a t-shirt and jeans. Beside him lay a black cloth bag with its contents spilled out all over the forest floor. All I could process was a few potions vials, a deck of tarot cards, and a bloody dagger.

The dagger caught my attention, but only briefly. It didn't cross my mind whether the person who'd done this was still lurking around. I was less concerned about finding out what had happened to him and more concerned about getting him somewhere safe. I didn't know how much time we had before he'd lost too much blood. Eric gave an involuntary shudder.

I quickly stripped my jacket off and tossed it over him. "Tell me how bad it is. Eric! Eric!"

He opened his mouth, but nothing came out. Forcing my quivering hands to steady, I cupped his face in my hands and slapped him a little to get his attention.

"Eric, look at me," I demanded, staring him dead in the eye. "We have to get help."

I grasped at the first thought that came to mind. Headmistress Verla's house was right on the edge of the cemetery. She was an Alchemist, one of the best in all the coven. At the very least, she'd be able to whip up something for the pain and stop the bleeding before the paramedics arrived.

I glanced in the direction of her house, though I couldn't see it from here. I quickly calculated how long it might take me to run there, get help, and come back. I didn't know if we had time for that. If Eric was going to make it, I had to get him to Headmistress Verla's the quickest way possible.

I rolled my jacket up until it resembled a long, thick rope.

"Eric, I'm going to need you to let me look at this," I said, tugging his hands away from the wound.

I expected him to protest, but he didn't. He must've been in too much shock. His hands fell away from his stomach, and blood poured faster out of the wound. I placed my rolled-up jacket over the wound and shoved the end between his back and the ground, wrapping it around his body. Then I twisted the two ends together and secured them tightly, creating a makeshift bandage to help slow the bleeding.

"Okay, Eric," I said, resituating myself. "I'm going to need you to—"

Eric looked at me with a blank expression, then his eyes rolled back into his skull.

Shit. Shit. Shit! We didn't have long.

I gave it everything I had. Taking one of Eric's limp arms, I wrapped it over my shoulder, then hoisted his body up onto my back. He was heavy, but it didn't matter. I'd carry him until he crushed me if I had to.

I knew I might regret this later—I was pretty sure it was the exact *opposite* of what they told you to do in emergencies like this—but it was the only option that made sense to me.

A small groan escaped my brother's lips as I began to carry him through the forest toward the gate at the front of the cemetery. The sound should've made me want to vomit, but it gave me hope. My brother was still alive. I could still save him.

We broke out of the trees to the wide expanse of the graveyard lawn. I almost stumbled over the nearest gravestone when I spotted a dark cloaked figure staring our way. Was it a reaper, here to take my brother's soul to the afterlife? No, that was silly. If it was, I wouldn't be able to see them.

When the dark figure began making their way toward us, I got the strangest feeling that they were not to be feared—that they were there to help. Was it perhaps the cemetery groundskeeper?

The figure reached me, then spoke before I could. "Lucas Taylor."

I didn't know why, but I was surprised to hear a woman's voice come from under the dark hood. Her voice was so melodic that it sounded like a song.

"Yes," I said quickly. "My brother. He's hurt. Can you help?"

The woman nodded once, then brushed her hand through the air. I felt the weight of my brother's body vanish. I whirled around, expecting him to be floating there behind me—I figured this witch was a Mentalist with telekinetic magic—but what I faced was entirely different.

Eric's features had been stamped into the fog like he was a ghost. Just as I caught a glimpse of ghost-Eric, his image washed away, like a cloud in the wind. Anger and fear coursed through me all at once. I spun on the woman in a flash, my nostrils flaring.

"What did you do!?" I cried. "What happened to my brother?"

"Relax, Lucas," she said kindly, like my harsh tone didn't bother her at all. "Your brother is fine for now."

For now? I wanted to ask, but she didn't give me the chance.

"You've impressed me," she said softly.

"I... what?" I asked. The anger had melted from my tone, replaced by confusion. What the hell was going on here?

She reached up to her hood. "It's me, child."

Her velvet hood fell to her shoulders, revealing her face. I'd never seen anyone so beautiful before. Her features were perfectly symmetrical, and her pale skin was so smooth that it looked airbrushed. She had dark eyelashes and red lips, though she wore no makeup. Her dark brown hair fell in loose waves around her shoulders.

My knees buckled beneath me, and I fell to the ground. I hadn't meant to do it, but I was so shocked I couldn't stop myself. I leaned forward to bow, because it seemed like the proper thing to do in the sight of a goddess.

"Mother Miriam," I said breathlessly, my eyes pointed toward the ground. "It's an honor."

"Lucas, my child." She bent to one knee. "There is no need to bow to me."

"But you're—you're..." I looked up to see she was smiling down at me. It was a truly loving gaze—the gaze of a mother. It was stupid of me to think I could argue with her. She reached out and helped me to my feet.

I straightened. "Is this real? Or is it part of my test?"

"It is in your mind," she said.

I sighed in relief. Eric wasn't in any danger. He'd only been an illusion.

"What happens now?" I asked our goddess. "What's my next test?"

She shook her head and smiled. "You only needed one, Lucas."

"Only one?" I asked breathlessly. Most people went through at least three or more.

"Walk with me," Mother Miriam said, offering her hand.

When I took it, the fog around the graveyard dissipated, and a warmth spread over me. The cool wind completely died down, and it felt like a warm spring night.

"In this test, there were many different choices you could've made," Mother Miriam explained. "Among the coven's Casts, the Mentalist would've made Eric comfortable and gone to find help. The Alchemist would've looked through the potions to see if there were any that could help. The Seer would've reached for the cards first—though most would never use them in such a dire situation, but whether they use them or not is not the important part."

"And Mortana?" I asked, looking over to her. *The Death Cast.*

"Most Mortana would've considered the dagger as a means to a merciful death," she said. "But you, my child, took a route most would not. You carried your brother's burden on your back. It's clear where you belong, Lucas."

"Where?" I asked, not understanding what she was saying. There was only one other Cast she hadn't mentioned—one that had died out years ago. But I didn't see how my choices would put me there. Could I be the first Curse Breaker of my generation?

"Where do you *want* to be put?" she asked.

I contemplated the question. No one had ever told me Mother Miriam offered a choice. I'd never really thought about it before. I always figured it didn't matter; I'd accept whatever gift she gave me, because I knew she'd choose the right one for me.

"I will do whatever you ask of me," I told her honestly.

I barely noticed that we had returned to the trees near the site of the mausoleum. I was too entranced by being in the presence of a goddess. This was a once in a lifetime opportunity. I couldn't take my eyes off her.

"*Anything* I ask, Lucas?" she asked.

I nodded. I couldn't think of anything she could ask that I wouldn't do. Her teachings were simple. *Protect the coven.* I'd do anything to protect the ones I loved.

"Anything," I confirmed confidently.

Mother Miriam led me up the rocks to the entrance of the mausoleum. Nothing had changed since I left.

She stopped and guided me around to stand in front of her. "I'm so glad you feel that way, Lucas. I know you'll make me proud."

When she said that, it felt like I was floating in the air again. My parents never said they were proud of me—not even Mom, though I knew she loved me. This was our goddess, the very deity we worshiped, and she thought *I* could make her proud.

"I'll do my best," I promised her. "Which Cast will I be placed in?"

"Shh…" She held an index finger to her lips. "You will find out soon enough. Have faith, my child, for I am always with you."

She shoved me hard in the chest, and my heart leapt up to my throat. The chill air returned, whipping by me as I tumbled backward. My body slammed hard against the concrete, sending an ache shooting through my body. My skull throbbed from where it impacted with the ground.

"Lucas! Lucas!" I heard Grant's voice, but it sounded like it was coming from a mile away.

Chloe's voice came a second later. "Here, let me try."

A small, cold hand slapped against the side of my face. My cheek stung as I shot upright. Grant was so close that we nearly knocked heads. He quickly jumped out of the way.

"Holy shit!" I cried, cradling my cheek. My friends were inside the burning candle circle now. "That was one helluva swing, Chloe."

She smiled proudly. "Told you I could wake him."

"Fuck," I groaned. "What happened?"

"You were floating there, and then your body just slammed to the ground," Grant said, sounding worried.

"That's normal, dipshit," I said, shoving him. "It signals the end of the ceremony. You didn't need to get the Wicked Witch of the West here to make me lose feeling in my face."

I made a show of moving the muscles in my face to test them out. Chloe didn't look concerned at all. She just beamed at the Wicked Witch comment, like she wore it as a badge of honor.

"So, which Cast were you assigned to?" she asked eagerly.

"I don't know," I admitted, turning my hands over for any sign of a mark. "Mother Miriam didn't say."

"What was it like meeting her?" Chloe asked. "Was she as beautiful as they say?"

"Slow down," Grant insisted. "Let's figure out which Cast he's in first."

I stripped off my jacket and tossed it aside, looking up and down my arms. The mark would appear as a tattoo, as if I'd just come fresh from the tattoo shop. I checked the back of my bicep, where Grant's mark was, but there was nothing there. It could be anywhere.

Chloe nudged me. "Take your shirt off."

I sighed and stood, then tugged my shirt over my head. I hoped I didn't have to strip down all the way to find the mark. It was cold as shit out, and I sure as hell wasn't giving Chloe a strip tease. She'd enjoy it a little too much.

"There it is!" she cried, pointing to my lower back. Her hand slapped over her mouth, and she stifled a giggle.

"What?" I asked, turning to try to get a good look. "What's wrong? Why are you laughing?"

"You have a tramp stamp!" Chloe cried, reeling back in uncontrollable laughter.

"Aw, fuck," I muttered. "I'm never going to live that down, am I?"

Even Grant had joined in on the laughter. "No, bro. You're not."

"Would you just tell me what it is?" I demanded. I hated being the last to know. "I can't see it."

"It's a skull," Grant said. "Here, let me get a picture."

He lifted his phone and took a flash photo of my backside.

"Let me see," I begged, and he handed the phone over.

I half expected him to be lying to me, but Grant sucked at lying. It was there clear as day, a skull mark tattooed along my spine just above my waistline.

"Mortana," I said breathlessly. I was a Death Warlock.

I backed up and steadied myself against the rock Chloe had been sitting on earlier. Being Mortana wasn't inherently a bad thing, but their magic was definitely seen as darker. Death magic was the touchiest of all. When it went wrong, it went *wrong*. Like, shit hits the fan wrong. Mortana were the kind of witches and warlocks who could reanimate the dead, kill with the touch of their hand, or see how people were going to die. I even knew one who could read the auras of a room and tell if a death had occurred there—and how bad it'd been.

The mark only told me my Cast, not which type of magic I'd inherited within that Cast. It could be days or weeks before I knew my specialty.

"You okay, bro?" Grant asked, rising to his feet and stopping beside me. He held out my shirt and jacket.

"Yeah," I said, shaking off the sinking feeling in my gut. I put my clothes back on, contemplating what this meant.

I didn't want to be the kind of guy who had magic everyone feared. But I'd been telling the truth when I told Mother Miriam I'd take whichever Cast she assigned me. Whatever my gift was, it was important to her.

I straightened. "I'm fine. It'll be great. Maybe I'm a necromancer. I'll raise an army of cat skeletons."

"That'd be badass," Chloe said.

I barely heard her as another voice cut through the silence. It came as if he was standing next to me, just beside Grant.

"I made a mistake. I don't want to die."

Every muscle in my body froze as my brother's voice invaded my mind. It took me a second to realize he wasn't here—that he hadn't just shown up out of the blue and spoken those soul-chilling words for all of us to hear. My friends stared back with a blank expression. They hadn't heard him.

It hit me so hard and fast that I suddenly became nauseous.

No! No, no, no… please don't let this be what I think it is.

I took off running before I could explain. I tore through the forest to the cemetery, then hurdled over gravestones as I sprinted toward the front gates. Chloe and Grant called from behind me, but I could barely process the sound of my own name.

Please, Mother Miriam, let this be a hallucination or something.

My feet carried me as fast as they could blocks away. My lungs were starting to burn by the time I reached home. I ran up the front steps so fast that I skipped several on my way. The door slammed into the wall when I flung it open. I pounded upstairs to my brother's bedroom. Commotion came from my parents' room as they were awakened by my loud entrance.

I skidded to a halt in the darkness of my brother's doorway. My heart race, and it only quickened when I saw that his bed was still empty.

"Lucas, what in the bloody hell is—?" my father started, but I didn't have time for questions.

I whirled around in the hall and shoved him out of the way. On any normal day, I wouldn't get close enough for him to touch me, but right now, I wasn't scared of him. I was terrified for my brother.

"Where's Eric?" I asked Mom, who had stumbled out of their bedroom behind my father, looking only half awake.

"He's not in his room?" she asked.

"No," I barked. "Something's wrong."

Eric should've been back by now. He didn't stay at school—since his professor of Seer Studies suggested it was best if he took the semester off—so he didn't have anywhere else to go.

I checked my bedroom, then ran back downstairs to check the kitchen, living room, and bathroom. Each room was as empty as the last. My parents followed behind me, trying to get an answer out of me, but I couldn't bring myself to tell them, not until I knew for sure what it meant.

I reached the door to the garage and flung it open. And that was when I knew...

I hadn't imagined a damn thing. Those words I'd heard in the mausoleum were real—and they were meant for me.

I stopped dead in my tracks as my blood ran cold. Every inch of my body shook as I took in the sight before me. Dad stumbled in the doorway, catching himself on the door frame.

"My boy!" he cried, his voice wavering in genuine agony. I'd never heard him use that tone before.

"What's going—?" Mom started, but I quickly cut her off.

"Don't look!" I spun around as she came closer. I threw my arms out and cradled her face to my chest. She didn't resist.

While I held my mother and let her tears soak into my jacket, my father rushed into the garage, like he could save Eric. But I already knew he couldn't. I couldn't explain it, but I could *feel* the void in the room. It wasn't just the gaping hole opening in my chest, either. It was a supernatural force telling me Eric's life was over. It was part of the gift I knew now with certainty I had.

Only one member of the coven inherited this power per generation. Mother Miriam chose me to carry the burden of the dead—to take their last thoughts to the other side with me when I died, where I'd become a reaper for the coven. I suddenly realized what a huge mistake I'd made promising her anything. I was now the Reaper's Apprentice.

And the first thought I'd carry was my brother's. It was the last thing that went through his head before he killed himself.

Mother Miriam thought I would make her proud.

She was wrong.

nadine
TWO

Two weeks ago, a darkness took over my life. Grammy promised things would get better as time went on, but so far they'd only gotten worse. My bedroom didn't even feel like my own. The walls were bare, and the sheets removed from the bed. All that was left were a few of my most prized possessions.

I ran my hand over the cover of the Agatha Christie novel Mom and Dad had given me for my birthday last year. The cover was already worn, and the corners tattered. I sat on my bed and opened the cover.

To Nadine, who always loved a good mystery. - Mom and Dad

A lump rose to my throat, but I forced it down. My parents liked to write me letters, but looking at their handwriting was a terrible reminder of what had happened. I quickly flipped the page. A small piece of paper fell out of the pages and fluttered to the ground. I leaned down to pick it up.

A ticket. I'd forgotten I used it as a bookmark the last time I read the book. It'd come from my ticket book that was filled with discounts to mysterious New England attractions. This particular ticket had been used when Mom and I drove five hours to Baltimore to visit the *Ripley's Believe It or Not!* Museum.

I placed the ticket back inside the pages and added the book to my last box on top of my *Clue* board game. The edges of the box were tattered and worn from the years Dad and I spent playing it every Sunday night.

I moved slowly, deliberately, because I wasn't ready to leave yet. Leaving only meant I had to admit I was never coming back. I couldn't move much faster anyway—not with the way my joints ached. I hadn't felt this awful in years.

I reached for a photograph propped up on my nightstand. It showed me and my best friends, Carly and Jessica, on the deck of a riverboat, each wearing a Sherlock Holmes hat. It'd been the night of the murder mystery riverboat tour we took last summer.

Tears pricked at my eyes as I thought of my friends. I'd already said goodbye to them at the funeral, because I couldn't stand to see anyone right now. I'd never forget our last fun night together, because it was the night I got the call—the one telling me my parents had died.

My life with Carly and Jessica was over. They were headed off to college together, and I knew the weekend sleepovers and Friday night bowling excursions had to end sometime.

I was *supposed* to be headed to the police academy. My goal had been to work the homicide division one day, but those dreams had been crushed when I'd been rejected from the academy last-minute. They told me there'd been an error in processing my paperwork, but I knew the truth. They didn't want me because of my *condition*. They were afraid I was more of a liability than I was worth.

Screw them.

After everything that happened—getting the letter from the police academy, only to lose my parents in a car accident days later—moving in with Grammy was my last option.

She'd made a pretty compelling argument when she invited me to come live with her. Mainly, offering to pay my college tuition—even though I was still undecided on my major. I didn't exactly have the money to live on my own right now, so I couldn't really refuse. I didn't *want* to live alone, either. Besides, I loved Grammy. Living with her would be great.

I just had one last thing to add to the boxes. My stomach twisted as I reached for the small wooden box on my nightstand. I hadn't had the guts to open it yet. If I did—if I looked at what was inside—all I'd think about was how my parents were gone. And though I knew what had happened was real, I couldn't face it yet. I couldn't truly say goodbye.

I shoved the wooden box deep within the packing box, covering it up with a few things inside so I wouldn't get tempted to open it. I couldn't deal with that right now.

A light knock came at my door, and Grammy stepped inside. Her footsteps seemed louder than they should in the empty room. Grammy was in her sixties, with short white hair, age lines, and the kindest smile I'd ever known. Like every day, she wore a long floral skirt that fell to the floor. She'd come to stay with me while we worked out the funeral arrangements and listing the house.

"Are you ready, Nadine?" she asked gently.

I closed my eyes and took a deep breath. It took me a moment to compose myself, but I finally lifted my head and nodded. "Yeah, Grammy. I think I'm ready to go."

I stood with my box and followed Grammy down the hall. The house didn't feel right, now that all the pictures had been removed as we prepared to sell. It didn't even smell right, as the scent of lemon cleanser masked the usual smell of baked goods and clean linens. Everything just felt... empty. Which was how I felt without my parents.

Sometimes, I forgot they were gone. I swore I could hear my dad working in the garage or smell my mom cooking in the kitchen. And then it all came crashing down on me again. I was glad I was moving in with Grammy. It was the fresh start I needed.

I loaded my last box in the front seat of my car. The back seat was packed to the brim, as was Grammy's vehicle. There was just so much I didn't want to leave behind.

"If you're not ready, Nadine, we don't have to leave yet," Grammy offered.

I took one last look at the white two-story house I grew up in. I knew this day would come eventually, but I didn't think it'd come like this. I couldn't keep dragging this out. "Let's go."

Grammy drove in front of me as I followed behind her in my car, where the music was on full-blast to drown out my thoughts. The drive wasn't long, only about an hour and a half, but it seemed longer.

I could tell we were getting close because the road narrowed and became more twisted as we drove through the foothills of the Appalachian Mountains. Tall trees rose on either side of the road, and the forest was bright green with summer foliage.

The road took another twist to the left, and I got my first view of the town in the valley below as we crested the hill. It was bigger than I expected, considering Grammy had always talked about the small, tight-knit community she came from. I was excited to see it was large enough to have at least a mall and a movie theatre.

The road twisted to the right, and the town disappeared from view as we dipped back into the trees. The forest seemed to close in on us, but in a comforting, warm-hug kind of way. We reached the base of the valley, and the trees slowly parted. A huge black sign read *Welcome to Octavia Falls*. Below that were various smaller signs advertising attractions like corn mazes, hayrides, and ghost tours.

Count me in on the ghost tours.

I took a deep breath as I slowed the car to match the speed limit. Tall maples and oaks lined the streets. My jaw dropped as we passed by beautiful homes. Each one was bigger than the last, and they all had a unique gothic charm to them. My favorite house had dark red siding with black trim and a tall turret. I turned the music off so I could take it all in.

I passed over a narrow bridge, and the beautiful houses gave way to four-story buildings. The lower levels were all small businesses, selling things like maple syrup and honey, as well as a cute coffee shop and a candy store.

The further we drove, the more crowded the streets became. It wasn't until the buildings parted and I spotted an expansive parking lot that I saw why. The lot was filled with canopies and people milling from one booth to the next like a farmer's market. I spotted vendors selling herbs, candles, and crystals—along with a booth advertising palm readings. The middle of the lot had been set up with a stage, where a woman sang a haunting melody and a group danced around her in a slow, beautiful display.

I barely caught a glimpse of it all before it was out of sight. We drove past more businesses, and I tried to get a feel for what was here in case I wanted to go shopping later, but it all passed by quickly. I noticed a few clothing stores, whose display outfits totally looked my style—dark top, skinny jeans, and my signature leather jacket. We passed by an apothecary and a metaphysical store before we came upon the industrial portion of Octavia Falls.

This part of town had every kind of drink manufacturer you could imagine—breweries, wineries, distilleries, and a cider mill. Grammy had told me about the orchards around here, and I was eager to check them out sometime.

I understood now why Grammy called this a small town. Despite the population in the tens of thousands, it had that quaint small-town charm to it.

I'd slowed to a crawl to take in the beauty of Octavia Falls, and I nearly missed Grammy take a turn ahead of me. Snapping back to attention, I picked up speed and followed behind her.

I expected the architecture to change as we moved into a new neighborhood, but it didn't. Every house looked like it should be hosting a Halloween party or something. I absolutely loved it.

Grammy slowed at the end of a street near a cluster of trees and a sign that read *Octavia Falls Park*. She pulled into the driveaway of the last house.

My eyes went wide. For eighteen years, we'd lived an hour and a half from my grandmother, and I'd never visited her. If someone had told me this was where she lived, I would've begged to visit sooner. Her house was huge, with pale yellow siding and white trim. A large porch wrapped around the front of the house, and a rounded turret reached three stories high. It already felt like it was calling me home.

I parked behind Grammy and opened my car door. My muscles ached from sitting so long, and my joints protested as I forced myself to step out of the car.

"Grammy!" I scolded as she made her way over to me. I still couldn't take my eyes off the house. "You didn't tell me you lived in a castle."

She chuckled. "Don't be silly, Nadine. It's just a house."

"A mansion," I corrected her. "When do I get the grand tour?"

"Now, if you'd like," she offered. "We can move your stuff in later."

I swung my purse over my shoulder and grabbed the box on the front seat. It was filled with odds and ends and pretty light.

"Here, let me take that," Grammy said quickly, stealing it from my hands.

I wanted to take it back and tell her I had it handled, but she turned quickly before I could. I knew what Grammy was doing. She was *coddling* me, because she knew how easily I got fatigued.

I didn't like being coddled. I could manage on my own.

I followed behind Grammy. My gaze traveled over the elaborate woodwork on the porch railing and the beautiful carvings in the front door. I seriously couldn't believe Grammy lived here. I'd kind of always wondered if Grammy was keeping a secret, since she'd come visit us on birthdays and holidays but we never came here. Plus, what was with a woman of her age having a cauldron tattooed on the inside of her wrist? Mom had the same one on her ankle. It kind of made me wonder if Grammy was part of a cult and that's why Mom never wanted to come back or something.

My imagination was getting away on me.

Grammy led me inside to a wide hallway. A sleek black cat ran down the stairs, then rubbed itself up against Grammy's leg, purring.

"This is Cornelius," Grammy introduced. "He's very friendly."

"Well hello, Cornelius," I said, bending to scratch him behind the ears. "You're just the prettiest kitty, aren't you?"

Cornelius tilted his head into my hand, showing his affection. I petted him a while longer, then stood to take in the rest of the house. To the right was a large living room with a beautiful brick fireplace and a welcoming, homey feel. On my left was a dining room with a display cabinet that stretched across the far wall. Inside sat endless vials of colored liquid. I had no idea what they were, but they shimmered beautifully in the light.

Grammy led me into a large kitchen. Back home, Mom was always in the kitchen, brewing up some sort of concoction that usually turned out better than the last. I knew she got the skills from Grammy, because my grandma couldn't come over for a holiday without a feast packed in her car—and it was always the *best* food. Her brisket was to die for.

Her kitchen just proved what kind of a cook she was. It was clean, but obviously used. Pans hung from a rack above the kitchen island, along with herbs that'd been tied upside down to dry. Her stove looked like it belonged in a restaurant, since it had six burners instead of the usual four. Plus, she had two of those built-in ovens on the wall, one on top of the other, and the fridge was big enough for a family of fifteen.

"Holy crap, Grammy," I said, trying to take it all in. "How many people do you feed?"

She waved her hand, like it was nothing. "Oh, I run a cooking business out of the home."

What the heck? Why didn't I know that? I was starting to sense there was a lot I didn't know about her.

"If you think this is impressive, you should see my garden." Grammy gestured to the back window, and I took a step closer to get a good look. Her yard stretched far back to a line of trees and over to the edge of the park. Almost half of the lawn was covered in a well-cared for garden. I recognized some of the plants, like lavender and sage, but others were more obscure. One of the bushes had big yellow flowers that looked like they were growing tentacles, and another had purple fruits that reminded me of radishes.

"You take care of all that yourself?" I asked.

She shrugged. "It keeps me busy. Do you want to see your room?"

"Yeah, of course."

Grammy pointed me down another hall and into the guest room. The walls were pale yellow like the outside of the house, and she'd made the bed with a light blue comforter. It was *so* not my style, but I was just glad to be here with her.

I stepped into the room, and my eyes caught a photograph of my mom on the nightstand. My heart sank. It looked like an old school photo, and reminded me a little of myself. Mom and I shared the same chocolate eyes, dark brown hair, and full lips. My guts twisted just thinking about her.

And how she was gone, along with my dad.

"I know you won't be here much, with college starting up soon," Grammy said, pulling me from my thoughts. She set my box on the bed. "But I want you to feel at home. Feel free to move things around."

I turned to her, picking at my nails. "Thanks, Grammy. About college, though. It's already the end of August. Isn't it a little late to enroll?"

I really didn't want to take the semester off. I was afraid if I did I'd fall into a deep, dark hole I couldn't pull myself out of. I needed something to distract me from my parents' death.

Grammy placed a gentle hand on mine. "It's all taken care of, Nadine."

I swallowed the lump in my throat, relaxing a bit.

The doorbell rang, stealing Grammy's attention. "Why don't you get settled in a little, then we'll talk about it? We have a lot to discuss."

I nodded, and the doorbell rang again.

"I have to get that," Grammy said. "Let me know if you need anything."

"I will," I said, then Grammy hurried off to answer the door.

I set my purse down, then sank onto the bed. I didn't lie down, because I knew that if I did I'd fall asleep for hours, and it was too late in the day for a nap. I started picking through my box instead. The first thing I pulled out was my yoga mat, which was rolled up on top. I hadn't used it in weeks, which was probably why my joints were so achy lately. That and the stress.

I closed my eyes and clutched the silver star necklace around my neck. My parents had given it to me when I was fifteen, on the day of my lupus diagnosis. When I started getting down on myself, I used it as a reminder of how far I'd come from that day. I was a completely different person from the "problem child" I used to be.

There was a saying we had in the lupus community. "I have lupus, but lupus doesn't have me." My mantra was more along the lines of, "Lupus can kiss my ass."

I repeated the phrase in my head until I started to relax. I told myself I'd get the yoga mat out before bed. Doing yoga before bed helped with the stiffness in the morning.

That was one of the drawbacks of having an autoimmune disease. My own freaking body couldn't help but attack its own healthy tissues. It was like my body couldn't help but destroy itself in every way it could for no good reason. Lupus liked to torture every patient differently, and my own brand of shit meant that I got joint pain every time I got a little stressed or spent too much time in the sun.

Check mark on the stress lately.

I sighed and pulled my journal from the box, then stood to place it on the dresser. As I crossed the room, movement outside caught my eye.

I stepped closer to the window and pushed aside the thin curtains. I became alert when I spotted a guy in a dark grey zip-up hoodie bent over Grammy's garden. His hood was up, concealing his features, but I could tell he was around my age, with long legs and broad shoulders. Every muscle in my body froze as I watched him, sensing he was nothing but trouble. What the hell was he doing out there?

He stood, and I noticed a collection of green leaves in his hands. When it hit me, a wave of heat washed over me, and my hands turned to fists. He was stealing from Grammy!

I quickly reached for the window and flung it open. "Hey, jackass!" I shouted across the lawn.

He turned and started walking toward the park.

"Hey!" I yelled again, louder this time. He just kept on walking, ignoring me.

Excuse me!? No one stole from my grandmother and got away with it!

I quickly turned from the window and ran out of the room, hurrying toward the back door in the kitchen. Grammy was still at the front of the house, talking to whomever was at the door, but I didn't hear what they were saying.

By the time I got outside, the guy was almost to the trees. The sky had darkened as storm clouds rolled in for the night.

"Stop!" I called to him. "What do you think you're doing?"

I knew I should've turned back and just let it go. I mean, it was only a couple of leaves, right? But I was curious to a fault and wasn't the kind of girl who avoided confrontation. I'd set anyone straight if they needed an ass whooping.

Besides, this was Grammy's livelihood. You couldn't just walk into someone's yard and compromise the health of their crop.

My breath grew hot, and my chest started to burn as I ran across the lawn. Screw the pain. This asshole wasn't going to get away with this.

I hurried into the trees behind him, but once I stepped inside the forest, it was like he'd vanished. I glanced around, looking for any sign of movement, but the forest was still. All I heard was the rustle of wind through the trees and the distant sound of an owl.

It was the time of day between sunset and nightfall, which left the forest cast in a dull light. The air felt chilly, and goosebumps broke out across my arms. It was class-A spooky-movie creepy. Most girls would turn around and run back home, but I wasn't most girls.

I continued forward, staying on high alert. My pulse thumped loudly in my ears, as if warning me to turn back—which only made me want to push on.

The narrow dirt pathway took me deep into the forest and past a steep ravine. And then I heard it—the sound of sticks breaking in the distance, like a pair of footsteps traveling off the path. The crunch of leaves came then, picking up in pace and intensity. I quickly realized I was listening to more than one set of footsteps.

I threw myself behind a thick tree as the footsteps came closer. One guy I could deal with. A whole group of them? Probably not.

I peeked around the tree to see four girls walking my way. They all looked my age, but they seemed anything but the kind of girls who would be walking in the woods after sunset. The vibe they gave off suggested they frequented the mall more than the outdoors.

The first girl was gorgeous, with sleek black hair and rich red lips. She wore a skin-tight black dress and low-cut boots with a heel to them. In her hands, she held what looked like a mini witch's cauldron the size of a softball. She had this look her face that said *get out of my way, bitch*, even though she faced nothing but trees. She was definitely the leader of the pack.

To her right walked a girl with porcelain skin, ruby red lips, and long white curls. Her legs went on for miles. The girl on her left had full lips and stick-straight dark hair cut just above her shoulders. It shimmered a deep red and had clearly been done at the salon.

The three of them looked like they could be Instagram models. They were enviously beautiful, with perfect hair and thin bodies. I was pretty sure if I got close enough, I'd see that their nails were done to perfection, too.

"Amy, get up here," the first girl snapped.

The final girl hurried forward. She looked the most down-to-earth of all of them. She was pretty, but in a different way than the Instagram-model chicks. She had jet-black hair and almond-shaped eyes, but she dressed more casually in jeans and a burgundy top.

"Sorry, Chloe," she said quickly, not meeting the main bitch's eyes. "I was just—"

"Shut up and grab the toad," Chloe snapped. "It's right there, or are you too blind to see it?"

Amy's eyes went wide for a second at Chloe's insult, but she quickly followed her instructions and bent to catch a toad I couldn't see from here.

It was clear Amy didn't fit in with these girls. She seemed timid around them, while they held up their noses at her. I wanted to cut in and rescue her, but I was too curious to break things up now. What the heck was going on? Was this some kind of hazing ritual, where they made the sorority pledge eat a live toad or something?

Amy caught the toad, and Chloe held out her mini cauldron. She nodded toward it impatiently. "Well…?"

Amy hesitated. "We really shouldn't be doing this."

Chloe rolled her eyes. "It's harmless. It'll wear off in twenty-four hours."

I furrowed my brow. What would wear off?

Amy bit her lower lip. "Yeah, but it's complicated. What if something goes wrong?"

"Will it?" Chloe asked, making it sound like a threat—like if something went wrong, Amy would be the one to blame. "Remember what we're doing here for you, Amy. You do this for us, and we'll help you find your cat."

The way she said it suggested Chloe knew *exactly* what happened to Amy's cat.

Amy looked torn. She glanced to the cauldron but held the toad close to her chest, like she was protecting it.

I watched curiously. What exactly was it they were asking her to do?

"It's not like we're going to hurt Mandy," the blonde girl said, though I didn't sense honesty in her tone.

"Gwen's right," the third girl added. "We just want to teach Mandy a lesson."

Amy swallowed hard. "What… what did she do to you?"

Yeah, I'd like to know that, too. It was like I was watching a drama TV show. I couldn't tear my gaze away.

Chloe pursed her lips, looking angry at the mention of this Mandy chick. "She's dating Ryan. This is her one and only warning."

"I thought you and Ryan broke up," Amy said.

Chloe took a swift step forward so she was up in Amy's face within an instant. Amy breathed heavily, like she was a little scared, but she held Chloe's gaze.

"You're not here to ask questions, Amy," Chloe snarled. "You're here to do the spell. I have eight months until my ceremony, so until I get my powers, you're going to help me. Now *finish it.*"

Hold up. Did she just say *spell*?

Amy took a step back and straightened a little. "No. I won't help you do this to her."

Chloe's featured hardened by the second. "You wouldn't want Mittens to… meet an untimely end."

"That's not her name," Amy mumbled, but Chloe ignored her.

"Besides, it's not like we're turning Mandy into a toad *forever*," Chloe said. "It's not permanent."

Turn someone into a toad? Was she serious?

Amy's jaw clenched. "You're a real bitch, you know that?"

Chloe tilted her head and sighed. "You say that like it's supposed to hurt my feelings."

Amy rolled her eyes. "Fine. I'll do it. But just know that I'm not here to be your on-call Alchemist."

Huh? Spells? Alchemy? Maybe I wasn't so far off with that cult idea. That, or these bitches were straight-up bat-shit crazy.

Amy gently placed the toad in the cauldron, then took it from Chloe's hands. She started mumbling words under her breath that I couldn't hear. I didn't know what to think at first, until I saw a dark blue light swirl out of Amy's hands, lighting up the cauldron. The tendrils of light swirled around it like some CGI shit, until they reached the open top and sank into the contents inside.

My eyes widened as I stumbled back from my tree. What in the living hell did I just see? A trick of the light? A hallucination? Swirling light didn't just come out of people's hands like that!

The girls hadn't noticed me, but I knew it was time to hightail it out of there regardless. What kind of crazy ass shit was going on here?

I ran away so fast that I lost track of the trail. I glanced behind myself to see if they were following, but they weren't. When I turned back around, my heart shot up into my throat as I stumbled over a rock. My body flew forward, and I went tumbling head over heels down the side of the ravine.

"Whoa!" I cried as I tried to catch myself, but my momentum didn't slow until I hit the bottom.

I lay on the ground, aching from the bruises I'd accumulated on the way down. The trees swayed in the wind above me, but I didn't move right away. I was half cursing myself for not watching where I was going and half just waiting for the initial shock to pass.

Finally, I pushed myself to my elbows—only to find a tall shadow standing over me, holding out a hand. He came as a beacon of safety. I didn't know what possessed me to take the stranger's hand, but I found myself reaching up to him. He pulled me to my feet, and I finally got a glance at his face.

Time seemed to slow when I looked into his mesmerizing green eyes. The sounds in the forest disappeared, and it felt like the world was spinning around me. For just the briefest of moments, my heart seemed like it was floating in my chest. It was a welcome change to the heavy weight I'd been carrying around lately.

It was *him*, the guy in the gray hoodie who'd been stealing from my grandmother's garden. He was hella attractive, with dark hair and cupid's bow lips, but his eyes were hooded in a darkness that both terrified and intrigued me.

I took a breath, and the world became normal again as time once again sped up. The weight on my chest returned, and the whistling of the wind became audible again.

I cleared my throat. "Um, thanks."

Above us, the sound of hurried footsteps rustled the leaves on the ground. He brought his index finger to his lips, signaling for me to be quiet.

"Follow me," he whispered. His voice was smooth, like a beautiful song.

Since he was still holding my hand, he kind of dragged me behind him. We ducked behind a large boulder that was big enough to conceal us both. We crouched low, our bodies almost touching. My hand tingled from where he held it. I could feel the heat coming off him in waves, and my heart pounded so hard I could feel it.

"What is it, Chloe?" I heard one of the girls ask—the one with the short brown hair.

The footsteps stopped at the top of the ravine. "Shut up, Camille," Chloe snapped. "I'm trying to listen."

"Listen to what?" Gwen asked.

"Didn't you hear it?" Chloe growled. "Someone's out here."

"Well, whoever it was is gone now," Camille said.

Chloe huffed. "I swear to our goddess, if Mandy is following us, I'll—"

"She wouldn't do that," Amy cut in.

"Whatever," Chloe said dramatically. "We got what we came out here for. Let's go."

Their footsteps faded as they distanced themselves from us. I didn't move until I could no longer hear them—and even then, I remained put for nearly a minute longer.

Finally, I relaxed, as did the stranger beside me. It wasn't until he helped me to my feet that I finally let go of his hand.

I crossed my arms and faced him. "Care to explain to me what's going on?"

He eyed me curiously, and I felt a blush rise to my cheeks. "What do you want to know?"

"Who were those girls? And why were you stealing from my grandma's garden?" I pursed my lips, waiting for his answer.

"You're Helena Tucker's granddaughter?" he asked, sounding a bit surprised.

"Yeah, I am. So tell me why you were stealing from us."

He crossed his arms and leaned his backside up against the boulder. "I wasn't *stealing*. Your grandma said I could take some leaves from her matus shrub whenever I wanted."

"Matus shrub?" I asked skeptically. I'd never heard of such a thing.

"You chew on the leaves to help relieve anxiety," he explained. "Anyway, will you be staying long?"

I hesitated, reluctant to give him too much personal information. "As long as I have to."

He pushed himself off the rock, then started for the edge of the ravine. I followed and climbed behind him.

"In that case, you'll want to steer clear of the Lucky Three," he said.

"What's the Lucky Three?" I asked.

He reached the top and held out a hand again. I almost didn't take it, because he seemed to be acting a little *too* helpful, but the ravine was super steep, and I didn't want to embarrass myself by falling down it again. He helped me onto level ground and quickly found the trail. We fell into step side by side as darkness began to envelop the forest.

He shoved his hands into his pockets, and I noticed a pair of earbuds hanging out of one. That must've been why he hadn't heard me earlier. "The Lucky Three are those girls you just had the pleasure of meeting."

"Seriously?" I asked. "Their gang has a name?"

He shrugged. "It was a nickname they got in high school that stuck. They always got lucky when it came to the popular vote. You know, student council, prom court, that kind of thing."

They got lucky, or they cheated. Something told me they were the kind of girls who'd stuff the ballot box.

"Are they, like, in some sort of cult or something?" I asked him.

He chuckled lightly and looked a little surprised. "A cult? What makes you say that?"

"They used some pretty cult-ish sounding words," I explained. "They were talking about spells and alchemy. And Main Bitch talked about *our goddess*."

He sputtered, like he was choking on air. "*Main Bitch*. I'm going to have to remember that one. It's a pretty accurate description of Chloe."

I smiled proudly.

We reached the edge of the trees. Grammy's house stood in front of us with the lights inside illuminating the garden.

"Anyway," he said, turning to me. "You should probably ask your grandma about the rest of it."

Way to stiff me on the details. I couldn't just leave my curiosity unchecked.

"Well, you're a big help," I said sarcastically.

He shrugged. "What can I say? It's a blessing."

I rolled my eyes at him. Fine. If he thought I should talk to Grammy, that's exactly what I'd do. I started across the lawn toward the house. "See you around."

"Wait," he called.

I stopped in my tracks and turned to him. I was once again taken off guard by the enchantment in his eyes. I didn't get it. I mean, yeah, he was a total hottie. But like, he was just *standing* there. What made *him* so special?

It was a rhetorical question, but a little voice inside my head told me I was going to find out eventually.

"What's your name?" he asked curiously.

I placed a hand on my hip. "Yours first."

"Lucas," he told me without hesitation. I half expected him to play back and demand mine first. *He's no fun.*

"I'm Nadine," I said.

An emotion I couldn't quite read crossed his eyes when I told him my name. I almost thought it was surprise, but there was a sense of familiarity there, too. I must've been reading him wrong, because it didn't make any sense.

"Anyway…" I broke the silence and gestured to my grandma's house. "I've gotta go. It was nice meeting you."

He nodded. "Yeah, you too. Stay safe, Nadine."

I laughed. "No promises."

I wasn't really the *stay safe* kind of girl. I was the *run into danger* kind. Life was more fun that way.

When I got back inside, I found Grammy standing at the kitchen window, looking out over the back lawn. Cornelius sat in her arms, purring. She raised a curious eyebrow that made me want to crawl into a hole.

"I see you've met Lucas Taylor," she said lightly, obviously teasing me.

I shrugged. "I guess."

"And…?" she pressed.

"And what?" I asked innocently. "He was fine."

"He's a nice boy," Grammy said. "Just be careful."

"Careful how?" I sensed there was more she wanted to say.

She shrugged, like she didn't have a real answer.

If she was trying to drive me away from him, she was doing it wrong. I liked a little mystery.

She sighed. "You look really tired. Why don't you turn in for the night and we'll move in everything in the morning?"

She was right. I was absolutely exhausted and wanted to crawl into bed and sleep for three days. But at the same time, I had questions that needed answering.

"Didn't you have something you wanted to talk to me about?" I asked. "Besides, I'm curious about a few things, and Lucas told me to talk to you."

Grammy waved her hand. "It can wait."

"But Grammy—"

"I'm not taking no for an answer, Nadine. You need to take care of yourself."

I really didn't need a babysitter, but Grammy was a little overprotective. Even though I tried to protest, she insisted I needed my rest.

I crawled into bed that night with a hundred burning questions on my mind. One thing, however, was very clear. There was something weird going on in this town.

And I intended to figure out what.

Lucas

THREE

Her name was a warm light within my cold, dark world. *Nadine.*

Of all the thoughts I'd collected over these past few months, there was one that stuck out. *Stay safe, Nadine. I love you.* There was more to it than that, but that was the part that hit me the strongest.

I didn't know who had died and why they mattered to her, but somehow I instinctively knew—there was no other Nadine. This was the girl who someone had dedicated their dying thought to.

And that was something special. There was this glow to Nadine that I bet she couldn't see. It was in the way she walked and the way she held herself. It was how she had this sarcastic, playful thing going on that I half wanted to be a part of. I had a hard time letting that side of me out.

I thought about her all night and into morning. I admit, I didn't have to cut through the park for what I had to do today, but I did anyway—if just for a chance to catch a glimpse of her. I watched her grandmother's house as I passed by, hoping I'd see her, but at the same time praying I wouldn't.

It wasn't until I was almost to the trees that I heard the sound of the back door slamming and her voice carrying over the lawn. My heart lifted, despite every warning bell going off that told me to leave this girl alone. She'd only get hurt getting involved with a guy like me. I couldn't taint the light within her with my own darkness. Besides, she was a curious soul—that, I could already tell. And there were things she would want to know that I could never tell her. It was best if I kept my distance, but apparently I'd decided that too late, because she was already crossing the lawn toward me.

"Lucas!" she called.

I put on my stone-cold expression so she couldn't read me. It was easier to keep my secrets that way. "Nad."

I didn't know why I called her that. Half her name slipped out, and the other half just didn't. She didn't seem to notice or care.

Nadine's eyes lit up when I turned to her, but the sparkle quickly faded as she took me in. "Wake up on the wrong side of the bed this morning?"

"No," I said. I hadn't even woken up in a bed, but I didn't tell her that. I'd been crashing at Grant's dad's place over the summer and sleeping on their couch, since the dorms were closed and I didn't want to live at home. I couldn't wait for school to start back up and be back in my old dorm room.

"Then I guess you won't mind if I tag along," she said brightly, swinging her arms and bouncing on her toes like she had no care in the world.

"Um, I kind of do." Or so I claimed. I wasn't exactly stopping her when I started down the path and continued on my way. Of course, she followed, which I was starting to sense was a Nadine thing.

Yesterday, I thought she'd come after me because she knew who I was—because she wanted to use me for my gift. It wasn't unusual. People came to me all the time to ask what their loved ones' last thoughts were. They tended to be brutal—regrets, secrets, and mixed emotions—but I liked to make shit up and tell people what they wanted to hear. It gave me less to deal with that way.

Nadine wasn't like that, though.

"Did you talk to your grandma?" I asked.

She waved her hand. "Nah, she blew me off last night and is still sleeping."

Nadine looked wide awake, like she'd been up for hours. She was the kind of girl who had a natural beauty and didn't have to wear a ton of makeup to impress a guy—the total opposite of Chloe. It only made her that much more appealing. She had big curls in her hair that seemed light and bouncy. I wanted to run my fingers through them to see how soft they were.

Okay, I was officially a creep.

"Anyway, I saw you and thought..." she started, before she trailed off.

"You thought?" I asked.

She shrugged. "I thought maybe we could hang out."

Girls and guys didn't just *hang out*. Not in my experience, anyway. Why would Nadine want to hang out with *me*?

I raised an eyebrow. "By *hang out*, you mean I can tell you things your grandma didn't."

She sighed dramatically. "Oh, come on! The suspense is killing me."

It was clear she didn't know about the coven, which her grandmother should've told her by now. Big mistake. But Nadine wasn't going to take no for an answer.

So what do I do? The stupidest thing I can think of, because apparently I'm an idiot.

"How about I show you?"

Nadine's face lit up, and for a brief moment, I felt like I'd made the right choice.

"What's in the bag?" she asked, gesturing to the backpack I was carrying.

I smirked. "You'll have to wait and see."

She squirmed. I was kind of enjoying how easy she was to toy with.

I led Nadine to the other side of the park. We stopped in front of an old house with paint so worn I could hardly tell what color it had originally been.

Nadine had been surprisingly quiet the last few minutes, but she looked skeptical as she stared up at the run-down house. "Is this where you take all your girls on the first date?"

I snorted—and immediately wanted to turn invisible. "Is this a date?"

She ignored the question and said, "You're not denying bringing other girls here."

A foreign feeling tugged at the corner of my lips, and I decided to play along as I started up the walkway. "Maybe I do. Does that scare you?"

Nadine hurried ahead and took the porch steps two at a time, until she was standing right in front of me, our bodies nearly touching.

"*Nothing* scares me, you hear?" She hesitated, then quickly added, "Even though this reeks of a kidnap scenario."

She narrowed her eyes at me, as if trying to judge whether I was going to tie her up in the cellar or not.

"Okay, then." I gestured to the door. "Ladies first."

I figured this could go one of two ways. One, she was fascinated by what she saw inside, or two, she'd be so freaked out she never asked to hang out with me again. Option two was probably best, because we could *not* be friends. She'd only get hurt.

I had enough on my plate already. It's why I was here. Professor Warren suggested I try to find some good in my gift. Okay, *suggested* wasn't the right word. He was pushing me—and pushing me hard. He said if I didn't find the good in my gift, things would just get harder from here on out. The sooner I found the light, the better. I feared I'd eventually cave to the pressure, and I was terrified of that. I wasn't ready to give up, not like Eric had. So I had to find some way to deal.

To do that, I was paying a visit to the recently deceased. I didn't know the guy; I'd only heard of him. Everyone in town called him Old Man Keller, and I knew he was a Mentalist with telekinetic powers. I never thought much of him until I heard his thoughts come to me. Since then, I'd heard rumors he hadn't moved on. He just blatantly refused to go with the reaper who'd come for him. Which meant he had some unfinished business. Maybe my gift was enough to help him resolve it and move on.

The door was unlocked, which I was a little disappointed about. I bet my magic would've impressed Nadine. It wasn't unusual to leave doors unlocked around here, though.

We stepped inside. If there ever was a haunted house, this was it. Even though it was early morning, it was dark inside. The curtains were all closed, and the whole place was in disarray, since someone had been moving things around to get the house ready to sell. A thin layer of dust covered everything, and the floorboards creaked under our weight. I swore the temperature dropped a few degrees, too. I wasn't a Seer, but I could feel the shift in energy as we entered the house. He was already here.

Nadine glanced around, peeking into the bathroom and then up the stairs.

"In here," I said quietly, like I might frighten the ghost.

Nadine followed me into the living room, and I plopped down right on the hardwood floor, even though there was a sofa nearby. The energy seemed stronger in here than it had in the entrance.

Nadine sat across from me. "What are we doing?"

I unzipped my bag and pulled out a Ouija board. It folded in half, which was the only way I managed to fit it into my bag. It was dangerous to use, since I could summon a demon by accident, but the chances were slim. I knew the ghost would be here, which meant he'd connect to the board before any demon could get his hands on it.

Nadine's eyes widened when she saw the board, but it wasn't like she was afraid. It was more like she was excited.

"You really know how to woo the ladies," she joked.

"Is that what I'm doing?" I asked. "Wooing you?"

Nadine smirked, but simply said, "You know I don't believe in Ouija boards, right?"

A smile tugged at the corner of my lips. "We'll see about that when we're done here."

I placed the board between us, then set the planchette on top. Nadine looked skeptical, but she placed her fingers next to mine anyway.

"Who are we contacting?" she asked.

"Everyone calls him Old Man Keller," I explained, pretending like she believed me. "I don't know a lot about him, other than I saw him walking the Black Circle every now and then."

"The Black Circle?" She made it sound like a biker gang or something.

I sighed. "Seriously, you need to talk to your grandma about this town the minute you get home. Anyway, the Black Circle is the trail that circles town. It's fifteen miles long, and Old Man Keller walked parts of it every day with his cat."

Nadine's eyebrows shot up. "His cat? Don't people normally walk dogs?"

"Pretty much everyone in Octavia Falls has a cat," I said. "Anyway, what I heard was that he was on the Black Circle Trail when he tripped and hit his head on a rock. No one found him until it was too late."

Nadine furrowed her brow. "And what happened to the cat?"

Good Goddess, was she serious? I just told her a man died, and she was wondering what happened to his *cat*?

"I don't know," I admitted. "Probably given to the family."

"Okay." She seemed satisfied with the answer. "Let's get started, then."

I took a deep breath, then called out to the dark room. "Old Man Keller? My name is Lucas Taylor. I'm here to talk to you about why you're here. I'm hoping I can help. Are you here with us now?"

The planchette began to move across the board. I could feel the spiritual energy pushing it and knew it was Old Man Keller's ghost, but Nadine looked shocked.

"You're doing that," she accused.

I just shook my head and focused on the board. The planchette stopped over the word *yes*.

Relaxing a little, I asked, "Do you remember how you died?"

The planchette wiggled a little, but it didn't move off the word *yes*.

"How can I help you?" I asked.

The planchette began to move again, stopping on the letter F, then moving on to the letter I. Nadine read the letters out loud until they started to form a sentence. I gritted my teeth as it began to spell out the word *find*.

Not this again.

For some reason, Old Man Keller held on to his last thought, and that's why he couldn't move on. If only he could say something—anything—else. But that's how ghosts were. They were confused and had a hard time communicating. Even a Seer couldn't help us now, not if he couldn't get anything out besides this nonsense.

That's all it was, really. Nonsense.

Find the crystal cave. Whatever that meant. It was the last thought I'd heard from him and exactly what he was spelling out now.

Nadine noticed my fallen face. "What do you think it means?"

It was almost like she kind of believed Old Man Keller was communicating with us. But I could still see the skepticism in her eyes.

I shook my head. "I don't know. Ghosts don't often make sense."

"Mm…" Nadine thought for a moment, then asked, "Are you confused about your death?"

The planchette moved again and stopped over the word *no*.

I furrowed my brow. "He's probably confused about that, too."

"Maybe it's a name," Nadine suggested.

"A name?"

"Yeah, like a woman. Crystal Cave."

"Then why say *the* crystal cave," I pointed out. "If it were a woman, he'd say *Find Crystal Cave.*"

Heat flared throughout my veins. I thought I could help him, but there was nothing I could do if I didn't understand his message. I wasn't a freaking interpreter. This whole thing had been a bust.

I snatched up the planchette and folded the board, then shoved both of them back in my bag.

"What's wrong?" Nadine asked.

Clearly, she thought we were just goofing off. But this was serious to me. My gift was fucking useless.

"Lucas," Nadine pressed as I got to my feet and started for the door. She stood but didn't move to join me.

I stopped and pressed my fingers to my eyes, then turned to her. "Look, Nad. I'm sorry I brought you here."

There I went again, calling her by half her name.

"We should just go—" I started.

Nadine cut me off with a terrified scream. I whirled around to where she was looking, only to come face to face with a ghostly figure. I couldn't make out his face. All I saw was a dark fuzzy outline of a body, like the shadowed imprint of a soul. The temperature in the room plummeted as he took shape.

"Find… the… crystal… cave…" His shaky voice filled the room.

I rushed over to Nadine, who was frozen in shock. She couldn't take her eyes off him.

I took her by the shoulders and shook her a little. "Calm down, Nadine. Ghosts can sense your fear. It might set him off."

"It's a… a…" She couldn't get the words out.

"Nad, look at me!" I demanded.

She did, but it was already too late. Old Man Keller let out a hauntingly high-pitched scream, then charged. I threw myself in front of Nadine, but his spirit swept straight through me like I was nothing but air. It chilled me to the bone, and I could feel the buzz of my magic wane as he stole a portion of my energy.

I whirled around just in time to see the ghost's figure slam into Nadine's chest. His hands solidified, and he shoved her. She went stumbling back. I tried to reach her, but I didn't have time. Her head slammed into the edge of the coffee table, knocking her out.

"Nad!" I cried.

I was at her side in an instant, cradling her head in my lap. Her whole body was limp in my arms. My chest twisted into knots.

"Nadine!" I slapped her face a little, until she moaned, but her eyes didn't open.

I quickly glanced around for signs of Old Man Keller, but he must've used all his energy up, because he was nowhere to be seen.

"I'm so sorry, Nad," I said, even though she probably couldn't hear me. "I didn't mean for you to get hurt."

I cradled Nadine in my arms and carried her out of the house, back through the park towards her grandmother's. The whole time, I couldn't stop staring down at her, thinking about how this was all my fault—because I'd gone searching for the good in my gift.

Right now, I hated being the Reaper's Apprentice more than ever.

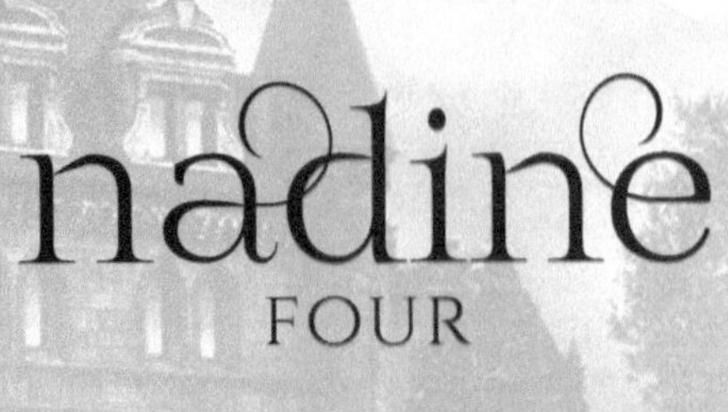

nadine
FOUR

Lucas's scent surrounded me. He smelled like spiced apple and pumpkin, and I felt a warmth and comfort in the scent. Someone moaned, and it took me a second to realize it was me. I tried to open my eyes, but they felt heavy.

"It's okay," Lucas said. "We're almost back."

Where? Everything that happened this morning came rushing back. Did I seriously just get attacked by a *ghost*?

"What happened?" a stern voice demanded. I thought it was Grammy, but I was still so out of it I could hardly tell.

"Haunted house," Lucas said coolly, like it was an everyday thing. "She hit her head."

"Set her right here," Grammy instructed. "I'll get some ice."

I felt my body being placed on a soft surface. My head pounded like a bass drum. Grammy placed an ice pack under my head, then I felt her part my lips and pour something down my throat. "Drink up, Nadine."

I barely processed the words. I didn't know what the liquid was, but it tasted sweet, so I drank it.

"What is that?" Lucas asked.

"A potion to cure the concussion," Grammy told him.

I was barely in my right mind, but did I just hear *potion*?

That was the last thing I heard before I slipped off into a dark oblivion.

Whatever Grammy had given me must've knocked me out for hours, because I woke up that afternoon in my own bed. I didn't know how I'd gotten there, but it just confirmed that everything that happened had been some wild, vivid dream—

Until I heard the sound of Lucas's voice coming from the kitchen. I touched the back of my head, where it was still tender. How could that be? What had *really* happened?

I wanted to jump out of bed and demand answers, but my joints protested as I slowly pushed myself to a sitting position. It took me ten minutes to drag myself out of bed. The world seemed to stay put instead of spin around me, so that was a good sign. I tried to listen to what Lucas and Grammy were saying, but they spoke so quietly that I couldn't make out their words.

I made my way to the end of the hall and stood in the doorway to the kitchen. Neither of them noticed me.

"It's almost done." Grammy stood over a huge pot that bubbled over a burner on the kitchen island. No, not a pot—a *cauldron*. What the hell?

Grammy stirred the solution. Small glass containers filled with herbs lined the counter beside her. "We'll tell her as soon as she wakes."

Lucas glanced over his shoulder in the direction of my room. His eyes brightened when he saw me standing there. He straightened from where he sat on a stool beside the island.

"Nadine," he said breathlessly. "You're awake."

"Am I?" I replied in a groggy tone. "What are you still doing here?"

The fact that he was still there sent a warm sensation to settle in my gut. It was like he *cared*. Which was stupid, because he didn't even know me.

Lucas stood. He looked like he was about to approach me, but he caught himself at the last second and stayed put. "I wanted to make sure you were all right."

Okay, I guess he did care. Cool.

"My head is better," I admitted, "but I'm going to need some answers."

"And that's exactly what I intend to give you." Grammy gestured for me to sit.

I took the stool beside Lucas, and he sat back down, so close that we were almost touching. I could feel the heat of his body, which made mine turn to mush.

I tried to ignore that. "What happened? Did I pass out?"

That had to be it. I hadn't passed out in years, but with my lupus in flare-up, it wouldn't surprise me.

Grammy set her stirring spoon aside on the counter. She looked at me with a grave expression. "No, honey. You fell and hit your head."

"I—I think I remember," I said cautiously. But no way was I remembering everything right. I must've imagined that ghost part when I'd hit my head. "What is it you need to tell me?"

Grammy took a deep breath, but she didn't speak right away.

"It's time, Helena," Lucas pressed.

Grammy shifted her weight between her feet. "I wanted you to rest first, since this might take a long time, but…" She sighed. "You'll find out one way or another, and I'd rather you heard it from me."

"What, Grammy?" I demanded, sitting up a little straighter. "Tell me what's going on."

Grammy gave me that look—the one Mom always had when she needed to talk over something serious. I half expected her to give me the sex talk right then and there.

Sorry, Grammy. Mom beat you to it.

The seconds ticked by at a snail's pace as I waited for Grammy's big reveal. She was obviously a woman of many secrets, but what could be so serious that she was looking at me like that?

"There's no easy way to say this, Nadine," Grammy started slowly. "You're a witch."

I was half tempted to make a Harry Potter joke and ask in my best British accent, *I'm a WATT!?*

But Grammy was looking at me like she was dead serious. So instead, I lightly scoffed and said, "Yeah, okay."

In the back of my mind, I was freaking out. I mean, I grew up reading about sparkling vampires and binge-watching supernatural shows on Netflix. The paranormal wasn't a completely foreign concept to me. But it wasn't *real*.

"Nadine," Grammy scolded. "I'm being serious. This town, Octavia Falls, has a secret. We're all members of the Miriamic Coven, and so are you."

She spoke with such honesty that it was starting to scare me. Did she seriously think she had magical powers? I looked to Lucas to see what he thought of this, but he wore the same serious look as Grammy did.

Holy shit. They weren't playing games.

"So, you're all Wiccans?" I asked, trying to make sense of what she was saying.

Grammy shook her head. "No. Wicca is a completely different religion from ours."

"So, what are you saying?"

"Octavia Falls is home to a coven of four different classes of witches and warlocks," Grammy explained.

"Five, technically," Lucas muttered.

"Yes," Grammy agreed, "but only four left. We can do magic, and so will you."

Now it was time for me to give *my* look. I scrunched up my brow and gazed at her sideways. Was my grandmother suffering from some sort of dementia episode? I didn't even know she *had* dementia.

Lucas caught my expression and said, "Your grandma's telling the truth."

"Oh, really?" I raised a challenging eyebrow. "Then prove it."

Lucas smirked proudly, accepting the challenge. "Okay."

He held his hand out, and a glowing white orb formed in it from out of nowhere. I recoiled, nearly falling out of my stool.

Holy shit! How did he do that?

I couldn't do anything but stare. Lucas tossed the orb into the air, and it burst into a hundred smaller orbs. They floated above our heads like lightning bugs, all orbiting in a uniform circle.

"What the...?" I was so entranced that I couldn't finish my sentence.

He watched the lights beside me. "It's a simple spell. Any witch or warlock can create orbs."

One of the lights floated in front of me. I reached out to touch it, but pulled back at the last second.

"Go ahead," Grammy encouraged. "It's not going to hurt you."

After a moment of hesitation, I reached out for the orb. It was warm, but it didn't hurt as my fingers went right through it.

"What is it?" I asked in wonder, still trying to convince myself what I was seeing was real and not just a trick of the light.

"They're magical lights," Grammy explained.

Lucas twisted his fingers, and the rotation of the orbs shifted to his command. They swirled around the room, weaving in and out of one another in a beautiful lights display. They blinked on and off, then joined and split like a kaleidoscope. I'd never seen anything so beautiful in my life.

Lucas waved his hands again, and the orbs floated toward me, surrounding my body but not touching me. I gazed at them, completely starstruck by what he could do. He closed his palm, and the orbs disappeared from where they hovered mid-air. He wore the slightest of smiles, like he enjoyed watching me view magic for the first time.

It took me a moment to find my voice. "Show me something else."

Grammy cleared her throat and held out her hand. In the blink of an eye, a box of chocolates appeared in her palm.

I nearly shit myself. "Grammy! What the hell? You can make chocolate appear out of nowhere?"

She chuckled. "Kind of. It's another ability all members of the coven have—conjuration. You'll learn all about it in school."

"School?" I balked, nearly choking on my words. I was still trying to wrap my head around the whole *my grandmother is a witch* thing! "There's a school?"

Lucas nodded. "Miriam College of Witchcraft. I'll be a sophomore this year."

"No," I said firmly, shaking my head. "This is insane."

Except I just saw my grandma materialize a box of chocolates from out of nowhere. And now she was eating them.

"Want one?" she asked, holding the box out toward me.

I eyed it skeptically. "Not really. What does magic chocolate do to you?"

Grammy laughed. "It's not magic chocolate, Nadine. It's normal chocolate. All I did was conjure it."

"Oh," I said flatly, because I didn't know what else to say.

The crazy thing was, I didn't just *believe* them. I *wanted* to. I mean, this was *magic*. If there was even the slightest chance they were telling the truth—which I still wasn't sure of, even though they'd just shown me things beyond explanation—I wanted to be a part of it.

"So, um... what else can you do?" I asked.

Grammy seemed pleased to see I was warming up to the idea. "We can all perform simple incantations and defensive magic, as well as use Ouija boards, read tarot cards, summon demons—"

"Summon demons!?" I cried. That sounded scary—and dangerous.

"Yes, but I *highly* advise against it," Grammy said firmly.

"What about séances?" I tapped my fingers against the counter, and my heart pitter-pattered as I eagerly awaited an answer.

Grammy's lips pressed into a thin line. "I know what you're thinking, Nadine, and the answer is no."

"But Lucas and I did one earlier!" I cried.

"And you got hurt," Grammy reminded me.

I raised a challenging eyebrow. "They're not going to hurt me."

She knew who I was talking about, but I was purposely vague since Lucas was sitting right there.

Grammy sighed and gazed at me with a soft expression. "We'll talk about this later, Nadine. Anyway, back to our discussion. Each Cast has a unique set of abilities."

She knew she could distract me by piquing my curiosity.

"What kind?" I asked.

Grammy cleared her throat, then picked up one of the bottles of herbs. She grabbed a pinch of dried leaves, then tossed them into the cauldron. The thick, milky solution bubbled more, then a puff of smoke rose into the air and swirled into the shape of a cauldron. It hovered in the air like a hologram.

"I'm an Alchemist." Grammy pointed to the tattoo on her wrist. "That's what my cauldron tattoo means. Alchemists infuse magic into potions to create things like magical medicine or love potions."

Ooh, love potions!

"Alchemists also grow their own magical herbs," Grammy explained.

My jaw dropped. "That's why you garden."

Grammy nodded proudly.

"So... Mom has that same tattoo," I pointed out. "Does that mean she was...?"

"An Alchemist, like me," Grammy confirmed.

I was so shocked I could hardly move. My mom... a witch?

"What other Casts are there?" I asked, eager to know more about all this.

Grammy tossed the herbs in again, and the smoke shifted into the shape of a skull.

Lucas leaned in closer, his elbows on the counter. He looked from the skull to me, then gave me this look I couldn't read. All I knew was it made my insides dance. "Mortana are known as the Death Cast. Their abilities vary, but they all have to do with death."

"Like necromancers?" I asked brightly. That'd be badass.

Grammy nodded. "Yes, some Mortana can reanimate the dead. Others might see how a person is going to die, or can read the auras of a location to tell if death has occurred there."

"And the other Casts?"

This time when Grammy tossed the herbs in the mixture, an eye took shape in the smoke.

"Seers are the Psychic Cast," Grammy explained. "Like Mortana, their abilities vary. Seers can get visions of the past, present, or future, talk to spirits, read auras, or get feelings through touch. It's the broadest Cast of them all."

She added more herbs, and the smoke turned into the shape of a tree. Grammy looked to Lucas, inviting him to finish the story.

"The last Cast is Mentalists," Lucas told me. "They can do anything relating to the mind."

"Like, read minds?" I asked. That'd be a cool ability to have, but I didn't want anyone else reading my mind. There were some dark and dirty thoughts there that I never wanted to escape.

"Yes, but it's rare," Lucas said. "Most Mentalists have telekinesis."

My jaw dropped. "Shut up! They can move things with their minds?"

Grammy and Lucas both nodded. I glanced to Lucas's wrist, trying to see which mark he had, but he wore that gray hoodie and his wrists were covered. I didn't see a mark anywhere else on him.

I shook my head. This was all too insane and fantastical. But I had just seen Lucas create light from nothing and Grammy conjure chocolate from out of nowhere.

My next question came out slowly as I calculated each word. "So, I'm going to have some of these powers?"

"Yes," Grammy said, tossing more herbs into the cauldron. The smoke transformed into tiny human figures. One of them lay down with five candles placed around them in a circle, while the other stood outside of the circle. The figures were so detailed that they were nothing less than a work of art. I was so entranced that I couldn't take my eyes off the scene playing out before me.

"On the eve of your nineteenth birthday, you will undergo an Evoking Ceremony. You will contact our goddess, Mother Miriam, and she will assign you to the Cast best fit for you." Grammy waved her hands, and the figure in the candle circle began to levitate. "She will awaken your powers, and you will receive your tattoo indicating your Cast."

"Receive your tattoo?" I asked. "How?"

She made it sound like you didn't just walk into a tattoo parlor for it.

"It appears once your ceremony is complete," Lucas explained.

Interesting… but I had so many other questions.

"So your goddess… she gives you magic?" I asked. "Can anyone get magic from her?"

"Yes, but it becomes a bit complicated," Grammy answered. "You must marry into the coven, and then you become eligible to join on the first anniversary of your marriage. You would be welcomed as a full member of the coven, but without Miriam's blood in your veins, your powers would be limited. Even so, you'd be eligible to live with Mother Miriam and our ancestors in Alora."

"Alora?"

"Our afterlife," Lucas clarified. "Think of it like our version of heaven."

I paused for a moment, absorbing everything they were saying. "So, if you don't marry into the coven, how do you join?"

Grammy brightened, like it was a good question. "You're born into it. All witches and warlocks born into our coven are descended from Mother Miriam. We are born with magic in our blood, which has the potential to become any type of magic—like a stem cell. But it's suppressed until your Evoking Ceremony. After that, it's up to you to exercise it. Like a muscle, it can be strengthened and improved upon."

"Are you the only coven with magic?" I was eager to know what else was out there—if anything. Witches had been mentioned all throughout history, even as far back as biblical times. What if there were others?

"There are many different magical societies around the world, each with their own gods and their own types of magic," Grammy told me. "We all remain secret, as exposing ourselves could lead to very dangerous consequences."

Lucas scoffed. "Yeah. Just look at the witch trials."

My eyebrows shot up. "Your coven was part of the Salem Witch Trials?"

"Those weren't the only ones," Lucas pointed out. "Our coven dates back before the Burning Times in Europe. And Salem's just one of the trials here in the states. The first execution for witchcraft in America took place right here in Connecticut. Fifty years later, and eleven people in our state alone were killed for witchcraft."

"All from your coven?" I balked.

"No," Grammy said firmly. "That's one of the reasons why we came together and formed Octavia Falls, and surrounded it with a protection spell. Just our mere existence caused fear and chaos. Innocent people were being hurt in our name. So… we went into hiding."

I went breathless for a moment. It was hard to wrap my head around everything. "I'm sorry you all feel like you have to hide."

Grammy waved her hand, like it wasn't a big deal. "Don't worry about it. We have two rules within the coven. One, do whatever pleases the Goddess. And two, protect the coven. If you follow those two rules in this life, you will be rewarded in the next. It's no inconvenience at all to protect our own people."

She sounded so noble when she said that.

Silence settled for a few seconds. I was still taking it all in, and they were waiting for my next question. I couldn't believe I was born a witch and would get magical powers in just a few months. It was like a fantasy I'd dreamed of my whole life, minus the sexy vampires. That said, I was sure this town had plenty of sexy warlocks—namely, the one sitting beside me.

"I just have two more questions," I said.

Grammy leaned in, looking eager to answer them.

"Why did Mom leave the coven?"

Grammy's spine straightened, and I didn't miss the fallen look on her face. She stilled for only a moment before quickly relaxing. "She met your father, and the rest is history."

There was a thickness in the air that left me feeling a little uncomfortable.

"What do you mean?" I asked, sensing there was something she wasn't telling me. "Couldn't Dad have stayed here with her?"

"They didn't want to. That's all," she assured me. "Your mother fell in love and followed him."

I guess it made sense. My parents weighed every decision carefully. They must've thought our family would be happier outside the coven.

"What's your other question?" she asked.

"This school… Miriam College of Witchcraft." I could hardly believe I was entertaining the idea that it was a real place. "That's the college you enrolled me in?"

A smile formed across Grammy's face. "Yes. The college was formed to ensure all Miriamic people have control over their magic and know how to use it, so we can avoid magical accidents. All students begin studying the year their magic will awaken, to prepare them beforehand and then teach them after."

"I can't believe I'm going to be studying magic." Even as I said the words, it felt like some make-believe role-playing game, not reality. But it was. I couldn't tell myself otherwise. It was like somewhere deep inside of me, I always knew I was a witch. It just made sense.

"It's nothing to be afraid of," Grammy assured me. "Besides, Lucas will be there to show you around. Won't you, Lucas?"

He looked shocked for a moment, but he quickly relaxed. "Yeah, sure. I'll show her around."

"Well…" Grammy spoke in a brighter tone as she turned the burner off. The cauldron stopped bubbling, and the smoky figures disappeared. "It's past lunch time. Are you hungry, Nadine?"

"Famished," I said quickly.

Lucas stood. "I think I'm going to go."

"Nonsense," Grammy insisted. "Sit down and eat something, Lucas."

He took a step away from the counter. "No, really. I'm not hungry. I should be getting home anyway."

Grammy frowned, but she didn't protest further.

"I'll see you two around." Lucas waved as he headed down the hall.

I hesitated a moment. There were still things I wanted to ask him. He reached the front door. If I was going to catch him, it was now or never. I scrambled out of my seat and down the hall.

"Lucas!" I called when I got outside.

He'd already started down the street. He turned to me with an expectant look on his face. "Yeah, Nad?"

No one had ever called me Nad before, but for whatever reason, it sounded good coming out of his mouth.

I stopped on the sidewalk in front of him. "How do you know my grandma? You two seem to like you're close."

They were on a first-name basis after all. The last thing I needed was for him to be my second-cousin or something.

Lucas shoved his hands into his pockets and glanced toward the house. "I guess you could call her my therapist."

Therapist? Was this guy hiding a deep, dark past or something? Not that I had any right to ask.

"Therapist? Is that what my grandma does?" I asked.

"She's more of a… magical pharmacist," he admitted. "She makes some of the best magical medicines in town."

"Right," I realized. "Because she's an Alchemist."

He nodded.

An awkward silence settled between us, but I wasn't ready to leave yet.

"So, you're going to be a sophomore," I said lamely. "That makes you a year older than me. Have you gone through your Evoking Ceremony?"

"Yeah, I have."

"What is it, exactly?" I asked.

He took a long breath. "It's a test from Mother Miriam. It's different for everyone, but you're going to have to prepare for it."

"Prepare how? If I can't even do magic yet?"

"Mentally and spiritually."

Wow. Less than four months to prepare for the biggest mental test of my life. That didn't sound like enough time.

I swallowed. "What happens if I don't pass this test?"

"If Mother Miriam doesn't find you fit…" He paused. I couldn't stand the suspense. "You'll be banished from the coven."

My blood ran cold at his words. Grammy was the last family I had left, and I couldn't be separated from her. Which meant I had to do everything in my power to pass.

Come hell or high water, I was joining this coven.

lucas
FIVE

The look Nadine gave me when I showed her the orbs stuck with me over the next few days. She had such wonder in her eyes that I'd never seen before. To her, magic wasn't an everyday thing like I'd grown up with. It was this beautiful new journey she had yet to discover—and I got to introduce her to that. It was like, for the first time in my life, someone actually appreciated that part of me.

Move-in day arrived on Saturday, and it was the first time in months that I woke up feeling positive.

"Rise and shine." I burst into Grant's room that morning and pulled open the shades. I had to be careful where I stepped, since his room was a complete disaster.

He shielded his eyes as sunlight streamed onto his face. "Dude, can't a guy get a little privacy?"

He pulled the blanket up over himself, since he was sleeping in nothing but his boxers.

"Not today," I told him.

He dropped his arm from his face and eyed me curiously. "You seem in an unusually happy mood."

I shrugged. "I get to sleep in a real bed tonight."

Grant suddenly seemed more alert. He propped himself up on his elbows and wiggled his eyebrows. "And you get to see that girl again, huh?"

"Shut up." I threw a pile of clothes at him from the foot of his bed and turned away so he couldn't see my face.

Yeah, I was excited. So sue me. If Nadine thought my light display was something, she was going to freak when she saw the mansion, and I wanted to be there when she did.

"I just want to move in before the rush," I told him.

I threw his clothes into a pile and waved my hands over them. *"Eye of frog and witch's brew, make these clothes as good as new."*

My magic glowed a dark purple as it intermingled with the threads. I lifted the shirt on top and smelled it. It had a fresh, clean linen scent to it, and all the dirt had disappeared. I tossed the shirt to Grant. "Your clothes are clean. Time to pack."

Grant sniffed the shirt. "Thanks, but seriously? *Eye of frog?* In what universe is that a cleansing spell?"

I shrugged. "Worked, didn't it?"

Grant rolled his eyes. "Yeah, I guess."

"Okay, then let's go."

Grant groaned as he rolled out of bed. "Give me a few minutes to wake up, dude. I need some breakfast before we leave."

Unlike me, who often forgot to eat, Grant needed to eat every two to three hours.

"Right," I said. "Well, let me know how I can help."

After a shower, breakfast, and three hours of packing—since Grant was *that* slow—we made it to campus. Miriam College of Witchcraft was situated on the edge of town in a mansion that, from the outside, looked ten times the size of the house I grew up in. It had sharp peaks, pointed roofs, and the gothic architecture shared with the rest of the town. Miriam Mansion was easily the coolest building in town.

Stepping inside was like coming home. It wasn't just the magic inside—like how it'd been enchanted to be bigger on the inside than the outside so it could house more dorms, a fitness center, and an Olympic-sized pool. It was the entire feel, like it was the one place I could be myself without fear of backlash.

At the same time, entering the foyer didn't bring the thrill and excitement as my first semester. Things were darker and more sinister. I was supposed to be here to learn about my gift, and so far, I was struggling with it. These wide, expansive halls were just a reminder of the endless nights I'd spent roaming them, trying to walk away my insomnia. The classrooms held memories of the magic I had yet to embrace.

Maybe I'd been wrong. Maybe this wasn't home. But it sure as hell was the closest I'd come, and I was going to have to live with that.

The school was already buzzing with activity. The foyer was crowded with students and parents. All around us, people were chatting away. One sophomore girl bragged to her friends about the Mentalist powers she'd gotten over summer break. She showed off by making her luggage float behind her up the grand staircase. The three other girls, who all bore the mark of an Alchemist, looked intrigued. At the top of the stairs, the Mentalist girl nearly bumped into a guy who looked to be in a heated conversation with someone I couldn't see. I caught a glimpse of an eye tattoo on his arm and knew he must've been a medium. Some ghost must've been asking for his help.

In the corner at a seating area, a group of freshman sat in a circle reading tarot cards. Beside them, two junior girls were changing their makeup at will and giving each other their opinions.

Grant and I walked across the foyer to the registration table, where we picked up our dorm keys and our class schedules. We climbed the stairs and took a left. There were so many people that we had to weave in and out of them, even though the hall was a good eight feet wide.

Our room was the same one as last semester, and not much had changed when we stepped inside. It was bigger than a normal college dorm, more like the size of a hotel room. There were two beds, two dressers, and two desks, with a couch between them facing a TV. Like the rest of the mansion, everything was decorated in dark tones.

Grant plopped onto the bed farthest from the door. "Dibs."

I shrugged. "Fine by me."

I conjured my bag and set it next to my bed, then turned around.

"Where are you going?" Grant asked. "Aren't you going to unpack?"

"Later," I told him. "I'm going to explore and find out where my classes are."

"Okay. I'll text you when I'm ready to hit the pool." In his next life, Grant was coming back as a fish, considering how much time he spent at the pool.

I stepped out of the room, glad he hadn't questioned me further. I hadn't exactly lied to him, but the truth was that I was only going to explore in hopes of running into Nadine.

I headed back down to the Main Foyer, but I didn't see her at registration, so I continued down the hall. I passed by endless classrooms, until I reached the Lounge. It was a huge room separated into different areas, with everything a student could ask for when they weren't in class—couches to sit on, big-screen TVs to watch, and games like pool and darts. There was even an arcade section and four bowling lanes, along with a restaurant. It was like the entertainment district all crammed into one room. Everything was cast in dim lighting, like a club but without the booze and pounding music.

I walked straight past the restaurant to the sitting area, then stopped dead in my tracks when I spotted a group of five guys in leather jackets gathered around the pool table. I tried to step away slowly before they noticed me, but Prime Asshole lifted his head and caught sight of me before I could make my exit.

"Well, if it isn't Lucas Taylor," he practically sang in the most condescending manner he could.

"Ryan." I nodded my head toward him.

The five of them stepped closer to me. Ryan came in close and wrapped an arm tightly around my shoulder so that even if I wanted to run, I'd have to put up a fight to do it.

"How you doing, *old pal*?" His hand tightened on my shoulder until it hurt.

I didn't let the pain show. These guys might have had the rest of the school fooled, but I wasn't scared of them. They were a gang of Mentalists, and despite their sophomore status, they had everyone else convinced they ruled the school. They called themselves the Treacherous Tarantulas, like they were some badass gang—and had a tarantula emblem on the back of their jackets like it proved something. It was a dumb name, and I was allowed to say that, since I was the one who came up with it.

"We're back to old pal now?" I asked casually. "Last time we talked, you called me a traitor."

"That's because you are," Ryan snarled.

He came in so close to me that I could smell the stench of his breath. I seriously didn't get why girls swooned over him. Sure, he had that tall, muscular, star-quarterback look going on, but underneath all that was garbage. My only guess was they liked him for his dick, but it couldn't be *that* big. I didn't care if it was two feet long; nothing could make up for his rotten personality.

"First, you leave the Tarantulas—"

"You stole Grant's insulin," I snapped.

The Tarantulas had never been a great group of guys. I should know. I used to be one of them.

I'd been thinking about leaving them for a long time, after some shit went down the summer before college. The final straw was when they decided to sneak into my dorm without my consent and take Grant's entire insulin supply in what they called a "harmless prank." I lost it. I traded in my leather jacket for this hoodie a year ago next week, and it'd been one of the best decisions of my life.

"And then you started fooling around with my girlfriend," Ryan continued, like he hadn't even heard me.

I resisted the urge to roll my eyes. "Seriously? We're back to that? How many times do I have to tell you that nothing ever happened between Chloe and me?"

I didn't find out until months later that the only reason Chloe asked to attend my Evoking Ceremony was to make Ryan jealous and get him to pay more attention to her. It worked for a while, I guess, but not before I was dragged into the middle of their relationship.

"You can tell me that all you want," Ryan sneered. "I'm still not going to believe you."

"What do you care, anyway?" I demanded. "You and Chloe broke up."

"Doesn't change the fact that you betrayed us." Ryan narrowed his eyes at me. "I don't want to see you coming around the Lounge anymore, you hear?"

"I pay my tuition, same as you," I said. It wasn't *exactly* true, since I was here on scholarship due to my parents' lack of funds. But Ryan didn't have to know that. "I'm free to use the Lounge as I please."

Ryan finally dropped his hand from my shoulder. "Do as you please, Lucas, but there will be consequences."

"Oh? Like what?" I knew Ryan was all talk and no action. He thrived on fear, and as long as I didn't give in to that, he couldn't touch me.

"Like this." Ryan flicked his wrist, and the cue ball flew off the table at full-speed toward my nose.

I flinched and ducked, but Ryan shot his hand out and caught the ball before it reached me. His posse laughed. I wasn't amused.

"Funny," I said flatly, straightening up. "Now if you'll excuse me, I have an appointment to get to."

I didn't give them a chance to respond. I turned and hurried out of the Lounge, the sound of their laughter echoing behind me. The truth was, I didn't want to get into it with those guys. As much as Ryan didn't scare me, if I swung, he'd swing back.

I *did* have an appointment, but it wasn't official. Professor Warren told me to stop into his office whenever I got settled in my room. It was on the way back to the foyer, so I figured it wouldn't hurt to swing by now.

Professor Warren's office was through his classroom. The door was open when I arrived. He sat behind his desk, his hand hovering over a dead mouse that lay in front of him. The mouse twitched, but it didn't get up and move like I'd seen Professor Warren do to creatures before.

I cleared my throat.

He jumped a little, then relaxed when he saw it was just me. "Lucas. Good to see you. Come in."

I stepped inside his office. It wasn't a very big room, but it was comfortable. One wall was made up completely of bookcases, while the other was decorated with various things that didn't seem to fit together at all—empty potion vials, an oil lamp, and several ships in a bottle. He even had a skeleton of a cat, which I found kind of creepy.

"Everything okay?" I asked, gesturing to the rodent corpse.

"Fine," he said quickly. "Just a little weak today is all. Take a seat."

I furrowed my brow, but I sat anyway.

Professor Warren stood to close the door, then returned to his chair. He was in his forties, with dark hair and a bit of stubble I guess the ladies liked or something. He was a widower and never had kids. He told me once his students were enough, though I wasn't sure I believed him. He seemed like a lonely guy.

"How was your summer?" he asked.

I shrugged. "Good, I guess."

Total lie. Honestly, I couldn't remember half the summer. I'd slept through most of it. The only parts I really remembered were disc golfing at Octavia Falls Park with Grant.

"And the task I gave you?" He gave me a curious look.

Professor Warren was a necromancer who taught Mortana studies. As my mentor, it was his job to help me understand my gift. The only problem? I was his first Reaper's Apprentice student. The last Apprentice in the coven died just days before my Evoking Ceremony. Rumor had it, he'd lived to be over a hundred. Professor Warren didn't exactly have a lot of experience in this area, and as much as I respected him, I wasn't sure he could really help me.

"I'm trying to find the good in my gift," I assured him. "But…"

"But what, Lucas?" he pressed.

I turned my gaze away from him and looked out the window, which was lined in red drapes. Not far from the window was a dark forest.

"I can't help you unless you talk to me," Professor Warren said.

I shook my head. "I tried to help Old Man Keller cross over, but it was a total bust."

"Oh?" He straightened in his chair. "I'd very much like to hear about that. What happened?"

I summarized the best I could. "By the end of it, the new girl got a concussion, and I'm not any closer to helping Old Man Keller," I concluded with.

Professor Warren didn't respond right away. He leaned back in his chair with his lips pressed together, like he was deep in thought.

"What?" I asked.

"You say your gift is nothing but a curse, but this girl…"

"Nadine," I said quickly.

He nodded. "Nadine. You sound fond of her."

"What?" I scoffed, my cheeks heating. Where'd he get that idea? "I don't even know her."

"Nonetheless, your gift brought you two together, correct?" Professor Warren raised a curious eyebrow.

"Um, I mean, not really."

If we were going to stretch it that far, I guess I could say my anxiety led me to Nadine, since I wouldn't have met her if I hadn't been picking her grandmother's matus shrub leaves. But we would've met at college anyway, so I couldn't say this was exactly a perk of my gift.

"If that's what you choose to believe, Lucas, that's up to you," Professor Warren said. "But I see no harm in taking this experience as a positive. Perhaps it's worth adding to your journal."

Professor Warren had given me a journal after my Evoking Ceremony when he started mentoring me. So far, I hadn't added anything to it. He only wanted me to add the *positive* about my gift. I told him it would be faster if I filled it with the negatives. He didn't like that.

"Yeah, I guess it'd be nice to finally add something to the journal," I stated flatly. "But what good is meeting a girl? She could become the Reaper's Shadow. I can't put that kind of burden on her."

He raised a curious eyebrow. "You realize you have complete control over the Reaper's Shadow situation, don't you?"

I sank further in my chair. "Things could get out of hand."

He frowned at my tone. "Lucas, I can't help you if you don't want to be helped."

A lump rose to my throat at the accusation. The bright mood I'd woken up in that morning suddenly seemed to darken. My lips tightened. "I *do* want help."

Professor Warren sighed. "I don't have a magic bullet. I can guide you, but you're the only one who can change your attitude."

"This isn't an attitude problem," I snapped. "This is a matter of circumstance. A fact. My gift sucks."

"That's your *perspective*," Professor Warren tried to convince me. I wasn't buying it.

"Would you think that if you were put in my place?" I challenged.

He shook his head and dropped his gaze. "Lucas, I can't say what I would feel in your situation. The only thing I can do is offer my support. If we don't sort this thing out, your powers are going to consume you."

He didn't say it explicitly, but I knew what he meant. If things kept going the way they were, Professor Warren worried I'd throw in the towel and off myself like Eric did. I wouldn't lie and say I hadn't thought about it more than once, but if he really thought I was going to do it, he didn't know me at all.

I crossed my arms. "That's not going to happen."

"It is happening, though," he pointed out. "You've cut yourself off from people. You've stopped doing the things you used to love."

I was quick to retort. "I cut myself off from people who are toxic. That has nothing to do with my gift. And the things I used to love? It's because my brother and I used to do them together."

Rock climbing, paintballing, kayaking—those were all mine and Eric's things, our means of escape when Dad got in one of his moods. The only reason I stuck with disc golfing was because it was the only thing I was comfortable doing on my own.

"I know you're still grieving," Professor Warren said.

I pressed my fingers to my eyes. "Can we not do this again? How many times are we going to have this conversation?"

Professor Warren paused for a moment, and a look of regret crossed his features. "I'm sorry, Lucas."

"I'm fine." If I said it enough times, maybe I'd start believing it.

"Okay, then." He nodded, accepting my claim, even if he didn't believe it. "I'll see you in two weeks."

I started to get up, but he stopped me.

"And Lucas." He gave me a pointed expression. "I want to see that journal."

"Right." The word felt dry in my mouth. "See you."

I left the room before I heard his goodbye. As soon as I stepped into the hall, a wave of nausea slammed into me. It was so strong that I stopped dead in my tracks. I resisted the urge to double over, because I knew nothing would come from trying to heave. This kind of thing happened to me daily now. I leaned up against the wall as sweat broke out across my body. I forced myself to control my breathing as the nausea worsened.

"I should've told her about the affair," a voice said in my mind.

It sounded like an old man's. Just another regret—a secret—for me to carry around for the dead. Not like I had a fucking choice.

The nausea passed as soon as the voice faded. I glanced around, wondering if anyone had seen, but there weren't very many people in the hall, and those who were here didn't look at me.

I breathed a sigh of relief, knowing the episode was over. I summoned an old leather-bound notebook—the kind used for recording spells and incantations. I wrote down the thought beneath the others. Professor Warren didn't know about *this* journal, the one where I kept track of everything I heard. I kept it just in case one day I needed to shove it in his face as proof of the shit I carried. Next week, I'd check the paper for the obituaries and try to match each thought with whoever had passed.

Maybe Professor Warren was right. Maybe I *was* focusing too much on the negative.

At least now I had one positive thing in my life. *Nadine.* I guess it was time to finally add an entry to the positivity journal.

nadine

SIX

ost mornings, I woke with a headache and stiff joints. Today was no exception. It took me over half an hour to get out of bed. While I waited for my joints to relax, I wrote my symptoms down in my journal.

Feel like shit. Joints ache. Another day in Paradise.

I'd been doing this since I was thirteen, so I could track my triggers. I knew most of them by now, but I figured it was still good to keep track. I poked at my phone for a while, then finally got out of bed to run myself an Epsom salt bath. After soaking in the tub, I finally felt like I could move.

Grammy knocked on the bathroom door while I was getting dressed. "How's it coming?"

"I fell in," I joked through the door.

She chuckled. "Do you need me to come in and rescue you?"

"Nah, I'll be fine."

"You sure?" she asked playfully. "I'll break down this door."

"I'd like to see that," I teased.

Grammy laughed. "Let me know when you're ready. Your ride will be here soon."

"My ride?" I asked through the door. "I thought you were taking me."

"I'll meet you there," she replied. "You don't want to miss the limo. It's a special opportunity for First Year students. Everyone looks forward to it."

I liked the sound of a limo, so I hurried up and got dressed. Twenty minutes later, Grammy stood at the front door with me. She picked a cat hair off my shoulder, then looked at me like she was proud.

"You're going to love college," Grammy assured me. "I just know it."

"I hope so," I said nervously. "This whole magic thing is really new to me."

"Pft," Grammy said, waving her hand. "You'll get used to it in no time."

"So… about that séance?" I said slowly.

Grammy's shoulders fell. "I know how hard this is for you, Nadine, but contacting your parents will be nothing short of emotional torture. I went through it with your grandpa, and believe me when I say contacting the dead makes it *much* harder to move on. I need you to trust me on this."

"I do trust you," I told her. I just wasn't sure I trusted her on *this*. It wasn't fair I never got to say goodbye to them. That was all I wanted.

Grammy glanced out the front window, and her eyes lit up. "Your ride's here. Now, remember, I'll meet you at the school to help you unpack. Have fun in the limo, and make lots of friends."

I chuckled lightly. "I'll try."

I gave Grammy a hug, and she squeezed me back tightly. I was glad she was meeting up with me later, because I didn't want to go through with this day on my own. I didn't take my bags with me, as Grammy would be coming with those later.

I stepped outside and walked to the end of the sidewalk, where a sleek black limo was parked. An old man dressed in a suit and cap bowed his head to me. "Miss Evers?"

I fiddled with the strap on my purse. "That's me."

He smiled kindly. "Welcome to The Hearse."

He reached out a white gloved hand and opened the door. I ducked inside and was shocked at what I found. I expected a few rows of seating and a couple other students, but there must've been a *hundred* people my age in there.

Holy crap! Inside, the limo was as big as a train! The ceiling was high enough for me to stand, and the red velvet seats stretched so far back I couldn't see the back window. It should've been impossible, since the limo only looked a dozen feet long from the outside.

The floor of the limo was all black carpet, and the seats ran the length of the windows. I could see houses passing by us outside, but the ride was so smooth I could barely tell we were moving. Every couple feet was a small table, and there were various counters with baristas behind them, serving up coffee and snacks. An *Evanescence* song played softly from the speakers. Students laughed and chatted with each other. Several people were stroking cats on their laps, or flinging strings around so the cats would chase them.

I noticed the Lucky Three a few seats down. They were surrounded by a big group of people and laughing like they were the life of the party.

No one noticed my arrival, except a girl with dark skin and black hair sitting closest to me. She was dressed in a trendy black skater dress, with red tights and high-heeled boots. She kind of reminded me of a gothic Princess Jasmine. Her nails were painted red, and her hair was twisted into braids. She obviously had a good sense of fashion, and there was this friendly, approachable air about her. She was all alone, and she smiled sweetly when my eyes met hers.

"Need a seat?" she asked kindly.

"Sure," I agreed. I sat beside her and glanced around.

"You've never been in The Hearse before, have you?" she asked.

I crinkled my nose. "That obvious?"

She chuckled. "A little."

"I'm told I'm a witch, but I'm a total magic virgin," I admitted.

She waved a hand and sat up straighter. "Don't worry about it. You'll catch on quickly. I'm Mandy, by the way."

Mandy? Could she be the girl I'd heard the Lucky Three talking about?

"Nadine," I introduced.

Mandy shook my hand, but she didn't let go right away. She turned my palm in her direction and looked down at it. "Wow, I love your hands."

I furrowed my brow. Was she hitting on me?

Mandy noticed my expression. "Oh, sorry. I just mean… I'm studying palm reading. I notice people's hands. Yours are really soft."

She ran her fingers over my palm. I should've found it creepy, but she came across as really friendly.

I laughed. "I'm flattered."

"Can I read it?" she asked.

My heart fluttered. I'd always wanted to get my palm read. "Sure."

Mandy inspected my palm closely. "Judging by the shape of your hands, you're really curious and have a lot of ideas, but you tend to worry a lot and are prone to stress."

My eyebrows shot up. "You're psychic, then?"

Mandy smirked, obviously proud that she'd hit it on the nose. "Nope. My ceremony's not until next semester. I just know my palms. The good thing about your hand shape is it means you're a good communicator, though you don't always share your feelings."

If she weren't a First Year, I wouldn't have believed she wasn't psychic.

Mandy ran her finger across one of the creases in my hand. "Your heart line suggests you fall in love easily, but your heart also breaks easily. If I'm reading your head line right, you're creative and spontaneous, and you love adventure. Now for the fun one…"

Mandy wiggled her eyebrows, but I was starting to get a little creeped out. So far, she was spot on.

Mandy touched the longest line on my hand. "This is your life line. Yours shows that you're tired a lot, but you're really strong. But—oh, no."

A shadow fell across Mandy's face.

"What?" I asked urgently.

Mandy sucked a breath between her teeth. "There's a circle on your life line," she said, and I sensed that was really bad.

I shifted in my seat. "What does it mean?"

Mandy's face fell. "It means you're either going to suffer a severe injury or be hospitalized."

I laughed, because it felt really ironic.

She furrowed her brow. "You don't believe me?"

"No, I believe you," I assured her. "It's just creepy how accurate you are."

Mandy looked uncomfortable, like she wanted to ask about my hospitalization, but she didn't. "Well, at least there are no surprises. Um… one more thing."

"What?" I asked.

Mandy cleared her throat. "I noticed your fate line is really prominent."

"What does that mean?"

"It means your life is controlled by destiny," she told me.

I tilted my head to the side. "You believe everyone has a destiny?"

Mandy shook her head. "Not everyone. But yours, Nadine… it seems pretty important."

We both went silent. Something about what Mandy said seemed really ominous. Mandy looked just as uncomfortable as I was, so she changed the subject.

"Since you're a magic virgin, it's my obligation to tell you to check out The Hearse for breakfast, lunch, and dinner," Mandy said. "And *definitely* visit after midnight."

"Why?" I asked.

She gestured around us. "In the morning, it's a coffee shop. At lunch, it becomes a café, and at dinner it's a fancy restaurant. It's at the witching hour that things get fun, though."

I leaned in, intrigued. "What happens at the witching hour?"

Mandy grinned. "The Hearse turns into a nightclub."

I bounced in my seat. "Ooh, sounds fun."

"Don't get me wrong," Mandy said. "The coffee shop is great, too. Come on, let's order something. Everything's free today on our ride to school."

Mandy and I stood and walked up to the barista. My eyes caught a vine plant wiggling on the countertop.

"Is that… alive?" I asked Mandy.

She chuckled. "All plants are alive, Nadine."

I scoffed. "Well, yeah. You know what I meant."

Mandy shrugged. "It's just a vitamort plant. Makes wonderful tea, but be careful. If you eat the leaves raw, it'll kill you."

I took a step away from it. "That sounds… dangerous."

Mandy shrugged. "Only if you eat it raw. What do you want?"

"Mm…" I continued to eye the menu. "A hazelnut cappuccino sounds good."

Mandy leaned against the counter and laughed. "Do you *want* to be awake for three days straight?"

"No," I replied.

"These aren't normal cappuccinos, Nadine," she told me. "They're made by Alchemists and infused with magical properties. You should try the vitamort tea."

"Didn't you just say it could kill me?" I asked warily.

"Not if you prepare it right," she said. "It's really good for nerves."

I couldn't deny that I was really nervous about today, so I went with Mandy's recommendation and got the vitamort tea. It was really sweet and had a hint of lemon to it. I finished it quickly and could already feel my nerves calming.

Mandy glanced out the window and inhaled a sharp breath. "We're here!"

Miriam College of Witchcraft was on the edge of town. I glanced out the window, and my jaw dropped when the campus came into view. A huge gothic structure stood towering three stories high. It was the kind of place that should be cast in a dark sky and a full moon, with the howl of a werewolf in the distance. Just one look, and I was already eager to get inside.

A large iron gate surrounded the property, with a thick forest behind the school. Inside the gates was an expansive lawn where groups of students were lounging under oak trees or playing Frisbee in the grass. A couple of girls sat on the sidelines and giggled as the Frisbee was sent off course. The guys started arguing about using their Mentalist powers unfairly, when it was clear from this perspective the girls were messing with them.

I was surprised to see how many cats were on campus—nearly one for every two or three students. If I had known we were allowed to bring pets, I would've considered adopting one.

The Hearse pulled up to the front of the school. When I stepped out, Grammy was already waiting for me with my bags at the front doors.

"Thanks for letting me sit by you," I told Mandy. "And for reading my palm."

Mandy waved her hand, like it wasn't a big deal. "No problem. Hopefully we'll run into each other soon."

"See you around." I waved to Mandy, then hurried over to Grammy.

"Did you have fun?" she asked when I approached.

"Yeah," I told her. "The Hearse was pretty cool."

Grammy smiled. "Told you."

"Come on, we're going to end up in the back of the line." I grabbed one of my bags and rolled it behind me. I could hardly get inside fast enough.

I stepped through massive double doors into a huge foyer two-stories high. Deep red carpet spanned the giant room and met up with a grand staircase painted in a black, glossy finish. Above our heads hung a black iron chandelier with burning candles on it. The walls were made of a dark wood and lined with beautiful sconces or elaborate mirrors. Everything was either red or black, and the lighting was dim, but I didn't mind. It was like we'd stepped into a vampire's lair, and I was down for that.

All around the crowded room were various plush sofas and chairs where students sat and chatted. One corner even had a huge fireplace, where a painting taller than me hung above the mantle. It depicted a beautiful woman wearing a corset dress. She had long flowing brown hair and beautiful bright eyes. Her skin was impeccably smooth, and her expression warm and welcoming. She was the kind of woman who you could go up and hug even though she was a stranger.

Grammy caught me staring. "That's Mother Miriam."

"Oh?" I asked, unable to take my eyes of the artwork. "She looks lovely."

I finally tore my gaze off the painting to look at the students. They performed magic out in the open like it was nothing. I witnessed someone conjure their class schedule and overheard one girl telling another her aura was off today. At the fireplace, a group of Alchemy students were cooking something sweet-smelling over the coals.

"This way, Nadine." Grammy led me over to a line behind the registration table. She stared straight ahead, like all of this beauty was an everyday thing. Meanwhile, I was still trying to take it all in.

"Is something wrong?" she asked.

I shook my head. "No, it's just that this foyer's so big. I'm wondering how much of the mansion is left."

Grammy smiled sweetly. "There's no shortage of room in this mansion. It was enchanted long ago with a space-bending spell to make room for new students. There's much more to this campus than meets the eye."

"Which Cast can do that kind of magic—the spacial thing?" I asked.

"All of them… and none of them," Grammy answered.

I furrowed my brow. "What do you mean?"

"When members of different Casts gets together, they're capable of extraordinary things— things we can't do on our own," Grammy said.

For the first time in weeks, I felt relaxed. "I can't wait to start classes to learn more about magic."

At the registration desk, they gave me a folder filled with information about my room, my schedule, and a map of campus. I also got a beautiful beaded bracelet that Grammy informed me was enchanted. It unlocked my dorm and acted like a credit card as long as I was wearing it. Every time I bought food on campus, the total would be deducted from my meal plan, which like my tuition, Grammy was paying for. Count me in on the magic credit card!

I groaned a little when I saw my first class was at 9:00 a.m. I wasn't exactly what you'd call a morning person. At least the classes sounded cool: Miriamic History, Demonology, Introduction to Tarot, and Conjuring Basics.

Looking at the map, I saw that Grammy was right. This place was *way* bigger on the inside than it looked on the outside. It was like an endless maze, one I wasn't sure I'd ever manage to learn. Great. The new girl was going to get lost on her first day.

"Come on, Nadine." Grammy cocked her head, and I followed her up the grand staircase, lugging one of my bags behind me. Grammy carried the rest of my luggage.

At the top, a huge, ornate window looked out over the forest. I glanced to the left, then to the right. Each hallway was identical to the other. They seemed to go on forever, as if someone had set up two mirrors facing each other. The same red carpet and dark walls from downstairs spanned in front of us. The walls were lined with beautiful sconces every few feet.

"The second floor is the dormitories," Grammy explained as she led me down the hall to the right. We weaved between other parents and students. Even though the hall was wide, there was so much foot traffic that it was a little crowded. "The first floor is where you'll find all your classrooms."

"Okay." I nodded along, but I kept my eyes on the doors as we passed by. Each was marked with a number, with the even numbers on the right and the odd numbers on the left. They started at 100. I was relieved to see that my number was 112. I didn't have long to walk.

When we reached my door, it was propped open. A haunting but upbeat melody played from somewhere inside. The beautiful noise spilled out into the hallway. I stepped up to the door and peeked inside. The room was bigger than I expected, with a huge closet and a bathroom right up front. A set of beds stood beyond that, with a couch between them. The furniture was all dark wood and smooth curves. Red drapes hung in front of the window and matched the bedding. I was pleased to see the bathroom had a tub, as I'd need that for my Epsom salt soaks.

A white cat lay curled up on the bed furthest from the door. In the far corner, a petite girl with brown hair, blue eyes, and smooth skin sat at a keyboard, playing the song. I noticed she didn't have sheet music in front of her, as if she was playing from memory. She looked up and stopped playing when she noticed Grammy and me in the doorway.

She cleared her throat, and her voice came out soft and a little higher than mine. "Oh, hello. You must be Nadine."

"Don't stop playing," I said quickly. "It sounded great."

She blushed a little and stood. "I was just practicing. I'm Talia, your new roommate." She walked over to the bed and picked up her cat. He stirred a little and blinked as she held him up. "And this is Gus."

I stepped further into the room. "Aw. He's precious."

I set my bags at the end of my bed and reached out to pet Gus. He nuzzled his head against my hand and purred.

"He likes you!" Talia said sweetly. She glanced behind me, as if searching for something. "Where's yours?"

"My cat?" I asked. "I, um, don't have one. Am I supposed to?"

"No, dear," Grammy replied. She set my largest suitcase on the bed and started arranging my clothes in the nearest dresser. "Cats are common in the coven, but not required. We believe them to be reincarnations of those who have passed on. Cornelius is actually your Grampy."

"Shut up," I told her. "He is not."

Then again, I just found out magic was real. Reincarnation wasn't totally out of the realm of possibility.

Talia furrowed her brow. "You don't know?"

I shrugged. "I'm new."

"Ah." She nodded. "That explains it."

"Explains what?"

"Why I didn't recognize your name. I know everyone in my class from high school. I figured you must've skipped a grade or something."

I shook my head. "Nope. Just new."

Talia's eyes brightened. "Oh my Goddess! You're going to love it here. First things first, we have to visit the Lounge. The restaurant there carries Barry's Enchanted Muffins. They're made by an Alchemist in town and can turn your hair purple or make you burp bubbles!"

I laughed. She seemed really excited to have a new person to show around. "That sounds amazing. Where's that at?"

"Downstairs," Talia said in excitement.

"I'd love to check it out after we unpack," I said. I noticed her bags were still full.

She glanced to them. "Yeah, I only got as far as the keyboard. I was going to unpack after my parents left, but the music was calling me."

"You're really good," I said as I started lining books up along the top of my dresser. "How long have you been playing?"

"Um, about thirteen years." She looked like she was trying to calculate it in her head.

"Wow." I'd never stuck with anything that long.

Talia shrugged. "It's always been a comfort to me. Ever since I was a kid, I struggled with reading because I'm dyslexic, but music makes sense. I can *feel* it. I don't have to worry about reading the notes."

"Wait," I said, glancing back at her piano. "You do all that without ever looking at sheet music?"

Talia offered a shy smile.

"Do you want this hung in the closet?" Grammy interrupted, holding up a slim black dress I'd never worn. I kept it just in case I ever happened to get invited out on a hot date—which would probably be never. She stopped in her tracks when she realized how short it was. "Good Goddess! You call this a dress? You'll bend over and everyone will see your cooch!"

"Grammy!" I exclaimed, covering my ears for show. Talia burst into laughter. "Don't ever let me hear you say that word again."

"Which word?" Grammy asked innocently. "Cooch?"

"*Grammy!*"

"Okay, okay," she sighed as he headed toward the closet to hang it up.

"I'll wear leggings under it," I promised.

It took another hour of moving around the room and giving introductions before we'd finished unpacking. Even though I'd paced myself, I was exhausted by the end of it.

Grammy picked up her purse and took a deep breath. "Well, I guess I'll leave you to it."

"Thanks for all your help, Grammy." I reached out to pull her into a hug. "I'll see you this weekend."

"I look forward to it. Bye, Nadine." She gave me one last squeeze, then turned to the open doorway.

"Oh!" Grammy whirled back to me like she'd forgotten something. "I meant to give you these."

She reached into her purse and pushed a pile of foil packets into my hands. I took them, not realizing what they were. She reached in for another handful and shoved them into my other hand, until they started falling onto the floor. When it hit me, I wanted to crawl into a hole.

"Grammy!" I cried, shooting a quick glance to Talia, who sat on her piano bench. She slapped her hand over her mouth and was trying not to laugh. She wasn't succeeding.

I turned beet red and hissed at my grandma. "Condoms!?"

Grammy shrugged, like it was no big deal. "You're in college. I want you to be safe."

"Grammy, I—I—" I couldn't find the words. It was too awkward.

"What?" she asked innocently. "You *are* going to be having sex, aren't you?"

"Oh my God," I groaned. Of course I was going to lose my virginity eventually—and probably in college—but couldn't she be a normal grandma and pretend I never would?

Grammy huffed. "Well, if you don't want them, give them back."

She reached for the pile of condoms, but I jerked away from her. Grammy raised a curious eyebrow. Talia could no longer contain her laughter. She doubled over, trying to catch her breath.

"I'll keep them," I told Grammy. "You know, just in case."

"That a girl," Grammy said proudly. "I'll see you girls later. It was nice to meet you, Talia."

"You too!" Talia called as my grandma left the room.

As soon as she was out of sight, Talia and I exchanged a wide-eyed look, then we both broke into a fit of laughter. I had to sit down on the bed, I was laughing so hard.

"Oh my God," I cried between laughs. "I can't believe she just did that."

"She's just looking out for you," Talia giggled, eyeing the pile in my hand.

"What?" I held them out to her. "You need one?"

She smirked. "Tell you what. We'll start a condom box."

"A condom box?" I asked.

She stood and bounced over to her dresser. She grabbed a jewelry box that opened from the top and turned to me. "We'll keep it stocked, and if anyone needs one, there will always be one handy."

I placed the condoms into the jewelry box, then leaned over to pick up the others that had fallen out of my hands. "Thanks, Talia. It's a good idea, considering you'll probably use most of them."

"Me?" she balked. "Uh, no…"

I snickered. "Then this condom box is going to last us a while."

She looked curious as she closed the box. "Wait. So you haven't…?"

I shook my head and quickly added, "Not that I don't *want* to. I've just never been in that situation."

"Shut up," she said with an eye-roll. "You're banging hot, Nadine."

I smiled. "Thanks, but I didn't have many options. I dated this guy in high school for two years, which kept me out of the dating pool. But it was just kind of puppy love, you know?"

For him, at least. I'd always wanted more, which made the break-up that much worse.

"Oh, I *know*," Talia said, like she'd had her fair share of crushes.

"Anyway, it didn't end well. He told me he was saving himself for marriage, but I guess he forgot about that when he fucked the head cheerleader."

Talia's jaw dropped. "He did not!"

My gut sank at the memory. Brandon made me believe he was saving himself for *me*. Nope. Just waiting for someone hotter to show up, I guess.

"Whatever." I brushed it off. We'd broken up months ago. I was over it. "I'm glad I never slept with him."

"Totally. I hope you whooped his ass," Talia said.

I chuckled. "I made a scene, all right."

In front of the whole lunch room, too. I dumped my entire milk carton over his head. Jackass.

I would've done a lot more had my friends not held me back. They had to remind me how much I'd regret it. I'd buried my dark side long ago. I wasn't the crazy bitch who started fist fights on the playground anymore.

Talia set the condom box on my nightstand and sat on the couch, leaning over the arm to face me. "I want my first time to be special, but like, I'm not the kind of girl who needs a ring first."

I laughed. "Me neither. Give me a loyal boyfriend, and I'll be good to go."

Talia made a crude motion with her hand and her tongue. I threw my head back in laughter.

"Oh, good." She gave a sigh of relief. "I was afraid my roommate would be a prude."

"Girl, you can make dick jokes all day long and it's not going to bother me."

"In that case…" Talia made another motion with her hands. I couldn't stop laughing.

A knock came at the door, which was still open. I leaned forward on my bed to peek around the bathroom at the door. A woman I didn't recognize stood in the doorway. She was at least my parents' age, with dark brown hair and hazel eyes. She wore a pantsuit and looked like she was someone important. A fat black cat followed at her heels.

"Excuse me?" she said kindly.

Talia shot to her feet and nodded politely. "Headmistress Verla."

Since I didn't know the proper protocol, I stood beside Talia.

Headmistress Verla smiled at the two of us. "Do you mind if I come in?"

"No, not at all," Talia said.

Headmistress Verla stepped into the room and extended her hand out to me. "Hi, Nadine. I'm Headmistress Verla, and this is Odin." She gestured down to her cat. "It's a pleasure to meet you."

I furrowed my brow. "How do you know my name?"

"I know all my students." She turned to Talia and said, "Talia Murphy."

Talia looked like she was going to pass out as she took Headmistress Verla's hand. You'd think she was meeting her pop star idol or something.

"To what do we owe the pleasure?" I asked. I glanced down to Odin, who was sniffing Gus curiously. Gus's hair stood on end, like he didn't like the other cat in his territory.

"I've come to welcome you to the school," Headmistress Verla said kindly. "I don't know if you're aware, Nadine, but I was friends with your mom. I know how hard things must be for you right now, especially after what happened."

Her expression turned sad. There was a genuine sorrow behind her voice that suggested she and my mom were very close, though I'd never met her. "I just want you to know that if you ever need anything, you can come to me. It's the least I can do."

"Thank you, Headmistress Verla," I said genuinely.

"Oh, please," she replied. "Call me Clarice."

Hold the phone. *This* was Clarice!? The friend from high school my mom always talked to on the phone? I'd heard so much about her.

She must've noticed the shocked look in my eyes, because she said, "I take it your mom has mentioned me?"

"Yeah," I said breathlessly, unable to believe I was finally meeting her. "She talks about you all the time."

It hit me that I'd said *talks*, like I still thought about my mother in the present tense. It was a hard habit to break.

Headmistress Verla gave me a smile, but it didn't quite reach her eyes. I bet she was thinking about how my mom was gone. I knew I was, and it was killing me inside.

Finally, she cleared her throat, and her eyes focused on me again. "I'm so glad to hear that. Well, I'll let you get back to things. I just wanted to come and introduce myself. It's great to meet you, Nadine."

"You, too," I said, feeling relieved that she didn't say anything more about my parents.

When she and Odin left the room, I turned to Talia. "She seems really nice."

Talia frowned. "Yeah. All the students love her. I just feel so bad for her."

"Bad?"

Talia dropped her gaze. "She's had it really rough these last few years. First she lost her sister. Then just a few weeks ago she gave birth to a stillborn."

"Seriously?" I asked, my heart breaking for her. I couldn't imagine. "She seems a little old for a baby, doesn't she?"

Talia shrugged. "I don't think it was planned. She's not married."

"That's still gotta be hard, though," I said. My guts twisted at the thought. She'd lost so many important people in her life in such a small amount of time. I couldn't imagine adding any more people I loved to the list of those I'd already lost.

"She said something happened to your parents?" Talia asked softly. It didn't sound like she was trying to prod, but rather make sense of what Headmistress Verla had said.

A heavy weight settled on my chest at the mention of my parents, so I sat on the bed to ease it. "Yeah. It was a car accident. That's why I came here."

Talia's frown deepened. "I'm so sorry, Nadine."

My breath wavered. "I don't really want to talk about it."

Talia's expression was soft, like she understood. "I could cheer you up."

I looked up to her and cracked a smile. I was glad my roommate was so nice. "You can try."

Talia sat on her piano bench and positioned her hands over the keys. Gus hopped onto the bench beside her and watched as her fingers began to move expertly, creating a soft, beautiful melody. I lay back in the bed, relaxing as I let the beautiful sound wash over me.

"This is the only way I know how to cheer people up," Talia admitted without missing a note.

"It's working," I told her.

"That's good."

She continued playing while I took deep breaths. My mind was on my parents now, which meant it could be hours until I stopped thinking about them. I loved them with all my heart, but sometimes it was easier to forget that they were gone. When I brought up their memory, a huge hole opened up in my abdomen, and it felt like it was trying to suck the rest of my body inside of it.

My head started to hurt, and my bottom lip quivered.

Suddenly, the music stopped.

"Can I help you?" Talia said.

My eyes shot open, and I pushed myself up in bed to see who she was talking to. I didn't get a look at the door before the voice came.

"I'm looking for Nadine."

That hole inside my stomach seemed to slam shut, and the tension in my head eased instantly. In fact, my whole body felt lighter as a fluttering sensation overtook my insides. Was that *Lucas* standing in my doorway?

I got to my feet and walked around the side of the bed where he could see me. His eyes seemed to light up, and the weight melted off my shoulders.

"Well, you found me," I told him. "Come in."

Lucas stepped into the room, followed by another guy I didn't know. Lucas must've noticed me eyeing him, because he quickly introduced us. "Nadine, this is my roommate, Grant. Grant, this is Nadine."

"Hey," Grant said, but his eyes remained locked on Talia.

Talia didn't seem to notice him, as she'd turned back to her piano and kept on playing. Grant smirked and stepped forward, leaning against the wall next to her.

"Well, *hello* beautiful," he said.

Talia didn't miss a beat on the piano. "Really? That's the pick-up line you go with?"

Grant stood straight up, looking shocked. "I'm sorry. Did it not work? Let me try again."

He leaned back against the wall and cleared his throat. "Did it hurt when you fell from heaven?"

Talia kept her eyes on her moving fingers. "Try again."

Beside me, Lucas chuckled. "Good Goddess, he's making a fool of himself."

"Really? I find it a little entertaining," I admitted.

Grant tugged at the collar of his shirt. "Is it hot in here, or is it just you?"

"Again," Talia said flatly.

Grant took a deep breath, like he was about to go in for the kill. "If I told you that you had a beautiful body, would you hold it against me?"

"No," she deadpanned. "Try again."

Grant groaned. "You're killing me."

Talia shrugged, but continued playing. "I'm going to make you do it again until you get it right."

Damn it. I loved this girl already.

Grant sighed, then stood up straight and spoke softly. "Hey, I'm Grant."

"I'm Talia," she introduced.

"Talia," he repeated, sounding pleased. "I couldn't help but notice that you're really talented. Is that *Dark Midnight* by the Wicked Warlocks?"

Talia glanced up at him with half a smile. "It is. You've heard of them?"

Grant beamed, pleased that she was responding. "Oh, yeah. I watched them play live last year."

Lucas leaned over to me and whispered, "The Wicked Warlocks are a local band."

"I figured," I whispered back.

"Have you seen them play?" Grant asked.

Talia's smile widened. "Considering my brother is their lead singer and I write half their songs, I'd have to say yes."

Grant's jaw dropped so low it was comical. "Shut up! Your brother is Tyler Murphy?"

"The one and only," Talia said.

"What would you think he'd say if I asked his little sister out on a date?" Grant asked.

"Smooth," Lucas mumbled.

Talia stopped playing, then looked up to Grant. "He'd probably castrate you for asking."

Grant's eyes went wide.

Talia snickered. "Good thing you don't have to ask him, seeing as I can speak for myself."

Grant relaxed and beamed at her. "So, what would you say to a date?"

Talia looked thrilled, but she was having too much fun. "How about we hang out with some friends first?"

Grant narrowed his eyes. "But, like, as a date?"

Talia laughed. "Let's start with this and maybe it'll turn into a date."

Grant shrugged. "I'll take it."

"Perfect." Talia stood and bounced over to her bed to grab her purse. "Nadine and I were talking about heading down to the Lounge to order some of Barry's Enchanted Muffins. She's never had them before."

"Sounds good," Grant said. He looked to Lucas for confirmation.

Lucas hesitated. "Oh, uh. I was just there and…"

He trailed off and looked to me. I was already reaching for my purse, excited about these magic muffins.

Lucas cleared his throat. "Never mind. Let's go."

We stepped out into the hall, and Grant took a right while Lucas went left. I followed behind Lucas, who kept walking without looking back. "This way, bro."

Grant whirled around and scrambled to catch up with us. "I swear to the Goddess, I'm never going to figure out this campus's layout."

"Is there anything that way, anyway?" I asked. "I mean, besides other dorm rooms?"

"No," Lucas said. "Unless you want to play Russian Roulette with the East staircase."

I tilted my head to the side. "What do you mean?"

"We call it the Vanishing Stairwell. There used to be a stairwell at the end of each hall, as well as the grand staircase in the middle," Lucas explained. "A few years ago, some girls in the room at the end of the hall wanted to expand their dorm, so they tried a space-bending spell. It clashed with the current spell and spread to the stairwell. Now it just kind of comes and goes."

"Huh. That's weird," I remarked. "What happens if it vanishes while you're inside?"

"Believe me," Grant said. "It's best to avoid it all together. Someone once got stuck in there for a month, and he starved to death. Rumor has it, he still haunts the staircase—when it appears, that is."

My eyebrows were raised so high I could feel the tension in my face. "Wow. Okay. Use the main staircase. Roger that."

The Main Foyer was quieter now that most students had been through registration. Lucas led us down the stairs and to a wide hall behind the staircase. He slowed as a pair of double doors came into view.

"Ladies, let me introduce you to the Lounge." He gestured to the doors and let Talia and me step inside ahead of him.

The Lounge was huge, with various walls sectioning off different areas. I couldn't see it all. The restaurant was straight up front, so I started for that first. Like the rest of the school, the lighting was dim, and there were various chandeliers that hung over the tables. It reminded me of an upscale bar, but without the liquor behind the counter.

There weren't very many people here. A large menu was hung above the main counter, so I assumed that was where we ordered. I couldn't take in the entire menu. There was a section of regular meals, then a menu of all different desserts that seemed to have magical powers—things like Glamour Gelato, Yodeling Yogurt, Slimming Sundae, and literal Humble Pie.

A girl with curly red hair who looked older than me stepped out of the back and up to the counter. I noticed the cauldron tattoo on her collarbone. Her name tag read *Darcy*. "Let me know when you're ready to order."

"Thanks," Lucas said. "We'll just be a minute."

"Is that Slimming Sundae for real?" I asked. Who wouldn't love to eat a sundae and lose a few pounds?

Talia crinkled up her nose, like it wasn't that great. "It only lasts for a few hours."

"In that case, let's stick with the muffins," I said.

Lucas stepped up to the counter. "We'll take a dozen of Barry's Enchanted Muffins. It's on me, guys."

"A dozen muffins?" I balked.

He shrugged. "They're pretty small."

The red-head girl turned to a rack behind the counter, where there were stacks of pre-packaged muffins. She handed the box to Lucas, who promptly turned and headed to an empty table. She never told him his total or gave him a receipt. It was like our bracelet-slash-credit-cards knew how much to charge to our account based on our order.

The four of us sat around a table next to a beautiful painting of a cat. Lucas sat across from me and opened the box. The muffins were bite-sized and all different colors. I didn't know which one to choose first.

"Try this one." Talia picked up one that looked like chocolate and slid it over to me.

"Talia, no," Lucas warned. "Maybe something a little tamer."

"What does it do?" I was intrigued.

Talia smirked. "Just try it."

I picked up the muffin and began peeling off the paper cup. I'd try anything once.

Lucas sighed. "Don't say I didn't warn you."

I popped the muffin in my mouth. A rich, chocolate taste filled my mouth, but it was better than regular chocolate, like I could taste the magic infused into it. Almost instantly, I felt this tingling in my chest. I looked down, then *bam!* My boobs were the size of watermelons. They almost ripped my shirt to pieces! My bra stretched tightly across the massive things.

"Talia!" I screamed, throwing my hands over my chest and ducking my giant boobs beneath the table. It barely did anything to hide them. If anything, leaning over just made my cleavage that much more obvious to the two guys across the table.

Talia burst into a fit of laughter. Across from her, Grant's eyes were glued to my chest, and he had his hand over his mouth as he tried not to laugh.

"My eyes are up here, buddy," I snapped at him, but it was all in jest.

Even Lucas cracked a smile. At least he was being decent and wasn't staring, though I caught him glance downward a few times.

"How long do these things last?" I asked. "I can't walk around like this all day!"

"They'll be gone in a minute," Talia assured me.

I relaxed a little. "Okay. Let's see what yours does."

Talia ate a muffin that looked like lemon-poppy-seed. Within seconds, her eyebrows started growing, until they formed into a single long, bushy unibrow. She leaned forward on one elbow and gave Grant a suggestive look while she wiggled her eyebrows. "Still want that date, sweetheart?"

He beamed. "Hell yeah."

She looked a little surprised and sat up straighter. "Well, let's see yours first."

Grant ate a banana muffin. I waited for something to happen, but several seconds ticked by and nothing changed.

"What does that one do?" I asked.

"I don't know," Grant said, but it wasn't in his own voice. It was at least an octave higher and sounded like he'd inhaled helium. His eyes went wide at the sound. "Dude, that is freaky!"

"Sing something," I encouraged.

"I don't sing," he replied in the comical high-pitched voice.

"Come *on*," Talia begged.

"Okay," he caved, then launched into a silly version of *Twinkle, Twinkle Little Star*.

Lucas rolled his eyes. By the time we got to him, my boobs had shrunk to their normal size and fit into my bra again.

"Your turn," I said, nudging him with my foot under the table. I didn't expect my foot to tingle at the contact, but it did. And then he looked at me, and my whole body was done for. It turned to mush. It was like he had this magic around him that did that every time we touched.

Lucas held up a red muffin like it was a shot and said, "Here goes nothing."

Except it never got to his mouth. He froze in place as his eyes locked on something behind me. I turned to see what he was looking at and found myself staring at three perfect girls strolling into the Lounge. They were the same girls I'd seen a few days ago—the Lucky Three. There was main bitch Chloe in front, followed by Gwen and Camille.

Talia frowned when she spotted them. "Not these bitches."

"You know them?" I asked.

"Yeah, we're in the same year," she said. "They were queen bees of our high school."

"Doesn't look like they've realized that doesn't make them king shit at the college," Grant whispered under his breath.

He was right. They walked in here like they owned the place.

Chloe didn't see us right away, as she had her eyes fixed to the front counter. But something must've caught her attention out of the corner of her eye, because she did a double take and looked straight at us.

Lucas groaned, but he'd already been spotted. Chloe changed course and started making her way over to us.

"Hey, Lucas," she practically sang, almost like the two had a thing. Judging by the way Lucas looked at her with disdain, whatever it was must've been one-sided.

"Chloe," he said politely.

"Why don't you introduce us to your friends?" The way she said it suggested that was the only reason she came over here.

Talia looked up to her with a raised eyebrow, which was back to normal now. "I'm Talia Murphy. You know me."

Chloe furrowed her brow and spoke with fake politeness. "Do I?"

Talia stared at her in disbelief. "Yes. We've been in class together since the first grade. I live on your street."

"Hmm…" Chloe mused. "I guess you just have one of those faces. You know, it blends in with all the others."

"On the contrary, I think she's beautiful and stands out," Grant growled.

Chloe looked down at him with a sneer. "Yeah, you would."

Whatever that meant.

Chloe turned her gaze on me. "I haven't seen you around before. And I know *everybody*."

"Apparently not," Talia mumbled under her breath, but Chloe ignored her.

"I'm new," I said.

"Huh. We don't get many new kids," Chloe shrugged.

"Well, we exist," I replied.

She glanced to Grant and turned up her nose. "Yeah, I can see that. I'm Chloe Olson, by the way."

"Mm…" I pretended to think. "Never heard of you."

She squirmed a little, like that bothered her. "And you are?"

"Nadine Evers," I told her, not really caring if she knew or not.

"Nadine Evers?" she repeated under her breath. "Why does that sound—wait! Are you Helena Tucker's granddaughter?"

"The one and only," I answered proudly.

Chloe's nostrils flared, like I'd just said something to seriously offend her. She slapped her palms flat on the table and leaned down to get right up in my face. She punctuated each word and spoke very clearly. "What the fuck are you doing in Octavia Falls?"

I leaned back in my chair, totally taken off guard. It was like she had something against me. I hadn't even done anything to piss her off yet… unless she'd seen me spying on her the other day.

Lucas shot to his feet and put a hand on Chloe's shoulder. "Back off, Chloe."

She slapped his hand away and whirled on him. "Don't tell me what to do."

She turned back to me, unadulterated hatred marring her features. I seriously had no idea what I'd done wrong. "You don't belong in Octavia Falls. You never should've come here."

I scoffed and crossed my arms. "Ominous, much?"

"I'm serious," she warned. "If you want to stay here, you won't go through with your Evoking Ceremony."

I rolled my eyes. All these basic bitches were the same. I'd handled them in the past. I could handle her. "Yeah, okay. I'll keep that in mind."

Chloe narrowed her eyes toward me, like she was trying to curse me with them. Lucas threw himself between us. "Seriously, Chloe, you need to leave."

She didn't take her eyes off me, but she started backing away. "This is far from over."

She whirled around, and her girl squad followed without a word.

I turned back to my friends. "Holy crap. What was that about?"

Talia shot a scowl at Chloe's retreating form. "No idea."

"She's just like that," Grant said. "I bet she's trying to scare you because you're new. She did the same thing when I first met her. She called me Hispanic scum."

I frowned. "I'm sorry."

Lucas sat back down, but he didn't take his eyes off Chloe, as if watching her for potential threats.

"Thanks, by the way," I told him. "She looked like she was about to curse my ass."

Lucas chuckled lightly. "No problem. She can't, though, because she hasn't gone through with her Evoking Ceremony yet. And if she did curse you, she'd get in trouble."

Something told me she'd find a way to talk herself out of repercussions.

"She's just threatened by you," Lucas assured me.

I gave him a skeptical look. "Threatened by me?"

He shrugged. "Yeah, because your grandma is such a powerful witch. Her family's powerful, too. Chloe's slated to be one of the best witches of her class. She doesn't want to lose her spot at the top."

I rolled my eyes. Like I said, all these basic bitches were the same. "Whatever. She has nothing to worry about."

Talia smiled. "Well, you already made the top of *my* list."

I reached for another muffin. "Good to know. I'll be sure to steer clear of Chloe from now on."

"A good idea," Lucas confirmed.

"Is this one any fun?" I asked, holding up a chocolate chip muffin.

Lucas smirked from across the table. "Will you still eat it if I told you no?"

I nodded firmly. "Absolutely."

I popped the muffin in my mouth, and my hair instantly changed to an I-don't-give-a-fuck bright blue.

"Ah," I said. "The perfect muffin to fit my mood."

Classes started on Tuesday, the day after Labor Day. Luckily, Talia and I had explored campus the day before, so we knew where our classrooms were. We had Miriamic History together, which I was grateful for, since I didn't want to attend my first class on my own.

The classroom was huge and set up like a movie theater, with big comfy chairs lined in rows. There must've been at least a hundred First Year students here. I noticed the Lucky Three up in front, but they didn't see us as we took our seats in the middle of the room.

"I'm totally going to fail this class," I groaned as I pulled out my laptop to take notes.

Talia scoffed. "You are not. What makes you say that?"

"Because everyone here knows all this history. It's brand new to me," I explained.

"You'll catch up in no time," Talia promised.

Our professor entered the room. He looked really old, like the history he'd be teaching would be told first-hand. His white hair was in stark contrast to his dark skin. He wore all black, including a silk black tie over a black button-down shirt. Though he looked ancient, he moved with grace down the main aisle until he came to the front of the room. The entire class quieted as all eyes turned to our professor.

"Good morning, students," he said kindly. "I'm Professor Richards, and this is Miriamic History. Welcome to your first semester at Miriam College of Witchcraft. Today, we will be studying the basics of our history. Later this week, we'll jump into more in-depth topics. There is no textbook in this class, so I suggest you don't skip my class, as you'll find it very difficult to pass your exams."

Professor Richards jumped into the lecture immediately. I rushed to start taking notes. "We're all familiar with Mother Miriam. She is the mother of all witches and warlocks within our coven, the very woman we are all descended from. The beginning of our coven starts with her story."

Professor Richards pointed his palms to the high ceiling. Small orbs the size of marbles floated up from his hands. They started out bright, then dimmed to various shades as he arranged them above himself in an intricate pattern. The orbs came together to form the image of a woman. Her face was identical to the painting that hung above the mantle in the foyer. It was clear he was a talented artist as well as a historian.

"Mother Miriam lived as a handmaiden in Europe during the fourteenth century," Professor Richard lectured. As he spoke, the orbs began to move to create a scene. The image of Mother Miriam began walking through thin air, performing chores like we were watching a play. "Her master was very mean to her. If she didn't do exactly as he asked, he'd lock her in the cellar for days without food or water. If she asked questions, he beat her."

The image of a whip came out of nowhere and slashed across her back. The orbs shifted quickly to make it look as if she was crying out in pain.

"You don't want to know some of the terrible things he did to her," Professor Richards said sadly. He took a deep breath and continued. "One day, she accidentally spilled a pail of water while doing her chores. He punished her by making her stand in the hot coals of the fire. The flesh burned clean off her feet."

Shudder.

"That night, she crawled from the house and fell to her knees, praying for someone to help her escape these terrible conditions."

The image depicted a woman on her knees with her hands folded in front of herself, looking toward the skies. My guts twisted as he told the story.

"She'd spent many nights praying to the gods, but they never answered her prayers," Professor Richards continued. "So instead, she summoned a demon to beg for retribution against her master. She was willing to do anything to escape his tyranny, including selling her own soul to a devil."

Silence settled over the room for a moment as we all took in the heavy weight of the story.

"A demonic god by the name of Santos appeared. As you all know, he is the father of all Miriamic people." More orbs floated up out of Professor Richards's palms and formed a second figure beside Mother Miriam. He seemed to look down upon her with mercy.

Professor Richards continued. "As he listened to her story, he became enraged. He traveled to the house of her master and killed him. It was after he sliced her master's head clean off his shoulders that he spoke his famous quote, *Even a demon would not be so heartless.*"

First of all, decapitation? Gross! Second, if this master guy was pissing off *demons*, there was a lot more about his treatment of Miriam that Professor Richard wasn't telling us. Part of me was curious to know, and the other part was grateful he'd spared us the gory details.

"In exchange for what he did, Mother Miriam pledged her soul to Santos, but he would not take it, for he felt she'd already given up enough to her master, that she didn't deserve an eternity in the Abyss," Professor Richards said. "To protect her, Santos remained on earth with Miriam, where they lived out the rest of their lives together. It was during that time that she taught him how to love, and they had five children together."

I gasped and leaned over to Talia. "Does that mean we're all part demon?"

She nodded.

Holy shit. Why hadn't Grammy mentioned this earlier? I had demon blood running through my veins!

"Each of these children had a different power," Professor Richards said. "With each child born, so was a new Cast. When Miriam died, Santos gifted her the power of the gods, and she became a goddess herself. Together, they formed Alora, our afterlife, and Mother Miriam became the sole judge of our people. Follow her, and you will be welcomed to Alora with open arms. Defy her, and you will be cast into the Abyss."

"The Abyss?" I whispered to Talia.

"It's basically hell," she whispered back.

"You have hell?" I asked.

She looked a little shocked by the question. "Well, yeah. Don't all religions?"

Touché.

Professor Richards went on to discuss the importance of Miriam's relationship with Santos and how together they had changed demonic principles that had been in place since basically the beginning of time.

"No demon, be it a demonic god or a lesser spirit, had ever created a utopia before," he continued. "It was the compassion Santos felt for Miriam that changed him, and her undying gratitude thereafter that helped them grow together. It was only because of their love for one another that they could create Alora in the first place."

By the time class ended, I had so much information to process.

"What is it?" Talia asked as we walked out of the lecture hall.

I shook my head. "I just can't imagine that kind of love—so strong and passionate that you can create an entire afterlife out of it. Can people really change like that?"

Talia cringed. "Don't let anyone else hear you say that. Santos's story is a beacon of hope for us. We believe in forgiveness and second chances."

I furrowed my brow. "But can't Mother Miriam kick you out of the coven as she pleases?"

"Yes," Talia confirmed. "But not without giving you a second chance."

I didn't know what a second chance entailed, but worry knotted in my gut as I wondered if that'd be enough—or if being an outsider had already doomed me for failure.

Lucas

SEVEN

The first week of classes passed by before I realized it. After Necromancy Safety on Friday, I waited until everyone else left the room before approaching Professor Warren.

"Lucas," he said brightly. "What can I do for you?"

I looked down to the positivity journal I clutched in my hands. My heart beat rapidly, though I couldn't explain why. This journal was *private*, and it felt like handing over a part of myself. I didn't like being vulnerable, but Professor Warren was my mentor. He'd said it more than once that he couldn't help me if I didn't help myself.

"I, um, wrote down a few things, if you wanted to take a look," I said.

He stood straighter, looking somewhat surprised. "Sure."

I handed over the journal. Professor Warren glanced at the first page, then flipped to the next to see if there was more. I hadn't even filled the first page yet, but at least I had a start.

Professor Warren didn't look at the journal long enough to read what I'd written. He closed it and handed it back to me, and I felt a weight lift off my shoulders. It eased my nerves to know he wasn't reading every entry. He probably wouldn't have made sense of what it all meant, either.

My gift led me to Nadine.

Muffins in the Lounge.

We met Talia.

Grant seems happy.

It wasn't sure if half that stuff counted. Technically, Grant meeting Talia had nothing to do with my gift, but if Professor Warren thought my gift led to Nadine—and meeting Nadine led to meeting Talia—then I guess it counted. Grant couldn't shut up about her since they day they met. He kept asking me when we were going to hang out with *the girls* again. I told him he had to give her time or he was going to suffocate the poor girl.

"I'm glad to see you taking this seriously," Professor Warren said. "I hope it's helping."

I shrugged. "I think so. I'm not sure yet."

"Well, we've only started," Professor Warren pointed out. "I want to see the next page filled by our next meeting."

I nodded. "I'll try."

It'd been like pulling teeth. I'd sat there for hours trying to think of one other thing besides meeting Nadine that my gift had done for me. It was only when I started playing off meeting her that the other ideas came to me. If I could tie everything back to that, I could probably have a page filled by next week—assuming things went well tonight.

"How have you been, Professor?" I asked.

He tilted his head in question. "I'm fine. Why do you ask?"

"You said you weren't feeling well the last time we talked," I reminded him.

"Ah, yes. I'm quite well now, thanks for asking. Whatever it was wasn't long lived."

"That's good to hear," I said. "I have to get to Afterlife Studies, but I wanted to keep you updated on my assignment."

Professor Warren nodded. "I appreciate that, Lucas. Keep up the good work."

I left the classroom feeling proud. None of my professors had called anything I did *good work*. In fact, I barely passed last semester at all.

Afterlife Studies was pretty easy so far. We were studying the many ways ghosts could communicate with us. We'd covered how ghosts speak to mediums, and we were moving on to Ouija boards next week. Later in the semester, we were supposed to conduct our own séance and write a paper about it.

After class, I went looking for Nadine, since I wanted to talk to her about tonight. I stuck my head into the Lounge, but she wasn't there. I considered visiting her room, but I didn't want to look overly eager, so I checked all the other common areas, like the pool and the foyer. Eventually, I headed outside. I swear to the Goddess my heart stopped when I saw her.

Nadine sat below a huge maple tree on the front lawn. Her back was leaned against the trunk while she typed on her laptop. She was wearing a black floppy hat with a wide brim that should've looked comical on her but was actually kind of hot, along with a dark long-sleeve shirt and matching skinny jeans. I thought she looked really good in all black. A gray tabby cat came up to her and started rubbing against her foot. She stopped typing to scratch it behind the ears.

I walked up to her casually, pretending as if I'd just been passing by. "Hey."

She glanced up, and a smile spread across her face. "Hey, Lucas. What's up?"

I shrugged. "I couldn't help but notice you were sitting alone. Did you want company, or were you busy?"

"No! Not busy at all." She shut her laptop and quickly gathered her books, then gestured beside herself in the grass. "Sit."

I took her offer and sat beside her in the shade. It was a beautiful day, and the lawn was crowded with people. "What's with the hat?"

She lifted her hand to touch it lightly, like she forgot she'd been wearing it. "Oh, uh, a fashion statement?"

I eyed her. She sounded unsure of herself, which was weird. I didn't know Nadine well, but she didn't seem like the kind of person who did things without a purpose. "A fashion statement?"

She wrinkled her nose, like she'd been caught in a lie. I found it kind of cute. "Okay, truth is, I don't like the sun."

I raised an eyebrow.

"I mean, I'm sensitive to it," she quickly added. "It's not a big deal."

She seemed like she didn't want to talk about it, so I changed the subject. "What are you studying?"

"Miriamic History," she said with a sigh. "It's a lot to take in."

I smirked. "Yeah, I can see that, if you didn't grow up with it."

Nadine groaned. "I told Talia I'd never be able to keep up, but she didn't believe me."

I chucked. "Who do you have?"

"Professor Richards," she said. "He's a great storyteller, but he moves so fast."

"Well, there's a lot to cover," I pointed out. "If you need help, I can slow things down for you."

Nadine's spine straightened. She was so excited that she grabbed my arm. "Really?"

"Yeah, why not? It's like, the one subject I'm actually good at."

"Shut up," she said lightly. "Are you serious? Because I have so many questions and I need to be caught up by next week."

"Absolutely," I replied. "Whenever you want."

"Are you free now?" she asked with bright eyes.

She had so much energy radiating off of her that I actually found myself smiling. I could tell I'd just made her whole day.

"Yeah, my classes are done for the day. I have a few hours until this party I'm going to tonight. But hey, why don't we study until then and you can come with me?"

Okay, I officially deserved some sort of award for slipping in that invitation so casually. I expected it to go a lot differently, mainly involving stumbling over my own words and fucking up the invitation.

Instead, Nadine smiled. "Yeah, that sounds great."

Score one for Lucas.

"So, what are you stuck on?" I asked.

"Just about everything," she joked. "Okay, so I get that the demon Santos saved Miriam and all that, but like, I don't get why he did it. He was a demonic god, so that makes him evil, right? How could he have any compassion for her?"

It was obvious Nadine was digging into things she didn't need to know for her exams, but it was a valid question.

"Demons aren't inherently evil," I explained.

Nadine tilted her head to the side. Damn it, she was so cute. "Then what makes a demon a demon?"

"Demon is a term for someone who lives in the Abyss," I told her. "There are a lot of reasons someone might end up there. Usually, they've either rejected their god or have been rejected *by* their god. Once cast to the Abyss, they usually band up with a demonic god and are gifted a set of powers to do that god's bidding. They make people do horrible things and turn them away from their religion so more people will join them in the afterlife."

Nadine furrowed her brow. "But Santos *was* a god."

"Right, but the other gods rejected him," I said. "All the demonic gods are outcasts."

"How'd he become a god?" she asked.

I was a little taken aback by the question.

She seemed to notice. "I mean, Santos made Mother Miriam into a god. Who made him?"

"There's more than one way to become a god," I explained. "You're either born a god or made into one by another god. Santos was a god at birth."

She looked more and more confused as I explained. "How many are there? Gods, I mean."

I shrugged. "I don't think anyone knows."

"So what makes a demon different from anyone else?" she asked.

"It depends on who they follow," I said. "Think of the afterlife like a big city, with endless gated communities. Each of these communities have rules in order to enter. If you don't pass or you leave, there's only one place left to go."

"The slums," Nadine said with a frown. "The Abyss."

"Right," I confirmed. "It's where the worst of the worst go. But it's just chaos—a constant war zone. Trust me, you don't want to end up there."

"Well, why don't all these demonic gods just go create their own communities?" Nadine asked.

I shrugged, wishing I had all the answers. "A lot of reasons, I guess. Some don't have the followers for it. Others want complete control and aren't willing to step aside and focus on their own people. Some are fighting their own wars with other gods. The whole thing is a mess, really. Anyway, back to your original question. You're right to assume demons are evil, because most of them are. But they're still capable of the same emotions we are. They just have to get past the bad first."

Nadine nodded, looking deep in thought. "I guess I can understand that. It must be hard for them, after being rejected and outcast like that."

Spoken like a true witch. No one else would show compassion for a demon.

"So, when people say we have demon blood, what does that mean?" she asked. "If Santos changed, does that mean he's no longer a demon?"

I shrugged. "Once a demon, always a demon, I guess."

Nadine glanced down to her textbook. "So, what happened after Miriam died? Like, to the coven, I mean? So far we've only talked about how she got her powers from Santos and they went on to create Alora."

I opened my mouth to explain, but I suddenly came up with a better idea. "Why don't I show you?"

Nadine's eyes widened in intrigue. "Show me what?"

I stood and reached out my hand to her. "It's a surprise."

She eyed my hand curiously, then took it and let me help her to her feet. She placed a hand on her hip and narrowed her eyes at me. "Just don't kidnap me, okay?"

I chuckled and pressed my hand to my heart. "Nad, I'm offended. I would never."

"Liar." She poked me in the side. It was the smallest of touches, but it made my insides flip. I swore to the Goddess, if she got any closer to me, my dick was going to give away just how I felt about her.

Shit. I shouldn't be thinking about that.

"Okay, okay," I teased back. "You caught me. I'm here to kidnap you. Are you going to put up a fight?"

She pretended to think about it. "Nah, I'll let you kidnap me just this once."

"Perfect. Let's go."

I helped Nadine gather her books, then led her outside the gates of Miriam College.

She hiked her backpack up a little. "Is it a long walk?"

I shrugged. "Not far. Less than a mile."

"Oh," she said flatly, but she kept her eyes forward and tightened her grip on the strap of her bag.

"Do you want me to carry those?" I asked.

"My books? No, I've got them," she assured me. "Tell me more about the coven's history."

"I told you," I reminded her. "I have to show you."

"Right," she said. "Then tell me more about you."

My body tensed. I didn't often talk about myself. There were a lot of things she probably didn't want to know.

"Like what?" I asked.

She shrugged. "I don't know. What do you like to do in your spare time?"

"Um, not much." Seriously, I didn't even know what I did with myself these days. Most times, I just felt like a shell of a human being. I'd rather sleep than anything, but Grant usually forced me out of bed and made me go outside. "I like nature, I guess," I admitted. "I like walking the Black Circle trail. Speaking of which…"

I gestured ahead of us to the trailhead that crossed the road to campus. "We'll be taking it to get where we're going."

"Cool." Nadine turned onto the trail. Her eyes went skyward, and she took in all the trees hanging over the path. It was really pretty out here, but I personally couldn't keep my eyes off her.

"There's a disc golf course close by that I like to play at," I told her.

"Oh, that sounds fun," she remarked. "I've never been."

"It's fun. You might like it." I didn't know why I said that, since I hardly knew her. "What do you like to do?"

She reached up to touch a leaf on a low-hanging branch. I noticed her pace slowed when she did it, and it never picked back up. I slowed my steps to walk alongside her. We were so close that we could've been holding hands. It was the first time I noticed that she smelled like roses, which I really liked.

"I like to read and binge watch TV, if those count," she said.

"No, they don't," I deadpanned.

Nadine shot me a look, and I couldn't hold in my laugh.

"I'm joking," I said. "They totally count."

"I do yoga, too, but not since…" Nadine trailed off.

"Not since what?" I asked curiously.

She sighed. "Not since I moved here. I really need to get back into it."

"Yeah, it sounds relaxing."

We walked for another ten minutes before we took another path and finally arrived. A small clearing spanned in front of us, where a massive, twisted oak tree sat in the center. Nadine's head tipped so far back that she had to hold her hat to keep it on. She stared at the tree in wonder.

The tree was huge and took five people hugging the base to reach all the way around. It reached up so high that you couldn't see the top when you were standing beneath it. The gnarly, twisted branches spanned so wide that the small clearing was completely shaded. The branches were heavy and hung low enough to climb onto them, though it was considered disrespectful among the coven to climb the tree. Huge leaves bigger than my hand fluttered gently in the breeze, and an assortment of acorns littered the ground. Several park benches were placed around the clearing. In the fall, the tree turned a rich, beautiful orange. It was the most beautiful tree in all of Octavia Falls.

"Wow." Nadine finally looked to me, and her expression was incredible. It was like I'd just given her the best gift in the whole world. "I've never seen anything like it."

"Come on," I said. "Let's sit."

Nadine seemed relieved as we took a spot on one of the park benches. She took her hat off and set it beside herself. The park was completely empty at this time of day, so we were alone.

"This is the Protection Tree," I told her, gazing up to its twisted branches. "It holds the power that fuels the protection spell around the town, which keeps out anyone who's not of Miriamic descent or preapproved into the coven."

"That's why it let me in," she guessed. "Because I have Miriamic blood."

I nodded. "So it sounds like Professor Richards left off with Mother Miriam's death?"

"Yeah, that's all I know so far."

"After she died, Mother Miriam's descendants spread across Europe," I told her. "A lot of them were accused of witchcraft, which led to mass hysteria and marked the beginning of the Burning Times."

"The witch trials?" Nadine asked.

"Right," I confirmed. "It lasted hundreds of years, and a lot of innocent people were burned or hanged for witchcraft."

Nadine dropped her gaze to her hands. She looked sad.

"The Miriamic people came to the States around 1600 to escape the trials," I continued. "But the trials only continued here. To protect themselves from further persecution, her descendants banded together and formed Octavia Falls in the early 1700s."

"Was that when the tree was planted and the protection spell made?" she guessed.

"The tree wasn't really *planted*," I clarified.

She tilted her head in question. "What do you mean?"

"The tree wasn't grown from seed," I told her.

Her eyes sparkled with intrigue.

"Ever wonder why we call our town Octavia Falls?" I asked her.

"I thought about it," she admitted. "Where exactly *are* the falls?"

I shook my head. "It's not *falls*, as in waterfalls. It's *falls*, as in a verb. Years ago when the town was formed, five priestesses came to this very clearing to perform the protection spell. But it was a very complicated spell, one that required the magic of four priestesses to flow through the fifth—the Curse Breaker. Her name was Octavia Barrows. The spell required more magic than she could give, and so she gave it all. Octavia fell right here in this clearing. The earth claimed her body, and out of her grave grew the Protection Tree, which activated the spell. She died to protect the coven."

"Wow," Nadine breathed. She looked back to the tree, and complete wonder crossed her eyes.

I noticed her shift a little. "What's wrong?"

She took a deep breath. "I'm still trying to wrap my head around all this. Some days I wake up and forget that magic exists."

I smiled. "Yeah, it's pretty cool, isn't it?"

Nadine looked up to me with those bright eyes, and I knew I was done for. I just wanted to reach out and touch her.

No. Yes.

Do it!

I didn't know what possessed me to do it. It just happened. I reached out and tucked a strand of hair behind her ear. As I pulled my hand back, I conjured a quarter, then held it up to her.

Nadine placed her hand over her mouth and snickered at me. She was obviously amused. "Oh my God. You're a real magician."

I rolled my eyes. "Warlock, but yeah."

Nadine seemed to relax as she dropped her hand from her mouth. "Thanks, Lucas."

I furrowed my brow. "For what?"

"For telling me about our history. It all makes more sense now. I just have one more question."

"What's that?" I asked.

A grin slowly spread across her face. "What should I wear to this party?"

It was ten o'clock, and I still hadn't spotted Nadine. The party was down at the lake, and the beach was packed, so I could've just missed her. But believe me, I'd been keeping an eye out. Grant and I sat in camp chairs close to the bonfire, and I'd been keeping watch for everyone who came and went from the parking lot. Music boomed across the beach, and the moonlight glistened across the water.

"Dude, you have to chill," Grant insisted, leaning back in his chair and taking a sip of beer. "They'll make it eventually."

I rolled my eyes at him. "Says the guy who just asked me for the third time in ten minutes if I'd spotted Talia."

We were both obsessed. Might as well admit it.

"I just hope they show up—" I started to say, but my words halted in their tracks when I saw her.

I'd told Nadine to wear a dress, since most of the other girls would, but I didn't expect her to come looking like *that*. My dick was practically trying to tear its way out of my jeans.

Fucking virgin, I chastised myself.

Nadine walked down the hill from the parking lot in a tiny black number that left very little to the imagination. It hugged her curves and showed so much skin—boobs, legs, and everything. There were even slits in the sides covered by see-through black fabric that showed the smooth skin along her torso. She wore her brown hair down in waves and fancy black sandals.

Grant stood. "Wow, she looks amazing, doesn't she?"

I was almost drooling. I swear I wasn't trying to objectify Nadine, but my dick kind of had other plans. It would *not* calm down.

"Yeah," I said breathlessly, rising to my feet beside him. "Nadine's really hot."

Grant elbowed me in the side. "Not her, lover boy. Talia."

I'd been so enamored by Nadine that I didn't even realize Talia was walking beside her. She was all dressed up and had on a dark pink dress, but she couldn't compare to Nadine.

"Hey, guys!" Talia called. She waved as they approached, then stopped in front of us. "Uh, Grant. You have a little something… there."

Talia touched the corner of her lip. Grant snapped his jaw shut and wiped the drool off his face.

I cleared my throat as Nadine met my eyes. "Glad you could make it."

"We're glad you invited us," she said, tugging at the bottom of her dress. She looked a little uncomfortable. I noticed Talia elbow her in the side. It was obvious Talia had made her wear the dress.

Out of respect, I forced myself not to look downward at her cleavage, which was fucking hard because her boobs looked amazing in that dress.

"Do you want something to drink?" I asked.

"Uh, no. I'm fine," Nadine said.

"Sure!" Talia answered at the same time.

Grant led Talia over to the coolers to get a drink, while I pulled up two chairs for the girls.

"Have a seat," I said. "The fire's nice."

Nadine took my invitation and sat. She crossed her legs, then uncrossed them, looking like she didn't know what to do with them. I quickly stripped off my hoodie and handed it to her. "Your legs look cold."

She blushed a little and took it. "Thanks."

Nadine draped the hoodie over her knees. I could tell she was only using it for modesty. I didn't want her feeling uncomfortable—ever.

Nadine relaxed into her chair and turned to me. "So, what are we celebrating?"

I took a sip of my drink and shrugged. I hated beer, so I'd mixed some vodka with soda. It wasn't very strong, though. "Do we have to celebrate something to have a party?"

Nadine smirked. I wanted to kiss the smirk off those lips.

Good Goddess, where had that come from? I wasn't even drunk yet. And I could *not* kiss her.

"Usually," she teased.

"I don't know," I said. "We're celebrating the first week of school, I guess. Ask Cody White. His parents are mega rich, and he hosts one of these parties almost every weekend."

She raised an eyebrow. "And no one gets caught? I mean, most everyone here is under age, aren't they?" She glanced around to take in the crowd.

I shrugged. "Everyone just kind of looks the other way, I guess. We won't get in trouble. Is that why you don't want a drink?"

"Oh, no," she said with a wave of her hand. "I just… don't drink."

I tilted my head a little to the side. "A witch who doesn't drink? That's a new one."

Nadine perked up as a new song came on over the speakers. Her eyes went a little wide at the upbeat tune. "Hey, I actually know this one."

I listened for a few seconds and realized what it was. I groaned. "Seriously? They play this at every party. It's getting kind of old."

Nadine poked me in the shoulder. "*Love Potion Number Nine* is a classic."

"You can't even dance to it," I argued. "And it's basically an insult to actual love potions."

"Oh, come *on*," Nadine said. "It's fun. And you *can* dance to it."

I raised a challenging eyebrow and leaned closer to whisper. "Then prove it."

Nadine pressed her lips together, contemplating my challenge. Finally, she grabbed my hoodie from her lap and handed it to me as she stood. And holy fuck, I was glad she did. I needed something to hide the boner that was quickly forming. When Nadine danced, it was like magic of its own. She held her arms in the air and got lost in the music as she swayed her hips from side to side. Her hands traveled down her body and landed on the side of her hips on the beat. She slowed her hips to make a circle as the song rang out its signature line.

Nadine winked at me as the song transitioned into the next verse. She moved in a slow circle. When her back was to me, she threw her arms out on the beat, then shoved them into her hair in the sexiest display I'd ever seen while she shimmied her ass in my direction.

Was she trying to turn me on? Because it was working.

Nadine glanced back to assess my reaction, and she totally lost it. She went into a laughing fit.

"Woohoo!" Talia called as she and Grant returned. "Shake that thang, girl!"

Nadine's face turned beet red, but she shook her butt one last time for show. She clammed up when she noticed she'd started drawing some eyes. She quickly returned to her seat.

"Hey, don't stop for us," Grant teased. "Some of us were enjoying the show."

"Well, it wasn't meant for you," Nadine shot back playfully.

Grant held up a hand in surrender. "Hey, I didn't say *I* was the one enjoying it."

I kicked him hard, though the girls didn't notice. I mean, he didn't have to blurt out my crush on Nadine and scare her away.

Though, maybe that was best.

"Forget it," Nadine said. "The song's almost over anyway—"

"What are *you* doing here?" a female voice sneered from behind us, cutting Nadine off.

The four of us turned to see Chloe standing a few feet away, though she wasn't talking to us. Camille and Gwen stood on either side of her, each of them wearing a matching look of disgust. Chloe was dressed in her usual attire—a dark dress and heels—and she was staring down a girl

I didn't know. The girl had light brown skin with red undertones, stick-straight black hair, and dark brown eyes. She seemed to cower under the weight of Chloe's stare.

"I, um, I…" the girl stuttered.

"I thought I told you not to come, you slut," Chloe growled.

Nadine's jaw dropped from beside me. Even I was a little shocked. Chloe was mean, but she usually kept her bitchiness in check around other people.

"You can leave me alone now," the girl said timidly, not meeting Chloe in the eye. "Ryan and I broke up."

"I don't care, Mandy," Chloe sneered. "It doesn't change that you slept with him."

Mandy's lips tightened. It was obvious she hated Chloe but was having a hard time standing up to her. "Yeah, well, that was his choice, not yours."

Chloe's hands curled into fists. She looked like she was about to start a girl fight. "Leave now."

Mandy's whole body shook, but she stood her ground. She lifted her head and looked Chloe straight in the eye. "Or what?"

Chloe didn't give second warnings. She raised her hands and shoved Mandy so hard that she stumbled backward and landed on the ground. Chloe reached down and grabbed Mandy by the ankle and started dragging her through the sand. "Then I'll make you!"

"Ow! Let go of me!" Mandy cried.

I leapt to my feet, but Nadine was faster than me. She rounded her chair so fast that it fell over, and sprinted over to Chloe, where she shoved her away from Mandy. I was only halfway there before Chloe was tumbling to the ground, kicking up sand.

"Leave her alone!" Nadine shouted.

At the same time, someone else had rushed over. She must've been one of Mandy's friends, because she helped Mandy to her feet like they knew each other.

Camille and Gwen turned their wicked gazes on Nadine. They looked like they were about to jump her. I threw myself in front of her, and they quickly backed down.

Chloe immediately recovered and pushed herself to her elbows. Shock crossed her face when she realized who'd tackled her. She pointed a manicured finger at Nadine as she got to her feet, like she willed a curse upon her or something. "You need to take a fucking seat, because this isn't about you."

Tons of people had stopped to look. Even though the music continued to play over the beach, and the bonfire crackled, all chatter had died down.

Nadine shoved her way past me to get up in Chloe's face. I wasn't going to lie, it kind of turned me on.

"Look at my face." Nadine's voice remained calm and steady as she pointed to her expression. "Does it look like I care? No. Because rule number one of the coven, we protect each other. So when I see someone being pushed around, I'm going to take a stand. That's what witches do. So maybe *you* need to take a damn seat and think about that for a minute."

Chloe's nostrils flared, and her lips tightened. It looked like the only reason she hadn't already punched Nadine was because so many people were watching. She held her head up high and said, "Bitch, this isn't even your coven. You're an outsider, and everyone knows it."

Nadine narrowed her eyes. "Oh, really? We'll see who the coven accepts when I'm the one standing up for them instead of beating them down."

"Okay," I said quickly, reaching for Nadine's arm. "That's enough."

I pulled Nadine away and stepped in front of her, creating a barrier between her and Chloe. "Chloe, this beach is big enough for everyone. Chill."

She narrowed her eyes at me. "Nobody asked you."

"Yeah, well, they didn't have to," I snapped.

By now, Grant was by my side, and Talia was right behind him.

Camille stepped forward and grabbed Chloe's elbow. "Let's go. This party's lame anyway."

Chloe didn't move for several seconds. She eyed me up and down, then shot daggers at Nadine. "You're not going to make it far in this coven. Sooner or later, everyone will see you for what you truly are."

"Fine with me," Nadine shot back.

Chloe turned on her heel and walked away. Camille and Gwen followed closely behind.

As soon as Chloe was gone, Nadine whirled around and went to Mandy's side. Mandy was standing beside her friend, looking relieved.

"Are you okay?" Nadine asked.

Mandy pushed her dark bangs out of her eyes. "I am now. Thank you."

Nadine offered a friendly smile. "It was no problem."

Mandy turned to the girl beside her. "Amy, this is Nadine. We met in The Hearse."

"Hi," Amy said with a wave.

"It's nice to meet you," Nadine replied. "Why don't you come sit by us?"

The girls glanced at each other and shrugged. "Yeah, why not?" Amy answered.

We found two more chairs for the girls and formed a circle not far from the fire.

"So, what's the deal?" Nadine asked boldly. "With Chloe, I mean?"

Talia leaned in a little closer to hear the gossip.

Mandy sighed. "It's dumb, really. I started dating her ex over the summer, and she's had it out for me ever since. We broke up because…" Mandy trailed off and looked to Amy.

Amy chuckled. "Because Chloe tried to turn her into a toad."

Grant's eyebrows shot up. "Did she really? How'd that go, considering she doesn't even have magic yet?"

Amy rolled her eyes. "She wanted *me* to do it, since I'm a Second Year. But I went to warn Mandy before Chloe could slip her the potion. It's how we met."

Mandy nudged her. "Yeah, and now you're not going anywhere. You're my soul sister."

"True," Amy replied with a smile.

"Anyway," Mandy said, "when I told Ryan, he laughed and said it would've been funny. So I broke up with him on the spot."

"That a girl!" Talia cheered, lifting her drink in celebration.

The other three girls joined in.

After about an hour, the girls were all getting a little tipsy, except for Nadine. But when Talia insisted they dance, Nadine joined them. The girls crowded around each other as they swayed their hips to the music. I just sat back and watched, because I wasn't much of a dancer. Plus, Nadine looked really nice.

"You gonna get in there?" Grant asked without taking his eyes off Talia.

"Nah," I said, sinking a little further into my seat. "You know how I feel about dancing."

"Bro, you need to get out and live a little," he insisted. "I want to see you smile for once."

"I *do* smile," I argued.

Grant looked at me sideways and spoke flatly. "Really?"

I suddenly realized how tense I was and that my arms were crossed. I dropped them to the armrests of my chair and sat up a little straighter. "Totally. See?"

I forced my lips into a smile, but it kind of ruined the mood. Forcing smiles was the worst. I'd been practicing it for almost a year now. You'd think I was a pro. But no. I hated it. But it kept people off my back.

"There you go." Grant clapped me on the shoulder. "Even though I can tell it's totally fake."

I shrugged. "Yeah, well, I wasn't trying very hard."

Grant looked back to the girls. Mandy and Amy were grinding on each other, and Talia was shaking her butt in Nadine's direction. Nadine threw her head back in laughter, then slapped Talia playfully on the ass.

"If you're not going to get in there, I am," Grant said eagerly. "See ya."

He gave me a salute, then stood and rushed over to the girls. Talia lit up when she saw him, then reached out for his hand. He spun her around, then caught her as she stumbled.

Fuck. I wanted to spin Nadine around like that. But I was a really, really bad dancer. I'd probably drop her rather than catch her.

Nadine shot a glance my way. I almost thought she was going to ask me to come join them, but she didn't. She smiled a little, then turned back to her friends. But that smile was enough. It warmed my heart in ways I didn't think possible.

I should just tell her I like her already.

The thought slipped into my mind before I could stop it.

No. I shot down the idea as soon as it came.

Friends was as far as we went. I shouldn't even be enabling that, but I just couldn't stay away from her.

I noticed Nadine's dancing slowed as the minutes ticked by. Her eyes kept darting over in my direction. I hoped she wasn't getting self-conscious because I was watching. Was I making it *that* obvious?

Eventually, she broke off from the group and came to sit beside me. She looked exhausted as she plopped down.

"Party pooper," she teased.

"I'm not a party pooper," I defended. "I just…"

She raised a curious eyebrow. "You're just…?"

My shoulders fell. "Fine. I'm a party pooper."

"I know," she chuckled. "But there's so much I *don't* know about you, Lucas."

"Like what?" I asked. "I'm an open book."

Mostly.

"What's your Cast?" she asked, like she was trying to figure me out.

It wasn't a secret. Everyone else already knew. But I liked the way she looked at me, like she was hungry for answers. So I decided to play with her.

"Guess," I said.

"Lucas!" She swatted my shoulder, but it was so light I barely felt it. "Unfair."

I shrugged. "You asked."

She eyed me up and down, like she was looking for my tattoo. Too bad she wasn't going to find it unless she wanted to strip me down.

Now that was something I wouldn't object to.

"Alchemist?" she asked slowly, like she was unsure of herself.

"No," I replied.

She pressed her lips together. "Seer?"

"You only get one guess."

"Hey! That wasn't part of the deal." She stuck her bottom lip out into a mock pout.

My gaze flickered down to her lips, and I started laughing. Damn, it felt so good to laugh. "You should've read the contract first."

She narrowed her eyes playfully. "Is this a sell-my-soul-to-the-devil kind of contract?"

"Do I look like the devil to you?" I teased.

"I don't know. You're all… mysterious."

I chuckled. "I'm not mysterious."

"You are! I still don't know your Cast." She paused for a second. "Or is that rude to ask?"

I shook my head. "Not rude. I just like watching you squirm."

Nadine squirmed in her seat for show, then said, "Seen enough?"

I smirked as my gaze flickered down to her cleavage. Damn it! I hadn't meant to do that. Not that I didn't want to, because Nadine was smoking hot. But I didn't want to be *that* guy.

"Not yet," I said.

Nadine went in to swat me again, but I grabbed her hand to stop her. Electricity sizzled between us when we touched. For a second, we both just sat there in silence, staring at each other. Her eyes were so soft, and she looked at me like she felt it, too. My stomach flipped in my abdomen.

Just friends, I reminded myself.

I dropped her hand before I let my feelings get away from me. Nadine cleared her throat and sat a little straighter in her seat. I noticed she was starting to look a little pale. She pressed her hand to the side of her face.

"Are you okay?" I asked, suddenly concerned.

"Yeah, it's nothing," she said softly. Her demeanor had quickly changed. "I'm just getting really tired."

It sounded like an excuse, but I didn't press her. "I guess it's getting kinda late. Do you want me to take you home? Back to school, I mean."

"What about Talia?" Nadine asked, glancing toward her.

"If she wants to stay, I'm sure Grant will get her home safely," I said.

"Yeah, okay," Nadine replied. "Let me go talk to her."

Nadine stood, though it looked like her knees were shaking. I didn't know why, since she hadn't drank anything all night. She made her way over to Talia and said a few things I couldn't hear, then returned.

"Grant's going to take Talia home in his car. Do you mind driving mine?" she asked.

"Not at all." I got to my feet and took Nadine's hand. My whole body lit up with nerves when I did. I didn't even know where it came from. It just seemed natural.

I was about to pull away and apologize, but Nadine leaned into me, like she was okay with it.

"Walk with me," she said.

I strolled alongside Nadine toward the parking lot. She pointed out which car was hers, then gave me the keys when I was in the driver's seat.

"Are you sure you don't mind leaving?" she asked. "I don't want to ruin any of your fun."

She had no idea I'd rather be right here in this car alone with her than anywhere else right now.

"You're not ruining any of my fun," I assured her as I shifted into drive. "I was ready to go anyway."

Nadine leaned against the door and stared out the window. "That's good to hear. You should wear your seatbelt, though."

I glanced to her for a moment, before turning my eyes back on the road. "We're just driving through town."

Nadine rolled her eyes. "You still need your seatbelt. It's like you have a death wish or something."

My whole body froze, and my hands tightened on the steering wheel. "I don't."

I said it harsher than I intended. She must've noticed, because she didn't say anything all the way back to the school.

"Lucas," she finally said after I'd parked. "Will you walk me to my dorm?"

"Yeah, of course," I answered before I could stop myself.

It was only when Nadine took my hand again that it struck me this might be some sort of invitation. How many times did I have to tell myself I couldn't get involved with her before I stepped away?

Too many, apparently.

But when we got to her room, she opened the door without inviting me inside. I was half relieved, but the other half of me really wanted to see what would've happened.

Nadine stood in the open doorway with her hand on the frame. "Thanks for making sure I got back safe, Lucas."

"Yeah, of course," I said. "I had fun tonight."

"Me too." She ducked her head and blushed a little. She paused for a few seconds, as if waiting for me to say something. Before I could come up with something clever, she said, "I'll see you later."

Disappointment washed over me. All I wanted was one more minute with her.

But instead, I said, "Bye, Nad."

And just like that, the door shut behind her and she was gone. My shoulders fell. It was like I could still feel her presence there, and I didn't want to let that feeling fade.

But eventually, I had to get back to my room. What would Grant and Talia think if I was still standing there pining after Nadine when they got back? Talia would tell Nadine for sure, and then she'd think I was a creep.

As I turned away from her door and headed down the hall, one thing became very clear. No matter how much I told myself I couldn't be with Nadine, my heart still wanted her.

I wasn't sure how long we had before I caved.

nadine
EIGHT

The party took a lot out of me. I loved to dance, and it was a lot of fun while it lasted, but I couldn't keep up the bright appearance forever. Eventually, I had to cave to my body's demands and admit it was time to call it a night. Lucas was like a blessing from Mother Miriam herself. He held my hand and supported me across the parking lot when I was getting too fatigued to walk on my own, and then he'd made sure I got home all right. I mean, he could've at least *tried* to kiss me at my door, but it was probably best he didn't. I might've passed out right there in his arms.

I didn't know why I didn't tell Lucas about my lupus. I guess I didn't want him to think less of me, like I was some burden who needed constant observation. Because I wasn't. I could handle myself. It was just nice to have someone around at times. And I was glad it'd been Lucas.

All I wanted to do Saturday was sleep, since I was totally wiped. Social outings did that to me. They were draining beyond belief, and it usually took a couple of days to recover. I lay in bed that morning, eyeing my yoga mat that was wedged between my bed and the nightstand. I thought about using it, but I couldn't find the energy. Gus was snuggled up next to me, and I didn't even want to lift my hand to pet him.

Across the room, Talia was picking out her clothes for the day. She glanced toward me and noticed I was awake. Her brow furrowed as she eyed me. "You okay, Nadine?"

"Fine," I lied. It was my go-to response, because it was easier than having people worry about me all the time. I still hadn't told Talia about my lupus either—not because I was hiding it from her, but it'd just never come up.

"Are you sure?" she asked. "I drank more than you, and I feel fine."

I took a deep breath. "It's not that."

Talia set her clothes aside and crossed the room to sit on the couch. She leaned over the armrest to look at me. "Did something happen last night? Between you and Lucas?"

"What?" I squeaked. "No. What about you and Grant?"

She shrugged. "Nothing happened, but I'm not so sure about Grant."

"What do you mean?" I asked. "He's nice."

"I don't know. He seems like he tries too hard. I don't really feel like I know the authentic him yet."

"I think that *is* the authentic Grant," I teased.

"I guess we'll see eventually," she said, before changing the subject. "Do you want to get some coffee or something?"

"No. I'm fine." I repeated my usual phrase without realizing it.

She narrowed her eyes at me. "You sure, Nadine? You seem tired all the time. Maybe you should see a doctor about it."

The comment was like a slap to the face. I knew Talia meant well, but she had no idea what I'd been through with doctors these past few years. It was like she thought I wasn't taking care of myself—and I was doing the best I could.

"I have," I snapped. I didn't mean to be so harsh. I quickly softened my tone. "I'm actually meeting my new primary care physician today."

Talia's eyes widened, and she sat straighter on the couch. "Nadine, I'm sorry. I didn't mean—"

"It's okay," I quickly assured her. "You didn't know."

She relaxed. "So, um…"

"It's called lupus," I told her.

My gut sank at the word, like it was some sort of curse. I always hated telling people about it, because they all got the same look on their face. The corners of their lips fell into a frown, and their eyes glistened. It was like they were watching a puppy being tortured or something.

Talia was shooting me the same look just now. I could see the moment her entire impression of me shifted. One moment, I was just Nadine, a regular girl with a thing for long baths and Netflix marathons. The next, I was this completely different person, a fragile girl you had to tiptoe around because if you made the wrong move, she'd crumble into a million tiny pieces.

"It's an autoimmune disease," I explained. "My body attacks itself. It makes me really fatigued all the time."

"I'm sorry," she said softly, like it was somehow her fault. "I didn't realize."

"Well, I didn't tell you," I said simply.

"Is there anything I can do to help?" she asked.

"No," I replied, before quickly adding, "I don't want you to think any different of me because of it."

Her shoulders fell. "Of course not, Nadine. What do you say I go down to the cafeteria and bring back some breakfast, then we watch a few episodes of that sexy vampire show you've been watching?"

A genuine smile crossed my face. "I'd love that, but there's something else I've been meaning to ask you about."

She tilted her head to the side. "What's that?"

I fiddled with a loose thread on the corner of my blanket. "What do you know about séances?"

Talia shrugged. "I come from a family of Seers, so I've done a couple. They're pretty easy."

"So you can do it before you get your magic?" I asked.

"It's like, the only thing we can do. Why do you—? Oh." Talia's face fell. She realized what I was asking before she finished the question.

"I just want to say goodbye to my parents," I said.

Talia took a deep breath, like the suggestion weighed on her. "This is up to you, Nadine, but… are you sure? We're always told not to contact loved ones unless it's an emergency."

I furrowed my brow. "Why not? If you have the power to do it, shouldn't you take advantage of that?"

Talia dropped her gaze. "Yes and no. Contacting someone once is one thing, but contacting your loved ones can become... addictive. It's not recommended as part of the healing process. It's taxing on you and on the spirits."

I couldn't believe the coven had this sort of power and didn't use it. "That's the problem, Talia. I'm *not* healing. I just want to see them one more time."

"It's more than that," she said. "Messages from the dead are ambiguous. You can't just call up the dead and talk to them."

"What do Seers do then?" I asked. "Don't they see and talk to ghosts?"

"Yeah, but they can't always choose who they see or who gives them visions," Talia explained. "When you do a séance, you're opening yourself to talk to anyone."

"Is it a problem if someone else shows up?"

"It can be," she said. "It's hard for spirits to communicate through words. More often than not, it's through signs and visions. Even Seers, who get messages more clearly, can't always make sense of them. Séances can be fun, but they're dangerous, too. It's like calling someone up on a shared phoneline. Anyone can answer. They could pose as your loved ones and use your grief to manipulate you."

My heart dropped. "I guess I see your point. But I still want to try."

Talia frowned. She looked deeply contemplative, like she wanted to help me but wasn't sure if she should.

Finally, she let out a breath she'd been holding. "I'll help you, but on one condition."

"Anything," I told her.

"We only do this once," she stated. "This is going to be really emotional, and I won't stand by and watch my friend hurt herself over and over. Do you understand?"

I nodded firmly. "I get it. Once and done. That's all I ask."

Talia's shoulders relaxed. "Okay. When do you want to do this?"

"The sooner the better," I told her.

She looked uncertain, but she walked over to the window and shut the curtains anyway, casting the room in darkness. "Let's get started then."

Talia had me gather my parents' belongings. I pulled a box out from under my bed, where I'd kept the things I hadn't been able to part with. I sat across from her on the floor and placed a photograph of my parents between us. For my mom, I chose her signature apron; for my dad, an old collector's license plate that came off the last car he and my grandpa restored together.

Gus curled into Talia's lap while she lit the candles. A chill traveled down my spine, and I swore I already felt an energy in the air that wasn't there before.

"Take my hands," Talia said softly. "Remind me of your parents' names?"

"Faith and Nathan Evers," I told her.

"You focus on them, while I call out their names," she instructed. "Deal?"

I nodded.

"Faith? Nathan? Your daughter wants to speak to you," Talia called out to the darkness.

I did my best to relax, but the more I thought about them, the heavier the weight in my gut became. I still couldn't admit they were gone.

But they weren't gone for good. At least, that's what I kept telling myself. I was going to see them soon. This *had* to work.

Talia continued to call out their names. The temperature in the room dropped, but nothing else seemed to change. I glanced around hopefully, expecting a spirit to be lurking nearby, but I saw nothing.

"Are they here?" I asked Talia.

She kept her eyes closed but pressed her lips together. "It feels like... like their energy is blocked or something."

My pulse quickened. I could practically taste their presence.

"Mom? Dad?" I called out to the quiet room. "Are you there?"

No response came.

I squeezed Talia's hands tighter, and the lump in my throat grew. I tried to picture my parents actually being here, and it tore a hole straight through me. "Dad, what do you say we play a game of *Clue*? Or maybe we can work on the Corvette this afternoon? Mom, how about a batch of cookies? We could head to the flea market and see if they have any of those old lamps you've been talking about."

Talia must've noticed the pained look on my face, because she said, "Maybe we should stop."

"No," I insisted. "We have to keep trying. Dad, if you're out there, please just let me know. Give me a sign."

Still, nothing came. My stomach twisted, and pain flared in my joints. I was starting to get a tension headache.

"Please?" I begged.

Then I heard it—the sound of my name. It was distant and distorted, but I swore it was a male voice.

I glanced around the room. "Dad?"

Talia's eyes darted every which way, but neither of us saw anything. She looked like she was holding her breath.

"Nadine..." Energy sizzled in the air like static electricity, and I heard a distant hum that seemed to distort the voice.

"I'm here, Dad!" I called out.

Talia gasped, and my gaze snapped to my right where she was looking. My heart lurched. A ghostly figure hovered in the air, but it looked like nothing more than a transparent smoky mass. I wanted it so badly to be my parents, but truth be told, I couldn't tell.

"Mom? Dad?" I asked carefully. "Is that you?"

"*Don't... careful...*"

The voice came in and out like we were tuning in to a distant radio station. I couldn't make out what they were trying to say.

"You're almost there!" I cried. "I'm right here."

The smoke swirled and started to dissipate. My stomach dropped to the floor.

"No!" I screamed, my voice cracking. "Come back!"

"*Sorry... go...*"

My heart felt like it was breaking into a million tiny pieces. That couldn't be it! My parents couldn't leave me yet!

"Don't go! Please!" I begged. My hands shook in Talia's. "I need more time—"

My breath stalled as the smoke disappeared and the room returned to its normal temperature.

"No," I sobbed. I turned to face Talia. "Bring them back! Please, bring them back! I didn't get to say anything I wanted to."

Talia's eyes shimmered, and she wore a look of sorrow. "I'm sorry, Nadine. I don't think I can."

I gaped at her. "That's it? That was all the time I got? I didn't say goodbye."

"I know, but we gave it our best shot," she said regrettably. "We actually got further than I thought we would."

"But we don't know if it was my dad." I let go of her hands and started gathering my parents things. "We'll try again. We'll get it right next time."

Talia shook her head. "We did nothing wrong, Nadine."

"We don't really know what we're doing," I insisted.

Talia sighed and wore a true expression of apology. "You agreed to do this once, remember? You'll always find another reason to contact them. Nadine, I really am sorry."

I blinked away the tears and wouldn't look her in the eye. I placed my parents' things back in the box and slid it under my bed. I wiped at my eyes. "I don't blame you. I just... I just want to be alone."

"I'm not leaving you alone," Talia promised. She helped me back into bed, then pulled the blanket up to my chin. "Let me know if you need anything."

I lay there curled in a ball. I stared at where the smoky mass had hovered during the séance, as if expecting it to return.

"I will," I rasped.

Talia left my side and went into the bathroom. I knew it was her way of giving me privacy without really leaving me.

I felt horribly sick that the séance didn't go well. It was as if a black hole had opened up beneath me and I was clawing tooth and nail just to hold on.

I suddenly knew what my grandmother meant by torturing myself. And the sad part was, I didn't know how to stop.

Getting to the doctor's office was hell. After the séance, I didn't want to go, but I forced myself to anyway. At least I didn't have to wait long in the waiting room.

"Nadine Evers," the nurse called, butchering my last name by pronouncing the *e* with a short vowel sound.

I stood and followed her into a long hallway with a bunch of identical exam rooms. She led me to the one on the end and gestured me inside. After taking my vitals and asking me a few questions, she told me the doctor would be in shortly.

I pulled out my phone to scroll through while I waited. It was usually a good fifteen to twenty minutes before the doctor came in. Which was why I was surprised when a knock came at the door less than a minute later.

The door swung open, and a man in his late forties stepped inside. He was good looking, with dark hair and a kind smile. He didn't wear scrubs like the nurse, but instead had on nice slacks and a black sweater. He reached out a hand to me. "Hello, Nadine. I'm Dr. Yonker. It's a pleasure to meet you."

"Hi," I said, shaking his hand. My grip felt weak, and it wasn't just from the flare-up. I was a little nervous about this whole appointment. Maybe as an Alchemist, Dr. Yonker had insight my other doctors didn't.

He sat in his chair in front of the computer and turned to me. "How are you feeling today?"

I shrugged. "Could be better."

My doctors were the only ones I didn't lie to about how I felt, because they might actually be able to help. The only thing anyone else could offer was sympathy, and I didn't need it. Plus, Dr. Yonker had this friendly thing going on that made me feel like I could trust him.

"Well, we're going to see what we can do about that," he said. "So, I heard you just moved here."

I shifted a little in my chair. I didn't want to explain everything, but he was my doctor, so he had to know. "Yeah. My parents passed away recently, and I came to live with my grandma. She helped me enroll in Miriam College. I've been having a lupus flare-up from the stress."

Dr. Yonker nodded in understanding. "I assume one of your parents is Miriamic, while the other is not?"

I furrowed my brow. "Yeah. How'd you know?"

He sat a little straighter in his chair. "Autoimmune diseases like lupus are very common among mixed children, though they don't all react in the same way. Some don't get ill at all."

Well, now it made sense why Mom pushed the doctors so hard toward an autoimmune diagnosis. She knew there was a chance I'd have it.

"When you're born, your magic is within you, but dormant," Dr. Yonker explained. "Your human side recognizes that magic as foreign and realizes something's not quite right. It triggers your immune system, usually in late childhood or early teens. However, since magic isn't a physical substance, your immune system can't find it, so it starts attacking your body."

"Do other magical races react the same way?" I asked curiously.

"Every society's magic is a little different," he said. "Their bodies react differently than ours."

So, witches were the only ones who had to deal with this shit? Good to know I'd been born into the wrong magical society and it was trying to kill me. But at least the coven had to have a cure.

"What can we do about it?" I asked hopefully.

Dr. Yonker sighed. "Well, we have a couple options—immunosuppressants, steroids, anti-inflammatories."

So basically everything I'd already tried. A wave of heat washed over me, and I held back from snapping at the doctor. Seriously? He had magic and was going to use the same drugs I could get anywhere?

"You mean, there's no potion that can help?" I asked in a small voice.

Dr. Yonker shook his head regrettably. "Magical healing works by enhancing the body's natural abilities inside of you so that you can heal yourself. Since your condition is a side effect of your magic, it will never balance out. Magical healing, however, is something the Miriamic Coven possesses in only small doses. Very few magical races have the power to heal on such a drastic level."

Great. What was the point of having magic if it couldn't heal me? Heck, it was *because* I had magic that I was sick in the first place. I was so frustrated that a heavy weight settled on my chest. I couldn't believe I'd gotten my hopes up for nothing.

Dr. Yonker's face fell. "I'm sorry, Nadine. There's nothing we can do until your magic awakens but keep you on the same medications."

"What happens when my magic awakens?"

He took a deep breath. Great. Sympathy. From my own fucking doctor. Could no one just treat me like a normal person? Was I walking around with LUPUS stamped to my forehead? *Hello, everyone! I'm hella sick. Feel bad for me!*

"In the Miriamic Coven, diseases like this often go into remission the more you use your magic," he explained. "You can train your body to recognize your magic as native."

I forced the lump down my throat, feeling my body lighten a bit. "So, once I have magic, it will act like a treatment?"

Dr. Yonker nodded. "In a way, yes. Symptoms will worsen at first, because your body will see the magic as foreign. Within a year or two, you'll be able to train your body to accept it. At that point, symptoms should go away completely."

"No more flare-ups?" I asked.

If that was the case, count me back in on the magic train.

"Most likely," Dr. Yonker said.

Relief washed through me. Dr. Yonker wasn't giving me a sure thing. There was no cure. And yet no doctor had ever given me so much hope in my life. I was always left hanging with, "We'll see what happens." To hear there was a treatment that could reduce my flare-ups was such a relief. I never thought it'd happen.

"In that case, I'll do whatever I have to do with my magic to get rid of these symptoms," I said.

Dr. Yonker gave a friendly smile. "I'm glad to hear that."

We spent the next half hour talking about my medical history. The weight gradually lifted off my chest as I told him everything. He was so different from my other doctors, who always seemed rushed and barely listened to what I had to say. Dr. Yonker actually listened and interacted with me, asking me important questions so he could get to know my case. He made me feel comfortable and at ease as I detailed my symptoms and concerns. By the end of my appointment, I was pretty sure I was in love with Dr. Yonker—as far as doctor-patient relationships went.

"Let's schedule an appointment for the end of the year, after your Evoking Ceremony," Dr. Yonker suggested. "I want to see how you're doing once your magic awakens."

"Sounds good," I agreed.

I could hardly wait until my Evoking Ceremony so I could start on the road toward remission.

"How'd your doctor's appointment go?" Grammy asked the following night when I came to visit for dinner.

"Really well, actually," I told her as I took a bite of casserole. "I really like Dr. Yonker."

"Good. He's a very talented Alchemist."

"You know him?" I asked.

Grammy gave me this side-eyed look. "Honey, I know everyone in my Cast."

"But there must be thousands," I argued.

Grammy tapped the side of her head. "I've got a great memory. Plus, he dated your mom for a while in high school."

My stomach sank at the mention of her. It was easy to forget Mom had a life before me and that she used to live in Octavia Falls. She never talked about her past, so I didn't know much. What hurt most was knowing she and my dad had no future.

The room went silent at the mention of my mom. Grammy dared to speak first. "You know what? I think I still have some photo albums of hers upstairs. What do you say we take a look after dinner?"

I wanted to tell her no. Acknowledging my mom's past was acknowledging the accident. It was easier to pretend it didn't happen.

But I didn't dare tell Grammy I felt that way. So instead, I just nodded.

Grammy finished her dinner quickly, but I poked at my food. Eventually, I finished, and I helped her with the dishes. Then she led me upstairs to a closet in the second guest room. She pulled out a big box and opened it. It was filled with at least a dozen scrapbooks.

"Wow, Grammy," I said, staring down into it. "That's a lot. I didn't know you were so into scrapbooking."

She grabbed one of them and flipped open to the first page. "It's nothing fancy. Come sit."

Grammy walked over to the bed and sat on the pink comforter with her back to the door. She patted the spot beside her, and I sat.

"Here's your mom at one month old." Grammy pointed to the first picture. It was a photograph of a baby in a studio setting. It didn't look anything like my baby pictures, though. The photo was faded, and my mom wore a frilly dress I'd never be caught dead in.

"She was really cute," I said, but inside, my guts were twisting.

"Of course she was," Grammy laughed. "She gets it from me."

I turned the page, wanting to get this over with as soon as possible. The next photos showed my mom in the grass, playing with an older woman I didn't recognize. "Who's that?"

Grammy leaned over to get a better look. "Oh, that's your great grandma."

I ran my fingers over the photo. "You look like her."

Grammy nodded.

"So, Mom *actually* got her good looks from Great Grandma?" I teased, trying to lighten my mood.

Grammy frowned. "Tread carefully, Nadine."

I laughed. "Right. Great Grandma got it from you. My bad."

"Now you're getting it," Grammy joked.

The doorbell rang, and we both looked up from the scrapbook.

"I'll get it," Grammy said as she stood.

I turned back to the scrapbook and flipped through the pages, but it felt like each flip of the page was another dagger to the heart.

She's gone, I thought. *This is all that's left of her… Pictures.*

Tears pricked at my eyes. I stopped on one picture where my mom must've been only a year old. She was standing on a step-stool at the counter, helping Grammy mix something in a bowl. She had a huge smile on her face, like she was enjoying herself.

I sighed. Mom had been preparing to become an Alchemist for years, and she'd left it all behind. It seemed really sad. It was hard to believe she gave it all up for my dad. Of course they loved each other, but she'd left behind her entire culture to marry him—

My thoughts halted in their tracks as a dark piece of fabric was thrown over my eyes from behind. I let out an earth-shattering scream as hands grabbed my shoulders and dragged me backward. My heart hammered against my rib cage.

"Grammy!" I shrieked.

No answer came. Oh, fuck! Whoever had been by at the door must've hurt Grammy.

I waved my arms and kicked my feet out, trying to get out of my attacker's grasp. My wrist broke free, and I hurled my elbow backward. It sank into my attacker's gut, and I heard them let out a pained *oof!*

Hold on. I knew that voice.

I stilled. "Grant!?"

"Let her go," Grant said in a strained voice.

The blindfold lifted from my eyes, and I turned to see Talia and Lucas standing beside Grant. They both had looks of amusement on their faces. Grammy was in the doorway, trying to hold back a laugh, while Grant was clutching his stomach.

"You've got a good swing," he groaned.

"Jesus Christ," I cried as I sat up straight on the bed. "What the hell are you guys doing?"

"We're abducting you," Talia said proudly.

I pushed my hair out of my eyes. "A little warning would've been nice."

"A warning wouldn't be any fun," Lucas replied with a smirk.

"What are you abducting me for?" I demanded.

"Your initiation." Grant's voice was back to normal.

"Initiation?" I looked to Grammy.

She waved her hand. "Go have fun. We'll look at the scrapbooks later."

Thank God! I needed a distraction.

I turned back to my friends. "Does everyone get an initiation?"

Grant chuckled. "Lucas did one for me, so I thought we should keep the tradition going."

"Why doesn't Talia get one?" I argued.

"I was born in Octavia Falls," she reminded me. "You weren't."

"Technically, I was, too," Grant said. "But I left and came back."

"Why would you leave?" I asked.

"My mom married into the coven," he explained. "When my parents split, my younger brothers and I left with my mom. I came back after high school to learn my powers."

"Dude, I miss your mom," Lucas said. "She was the best cook ever."

Grant chuckled. "Why do you think she opened her own restaurant?"

"Grant's a good cook, too, by the way," Lucas said, obviously for Talia's benefit. "His mom's family emigrated from Costa Rica, and she runs a Latin American restaurant. Grant spent high school working there, so he knows all the secret recipes."

"Well, you'll have to cook for us sometime," Talia suggested.

Grant's eyes lit up.

Talia turned to me and held out the blindfold. "Now put this on."

I groaned. "Do I have to?"

"Yes," Lucas insisted. "It's part of the ceremony."

"A *fake* ceremony," I shot back. I knew my friends were only trying to have fun, but they could've gone about it another way. My heart was still racing.

"Please," Talia begged. "It'll be fun."

I glanced to Grammy. She had this knowing look on her face. Had she been involved in planning this? Well, she should've told them abducting me wasn't a good idea. I'd have drawn blood if I had to.

I caved. "Okay."

"You have to wear the blindfold, though," Lucas insisted.

"How will I know where I'm going?" I asked.

Talia let out a fake evil laugh. "You won't. That's what's fun about it."

I rolled my eyes. "Let me at least walk down the stairs by myself."

Lucas nodded. "Agreed."

I took the blindfold and started for the door. Grammy stepped aside to let me through, but I leaned over and hissed at her. "No cool, Grammy. Not cool."

Talia heard me and patted Grammy's shoulder on the way out of the room. "She's a liar, Helena. You're the best."

"I appreciate your vote of confidence," she replied playfully. "Can't say the same about my granddaughter."

I didn't look back as I flipped Grammy off while I descended the stairs. Her laughter rang out through the house.

"Love you, Nadine," she called.

"Love you too, you traitor!" I said with a chuckle.

"Have fun." Grammy waved from the top of the stairs.

That was all I saw before Lucas took the blindfold from my hands and pulled it up to my eyes. My heart fluttered as his fingers brushed across my hair.

"You ready?" he asked, placing one hand on my shoulder. His touch sent tingles all throughout my body. I wondered what it'd be like if he touched me other places…

I cleared my throat, pushing the dirty thoughts from my mind. "Yeah, let's go."

Lucas kept hold of me as he guided me outside and down the porch steps. It was dark outside, so I couldn't see anything behind the blindfold. Lucas took my hand to keep me from falling. At the bottom of the stairs, neither of us let go of each other, so he led me across the lawn holding my hand. It was kind of weird, but felt natural at the same time. I felt a little light-headed and disoriented as we walked, and it wasn't just from the blindfold. Lucas's scent surrounded me, and all I wanted to do was sit under the stars while he held me.

I was getting ahead of myself. He probably didn't even like me that way. I wonder if he thought I was at least bangable. Apparently my ex didn't.

My thoughts were interrupted when Lucas spoke. "We're headed into the forest. Watch your step."

"Watch my step?" I asked. "I can't see a damn thing."

Talia snickered from up ahead. "That's the point."

I rolled my eyes, even though none of them could see it. "This better be worth it."

We walked for another ten minutes or so. The whole time, Lucas held me close so I wouldn't trip over anything. Grant was trying to flirt with Talia, but I missed most of what he'd said because I was so focused on Lucas next to me. My mind was fighting a fierce battle on whether or not I should ask him out.

Don't do it, the dominant voice argued. *It could ruin your friendship. What if he doesn't like you back?*

Screw you. I can do whatever I want, I shot back at the voice.

"We're here," Talia announced.

Lucas leaned over to whisper in my ear. "Sit down."

"What? Right here?" I asked. I could still hear the sound of the wind in the trees above us and feel the cool air on my skin.

Lucas guided my hand over, and I felt the back of a chair. It was soft fabric, like a camping chair. He helped me sit, then said, "Don't take your blindfold off yet."

Lucas's hand disappeared from mine, and cool air rushed in to take his place. I could hear the shuffling of feet and the soft rustle of fabric.

"What's going on?" I asked.

Nobody answered for a few seconds, until Talia spoke in an ominous voice. "You may now remove your blindfold."

I reached up and tugged the blindfold off my eyes. In front of me stood three cloaked figures. Their hoods shaded their faces, and it was so dark out that I couldn't see their eyes. I could still tell who was who by their height. Behind them, a fire burned in the forest, and a cauldron bubbled above the flames.

I couldn't take my eyes off Lucas, who stood on the right. He looked so mysterious. It was fucking hot. I just wanted to rip that cloak off and see what was underneath…

"Nadine Evers," Grant said in a deep voice, like he was trying to sound like someone else.

"Um… yes?" I said.

Grant cleared his throat. "You have been called by the Goddess to join the Miriamic Coven. How do you respond to this request?"

"Um, I accept?" I said it like a question. My friends were acting really weird.

Grant dropped his shoulders and spoke in his normal voice. "Nadine, come on."

I sighed and made my voice serious. "Fine. I accept."

"You will be gifted magical abilities unlike any other," Grant said in his deep voice. "But you must undergo grueling obstacles to prove yourself worthy. Are you willing to undertake the task?"

I sat a little straighter and played along. "I am."

Grant's voice grew in intensity. He was starting to sound like a drill sergeant. "Are you willing to do anything to serve the Goddess, no matter what she asks of you?"

"I am."

"Will you protect and serve the coven, no matter the cost?" Grant practically yelled.

"Yes," I replied.

The three of them took a step back and bowed their heads in unison.

"Then you may step forward and drink from the Cup of Life," Grant said. "Pledge yourself to Mother Miriam, and drink the blood that flows through her veins."

I stood and followed my friends to the fire. Inside the cauldron was a bubbly liquid that looked a lot more like soda than blood.

"Is this for real?" I asked.

Lucas pushed his hood back. "Consider it a perk of being friends with Grant. He has a wild imagination. There is no Cup of Life."

"Shut up and put your hood back up," Grant scolded. "We're not done."

"Can we be? Please?" Talia asked, dropping her hood. "I can't see under this thing."

Grant sighed and stripped off his robe, then tossed it aside. "Fine. You're all losers. You're no fun."

"You say that now," Talia teased, raising an eyebrow at him. She was totally joking about getting into bed with him. Once she stopped lying to herself about liking him, it was only a matter of time before that condom box was empty.

Talia and Lucas took their robes off and put them on top of Grant's. We all sat on the ground in a circle around the fire. Talia sat across from me, and Grant and Lucas were on either side.

Grant reached for the ladle in the cauldron and conjured a plastic cup in the other hand. He ladled one scoop of the potion into the cup and handled it to me. "The blood of Mother Miriam, in the Cup of Life."

"Wow," I said flatly. "I thought the Cup of Life would be… prettier."

Grant laughed as he ladled another cup. I started passing mine around the circle toward Lucas.

"Whoa!" Talia exclaimed, while everyone else froze. Lucas held his hands up, like he was refusing the cup.

I pulled it back toward myself. "What? What's wrong?"

Lucas relaxed. "It's customary to only accept a potion from an Alchemist. It's how you know it's safe."

"Oh," I said. "I didn't realize sharing was sacrilegious."

Talia snickered from across the circle. "I wouldn't go that far. It's just considered bad luck to take a potion from a non-Alchemist."

The way everyone looked at me, you'd think I'd just sacrificed a cat or something. I ducked my head. "Sorry."

Grant shrugged as he handed Lucas a cup. "You didn't know. Now you do."

I relaxed. "So, what is this anyway?"

I looked down at my cup and sniffed it. It smelled sweet.

Grant handed Talia the next cup, then sat back on his heels and smiled. "I call it Fizzy Bubbly."

I raised an eyebrow. "Sounds good, but that doesn't really answer my question."

"It's a little concoction I made myself," Grant said. "It tastes great without affecting your blood sugar."

"Is it alcoholic?" I asked.

"Nope," Grant said. "That's the beauty of it."

I didn't drink alcohol because of my lupus. Maybe this would be different.

"But it does have a little kick that'll make you tipsy after a few," Grant warned.

At that, Talia threw her head back and chugged her drink. She smacked her lips and held out her cup. "In that case, pour me another one."

Grant smiled. "Gladly."

I leaned over to Lucas. "Is it safe?"

He took a sip. "Would I drink it if it wasn't?"

"Depends," I said. "Are you trying to get me drunk?"

He smirked. Good God. I loved that smirk. "What would happen if I was?"

Hopefully a make-out session, I thought.

I brought the cup to my lips. "I don't know. Let's find out."

I figured it didn't hurt to try. I kept it to one drink for now just to be safe.

The drink was sweet, with hints of citrus to it. It bubbled on my tongue but was smooth at the same time.

"What do you think?" Grant asked after I'd tried it.

"Really good," I said.

Grant took a swig. "You're lucky. When Lucas *initiated* me, he made me strip down and skinny dip in Lake Santos."

"Lucas!" I scolded.

His jaw dropped. "I did *not*. You're the one who decided to go skinny dipping. You're all like, '*I'm such a fast swimmer. Look how fast I can go naked.*'"

Grant snickered. "Whoops. I forgot."

"Hey, that's a great idea!" Talia cried, lifting her empty cup. "Let's go skinny dipping."

"Talia—" I started, but Grant cut in before I could finish.

"That sounds fantastic. I can show you how fast I can swim!"

Lucas groaned. "Guys, I'm not stripping down."

"Good," Grant jabbed at him. "No one wants to see that."

"I do," I blurted. My face went beet red as all eyes turned to me. Lucas's eyes widened in shock. I tore my gaze off his and glanced to my drink, which was almost gone. "Holy shit. What's in this thing?"

Grant nearly died laughing. "That was all you, Nadine. I don't make my drinks that strong."

Talia stole Grant's attention by holding her cup out. "Can I have another?"

"You might want to slow down," he warned her.

"I thought you didn't make it *that* strong," I teased.

"Can't slow down," Talia said. "I need the courage if we're going skinny dipping."

"You don't have to," Grant assured her in a genuine voice.

She shrugged. "I want to. It'll be fun. I've never been. This is college, isn't it?"

Grant shrugged, like he couldn't argue. "It is."

As Grant filled Talia's cup a third time, Lucas leaned over to me to whisper softly. "So, you want to see me naked, huh?"

My gaze traveled down his torso. *Hell yeah!*

"It's the Fizzy Bubbly talking," I claimed.

"Doesn't make it untrue," he pointed out.

I took another gulp. It was really tasty and actually might've been making me feel better. "Perhaps."

"So what's the answer?" he challenged.

"Mm… I think I'm gonna keep you guessing," I teased.

He frowned. "Not fair."

"Totally fair," I shot back. "You didn't answer my question."

"What question?" he asked.

It was only a moment later that I realized I hadn't asked him anything. Tipsy my ass. Grant's Fizzy Bubbly was some strong shit.

I went for it anyway. "Do *you* want to see *me* naked?"

Lucas stilled, and his eyes flickered toward my boobs. I leaned over a little, making my cleavage more obvious.

"I'm, uh, not answering that," he said breathlessly.

"Why not?" I pouted.

"Because if I answered like a gentleman, I'd be lying."

Holy shit. He *did* want to see me naked! Every nerve in my body came to life as heat spread over my skin. This Fizzy Bubbly was seriously messing with my courage. I'd kiss him right then and there if he let me.

"Nadine..." Talia dragged out my name. I'd been so focused on Lucas that I didn't realize she'd come up behind me. She tugged on my arm. "Let's go."

I didn't take my eyes off Lucas as I shot him a smirk. The challenge was on!

"How far is the lake?" I asked.

"It's right down there." Talia bounced on her toes and pointed down the path. "Let's go!"

Talia and I ran off giggling. I glanced back to see if the guys were following us, and they were. They whispered to each other, though I didn't know what they were saying.

Talia's version of "right down there" was at least ten times longer than mine. It felt like we were walking for a mile before the trees parted and a clearing gave way to a rocky beach. Beyond that was a huge lake that reached nearly halfway to the horizon. It must've been a couple miles across. I was exhausted by the time we arrived.

"I'm going in!" Talia sang as she stripped off her top.

"Oh my God. Talia!" I shouted at her as she sprinted toward the water. "You're drunk."

"Am not!" she shot back. "I'm just having fun."

The quarter moon illuminated her silhouette. I caught a glimpse of her breasts before I quickly looked away. The guys were still in the trees, thank God, so they didn't see anything.

Talia squealed as she entered the chilly water, but it didn't seem to bother her, because she dove in a second later. Her head broke the surface, and she inhaled a big gulp of air. "Come on, Nadine. The water's great."

I glanced back to the trees. I could hear the guys' distant voices, but I didn't see them yet.

"Don't be nervous," Talia said. "I have a sister, and we shared a bedroom. It's no big deal."

I looked back to her, trying to work up the courage to slip my clothes off. It *did* look like fun. But we were talking about being naked in front of Lucas. It was one thing to dream about and another to actually do it.

"Quick!" Talia said with a laugh. "They're coming."

I decided to go for it. I kicked off my shoes and unbuttoned my jeans. They fell to my ankles, and I stepped out of them. I pulled my shirt over my head and reached for the waistband of my panties, before I heard a loud whistle from behind me.

I whirled around to see Grant and Lucas frozen at the edge of the trees. Lucas's eyes were glued to my ass, but it'd been Grant who'd whistled.

An involuntary squeak left my throat, and I suddenly lost all my courage. Instead of throwing my clothes back on like a normal person, instinct took over. I ran to jump into the water to hide myself, but I tripped on a rock and face-planted into the water. I inhaled a deep breath, and water filled my nostrils, burning my nasal passages.

I pushed off the shallow bottom with my arms, and my head broke the surface. I inhaled a greedy gulp of air. Suddenly, a pair of hands were on me, helping me out of the water.

I looked up to see Lucas's green eyes staring down at me. "Nad, are you okay?"

"Fine," I said, though I was still sputtering.

His hands left mine, and I sank deeper into the water so it would conceal me. My eyes traveled downward, and I started laughing. Lucas was standing in the water fully clothed, and his shoes were completely soaked.

"What?" he asked in alarm.

"You're funny," I giggled. Okay, the Fizzy Bubbly was officially hitting me. "It's not like I was drowning."

Lucas stood up straighter and shrugged. "Better safe than sorry."

I leaned into the cool water and floated on my back, then ran my hands through it to pull me out deeper into the lake. "You should come in. The water feels nice."

"Cannonball!" Grant shouted.

I glanced over, only to see a naked ass right next to me. Grant landed a few feet away from me, spraying water up into my face. I shrieked at the cold shock and stood up straight. The water came to my belly button.

Grant came up for air and wiped his eyes, then rubbed his tailbone. Thank God the water reached his hips. "Ow. A little shallow for a cannon ball."

"Dude, personal space," I snapped.

"What? You don't want my naked ass anywhere near you?" he teased.

"No, I don't," I said.

"I want it over here!" Talia called. She was low in the water so that it covered her shoulders.

Grant smirked and started wading through the water over to her. He stopped a good ten feet way to respect her space.

I turned back to Lucas, who was sitting on the beach and stripping off his wet shoes. "Are you coming in?"

"I don't want to get naked," he said.

"Come in with clothes on," I encouraged. "Like me."

Lucas sighed and rose to his feet. "If I *have* to."

He reached for his jeans and started unbuttoning them. Heat pooled between my thighs. Pretty sure I was making the lake even wetter than it already was. I couldn't take my eyes off him as he pulled his shirt over his head. Holy hell. He was toned as fuck. All I wanted to do was run my hands across those muscles. To kiss him. To… do other things to him.

Lucas stripped down to his boxers and stepped into the water until it was up to his knees. "There. I did it."

I rolled my eyes and swam closer to him. Grant and Talia were in their own little world splashing each other. They didn't notice Lucas and me.

"That doesn't count," I claimed. "You have to get wet."

He glanced down to the water beneath him. "I am wet. This counts."

"Does not." I splashed him, and the water landed on his stomach. Droplets dripped down his toned abs to his waistband. I couldn't help but think what *I* wanted to do to that waistband.

Lucas dropped his jaw dramatically, then bent down to splash me back.

"Hey!" I cried, wiping my eyes of the water. "I'm already wet."

In more ways than one. I was fucking swimming, and I didn't mean in the lake. Lucas was hot as hell.

"Turnabout's fair play," he teased.

"In that case…" I swam straight up to him and reached out for his wrist, then tugged him into the water.

Lucas stumbled and landed right on top of me. My heart lifted in my chest as his body pressed against mine. I didn't even care that my head had dipped below water. I'd hold my breath forever just to stay in this position.

Lucas's arms wrapped around me, and he pulled me out of the water. I pushed wet strands of hair out of my face and giggled. I couldn't help it. He did things to me that no one else ever had. I felt like I was floating, even though the water was so shallow that we were both on our knees.

Lucas didn't let go of me, even though I was no longer in danger of drowning. I figured it was some sort of signal, so I decided to play along. I wrapped my arms around his neck.

"See?" I said innocently, like we weren't sitting here in an intimate embrace. "The water's nice, isn't it?"

He stared down at me, never taking his eyes off mine. His chest rose and fell rapidly in shallow breaths. "Yeah, it is nice."

His gaze flickered down to my lips, then further down to my breasts. I inhaled, purposely lifting my chest out of the water a little so he could get a better look. In the cool water, my nipples were rock hard, though he couldn't see through my push-up bra. My mouth went dry as my eyes roamed over him. They locked on his lips, and my whole body felt magnetized toward him.

The Fizzy Bubbly had made me bolder than normal—a helluva lot bolder. I dragged myself closer to Lucas and wrapped my legs around his middle, until our bodies were pressed tightly against each other. Lucas seemed like he was in another world, totally oblivious to Grant and Talia's laughter across the beach as I drew closer. My hips pressed into his, and I could feel his erection through my panties. My heart was hammering so hard that I was sure he could feel it. I could hardly believe this was actually happening.

"You're so warm," I whispered.

Lucas's arms tightened around me. He licked his lips, staring at my mouth like he was in a trance. "You, too."

"Well, what are you going to do about it?" I asked.

His hands trembled on my back, like he wanted to move them across my body but was too scared. He swallowed. "I, uh, I…"

I leaned in closer. My breasts pressed up against him, and my heart hammered so hard it rocked my entire body. I didn't know how I could feel this way when we hadn't even kissed yet. All I knew was that I wanted Lucas more than I ever wanted anyone. It wasn't just because he was hot, either. I really, *really* liked him.

"You could kiss me," I whispered in his ear.

He shook his head. "Nadine…"

"What's wrong?" I asked. "Are you nervous?"

Then, because I had absolutely no inhibitions at the moment, I pressed my lips to the corner of his jaw. Lucas froze against me, his breath cooling the side of my neck. Testing his limits, I ran my lips along his jawline and pressed a kiss to his cheek. My pulse quickened. I was so close to kissing him for the first time.

Lucas closed his eyes and turned his head, until his warm lips brushed across the side of my face. He was so close to my lips that he almost touched them. My heart skipped a beat. I burned for more, to have his lips all over me, his tongue inside my mouth. I tilted my head toward him, anticipating the kiss.

But it never came. Lucas's eyes snapped open. In an instant, his hands left my back and pressed against my shoulders. My stomach dropped as he pushed me away from him.

Lucas gazed at me with sad eyes. His face had paled, and he looked like he was going to be sick. Because of me? "I'm sorry, Nad. We can't."

That floating feeling in my chest disappeared as a heavy weight came crashing down. What just happened?

I dropped my legs from around his waist and pushed away from him in the water. "What's wrong?"

Lucas turned away from me. He wouldn't look me in the eye. "I can't do this, Nad. It isn't fair to you."

"Wait, Lucas."

He stood and started for shore. My limbs felt so heavy that I couldn't bring myself to follow him. I thought we were having a good time. Wasn't he flirting back? Or had I misread his signals?

"Lucas, what's wrong?" I asked in a small voice. I barely noticed that Talia and Grant had stopped goofing off to stare at us. "What did I do?"

Lucas stopped on the shore to look back at me as he reached for his jeans. "Nothing, Nad."

My eyebrows knitted together as I searched his expression for explanation. But I couldn't find any. A thousand thoughts ran through my head. Was he not attracted to me? Did he already have a girlfriend? Had he promised Grammy he wouldn't get involved with me?

No, that was all stupid. So what was the problem?

I blinked a few times, feeling the weight of the rejection getting heavier. God, I was so immature. It's not like we were breaking up. We weren't even dating!

Lucas sighed. He dropped his jeans and stepped back into the water. He reached out for me. "Nad…"

I pushed off the bottom of the lake and swam around him. "Whatever. It's cool."

I tried to keep an even tone, but it didn't come out that way. "I didn't realize… I thought…"

I couldn't finish my sentence. Instead, I started toward shore, barely caring that my panties were on display for him. *Maybe it'll get him to change his mind.*

"Nadine, please," Lucas begged. "Let me explain."

"Lucas, it's fine," I practically snapped, though I didn't mean to. "We're just friends, and I'm not myself right now. Neither of us are. So let's just forget this happened and go back to normal tomorrow?"

It wasn't true. I was being myself, just with a little extra courage. I *wanted* the kiss to happen —and so much more. I was stupid and crazy. There was still so much I didn't know about him —which incidentally only drew me closer. I wanted to know it all.

Lucas stared at me like a deer in the headlights. "Nad, I just don't think—"

"You don't owe me an explanation," I said as I started pulling on my clothes. I didn't know why I told him that, considering an explanation was all I wanted. I just wasn't sure I could hear it right now. What if it was worse than I was thinking?

"If that's what you want," Lucas said softly.

It wasn't, but I nodded anyway.

Talia and Grant had come to the shallow end, though they kept their distance from each other.

"Hey, guys," Talia said softly. "What happened?"

"Nothing," I told her as I put my shoes on. "I think it's time to go."

"Yeah, sure." Talia sounded more like herself now. "Can you toss me my clothes?"

I gathered her clothes and held them out to her where she was crouched down in the shallow end. The guys turned their eyes away as she got out of the water and started to dress. I averted my eyes out of respect.

The whole time, I couldn't stop replaying what had just happened in my mind. It was obvious Lucas and I had chemistry. He clearly wanted to kiss me back, and yet he insisted on pushing me away. The only explanation I could think of was that Lucas was playing some sort of game with me.

A game that I was going to win.

I hated my fucking gift. I had Nadine in my arms. I was going to kiss her. If we'd been alone, we probably would've gone a lot further, too. The second my lips touched her cheek, the nausea hit, and a thought from the recently departed came to me, shattering the moment.

"We were never right for each other," the female voice said. She sounded younger than most, but I didn't want to think about how she died. I hoped it was an accident, but there was a hint of fear in her voice that suggested something more was going on.

And that chilled me to the bone. What if it was some sort of sign? I had to admit, it couldn't have come at a worse time. It was like a reminder that I wasn't any good for Nadine. And so I pushed her away, because if I let this happen once, I didn't think I could ever stop. She deserved better than me—better than someone whose mere existence could hurt her in ways I couldn't imagine.

So as much as it killed me to do, I kept my distance from her.

It was literal torture. I didn't know why, but when I was around Nadine, the weight of my gift seemed to ease. Now that I was avoiding her, it seemed to weigh heavier and heavier.

The voice I'd heard at the lake ended up being a woman named Emily Robinson, who'd died after being pushed down the stairs. The jackass who'd pushed her had already been arrested, but that didn't bring me much peace from the thought, if any. That one stuck with me for days, because every time I pictured the girl, I saw my mom. I'd even called Mom to check up on her, and she assured me she was fine. I wasn't sure I believed her.

Over the next few days, the nausea grew worse. On Thursday after lunch, I was taking a piss at the urinal when another thought struck.

"Is it playtime?" a child's voice whispered in my mind.

Though it was quiet, the weight of the thought crashed down on me like a tidal wave. I swayed on my feet, spraying urine all over the floor. I quickly shoved my dick back inside my pants, then made a beeline for the stall behind me. I fell to my knees so quickly that a sharp pain shot up through my legs. But I barely noticed as my attention was stolen by the ache in my gut. It felt as if someone had stuck a fork into my stomach and twisted my intestines around like spaghetti. I hunched over the toilet, waiting for my lunch to come back up, but all that came out were dry heaves.

"Shit," I groaned as I curled up into a ball on the floor. I was hot all over, but freezing cold at the same time. A sheen of sweat covered my body, and I shivered. The child's voice just kept echoing over and over again in my mind.

"Is it playtime? Is it playtime?"

Fuck, the kid didn't even know he was going to die. I wish I could've taken his place.

No! You're not allowed to think like that, I reminded myself. In times like this, it was difficult not to.

It took another half hour for the nausea to pass, which was unusual. Usually it was gone in only a few minutes. I pushed myself up off the cold tile, my arms shaking. Taking a deep breath, I leaned my head back against the stall door, waiting for the last of it to fade. Eventually, I felt like I could move again, so I conjured my journal and added the thought to it. I wished I could've added something to the positivity journal Professor Warren was forcing me to make, but all I wanted to do was rip the pages out of it and tell him to go screw himself. Listening to little kids die was the furthest thing from what I'd call a *gift*.

I did a quick scroll through my social media accounts to see if anyone had reported on the death yet, but it was too soon. My stomach sank when I noticed the time on my phone. I only had a few minutes to get to my Introduction to Incantations class.

Ugh. I forced myself to my feet—I was a little shaky, but stable—then started for my Incantations classroom. I took a seat in the back row of the lecture hall, so I could slip out easily if the nausea hit again. I spotted Ryan and the other Tarantulas sitting toward the middle of the room. They were laughing loudly and shooting spitballs through a straw.

Our professor walked in just as one of the balls was flying toward the front. She waved her hand, and the spit wad changed course and snapped back in the direction of the Tarantulas. It landed square on Ryan's forehead. He swatted it away and mumbled a few crude words about Professor Loren under his breath.

Professor Loren strolled to the front of the room without even glancing back at Ryan. She was an older woman with long silver hair who frequently wore flowing black dresses. She was wise and pretty much knew everything about everything—and she didn't take anyone's shit. Everyone really loved her classes, unless they were the one causing trouble.

"Last week, we covered basic incantations all witches and warlocks should know," Professor Loren began her lecture. For a woman as old as dirt, she had a surprisingly strong voice that projected all throughout the lecture hall. "You've learned basic defensive magic, like stunning spells."

Nolan, one of the Tarantulas, raised his voice. "When do we learn battle orbs and shields?"

Professor Loren frowned. "Not until you're much more mature with your magic, Mister Kowalski. Those spells are far too advanced for this class."

She turned toward the other side of the room, ignoring him. "Today, we will be talking about the theory behind incantations. Why do you think incantations work for all Casts and not just a select few?"

Felicia Green's hand shot up at the front of the room. She was in all my classes last semester and always had an answer for everything. She was the real Hermione Granger of Miriam College. She was pretty, with long blonde curls and nice skin, but her lack of humility left a lot to be desired.

"Yes, Miss Green?" Professor Loren called on her.

Felicia spoke like she was reading out of a textbook. "Incantations are universal to all Casts, because the *tasks* generated by them are universal. Incantation magic comes not from the incantation itself, but from within you."

"Exactly," Professor Loren said proudly.

Ryan leaned forward in his seat and shot another spit wad at the back of Felicia's head. Her hand slapped over it, and she whirled around to shoot daggers Ryan's way. "Do that again, and I'll incant your ass all the way to the Abyss, dickhole."

A chorus of *oohs* traveled around the room. I couldn't see Ryan's face from here, but he sounded amused. "Savage, Felicia. I like it. You wanna take the trip with me?"

"Screw you," she spat.

"Yeah, I bet you'd like to," Ryan teased.

Felicia shot him a look of disdain before turning back around in her seat.

"Let's behave ourselves," Professor Loren scolded. "You're not children anymore, for Alora's sake!"

Ryan leaned back in his chair, and his buddies laughed around him. What a fucking loser.

Professor Loren turned away from them and continued her lecture. "Incantations serve to alter your mindset. Later in the semester, we'll be writing our own incantations for simple tasks. By the end of your senior year, you should be able to perform the same tasks without incantations at all."

Felicia's hand shot into the air again, and the Tarantulas shared a collective groan. "What about group spells? Isn't it dangerous to try them without an incantation?"

"Yes," Professor Loren responded. "We'll be getting to that unit later in the semester, but since you asked, I will warn you all that group spells should always use incantations. It's the only way to ensure you're all on the same page. If not, your magic could clash. Any other questions?"

Another hand raised at the far corner of the front row.

"Yes, Mister Walker?" Professor Loren said.

Gregory Walker was a straight-A student like Felicia. If the school had some sort of geek squad, they'd both be on it. Gregory was a tall, skinny guy with a long neck and glasses. His hair stood up in all directions. I wasn't sure if it was some sort of fashion statement or what, but it looked like a mess.

"What about curses?" Gregory asked. "Can those be cast through incantations?"

Professor Loren's face fell. "Curses are very dangerous, Mister Walker."

"It's all theoretical, of course," Gregory quickly clarified.

Professor Loren's lips pressed into a thin line. Finally, she spoke softly. "A curse—or a spell cast with malicious intent, to hurt someone else—can be cast through incantations. However, curses are difficult to cast. They stem from hatred and very deep, terrible emotions. Curses are against Miriamic law. Since the Curse Breakers died out, there isn't a witch or warlock in the world who can break them. It's best if you never utter a curse at all."

Everything in the room seemed to come to a chilling halt. It was so quiet I couldn't even hear the people beside me breathing.

After a moment, Professor Loren cleared her throat and returned to her lecture. She covered things I already knew, so I took to ignoring her. Instead, I conjured my positivity journal and opened up to the first page. That child's voice was still nagging at me. Maybe if I could find the positive in it, it wouldn't hurt so bad.

I sat there the rest of class, staring down at a blank line on the page and waiting for something to come to me. But nothing did. I was so engrossed in my own little world that I didn't even realize when class ended. Ryan and his gang were headed out of the lecture hall when he stopped beside me.

"What's this, Taylor?" he asked in a harsh tone.

My gaze snapped upward to see him peering down at me. His massive arms were crossed over his chest, and he looked like he was about to start something. I bet he needed to let out some of his anger after Felicia called him out in class. And I was an easy target.

I brushed the hair out of my eyes. "Nothing. Get lost."

"Nothing, huh?" Ryan pressed. "Then why don't you let me see it?"

Before I could jab back, his hand shot out and snatched the journal out from under my hands. I was on my feet in a second, reaching for it. "Give it back!"

Ryan shoved an arm in my direction, holding me back. Using his magic, he made the journal hover just out of my reach, while he commanded the empty pages to flip. He hadn't noticed the writing on the first page, so the notebook just looked empty.

I grabbed for the journal again, but Ryan tossed it to Nolan, one of his gang members, who then passed it to Finn. The five of them laughed as they passed it around out of my reach. I bet they were so fucking proud of themselves.

I backed off and crossed my arms. By now, we were the last ones left in the classroom. "Aren't we a little old for Monkey in the Middle?" I snapped.

Ryan let out a deep belly laugh. "We're never too old to piss you off. What's so special about this stupid little notebook?"

My hands turned into fists, and my jaw tightened. "None of your damn business, that's what it is, jackass."

Ryan fucking lost it. He grabbed me by my shirt and shoved me up against the wall in the back of the room. He landed a heavy forearm to my chest to hold me there.

"Talk to me like that one more time, Lucas," he dared. "It'll be fun showing you what I can do about it."

Ryan raised his other hand, and magical swirls the color of night rose out of his palm. His magic twisted like smoky, burnt fingers. One of the fingers elongated until it reached my jaw, then skimmed along it threateningly. A magical chill spread where it touched me. I wanted to open my mouth to give him a piece of my mind, but my jaw was clamped shut tight by his Mentalist powers. My nostrils flared.

Fuck you, asshole!

I didn't take my eyes off his. Time and time again, I'd watched warlocks drop their gaze in submission to this sorry excuse of a human being. I wouldn't let him win like that.

Ryan stared me down, until his buddy Declan said, "Hey, look at this."

Ryan turned and snatched the journal out of Declan's hands. He started reading off my list. "*My gift led me to Nadine. Muffins in the Lounge. We met Talia. Grant seems happy.* What the fuck is this, Taylor? Some sappy poem? Sounds like garbage to me."

He released his magic on me, and my jaw finally freed.

"Yep," I said through gritted teeth. "That's me. A bad poet."

Ryan scoffed and shoved the journal at me. "At least you're right on that one, loser. Have fun with your sucky poetry."

Ryan walked off without looking back. The rest of the Tarantulas followed him. They all laughed like it was the best insult they'd heard all week. Probably was, considering Ryan's complete lack of creativity.

Whatever. I didn't have time for idiots like them. I had real problems to deal with.

Like my gift. This was one of the reasons I hated it. When I wasn't on the verge of vomiting, it was getting me into trouble in one way or another.

I subconjured my journal. It disappeared out of my hand and went into my stash, where I kept all my junk so I wouldn't have to carry it around.

I decided to head to the disc golf park to take my mind off everything. I was so stuck in my own head that I nearly walked straight into Professor Loren on my way out of the classroom. She was standing in the hall talking to Professor Richards, who was an Alchemist.

"Do you think you could brew me something?" she asked him a moment before I nearly trampled her.

"Sorry," I mumbled.

She grabbed my shoulder to steady me. Her face immediately fell. "Lucas, are you okay? You look a little pale."

I shook my head. "I'm fine. Are *you*?"

She furrowed her brow. "Yes, of course. Why do you ask?"

"You said you needed something brewed," I pointed out.

Professor Loren waved her hands. "It's nothing but old age, I'm sure. Just a little blip of magic waning here and there. Nothing to be worried about."

I narrowed my eyes. "Is that usual? Professor Warren wasn't feeling well a few weeks ago. He said his magic was weak, too."

Professor Loren and Professor Richards shared a glance, but it was Richards who spoke. "I'll be sure to check on him, Lucas. Thank you for letting us know."

"Yeah, no problem," I said before heading on my way.

The way they looked at each other worried me a little, but there wasn't anything I could do about it.

I headed toward the Main Foyer and stopped dead when I spotted Nadine. My heart fluttered before I could tell it to calm down. I'd nearly forgotten I wasn't supposed to be drawn to her.

She was walking toward me with a pile of books in her hands, as if returning from outside after a study session. She wore long sleeves and a wide-brimmed hat. Her hair spilled around her shoulders, and she looked really nice, but I'd promised myself I'd keep my distance.

I took a second to admire her. She radiated beauty as she smiled and waved to Mandy and Amy across the foyer. I tried to slip back down the hall before she saw me, but I didn't make it fast enough.

Nadine's eyes met mine, and the bright look on her face darkened. She hurried over to me before I could slip down the hall.

"Lucas," she greeted coolly. Her lips pressed into a thin line. She was obviously upset with me. I couldn't exactly blame her, after the way I blew her off.

"Uh, hi." I shoved my hands into my pockets. *Awkward.*

"Can we talk?" she asked.

I shrugged. "Yeah, sure."

What else was I supposed to do? Tell her no?

Nadine led me to a secluded sitting area in the corner where no one would hear us, and I took a seat on one of the plush red chairs. Nadine set her books down on the coffee table next to us and removed her hat. It caught on her hair, which made it stick up in a couple places. I found the messy look kind of hot. She tamed it with her fingers, then sat across from me with the hat in her lap.

"What's up?" I asked casually, even though I already knew what she wanted. It was obvious we were going to have to talk about the night at the lake eventually.

Nadine sat up straight in her chair. "Look, we're friends, right?"

I nodded, though I wasn't sure. Were we?

"And friends tell each other the truth?" she asked.

Fuck. I already knew where this was going. "Yeah, they do, Nad."

Nadine looked me straight in the eye. "Then tell me what happened at the lake, Lucas. Why have you been avoiding me?"

I dropped my gaze. There were a million reasons I couldn't get involved. Even if I weren't the Reaper's Apprentice, she wouldn't want me once she figured out who I really was. Who would be happy with me if I wasn't happy with myself? Worse, I couldn't put the burden of my gift on her, and it was inevitable if we got together.

Shit, look at me getting ahead of myself. Who said we were going to get together?

"Nad, it's not you," I assured her.

She frowned and gave me a disappointed look.

Hell, was I seriously going to go and make things worse? *It's not you, it's me.* How lame could I get?

I was quick to clarify. "I can't get into a romantic relationship. There's stuff you don't know."

"Then tell me," she begged, her tone softening.

I sighed. "Nad…"

"At least give me something, Lucas." She looked at me with these big puppy dog eyes I couldn't refuse.

"What do you want to know?" I asked.

There was so much I wasn't ready to talk about. My parents. My brother. My gift. And worst of all, the dying thought I'd heard about her. That secret was something I'd have to take to the grave.

"Your Cast, for starters," she said sheepishly.

I smirked. "Isn't the mystery a little fun?"

She shook her head. "Not for me. You're a mystery I can't figure out, and I want to know everything, Lucas."

"Really?" My voice was a few pitches higher than normal.

"Yes." She blushed a little.

My smirk turned into a light smile, and tension eased out of my shoulders. It was hard to leave her alone when it felt this good to be near her.

"Maybe we can start with what everyone else already knows about me," I offered.

Nadine's eyes lit up, and she sat straighter. "Okay."

I took a deep breath. "My Cast is Mortana. I'm the Reaper's Apprentice."

Nadine blinked a few times, but otherwise, her face remained blank.

"You know what that is, right?" I asked.

She cleared her throat. "I, um… think I heard about it?"

Good. I didn't have to explain it to her. Talking about my gift was almost as bad as experiencing it.

"That's why we can't get involved," I told her bluntly. "Even if I liked you, I couldn't be with you."

Nadine swallowed. "O-okay," she stammered.

It was obvious she *wasn't* okay with it, but I couldn't find the words to explain myself. Instead, I found myself saying, "Thanks, Nad. Why can't everyone be like you?"

She chuckled nervously. "Because I'm perfect."

She placed her hat back on her head, then rested her chin on her fist and fluttered her eyelashes like she was posing for a camera.

Damn it all if that didn't make her look even sexier.

I laughed. "The hat suits you."

She touched the brim. "You think? I thought it was ugly."

I furrowed my brow. "Then why do you wear it?"

Nadine's face fell, and she set the hat aside on top of her books. "I wasn't going to tell you this yet, but since you asked…"

My heart slammed against my rib cage. The sad look on her face had me worried, like she was about to break some terrible news. I had no idea what it could possibly be.

Nadine knotted her hands together in her lap and took a deep breath. "I have something called lupus."

Her words knocked the wind out of me. I didn't wish a chronic disease like that upon anyone. "Nad…"

"If you tell me you're sorry, I might lose it," she threatened playfully.

My mouth slammed shut.

She laughed lightly as she watched my eyes go wide. "I just mean, it's what I hear every time I tell someone. You don't have to be sorry. It's not your fault."

"Well, I don't feel good about it," I admitted. "Nadine, I had no idea."

She shrugged. "Why would you? Most people don't even know what lupus is."

"If there's anything I can do to help, you have to tell me," I said.

Nadine forced a smile. "Thanks for being nice about it. Most people just tell me I don't look sick, then throw their pity at me when I explain it to them."

"My cousin has lupus," I said. "So I know a little about it."

It didn't mean I understood what she was going through, though, because I didn't.

She seemed relieved, like she didn't want to have to explain it all. "So you must know I'm sensitive to the sun."

I nodded. Inside, my guts sank. I wished there was something I could do to help her—some way to take all the pain and symptoms away.

"That's why I cover up when I'm outside," she explained. "When I get too much sun exposure, my symptoms flare up. Like, right now my joints are really sore."

She held one hand with the other and flexed her fingers. The way they moved in a stilted way suggested she was in more pain than I knew. My instinct hit, and I reached out for her. She didn't protest as I took her hand in mine and gently massaged her joints. The warmth from her hand seemed to consume me, radiating up my arms and all throughout my body. Once I started, I couldn't stop. I just wanted to be near her, to touch her.

She shot me a nervous smile. "That actually doesn't hurt."

I shrugged. "My mom broke her hand when I was a kid, and it never quite healed right. She used to ask for massages all the time, so I kind of got good at it."

I didn't tell her how Mom had broken it during one of Dad's fits.

Nadine relaxed into her seat as I continued massaging her hand. She closed her eyes and rolled her head back. "Oh my God. Can I pay you to be my personal masseuse?"

I chuckled. "What are friends for?"

"Most of my friends wouldn't do this for me," she joked.

I couldn't take my eyes off her perfect skin as I stared down at my fingers moving over her. Her eyes were closed, so she couldn't see me admiring her beauty. There was so much I wanted to do with these fingers—for these hands to do to me.

I dropped her hand before my imagination could run too wild on me. But even that didn't slow my heart. Just being this close to her and smelling the rosy scent on her skin, it made my body go wild. I longed to be back in that position at the lake. I'd freeze the moment in time as her legs boldly wrapped around my waist, her half-naked body pressed tightly against mine. Maybe instead of pushing her away, I'd actually kiss her…

In a perfect world, where the Reaper's Shadow didn't exist.

Nadine cleared her throat, calling me back to reality. "Thanks, Lucas. That really helped."

I sat up straighter. "Are there other things that help with your symptoms?"

"I already told you about the yoga," she said, "but someone needs to kick my ass, because I haven't been doing it lately."

"Why not?" I asked. "If it helps?"

Nadine's shoulders dropped. "It's hard to convince myself to do it with all the stress."

"What do you mean?" I asked.

Nadine eyed me curiously. "You don't know, do you? I thought everyone knew."

"Know what?"

She swallowed, and her voice came out small. "Lucas, my parents died."

If her telling me she had lupus knocked the wind out of me, this one was a double whammy. Why hadn't Helena mentioned it to me?

I knew someone in her life had died recently, because I'd heard the woman's last thought, which was about Nadine. But I didn't know it'd been her mom. I should've put the pieces together. And now I'd learned that her *dad* died, too. Holy shit!

Her mom's last thought echoed through my mind. There was more to her last thought than I could ever tell Nadine... a dark, ominous warning that could get Nadine hurt. Which was why I hadn't spoken of it—and wouldn't.

What could I possibly say to Nad if she didn't want to hear *I'm sorry*?

Like an idiot, I spat out, "My brother died, too."

What the hell? Why was I making this about me?

"I just mean, I get what it's like to lose a family member," I quickly added.

Her expression softened. "It's nice to have someone my age around who understands. Most people don't get it."

"Tell me about it," I said, feeling a little more of that weight on my shoulders lift.

She played with a thread on the chair and didn't meet my eyes. "How long ago?"

"Almost a year," I answered.

"Mine was this summer. It was a car crash." She didn't say anything more than that. She just stared down at the loose thread, poking it with her finger while we sat in silence. It killed me to watch. I wished that I could shoulder all that pain, just to see her happy.

I decided to change up the subject. "Well, if you're looking for help with your yoga, you should check out the fitness center."

She finally looked to me. "They have yoga?"

"Yeah. We could head over there and pick up a schedule if you want," I offered.

Damn it. I was supposed to be staying away from her, not inviting her on walks with me.

Screw it. This one time wouldn't hurt anything.

"Okay," she agreed.

She reached for her hat, but I grabbed her books for her before she could get them.

"I can carry those," she protested.

I shrugged. "So can I."

Nadine huffed a little, but she didn't put up a fight.

"This way." I cocked my head, and we started down the hallway toward the pool and fitness center.

She walked a step ahead of me, so she didn't see how I was eyeing her from the side. She had a beautiful profile, and that hair... I couldn't stop staring at that long brown hair that looked so soft. I just wanted to run my hands through it and—

Nausea hit me.

Aw, fuck.

I didn't want Nadine to notice, so I kept up pace beside her.

"Five more minutes…" the thought said.

The thought was there and gone in a matter of seconds. I'd collected a lot of thoughts like that over the months. Most people would sell their souls just for a few more minutes with their loved ones. This guy was no exception.

It was only when the wave of nausea passed that it hit me how smoothly that one had gone. It was nothing like earlier. I didn't even have to double over and catch myself against the wall. How could that be when just a few hours ago I was writhing on the bathroom floor?

And then it hit me.

The difference was Nadine. I didn't know what it was about her, but being around her made everything better. I didn't feel as hopeless when she was nearby.

I quickly conjured my journal and a pen, then scribbled something down on the next line before Nadine saw.

She makes it all bearable.

She looked in my direction, but I'd already sent the notebook away to my stash.

"What?" I asked innocently.

She shrugged and offered a kind smile. "Nothing."

Well, fuck. How was I supposed to stay away from her now?

nadine

TEN

I was a filthy liar. I don't even know why I lied to Lucas. It just slipped out.

Oh, yeah, Lucas. I totally know what the Reaper's Apprentice is.

Ugh.

I guess I didn't want to sound totally clueless around him. And then I had to tell him I understood? WTF? I didn't. Not really. I just couldn't bear to see him looking all sad like that and everything.

I was still thinking about it days later on my way to my Introduction to Tarot class. It was a small class with only thirty students. The subject was interesting, but Chloe was in this class, and I couldn't stand her. She always had to call people out for their interpretation of the cards, even though Professor Wykoff said in our first lesson there were no right or wrong interpretations.

We'd already covered the basics of Tarot, how there were twenty-two Major Arcana cards in a deck that spoke to your life-long spiritual journey, and fifty-six Minor Arcana cards that represented everyday challenges. We learned about the four suits—that cups represented emotions and relationships, swords referred to behaviors and the mind, pentacles were about finances and career, and wands were about spirituality. From there, Professor Wykoff said, all we had to do was interpret the images.

Professor Wykoff was younger than most of my other professors. She must've been in her thirties. She had long caramel-colored hair and always wore multi-colored dresses and sandals. She spoke in a soft tone so that the class had to be dead silent to hear her.

Today, she stood at the front of the room, shuffling the cards in mid-air with her telekinetic abilities. "I'd like to start our lesson today with a fun exercise. Each of you will come up and pick a single card that represents *you* and your life's journey. As a class, we will work to interpret the card together. Who'd like to go first?"

Chloe's hand shot up at the front of the room. I sank down in my seat. I wasn't looking forward to getting up in front of everyone else. They all knew tarot way better than I did.

Professor Wykoff smiled brightly. "Miss Olson, come on up."

Chloe breezed to the front of the room. As much as I hated to admit it, she looked graceful in her high heels.

Professor Wykoff held out her hand, and the cards fluttered out of the air into a neat pile. She held it out to Chloe. Chloe tilted her chin up confidently and split the deck, then pulled a card from the middle. She smiled proudly as she turned it over.

"Hold it up so everyone can see," Professor Wykoff encouraged.

Chloe held the card high over her head and announced, "I got the Hierophant."

I remembered him from our readings last week. He was like a priest, a spiritual leader. He sat on a throne in front of two subjects, with a set of keys placed at his feet.

"An excellent card," Professor Wykoff said. "What do you think it means?"

Chloe lowered the card to study it closely. "Well, I know he's a teacher. The keys represent his ability to unlock the mysteries of the world, and these two guys here represent a group identity."

Damn, I was hoping she'd be wrong, but she sounded like she knew what she was talking about.

"How do you think that fits into your life?" Professor Wykoff asked.

Chloe held her head up confidently. "It must mean that I'll become a spiritual teacher some-day. Perhaps I'll serve on the Imperium Council like my grandmother."

Professor Wykoff nodded. "Very good. Would anyone like to challenge this interpretation?"

I sat a little straighter. Last week, Professor Wykoff had told us each card had multiple different meanings. Chloe didn't really come off to me as the *teacher* type. Maybe the card had a different meaning for her.

"Nobody?" Professor Wykoff prodded. Her eyes turned to me. "Miss Evers?"

I didn't know why she called on me. Maybe she sensed something in my expression. My pulse quickened, but I answered anyway. "Well, I was just thinking... the card could mean that you *need* a teacher, instead of becoming one, right?"

Professor Wykoff nodded, but Chloe's features darkened.

I tried my best to ignore her. "Or perhaps it's not about the teaching aspect at all. Priests are all about tradition, aren't they? So couldn't this card be encouraging you to honor your tradi-tions, to not break the rules?"

"I'm not breaking any rules," Chloe snapped.

"Turning someone into a toad sure sounds like breaking the rules to me," I snarled back.

Gasps traveled around the room, and it took me a second to realize what I'd said. I didn't mean to. It just slipped out.

Chloe narrowed her eyes at me, as if trying to figure out how I knew about that. "I don't know what you're talking about."

Liar.

"Ladies," Professor Wykoff quickly stepped in, pretending like she didn't notice the hostility between us. "These are both very valid interpretations. Miss Olson, I suggest you take into consideration Miss Evers's suggestions as you weigh the possibilities of this card on your life."

Chloe looked Professor Wykoff up and down, then scoffed as she tossed the card back at her. "I know my tarot. I'm not wrong."

She stomped back to her desk and flipped her hair over her shoulder while she sat.

Professor Wykoff turned her gaze back to me. "Miss Evers, perhaps you'd like to go next?"

It didn't sound like a suggestion. Taking a deep breath, I stood on shaky knees and walked to the front of the room. Professor Wykoff shuffled the deck again, then held it out to me. I cut it as Chloe had and picked a card out of the middle. I was a little taken aback by what I got.

After a few moments, Professor Wykoff said, "Hold it up for everyone, please."

My pulse raced as I flipped the card over and showed the class. "The Eight of Swords."

This card depicted a woman bound in cloth, with a blindfold over her face. Eight swords were sticking out of the ground around her.

"What do you think it means?" Professor Wykoff asked.

I studied the card before answering. "Well, we know that swords represent behaviors. She's bound and can't see where she's going. So it might mean that my behaviors and mindset are holding me back."

"Very good," Professor Wykoff praised. "This is the card of negative thoughts."

I furrowed my brow. "That doesn't sound good."

Chloe's hand shot into the air.

"Yes, Miss Olson?" Professor Wykoff called on her.

Chloe straightened her spine. "On the contrary, this card is quite positive if you look at it correctly." She shot me daggers as she emphasized the word *correctly*. "Notice how her feet are unbound. She has the ability to go in any direction she chooses. The woman in this card is bound by her own doing. All she has to do is stop playing the victim."

Chloe glared at me. Was she seriously accusing me of victim mentality when she didn't even know me? Yeah, my life sucked, but I wasn't a victim. I dealt with my shit.

"Excellent," Professor Wykoff said. With her, I didn't think anyone could interpret the cards wrong. "It seems the power to escape your issues is in your hands, Miss Evers. Remove the blindfold, and everything shall be made clear."

I gave her back the card and returned to my seat. The whole time, Chloe's eyes followed me. I sat, wondering if maybe I'd chosen the wrong card. Was I really holding myself back? I didn't play the victim, did I?

I was contemplating it all class, so I didn't really pay attention to the rest of the readings. All I knew was Chloe had to challenge them all, and Professor Wykoff praised her each time.

As I was walking out of the classroom, Chloe grabbed my wrist and dragged me down the hall. I ripped my arm out of her hold and glared at her. "What the hell?"

She lowered her voice, but her tone was as harsh as ever. "You think it's funny challenging me like that?"

"Professor Wykoff called on me," I growled. "I followed the assignment."

Chloe pointed a manicured finger in my face and leaned close. "Don't *ever* insult me like that again. Understand?"

"I'm so scared," I said flatly. "Try not to act so offended next time... unless it's true?"

Her lips tightened. "Screw you, Nadine. No one wants you here anyway. Why don't you just leave?"

"I don't know. Why don't you come up with a better insult? I've heard that one before," I said coolly.

Chloe didn't like that. She stepped closer, until she was looming over me. "I'm going to have so much fun driving you out of town."

I raised an eyebrow. "Yeah? I'd like to see you try."

Chloe scoffed. "You're on."

She breezed away. I stared after her, narrowing my eyes at the back of her head. It wasn't until she turned the corner that I breathed a sigh of relief. Whatever. She didn't deserve my attention anyway. What I really needed right now was a nap.

I turned and started back toward my dorm room. When I got there, the door handle didn't move. I twisted harder, but it wouldn't budge.

"What the...?" I glanced down to my wrist, and my gut sank. My bracelet! It was gone! That was the key to my room.

I pounded on the door, feeling a red-hot energy rise inside of me. How could I have lost my enchanted bracelet?

Talia answered a few moments later. She furrowed her brow and tilted her head. "You didn't have to knock."

"I did." I held up my wrist to show her it was empty.

She gazed at my wrist in shock. "What happened to your bracelet?"

I entered the room and plopped down onto my bed. It felt really good to lie down. "I don't know."

Talia sat on the couch. "When was the last time you saw it?"

I racked my brain, trying to recall. "I definitely had it at lunch. I fell asleep in the study area outside the fitness center between classes, but I'm pretty sure I still had it on me when I woke up. Which means I must've gone to my tarot class with it on."

"Should we retrace your steps?" Talia asked.

I was too tired to move. I shook my head. "Maybe in a bit."

Talia's face fell. "You know what? I'll go look for it."

"No, Tal," I said quickly. "You don't have to do that."

She grabbed her bag. "Well, I'm going to go for a walk. If I happen to stumble upon it, I'll let you know."

I'd already closed my eyes. I was drifting off so quickly that I barely heard her. "Yeah, okay. Have fun on your walk."

I was out before I heard the sound of the door shut.

I woke at least an hour later to the sound of three voices entering the room. It felt like I'd barely slept at all. I pushed past the pain in my joints and sat up in bed to see Talia, Mandy, and Amy entering the room. Mandy wore a plum dress with a plaid skirt that fell to her knees, with dark tights and high heels. Amy dressed more casually, in jeans and a *Miriam College* hoodie.

"Bad news," Talia said. "I didn't find your bracelet, but I *did* find these two wonderful ladies who want to go shopping with us and take us out to dinner."

"Anywhere but the Chinese buffet," Amy said. "I'm sick of rice and egg rolls. My mom hasn't stopped making them all summer. She's trying to replicate my grandmother's famous recipe."

"In that case, no Indian food, either," Mandy added. "Curry's the only thing my mom knows how to make."

"Your family has a secret recipe?" Amy asked her.

"Just the one," Mandy replied. "That recipe was the one thing my grandma brought with her from India."

"Same," Amy said. "Except my grandma came from China."

Mandy turned to me. "So, what do you say, Nadine?"

I forced a smile. As much as I loved shopping, it was beyond tiring. I hated to miss out, though. "Sounds like fun. You'll have to give me a few minutes to get ready."

"Sure," Talia said, before walking over to her bed to pick up her cat. "Hey, you guys want to meet Gus?"

"Oh my gosh! He's sooo cute," Mandy raved. "Nadine, do you have a cat?"

I grabbed my hairbrush and started brushing my hair into a high ponytail. "No, not yet."

The girls either didn't notice how slowly I moved, or they didn't care, because they didn't rush me. It was kind of nice.

Talia leaned against the bathroom door while I was fixing my makeup. "I can't wait until we get our magic. Hair and makeup will be so easy."

"We can do magic makeup?" I asked as I smeared mascara across my eyelashes.

She nodded proudly. "Makeup and hair. It'll make my morning routine super fast."

I tightened my ponytail and turned from the mirror. "It will definitely be a perk of magic."

We took Mandy's car into town and parked along a street with a bunch of cute shops. I noticed various signs advertising free samples of things like honey, maple syrup, and apple cider. There were plenty of cute clothing shops and metaphysical stores. I didn't know where to start.

Amy noticed me eyeing the street curiously as we stepped out of the car. "Haven't you been here before, Nadine?"

I shook my head. "I haven't had the time yet."

Mandy inhaled a sharp breath. "Girl, you're missing out! You *have* to try Grandma Dee's Apple Cider. It's the best."

"We could start here and work our way to the end of the street," I suggested, pointing to the closest store, which sold crystals.

"Good idea." Talia looped her arm through mine, and we entered the shop.

It was quiet inside, though a soft melody played over the speakers. Various incense smells hit my nose all at once. Beneath the counter in the middle of the shop, crystals big and small glittered under the light. There was an entire section dedicated to different tarot decks, and another for candles. The entire ambiance soothed me…

Until I caught sight of Gwen and Camille. They were filling small draw-string bags with different colored stones. I was pretty sure I saw Gwen slip one of the smaller ones into her pocket. The two of them shot daggers my way when they noticed my eyes on them. I quickly glanced away and followed my friends to the other side of the store.

I pulled a box of tarot cards from the shelf. "I should probably get myself my own tarot deck. It's not required for my class, but it might help me study."

The artwork on this deck was beautiful, but I didn't recognize the cards shown on the back.

"Those are oracle cards," Talia said.

"What's the difference?" I asked.

"Tarot is more standard," Talia explained. "Tarot decks should have seventy-eight cards, with Major and Minor Arcana, and four suits. Oracle cards can basically be anything the creator wants them to be. There's more flexibility in the oracle cards."

"Interesting…" I mused as I studied the artwork on the front. It depicted a beautiful woman with the full moon behind her. She looked as if she was praying. I didn't know why, but I felt drawn to her. "I think I'm going to get these ones."

"Oh my gosh! Check these out," Mandy cried. She was hunched over the front counter looking down at one of the crystals inside. The three of us came over to join her. Below her was a beautiful orange and red crystal set into a silver ring. It shimmered in the light. "It's beautiful, isn't it?"

"I like this one," Amy said, pointing to a midnight blue crystal. "Don't let me buy it, though. I have at least a dozen of these already."

"Seriously guys?" Talia teased. "It's pink all the way."

"Check this out!" Amy cried, flapping a hand. She pointed to a green stone beneath the glass. "This is supposed to ward off curses. I hear it's the best thing since Curse Breakers."

"Curse Breakers?" I asked.

Mandy's face fell. "Oh, honey. You have so much to learn. Curse Breakers are the fifth Cast."

My eyebrows knitted together. "They died out, didn't they?"

Mandy nodded. "Yeah, I think… well…"

She hesitated.

"What?" I pressed.

Mandy played with the strap on her purse. "I'm just surprised no one mentioned it to you. I'm pretty sure your grandpa was the last one."

Shock hit me. Why hadn't Grammy told me?

"What exactly is a Curse Breaker?" I asked carefully.

"Exactly what they sound like," Mandy said. "Witches who break curses."

"There's more to it than that," Amy added. "They could transfer magic from one place to another. That's how they broke the curses. Plus, they can absorb magic."

"That sounds really cool. I wonder why there aren't any left," I mused.

"It's always been kind of rare," Talia explained. "I mean, being able to absorb magic takes a lot of responsibility. Mother Miriam wouldn't want that kind of power to be put in the wrong hands."

"I guess that makes sense," I said.

Talia gestured to the stones below us. "Which one is your favorite?"

I peered into the glass. They were all so gorgeous. Some shimmered like diamonds, while others were smooth. I was drawn to a light blue one, but it was hard to pick a favorite.

"Will that be all for today?"

My thoughts were interrupted by the sound of the cashier checking out a customer. I looked up to see Headmistress Verla setting a huge crystal on the counter next to us. It was orange and reminded me of a Himalayan salt lamp, but it was solid and looked hella heavy. She had a large bag draped over her shoulder, and Odin's black head poked out the opening.

She brushed her brown hair out of her eyes. "Yes, that's it."

The cashier started ringing her up. Headmistress Verla lifted her head and caught my eye. "Girls, how are you?"

"We're good," I said.

"Nadine, I'm actually really glad I ran into you," Headmistress Verla said. "I wanted to talk to you about your Evoking Ceremony training."

"Oh?" I pushed my hair behind my ear. "How exactly does that work?"

She gave a polite smile. "Each freshman is assigned a mentor who will help prepare them for the ceremony."

"Have I been assigned?" I asked eagerly. I was excited to hear who I'd been assigned to.

"Yes," she said brightly. "Me."

I blinked a few times. "You're my mentor?"

"You sound surprised, Nadine."

"I just thought it'd be one of my professors," I said.

"Well, it was, but there were some… reassignments." I didn't know what she meant by that, but I sensed something in her tone.

"What do you mean?" I asked curiously.

She waved her hand nonchalantly. "It's nothing. I just thought… maybe we could get to know each other. You know, since I was so close to your mom."

"Yeah, I'd like that," I told her.

"Excellent," she said brightly. "I suggest we meet at least three times before your Evoking Ceremony. How does the first week of October sound?"

"Sounds great."

"I'll see you then." She paid for her crystal, then left the shop with it cradled in her hands.

Talia, Mandy, and Amy all turned to me with wide eyes.

"What?" I asked innocently.

"You're so lucky," Talia said. "She never mentors anyone."

I furrowed my brow. "She doesn't?"

"No," Mandy confirmed. "She's super good, too. You'll pass your Evoking Ceremony for sure."

Relief washed over me. "That's encouraging."

"You should get a crystal to celebrate," Amy suggested.

I eyed Talia and Mandy. "Is that what witches do?"

Amy laughed. "No. I just *really* like crystals."

Mandy frowned. "I feel so bad for the headmistress."

My heart sank. "Me, too. Talia told me what happened. She lost her sister *and* her baby."

Mandy leaned in to whisper. "It wasn't just any sister, either. It was her twin."

"Wow, that must've been hard," I said in a soft tone.

Talia shook her head. "Worse than that. Identical twins share a soul. She literally lost half her soul."

My jaw dropped. There were no words for this kind of thing. "Is there anything we can do?"

Talia shook her head. "There was a memorial for her baby after it happened. The whole town came. I would hate to reopen old wounds."

"You're right," I told her. I felt the same way with my parents. The grief was personal. I didn't want to talk about it, and I bet Headmistress Verla didn't want to, either.

Mandy seemed to sense the tension in the air and made a point to break it. "Well, I'm going to get this ring and another palm reading book for my collection. Anyone else getting anything?"

I bought the oracle cards, then we went next door to a cute shop that sold fudge and salt water taffy.

I chuckled as I read through the names of the taffy flavors. "These are great. Eye of Newt. Witch's Brew. Midnight Reaper."

I stopped in my tracks when I saw the one labeled *Midnight Reaper*. It was a deep black and probably licorice flavored, but the name reminded me that I'd been meaning to ask Talia about what Lucas had said.

"Midnight Reaper tastes amazing," Talia said. She reached for a bag to start filling it with candy.

I cleared my throat. "Speaking of reapers, I heard of something called a Reaper's Apprentice, but I'm not sure what it means."

Mandy paused as she reached for a taffy labeled *Pumpkin Spice*. "You hang out with Lucas Taylor, don't you?"

I nodded. "He told me he was the Reaper's Apprentice, and I said I knew what he meant, but I didn't."

Amy came up close to me to explain in a low voice. "There's one Reaper's Apprentice every generation. They collect the last thoughts of the dead, so that the spirits can move on to the afterlife. When he dies, he'll become a reaper."

My eyebrows shot up. "Like the Grim Reaper? A scythe and everything?"

"There is no Grim Reaper," Talia said. "Just reapers. Lots of them."

A heavy weight settled on my chest, and I suddenly felt for Lucas. He dealt with death day in and day out. It sounded like a huge burden to bear.

I quickly became intrigued. "Do all magical races have reapers?"

Talia shrugged. "Depends on what you call it. In some societies, their ancestors come to lead their spirits to the other side. In ours, specially trained reapers help you cross over."

"Mm…" I mused thoughtfully. "So, why can't a Reaper's Apprentice have a girlfriend?"

Amy tilted her head to the side. "What do you mean?"

"Lucas said we couldn't get involved because he was the Reaper's Apprentice," I explained. "Any idea why?"

The three of them stared back at me blankly.

"It sounds like an excuse to me," Talia said bluntly.

"Totally," Amy agreed. "I bet he's scared or something."

My teeth gritted. "If he doesn't like me, why doesn't he just say that?"

No one had an answer for me.

We bought our candy and left the store. As we were leaving, two women in beautiful velvet robes passed by us. In unison, Mandy, Amy, and Talia all bowed their heads and politely said, "Priestesses."

The women bowed their heads back, then continued on their way. My eyes followed them. They were both decades older than us. One had salt and pepper hair, while the other had a mane of red hair tied into a long braid. They held their heads high, like they were important. I noticed a cauldron tattoo on the back of one lady's neck, and a skull on the other's wrist.

I turned to my friends. "What was that about?"

Mandy and Amy exchanged a glance, but it was Amy who spoke. "They're Imperium members."

"Imperium?" I asked. Chloe had mentioned the Imperium Council, but I hadn't asked what it meant.

"Our government," Amy explained as we entered the next shop down, which was a cute boutique that sold dresses. "The Imperium is made up of one High Priestess from each of the coven's Casts."

I smiled. "The coven's run by women?"

Talia ran her hands down a pink dress. "Absolutely."

"Awesome," I said. "How are the priestesses chosen?"

"Oh! We just talked about this in my sociology class," Amy piped up excitedly. "When a priestess dies, the remaining Imperium members nominate and vote on the next priestess to take their place. Usually, they choose the strongest members of the Cast."

"What if there's a disagreement or a tie vote?" I asked.

Talia's gave me this dead serious look. "Then it's a fight to the death."

My face fell. Talia and Amy burst into a fit of laughter.

"I'm kidding!" Talia giggled. "I don't think there's ever been a tie vote. They definitely pray to Mother Miriam before they vote, so it's usually unanimous."

I pulled a black floral dress off the rack and held it up to my body. "It sounds so easy."

"You should try that on," Talia encouraged.

"You think?"

"Yeah, and I'll try this one." She grabbed the pink dress she'd been eyeing. "This would look hot for the Midnight Formal."

"Midnight Formal?" I asked.

Mandy beamed. "A winter tradition! It's the best dance of the year."

"I didn't know colleges held dances," I said.

"You think we're all done dancing after senior prom?" Mandy asked. "No way. We love our dances around here."

"Okay, so which one of you can I take?" I joked. "I doubt I'll find a date."

"Don't talk that way, Nadine," Amy scolded. "I'm sure there are tons of guys who would love to take you."

Problem was, there was only one I wanted to go with.

I shrugged. "I guess we'll see."

We made our way back to the fitting rooms. The black dress was light and flowy on me. It was a little too girly for me, but my friends liked it, so I decided to buy it. Mandy bought three, all in different colors. We stopped at a dozen more shops before we ordered dinner at a cute café that was famous for its assortment of pies. I got to try some of the cider I'd heard so much about, and it was amazing. Finally, we decided to call it a night. By the time we got back to campus, my arms were full of shopping bags.

"You think those shoes I wore yesterday will go with my new dress?" Mandy asked Amy as we crossed the foyer.

Amy thought about it for a second. "The black sandals with the strap?"

"Yeah. I don't know if those will work or if I should buy new ones," Mandy said.

Amy scrunched up her nose. "Buy new ones anyway."

Mandy's jaw dropped dramatically. "Girl, you are no good for my credit card."

Amy flipped her dark hair over her shoulder. "What do you think I'm here for?"

I gripped hard to the banister as we climbed the stairs. All the walking we'd done had really tired me out. Talia noticed, but she didn't say anything. She made a point to walk behind me, in case I passed out or something.

"Bad Mandy," Talia snickered. "You already spent too much today."

Mandy groaned. "I know. My parents are gonna kill me."

We reached the top of the steps, and my stomach sank when I saw Chloe, Gwen, and Camille standing there. They were huddled in a small group and giggling about something I couldn't hear. Their laughter instantly died when Chloe lifted her head and caught me staring. I was pretty sure she was trying to flip us off with her eyes.

Mandy shot her a disgusted look, then flipped her hair over her shoulder and continued on her way. "Sorry, guys," she said when we were out of earshot of the Lucky Three. "I kind of attract hostility from that chick."

I scoffed. "Believe me, it's not just you."

I reached for the door handle on room 112, but when I twisted, nothing happened. "Whoops. I forgot I lost my bracelet."

"That's okay. I've got it," Talia said.

When the door swung open, my jaw dropped.

Talia's hand shot over her mouth. "Good Goddess."

The room had been totally trashed. I was too shocked to say anything. All the dresses in our closet had been ripped out and were strewn across the entryway. In the bathroom, my Epsom salts littered the floor, and Talia's shampoo had been poured over every surface. All the books from my dresser were on the floor. Some of them lay open, with the pages crinkled at the corner. Our bedding was all messed up, and the cushions were thrown off the couch. Dresser drawers were open, and our clothes were scattered all around the room. All the condoms from Talia's jewelry box had been ripped open and were hung from the knobs on our dressers. A small cry came from under the bed.

"Gus!" Talia screeched. She rushed over and dropped her shopping bags at her feet, then reached under the bed to pull out her suitcase. She flipped the top up, and Gus jumped out. He purred as she set him free.

My hands shook as I leaned down to pick up my books.

"Oh my gosh," Mandy said breathlessly. "Who would do this?"

Talia held Gus close and gently stroked his white fur. "I don't know."

I placed one of the books back on my dresser, and that's when I noticed it. My enchanted beaded bracelet sat neatly on the middle of my dresser. I picked it up and turned to Talia. "This definitely wasn't here when we left."

Talia's jaw dropped. "Someone must've found it and done this…"

Red hot rage tore through me. Something from earlier flickered through my mind, how Chloe had grabbed my wrist after our tarot class. My nostrils flared. "I don't think they found it. They *stole* it."

"Oh, no," Amy whispered as she reached down to pick up one of my books. She flipped it over, only for me to see that the cover had been ripped off of my Agatha Christie paperback. Amy held it up in two pieces.

That's when I fucking lost it. I tore the book out of her hand and stomped out of the room. Screw my fatigue and aching joints. I didn't care how much it hurt to punch this bitch in the face. She deserved it. She was going to pay for this!

I ignored Talia's voice calling my name as I marched down the hall. Chloe looked to me with false shock in her eyes, but I could tell she was holding back a laugh.

"Oh, no, Nadine," she feigned. "What happened?"

I thrust my arm out and shoved Chloe so hard that pain shot through my wrist. She stumbled back a step, but quickly straightened.

I shoved the book into her face. "Look what you did, you fucking bitch!"

"I have no idea what you're talking about," Chloe said coolly.

Gwen and Camille snickered from behind her. Chloe just looked amused. In the foyer below, all eyes turned to us.

"This was the last thing my mom gave me before she died!" I shouted, my hand curling into a tight fist. "And you've ruined it!"

Chloe's eyebrows knitted together. She spoke loud enough for the onlookers in the hall to hear. "But Nadine, how could I have gotten into your dorm?"

"You know damn well how you did it!" I snarled, getting up in her face. "You stole my bracelet and went in while Talia and I were in town. I bet you sent your back-up bitches to keep an eye on us."

Gwen and Camille only laughed harder—like they took the insult as a badge of honor.

Chloe crossed her arms and leveled me with a challenging gaze. "Prove it."

"Nadine." I felt Talia's hand on my elbow, but I shrugged her off.

"Are you seriously going to stand here and tell me it wasn't you?" I growled at Chloe. "No one's going to believe you!"

She leaned forward and spoke in a low voice. "Leave town, and it won't happen again."

"Leave town...?" My fist tightened. "How about you tell me what the fuck it is you have against me?"

Chloe eyed me up and down, then scoffed. "You don't know, do you?"

"Know what?" I snapped.

She smirked. "Maybe you should ask your grandma. Anyway, good luck cleaning up."

Chloe turned on her heel and started walking away from me, but I dropped my book and lunged forward. My fingers tangled in her hair, and I jerked so hard that she stumbled backward and landed on the ground. I was about to jump on top of her when three pairs of hands held me back.

Chloe cradled her head where it'd hit the ground and quickly got to her feet. "You're crazy!"

"And you're a fucking liar!" I seethed. Tears began to stream down my face as I struggled out of my friends' hold. But I couldn't get away from all three of them. "That was my mom's book, you bitch!"

I screamed more obscenities at her, but they flew out of my mouth without me really realizing what I was saying. I was pretty sure I called her a bitch at least three more times. It was loud enough for practically the whole school to hear. I probably looked insane as spittle flew from my mouth and I struggled away from my friends. But I didn't care. I just wanted her to pay.

Professor Wykoff rushed up the stairs. "Nadine, Nadine," she said softly. "You need to calm down."

"Calm down!?" I shrieked. "Did you see what she did?"

Professor Wykoff didn't raise her voice at all. I had to quiet down to hear her. "Why don't you show me?"

I was still seething, but it was enough to get me to stop struggling. My friends let me go, and I led Professor Wykoff back to our room.

"Oh, dear," she said once she saw the mess. "Let's... let's get some help."

She turned from the room, presumably to find some other professors. Talia led me over to my bed, and I sank into it.

"Nadine, what *was* that?" she asked.

I took a deep breath and wiped the tears from my eyes. "Don't you want to punch her, too?"

"Yeah, of course I do, but that…" Talia hesitated. "That didn't seem like you at all."

I sniffled as Mandy handed me my book that I'd dropped in the hall. I hugged it close to my chest. "I just… get that way sometimes. I can't explain it. It's like…" I choked up as a sob rose in my throat. "It's like I have this darkness inside of me. Most of the time it's fine, but other times it's like… like I want to rip somebody's head off."

Amy's shoulders fell. "We all get that way sometimes, Nadine."

I shook my head. She didn't understand. When I got this way, I could get downright murderous. It was way overly dramatic, and I knew I was totally out of line, but I couldn't control myself. I was beyond furious.

"Deep breaths, Nadine," Mandy encouraged.

"No." I got to my feet, but I stood too fast. The room spun around me, and I flopped back onto the bed.

"Nadine, you need to slow down," Talia insisted.

I pressed the heel of my palm to my forehead, waiting for the dizziness to pass. "I don't want to calm down, Tal."

"Okay, but you can't keep acting like this," she stated sternly.

I dropped my hand and looked her in the eyes. "Fine. Then I want to go see my grandmother."

Talia exchanged a nervous glance with the other girls.

"We'll stay and clean up," Amy offered.

Talia turned back to me. "Okay, Nadine. We'll go visit your grandma."

I was still fuming on the car ride over, but Talia had insisted she drive, so I managed to cool down a little by the time we pulled into Grammy's driveway. Grammy rushed out of the house when she saw my car pull up.

"Nadine, what happened?" she demanded. There was a look in her eye that told me she already knew.

"Who told you?" I asked as I stepped out of the car.

Grammy frowned, but she wrapped an arm around my shoulders and led me up the walkway. Talia followed close behind.

"Clarice called," Grammy admitted.

I groaned. Headmistress Verla knew? Was I going to get suspended or something?

"I heard you made quite a scene," Grammy stated. I expected her to sound disappointed, but her tone was impossible to read.

"It was justified," I said bitterly.

Grammy led me into the living room, and I took a seat on the couch. Talia sat beside me with a worried look on her face.

Grammy sat in the chair across from us. She adjusted her long skirt and folded her hands in her lap. "Why don't you tell me what happened?"

My blood heated as I pictured that satisfied look on Chloe's face. What a fucking bitch. I took a deep breath before jumping into my explanation. "There's this girl at school who hates me—I don't know why—and she broke into our dorm room and tore the whole thing apart."

My hands shook the longer I spoke. "She ripped the book Mom and Dad gave me for my birthday, and I just… I lost it. She's lucky I'm going through a flare-up, or I would've pummeled her fucking—"

"Nadine." Grammy held up a hand to stop me. She spoke so calmly, like my anger didn't faze her at all. "I understand that you're upset, but getting into fist fights is not the answer."

I groaned. "What was I supposed to do, Grammy? Sit there and take it?"

Grammy sat silently, unmoving, though Talia shifted uncomfortably beside me.

Finally, Grammy's stoic features turned into a frown. "I'm sorry about your book, Nadine. Perhaps we can get you a new one—"

"I don't *want* a new one," I snapped.

Grammy's eyebrows tightened.

I quickly adjusted my tone. "It's not just any book, Grammy. Mom and Dad signed it to me. It's... it's—"

I choked up again.

Talia inched closer to me and pulled me into a hug. "It's going to be okay, Nadine. No one got hurt, and that's what's important."

I melted into the hug, letting it cool some of the heat raging through my body. Slowly, the tension in my shoulders began to ease. Finally, I drew away from Talia, feeling like my head was a little clearer. "I'm sorry. I know I could've reacted differently. And you're right, Tal. No one got hurt. I just don't get why she did it in the first place."

I turned my gaze back to Grammy. "She told me to ask you."

Grammy's face fell, and she completely froze up. "Me?"

"Yeah, she acted like there's something I should know, and she thought you might be able to tell me," I said.

Grammy furrowed her brow. "What's this girl's name?"

"Chloe." I cleared my throat. "Chloe Olson."

Grammy huffed, but it was barely audible. Her lips pressed together tightly, and her eyebrow twitched, but I couldn't read the look in her eyes. It was like she was trying hard not to give anything away. "I have no idea what she meant."

I crossed my arms and glared at Grammy. It was obvious she was lying to me. "Are you sure? Because she seemed pretty certain you knew something."

Grammy sucked on her teeth and hesitated. "I know that years ago, before Grampy died, he didn't get along well with the Olson family. But that's over now."

My eyebrows knitted together tightly. That couldn't be what this was about. Grampy had died over forty years ago, when Grammy was still pregnant with Mom. Whatever she was talking about had nothing to do with Chloe and me.

"What did they fight about?" I asked.

Grammy shot to her feet. There was anger etched in her eyes, like she was furious I had the nerve to ask. "That's in the past, Nadine. There's no reason to go opening old wounds. Stay away from this Olson girl, and you'll be fine. Now come eat some cookies. They're fresh."

I gaped up at Grammy. "Actually, I'm not hungry—"

"I'm not going to ask you again, Nadine," she snapped. "I made too many, and I need your help eating them."

Holy crap. Grammy could get sassy when she wanted to. Talia and I shot each other wide-eyed gazes, then quickly got to our feet to follow Grammy to the kitchen. It was obvious Grammy wasn't willing to talk about this thing with Grampy. But she couldn't keep it from me forever.

One way or another, I'd figure out what she was hiding.

Grammy's secret hovered at the forefront of my mind during classes the next day. I could hardly concentrate knowing she was keeping something from me, but I knew how stubborn she could be. She wouldn't spill unless she wanted to, and it drove me nuts.

Talia and I had returned to school the night before to a clean dorm and a note from Amy and Mandy that said we could thank them with an order of Barry's Enchanted Muffins. We'd left a dozen outside each of their dorm rooms that morning, along with a personalized thank-you note to each of them. Talia had made some inappropriate drawings inside that she assured me they'd both appreciate.

At lunch, I was filling my plate in the buffet line when I caught sight of Lucas and Grant entering the cafeteria. The school's cafeteria wasn't like the lunch room back at my old high school. Instead of long tables with benches and bright, fluorescent lighting, the college's cafeteria was set up more like a restaurant, with red carpet, dark walls, and dim lighting. The room was so big that it had three full buffet lines, and the high ceiling featured beautiful black chandeliers.

Seeing Lucas brought a whole other issue to mind—one that I *was* going to get answers to.

I abandoned Talia and intercepted Lucas on his way to grab a plate. "Hey."

My tone was less than friendly, but his eyes lit up when he saw me. "Hey, Nad. What's up?"

"I need to talk to you." I wasn't giving him a choice this time.

Lucas shot a glance to Grant. "Um, sure…"

He filled up his plate, then followed me to a secluded corner of the room at a table set for two. Grant looked more than eager to share Talia's company for lunch, so he didn't seem bothered that I dragged his friend away from him.

"What do you want to talk about?" Lucas asked. His voice was steady, but I sensed a hint of uncertainty in his eyes. He wouldn't look at me directly.

"I want to know the truth," I stated.

He finally looked at me. "The truth about what?"

I sighed. "If you don't like me, just tell me."

"Whoa." Lucas's spine straightened. "Where's this coming from, Nad?"

I gaped at him. Was he serious? "You said we couldn't be together. I want to know what that means."

He furrowed his brow. "I thought you said you knew."

I swallowed. "I lied to you."

His face paled. "What do you mean you lied?"

Now I was the one who couldn't meet his gaze. I poked at my food. "When you told me the other day that we couldn't be together because you're the Reaper's Apprentice, I said I understood, but I didn't. Not really. And my friends… they don't seem to understand either."

When I finally lifted my gaze to his, he had this sad look on his face. It was barely there, but I could sense it.

"Nad, I'm sorry," he said softly. "It's something we cover in Mortana Studies. I assumed others knew."

"What does it mean?" I begged. If I couldn't be with him, I wanted a good reason.

Lucas glanced around, and although no one was seated near us, he leaned in and lowered his voice anyway. "Nad, you have to understand that being the Reaper's Apprentice is a very difficult calling. There's a reason the dead leave their last thought behind with me. It's because…"

"Because?" I pressed.

Lucas swallowed. "The nature of what I do can be a bit… morbid. Dark. And sometimes, that darkness is passed on."

"Passed on?" I asked.

"Like, to children," he clarified.

"Whoa!" I held my hands up and leaned back in my chair. I mean, I liked Lucas, but I wasn't seriously thinking about having his babies just yet.

"Goddess, no," Lucas said quickly. "I didn't mean us. Around two hundred years ago, a Reaper's Apprentice fathered a child, and that child was born with a darkness inside of him that no child should be burdened with. As he grew, so did that darkness. He was literally pure evil."

I could feel the crease between my eyebrows deepening. "So you're afraid of having kids? Lucas—"

He held up a hand to stop me. "Let me finish."

I snapped my jaw shut and listened.

"Anyway, this kid, he grew up to resent his parents," Lucas continued. "I don't know the full story, but I guess all those bad emotions built up, and one night, he lost it. He…"

I leaned in closer, intrigued.

Lucas swallowed. "He snapped and murdered his own mother."

I audibly gasped.

Lucas shuddered. "Apparently, it was so brutal that he accidentally cast a curse upon all future Reaper's Apprentices."

My stomach sank. Lucas was cursed?

"There must be a way to break the curse," I said hopefully.

Lucas shook his head. "There isn't. Without a Curse Breaker, it's impossible. Even with one, it'd be tricky."

A beat passed as I considered the weight of his words. "So, what does the curse do?"

"If I was with you, Nadine, you'd…" He hesitated and glanced down at his food.

"What, Lucas? I'd what?"

He cleared his throat. "You'd become the Reaper's Shadow. I couldn't do that to you."

A shiver ran down my spine. "What—what's the Reaper's Shadow?"

He took a long breath. "The Reaper's Shadow is the mate of a Reaper's Apprentice. The sacrifices involved are too much."

"What sacrifices?" I shifted in my seat. I was burning for all the answers.

Lucas hesitated, like it was too painful to even think about. "There are three stages. If the Reaper's Apprentice has sex with the Reaper's Shadow, she will experience a great illness."

I snorted, and Lucas gave me a strange look. I was already sick enough to fit that description. So I was keeping sex on the table. Yeah, like, on this table. I'd like to do him on it.

What the hell? That came out of nowhere.

"Go on," I encouraged, pushing the dirty thoughts aside.

"If the two get married, the Reaper's Shadow will experience severe trauma," he explained.

Nothing I hadn't gone through before. So far, he wasn't exactly scaring me off.

"And the third stage?" I asked.

Lucas closed his eyes. He didn't answer for a moment. "If the Reaper's Apprentice fathers a child… the child will have no choice but to kill the mother."

My breath stalled in my chest. So Lucas was saying that if this turned into something serious, I'd either have to give up kids or die.

That was a big decision to make, but we *weren't* serious. There wasn't any reason to worry about that right now.

"Okay," I said slowly, mulling it all over. "I can see your hesitation. But I mean, the first stage only starts at sex. That doesn't mean you can't have a girlfriend—and I'm not just talking about me," I added quickly when he looked at me.

He scoffed. "What do you think boyfriends and girlfriends do, Nad?"

"What? You're never going to kiss someone?"

"I've kissed people," Lucas grumbled. "And I've done enough to know that kissing leads to other things. *We* almost kissed. I'm not going to risk it, Nad. I don't care how much I want you."

He pressed his fingers to his lips, like he hadn't meant for the confession to spill out.

I blushed a deep pink. "You… you want me?"

Lucas's lips twitched, but the rest of his body had gone still. "I just meant… in general."

Fucking liar! Lucas liked me. I'd bet my ass he wanted to take me right here on this table, too. Damn it. His confession only made me want him more.

"Nadine," he said softly. It caught my attention, because he'd used my full name.

"Yeah?" I responded past the lump in my throat.

"You have to understand why I've chosen to remain celibate." He ran his fingers through his hair, looking flustered. "It's not because I don't want… it's not because…" He took a deep breath. "Look, the truth is, I—"

He cut off, like he couldn't bear to tell me the truth.

"You what?" I asked. I was dying to hear the last half of that sentence.

He dropped his hands to the table and looked me straight in the eye. "The truth is, I'll never have a real relationship like that. I can't do that to someone."

There was such sorrow in his eyes. The way he looked at me, it burrowed deep down into my soul. I felt my own sadness streaming out from my chest. I just wanted to hold him in my arms and tell him that it was all going to be okay. That even if he couldn't have someone *like that*, there were still people who would love him.

But I choked up, and I couldn't say any of that. Instead, I simply smiled and said, "If that's what you really want, Lucas."

Even as I said it, I heard the lie in my voice. I wanted more. Lucas wanted more.

Lucas shifted in his chair, looking like he had more to say. Finally, he lifted his gaze and whispered, "All I want is for you to be safe, Nad."

My heartbeat quickened, and my body heated. The room spun, but not in the scary kind of way. It was exhilarating, like the thrill of reaching the crest on a roller coaster. The problem was, once you stepped onto a roller coaster, you had no choice but to ride it to the end.

Something told me Lucas and I had a long ride ahead of us.

alking to Nadine about the Reaper's Shadow wasn't easy.

I'll never fall in love or have sex.

Total pick-up line. I bet she wanted me so badly right now.

At least I'd managed to finish the assignment Professor Warren had given me, to fill the page in my journal. It was all bullshit, but he didn't look at it long enough to make sense of what I'd written.

"Good job, Lucas," he said proudly before class one day. He handed the book back to me. "I'm glad to see you're making progress."

Ha! Progress.

If anything, I'd gone backward this past week. I'd considered skipping classes just to sleep all day. If it weren't for Grant literally dragging me out of bed, I would've.

Professor Warren clapped me on the shoulder. "Take a seat."

I sat in the back of the classroom as the rest of my classmates filed in for Necromancy Safety. Professor Warren started the lecture right away, while I pulled up the *Miriamic Messenger* on my phone.

This week had been hard on me. I never did find out how that kid died. The family probably wanted their privacy at this time.

I was scrolling through the obituaries, not really paying attention to the lesson. Professor Warren was going on and on about how necromancers had to be careful to only reanimate a soulless being. If you started playing around with the body before a reaper came to take their soul, bad things could happen. It was like that with all Mortana. Our magic was touchy, and if you didn't do things the right way, it could backfire.

Honestly, I wasn't even sure why I was in this class. I wasn't a necromancer. I couldn't create an army of zombie rats or whatever. But they didn't have a class for reapers, and Professor Warren was my mentor, so I guess they just threw me in here with him.

I was hardly listening when a hand shot up at the front of the room.

"Theoretically, could a necromancer bring someone back to life?" a girl asked. It was Lena, my ex-girlfriend from high school. We were on good terms, but I didn't care about her like that anymore. We'd only dated for a few months and never got past second base. "I mean, if they tried reanimating them before the reaper got there."

"No," Professor Warren said firmly. "It's been tried many times, and each time, it fails. You are forbidden from even attempting it. That kind of magic can do great damage to the soul—and bind it here on the earthly plane."

Another hand went into the air. This time, it was a girl named Samantha. "I heard there was a guy in the coven who was brought back to life like, two hundred years ago or something. So there must be some Mortana who can do it, right?"

Professor Warren hesitated. "I'm sure that's just a story."

"But if someone could do it, who's the most capable?" she pressed.

Professor Warren paused, but I barely processed it since I was still reading my phone. "*If* someone could do it, it'd be very difficult—almost impossible. And they'd have to do it before the soul crossed over."

"Who?" Lena demanded.

The room went dead quiet until Professor Warren cleared his throat and said, "The Reaper's Apprentice."

That finally got my attention. All eyes turned to me, and a chill ran down my spine.

"Of course, it's just a theory," Professor Warren was quick to clarify. "A theory one would hope they never have to test."

His stare felt as if it bore a hole in my forehead. The look he gave me was so intense—like he was warning me not to even think about it. *Of course* I wasn't thinking about it! Like hell I wanted someone to die in front of me just to see if I could bring them back. No, thank you.

Samantha raised her hand again. "So let's say the Reaper's Apprentice *could* do it. How would that work? Could they do it to anyone, or does it have to be at a special time, like during the Reaper Moon?"

My spine straightened. I'd never heard of the Reaper Moon before, but it sure sounded important. "What's the Reaper Moon?"

Professor Warren's lips tightened. "We don't cover reaper lore in this class."

I leaned forward in my seat, my hands tightening into fists. This was so unlike Professor Warren. He was the kind of guy who'd give you a lecture about anything just to hear himself talk. It was almost like he was hiding something from me.

"Tell us what the Reaper Moon is," I demanded.

Samantha tossed her long black hair over her shoulder as she turned to me. "It's an astronomical phenomenon that happens every hundred years or so—"

"It's nonsense," Professor Warren insisted, cutting her off.

Samantha acted like she didn't hear him and continued. "When the moon aligns just right, the Reaper Veil lifts and—"

"Miss Stone!" Professor Warren snapped.

Samantha's face paled, and she turned around to face the front of the room again.

Professor Warren crossed his arms. "The Reaper Moon is nothing more than myth, Miss Stone. You're wasting our class time by discussing it. Now let's get back to business."

I didn't hear the rest of the lecture, because I was too hung up on what Samantha said about the Reaper Moon. I wanted to know more, especially since Professor Warren thought I shouldn't. I tried searching for it on my phone, but nothing came up.

The second class let out, I shot out of my chair and ran into the hall to catch up with Samantha.

"Hey, Samantha!" I called.

She turned. Her face fell, and she held her textbooks tight to her chest. "Hey, Lucas. Sorry about bringing up the Reaper's Apprentice in class. I didn't mean to embarrass you."

I shook my head. "You didn't embarrass me. Can you tell me more about the Reaper Moon?"

Samantha glanced back to the open classroom door, then nodded. "Yeah, but not here. Come on."

I followed her to a small study area off the main hall. It was nothing more than an alcove with three plush chairs. I sat across from her and leaned forward, resting my elbows on my knees.

Samantha set her books on her lap and pushed her hair behind her ears. "Let me preface this by saying I don't know all the details about the Reaper Moon. I only know what my grandpa told me. He used to be a history professor here before he retired."

"I want to know everything," I said.

"The Reaper Moon is pretty rare—a once in a lifetime kind of thing," she explained. "Usually, reapers can only step through the Reaper Veil on assignment—when someone dies and they have to step onto our plane to help them to the next."

"Right. I know that," I told her.

Samantha sat up straighter. "Okay, so the Reaper Moon does away with the Veil for just that night. All the reapers are free to roam our plane. Think of it like Halloween, but for reapers."

I furrowed my brow. "Why haven't I ever heard of it? Why isn't there a big celebration for it?"

She frowned. "Well, because it's rare, and most people, like Professor Warren, don't think there's any truth to it."

"Why not?" I asked. It didn't seem that implausible.

"Because people don't believe things they can't see with their own eyes," Samantha asserted. "On Halloween, Seers can see the spirits, speak to them, sometimes even touch them. The Reaper Moon's not quite the same. The only one who can see the reapers is—"

"Is me," I finished for her. "The Reaper's Apprentice. But why would I be able to see them during the Reaper Moon when I can't see them all the time?"

She pressed her lips together. "I'm not entirely certain. I would guess it has something to do with the Veil."

Her eyes brightened. "You'll get to see for yourself, though. It's been a hundred years since the last one. The next Reaper Moon is coming soon—on December twelfth."

My eyebrows shot up. "So soon?"

She frowned. "Yeah, which is why I don't get why Professor Warren wouldn't talk about it."

"Yeah," I agreed. "It doesn't sound dangerous. Unless there's a reason he doesn't want me to see the reapers or get in contact with them."

Samantha glanced down to the books in her lap, but she didn't say anything.

"Wait, do you know something else?" I asked.

She bit her lower lip. "I have a theory."

"What is it?" I didn't like that Professor Warren was keeping something from me.

Samantha hesitated before answering. "Well... my grandpa told me this story about the last Reaper Moon."

I practically squirmed in my chair. The anticipation was killing me. "And...?"

"The Reaper's Apprentice who was alive at the time... he went to one of the reapers, and he asked them to take away his power and assign it to someone else."

I gasped. "Is that even possible?"

No wonder Professor Warren didn't want me to know about the Reaper Moon. He wanted me to suffer with this gift forever. He knew if there was a chance to get rid of it, I'd take it.

"It must be, because it worked," Samantha said. "The reapers all came together and used their magic to take the gift away from him. He lived another forty years or something without ever hearing another person die."

My mouth had gone dry, and I stared blankly ahead. I couldn't believe I had a chance to get rid of this thing—to silence the voices!

"Lucas, are you all right?" Samantha waved her hand in front of my face.

I snapped out of it and shot to my feet. "Yeah, I'm fine. Thanks for the information. You're a lifesaver."

I abandoned Samantha and rushed back to Professor Warren's classroom. The room was empty and silent, but I found him sitting behind the desk in his office. The curtains were closed, and it was a little eerie.

"I know what the Reaper Moon is," I stated as I burst into the room.

I fell down into the chair across from him without so much as a hello. The dick didn't deserve it. He'd been lying to me for months. *Find the good in your gift, Lucas. You're stuck with it for the rest of your life.*

What a load of crap!

Professor Warren looked shell-shocked as his gaze followed me to the chair.

"Why didn't you tell me there was a way to get rid of this… this curse?" I demanded.

Professor Warren leaned back in his chair. "For one, the Reaper Moon is nothing but fiction."

"You don't know that," I snapped. "Most would say that about our magic."

Professor Warren tilted his head as if to say *touché*. "The truth is, Lucas, I didn't want to put ideas in your head. Even if it worked, it would have great consequences."

"Like?" I challenged with a raised eyebrow.

Professor Warren sighed and sat up straight. "For one, your powers would be passed on to someone else."

"Yeah, to someone who wants it," I shot back.

He raised an eyebrow. "How can you be sure of that? Are you truly willing to take that risk and let someone else carry this burden?"

My jaw tightened. Honestly, I didn't really care. Let them have it.

"Mother Miriam chose you for a purpose," Professor Warren reminded me.

"Yeah, yeah," I grumbled. "I've heard that one before."

His lips tightened. "Don't you think it's a little… *dishonorable* of you to refuse the gift she's given you?"

"That's what I'm saying!" I cried. "This isn't a gift. I can't do cool shit like the rest of you. I can't brew potions or see the future. I hear people *die*, Professor Warren! Every single day, I take their secrets and their regrets, and I shove them as far down as possible so they can't hurt anybody anymore!"

I shook, but Professor Warren barely seemed fazed.

"Perhaps that's the problem, Lucas."

I gaped at him. "Excuse me?"

"You're pushing them down, instead of facing them—*accepting* them."

I slammed my hands down on his desk, my nostrils flaring. "Don't tell me what I'm facing. You don't know shit."

Professor Warren backed off a few inches. "Please understand, Lucas, I'm only trying to help. If you refuse Mother Miriam's gift, she won't let you into Alora."

"Who says?" I growled. "Giving my gift back isn't a sin."

Professor Warren sighed. "That depends on how Mother Miriam sees it. If you displease the Goddess—"

"This isn't about her!" I roared.

Professor Warren's eyes went as wide as golf balls. It was like he couldn't believe I had the gall to take a jab at my own goddess. For a second there, I couldn't believe it, either.

But she's the one who wanted me to spend the rest of my life under the weight of this mental trauma. She hadn't sent me a real mentor—someone who actually knew shit about reapers. She hadn't told me what to do, or given me any real way to deal with it. Professor Warren's attempts be damned. Maybe I'd take my chances in the Abyss.

I whirled around and stomped out of his office, but his voice followed behind. "The coven needs a reaper, Lucas!"

I grumbled on my way out of the classroom. "The coven's got enough."

"Hold up. You're telling me there's a way to *stop* being the Reaper's Apprentice?" Grant asked.

"Yep." I stepped up to the concrete disc golf platform.

Grant let out a puff of air. "And I thought *my* day was bad."

"What happened to you?" I asked.

Grant frowned. "The whole Alchemy department's in an uproar because someone broke into the supply closet and stole a shit ton of potion ingredients."

"I hope they caught the idiot." I threw my disc as hard as I could. I held my breath as it flew through the air, praying it wouldn't land in the trees on either side of us. It soared in a perfect arc and landed five feet from the basket.

"They haven't caught him yet. Good throw, man," Grant said as he stepped up to the platform. He took a running start and threw his disc, flicking his wrist at the last second. His disc landed in line with the basket but too far away to make it in the next shot. "Anyway, I can't believe Warren didn't tell you about the Reaper Moon. Like, the dude just *forgot*?"

"No." My teeth ground together as we walked down the fairway. "He purposely didn't tell me. *The coven needs a reaper, Lucas.*"

Grant laughed. "That's a pretty good impression of him. Why are you so desperate to get rid of it, though? I mean, if Mother Miriam wanted you to be the Reaper's Apprentice..."

I shook my head. "I'm not cut out for it. I'm too weak."

"You're *not* weak," Grant insisted, punching me lightly in the shoulder.

I dropped my gaze to my feet. "I don't know. Maybe I am."

Grant stopped beside his disc and picked it up. "You know what I think? I think this has less to do about your gift and everything to do with a certain someone whose name starts with an N and ends in an Adine."

I let out a puff of air and rolled my eyes. "This isn't about Nadine. But I'm not going to lie to you, it's definitely crossed my mind. Fuck man, I'm cursed to be a virgin my whole life."

Grant chuckled and tossed his disc. It bounced off the corner of the metal basket and ricocheted back at him.

"That's what you get for laughing at me, douche," I teased.

Grant stepped forward and swapped out his driving disc for a putting disc. This time, the chains *clanged* as he landed it inside the basket. "Technically, you're not cursed. You could fuck whoever you wanted and be fine."

"Yeah, but at their expense!" I conjured my putter and tossed it into the basket. "I'm not going around fucking girls I don't care about just to get laid, only to curse them with a terrible illness."

We both grabbed our discs and headed to the next platform.

"You're too soft," Grant accused.

"Dude, you're awful," I shot back.

Grant rolled his eyes. "It was a joke, Lucas. So, what are you going to do about Nadine? Are you going to get rid of this thing so you can date her?"

I frowned. "I don't even know if she wants to date me."

"What are you talking about?" Grant asked. "She totally likes you."

"I don't get why," I grumbled.

Grant stepped up to the platform, flipping his disc in his hands. "Well, you could ask her."

"I'm not going to ask her!"

Grant rolled his eyes. "Say she wanted to date you. Would you contact the reapers at the Reaper Moon?"

I hesitated. My instinct was to say yes, but Professor Warren had made some good points. Now that I had time to consider what he said, I feared he might be right. Mother Miriam trusted me with this gift. If I gave it back, I'd be banished and sent to the Abyss. So my choices basically came down to Nadine or Alora.

Fuck.

"I don't know," I admitted. "It's kind of a big decision. I've got to weigh the pros and cons. To be honest, it's looking pretty appealing right now. I wouldn't have to carry these thoughts around anymore. And I know there's no way to break the Reaper's Shadow curse, but this is the next best thing if I'm ever going to date. But… the Abyss, man."

Grant shuddered. "Yeah, that's tough."

I gaped at him. "That's all you have for me? *That's tough*?"

He shrugged, then threw his disc and watched it soar through the air. It hit a tree and bounced into the forest. He sucked a sharp breath between his teeth, then turned to me. "If it were up to me, I wouldn't risk the Abyss. An eternity of damnation? No thanks. But I can't make that decision for you."

"Why not?" I joked. "It'd be easier."

Grant frowned. "Nothing about this is easy. If you're not going to go through with the Reaper Moon, you need to stay away from Nadine."

My eyebrows slammed together. "What? No way. She makes me happy. I actually smile around her, and the voices are quieter when she's around."

Grant frowned. "You know that never works. One of these days, you're going to cave."

I narrowed my eyes at him. "And what do I do if she wants to stay friends with me? I can't just avoid her."

Grant shrugged. "Be an asshole, and *she'll* be the one avoiding you."

I scoffed and stepped up to the platform. "Uh, no thanks."

I swung my arm around and flicked my wrist, and my driver went flying toward the basket. It narrowly missed a tree and landed just a few yards from where I was aiming.

"How about I tell her you've been keeping secrets?" Grant suggested.

"You promised!" I growled.

It'd been weeks ago that I'd told Grant where I'd heard Nadine's name before—in her mom's last thought. Nadine didn't know, and I couldn't tell her. It could put her in danger.

Grant held his hands up in defense. "I'm not going to tell her! Not unless you decide you want to drive her away. What'd this last thought say, anyway?"

I shook my head firmly as we started toward our discs. "Nope. Not telling. Reaper's Apprentice privileges only."

"It's killing me why you won't tell her," Grant said. "What's the big secret?"

"I've already told you too much."

"Fine," Grant sighed. "Your secret is safe with me. So, can we invite the girls out for a round of golf?"

"What's with you, man?" I complained. "One second you're telling me to stay away from her. The next you're inviting her to our bro day."

Grant cocked an eyebrow. "Bro day? You *just* said you're not going to avoid her. So pick one."

"Whatever. Invite them if you want."

Grant conjured his phone and started poking at the screen.

Grant and I worked our way through the rest of the course. The last hole ended close to the parking lot. Grant chucked his disc above a wall of tall bushes, and we heard it skid along the gravel.

When we stepped out of the forest and into the parking lot, my blood ran cold. Next to our vehicle sat a sleek black sports car. It was the only car here besides ours. Just thinking about all my rides in that thing made me want to hurl. I couldn't believe I was ever friends with those assholes.

Grant turned up his nose. "What are the *Tarantulas* doing here?"

I frowned. "Dunno. But I guarantee it's not disc golf."

I'd only ever seen Ryan play once, and I kicked his ass so badly he made a big deal out of how disc golf wasn't a real sport and I was a sissy for playing instead of working out in the gym like a "real man." I can't believe I took that jerkwad's verbal abuse. I guess growing up with my dad, you just learned those kinds of things were normal.

Grant chuckled. "I bet their drug drop-off is somewhere around here."

The sad thing is, he wasn't kidding.

"Let's find my disc and get out of here before they come back," Grant said. He still hadn't forgotten the prank they'd pulled on him last year. Neither of us wanted to face those losers.

Grant and I glanced around the parking lot, but his disc was nowhere in sight.

"That's weird," Grant remarked. "I didn't think I threw it *that* far."

He walked to the other side of the parking lot to see if his disc had landed in the grass. Meanwhile, I bent over and tilted my head to look beneath the cars. Sure enough, Grant's green disc was lying in the gravel beneath Ryan's shiny black car. I groaned and lowered myself onto my stomach to reach under the car for the disc.

"Hey!" a deep voice boomed across the parking lot.

My whole body gave a jolt. Several pairs of footsteps began racing across the gravel all at once. I quickly pushed myself out from under the car and tried to get to my feet. But I didn't get there before Ryan dropped a backpack beside his car and grabbed me by the collar.

"Stop!" Grant cried as he sprinted over to me. Nolan and Finn stepped in front of him and held him back.

"What the fuck were you doing to my car?" Ryan roared. Spittle flew onto my face, and his nostrils flared.

My whole body shook in rage. What I wouldn't give to punch this jerk in the face. I shoved him away with my forearm so hard that he stumbled backward and let me go. "Get off of me, man. I didn't touch your damn car. We lost a disc."

I held up the disc as evidence, but Ryan didn't seem to buy it. He was back on me in less than a second, his forearm pinning me to the side of the car.

"I don't believe you," he growled, his dirty breath skimming along the side of my face.

Grant tried to side-step the other Tarantulas, but the third and fourth gang members stepped forward to block his path.

"Now tell me what you did to my car!" Ryan shouted in my face.

My lips tightened, and I held his gaze. "I told you. We lost a disc. That's all. I wouldn't touch that filthy thing anyway."

Ryan's lips curled into a sneer. He grabbed a fistful of my shirt with each hand, then slammed my back against the car again so hard it nearly knocked the wind out of me.

"I'm not in the mood today, Taylor," Ryan threatened. "If you cut my brake lines or some shit like that, there's going to be hell to pay."

I scoffed. Did this loser really think he could scare me? The only time we'd ever gotten into a fist fight, I'd won. "I've already served my time. Being friends with you was hell enough."

Before I saw it coming, Ryan's fist slammed into my mouth. A shock wave went through my teeth and down my jaw. Warm liquid and the taste of copper filled my mouth. For a second, I couldn't believe he'd actually done it.

I was done. I was *so* done with this asshole. I dropped the disc and retaliated quickly.

"I've had enough of your mouth—" Ryan started.

He was cut off by my fist cracking into the side of his jaw. Pain shot through my knuckles, but I didn't care. It was totally worth it to watch him stumble to the side clutching his face. A wave of pride washed over me, but it was short lived.

Ryan righted himself and shot daggers my way. "You're gonna pay for that, Taylor."

Ryan gathered midnight blue magic in his hands and muttered an incantation under his breath. He thrust the defensive magic forward. I ducked and lunged, slamming my shoulder into his middle. We both fell to the ground the same time the sound of shattering glass came from behind us. The idiot had smashed his own window.

Everything moved so fast that I barely knew what was going on around me. All I heard was the sound of feet slamming into flesh and Grant's pained grunts not far from me. I had to get to him pronto, but I couldn't while Ryan was trying to rip the flesh off my face. Fingernails dug into my skin as he muttered an incantation and ran his nails down my cheek. A burning sensation—like acid—ignited across my face. Whatever magic he was using wasn't anything we'd learned in class. It was probably illegal.

I gathered magic in my hand to retaliate with a defensive spell, but Ryan was quicker than me. He shot his hands out and used his telekinetic powers to throw me backward.

My elbows skidded along the gravel. Ryan was quick to get to me. He jumped on top of me to hold me down and punched me straight in the nose. Red flashed across my vision, and blood spurted everywhere.

I grabbed him around the neck and threw him off of me. I used the momentum to slam his body into the dirt. I jumped on top of him and wrapped my hands around his throat. I squeezed tightly, enjoying the satisfaction of shock cross his features. He grabbed my wrists and tried to twist them off him, but I wouldn't budge. His lips curled into a rage-filled sneer.

A second later, an invisible force slammed into my wrists, throwing my arms outward and catching me off guard. Damn Mentalist powers.

I could feel Ryan trying to lift me off him with his magic, but he wasn't strong enough yet to do it. I regained control of my hands and grabbed his shirt.

"What the fuck's your problem?" I shouted.

"You are," he spat. "I'm not letting you ruin this."

"Ruin what?" I demanded.

Ryan never got a chance to answer. A foot slammed into my guts, launching me off of Ryan. I rolled a couple of times in the gravel. When I looked up, Declan was standing over me, fury etched in his features.

"Traitor!" he snarled, cracking his knuckles.

Why were these idiots still hung up on that? So I left their group. Why couldn't they just leave me alone?

I swung my leg out and knocked Declan off his feet, but I didn't have time to stand up before all five of the Treacherous Tarantulas were surrounding me. One quick glance toward their car, and I saw they'd finished with Grant. He was lying there clutching his stomach and groaning in pain.

I held my hands up in surrender. "Guys, please. We were really just—"

A heavy boot smashed into my face. All I saw was a shadow coming closer and closer, then felt the ungodly pain shooting through my face. A *crunch* sounded, and my ears rang. When the darkness cleared from my vision and refocused, Ryan's bruised face was right in front of me.

"This beating's long overdue, Taylor," he seethed. "And for once, your brother's not here to stop it."

Heavy footfalls began to rain down on me from all directions as each of the Treacherous Tarantulas took their turn beating me to a pulp. It was hard to tell where the pain was coming from. Everything hurt.

"How's it feel, Lucas!?"

I squeezed my eyes shut tightly and brought my hands up to protect my face, but Ryan's voice sounded like it was coming from all around me.

"How's it feel to finally be the one on the ground?" Ryan taunted. "I bet Eric's looking down on you from Alora thinking what a pussy you are. He was a pussy, too—"

The sound of tires crunching across the gravel was like music to my ears. All five of the Tarantulas halted at once. They whirled around, but I just lay there trying not to spew my guts.

Ryan started laughing, and the other four quickly joined in. I finally peeled my eyelids back to see what was going on. My heart lifted at the sight of Nadine's silver sedan stopped in the middle of the parking lot. Nadine and Talia shared a similar wide-eyed expression, like they couldn't believe what they were seeing. Nadine's gaze met mine from behind the wheel, and her features quickly shifted. Her eyebrows dropped over her eyes, and her lips pressed into a thin line.

Ryan chuckled and stepped in front of the vehicle with his arms held wide. "What are you going to do, bitches? Come at me?"

Nadine shot one look at Talia, and Talia gave her a subtle nod. Without hesitation, Nadine narrowed her gaze on Ryan and stepped on the gas. The car hurled through the parking lot, speeding straight toward the Tarantulas.

Ryan must've thought Nadine was playing chicken with him—or he was trying to stop the car with his powers and failing miserably—because he didn't back down until the very last second. Ryan and his cronies leapt out of the way.

"What the fuck, you crazy bitch!?" Ryan screamed as he jumped back to his feet and dusted the dirt off his leather jacket.

Nadine yanked on the wheel, and the tires spun as she turned the car around back in Ryan's direction. She shot him the finger, then placed her hands firmly back on the wheel.

"Crazy hoe!" Finn yelled.

"Let's get out of here!" Ryan shouted at the same time.

Ryan grabbed the bag he'd dropped, and the five of them scurried into his vehicle. Nadine's car hadn't moved an inch, but she kept her narrowed gaze on them and her hands tight on the wheel. The Tarantulas tore out of the parking lot without so much as a glance back.

Grant groaned and pushed himself to his knees, shaking a fist in the air. "Not so tough now, are you?"

Of course, they didn't hear him.

Nadine shifted into park, and she and Talia jumped out of the car before she'd even cut the engine.

"Lucas!" Nadine cried as she ran over to me.

I clutched my stomach and pushed myself to a sitting position, but it was difficult. It felt like I was bleeding out everywhere.

Talia sprinted toward Grant. "Goddess, let me help you. We should get you to the hospital."

Talia pulled Grant to his feet and supported him as he limped over to Nadine's car.

"Lucas," Nadine said breathlessly. She dropped to her knees beside me and gazed into my eyes with deep concern. She placed her hands on either side of my face.

When Nadine laid her hands on me, it was like magic. My heart lifted, and all the pain seemed to melt away. I couldn't even feel the gravel beneath me, as if I was floating.

"Nad…"

"Shh, Lucas." Nadine stripped off her zip-up sweatshirt and balled it up to place beneath my head like a pillow.

I must've been really out of it, because when I lay back and looked up at her, it looked like there was a halo surrounding her. She truly glowed.

Without thinking about it, I reached out and ran my fingers across the side of her face. "Nad, you're here."

"Yes, I am," she said in a rush. "And you have a broken nose. We're going to the hospital."

"We will," I assured her. "Just let me rest a moment."

"Lucas, what hurts?" she asked frantically. "Tell me what hurts."

I shook my head. "Nothing, Nad. It's all good now."

Nadine threw herself over me and buried her face into my shoulder. Her knee brushed up against a bruise forming on my hip, but I didn't care. She was hugging me, and that made everything better.

"Lucas, I was terrified for you." Her voice was muffled in my hoodie. "When we drove in and saw them, I…" Nadine drew away to look me in the eyes.

I grabbed the sides of her face. "You got here just in time."

Her eyes began to sparkle with tears. "If we'd gotten here just a little sooner—"

I swallowed. I was pretty sure I was swallowing blood, but it didn't really register. "No use in worrying about what could have been. Thank you."

Before I knew what I was doing, I dragged Nadine's face close to mine, and I pressed my lips to hers.

Kissing Lucas was beyond anything I ever imagined it would be. You know in the movies when the guy gets the girl and he sweeps her off her feet, then everyone starts clapping and this beautiful, teary-eyed music starts playing? Then they cut forward a few months and he's carrying her out of the church on their wedding day, everyone's throwing rice and is all happy, then they drive off into the sunset and nothing can ever hurt them again?

That's what Lucas's kiss felt like, but better. It was like nothing bad could ever touch me.

Lucas's hand came up to cradle the back of my neck. A fire ignited deep within my belly, and I relaxed into the kiss. My lips parted, and his tongue slid inside my mouth.

It felt as if the ground had dropped away, like we were spinning in midair and the whole world had ceased to exist around us. My heart lifted in my chest before the adrenaline settled in and sent my heart pummeling against my rib cage.

My hands tangled in Lucas's hair, and I dragged him closer to me. He kissed me harder, like I was the very breath he breathed. My nipples hardened beneath my shirt, begging for more.

Lucas drew away, and his soft eyes roamed over my face. I was frozen in place, unable to move, blink, or breathe. Several quiet moments passed as we stared deep into each other's eyes, until I thought my lungs might burst.

It was the only indication I had that time was still moving forward.

"I'm sorry," Lucas whispered. "I shouldn't have done that."

I shook my head and finally took a breath. "It's okay, Lucas. I'm glad you did."

I hesitated as my gaze roamed over his bruised features. I longed to kiss him again, but right now wasn't the time. "Let's get you to a hospital."

The next few hours passed at an ungodly slow pace as Talia and I waited in the emergency room for Grant and Lucas. When they were finally released, Grant had four stitches above his eyebrow, and Lucas's broken nose had been set. We took the guys back to their dorm room, then brought them ice cream before turning in for the night.

We didn't see them the rest of the weekend. I tried visiting Lucas on Saturday, but no one answered the door, even though I was pretty sure I heard footsteps behind it. I could hardly sleep over the weekend as the kiss replayed over and over again in my mind. Every time I thought about it, my heart lifted in my chest.

And then I remembered that I hadn't seen Lucas in days, and my pulse quickened for entirely different reasons. He was obviously avoiding me again, and I was ticked off about it. One minute he's kissing me like his life depends on it, and the next he falls completely off the map. I was getting really sick of his mixed signals.

Tuesday morning, I awoke with a terrible shooting pain in my left hand. My whole body was stiffer than normal, and it took at least fifteen minutes of lying in bed trying not to scream before I could shift and get into a more comfortable position.

Lupus was like that sometimes. I had good and bad days, and it was all totally unpredictable.

Talia noticed I was lying in bed longer than usual. "Hey, girl. Are you going to take your bath this morning?"

My neck was so stiff I couldn't even work up the strength to shake my head. Screw my body. Why did it hate itself so much?

"Eventually," I told her.

"Well, you better hurry up," she said as she brushed her hair. "Miriamic History is in half an hour."

I groaned and reached for my phone on my bedside table. She wasn't lying.

"I think I'm going to skip today," I said. I didn't want to, since it was the one class I struggled the most with, but I hadn't skipped all semester, and I figured I deserved a pass at least once. Today just wasn't happening.

Talia turned from the mirror and shot me a concerned expression. "Are you going to make it to Conjuring Basics later today?"

"Yeah, I'll make it."

Talia frowned and grabbed her bag. "Okay. Feel better."

I scoffed. "I'll try."

It was another hour before I got out of bed, and another hour after that before I finished my bath and got dressed. I was feeling a lot better, but all I wanted to do was go back to sleep. I had a few hours before Conjuring Basics, and I needed to get some homework done before I went, but I couldn't bring myself to work up the energy. I couldn't recall a day this bad since before my diagnosis.

Eventually, I got so hungry that I knew if I didn't head down to the cafeteria soon, I'd end up passing out before I got there. I ate, then headed off to Conjuring Basics.

"Before we jump into our next lesson," Professor Carlisle said, "let's review what we already know about conjuring."

Professor Carlisle was a short, elderly Seer with salt and pepper hair and an equally gray cat who looked like he was on his last life. You'd think at first glance Professor Carlisle was too, but he had this energy about him that suggested he had many years left.

He continued. "Earlier in the semester, we learned that conjuring is bound by many rules. You can't conjure something out of nothing, and you can't make one thing disappear from somewhere and end up in another. Imagine a pocket universe that follows you around everywhere you go. To *subconjure*, you take an object from your hand and place it into this pocket universe. To *conjure*, you take something from that universe and place it into your hand."

Professor Carlisle held out his hand, and a cane materialized out of nowhere. "Conjured."

He smiled brightly and did a little tap dance at the front of the room. At the end, he kicked the cane and made it spin around in his hand. It disappeared right in front of our eyes. "Subconjured. See? Simple."

A few people clapped at the demonstration, but it was half-hearted.

I couldn't wait until I had magic so I didn't have to lug around my textbooks wherever I went. It'd be so convenient to have my wallet at my fingertips without having to actually carry it around. I mean, I'd be fine with it if the fashion industry just gave women pockets, but I guess that was more of a stretch than actual magic.

"What we haven't talked about yet this semester is conjuring's limitations," Professor Carlisle said. "Let's say I wanted to fill my pocket universe to the brim. How many items do you think I could take with me?"

A hand raised at the front of the room. "Five?" the girl guessed timidly.

Professor Carlisle pressed his index finger to his lips. "Mm… not exactly."

"Ten!" someone else shouted, but Professor Carlisle shook his head.

"A hundred!" another voice came.

Professor Carlisle didn't stop shaking his head as more and more students piped up with their guesses, the numbers growing each time. I couldn't help but think that my classmates were idiots. This obviously wasn't the kind of answer Professor Carlisle was looking for.

I raised my hand, and his eyebrows shot up. "Miss Evers?"

The room went quiet, and I cleared my throat. "Wouldn't it depend on the size of the objects and not the amount?"

His eyes brightened, and he smiled. Professor Carlisle had one of the most expressive faces I'd ever seen. "Precisely. But how big do you think our invisible bag is? Could I, say, fit a car in it? Or an entire library of books?"

He looked directly at me, but I didn't know how to answer his question.

Professor Carlisle clicked his tongue. "No guesses?"

Some jock in the front row leaned back in his seat. "I bet you could fit a car."

Our professor cocked an eyebrow. "You think so, Mister James?"

"Sure," he claimed. "I'll betcha ten bucks after my Evoking Ceremony I'll subconjure a car."

Professor Carlisle smirked and stepped up to him with his hand out. "You're on."

The two of them shook on it, then Professor Carlisle turned to the door at the front of the lecture hall. He stepped behind it and put a door stopper in front of it to keep it open. Practically the whole class craned their necks to see what he was up to. I couldn't see anything, until he shot back into the room sitting on a chest of drawers that was on wheels. He sat with his knees crossed and his arms held in the air, like he was making a grand entrance to a Vegas show or something. The chest of drawers spun once. He jumped off and nearly stumbled over his cat, but he made a clean landing. The class clapped and cheered for him.

"Ladies and gentlemen, a chest of drawers!" Professor Carlisle gestured to it. It was dark mahogany and looked a lot like the dressers we had in our dorms, except it was longer and shorter. "This is approximately the size of your unique pocket universe. So by all means, Mister James, if you manage to subconjure a car, I'd be very interested to see that."

Professor Carlisle turned back to the chest of drawers and conjured his cane, then started tapping it against the drawers. "This is all the space you get, ladies and gentlemen. In my opinion, it totally beats a duffel bag, and it definitely saves you money when you fly."

The class chuckled.

A girl at the front of the room raised her hand. "What happens if you try to subconjure too much, if your space gets full?"

"Let me ask you this," Professor Carlisle replied. "What would happen if I tried to fill this chest of drawers too full?"

"Well… the drawers wouldn't close, obviously," she said.

"Exactly," Professor Carlisle said. "It'll push back. Things will start spilling out. Simple as that."

The jock eyed the chest of drawers. "So, what happens if you subconjure a person?"

Professor Carlisle raised an eyebrow. "Why, Mister James? Do you have plans to kidnap somebody?"

James sent a nervous glance around the room at the people who were laughing. "No. I just wondered, you know, could you survive it? The pocket universe?"

"I don't know," Professor Carlisle answered. "That's another limitation to conjuring. You can't subconjure a living thing."

One of James's friends leaned over to him. "There goes your kidnapping plans."

"Shut up." He shoved his friend.

I raised my hand, and Professor Carlisle called on me. "I'm curious, can things get lost? Like, if I wanted to subconjure something to hide it from someone, would they ever be able to find it? Or say I subconjured a valuable family heirloom, but I died before I had a chance to pass it on. Would it be lost forever?"

Professor Carlisle pressed his lips together firmly. "That's a very good question, Miss Evers. And this is why I advise you never subconjure anything of value. That said, there *are* ways to retrieve items from someone else's personal stash. However, it is a very complicated spell that requires more than one individual to perform and is only done on rare occasions. Why, Miss Evers? Is there something you'd like to retrieve?"

I shook my head. "No. I was just curious how it works is all."

"Snooping into someone else's pocket universe is dangerous," Professor Carlisle warned. "You may not like what you find. Don't let your curiosity get you into too much trouble, Miss Evers."

I chuckled under my breath. Professor Carlisle didn't know me at all.

After class, I made my way to Headmistress Verla's office for my first Evoking Ceremony training session. I turned down a short hall, but it was deserted. I glanced down to my campus map to confirm I was in the right hall, then walked to the end. There sat a pair of double doors with a plaque that read *Headmistress Clarice Verla*. I raised my fist to knock when I heard a deafening *bang* sound from the other side of the doors. My heart leapt up to my throat, and I swayed on my feet as the ground shook beneath me.

I heard the sound of doors swinging open from the adjacent hall, then came the many footsteps. A second later, white smoke began to billow out through the cracks around the doors. It was unusually thick and didn't smell of fire. I eyed the smoke curiously and reached my fingers out to touch it. A stinging pain shot though my fingers, and I jerked away like I'd been burned.

Professor Wykoff—my Introduction to Tarot professor—rounded the corner. Her usual calm demeanor was replaced by a terrified look in her eyes.

"Dear Goddess!" she cried. "What's happened?"

"I-I don't know," I stammered, stepping away from the smoke creeping out into the hall. My fingers stung like I'd been attacked by a bee.

Professor Wykoff whirled around as two other professors came running. "Get Professor Richards."

The other professors went running to get help, while Professor Wykoff turned back to me. She grabbed me by the elbow and spoke gently. "Come, child. You must stay away."

"Wait, what's going on?" I asked, terrified that I'd just encountered some sort of chemical weapon. "Is Headmistress Verla going to be okay? What is that?"

Professor Wykoff pulled me into the next hall and guided me to stand next to the wall to let a group of professors pass. I noticed Professor Richards among them, clutching a flask full of a blue liquid.

"Tell me what you saw," Professor Wykoff instructed.

My jaw dropped, and I rubbed my aching fingers with my thumb. I think I was still in shock. "I-I didn't see anything. I'd just walked into the hall when I heard a bang. Then I saw the smoke, and you were there a second later."

Professor Wykoff grabbed my wrist and inspected the ends of my fingers. They were bright red, but otherwise looked fine. She breathed a sigh of relief. "Child, what are you doing in this part of the school?"

Voices yelled down the hall, and it took me a second to process her question. "I came to meet Headmistress Verla. We have an appointment."

"Okay," she said with a frown. "You stay right here, Miss Evers."

I didn't really know what was happening, so I did as I was told. After Professor Wykoff turned the corner to join the other professors, I heard them start to argue.

"We need to figure out who did this," a male professor said.

"Agreed," Professor Wykoff replied. "This is a threat."

"How do we know it's not just a prank?" a second female professor asked.

"We don't," the first guy responded in a clipped tone. "But until we know, we must treat it as an attempt on the headmistress's life."

Professor Wykoff gasped. "Who would do that?"

I was breathing heavily, unable to process what they were saying. Was someone out to *kill* Headmistress Verla?

"Relax, I've got the perimeter secure," Professor Richards said. "The antidote is working, but it will take a few hours."

The sound of clicking heels caught my attention. I looked up to see Headmistress Verla breezing down the hall. Her black cat ran behind her, but he was so fat that he more or less waddled. I breathed a sigh of relief, grateful that she hadn't been in her office when that thing went off. Her eyebrows hung low over her eyes, giving her this dark look that seemed strange on such a beautiful woman. She walked past me, like she didn't even see me, and stomped straight up to the other professors. I inched my way along the wall to peek around the corner and get a good look at them.

"What in the name of Mother Miriam is going on here?" she cried.

"A sting bomb," Professor Richards said. "But not to worry, Headmistress. This potion should take care of it in a few hours."

He held up the blue potion I'd seen him run past with. Most of it was gone.

Professor Wykoff's jaw dropped. "A stink bomb?"

"No," Professor Richards replied. "A *sting* bomb. It's a defense potion brewed using stinging nettle. It's fairly harmless but hurts like a son of a bitch. Thank Alora Headmistress Verla wasn't in her office when it was set off."

"Did anyone see who did it?" Verla demanded. Odin stepped toward the cloud of smoke and hissed.

The professors all glanced to each other and shook their heads. Professor Wykoff's eyes brightened, and she looked to me. My face paled as I was caught eavesdropping.

"There was a witness." Professor Wykoff gestured to me.

Headmistress Verla's face fell as she turned to me. "Nadine, tell us what happened."

Timidly, I stepped out from around the corner and joined the professors. The double doors were open. All I could see behind them was a wall of white smoke, but it just hung there in the air instead of creeping into the hall.

"I actually didn't see anything," I admitted. "I only just arrived when it went off."

An older male professor who looked cocky as hell gazed down his nose at me. He wore an ironed suit, and his gray hair was combed into a neat style. "Who's to say *you* weren't the one who set it off?"

He reached out and snatched my wrist.

"Ow!" I cried.

"Oh, please," he sneered. "I barely touched you. Proof!"

He held my hand up to all the other professors to show them my red fingers. He pointed an ugly finger at me. "You've been caught red-handed! Did you think this was some innocent little prank, half-blood?"

I gaped at him. Did he seriously just have the nerve to call me a half-blood in front of all these other professors?

"Professor Daymond!" Headmistress Verla shouted.

He dropped my hand, and I held it to my chest protectively. If I had any strength in it at the moment, I might've curled it into a fist and sucker-punched that smug sneer off his face. I prayed to Miriam I'd never have this professor. He seemed awful.

Headmistress Verla stepped forward to get up in Professor Daymond's face. "How dare you accuse a *student* of this. She is my mentee."

"Well, I-I," he stammered.

Headmistress Verla scoffed at him. "Go do something useful with your time, Archibald."

Professor Daymond narrowed his gaze at her before huffing and stomping off.

Headmistress Verla turned to me. "I'm very sorry, Nadine, but I'm afraid we're going to have to reschedule while I deal with this. I'll get back to you on our next session."

"Okay," I said. "I'm sorry this happened."

Headmistress Verla shook her head. "Don't worry about it. Unless you saw something happen…"

She eyed me, like she too was a little suspicious. If she was, I wasn't sure why she'd stood up for me.

"I didn't," I said. "I swear."

Headmistress Verla looked at me a moment longer, then dropped her shoulders. "You may go."

I walked away feeling really confused. Did Headmistress Verla seriously suspect me of trying to sabotage her? Why would I do something like that? The only person in this school I knew who had the balls to sabotage someone like that was Chloe.

Speak of the devil…

I exited a long hallway to see Chloe, Gwen, and Camille huddled in a group and snickering at each other. Can you say *déjà vu*? They'd done the exact same thing after they broke into my dorm room.

I stomped straight up to them. Chloe noticed my approach and shot me a death glare. She placed her hand on her hip. "What's *your* problem?"

I crossed my arms and stood just inches from her. She was a lot taller than me in her heels, but I liked to think I intimidated her nonetheless. "A sting bomb just went off in Headmistress Verla's office. You don't happen to know anything about that, would you?"

Chloe scoffed and rolled her eyes. "Please. I've been standing here for the last ten minutes. My girls will back me up."

Camille pursed her lips in my direction. At the same time, Gwen tossed her blonde hair over her shoulder. It was the first time I noticed a cauldron tattoo on her chest. It definitely wasn't there before, which meant she must've gone through her Evoking Ceremony recently—and that Chloe now had a right-hand Alchemist to do her bidding.

"So, what? You put it on a timer or something," I accused.

Chloe shot an innocent look to the other girls. "I don't know. Can you do that with potions?"

The other two shrugged in unison.

Chloe leaned forward so I could feel her breath on my face. "You don't know *anything* about this coven, Nadine. You don't want to leave on your own? Then I'll *make* you."

My hands tightened into fists, but my fingers were still burning from the sting bomb. "Is that a threat?"

Chloe stepped away without acknowledging my question. "Good luck passing your Evoking Ceremony without any training."

She flipped her hair over her shoulder and started walking in the other direction. I gaped at her. That was a confession if I'd ever heard one. No one had tried to hurt Headmistress Verla. Chloe had set off that sting bomb to sabotage my lesson! She knew I had it this week because Camille and Gwen had been in the metaphysical shop when Headmistress Verla and I talked about it. That bitch would do anything to drive me out of town, including ensuring I failed my Evoking Ceremony. And all for… what? A dead feud between our grandparents?

"Get a life and stop trying to ruin mine!" I shouted down the hall.

Chloe continued on her way, swaying her hips as if she never heard me. I'd bet anything she was the one who'd raided the Alchemy lab last week, too.

"Gah!" I screamed, turning on my heel and storming in the opposite direction.

I was passing by the cafeteria when I caught sight of Grant sitting alone at a table near the door. I walked in and plopped down across from him. He glanced up to me, but he didn't have any food in front of him. I shot him a curious expression.

"What's got your panties in a bunch?" he asked.

I huffed. "Chloe's at it again."

Grant frowned while he poked at something beneath the table. "What'd she do this time?"

"Well, I don't have any proof, but I'm pretty sure she's responsible for setting off a sting bomb in Headmistress Verla's office to sabotage my Evoking Ceremony training," I said.

"It *does* sound like her." He winced, then stuck his finger in his mouth and sucked on it like it hurt.

I eyed him curiously. "What are you doing?"

"Oh, this?" Grant held up a small device with digital numbers on it. "I'm checking my blood sugar before I eat."

I tilted my head, and the knot in my chest loosened. "You have diabetes?"

He nodded as he took his bag from his lap and placed it on the table. It opened flat like a wallet and was filled with his medication. "Not a big deal. I can hardly remember a time I didn't have it."

I suddenly felt an instant connection with Grant that wasn't there before. Obviously diabetes and lupus weren't the same thing, but I always got a jolt of excitement when I met someone with a chronic illness. It was like they were the only people who even remotely understood what I went through.

"How long have you known?" I asked.

"Since I was fourteen," he replied as he grabbed a needle and started filling it with insulin.

"I was fifteen when I was diagnosed," I blurted. I usually didn't talk about my disease to just anyone, but I felt like Grant would understand.

He raised a curious eyebrow. "Diabetes?"

I shook my head. "Lupus."

"That's autoimmune, isn't it?" he asked casually.

I smiled. Usually I was met with, *"Oh, Nadine, I'm so sorry,"* or, *"Have you seen a doctor about that?"* But Grant just wanted to know more, like I was telling him about one of my classes.

"Yeah, my doctor says it's common in the coven," I said.

He injected his shot, then nodded. "Yeah. It comes with being half human."

A silent beat passed between us, but I broke it. "Do you want to get dinner together?"

"Sure. I just have to wait a few minutes for the insulin to kick in," he said.

I folded my hands in my lap. "I can wait. Are Lucas or Talia joining us?"

He shook his head. "Lucas is meeting his mentor, and Talia has a study group."

I frowned. I wasn't sure if Grant was covering for Lucas or if it was the truth.

"What's wrong?" Grant asked, sensing my discomfort.

I hesitated a moment, but I couldn't stand not knowing. "Does Lucas *really* have a meeting with his mentor?"

"Yes," Grant answered honestly. "Why wouldn't he?"

I pressed my lips together. "Well, I haven't seen him since…" *Since our kiss,* I wanted to say. Instead, I said, "Since the hospital. He has a habit of avoiding me, and I'm worried—"

"Don't worry, Nadine," Grant assured me, but I sensed uncertainty in his tone. "Lucas just needs… time."

My stomach sank. *Time to decide how he truly feels,* I thought.

I tried not to let my disappointment get to me, but it was hard when all I could think about lately was that kiss. Lucas said he didn't want to be with me, then he kisses me like that—the best kiss of my entire life. What the hell was his deal?

"Well, I guess it's just us two then," I said.

"Yep, just us." After a moment of silence, Grant said, "Hey, do you think if we put our immune systems together, we'd have a working one?"

I laughed. "I don't know about that. Mine's trying to kill me."

"Mine, too. But in a different way." He started putting his supplies away in a bag that held it all. "I've got Type 1 diabetes. My immune system attacks the cells in my pancreas that produce insulin. I have to eat regularly and inject myself to regulate my blood sugar. There's no cure, but at least life's pretty normal, as long as I plan ahead."

"Same here," I said. "Do you have to use an insulin pump?"

I was too curious not to ask questions.

Grant subconjured his supplies, and they disappeared from the table. "I could if I wanted to, but then I'd have to wear it all the time, and I'd have to take it off when I'm active, which is a pain, especially with how much I swim. With the shots, it's in, out, and done, and there's a lower risk of infection."

"That makes sense. So, I'm curious about something. If mixed kids in the coven like us end up with autoimmune diseases, how'd the first generations survive?" I asked. "I mean, there was no treatment for this type of thing back then, and I'm pretty sure they weren't all purebred."

Grant leaned forward, looking interested by the question. "Back then, they didn't have their magic suppressed in childhood like we do now."

"They didn't?" I asked.

"No," Grant said. "Mother Miriam started suppressing our magic when she saw what a danger it could be to children. That's when the Evoking Ceremonies began. Anyway, back before the kids had their magic suppressed, their bodies became accustomed to the magic faster, before their immune system could be triggered. But…"

Grant sighed. "Mother Miriam had to make a trade-off to control children's magic. In the long run, I guess a few sick witches and warlocks are better for the coven than hundreds of kids running around with unpredictable magic."

I chuckled. "Yeah, I guess it is. Turns out we just drew the short straw."

Grant rolled his eyes. "I always seem to draw the short straw. It's like I'm cursed or something."

"I guess you could be," I joked, "considering curses are real."

Grant pressed his hand to his heart and dropped his jaw. "Now who would want to curse me? I'm a darling."

I cocked an eyebrow. "Are you? I've heard horror stories from Talia."

He dropped his jaw further. "What did she tell you?"

I threw my head back and laughed. "Nothing. I was joking."

Grant blew out a breath of relief. "Oh, good. Hey, maybe you can work in a good word for me."

"With Talia?" I asked.

He nodded.

I scoffed. "Uh, you're going to have to do the work yourself."

"Come on," he begged. "At least give me a hint. How do I get the girl?"

"I don't know. Serenade her?" I joked.

Grant tapped his chin. "That just might work. You're a genius."

I pressed my palm to my forehead. "I wasn't serious."

"Well, it's worth a try, isn't it?" he asked.

"Yeah, I guess," I admitted.

The truth was, I was pretty sure Talia enjoyed the chase. Eventually, she'd cave, but not before Grant jumped through hoops to get to her.

Grant finally said he was ready to eat, so we made our way through the buffet line. He went straight for various dishes instead of contemplating them, like he'd planned out his meal beforehand. We returned to our table and chatted. Halfway through dinner, Grant's eyes focused on something behind me.

I turned to see the gang of idiots who'd beat up him and Lucas sitting at a table in the corner of the room. They were wearing their stupid Treacherous Tarantula leather jackets, and one of them was trying to see how many peas he could shove up his nose. Totally badass.

Not.

Heat flared in my bones, and my eyes narrowed their way.

"Idiots," I mumbled under my breath.

Grant scoffed. "No kidding. Did you know the Imperium did nothing to punish them?"

My jaw dropped. "You're kidding! There were witnesses. You have *stitches* above your eye."

Grant shrugged. "Yeah, well, apparently they have better things to worry about than *some petty fight.*"

My nostrils flared. "That wasn't a petty fight! That was battery!"

"Shh…" Grant glanced around the cafeteria. "I know. I'd like to get back at them too, but I can't justify going after them when they could just beat me to a pulp again."

"It was five against two," I said. "It was hardly a fair fight."

My hands clenched into fists as I thought about all the terrible things I could do to get back at them. The gears started turning in my head, and a wide smile spread across my face.

Curiosity filled Grant's eyes. "What's going on in that pretty little head of yours, Nadine?"

I leaned forward. "Tell me, Grant. How badly do you want to get back at them?"

He eyed me. "Depends on what you have in mind."

I crinkled my nose. "I've got a plan."

"This is dangerous," Grant hissed at me. "Lucas would kill us if he knew we were doing this."

I smirked. "Why do you think I didn't invite him?"

He grabbed me by the arm and pulled me behind a black sedan. I kept my gaze on the five

Tarantulas across the school parking lot. They were piling into Ryan's black sports car. It was past nightfall now, and the only light we could see by was the moon.

I cocked an eyebrow at Grant. "So what? I thought you wanted to get back at them."

"Not by *following* them," he said. "Nadine, you don't know these guys."

I rolled my eyes and zipped my leather jacket all the way up. "I've known enough guys like them. Now let's go before we lose them."

I hurried out of my hiding spot and raced a few cars down to my own vehicle. I unlocked the doors and tossed my backpack on the floor below the passenger seat. Grant hesitated, then ran after me and climbed in beside me.

I threw the car into reverse. "Did you see where they went?"

Grant pointed to the right. "That way."

I tore out of the parking lot and followed the Tarantulas down the road. I caught up quickly, but was careful to keep my distance so they wouldn't notice my headlights following them.

"Lighten up, Grant." I nudged him in the side. "I thought you of all people would be thrilled to get back at them."

"Hell yeah, but I don't want *you* getting in the middle of it," he said.

I smirked. "You have a lot to learn about me."

Grant looked at me for a few seconds, then caved. "Okay, Nadine. I'm all in, as long as you understand what you're getting yourself into."

I scoffed. "I'm not scared of these assholes."

Grant clicked his tongue. "I think we need to hang out more often. I already like you ten times more."

I chuckled. "That's because I'm awesome. Where are these guys going, anyway?"

"I don't know," Grant said, "but it looks sketchy to me."

I glanced to either side of the road, but there was nothing but trees. I didn't recognize where we were. Wherever the Tarantulas were going, it wasn't into town.

The Tarantulas turned into a long driveway. I slowed and tried to take in as much as I could about the property, but we could hardly see anything from the road. All I saw were more trees.

"What the...?" I whispered. Hairs rose on the back of my neck, and I was getting a little creeped out. Whatever this was couldn't be good. Which meant I definitely had to check it out.

I pulled off to the side of the road and cut the engine.

"What are you doing?" Grant glanced back to the dark driveway.

I smirked at him as I opened my door. "We're going to check it out, of course."

Grant frowned. "You sure, Nancy Drew?"

I smiled at the nick name. "Positive."

I shoved my car keys in my pocket, then grabbed my bag and swung it over my shoulder. Grant stayed by my side as we entered the woods and crept through the trees.

"What do you think they're doing back here?" he asked, looking amused.

I shrugged. "Sacrificing babies?"

Grant chuckled. "Probably."

I half expected to walk in on them around a bonfire conducting some dark ritual. Instead, we came upon a run-down house with their car parked out in front. It looked like nothing more than a small weekend cabin, no bigger than two bedrooms. I'd kill to know what they were doing inside.

I swung my bag off my shoulder and opened it. Contents clinked together and fell to the ground. My heart lurched at the noise. I froze and glanced to the house to make sure no one had heard.

"Shh..." Grant hissed. He looked down to all the boxes and aluminum spray cans I'd run back to my room to get after dinner. "What *is* all this, Nadine?"

I gathered the contents and shoved it all back in my bag, then handed him a can of spray paint. "I bought it at the joke shop in town after Chloe trashed my room—just in case."

Grant read the spray paint label in the moonlight. He smirked and started shaking the can like he had a good idea for it. "What else have you got in there?"

I started digging through my bag to show him. "Unpoppable bubbles, multiplying silly string, and these beads that smell awful when you touch them."

An evil grin spread across Grant's face. "I like how you think, Nadine. Like an Alchemist."

I shrugged. "I have my moments."

"I might have something we can use, too." Grant conjured a collection of firecrackers.

"Put those back," I whispered. "We don't want to let them know we're here. Now let's go before they come back out. I want to get those jerks back for what they did to Lucas's face."

Grant's jaw dropped. "What about mine?"

I smiled. "Yours too. For you and Lucas."

"For me and Lucas," he repeated.

Grant and I crept through the shadows toward Ryan's car. Grant started spraying the back window with hot pink paint, while I threw the stink beads through the open driver's side window. They scattered across the front seats. I threw the rest of the container in the back. When that was empty, I pulled out a can of unpoppable bubbles. They rushed out of the container like spray paint, covering the seats with big, soapy-looking bubbles.

I smiled proudly as I emptied the can. Adrenaline pulsed through my body, and my heart slammed against my rib cage. It was exhilarating.

Next, I pulled out the can of multiplying silly string. I sprayed that all over on top of the bubbles, then touched it just for fun and to test it out. Beneath my fingers, the silly string started growing, twisting into new strings everywhere I poked it. Grant snickered as he sprayed the tires with paint.

"I think that's good," he hissed through the darkness.

"Hang on," I said. I pulled my keys from my pocket and dragged one along the side of Ryan's car. It made a satisfying *screech* as it dug into the shiny black paint.

I smiled proudly. "Okay, let's go."

We shoved our supplies back in the bag and started toward the forest. But we didn't make it there before the front door of the house banged open.

"Hey!" one of the Tarantulas shouted, making my heart leap up into my throat.

Grant grabbed me by the hand, and we sprinted into the trees. My knees groaned in protest, and I couldn't keep up with Grant. I slowed and caught myself on a nearby tree. Not far from us, we could hear the Tarantulas screaming about what we'd done to their car.

Grant tugged at my hand. "Come on, Nadine. We've gotta go."

I knew he was right, despite my body telling me otherwise. I suddenly regretted following the Tarantulas on a day I was so wiped I could hardly walk.

"Give me a second," I gasped.

Grant seemed to realize I wasn't completely myself, because a look of concern came over his face. "Get on my back, Nadine."

I didn't have a moment to question it, because Ryan was shouting at his Tarantulas to split up and find whoever vandalized his car. If I didn't get moving fast, they were going to catch up with us.

I climbed onto Grant's back, and he started moving through the woods. He stopped in his tracks when he turned toward the road and we saw orbs hovering in the forest ahead of us.

"They're going to see us if we go that way," I said.

"I have an idea," Grant whispered.

He turned around in the opposite direction and doubled back toward the house.

"What are you doing?" I hissed.

"They're not going to look for us over *there*," he pointed out.

"Good point."

Grant moved quietly through the trees toward the back of the house. From what we could see, Ryan was angrily trying to clean out his car, but the multiplying silly string was getting tangled in his hands. He swore and flailed his arms around angrily, making it clear he was going to strangle whoever had done this. I thought it was hilarious. The other four Tarantulas were in the trees looking for us, without a clue that we'd slipped past them.

Grant set me down. I steadied myself against a tree and sat on the ground. He crouched beside me, keeping close watch on all the Tarantulas.

"Are you okay?" Grant asked.

I was a little lightheaded and could feel that the blood had drained from my face. I felt like curling into a ball and falling asleep right there. But I couldn't say that to Grant. My disability never gave me any rational reason to feel the way I did. These waves of fatigue hit randomly, and there wasn't much I could do about it.

"I'll be fine," I told him. "Thanks for asking."

We sat there for another ten minutes, and I started to feel the blood return to my face, which was a relief. Ryan had managed to pull most of the bubbles and silly string out of the car, and it just lay there on the gravel in a heap around the vehicle. He was still pissed about the spray paint.

The four Tarantulas returned. "Whoever it was got away," one of them said.

"Shit!" Ryan growled in rage and kicked one of his tires. "Incompetent fucks. Get in the car. We're leaving."

Grant and I breathed a sigh of relief at the same time. He turned to me with a smile. "Good work, Nadine. You've successfully pissed them off."

I shrugged. "It's a gift."

Ryan tore out of the driveway like he was ready to raise some hell of his own. I snickered as we watched their lights disappear through the trees, but I held my breath when they reached the end of the driveway. I prayed they wouldn't turn to the left, where my car was parked. Luckily, they took a right back the way we came. We were safe.

"Come on." I gestured to Grant and got to my feet, then crossed the small clearing to the side of the house.

"Nadine!" he hissed through the darkness. "What are you doing?"

I reached for the side door and turned back to him. "Aren't you the least bit curious?"

"Someone could be in there," he pointed out.

I shrugged. It was unlikely, since there weren't any other cars here and the lights were off. "Don't you at least want to find out?"

I turned back toward the door and twisted the handle. It didn't budge.

"Guess we're not getting in," Grant said.

I eyed him. "Don't you know a spell to unlock it or something?"

Grant glared at me, like he wasn't using it even if he did.

"Not a problem," I said. "I brought my lock pick set."

I pulled my lock pick out of my bag, and Grant's eyes went wide. "What do you have *that* for?"

I shrugged. "It's a hobby."

Despite Grant's obvious unease, he looked impressed when I picked the lock in under a minute. "I didn't know breaking and entering was a hobby."

"I really am a bit of a Nancy Drew," I teased. "Come on."

Grant groaned and followed behind me.

"A little light?" I suggested.

An orb formed in Grant's palm, lighting up the stairwell in front of us like a flashlight. We were standing on a landing, where a few stairs went up to a kitchen on our left and the rest went downward to the basement.

"Come on." I waved my hand, and Grant and I started upstairs to the main level.

Like I guessed, there was no one here. It was eerily quiet, and apart from a few empty soda cans and a bag of chips lying on the ground, it looked like no one had been here in years. There was hardly any furniture—just a couch in the living room and an old mattress in one of the bedrooms. Everything was covered in a thick layer of dust.

"Why do you think they came here?" I whispered to Grant. We were alone, but the place gave me the creeps, so I kept quiet.

"I don't know," he replied. "To hide a body? To talk to the ghost who haunts this place?"

"You think it's haunted?" I asked.

He shrugged. "I'm not a Seer."

I glanced into the second bedroom, but it was empty. "Let's check out the basement."

Grant stopped me at the top of the stairs. "Let me go first, Nadine."

I stepped out of his way, and Grant took the stairs first. I followed close behind. When we got far enough down the stairs to see in the light of his orb, I inhaled a sharp breath. The basement was nothing but endless counters, all covered in various alchemy supplies. There was even a huge shelving unit in the corner with tons of ingredients packed haphazardly into it.

Grant's eyes grew wide. He tossed his orb into the air, and it split into a million tiny stars, lighting up the room like it was daytime.

It took me a second to find my voice as I took in all the cauldrons and vials. "What is all this? Those guys aren't even Alchemists."

Grant was too shocked by what we'd found to say anything. He walked over to the supply shelf and started reading the labels. "Dragon scale. Breath of a kirin. Hunpedskin venom. I don't even know what that is or what it's used for, but it's definitely not something these guys should be able to get their hands on."

Grant continued talking while I walked around the room inspecting all the supplies. "Mermaid scale. Blood of a vampire. *Wolven tooth*? Nadine, none of this stuff comes from the coven. These are all from other magical societies—like the Elementai and Arcanea. To get your hands on this stuff… Goddess, you'd have to be the Imperium. Or at minimum, the alchemy supplies director at school."

I came up behind Grant to look at all the vials. I could hardly believe what I was seeing—a real phoenix feather, and a hair from a unicorn. And to think. Just a few months ago I thought *witches* were nothing but fiction.

"You mean you can find this kind of stuff at school?" I asked.

Grant nodded.

I raised an eyebrow. "Isn't it obvious, then?"

Grant's jaw dropped. "Nooo. You think *they're* the ones who raided the Alchemy lab?"

I gave him a bored frown. "No. It's too unlike them," I said sarcastically.

Grant picked up a vial that had a thick blue liquid in it. "What do you think they're going to do with all this?"

I pressed my lips together. "Well, they're not Alchemists, so my guess is they're going to try reselling it."

An evil grin spread across Grant's face. "They can't sell it if there's nothing to sell."

I was instantly intrigued. "What are you suggesting? We steal it back?"
Grant rubbed his hands together mischievously. "I've always wanted to play Robin Hood."
"Steal from the rich and give to the poor?"
Grant crinkled his nose. "More like steal from the assholes and put it back where it belongs."
I smiled. "Count me in."

Lucas

THIRTEEN

"You. Did. *What?*" I growled.

Grant sat on his bed and sucked air through his teeth. He knew he was in deep shit with me. "Nadine and I followed the Tarantulas to an abandoned house and robbed them…?"

I paced around the room, my hands fisting at my sides. "Is that a question, Grant?"

He shook his head. "No. We definitely robbed them. But we only did it to give the stuff back to the Alchemy department. We dropped it off in Professor Richards's room. No one saw us."

I raked my fingers through my hair. "So you put Nadine in danger?"

Grant gaped at me. "It was her idea."

"When did this happen?" I demanded.

Grant shrugged. "Over a week ago. I wanted to tell you, but…"

"But?" I cocked an eyebrow.

Grant frowned. "I thought you'd be mad."

"Of course I'm mad!" I yelled. "I don't want Nadine anywhere near Ryan—or any of the Tarantulas. What were you doing hanging out with her, anyway?"

"I don't know," he said vaguely. "She wasn't feeling well, and I guess she just—"

My jaw dropped. "She wasn't *feeling* well? Like how?"

Grant furrowed his brow. "I don't know. She didn't give me a detailed list of her symptoms."

I covered my mouth with my hand as realization struck. "It's my fault," I muttered, thinking back to the kiss.

"What's your fault?" Grant asked.

My teeth ground together. "The kiss. I never should've kissed her."

"About that…" Grant hesitated.

I stopped pacing and faced him. "About that, *what?*"

Grant sighed. "Well, Nadine's kind of upset you haven't talked to her since then. She thinks you've been avoiding her."

616

"Oh, so now you've been talking to her behind my back?" I fumed. Today was *not* a good day. My temper was all over the place.

"Come on," Grant said. "You know it's not like that."

I *had* been avoiding Nadine, but I only did it to protect her. I still hadn't decided if I was summoning the reapers at the Reaper Moon and risking the Abyss. And if I didn't, I couldn't take things any further with Nadine and make her the Reaper's Shadow.

"I have good reason," I said.

"*I* know that," Grant told me. "But Nadine doesn't. You should talk to her."

I groaned. "You know what happens when I talk to her."

"You turn into a love-sick puppy?" Grant teased.

"Shut up." I grabbed my pillow and threw it across the room at him.

Grant checked the clock on his nightstand. "It's almost noon. You should go ask her out to lunch."

"*You* should go ask Talia out to lunch," I shot back like a child.

Grant crossed his arms. "Tell you what. I'll one-up you. I'll *serenade* Talia if you have just one lunch with Nadine."

I scoffed. "*That*, I'd like to see."

Grant shrugged. "The sooner you go ask Nadine to lunch, the sooner I can get to serenading."

I groaned, but I snatched my hoodie up off the bed anyway. "Fine. I'll do it."

I could hear the sound of Grant laughing in delight as I left the room. I shoved my arms through the sleeves of my hoodie and sauntered down the hall with the hood up. This was going to go absolutely fantastic.

Not.

I raised my hand to knock on Nadine's door, but I hesitated. After waiting two weeks since the kiss to talk to her, she probably never wanted to see my face again. Goddess, what was I thinking? Girls were so emotional. She probably took it super personally, which I guess I couldn't blame her for.

Before I could talk myself into knocking on her door, it swung open. The sound of piano music spilled out into the hall, and Nadine's bright eyes stared back at me.

When I saw her, it was like a dark storm cloud lifted from above my head. My hood fell to my shoulders. She was so pretty, with her hair down in waves and tight skinny jeans hugging her curves. How had I managed to steer clear of her for two weeks? This girl drew me in like a magnet.

She stumbled back a step, surprised to see me standing there. "Lucas?"

"Nadine, I, um…"

Fuck, why couldn't I talk? I spit it out before I could make a total fool out of myself. "I came to see if you wanted to come to lunch with me."

Nadine's features hardened. She didn't say anything for several long seconds. I half expected her to yell at me considering the death glare she shot my way. It was preferable to the silence. I had no idea what she was thinking.

"So you're not avoiding me?" she finally asked sharply.

Ouch.

"Well, I'm here," I replied.

Nadine hesitated, but her tone softened. "I was just headed down there anyway. Hang on."

She left the door open and hurried back inside the room. Talia sat at her piano bench playing the keyboard, and she hummed under her breath. Nadine returned moments later.

"Is Talia coming to lunch?" I asked, holding my breath. I liked Talia, but I kind of wanted to be alone with Nadine.

"No," she said as she shut the door behind her. "She's stuck in the zone."

We started down the hall side by side. I noticed she was clutching her fist tightly, like she was holding something. "What's that you've got there?"

She bit her lip and looked up at me. "It's for you."

Nadine held her fist out, and I placed my hand beneath it.

"For me?" I asked in surprise.

Nadine opened her hand and a small, cool object fell into my palm. It was a blue stone.

"Um… thanks," I said lamely.

Nadine raised an eyebrow, like my indifference amused her. She stopped at the top of the stairs and turned to me. "It's celestite, Lucas."

I blinked at her a few times. I knew that was supposed to mean something, but I hadn't taken Crystal Studies yet.

"It's a calming stone," Nadine explained without me having to ask. "You know how you can't sit still and you're always fidgeting?"

"I am?" I asked. I'd never noticed, but I guess she was right.

She nodded. "I bought it for you at the hospital gift shop, but I haven't had a chance to give it to you. I thought it might help you feel better."

My heart instantly melted at the sentiment. I didn't care what the stone was meant for. The fact that it came from Nadine made all the difference.

"Thank you," I said genuinely as I curled my hand tightly around the celestite. "That's very thoughtful."

That's very thoughtful? Who was I? The pope?

I wanted to say something more, but Nadine turned away and started down the stairs. She gripped tight to the railing—like she was afraid she might fall.

"Are you okay?" I asked.

"Fine," she told me. "Why?"

We reached the bottom of the stairs, and I breathed a sigh of relief. "It's just… Grant told me you weren't feeling well."

Nadine scoffed and continued toward the cafeteria. "I never feel well. I have my good days and my bad."

"What's today?" I questioned. "A good day or a bad day?"

A weight like a rock settled in my stomach. I dreaded the answer.

Nadine frowned. "How about we don't ask questions we don't want to know the answers to?"

Now *that* pissed me off. I grabbed Nadine's hand and stopped her just outside the cafeteria. She scowled at me and jerked away. I gaped down at her for a second, shocked that she was so offended by my touch. I guess after avoiding her so long, I deserved that.

"I *do* want to know the answer," I assured her. "I always want to know how you're feeling, Nad."

She crossed her arms, and her eyes darkened. "Really? Is that why you haven't spoken to me in two weeks? You want to know how I feel, Lucas? I feel confused. I feel abandoned."

Holy shit.

"Nad, I—"

"I feel like I did something wrong, and I don't know what it was." Angry tears rose to her eyes, and it was like a knife through my heart. "I feel like we had something going, but when we kissed, it was like… like you just decided I wasn't worth your time anymore."

Fuck, I'd really screwed up. That stone in my stomach grew heavier and heavier by the second.

"That's not it at all," I insisted.

A few people slipped by us on their way out of the cafeteria, and I realized we were blocking the doors. I took Nadine by the shoulder and led her down the hall where we could talk in private. She didn't shy away from me this time.

"Look, Nad." I pressed my fingers to my eyes. "The reason I've been staying away is because I'm concerned about you."

She scoffed. "For real, Lucas? Because you say stuff like that, but it doesn't *feel* like it."

"It's true," I promised. "You already know we can't be together because of the Reaper's Shadow."

"Screw the curse!" Nadine shouted, earning us a few stares from people in the hall. She quickly lowered her tone. "The curse has nothing to do with you not talking to me."

My face began to heat, and my lips pressed tightly together. She didn't get it.

"Yes, it does," I snapped.

I hated myself for the harsh tone I was taking. I never wanted Nadine to be on the receiving end of one of my freak-outs. But if this was what made her understand—and kept her away from me—then maybe I had to hurt her a little. Maybe I had to be the asshole to save her.

"The curse has everything to do with this," I said. "Because every time I'm near you, I just… I just…"

"You just, what?" Nadine snapped.

Before I knew what was happening, I grabbed her face and pressed my body up against hers, pushing her back against the wall. My lips swooped down, but I stopped a millimeter away from her mouth. I was dying to claim it as my own, to kiss her one more time, but I became a statue stalled in fear.

Nadine's chest rose and fell rapidly. Her eyes were practically begging for it. My dick wasn't cooperating either, as it hardened in my jeans. What I wouldn't give to get rid of the clothes between us.

I swallowed, and my voice lowered to a soft whisper. "Every time I'm near you, Nadine, I just want to kiss you."

Nadine inhaled a sharp breath. She wrapped her hands around my back, pulling me closer until her breasts were pressed against my chest. Images of the night at the lake flashed through my mind. I wanted to be back there—to feel her skin on mine again.

Nadine's breath wavered. "So kiss me, Lucas."

By the Goddess, I almost did. Then all these warning bells went off in my mind, and I couldn't bring myself to do it. I couldn't keep hurting her.

I stepped back and dropped my hands from Nadine's face. "I'm sorry, Nadine, but I can't. Look what happened last time I kissed you."

Nadine laughed—but it wasn't the kind of laugh where she was having fun. It was like she couldn't believe what I was suggesting. "You mean I got sick?"

"Exactly," I said. "The curse causes illness the closer we get physically."

Nadine blew out an exasperated breath and spoke firmly. "Let me make something very clear. I have lupus. I am sick *all* the time. Nothing you do—now or ever—will change that. This is not your fault."

"But what if—?"

"Exactly, Lucas," she cut me off. "You're basing this all on *what if*. Well, I have a question for you. What if Lucas Taylor just wanted to be my *friend*? What if we just hung out and—gasp!— he *didn't* expect sex from me?"

I gaped at her. Is that what she thought? That I believed hanging out with her meant she *owed* me sex? I didn't expect a damn thing from her.

"I'd love it if we could just be friends, Nadine," I said harshly. "But how can we do that when you keep leading me on? You're the one who tried to kiss me at the lake. You just asked me to kiss you now. Do you get some sort of thrill out of this?"

"Thrill?" she bit.

Aw, fuck. I was making this worse. Right now, it was hard to keep my mouth shut after what she just accused me of.

"It's like you're addicted to danger or something," I accused. "Like you're trying to see just how far you can push it. Just like you did when you followed the Tarantulas!"

Her eyes went wide, like she couldn't believe I'd throw that in her face. "I went after them because of what they did to you. Because I care."

I rolled my eyes. "Don't say stuff like that, Nad."

She scoffed. "Why not? It's true."

I raked my fingers through my hair. For the first time since I met her, I was seriously frustrated with Nadine. "It's *not* true," I insisted. "People don't care about me."

She gaped at me, like I'd just insulted her. "Are you serious right now? Grant cares! Professor Warren cares! I'm standing right here telling you I care, and you still can't believe it?"

"No, I can't," I growled. "I can't believe you would put yourself at risk just to be with me."

She pursed her lips. "Maybe I would."

"Why?" I cried. "You know the risks of getting involved with me. And you still want to take things further."

"Maybe you're worth it," she argued, fuming.

"But I'm not! The further we go, the sicker you get. You must love the pain!"

The hall went dead silent. For a second, it was as if time stood still. Then I realized what I said, and my stomach dropped.

Nadine's lips pressed into a thin line. "You think I like being in pain? You think I *like* being disabled?"

I sighed. "Come on, Nad. I didn't mean—"

"Screw you, Lucas," Nadine spat. "You don't know me at all."

Nadine slammed her shoulder into mine as she stomped off into the cafeteria to eat lunch alone. My heart felt like it was breaking into a million pieces, and that heavy stone in my stomach had all but consumed me.

I guess I didn't have to worry about avoiding Nadine anymore. I'd done exactly like Grant suggested and been a complete ass. Nadine would be the one to avoid me from now on.

I tossed and turned all night. How could I have acted like such an idiot?

Jerk. Total and complete asshole.

That's what I was, and I hated myself for it. I wanted to do better. I wanted to be a better person. But I didn't know how.

My eyes shot open in the darkness to the most excruciating nausea I'd felt since I'd heard the kid. I curled into a ball on my bed, waiting for the thought to come and the nausea to pass.

"I bet no one will notice. They never cared anyhow."

Aw, fuck. Not another suicide.

I tossed the covers off myself and made a beeline for the bathroom, but I didn't make it that far. I doubled over at the trash can and heaved. The stench of puke filled the room, and Grant stirred in his bed as I made gagging sounds.

I'd never handled suicides well, but this one was particularly taxing. It echoed the exact thoughts I'd had when I considered offing myself.

No! I screamed at myself internally. I didn't let myself think about that. I'd decided long ago I wouldn't go back down that road.

I had to take my mind off it somehow, so I crawled back into bed and put my headphones in to listen to music. But tonight, even the heavy beats that usually drowned out my thoughts didn't work.

I hated myself, and it wasn't just because of my gift. Even if I got rid of it, it wouldn't fix the way I felt about myself. Nothing could.

In that moment, I truly meant it. I had no hope. I didn't want hope. Without it, I could never be disappointed.

I wished I could've said I slept that night, but I didn't. I just lay there, shivering in a ball as the darkness of my own mind closed in around me. I hated feeling this way, but I deserved it.

I didn't know how much time passed, but eventually, I heard the sound of the door slamming and Grant squealing as he came into the room. I hadn't even noticed he left.

I groaned as I pulled the blanket down from my head. The daylight coming through the window was blinding. "What the...?"

Grant ran across the room and jumped on his bed a few times. He didn't even notice me. He ran back to the door and double checked the peephole for Goddess knows what.

"Grant, jeez," I sighed, still trying to find my bearings as I stirred awake. "What's going on? You're acting like a girl."

Grant's eyes went wide. "What are you still doing in bed?"

I pressed my hand to my pulsing forehead. "Don't feel well. What happened?"

Grant bit his lower lip. "I was going to serenade Talia. I had everything set up in the Lounge and was going to play the grand piano and everything—"

"You can't play piano," I reminded him flatly.

"But I chickened out!" Grant groaned, like he hadn't even heard me.

I rolled my eyes and threw the covers back over my head. "So try again and don't chicken out this time."

"You don't get it," Grant said. "Ugh, I'm a total fool."

I shrugged. At least he and Talia were still on good terms. He wasn't a total loser like me. He didn't know how good he had it.

Grant sighed and stomped out of the room. Thank the Goddess for some peace and quiet.

Except I quickly realized the peace and quiet was just as excruciating, if not more. My thoughts were racing far too quickly, burying myself into a deeper, darker hole than I was already in. I knew the only way to drag myself out of it was to get out of bed. I told myself that all I had to do today was take a shower, but I couldn't even manage to do that much.

It wasn't until late afternoon when I finally decided I couldn't hold my piss any longer and dragged myself out of bed.

After showering, I eyed the bed. It called to me, but I knew if I crawled back under the sheets, I might not get out for a week. I decided to leave my room and grab some takeout from the cafeteria. I wasn't really hungry, but I could practically hear my mother's voice in my head.

"Do they feed you at that college, Lucas? You're getting too skinny."

Speaking of my mother, today was as good a day as any to visit her. I hadn't seen her all semester, and I knew Dad would be down at the bar drinking away his troubles before he had to go back to work for the week.

I left the school and let my feet carry me home. I wasn't really watching where I was going or paying attention to how long it took me. Even the chill of the October air didn't register.

Eventually, the small black house came into view. My family's little three-bedroom was nothing compared to the elaborate gothic houses along the main stretch of road through town.

Ours shared the same architecture, but was practically a dollhouse compared to the other houses in town.

I breathed a sigh of relief when I didn't see Dad's car in the driveway. Mom didn't have her own car, but I bet she was home anyway. Dad never let her go anywhere on her own.

I didn't knock. Even after all this time, it didn't seem right. I opened the front door and—

My mother gasped. "Lucas, don't come in!"

But it was too late. I'd already witnessed the damage. Across the living room and through the kitchen doorway, I saw my mother on her knees. Huge chunks of glass lay at her feet, surrounded by a giant splatter of Shepherd's pie and little drops of blood.

My stomach bottomed out. I rushed over to her, kneeling at her side to help clean up. By the looks of things, I'd just missed my father.

"Mom," I sighed, looking down to the broken dish and her wrapped-up hand. "A casserole dish? What was his problem this time? The casserole was too salty? Not salted enough?"

"No," she said, wiping her gauzed hand across her nose. "It was my fault. I dropped it and cut my hand cleaning up."

She could tell me that all she wanted, but I'd never believe it. What terrified me was that she actually believed it herself.

"You don't have to lie to me, Mom," I said as I placed broken bits of glass in the garbage beside us. "I remember how he is."

My mother pressed her lips together, but she continued to clean up as an excuse not to meet my gaze. "You don't remember him as well as you think, Lucas. We had good times, too, but you choose to focus only on the bad. Why do you demonize him so much?"

I gaped at her as I tore a wad of paper towel from the roll. "Because he's a jackass, Mom."

Before I could blink, my mother huffed and snatched the paper towel from my hand. She looked as if she might slap me, though I knew she'd never lay a hand on me.

"How dare you!?" she snapped, catching me off guard. "How dare you talk about your father like that. You know he can't control it."

My breath grew hot. How could she keep telling herself that after all this time?

"Of course he can, Mom," I shot back at her. "He tells you that so you'll excuse his behavior."

"I do not excuse it," she argued.

I sighed. Mom hadn't changed at all these past few months. She was still in denial, and no matter how much I tried to tell her otherwise or how much space I gave her, there was nothing I could do. I guess I thought that I could change her mind somehow. It was just another person's burden I carried. She was so deep in denial she didn't even know the burden was there.

I took a deep breath and placed my hand on Mom's shoulder to get her to look at me. She sniffled and glanced up. "Mom... you know I'll always be here for you, right?"

The crease between her eyebrows deepened. "No, Lucas, I don't. I haven't seen you in months, and then you show up here out of the blue just to insult your father? I don't want to hear it."

I froze in place. My own mother didn't want me around? She preferred my sorry excuse of a dad to me? Tears brimmed Mom's eyes, and she placed a hand over her mouth so I wouldn't hear her sobs.

"Hey, Mom," I said softly, reaching out for her.

She shrugged me off. "It's just so hard to see you here, Lucas," she admitted. "I've already come to terms with the fact that my son is dead."

My guts twisted. "I know, Mom. We've all dealt with Eric's death in different ways."

Mom shook her head and placed her hand on the side of my face. "Not Eric, Lucas. You. The night we lost Eric, it was like... like we lost you, too."

Every muscle in my body tensed. Her words were like a knife through my heart. Maybe I hadn't been lying to myself all this time.

Maybe it was true that no one wanted me around anymore.

Lucas Taylor was a jerk.

I couldn't believe I fell for him. And yet, at the same time... I couldn't stop thinking about him. I flipped between the two moods so quickly it could give me whiplash.

No, no. He's *definitely* a jerk.

I tried to put him out of my mind in Demonology the following week.

"Today, we move into our unit on demon deals," Professor Daniels announced. She was a middle-aged woman, with flowing brown hair and a beautiful Bengal cat that lounged on her desk during every lesson. "Before we begin, let me lead off with a warning. The one and *only* reason we cover this unit is to warn you of the dangers of making deals with demons. I will not be teaching you how to summon a demon, and I *strongly* advise you never do so. The consequences can be... dire."

A shiver ran down my spine. Though I'd never seen a demon before, my mind brought up horrible images of creepy, black-eyed men—the spirits of those who followed evil gods. In my head, they were followed by demonic monsters. Professor Daniels had shown us drawings of some of the monsters, and I hoped to never encounter one in my life. They were terrible creatures created by the gods or mutated from magical creatures. There were canines that were nothing more than skin and bones, creatures with the skull of a deer for a head, and three-headed lions with black manes and golden eyes. She didn't have to tell me twice. I wouldn't be caught dead summoning one of those things.

"As we all know, our history is rooted in the summoning of demons," Professor Daniels continued. "With demon blood in our ancestry, it is easier for Miriamic people to summon demons than it is to summon other spirits, as the demons are more willing to show up. That said, demons only appear when they can strike a deal that will benefit them."

Someone spoke up from behind me, though I didn't see who. "But what about Santos? He helped Mother Miriam, even though there was nothing in it for him."

Professor Daniels cocked an eyebrow. "Is that something you'd wish to risk? Demon deals always come with a price."

I raised my hand. I was too curious not to get in the middle of the discussion. "What kind of price? Can you give an example?"

Chloe shot me a scowl from across the room. What? I wasn't allowed to talk now? I ignored her.

Professor Daniels hesitated, then cleared her throat. "An extreme example might be making a deal for more magic. This kind of deal would require..."

She hesitated and got a faraway look in her eye. "Well, it'd require a soul."

My muscles tensed. There was something deep and dark in her tone that suggested such a thing was worse than giving up your own soul. Almost like... like you'd have to *kill* to make the deal.

Who could do such a vile thing like that?

Headmistress Verla called me into her office that afternoon. She stood from her desk and straightened her blazer when I walked in. Odin purred from his spot on her desk. "Nadine, I'm so glad we finally get to prepare for your Evoking Ceremony. Have a seat."

She gestured to a chair across from her. My hands shook as I sat. I shouldn't have been so nervous, but I was. My Evoking Ceremony would determine my magic and where I fit in within the coven. I couldn't mess this up.

Headmistress Verla rounded her desk and leaned against the corner, placing her hands in her lap. "I'm sorry we had to cancel our previous lesson. How are things going here at school?"

I relaxed a little as she spoke in a casual tone. "They're fine. My history class is a lot to take in, but I'm really enjoying all the others."

The corners of her lips turned into a frown. "Is that something I can help with? I could set you up with a tutor."

"No," I said quickly, though I appreciated the kind gesture.

"Let's get started then." She returned to her seat behind her desk and stroked Odin's fur. He closed his eyes and swished his tail, enjoying the gentle massage. "Let's begin with any questions you have. It'll help me get a feel for what we need to cover."

Headmistress Verla spoke to me like I was her equal. I should've felt better about it, but it put me on edge. Did I perhaps remind her too much of my mother?

I didn't want to think about my mom, so I pushed the thought out of my mind.

"What exactly happens during an Evoking Ceremony?" I asked.

Headmistress Verla gave a bright smile, like she was happy to answer the question. "It's quite simple, really. You'll lie on the ground in a circle of five candles—one to represent each of the Casts. Another witch will perform the ceremony by repeating an incantation."

"Who will that be?" I asked. "You?"

She gave a slight nod. "If you want it to be, but you can ask anyone you choose, as long as they've already been through their ceremony. Your grandmother, for instance, would be a perfect example."

I let out a deep breath. I'd really like for Grammy to be there with me. "Can other people be there, or just the one witch?"

"You can invite anyone," she answered. "Some witches throw huge parties for their ceremonies, while others prefer to keep it strictly to family and friends."

I was already forming a list in my mind of who I wanted to be there, but the list pretty much stopped at Grammy, Talia, and Grant. Lucas's face flashed through my mind for a second, then I remembered that I was mad at him.

I shifted in my chair. "What happens after the incantation is spoken?"

"You will fall into a trance," Verla explained. "This trance is so deep you won't even realize you're in it."

"Then how can I prepare?" I balked. Nerves ignited deep within my belly. How could I pass the test if I didn't know I was being tested?

Verla held up a hand to calm me down. "Not to fear, Nadine. If your heart is in the right place, you will pass."

I swallowed. What if my heart *wasn't* in the right place? I didn't even know what that meant.

"What if...?" I trailed off. I had so many questions I didn't even know which one to start with. Verla raised a curious eyebrow, and I knotted my hands in my lap. "What if I decide not to do it?"

Verla frowned. "Why wouldn't you go through with your Evoking Ceremony, Nadine?"

Because I'm scared. I don't want to fail. I can't let Grammy down.

Instead, I just shrugged.

"If you don't go through with this, you won't receive your powers," Verla stated.

"Is my birthday my only chance?" I asked.

Verla pressed her lips together and nodded regrettably. "It's the one and only night the veil lifts for you and allows you to contact Mother Miriam. Contacting her on any other night would be nigh on impossible."

A knot formed in my chest. Usually I wasn't so afraid to take chances, but this was different. This was terrifying.

Verla eyed me, and her features softened. "Nadine, what's wrong? Perhaps I can ease some of your worry."

My eyes locked on her cat so I wouldn't have to meet her gaze. I took a moment to breathe, then forced the confession out. "What if... what if I don't have the power to be part of the coven?"

Verla furrowed her brow. "What do you mean?"

I forced down the lump in my throat as my anxiety reached the surface. "Well, I'm only half witch. My mom was a witch, and my dad was a human, right? So what if I don't have enough power to pass Mother Miriam's test?"

Amusement crossed Verla's features for a moment before settling into a sympathetic expression. "I assure you, Nadine, Mother Miriam doesn't work that way. As long as you have her blood running through your veins, she will accept you as any other. When a witch has a child with a human, their children have the same potential as the parent. You can be just as strong of an Alchemist as your mother, Nadine."

"You think I'll get Alchemy?" I asked.

"It runs in your family," she stated. "Mother Miriam almost always assigns families to the same Cast, as the coven is very family-oriented. In some instances, she may assign you a different Cast if she sees fit, but it's quite rare."

"What about if the parents are from different Casts?" I questioned. "Can you end up in two?"

Verla shook her head. "No. There's never been a witch or warlock assigned to more than one Cast. Mother Miriam will pick the one that's the best fit for you regardless."

"So, what do I have to do to become an Alchemist?" I asked.

"I'd like to run you through a few scenarios," Verla said. "Of course, we can't predict what scenarios Mother Miriam will put you in, but we can—"

Screeeech!

My heart leapt into my throat as Odin jumped to his feet and let out a terrifying meow that sounded more like a scream. His back arched, and his hair stood on end. Verla gasped as Odin jumped off the desk and tore across the room like he was being chased. He ran around in circles, crying out like he was in pain. My stomach bottomed out as I watched the creature sprint from one end of the room to the other. A chill ran down my spine as he yowled.

Before I could really process what was happening, Odin's head slammed into the wall, and he slumped to the ground.

"Good Goddess!" Verla cried. She leapt out of her chair and rushed over to Odin's limp form. She cradled him in her arms.

Meanwhile, I was still trying to process what had happened. It was like he'd been possessed or something.

I cautiously stood and draped my bag over my shoulder. "Is he okay?"

Headmistress Verla kept her head down, and she stroked Odin's black fur. She shook him, but he didn't move. "I—I have no idea what happened."

She lifted her gaze to mine, and her features were so heartbreaking it made me want to cry. "I'm sorry, Nadine, but I've got to get Odin to the infirmary. We'll have to reschedule again."

"Don't apologize," I said, my heart still hammering. "Go take care of your cat!"

Headmistress Verla hurried out of the room with Odin cradled in her arms. I slumped out of the office behind her, thinking how strange and out of the blue that all was.

And then it hit me. Maybe it wasn't so random after all.

Curling my hands into fists, I headed down the hall in the opposite direction that Headmistress Verla had gone. When I passed by the Lounge, I spotted the Lucky Three inside. They were sitting in the coveted chairs around the biggest TV. Chloe had her feet up on the coffee table and was inspecting her nails.

"It's been two weeks since my last manicure," she complained. "I totally need a new one."

"Let me see," Camille offered, holding out her hand.

My nostrils flared as I stomped into the Lounge toward them. "It was you, wasn't it?" I growled.

Chloe turned from Camille and looked up at me with utter disgust. "What are you going on about?"

A few people in a nearby seating area looked our way, but I didn't care.

I crossed my arms. "What was it this time? Some poison slipped into Odin's food bowl this morning? A curse one of your friends cast on him?"

Chloe rolled her eyes and stood so that she was a mere step away from me. "I seriously don't know what you mean."

I narrowed my gaze at her. "I know you had help. You don't have magic of your own yet."

Chloe faked a frown and spoke in a mocking tone. "Oh, dear. Didn't you know I don't *need* magic to get my way?"

"Screw you," I growled. I wanted to rip her hair out, but with two other girls behind her, I didn't think it'd get me anywhere. "You can mess with me all you want, but you don't get to touch other people—or their cats."

Chloe chuckled, but her laughter instantly died as she stepped forward. She was so close that our noses almost touched. "You don't make the rules."

"Oh yeah?" I growled. "We'll see about that."

I turned on my heel and stomped away from her, fuming.

Chloe's laughter echoed through the room. "You can't touch me, Nadine. But have fun trying."

Oh, bitch. I will.

I didn't really know where I was going, until I passed through the Main Foyer and saw Talia. She clutched her books tightly to her chest with one hand. She held the other out in the direction of a very tall, very handsome warlock. He must've been a senior, but she looked up at him with dreamy eyes like he was a god. He had dark hair that fell into his eyes and a strong jawline. He traced his finger over her hand as she giggled.

"And this line here means you've got a hot date coming up," he teased. "On Friday night. With me."

Talia snickered. "Well, the palm doesn't lie. I guess I can't say no."

I furrowed my brow as I approached. "What's going on?"

Talia finally tore her gaze from the guy. "Oh, Nadine. This is Cody. He was just…"

"I was just enjoying Talia's company," he said slowly, deliberately. He didn't take his eyes off her when he spoke. She practically drooled.

"That's great, but I kind of need you right now, Tal," I said.

Talia's face fell when she noticed my tight expression. "Yeah, sure. I'll see you later, Cody."

"See you." He winked at her and walked away.

Talia turned to me. "What's wrong?"

"Wrong with me?" I balked. "Who is that guy? What about Grant?"

Talia shrugged. "I can't wait around for him forever. Cody asked me out, and I said yes."

I frowned. That was too bad. I was rooting for her and Grant.

"Never mind that," she said. "What's up with you?"

"Chloe," I scoffed, like that explained everything. I looped my arm through hers. "We need to gather the girls. It's time to raise some hell."

"Are you sure this is safe, Amy?" Mandy asked as the four of us gathered around a cauldron in one of the Alchemy labs.

"Totally," Amy assured us. She pulled her dark hair into a ponytail. "Though that depends on your definition of *safe*."

Mandy was sitting on one of the tables, swinging her feet beneath her and tapping the table top with her long, manicured fingernails. She blew a bubble with her gum, and the *pop* sounded throughout the empty room. "What's your definition?"

Amy chewed her lower lip. "Well, it's not going to *hurt* Chloe, but it will give her some serious nightmares."

I picking up various ingredients Amy had signed out from the supply closet and began reading their labels. My guts twisted as I thought about what we were going to do to her. I mean, Chloe deserved it, but was it worth it to stoop to her level? She'd done the same thing when she asked Amy to help her brew a revenge potion.

My hesitation passed quickly, as I reminded myself that getting back at Chloe was the only way to stop her from sabotaging my lessons. If I didn't ruin this bitch, I wasn't going to make it through my Evoking Ceremony.

"How does it work?" I asked.

"Once it's brewed, we'll sprinkle the potion in front of her dorm room door," Amy explained. "When she crosses the line, it will trigger night terrors."

Talia rubbed her hands together and smiled mischievously. "How long does this stuff last?"

Amy pressed her lips together in thought. "A few weeks, maybe?"

"Perfect," I said. "Let's make it real potent. I want to scare her panties off."

"Ew. No," Mandy joked. "Let's keep those on. I've heard horror stories from Ryan."

Talia chuckled. "Do you think this is good enough payback? Or should we like, make her hair fall out?"

"In patches," I added.

"Or boils," Mandy teased. "She could cover up the bald spots with a wig. Let's give her something she can't hide."

"Ooh, or hair like, all over her body," Talia laughed. "Like Bigfoot."

I snickered. "How about a beard?"

"Come on now," Amy joked. "You're getting a little out of my paygrade here."

I calmed my laughter. "Okay. Nightmares it is."

"Perfect," Amy said. "Nadine, I need an extra hand. Talia, can you get me a spoon from the wall over there?"

"What about me?" Mandy asked.

Amy smirked. "You can just sit there and look pretty."

Mandy lay on the table top with her head propped up on her elbow and the other hand on her hip. She batted her eyelashes. "Like this?"

Amy's eyes roamed over her. "That's perfect. Here, Nadine. I need you to pour these two vials into the cauldron the same time I do these two. We have to pour at the same rate. Got it?"

"Got it." I took the vials of liquid from her hands. One vial read *Basilisk Venom* while the other read *Cockatrice Blood*. A shiver ran down my spine. Neither of those sounded like friendly creatures.

"Here you go." Talia returned holding out a big wooden spoon.

"Perfect," Amy said. "Can you stir while we pour?"

"Sure." Talia stood beside me and placed the spoon inside the cauldron. As Amy and I poured our vials together, Talia began stirring. A strong, putrid stench filled the lab, and dark gray steam started to rise from the cauldron.

Mandy sat up straight and pinched her nose. "Is it supposed to do that?"

"Sure is," Amy said brightly, looking proud. "The smell will go away once we've finished brewing."

She picked up another container full of dried herbs. She took a pinch and sprinkled it into the brew. It turned a thick, murky black, and big bubbles started snapping in the bottom of the cauldron like tar. A thrill went through me when I realized I was brewing my first potion.

Amy added another spoonful of dried herbs, and the potion instantly cleared. It became thin and looked a lot like tomato juice. Amy took the spoon from Talia's hands and stirred while she waved her hand over top of the steaming cauldron and muttered an incantation under her breath.

Mandy watched in deep interest. She noticed my eyes on her and said, "She's really good, isn't she?"

I nodded.

Amy finished the incantation. She leaned over the cauldron and inhaled deeply. "That's more like it."

"That was it?" Talia asked, looking impressed.

Amy scooped a spoonful of potion into an empty vial and held it up. "That's all there is to it. Who wants to do the honors?"

To say I was excited to see Chloe get what was coming to her was an understatement. She'd used Amy to try to turn Mandy into a frog, torn apart mine and Talia's room, sabotaged my lesson with Headmistress Verla, then went after Verla's cat. She deserved every ounce of terror she got in her sleep tonight.

I'd been given the honors of pouring the potion over the carpet in front of Chloe's dorm while my friends kept watch. No one spotted us, and we hurried away before we could get caught. Talia and I invited Amy and Mandy to stay in our dorm in case anything interesting happened. It turned into a full-on slumber party, with pizza, manicures, and guy talk. Amy's cat, Stormy, and Talia's cat, Gus, snuggled up together on Talia's bed.

Mandy had twisted my hair into a pair of French braids, and she was working on painting Amy's nails. Talia stood in front of the mirror, pushing her boobs up to see how much cleavage she could get out of them.

"Do you guys think I should wear a push-up bra on my date with Cody on Friday?" Talia asked. "Or is that just setting him up for disappointment?"

Mandy laughed. "That depends. He can only get disappointed if he sees what's underneath the bra."

"Or feels it," Amy added.

"See, that's the thing," Talia said. "I don't know if things are going to go that far or not. Should I play it safe?"

I looked up from filing my nails. "If you want to play it safe, you're going to want to bring the condom box with you."

Talia's jaw dropped. "The whole box?"

"Hold up," Mandy said. "Condom box?"

Talia smirked and went to her dresser. She opened her jewelry box, and a bunch of condoms spilled out. "Yep. We had to restock after the Lucky Three trashed our room."

"Oh, *that* explains all the condoms," Amy said.

"Either of you need one?" Talia offered.

Mandy scoffed. "That would be a miracle right now. I'm going through a serious dry spell."

"You?" Talia held out a condom toward Amy.

Amy crinkled her nose from where she sat on the floor. "That's kind of useless for a girl like me."

"What do you mean?" Talia asked.

Amy raised her eyebrows. "I thought you knew."

Talia tilted her head to the side. "Knew what?"

"That I like girls." Amy glanced from Talia's shocked face to mine. She burst out in laughter. "Oh Goddess, you guys. You should see your faces."

I quickly righted my expression. "I didn't mean to assume anything."

"No, it's fine," Amy assured me. "I really thought you guys knew. Just as long as you're still my friends."

"Of course we are," Talia said, placing the condoms back in the jewelry box. "It just means more condoms for us."

Amy chuckled. "You can have all the condoms you need, girl. I'm not going to use them."

Before anyone else could say anything, a high-pitched scream echoed down the hall. It shocked me at first, but my pulse quickly slowed as a proud smile spread over my face. "Looks like it's show time."

Talia smiled mischievously and headed for the door. Mandy screwed on the cap to the nail polish, and Amy blew on her fingers. We all followed behind Talia as she opened the door. Down the hall, we could hear the sound of doors swinging open.

Gwen rushed out of one of the dorm rooms as the scream came again. She pounded on the door next to hers and shook the handle. "Chloe!? Chloe, what's going on?"

Camille stepped out of the room behind Gwen in nothing but tiny shorts and a skimpy tank top. "What was that?"

"Chloe!" Gwen screamed again, pounding on the door.

Chloe's door swung open. She looked like a total mess, with no makeup on and her hair in disarray. Her silk nightgown hung off her at an odd angle. "What the hell are you doing, Gwen? It's like, one in the morning."

Gwen blinked a few times in shock. "You were screaming. I thought—"

"You thought wrong," Chloe snapped. Her eyes scanned the hallway, and she noticed a bunch of girls watching curiously. She raised her voice. "What are you looking at? Go back to sleep, losers."

A few people murmured to their roommates as they shut the doors. I, on the other hand, stepped out into the hall and crossed my arms. I leaned against my door frame, proudly admiring our handiwork.

"Are you okay?" Camille asked Chloe.

"Yeah, just a bad dream," Chloe admitted. "I haven't had a dream like that in—"

She cut off as she noticed me standing there. She pushed past Gwen and Camille, her nostrils flaring. "What did you do, Nadine?"

"Me?" I asked innocently. "What ever do you mean, Chloe?"

Mandy and Amy snickered from behind me.

"You cursed my sleep!" she accused, pointing a finger in my direction.

A few girls were still peeking through the cracks in the doors. Good. Let them enjoy the show. I hoped Chloe looked as crazy to them as she did to me in that moment. It was *so* satisfying to watch her stand there shaking.

I tilted my head to the side. "How could I do that, Chloe? I don't have magic yet."

She turned her angry gaze on Amy. "It was her!"

"Me?" Amy feigned. "You really think I'd do anything to you, after you kidnapped my cat and threatened to kill her?"

Chloe's eyes darted from door to door. She noticed a few onlookers. "I would never threaten a cat, Amy. Everyone knows that."

Heat flared deep in my belly. No way was she getting away with such a bold-faced lie. I straightened and stepped forward. "Really? Is that why Headmistress Verla's cat is in the infirmary? Oh, wait. Let me guess. That wasn't you, either?"

Chloe cocked an eyebrow, but she couldn't hide the fury etched in her features. "I told you I don't know anything about that."

"Too bad you're not a very good liar," I said.

Chloe's features hardened. She seemed to forget about all the other onlookers. "Fine, Nadine. You want to curse me with nightmares. I'll show you just how much of a nightmare I can be."

She whirled around and stomped back toward her room. Camille and Gwen stepped forward to join her, but Chloe slammed the door in their faces.

When I turned back to my friends, Talia's eyebrows were raised. "Wow. She's really intense, isn't she?"

I shrugged. "Doesn't matter to me. I'm not scared of her."

"I heard you and Chloe went at it the other night," Grant said to me after class on Friday. I hadn't meant to meet up with Grant again, but he happened to be sitting in the same study area in the Main Foyer I usually sat in after Introduction to Tarot.

I scoffed as I settled into one of the plush red chairs. "Believe me, if we *went at it*, she'd have a chunk of hair missing."

Honestly, I couldn't believe she'd gone all week without retaliating. At least Verla's cat was back to normal, but I still didn't know what Chloe might do next. I'd been watching my back for days, and she had yet to strike. I figured it was all part of some elaborate plan to put me on edge. It was working. Between my feud with Chloe and everything going on with Lucas, I barely had a chance to breathe all week.

I didn't want to ask Grant about Lucas, so I asked about Talia instead. "So when are you planning to ask Talia out?"

Grant frowned. "About three weeks ago. Every time I get close, I chicken out."

"Why?"

"Because she already rejected me once," he admitted.

I sat straighter in my chair. "What? When?"

"On move-in day," he reminded me. "I asked her out, and she said we should all go out for muffins instead. I'm afraid she'll reject me again."

"I wouldn't call that a rejection," I told him. "She's been waiting for you to ask you out again and has gotten sick of waiting. She's got a date with some guy named Cody tonight."

Grant groaned. "Cody White. Are you kidding me? How am I supposed to compete with *him*?"

Grant sank down in his chair. "She never would've gone for me anyway if she's got guys like *Cody* asking her out."

"Hey, don't say that," I scolded.

Grant ran his fingers through his dark hair. "Damn it. I missed my chance, didn't I?"

"No," I reassured him. "She can't date him forever."

"You don't know that," he grumbled.

Grant's eyes went wide as they connected with something behind me. He sank even further in his chair until he was practically hiding.

"What?" I turned around to see what he was looking at.

"Speak of the devil," he murmured.

My eyes landed on Talia. She looked really cute in a casual red dress that fell to her knees and black boots. She wore her hair up in a high ponytail. Cody walked alongside her and tugged playfully at the ponytail.

"You look like a freshman with your hair up," he told her. "You should wear it down."

Talia reached up and touched her ponytail. "You think so?"

"Yeah, you'd look so much hotter," he said. "Here, let me show you."

He reached into her hair and pulled the elastic out of it. Talia's hair fell around her shoulders. She ran her fingers through the strands to straighten them. "How's this?"

"Perfect," Cody said, shooting her a smile. "Let's get out of here."

"Can I have my elastic back?" Talia asked.

Cody looped it over his wrist. "And risk you putting your hair back up? No way. It's mine for the night."

Talia walked alongside Cody toward the doors. She noticed us as she was passing and waved. *Good luck*, I mouthed.

As soon as Talia was out the door, Grant straightened. "What a jackass."

I raised an eyebrow at him. "Is someone a little jealous?"

Grant's face fell. "That's not what I meant. The way he took her ponytail down like that… It's an asshole thing to do."

"It was harmless," I argued.

Grant crossed his arms. "If I were dating Talia, I'd let her wear her hair any way she chooses."

Before I could respond, Grant's face fell as his eyes connected with something else across the foyer. "Uh oh."

I turned to see Lucas across the room. My heart lifted in my chest, then started pounding furiously. I hadn't seen him since that day I snapped at him by the cafeteria. I hoped he didn't come over here to talk to Grant. I didn't know what to say to him.

And then I saw *her*. I didn't know who she was, but she was walking alongside Lucas and laughing. She was a tall blonde, with legs that went for miles and a tiny little waist. Her hair flowed around her in perfect curls. She looked like she belonged on the runway.

"Who's that?" I asked Grant before I could stop myself.

"Lena?" he asked. "She's nobody. A necromancer in one of his classes. They're writing a paper together."

Grant said it like it should've eased my nerves, but it did the exact opposite.

"If she's nobody, why did you say *uh oh* when you saw them?" I demanded.

Grant bit his lower lip. "Because Lucas told me you two got into a fight. If you want my opinion—"

"I don't, thanks," I snapped.

I felt bad as soon as I said it. I didn't mean to take my frustrations out on Grant, but seeing Lucas with Lena made this red-hot jealousy ignite inside of me that I didn't know was there. I'd never met Lena, and already I wanted to slip a potion into her lunch that would turn her into a frog. I mean, the girl was too pretty for her own good. There was no way she and Lucas were just *writing a paper* together.

"They look awfully comfortable together." I tried to keep the bitterness from my voice, but it didn't work.

Grant shrugged. "Well, yeah. They went out in high school."

My body went rigid, and Grant noticed. He was quick to add, "But they weren't serious. Not like *that*."

I wasn't sure I believed him. The way Lena looked at Lucas, it was like she still had feelings for him… Fresh feelings.

Lena threw her head back in laughter at something Lucas said, though I didn't hear what it was. She reached out and casually touched his arm. My teeth ground together. Lucas's gaze darted in my direction, and my heart jumped as our eyes locked. He looked away quickly and pretended like he hadn't seen me, but it'd been as clear as day.

Lucas reached out for Lena's hand, and my jaw dropped. He entwined his fingers in hers and whispered something I couldn't hear. It felt as if time stood still, but I must've been the only one frozen in time, because Lucas and Lena continued up the grand staircase hand-in-hand. Grant gasped from beside me.

Lucas shot one last glance over his shoulder, and he looked straight into my shocked eyes. It was in that moment that I realized he'd done it on *purpose*. I could feel a fault form in my heart at the blatant rejection.

I took back what I said about Lucas being a jerk. Rubbing this rejection in my face to intentionally hurt me entered entirely new territory.

Congratulations, Lucas Taylor. You've just graduated to full-level asshole.

I saw the way Nadine looked at me when I passed through the Main Foyer with Lena. Her expression was full of longing, but it quickly shifted to unadulterated loathing when she spotted Lena at my side. I couldn't explain it, but that look in her eyes tore my fucking heart in two. I hated how much I'd hurt her, but I had to protect her.

And so I did what I had to do to keep her away. I grabbed Lena's hand.

Nadine's features darkened, and a heavy weight dropped on my stomach. But I couldn't back down now. Nadine had to know we could never be anything more than friends. If acting like the asshole was what got her to get over me, then I'd do it.

"Just go with it," I leaned over and whispered to Lena.

Lena smiled back at me as we started up the stairs. "Just go with it? Lucas, are you *flirting*?"

"Believe me," I said. "You'd know it if I was flirting."

Lena batted her eyelashes at me, and my stomach sank. I didn't want anything to do with Lena. But here I was, holding her hand.

I really was a jerk, wasn't I?

I watched for Nadine over the following week, but I didn't see her. I was pretty sure *she* was the one avoiding *me* now. It was probably for the best.

On Thursday, I stayed in bed, my head buried under the pillow. It was Halloween, a sacred holiday for the coven, which meant we had off school for the festivities, but all I wanted to do was sleep.

"That's it," Grant said from across the room.

I was awake, just not moving.

"It's time for you to get out of bed." Grant grabbed my ankle and tugged.

I jerked it away. "Get off me, man," I snapped. "You're not my mother."

Not like I'd let my mom drag me out of bed, either.

"It's *Halloween*," Grant emphasized. "You have to get out of bed."

I pulled the pillow off my head and rubbed my eyes. Grant stood beside my bed in a suit and cape. His hair was slicked back, and he wore fake vampire fangs.

"You're ready already?" I groaned. "The festival isn't until dark."

Grant shrugged. "No, but there's plenty to do before then. We could hit up Main Street and shop the sales."

"That crowd is worse than Black Friday," I complained.

"But we can get free cider!" Grant exclaimed.

He was way too fucking cheerful. Didn't he realize this day was all about the dead? It was too depressing to handle.

"I don't want free cider," I grumbled, putting the pillow back over my head.

Grant yanked it off me. "You have to at least *eat* something today."

"Not hungry," I told him. My stomach felt hollow, but I didn't want to eat.

Grant eyed me curiously, and his tone softened. "Dude, what's up with you? Last year you couldn't wait for Halloween."

I pulled the blanket up over my head. "Last year was different."

"Why?" Grant asked.

I didn't answer.

Grant huffed. He grabbed my blanket and tore it off from me, throwing it on the floor. It was really cold without it, so I curled up into a ball to stay warm.

"Lucas, talk to me," Grant demanded in a harsh tone.

"I don't want to talk about it," I told him.

"I'm your best friend, man," he said. "Let me help you."

I swallowed the lump in my throat and turned my gaze up to him. Thinking about what this day meant only made my guts twist. But Grant wasn't going to give up until I gave him something.

I pushed myself upright in bed. "I'm not sure I want to attend the festival tonight."

"Is this about your gift?" Grant asked.

It was obvious by his tone. He worried I'd faced too much death this past year and didn't want to celebrate. But that wasn't it at all.

I shook my head.

"Then what?" Grant asked, spreading his arms out in question. "You love Halloween. The hay rides, the apple bobbing, the costume contests. You could even go to one of those Seer booths and—"

Grant stopped in his tracks, and realization crossed his eyes. "Oh," he said flatly, eyeing the fallen expression on my face. "You don't want anything to do with spirits today."

I curled my arms around myself, because it felt like my guts would spill out otherwise. "There's a reason I haven't gone to a psychic since he died."

The words felt heavier than I thought they would. *He died.* Eric was gone. I knew it, and still it was hard to wrap my head around. Because he wasn't totally gone. His spirit was out there somewhere. I was just too afraid to figure out where.

"You don't want to talk to him," Grant whispered, sinking into a spot on the couch.

"It's not that," I told him. "It's just…"

I hesitated. I wasn't good at sharing my feelings. With Grant, we could talk about girls and crap like that, but I couldn't talk about the heavy stuff. I couldn't talk about my brother.

The truth was, Eric hadn't reached out to me in the past year. If he wanted to talk to me, he could've contacted a medium and relayed a message. But he hadn't. Which either meant he was at peace with everything that happened… or he'd ended up in the Abyss.

It was easier to believe he was at peace. I'd rather not seek out confirmation.

"You don't have to visit a Seer," Grant said. "Just dress up and go to the festival with me. That's all I ask."

I shrugged. "I don't know, Grant. I'm not feeling very festive."

"Here's an idea," Grant said brightly. "The veil's thin tonight, which makes séances super easy. You'll get an A for sure."

I cocked an eyebrow at him. "You want to help me do a séance for my Afterlife Studies class?"

"For sure," Grant said. "It'll be fun, and you have to do it sometime this semester."

I sighed. "I guess you're right. But I don't have a costume."

Grant smiled. "I have the perfect thing."

Grant's idea of *perfect* was far from my definition. I lifted the hem of the robe I wore, ready to tear the freaking thing off because I couldn't stop tripping over it. It was one of the black robes we wore the night of Nadine's initiation. Grant said I should dress as a reaper.

"Not cool," I'd told him, rather harshly.

"I didn't mean it as a joke," Grant promised. "It's an easy costume."

I grumbled about it all day, before finally giving in. At least I could hide beneath the hood.

It was dark by the time we finally left the dorm. I held the celestite stone Nadine had given me in my hand. It was supposed to calm me, and our goddess knew I needed some serious help in that area. So far, it didn't seem to be working. I slipped the stone in my pocket and instead focused on not tripping over my robe. Who the fuck were these things made for? The Harlem GlobeTrotters? I wasn't exactly a short dude.

"Dear Goddess," Grant groaned. He stopped in the middle of the sidewalk and knelt down. He grabbed the hem of my robe and tied the corner into a knot, so that it hung just above my feet.

"There." He stood and cocked an eyebrow at me. "Can we get to the festival now?"

"Geez," I said. "Someone's in a hurry."

"Trick-or-treating is already over," Grant pointed out, gesturing around the dark street. There were cars parked in every slot, which was why we decided to walk. "I don't want to miss the bonfire, too."

"So, you're gonna dance?" I asked.

"Hell yeah," he said as we started walking again. "What do you think Halloween's about?"

We turned the street corner, and it was like stepping into an alternate dimension. The last street was so quiet and deserted, but Main Street was bursting with life. All the shops were open, and there were strings of orange and white lights above us.

People walked up and down the road, since it was blocked off to cars. They were dressed in creepy costumes like ghouls, demons, and scary clowns. I saw at least a dozen people in costume as slasher film villains, and there was an entire family dressed up as characters from the *Addams Family*. One girl had done her makeup to look as if her skin was falling off. Her boyfriend made it look like his head had been severed. Everywhere I looked there was some sort of dead something or other—a dead bride, dead prom queen, and a dead nurse. One kid walked around looking like a talking ventriloquist doll, which was creepy as hell. I even saw a girl dressed up as a Ouija board, with the planchette painted on her eye and the letters on her chest. A trio of girls from school had dressed up as the Sanderson Sisters from *Hocus Pocus*. I noticed Lena was the one dressed as the pretty blonde.

Up and down Main Street, the shop owners had gone all out with decorations. Skeletons hung from signs, and cobwebs had been stretched across windows. Jack-o-lanterns of all shapes and sizes were set up along shop stoops or on bales of hay in front of windows.

We passed by the four Imperium priestesses. They wore long, flowing robes and were handing out suckers shaped like their Cast's symbol to all the kids.

As Grant and I made our way through town and to the park, the Halloween decorations only became more prevalent. Plastic bats had been hung from the trees, and fake blood was smeared all over tree trunks. The vendor booths in the park were even more elaborate than the shops on Main Street. One looked like a gingerbread house, and a lady dressed as an ugly old witch invited kids inside for candy. A haunting melody came from the bandstand, and I could see the bonfire burning down by the river.

"Candy!" Grant cried. He ran over to the first booth and grabbed a handful of chocolate from the bowl sitting there. He subconjured it, then grabbed another handful and shoved it in his pocket.

I eyed him with a frown, and he stopped dead in his tracks. He pulled the candy from his pocket and held a piece out to me. "Sorry, bro. Did you want some?"

"No, thanks," I said.

Grant shrugged. "More for me. So, you want to start with apple bobbing, or the hay bale maze?"

"They're both for kids," I pointed out.

Grant clapped me on the shoulder. "There's a kid inside all of us. It's your fault if you refuse to embrace it."

Grant really wanted to do the apple bobbing, so we wove through the maze of booths to find it. Each booth had a different activity, like pumpkin painting or pumpkin carving. There were photo booths, pumpkin tosses, and all sorts of carnival games with Halloween themes. One booth had aisles made out of hay bales, and people were rolling pumpkins down them at plastic bowling pins. Beside that, miniature pumpkins had been set up on a giant checkerboard. Not far from us, a Halloween movie was playing on a projector, and kids were snuggled in blankets on the grass watching.

If the booths weren't hosting some activity, they were selling food. My favorites were the hotdogs wrapped in dough and made to look like miniature mummies, and the Jell-O shaped brains.

Grant stopped at the apple bobbing booth and rolled up his sleeves. "Watch the champion at work."

"Yes, Grant, because they give out trophies for apple bobbing," I teased.

He frowned. "They should—oh my Goddess."

Grant's eyes locked on something across the way, and he ducked behind me. I looked to where his gaze had gone, but I didn't see anything. I turned toward him, but he just moved with me to stay hidden.

"Hey, dude, what's up?" I asked.

Grant hid his face. "Talia's coming. Hide me."

I scanned the crowd again, and sure enough I spotted Talia and Nadine coming our way. Talia was dressed in a short green dress and faerie wings. Her cat wore a sack with something written across the side, though I couldn't read it.

Nadine looked absolutely stunning in a plaid shirt, overalls, and a straw hat. Her hair had been twisted into braids, and her makeup was done up to look like a scarecrow. I didn't know what it was about her outfit—maybe the way the overalls hugged her curves—but she looked amazing.

It took me a few moments to tear my gaze off of her.

"Relax," I told Grant. "They're not coming over *here*."

Except they were. They hadn't seen us yet, but they stopped beside the booth next to us, where a dozen other college girls were giggling. At first I didn't know why, until Grant inhaled a sharp breath.

"That's the matchmaker booth," he pointed out. "Do you think Talia will get me?"

I shot him a side-eye look. "You'd have to be dating her first."

"It could happen," Grant shot back.

"Come, come, ladies." Professor Wykoff gestured Nadine and Talia forward. She was dressed in a medieval Celtic dress and was running the matchmaker booth. The booth drew in high school and college girls, and they performed various rituals that would tell them about their future relationships.

"Come," she said again. "Open your minds, and your future husband shall be revealed."

Nadine shot Talia a skeptical look, but she giggled like she was having fun. She stepped up to the booth. "How does this work?"

"Well, my dear, there are many rituals performed on the night the veil is thin," Professor Wykoff said in a mystical voice. "The spirits of our ancestors will guide you and tell your future."

Talia nudged Nadine forward. "It's worth a shot."

"Okay," Nadine agreed, though she didn't sound sure of herself.

"Start with the mashed potatoes," Professor Wykoff said, holding out a small bowl to each of them.

"Oh, this one's fun," Talia said chipperly.

"You've done this ritual before?" Professor Wykoff asked.

Talia's cheeks blushed pink. "Once, but I didn't get the ring."

"What do you mean?" Nadine asked. "What's supposed to happen?"

"We've made a large batch of mashed potatoes," Professor Wykoff explained. "And I've hidden a ring inside. Whichever young lady finds the ring is said to be married by next Halloween."

Nadine chuckled. "If I find the ring, I think it'll come as a shock to all of us. I don't even have a boyfriend."

Professor Wykoff smiled. "Well, you never know, my dear. Things can move quickly when they're meant to be."

She handed each of the girls a spoon, and they both took a scoop of mashed potatoes. I didn't know why, but I found myself holding my breath. I breathed a sigh of relief when Nadine swallowed—no ring to be found.

Nadine handed back the bowl. "No ring, but that was delicious."

"Thank you," Professor Wykoff said. "Not to worry, my dears. We have plenty of other rituals for you."

Professor Wykoff offered them a bowl of hazelnuts. "In this ritual, you'll name each hazelnut for each of your suitors. You'll place them into your fire at home. The nut that burns to ashes will represent your future husband."

Nadine hesitated. "Oh, um... I don't really have any suitors right now."

Grant stiffened beside me, like he hoped Talia might take a hazelnut and name it after him. But she refused the bowl as well. "We don't have a fire in our dorm."

"Not to worry, not to worry," Professor Wykoff said. "Let's try the apple peels."

Professor Wykoff held out another bowl, which was filled to the brim with apple peels.

"What do we do with these?" Nadine asked.

Talia bounced on her toes. "Oh, I like this one. I never got a good reading on it, though."

"It's simple," Professor Wykoff told them. "Take a handful of apple peels and toss them over your shoulder. The shape they land in will reveal to you your future husband's initials."

Nadine laughed. "I guess I'll try it."

She and Talia both took a handful of apple peels and tossed them over their shoulders on the count of three. Grant grabbed my robe and tugged on it, but when I glanced over to him, his eyes were locked on Talia. He didn't seem to notice he had a hand on me at all.

"Mine doesn't look like anything," Nadine said.

She was right. It just looked like a mess.

"I think mine worked!" Talia exclaimed.

Grant tugged on me harder, until my robe was practically choking me. I coughed, and he let go, but he couldn't tear his eyes from Talia.

"That could be a G…" Talia said thoughtfully, pointing down to her apple peels.

Grant gasped.

"Or a C," Nadine added.

Grant sighed.

Talia tilted her head to the side, inspecting the peels. "True. I can't make out the last initial, though."

"Did you hear that?" Grant said to me. "*It might be a G!* That's me!"

"Or a C," I reminded him. "Could be Cody."

Grant frowned. "Screw that asshat. He doesn't deserve her."

I shrugged. "Then ask her out."

Grant ignored my suggestion and tugged on my sleeve again. "Good Goddess, Nadine's doing the mirror!"

I looked back to Nadine, and sure enough, Professor Wykoff had guided Nadine in front of a full-length mirror. It was pointed in our direction, so I could see her reflection perfectly. She looked nervous as she stepped up to it, but there was curiosity in her eyes, too.

"Take this and concentrate on the spirits around you," Professor Wykoff instructed. "Ask them to guide you to see your future husband's face."

Professor Wykoff placed a lit candle into Nadine's hand. Nadine took a deep breath and closed her eyes. Talia stood off to the side, peering curiously at Nadine.

"What if Talia sees me?" Grant whispered from beside me.

"Shh…" I hissed at him.

I shouldn't have cared what Nadine saw in that mirror when she opened her eyes. Whichever guy she saw, it wasn't going to be me. That shouldn't have bothered me, since I knew we'd never end up together, but for some reason, it did.

Nadine's eyes shot open, and she gasped. "Lucas!"

My heart jolted in my chest. No, she didn't see me. She couldn't have.

She whirled around, and her eyes locked on mine. Shock was etched into her features for a moment, until a darkness akin to anger took over.

"Lucas," she snapped. "You ruined my spell!"

I was so stunned by the accusation that I just stood there for a moment. "I—I what?" I stammered.

"What are you doing standing there?" she demanded.

It was only then that realization hit. She *had* seen me in the mirror, but it wasn't because of the spell. It was because I was standing right there, the mirror pointed straight at my face.

"I didn't *try* to mess up your spell," I defended. "Grant wanted to apple bob." I gestured to the booth we stood next to.

"No, I didn't," Grant said quickly, shooting a glance over at Talia. "Apple bobbing is for kids."

Talia chuckled. "No, it's not. It sounds fun."

Grant's features brightened. "Oh, well… I'm pretty good if you want to challenge me."

Dear Goddess. I resisted the urge to roll my eyes.

Talia stepped toward him and raised a challenging eyebrow. "Maybe I will."

"Don't forget these!" Professor Wykoff shoved a small bag of treats into the girls' hands.

"It's walnuts, hazelnuts, and nutmeg. Eat it before you go to bed tonight, and you'll dream of your future husband."

"Um… thanks," Nadine said, glancing down to the bag. She eyed it like she wasn't quite sure of this *future husband* ritual, since I'd screwed the last one up.

"Maybe after apple bobbing, we could dance around the bonfire?" Grant suggested to Talia.

"Sure, that sounds great!" She sounded really excited.

Grant suddenly didn't sound so shy. "Cool. So, what are you supposed to be? An Arcanea?"

Grant was careful with his words. It was offensive to dress up as other races for Halloween, and we all knew it.

Talia frowned. "I'm Tinkerbell. Gus is my bag of fairy dust."

Gus was licking his paw. He stopped when he heard his name.

"You're not a Midnighter, are you?" Talia asked, eyeing Grant's costume.

He looked disappointed she didn't recognize him. "I'm *Dracula.*"

"Ah, I see it now," she teased. "You're missing the receding hairline."

"I know, my hair's just too perfect for Dracula," Grant joked, running his hands through his gelled hair. "Anyway, shall we?"

Grant and Talia ditched us to take their turn apple bobbing, leaving Nadine and me alone. Neither of us said anything. I couldn't stand it. I think I would've rather stabbed myself in the stomach with a chef's knife than stand there in awkward silence.

"So, um… a scarecrow?" I said to kill the silence. If anything, I only made it worse.

"Yep," she said, popping the P at the end of her word. She shoved her hands into her pockets. "And you're… a reaper?"

I nodded. I couldn't look at her, so I kept my eyes on Grant and Talia as they dipped their heads into the water.

"Creative," Nadine said flatly. I couldn't read her tone, but it sure felt like an insult.

Several minutes passed, and we just stood there. I swear I'd never waited longer in my life. Grant was taking forever. I thought about saying more to break the silence, but Nadine hadn't said anything, either. I got the feeling she didn't want to talk to me. I wanted to apologize, but I could hardly find my tongue. Something told me that'd just end in a fight, and I didn't want to ruin her night.

Finally, after what felt like seven hours of excruciating silence, Grant and Talia returned. They were both laughing, and Talia was running her fingers through her wet hair.

"You were right, Grant," she said. "You *are* good at apple bobbing."

Grant puffed his chest out proudly. "Got one on my first try."

"So, Talia, you wanted to dance?" Nadine said quickly, like she was dying to escape as much as I was.

"Yeah," Talia said brightly. "It's the best part of Halloween."

Nadine looped her arm through Talia's and said, "Show the way."

Grant practically skipped behind them, and I followed along at a distance.

"Come on," Grant hissed at me.

Ugh. Why'd he have to invite Talia and Nadine of all people? This was too weird.

We reached the bonfire, where people in costume were already dancing and having a good time. There were large logs set up around the perimeter. I took a seat on one, because I wasn't much of a dancer.

"Party pooper," Grant joked, before running off to dance with the girls.

Grant took three stocks of dried yarrow off one of the picnic tables. St. John's Wort flowers were woven around the stems. He handed one to each of the girls.

"What's this for?" Nadine asked.

"We dance with it, to keep the faeries away," Grant explained.

Nadine raised an eyebrow. "Faeries? Like the Arcanea?"

"Yes, but also their ancestors," Grant clarified. "The veil between all realms is thin tonight. We don't want any tricksters in our midst."

The three of them hurried off to join the dancing. From the bandstand, a female voice sang a slow, melancholy tune played in a minor key. She was backed by a piano and bells. Everyone danced to their own muse. There was no choreography, except they all moved around the fire in a counterclockwise rotation. Talia and Nadine swayed their hips slowly to the music, while waving their arms seductively. Grant looked like he was doing a poor rendition of *Swan Lake*, though at least he looked like he was having fun.

I couldn't take my eyes off Nadine. It was like that every time we were together, but tonight especially. She smiled and laughed, like she was having the time of her life. It made my heart lift, even though I wasn't participating. All I wanted was for her to be happy.

After a while, Nadine stepped away from Talia and Grant. She breathed a heavy sigh as she came to sit beside me. She looked totally wiped.

"You okay?" I asked.

I could pretend to be an asshole, but I still *cared*. So sue me.

"Just need to catch my breath," she said.

"Are you having fun?" I asked.

"I am," she replied. "So, what's the deal with Halloween around here?"

"What do you mean?" I asked.

She waved her hand and gestured to the people dancing around the bonfire. "You guys seem to take it really seriously. I thought Halloween was all superstition."

I chuckled lightly. "You're a witch, and you think superstitions aren't real?"

She shrugged. "I don't know. *Is* it all real?"

"Most of it," I told her.

She raised an eyebrow. "So, do the gates to hell open on Halloween or something?"

I rolled my eyes at her. It was cute how little she knew. "No, but the veil between the living and dead is thin."

She turned to face me, looking intrigued. "Why tonight, though, on All Hallows Eve?"

"We don't call it that," I stated.

She furrowed her brow. "Really? I thought that was the traditional name of Halloween."

"Our traditions date back *way* further than that," I said. "All Hallows Eve ties into All Saints Day, which is a Christian tradition that coincided with Halloween. Our traditions date back to Celtic culture and the Samhain festival."

Nadine tilted her head. "The coven isn't Celtic, though, is it?"

"No," I told her. "But we adopted the traditions of Samhain because they were so effective."

"Effective at what?" she asked curiously.

It was weird that she was talking to me so casually again after I'd been such a jerk to her. But she always got this way when she was curious about something. Her curiosity was one of the things that drew me to her.

"At keeping away the evil spirits," I told her simply. "The end of October marks the end of the harvest. It's the midpoint between the fall equinox and the winter solstice. Cultures around the world believe that this is the day of the year when the veil between the living and the dead is the thinnest. That's why Professor Wykoff was making you do all those rituals at the match-making booth—because they work best when the veil is thin."

"So, evil spirits can really get through to the land of the living on Halloween?" she asked.

I shrugged. "Sure. They all can, if they want to. The point of all these Halloween traditions is to scare away the evil spirits and welcome the good ones."

"Scare them away? That's why everyone dresses up so scary and people hang creepy decorations?" she asked.

I nodded. "Right. It's why we dance and sing around the fire and burn our crops, too. Ages ago, we used to burn cattle, but we don't do that anymore."

Nadine's eyebrows shot up. "If you do this all to ward off spirits, how do you welcome the good ones?"

"A lot of people will set an extra plate at dinner so their ancestors can dine with them," I explained. "After the festival, people will bring flames from the bonfire back to their houses to light their own fireplaces. Then we'll all light candles so the spirits can find their way back to the afterlife when the night is over."

It was actually cool to explain this all to her, because her eyes lit up with intrigue with every little piece of information I gave her. She was obviously a really big fan of Halloween.

"What's the deal with all the candy and crafts, then?" she asked, gesturing to the booths in the park behind us.

I shrugged. "That's just for fun. The Seer booths are real, though. If you want to talk to anyone who's crossed over, now's the best time."

Nadine's features fell, and she stared into the bonfire. I couldn't read her expression, but she looked deep in thought.

She cleared her throat. "I, um… think I might prefer the haunted house tonight."

Nadine got really quiet after that.

"There's no one you want to talk to?" I asked.

I could've sworn I saw tears in Nadine's eyes, but I couldn't tell for sure because she wouldn't look at me. Great. I was the asshole *again*.

"Thanks for telling me about Halloween," Nadine said without looking at me. "But I'm going to get back to dancing."

Nadine stood and walked over to Talia and Grant. She barely danced, though. She picked up Gus and made it look like he was the reason she wasn't dancing, but I could tell she was really tired.

"Lucas," a voice hissed through the darkness. It was so chilling that it made me freeze on the spot. I glanced around, wondering if anyone else had heard it, but everyone kept on dancing and laughing.

"Lucas," the female voice sounded again, louder this time.

I whirled around, and I nearly fell out of my seat when I saw a woman dressed in black crouched at my level. Her face was only inches away from mine. She was dressed as a night hag —a creature of lore who could invade your dreams and caused sleep paralysis. She wore a black veil over her face, but red eyes glowed from beneath it.

"W-what do you want?" I asked.

"Fear not, child, for I am only a Seer," she said.

I knew it was a costume, but I'd be damned if it didn't scare the living daylights out of me.

"A spirit has visited me tonight," she whispered. "He has seen the future, and he has a message for you."

The woman reached out and pressed a piece of paper into my palm. When I glanced down at it, I saw it was a tarot card. Not just any card, either.

Death.

My stomach dropped to my toes. I glanced back up at her. "Is this some sort of joke?"

She shook her head. "Death follows you wherever you go, Lucas."

A shiver ran down my spine.

"Of course it does," I snapped at her. "I'm the Reaper's Apprentice. What does this mean?"

The card could literally mean anything. I dealt with death on the daily, but I knew the Death card had many other meanings. Usually, it wasn't literal.

"You must stop this," the Seer warned.

"Stop what?" I demanded.

"Lucas!" Grant called.

Instinctively, I looked toward him. He waved his hand in my direction as he passed by me. "Come dance! It's fun."

Grant turned back to Talia and grabbed her around the waist. She giggled as he bared his fake fangs and pretended to bite her neck.

I ignored him and turned back toward the Seer... but she was gone. The card still sat in my hand, but it was as if the woman had never existed.

Whatever. I was sure it was nothing more than a joke.

I tossed the card into the grass behind me, and it tumbled in the wind.

Even after the card disappeared from view, I still had this feeling of dread settled deep in my stomach. What if the Seer had really meant something by it? The whole encounter had me shook.

Grant and the girls made it around the bonfire again, then plopped down on the log beside me. "Man, is it fun warding off evil spirits!" Grant exclaimed.

"Gus had fun," Talia said, stroking her cat's head.

Nadine shot a glance my way, but she didn't say anything. Silence settled over our group, and I could feel the awkwardness creeping in again. I just wanted to get out of there—away from the creepy Seer, and away from this awkwardness with Nadine.

I cleared my throat. "Well, Grant. We should probably get going."

"Get going?" he balked. "But I'm having so much fun."

"And I have that paper to write," I reminded him.

"Right. The séance." Grant's shoulders fell. He didn't sound as enthused about it as he had been earlier.

Nadine's spine straightened, and her eyes lit up. "You guys are doing a séance?"

"Um, yeah," I said nervously. She sounded like she wanted to come, but I'd been using it as an excuse to leave.

"Yeah, Lucas needs to do one for his Afterlife Studies class," Grant said. "Do you two want to join us?"

I pinched his arm the same time Talia and Nadine answered in unison, "Yes!"

"That's not necessary," I said. "You guys enjoy the festival. Grant and I are fine on our own."

Grant shot me a look the girls didn't see. *Come on, bro!*

"Ooh, I'd love to see it!" Nadine's eyes were so bright and hopeful.

I still felt bad about the first séance we did. I supposed I owed her a descent séance that didn't end in her getting hurt.

I spoke before I could talk myself down. "If you want... you can come," I offered timidly.

My guts twisted as soon as I said the words. Something told me I was about to regret this decision.

The cemetery was creepy at night, but it was particularly chilling on Halloween. The front gates had been left unlocked, and they creaked on their hinges. The moon was nothing more than a sliver, which cast the cemetery in almost complete darkness. Cold air brushed across my skin, raising the hairs on the back of my neck. There wasn't a soul in sight, but I could feel death in the air.

Nadine and Talia clutched each other, and Gus took cautious steps forward.

"Is there a reason we're doing this in the cemetery?" Nadine asked. If it were any other girl, I'd expect her to sound terrified, but Nadine wasn't. Her voice was steady, and she sounded intrigued.

"It's easier to contact someone who's recently deceased," Grant explained. "And since we don't have anything personal, we figured a grave would do."

"Who are we contacting?" Nadine asked.

I shrugged and gestured to the newest plots. "Take your pick."

Nadine walked up to a fresh gravestone. The ground sank a little beneath her feet. The grass hadn't even started growing over the plot.

"Nadine!" Talia exclaimed. She grabbed Nadine by the arm and dragged her back onto the grass.

"What?" Nadine asked innocently, glancing between the three of us.

"It's rude to step over someone's grave," Talia told her.

Nadine pressed her fingers to her lips, and her eyes went wide. "I'm sorry. Did I already ruin the séance?"

I shook my head. "No. We can still contact… Emily Robinson."

My heart stopped when I read off the name on the gravestone. It was the girl who'd died in that domestic attack a few weeks ago. I thought for a moment it'd be better to contact someone else—someone who hadn't left with such a sad last thought. But then I realized pretty much everyone died with some sort of baggage. Emily was as good of spirit as any to contact.

I eyed the date on the stone, then glanced down to the freshly turned earth. Something about it made me uneasy, though I couldn't put my finger on it.

Talia's face fell. "What is it, Lucas? Do you know her?"

I cleared my throat. "No. Let's get this over with."

The four of us sat around the gravestone, being careful not to sit directly on Emily's grave. Gus snuggled up in Talia's lap, looking positively content.

"Anyone happen to have a candle or two on them?" I asked. I'd totally forgotten about it before we left.

"Yeah," Nadine said, grabbing at her pockets. "I've got a whole stash right here in my overalls."

I looked at her hopefully, then realized she was joking. She chuckled, and I rolled my eyes at her.

Not amused.

"I've got you." Grant conjured a candle and set it at the base of the grave marker, then lit it with a lighter. He looked to me for further instruction, since this was my class assignment.

"Everyone join hands," I said. I hesitated when I realized Nadine had sat on my left, which meant I had to hold her hand.

She noticed my hesitation and frowned at me. "I'm not contagious."

"Didn't say you were," I replied, a little harsher than I meant.

Nadine's eyes narrowed. She looked like she was about to say something, but thought better of it. She didn't want to get kicked out of the séance.

I took her hand, but I must've squeezed a little too tight, because she winced. I let up a little, until I was just barely touching her, but it didn't matter. Her touch sent an electric shock straight through me. It took me a few moments to find my voice.

"Try to relax," I told everyone.

Pft. I was one to speak. I really didn't care for this assignment. I mean, who was I to disturb the dead? But I was barely scraping by in Afterlife Studies. If I missed this assignment, too, I'd have to repeat the semester.

"Focus on Emily," I instructed.

Nadine peeked an eye open. "Focus how? We know nothing about her."

I shrugged. "Think about how she loved her Grandma Bea. Or how she used to weave blankets and loved singing karaoke."

Nadine furrowed her brow. "I thought you didn't know her. Did you just make that stuff up? I don't think that's how séances work."

Grant shot me a knowing look. I'd never met Emily in my life, but I'd read her obituary at least fifty times. I knew enough about her to summon her.

"Just go with it," I said flatly.

Nadine closed her eyes again, and the four of us inhaled a collective breath.

"Emily," I called out to the darkness. "We seek to contact you. If you can hear us, please make your presence known."

A light breeze rustled through the trees, but nothing about it felt particularly spiritual.

"Emily," I repeated her name. "All we want is to know how you are. Show us a sign—any sign—that you've made it to the other side all right."

Nothing but silence met us in the night. After several minutes of calling Emily's name, I was starting to wonder if I was doing it wrong. But I couldn't be. Séances were easy. It should've been simple tonight of all nights.

"Emily?" I called again. I tried not to let the irritation in my tone show, but something told me this wasn't going to happen tonight. Emily's spirit wanted nothing to do with us. She was probably hanging out at her Grandma Bea's house. Why would she bother visiting us when she could go anywhere tonight? This was a dumb idea.

I tried one last ditch effort to get her to appear. "Emily, please show yourself—"

An earth-shattering scream cut through the night, sending my heart up into my throat. My eyes shot open, and I jumped away from Grant and Nadine.

Talia sat across from me, screaming like a banshee. Her face had gone paper white, and she pointed to something behind me. Grant scrambled away from where he'd been sitting, looking like he might've shit his pants. Nadine's eyes went wide.

I whirled around and nearly dropped dead at what I saw. A woman in a black dress limped toward us through the shadows. Her face was pale as death, and there was a sickening gray tone to her skin. Her eyes stared forward without focusing on anything. At first, I thought it was some chick from the festival dressed as a zombie, until the moonlight crossed her face. I realized I recognized her from her obituary picture.

Holy shit! It was Emily, but this was no fucking ghost. She was here in the flesh.

How the hell was that possible?

I shot to my feet, my heart racing. "Stand back, everyone!"

I threw my arms out to push everyone behind me.

Emily limped forward. She moved her lips, but nothing came out. I'd seen Professor Warren reanimate animals in Necromancy Safety, but I'd never encountered a human corpse. To say it chilled me to the bone was an understatement.

Nadine grabbed my robes and peeked over my shoulder at Emily. Unlike my hands that were shaking fiercely, Nadine's held steady.

"Emily?" I asked the walking corpse.

She reacted by twitching her head at me. It moved unnaturally, like a creepy demon child from a horror movie. She was almost close enough to touch now, but I didn't want to freak her out—especially if I wanted answers. How was this happening? Was there a necromancer hiding in the trees laughing at us right now or something?

"Emily, what happened to you?" I asked. I didn't know why I was asking. If this was a necromancer's prank, she wouldn't be able to speak. But it was too much of a coincidence that we'd been trying to summon her spirit and her body showed up. Something deeper was happening here. The thing was... did I really want to stick around and figure it out?

Emily reached out for me. Two things happened at once. Emily's cold, dead fingers brushed against my robe, and it was like death itself had touched me. I felt the emptiness of death within my gut.

At the same time, Emily parted her lips. Black smoke began billowing out of her mouth. I'd never seen anything like it. All I knew was that it could only mean something bad. Like, *black magic* bad.

Nope!

We were out of here. To hell with answers.

"*Debilito!*" Grant cried. Green magic shot out of his hands and slammed into Emily's chest. It was a simple defense spell meant to cripple your opponent.

Emily's body crumbled to the ground, but that black smoke continued to billow out of her mouth.

"Run!" I shouted to my friends.

The four of us whirled around and started sprinting toward the cemetery gates. My heart pummeled against my rib cage. I didn't think I'd ever run so fast in my life.

We only made it a few gravestones down when I heard Gus screech. I took a few more paces before I realized Nadine had disappeared from my side. I spun back around and gasped.

Nadine had tripped over Gus and lay in the grass, groaning. Emily's corpse had risen from the ground and had gone straight for her. Nadine rolled over, and Emily reached out toward the silver star necklace Nadine always wore. She tried to say something again, but it was nothing more than a chilling moan.

"Nad, get up!" I shouted as I raced back toward her.

But Nadine hardly needed my warning. She lifted her foot and slammed it into Emily's gut. Talia and Grant gasped in unison as Emily went stumbling back. I reached Nadine and grabbed her under the shoulders to drag her to her feet.

Nadine held on to me, but she didn't move. She inhaled several breaths and stared at the live corpse like it was the most fascinating thing she'd ever seen.

"*Iactus!*" I screamed. My purple magic sent Emily flying back a few feet, but it barely fazed her.

"Nad, come on." I tugged at her.

I was about to toss her pretty little ass over my shoulder to get her out of there, but I didn't act in time. Emily recovered and lunged toward Nadine again.

Nadine screamed and curled into me. I wrapped my arms tightly around her. I expected Emily's body to slam into both of us, but she didn't reach us before a sleek black cat as dark as midnight sprinted into view. It hurdled over the nearest gravestone and hissed as it jumped through the air. The cat's claws sank into the flesh on Emily's face.

Nadine's eyes went wide, but we didn't have time to sit around questioning it. I grabbed her around the waist and tossed her over my shoulder.

"Let's go!" I demanded.

Talia and Grant were holding each other, and Gus had scurried on ahead. They both wore a deer-in-the-headlights expression, but they quickly snapped to attention when I hurried past them.

"Lucas!" Nadine protested, slapping me on the back. "Lucas, we have to go back!"

"Screw that!" I cried. We were almost to the front gates now, and there was no way I was going back to face that dark zombie. Sure, she moved slowly, but there was something terrifying about her. Whatever this was was way out of our paygrade.

"Lucas, you don't understand," she cried, kicking her feet.

We passed through the front gates, and I set Nadine on solid ground. I noticed she'd lost her costume hat at some point.

She brushed the hair out of her eyes. "We have to go back for—"

"We don't have to go back for anything," I stated firmly. "Whatever that was wasn't just some everyday reanimant. There was something dark."

"Necromancy gone wrong?" Talia asked curiously. Gus approached her, and she bent down to pick him up.

Grant pulled the gates to the cemetery shut and whispered an incantation to lock them.

"I'm not sure." My heart continued racing as I stepped up to the gate and wrapped my hands around the bars. My pulse slowed as I looked over the cemetery. I didn't see the zombie anywhere.

"Lucas," Nadine pressed.

I whirled around and pressed my fingers to my eyes. Usually, her curiosity turned me on, but right now, it was downright irritating. "I don't care what you want to go back for. Want to see if she's really dead? Want to know what that black smoke was coming out of her mouth? Too bad."

Nadine placed her hand on her hip and looked at me with a pissed expression. She raised an eyebrow. "You done? I was *going* to say, we have to go back for the cat. She saved us."

"Are you kidding me?" I balked. "That cat can clearly take care of itself—"

The rattling of the cemetery gates startled all four of us. Emily had returned from seemingly out of nowhere, and she was violently shaking the cemetery gates. Her features twisted into rage, and she moaned at us like she was some sort of rabid animal trying to escape.

The four of us took a collective step back.

"She can't get to us," Talia stated, though her voice shook.

Grant reached for Talia and stepped in front of her protectively. "Who knows? Our stunning spells didn't work."

"Well, we have to do *something*!" Talia insisted.

"We trapped it," Grant pointed out. "What more can we do?"

Nadine huffed, then stomped over to the side of the road. She grabbed a thick stick and started toward the zombie.

"Hold up." I grabbed for the stick before she could get too far. I didn't want her anywhere near that thing. "I'll do it."

Nadine stepped back. "Be my guest."

I hesitated as I walked up to the corpse. She continued to rattle the gates like a madwoman. My stomach felt hollow as I considered what I was about to do. But it wasn't like she was *alive*. I wasn't going to *hurt* her.

I flexed my fingers around the stick, testing how it felt in my hand.

"Grant?" I cocked my head at him, though I kept my eyes on the raging zombie.

He stepped forward. He kept his voice steady, and I guessed it was for Talia's benefit. "What do you need, man?"

"A little help with the *validus* incantation," I told him. "I can't do it myself."

"I've got you." Grant wrapped his hands around the stick with me.

"*Validus,*" we spoke together.

The stick glowed purple and green as we pooled our magic to make it stronger. It felt like a steel rod in my hands, and I could feel the power emanating from it.

"On three?" I asked.

Grant and I stepped closer to the corpse.

"One…" he said.

"Two…" I added.

"Three!" we cried together.

We lifted the stick and aimed it between her eyes.

"Sorry," I whispered to her.

Grant and I slammed the end of our enchanted stick straight forward through the bars. It connected with Emily's face so hard that it snapped her head back, and her moaning ceased instantly. Her eyes rolled back into her skull, and she collapsed onto the ground.

I thought that was the end of it, until her back arched instantly. The sound of bones snapping met my ears, and black smoke erupted out of her eyes, mouth, and ears. It swirled into a ball above her head, and a high-pitched shriek that wasn't quite human echoed across the cemetery.

"Get back!" I screamed, my heart racing. The four of us stumbled down the road, but we couldn't take our eyes off the strange phenomenon happening in front of us.

Then all at once, the smoke dissipated, and the shrieking stopped. I gasped for breath as my heart rate slowed.

"Let's get out of here," Grant said.

"Wait." Nadine grabbed Grant's arm to stop him. "We can't just *leave* her here."

"Well, we can't touch her, either!" I pointed out. "We don't know what that was."

"Then we need to tell someone," she insisted.

"Yeah, let's freak *everyone* out," Grant said sarcastically.

She frowned. "Someone has to take care of this."

She had a point.

"Headmistress Verla's house is just ahead," Talia said. "We can tell her."

I glanced to each of them, and they all looked in agreement. "Okay."

Headmistress Verla's house was tucked back in the trees. It was pretty elaborate for just one person, with two stories, a three-car garage, and a balcony at the top of the gothic turret. Verla owned like, twenty acres out here at the edge of town, but she was headmistress. She was loaded.

The house was dark when we stepped up to the front door. There was a chill in the air that was even more apparent here in the trees. Two huge door knockers hung from the black double doors. They were shaped as skulls and kind of creepy.

"She's probably not home," I said, like the pessimistic guy I was. "I bet she's at the festival."

Nadine rolled her eyes. "It doesn't hurt to check."

She stepped forward and grabbed the door knocker shaped like a bone. She slammed it hard against the door.

Silence.

I glanced around the forest, as if searching for any signs that the corpse would reappear.

Nadine knocked again, but no one came to the door.

"Maybe we should go," Talia suggested, eyeing the trees. "There are lots of people in town we can tell."

"Yeah," Grant agreed. He seemed eager to get out of here.

Nadine turned from the door. "Okay, let's go."

The four of us stepped off the porch, but the sound of a door swinging open caught our attention. We turned around in unison.

Headmistress Verla stood in the doorway, looking positively surprised to see us there. She wasn't wearing a costume, just a black cardigan she pulled around herself. Her eyes fell on Nadine. "What are you doing here?"

Nadine cleared her throat and spoke like this was an everyday thing. "There's a zombie in the cemetery. We thought you should know."

Headmistress Verla's eyes went wide.

"I think we killed it," Nadine added. "But the corpse is lying by the entrance, and we didn't want to touch it."

Verla's face paled. "Necromancy?"

I stepped forward. "It was something different. Something... *dark*. Black smoke came out of the corpse's mouth."

"I'm sure it's nothing more than a harmless Halloween prank. I'll handle this." But there was something akin to recognition in her eyes, like she knew there was more to what we'd just encountered than that. It was like she recognized the magic we spoke of, but couldn't tell us because we were students.

I realized then what had made me uneasy about Emily's grave. The plot was too fresh. Someone had intentionally grave robbed her and raised her tonight.

The question was who, why, and how the hell were we getting those answers?

The events of Halloween had me shook. I didn't know what to make of what we'd seen.

"Verla's probably right," Talia said as we headed back to our dorm after midnight. Grant and Lucas had walked us back to school, and we split up at the top of the stairs. "It was just a harmless prank... right?"

"Yeah, but who would do that—?"

Talia raised an eyebrow.

"Chloe!" I realized.

Talia shrugged. "I wouldn't put it past her."

My lips pressed into a thin line. "She *would* find a necromancer to freak us out."

"Well, there you go," Talia said. "Mystery solved—"

Talia cut off when Gus jumped out of her arms. He ran down the hallway toward a black cat that sat just outside our door. He crept toward it and sniffed it curiously. The black cat sniffed him back and started purring.

"Um, Talia?" I said as we got closer. I couldn't take my eyes off the cat—or rather, kitten. It looked only a couple months old. It had a short black coat, and there were no unique markings on it. But there was something about those piercing green eyes. "Is that the cat from the cemetery?"

She took a cautious step forward. "I think it is."

"What's it doing here?" I asked. It had to be more than coincidence. There was something about this cat that left me enamored. I had the strangest feeling the cat felt the same connection with me.

It looked up at me, then walked over and started rubbing itself against my leg. My heart melted, and I bent down to pet it. A warm sense of peace settled over me. "She's *so* sweet."

Talia eyed me curiously. "Nadine, can you describe to me what you feel?"

I stroked the kitten's fur. "I don't know."

I couldn't put it into words. There was a sense of familiarity there that didn't make any logical sense. I wanted to dress her up in little aprons and decorate sugar cookies with her. I could practically taste the dough melting in my mouth when I touched her. And there was this scent to her that made my mouth water—like the delicious scent of baking bread. I wanted to snuggle her tight and never let her go.

And then it hit me. I gasped and threw my hand over my mouth. Talia smiled from above me, like she already knew.

I let out a shaky breath and dropped my hand. "Talia, could this cat be reincarnated?"

"I think you already know," she replied softly.

Tears pricked at my eyes. "Is this cat my mom?"

Talia shrugged, but she looked happy for me. "Only you can tell."

"But… how do I know?" I asked.

"You just… *feel* it," she said. "Like when I first met Gus, he came to me with a chickadee in his mouth."

"What does that mean?" I asked.

"My grandpa Jimmy was a birdwatcher," she told me. "He taught me bird calls, and he called me Little Chickadee. I just *knew*."

I couldn't explain it, but something deep within my soul knew this cat was my mother. I picked her up and cradled her in my arms. She nuzzled against me, and my entire body felt warm with love. "I'm keeping her."

Talia and I entered the room, and I sat on my bed and stroked the kitten. "Does she remember me?"

"Not quite in the same way," Talia explained as she began to strip off her costume. "It's the same soul, but she's still a cat. She'll have a strong connection with you that spans lifetimes, but you'll create new memories with her."

"A strong connection?" I questioned.

"Why do you think she protected you in the cemetery?" Talia pointed out. "And that you wanted to go back for her? It's probably how she found our dorm room, too. Reincarnated cats are different from regular cats. They have a high sense of intuition that will draw them to their loved ones, and they'll act to protect them."

I pressed my nose into the kitten's fur, inhaling the sweet scent that reminded me of my mom. A tear fell from my eyes and soaked into her fur. For a moment, all my fatigue washed away, and I knew without a doubt that my mom had returned. She was here to take care of me again.

I sniffled. "I guess that's why the séance didn't take. My parents souls must've been reincarnating or something."

Talia looked thoughtful as she placed her costume on the hanger. "That might explain it."

The kitten began kneading my stomach. I swooned. "Aww… so, what do I name her? Do I name her after my mom?"

Talia pulled an oversized t-shirt over her head. "It's customary to give them a new name. It differentiates this life from their last."

"Mm…" I mused. "Then I think I'll call her… Isa."

Talia sat on her bed and stroked Gus. "Isa? That's pretty."

"It's my mom's middle name," I told her. I squeezed Isa tight to my chest. "I'm so happy to have her back."

Isa turned out to be a godsend over the next week. My symptoms had flared so bad I couldn't get out of bed and ended up missing a few days of class. She kept me company while I waited for the pain to settle.

By Friday, I was feeling better. I went to Demonology in the morning, then headed to Introduction to Tarot after an early lunch. I noticed Chloe walking my way. I slowed my steps so I wouldn't run into her, but she did the same thing. We ended up at the classroom door at the same time. Chloe stepped in front of it so I couldn't pass and placed a hand on her hip. At my feet, Isa hissed.

That a girl.

"I heard you were sick," Chloe sneered.

I shrugged. "I'm always sick. What's your point?"

She narrowed her eyes. "You don't look sick to me."

Good Goddess, didn't this girl have anything better to do than to torment me?

"If you could tell I was sick, it wouldn't be called an *invisible illness*," I snapped.

"If you want to be invisible, you might as well just leave Octavia Falls," she said. "It's too bad. I'd kind of been hoping that's what happened to you."

I scoffed. "You really think your stupid Halloween prank could scare me away?"

Her lips tightened. "I don't know what you're talking about."

"You said the same thing about Verla's cat," I reminded her.

She rolled her eyes. "Okay, *maybe* I slipped something into his food. But I didn't do anything on Halloween. I take Halloween *very* seriously."

"Right," I said sarcastically, dragging the word out. I didn't believe her. "You would *never* break the rules. Black magic's *way* outside of your comfort zone."

Chloe's gaze darted up and down the hall, as if making sure no one else heard, then she narrowed her eyes at me. "Go die in a ditch, Evers."

She whirled around and entered the classroom. I just laughed from behind her, while Isa let out another hiss.

"That a threat, Chloe?" I called. "Or are you working on casting a curse?"

She ignored me and pulled her tarot cards out of her bag. She started shuffling through them as I took my seat. She pulled a card from the top and started laughing so loud that the other students stopped talking to look at her. Chloe turned the card toward me and beamed.

It was the Death card, but I didn't really care. I knew she'd picked it deliberately to try to freak me out, but I was totally at ease. I pretended I didn't see it and faced the front of the room. Isa purred in my lap.

Class continued like normal. We were studying the symbolism in various cards within the suit of Wands, which was all pretty easy to pick up at this point in the semester.

At the end of class, I waited until everyone else had left, then approached Professor Wykoff.

"Nadine," she said brightly. "What can I help you with?"

"I missed a couple days of class, and I was wondering if there was any makeup work to do," I said.

"I noticed you were out of class," she said solemnly. "Is everything okay?"

"Fine," I told her. "Just been feeling a little under the weather."

She frowned. "Must've been a nasty little bug."

I chuckled under my breath, though she didn't notice. "Yeah, it's pretty awful."

"At least you're better," she said. "I mean, it could be worse. Could be chronic."

My stomach sank at her words. She had no idea.

"Yeah," I said flatly. I didn't have the energy to explain to her it *was* chronic. I quickly changed the subject. "So, is there any makeup work?"

"We studied the Ace of Wands through the Ten of Wands," she told me, "but there's no homework."

"Okay, thanks." I turned and left the room with Isa in my arms. I knew Professor Wykoff had been trying to make me feel better, but I couldn't get her comment out of my mind. Who was *she* to assume what I went through?

I was walking back to my dorm, barely paying attention, when I passed through the foyer. Tons of students were hanging around, but it wasn't until Isa growled lowly that I actually paid attention.

I lifted my gaze and saw Lucas chatting with that blonde chick, Lena, next to the fireplace. She laughed at something he said, which was dumb, because he wasn't even that funny. When she laughed, she reached out and touched his arm. He glanced down at her fingers, but he barely acknowledged that she touched him, like it was totally natural for those two.

Lena pushed a strand of hair behind her ear and fluttered her eyelashes at him. I just stood there frozen, watching, my stomach turning into knots. If he held her hand again, so help me…

Lena's eyes darted around the foyer, and for a second, they landed on me. She didn't look at me long, but something sparked in her eyes when she saw me. I couldn't even explain what it was. Jealousy, maybe?

Which made no sense, because if anyone was allowed to feel jealous, it was me. Lucas clearly didn't have a problem hanging out with *her*.

Lena said something I couldn't hear. The next second, she reached up and placed her hand on the side of Lucas's face. She leaned in and planted a kiss right on his lips. *In the middle of the fucking foyer!*

I went completely still, and the room spun around me. Rejection settled like a knife in my gut. This was a hundred times worse than when he held her hand. This was confirmation of everything I'd worried about the first time I saw them together.

Lucas didn't want me.

But apparently, he didn't care about the Reaper's Shadow curse when Lena was involved. Those two could have it *all*.

How could I have been so stupid? Why had I fallen for Lucas in the first place? And why the hell was I so mad that he was kissing Lena? It wasn't like I *owned* him.

Rationally, I knew that. But deep down, I felt a connection there that screamed of possession. He was mine, and I was his. We were two broken puzzle pieces that fit perfectly together—if only he wanted to.

Except Lucas didn't want that with me. He wanted it with *Lena*.

Screw him! He didn't know what he was missing out on. I was going to have to get him to see that for himself.

I couldn't make sense of what dark energy overcame me in that moment, but I felt nothing like myself. Jealousy, rage, and revenge bubbled up inside of me. All I knew was I had to do *something* to let off some steam.

I whirled toward the stairs. One second, I was stomping toward the banister, and the next, I was in my room. I hardly knew how I'd gotten there.

Talia was playing music at her piano but stopped abruptly when I entered the room. "Is something wrong?"

A maniacal laugh bubbled out of my throat. "Try everything. I just saw Lucas kissing that *bitch* Lena."

Talia's jaw dropped. "He didn't."

"He did," I stated. "And I'm getting back at him."

I dropped Isa off on my bed, then flung open my dresser and went for the skimpiest outfit I could find. I pulled on a black crop top and matching shorts that showed off my ass cheeks. I didn't even know where the outfit had come from, but I felt empowered in it. I let my hair down and slipped on a pair of high heels.

Talia's jaw dropped. "Nadine, are you sure about this? You're really emotional right now."

"Hell yeah, I am!" I cried. "Lucas can reject me all he wants, but he can at least tell me the truth, jackass. See you later, Tal."

I waved over my shoulder and left the room.

"Nadine, wait!" she called, but the door was already closing behind me.

I didn't know where I was going—just that I was looking for trouble. I passed through the foyer, expecting to show off my new look to Lucas, but he was gone.

Shame.

I swayed my hips as I walked down the hall as if I was on the runway. I could practically hear the bad-chick music in my mind. I pursed my lips and floated down the hall like a hella confident goddess. All eyes turned my way, and power exuded out of me. I felt like I could lift a mountain.

I stepped into the lounge, where my gaze narrowed in on what I was looking for—the one thing that would piss Lucas off the most.

Ryan.

He sat alone in the corner by the TVs, his arms stretched across the back of one of the couches. There was something in the way Ryan sat that made it look like he was on a throne. Confidence rolled off him in waves. He seemed like a king turning his nose up at all his peasant servants.

He was the total opposite of Lucas, and right now, it totally turned me on.

I walked straight up to Ryan, and let me tell you, when he noticed me, he *noticed* me. His eyes roamed up and down my body in such a seductive way that it already felt like his hands were on me. I should've felt dirty—and I did, in a way. But something about it exhilarated me, too.

Well, hellooo, danger.

"Mind if I sit?" I asked in a tone that wasn't my own.

Ryan straightened his spine, and his eyes traveled straight down to lock on my breasts. "Go ahead, sweetheart."

He gestured to the cushion beside him, but I didn't take it. I caved to the bad girl inside of me and sat straight on his lap, wrapping my arms around his neck.

"Where have you been hanging around, handsome?" I asked.

Ryan wrapped an arm around my waist. "I could ask you the same thing. Have we met?"

I found it hilarious he didn't recognize me, considering I nearly ran him over with my car. But that was the kind of guy he was. He only noticed a girl if she was spewing sex pheromones his way.

I ran a finger across his chest. "I think I'd remember *you*."

Ryan smirked. "I'll give you something to remember."

"How about a broken jaw?"

My heart fluttered at the sound of the voice, and I couldn't help it when a smile spread across my face. I turned to see Lucas standing there, his hands curled tightly into fists. A dark shadow crossed his eyes, and he looked like he was about to strangle Ryan.

My, my, my… looks like Lucas couldn't handle a little jealousy after all.

And it *thrilled* me.

Lena was kissing me. What the hell?

One second we were talking about our class assignment, and the next her lips were on mine. I'd kissed Lena before, back when we were dating in high school, but this was different. This was empty.

I felt nothing—absolutely *nothing*. Her lips were cold, and her hand felt like ice on my face. For all I knew, she could've been a ghost.

It took me a few seconds to realize what was happening, because no *way* was Lena fucking kissing me. But it was happening, and I totally wasn't okay with it.

I pressed against Lena's shoulder and pushed her away from me. "Lena, what the hell?" I hissed, glancing around the foyer. No one seemed to notice—or simply didn't care.

Lena tossed her blonde hair over her shoulder. "What's wrong, Lucas? We've kissed like, a million times before."

"When we were *together*," I snapped.

She pursed her ruby red lips and shrugged. "I thought you'd like a taste of what you were missing."

I scoffed. "I gotta say, Lena, it wasn't that sweet."

"So, what?" she challenged. "You've had sweeter?"

I raked my hands through my hair. "Come on, Lena. You know I don't date."

She lifted a manicured eyebrow. "Really? Because word around these halls is you have something going on with that Nadine girl."

"There's nothing going on…" I trailed off. Lena wore a pleased expression, but I didn't understand it at first.

Then it hit me. She'd kissed me because of Nadine.

"She saw, didn't she?" I growled. "You made sure of it."

Lena shrugged. "I don't know. Why don't you go ask her?"

"Lena," I groaned. I started to walk away—because I just couldn't take her right now—but I realized a second later I had more I wanted to say. I whirled back toward her. "You know what? I'm not some piece of property you can go around *marking*."

"You know I don't think that," she said, but there was no emotion behind her voice. She was as cold as ice—always had been.

"What do you want with me anyway?" I demanded. "You know nothing will ever happen between us."

She just stood there staring at me with complete confidence written across her face. Then it hit me—if she couldn't have me, no one could.

To hell with her. I could hang out with whomever I pleased.

I stomped away from Lena and headed down the hall in search of Nadine. I'd never seen her in the foyer, so I didn't know which way she'd gone. Heck, I didn't even know for sure if she'd seen. It could all be a stupid manipulation tactic from Lena to get me to tell Nadine I kissed another girl.

Yeah, I got that I was supposed to be playing the asshole, but I wasn't *that* kind of asshole. I had to explain to her what happened.

I wandered down the hall and checked the cafeteria, then tried a couple study areas, but I didn't spot Nadine. I turned around and headed in the other direction toward the Lounge.

My stomach flipped when I caught sight of her, but it immediately dropped when I noticed everything else about the scene. It was all *wrong*.

Nadine was dressed in sexy little number that left little to the imagination. It seemed like something Chloe or Lena would wear—not my sweet Nad. I barely recognized her.

It wasn't just the outfit she was wearing, either. It was this look in her eyes I'd never seen before. Something dark and sinister lurked beneath the surface—like she was under some sort of spell.

The worst part, though, was Ryan. Nadine sat in his lap, her arm draped around his shoulder. His hand rested so low on her hip he was practically touching her ass.

"I think I'd remember *you*," Nadine said in a voice that wasn't quite her own.

Ryan practically undressed Nadine with his eyes. "I'll give you something to remember."

Red-hot rage ignited inside of me. "How about a broken jaw?" I snapped.

Nadine turned toward me, and she smirked proudly.

Ryan chuckled. "You really think you can take me, Taylor? Don't forget what happened last time."

"Your backup's not around this time," I pointed out. "Let Nadine go."

Ryan smirked, like my attempt to rescue her was nothing short of amusing. "You act like I'm the one who initiated this. I think the girl can speak for herself."

I crossed my arms and looked to Nadine, a single eyebrow raised. "Nad?"

She practically beamed. "Ryan and I were just hanging out."

Ryan and Nadine would never just *hang out*. Someone must've slipped her a potion or something.

"You're not thinking straight," I insisted. "Let's go."

I reached for Nadine's wrist, though I was careful to be gentle with her. Nadine got to her feet, but so did Ryan. He took her other wrist, like he was laying his claim on her. She glanced between the two of us, looking mildly pleased.

Ryan puffed out his chest. "You're gonna have to fight for her—"

Thwack.

My fist connected with Ryan's jaw before he could finish his sentence. Hell yeah, I was going to fight for Nadine! And I was going to get a good swing in before he went all telekinetic crazy on me.

Pain shot through my knuckles, but it was worth every ounce. Ryan's head snapped backward, and his eyes rolled into his skull. His body slumped onto the couch. A girl sitting nearby gasped, while the guy next to her beamed at the sight of a fight.

Nadine's eyes went wide as she looked down to Ryan's unconscious body. "Lucas!"

At first, I thought she was scolding me, but she turned to me with an expression of exhilaration written on her face.

I shook my hand out. "Lucky shot, I guess. Let's get out of here."

I took Nadine's hand, and we hurried out of the Lounge. She followed without resisting. I dragged her into a dark, empty room down the hall and took her face in my hands. I searched her eyes for dilation, but they looked normal.

And yet, I couldn't help but get lost in them. Once my eyes began to roam her features, I couldn't look away.

Nadine shot a glance toward the door. "Um, Lucas. What are you doing?"

"I'm checking to see if you've been drugged."

"What!?" Nadine slapped my hands away. "I haven't been *drugged*."

"Then what the hell is wrong with you, Nad?" I snapped. Heat flared deep in my belly just thinking about her with Ryan.

She crossed her arms. "Nothing's *wrong* with me. That was all me back there."

"This isn't you," I argued. I eyed her up and down. The new look was... stunning... but it wasn't her. I much preferred her usual look—tight jeans and long sleeves. "You don't dress like this, and you don't act like *that*."

"I could say the same about you!" she yelled. "I thought you didn't date."

My breath caught. I didn't need any more confirmation than that. She'd seen Lena kiss me.

I raked my fingers through my hair. "Nad, it's not what you think."

She raised an eyebrow. "Oh? What is it that I think?"

I frowned. "I know you saw me and Lena in the foyer."

She pursed her lips. "Yeah. How *is* the new girlfriend?"

"She's not my—" I blew out a breath of exasperation. "Lena kissed *me*, okay? I didn't kiss her back, and I'd never want to."

Nadine's features fell, and she blinked a few times. "Oh. Well, that's..."

She trailed off, looking deeply contemplative.

A few moments passed before I broke the silence. "So, do I get an explanation, or—?"

"Where is that motherfucker!?" a voice sounded down the hall, cutting me off.

Instinctively, I grabbed Nadine's shoulders and pressed her up against the wall, pushing both of us deep into the shadows.

The two of us held our breaths as we listened to the sound of Ryan's footsteps pound down the hall toward us. I finally let out a breath when he passed. It was only then that I became acutely aware of how close Nadine and I were. I'd sandwiched her between myself and the wall, and I could feel her heartbeat against me. Her breasts were pressed firmly against my chest, and my jeans started to tighten.

I jumped away from her quickly, and I cleared my throat. My eyes darted around the room —anything not to look her in the eyes while my dick calmed the eff down.

It was the first time I noticed what room I'd dragged her into. It was one of the fitness rooms, complete with those big yoga balls, towels, and a shelf packed full of rolled up yoga mats. My eyes fell on a box marked *Lost and Found*, and I noticed a black fleece and yoga pants inside.

I grabbed them and shoved them at Nadine. "Put these on."

She gaped at me. "I'm a big girl. I can wear whatever I want."

I looked to her arms, which were covered in goosebumps, then shrugged. "Suit yourself."

She wrapped her arms around herself, like she'd just noticed how cold she was. She glanced to the clothes, then narrowed her eyes at me. "I'm only doing this because I'm cold."

She snatched the clothes up and started putting them on. I peeked out into the hall. Ryan stood at the end of it, his hands curled into fists. He twitched his fingers, and the door next to him swung open. A loud *bang* sounded through the hall.

I whirled back to Nadine. "Ryan's coming."

She zipped up the fleece and shrugged. "Then we're going to have to make a run for it."

My gaze roamed over the room. "Want to take the window?"

Nadine smirked. "I *do* love sneaking around."

"Then let's hurry." I started across the room with her, but I stopped mid-stride. Something about the yoga mats called to me. I remembered how much Nadine said she liked it. I turned back to the shelf and grabbed two mats, then sub-conjured them.

"Lucas," she hissed. She already had the window open and was straddling the sill. "That's stealing."

Bang!

Another door crashed open, closer this time.

"We'll bring them back. Let's *go!*"

I nudged Nadine out the window, and she jumped to the ground. I stuck my head out the window to see her catching her balance.

"You okay?" I asked.

Nadine didn't get a chance to respond.

"Taylor!" Ryan growled from behind me.

We hadn't been quick enough.

I whirled around just in time to see Ryan lifting his hand toward me. A dark ball of defensive magic formed inside of it. I wasn't sticking around to see which spell he wanted to use on me. I jumped out the window and landed in the grass beside Nadine.

"Hurry!" She chuckled under her breath, like running from a madman thrilled her.

Nadine and I locked hands and ran toward the forest. A ball of magical energy whizzed past us, missing my head by a hair. Ryan was pretty set on revenge, but the trees were thick and made good cover.

"This way," I said.

I tugged on her hand and pulled her behind a thick tree. The two of us crouched down beside each other. I braced myself against the tree, and Nadine pressed her back to it. I couldn't help but notice how close we were again. Her chest rose and fell rapidly, and her breath touched the side of my face. It sent my heart beating double time. While Nadine's eyes darted around the forest, I kept my eyes on her.

What I wouldn't give to lean in and kiss those sweet, soft lips of hers…

"I think he's gone," she whispered.

I breathed a sigh of relief, though all I wanted was to stay in this position—to be as close to her as I could without touching her. If only I could, I wondered where we'd be now. The images that crossed my mind were dangerous.

I cleared my throat and stood. Now that I had a moment to calm down, I realized how cold it was. There'd been snowfall after Halloween, but it was nothing more than a light dusting. Still, tonight was pretty chilly.

I reached out to help Nadine to her feet. "You okay?"

She brushed her hair out of her eyes. "Yeah, I'm fine. You?"

"Good… for now," I told her. "Ryan's not going to rest until I pay for that."

She winced playfully. "Yeah, it must've really hurt his pride."

"What were you *doing* with him?" I asked.

She dropped her gaze. "Honestly?"

I nodded. "Honestly."

She bit her lower lip, which only made me want to kiss her more. "Honestly, I don't know."

My eyebrows shot up. "You don't know?"

"Yeah," she snapped. "I'd really like not to talk about it right now."

My heart dropped. I didn't know what she meant by that, but she sounded pretty serious. Her face fell, and I realized in that moment that a lecture from me was the *last* thing she needed. I didn't know what was going on with her, but I could see it in her eyes. Right now, all she needed was a friend.

"Okay, we won't talk about it," I agreed.

The sound of leaves crunching in the distance caught my attention.

"We should hide," Nadine suggested.

I placed my index finger over my mouth. "Shh… you like haunted houses, don't you?"

Her eyes lit up, but her features quickly turned into a mock scowl. "Not if it's anything like last time."

"It won't be," I promised with a smirk. "This one's not actually haunted."

She narrowed her eyes, like she couldn't figure out what I had in mind. But like the curious soul she was, she agreed to come with me. "I want to see it."

Good Goddess, this girl would do anything to satisfy her curiosity. It was going to come back and bite her in the ass some day.

"This way." I cocked my head, and Nadine followed beside me.

I navigated through the woods by sheer intuition and a vague memory. We walked for at least fifteen minutes, until I finally spotted the clearing in the trees.

"Is this another kidnapping attempt?" Nadine teased as she ducked under a tree branch.

"Indeed," I told her.

She rolled her eyes. "You've gotta stop doing that, Lucas."

"But you're just so easy to kidnap."

She shrugged. "You know how to intrigue a girl."

I turned serious again. "You're free to go whenever you want, but we're here."

I pulled back a tree branch, and Nadine's eyes sparkled in wonder. In the clearing stood an abandoned gothic mansion. It looked a lot like the school, with the sharp, peaked roofs, tall turrets, and thick wooden doors, but it was smaller. The walls were made of stone, which was probably why it'd stood so long. Ivy grew up the side of the house. This place was absolutely stunning when the clearing was in full bloom and the ivy blanketed the house in green, but right now everything was just kind of dead and sad.

And yet Nadine couldn't take her eyes off it. It was like she saw beauty in the house I couldn't quite see myself.

"Wow," she breathed. "This place is amazing. Can you imagine if someone fixed this place up, how beautiful it would be?"

"Yeah. I bet it was really nice when it was built," I said. "Want to see the inside?"

Nadine nodded eagerly.

We stepped up to the house and entered through the front doors. Hardwood floors spanned in front of us, and the banister that led upstairs was intricately carved, interweaving all the five Cast symbols in a beautiful work of art. There wasn't any furniture, and all the cupboards were empty. Like on the outside of the house, ivy grew on the inside, too, weaving its way through broken windows and overtaking practically everything.

Nadine's jaw dropped. "This architecture is amazing. Look at the archways and crown molding. What is this place?"

I explained as we walked through the rooms. "It used to belong to one of the headmasters of the school. It was abandoned when he died. Legend has it, the house will only reveal itself to those who wish not to harm it."

Her eyebrows shot up. "I guess that's why it makes a good hideout from Ryan."

"Exactly," I stated. "That idiot would fuck this place up. Anyway, Grant and I found it last year."

Nadine reached out a hand and ran her fingers across the wall. "How often do you come back?"

"I haven't been back," I admitted. "We explored, saw what there was to see, and left."

"But this place is just so beautiful," she whispered.

It was, but it was just a *house*. And it was on the cusp of collapse.

Nadine's eyes continued to wander as we entered the sitting room. It was my favorite room in the house because of the massive fireplace. The black mantle was intricately carved, making it the clear centerpiece of the home.

The rest of the room was empty, save for a pile of firewood someone must've brought in a few years ago. There was a thick layer of dust over all the firewood, though it hadn't started to rot.

Nadine drew a breath when she saw the fireplace, then turned to me. "Are you sure the house isn't haunted?" She sounded a little disappointed.

"I'm sure. Let me show you." I took Nadine's shoulders and guided her to stand in the middle of the room. "Close your eyes."

Nadine did as I instructed and inhaled a deep breath. I found myself walking in a circle around her, inspecting her features from every angle. She looked so at peace, so alive and eager for answers. There was this spark inside of her that glowed bright—and like a moth to a flame, I couldn't resist being drawn in.

She took another calming breath. "Now what, Lucas?"

I stopped behind her. We were so close we nearly touched. My pulse quickened, though I resisted the urge to pull her into my arms.

"What do you feel?" I whispered in her ear.

I could've sworn I saw her shiver, but it must've been from the cold.

"I feel… at peace," she finally said. "I feel like I could be happy here forever. There's this warmth inside the house, like it was built on happiness. But… there's something missing. It's like it's fading, like it's losing its memory. All it needs is someone to nurture it."

I stepped around her to look at her from the front again.

Her eyes opened, and her cheeks blushed pink. "Was that the wrong answer?"

I shook my head. "There are no wrong answers."

"What does it mean?" she asked.

"For one, you're intuitive," I said.

She tilted her head to the side. "Aren't most witches?"

I nodded. "True. It also means there are no malevolent spirits hanging around."

"I'm not a Seer, though," she pointed out. "I can't tell when there are spirits around."

"Not the way a Seer can, but even humans can feel the negative energy of a malevolent ghost," I explained.

"Good to know we're in the clear." Nadine spun around again, taking in all the little details she didn't see the first time. "It's a shame that no one is taking care of this place. I just want to… sweep it or something."

"I've got it." I stood in the middle of the room and raised my hands. "*Peppermint patty and grass so green, make this room sparkling clean.*"

Purple magic swirled out of my hands, causing dust to rise off of the floor. It gathered into a cloud at the base of the fireplace, then swept up through the chimney and out of the house. I looked to my feet and ran the tip of my shoe across the floor. It was totally clean.

Nadine's eyebrows shot up. "I can't wait until I learn cleansing spells."

I shrugged. "Cleansing incantations are easy. You just make shit up."

She looked amused. "Oh, so you're a poet now?"

"You get a feel for it," I said.

Nadine wrapped her arms around herself.

"You cold?" I asked.

She nodded. "November's not exactly known for its warm temperatures."

"Hold on." I knelt at the fireplace and started building a fire with the bits of tinder next to it. I conjured a lighter and lit it, then added bigger pieces of wood.

Nadine knelt beside me and warmed her hands. She breathed a sigh of relief. I watched her for several moments, until she lifted her gaze and caught me staring.

I cleared my throat and stood, then did the only thing I could think of to keep my hands busy. I conjured the two yoga mats I'd borrowed from school and laid them out on the floor in front of the fireplace. Nadine talked so much about how she liked yoga and needed to get back into it. Maybe this would help her—or at least give me a chance to apologize.

She eyed the yoga mats. "What are you doing?"

I kicked my shoes off and stood on one of the mats. I placed my hands together at my heart and closed my eyes. I lifted one foot and tried to balance on the other, but my balance was shit. I stood back on two feet and peeked an eye open. "I'm doing yoga. What does it look like?"

Nadine laughed and stepped onto the yoga mat beside me. "Need some help?"

I resisted the urge to smile. I really liked that we were getting along for once. "You're the expert."

Nadine lowered herself onto the mat and crossed her legs. I mirrored her posture.

"Let's just breathe for a minute," she suggested.

Nadine went silent. For the first minute or so, it was really hard not to let my mind wander and my body wiggle. But the longer Nadine just sat there breathing, taking in the moment, the more I came to appreciate it, too. I felt grounded, rooted right here with Nadine. My mind wasn't on my gift, my brother, my mom, my classes—any of that. I was just right here, drinking in every second I could with Nadine.

How could I have been such a jerk to her? She didn't deserve any of that. She deserved to be loved.

Nadine shifted and got onto all fours on the mat. She arched her back, pointing her belly toward the floor. I couldn't help but steal a glance at her ass, which made my pulse quicken.

"Do you know any yoga?" Nadine asked, snapping me out of it.

My eyes shot back up toward her face. "No."

"This is cow pose," she told me. "Then you arch your back the other way…" She brought her chin inward and curled her spine. "And you have cat pose."

I tried it along with her, and I was surprised at how much it stretched my back. It actually felt really good, like I could breathe easier.

Nadine walked me through several other simple poses—downward facing dog, cobra, and my favorite, mountain, since we just stood up and it was really easy. She explained each one, until she seemed to disappear into her own little world. Soon, she was moving slowly to her own muse without speaking to me at all.

She stopped in a pose that had one foot forward and the other pressed firmly to the floor. She held both arms out parallel to the floor.

"What's this one?" I asked.

She inhaled a deep breath, like she was enjoying herself. "Warrior two. Feels good, doesn't it?"

"Yeah," I whispered. It felt *really* good to be around her.

Nadine opened her eyes, then stepped out of the pose. She straightened her fleece and sat on the ground again. "Thanks for doing this, Lucas. I forgot how much it helped."

I didn't even realize what I was doing when I sat beside her and took her hand. I began massaging it like she said she liked. I knew her joints always hurt, and I just wanted to help.

I shrugged. "I didn't do anything."

She got really silent after that, but she didn't pull away from me. She just let me run my fingers over her hands. They were so soft and small. She seemed so fragile.

"Do you have any other poems?" Nadine asked to break the silence.

"Poems?" I asked. Then I realized she was talking about spells. "You mean incantations?"

"No," she replied. "Like, actual poems. You seem like you'd be good at them."

I kept my gaze on her hands and shrugged. Deep down, my heart warmed. No one had ever said I'd be good at poetry, and I really wanted to impress Nadine. I knew whatever came out was going to sound like shit, but I just started spewing words without thinking about it.

"Your eyes are like the stars, twinkling so bright. Your smile is like the sunrise, bringing light to night. Your laugh is like the soundtrack to Alora's great divine. But if one thing lights the world at all, it's your soul that really shines."

My cheeks flames when I realized what I just said. Did I seriously just improv poetry in front of Nadine? She must've thought I was such a nerd.

She didn't say anything at first, which made me really nervous. I lifted my gaze to hers, and that's when I noticed her eyes sparkling with tears.

My stomach twisted into knots. "What's wrong?"

She shook her head and pulled her hand away from mine to wipe her eyes. "Nothing. It was really good."

I was stunned. Was she just staying that?

Nadine looked like she was going to add something, but she hesitated.

"What is it?" I asked. I was dying to know her every thought.

She took a few moments to respond. "Why do you act like such a jerk?"

My heart fell. That wasn't exactly the kind of thing a guy hoped to hear.

"I don't know," I lied. The truth was, we both knew exactly why. But it was hard to be a jerk all the time, because that wasn't who I was. Apparently, I was somewhat of a poet-writing romantic. Who knew?

"You're not a jerk, though," she said softly. "Not for real."

My heart felt like it was turning to stone in my chest. I felt really guilty for the way I'd treated her. "Well, I act like one. Doesn't that make me one?"

Nadine swallowed. "It depends on the intentions."

Fuck, even Nadine could see straight through me. Was it this connection we had, or was I really that transparent?

The truth was, I was sick of pretending to be a jerk all the time when all I wanted to do was be near her. But could we really just stay friends?

We had to, because there was no other alternative. By the grace of Mother Miriam, I couldn't stay away from Nadine. It was like we were pushed together by some divine force that wouldn't freaking give up. I wasn't sure I really had a choice anymore. I was just making it harder on both of us.

"I'm sorry." My voice came out so small I wasn't sure Nadine heard me.

She perked up. "What?"

I shoved my pride deep down inside of myself and cleared my throat. "I'm sorry," I said more clearly this time. "I'm sorry I was such a jerk to you. It wasn't fair to you, and I said things I never should've said."

She took a deep breath. "So did I."

"What you said was fair, though," I pointed out.

Her lips tightened. "Why do you do that?"

"Do what?" I asked.

"You just… I don't know… *accept* the worst-case scenario," she said. "You put yourself down and focus on the negative."

"That's not true," I argued.

"Really?" She raised an eyebrow. "When was the last time you focused on the positive?"

I opened my mouth to answer, but the words halted on my tongue. It seemed the only time I was ever positive was around her.

That was the moment it hit me, why I craved Nadine's company so much. When I was around her, I felt a positive spark in my heart. She literally brought to life parts of me I long thought were dead and buried. I wasn't just bull-shitting with that poem earlier. She literally brought light into my life.

I didn't know how to tell her that, so instead, I answered her first question. "I guess I act like a jerk as a defense mechanism."

Nadine's shoulders dropped, and sympathy crossed her face. "I wish you didn't feel like you had to defend yourself."

The knots in my abdomen eased. Her words were a relief, an invitation to let life flow through me instead of bottling it up all the time. It was strange—like she was going against everyone else's unwritten rules. Another reason why I couldn't keep myself from falling for her.

"It's okay, Lucas," she whispered. "You don't have to defend yourself around me. You don't have to hide."

"Neither do you," I assured her softly.

She knotted her hands together in her lap. "So, you've noticed?"

"Noticed what?" I asked curiously.

Her voice cracked, and it broke my heart. "That I hide. That there's this piece of me that I push deep down inside until my walls crack and she comes flooding out."

"She?" I wasn't sure where she was going with this. Sure, sometimes Nadine acted out of character—like earlier with Ryan—but she spoke as if she was hiding a secret identity or something.

Nadine didn't look at me when she spoke. "She doesn't have a name. I just know she's not… me."

Oh, shit. I had no idea that Nadine was hurting this much. I didn't know what kind of secrets she was hiding. But that was the thing about this coven… it was full of secrets.

If there was one thing I learned as the Reaper's Apprentice, it was that everyone had secrets. I wanted to know Nadine's, but I feared if I pressed her, it'd only push her away.

"In what way?" I asked, trying my best to be gentle with her.

Nadine kept her gaze on her hands. "I've learned to control it… mostly. But sometimes, this dark side of me just comes out, and I can't stop it until she's satisfied."

All I wanted to do was rip the demons out of her and make them my own. I reached out and gently brought her chin up so she'd look at me. Our eyes searched each other's for several long moments before I finally spoke.

"Don't hide from me, Nad," I said. "I'll never judge you."

A smile touched the corners of her mouth, then suddenly, the confessions started spilling out. "It's hard to explain, but I've always felt like I had this darkness inside of me. When I was a kid, my teachers called me a *problem child*. If I got upset, even over the littlest thing, I'd freak out. Someone sat too close to me? I'd hit them. Someone took the jump rope I wanted at recess? I'd pick a fight. I can't tell you how many times I was sent to the principal's office. I got kicked off the bus for pulling a girl's hair out. My parents eventually started homeschooling me when I stopped doing my work."

She continued like she couldn't stop herself. "I went through a couple years of therapy, but it was really my lupus that changed me. I guess on some level, it was sort of a blessing. My diagnosis was a huge wake-up call. I had to learn to control myself to keep my symptoms from flaring. It was like the angrier I got, the more pain I felt."

She took a breath. "Eventually, I returned to public school for high school. I learned how to control my temper, but it still comes out sometimes. I just wish I could get rid of it, you know? It's not me. Like when I almost ran Ryan over with my car. Or how I acted with him today. I don't even know why I did it. It already feels surreal—like a dream."

I pressed my lips together, contemplating her story. That darkness she spoke of was far from the Nadine I knew.

"I'm sorry, Nad," I said. "No one should have to deal with that."

She shrugged, like it wasn't that big of a deal, but I knew she was underplaying it. Constantly watching her own behavior had to be taxing on her.

"It is what it is," she said. "Can I ask you something?"

"Anything," I replied.

She spoke slowly, like she was choosing her words with care. "What's the deal with you and Ryan? Do you two have a history or something?"

Oh, boy. Here we go.

I didn't really want to talk about it, but Nadine didn't want me to hide around her. Just the opportunity to lay it all out there on the table was freeing. I wanted her to know everything. I just hoped it didn't change her opinion of me.

I sighed. "Ryan and I were buddies in high school. We formed the Treacherous Tarantulas together."

Nadine's eyebrows shot up. "You were a Tarantula?"

I chuckled. "I wasn't just one of them. I was their *leader*."

Nadine's jaw dropped further. "Lucas Taylor, the lone wolf, in a gang. Who would've guessed?"

I was shocked by her reaction. She didn't look like she thought less of me. In fact, she eyed me up and down like the thought intrigued her, maybe even—dare I say it?—*turned her on*.

"I wasn't always a lone wolf," I said. "But the Tarantulas weren't always the low-life gang they are now. When we formed, it was about brotherhood. We stood to protect other people. When we saw something we didn't think was right, we'd stand up to it—you know, guys pushing other people around in the locker room, pressuring girls in the hallways, that sort of thing."

"That sounds incredible," Nadine praised. She looked at me with dreamy eyes, like she was picturing me walking down the halls in my leather jacket and whipping other kids into shape. "What happened to the group?"

"After graduation, Ryan got into the drug scene," I explained.

"Shocker," she said flatly.

"Right?" I chuckled. "Anyway, he got the other guys to agree to dealing. They were all enticed by the money—and the drugs—but I couldn't do it. I tried to stick it out, but then they pulled this sick prank on Grant and stole his insulin. That was the last straw. I left the group, and they've had it out for me ever since. They call it a betrayal, but I call it a mutiny."

Nadine frowned. "I'm sorry, Lucas. I had no idea."

I shrugged. "It's good, I guess. I've got Grant now, and he's a better friend that all five of the Tarantulas put together."

"He *is* cool," she agreed.

A silent beat passed. Neither of us knew what to say next.

Nadine hesitated, then broke the silence. "So, what were you like… before the Tarantulas ditched you? Were you happier?"

The question hit me hard in the gut. *Was* I happier? Yes and no.

"In a different way," I admitted. "But a lot has happened since then. There are other reasons that I'm so… I don't know… *me*."

"You can tell me," Nadine offered. "You didn't judge me, and I'm not going to judge you."

I knew Nadine was being honest, but I had a hard time talking about this at all. I pretty much tried not to think about it myself. But pushing it down made the memories stew, made them that much more painful. I knew it, and yet I couldn't face them.

Nadine reached out and touched my hand. My breath caught.

"It was my brother." The words spilled out. "I loved him so much, and when he left, it was like… like a part of me left with him."

"I get it," Nadine whispered, her eyes twinkling with tears. "I feel the same way about my parents."

A lump rose to my throat. I started talking to get it to budge, and I just couldn't stop after that. "My brother and I were really close growing up. My dad was a total asshole, always yelling and starting fights with my mom. She excuses his behavior because he never touches her, but he gets his work in. He's a Mentalist—has telekinesis. When he gets mad, glasses break, things start flying around the room, and… he takes it out on Mom."

Nadine's hand went to her mouth.

"The worst one was when Dad got in one of his fits. Mom *says* she tripped, but Eric and I both knew Dad used his magic to push her down the stairs. She broke her hand."

"Lucas, I'm so sorry you had to grow up with that," she said.

"Don't be," I told her. "It's not your fault. Anyway, Eric and I bonded over our fear of our father. We didn't spend a lot of time at home, since he didn't want us around anyway, so we spent all our time together."

My entire body tensed at the memories. "Things changed after his Evoking Ceremony. He became a Seer. He couldn't see ghosts, but he could hear their thoughts. He described it to me as this constant, annoying chatter he couldn't turn off. I mean, maybe I should be grateful. At least I only hear a couple thoughts a day. With Eric, it was constant. I guess he just couldn't take it anymore. The night I did my Evoking Ceremony…"

My breath halted. I didn't know if I could say it out loud. But maybe it would help.

"That night, Eric hung himself in the garage," I spat out.

Nope. Not better. Not better *at all*.

The confession was like knives through my heart. I didn't think I'd ever said it out loud. I knew that Eric was gone, but I didn't think I'd come to terms with the fact that he killed himself. It wasn't like it was an accident. He left me by choice.

That single thought made me want to hurl. It was selfish to think that way. Eric had been struggling, but I couldn't help him. Yet here I was blaming *him*. I wasn't being fair.

I didn't even know I felt that way until now. I pressed my face into my hands to hide myself from Nadine. I was supposed to be strong, not some emotional wreck for her to piece back together. This was why I didn't open up—because when I did, it all came flooding out all at once.

"Lucas…" Nadine's voice was like a song—a soft, comforting song that kept me grounded to reality.

She reached out and took my wrists, then pulled them down from my face. I was embarrassed for her to see tears dotting my eyes. But she stared straight at me like she saw past them —like she saw *me*.

"You don't have to hide from me, remember?" she asked.

I choked back a sob. "You don't know the worst part, Nad."

"I want to," she whispered. "I want to hear it."

I turned my head away from her. She waited. The silence was almost more agonizing than the confessions.

"You know how I hear the last thought of the dead?" I asked her.

She nodded.

I forced down the lump in my throat. "Well, the night my powers awakened, Eric's last thoughts were the first I heard."

Tears spilled over Nadine's lids, which only caused mine to flow. I dashed them away.

Sure, open up to Nadine. See what she thinks of you now.

I bet she thought I was a freaking *joy* to be around. If I wanted to chase her away, I should've started crying sooner. Who wanted to be around the guy who was so weak he couldn't even hold his tears in?

Nadine reached for my hand again. She pulled it away from my face so I couldn't wipe the tears.

"Don't do that," she said.

"Do what?" My voice cracked. "Cry?"

She shook her head. "No. Don't push it back in."

"I have to," I argued. "Otherwise, I'm weak."

She ran her thumbs across my face and wiped the tears for me. They only continued to fall harder.

"Crying doesn't make you weak," she said. "It's an opportunity to grow."

I laughed nervously. "And you call *me* the poet."

"Shh..." Nadine whispered. "Let's not talk."

And then the strangest thing happened. Nadine crawled into my lap. I didn't know where it came from, but here she was snuggling close to me, not because she wanted something from me —but because she wanted to comfort me. I wondered for so long what that might feel like—for someone to love me unconditionally and expect nothing in return. It was the most amazing feeling in the world, but it felt wrong, too. It felt like I was stealing from her. Stealing what, I didn't know. This moment, perhaps. She could be anywhere doing anything right now, and she chose to be in my arms.

I wrapped her close to me, holding her to my chest. And yet somehow, it felt like *she* was holding me.

Nadine's rosy scent surrounded me, and her warm body sent the chill away. Though my eyes were closed and my nose pressed into her hair, I could swear I could *see* the light radiating off of her. Peace washed over me, and for the first time in my life, the tears stopped on their own. I didn't have to force them.

I drew away from her and whispered, "Why are you doing this, Nad?"

She looked into my eyes, which made my heart melt. I never knew how freeing it would be to hold her in my arms like this.

"Doing what?" she asked.

"Why are you here with me?" I questioned. "Why do you like me?"

Nadine shrugged, but it was obvious she was stalling. There was an answer behind her eyes. I just couldn't read it.

"I like being with you, Lucas," she finally said.

"But why?" I pressed.

She sniffled. "When I'm with you, I forget that my parents aren't alive."

It was such a simple answer, but I felt it deep within my soul. Maybe Nadine and I were more alike than I thought. Maybe we weren't total opposites—light and dark.

Maybe I brought a spark of light to her darkness, too.

No, that was ridiculous. I had no light to share.

"But I'm broken," I told her.

"Not broken," she said softly. "Just growing."

No one had ever put it that way before. If I wasn't broken, maybe I didn't need to be fixed. If I was growing, then maybe the wounds would heal. Maybe it wasn't about putting the shattered bits back together and hoping the glue would stick. Maybe it was about growing new branches.

I pressed my face back into her hair. I was quickly realizing it was the one place in the world where I felt my problems couldn't touch me. "You have no idea what it means to hear you say that."

Nadine wrapped her arms tight around me. "There's more, you know."

"More what?" I mumbled into her hair.

"More reasons why I like you," she said.

"There are?" I asked curiously.

Nadine reached up a hand and started running it through my hair. "I like to think I see the real Lucas beneath the layers."

I didn't even know what that meant. "I *am* the layers."

"No," she said. "You're not your past. You're not your darkness. That's what my therapist always told me. You, Lucas… you're kind and protective and fun. You have a heart so big it should have its own satellite."

I chuckled lightly. Part of me actually believed what she was saying.

"You are selfless," she continued. "You have this desire to take on everyone else's pain just so they won't suffer. If you could, you'd take on the sins of the world."

I stared down at her. I searched for the lie, but it wasn't there. She really believed everything she was saying.

"You… you *see* all that in me?"

She nodded. "I just wish you did, too."

I told myself I'd resist, but I couldn't anymore. Everything Nadine had said was what I needed to hear and more. She was beyond anything I could ever imagine, and I'd be damned if I hadn't fallen head over heels in love with her.

I brought my lips to hers. She melted into my kiss like ice on a warm summer's day. The thought to pull away, to resist, never crossed my mind. All I wanted was this moment. If I was to steal anything from her, it was this kiss, right now.

Kissing Nadine was like standing on top of a cliff. My toes lined up with the edge, and my arms opened wide. She was that moment as I raised my heels from the ground and tilted forward—the split second you thought you had before you could stop the freefall. Her kiss was that wild adrenaline rush, suspended in time. I was safe here—and I was free.

Nadine parted her lips, and my tongue slid into her mouth. My heart beat frantically, and my jeans tightened. She was so warm in my arms that I never wanted to let her go.

I thought I'd have to, but the kiss didn't end. Nadine wrapped her arms around my neck and continued making out with me. Her breasts pressed tight against my chest, and that was the moment I lost it. I went free falling down that cliff, and I couldn't catch my balance.

The room spun around me, and I couldn't hold Nadine up any longer. I gently lowered her to the mat beneath us. She moaned as my kisses continued across her lips. Her noises were like a symphony to my ears. I loved every sound she made.

Nadine's hands continued to roam through my hair, and it felt amazing. I couldn't stop my hands from running up and down her sides. I wasn't on top of her—more or less propped up at her side—but I wanted to be. I wanted to be with her in every sense of the word. I wanted to fight for her tooth and nail.

But I couldn't. And I knew that.

In this moment, though, it didn't seem to matter. I didn't push her away like all the other times. Because if this moment was all I ever had with Nadine, I was going to bask in the warmth of every second I could get from it. I wasn't going to ruin it this time.

Eventually, Nadine pulled away. I pushed myself onto my elbow and hovered above her. The light from the fire flickered off her face, and I'd be damned if it wasn't the most beautiful thing I'd seen in all my life.

"Is something wrong?" I asked.

"No," she said softly. "Would you just… hold me?"

She didn't have to ask twice. Nadine rolled onto her side. I lay next to her, my front pressed against her back. I draped one arm over her. She fit so perfectly into my arms, like it was where she was meant to be.

Nadine went quiet for a long time. After a while, I noticed she was shivering.

"Are you cold?" I asked. I didn't know how. I was radiating so much heat I was practically sweating. Being near her made me hot all over.

"No," she said. "I just… want to ask you something. I don't know how."

"You can ask me anything," I told her.

She shifted and rolled over to face me. She rested her face on her hand, and her hair spilled across the floor. We just lay there staring at each other. It was a beautiful moment I wished would never end.

"I've wanted to ask you for a while, but I know you don't like to talk about your gift," she said.

"Ask me anything," I offered. I wasn't so scared to share with her anymore.

She took a deep breath. "I know it's a long shot, but… did you hear my parents when they died?"

My body tensed. This wasn't the first time someone had asked what their loved ones' last thoughts were. I didn't like to answer, because it usually wasn't what they wanted to hear. That, and last thoughts were Reaper's Apprentice privileges only. It violated the integrity of the job if I went around telling everyone what I heard.

But this was Nadine. I didn't want to lie to her.

I answered carefully. "Your father was never part of the coven, so I didn't hear him."

"And my mother?" she asked.

I nodded slowly. "I heard her."

Her eyes filled with hope. "Can you tell me what she said?"

This was where things got hard. Her mom's last thought was complicated—a mix of good and bad all wrapped into one.

The coven's in danger. Stay safe, Nadine. I love you.

This thought had been weighing on me for months. I didn't know what it meant. I couldn't investigate, either, because I didn't know where to start. For all I knew, her mom was as confused as Old Man Keller.

I couldn't tell Nadine. I didn't want her to know her mom died worrying about her. If I told her the truth, she'd want to fix whatever danger her mother spoke of. She'd get herself hurt looking for answers.

I wanted to tell her, but I couldn't until I knew what it meant.

"She said she loved you," I told her honestly. It was only half of it, but it was true none-theless.

Nadine's eyes glistened. "Is that true, or is that just what you tell everybody?"

"It is what I tell everybody," I admitted. "But in this case, it's true."

She sniffled. "Thank you, Lucas. I love her, too."

I couldn't bear to see her upset. I leaned forward and kissed her again. She reached up and placed her hand on the side of my face, and that warmth ignited in my heart all over again.

The kiss didn't last long, though. A few moments later, she drew away.

Her eyes searched mine. "Why are you kissing me, Lucas?"

I was struck by the question. "Don't you want me to?"

"I do, but… you're kind of sending me mixed signals," she said. "Do you want this or not?"

I hesitated. Of course I did. I wanted every moment with Nadine and more. But I didn't want her to get hurt.

"I do," I told her honestly. "I wish there was a way we could be together, but…"

"But if we were, this is as far as we could go," she finished for me. "We can't have what every other couple has."

Her voice was so sad, so melancholy. When we first met, I thought she was just chasing me for the thrill of it. I thought she'd get over me once I turned her down. But it wasn't like that between us. Nadine and I were drawn like magnets. And now that we'd come together, nothing could come between us, not even this stupid curse.

"Are you okay with that?" I asked.

I held my breath, awaiting the answer. Part of me feared both options.

"I don't know," she finally said. "I think I need time to figure that out."

"Then we won't make any decisions right now," I promised.

"Okay," she agreed. "At least now we can be friends."

I smiled—a real, genuine smile. I didn't know how she did that to me. "Agreed. We're done arguing. I'm done pushing you away."

She closed her eyes and sighed blissfully. "That sounds good."

I reached out and took Nadine's hand. She lay there, looking perfectly content, while I ran my thumb across the back of her hand.

It was in that moment that I realized it didn't matter which decision Nadine made. There would never be anyone else. Nadine would always be it for me.

I just hoped I could handle her decision.

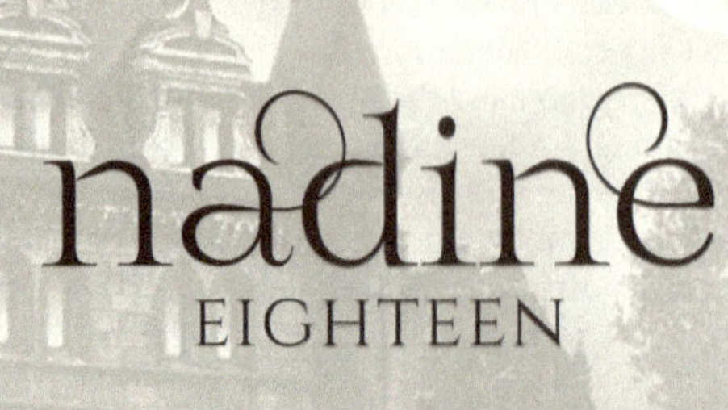

I needed Lucas in my life. It didn't matter that we couldn't be together in the way that I wanted. I needed him near me the way I needed the very air I breathed. Without him, I was caged. But when he was around, I was a free bird soaring the skies. I could almost believe the two of us were capable of anything together.

Something changed when Lucas brought me to that abandoned house. I didn't know if it was a change in him, or me, or both of us. It was like we could finally breathe again.

The house was gorgeous, and there was a beautiful energy surrounding it that made it feel like home. It was crazy, considering the state of the place, but I just felt like I didn't have to hide anything there.

I'd never felt so close to Lucas. When he stood next to me, I couldn't help but shiver. When he kissed me, the world seemed to tilt on its axis. It was magic.

I walked through the school hallways the following week on this amazing, magical high. I felt energized, and my joints moved with ease. It was like Lucas's touch had a way of healing me.

He was still waiting for an answer from me. Truth be told, I didn't want to think about that right now. We could figure out where we wanted to go with this later. Right now, I just wanted his company.

Lucas met up with me in the hall after class on Wednesday. He carried my books, and I took his hand. It was instinctive now. It was like we couldn't be together without attaching ourselves. It turned a few heads, but I didn't care. Screw the haters.

Let it be known that Lucas Taylor and Nadine Evers were a thing.

A non-official thing, but a thing nonetheless.

"How was class?" Lucas asked.

I shrugged. "Chloe drew the Seven of Swords. I think that means she's planning to act on her threat soon."

Lucas's face paled. "That's not good."

"It's okay," I said honestly. "Now I have some warning. I can't say I'm surprised, though. I have a meeting with Verla today. I expect Chloe to do something."

"Yeah, she's kind of predictable," Lucas said. "But I'm not going to let her hurt you."

My heart fluttered. "Oh? How are you going to do that?"

He smiled. "By not letting you out of my sight."

"I don't think Verla's going to let you in on my lesson," I pointed out.

He shrugged. "Then I'll stand outside the door."

"For how long?" I asked, though I was really enjoying his offer.

He slowed his step and turned to me. He pushed a strand of hair behind my ear, which made butterflies dance in my stomach. "However long it takes. Consider me your personal guard for the day."

My heart totally melted. "Thank you."

"No need to thank me," he replied gently.

Lucas and I returned to my room to put my books away. Talia, Amy, and Mandy were there. Amy and Mandy poked at their phones, while Talia flung around a string for Gus, Isa, and Stormy to chase.

"Hey," I greeted as I entered the room. "What are you guys up to?"

Mandy looked up from where she lay on the couch. "Looking at dress ideas for the Midnight Formal. I'm thinking full-on gothic."

"I was thinking of going with something white and sparkly," Amy said.

Mandy's eyes lit up. "Ooh, it could be a theme. You could be like, the good witch, and I'll be the bad witch."

Amy laughed. "I love it."

"Consider me the Good Witch of the South," Talia said. "I've got my pink dress picked out already. Do you have any ideas yet, Nadine?"

I shook my head. Lucas looked oddly uncomfortable with all the dress talk.

"I'll figure something out," I said. "In the meantime, I have a meeting with Verla today."

Talia's spine straightened. Isa grabbed ahold of the string with her paw and ripped it out of Talia's hands. She barely noticed. "Uh oh. Does that mean another sabotage?"

I crossed my arms and smirked. "I was thinking so. Except this time, maybe we could be the ones doing the sabotage."

Mandy beamed as she stood and gave me a salute. "We're on it, girl."

Talia and Amy jumped to their feet. "You don't have to worry about Chloe," Talia promised. "Go have fun at your lesson."

"Wait," I said. "You mean I don't get to watch?"

Talia frowned. "That would beat the point of distracting her for your lesson."

I made a face. "True. Any ideas?"

Amy stepped forward and patted me on the shoulder. "You let us take care of that."

"You guys are the best." I reached out to hug each of them in turn, then turned back to Lucas.

"Are you ready?" he asked.

I took a deep breath. "Yep. Let's get this over with."

Lucas took my hand and walked me to Headmistress Verla's office. Isa followed at my feet. She seemed to sense my discomfort. The whole time, I kept watch for Chloe, but I didn't see her anywhere. Maybe she'd finally given up.

I knocked on Verla's office.

"Come in," she called.

Lucas stood guard outside while I stepped inside.

Verla shot me a kind smile, but she wasn't the only one there. Professor Daymond, the jerk who'd called me a half-blood, sat in one of the chairs next to her desk. He barely looked my way.

"I hope I'm not interrupting," I said as Isa and I approached the desk. "I'm here for my lesson."

Verla gestured to the chair next to Professor Daymond. "You're not interrupting anything at all. In fact, we were waiting for you."

I couldn't keep the disgust from my voice. "What's *he* doing here?"

"I'm here to help," he replied in a less than friendly tone. Something told me he wasn't very interested in helping me.

I sat but remained at the edge of my seat. "How?"

Isa looked to Odin, who was perched on a cat tower beside Verla's desk. She gave a low growl, then jumped into my lap. I stroked her to calm her down, but she kept throwing glances at Odin.

"I'd like to start where we left off last time," Verla said. "I've invited Professor Daymond here to help run us through some scenarios. Hopefully we won't be interrupted."

"I think we'll be okay," I told her. I trusted my friends to deal with Chloe.

Verla straightened in her chair. "Excellent. As you know, an Evoking Ceremony tests your emotional state. Everyone is tested differently, based on their strengths and weaknesses. I thought we could talk about that before we try out some scenarios."

I looked to Professor Daymond, who held his nose high. I wasn't really interested in talking about my strengths and weaknesses in front of him.

I scratched Isa behind the ears to keep my hands busy. "Isn't that, um... kind of private?"

"Well, yes, but—" Verla started, but Professor Daymond spoke at the same time.

"You want to pass your Evoking Ceremony, don't you?" he sneered.

What a prick.

"Yes," I said.

"Then let's get on with it," Professor Daymond said.

Verla looked a little shocked by his tone, but she brushed it off. She picked up a tablet on her desk and began scrolling through it. "Nadine, I want you to rate the following statements from one to five, one being strongly disagree, and five being strongly agree."

"Okay." That didn't seem too hard.

Verla cleared her throat and began reading off the list of questions. *"When I see someone being bullied, I feel the need to step in."*

"Five," I answered automatically.

Verla pressed her tablet, then moved on to the next question.

"I find it easy to forgive other people."

I thought about that for a moment. "Um... four."

"I often feel like other people don't like me."

"One," I said. I was a joy to be around.

"I get envious of other people easily."

I paused for a moment. Usually, I'd answer one to this question—strongly disagree. But I couldn't help but recall how I felt when I saw Lena kissing Lucas.

"Three," I decided on.

Verla went on like this for at least another fifteen minutes. Most of the questions I felt pretty comfortable with. Professor Daymond's lips pressed into a thinner and thinner line as the minutes ticked by. It was almost like he was unhappy I wasn't a total train wreck.

It wasn't until Verla neared the end that I started to feel the questions weighing on me. *"I find it easy to bounce back from hardship,"* she said.

My stomach twisted into knots. I *wanted* it to be true, but I'd be lying if I said it was.

"Two," I told her.

Professor Daymond seemed pleased by that, though I didn't know why. Wasn't he supposed to *support* his students?

"*My moods are greatly affected by my situation,*" Verla continued.

"Five," I answered. I mean, who *wasn't* affected by their situation?

"*I feel lonely when my loved ones aren't around.*"

My gut sank at the mention of *loved ones*. All I could think about was my parents, and Verla's statement felt shockingly true in that moment. I sank deeper into my seat.

"Five," I said in a small voice.

Verla eyed me, like she sensed my discomfort. "Just one more, Nadine. *Memories of the people I've lost upset me.*"

Okay, now it felt like she was doing it on purpose.

"Of course memories upset me," I said, suddenly feeling very defensive. "I mean, who wouldn't be upset by losing someone?"

Verla kept her eyes on the tablet. Her expression didn't give anything away. "So, where would you rate that?"

I hesitated, though I knew the answer. Finally, I spoke so soft I wasn't sure she heard me. "Five."

Verla took a deep breath and set the tablet aside. "I think it's clear what we need to work on."

"What's that?" I asked, a little scared to hear the answer.

Verla gave me a sympathetic look. "Your grief."

My breath halted. I knew I had work to do, but the way she said it... it was like I shouldn't be allowed to feel this way. But I should! I lost my parents, for Alora's sake.

Unless... unless Mother Miriam didn't want people like me in the coven.

"Am I not allowed to grieve?" I asked in a small voice.

"Of course you are," Verla said kindly. "But you can't shove it aside. You must work through it."

I didn't want to. I wasn't ready.

"And I have to do that before my ceremony?" I asked.

Verla nodded. "Mother Miriam will test your weaknesses."

My bottom lip quivered. It felt as if the air was being sucked from the room. "So, if I can't get over it by then, that's it? I'm banished?"

I couldn't be! This was the only place where I had family and friends. I wasn't leaving the coven.

"Relax, Nadine," Verla said softly. "I'm not asking you to get over it. All I'm asking for is progress."

"But I'm not ready." My voice cracked.

Beside me, Professor Daymond smirked, like he was getting great joy out of this. What the fuck was his problem?

"You must try," Verla said. "You must trust that Mother Miriam has a plan. If you don't show her that you're willing to change, your magic won't come."

Headmistress Verla was really starting to scare me. How could I be asked to get over my parent's death so quickly? Surely, Mother Miriam would understand.

Yet part of me feared she wouldn't.

I swallowed. "I'll do anything to pass my ceremony."

"Then let's try our first scenario." Headmistress Verla gestured to Professor Daymond. "Professor Daymond is a unique type of Mentalist. He can imprint pictures into your mind. It's a lot like the visions you'll see during your Evoking Ceremony."

I turned to him, clutching the armrests of the chair so hard my knuckles turned white. I had to believe he was here to help me, because there was no alternative. Either he helped me get past this block, or I failed Mother Miriam's test.

That wasn't an option. I'd do anything to stay here with Grammy, Lucas, Grant and Talia.

"Okay," I said, my voice strong. "How does this work?"

Professor Daymond reached out a hand. "My powers work through touch."

I hesitated. "Is it just visions, then? Or can you see other things in my mind?"

I wasn't about to let this stranger poke around in my head.

"I can project visions using memories of your past," Professor Daymond explained. "But I can't see anything you don't want me to see."

"It's perfectly safe, Nadine," Headmistress Verla assured me.

I trusted her, and I really wanted to pass my ceremony, so I placed my hand in his.

Immediately, the room around me disappeared. Instead, I stood at the edge of the road. It was nighttime, with nothing but the moon and stars above to light the landscape. Forest surrounded me at several angles, save for a clearing that gave way to a cliff. Below that spanned a large lake. The road curved along the outer edge of the lake, and a guardrail bordered the edge of the cliff.

I glanced around. There was no motion, no sound.

"I don't get it," I called out to the darkness. I didn't know if I said the words aloud, but I sensed that Professor Daymond could hear me.

I waited another beat, and then I heard the sound of a vehicle approaching at high speed. The headlights flickered past trees in the forest, and the vehicle twisted and turned with the road. I expected the driver to slow, but they didn't. They just kept picking up speed. I knew that if they didn't hit the brakes soon, they wouldn't make it past the turn I stood at.

I have to stop this, I thought.

That was the answer to the test, right? Professor Daymond wanted to see if I'd save them.

Except there wasn't anything I could do. There wasn't enough time. I began running up the road. My heart slammed against my rib cage. I began to wave my hands in the air.

"Slow down!" I cried, even though the driver couldn't hear me. "There's a turn up ahead. You won't make it!"

The car sped by me so fast that it was there and gone in the blink of an eye.

"No!" I cried hopelessly, running out into the middle of the road as I watched the car speed away.

Horror struck when I spotted the license plate. It was so familiar, and it left this gaping hole in my heart. Professor Daymond had dug into memories he shouldn't have!

"Mom! Dad!" I screamed.

I could hardly hear the sound of my own voice over the screech of the tires. Red brake lights lit up the night—a color that I sensed would haunt me for many nights to come.

It was already too late. The car lost control and slammed into the guard rail. My stomach ached so badly, it was like the car had hit *me*.

The guard rail crumpled like a piece of paper, and the car launched over top of it.

"STOP!" I screeched. I threw my hands over my ears, but the sound of my parents' screams filled the vision. I heard the car hit the water, and then… silence.

My ears rang, and my vision blurred. I didn't want to witness the aftermath, but my feet moved beneath me involuntarily. I stumbled toward the edge of the cliff. Somehow, I made it to the guard rail, and my hands splayed across the cool metal to steady myself. I leaned over to look, but I couldn't bring myself to do it. Bile rose to my throat as I squeezed my eyes tightly shut.

"Stop it!" I cried. "I want out. Get me out of here!"

"Nadine? Nadine!" Verla's voice sounded just feet away from me.

I felt the weight of Isa in my lap again, and I opened my eyes to see I was back in Verla's office. Sobs bubbled out of my throat, and my head pounded.

Verla shot Professor Daymond a hard look, but he wore an expression of indifference.

"That was horrible," I spat.

"What did you do, Professor Daymond?" Verla demanded.

"My job," he told her simply, before turning to me. "Believe me, Miss Evers. If you can't handle a simple vision such as this one, you won't pass your Evoking Ceremony."

My hands trembled. "I doubt Mother Miriam would be so heartless. That's not something *anyone* should ever witness."

Professor Daymond smirked. "This just goes to show you're not ready, Miss Evers."

I shot out of my chair so fast that Isa fell to the ground. "Who are *you* to judge that?" I snapped. "You're cruel!"

"Nadine, calm down," Headmistress Verla said softly. "Let's discuss what happened."

I opened my mouth, but nothing except a sob came out. I covered my mouth with my hand. I thought closing my eyes would help get rid of the image I'd just seen, but it only made it worse. The vision of the car falling off the road assaulted me. Then came flashes of other memories—real memories. I saw the caskets, then the gravestones, then the empty house.

Even if I wanted to talk about it, I couldn't. My chest wound so tightly that I couldn't get a word out.

"Nadine?" Headmistress Verla pressed.

All I could do was shake my head. This was so embarrassing. I just wanted to hide in a hole. It felt like I was being buried in one already.

"I'm sorry," I managed to get out. "I-I can't."

I whirled around and ran for the door. Isa followed at my feet as I flung the door open and stormed out of the room.

"Nadine!" Headmistress Verla called, but I ignored her.

Lucas was leaning against the wall outside her office. I'd almost forgotten he was waiting for me.

He straightened when he saw me and reached out for my arms. "Nad, what's wrong?"

I heard the sound of Headmistress Verla's heels against the carpet, and I knew she was on her way across the room to follow me.

I grabbed Lucas's hand. "Let's go."

Lucas didn't inquire any further. He followed me as we rushed away from Verla's office. It wasn't until we turned two other halls and I was certain we'd lost her that I finally slowed. Isa purred and rubbed herself against my leg.

Lucas turned to me and took my face in his hands. "Nad, what happened?"

I wiped my nose and sniffled. I tried to keep my voice steady, but it cracked. "Professor Daymond showed me a vision. It was supposed to be like one of Mother Miriam's tests, but it was awful."

Lucas frowned. "I'm so sorry, Nad."

I took a breath, but I could hardly breathe. "Lucas, he made me watch my parents die."

His eyes went wide, then he wrapped me into a tight hug. His spicy scent surrounded me, and his chest felt warm against my cheek. After a few moments, I felt like I could breathe again.

"I wish I could make it better, Nad," Lucas whispered.

"You *are* making it better," I replied. "Just being here with me is enough."

My heart rate slowed, and I finally drew away to look up at him. "I'm sorry I freaked out. I didn't mean to."

"Don't apologize," Lucas said. "You're allowed to feel upset over this."

I sniffled and wiped my nose again. "Yeah, but if I can't handle this, how am I going to handle the ceremony?"

Lucas squeezed my hands. "One step at a time, Nadine."

The sound of heavy sobs came from down the hall. Lucas and I looked up to see Amy and Mandy walking our way. Mandy was hunched over and sobbing uncontrollably, while Amy supported her.

"How did this happen?" Mandy wailed.

"I don't know." Amy's voice cracked. "We're going to get answers. We just need—"

Amy lifted her gaze, and she stopped dead in her tracks when she spotted Lucas and me. Her eyes widened, and her jaw dropped. She looked like she'd seen a ghost.

I glanced around the hall briefly, wondering if she really *had* seen a ghost. The hall was empty.

"Hey, guys," I said. "What's wrong—?"

I barely got the question out before Mandy squealed and raced over to me.

"Nadine!" She flung her arms around my neck and drew me close.

Amy came up beside her and pulled me into a group hug. "Goddess, Nadine! You're okay!"

I drew away from them. Lucas looked just as confused as I was.

"I'm fine," I assured them. "What's going on?"

Amy and Mandy exchanged a grave look.

My face fell. "What did Chloe do this time?"

Mandy wiped her tears. "We're not sure if it was her, but considering you're standing right here…"

Lucas crossed his arms impatiently. "Will you guys tell us what's going on?"

Amy hesitated. "It's probably better if we show you. Just… don't freak out."

Yeah, because that was *totally* the way to stop me from freaking out.

"We can't make any promises," I told them.

Amy and Mandy led us toward the foyer. When we got there, we saw that the front doors were open. Cold air rushed into the room, and the flames in the fireplace flickered. A huge crowd had gathered outside, and we couldn't see anything beyond them.

I craned my neck. "What's going on?"

Mandy took my arm. "Come on. They'll make way for us."

Mandy led me out the front doors and through the crowd. People murmured quietly, but they went dead silent when their eyes turned toward me. The sound of a woman's wail traveled across the yard. Above us, the clouds were dark, and the air was so cold it made me shiver.

"Mandy, what's going—?"

I stopped dead in my tracks. The crowd parted enough that I finally caught a glimpse of what was happening. Two figures knelt at the base of a large oak tree. They were both sobbing. That's when I realized the wailing was coming from Talia.

For a split second, I didn't realize why she was crying, or why Grant was next to her, trying to comfort her. Then my gaze lifted, and I saw what everyone was staring at.

I saw the boots first—black boots, just like mine. Then came the ripped skinny jeans, then the leather jacket, and then finally… my own face.

I didn't know how it was happening, but my body hung from a noose in the tree. I was standing right here, and yet my lifeless body was spinning in the tree. Isa hissed and ducked behind me.

I got so suddenly nauseous that I could hardly stand. I braced myself against Lucas, but he seemed equally weak on his feet. He turned his gaze away from the hanging body and kept his eyes on me. I was almost certain I'd just witnessed my own death, but it didn't make any sense.

"It isn't real, Nad," he said, but it sounded more like he was trying to convince himself.

"Is this another test?" I asked. "Did I ever leave the vision?"

"*This* is real," he assured me, gesturing between the two of us. "We're standing here for sure. But whatever *that* is…" He pointed to the hanging corpse, but wouldn't look at it. "That's not you."

"Then how is this happening?" I asked, my heart racing. I wasn't sure which was worse—watching my parents die, or seeing myself hanging from a noose. Both were equally horrifying.

"I don't know," Lucas whispered.

I swallowed hard and looked back to Talia and Grant. Their backs were to us, so they hadn't spotted us. It broke my heart to hear Talia cry like that.

"Give me a minute." I stepped away from Lucas and walked over to Talia. I didn't know how to break the news to her that I was still alive. I feared I'd only scare her, but she had to know this wasn't real.

I stopped behind her and cleared my throat. Grant turned first, but he more or less looked *through* me. He turned back to Talia to comfort her, before doing a quick double take.

"*Nadine!?*" he cried.

Talia turned, and her sobs instantly ceased. She went totally still, like she couldn't believe what she was seeing. After a moment to let it sink in, her gaze darted between me—the real Nadine—and the other me—the fake, dead Nadine.

Her eyes grew wide, and she scrambled to her feet. "Nadine! What's going on?"

"I could ask you the same thing," I told her.

She threw her arms around my neck and hugged me so tight it practically choked me.

Grant got to his feet beside her and wiped the tears from his face. "We thought—"

"I know," I said, cutting him off. I didn't want to hear him finish that sentence. "But I'm here."

Talia's eyes darkened, and she looked out toward the crowd, who still hadn't taken their eyes off us. There must've been a hundred people gathered around, like my life was some sort of freak show.

"Who did this?" Talia demanded. I'd never heard her talk in such a loud, stern voice.

Nobody responded. They all looked as shell-shocked as we did. Isa growled at the onlookers.

Mandy's nostrils flared. "You fuckers better start talking!"

She stomped up to the nearest guy, whose face was hidden in his jacket. She grabbed the back of his hood and yanked it down, then got up in his face. "Are you enjoying this, Gregory?"

He was a lanky guy with glasses and messy hair. His hands instantly shot up in surrender, and he cowered away from her. "I don't know anything, I swear."

Lucas crossed his arms and loomed over Gregory. "What do you know about this kind of magic?"

"Nothing!" he repeated. "I said I don't know anything."

A muscle popped in Lucas's jaw. "Come on, Gregory. You know everything."

Gregory's eyes twinkled for a second, like he appreciated the compliment, but it was gone a moment later. He shot a dark look at Mandy, who still had a tight hold on his hood. "Let me go and I'll talk."

Mandy narrowed her eyes at him, then finally dropped him. As Gregory straightened out his jacket, Mandy looked out to the rest of the crowd.

"Well?" she growled. "What are you all still doing here? Show's over!"

The crowd started to disperse. We turned back toward Gregory, awaiting his explanation.

"M-my guess is it's an illusion," Gregory stammered. "It's the only explanation."

"Witches can't cast illusions," Lucas stated bluntly.

"No, but the Arcanea can," Gregory reminded him. "The school's got enchanted objects from all over the world. I wouldn't be surprised if they had a fae object from Malovia that could do this sort of thing."

"But why would anyone want to make it look like Nadine…?" Grant started to ask, but he trailed off. The six of us looked at each other, and it was as if we all already knew the answer.

Talia's hands curled into fists, and her nostrils flared. "*Chloe,*" she snarled, like the name was poison.

"I thought you guys were keeping an eye on her," I said.

"We *were,*" Talia replied. "Then this happened, and…"

Her eyes locked on something toward the front doors, and her features darkened. I turned to see the Lucky Three standing in the open doorway. Chloe's hands were on her hips, and she stared toward the oak tree with unadulterated pride on her face. I bet she fucking *loved* watching my friends and I squirm like this.

Chloe's proud stance lasted only a moment, just long enough for us to spot her and pin her as the evil mastermind behind the illusion. Once her eyes connected with mine, she turned back into the school, her two side bitches following behind her.

Amy gasped from behind me, and I turned to see the illusion was gone. A stuffed dummy hung from the tree, but my face was no longer on it. It wore clothes like mine, but that was it. There was no hair or face—just stuffed canvas.

"She's not going to get away with this!" Talia yelled. She started across the lawn faster than any of the rest of us could react.

We hurried behind her, but Talia sprinted so quickly she was inside the school before I made it halfway back. When the rest of us reached the doors, Talia was running up the grand staircase behind Chloe. She flung herself forward and grabbed Chloe around the neck, then yanked her back.

My hands flew over my mouth as the two went tumbling down the stairs. Gasps traveled around the crowd that continued to linger. The two girls landed at the bottom of the stairs, but Talia barely seemed fazed. She scrambled to her knees and pulled her arm back, like she was about to pummel Chloe's face.

But her fist never made it. She just froze.

Her face contorted in anger, like freezing up wasn't of her own free will.

"You think you can threaten my best friend like that!?" Talia shrieked. "You think you can go around doing whatever you—*who the fuck is doing this to me*!?"

Several things happened at once. Grant, Lucas, and I rushed over to Talia the same time Ryan stepped forward with a proud smirk on his face. He held his hands up toward Talia, and I knew he was the one controlling her. Poor Talia was so petite that she wasn't strong enough to push past his telekinetic hold. Before I reached her, Ryan twitched his wrist, and Talia's fist shifted course, slamming straight into her nose.

At that, the room broke into utter chaos. Chloe scrambled backward, laughing like a maniac. I grabbed Talia and dragged her behind the stairs, and Isa followed. Grant threw his arms out around us and acted like a human shield. I couldn't really see what else was going on, though I saw purple sparks erupt from Lucas's hands.

Screams filled the foyer, and footsteps pounded above us on the stairs as students scattered. I heard the sound of glass breaking and people screaming. The sound of cats screeching and hissing came from all angles. Isa crouched in front of me, like she was standing guard. Her tail stood on end, and a low growl came from her throat.

A figure ran from the fight and ducked beneath the stairs with us. I didn't realize who it was at first until he spoke.

"Talia, babe. You okay?" Cody pushed past Grant and cradled Talia in his arms.

She curled into him. "I'm fine. But I need to get back out there and kick Chloe's pretty little—"

"No," Cody said sternly. "I'm not letting you go back out there."

Grant shot Cody a look of disdain. My heart hammered. I wanted to get back out there, too. I couldn't let Lucas fight by himself. I started to get up, but Grant grabbed my hand.

"Nadine, stop. You don't have magic."

"I have to do *something!*" I didn't care what it was. All I wanted was to get back at Chloe.

I ripped my arm out of Grant's grip and rushed out from beneath the stairs before he could catch me. My eyes locked on Chloe, who'd ducked into the corner. I barely noticed magic flying around me as I stomped over to her. She didn't notice me at first, as she was preoccupied by the fight, but I sure as hell got her attention when I grabbed her by the shirt and shoved her up against the wall. Isa came streaking out from under the stairs after me. She stood at my feet and hissed at Chloe.

"What the hell is your problem?" I snapped. "Come after *me*. Don't hurt my *friends*."

Chloe shoved me, and I stumbled back a few steps. "Get off me, bitch!"

"*I'm* the bitch!?" I snapped. "I didn't start this!"

"You did!" she yelled. "The second you came to Octavia Falls."

"I didn't do anything to you," I growled.

"You didn't have to," she spat. "It started long before either of us were born."

Was she fucking serious?

"I know our grandpas had it in for each other, but that's no reason for you to act so evil," I snarled. "There's enough room in Octavia Falls for both of us."

"That's just it, Nadine!" she screamed. "There *isn't* enough room for the both of us. That's why you need to leave!"

She shoved me again, and I shoved her back harder.

"I'm not going anywhere," I promised.

"You really want to risk it?" she asked harshly. "How badly do you want to die for this?"

My eyebrows shot up. "Die for it? What, you're going to *kill* me if I don't leave?"

She glared at me. I'd never seen so much hatred in someone's eyes before. "*Someone* has to die. Don't you get it, Nadine? Once we both go through with our Evoking Ceremonies, that's it. That's all the time we have. One of us has to leave."

"Why!?" I yelled. "What has you so fucking terrified of me?"

"*We're cursed!*"

Chloe's words stopped my heart. I swayed on my feet, but I barely had a chance to process what she said before another voice boomed throughout the foyer.

"EVERYBODY STOP!!!"

Chloe and I both turned to see Professor Richards standing in the center of the room. He held up a large vial of green liquid. Everyone had gone totally still. Ryan and Lucas both had each other by the collar, and they'd stopped with their fists pulled back. Amy and Mandy were on the ground with Camille and Gwen. Mandy had a fistful of Gwen's white hair, and Amy had twisted Camille's arm around her back.

All eyes turned to Professor Richards.

"Make one more move, and I'll set off this sleeping potion on the whole room," he threatened in a stern voice.

Nobody said a thing. All I heard was the click of heels down the hall, then Headmistress Verla stepped into the foyer. She wore a look of utter disapproval. It was so intense it could cut straight through you. For a moment, she actually sort of scared me.

"Everyone back to your dorms," she commanded. "*Now.*"

People started to hurry up the stairs and scatter in either direction. Chloe stomped past me, purposely slamming her shoulder into mine on the way. I moved slowly, still trying to grasp what she'd said.

I was cursed.

Why had Grammy hidden this from me? Why had she written it off as some dead feud?

I ended up in the back of the crowd. Ahead of me, Cody was helping Talia up the stairs, while Grant glared from behind them. Amy and Mandy made faces at Gwen and Camille while they headed back to their room. Isa joined me at my feet.

Lucas found his way over to me. A bruise was forming beneath his eye, but his knuckles looked raw, like he'd gotten in a few good punches. Shit. I didn't want this for him. I didn't want him getting hurt because of me.

"You okay, Nad?" he asked softly.

I swallowed. I couldn't lie to him. Today had been one shit show after another. I was beyond exhausted.

"There's something I need to tell you," I whispered under my breath. I didn't want to tell him about the curse out in the open, though.

"Nadine?" Headmistress Verla cocked an eyebrow in my direction. She looked less than happy.

I scooped Isa into my arms, then looked to Lucas. "Come with me."

We walked over to Verla. The room had been cleared out, so no one heard us.

Verla placed her hands on her hips, like a mother disappointed in her children. "What happened here?"

Though she looked at Lucas and me with tight lips, I realized she wasn't mad at *me*. She'd asked me over because she trusted me to tell her the truth.

"It was a prank, Headmistress," I told her. "Someone used illusion magic to make it look as if there was a dead body hanging from the tree outside. People got upset, and a fight broke out."

I didn't know why I didn't tell her it'd been my body hanging from the tree. Something didn't feel right about telling her about Chloe and me. If Chloe got in trouble for it, it'd only make things worse between us, and they were bad enough already.

Verla breathed a heavy sigh, like she couldn't deal with such pettiness today. "Very well. You may return to your dorms."

Lucas and I turned, but Verla stopped us once more.

"Oh, and Nadine?"

I stopped to look at her. "Yes?"

Her shoulders fell. "I'm very sorry about earlier. We'll get this worked out, and you'll pass your Evoking Ceremony."

I nodded, though deep down in my gut, I wasn't sure. I only had a few weeks left. On top of it, there was this curse Chloe just told me about.

"You don't look well, Nad," Lucas pointed out as we climbed the stairs. "Is there anything I can do?"

"No," I told him. "But there's something *I* have to do."

"What is it?" he asked. "Let me help."

I shook my head. "I have to do this by myself. My grandmother has some explaining to do."

"Nadine." Grammy sounded pleased to see me when I arrived at her house that night. "What a pleasure!"

"Cut the crap, Grammy," I snapped.

She gaped at me. "Is something wrong?"

I narrowed my eyes at her. "You could say that."

Grammy's eyes widened in concern, and she stepped aside to let me in. She gestured to the living room, but I just stood there in the hallway, my arms crossed. I felt weak on my feet, but I was too angry to sit down. Cornelius rubbed up against my leg, but I wasn't interested in his affection.

"What's wrong?" Grammy asked.

"Why didn't you tell me about the curse?" I demanded.

Grammy's features immediately darkened. She looked pissed that I'd brought it up. "I didn't tell you because there *is* no curse, Nadine."

"Then why does Chloe Olson insist there is?" I shot back. "I knew you were hiding something from me the last time I mentioned her."

Grammy sighed. "Nadine, please sit down and let me explain."

I threw my hands up. "I don't *want* to sit down. I want you to tell me everything."

"I will," Grammy promised. "Let's talk about it over a cup of tea."

Please. Like I wanted *tea* right now.

Grammy's lips tightened. "Sit *down*, Nadine."

She spoke in a tone I'd never heard her use before. I felt like I had no choice but to sit. It seemed to be the only way I was getting answers.

While I stepped into the living room, Grammy went down the hall to brew us some tea. I was fuming so badly I could hardly sit still, which was saying something considering how exhausted I was.

Assumptions raced around in my head while I waited for Grammy to return. Did Grammy *want* the curse to hurt me? Did she think I was better off dead?

Or had Chloe been lying to me?

Somehow, I doubted that.

Grammy returned to the living room with a tray. She set it on the coffee table, then pushed a cup of tea into my hands. "Drink, Nadine."

I started to sip it, and I noticed my anger begin to wane immediately. I realized what horrible things I'd just thought about Grammy, and it killed me to think them. She loved me to death. Surely she had a good reason for not telling me.

Suddenly, I felt angry for a different reason. I set my cup back on the table and glared at her. "If you're going to serve someone a potion, you should probably tell them first."

"It's nothing more than a calming tea," Grammy assured me.

My lips tightened. "Forgive me if I'm having a hard time trusting you right now."

Grammy straightened in her chair. "Look, Nadine. I'm not going to lie to you. There *was* a curse."

Well, at least she was starting to be honest with me.

"What was the curse, exactly?" I asked. "What were our grandparents fighting over?"

Grammy took a long breath before diving into the story. "Years ago, when I was pregnant with your mother, your grandfather served on the Imperium Council. He was the last Curse Breaker and the only male to ever serve. Chloe's grandfather stole a valuable item from the council, and though he denied it, the two of them fought over it. Chloe's grandfather wanted to get rid of yours, so he cast a curse upon him and his descendants. This curse would allow only one of the families from each generation to remain in Octavia Falls. The other either had to leave… or die."

"Wait…" The pieces began falling into place. "Is that how Grampy died?"

Grammy's eyes watered. "Nadine… your grandfather was murdered. Chloe's grandfather killed him."

The air left my lungs. "Mom didn't leave the coven for my dad, did she?"

Grammy shook her head regrettably. "She left to outrun the curse."

"How exactly does this curse work?" I asked.

Grammy sighed. "According to what your mother learned before she left, the curse only touches you once you're accepted into the coven. Since you haven't gone through with your Evoking Ceremony yet, it can't hurt you."

"But it has," I argued. "Grammy, it's been there my whole life. I can feel it inside me."

Grammy dropped her gaze. I'd never seen her look so guilty.

"Why didn't you tell me?" I demanded. "Why would you keep any of this from me?"

"Because the curse is over, Nadine!" Grammy cried.

"How do you know that?" I asked. Chloe sure seemed to think it was alive and well.

Grammy's breath caught. "I refuse to believe your grandfather died without breaking it. He was a Curse Breaker."

"Oh my God…" I pressed my hand to my forehead. She was seriously basing this off… nothing?

"Why would you even take this chance?" I snapped at her. "If this could cost me my life—"

"It's going to cost me my granddaughter!" she erupted. "I already lost my husband and my daughter. I'm not going to lose you, too!"

The room went dead silent.

After a few moments, I finally spoke. "It wasn't right of you to hide this from me, Grammy. You have no proof that the curse was broken."

"And you don't know it wasn't," she said softly.

"Is that something you really want to risk?" I asked. I was offended she'd play with my life like some sort of slot machine. "The curse isn't broken, Grammy. And I think deep down, you know that."

Grammy's face paled, and her voice quivered. Slowly, she rose to her feet and came over to sit beside me on the couch. Her eyes watered, and a pang of guilt hit me. I felt bad about lashing out at her.

"Nadine, I'm sorry I didn't tell you," she said softly. "It was selfish of me. All that really matters is that you're safe. Can you forgive me?"

I hesitated. "I want to, but…"

My unspoken words hung in the air. *But she broke my trust.*

Grammy reached up and pulled a chain out from beneath her shirt. An antique skeleton key I'd never seen before hung from around her neck. It looked really old, and had a pretty swirly design on the end.

"I want you to have this," she said.

I furrowed my brow. "What does it go to?"

"It's not what it goes to," she told me. "It's what it does. I've worn this key for over forty years. Your grandfather gave it to me just before he died, in the midst of his feud against Jeb Olson. He said it was enchanted to protect the owner."

"Is that true?" I asked. "Is it really enchanted?"

"It's served me thus far," Grammy answered. "I should've given it to your mother ages ago. I want it to protect you now, Nadine. I can't lose you. You're all I have left."

She pulled the necklace over her head and handed it to me. My heart warmed at the kind gesture, and I wrapped the key tightly in my hand.

"This should protect you from the curse," Grammy said, though she looked uncertain.

Silence settled between us, until I finally spoke. "What happens once I go through with my ceremony?"

"If the curse is still alive, you have until Chloe goes through with hers, since you two are the only descendants of your generation."

"And if we both joined the coven?" I asked. "How long would we have?"

"Your mother guessed a month, tops," Grammy said. "But she didn't stay that long. She left the night of her ceremony."

"My ceremony is before Chloe's," I pointed out. "That puts me at an advantage."

Chloe would have to forfeit her own ceremony if she wanted to stay. Otherwise she'd be submitting to a game of Russian Roulette with this curse. The only other option was to kill me and save herself, but she hadn't done it yet. To be honest, I didn't think she had it in her.

"Please don't leave me like your mother did," Grammy whispered.

"I won't," I promised. "I'm going through with my Evoking Ceremony. I'm going to pass, and I'm going to show Chloe that I belong here."

If anything, she'd be the one that would have to leave. Because I wasn't going to.

The following night, I couldn't sleep, even though I was really tired. After I told Lucas about the curse, all I wanted to do was be by him because he made me feel better about the whole thing. My heart yearned to be in his presence, and I couldn't stand to let my hunger for him go unchecked.

To hell with it. I was going to be spontaneous tonight.

I crawled out of bed as quietly as I could so I wouldn't wake Talia. I changed into a swimsuit, grabbed a towel, and then quietly left the room. I tiptoed down the dark, quiet hall and stopped at Lucas's door. I knocked lightly, but no answer came, so I tried again.

A few moments later, the door swung open. A sharp breath passed my lips when I saw him standing there. He wore nothing but sweats that hung off his hips in a way that made me want to drool. His abs were freaking amazing. I just wanted to reach out and touch them. His hair was tousled and looked really sexy. Just seeing him standing there shirtless did things to my body I couldn't control.

"What's this?" he teased in a low whisper so he wouldn't wake Grant. "A booty call?"

I laughed lightly. "No. Did I wake you?"

He shook his head. "Nah, couldn't sleep."

"Me either," I admitted. "I'm going swimming and wondering if you wanted to come along."

He hesitated. "The pool's closed this time of night."

I shrugged. "You think that's going to stop me?"

"Um… it should," he said, sounding equally curious and confused.

"Well, if you don't want to come, I'll just go myself," I said.

I turned from the door and started down the hall, but I was totally bluffing. I knew he wouldn't be able to resist his curiosity.

"Wait, Nad," he hissed.

I smiled brightly and turned back to him. "You're coming?"

He groaned, though he didn't sound upset. "Hold on a minute."

Lucas ducked back into the room and changed into his swim trunks, then grabbed a towel. He emerged looking hella sexy. The light from the sconces along the wall accented the hills and valleys of his abs. It took all I had not to stare.

"What?" he asked innocently.

I forced my gaze away from him, hoping he hadn't seen me blush. "Nothing. Let's go."

Lucas and I tiptoed quietly down the stairs and to the rec center. The door was locked, but all it took was one tiny incantation from Lucas, and we were in. The air was warm and thick inside, but it felt really good. The room was dark, but a light streak of moonlight came in through the tall windows that faced the forest, glistening off the water.

"Do they have some sort of magical alarm system for this?" I asked, though I didn't really care. The threat of getting caught was all part of the fun.

Lucas shrugged. "Security isn't a huge deal around here. Most people aren't brazen enough to sneak in."

"I'm *brazen*?" I teased as I dropped my towel on one of the pool chairs.

Lucas laughed and tickled me in the side. "Why do you think I like you?"

My heart fluttered at those words. I mean, I already knew he liked me, but hearing him say it got me every time.

"Don't tickle me," I snickered. I reached out and tickled his side. An electric shock traveled through my fingertips and up my arm when I touched him. I didn't think that would ever get old.

"Hey!" Lucas cried, his voice echoing throughout the pool. "Tickle me again, and I'm throwing you in."

My jaw dropped dramatically. "You wouldn't dare!"

He cocked an eyebrow. "You wanna bet?"

I shrugged and tugged at the string on my robe. The flaps fell open, revealing my black bikini. Lucas's gazed dropped and roamed across my body. His eyes lingered on me a few moments, like I wouldn't notice.

"My eyes are up here, buddy," I joked, reaching out to tickle him again.

"Hey! I said no tickling," he teased. "That's it. I'm throwing you in."

I smirked. "You'll have to catch me first."

I started running away from him. Lucas caught me around the waist, and I yelped. My voice echoed through the room, as did Lucas's laughter.

"No!" I yelled through my laughs.

I locked my arms around Lucas's neck. He tried to throw me in, but I didn't let go. Instead, we both went tumbling down into the water together.

I held my breath as my head dipped below water. My feet touched the pool floor below me, and I pushed upward. My head broke the surface, and I inhaled a large breath. Lucas came up a second later, gasping.

"That's what you get," I laughed, splashing him.

"Hey!" he splashed me back.

That turned into a full-on splashing war. Our laughter filled the entire pool. I couldn't remember the last time I'd had this much fun.

"Your splash game is *weak*," I told him.

"Is it?" he challenged.

He kicked forward and glided through the water, until he was right in front of me. I tried to splash him, but he grabbed me around the middle and tossed me upward out of the water.

I screamed playfully as I went flying, then landed safely in the water a few feet away. "Not fair!" I cried, wiping my eyes.

"Totally fair," he countered.

I raised an eyebrow. "Oh, so we're playing dirty now?"

He smirked. "That's the only way to play, isn't it?"

That sounds like a challenge!

I ducked my head below water and swam forward, until my shoulder met his knee. I wrapped one arm around his leg, then pushed off the bottom of the pool. He was light in the water, but as more of his body got out of the water, he got really heavy. I pushed with all my might, until my head broke the water. Lucas flailed as he went tumbling backward, kicking up water.

I laughed uncontrollably as he shook the water from his hair. Droplets splashed my face, but I was having so much fun I didn't care.

"Come here," Lucas growled playfully.

I splashed him lightly. "Stay away."

He grabbed my arm and dragged me through the water. My laughter instantly died when he wrapped his arms around me. Suddenly, I felt really hot—like the water might start sizzling on my skin at any moment. Our chests pressed together, though he held my arms tight at my sides.

Lucas's gaze flickered down to my lips, and he spoke softly. "Try to get me now."

I struggled out of his hold and wrapped my arms around his neck. "I've already got you," I whispered.

Lucas chuckled under his breath, but I felt like we weren't joking around anymore. Images of the night at Lake Santos flashed through my mind. It felt like we were back there—holding each other, ready to kiss.

My breaths grew shallow, making my breasts rise and fall from the water rapidly. His gaze darted downward, first to the key around my neck, then to my breasts, before landing on my eyes again. My heart pummeled against my rib cage. Being this close to him made every nerve in my body come to life. I wondered if he could feel me shaking.

"So, what's this?" I asked. I didn't mean to lean closer to him, but I felt my lips magnetize to his. "Is this a continuation of where we left off at the lake?"

Lucas leaned closer. His lips were barely an inch from mine. His sweet, warm breath brushed across my cheek. My pulse quickened.

"I-I…" Lucas stuttered.

He sighed, shattering the whole moment. My heart dropped.

"I don't know, Nad," he finally said.

I drew away. "I thought you wanted this."

"I do," he said quickly. "But do *you*?"

Truth be told, I wanted Lucas so bad it hurt. Problem was, the future scared me. Would this relationship work if the Reaper's Shadow curse kept us at a distance?

I couldn't think about that. So I resolved to enjoying every moment with Lucas that I could.

"I don't know what the future holds," I admitted. "But I know that I want you right now."

Lucas's expression softened, like my words warmed his heart. I waved my hands through the water and stepped closer to him. With each step I took, he took a step away. It wasn't like he was running from me—more like he was giving me a choice to pursue him.

"Why worry about the future when all we need to do is live in the moment?" I questioned.

Lucas stilled when his back hit the edge of the pool. His breath wavered. "Because our choices in the moment affect the future, Nad."

I shrugged, like none of that mattered, though I knew deep down that it did. "Let's pretend like there is no Reaper's Shadow curse," I suggested. "What's a witch gotta do to get you to ask me out?"

Lucas sighed and hoisted himself up out of the pool to sit on the edge. Water dripped from his dark hair, and the moonlight accented the deep shadows of his muscled chest.

He looked down at me with those bewitching green eyes, sending my heart pummeling against my rib cage. "Are you sure you want to be with me, Nad? You deserve to be happy."

"We can be happy together," I promised.

He raised a curious eyebrow. "How do you know?"

I pressed my hands to the edge of the pool on either side of him and pushed myself upward so that only my legs were in the water. My hips rested on the edge of the pool between his legs. Heat pooled between my thighs as I came in so close we were practically touching. Energy sizzled between us, and I saw it in the way he looked at me that he felt it, too. The sexual tension was palpable.

"Why don't you kiss me and find out?" I whispered.

A moment passed where I didn't know what might happen next. We felt frozen in time, and I held my breath.

Then Lucas's hand came up to cradle the back of my neck, and he drew me to him. My whole body felt like it was melting into the water as his warm lips moved over mine. My lips parted, and he deepened the kiss.

My arms suddenly became weak, and I lowered myself back into the water. That didn't stop Lucas from kissing me deeper, though. His lips never parted from mine as he followed me into the water. He took my face in his hands and ran his tongue over my bottom lip. I moaned as I wrapped my arms and legs around him, pressing myself so close to him that it should be a sin.

Lucas's hands roamed downward, until they were cupping my ass. I gasped and pressed my hips into him, until I could feel his erection pressing up against my most sensitive areas. My fingers trembled as I ran them through his hair. He made little noises of pleasure that sent waves of heat all over my body. A glorious high filled me, like I was mere meters away from cresting the top of a mountain. This was how it should be with us. This was what it should feel like to be with the person you loved. To be denied of that was a curse… literally.

I wanted more with Lucas—as much as I could possibly get. We were two lost souls who found each other in the darkness. Somehow, we had created a spark out of nothing. When he kissed me like this, it was as if the spark could never die. The very air he breathed was mine, and as long as we were together, the fire we shared could never die.

Boldly, I reached up and tugged on the string of my bikini top. The fabric fell away, and I pressed my exposed breasts to Lucas's chest. My nipples hardened beneath the coolness of the air.

Lucas's entire body quivered. I half expected him to draw away, to tell me to cover up and remind me we couldn't touch like this, but he didn't. Instead, his hands traveled up my body, before settling on the curve of my breasts.

My heart hammered so hard I was sure he could feel it. The air around us seemed heavy with hormones so thick I could hardly breathe. Lucas's hands massaged my breasts as mine tangled in his hair. Our lips moved in perfect sync as we made out passionately. The room spun around me so fast I didn't know which way was up or down. The only thing rooting me in place was Lucas's body against mine. We could've been making out for only a minute, or it could've been hours. All I knew was that it'd never be long enough.

Bang!

A noise like the slamming of a door startled the two of us apart. I grabbed for the fabric of my bikini and pressed it over my breasts. Lucas and I shared an expression of total horror.

"We should probably go," he suggested.

I quickly agreed as I tied my bikini back on. We jumped out of the water and gathered our things, then snuck quietly out of the pool. Lucas took my hand as we ducked through the shadows in the hall. We didn't see anyone, but we made our way back to the dorms slowly and carefully. My heart pounded in exhilaration. I didn't think either of us wanted to leave the other.

My heart sank when we arrived back at my dorm. I stuck my arms through the sleeves of my robe and draped my towel around my neck.

"That was a lot of fun," I whispered to Lucas. "It helped take my mind off things."

Lucas's face fell. "You mean the curse?"

I nodded.

"Any ideas what you're going to do about it?" he asked.

"I think it's pretty obvious," I replied. "Either me or Chloe has to leave Octavia Falls. I'm staying."

"You're playing a game of chicken, Nad," he pointed out. "Chloe's not going to cave."

"She's going to have to, because I won't," I promised.

Lucas frowned, like what he was about to say pained him. "Or she'll kill you."

I rolled my eyes. "If she was going to kill me, she'd have done it already."

Lucas's eyes roamed over me, and he took my hand. "Maybe you don't have to go through with your Evoking Ceremony. If you don't do it, the curse would never activate. You could stay."

"And then I'd never be a true member of the coven," I reminded him. "That's what Chloe wants. She wants to prove I don't belong. And I do, Lucas."

"I just want you to be safe," he said.

"This isn't up for discussion," I stated firmly. "My mind's made up."

Lucas sighed.

"Let's forget about that," I suggested, before wrapping him in my arms. "I don't want to ruin the amazing night we just had together."

Lucas pressed his nose into my hair. After a long moment of silence, he spoke. "What's your secret?"

"My secret?"

"Yeah. You're so positive lately. How do you do it?"

"I don't know. It might have something to do with this." I drew away and lifted the key around my neck.

"What is it?" he asked.

I shrugged. "Something my grandma gave me. It's supposed to be enchanted."

Lucas's eyebrows shot up. "Then it must be rare. We aren't so great at enchantments in the Miriamic Coven. Can I see it?"

"Go ahead."

He reached out and lifted the key in his hand. Though it was dark in the hall, he inspected it closely. As I watched his eyes roam over it, I saw something in them. It was like *he* needed protection. What from, I wasn't sure—whether it was from himself or some darker force. All I knew was Lucas seemed to need it more than I did.

I didn't realize what I was doing until I did it. I reached up and undid the clasp on my necklace. I started to fasten it around his neck.

"What are you doing?" he asked.

"I want you to wear it," I said.

"Nad, I can't," he declined, but I'd already placed it around his neck. "It's from your grandma."

"So?" I challenged. "You want to try being more positive? Let's see if it helps. I want you to have it."

"I can't," he insisted. He reached up to start taking it off, but I placed my hands on his to stop him. My skin tingled where I touched him.

I looked him straight in the eyes. "You know I don't take no for an answer. Consider it an early birthday present. It's yours."

Lucas relaxed. He came in close and pushed a strand of wet hair behind my ear. Butterflies danced around in my stomach. "Thank you, Nad."

Lucas just hovered there, neither of us wanting to move. He was barely a foot away, just staring down at me. My mouth grew dry as I awaited another kiss. I wished I could invite him inside, but Talia was sleeping.

I licked my lips, but my voice wavered. "Thank *you* for tonight. We should do it again some time. It'd be fun."

He nodded as his eyes roamed my face, before traveling down my body. He reached out and ran his fingers down the arm of my plush robe. "You know what else would be fun?"

My whole body trembled. I could think of quite a few things. "What?"

Lucas looked like he was holding his breath. Then all at once, the question spilled out of him. "Would you like to go to the Midnight Formal with me?"

I went speechless. Instead of jumping at the chance, I spat out like an idiot, "I... I thought you didn't dance."

He smiled sweetly. "I'd dance for you, Nad."

My heart never felt as warm as it did in that moment. Lucas made my heart sing in ways no one ever had before. That was when I knew—no matter the limitations, I wanted to spend my life with Lucas. I'd walk to the ends of the earth and back for him.

I became so overwhelmed with joy that all I could do was throw my arms around his neck to keep it from bursting out of me. "Yes, Lucas," I whispered. "I'll go to the dance with you."

I drew away and took his face in my hands. He looked down at me with a blissful expression in his eye.

I smiled back. "And I'll share every dance with you after."

His eyes widened, and he went breathless. "Is that a decision?"

I nodded eagerly. "Yes. I want to be with you."

Lucas wrapped me in his arms, and I felt so warm and safe there. "I'll find a way around this curse, Nad."

"I hope we can," I whispered back. "I'd do anything to be with you."

He shivered, but I thought it was a good shiver. "Anything?"

"Yes," I said. "Wouldn't you?"

He let out a deep sigh and pulled me tighter. "Absolutely."

The night at the pool was the most fun I'd ever had. Kissing her like that was beyond incredible. I'd never kissed someone like that, and no one had ever kissed me back with such passion. And her breasts… oh my Goddess. There were no words. I could hardly believe she'd let me touch them. It felt like a dream.

But it was real, and I couldn't stop playing it over and over in my mind. Nadine wanted to be with me, no matter what.

She had no idea how much it meant to me that she was willing to give up her grandmother's necklace. I didn't think she understood how valuable an enchantment like this was in the magical community. When Nadine gave me that key, it was like she gave me her heart.

It was in that moment that I realized I was done for.

As long as Nadine was staying in Octavia Falls, I was going to be with her.

One day, I flagged Samantha down after Necromancy Safety.

"Lucas?" She looked surprised to see me. "What's up?"

I glanced around the hall to make sure no one was around to hear. "I have some questions about the Reaper Moon. Mind if we talk?"

She looked a little hesitant. "I already told you everything I know."

"I just want to know how the last guy did it," I begged. "How'd he get in contact with the reapers on the Reaper Moon? I mean, did he just walk up to them and ask?"

She bit her lower lip. "I think it requires a ritual."

That's what I was afraid of.

"What kind? How?" I asked.

She shot me a look of apology. "I'm sorry, Lucas. I don't know. You're going to have to ask someone else."

And that's exactly what I was going to do until I found answers. Who better to go to than the last guy who figured it out?

I didn't tell Nadine what I was up to. I knew it wasn't right to keep secrets from her, but I didn't want her talking me out of it. I could already hear her voice in my head.

"I'm not worth risking the Abyss," she would say.

But she was. She totally was.

Friday night arrived, and I ducked out the back door of the school before Grant or anyone else could find me. It was my twentieth birthday, and I was pretty sure Grant wanted to go party or something dumb like that, but I had other plans in mind.

As I rounded the side of the school, I heard Ryan's voice. "Where's the money you owe me, Gregory?"

"I'll get it," Gregory replied, his voice shaking.

"You better," Ryan spat. "Now get out of here!"

I heard Gregory scramble off in the other direction. I spun on my heel and rounded the other side of the school. I didn't need another confrontation with Ryan. I felt bad for Gregory, but at least Ryan seemed distracted enough that he was off my back for a while.

I left campus and walked into town. It wasn't far, and I didn't have my own car. Snow fell gently from the sky, but the air actually felt nice. I stopped at a psychic shop along Main Street and went inside.

The shop was really small and had only a handful of products on display—things like tarot cards and herbs. It was dark inside, with black walls, dim lighting, and a deep red curtain separating the main room from another room in the back. There was no one there when I walked in, but I suspected the Seer who ran the place could sense my presence. She was supposed to be one of the best in town —slated to be the next on the Imperium Council. I'd never met her, but I'd heard of her. So when I decided to visit a Seer to figure some shit out, I thought she might be the best person to ask for help.

I barely waited a minute before the curtain behind the counter opened. A woman stepped into the room. She was at least twice my age and had beautiful tight curls framing her face. She wore dark clothes and a purple shawl over her shoulders.

She smiled kindly. "Lucas, I thought I'd be seeing you again."

I hesitated. "Um… I don't believe we've met."

"Right," she said, like she just remembered. "I was in costume. I'm Everly Hall."

She reached across the counter, and I shook her hand. "Nice to meet you. Were you… were you the night hag on Halloween?"

She smiled. "I was."

Creepy…

"What did the card mean?" I asked.

She gestured to the curtain. "Why don't we sit down and talk about it?"

I followed her into the next room, which was just as small as the first. There were candles lit around the perimeter. In the center of the room stood a round table covered in black cloth. A crystal ball and tarot cards sat neatly on top of it.

"Please, sit," Everly said, gesturing to one of the chairs.

I took a seat, but I shifted uncomfortably. I'd come here to get answers, but now I had no idea what to expect.

"What can I do for you, Lucas?" Everly asked as she sat across from me.

I cleared my throat. "First of all, you can tell me about Halloween."

She shook her head and wore an expression of regret. "I'm afraid I can't always make sense of the messages I receive."

"Do you know who sent you the message?" I asked. "What did they say, exactly?"

Her shoulders fell. "I don't know. I did as I was told to do. I found you, gave you the card, and…"

She trailed off and stared into the distance. After a few moments, she shook her head, like she couldn't remember. "I gave you a warning, didn't I?"

"Yeah," I told her. "You said I needed to stop… something. You don't remember?"

She looked at a loss for words. "The way my powers work, I don't always remember the messages I relay. It's automatic."

Well, that was a freaking dead end. I decided to focus on the real reason I came.

I leaned my elbows on the table. "I'm not actually here about Halloween. I'm looking for answers about my future."

"Knowledge can be a dangerous thing, Lucas," she warned.

"It's not like that," I assured her. "I just need some guidance."

She straightened in her chair. "I may be able to help with that."

My shoulders relaxed, and I felt at ease. "The thing is, there's this girl."

Everly's eyes brightened. "Ooh, tell me about her."

"Nadine is… amazing," I stated. "She's just so curious about life, so full of this amazing energy that lifts me up every time I'm around her. I want to be around her all the time. I want to be… *with* her. But…"

"But you're the Reaper's Apprentice," Everly finished for me. "Which means you can't be with her without hurting her."

"See? You understand," I said. "Apparently that's not common knowledge around school. The thing is, to be with her, I'd have to get rid of my gift."

Everly looked thoughtful. "And you're wondering whether you should or not?"

I shook my head. "No. I'm wondering *how*."

Her face fell. "Do you realize what you're saying? Rejecting your powers like that—"

"I know," I said quickly. "I'm not here for a lecture."

"It's not my job to give you one," she stated simply.

"I have to get in touch with a reaper, which I can only do on the Reaper Moon," I said. "Problem is… I don't know how to do it. I mean, it might be as easy as walking up to them, but if I have to do a ritual, I want to be prepared. I heard a story about a guy who did this years ago. Do you think we can contact him?"

Everly sighed. "I'm sorry, Lucas, but my powers don't work that way. The messages I receive are powerful, but I can't decide who gives them."

"Can we at least try?" I begged.

She narrowed her eyes. "You do realize what you're getting into, don't you?"

"Yes, and I've thought it over pretty extensively. Will you help me or not?"

Silence settled over the room for several long seconds. I held my breath.

Finally, Everly sighed. "I'm not one to refuse help when it's asked of me, so long as you understand what you're doing."

I nodded firmly. "All I want is information."

She raised an eyebrow. "You realize I can't guarantee that, don't you?"

"Yes, but I want to try," I told her.

She took a long breath. "Okay, I will help you. My fee is a hundred dollars per page."

"Page?" I asked curiously.

She reached over to a nearby shelf and pulled out a stack of paper and a pen, then placed them in front of her. "I'm an automatic writer, Lucas. It's how I receive the messages."

I shifted in my chair. I was probably going to have to borrow money for this, but to hell with it. I'd pay it back. Anything for answers.

"I'll pay whatever you charge," I finally said.

She nodded. "Then let's get started."

Everly closed her eyes and positioned her pen above the paper. She breathed in and out, barely making a sound. A creepy clock with skeleton-shaped fingers ticked on the wall. I wondered if I was supposed to do something, but Everly didn't give any instructions. I just sat there... waiting.

At least if she didn't write anything, I didn't owe her anything, right?

After two minutes that felt like two hours, the temperature in the room dropped. The hair stood on the back of my neck, and I shivered. I should've been creeped out, but I wasn't.

Without warning, Everly's eyes began to move rapidly beneath her lids. Her eyelids fluttered open and closed the tiniest bit, and it really freaked me out. She was obviously in a really deep trance.

Everly started scribbling on the paper, and the pen made chilling scratching noises against it. My heart leapt to my throat in anticipation. I jumped to my feet and rounded the table to read what she was writing. She didn't respond at all, just kept writing like she was possessed.

So you want to know about the Reaper Moon? she wrote in smooth, clear handwriting.

I glanced around the room, as if expecting to spot a ghost hovering somewhere nearby, but I didn't see a thing.

"Yes," I said aloud. I spoke quickly, like I feared the spirit may leave us at any time. "What can you tell me about contacting the reapers? Is there a ritual involved?"

Everly began scribbling on the next line. *Yes, but why would you want to do it?*

"That's private," I said.

Won't you confide in your brother, Lucas?

I gasped. My eyes went as wide as saucers. The spirit that spoke through Everly was *Eric*?

Maybe, I thought. I didn't want to get my hopes up if this was some sort of trick. I *hoped* it was him, though.

"E-Eric?" I asked, stumbling over the word. My throat closed up as I spoke his name. It'd been so long since I said it out loud.

It's me.

My heart began to hammer fiercely. I wasn't sure if I was excited to talk to him again or pissed this might be an attempt at manipulation.

"How do I know it's you?" I asked. My eyes darted around the room, even though I couldn't see anything.

We had a code word. Remember?

I furrowed my brow. Code word?

Then it hit me. Years ago, when my brother and I were just kids, we lay out under the stars one night talking about death. We decided that if one of us croaked off before the other, we'd contact the other using a code word. It was how we'd know we weren't being punked by some mischievous spirit. I couldn't believe I'd almost forgotten.

"I remember," I said.

I gripped on hard to the back of Everly's chair as she began scribbling on the next line.

Mystic and Midnight.

They were the names of the two cats we had when we were kids. My knees became weak beneath me. Before I collapsed, I dragged my chair around the table and sank into it beside Everly. She kept on writing while I tried to catch my breath and wrap my head around the fact that my brother was back in the same room as me.

Do you believe me now? she wrote on the next line.

That snapped me back to attention. I realized I may not have a lot of time left with Eric, and I wanted to get in as much conversation as I could.

I straightened in my chair. "I can't believe it's you. I mean, I do, I just..."

I couldn't find the words.

"W-what's it like where you're at?" I asked.

I held my breath, awaiting the answer. I hoped to our goddess he wasn't where I thought he was. I didn't know if I could handle that. He took his own life, but he didn't deserve an eternity in the Abyss for it.

Alora's wonderful, Eric answered.

My jaw dropped open. I never thought I'd feel such relief to hear Eric was safe and happy with our ancestors.

"You're in Alora?" I asked breathlessly. "That's great."

There's no time for small talk, the next message read.

"You're right," I said. "Do you know anything the Reaper Moon?"

I leaned over Everly's shoulder and watched carefully as she wrote out the next message.

The people here talk a lot. I've picked up a lot of information. I've come to tell you not to do it.

I gaped like a fish. "Wha—why?"

My own *brother* wasn't going to support me?

Mother Miriam gave you this gift for a reason. Don't give it up like I did.

"This isn't the same thing!" I cried. "Please, just tell me how to do it!"

Everly's pen paused above the paper, though her eyes continued to move rapidly—like she was still in the trance.

"Eric, please!" I begged.

Finally, Everly placed her pen back to the paper and wrote, *You must go to the cemetery and find the grave of Caesar Peppertrine. It is there where you'll find the scroll that tells you how to contact the reapers.*

"Caesar Peppertrine?" I asked.

Everly was already writing another message.

Be careful, Eric cautioned. *You must heed the warning from the card I gave you on Halloween. The choice is yours, Lucas.*

I swore my heart stopped for a couple seconds as I read the message. "*You're* the one who sent me the Death card? What does it mean?"

Everly's pen didn't move.

"Eric!" I shot to my feet and looked around the room, but I couldn't see him. "What does it mean!?"

Everly cleared her throat, and my stomach dropped. I looked to her to see her eyes were wide open. She swayed a little, like she was dazed.

"No!" I cried, my heart racing. "You can't be done. I have more questions!"

Everly set her pen down and spoke calmly. "I'm sorry, Lucas. I did what I could. You must recall I did not promise you *any* answers."

I slammed my hands down on the table, making the pen jump an inch into the air. "Then bring him back!"

She shook her head regrettably. "I'm afraid he's already gone."

I couldn't explain the wave of anger, disappointment, and sadness that washed through me. All three emotions hit me at once. All I wanted was a few more moments with Eric.

Like a brick to the gut, I realized how dangerous that thought could be. It was like all the other thoughts I heard, and I didn't want to be that guy.

I was going to live my life, and I was going to die happy.

And that meant going down this road so I could be with Nadine.

Caesar Peppertrine didn't exist.

At least, that was the conclusion I was coming to. His name was nowhere in the coven's records. For the last week, I'd been leaving campus between classes to search the graveyard, but it was so huge it seemed to be taking forever. I entertained the idea that Caesar Peppertrine's grave wasn't on coven grounds, but it made no sense. Eric had specifically told me to go to *the cemetery*, which could only mean ours here in town; otherwise, he would've specified.

I wondered if this was Eric's way of throwing me off—of keeping me busy until the Reaper Moon had passed. But I couldn't believe my brother would lead me astray like that. He'd given me the choice to make for myself. He wouldn't lie to me.

Which only meant one thing. Caesar Peppertrine's grave was out there—and I was going to find it.

But it was going to have to wait until after tonight. Tonight, I had other plans.

I stood in front of the mirror on Saturday night, straightening the tie on my suit. The last time I'd worn it was at Eric's funeral. I expected to feel ill putting it on, but I didn't. Instead, I felt comforted, like Eric was here with me.

Grant poked his head through the open bathroom door. "You ready?"

"Almost," I said, combing my hair back one last time.

"Wow," Grant said. "Haven't seen you clean up this nice since—"

He cut off. I could already hear what he was going to say. *Since your brother's funeral.*

"It's okay." I clapped Grant on the shoulder. "You don't have to tread lightly around me anymore."

Grant gave me this confused look. "Who are you and what have you done with Lucas?"

I got it. The *old* me would've been pissed for any reminder of Eric. But now that I knew Eric was in Alora, I felt like I could breathe at the mention of him again.

I hadn't told Grant about the night with the Seer and how Eric had given me a message. I didn't want to chance anyone trying to talk me out of the Reaper Moon. I was going through with it, and that was final.

I mean, I hadn't found the scroll, but I had a week left. I wasn't giving up.

"I haven't gone anywhere, buddy," I said. "This is the old me coming back. Should we go find our dates?"

Grant frowned. "You mean *your* date."

I furrowed my brow. "What happened to yours?"

Grant raised his eyebrows, like he was *really* starting to worry about me. "Have you listened to anything I've said at all this past week? If I can't go with Talia, it's totally not worth going out with someone else."

"But you're still going," I pointed out.

Grant shrugged. "I'll be there to swoop in when Talia realizes Cody's a total douche. Plus, I'm not missing a dance, man."

"Then let's get going." I could hardly wait to see Nadine.

Grant and I took the grand staircase down to the Main Foyer.

"You go on ahead, man," I said. "I told Nadine I'd meet her here."

He gave me a salute. "See you soon."

I felt pretty awkward just standing there. I shot a glance around the foyer to see other couples chatting or sipping drinks. I was about to go sit down when movement caught my eye.

Nadine stood at the top of the stairs, looking like a radiant goddess. It nearly knocked the wind out of me. She had her hair in long, beautiful waves around her shoulders, and wore a floor-length dress that had lots of sparkly diamonds on the bust and exposed part of her midriff. It was a deep, dark purple, like the color of my magic, and it looked really good on her.

She glanced around the foyer, until her eyes fell on me. Her face lit up. My heart started pounding, and it was as if all time had stood still. I was rooted completely in place, and the only thing that moved around me was Nadine. She reached for the banister and started down the steps. I couldn't take my eyes off her.

It wasn't until she reached the bottom of the grand staircase and cleared her throat that I snapped back to attention. She blushed. "Everything okay?"

I quickly reached my hand out and took hers. "You look… absolutely perfect."

She smiled brightly. That smile lit up my whole world. "Thank you."

After a few moments of silence, I realized it was my turn to speak again. "I'm actually really glad you picked that color. It's, um, it's my favorite. I didn't know what color you'd wear, but…"

I cupped my hands together and conjured the corsage I'd bought her. I opened my palms to reveal a velvety purple rose. "It's for you."

Nadine gazed down at it, speechless. "Lucas, it's beautiful."

She held her wrist out, and I placed the corsage over her hand. She ran her fingers over the petals.

"It's not as beautiful as you," I said.

She chuckled under her breath. "That's sweet of you. You don't look too bad yourself."

"I have my moments." I took a step back and held my elbow out to her. "May I escort you to the dance?"

She beamed and hooked her elbow through mine. "You may."

I led Nadine down the hall. We walked past the cafeteria and to the end of the hall, where a pair of double doors opened to a magnificent ballroom.

Nadine's jaw dropped when we stepped inside. The ballroom walls were a midnight blue, and the carpet was a deep black. The room was cast in moonlight streaming in through the tall, arched windows. Candles hovered above our heads. They weren't attached to anything, but they bobbed up and down with ease, like one of the professors was using their Mentalist powers to set the ambiance. Tarot cards spun between the candles. I looked up and noticed they were all Major Arcana cards that spoke of good fortune and abundance. The Death card was nowhere to be seen, thank the Goddess.

A live band played at the opposite end of the room, filling the space with a punk-rock melody. On stage, two skeletons jived to the beat in a coordinated dance. It was obviously the work of a talented necromancer. Grant was already on the dancefloor busting his moves. Amy and Mandy danced alongside him in black and white gothic gowns.

"Would you like something to drink?" I asked Nadine.

"Sure," she answered with a shrug.

I led her over to the refreshments table. A sweet scent emanated from a bubbling cauldron.

"Two, please," I said to the Alchemist behind the table.

As he started serving us drinks, Nadine hesitated at my side. "What's in it?" she asked.

I could tell by the way she eyed it she worried it might flare her symptoms.

"It should be okay," I said. "It's just a hydration potion. Helps you go longer on the dancefloor."

"Oh," she said brightly, sounding intrigued. "I'll have to try it then."

We sipped our potion, which tasted fruity and sweet, with a hint of carbonation. My gaze roamed over the ballroom and stopped on the doors as Talia entered on Cody's arm.

"Uh oh," I said under my breath.

"What?" Nadine followed my gaze, and she realized what I was talking about. "What's wrong with Cody?"

I almost snorted. "Grant wants to kick his ass."

Nadine sighed, but she smiled in amusement. "Okay, he can't be *that* bad. Talia really likes him. What harm is there in letting her enjoy his company?"

The question was rhetorical, but it made me think of my mom. *She* claimed she enjoyed my dad's company. Sure, there were times when he could be fun, but they were few and far between. Not that Cody was anything like my dad, but still.

I took another sip of punch. "Depends. Want to get out there?"

She beamed. "You're really going to dance with me this time?"

I tossed my empty cup in the trash nearby, then took her hand. "I told you I would, didn't I?"

Nadine threw her cup away before she'd finished, then followed me onto the dancefloor. The song had changed since we came in, but it was the same punk-rock type of music. Nadine started swaying her hips right away, but I just sort of stood back awkwardly. I was *not* a good dancer.

"Woohoo!" Grant cupped his hands around his mouth and shouted. "Nadine is on the floor! Let's get this party *started*!"

"Get in here, girl!" Amy cried, gesturing her forward.

"Shake it!" Mandy added. She spun around and started twerking in Nadine's direction.

Nadine giggled as Grant swirled an imaginary lasso above his head. He threw it over her and reeled her to the center of the dancefloor.

"Hey there, buddy," I cut in, stepping between them. "I'm gonna have to take that from you. She's mine tonight."

Grant shrugged and stepped aside, then pretended to place the invisible lasso rope in my hands. "Go wild."

Nadine threw her head back in laughter as I pretended to reel her in. She ended up so close to me that I grabbed her around the waist. She kept dancing, so I just went along with it, moving my body to the beat. I probably looked like a total fool, but I didn't care. I had Nadine Evers in my arms. My attention was so laser-focused on her that we could've been the only two people in the room for all I knew. When she laughed and danced, it was like my whole dark world lit up, but there was only one thing to see—*her*.

"You're *dancing*!" she exclaimed.

"Don't go teasing me, now," I warned. "I might stop."

"I'm not teasing," she countered. "I'm enjoying it."

"Well, enjoy it while it lasts," I said, though something told me Nadine and I would be sharing many dances in years to come.

"Heeey!" Talia shouted as she came onto the dancefloor, dragging Cody behind her.

"Talia!" Mandy squealed. She reached out for Talia's hand, then spun her around.

Talia giggled, then returned to Cody's side. The two started grinding like they were animals. Good Goddess, I did *not* expect that out of Talia.

Nadine noticed me watching them, but she must not have noticed the look of disgust on my face. "You want to dance like that?" she teased.

I shot a glance around the crowded dancefloor. "With all these people around?"

She shrugged. "Yeah, what could it hurt? All you have to do is stand there."

I liked the sound of that. Nadine started to demonstrate. She turned around and pressed her backside against my front, then dipped down a little before coming back up.

I gasped. If she kept this up any longer, it was going to be pretty obvious to everyone just how much I liked it. But I didn't want her to stop, either.

"You okay back there?" she asked as she continued rubbing herself against me.

"Peachy," I said. I wanted to slap myself. Was that really the best I could come up with?

"Good," she teased. "Because there's more where that came from."

To my surprise, Nadine bent at the waist, pressing her ass against my dick. And no, that *wasn't* a roll of quarters in my pocket. I was *very* happy to see her. Damn, I just wanted to reach out and grab her ass, but I couldn't with all the people around. She flipped her hair, then shoved her hands into it, letting it flip around in a really sexy way.

"Woo!" Talia cheered. "Nadine's got *moves*."

Nadine turned back toward me, blushing. She placed her arms around my neck and continued swaying her hips to the music. "I should maybe save that for when we're alone, huh?"

My eyebrows shot up. "Are you offering me a lap dance?"

Her lips twitched at the corners. "Depends. Are you accepting?"

Once this fucking curse was gone, she could give me all the lap dances she wanted. Nadine and I started dancing like normal again, and my eyes scanned the crowd. I realized for the first time that Grant had practically stopped dancing. His eyes were locked on Talia and Cody. He looked about ready to bare his teeth and growl.

I cocked my head to Nadine, and we danced a few paces over toward Grant. He didn't notice us until I nudged him with my elbow. Finally, he snapped back to reality.

"What?" he asked.

"Chill," I warned. "No one wants to see a fist fight tonight."

Grant scoffed. "Then let's pray he doesn't give me a reason."

Just then, Cody reached down and squeezed Talia's ass. It wasn't cute and sweet, either. It was a very obvious, full-on ass grab for the whole dancefloor to see.

Talia squealed and jumped away from him. She looked shocked at first, but a smile came across her face. "Cody, what'd we talk about?"

She made it sound like she was joking, but the whole thing made me uneasy. It definitely riled up Grant, because he stomped over to them.

"What the hell do you think you're doing, man?" Grant snapped.

Cody scowled. "Me? I don't even know who the fuck you are. Get out of here."

"You get out of here!" Grant countered. He shoved Cody in the shoulders, and he stumbled back into another couple.

"Grant, don't!" Talia shouted.

Cody's nostrils flared, and he looked ready to punch Grant in the face.

Talia threw herself between them. "Cody, forget about Grant. He's just a friend. Grant, it's fine. It was harmless."

"Didn't look that way to me," Grant sneered without taking his eyes off Cody.

"The girl says she's fine," Cody snapped. "Now back off."

Nadine went to Talia's side. "You okay?"

The two exchanged a few words in whispers.

Grant looked to Talia, as if expecting her to call Cody out. "Tal, come on. Don't tell me you're okay with that."

"I'm fine," she insisted. "Let's not ruin the night with a fight, okay?"

Cody scoffed as Talia turned back to him. They started dancing again, though Cody dragged her further away from us. "What a loser," he said to her, though it was loud enough for us all to hear. "You're really friends with that guy?"

"Is she really okay?" I asked Nadine as she returned to my side.

She shot a glance at Talia. "She says she is. She thinks Grant's overreacting."

"Do *you* think he is?" I asked.

"I don't know." She frowned in contemplation. "She looks okay now."

Talia twirled on the dancefloor in Cody's arms, beaming up at him. Grant still hadn't backed down. He stood there, his hands curled into fists.

Mandy stepped in front of him and raised an eyebrow. "Are Amy and I going to have to drag you off the dancefloor? Let Talia have fun with her date."

Grant narrowed his eyes at Cody. "Do I have to?"

"Yes," she insisted.

Grant groaned, and Mandy shot him a pointed look. "Do you want Amy and me to dance around you and try to make her jealous?" she suggested.

Grant's eyes lit up at that. "Mandy, I think you just became my new best friend."

Nadine gasped dramatically. "I lost top spot?"

"Don't worry," Grant played along. "You're top five for sure."

She laughed as Grant turned to dance with Mandy and Amy. Just as they were getting into it, the song changed to a slow melody. Now this, I could do.

I stepped back and offered Nadine my hand. "May I have this dance?"

She curtsied. "Why yes, kind sir."

I couldn't help but beam as Nadine took my hand and I wrapped my arms around her waist. We swayed on the dancefloor, and my heart swelled. I loved holding her in my arms.

"I'm glad we still get dances in college," Nadine said. "I'm having lots of fun."

"Good," I replied. "I am, too."

"Even though you're dancing?" she asked playfully.

I nodded. "I mean, you basically twisted my arm, but it'll heal."

She snickered, but she went quiet a few moments later and rested her head on my chest. This moment was incredible. I wanted a million more like it, and then some.

My eyes roamed the ballroom again. Across the room, I noticed Chloe dancing with Finn, one of the Treacherous Tarantulas. She kept throwing glances toward Ryan, who sat slumped in one of the chairs and looked out at the crowd like he was too good to be there. His bowtie was already undone, like he was totally wasted already.

Fucking loser.

At least all Chloe's attention was on him and not on my precious Nadine. If she ever tried hurting her again, she was going to have to deal with me. The consequences be damned, I'd curse that bitch's ass to protect my girl.

I continued to look around the room and noticed Lena dancing with Gregory. She really had to be desperate for a date if she'd come with him. The poor guy looked at her like he was a lost puppy, but she kept pulling her head away, like she couldn't stand him breathing on her.

She shot a glance my way, but I ignored her. If she was trying to make me jealous or something, it wasn't going to work.

Finally, my eyes landed on Professor Warren and Headmistress Verla standing in the corner. We didn't need chaperones, but they were there no doubt to make sure no one spiked the punch bowl or started any fights. It wouldn't be the first time.

Verla sipped her drink slowly while Professor Warren talked to her. Whatever he was saying must've been pissing her off, because she didn't look him in the eyes. She kept her gaze on the students and pursed her lips. I couldn't tell what he was saying, but he looked somewhat annoyed with her. I hadn't realized the two were on less than friendly terms.

"What's wrong?" Nadine asked.

"Nothing," I said, turning my gaze back to her. "Professor Warren and Headmistress Verla look mad at each other."

She looked toward them and frowned. "It definitely looks like something's going on. I saw her twice this week for make-up sessions, and she seemed fine then."

I spun Nadine around, then pulled her back into my arms. "What day is your ceremony again?"

She gasped playfully. "You don't remember my birthday?"

"I don't think you ever told me," I pointed out. "I know it's next week."

She snickered lightly. "It's the thirteenth. You're coming to my Evoking Ceremony, right?"

My whole body stilled. I must've looked like a statue as it hit me. That would make the eve of her birthday, and her ceremony… the same night as the Reaper Moon.

"I know what you're thinking," she said, pushing her hair behind her ear. "Friday the thirteenth is really not the best time for a ceremony."

She chuckled nervously, but I didn't respond.

"Lucas?" Nadine asked.

I snapped out of it. I couldn't miss the Reaper Moon, but I couldn't ditch her ceremony, either.

"I'll be there," I promised.

I had to be. As for the Reaper Moon, I'd be in, out, and done before the witching hour. I'd make it to her ceremony…

I hoped.

After the slow song ended, Nadine announced that she was going to sit out the next song. I started to follow her, before Grant grabbed me by the elbow and dragged me away from her.

"Sorry," Grant said to Nadine. "I've got to steal him for a second."

"Dude, what the hell—?" I started.

Grant dragged me out the doors and turned on me as soon as we were in the hallway. He pointed a finger in my direction. "I saw that look!"

"What? What look?"

"Nadine told you the night of her ceremony, and you totally froze up," he accused. "You ditched us the night of your birthday, too. And don't think I haven't noticed you sneaking off campus. What's up with you lately?"

"Nothing," I lied, but my voice rose several pitches.

Grant gave me a stern look. "Don't lie to me. We've lived together long enough that I know your tells."

"My *tells*?" I asked.

"Your eyes narrow when you lie," Grant pointed out.

"They do not!" I defended, but I suddenly realized they *were* narrowed just a bit. I consciously widened them.

"Don't tell me you've gotten wrapped up in something bad," Grant said.

"Goddess, no," I hissed. "It's not like that at all."

He crossed his arms. "Then tell me what's up."

"Nothing," I lied again. "I swear."

Grant tapped his foot. "I'm not letting you go back in there until you tell me."

I rolled my eyes. "Then you're going to be waiting here a while."

He shrugged. "I don't have a date waiting for me. I've got all night."

I groaned. He had me there. I couldn't let Nadine think I ditched her.

"What is this? Some sort of blackmail?" I asked.

Grant pursed his lips. "It's a threat for sure."

"Come on, Grant," I complained. "Is this for real?"

"You're hiding something," he accused. "Am I going to have to save you from yourself?"

"No," I promised. "I have it handled."

He sighed and dropped his arms. "Then let me help."

I shook my head. "I don't think you're going to want to help on this one."

Grant frowned. "That's what friends do, Lucas."

I pressed my lips together. They were officially sealed. If I said any more, he'd know what I was up to.

But I didn't have to say any more. Apparently, my silence was enough.

Grant's eyes widened. "That's the night of the Reaper Moon, isn't it? You're going to do it."

"Yes," I snapped. "And you're not going to talk me out of it."

Grant gaped at me. "You're talking about the Abyss. If you give up your powers, you'll be condemned by the Goddess forever. You'll never be able to enter Alora."

I shrugged like it wasn't a big deal, but to be honest, the thought of going to hell scared me.

But not as much as being with Nadine for the rest of my life thrilled me.

Not to mention getting rid of all these thoughts—ditching the responsibility of the Reaper's Apprentice. Carrying these thoughts around was too much. I'd risk the Abyss if it meant I didn't have to carry around these secrets anymore.

"You said I had to make a decision," I reminded him. "I decided."

"Well, you're deciding wrong!" Grant exploded.

A few people at the ballroom entrance looked our way. I grabbed Grant by the shoulder and dragged him further down the hall, where we couldn't be heard.

"In all fairness, this isn't your decision to make," I snapped at him. "As soon as I figure out how to do the ritual, I'm doing this. All I need is to find the grave of some guy named Caesar Peppertrine—where there's supposed to be scroll waiting for me."

Grant raked his fingers through his hair. "Are you shitting me, Lucas? You're doing this all for... what? A girl."

His words were like a slap to the face.

"Nadine's not just *any* girl," I growled. "She's *the* girl."

"Then shouldn't you want to spend the rest of eternity with her?" he argued. "You're trading your soul to... to get laid!"

Was he fucking kidding me?

"That's not what this is about," I argued. "I hate my gift, and you know that. This is my one chance to get rid of it."

"So that's the real reason?" he mocked, crossing his arms. "You're not just upset about this sex curse?"

"It's not a *sex curse*," I shot back, fuming.

"It sure sounds like your dick's making the decisions right now," Grant snapped.

A couple walked by just then and shot us an odd look.

My teeth gritted as I exploded on Grant. "This curse isn't about my dick! It's the whole fucking package! As long as I'm the Reaper's Apprentice, I don't get to be in a relationship. I never get married; I never have kids. Nadine deserves all that."

Grant looked disgusted with me. "That's noble and all, but you're talking about eternity. Our lives here are just a blip on the map."

"Then what are we doing here?" I countered. "Our lives matter, Grant. I'm going to make mine count. Nadine actually wants to be with me. She deserves the fucking world. So yeah, I'd gladly trade my soul to give her that. You wouldn't know what that feels like because the girl you're pining for doesn't want you back!"

Grant's jaw dropped. He stood there for a moment in total silence. To be honest, I was pretty pissed at him. I didn't care.

Finally, he found his voice again. "Fine," he snapped, opening his arms wide. "You want to do this, be my guest. Just don't expect me to supply the sledgehammer when you're fucking up this asshole's grave marker."

I rolled my eyes. "Very mature."

Grant started to walk away, but he paused and turned back to me. He got up in my face and pointed a finger at me. "You know what? I hope the mausoleum *is* haunted! Maybe the spirits will make you think twice about stealing that scroll."

With that, Grant stormed off. I paced back and forth, raking my fingers through my hair. What the fuck just happened?

I ran the conversation back in my mind, wondering where everything turned to shit. Then something Grant said hit me.

The mausoleum.

He *knew* where Caesar Peppertrine's grave was. And he had no idea he'd just helped me find it.

It must've been three in the morning before Nadine and I finally left the dance. I walked her back to her room, since she looked exhausted. I wanted to make sure she got back all right.

When I made it back to my room, Grant still wasn't back yet. He was probably off somewhere being pissed at me for what I said. I changed back into my street clothes and left campus. It didn't matter how late it was; I wasn't going to sleep anyway until I found that scroll.

I had an eerie sense of déjà vu as I broke into the cemetery using my magic. I formed an orb in my hand and used it to light my path. I must've passed a thousand headstones before I reached the trees at the back of the property. Snow coated the ground, and it was really chilly out, but I barely noticed. My heart was pounding so hard at the thought of being so close.

I entered the trees and pushed through the brush until I came upon the abandoned mausoleum where I'd had my Evoking Ceremony. I climbed over broken bricks and stepped inside. Nothing had changed since the last time I'd been here, except there was a light dusting of snow covering the ground.

I glanced around at the grave markers, though there were few that were still in-tact. My eyes fell upon one that read *Caesar Peppertrine*.

"I'll be damned," I whispered as I approached. Grant must've noticed the name the night of my Evoking Ceremony.

I knelt beside the marker and ran my fingers over the engraved letters. Something about the name seemed… off. According to coven records, this grave shouldn't even be here. In fact, there were no Peppertrines listed *anywhere* within the coven records. So where had this guy come from?

"Who are you, and what are you doing with a Reaper's Apprentice scroll?" I said under my breath.

That's when it hit me. As my eyes roamed over the letters, my brain started to notice a pattern. I quickly conjured one of my notebooks and scribbled his name down on the paper, then started crossing off letters. When I finished, it became very clear.

Caesar Peppertrine wasn't a man at all.

It was an anagram for *Reaper's Apprentice*.

This grave marker was nothing more than a message. A message for *me*.

Heart pounding, I got to my feet.

Well, there's only one way to find out what that message is.

I conjured the sledgehammer I'd brought along and started smashing it into the stone. I expected the stone to resist, but it cracked on the first swing. I put all my strength behind the hammer and swung as hard as I could.

Smash!

The stone gave way just a little more.

Smash, smash, smash!

With every swing, a little more of the marker crumbled away. Even though it was cold out, I started to sweat.

Smash!

I swung again.

Finally, I broke through. My heart lurched, and I stepped back and set my hammer aside. I stared into an open hole in the wall, trying to catch my breath.

There was no casket inside like there should have been—just utter darkness.

I stepped forward and knelt down next to the opening. An orb formed in my hand lighting the cavity in the wall. Utter relief flooded through me when my light touched an ancient scroll sitting in the center. It looked as if it'd gone untouched for years.

"It's here…" I whispered.

I reached into the cavity and pulled out the scroll. It felt really old and fragile. My pulse quickened as I unrolled the scroll, but my stomach dropped the further I read.

I was naïve to think this was going to be simple.

I'd be lucky if I managed to pull this off at all.

nadine
TWENTY

I couldn't believe my Evoking Ceremony had arrived so quickly. I shook as I thought of what the night would bring. After tonight, I would either be welcomed into the coven, or banished. I would cement my life here with Grammy, Lucas, and my friends, or I would be forced to leave.

Part of me worried that Chloe had won—that she'd sabotaged enough of my lessons that I wasn't prepared enough.

I forcefully pushed the thought from my mind. She hadn't won yet. I couldn't start getting down on myself before I even began.

"Where's Lucas?" I demanded of Grant. "Why isn't he here yet?"

I sat in Grammy's living room, with Isa purring softly on my lap. The coffee table had been removed, and in its place were five candles set in a circle on the floor. I was surrounded by three of the people I loved most in the world—Grammy, Talia, and Grant.

But the one person I really wanted to be here wasn't. I was really worried about him, because I didn't think he'd bail on me. I brought his number up on my phone again, but before I could call him, Grant reached out and took my hand.

"It's not going to help," he said with a frown.

"We should check on him," I insisted.

"Yeah, it's really weird he's not here yet," Talia agreed.

"There's no time," Grammy argued. "The witching hour is approaching. This is Nadine's one chance to contact Mother Miriam. We must go through with the ceremony, no matter what."

"What about Chloe?" I asked, my guts twisting.

Grammy cocked an eyebrow. "What about her?"

"She sabotaged all my training lessons," I pointed out. "I wouldn't put it past her to sabotage this as well."

Grammy shook her head. "She can't touch you tonight, Nadine."

"What do you mean?" I asked.

"Mother Miriam protects you on the night of your ceremony, so you can go through with it in peace," Grammy explained. "That's why Chloe tried to hurt you during your training—because she knew she couldn't get to you tonight."

I dropped my gaze and muttered, "Well, she might've had the right idea."

I wasn't ready for this.

"Don't say that," Grammy demanded. "You must not let Chloe get to you, especially tonight."

She was right. I had to go into this with a clear head.

"Maybe I need more of that calming tea," I suggested.

I set Isa aside and started to get up, but Grammy stood at the same time. "Let me get it for you, Nadine."

She was coddling me again, which was unnecessary. I'd napped most of the day so I'd have enough energy for tonight. I could get my own tea.

She started for the kitchen, but I didn't sit back down. I followed behind her. Grant and Talia immediately started whispering, and I didn't miss the look of concern in their eyes before I left the room. It was almost like one of them knew something was up.

Grammy poured me a cup of tea. When she turned, she looked surprised to see me there. "Here you go."

She handed me the cup, and I began sipping on it. Neither of us moved from where we stood.

"How's that feel?" Grammy asked.

I didn't feel any change, to be honest. "Getting better," I said, mostly because I wanted it to be true.

Grammy sighed. "Whatever happens tonight, Nadine, you will complete your Evoking Ceremony."

I furrowed my brow. What was she getting at? "I know."

She tilted her head to the side. "Then why are you letting yourself get so nervous about it?"

"Um... because it's nerve-racking?"

Grammy reached out and placed a hand on my shoulder. "Tonight is a special night. You only get one chance at this. Embrace it."

A lump formed in my throat, and even the tea didn't help wash it down. "Grammy, I don't know how," I admitted.

"I'll show you," she said kindly. She reached out for my tea and set it on the counter beside her, then she wrapped her arms around me. I melted into the hug. "See? Embraced."

I chuckled lightly under my breath, but I didn't move to pull away. Her hug was so comforting, and it instantly helped wash away some of my worry. "What do you think is going to happen?"

"I don't know," she said quietly. "It's different for everyone."

I finally drew away, but as soon as I did, a knot in my chest tightened. "I know. How do you think Mother Miriam will test me?"

Grammy's features softened. "Well, Nadine... you're very curious. Why don't we wait and find out?"

I frowned, but a smile twitched at the corners of my lips. "Grammy, that's not helpful."

She smiled back. "The truth is, there is no magic formula, Nadine. Sometimes, people who seem to be the best among us end up banished, and others are accepted. It's not the actions you let others see that makes you a part of the Miriamic family. It's the intention that's in your heart."

The knot in my chest eased ever so slightly. I'd said something similar to Lucas at the abandoned house in the woods. He'd acted like such a jerk to me when all he wanted to do was protect me. Were my own intentions enough to get me into the coven?

"Headmistress Verla seems to think Mother Miriam will try to address my grief," I told Grammy. "I don't know if I'm ready for that."

Grammy's gaze dropped, like she was really contemplating what I said. Finally, she sighed. "Nadine, do you think Mother Miriam only accepts perfect souls into her family?"

I hesitated. Of course not. There were people like Ryan and Gwen who'd already gotten their powers. Obviously Mother Miriam chose them for a purpose.

"No," I admitted.

"She will not banish you for the grief that's in your heart," Grammy promised. "She's there to *help* you with that."

I swallowed. "How did you get over Grampy's death?"

Grammy took a few breaths before answering. "That's not something you get over."

"Oh," I said flatly. That wasn't at all the answer I expected.

Grammy reached out and guided my chin upward to look her in the eye. "It's something you *accept*, but not forget."

"I don't understand," I admitted.

"Death is not an end for us, Nadine," Grammy reminded me.

"I know," I said. "We go on to live in Alora."

She shook her head, like that wasn't what she meant. "Your parents live on in your heart. Every hug, every kiss, every moment they supported you—it filled your heart with love, Nadine. And every action you've had from the moment they died has been a chance to spread that love they showed you. Your parents left you with a gift. You must not wrap it up and try to give it back. You must open it and let your love pour out to the world."

I got so choked up I could hardly get the words out. "Thank you, Grammy."

She smiled. "Anytime. The witching hour is almost here. Shall we get started?"

"But what about Lucas?" I asked. "He's coming. He promised me he'd be here."

Grammy frowned. "I'm afraid we'll have to start without him."

I couldn't do that. Lucas would make it. He'd be at my side while I went through my trials. He had to be.

I narrowed my eyes at Grammy. "Is this one of my tests? To see what I'd do without him?"

Grammy threw her head back and laughed. "This is not a test, Nadine. This is real."

"Well, how am I supposed to know that?" I asked.

"You can't," she admitted. "But here's what you need to remember…"

Grammy got a really serious look on her face. "Don't live your life like it's a test, Nadine. Live your *test* like it's your life."

Grammy started back toward the living room, but I just stood there, contemplating what she said. It took me repeating it several times in my mind to realize what she meant.

This test wasn't about doing the right things to get into the coven. It was about showing Mother Miriam who I was on a deeply spiritual level. All I could do was strive to make her proud.

"Nadine?" Grammy called from the living room.

"Coming," I called back.

I took another sip of calming tea, before leaving it on the counter and returning to the living room. I was disappointed to see that Lucas still wasn't there.

Grant must've noticed my unease, because he quickly stood and grabbed my shoulders. He looked me straight in the eye and said, "It's going to be okay, Nadine. Focus on the ceremony."

I searched his eyes. "You know something, don't you?"

Grant pressed his lips together. "I know that if Lucas can't make it, he has a good reason."

"Or something bad happened to him," I pointed out.

"Worry about your ceremony," he insisted, "then we'll worry about Lucas."

I sighed. I didn't have any other choice, did I?

Grant stepped aside, and Talia stood to pull me into a hug. "You're going to do great, Nadine," she encouraged. "You've got this."

I squeezed her back. "Thanks, Tal. I'm really glad you're here."

She smiled brightly. "I wouldn't miss it for the world."

At my feet, Isa purred and rubbed herself against my leg. I bent to pick her up, then pressed my nose into her fur.

"I'll be all right," I whispered to her. "I'm ready, Mom."

Deep down, I didn't feel like it was true, but I couldn't back out now.

"It's time, Nadine," Grammy said.

I handed Isa to Talia, then stepped into the middle of the room. The candles weren't even lit yet, but I swore I could feel a heightened sense of energy inside the circle. I lay on my back on the carpet and closed my eyes. No sooner had I laid my head down did I hear the sound of Grammy's clock striking midnight from the hall.

"The witching hour has arrived," Grammy said in a grave tone. "We can begin."

I heard the sound of Grant striking a lighter, but I kept my eyes closed. My whole body quaked in anticipation. Isa meowed from Talia's lap, but I shut out all external stimuli and focused on keeping my body relaxed.

Grammy began to recite an incantation. *"The clock has struck the witching hour. It's time to wake this witch's power."*

A shiver traveled down my spine. Grammy spoke in a voice I'd never heard her use before. It was so full of finite clarity. At first, it was strange, but her voice began to soothe me the longer she spoke.

"We call our goddess down to earth. To bear witness to this new rebirth," she continued. *"A series of tests she shall partake. And join the coven before day breaks."*

I felt my body begin to rise from the floor, and then—

Darkness enveloped me. I didn't know where I was or how I'd gotten there. I lay on a warm, hard surface. When I tried to move, I went nowhere. I was paralyzed.

"Hello?" I called, my voice wavering. "Is anyone there?"

As I spoke, I realized the weight of a blindfold around my eyes. I started to struggle even more, and I found that I could move my feet, but my arms were bound to my sides. I began to panic.

"Help!" I cried. "Somebody help me!"

A million questions raced through my head all at once. Where was I? What had happened to me? Who had done this?

The sound of echoing voices met my ears. Three girls giggled in unison, and a knot in my stomach twisted so tight I could swear the ropes around my arms tightened as well.

The Lucky Three.

"Chloe!?" I demanded. "Let me go! This isn't funny anymore."

I heard the sound of footsteps approach. They were soft, as if she walked on the carpet.

"Oh, Nadine," Chloe scoffed. "But it *is* funny."

"Chloe!" I screamed as I listened to the sound of her footsteps retreat. "What did you do to me? Let me go!"

She chuckled again. "I didn't do this to you, Nadine. *You* did this."

Suddenly, I stopped struggling. I tried flipping back through my memory to figure out how I'd gotten here, but I couldn't remember. Though I had every reason to believe Chloe had done this to me—given her track record and complete and utter disdain for me—I had no proof. I couldn't say with certainty that she was wrong, either. But how could I tie myself up and blindfold myself?

I wracked my brain, trying to come up with an answer. What bothered me more than being tied up was that I couldn't recall the events leading up to it.

"Hello?" I cried. "Can anyone hear me?"

Chloe cleared her throat. I gave a start—as I hadn't realized she was still there.

"No one's coming to your rescue," Chloe said.

"You could help," I bit at her.

"Why would I do that when you can just untie yourself?" she asked.

I scoffed. "Untie myself? How am I supposed to do that?"

"I don't know," Chloe said, like she didn't care one way or another. "Get creative."

It was in that moment that I realized I didn't have a single idea. I'd been here for several minutes already, and all I could do was question how I got here. I needed to look for the solution. Once this blindfold was off, maybe then I'd find my answer.

I began to struggle more, but the more I struggled, the tighter the rope held on me. My whole body ached, and I thought the circulation in my arms might stop dead at any moment.

"I can't move," I sobbed. "Please, somebody help."

Chloe chuckled. "Stop playing the victim, Nadine."

My whole body stilled. I'd heard Chloe say that before. It was in Introduction to Tarot, when I drew the Eight of Swords card.

"Her feet are unbound. She has the ability to go in any direction she chooses. The woman in this card is bound by her own doing. All she has to do is stop playing the victim," I recalled Chloe saying.

And that's the moment it became clear to me. My feet *were* unbound. I could go anywhere I wanted.

"I. Am. Not. A. Victim," I stated with every ounce of conviction I had in me.

Once I realized that, the solution was simple. I pulled my knees to my chest and rolled over. All I had to do was get to my knees, then stand on my own two feet. The moment I stood upright, the rope that bound me loosened and fell away. I reached up and tugged the blindfold off my eyes.

I glanced around to see that I was standing in the middle of the Main Foyer. It was really dark, except for a small fire that burned in the fireplace. I looked around for Chloe, but she was gone.

Before I could take another breath, an earth-shattering scream tore through the night. I whirled around and saw that the front doors of the school were wide open. A strong breeze swept past the doors, blowing leaves all over the place. I could barely see anything through the darkness of the night.

I ran outside in the direction of the scream, but I stopped dead when the scene came into view.

I stared up at a tall oak tree. Chloe's feet hovered just above the ground, kicking frantically and searching for a foothold to save herself. Her hands grasped her neck, where a tight noose had been slung around her throat.

For a moment, a pang of satisfaction hit me. I didn't dare admit to anyone, but watching Chloe hang like that made me feel a bit... triumphant.

I knew immediately it was the devil on my shoulder talking, because I felt the sudden urge to punch that sucker out. I didn't care what Chloe had done to me in the past. She didn't deserve a death like this.

Chloe clawed at the rope around her neck. "Help!" she gasped, though I could barely understand the word.

Screw the dark side of me that enjoyed watching her hang. The real Nadine found it sickening.

I raced over to her and got beneath her, my heart racing in panic. I lifted her onto my shoulders, though it took every ounce of my strength to keep my aching knees from collapsing beneath me.

"I've got you, Chloe!" I called up to her.

Her center of gravity shifted from side to side. I assumed it was because she was struggling to get the noose off her neck.

"Are you okay?" I asked, since I couldn't see anything. "Can you—?"

Chloe's weight gave way, and we both went tumbling to the ground, screaming. She pressed her hand to her bruised neck and gasped for breath.

"W-why did you save me, Nadine?" she managed to choke out.

Our eyes connected, and for the first time since I met her, I saw a look of pure gratitude in her eyes.

"I had to," I told her.

"No, you didn't," she argued, like she couldn't understand me at all. "I've been awful to you. You should've enjoyed watching me hang."

I shook my head. "Not like that. We're part of the same coven. We help each other, even if you're my enemy."

Chloe opened her mouth to say something, but she never got the chance. The sound of a woman's maniacal laughter reached us. I gave a start, and both of us looked in the direction of the voice. It was coming from somewhere inside the school.

"What's going—?" I started to ask, but I cut off when I looked back to Chloe.

Except she wasn't there. I glanced around frantically, wondering where she'd disappeared to. She couldn't have run off that fast.

My heart started pounding fiercely as the laughter continued. Something about it sounded chillingly familiar, though I couldn't put my finger on it. Curiously, I rose to my feet and stepped toward the school. I followed the sound of laughter through the dark hallways of Miriam Mansion. Light flickered from the sconces on the wall, and the hair on the back of my neck stood.

"Hello?" I called down the hall.

No answer came.

Cautiously, I stepped forward until I came to the double door entrance to the school's ballroom. I peeked inside to see a woman sitting cross-legged on the ground, her back to me. She wore all leather and had long brown hair flowing down her back. The room was almost entirely black, except for the light coming from five candles set around the girl. Each candle was connected by a line of salt that created a pentagram. Another salt line surrounded that, enclosing everything into a circle. The woman looked like she was doing something with her hands, but I couldn't see what it was.

"Are you going to stand there all day, Nadine?" she asked bluntly.

I hesitated. How'd she know I was here?

"I know you're out there," she called without turning her head. "Come see what I've made for you... for *us*."

Her voice sounded so familiar. Something told me I knew this woman, but I couldn't place her.

Carefully, I took a step forward. "Do I know you?"

She chuckled, like the question amused her. "Oh, Nadine. Don't you recognize yourself?"

Finally, she turned toward me, and my heart lurched into my throat. My own face stared back at me.

But at the same time, it wasn't *me*. She was more like my evil twin—with dark makeup around the eyes and a smirk of unadulterated pride I'd never be caught dead wearing. I had more self-respect and humility than that.

"What the hell is going on?" I demanded. This had to be another one of Chloe's illusions.

She gave me a sinister smile. "Come look."

I hesitated, but I was too curious to see what she was holding. I stepped around her and saw that she had a small stuffed doll in her hand.

A voodoo doll.

My knees shook as I stared down at the doll. The coven didn't practice voodoo. Hell, I didn't even know if voodoo was *real*.

Two other dolls lay on the ground in front of my doppelganger. Each was faceless and dressed only in black fabric, except they each had a different color of yarn sewn onto their heads. The one on the left depicted a girl with short brown hair. The one on the right had long white-blonde hair. And the one she held had black hair.

"Are those the Lucky Three?" I asked, but my voice came out scratchy and dry.

She smirked proudly. "What do you think of them? I made them for you."

"Well, I don't want them," I snapped. No good could come of this.

She tilted her head. "I thought this was what we *both* wanted, Nadine. *Revenge.*"

"I just want them to stop tormenting me," I stated. "I don't want to hurt anyone."

She smirked. "But it'd be *so* fun."

She set the Chloe doll between the other two and picked up a dagger that lay at her side. I hadn't seen it before. She brought the blade to the pad of her thumb and pressed until thick red liquid began to drip down the blade.

"For Gwen, I was thinking poison." She pressed her bloody finger to the Gwen doll's mouth and wiped the blood across it. "Killed by her own Cast."

She set the blade aside and picked up a pin. "For Camille, a heart attack."

She stabbed the pin into the brunette doll's heart. Her eyes widened in pleasure. "It should go undetected. Finally, for Chloe, I've saved something special."

An evil smile spread across her face as she picked up a red string of yarn and began to tie it around the Chloe doll's neck. She held the doll up by the string and smiled down at it with crazy eyes.

"Hanging," she chuckled.

My guts twisted, and I took a step back. "This isn't what I want."

"No?" My doppelganger tilted her head. "But it's the only way to save ourselves, Nadine."

"I'm no killer," I spat.

"But you are," she reminded me. "You let Rocky outside without his leash."

Rocky had been our neighbor's dog. They'd hired me as a kid to dog sit when they went on vacation. One day, I accidentally left the door open, and he slipped outside and was hit by a car. It'd been so long ago that I barely remembered Rocky.

"How do you know about that?" I demanded.

Her lips curled into a sneer. "Because *I'm* the one who left the door open! That dog was a fucking nightmare! We did it on purpose."

"No!" I cried. "It was an accident."

She got to her feet, and I backed up another step. She stared at me under dark lashes as she stepped out of the pentagram. "Tell yourself that all you want, Nadine. It doesn't change what you did."

"I'm not like you!" I cried. "Killing people isn't how I handle things. It'll only get me banished from the coven."

"But you *want* to," she accused, taking another step toward me. "You *want* to get rid of Chloe. We both do."

"Not like this," I insisted. "There has to be another way."

"There *is* no other way!" she exploded. "Let me out to play, and I'll do my worst."

I took another step back. "No."

I hadn't realized how far we'd moved across the ballroom until my heel touched the wall. I ended up pressed flat against it.

Dark Nadine got so close to me that I could feel her breath on my face. "Admit it, Nadine. You're *weak*."

"That's not true," I said.

"It is," she growled. "You're so weak even your body's rejected you. It hates you so much it's trying to kill itself just to get rid of you."

"You're wrong," I stated. My hands shook and curled into fists. Who the hell did this bitch think she was?

She narrowed her eyes. "How do you expect Lucas to love you if he has to take care of you all the time? You're *weak*, Nadine. Let me take over, and I'll make you strong."

Strong. I'd do anything to be strong again—to live a life where the constant joint pain and debilitating fatigue didn't drag me down.

She reached out and lifted a strand of my hair. She spoke in a smooth, alluring voice. "You're a burden, Nadine. I can change that."

The more she spoke, the more I became entranced by her.

"And our parents?" she continued. "I can make you forget all about them."

I swallowed. "I don't want to forget about them."

"Yes, you do," she snapped, her eyes suddenly darkening again. "You want to forget the pain! You want to get rid of the memories and forget they ever existed! You don't want them anymore! Why do you think they died? They couldn't stand being your parents. They left because of *you*, and you want to leave, too. Don't you, Nadine!?"

"No!" I screamed. "I want them back! But I can't! So I'll live with the pain, because it reminds me that they were there to begin with. I loved my parents, and they loved me. I. Am. Not. Their. *Burden!*"

I shoved Dark Nadine as hard as I could, and she went stumbling backward. I made a run for it, but I barely made it a few steps before something hard slammed into my back.

The air left my lungs, and I went tumbling down. I threw my hands outward to catch myself, but I saw stars. I quickly rolled over to see her coming at me. Dark black magic crackled in her hands.

She threw her head back and laughed as she approached. "Try to run, Nadine. I will *always* be with you. You and I are one in the same."

"We're not!" I screamed.

She came close enough to touch. I kicked my heel into her gut. She stumbled back, and the magic in her hand fizzled out. She gasped for breath as I scrambled to my feet and ran across the ballroom.

But Dark Nadine moved faster than me. She sprinted in front of me and cut me off on my way to the door. With a single wave of her hand, the doors swung shut, slamming so hard against the frame it shook the room.

"There's nowhere to go," she mocked. "You can't outrun me."

My gaze darted to my left, toward the pentagram circle. The dagger still lay in the middle of it next to the dolls.

"I can try," I spat.

I jumped away from her and sprinted toward the dagger. I heard her footsteps behind me and dove for the knife. She caught me by the legs and landed on top of me. I was barely six inches from the dagger and couldn't reach it.

"Get off me!" I cried, struggling out of her hold.

I managed to yank one of my feet away, then slammed it into her face. Her head snapped backward, but she grabbed tighter to my leg, until I thought it was going to bruise. Her eyebrows slammed together, and her nostrils flared.

"Bitch!" she snarled.

She pulled me backward with all her strength, dragging me through the salt circle and away from the dagger. I clawed at the carpet, but it was no use. There was nothing to hang on to.

Then my hands found something—one of the candles. I curled my fingers around it and swung my arm toward her. I shoved the flame up into her face. Her shrill cry echoed off the walls of the empty ballroom.

As her hands came up to cradle her burnt skin, I took my chance and dove for the dagger again. My fingers touched the cool handle. I was just about to use it against her when a black heel stomped on my wrist.

"Gah!" I screamed as my bones crushed into the ground. I heard a horrifying *snap*, and pain shot up through my arm and down to my fingertips. And still, she didn't let up.

Dark Nadine bent down, her chest heaving with shallow breaths. A burn red with blisters marred the side of her face. "I told you that you can't outrun me."

She reached over and picked up the Chloe doll, then ripped the hair from its head. I tried to struggle away from her, but each time I moved, an ungodly pain rippled up and down my arm. She placed all her weight on my wrist and laughed maniacally.

"See this doll, Nadine?" She held it in front of my face and smiled proudly. "That's *you*."

She held the doll over one of the candle flames.

"No!" I cried, horror twisting deep within my gut. My toes started to heat, like there was a fire burning beneath me. "Don't!"

She chuckled, as if she enjoyed the sound of me begging. "Too late."

She lowered the doll, and the fabric caught fire. A shriek so loud it could wake the dead erupted out of my lungs. Though there was no fire at my feet, I felt the flames licking up my legs. It was like my skin was searing straight off my bones.

Dark Nadine rose to her feet and took a step back. I wished I could say it was a relief when she released my wrist, but I barely felt the pain of broken bones anymore. All I could feel was the fire consuming my body. I writhed on the ground, as if I could outrun the red-hot pain consuming me. It was as if a million heated pins had pricked my body all at once. My vision started to blur as the invisible flames licked up my body and began to sear the skin from my face.

"I was right about you, Nadine!" Dark Nadine mocked. "You're weak! Always have been. You can push me down. You can try to control me. But I will *always* win."

I gritted my teeth. Pushing past the fiery inferno, I lifted my arm. "Not this time."

I took the dagger in my good hand and forced all of the strength I had through my arm. I lifted the dagger and plunged it downward... straight into Dark Nadine's foot. It sliced through her boot, into her skin, and out the bottom of her sole. It embedded so far that the blade didn't even show—it had stuck straight into the floor and rooted her in place.

She screamed a chilling cry and dropped the doll. It fell within my reach, and I grabbed it, stomping out the fire with my hand. Relief washed over me as the pain stopped spreading. I could've sworn if I looked at myself, skin would be hanging off my bones, but I pushed past it and scrambled to my feet. I backed up several paces.

Dark Nadine tried to come for me, but the dagger kept her in place. She screamed in frustration and pain as her foot tugged on the dagger, ripping into more flesh as she tried to come after me.

"I'm not weak!" I yelled at her.

I whirled around and ran for the doors.

"You're nothing without me!" she shouted from behind me.

I flung the doors open and stumbled out into the hall. As quickly as I could, I closed them again. My heart slammed against my rib cage as I glanced around. My eyes landed on a branched candlestick sitting on a table in a nearby alcove. I ran for it and snatched it up, then returned to the doors, where I shoved the candlestick through the handles to trap my darkness inside.

She screamed again, louder this time. Her shriek echoed down the hall, and I guessed she must've ripped the dagger from her foot.

"I'll come for you, Nadine!" she raged through the closed doors. "I'll come for you!"

My heart raced as I whirled around and sprinted away from the ballroom and the evil woman locked inside. I glanced back to make sure she wasn't coming for me, but the hall was empty. As I turned forward again, my toes caught on the hallway rug, and I stumbled forward. I threw my hands out to catch myself...

But instead of landing on carpet, my hands sank into the earth. One second I was running away from my darkness in the halls of Miriam Mansion, and the next, I was lying in the grass, the daylit sky overcast above me.

Dark Nadine completely fell from my mind, as if the moment with her had never happened. The pain of a broken wrist vanished. My attention became completely wrapped in the scene before me.

The first thing I saw was a stone—a smooth, polished stone. I lifted my head to see that it was a gravestone, one of many throughout the graveyard. My eyes drifted over the two names etched into the grave marker.

Nathan Evers. Faith Evers. Loving father and mother.

Somehow, I'd ended up at my parents' graves.

LUCAS
TWENTY-ONE

The setting sun lit the sky in a bright orange hue as I approached the gates to the cemetery. The Reaper Moon would rise soon, and then I could begin the ritual. I was excited by the idea—to get rid of the voices, to ditch the curse. It would be a dream come true.

And yet another part of me feared I might not have what it takes. This was my one and only shot, and if I couldn't summon the reapers by night's end, Nadine and I would always be kept at arm's length.

I steeled my shaking nerves and stepped into the cemetery. I trudged through the snow until I came upon a tall statue at the center of the cemetery. It depicted a reaper at least ten feet tall, clothed in a dark, flowing robe. Where his face should be was nothing but a dark hole. His fingers were only bone. One of his hands reached outward, as if inviting me closer. The other held on to a tall scythe.

At the base of the statue was a name carved into the stone. *Edgar Nowak. Reaper's Apprentice.*

He'd been the one before me.

Beneath his name were his birth and death dates. The rumors were true. The poor bastard had lived to be over a hundred. I didn't want to do the math to figure out how many thoughts he'd carried with him to the afterlife.

I took a deep breath as the sun dipped below the horizon. "Almost time…"

I knelt at the head of Edgar's grave and waited. As I waited, I tried to calm myself, to push all doubt out of my mind.

I can do this, I told myself. *I will summon a reaper.*

I didn't know if I meant it, or if it was just wishful thinking.

Darkness continued to fall over the night, until finally the last few rays of sunshine disappeared. Above me, the full moon shone. I liked to think the clear skies were a beacon of hope, as if opening me to Alora above. But somehow, the stars seemed dimmer than they should, like there was a darkness cutting me off.

My gaze darted around the cemetery. The shadows of the gravestones were ominous. A shiver ran down my spine, but I knew my unease was all in my head. Tonight, there were no zombies that were going to jump out of the bushes. Tonight, the only enemy was myself. Though I was on my knees, my legs shook beneath me.

I summoned the scroll I'd stolen from the mausoleum and read over it again for the hundredth time. It shook in my hands. I had to get this right. It had to be perfect.

Give up your blood to a reaper's grave. Shed doubt, fear not, stand firm and brave. Face the thoughts that you've neglected. Accept and let go of all you've collected.

The interpretation was clear. I had to revisit all the thoughts that'd been given to me as the Reaper's Apprentice before handing them over.

This was going to be a long fucking night.

"Well," I sighed to myself. "It's now or never."

I summoned a knife and pressed the blade to my opposite palm. I winced as the knife sliced into my skin, but after the initial shock, I didn't mind. The stinging pain was sort of welcome.

Blood dripped out of my palm and stained the snow below me. I reached out and smeared the blood across the base of the reaper's statue, straight across his name. Then I shoved my hand into the snow to numb the sting. It eased it, until my hand became so numb I couldn't feel anything at all.

With my good hand, I summoned the leather-bound spell book where I recorded all the thoughts I'd heard. I didn't have to open it to recall the exact wording of the first thought I'd ever collected.

"*I made a mistake,*" I repeated Eric's last thought, though it barely came out. I'd never spoken his words out loud, and I knew why. The words cut deep into my chest, tearing deep, sharp holes in my heart. I hated that he'd died with this last thought on his mind. He should've died happy.

But it was done now. He'd moved on. It was time I did, too.

I swallowed the lump in my throat and continued. "*I don't want to die.*"

Tears pricked at my eyes. Fuck, I was only on the first one. How was I going to make it through hundreds?

The hard part is over, I told myself. *You've faced Eric's last thought. You can handle a handful of strangers' thoughts. Let's get this over with.*

I opened my book and began to read the words I'd recorded. Some thoughts were easier than others. Some didn't make sense at all. Every now and then, there were those that tore me to the very core. I couldn't help but wonder if these people had crossed over all right. Had I done right by holding on to their thoughts so they could make it to the other side? Or had their dark past behind those thoughts held them back?

"*I hope she got what she deserved,*" I read.

The thoughts just kept going like that—revenge, regret, anger, sadness.

I'm not ready to go.

I should've stopped him from hurting her.

I'll get my revenge in the afterlife.

I tried not to think about how much time had passed. The coldness of the night brushed across the back of my neck and seeped through my jacket. My fingers became numb, and I curled my arms around myself to try to keep warm. It barely helped though. I shivered, and my breath turned to fog each time I breathed out.

I'll miss you.

I hope you keep your promise.

Is it playtime?

Page after page, it kept going. Hundreds of thoughts piling up. The more I read, the harder it became. It was like each thought I read added another ten-pound weight to my chest.

Finally, after an eternity of reviewing each and every thought in my journal, I reached the last page I'd filled in. I read out the last thought and breathed a sigh of relief. I'd done it. I reached the end!

I glanced around the cemetery, waiting for the reapers to appear, but I saw nothing.

"Hello?" I called out to the darkness. "Anyone there? I did like the spell said. I faced the thoughts! Where are you!?"

No answer came.

My guts sank. Frantically, I flipped back to the front of the journal and read the thoughts over again.

Still nothing.

"This is what I'm supposed to do, isn't it?" I shouted. I was a fool if I actually thought someone was going to answer.

"I must be doing something wrong," I muttered to myself. I turned back to the scroll and unrolled it all the way. I flipped it over once, then twice, to make sure I hadn't missed anything. "This is it… that's all I have to do. What am I doing wrong?"

That was my only explanation. I wasn't doing it right.

Face the thoughts…

Maybe reading them wasn't enough. Maybe it was about *feeling* them.

I took a deep breath and started at the beginning again for the third time. This time, I didn't just read the words on the page. I took a breath for each thought and allowed the messages to seep deep into my soul. I gave each of them the time and consideration they deserved.

By the time I was done, hours must've passed. Fuck, if this took me much longer, I was going to miss Nadine's ceremony.

I held my breath and looked around the cemetery again. I could swear I felt a presence there, but it must've been wishful thinking, because there were no reapers. No… anything.

"Come on…" I gritted my teeth and muttered under my breath. I reread the ritual again, and something jumped out at me.

"I have to let the thoughts go," I realized.

It was so simple.

I conjured a lighter and held the edge of my journal above the flame. The pages caught fire instantly, and the flames eagerly ate away at the paper. Once the flames came too close to my hands, I tossed the journal to the snow in front of me. I watched as the flames ate away at the words on the page. Pieces of burnt paper broke off and drifted away in the wind, tumbling across the surface of the snow.

I wish I could say I felt something, but I didn't. It should've been a relief, but the weight on my chest only became heavier.

Nothing within the cemetery changed. It was just shadows, just cold, just emptiness!

"Fuck the reapers!" I shouted to the skies. Frustration curled its evil arms around me, squeezing me so tight it was the only thing I could feel. My eyebrows knitted tightly together, and my lips pressed into a firm line.

Was this some kind of sick joke they were playing on me? Was this fucking ritual even real?

I got to my feet. "Where are you!?" I screamed, my voice echoing over the cemetery. "You're supposed to be here! I summoned you! Come and take this curse from me!"

I reacted without thinking about it. I curled my hand into a fist and slammed my knuckles against the base of the reaper statue. A sharp, unbearable pain shot across my hand.

"Fuuuck!" I cried. I sucked air through my teeth and tried to catch my breath. "Is this what you wanted? Is this what the ritual needs? Blood and broken bones? Have them. I don't fucking care anymore."

Heavy, shallow breaths racked my chest, and my arms quaked. I held my hand tight to my abdomen, but the pain started to ease quickly. I flexed my hand to find it wasn't broken. Hurt like a son of a bitch, though.

"Face the thoughts you've neglected. Accept and let go of all you've collected," I spat. "You want to know the truth of what I've neglected? You want to know!?"

I was raging like a mad man at nothing but a lifeless statue, but I didn't care.

"I fucking *hate* myself!" I screamed. "Is that what you want to hear? Let's see… what have I collected? Shame! Guilt! Depression! You need a longer list? *I* didn't see the signs that my brother was at the edge of his life. *I* could have stopped it if I just took a second to understand what he was going through—to listen to his cries for help. I should've known when he didn't show up for my ceremony that something was wrong. I should've helped!"

I barely took a breath before I continued raging. "And guess what else? I made a promise to the highest power of all the coven, and I broke it. I said I'd accept whatever Mother Miriam had in store, but I rejected it the night she gave it to me. I *should* feel guilty about that. You want to know why I'm doing this? Because I'm damned to the Abyss anyway! Might as well try to enjoy the one chance at happiness I'll ever get. But I don't deserve even that! We all know it. That's why you're not here, isn't it? I'm not worthy! You think so, too; otherwise you'd be here!"

I plopped my ass on the ground and leaned my back against the base of the reaper statue. I pulled my knees to my chest and buried my face in my arms. My whole body shook, but I'd be damned if it didn't feel good to get all that out in the open.

"Lucas."

My gaze snapped upward at the sound of the voice. The blood drained from my face when I saw a cloaked man standing there. He was as solid as I was. I could hardly believe what I was seeing.

It worked!?

My heart began to pitter-patter against my rib cage. "You're a reaper?" I questioned cautiously. Part of me worried this might be some sort of joke. My eyes roamed over him, looking for signs of death, but his hands were covered in dark gloves, and I couldn't see his face.

"I'm Edgar Nowak, the newest member of the Reaper Order," he stated. "I take it you've summoned me to remove your power."

"So it's true?" I asked hopefully. "You can do it?"

"Yes," he said, but a grave warning lurked in his tone. "You understand what this means, don't you?"

"I know," I said desperately. "Refusing Mother Miriam's gift will damn me to the Abyss. But I want it gone."

"The Abyss is not a damnation to be taken lightly. Abandoning Mother Miriam is a sin that can never be forgiven," he warned. "You will burn for all eternity. The flesh will be seared from your bones, regrown, and burned off again and again. Splinters will be shoved beneath your fingernails, before each fingernail is ripped from your nail bed one by one. Red-hot rods will be shoved into your eyes. You will not feel a moment of relief, young reaper. You will be faced with a nightmare most cannot even begin to imagine. You will suffer in ways men have never suffered before. Are you sure you want to do this?"

Nothing he said scared me. The real hell was never getting a chance to live a full life with Nadine.

I stood and planted my feet firmly beneath me. All the shaking that had rocked my body moments ago had vanished. I held my head high as I answered. "I'm sure. Tell me what to do."

nadine
TWENTY-TWO

My heart jumped into my throat, and I scurried backward until my back hit the gravestone behind me. My stomach felt as if a gaping hole were about to erupt open. I pulled my knees to my chest and curled myself into a ball. I buried my face into my knees, because I couldn't stand to look at my parents' graves.

I shouldn't be here, I thought. Why had I come? I knew I'd never be able to handle it—seeing their names on the headstone, knowing their bodies had been placed into the ground at that very spot.

Your parents are dead.

I didn't know where the voice had come from, but it must've been my own. It was a dark, cruel reminder of everything I'd been through after losing them. I wanted them back. I wanted them back more than anything. And I never would…

"Nadine," a woman's voice said.

I must've been hallucinating, because she sounded just like my mother. I lifted my gaze. I nearly dropped dead right then and there. Two figures stood above me, but it was like looking at ghosts.

"Nadine?" Dad asked, reaching out his hand.

Nothing about him had changed. He had brown hair, electric blue eyes, and a graying beard. Yet something felt… off.

Of course it does! He's dead! I reminded myself.

"It's okay, Nadine," Mom encouraged. Her voice sounded like a song. She was so pretty. Why hadn't I ever realized how pretty she was before?

My parents held their hands out to me, waiting for me to accept them.

"Is it really you?" I asked, my voice cracking.

Dad nodded. "It's us, baby girl."

Sobs began to rock my shoulders. I reached out and took each of their hands, and they helped me to my feet. I wrapped an arm around each of them, until the three of us were locked into an embrace. They felt so real—so solid. I didn't know how, but they were here with me. Hot, heavy tears streamed down my face, but the hole in my belly started to close. I felt like I could breathe for the first time in months.

"How are you here?" I asked. I wished I could keep them here forever. "This is impossible."

Mom drew away from me and tilted her head. "Impossible how, sweetheart?"

I sniffled and wiped the tears from my eyes. "You know."

Mom and Dad exchanged a shocked expression. They *didn't* know.

"We know what?" Dad asked. "What's going on?"

A weight settled on my chest. How could they pretend like they didn't know what happened? Tears fell down my cheeks. I wrapped my arms around myself because it was all I could do to hold myself together.

"You don't remember?" I asked.

Mom tilted her head to the side. "Remember what?"

"You're really going to make me say it, aren't you?" I sobbed.

"We don't understand," Dad insisted. "Tell us what's wrong, Nadine."

My bottom lip trembled. I wanted to tell them, but I couldn't get the words out. I just totally froze up.

Mom stepped forward and took my arm. I couldn't believe how warm and real she felt. All I wanted to do was wrap her in my arms again.

But I couldn't. Because no matter how much I wanted my parents with me, it couldn't happen. I didn't know how it was happening now, but it wasn't real.

"Let's go home," Mom suggested. "We'll get this all sorted out."

I jerked away from her, but my voice came out really small. "I can't go home with you."

"Of course you can," Dad said, like this was any old day. "We had plans to work on the car this afternoon."

"And you and I were going to make cookies," Mom reminded me.

My stomach dropped. I wanted to do all of that so badly. I'd love to drop everything and go home with them. But instead, I took a step back.

"I'm sorry, but I can't," I told them. "You don't belong here. I have to go back home to Octavia Falls."

Mom's brow furrowed. "You don't live in Octavia Falls, Nadine. You've never been there. Are you having an episode?"

"No, I'm not having an episode," I snapped. Why couldn't they see? How could I make them understand?

"Then tell us what's wrong," Dad demanded.

"You're *dead!*" I burst.

The world seemed to stop spinning. The entire cemetery went silent, though my voice continued to echo in the distance.

Dead. My parents were dead.

I'd said it aloud so many times before, but I never *felt* it like I did in that moment. They were truly, honestly, one-hundred-percent gone from this earth. And nothing I could do—no amount of praying, séances, necromancy, or potions—could bring them back.

Dad looked at me. His eyebrows knit together, creating deep lines of concern on his forehead. "What do you mean, baby girl? Your mother and I are fine."

"No, you're not!" I cried. "You died last summer. I planned your funeral. I watched your caskets be placed into the ground right—"

I cut off. As I gestured to their grave plot, I realized their names had been removed. There was nothing but smooth stone where their names had been carved.

"Nadine?" Mom asked, worry lacing her tone. "Are you okay?"

"No!" I cried, rounding the gravestone to inspect it from every angle. "No, I'm not okay. This is where I buried you. You're not real! You're ghosts!"

And that's when it truly hit me. This was it for us. The next time I'd meet them would be in Alora.

"You're ghosts," I repeated in a low whisper. As I said it—as I felt it deep down within my soul—the names on the gravestone began to appear again. Bits of stone sank inward in the shape of letters, until it showed my parents' names again.

Warmth spread throughout my heart when I realized what this meant. I'd been given a second chance to speak to them. I could say all the things I didn't get the chance to say!

"Nadine—" Mom started, but I cut her off.

"We might not have much time," I said quickly. "Please let me get this out before you leave."

I walked over to my father and pulled him into a tight hug. "Dad, I should have said thank you more. You supported me in *everything*. Do you remember when I was eight and snuck DVDs to my room to watch those homicide detective shows you and Mom thought I was too young for? You caught me one day, and I thought I would be grounded for life. But instead, you came into my room, sat next to me on the bed, and started watching with me. You didn't say a thing, just held me in your arms and kept watching."

Sobs bubbled up in my throat, but I continued. "When I was ten and told you I wanted to be a homicide detective, you didn't think that was too off-the-wall. You bought me my first *Clue* game for my birthday, and you played every Sunday since. You taught me more about cars than most girls will ever know, and you made me fight when I thought there was no fight left in me."

I drew away and wiped at my nose. Dad stared down at me with the softest, kindest expression. That was one of the things I missed most about him—the kindness.

"You taught me how to be good to other people," I told him. "And I'm never going to forget that."

Tears welled in my father's eyes. "I love you, baby girl."

"I love you, too."

Dad and I shared another embrace. I didn't want to pull away, but I had more to say to my mother.

I turned to her. "Mom, I wish I'd listened to you more. You are *so* wise. Especially about boys."

Mom chuckled, but she couldn't hide the tears. "I *do* have some experience in that area."

"I miss everything about you," I said. "The smell of your hair, and the way you'd dance when you were doing dishes. I miss coming home to the smell of freshly baked bread and cookies on the counter. Sometimes, I want to crawl into your bed like I did when I was a kid— because when I lost you, it was just one huge nightmare. But I know everything is going to be okay, because you taught me how to be independent in ways I didn't realize."

Mom pulled me into a hug before I was done telling her how much I missed her. I hugged her back so hard that it made my arms hurt.

Finally, we drew away from each other, and I looked to both of my parents. "You have both been wonderful to me. You had to put up with me when I acted out, and stood by me with unwavering faith when I was in and out of the hospital. You two have just been amazing. I couldn't have asked for better parents. I'm so lucky to be your daughter. And just because you're gone doesn't change that. You'll always be my parents, and you'll always be with me… right here."

I placed my finger to my heart, and Mom and Dad totally lost it. The three of us started sobbing together. But they were beautiful, wonderful tears. A huge weight lifted off my shoulders, and I felt so light I could float to the stars.

I wiped my eyes. "I have to admit. This is probably the hardest thing I've ever had to do—and that's saying a lot."

I took a deep, wavering breath. For a moment, I worried that the words wouldn't come out. And then they just… did. And it was the most freeing, beautiful moment of my life.

"Goodbye," I said.

Mom and Dad shared a smile. "Goodbye, Nadine. We love you."

Peace washed over me as my parents faded from view. I should've run after them. I should've sobbed and begged them to come back. But I didn't, because somehow, I was finally okay with letting go. It didn't mean I didn't love them. It didn't mean I didn't care that they were gone.

It just meant… everything was going to be okay.

"You've done well, my child."

I whirled around at the sound of an unfamiliar voice. The cemetery had transformed around me. Instead of being day, it had instantly transformed into night. I wasn't standing near the same plot as I was before. In fact, I wasn't even sure I was standing in the same cemetery. The air was cold, and snow covered the ground. The full moon glowed above us.

A woman stood several feet away from me, cloaked in a velvet hood. I tilted my head to try to get a better look, but the hood fell so far over her eyes that even the moonlight didn't touch her face.

"Excuse me?" I asked.

She reached up and lowered her hood. My heart stalled in my chest when I saw her. I'd seen those high cheekbones, full lips, and beautiful eyes before—in the painting that hung above the mantle at school. It was Mother Miriam.

I found myself rooted in place as I took her in. Positive energy radiated off of her in waves, and she seemed to glow slightly in the moonlight. The cool air around us warmed, and I truly felt like I was standing in the presence of a goddess.

"Mother Miriam?" I asked breathlessly, just to see if it was real.

She nodded lightly, then stretched out her hand. "Come with me, child."

I hesitated a moment. Was I worthy enough to take her hand?

I wanted to be. And she was offering. So I took it.

All the pain in my muscles and joints washed away. When I touched her, it was like taking the hand of someone I'd known forever. All my hesitation fell away, and I felt totally at ease in her presence.

"What's going on?" I asked as she led me through the cemetery.

Mother Miriam spoke slowly, like we were in no rush. "There's something you must see, Nadine."

Though I'd never heard her speak my name before, something about it seemed so familiar. It was like I'd known her my whole life.

We passed by gravestone after gravestone, until I spotted a shadowed figure in the distance. He sat in the snow, his back pressed against the base of a tall reaper statue. His knees were curled to his chest, and he shook in the cold.

"Who is that?" I asked Mother Miriam.

"I think you already know," she said kindly.

My pulse quickened as we came closer. I began to make out the shape of his shoulders.

"Lucas?" I realized, before raising my voice so he could hear me. "Lucas!?"

He didn't respond.

"He can't hear you," Mother Miriam told me.

I looked to her as we came to a stop several gravestones away from him. "What is this, then? A vision?"

"Of sorts," she said with a nod.

"Is it real?" I asked.

She gestured around us. "Everything you see here is happening, Nadine."

She was like the Ghost of Christmas Present.

I furrowed my brow. "What are we here for? What's Lucas doing?"

Mother Miriam's breath wavered, and my stomach dropped. Though she hadn't answered, I sensed that it was something dark and dangerous. I gazed closer at Lucas, and that was when I noticed the pool of blood in the snow beneath him.

"Lucas is summoning the reapers," Mother Miriam said solemnly.

"Summoning them… why?"

"Because their power can take his away," she explained.

"He's not going to be the Reaper's Apprentice anymore?" I asked.

I wanted to be excited about it. It meant the Reaper's Shadow curse couldn't touch us. We could be together.

But I sensed something deeper in the way Mother Miriam spoke. She obviously cared very deeply for Lucas.

"If he completes the ritual, he will be washed of his gift," she explained.

"Why's that bad, though?" I asked. "He doesn't want it."

She turned her gaze back to Lucas. She got this faraway look in her eyes—like she was recalling a special memory. "Because he made a promise to me, Nadine. When I offered him his power, he agreed to accept whatever gift I gave him. And now he is refusing that gift. He went back on his word. I can't accept him into Alora if he does that."

The air in the cemetery seemed heavy as a rock. I couldn't breathe it in. I just stood there, completely frozen and trying to wrap my head around her meaning.

"You're saying if he goes through with this, he'll be cast out of the coven?" I asked. "He'll be damned to the Abyss?"

Deep, unsettling worry twisted around my heart. Mother Miriam nodded solemnly.

"Then we have to stop him!" I insisted. "Lucas!"

Mother Miriam placed a gentle hand on my shoulder to stop me. "I'm afraid we can't stop it, my child."

A thick lump rose to my throat. "You don't have to send him to the Abyss. I-I thought the coven granted second chances."

"I *am* offering him a second chance… through you."

"W-what do you mean?" I asked, but my throat closed so tightly around my words that it barely came out.

"Lucas is doing this for you," she stated. "As long as you're around, he will give up his gift to be with you. Once his magic is gone, he's condemned himself, and his soul can't enter into Alora… not without a trade."

My knees grew weak as I realized what she was offering. "I can trade my soul for his?"

"These last few months, your souls have intertwined," she explained. "I can take one, but not the other."

"We'll be apart," I realized with sinking clarity. "No matter what, we'll never be together."

"Yes," Mother Miriam confirmed. "There are only two outcomes, Nadine. If he gives up his gift for you and you live out your lives together, he'll end up in the Abyss. Or you can trade your soul for his. I will take away his gift, and he will live his life without the voices, but I will accept him into Alora with open arms. Yet you will be condemned to the Abyss in his place, forever."

The fact that those were our only two options burned me to the very core. All I wanted was to be with Lucas.

But we couldn't have that.

If I did this for him, it meant giving up my life and my magic. It meant leaving Grammy behind and never seeing my parents again in Alora. I'd be banished to hell. I'd have to give up absolutely *everything* for him.

"Time is running out, Nadine," Mother Miriam stated. "Will you give up your soul to take Lucas's place?"

Lucas

TWENTY-THREE

"Take my hand."

That's all the reaper said. I couldn't believe it was that simple.

"That's it?" I asked.

Edgar's robes billowed in the wind. "That's all. I will take the thoughts you've collected with me. You will be relieved of your duties. Your power will be taken from you, and you will be sentenced to the Abyss."

I took a step forward and reached for him. My hand just barely grazed his before he jerked away. His head snapped to the side, like he heard a noise in the distance that had caught his full attention.

I looked in the same direction, but I didn't see anything. "What is it?"

Edgar turned to me, though I still couldn't see his features beneath his hood. "I'm sorry. I must go. I have a soul to collect."

"Wait!" I cried, but he was already backing away from me.

The reaper whirled around. His body glided above the snow and left no prints. I started sprinting after him, but he moved so fast I couldn't keep up.

"Come back!" I screamed.

The air seemed to suck out of the cemetery the faster I ran. It was only moments before he had vanished from sight.

Panic swept through me. Had I lost my chance? Had he totally abandoned me? Was he coming back?

I slowed and stared after the reaper where he'd disappeared into the trees. A feeling of hopelessness settled over me. I'd missed my chance, hadn't I?

"I thought we had an agreement!" I shouted.

A leaf tumbled in the wind and caught on my shoe. I kicked it off, but the wind swirled around me, sending the leaf back into my leg. I tried twice more to shake it off, but each time, it came back. Frustrated, I bent to grab it, ready to tear the freaking thing to shreds—

But it wasn't a leaf at all. I took it in my hands and lifted it. My stomach dropped out of my abdomen. It was a tarot card, the *Death* card—perhaps the very one I'd thrown into the wind on Halloween. Somehow, it'd come back for me.

It had to be a message. My eyes went wide. I glanced around, like I expected to see someone standing there willing to explain.

"Eric?" I called out to the darkness. "Is this yours? What does it mean? What do you want me to do?"

The voice that answered was the last one I'd ever expected to hear.

"I did it to save you, Lucas. I will always love you."

I whirled around, expecting *her* to be standing there, but there was nothing but tombstones beside me.

I'd heard her last thought.

The heart-wrenching realization hit me like the weight of a thousand stunning spells. For a moment, I couldn't move, couldn't think. All I could do was stand there as my entire world stopped spinning.

Not my Nadine.

The second her name passed through my mind, I snapped back to attention. *No one* was taking my Nadine from me!

I started sprinting. I'd never run so hard and fast in my life. The only time that came close was the night of my Evoking Ceremony when I'd rushed home to Eric. It struck me how frightening similar this was. Hurdling over grave stones and sprinting out of the cemetery was a sick form of déjà vu.

I just hoped this time I wasn't too late…

My sliced palm stung as I pumped my arms. My legs protested as I pushed them harder than I'd ever pushed before. My chest burned with the need for air. But none of that mattered right now, because the thought of losing Nadine hurt more than any other pain I could imagine. I'd gladly welcome a thousand eternities of flesh-burning torture for her.

Houses blurred past me as I ran through town. I sprinted down her grandmother's street— and stopped in my tracks when I caught sight of the scene in Helena's living room. I had a mere split second to take it in.

Through the window, I saw Helena, Grant, and Talia seated around Nadine's body. She hovered in the air as if she was lying on an invisible table. Everyone watched on silently, oblivious to the fact that there was a fucking *reaper* standing over her! He stood beside her like he was hungry for his next meal.

The only one who seemed to notice something was amiss was Isa. She stood on Talia's lap, her hair on end, hissing.

The reaper reached out for Nadine and scooped her up. Suddenly, I was seeing double. Nadine's body remained hovered in the air, but a transparent figure identical to her lay cradled in Edgar's arms. I didn't know how I was seeing her soul, but I sensed it was because the reaper had touched both of us tonight.

"Stop!" I screamed.

But no one heard me. Nadine's body dropped out of the air, slamming to the ground beneath her. All at once, Helena, Grant, and Talia leapt to their feet. Sheer and utter worry marred each of their faces.

I barely had a chance to process it before the reaper was on the move. He stepped through the wall and onto the porch like a ghost. My precious Nadine's spirit lay lifeless in his arms.

"You can't do this!" I demanded.

He looked toward me, but he must've decided I meant nothing, because he turned away and started toward the trees at the side of Helena's house. I didn't know how far I'd already run, but I knew one thing for certain: I'd race to the ends of the earth for Nadine.

I followed the reaper as fast as my legs could carry me. I trampled over dead plants in Helena's garden and crunched down snow as I raced over the lawn. I followed the reaper into the forest, where the snow was minimal and a clear dirt path paved the way.

"Come back!" I shouted.

Edgar didn't slow, but somehow, I was catching up.

I heard him mumble something under his breath, and then something frightening happened. I could barely believe my eyes.

In the middle of the forest, a portal opened. One moment, all I saw was shadows of trees in the moonlight. The next, a wide, swirling archway grew from nothing. It expanded until it was large enough to step through. At first, all I saw was blackness around the edges. Then came the distorted image of the horrifying landscape beyond. In the flickering of the portal, I could make out fires that went for miles across a dark, desolate landscape.

The Abyss.

He was taking my Nadine to the Abyss! This was either a sick joke, or a horrible mistake. I had to stop this!

I didn't know if it was sheer willpower or by the fate of the Goddess, but I finally reached him. My hands shot upward, and my fingers wrapped around the dark fabric of his hood.

I yanked downward, and his hood fell away. He whirled around and thrust his arm outward. A blast of red magic shot out of his hand and slammed into my chest. I went flying backward but hardly made it three feet before slamming into a tree. I slumped to the ground, gasping for air.

It barely fazed me, because what I saw next shook me to my very core. The reaper turned, and I caught sight of his face—his true, deadly form. The legends of the reapers were true. They walked the earth as a shadow of death. His face was nothing but a skull. There were no muscles, no skin—just pure white bone. His eyes were completely hollow—a deep, dark black that seemed to suck my life energy just looking at them. He was the very embodiment of death.

"You can't save her," he snarled. "She's *my* assignment."

His jaw moved, but he had no lips to form his words. Somehow, they came out sounding clear.

"I'd be damned if I didn't try," I growled.

I raised my hands, and purple magic shot out of my palms. A stunning spell slammed into his chest. His feet swept out from under him, and he went tumbling backward. Nadine's spirit fell from his arms, and she hovered in the air limply.

I jumped to my feet. At the same time, the reaper sliced his hand through the air, and I felt a sharp pain on my face, as if an invisible dagger had cut my skin open. The warmth of blood trickled down my face, but I didn't stop to assess the damage. I hurdled over the reaper and reached out for Nadine. I nearly touched her soul, but I didn't get there before a cold hand grasped my ankle.

"Let me go!" I shouted.

I drew my foot back and slammed my heel into his face. A satisfying *crunch* met my ears, though it didn't seem to slow him down. He squeezed my ankle tighter and yanked me backward, dragging me through the snowy dirt. My hands clawed desperately outward, but I couldn't find a handhold.

"You can't stop this," he warned, before drawing his arm back and slamming it into my cheek to slow me down.

Ever been punched by a reaper? Turns out, their swing is fucking *strong*. He had the punch of a freaking heavyweight champion, yet he didn't have a single muscle on him. Pain radiated across my face, and a blast of red flashed across my vision. The world spun around me. I was half surprised he hadn't knocked me out right then and there.

The reaper left my side to go to Nadine, but there was no way I was giving up now. I jumped to my feet, though it felt as if the earth was rocking beneath me. I forced my eyes open, but only my right one followed my command. The left was completely swollen shut.

He reached out for Nadine. I couldn't stand the excruciating thought of death touching her. Not today.

I totally and one-hundred percent lost it.

"You're gonna have to try harder than that," I growled.

Fury swept through me, and I threw all of my anger into my magic. A sizzling ball of magic swelled in my palms. As the magic came too much to hold on to, it shot from my hands and went spinning toward the reaper. My battle magic landed at his feet and exploded, sending him blasting away from the portal and my Nadine.

It disoriented him enough that I gained the upper hand. I threw all my weight at him and grabbed him by the back of the robes. I gritted my teeth and screamed as I spun him around. I intended to use his moment to smash his head into a tree, but I guess I forgot we were fighting on different planes. My magic worked against him, but other weapons didn't. His skull went through the damn tree. I swung him to the ground and threw myself between him and Nadine.

"You can't have her!" I cried.

He pushed himself up, like he hadn't felt a thing. How the hell was I supposed to fight a freaking *skeleton*? He didn't feel pain. He couldn't be choked or bruised or knocked out. Plus, he was fucking strong. I was at a total disadvantage, but I'd still do anything to defeat him.

Just as I was about to speak another incantation, the reaper reacted. Red magic slammed into my ribs. It was so heavy and strong that it knocked me on my ass in no time flat. My vision blurred. I tried to push myself up, but a sharp, searing pain like a sword in my side shot through my ribs.

Broken.

"Shit," I growled beneath my breath as I pushed myself to my feet.

Edgar yanked his glove from his hand and thrust his palm out in my direction. Suddenly, excruciating pain assaulted me from all angles. Every muscle in my body seemed to twist at his command, and my skin felt like it was separating from my body. The pain permeated deep into my bones.

It was battle magic like I'd never seen before.

"Gah!" I screamed as blinding pain overtook every nerve ending.

My knees buckled beneath me, and my back arched as I cried out. I tried to move my hands, to force defensive magic out through them, but they stayed curled into fists at my side. My scream echoed through the forest, laced with the chilling overtone of torture.

"You don't know what you're doing, Lucas," Edgar warned. His boney fingers twisted, like he intended to crush me by sheer will. "She's dead. You can't bring her back. It's against the rules."

"Screw the rules!" I spat. It took all my energy to push past his magic and speak. "Let her stay."

"It doesn't work that way," he insisted. "I need a soul."

"Then take me instead!" I begged through gritted teeth. "I've got a soul. I haven't been damned yet."

"And you won't be," he stated coolly.

The pain intensified as the realization hit me. "She did this for me. Didn't she?"

At this point, the reaper's spell might as well have been a mere tickle across my skin. The excruciating pain was nothing compared to the heartbreak that crushed my very soul in that moment. Nadine gave herself up for me, and that's something I would eternally blame myself for. I would never forgive myself for being the reason she was damned.

Edgar nodded. "She gave up her life to stop the ritual. She gave her soul in place of yours. She is sentenced to the Abyss. I must take her and leave now."

Pure fury rocked my body. I'd do anything to save Nadine from damnation. She was the sun my earth moved around, the gravity that kept me grounded, and the force that kept my world from spinning off its axis. She was the air in my lungs and the magic that flowed through me. I loved her like the night sky loved the stars. She was mine, and I was hers. Forever.

"You're not going *anywhere* with her," I growled.

"Only a reaper has control over the life and death of a soul!" he yelled furiously. "If you restore this soul, you accept your reaper magic, and it will bind itself to you once and for all. After that, I can't take that magic away. If you wish to continue with our agreement from earlier, you must let me take her soul to the Abyss."

So I either give up my gift, or save her life?

The answer was simple. Her soul was staying.

Magic like I'd never felt before ignited deep within my belly. I gathered it tight within my chest and pushed outward with all my might. Darkness clouded my vision as the magic passed through me. Then…

Boom!

My magic exploded, whipping through me like a tidal wave. By some miracle, my magic overpowered his, counteracting his spell. The pain washed away, and I fell onto my hands and knees, gasping. One hand clutched my broken ribs as I waited for my vision to return.

When it finally did, I looked up to see an empty forest. I immediately whirled around toward the portal to see Edgar hovering over Nadine's spirit. He bent beside her and touched her.

Not today, motherfucker!

I scrambled to my feet and ran forward. My foot swung outward like I was about to kick the field goal of the century. I kicked as hard as I possibly could, and my foot connected perfectly with his skull.

Edgar's vertebrae snapped, and his head flew off his skeleton. It went soaring forward straight toward the portal, his scream echoing through the forest. And then…

Silence.

His head was gone, lost to the Abyss. I could hardly believe what I'd done.

But we weren't finished. Edgar's body whirled toward me. It was kind of creepy to see a headless guy moving through the forest. His arms raised, and his shoulders heaved as a spell formed in his hands.

On instinct, I threw my hands upward. I had no intention, no clue what I was doing. All I knew in that split second was I had to protect myself.

A battle orb shot out of Edgar's hands…

But it never reached me. The magic bounced off an invisible shield and ricocheted back at him.

The battle orb slammed into his chest and exploded. His headless body blasted backward. His heel teetered on the edge of the portal, and his arms desperately reached out for something to grab on to—but they found nothing. He went tumbling backward, and the portal swallowed him up.

The reaper was gone.

I gasped, utterly shocked by what just happened. Did I just send the reaper to the Abyss? Had I just used *shield* magic?

I barely had time to question it before the ground began to shake. The earth rumbled around me, and I could barely stay on my feet.

Oh, fuck.

Lightning crackled out of the portal, and thunder boomed through the forest. My stomach twisted into tight knots. I didn't know how much more I could handle. For a second, I thought I was going to have to deal with this damn reaper clawing his way out of the depths of hell.

Then suddenly, the portal slammed closed.

Utter silence settled over the forest, and the image of the trees became clear again. It was as if the portal had never been there in the first place.

Relief washed over me. It was over. I'd defeated the reaper. I'd saved Nadine.

I rushed over to her floating spirit, my heart racing. I reached out and touched the side of her face. My fingers didn't move through her spirit like I expected them to. They touched solid skin—I guess for the same reason I could see her.

I scooped Nadine in my arms. She was as light as air, but she was warm and solid in my arms. I could feel the life inside of her as I cradled her to my chest.

I pressed my lips to her forehead and wept as I lifted her. "Hang on, Nad. We're going to get you home."

Carrying Nadine's spirit back to the house was like stepping out of a fire a hero. I had a sliced hand, at least two broken ribs, and one hell of a black eye. But most of all, I had Nadine.

I didn't take my eyes off her as I carried her limp spirit back to the house. I could've sworn we moved in slow motion. The relief I felt made my heart sing. Nadine was so perfect it was enough to stop time just looking at her.

I climbed the stairs to Helena's front door. It was only when I opened it and heard the panicked shouts inside that time seemed to speed up again.

"She's still not breathing!" Grant cried.

"I'm working as fast as I can!" Helena shouted back.

"How could this happen?" Talia sobbed.

I stepped into the living room, my heart hammering like a bass drum. I hoped I wasn't too late. Grant knelt over Nadine's lifeless body, performing CPR, while Helena clutched a mortar and pestle—an ancient herb crusher. She ground herbs into powder that I assumed were meant to heal. Talia was pacing back and forth, stroking Isa's fur.

I cleared my throat, and all eyes turned toward me. Grant's eyes grew as wide as saucers, and Talia's jaw dropped. Helena was so shocked she dropped the mortar and pestle, and the herbs spilled all over the carpet.

It was clear as day—they could see Nadine's spirit in my arms. It must've had something to do with me touching her after I'd touched a reaper.

I felt death in the room. It was like a dark hole that nothing could enter and escape. It was just... nothing. And that feeling centered over Nadine's heart. Her body wasn't going to last much longer without her soul in it.

"W-wha… How did you…?" Helena stuttered.

"I'll explain later," I said. My knees quaked as I rushed to Nadine's side.

Grant scurried out of the way.

"*What* am I seeing?" Talia asked breathlessly.

"I could ask the same thing," Grant said in astonishment.

"You saved her?" Helena breathed.

I swallowed. "Not yet."

I pressed my lips to the side of Nadine's spirit cheek, then positioned her spirit over her body. A single tear ran down my face and dripped onto her chest.

"I love you, Nad," I whispered. "Now and forever."

I gently lay her spirit back into her body… and waited…

nadine
TWENTY-FOUR

Lucas Taylor couldn't see the light within himself, but I could. Though dark cloud after dark cloud had swept into his life to block out the light, it continued to burn bright. The world would be a much better place with him in it. *My* world had been made better with him in it.

He didn't deserve an eternity in the Abyss. He deserved to be with his brother and the rest of the coven in Alora, where he would be happy.

I loved him. I loved him more than the grass beneath my feet, more than the stars in the sky, more than the very air I breathed. My heart beat for him, and my world moved with him. I didn't know how much I truly cared about him until that moment. I was unconditionally and undeniably in love with him.

I turned my gaze from the nearby gravestones to look at Mother Miriam. "I'll do it."

The scary part was, giving myself up for Lucas didn't scare me at all.

A proud smile crossed Mother Miriam's face. "Then it is time."

She formed a ball of magic in her hand. It was the whitest, most pure magic I'd ever seen. A mesmerizing rainbow of colors swirled within it. She threw the magic upward, and it exploded into a million tiny little stars above my head that rained down on me like snowflakes. The flakes of magic touched my skin, and my whole body started to glow.

"Wait, this is it?" I asked. "I don't get to say goodbye?"

"You have one chance," she reminded me.

Right. Lucas would hear my last thought.

"I did it to save you, Lucas. I will always love you," I thought.

The glow of my skin brightened, until a blinding white light completely consumed my vision. Even as I squeezed my eyes shut, it was all I could see.

The last thing I heard was Mother Miriam's soft, calming voice. "Just remember, Nadine. You are not defined by what happens to you. You are defined by how you react to it."

The light became too bright to bear, and then... nothing.

729

I saw nothing. I felt nothing. There was no light or dark, no pain or comfort, no sense of time or space. Just… nothing. I could've been stuck in this state for eternity and never known it.

Then something happened. A voice called out to me like a beacon in the darkness.

"Nad!"

It took me a few moments to make sense of my name. I couldn't remember what had happened to me or why I was here. Then it all came rushing back.

The Abyss!

My heart lurched to life in my chest. My eyes shot open, and I sprang upward. A high-pitched scream pierced my ears. It took me a moment to realize it was my own voice.

"Nad, it's okay!" Lucas's soothing voice came from beside me.

As my vision focused, I saw his beautiful face in front of me. His left eye was black and swollen, but he was incredibly beautiful nonetheless.

"Lucas, you're hurt," I said breathlessly.

He shrugged. "Totally worth it."

My heart raced, and my whole body quivered. Frantically, I glanced around the room to see I was sitting on the floor in Grammy's living room. The candles that had surrounded me had been burnt out. Grammy, Grant, and Talia all looked down on me with wide-eyed expressions of disbelief. Isa jumped out of Talia's arms and purred as she rubbed against my side.

It was all a test, I realized. *None of it was real.*

I placed my hand to my thumping heart as it started to slow. "Oh my God. I thought I died!"

Lucas's features fell. "Nad… you did."

"W-what?" I nearly choked on the word.

Grammy knelt beside me and swept me into her arms. She kissed me on the cheek over and over, and squeezed me so tight I thought she might suffocate me. Tears streamed down her face.

"I'm so relieved that you're okay, Nadine," she whispered. "I thought I'd lost you."

As Grammy drew away, Grant and Talia threw themselves at me. They both curled me into a tight group hug.

"We're not losing you, you hear me?" Grant said pointedly.

Talia swatted me on the shoulder. "Don't *ever* do that to us again."

"Do what?" I asked. "What happened?"

Everyone stared back at me like they didn't know where to start. The only one who looked remotely understanding was Lucas. I looked to him for an explanation.

Grammy cleared her throat. "We'll just… give you two a moment."

Grant and Talia nodded in agreement, and the three of them quietly left the room.

Tears welled in Lucas's eyes as he stared at me like I was the only girl in the world. He took my face in his hands. They were so warm and comforting.

"You gave up yourself for me," he reminded me. "I had to fight a reaper to get you back."

My breath caught in my chest. Lucas had saved my life?

His eyes sparkled in a mix of pain and relief. "Why'd you do it?"

I placed my hand over my mouth to keep the sobs from spilling out. My eyes searched his. After taking a moment to breathe, I dropped my shaking hand.

"Don't you get it, Lucas?" I asked. "I love you."

"I know," he said. "But—"

"No," I cut him off. "I really, *really* love you… Enough to go to hell in your place."

Tears spilled over Lucas's lids, and my heart swelled. "I love you, too, Nad."

Lucas swept me into his arms, and we kissed with a passion like never before. His love poured into me like pure, warm water filling my soul, and mine poured back.

The roller coaster ride we'd been on slowed in that moment, reaching its peak at the highest point of the track. My heart lifted in anticipation of the freefall.

I parted my lips, and Lucas kissed me deeper. I went spiraling downward, my stomach flipping in my abdomen.

But it didn't feel like we were on a roller coaster anymore. The safety harness had given way, and I'd grown wings. I was safe here with Lucas, because he was my wings, and he would never let me fall.

Lucas drew away from me and pressed his forehead to mine. Desperation filled his tone. "I never want to lose you, Nad."

Tears rolled down my cheeks, and a sob broke in my chest. "I never want to lose you, either."

"I don't care about the Reaper's Shadow curse," Lucas said. "I'll tip-toe around it for eternity just to be with you every single day for the rest of my life. I'll do everything in my power to protect you from it."

I wiped the tears from my cheeks. "I agree. If we can't be together fully, we'll take what we can get."

Lucas's gaze dropped, and his fingers ran over my arm. His voice trembled when he spoke. "Can I have *you*?"

My heart pitter-pattered against my rib cage. "For as long as I can have you," I whispered.

His lips pressed to mine again, and we shared an amazing kiss that made my head spin.

I didn't know how long we were kissing, but we were interrupted by the sound of Grant clearing his throat. We drew away and glanced toward the entrance to the living room. Grant stood there holding an ice pack.

He smiled. "You two make me want to cry."

"Spying on us?" Lucas teased.

Grant chuckled. "No. Just wondering when we can come back in to see what Cast Nadine got."

I gasped. I'd nearly forgotten!

"Yes!" I cried. "Everyone, come in."

My heart pounded fiercely as I got to my feet. Grant handed Lucas the ice pack, and he pressed it to his swollen eye. Grammy and Talia entered the room behind him.

"Well, come on," Grant encouraged, nudging me in the side. "What's your Cast?"

"I don't know. Let's see."

I stretched my arms out and flipped them over, looking for any signs of a tattoo. Grammy started spinning me around so we could look at all angles. Isa rubbed against my leg, so I took off my shoes and checked my feet, then lifted my pants legs to check my calves.

"Lucas might have to strip you down to check," Grant teased.

Talia and Grammy both chuckled under their breath, but Lucas looked thoroughly unamused. He'd taken a seat on the couch and clutched his side with one arm, holding the ice pack to his eye with the other. I noticed for the first time he was sweating a little.

"Will you be okay?" I asked him.

"Fine," he said, waving a hand. "Find your mark."

I lifted the hem of my shirt to check my stomach, and that's when I saw it. Just above the inside of my hip lay a black mark.

My whole body gave a start. I gasped and dropped my shirt.

"What is it?" Talia asked, looking intrigued.

"Come on, Nadine. Let us see," Grammy begged.

Grant eyed me curiously. "Judging by your reaction, I'm guessing Mortana."

I felt the blood drain from my face. I swallowed and lifted my shirt to show everyone the tattoo. "I got… Curse Breaker."

I let out a wavered breath. All eyes locked on the crescent-moon tattoo on my hip.

Grammy's hand shook as she brought it to her mouth. I wasn't sure if she was terrified or delighted by the news. Talia and Grant shared a confused expression. Lucas had gone totally still. The room was dead silent.

"How is this possible?" I asked. "The Curse Breakers died out."

Grammy finally found her voice. "Yes, but Mother Miriam can assign you *any* Cast she sees fit. She must think you're worthy, Nadine."

I gaped at her. "Me?"

"What'd she test you on?" Grant asked eagerly.

"I started out tied up in the Main Foyer," I told them, before diving into an explanation of everything else that happened.

By the time I was finished, we'd all taken a seat. I was sitting beside Lucas, and Isa was purring in my lap.

Grammy leaned forward in her chair and rested her elbow on her knee. "It sounds like you impressed Mother Miriam. You showed her you're willing to take responsibility."

"And you showed some serious integrity saving Chloe's life," Talia added.

"Also strength and resilience," Grant said.

"Yeah," Talia agreed. "You fought the darkness inside of you instead of giving into it. You didn't let it consume you, which means you'll be able to fight the darkness of any curse you break."

My heart melted.

"And then you traded your soul for mine," Lucas pointed out. "You're pure of heart, Nad. Something no other witch has been since the Curse Breakers died out."

"Wow," I said breathlessly. "I guess I didn't realize what I was capable of."

"You're capable of anything you put your mind to," Grammy encouraged. "But you must be careful, Nadine."

I tilted my head to the side. "What do you mean?"

"You're the only Curse Breaker of your generation," she pointed out. "Just as your grandfather was. People will try to use you."

I shot a nervous glance around the room. "To break curses?"

Grammy dropped her gaze and shook her head. "For much more than that, I'm afraid. Recall that when a member of each of the five Casts comes together, they can create elaborate spells."

"Like the space-bending spell that expands the school," I stated, remembering how she explained it to me on my first day at Miriam College.

She nodded. "I'll be honest, Nadine. If your grandfather were here, he'd tell you this is as much a curse as it is a blessing."

I looked to Lucas, then to my friends, as if expecting one of them to counter her claim. Everyone wore the same uncertain expression. I suddenly felt worry knot deep within my belly.

"So I pose a threat," I realized.

"Or people will threaten *you*," Lucas added, looking terrified for me. "They're going to want a piece of your magic."

My stomach dropped. How could I get this wonderful gift, only for it to put me in the line of fire? Octavia Falls was my home. I should be safe here, but I wasn't. I hadn't been since the moment I stepped foot in town. Something told me Chloe was just the least of my coming threats.

But I'd be damned if I didn't fight for my right to stay.

"Then I'll hide it," I stated, my mind made up.

Talia tilted her head to the side. "Hide your powers? How?"

"I don't know," I admitted. "We could tell people I didn't go through with the ceremony."

"But you need to stay in classes to learn how to control your magic," Grant pointed out.

I sighed. "True."

Lucas looked deeply contemplative, then his eyes lit up. "I know how to hide it."

"You do?" I asked.

He smirked. "You can pose as an Alchemist."

I frowned. "But I don't have Alchemy powers."

Grant's jaw dropped. "That could actually work."

"What?" I asked. "How can I possibly pull that off?"

"It's a good theory," Grammy agreed. "Curse Breakers' powers work by transferring magic from one place to another. You can use Alchemy crystals to brew potions."

"Alchemy crystals?" I asked.

"It's like this," Grammy explained. "I transfer my Alchemy magic into a crystal. You take that magic and transfer it into a potion."

"Couldn't anyone do that?" I asked.

She shook her head. "Only a member of each Cast can access the crystal magic of that cast. Alchemists can use Alchemy crystals, Seers use Seer crystals. But as Curse Breaker, you can move magic from one place to another."

"So I could use crystals to pose as any Cast?" I asked.

Grammy shook her head. "Not quite. It gives you no powers. A Seer crystal wouldn't allow you to see or hear spirits. You couldn't control a corpse with a necromancy crystal. Your power lies in the *transfer* of magic. And that's the beauty of Alchemy. Brewing potions is a simple transfer of Alchemy magic. We're actually not the only race who can do it."

"So... as long as I had Alchemy magic to draw from, I could fool everyone," I realized.

"It's our best shot," Talia said.

"It could be the only way to protect you," Lucas added.

"Then I'll do it," I said. "I'll let everyone believe I'm an Alchemist."

"What about your tattoo?" Talia questioned.

"I'll get a fake one," I decided. "I'll put it somewhere that's easily noticeable, so no one will question it."

"You'll have to practice your Curse Breaker powers in private," Lucas pointed out.

"I will," I agreed. "For as long as I can manage, I'll remain a secret."

"One of the coven's greatest secrets of all," Lucas whispered ominously.

I nodded, accepting my new title. "I'll be the coven's secret."

I had so much to process from that night that I didn't even know where to start. Since it was really late and everyone was tired, Grammy invited all of us to stay the night at her house. I was relieved, because I could hardly keep my eyes open anymore.

I stood from the couch and tugged on Lucas's arm. "Let's go to bed."

"In a minute," he argued.

I tugged him a little harder, and he winced. I immediately dropped his arm. "What's wrong?"

"Nothing," he said, but I heard the lie in his voice.

I gazed down at him sternly. "Don't lie to me. Let me see."

"I'll be fine, Nad," he said.

"If that's true, let me see it," I demanded. "No secrets, Lucas."

He sighed and stood. Everyone else was already moving out of the living room, but when he lifted his shirt, we all stopped dead. A huge purple bruise marred the side of his torso.

My stomach plummeted to my toes. "Why didn't you say something!?"

Lucas dropped his gaze. "I didn't want you to worry."

"You need help," I stated. "We're going to the hospital. No objections."

Lucas sighed. "Nad, come on. It's way too late for that."

"It's never too late to get you help," I replied.

"The doctors aren't going to do anything but tell me to rest," he argued. "Besides, you're too tired for an emergency room visit."

Yes and no. I was exhausted, but I wanted to be with him.

Grant quickly stepped in. "I'll take you, bro."

Lucas frowned.

"Lucas, you're going," I repeated. "You're not burdening anyone by getting medical treatment. Please accept that."

He sighed. "Okay. But you need to rest. I'll see you tomorrow."

I protested a while longer, but Lucas insisted he was only going to the ER if I went to bed. As long as he was getting medical attention, that was good enough for me. Talia went to the guest room upstairs, while I took the guest room next to the bathroom. My moving boxes were still piled in the corner. I found some pajamas in one of them and changed. I tossed my dirty clothes into one of the open boxes on the top, but they caught on the corner and knocked it over.

Isa meowed from where she lay on the bed.

Sighing, I bent to clean up the contents. As I reached for the last item that had spilled out, my breath caught. It was a small wooden box I hadn't opened since my parents died. I took a deep breath and reached out for it. When I held it, I was surprised to realize I no longer felt a deep black hole within my gut when I thought of them.

I took the box and crawled under the covers with it. The lamp beside my bed illuminated the soft curves of the box and the glossy finish. I reached up and lightly touched my silver star necklace.

Isa walked across the bed and curled up next to me.

I took a deep breath. "I'm not scared anymore, Mom."

I opened the box, and my heart warmed. A pile of envelopes sat inside, each one of them a different color from the last. My name had been scrawled on each one in my mother's smooth handwriting.

I swallowed and pulled the first envelope from the top. I flipped open the card to read the letter my parents had written me.

Happy eighteenth birthday, Nadine!

    This year has been crazy. Remember the escape room, when we almost lost because of your dad but you turned it around and got us out in the last minute? We'll never forget the trip we took to Washington D.C. this summer. We got lost for three hours looking for the Washington Monument. How's that even possible? Don't forget when your mom tried skiing on that spontaneous trip we took this winter. Miserable failure! We hope this year will bring many bright beginnings. Never stop enjoying the mystery in life.

    We love you, Nadine.

    - Mom and Dad

Tears welled in my eyes. The past year brought the worst of the worst endings.

I set the birthday card aside and pulled out the next one.

Happy seventeenth birthday, Nadine!

They all started out like that, each one sharing memories from the previous year and wishes for the year to come. It hurt that it was my birthday and I wouldn't be getting a card from them this year.

I finished reading through all the letters and was placing them back in the box when a knock came at my door. I cleared my throat. "Come in."

Grammy opened the door. "You're still up."

I nodded. "Just looking over some old keepsakes."

She eyed the box I held in my lap. "Are those your birthday letters?"

I nodded.

She held up a finger. "Give me a minute."

I furrowed my brow as Grammy left the room. She came back in a minute later holding a piece of paper in her hand. She crossed the room and sat at the edge of my bed.

"I found this while we were cleaning out the old house," she admitted. "I was saving it for your birthday. And since it's your birthday now…"

Grammy handed over the piece of paper, and I realized it was an envelope like all the others. My name was written across the front in my mother's handwriting.

I froze in place, unable to breathe. "Grammy, what is this?"

She shrugged. "I didn't read it. It's for you."

I swallowed and took the letter from her hand, then opened it. My quiet tears turned into full-on sobs as I began to read the letter.

Nadine,

We know we usually save these cards for your birthday, but we have so much to say. We know you're upset about the police academy. We know it's all you ever wanted. But there's a saying we want you to remember. You've heard us say it many times before. 'When one door closes, another one opens.' We know that's not what you want to hear right now, but you'll realize one day when all of this is over that it's true. Everything happens for a reason. We believe that bigger and better things are in store for you. All you have to do is look for the blessing and be willing to receive it.

We will always be here for you and love you no matter what.

-Mom and Dad

A beautiful swelling of joy grew in my heart. I didn't feel sad when I thought about them. I felt *joy*. I had eighteen wonderful years with them. I was the luckiest girl in the world to be their daughter. I couldn't ask for anything more than that.

It was true this year had been rough, but wonderful things had happened, too. My parents' death had led me to Octavia Falls, and I couldn't imagine being anywhere else.

I sniffled and closed the card, then added it to my box. "Thank you for saving that for me, Grammy."

"What's it say?" she asked curiously.

I smiled. "It says everything is going to be okay."

In that moment, I truly meant it.

But I never would've said it, had I known the types of dark and sinister trials awaiting me next semester.

I lay on the bed in my hospital room. It was still dark outside, but the sun would rise soon. It'd been a really long night, but I didn't sleep. I lay there thinking of Nadine, how she was alive against all odds. I was the luckiest guy in the world.

"I was wrong," I admitted quietly without turning my gaze from the window.

Grant sat in the chair next to my bed. I was surprised he hadn't gone home yet.

"Wrong about what?" he asked.

I sighed and finally turned to look at him. "I was wrong about trying to give my gift back. You were right. I never should've risked it."

Grant eyed me solemnly, and his shoulders fell. "I'm just glad you didn't trade your soul. I was really looking forward to fucking shit up with you in Alora."

A half-smile crept across my face. "Well, we still have our chance. Bring it in, man."

Grant stood from his chair and leaned over my bed to give me a hug.

I clapped him on the back. "I'm sorry for what I said to you."

"I'm sorry, too," he said. "Friends?"

"Always."

Just then, a knock came at the door. Grant turned as an older man stepped into the room.

"What's the verdict, doc?" Grant asked.

The doctor adjusted his glasses and looked down to the clipboard in his hands. "I'm afraid it's not good. We're looking at two broken ribs and a fractured occipital bone."

Grant cocked an eyebrow at me. "You're lucky that's all you walked away with."

I smirked. "Still totally worth it."

The doctor furrowed his brow. "If you don't mind me asking, what were you boys doing to cause this?"

Grant and I shared a look, but I answered. "I beat the shit out of a reaper."

The doctor laughed lightly. He thought I was joking. "Okay, well, let's talk treatment. Unfortunately, there's not much we can do but send you home with pain meds and advise you to get plenty of rest. No sports until you heal. It should take about six weeks until you're good as new."

"Thanks, doc," I said.

"I'll have the nurse get your discharge papers," the doctor said. "Have a good night, boys."

He left the room, and I looked sideways at Grant. "Told you they wouldn't do anything."

He shrugged. "You get pain meds."

I chuckled. "I'm sure you could brew me something better."

Grant yawned really wide, then stood. "I'm gonna take a piss."

"Thanks for announcing it," I joked.

Grant walked off, and I turned back to the window. I really hoped Nadine was resting right now. She needed it after everything she'd been through tonight. I missed her so much already.

Part of me was disappointed that the night hadn't gone as planned. Another part of me was glad Nadine had saved me from the Abyss. I was stupid to try to contact the reapers in the first place. I mean, how could I think the Abyss was preferable to any sort of life with her—and an eternity thereafter?

It was the voices, the thoughts I carried. The weight of the coven's secrets had pushed me to do the unthinkable. But the weird thing was, after burning the journal where I wrote them all down, I didn't feel their weight as heavily anymore. It was like holding on to those thoughts in the journal was the real thing that was weighing me down.

A thought struck. I conjured my positivity journal and a pen. I opened up to the next page and started scribbling down the greatest perk my gift had ever given me:

I saved Nadine's life.

Once I started writing, I couldn't stop. For the first time since Professor Warren gave me this notebook, the positivity just flowed out of me. I pictured all the wonderful things that saving her life meant. She'd live on and would bring beauty into the world everywhere she went.

But it wasn't just about her, either. Suddenly, all these other things started rushing through my mind.

I help others cross over.

I serve the coven.

I'm ready to start doing better.

I felt totally at peace as I closed the journal and subconjured it. That last thought stuck in my mind. I'd admitted my faults tonight. I realized things about myself that I never knew before. For the first time in a year, I could finally face myself, instead of shoving everything down and ignoring it. I wasn't *there* yet, but I was ready to try.

I closed my eyes and relaxed into the pillow as Grant came out of the bathroom.

"You okay, man?" Grant asked.

A smile touched the corners of my lips. "Nadine's alive. We're together now."

"I would hope so, after tonight."

My eyes shot open and darted to the doorway. Nadine stood there, twisting her purse strap around in her fingers.

"Nad," I said breathlessly. "I thought you were at home resting."

"I couldn't sleep," she admitted.

That was so unlike her.

Grant cleared his throat. "I'm gonna go see what I can find in the vending machine."

He left the room, leaving Nadine and me in private. The door swung shut behind him, and Nadine stepped forward. She pulled a chair to the side of my bed and sat down, then took my gauze-wrapped hand in hers.

"Tonight was… crazy," she breathed.

"I know," I whispered, unable to take my eyes off her. "But we made it."

Silence settled over the room for a few moments, until she finally spoke. "I can't believe you'd go to hell just to spend your life with me."

I placed my good hand over hers. "Nad, you know I'd do anything for you."

"And I for you," she whispered. "Which is why—"

"Hang on," I said, suddenly realizing something.

She tilted her head curiously as I raised my hand and curled it into a fist.

"It's your birthday," I pointed out. "I got you something."

I conjured her present and unfurled my fingers. It was a brass key, but it wasn't like the antique one she'd given me. This was old, but still modern.

She reached out and took it. "What does it go to?"

A smile spread across my face. "The abandoned mansion behind the school."

She stared down at it, gaping like she couldn't believe it.

"I went back after that night," I admitted. "I found it upstairs in one of the bedrooms. It works on all the doors."

She blinked a few times. "I don't get it, Lucas. Why are you giving me this?"

"Because that place is ours, Nad," I said. "It's our special place, and this is me promising you we'll be making lots of memories there."

Her eyes sparkled, and she curled her fingers around the key.

"I love it!" she cried, before throwing herself over me. I winced as her weight pressed into my broken ribs.

Nadine kissed me gently, and my stomach flipped in my abdomen. Kissing her was never going to get old.

"This is amazing, Lucas," she said as she drew away.

I smiled. "I'm glad you like it."

Nadine sat back down and took a deep breath. "Look, there's a reason I couldn't sleep—a reason I came to visit you."

"Uh, oh," I said, my guts sinking.

"It's not bad," she said quickly, and I relaxed. "It's… complicated, I guess. I was lying there in bed, thinking about being a Curse Breaker, when it hit me."

"What hit you?" I asked when she paused.

Her eyes brightened. "Lucas... we could break the Reaper's Shadow curse."

Her words thrilled me. What a blessing that would be!

But my thrill only lasted a split second. This curse was one of the darkest I'd ever known. She couldn't break it on her own—especially as a novice. Breaking this curse… well, it could consume her before she managed it. The magic was so strong and so dark, it could overpower her. She could die in the attempt, and I'd lose her all over again.

That wasn't a risk I was willing to take.

"Nad, I don't think that's possible," I said solemnly.

"Why not?" she argued. "I'm a Curse Breaker."

"Yes, but you're the *only* one," I pointed out. "A curse this big could hurt you. I don't want you getting mixed up in magic you can't handle."

"I'll practice," she promised.

"I don't want to lose you," I replied firmly. "I thought I was going to lose you tonight, and I don't want either of us to go through with that again. Magic like this… it could be too much for you. You could get yourself killed."

"I was willing to go to the Abyss for you," she reminded me. "I'll risk this, too."

"But you don't have to," I assured her. "We agreed we'd live with the curse, to work around it."

"That was before we knew I was a Curse Breaker," she said. "The least we can do is *try*."

My heart sank. The last thing I wanted to do was risk losing my Nadine again. She didn't know how much magic she could handle or what breaking this curse could do to her.

"Curse breaking is a complicated process, Nad," I said.

She tilted her head to the side. "Don't you want to get rid of it?"

"Of course I do," I insisted. "I just don't want you to get hurt."

"I won't," she promised, but I wasn't sure I believed her. "I'm going to figure out this curse, and I'm going to break it. I don't care how long it takes me."

My lips tightened. "You're going to do it with or without my help?"

"I *hope* you'll help me," she said quietly. "I want this for both of us."

"I do, too," I replied. "I just... I can't watch you put yourself in danger."

She stared at me under long lashes and spoke softly. "You know me, Lucas. I don't run from danger."

"And that's why I'm here—to drag you away from it," I teased.

Nadine dropped her gaze. Apparently, she didn't find that funny. "Maybe we should take some time to think about it."

"Agreed," I stated, though I wasn't planning on changing my mind. I just hoped *she* would.

"I don't think I'll be around for winter break," she announced, finally lifting her gaze to meet mine.

"What?" I gasped. The thought of being away from her killed me. "Why not?"

"I need to go home," she said.

"Octavia Falls *is* your home," I reminded her.

"I know. But I want to visit my parents' graves." Before I could suggest coming along, she added, "It's something I need to do by myself."

"Are you sure?" I asked. I didn't want her going *anywhere* alone, but I couldn't force her to take me with her.

She nodded. "I'll be fine. I'll stay with a friend from high school. When I get back, we can figure out this curse and what to do about it."

"Okay," I heard myself agree, though I was thoroughly against all of this. "I'm going to miss you."

"I'm going to miss you, too," she said, choking up.

I couldn't stand to see her like this. All I wanted was to make her happy.

I reached an arm out. "Come here, Nad."

She leaned onto the bed and curled into me. Her head rested on my shoulder, and though her weight put pressure on my ribs, I didn't care. Because I had my Nadine with me. We could handle this curse later. Right now, all I could do was be grateful that Nadine and I had both survived the night. All was good in the world.

Or it would've been—if I hadn't been hit by the most debilitating nausea in the next moment. A brick slammed into my guts, and bile shot up my throat. I sprang upright in bed, throwing Nadine off of me. I leaned over and heaved. A sharp, searing pain radiated across my side.

Nadine gasped. "Lucas!"

I was pretty sure she said something else, but I didn't hear her over the high-pitched ringing in my ears. I'd never felt anything like it in all the time I'd been a Reaper's Apprentice.

A child's voice played in my mind as if he was sitting at my side.

"Playtime is over. No child in the coven is safe."

The air sucked out of the room. This thought was shockingly similar to another I'd heard months ago—the one that left me curled on the bathroom floor between classes. *Is it playtime?*

But this new one came with a warning.

A dark, ominous cloud seemed to swirl around me as realization hit. These two kids' deaths were connected. The warning was clear: someone had murdered these kids.

And there was no telling who they'd come for next.

END OF BOOK ONE

Continue Nadine and Lucas' story in The Reaper's Shadow (Hidden Legends: College of Witchcraft, Book Two).

PRISON FOR SUPERNATURAL OFFENDERS BOOK ONE

MEGAN LINSKI & ALICIA RADES

charlie

ONE

I'd often heard the world was black and white, but I didn't believe the lies. Bad things happened to good people all the time. There were no rules when it came to what was fair and just. We lived, we died, and everything else just *was*. Right, wrong— it didn't matter, as long as you made it to tomorrow.

Right now, two hundred bucks would get me a hell of a long way toward tomorrow. Rent was due, and if I didn't want to end up on the streets again, I had to find a way to come up with the money.

Hustling assholes down at *Flying Phoenix Inn*, a pub on my side of Detroit, was a sure-fire way to make the money. To be honest, I wasn't sure how the owners managed to fit so much ego into one building. The place attracted quite the arrogant crowd.

I entered the pub, and a musty scent covered by beer hit my nose. I stepped in a puddle of something wet and sticky— someone's spilled drink. To be honest, I'd be surprised if the floors were *clean* in this dump. The place was almost deafening with chatter and music, and sports-enthusiasts complained loudly at the game on TV. Someone bumped into me and kept on walking, as if being blind made me invisible.

I didn't like to drink— I had to keep my head clear— but it was part of the con. I had to blend in. I ordered a whiskey and took a seat close to the dart boards, sipping on my drink to make it look like I was busy.

Three sets of footsteps approached, and each fell in a heavy, overly confident beat.

Target acquired.

The tap of beer bottles being set down on a table nearby met my ears.

"Who wants to lose first?" the first man asked while cracking his knuckles. He had a deep, smug voice.

"If you go up against me, you'll be the first to lose, bud," his friend said, clapping him on the back.

"Oh, really?" the deep voice responded. "We'll see about that."

A chair screeched across the floor, and the third guy laughed as he sat. "He's not wrong, you know."

"Shut up," the first guy snapped. "Challenge me to darts any day, and I'll kick your ass."

His friend laughed. "Oh, I'm sure you would… after I won."

"You'll be eating your words once this is over."

The third friend was obviously amused by their trash talk. "How about we let the score speak for itself, huh?"

The guy with the deep voice huffed. "Fair enough."

The men scuffled around, until they retrieved their darts. They went quiet, and heavy footsteps walked up to the starting line. The man took aim, and the dart flew from his fingers. I knew the second it began spinning through the air, because I could feel the flutter of current coming off the fletching.

I didn't know how I could do it, but I could *feel* things in the air that other people couldn't. It was almost like my body was making up for my lost vision by tuning into the smallest shift of air current around me. I could feel every person as they moved through the bar, just by the shifts in the air currents around them. I could feel the air as it moved around items, feel what took up space. You could call it my own personal echolocation, just with air instead of sound. It was how I got around so easily and fooled people into thinking I could see.

The dart landed somewhere near the corner of the dartboard, and the guy groaned. His opponent laughed. "Better luck next time."

"Screw you," he responded.

The game continued like that— nothing but trash talk. Neither guy was any better than the other. It was like watching two losers compare dick size when they both had a micropenis. It was honestly a total bore to listen to… until one comment caught my attention.

"You're so bad, even a blind guy could beat you," one of the friends said to the other.

The man with the deep voice chuckled. "Too bad there's no one around to test that theory."

I smirked and set my whiskey aside. "I'll give it a shot," I offered.

The three men turned to me. The first guy must've been sizing me up, because he scoffed a moment later. "You think your blind ass could beat me at *darts*?"

I shrugged. "I'll bet you a hundred bucks I can hit the bull's eye."

All three of the men laughed, but the man with the deep voice responded. "You don't *look* blind."

It wasn't the first time I heard that one. My foster families had told me that my whole childhood.

"I don't have to look blind for it to be true," I said. "But hey, if you're afraid a blind guy will beat you—"

He huffed. "I'm not afraid of *anything*, hear me?"

I took a step forward. I felt the air currents around his form. He was bigger than me, so much that his breath passed the top of my head. He must've been at least six-five, but I wasn't scared of him. Marty had taught me how to hold my own in a fight.

"Then prove it," I challenged. "If it helps, I'll even close my eyes— not like I need them anyway."

Air moved through his nose quickly, like his nostrils were flared. "Fine," he conceded. "A hundred bucks for the bull's eye."

His friends laughed, and someone placed a dart in my hands. I ran the tip of my shoe along the hardwood floor to feel for the line of tape, then stood behind it. I drew a deep breath and squeezed my eyes shut tightly. I couldn't see the dartboard, but I'd sat in this pub listening to the sounds of darts hitting the wall long enough to know exactly where the board hung.

I thrust the dart forward, and it flew out of my fingertips. Ripples of air rushed past the fletching, and I knew I'd aimed slightly off course.

I didn't know how I could do it, but when I prayed for the air to follow my command, miracles happened. I could feel the air particles shift around the dart, nudging it back on course in mid-air.

A *thud* came, then cries of disbelief. The man I was challenging must've been gaping like a fish, because I could feel the air coming out of his mouth in waves.

"That-that's impossible," he sputtered. "He's *blind!*"

"Oh, come on," one of his buddies encouraged. "Pay up."

"*Told you* a blind man could beat you," the other taunted.

My opponent huffed his disapproval, then reached into his back pocket. "A deal's a deal, I guess."

He sounded more willing than I'd anticipated. I was expecting a double or nothing deal here. I heard the sound of a bill sliding over another, and I held my hand out for payment. He placed a crumpled bill in my hand, and his friends' laughter grew. They tried to hide it, but it was pretty apparent. I knew immediately that I was being swindled.

"We agreed to a hundred," I snapped.

The man scoffed. "We also agreed you couldn't see."

I'd only been guessing about the swindling, but that was all the confirmation I needed.

"I can't, jackass!" I fumed. I really needed that money. "I just happen to know when I'm being taken advantage of."

The man laughed and grabbed his beer off the table. He took a swig before responding. "Oh, go walk off a bridge… if you can find one!"

He and his buddies roared with laughter.

Anger bubbled up inside of me. *No one* used my blindness against me. I curled my hand into a fist, crumpling the bill even further. I brought my fist down onto the table, startling the three men.

"We had a deal!" I growled.

The man stepped closer. I could feel the heat rolling off of him. "It was all just fun and games. Now run along. Don't walk into the door on your way out."

"I want my money, dipshit!" I demanded.

Apparently, that was the wrong thing to say, because the next thing I knew, air rushed toward my face. I was so furious that I caught it too late. The man's fist cracked across my jaw, and I went spiraling toward the table. I grabbed the edge to catch myself, but I couldn't slow my momentum. The table crumbled beneath my weight, and I crashed to the floor. Bottles shattered, and liquid seeped into my jeans. The smell of beer hit my nose, but it barely registered. I was freaking *pissed.*

I took just a moment to process the assault. The whole bar was in an uproar, so much that I could barely hear the music. Chairs screeched across the hardwood, and people started yelling. The main asshole laughed with his buddies. He didn't even realize when I pulled myself to my feet— must've thought a blind guy wouldn't fight back or something. I knew exactly where he was by feeling the air around his form.

I launched myself at him and tackled him to the ground. My fist connected with his face three times, each one as satisfying as the last. Then a hand clamped around my wrist, dragging me backward.

It was one of his friends. He yelled obscenities at me, but my breath had grown so ragged they didn't register. As I was being hauled to my feet, I reached my hands out and swiped the man's wallet from his pocket, then slipped it into my jacket. He threw me backward, but I'd been so smooth about it he didn't notice the wallet missing. I crashed into another table, but this one didn't crumble beneath my weight.

"Get out of here!" the jerk shouted. "We'll beat your ass!"

I was more than happy to oblige. I wiped blood from my lip, then held my hands up in surrender. "No need. I'll show myself out."

One of the men huffed, but at least he didn't come at me. I turned and started toward the door. The bar had quieted, but I could feel the patrons' eyes on me as I left.

Just as I reached the door, I heard, "Where the hell is it? He stole my wallet!"

That's when I knew it was time to get the hell out of there. I took off, sprinting out the door, pumping my arms as fast as I could as I ran down the sidewalk. I sensed the air pressure around me, filling in the cracks between streetlights and cars, which allowed me to create a mental map of the street ahead. I dodged around someone heading my way, and I turned the corner. The sound of heavy footsteps and shouts followed me. They weren't far behind.

Something made me slow. It was like running into a mental wall— something that just told me to dig in my heels and stop right there in the middle of the sidewalk.

I skidded to a halt. Someone coming from the opposite direction bumped into me. I stumbled sideways into an alley. The sound of car horns echoed off the brick buildings squeezing in around me, and the air felt damp and smelled of garbage.

I should've kept on moving, but I remained rooted in place. Call it intuition, but I could sense something ahead. I didn't know what it was, but I knew it wasn't dangerous. It was more like a beacon calling me forward, offering me sanctuary.

That was saying a lot, considering sanctuary was tough to come by in my experience. I could barely make sense of the feeling.

I focused on the alleyway, trying to map it out in my mind using the sounds of the city and the air pressing in around me. The best I could tell, the alley was empty. I must've been imagining things.

"Where'd he go!?" one of the men from the bar shouted, snapping me out of my daze.

My heart leapt. I wished I could say I was in this for the thrill, but these things didn't excite me anymore. Not after what happened to Marty.

"There he is!" someone shouted.

Hell.

I knew I wasn't getting out the way I came without getting my ass kicked, so I turned and hightailed it in the opposite direction. I could make out the sound of cars on the street ahead, coming closer and closer as I ran—

Then something tangled around my legs, and I smashed to the ground. My face hit the asphalt so hard, I couldn't make sense of which way was up and which was down. It took me a moment to realize someone had tackled me. Before I could react, a foot connected with the side of my ribs, and I grunted.

I didn't stay down long. When you grew up the way I did, you learned pretty fast how to defend yourself. I swung my leg out and knocked one of the men on his ass. I jumped to my feet and kicked my elbow back into the second guy's nose. He yelled as he went stumbling backward. I stood my ground, surveying the air for the next attack.

Heavy footsteps approached, and I forced my breathing to slow so I could listen carefully. A threatening laugh bubbled up from the man's throat. It was the guy with the deep voice. Something smacked into his palm, like he was carrying a weapon and was showing it off. A baseball bat, perhaps? *No*, I realized. It was one of the legs of the table I'd broken back at the bar.

"Normally, I wouldn't hurt a blind guy," he said sardonically. "But I'm going to get real pleasure beating you—"

He cut off as a deep growl came out of the shadows. Air rushed past me as a large figure leapt toward the man. I didn't know what it was at first, until my attacker began to scream. Angry barks and the snapping of jaws echoed down the alleyway. It was a *dog*.

I was so dumbstruck at its sudden appearance that I took a few steps back. The other two men scrambled forward, trying to save their friend from the canine attack. The dog snarled, and one of the men screamed like he'd been bitten.

"Get the fuck off of me!" the man with the deep voice yelled.

I heard a loud *smack*, then a whimper from the dog. Best I could tell, the man had used his weapon against the creature. The air knocked out of my lungs, as if he'd just swung the weapon straight into my abdomen, though I hadn't been touched.

My hands curled into tight fists, and my arms shook in rage. I couldn't explain the primal instinct that took over me in that moment. All I knew was I had to protect that creature— or die trying.

I jumped forward. "Leave him alone!" I shouted.

A second *smack* came as the dog slammed into the side of the building. Another whimper escaped the poor creature's throat, and my stomach plummeted to the asphalt.

"Or what?" one of the men threatened.

He took a step forward, and I threw myself in front of the dog. "You don't want to know the answer," I growled. I reached into my pocket for my knife and flicked it open. "Get out of here while you still have the chance."

The man laughed. "Your little switchblade doesn't scare me. Three men against one blind guy and his dog? Who do *you* think is going to win?"

Me, I thought instantly.

The man stepped forward and swung the table leg at me. It connected with my hand before I could pull away, and my knife went flying across the alley. He took another step, but I was so enraged I wasn't willing to let him get any closer.

"Fuck off!" I screamed.

I threw my hands outward. I meant to shove him away from me, but something else happened entirely. A strange power unlike anything I'd ever felt before surged through my body and shot out of my palms. I could feel the shift in the air as the blast sent the men flying a dozen feet away from me. They crashed into the ground next to the dumpsters nearby.

My hands shook. I couldn't even process what had just happened.

The men warily got to their feet, but they didn't advance on me. One of them whispered something to the others, but I couldn't make it out. My pulse pounded in my ears as I tried to understand the power I'd summoned. Had it been *me*? No, that was ridiculous. There had to be some other explanation.

But the way the men huddled together, they seemed terrified of me.

"I said *leave*!" I screamed, raising my hands threateningly.

That was all it took for the men to scramble away with their tails between their legs. Wood clanked to the asphalt, then came the men's retreating footsteps. Whatever had happened had scared them off.

Satisfied they were gone, I turned to the dog behind me. I could hear its labored breathing, but more than that, I could sense its heartbeat as if it were my own. I'd never had a pet before, but the urge to protect this poor animal was so strong I might as well have been tending to my own broken leg.

I stepped toward the creature and held out a cautious hand. I wasn't sure whether it would attack again, but something told me it wouldn't— as if the dog had been protecting me from those men.

"Don't worry, boy," I said. "I'm not going to hurt you."

I lowered myself to my knee and touched the top of the dog's head. The second my fingers sank into his soft, thick coat, the alleyway spun around me so quickly I couldn't make sense of it. The asphalt might as well have dropped out from under my feet. It was as if nothing in this world existed outside of me and the dog. Color blasted across my vision, though I could hardly remember what colors *were* from before I went blind. The air smelled like fresh rain, and the smooth, sweet taste of lemon meringue pie swept over my tongue. The sounds of the city faded and were replaced with the rustling of trees in the breeze and the sound of bird calls. I swear I could even hear the ocean waves in the distance. The feeling of sunlight hit my skin, and I felt as if I was being embraced in a warm hug.

None of it made any sense, and yet... I couldn't bring myself to question it. Something about it felt right. More real than the city ever had.

Soon, the strange sensations settled, and I was pulled back to the present in the alleyway. I couldn't help the smile that spread across my face. There was no explanation, and yet for the first time, I felt like I'd visited a place that was my first true home.

I didn't have extra money for food to feed this guy, but it didn't matter. I already knew I wanted him.

"Did you do that?" I asked the dog aloud, though I knew he wouldn't respond.

I stroked the dog's fur as he got to his feet. He was big and strong. The shape of his ears suggested he was a husky, or a similar breed.

"You're a nice doggy, aren't you?" I said, scratching him behind the ears. I checked his neck for a collar, but didn't find one. "You were protecting me from those bad guys. I think I might just keep you. What's your name?"

Oberi, a voice responded in my mind.

Given the last few minutes, I should've been halfway to a mental institution by now. But something about that voice seemed so familiar... like I'd been listening to it my whole life. Hearing it inside my head didn't seem unusual at all.

"Oberi," I repeated. "It was you calling me down this alley, wasn't it?"

The dog didn't respond with words this time. Instead, he licked my hand, and in that moment, I *knew*. This dog was special. This dog was *mine*.

This dog was my sanctuary.

Days passed, and Oberi never once left my side. I didn't know where he'd come from, and I didn't question it, either. Somehow, I knew he was meant to be mine.

The wallet I stole had enough money to cover rent, plus extra to buy supplies for Oberi. I always avoided credit cards if I could, because I knew that was a good way to get caught. I was the kind of guy who liked to stay *off* the radar. Learned that one the hard way.

Oberi became an asset when it came to making money. Turns out people had a sweet spot for dogs. All I had to do was sit on the sidewalk with a cup at my side and people would drop money in like a slot machine. Oberi was quite the charmer, and I brought back double my usual haul over the next three days.

My grocery run that week was phenomenal. I managed to afford the cheesy chips I loved so much— the definition of pure luxury. The employee helping me shop seemed annoyed by how long I took to decide, but it was hard when I had so many choices in front of me. Oberi followed behind me as I climbed the stairs in my apartment building.

The place was nice— well, as nice as a cheap Detroit apartment got. The rug on the stairs had holes in it that I'd nearly broken my neck on more than once, the creak of the pipes kept me up at night, and there was a constant unidentifiable smell that was less than pleasant. But it was a roof over my head... for now, anyway.

Mrs. Miller, the old lady subletting me the place— illegally, mind you— had been on an extended vacation to visit her daughter in Florida. She never gave me a time frame on when she'd be back, so I knew my stay here was limited. I could be kicked out any moment. But that's how things had always been with me. My life had been uncertain since the day I was born.

I reached my door and stuck the key in the lock, but was surprised when the key turned smoothly and without resistance— as if the door was already unlocked. I twisted the handle, and sure enough, the door swung open with ease.

"Mm…" I mused. "I thought I'd locked it."

I shrugged, and Oberi stepped into the apartment in front of me. I stopped dead in my tracks the second I walked in the door. I didn't know what it was at first, but something was *wrong*. Oberi came to a halt beside me and sniffed the air.

I smelled it, too. I couldn't put my finger on it, but it was something akin to ocean water— totally out of place. Then I heard it, the sound of footsteps in the kitchen.

An intruder!

I held my breath and motioned for Oberi to stay quiet. Slowly, I set my bag of groceries on the ground, careful not to make a sound. I pressed myself to the wall and inched closer to the kitchen.

A man began humming a tune I was sure I'd never heard before, but sounded vaguely familiar. He had a roughness to his voice, and his footsteps moved slowly, like he was old.

I listened for signs of other intruders, but he seemed to be alone. There came the sound of something scratching, then metal hitting the counter. Silverware, perhaps? Was the guy making himself a *freaking sandwich* in my kitchen? What the hell, man?

I reached into my pocket and pulled out my knife. I flicked it open just as I heard the man open the refrigerator. When he turned his back, I lunged out of my hiding spot and into the entrance of the kitchen.

"What the hell are you doing!?" I demanded, holding my knife out threateningly. It was pretty clear I'd use it if I had to. The old man better not test me. I wasn't afraid to use this damn thing.

The man paused a second. It went so quiet I wasn't sure if I'd given him a heart attack or something. "Come now, Charlie," the old man said. "There's no reason to fear me. Put the knife away."

"Put it away?" I balked. "I don't know who the hell you are. How do you know my name?"

"I've known about you for a long time, Charlie," he said.

I racked my brain, trying to place the voice. I knew a lot of people from being shuffled around between foster homes when I was a kid, but surely none of them cared enough to come find me. Not like anyone had a reason.

"You're not a cop, are you?" I accused.

The man chuckled. "No, not a cop at all. Just a hungry old man looking for a sandwich. You hungry?"

He took a bite, then held the sandwich out so close to me I could feel him.

I curled my nose up. "No, thanks. Who are you—?"

Oberi cut me off by giving a happy bark and skirting around me into the kitchen. He went over to the man like he knew him, making gross licking noises with his tongue.

"Oh, this must be your Familiar!" the old man said, like we were two old friends catching up. I was caught off guard, to say the least.

"Familiar?" I questioned. What was he talking about?

The man spoke to Oberi like he hadn't heard me. "You want a sandwich, buddy? Here you go. Just a bite."

"Hey, don't feed my dog that," I objected, but he must've not heard me, because Oberi wolfed the thing down in seconds.

He scratched Oberi behind the ears. "You're a long way from home, aren't you? Yes, you are."

The man seemed harmless, and Oberi appeared to trust him, so I lowered my weapon.

"Will you stop talking to my dog like he's an infant?" I demanded. "What are you doing here?"

The man straightened. "Yes, of course. You must be so confused. Why don't we sit down and talk?"

"I don't want to *sit down*," I growled. "Tell me what the hell's going on."

The man took a deep breath, then tapped his fingers on the counter. "Let me ask you this. Have you noticed anything strange lately?"

"Yeah. There's a weird old dude in my kitchen," I stated flatly.

"I mean since your Familiar arrived," he said.

I furrowed my brow. "My Familiar?"

"Yes. Perhaps you've noticed… powers."

"Powers?" I repeated. "Okay, grandpa. You gotta go."

"But you need to hear this, Charlie!" he protested. "Your father had the power to control Air, which means you can, too!"

I was just about to grab the guy and shove him out the door, but what he said made me pause. I instantly thought of what happened the night I found Oberi, how I'd blasted the three men back with no explanation. Had I been controlling the air around them?

"I don't know what you're talking about," I said.

"Yes, you do," he argued. "I saw it in your eyes just now. You've used your Air magic before, haven't you?"

"I don't believe in magic," I told him, but it felt like coughing up rocks. Something about saying that out loud felt wrong.

"Please listen to me, Charlie," he insisted. "My name is Professor Elliot Baine. I'm an Elementai, like you."

I took a step back. "Elementai?"

The man was talking crazy. And yet… I swore I'd heard the word before.

"Please, if you'd just sit down, I'd like to explain. I want to help," he assured me.

Like hell. The only people who ever said *I want to help* only wanted to help themselves. Another lesson I'd learned the hard way. Marty had been the only person I ever met who meant it. He was a true friend up until the day he died.

But this old man was a stranger. Surely he had ulterior motives.

And yet… he had me intrigued. Something *had* happened the night I met Oberi, and I hadn't been able to explain it. Hell, there was a lot about my life I couldn't explain.

"Let me prove it," he insisted. He walked over to the sink and turned on the faucet while he spoke. "I'm Toaqua, which means I can control Water."

I jumped when something cold touched my arm. I swiped at it, only to realize that it was water. The water droplets washed away, only to return a moment later. They crawled over my skin, then soaked into my shirt. It was freaking eerie, like the water had a mind of its own. A moment later, the water was being sucked out of my shirt, and the fabric went dry again. The water wrapped around my arm like a snake. As it slithered away, I reached out a hand and discovered that it was floating in mid-air.

I stood there, mouth agape, unable to believe what he'd just done. Magic? Could it be true?

"Fine," I agreed. "Tell me everything."

I couldn't believe I was actually welcoming this stranger into my home. Had I gone insane?

The old man— Professor Baine— and I left the kitchen and sat in the living room. Oberi lay at my feet.

"Like I said, I'm an Elementai," Professor Baine started. "We're a group of supernaturals who are able to manipulate the elements— Fire, Water, Earth, Air, and Spirit."

I scoffed. "Spirit— like healing?"

"Exactly."

"If you're offering to heal me, you can go fuck yourself," I snarled. I didn't need to be able to see to have worth in this freaking world. I was blind, but that didn't matter. I still meant something.

"No, no, you misunderstand," he said calmly. "Even if we wanted to, our healing wouldn't help with your... condition. It doesn't work that way. I'm here because you were born in our society, Charlie, and we've been looking for you for a long time."

"I... what?"

"You were taken away and put into foster care when you were only a toddler," he continued. "That was back during the Hawkei Civil War, when your parents were arrested for treason—"

"Hawk-eye *what*? Back up, old man," I insisted. "You'll have to start from the beginning— if I'm even going to entertain what you're saying at all."

Professor Baine took a deep breath. His words came out sounding thoughtful. "The beginning... okay. The Hawkei are a Native American tribe living in Northern California. Long ago, when the colonizers waged war on us, our ancestors granted us magical powers to protect ourselves. We were split into five Houses, named for each of the five elements. Children are born into the House of their parents, as they will inherit the same type of magic. With this blessing also came magical creatures, which we were tasked with protecting and caring for. Some of these magical creatures bond with us. They are our other halves, our soul and the source of our powers. We call them Familiars."

My brow furrowed the more he spoke. It was a fun story, but it couldn't be true. "And Oberi is my... Familiar?" I questioned hesitantly.

"Yes," Professor Baine confirmed. "He is bonded to you now. If one of you dies, you both die."

My heart jumped at the thought. I could be gone tomorrow, and Oberi would perish with me? That didn't seem fair.

"But I'm not Native American," I argued. Truth be told, I didn't know *what* I was. I knew I had darker skin, but people had treated me like dirt my whole life. I didn't think I belonged anywhere.

"Of course you are," Mr. Baine said. "Not all Hawkei look Native American. After we were gifted our powers, we sought to expand our tribe. Men and women from all over the world joined us, and so our culture is very diverse, influenced heavily by both our Hawkei and non-Hawkei ancestors."

"Where's *your* Familiar?" I asked rather harshly. I wanted the proof.

"I'm afraid Thalassa is too big to bring on such a journey," he said, before continuing with his story. "Twenty years ago, the Hawkei underwent many disagreements, one of them being whether couples from separate Houses— or those with different powers— should be allowed to mate. At the time, it was thought that mixed-House children would have diluted powers, and many feared losing our magic. Interhouse relationships were outlawed, and anyone found to break that law was sentenced to prison— or death."

I shuddered.

"I'm afraid your parents were among those sentenced," he said sadly. "Your mother was

Nivita— an Earth Elementai— and your father was Yapluma— an Air Elementai. People from those two Houses were not allowed to be together. Or have children."

My hands curled into fists. How dare he try to use my parents against me! I blew a breath and spoke sarcastically. I didn't believe him. "And that's why I was taken away and put into foster care?"

He took a deep breath, like it pained him to admit the truth. "Yes. Unfortunately, the Elders — our government— did not think you worthy of the tribe. But things have changed, and the Hawkei have been trying to get these interhouse children back."

My body went rigid. Holy shit. He was serious.

"Why?" I asked in disgust. "Why would I go back to a society that thought me worthless?"

"We're not like that anymore," he insisted. "But you've been very hard to find, Mr. Wahkin."

"How *did* you find me?" I demanded.

"Remember that break-in you were wanted for last year?" he asked.

I crossed my arms. I couldn't believe he'd bring that up. I didn't do break-ins— not anymore. But since Marty died, I was desperate. I fell into the wrong crowd, and they convinced me to get in on a burglary job. It ended in five arrests, and only three of us got away. It hadn't been pretty— hence why I preferred to stay *off* the radar.

"Yeah, I remember," I bit.

"Well, there's been a warrant out for your arrest ever since," Professor Baine explained. "You were caught on camera in a bar fight a few days ago. It tipped off our officials on your whereabouts."

"Okay, I get that, but seriously, how did you find me *here*?" I asked. "My name's not on the lease."

It was one of the reasons the police hadn't arrested me on that warrant yet. They didn't know where to find me.

"Ah, yes. That was a tricky one," Baine said. "Once I had a general idea of where you were staying, all I had to do was follow the scent of magic."

"Scent of magic?" My eyebrows shot up.

"Well, not literally," he said. "I'm a particularly gifted Elementai. I've mastered techniques many others have not. Among them, I'm able to siphon magic from creatures who are not my own Familiar."

I went rigid, and I instinctively placed a leg in front of Oberi's lounging form.

"Not to worry, Mr. Wahkin," Mr. Baine said. "I have no reason to draw from your Familiar. However, the technique allows me to sense the magic around me. Since Oberi is the only magical creature in the area, I was able to sense her from a great distance."

"Him," I corrected.

Mr. Baine hesitated, like he was confused. "Yes, of course. Sense *him*."

Silence settled between us for a few moments. I was still trying to absorb everything he'd said. I could feel Mr. Baine's eyes on me.

"You do believe me, don't you, Charlie?" he asked.

I contemplated it. Did I believe him? It was all so crazy... yet seemed to make all the sense in the world.

"I don't know," I admitted. "For the last couple of years, I've been able to... I don't know how to explain it. I can *sense* the world around me through air pressure. It's like my eyes don't work, but I can get an idea in my mind of what a room looks like just by how the air moves."

"That makes perfect sense!" Baine sounded delighted. "You came of age, so your magic started working. Now that you and Oberi have bonded, you will begin learning magic at a rapid rate. Soon, you'll be able to control the Air itself."

I gaped, and he must've noticed.

"What is it?" he asked.

"Well, I-I think I already did that." And it wasn't just that blast in the alleyway, either. I could do it playing darts and things like that, though on a much smaller scale.

Holy shit. This guy wasn't lying. There really was a society of magical people who could control the elements… and I was one of them.

"What do you want from me?" I finally asked.

"Nothing." He sounded genuine. "I only want to help."

"But why me? I'm nothing special."

"You are very wrong about that, Mr. Wahkin," he countered. "You are an Elementai, a member of the Hawkei tribe. You belong in Kinpago with the rest of us. There, we can teach you how to use your element and strengthen your bond with your Familiar. There's a school, Orenda Academy of Magical Creatures—"

"A college?" I balked. "No, I'm too old for college. Besides, I don't even have a high school diploma."

"Precisely why we will give you an education. You can get your GED *and* a college degree. All Hawkei deserve that much."

"Wait… give it to me?" It took a moment for what he was saying to sink in. "Like, a scholarship?"

"All Orenda Academy expenses are paid by the tribe," he explained. "You will have room and board, food, money for supplies—"

"Thanks for the offer, but this all sounds too good to be true," I said bitterly. "What is it you *really* want in return?"

Baine took a long breath. "We want to make amends, Charlie."

I scoffed. "Then the Elders who threw me out can go drop dead."

Baine got really quiet. "They are. The council is new now, full of people who want to restore balance to our tribe, instead of tear it apart like the ones who came before. Reaching out to our outcasted members is one way for the tribe to atone for its many sins."

My blood ran cold. I still didn't want to go. "Why would I go back to a society that executed my parents and made me an orphan? You abandoned me."

"You can't stay here," he pointed out. I opened my mouth to protest, but Baine continued. "Sooner or later, your warrant will catch up to you. We can provide you with a good home and proper education. If you stay here, you'll end up in prison… or worse."

Hell, this old man was right. I was basically holding my breath waiting for an arrest or to bleed out in a gunfight.

Maybe I could use this new place to my advantage. It'd be a new playground for my cons, and I could plot my revenge on the tribe while I was at it.

I wasn't sure I had a choice.

"Okay," I said. "I'm in."

ava-marie

TWO

The day I was born, the world went mad.

And I went mad with it.

The pounding of the hippogriff's hooves beneath me was like a war drum beating a prayer song. I could feel the music that resonated through the earth as it sent power flowing through my blood. The valley ahead of me was green and open, welling with sunlight on a fresh August morning. The hippogriff herd pressed around me as the mountains of Northern California rose in the distance, redwoods like soldiers standing tall against the blue sky.

I could feel everything that was alive, smell the resonance of life as energy ricocheted through the air. I could see the entire universe, spread out like a map that was mine for the taking. I rode upon a euphoric high, feeling more powerful than a god and never wishing to come down as the colors began to bleed together into a watercolor painting.

I dug my hands into the creature's feathers and held on tight, pressing myself to the bird's neck and urging it to go faster. The half-horse, half-eagle creature let out a low whinny, enclosing its wings around my legs. I laughed along, giving a sound that was shrill and ignited the world.

Eventually, the valley came to a close as the mountains grew higher above us. The hippogriff slowed, until it jogged to a stop by the opening of a cave entrance. I slid off and patted the hippogriff's neck as the colors of the world bled away and became normal once again. "Good girl. Thanks for the ride."

The hippogriff snorted, blowing back my hair before taking off into the sky. The herd followed, spreading their wings to follow the lead mare into the clouds.

I looked back. My brother was clinging to the back of the slowest hippogriff, who rounded up the last of the herd. His black hair was wild and stuck up on one side, and his cheeks were bright red.

"Ava-Marie, wait up!" he complained. His hippogriff skidded to an abrupt halt. Ezekiel yelled as he was tossed forward and sent sprawling into the ground, tearing a hole in his jeans.

I put a hand over my mouth and laughed again as Ezekiel spat out dirt. The hippogriff huffed and kicked up its hooves, flying into the sky with the rest of them.

Ezekiel gave me a sour look. "You could wait for me every once in a while."

"You wouldn't fall behind if you were a better rider." I reached out a hand to pull him to his feet. Ez and I often raced hippogriffs, but he rarely beat me. He could never tell which ones would be the fastest. I could.

We turned toward the cave entrance. Ezekiel's mouth fell open as he gazed upward, taking in the sight of the cave— and the various signs around the entrance warning that further venturing would be trespassing on government property. As this cave was outside the Hawkei reservation, whatever was found within it was free for anyone to take— as far as the colonizers were concerned.

"Are you sure we should be doing this?" Ezekiel asked. "It definitely counts as illegal activity."

"Stop being such a baby." I reached into my backpack and took out a headlamp, fastening it before clicking on the light. "It's the weekend. No one's at the worksite."

"If we get caught here, it's a federal crime," Ezekiel said, pointing at the cords roping off the entrance.

I rolled my eyes. "What, like the colonizers committed a crime by *stealing our land*? Those artifacts are Hawkei property, Ez. They belong to the tribe. Now we're going to get them back. Do you really want the colonizers to put our heritage in one of *their* museums? It's not right."

"No, but—"

"Then what's the issue?"

Ezekiel's tone was flat. "I don't feel like going to jail."

"You're such a goody-two-shoes. Let's go."

"Ava-Marie!"

I'd slipped under the ropes before he had a chance to stop me. Ezekiel fastened on his own headlamp and hurried in behind, like I knew he'd always do. The sunlight vanished as we wandered further into the cave.

I got that Ez was nervous, but he needed to chill. This was the *right* thing to do. The supernatural world had suffered enough from humans in the past— the Hawkei being one of their greatest victims.

The Hawkei were an indigenous people who'd lived in California for thousands of years. We'd nearly been exterminated when the colonizers came to our territory and began terrorizing our tribe. We'd pleaded with the ancestors for help, and they'd answered our prayers, and gifted us our powers— the magic of the elements.

We became the Elementai— elementals— and grew strong enough to defend ourselves from the humans. We separated into five Houses for each of the five elements— Koigni, for Fire; Toaqua, for Water; Nivita, for Earth; Yapluma, for Air; and Anichi, for Spirit.

Though we had to keep our magic a secret, I wasn't about to let some colonizers get their filthy hands on what belonged to us. I was doing the right thing. They were trying to steal our culture. Now I was stealing it back.

The headlamps didn't provide enough light, so I lifted my hand. A ball of fire burned within it, illuminating the path ahead with light.

Ezekiel looked on in awe. "I'm so jealous. I can't wait to get my powers."

"You're eighteen. They'll show up soon."

Supernaturals got their abilities when they came of age, but Ez hadn't shown any magic yet. I was over a year older than him, but I'd gotten my Fire magic the day I'd turned eighteen.

Though Ezekiel's powers would be different from mine. Our parents were from separate

Houses. My mother was Koigni. My father was Toaqua. Elementai always inherited their powers from their same-sex parent, so Ezekiel would have Water magic instead of Fire like me.

Ezekiel scowled as the walls of the cave began getting narrower. "You could at least tell our parents where we're going. I don't like lying all the time. If he finds out we're here, Dad will be madder than when you got your tongue pierced."

I waggled my piercing at him. "Well, someone's gotta be the rebel."

"Not all the time. Can't we have a *normal* day for once?"

"I do what I want."

I held my arm out as the cave path came to an abrupt halt, leading to the edge of a cliff. I sent the fireball sailing downward. It landed on the cave floor twenty feet below, where it shone light on piles of pick axes, shovels, and wheelbarrows full of dirt. The fireball fizzled out, leaving the area below in darkness.

"There's the excavation site." I slipped off my bag and began pulling out my gear. I pounded an anchor into the floor and strung a rope through the safety clips before slipping on my harness. I was rappelling down the side of the cliff before Ezekiel even had his harness on. I landed on the ground safely and unclipped myself while Ez clumsily— and fucking *slowly*— descended.

Ezekiel got tangled up in his climbing gear a foot above the ground. He struggled with the ropes and glanced at me helplessly as he spun in circles against the rock.

"Um, can you help? This harness is strangling my balls," he whined.

"Ancestors, Ez, you're so clumsy." I got Ez loose, and he staggered against the wall. I had to resist rolling my eyes again.

"Hey, I'm a fat kid. I don't do things like this."

"You're not fat, Ez, you're fluffy."

"Easy for you to say. You can't weigh more than a hundred pounds."

"Shut up."

I called another fireball into my hand as I observed the excavation site. There were footprints in the dirt, and a lot of tools, but I didn't see anything of value.

"They must've not found it yet," I reasoned.

"Do you hear that?" Ezekiel tilted his head. There was a trickling sound. I followed the source of the noise across the area until my boots splashed upon mud and water. The fireball in my hand displayed a river ten feet wide, and probably just as deep.

"It's an underground river," I said. "How fascinating."

I reached into my bag and pulled out a leather guidebook. I scribbled a few things down while Ezekiel groaned. "Ava, can we go? I don't want to get caught down here."

I snapped my guidebook shut. "Look. When you're navigating ruins, you're supposed to document *everything*. Otherwise, you could miss a crucial clue that's important later. I have to practice; otherwise, I'll never be—"

"*A real explorer*," Ezekiel echoed for me, like he'd done a million times. "I get it. Where is this thing, anyway?"

"Grandpa said the artifact would be down here." I followed my instincts and began navigating the river. Ezekiel nearly slipped into it, before I caught him.

"Grandpa's wrong about a lot of things," Ezekiel grumbled, but I ignored him. We moved ahead, leaving the excavation site behind us.

We walked for half a mile in silence. The walls of the cave narrowed. Eventually, the river ended, but not before I noticed a small slit in the cave wall near my feet. I'd fit through it, but not Ez.

I had a feeling there was something lying beyond. Ezekiel frowned when he noticed it. "You can't be serious."

"Where's your sense of adventure?" I asked. I had already dropped to my knees and began squeezing myself through the hole. "I won't be long."

Ezekiel danced nervously by the gap as I pushed myself through the claustrophobic space. For a moment, I did get stuck— momentary panic struck me, but I shoved it aside. Fear was a useless fucking emotion. It wouldn't get me what I wanted.

I finally slipped through. As I did, I was able to stand and light a fireball. I stood in a small circular area, and lying on the floor was exactly what we'd come here for.

I reached out and picked up a small gold sculpture in the shape of a person. It was as big as my hand, and depicted each of the five elements throughout. The face showed half the face of a man, and half of a woman. It was meant to be a carving of one of the Hawkei gods— a piece of the Great Spirit we worshiped alongside our ancestors.

After a quick inspection, I rendered it had to be authentic. A piece like this was invaluable. To the colonizers, such an item would sell for millions at auction, but to our tribe, it was priceless.

I wriggled out from underneath the gap, and Ezekiel sighed in relief. His smile brightened when I showed him the figurine.

"Finally. Let's head out." We turned to go, but as we did, the idol in my hand started to burn. I let out a gasp. Being Koigni, it shouldn't have hurt, but the statue was actually able to singe my skin. Both of our mouths dropped open as we realized the idol was glowing bright red. From the mouth of the idol streamed black smoke, which formed into a transparent man with a malicious grin.

Shit. The idol was a piece of Spirit Art. Grandpa had told me about these things. If a supernatural cared about their creation enough, they could actually seal a piece of their soul inside it, preserving their spirit forever within an item they treasured here on this earth. Usually, people who made Spirit Art were benevolent and kind beings, meant to help others.

But whoever had made this piece of Spirit Art was a fucking asshole, because this spirit was obviously not here to help. Dark magic like whips began gathering at his sides as the entity readied to attack. I saw fire flickering on the spirit's form— this man had been Koigni in his former life.

"Ava, run!" Ezekiel cried. He grabbed my wrist, but the dark entity lashed out, knocking him to the ground. His headlight went out, and I heard glass crack.

The spirit smacked me across the face. My helmet went flying off, and the light broke against the stone.

We were locked in darkness. I threw a fireball in the direction I thought the dark spirit might be. It sailed right through him. I saw with horror that the monster was advancing on Ezekiel, who was scampering backwards trying to get away from it. The evil spirit reached out its dark tendrils, wrapping them around Ezekiel's form and squeezing him tight. He gasped, pulling at the tendrils around his neck as they suffocated him, his feet kicking at the water of the river as he tried to escape.

When I saw that my brother was in danger, I didn't think. I reacted. I flung out my left hand, expecting flames to shoot out my fingers at the entity, though I knew it wouldn't do any good.

That's not what happened. A shiver ran from my core all the way out to the tips of my fingers as I felt my skin turn cold, not hot. I'd never experienced such a chilling feeling before. When I cast Fire, there was anger, passion, exhilaration— nearly on the bounds of being out of control.

This magic was different. It was calming. Cool. And had an ancient power within it that scared me.

The water in the river rose upward. The riverbed drained. Ezekiel gasped. The spirit just had time to look up before the wave crashed into him. The dark entity gave a wicked cry as the water smashed into his body, putting out the flames licking his form. There was a sizzling sound, and the spirit dissolved, leaving the idol silent and immobile on the ground. The water trickled back into the river, and I was left completely dumbfounded.

What did I just do?

Ezekiel shook, but it wasn't because of the entity. "Ava, you— you just used Water magic!"

I clambered to my feet. "No... it isn't possible."

"It has to be." Ezekiel got up, and his feet splashed on the stone. "I saw you do it. You're not just Koigni. You're Toaqua, too."

Denial flashed in my mind. I was a Fire caster, through and through. I had the fiery temperament for it. The ability to call upon Fire was as easy for me as breathing.

And yet... I'd told the river to protect Ezekiel without any effort whatsoever, and it'd obeyed.

I wouldn't accept it. It wasn't real. I couldn't have inherited my father's powers, too. This had to be a fluke.

I wouldn't have one more thing that made me more different than I already was.

"Ez, you can't tell Mama and Daddy about this," I said as he approached. "It has to stay between us."

His face fell. "If you're both Houses, it's important for them to know."

"No! I want to be Koigni— I want to be normal," I pleaded. "I'm already a fucking freak."

Ezekiel's eyes turned sad. "You're not a freak, Ava."

I let out a snort. Yeah, right. I'd been the weird kid at school. And weird was putting it lightly. People were afraid of me.

It was exceptionally rare— nearly unheard of— for an Elementai to have the ability to cast more than one element. Most could only cast the element of the House they were born into. Sure, there were exceptions, like my mother, who could use both Fire and Spirit magic.

But there'd never, in the history of all the Hawkei, been an elemental who could use both Fire and Water. The elements were total opposites. And I didn't want to be the first anything.

I picked up the idol and shoved it into my bag. "Come on. Let's go."

"Ava!"

Ezekiel protested all the way behind me— even as he struggled to climb the wall that led back out of the cave. When we burst out into the sunlight, he grabbed my shoulders to stop me.

"This isn't something we can hide," he said. "Nor should you."

Ezekiel was stubborn. He wouldn't give up.

"Let's just drop the idol off at Grandpa's," I said with a sigh. "Then we'll talk about it."

Or like, never.

Ezekiel's shoulders sagged. "Okay. We can stop by on the way home."

"Like hell! I *need* makeup." I could deal with jeans just fine if I was running around in a cave, but any other time of day, I wanted a dress on. Crawling in the mud was no excuse for not looking fabulous— and I was *not* walking through town with my hair like this.

"Ugh. Fine. I guess I'm hungry, anyway."

"You're always hungry."

The hippogriff herd had returned by this time. They were grazing in the valley beyond. The lead mare lifted her head as I walked toward her. I pulled myself onto her back, and Ezekiel climbed onto the same tawny stallion he'd fallen off of earlier. I nudged my heels into her sides, and the hippogriff spread her wings, taking off into the air.

There was nothing like feeling the wind on your face while you were flying on a hippogriff. I looked down, and as the valley shrank beneath me, I turned my gaze toward the city beyond.

Kinpago was my home, and always would be. I admired the beautiful skyline as the hippogriff tilted in the air, directing us toward an island that sat surrounded by the crystal clear ocean.

The two hippogriffs landed on the sandy beach of the island. Ezekiel and I fed them treats before bidding farewell and walking up the brick pathway to the grand stone mansion beyond.

I loved our house. It was open-concept, decorated in white and blue tones with a crystal chandelier hanging in the main entrance. The kitchen connected to the living room, and the porch doors were open, letting in the breeze from the beach. Some would say it was too big, but I had such a large family, it always felt warm and welcoming to me.

My younger sister sat on the couch, reading, like usual. Her red mane of hair fanned out behind her on the pillows. She looked up as we entered.

"Where've you guys been?" Alana asked. She was only fifteen, but she was fucking sharp— nothing got past her. She got off the couch and threw her book aside as Ezekiel began rummaging through the cupboards to make a sandwich.

I took the idol out of my bag and set it on the counter. "Getting this."

"No way. You found it?" Alana's eyes widened as she took in the statue.

"Yeah. It only took vanquishing an evil spirit out of the statue," Ezekiel said with a mouth full of food.

"Really? How'd you do that?" Alana asked.

I glared at Ezekiel, and he shut up as Alana inspected the idol.

I could hear swear words coming from the garage. I poked my head in.

My eleven-year-old brother, Maverick, was sprawled on the floor, surrounded by tools as he messed around with an old motorbike. The bike was an antique. It had been my grandfather's, passed down to my dad, then passed down to me. I took it to the mainland sometimes to ride it around. Maverick was itching to be old enough to drive it. I'd told him he could tinker with it. He was good with mechanical things. His brown hair was matted with oil as he tightened loose bolts.

"You got it, Mav?" I asked.

Maverick threw a wrench down. "Stupid chains are busted."

"Well, if you need help, ask."

Ez and I took after our dad— Alana and Maverick our mom. Ezekiel and I had tan brown skin, while Alana and Maverick's was lighter. Ez and I looked native, and the other two didn't — even though we had the same Hawkei blood running through our veins.

I returned to the kitchen. "Where are Mom and Dad?" Ezekiel asked Alana before he chugged a glass of milk.

"Dad's at the office," Alana said. "I guess Mom went with him for some reason."

Thank the ancestors that Mama and Daddy weren't home. Ezekiel had a big mouth.

"If they're both there, it must be important," Ezekiel said.

Alana shrugged. "Maybe."

Daddy was the chief of Toaqua, and responsible for everyone in the Water tribe. Mama was on the Koigni Elder Council, working alongside him to maintain peace amongst the Houses. During the Elementai Civil War twenty years ago, there'd been a prophecy about my mother and how she would save the tribe. I'd only been a baby then, but according to my parents, it'd been a terrible time of war and suffering amongst the Houses. As the chosen one, my mother had led the tribe into a new age of peace— but not without a lot of sacrifice.

Because I was her firstborn, I was expected to live up to her incredible story. And I'd thoroughly disappointed everyone.

As if being the daughter of the Water chief wasn't enough publicity. My parents were tribal heroes. Me being able to cast magic from two different Houses would cause more undue attention to our family.

Like I hadn't done that enough already.

While Ezekiel ate, I ran upstairs. I showered, dried and curled my hair before flinging open my closet door— which was packed to the brim with poofy dresses, bedazzled jean jackets, and six-inch pumps.

I stood at the door and tapped a finger against my chin. What was I in the mood for today?

I had this fabulous pink tulle skirt I'd sewn myself that fell around my knees, with a cut-off cream shirt. They'd go perfect with a white pair of heels. I slipped them on, then sat at my vanity and began applying primer and foundation before working on contouring my cheekbones. I tossed lipsticks and eyeliner around my messy room carelessly, looking for the right one.

I was nothing more than thinly organized chaos. Everything in my room was pink— I *loved* pink— though you could barely tell under the piles of clothes I had lying around. My bedroom had a theme; unicorns. I had a unicorn bedspread, unicorn posters, and unicorn lamps.

I collected unicorns. I was fricking obsessed with them. I even wanted a unicorn tattoo one day. It was all so pink and girly, and it made me feel fabulous. Anyone who thought my room looked like a five-year-old's could suck a dick, because I liked it, and that's what mattered.

I had a wardrobe full of makeup products. I didn't need them as much anymore... not since I quit my beauty vlog, but it felt like a sin to throw them out.

Mama and Daddy wanted me to pick it back up again. But I hadn't made a video since Monica died. It felt like a betrayal to make one without her.

Thinking of Monica always made a pang run through my chest. I threaded my fingers over the bracelet she'd woven me, which I never took off. Red and green, for Koigni and Nivita.

It was the last piece I had left of her. Sometimes, I still heard her laugh echoing through the house. The memory of her smile got me through my bad days.

I had a lot of those.

I rummaged through my vanity drawer, looking for the final touch. If Uncle Jonah had taught me one thing, there was never enough glitter. I dusted a tiny bottle of it over my arms and cheeks before I posed in the mirror.

I looked *so hot*. Looks were everything. People judged with their eyes. I loved makeup, because there was nothing you couldn't hide with it.

Ezekiel was messing around with his guitar when I came downstairs. "Finally."

He put his guitar aside. Alana gave a wave as we headed out. We'd asked her to come with us, but she was an introvert and liked her alone time.

We took the motorboat into town. I watched as dolphins and whales swam between hippocampi— half-horse, half-mermaid creatures. Their scales sparkled in the water, making me wish to reach out and brush my fingers over their spiny manes. Everything about my world was magical, and I savored each moment of it.

We docked the boat before walking up the winding path to Kinpago. As we entered the city, another invigorating sense of *home* struck me. I watched from the streets as dragons flew overhead, twirling with griffins and birds with rainbow feathers that were bigger than buildings. The streets were packed with Elementai walking side by side with direwolves, basilisks and three-headed animals like chimeras.

The perytons were always my favorite. The winged deer had such spirits as they bounded through the streets, bobbing their antlered heads.

The Elementai had the most important job in the world— protecting and defending magical creatures. We were their caretakers as designated by the ancestors themselves, and the creatures depended on us for survival. Every magical creature imaginable that existed in the world had a species based here in Kinpago. More often than not, we were the only thing that prevented them from going extinct. As a result, many of them became our Familiars.

A Familiar was an Elementai's soul, the part of their spirit that existed outside of their body. Every Elementai was bonded to one, and you usually met them sometime after you got your powers. Elementai couldn't live without their Familiars, as they were the source of our magic, our life energy. If you died, so did they.

I hadn't gotten my Familiar yet. I'd desperately looked for one the first day I could cast my element, but I hadn't found them. Somewhere, I knew my soul was out there waiting for me, and the longing to join the pieces of myself together was almost like an obsession. What would they be, and what would my Familiar mean to me?

There were so many colors in Kinpago. Streamers hung from buildings, and Hawkei music played as people danced in the streets beneath the skyscrapers and shops. I smelled fry bread, cinnamon, and freshly baked pizza. Vendors on the street sold beads for making jewelry, white sage and woven baskets.

I wanted to stop and look— shopping was my favorite activity— but Ezekiel pulled me along in the direction of my grandfather's house. He knew once I went on a shopping spree, I wouldn't stop until I was flat broke.

In the distance, I saw the spires of a white castle rise into the clouds, and my heart thudded with just a little bit of magic.

Ezekiel nudged me knowingly. "Are you ready? Just a few more days now."

Excitement welled in my chest. I couldn't wait to attend Orenda Academy of Magical Creatures. I'd heard so many stories from my parents about how amazing it was when I was growing up. I wanted to have those incredible experiences, too.

"I'm glad I'm going with you," I told Ez. I'd taken a year off after graduating from high school and postponed my enrollment because... well, Monica.

And something else I didn't want to think about.

But now I was ready. I was sure of it. And Ez would be there, right alongside me in the same grade. I could handle it.

Ezekiel came to an abrupt halt. I nearly slammed into him, but held myself back at the last minute.

An annoying laugh caused a twinge of irritation to pass me by. I saw the bleached blonde mane of hair before anything else. Ezekiel's mouth became thin, though I felt the hints of desperation oozing out from him.

I grabbed Ezekiel's arm and steered him in a different direction. "Just ignore her. She's not worth it."

His eyes remained glued to the back of blondie's head. I took another glance back. When I saw who she was talking to, my mouth ran dry.

I *really* didn't like Rosary, but it was the sight of the person beside her that churned my gut. I took a short look before I set my eyes forward. The small movement was just enough to make a smirk cross John's face.

Fuck him. I *hated* him.

I forced my hand not to shake on Ezekiel's arm, and we took a different path. Even when we were well out of John's sight, I still felt sick to my stomach.

I wouldn't acknowledge it. I'd forgotten. That was that.

Ezekiel hadn't noticed my momentary panic. He was still miserable. "Do you think there's a chance she'll take me back?"

I focused on the conversation with Ezekiel, to redirect my nauseated feelings. "You've gotta let her go, Ez. She's no good for you."

"I know." His shoulders slumped. "Just wish things would've turned out different."

Rosary had completely broken my brother's heart. He'd never been the same after she dumped him.

Good riddance. I thought of wrapping my hands around her neck and squeezing, and a smile crossed my face. "She was abusive. You can do so much better."

Rosary had hit my brother once. I'd made sure she'd never do it again. The burns were so bad she still had a scar on her arm. *Nobody* fucked with my little brother.

"I'm sure things would've worked out." He dropped his head. "If the baby would've survived."

Okay, Ezekiel was a goody-goody until it came to one thing— girls. He thought with what was in his pants instead of in his head. I guess the condom broke one time. Not gonna lie, it was kind of nice when Daddy and Mama found out. They'd grilled Ezekiel's ass instead of mine, for once. He and Rosary were set to become teen parents— until Rosary had lost the pregnancy last year, and dumped him right off the bat.

My brother had taken the miscarriage harder than Rosary had. Ez had such a sweet heart— he'd cried for days. My whole family had just managed to bring him out of it. And as much as I despised her, I felt sorry for Rosary. No one should lose a baby, but the way she'd treated Ez after the fact was just plain cruel.

I felt the tension in the air alter as Ezekiel changed the subject. "Maybe you should try talking to Johnny again. I know you guys had a falling out after Monica died, but you two were really close. It's sad you don't talk anymore."

A pit in my stomach opened up and devoured me. He wasn't Johnny anymore. He was John. And Ezekiel didn't know what happened between us. Nobody did.

Thoughts came rushing back. I tried so hard to push them out of my head, but they kept coming, pouring over me like an endless waterfall. I literally felt the color from my face drain. I let go of Ezekiel's arm, so he could no longer feel my hands quiver.

"Ava, are you okay?" Ezekiel noticed my pale expression. "Did you take your pills this morning?"

"I always take my pills." Not that they helped. I was still three fries short of a Happy Meal.

Ezekiel watched me carefully. "Are you sure you'll make it to Grandpa's? Maybe you should go back home."

"You're probably right. I'm not feeling great," I mumbled. I reached into my purse and gave him the idol. "Take this to Grandpa's. I'll meet you later."

He eyed me up and down. "It might be a good idea to walk you back."

"I'm fine, Ez. I promise."

I was not fine. Yet Ezekiel knew I hated it when people hovered over me, so he stepped back to give me some space. "Okay. You can take the boat back. I'll grab the ferry. See you."

Ezekiel started down the road. I turned the other way, though I didn't go back the way we came.

I needed to take a different path. I had to be alone.

As I wandered down the city streets of Kinpago, I felt a burst of energy fizzle through my brain. It felt like I could run a hundred marathons without breaking a sweat. I wanted to run right now— get all these eyes off of me. Dozens of people were passing me by, and it felt like all of them were staring right through me.

They're spying on you, Ava.

They're following you.

You're not safe.

Run!

"Shut up," I whispered under my breath. I shut my eyes for a few moments to make the voices stop, but they kept coming, so numerous I could no longer make out what they were saying. It was like an entire auditorium was screaming at me all at once, amplifying the volume with every word.

I could taste metal. I could smell blood. It was so overpowering it made me want to vomit. All those eyes were still on me. The buildings were leaning inward and threatening to topple over. I diverged from the main street and began jogging down a deserted alley, trying to escape the ringing in my ears.

"It's just a hallucination. Ignore it," I told myself.

Yet I couldn't. Voices. So many voices echoing in my head. There was no way of escape—

I was thrown off balance as someone slammed into my side. I thought it was another part of the hallucination, until I felt a strong hand on my arm keep me from falling over. I tottered on my heels and my purse slipped off my arm, falling onto the pavement. The voices abruptly stopped as I turned to face the person I'd accidentally run into.

"Easy there, pidge," a cool, smooth voice said. "Don't want to scrape up those pretty little knees."

I caught the flash of a remarkably cocky smile, and for no reason at all, it instantly put me at ease. My eyes roamed up and down the man who'd caught me. He had to be in his early twenties. He was a few inches taller than me, around six foot two. His dark hair fell into his murky eyes. We were so close together I could see the emerald flecks within the hazel tones, which appeared to be honey pools I could dive into. His skin was brown, darker than mine, and his body was corded with muscle. His ripped jeans and tight t-shirt was like something straight out of a magazine.

A bad boy. I liked bad boys. At his side, a gray husky with a star marking on its forehead sat panting in the sun.

I tried to place what ethnicity the guy might be. He had to be Hawkei, like me— he had a Familiar after all— but besides being an indigenous North American tribe, the Hawkei had been intermingling with other races for centuries. I thought I could place him as Latino, but I could see some Middle Eastern features as well, mixed in with African traits.

Hey, I liked multicultural guys, and this dude looked like a world tour. For my vagina.

Then I noticed something— how the man's gaze didn't quite connect with mine. The dog eyed me with a shining expression, one that was confusing to put together.

The man was blind. I felt stupid for not noticing sooner. Should've paid more attention instead of ogling over him like the god he was.

Which is why what came out of my mouth next was just as stupid. "How... how can you tell I'm a girl?" I asked. I didn't know if it was a rude question, but he couldn't see me, right?

The man smirked again. This time, I noticed he wasn't actually looking me in the eye— he stared in my direction, but his gaze went right through me, confirming my theory he was blind. "Most men don't wear perfume, pigeon. Or dresses that make that much noise. Your heels click on the stone."

His hand was still on my arm. The feel of his touch smoldered against my skin. I knew he couldn't see me, but when I looked into his eyes... I don't know. I felt a powerful connection, something that drew me in and absorbed my thoughts, making everything in my universe center upon this one man.

I didn't like being alone with guys, but this was different. I had an immediate knowledge that this stranger wouldn't hurt me. I noticed there was a jar on the ground, filled with a collection of coins and a few dollars. He'd been panhandling.

Sympathy filled my chest. I came from a rich family, so I'd never known what it was like to suffer financially. And however this guy had ended up in his situation, I didn't feel he deserved it.

"You dropped your purse." The guy took my purse from the husky's mouth. The dog must've fetched it, but I hadn't seen.

I took my purse back from him, still fixated on the sight of this guy. What was it about him that drew me in? "Thank you."

"No problem, pidge."

I felt like doing backflips. "Why are you calling me that… pidge?"

"Short for pigeon." He flashed another attractive smile. "Old timey slang for a hot dame."

He thought I was hot? I mean… he couldn't see me, but he had to be attracted to me all the same, to say something like that. Butterflies fluttered in my stomach. I *loved* vintage movies. I'd grown up on black and white films from the 1940s my Grandmother Eleanor loved. I thought the nickname was cute. "You new around here? I've never seen you before."

"Charlie Wahkin, ma'am," he drawled. "And you?"

"Ava-Marie." I knew better than to give him my full name. And yet we were like two magnets, drawn together as if by fate. Charlie. I liked it.

"You might want to be a little more careful next time," he said. "There are worse things in these alleyways than me."

I laughed. "Now why do I doubt that?"

He cocked his head a little. "Just mind what I told you, pidge. The back parts of any town are no place for a lady."

Charlie's smile smoldered, and my eyes went immediately to his lips. I had the thought of pressing mine against his… just to see what he would taste like. Gunpowder and lead came to mind. It would be explosive. I mean, it was insane to think of kissing a homeless guy, even one that was really, really cute. Hot damn, this guy was a full-course meal with dessert on the side. Could I put in an order for delivery? Because I'd totally eat him up.

I brushed off my skirt— it'd gotten some dirt on it when Charlie had grabbed me. "Well, Charlie, I hope I see you again soon."

"Don't count on it, miss. I don't stick around."

He inclined his head. The tiniest movement he made was sexy. I smiled back, though I realized he couldn't see it, so instead I said, "Thanks again, Charlie."

When I was at the end of the alleyway, I dared to turn around. Charlie was gathering the few things he had, stuffing them into a backpack before he and his husky wandered the other way.

Once Charlie was out of my sight, cold deadness settled back into my chest, bringing my heart down with a heavy weight. As I left the man behind me, the hallucination came pouring back into my thoughts. If I hadn't run into Charlie in the alley, and stopped the hallucination, no telling how far I'd fall into it this time.

I suffered from psychosis. Often. It was a symptom of my bipolar disorder. Not all people with bipolar saw and heard things that weren't there, but I did. I'd talked to invisible people long after it was appropriate to have imaginary friends, and described things I could see that other people couldn't. Sometimes, it happened in school and I'd scared my classmates. By the time my doctors had put together a medication regimen that lessened the severity of the hallucinations, my reputation had already been tarnished. Crazy Ava-Marie. That's what people called me.

Growing up, the response to that would always be I *wasn't* crazy, but now I wasn't so sure they were wrong. I'd been in and out of therapy all my life. I wasn't going now, because I'd been crafty enough to convince my parents I didn't need it. The truth was, I'd just given up hope, and didn't see how talking to someone would help me now if it hadn't in the past. The hallucinations had been under control, before Monica died.

Ever since? They were worse than they ever had been.

I got back on the boat so I could head home. I rummaged through my purse to find the boat key. I found it, but not much else. My guts bottomed out when I realized my wallet was missing.

What the hell? How did I lose it? My mind raced. I hadn't touched my wallet once since we'd left the house. I had no idea how it could be missing.

Then I pieced things together. My purse had fallen off my arm when I'd stumbled into Charlie. His Familiar was the one who retrieved it for me. The dog must've snatched the wallet before Charlie had given me back my purse! I'd had over a hundred dollars in there. This was bullshit!

I let out a huff and rolled my eyes. What the fuck ever. I never carried my credit cards with me, anyway, so those were safe. If that guy was lousy enough to steal, he needed the money more than I did.

Geez, what a loser. I thought that guy was hot. I had the shittiest taste in men.

I drove the boat back to the house in a bad mood.

It was a Sunday, so like always, my giant family was here, getting ready to have our afternoon get-together. My Uncle Cade was at the grill, while my Aunt Imogen was doing the hula to tropical music that played on the radio. Her fox Familiar, Sassy, rose up on her hind legs to sway to the beat. Four of their boys, all various ages, were playing football on the beach. Their fifth son— the oldest, same age as my younger sister, was talking to Alana as he swam around the pool. Alana never swam— she was afraid of water. She sat on one of the lounge chairs and screamed as Luis tried to splash her and missed. I kicked off my heels in the boat and walked barefoot to the house.

"Ava, my darling!" A wet kiss was placed on my cheek as I felt arms the size of tree trunks wrap around me and squeeze.

"Can't breathe," I gasped. I fell several feet as my Uncle Jonah let me go. He was a giant of a man, but he had the biggest heart.

"You'd better be taking my dance class this semester," Uncle Jonah said as he waggled his finger at me.

"I've already signed up." Jonah was the Dean of Yapluma at Orenda Academy. He mostly taught Air magic and psychology classes, but his dance class was not to be missed. His Familiar, a hippogriff named Squeaks, trotted up to me and nudged me with her head.

Her offspring were a part of the hippogriff herd I'd gotten a ride from that morning. I scratched her shoulder feathers, and she cooed happily.

"Don't expect to get by so easily because you're my niece. I fully expect you to shake that booty until it falls off," Uncle Jonah teased, and his eyes sparkled.

I laughed. "Yes, Auntie."

Whether we called Jonah auntie or uncle depended on what personality he'd decided to put on that morning. He was fine with either. He crushed the beer can he was holding against his head and ran down the beach, screaming, "Save a touchdown for me, boys!"

His husband, Jake, was tossing the football. Jonah hurtled toward him and tackled him onto the sand, where they wrestled for dominance. Squeaks danced around them awkwardly, until her tail swished and knocked a tray of hot dogs off the picnic bench and onto the ground.

Jonah's daughter, Josee, was messing around with a soccer ball like always. She kicked it to Maverick, who tried to navigate it around her to score a goal. He failed when she snatched it out of the air effortlessly.

Josee was a total tomboy. All she cared about was sports. Not me. I liked looking pretty, thank you very much. She waved me over to join them, but I shook my head no and continued onto the porch.

Mama was there, taking pictures with her professional camera. The cutest little creature sat on her shoulder. It had big eyes, with fluffy brown fur, a poofy tail and long ears like those of a fennec fox. Her name was Buttercup, and she was a kurble— a type of marsupial. Buttercup trilled when I climbed the porch steps, and Mama looked up.

I always thought Mama was one of the prettiest women alive. She had long brunette hair with eyes that were always welcoming and kind, and she held herself in a dignified way I never thought I could imitate, or achieve. My mother radiated power like the sun radiated heat, and people respected her for it.

Mama put the camera down and smiled as I came by.

"Did you and your brother have a nice hike?" she asked.

"Yeah," I lied. "He's still out there. Wanted to stop by Grandpa's for a minute. What did you and the council talk about?"

Mama's smile faltered for a brief moment. "It was nothing important."

Nothing, huh? I wasn't the only one telling tall tales.

Just then, a dragon's roar rang across the wind. I looked up. A ruby red dragon, with scales glistening in the sunlight, spiraled down from the sapphire skies. The dragon was massive, and was almost as large as our house. As the dragon landed, shock waves resonated across the beach, and a man slid off the dragon's back.

"Watch your tail, Julian," Daddy said. "You nearly knocked down the house."

Julian grumbled and curled his tail the other way. It hit Squeaks and sent her flying into the water. The hippogriff made an angry sound, while Julian grumbled an apology.

Daddy was tall, with long black hair and a strong jawline that made him appear proud. The chief of the Water tribe always looked strong, even when he was at his weakest.

I wished I could emulate that kind of confidence. My dad had never been a fish out of water.

Unlike my Mama, Daddy was very sick. I could see it clearest when he was trying to hide how he really felt. Daddy suffered from a rare disease that caused his magic to weaken his bodily systems, his immune system getting the brunt of the illness. It was genetic, but so far, neither me nor my siblings had developed it.

And I hoped none of us ever did. It was tough growing up, watching your dad be in and out of the hospital. A few times, he'd barely pulled through. But I'd never have it any other way, because I really loved my Daddy, and I didn't care if he was sick, so long as he was here.

As he drew closer, I noticed the bags under his eyes, and the way his steps faltered slightly on the sand. He could smile, but I wasn't fooled. He was tired today.

Still, he put out an arm and drew me into a hug. "There's my peanut. I missed you this morning."

My stomach wiggled uncomfortably. I'd left before Daddy had gotten up, to retrieve the idol. "Ez and I wanted to get a head start on the hike."

"See anything interesting?"

I swallowed. Lying to Daddy was always the hardest. "Nah. Nothing out of the ordinary."

Daddy gave me a warm smile. Before he could ask anything else, I said, "You and Mama were gone for a long time. You don't work on weekends. Is something up?"

He frowned slightly. "You know tribal business can happen at any time. It's nothing to be worried about."

I knew exactly when Daddy wasn't telling the truth. He blinked twice.

It was strange Mama and Daddy were being shady about the Elder meeting this morning. Why didn't they want me to know about it?

I decided I didn't care. I trusted Daddy with everything. If he was keeping something from me, it was for my own good. He wouldn't lie to me about something important. He never hid secrets from me that mattered.

Mama bit her lip as she took in my father's appearance. "You look tired, Liam. Come inside."

"Only for a moment." Daddy's eyes crossed to Aunt Imogen and Uncle Jonah, who were shaking their butts on the beach to the music. It was very typical of them. That was my crazy aunt and uncle.

Daddy shuffled slowly up the steps. I walked behind him, to catch him just in case he fell.

"I don't need to be nannied, you know," Daddy said crossly as he sat on a kitchen chair. He sent a surly gaze to me as Mama placed a glass of water on the table.

"What kind of daughter would I be if I didn't?" I asked. I hovered beside him, but not too close. Buttercup perched beside the glass of water and tilted her head before Daddy took a sip.

Mama sat across from Daddy and laid a hand on his chest. As she did, a white glow emitted from her fingertips and spread over Daddy's body. I watched, entranced by the silvery strands that wrapped around Daddy's form.

Mama could treat Daddy's disease with her Spirit magic. She couldn't cure him, but she could heal him partially, and treat his symptoms. Her powers were the only thing that kept him going most days. Watching her use her magic on him was always beautiful. Spirit magic came from love, and I could really tell that Mama loved Daddy.

All at once, the color in Daddy's face brightened, and he sat taller. It was like I could see his illness visibly ebbing away from him as Mama's Spirit powers worked their magic. When she was done, the glow faded and Daddy's voice was stronger.

He turned toward me. "So, what path did you and your brother take today?"

Before I could answer, the door burst open and slammed against the wall. I heard footsteps run into the kitchen as Ezekiel screamed, "Ava's got Water powers!"

Fucking dammit. Couldn't trust Ez to keep a secret to save his life.

Ezekiel skidded to a halt. The color drained from his face as he realized I'd gotten back first. My lips formed into a sneer. Mama and Daddy's mouths dropped open at the same time, looking from me to my brother in surprise.

I pounced. I jumped on Ezekiel's back and locked my arm around his neck. "You little snitch!"

Ezekiel grabbed my arm as he fell to his knees. We struggled violently before he wrenched me off. I went tumbling to the floor. I went to launch myself at him again, but Daddy held me back.

"Ow! You kicked me in the face!" Ez complained, holding his eye.

"Good, you probably look better," I shot back at him.

"Enough," Daddy said firmly. "Ava, what's this about?"

I took a few ragged breaths and refused to answer. But Ezekiel, who went to pieces under any sort of interrogation, blurted, "Ava and I were at the dig site, and—"

"You two went to that excavation?" Daddy leapt up from his chair. "I specifically told you not to mess around in those caves— don't roll your eyes at me, young lady!"

He'd caught me at it, but come on. This was stupid.

"Forget about that," Mama said quickly. "Ezekiel, you said Ava used Water powers."

"Uh-huh." Ezekiel's head bobbed like he was a little boy. "We found the idol, but it turned out to be a malevolent Koigni Spirit Art. It was going to kill me, until Ava commanded the underground river within the caves to attack it. I watched a wave rise up and destroy it."

"Honey, is this true?" Mama's eyes were wide. Buttercup mirrored her expression.

"I mean..." I shrugged. "Yeah, it happened, but it must've been a one-off thing. I don't have Water powers. I'm Koigni!"

"That's not what she asked," Daddy said. I was trying his patience.

"Look, I just did it to protect my brother! I don't know if I could do it again!" I said.

Mama nodded. She'd first discovered her powers doing something similar, defending her sister from an attacking lion years ago.

I fisted a hand in my hair. "Maybe we shouldn't have gone to the caves. But whatever happened this morning, it won't happen again. I've never felt partial to Water. I like Fire. I'm a Koigni through and through, and—"

As I was rambling, Daddy purposefully knocked over the glass of water that was sitting on the table. I gasped and reacted instinctively. My left hand shot out. The water that was about to hit the floor suspended in the air, hovering at my command.

I was so shocked that the spell broke, and water splashed all over the hardwood. Nobody moved to clean it up. Everyone stared at me, like I was some sort of freak animal.

Daddy took in a breath. "Ava, you're incredible." Daddy was fit to boasting. He was proud I'd inherited his side of the magical spectrum. But why were they all so happy about this? I didn't feel like it was anything to celebrate.

There was no denying it. Or hiding it. I did have Toaqua powers. I just didn't understand why.

"How could this have happened?" I asked. "I thought Elementai always inherited the powers of their same-sex parent."

"Ava, you have multiple generations of Fire and Water running through your veins. The same-sex parent rule must be canceled out once your genetics become diluted enough. Fire and Water are both dominant traits in your genes," Mama said, marveling at her own words.

"Does this mean I might get Fire powers, too?" Ezekiel asked in excitement. He was thrilled about becoming a dual-caster, but he didn't get it. It wasn't a gift to be different. It was a curse.

"It depends on what traits are dominant. My traits are from my Spirit and Fire side, but they can co-exist peacefully. But I've never heard of Fire and Water traits being dominant at the same time," Mama said.

"Exactly. It's never happened before." I couldn't keep the bitterness out of my voice. This was just one more thing that would set me apart from everyone else.

"Ava, the ancestors chose to give you this gift," Daddy said. "Why not use it for good?"

"Because I just want to be normal, that's why!" I burst. "People already think I'm crazy. What are they going to say when they find out I'm a dual-caster? The press is going to go nuts!"

As the daughter of the Toaqua chief and the chosen one, I'd been the subject of Hawkei tabloids multiple times. Most of the articles weren't very kind. I couldn't imagine this one would be, either.

Mama's eyebrows scrunched together. "You're not crazy, sweetheart. You have bipolar."

I blew a lock of hair out of my eyes. "Big difference."

Ezekiel came close to me. This time, he looked a little bothered. "Are you okay, Ava? I was worried about you when you left earlier."

"I told you I was fine." Did he really have to bring this up in front of our parents? He could've asked me later.

"I just... I don't know." Ezekiel shrugged. "You had that look in your eyes you used to get when you were hearing things."

Daddy and Mama went rigid. I suppressed a groan. "You're hearing voices again?" Mama's eyes narrowed in concern.

"No," I lied. "I haven't heard anything. I was just tired earlier."

"Ava, you'd better be telling the truth," Daddy warned.

"Not a single sound."

I couldn't let them know the voices were back. They'd give me a kiss and ship me off to the loony bin before I had a chance to pack my designer heels. I'd told them the voices had stopped years ago, to keep them from worrying, when in reality they never had.

Ezekiel gave me *the look.* It was a secret gesture only we understood, and he was telling me I was full of shit.

"Ava, whatever happens, we're here to help you," Mama said gently. She took my hand, like she was good at doing, and squeezed it tight. "If you're hearing voices, or if you don't understand your magic, we can work it out. There's nothing we can't do together as a family."

Tears started to bead at the corners of my eyes, but I pushed them back down. I didn't cry.

"You guys don't understand. I'm tired of being different. My magic was one thing that felt safe. And it doesn't feel like that anymore."

I turned away from them and ran. My parents called after me, but I ignored them. Everyone on the beach looked up as I bolted to the shoreline.

I didn't think about what I did. Just like my Fire, my Water magic erupted from me by feeling. I didn't know how I did what I did, but one moment, I was on the sand, and the next, a wave had risen up to catch my feet. I continued running, and the Water crashed upward to support my weight. I fell into the water and surfed across the waves like I would on my surfboard. People gasped when they saw me riding upon the water. I heard more cries, but I pretended like I didn't hear them, keeping my eyes on the horizon.

Soon, the island was long behind me. I collapsed on the shore of the mainland on all fours, breathing heavily. My shoulders shook. My clothes were soaked, but I didn't care.

I felt like I was going to crack. If I didn't maintain control, I *would* crack, and everything I was holding inside would break free. I had to get it together. I forced myself to stand and slicked back my wet hair, eyeing the span of the empty beach.

I was so empty inside. The hollowness just wouldn't go away, and I didn't know how to fill it.

I was Toaqua now. Maybe I could drown it.

As the dark thought crossed my mind, I heard a rustle in the trees coming from the forest beyond the beach. I stood up slowly as a creature emerged.

By the ancestors, she was beautiful. The creature was a tall and slender unicorn, with a coat dark as night and an obsidian horn rising out of the center of her forehead. The mare's eyes were black, and her mane and tail burned with flame, sending embers to the ground as the fire that made up her hair trailed over her neck and withers.

A Fire unicorn. I'd heard of them, but I'd never seen one before. She was looking right at me.

I advanced toward the Fire unicorn. As I drew near, my clothes and hair dried automatically at the presence of her heat. The air around her was hot, but I didn't mind at all. The unicorn was completely still as she faced me head-on. In the middle of her forehead was a singular white mark— a seven-pointed star. She nickered as I dared to reach out a hand. I placed it on her velvety nose.

The moment I touched her, the entire world opened up. I saw so many colors at the edges of my vision, colliding together in a gorgeous rainbow. The purpose of my life entwined together with this creature, sucking me in and holding me in an embrace that was welcoming and home. I felt the fires of her passion burning away at me, taking away anything that was bad and leaving behind only what was right. This wasn't like the visions I experienced during psychosis. This was real, and it was comforting. I smelled sandalwood, the ocean, and the remnants of a burning fire. I heard my brother's laughter and the sound of Monica singing. The song continued, wrapping around me as I felt Daddy's hug and Mama braiding my hair. I imagined sunlight hitting my face, and the glow of a candle in the dark. Images flashed before my eyes, like they would if I was experiencing my last moments before death; but instead of death, this was a new awakening.

The unicorn placed her nose to my chest. When she touched my heart, I felt such a powerful wave of emotion that my knees buckled beneath me and I cried out.

As the music faded and Monica's voice ebbed away, I knew immediately that I had bonded. I didn't need to question it. This unicorn was my Familiar. My soul. Familiars always came to you at your weakest point— and she had known I needed her now.

"Who are you?" I whispered. I was completely enchanted by her.

The mare blinked. She didn't speak to me, but I felt a strong feeling in my heart, and a name popped into my head… *Oberi.*

"Oberi." That was her name. I reached out and wrapped my arms around her neck. The unicorn turned her head inward and nuzzled me, as if hugging me to her chest.

The hollowness inside me went away, and I reveled in the feeling of touching my Familiar for the first time. I had found who I was. I'd discovered myself. Everything in my life tied me to this creature, and I knew then that I wasn't alone.

As I pulled away, the unicorn turned to me, offering me her back. I reached up to take her mane in my hands. Though it was made of Fire, the flames didn't burn me. I pulled myself onto the unicorn, and Oberi gave another knicker. She bounced a few times on her hooves before giving a tiny rear, then bolted forward.

Her feet kicked up sand as she galloped down the beach. My hair was blown backward by the wind, and I gave a cry of joy. This was entirely different than riding the hippogriffs. It was like Oberi and I were one, a singular being with no start and no end. Her flames blew by as I twisted them in my hands. It was like my spirit left my body as I felt her powerful strides pound the earth, creating a song in my heart as we splashed against the waves. As we ran, I saw other unicorns made of Water rise out of the ocean, charging alongside Oberi.

I had done that out of my emotion. My magic. Maybe being Toaqua wasn't such a bad thing after all.

Oberi slowed to a halt, and I took deep breaths to stabilize my shaking form. I slid off her back, still winded. My mind calculated the possibilities as I stroked Oberi's midnight coat.

I'd bonded with a Fire creature. This proved I was Koigni, right? Maybe I could hide my Toaqua side. Nobody needed to know about it, right? They'd never guess, not with a Fire unicorn at my side.

As I was still taking in the incredible moment, an angry cry rang out across the beach. "Get away from my Familiar!"

I turned around. My stomach bottomed out when I realized who was shouting at me. It was Charlie— the blind man I'd run into earlier. The one who'd taken my wallet. He stomped up the beach, his bag thrown over his back.

Anger rose within me. This guy was a piece of work. What the hell was he doing, bothering me and Oberi? How did he even know where we were? He couldn't see us.

"You're going to get a fireball to the face," I snarled. I conjured one and drew back my hand to throw it.

Before I could, Oberi gave a high-pitched whinny. She ran toward Charlie, tossing her head. The fireball dropped out of my hand and fizzled on the sand as I watched Oberi change. In seconds, she'd morphed from a female Fire unicorn... into the same male husky I'd seen with Charlie earlier.

The husky barked and wagged his tail at Charlie's side. Shock twisted my guts when the husky turned to look at me. I noticed the same seven-pointed star on his forehead that Oberi had.

This was impossible. How could Oberi have two different *genders*? Two different *forms*? I'd never heard of such a Familiar before.

My heart twisted sickly as I watched Charlie pet the husky. Then I knew.

I wasn't just bonded to this creature— to Oberi. I was bonded to *Charlie* as well. His Familiar was also my own.

My spirit was split into two pieces. And the other half belonged to him.

I shared a soul with a complete stranger.

I wasn't even here for a freaking *day*, and already I'd run into trouble. *Ava-Marie.* The sound of her voice was irritating. How *dare* she touch my Familiar!

Apparently, first impressions weren't all they were cracked up to be. At first, I felt bad for stealing from her. Now I knew it was karma at its finest.

Ava-Marie stomped her foot into the sand. *Real mature.* "This *can't* be happening."

"What?" I bit. "Getting caught trying to kidnap my Familiar?"

"Kidnap!? As if," she growled. "Oberi and I just bonded."

I went still. "How do you know his name?"

"*Her*," Ava-Marie countered. "Oberi's a *girl*. And I know because I just bonded, like I told you, jackass!"

No way. Professor Baine said Oberi and I shared the same soul. I wasn't about to give joint custody to this stranger. I wanted to snap back at her, but I hesitated. I didn't know much about this world. I needed answers.

"Does that happen often?" I asked.

"What? Two people bonded to the same creature? Of course not!" she cried. "Is this your first day in Kinpago or what?"

I crossed my arms. "Actually, yes."

"You—" Ava-Marie cut off, like it took her a second to process what I'd said. Her tone softened. "This is seriously your first day?"

"Yeah. Some guy named Professor Baine showed up at my apartment and said I had to come learn my powers," I explained.

"*Professor Baine*?" Ava-Marie huffed, before lowering her voice to a mumble. "What the fuck is Grandpa up to now?"

"Excuse me?" I balked. "Did you just say Professor Baine is your *grandfather*?"

Ava-Marie didn't answer. I heard a subtle vibration, and realized she was punching the screen of her phone. I could practically hear smoke coming out her nose as she spoke. "Hi,

Grandpa. Care to explain what some guy named Charlie is doing on the beach claiming he's bonded to *my* Familiar?"

Professor Baine's voice came from the other end. "Ancestors, Ava. You've *bonded*?"

Ava's voice was seriously irritated. "Kind of not the main issue here. Can you please get down to the beach and convince this… *impostor* how bonding works? We can't be bonded to the same Familiar. It doesn't work like that!"

"I'll be there right away," Professor Baine said. "Don't go anywhere."

Ava-Marie scoffed. "As if. I'm not going anywhere without my Familiar."

Ava's phone vibrated as she hung up, before she directed her anger back at me. "You have real nerve showing up here thinking you can just bond with whomever you want!"

"You say that like I planned this," I shot back. "Oberi came to *me* first."

"*You're* the one who came to Kinpago," she accused. "You should've stayed in whatever hellhole you crawled out of."

My hands curled into fists. Had no one taught this girl manners?

"That hellhole's better than standing here arguing with you," I snapped. "Besides, Oberi didn't find me in Kinpago. He found me in Detroit."

"Sure she did," Ava-Marie said sarcastically. "Because magical creatures just leave the boundaries of the reservation every fucking day."

"Well, *he* left to find me!" I countered.

She gave an obnoxious noise. "There has to be a way we can figure this out fair and square," Ava-Marie insisted.

"What, like put Oberi between us and see who he runs to?" I replied flatly. "That sounds like a great idea."

"Yeah, it does," Ava-Marie sneered. "Oberi, come."

Oberi stood, but I placed a hand on his neck. "No, Oberi," I commanded. "Stay."

He hesitated. I hadn't heard his voice in my head since the night I met him, but I could feel his emotions ebb and flow through the bond. He was conflicted.

Eventually, Oberi settled and obeyed my command, but Ava-Marie wasn't happy about it. "You're being unfair!" she huffed. "Oberi is *my* Familiar!"

Air began rushing toward me a second later. On instinct, I reached out and caught Ava-Marie's wrists before she could shove me backward. She stumbled forward until we were so close I could feel her heartbeat against my chest.

Warmth swelled throughout my abdomen, though I couldn't explain it. I hated this girl, yet something told me to wrap my arms around her and pull her close. The conflicting instincts were enough to make me want to throw up from nausea. Ava-Marie blew a breath of disbelief.

"I wouldn't do that if I were you, pidge," I warned.

"Oh, yeah?" she challenged. "What are you going to do about it?"

I opened my mouth to answer, but I was cut off by the sound of Professor Baine's voice carrying across the beach.

"Ava!" he called.

She shoved herself away from me. Spite filled her voice. "Oh, good. My *gran-pataa* and Aunt Imogen are here. We can finally get some answers."

Professor Baine approached, along with another pair of footsteps. This must've been Ava's aunt. The woman barely made a sound in the sand, like she was walking barefoot. A four-legged creature followed beside her, though I couldn't tell what it was at first. It came up to sniff my feet, and I bent to pet it. The creature was the size of a small dog, with a short nose and pointed ears— a fox.

"What seems to be the problem?" Professor Baine asked.

"Charlie *stole* my Familiar!" Ava-Marie accused.

"Stole?" I nearly choked on my words. "I bonded to him first!"

"Well, I bonded to her, too!" Ava-Marie shouted.

"Oh, dear," Professor Baine mumbled. "This is quite the conundrum, isn't it?"

Ava-Marie blew a breath. "Understatement of the century. Charlie must be lying."

I gritted my teeth. This girl was really starting to get on my nerves.

"Professor," I begged. "You must know I bonded with Oberi. You said yourself it's how you found me!"

"Yes, yes, of course," Professor Baine said, sounding thoughtful.

"Auntie Imogen." Ava-Marie turned to her. "Tell me this isn't possible."

Her aunt sounded intrigued by the whole ordeal. "I've never seen it, but there's a way to find out the truth."

"There is?" Ava asked, relieved. My chest felt lighter.

"Yes," Imogen said. "Professor Baine knows a ceremony that will reveal the truth of the bond. Let's find somewhere comfortable to sit."

Their footsteps shuffled through the sand ahead of me. Oberi nudged my hand, and I placed it on his back. He led me forward, and I followed the three of them to an outcropping of rock.

"It's not far, Charlie," Professor Baine said. "Just a few more steps."

"Thanks," I mumbled, but I was less than grateful. I didn't need to be treated special just because I was blind. I could navigate my own way through this world. Rock and earth were especially easy to maneuver. It was like I could sense them as an extension of myself. They had a vibration of their own, like the air did.

My hand moved over the rock, and I sat down. I listened as Ava plopped onto the rock beside me, and felt Oberi's fur as he sat in the sand between us. Imogen cleared her throat on the other side of her.

"So, how does this work?" Ava asked impatiently.

"It's an ancient Hawkei ceremony," Professor Baine explained. "I will ask the ancestors to reveal the true nature of this creature's bond. You can both relax."

I let my shoulders fall, but it was difficult *relaxing* beside Ava-Marie. I worried she might grab Oberi and run off with him. She was the kind of dame that would do that.

But she seemed totally chill beside me— like calling upon the ancestors calmed her. To me, this was uncomfortable. I didn't know what the hell to expect.

Professor Baine began speaking in a language I didn't recognize. After a few moments, Ava gasped.

"What?" I asked breathlessly. "What is it?"

"Oh, it's *beautiful*," Ava practically sang. She leaned toward me slightly and spoke lowly, as to not interrupt her grandpa. "Ancestral light is swirling around Oberi. It has so many colors... like a watercolor painting. I wish you could see it."

I scoffed. Fat chance of that.

Professor Baine continued the strange incantation. The wind picked up around us, and Oberi barked. Goosebumps broke out along my skin, and a shiver traveled down my spine.

"What's happening now?" I asked Ava-Marie.

"The Spirit magic is shifting. It's breaking into two long tendrils and— ah!"

I felt it the same time she gasped. A warm energy shot straight into my chest. I jumped at first, until I noticed a calm wind wash over me. It was like touching Oberi for the first time all over again. I reached my fingers up to my chest, and they passed through a strange energetic current.

"What the hell?" I muttered.

"It's Spirit magic," Ava explained, but she sounded angry. "And it's connecting *both* of us to Oberi!"

"Ancestors!" Imogen breathed. "Professor, do you know what this means?"

"Th-this can't be," Professor Baine stuttered.

"How is this possible?" Ava demanded.

"What?" I asked. "What's going on?"

"You were right," Imogen said. "You're *both* bonded to Oberi."

"Which means you are part of the same soul." Baine sounded like his head was in the clouds. I didn't think he'd ever seen anything like this before. He kicked sand forward onto my shoes as he stumbled and steadied himself on the boulder beside me.

"This makes no sense!" Ava protested.

"It does," Imogen insisted, like she'd just realized something. "Many supernatural races have legends about people sharing the same soul. They call them twin flames. In the Miriamic Coven, identical twins share a soul. In the Hawkei world, you are what's referred to as *minai*."

"But what does that *mean*?" Ava asked. "How could we share a soul?"

Imogen sighed. "The mechanics are unclear. I presume Charlie's older, so when he was born, his soul must've fractured. And you, Ava, are the physical manifestation of what was left of it."

It was too much to wrap my head around. I'd gone speechless. I shared a soul with this strange girl? That couldn't be true.

"What, so I got the shitty half?" she questioned.

Imogen sounded disappointed. "Come on, Ava. It doesn't work that way. You're still your own person, but you and Charlie are connected. Just as your spirit was never complete without your Familiar, you and Charlie are not complete without each other."

I got a sour taste in my mouth. She sounded like she meant it *romantically*.

"So, Ava's like a second Familiar to me?" I asked.

"Don't say it like I'm some sort of *pet*," she growled.

"That's not what I meant," I snapped. God, she knew how to get on my nerves.

"Calm down, children," Professor Baine said. "I believe all Charlie meant was that you two are connected the same as you are connected to Oberi."

"It's not the same thing," Ava insisted.

Professor Baine didn't seem to hear her. "You two must learn to get along, as you will be sharing a Familiar for the rest of your lives."

"I don't want to *share her*," Ava whined.

I'd be damned if I didn't feel the same way. I didn't know Ava. I hadn't had Oberi long, but he meant everything to me. I didn't want to give any of my time with him to this stranger I'd just met.

Ava shifted on her rock, and she leaned down for Oberi. The moment I heard the rustle of his fur, something changed. I felt it deep down in my belly— like sensing a shift in the air. Oberi's energy suddenly felt less playful and became serious. There was a passion to our connection that felt different from anything I'd ever known.

Imogen and Professor Baine both gasped in unison.

"There's my Oberi I bonded with," Ava-Marie sang in a baby voice. "You're a good girl, aren't you?"

"What happened?" I growled, shooting to my feet. "What'd you do to him?"

"I didn't *do* anything," Ava countered. "Oberi shifted. Come here."

Ava grabbed my hand and yanked me forward so hard, I nearly fell over. She pressed my palm against something warm and soft. Oberi's energy pulsed through my hand, and I splayed my fingers over his form. But he was different. He was taller than I was, and his long husky coat had shrunk to short, velvety fur. I ran my fingers up his snout and felt his ears.

"A-a horse?" I questioned.

"A *unicorn*," Ava corrected. "And she's a girl now."

Curiously, I moved my hand over her forehead, and my fingers curled around a warm, smooth horn. It was enough to nearly knock me off my feet. It felt like some sort of trick, but I knew it was real.

"Oberi's a shifter," Professor Baine said aloud, though it seemed like he said it more for himself than anything.

"Ancestors, this is amazing!" Imogen squealed.

"You've heard of shifting Familiars?" Ava asked, like she'd never heard of one herself. "Does it have to do with sharing a soul? Like she takes one form for Charlie and one for me?"

"No," Imogen said. "I believe Oberi may be a *mutabeecha*."

"A muta-what?" I asked.

"*Mutabeecha*," Imogen repeated. "They're shape-shifting creatures known only to lore. Legend says they can only be found in the spirit realm as a companion to the Great Spirit. I never thought I'd see one with my own eyes."

"Yeah," I deadpanned. "Me, neither."

Ava-Marie was the only one to catch my sarcasm. She scoffed, like it wasn't that funny.

Imogen continued. "*Mutabeecha* take on a single form for every element. The Fire unicorn is obviously for Fire, and the husky must be for Air. She must've appeared to each of you in those forms, because they're your element."

Ava stroked Oberi's nose. "So Oberi has more than *two* forms?"

"If she is, in fact, a *mutabeecha*, she could have as many as five, for each of the five elements," Imogen said.

"*If?*" I asked. "Are there other possibilities?"

"Not that I know of," Imogen admitted. "But it's just so strange to see one. No one's ever encountered one on earth before. They exist only in the afterlife— in spiritual realms."

"The spirit realm?" I asked.

"Don't tell me you've never heard of the Ancestral Lands," Ava said.

What part of *I'm new here* did she not understand?

"Can't say I have," I stated flatly.

Professor Baine was the one to explain. "The Ancestral Lands are our afterlife. It is where the ancestors and the Great Spirit Himself reside."

"So if these… *mutabeecha* only exist in the spirit realm, how does anyone know they exist?" I challenged.

Ava elbowed me lightly in the side. "The ancestors speak to us. We're not totally clueless about the Ancestral Lands."

"Still new to all this, remember?" I sneered.

"Well, you have a lot of catching up to do," Ava-Marie said. It wasn't an insult, but this girl could come across rather harshly.

Professor Baine piped up then. "Which is *precisely* why Ava should show Charlie around."

"*What?*" the two of us yelled at the same time.

Imogen laughed, like we were amusing. I found the whole thing fucking annoying.

"Well, why not?" Professor Baine said, like it was the best idea he'd ever had. "You two share a Familiar. You'll be spending a lot of time together. Ava-Marie can show you around Orenda Academy and get you acquainted with our history."

"More like she'll snatch my Familiar and run off," I accused.

"That's actually not a bad idea," she shot back.

"Ancestors," Imogen groaned. "You sound like your mother, Ava."

"Is that a bad thing?" Ava challenged.

"Unfortunately, you don't have a choice," Professor Baine said. "I may be retired, but as an honorary Head Dean of the academy, I appoint you as Charlie's student guide."

"Student guide!" Ava nearly choked. "That's a pretty hefty demotion from *granddaughter*."

"I don't like this, either," I interjected. "I don't need a guide."

"I'm not doing this to punish either of you," Professor Baine assured us. "But Charlie needs a peer mentor, and you *both* need to learn how to share a Familiar."

"But Grandpa—" Ava started.

"No buts," he said. "My mind is made up. You two will either work together— or compromise the bond with your Familiar. The choice is yours."

Screw Professor Baine. Who the hell did he think he was to make me work with *Ava-Marie*? The girl was insufferable.

We walked along a path toward Orenda Academy— or I assumed that's where we were going. Ava-Marie casually mentioned tar pits in the area. Wouldn't be surprised if she lured me to them and threw me in just so she could have Oberi all to herself.

Then again, the tar pits were probably a lie. Everything else she said sounded like one.

"Grotesque monsters roam the grounds of the school, so you have to be careful which corridors you use," Ava-Marie said. "And don't get caught out at night. That's when the ghosts come out."

I tried to ignore Ava and instead focused on the sound of Oberi's hoofbeats on the path. But her voice was like a mosquito trying to fly into my ear. It wouldn't go away.

"Stop messing with me, pidge," I demanded. "I don't believe in ghosts."

"Why not? You didn't seem to have a problem believing in the ancestors. What's the difference?"

I hesitated. "I don't know. I don't know *what* I believe yet."

"Well, you better believe it, because it's true," she said.

A silent beat passed, and I waited for the confession I knew was coming.

"Okay," she caved. "Maybe I made up the thing about the monsters. And we don't really get ghosts in Kinpago. That's more of a witch thing. But rumor has it the old tower of Orenda Academy is haunted. Most of the castle is new, after it burned down twenty years ago."

"Yeah, okay," I said, still not believing a word she said.

"*Hey*," Ava-Marie snapped. She stopped ahead of me on the trail. I nearly ran into her, and Oberi stopped at our side. "I may have joked about the monsters, but I do *not* joke about Hawkei war history. My Grandfather Liwanu *died* when the castle burned to the ground. I never even got to meet him. Don't go make me out to be a liar when it comes to shit like this."

My shoulders relaxed, and my tone softened. "Okay, I believe you. What exactly happened in the war?"

Ava huffed and started walking again. "Forget it. It's not like you'll listen to me, anyway."

"That's not true," I countered. "If I'm going to live in this world, I want to know its history and all about the magic."

"Why? So you can challenge me in a magical duel over who gets Oberi?"

I pressed my palm to my face. "Oh, my god. You're impossible. Maybe I *will* battle you if it gets you to shut up."

"How dare you!" she gasped.

Ava seemed less than pleased with me. She quickened her pace and stomped ahead of me on the trail. I stayed close to Oberi, so she could lead me through this unfamiliar terrain.

I got a whole five seconds of reprieve from Ava, before she whirled around and stomped back toward me. "I'm not leaving Oberi."

Neither am I, I thought, though I didn't say anything. The last thing I needed was to fuel this girl's fire. I mean, she literally had Koigni powers. She could fry me in one blow.

We didn't talk again until we made it to the castle. I could tell when we arrived, because the air seemed to expand, giving way to a wide-open courtyard. The sound of students chatting met my ears, and I could sense the air currents of Familiars prowling through the courtyard. Strange animal calls I'd never heard before filled the area. A roar sounded, and I could've sworn it was a lion, but no way were there just *lions* walking around school grounds... right?

There were so many creatures that it was hard to make out all their sounds. I heard the whinny of a horse and the cry of an eagle. Wings flapped overhead, but it was unlike the wings of any bird I'd ever heard. Whatever it was must've had a twenty-foot wingspan.

I reached my senses out wider, and my magic stopped at a tall stone wall a hundred feet ahead of us. Ava hadn't been lying when she called Orenda Academy a castle. It was huge— I could tell by the way the wind currents moved around it.

"Ancestors, I love it here," Ava breathed.

"Is it that great?" I questioned.

"*That great*?" she repeated. "It's the most beautiful building in the world. It's too bad you can't see it."

For once, she actually sounded genuine. It made my insides soften. I caught it immediately, and they went right back to rock solid. I didn't fuck around with emotions. That was a good way to get hurt.

"Can you describe it to me?" I asked, hoping she'd say yes.

"Sure, but you'll have to keep up." Ava spoke as we walked across the courtyard to the castle. "The castle was built long ago by a friend of the Hawkei. The guy was mega-balls rich. After three-quarters of the castle burnt down, they tried to keep the same aesthetic in the rebuild. My parents say they can hardly tell it burnt down. Outside, the walls are made of stone. There are four main towers, and so many beautiful stained-glass windows. I love coming out here around sunset because the dragons like to perch on the spires and watch the ocean."

"Dragons!" I gasped. "There are really dragons here?"

"Well, yeah," she said like it was obvious. "This *is* the Academy of Magical Creatures."

"What other creatures are there?" I asked, intrigued.

Ava stopped just as we started climbing the stairs to what I figured must be the main entrance. She seemed to be taking a calculating survey of the courtyard. "Literally everything. Chimeras, manticores, phoenix, alicorns, griffins— take your pick."

The sound of hooves approached, and warm feathers brushed by my arm.

"Oh, and that was a hippogriff," Ava said.

I couldn't help but gape. I never in a million years would've thought these creatures were real.

Ava-Marie must've noticed the longing in my features, because she whistled and called out to someone she knew. "Hey, Josee!"

A few moments later, sneakers sounded in the grass as someone jogged over. "Hey, Ava. What's up?"

The voice was female— probably a girl around our age.

"I've got a peer mentee," Ava said. "He's blind and has never seen a magical creature before."

Yeah, just go announce it to the world, why don't you? I despised her.

"Could he hold your dracavern?" Ava-Marie asked.

"Yeah, of course," Josee answered, and I heard something preen. "I mean, I don't let just *anyone* hold Cassie, but I can already tell she likes you."

Josee set something warm in my arms. It was barely the size of an infant, but as I ran my fingers over the creature, I realized that it was shaped like a small reptile. It had scales that were cool to the touch, and soft leathery wings that folded over its back. Spines ran along its back and down its tail, but they didn't hurt to touch.

"What's a dracavern?" I asked. "I've never heard of one."

"They're cave dragons," Josee explained. "They're really small, so they can fly through tight caverns."

I stroked Cassie's nose. She sneezed, sending air as cold as ice across my fingers. I jerked my hand away.

"Don't worry. She's harmless," Josee said.

"That was really cold," I said, shivering.

Josee reached out for Cassie and pulled her back into her arms. "Cassie's an ice dracavern."

"I thought dragons would breathe fire," I said.

"Some can," Ava replied. "Depends on the dragon. Come on, Charlie. I'll show you inside the school."

For a second, it was like Ava had forgotten our disagreement. She was too wrapped up in the magnificence of the academy as we said goodbye to Josee and moved on.

"This is the Grand Entryway," Ava-Marie explained. "You might be able to feel it with your Air magic, but the foyer reaches up five stories. There's a balcony on each one. What you may not be able to feel is the *ah-mazing* chandelier above us. It's gold-plated and has real diamonds!"

"Holy shit," I breathed. That chandelier sounded crazy expensive. How did the Hawkei afford it?

"I know, right?" Ava said. "It took the Hawkei ages to rebuild that after this section burnt down. It wasn't cheap."

"No kidding. You aren't lying to me again, are you?"

Ava scoffed. "About Orenda Academy? Fuck, no!"

"How do the Hawkei afford it, though?" I questioned. "This isn't exactly what I pictured when I was told I was coming to a reservation."

I'd never been to a native reservation before, but from what I'd heard, most indigenous nations were deep in poverty. It was common to experience overcrowded and inadequate housing, without luxuries like running water and electricity— along with underfunded healthcare.

"Don't get me started on the living conditions of Native Americans," Ava growled. "It's disgusting the way the government treats us. Luckily for us, the Hawkei have money."

"But how?" I asked. "Casinos, or what?"

Ava-Marie laughed. "No. We make our money on magical exports. It makes for a very comfortable lifestyle for the tribe."

"Magical exports? You don't ship off magical creatures, do you?"

"What? No." Ava sounded offended. "We sell things like unicorn hair and dragon scales to other magical societies. It's harmless, but we're the only suppliers, so we can charge whatever we want. The tribe makes bank off it. Anyway, shall we move on?"

Ava continued leading me through the castle. She spoke fast and skimmed over details, like she expected me to already know them. We turned so many hallways I couldn't make sense of where I was, and I was usually great at mapping out my surroundings. I had to be.

Eventually, Ava led me outside. Floral scents hit my nose, and the air seemed clean. A few people walked around, but their footsteps were quiet and serene. Even Oberi's hoofbeats beside me seemed calmer.

"What is this?" I asked. "A garden?"

"Are you *sure* you're blind?" Ava sounded skeptical.

"There's more to seeing than looking with your eyes," I told her.

"What do you mean?"

"Come here." I reached out for Ava's shoulders and situated her in front of me. Gently, I placed my hand over her eyes, just to make sure she wouldn't cheat. "Stand here and close your eyes."

"Um… okay."

"What can you see?" I asked.

"Not a damn thing," she said flatly.

"What about the bee buzzing near the rose bushes?" I questioned.

Ava shrugged. "A wild guess, perhaps? How do you know those are rose bushes?"

"I can smell them," I told her. "The flap of the bee's wings is unique— unless you have some weird magical insects around here, too."

"No, just bees," she said.

"What else can you see?" I pressed.

Ava quieted. A nice few moments, for once.

"I hear heavy hooves two paths over," she said. "Someone's Familiar… a unicorn, maybe? And there's laughter outside the garden. Two people… a boy and a girl. I think they're flirting."

Ava went quiet again. In the silence, it was actually really nice to be around her. Her shoulder was warm under my hand, and her eyelashes tickled the palm that was covering her face. A light breeze passed by us, and her hair brushed across my cheek. She had a really nice scent— like raspberries.

"I smell all kinds of flowers, but there are too many to make out the varieties," Ava continued. "In the middle of the garden is a fountain. I can hear it trickling, but it's muffled by the bushes around us. There's a bird perched atop the totem pole."

I could hear the bird chirping, but I'd missed the totem pole altogether. "How do you know what it's sitting on?"

Ava shrugged again. "I've visited the gardens before and know the layout. The totem pole is the most important part of the gardens. It was built after the fire as a memorial to those who died."

I listened closer and realized she must be telling the truth. The bird's call was high above us, but wasn't muffled by any branches or leaves.

"And where's the path?" I asked.

Ava swallowed. "Straight ahead."

"How would you know that without seeing it?" I wanted to get her to think. If we were going to be spending time together like Professor Baine said, I needed her to understand how I saw the world.

Ava-Marie thought about it for a few beats. "I can tell where the bushes are because of the way sound travels through the gardens. They absorb it— like you can sense a wall there."

Ava's shoulder moved, and she reached out to the nearest flower bush. "And I can feel the bushes, too. I don't have to see them to know they're there."

I leaned into her without realizing it. My nose was only an inch from her hair. That sweet scent of hers filled my nostrils. I came in so close my front pressed against her backside. Adrenaline surged through my chest and downward.

Holy shit!

I leapt backward, nearly tripping over Oberi's hoof. Ava cleared her throat and broke the spell. All the serenity within the garden seemed to wash away. It didn't seem like a calm place anymore, not the way my heart was racing.

"Get it now?" I asked. "I don't need my vision to see the world around me. You might be surprised at how much I see. Perhaps sometimes more than you, pidge."

Ava stayed far away from me near one of the rose bushes. She snapped a flower off and started picking at the petals. I could feel each one flutter to the ground when she dropped it.

"That was a nice lesson, but I think the tour's over," she said. "It sounds like you can navigate the academy just fine yourself, so we can go our separate ways now."

One semi-nice moment with her, and she was already back to her normal self. *Great.*

Fine. If she didn't want me around, I didn't have to be here.

"Oberi and I will just find our way back to my dorm room, then," I said. "Professor Baine hooked me up with a sweet room this morning."

"No way!" Ava protested, grabbing me by the arm before I could get anywhere. Her hand was scalding, which I mistook as some sort of passion at first— until I remembered she had Fire power. "You're not going anywhere with Oberi."

"Well, I'm not leaving her!" I insisted.

Ava-Marie dropped my arm. "I can't be left alone without her. I just bonded."

"She has to sleep somewhere. She can't stay with us both tonight," I argued.

"You're right." Ava put herself between Oberi and me. "Oberi will stay with me."

"That's not fair! I bonded first."

"Like that makes you special," she spat. "How am I supposed to secure my bond with my Familiar if you're always around?"

"What do you mean, *secure your bond*?" Professor Baine had never mentioned it.

Ava sighed, like she didn't care to explain. She did anyway. "When you bond, you make a magical connection, but the emotional one isn't there immediately. Every Elementai has to go through something difficult— usually traumatic— with their Familiar to make that emotional bond. Only then will your powers reach their full potential. I can't fully bond with Oberi with you in the way."

I raised my eyebrows. "We have to go through something traumatic? Oberi and I should be good after a few days listening to *you* talk."

Ava gasped. "You're an asshole, you know that?"

I leaned in to whisper to her. "And proud of it, pidge. I'd rather be an asshole than spend another minute with you."

"You *jerk!*" Ava shoved me backward, though I barely moved. "We can't share a Familiar. This is never going to work."

Oberi huffed and stomped her hoof, like our fighting was bothering her.

"Great, now you've upset Oberi," I growled. "We obviously don't like listening to you *whine.*"

"I do not whine!" she protested.

"You're the definition of a cry baby!" I shot back.

"You're just mean," she snapped. "You've already had plenty of time with Oberi. It's my turn. I need her tonight."

"You're a stranger," I argued. "It will scare Oberi to be without me."

Ava started leading Oberi down the path, but I grabbed her hands to stop her. She shrugged me off. "Oberi is *my* Familiar. We may have just met, but I've known her my whole life!"

"That makes no sense. We need to figure something out."

"Like what?" Ava challenged. "Neither of us wants to leave her. We can't just sleep on the couches in the Commons all semester. She'll sleep in my dorm tonight. It's my turn with Oberi."

I groaned. "*Your turn.* What the hell do you think Oberi is, a toy?"

Oberi whinnied to get our attention, but neither of us responded.

"I'm just trying to protect my Familiar," I insisted.

"Don't forget she's *mine*, too," Ava hissed. "I can do with her whatever I like."

Ava-Marie started walking away again. Oberi seemed indecisive for a moment, then I heard the sound of her hooves beneath her.

"Ava, wait!" I reached out for her arm again.

"Back *off!*" Ava's skin turned red-hot, burning my hand.

I jumped back. That freaking *hurt*.

"Don't touch me, or my Familiar!" Ava shouted.

I heard the crackle of the fireball before it left her hand. Instinctively, I shot my hands up in front of my face. I didn't know how I did it, but the air followed my command. It blasted backward, and the fireball changed direction. It crashed into a bush nearby, and my stomach plummeted. Heat rolled off it in waves as the whole thing lit aflame in seconds.

My nostrils flared. "Pidge, what'd you do?"

"Me?" Ava-Marie sputtered, like she couldn't believe her eyes. "You should've let the fireball hit you!"

"Yeah, because that was the smart idea," I said sarcastically. "Can't you put it out? You have Fire power."

"I'm trying!" she growled through gritted teeth. "I can't work my magic when you're yelling at me. Fuck!"

I knew what was wrong the moment Ava-Marie cursed. The fire was getting hotter and louder. I didn't know how many bushes it'd consumed already, but the magical Fire was spreading quickly, eating away at the garden far faster than any normal flame.

"Oberi's a Fire creature!" I realized. "Oberi, help!"

Oberi whinnied, as if to tell me she was doing her best.

My pulse pounded in my ears. We were in so much fucking trouble.

Polluted air filled my lungs. My eyes burned, and I struggled to breathe. I tried commanding the air around the Fire. Maybe if I could pull the oxygen away, the Fire would die out. But I barely knew how to control my element. My magic did nothing but make it worse.

"Ava, we have to go!" I yanked on her wrist, but she stayed put.

"I can do this!" she promised. "I can put it out!"

"If you could put it out, it'd be out already," I argued. "We have to go get help!"

"*Fuuuck!*" she shouted.

"What now?" I groaned.

"The Fire's heading toward the totem pole!" she screamed. "We have to— ancestors!"

Ava-Marie went totally breathless. I thought she might collapse beside me. I knew by the sound of her voice that the totem pole had caught fire. My stomach plummeted as the sound of Fire crackled. The smell of paint and burning wood filled my nostrils.

"No!" Ava-Marie wailed. It was obvious the totem pole meant a lot to her— to the tribe.

Across the garden, people began to scream. Some were fleeing, while others were calling for help.

"Ava... there's nothing... we can do," I said through coughs.

Just then, the doors to the school burst open. Heels clicked against the stone path. Air billowed around the newcomer, as if she wore a long velvet dress. Two other sets of footsteps followed her.

"Ava-Marie!" the woman sounded worried. "What happened?"

"It was an accident," Ava said. At least she was telling the truth.

I barely sensed the woman flick her wrist, and I felt the heat in the gardens recede as the Fire started to die down. She must've been a very powerful Fire Elementai to control such a large fire, whoever she was.

I drew in a deep breath, happy to be able to breathe again. Being without air was literally one of my worst fears.

"I don't *believe* this," the woman gasped. "The memorial totem pole... it's been destroyed!"

"You don't understand, Grandmother," Ava pleaded.

"Grandmother?" The word slipped out of my mouth.

The woman turned to me and snapped, "That's Head Dean Doya to you, *boy*."

My jaw dropped open. Ava and I had nearly burnt down the entire Orenda Academy gardens, and we'd been caught by the Head Dean? Could this day get any worse?

"I understand more than you know," Head Dean Doya said. She spoke in such a refined and dignified way, it was nearly off-putting. "Your grandfather just stopped by. Care to explain?"

When Ava didn't respond, I realized she wasn't asking her. "Me?" I questioned.

"Yes, you," Doya snapped. "What could possibly possess you to light the school grounds on fire?"

Whoa. This woman seriously thought *I* was to blame?

Of course she did— because her precious granddaughter could do no wrong.

"It wasn't me," I said. "I don't have Fire power."

Head Dean Doya gasped. "Ava-Marie. You *didn't*!"

"Charlie made it worse with his Air magic!" she said, like that helped the argument.

One of the people who'd followed the Head Dean outside stepped forward. "Head Dean, if I may," a man cut in. "Student duels are against school policy outside of class. Precisely for the danger they pose, such as in this instance."

"Come *on*, Bren," a second man with a much deeper voice said. "I'm sure Ava-Marie didn't mean it."

"Uncle Jonah's right," Ava said. "I didn't mean it."

Seriously, was this girl related to half of Kinpago or something? She had connections everywhere.

"You threw a fireball at my head, pidge," I reminded her.

"Ava's only nineteen," Jonah said. "We can't expect her to control her powers at all times. I'm sure it won't happen again."

Head Dean Doya sighed. "Forgive me, Dean Chanee, but I believe Dean Emberly is right. I can't be seen playing favorites as the Head Dean."

Her voice became even more stern. "Accident or not, what happened here must have consequences."

"You can't seriously be punishing me, Grandmother!" Ava said. "I only just got here! Can't I be let off with a warning?"

"Oh, I think you misunderstand me, Ava-Marie," Head Dean Doya said. "*I* will not be punishing you at all. It would be a conflict of interest, and unfortunately, destruction of tribal property— even on school grounds— is within the Elders' jurisdiction. You will have to appeal to them regarding what happened here today."

I smirked and gave Ava a salute. "Nice knowing ya, pidge."

"This isn't fair!" Ava-Marie shouted.

"Ava, I have let you slip up too many times without any consequences," Doya barked. "Do not expect me to keep making allowances for you."

Ava-Marie didn't give any backtalk, for once in her goddamn life. It was clear she respected this woman.

"And *you*," the Head Dean added. "Mr…"

"Wahkin," I told her. "Mr. Wahkin, ma'am."

"Mr. Wahkin," she repeated. "Don't think that you're getting off scot-free. It seems that you had just as much a part in this duel as my granddaughter."

I could hardly believe my ears. I get attacked, and *I'm* the one being blamed for the arson? What kind of messed up society was this?

"You will both appear before the Elder Council," Head Dean Doya said. "You are both responsible, and therefore, whatever the Elders have in store for you, you shall both endure. You better get used to it."

That was all she said before she turned on her heel and started back toward the castle. My body gave a shudder in the silence that stretched between Ava and me.

Something told me Head Dean Doya was referring to far more than this minor infraction. Ava-Marie and I shared a soul— and a Familiar. Whatever happened to one of us happened to us both.

I wasn't eager to find out what sort of trouble Ava-Marie might get us into next.

Three days passed before our hearing, and Ava-Marie was getting on my nerves more than ever. We couldn't agree on how to handle this situation, so Oberi more or less came and went as he pleased. Kind of pissed me off when he disappeared to go find Ava. My first companion, and he was already ditching me on the daily. Made me want to stay here *so* bad.

Professor Baine claimed Kinpago was where I belonged, but I didn't feel like I fit in. I was more comfortable sleeping under a bridge than in the private suite in the Yapluma dorms they'd given me they called a "dorm room." It all felt like some sort of joke— like they were going to come knocking on my door one day and ask for their hundred grand to cover my tuition.

I wasn't used to staying in fancy places. I'd gone from a shitty apartment in Detroit to living in a palace. It was too much too soon.

It felt somewhat appropriate to find myself in a courtroom my first week here. Honestly, being prosecuted felt like the most familiar thing I'd experienced in Kinpago. I'd frequently gotten into trouble with the law before, for minor infractions, so going in front of a judge was something I was used to— so much so that it was nearly comforting.

I hadn't really thought things would go this way, though. Had someone told me a week ago this is where I'd be sitting, I would've thought it'd be for petty theft— not whatever the hell this was.

"Ava's late," Professor Baine grumbled. He sat beside me in the courtroom, tapping his foot impatiently. He was the only person I really knew in Kinpago, so he'd offered to accompany me to the hearing. He never outright said it, but I think he felt bad for me, because he knew this was all Ava's fault.

Oberi sat near my feet, licking his paws. He'd shown up that morning in my dorm room after I'd woken up. I stroked the top of his head to calm myself. There were others in the courtroom, too, but everyone spoke in low whispers. In the row just behind me, a man and a woman sounded worried for Ava. I guessed those to be her parents. Someone fidgeted beside them— a sibling, perhaps?

Not far from them, I recognized her Aunt Imogen and Uncle Jonah's voices. There were two other men with them, but I couldn't tell who they were. I didn't think I'd met them. At the table across from us, a man kept clearing his throat impatiently. I could hear the occasional pound of hooves on the hardwood floor.

"Don't worry," Head Dean Doya said to Ava's parents. "You know the Elders never go too hard on Ava."

"They're too scared of Liam," her mother joked.

"I'm *not* scary," her father argued.

"When it comes to your daughter you are," Ava's mother said.

"This isn't Ava's fault," her father huffed. "It's *that boy's*."

I whirled around in my chair. *"That boy* is innocent. If your daughter told you otherwise, she's a liar."

"How dare you speak of my daughter like that!" the man boomed.

"Liam," Professor Baine warned. Somehow, he was able to calm the situation.

After a few moments to steady my breath, I turned to Professor Baine. "What should I expect?"

"You and Ava will get a chance to plead your case," Baine explained. "Then the Elders will read you your sentence."

"Who are the Elders, exactly?" I asked.

"In Hawkei society, each House has a chief and four Elders to represent them, for a total of twenty-five members on the Elder Council. This is a minor case, so you'll appeal to a panel of three Elders who will determine your sentencing. The panel has been chosen to avoid any bias, so you won't see any Toaqua behind the judge's table."

"Why not?" I questioned.

"Well, because Ava's the daughter of the Water chief," Professor Baine said simply.

"Seriously?" I gaped. No wonder she had so much privilege.

Professor Baine sounded confused. "I thought she would've told you."

I scoffed. "Believe me, Ava doesn't say much."

"Huh. She's usually quite the chatterbox."

"Oh, hell yeah. She just doesn't say anything that matters."

Just then, the doors to the courtroom burst open dramatically. It got loud as everyone turned and started whispering.

"I hope you haven't started without me," Ava announced loudly, her heels clicking as she walked to the front of the room. God, she sounded like she was the guest of honor, not some criminal about to be read their sentence. How did I get wrapped up with a girl like her?

"I had a minor wardrobe malfunction," Ava said, like that excused her late arrival. "Nothing to worry about. I got it all sorted out."

The whispers quieted down as Ava took a seat beside the man at the other table. "Ava," he hissed. "That outfit is hardly appropriate for the courtroom."

Ava's fingers brushed across the fabric. "What's wrong with pink, Sean?"

"For the last time, I am your lawyer. You may call me Mr. Andre."

Lawyer? I hardly thought she needed one for this.

"With all due respect, *Mr. Andre*, I love pink. I think this power suit is fantastic on me. My ass looks great."

"Ancestors help us," Mr. Andre mumbled.

A voice came from near the judge's table. "All stand in honor of the Elder Council— Koigni Chieftess Vanessa Emberly, Yapluma Elder Riley Brandt, and Nivita Elder Sam Gardner."

I stood with everyone else. Doors at the corner of the room opened, and three Elders came breezing in. Air billowed off their judge's robes, and their footsteps echoed as they climbed the steps to their table.

"You may be seated," the female chieftess said. Once the courtroom quieted, she spoke again. "We are here today to address the case of the Hawkei Tribe versus Ava-Marie Mitoh and Charlie Wahkin. Both are charged with co-perpetrating an underage magical duel, destruction of tribal property, and vandalism."

Ava-Marie shot out of her chair. "Objection, Your Honor!"

Chieftess Vanessa spoke calmly. "Please, Ava. There is no need. You will have a chance to plead your case. First, the Elder Council would like to hear from Mr. Wahkin. Mr. Wahkin, can you tell us exactly what happened regarding the events of August twenty-fourth?"

I leaned over to Professor Baine. "Do I have to go to the witness stand?"

"No, no," he assured me. "Just stand right here and tell your side of the story."

I nodded, then cleared my throat and stood. "Your Honors, the events of August twenty-fourth began as a disagreement between Miss Mitoh and I over my Familiar." I gestured to the husky beside me. "She threw a fireball at my head, and I deflected it with my Air. It was pure instinct."

"See? He *admits* it was his fault!" Ava cried.

I kept my cool. "On the contrary, just the opposite. Miss Mitoh was the one to attack. I was only acting in self-defense."

"I see, Mr. Wahkin," Chieftess Vanessa said. "We will take that into consideration. If I may, what exactly was the disagreement about your Familiar about?"

I cleared my throat, stalling. I waited for Professor Baine to give me some sort of advice, but he remained silent. "Well, you see, Your Honor… Ava and I *both* bonded to Oberi."

Gasps traveled around the courtroom. One of the Elders smacked their gavel at the front of the room.

"Order!" Chieftess Vanessa yelled. "Mr. Wahkin, that's impossible."

"I'm afraid not, Chieftess," Professor Baine piped up. "I performed the identification ceremony myself. Ava-Marie and Charlie do, in fact, share a Familiar."

"O-oh," Chieftess Vanessa stammered. "Well, this is… new. I'm afraid it won't impact the outcome of this hearing, but we will certainly take note of this. Miss Mitoh, is there anything you'd like to add?"

Ava's chair screeched across the floor as she stood. Her lawyer cleared his throat, but Ava stopped him. "I've got this, Sean. I can speak for myself."

Ava's heels clicked against the floor as she stepped out from behind the table. She began pacing in front of the judges. "August twenty-fourth was meant to be the greatest day of my life — the day I bonded. It was a beautiful, brisk day. The ocean waves were rolling across the sand, and the sun was shining its beautiful blessing down upon me, when to my surprise, a magnificent creature stepped onto the beach. The moment I touched her, my whole world titled on its axis. It was as if a Vincent van Gogh painting had come to life, or an original Shakespeare play was happening before my eyes. It was like—"

"Ava, we don't have all day," Chieftess Vanessa said calmly. "Can you just tell us what happened?"

Ava turned on her heel and finally stopped pacing. "Chieftess, do you remember what it was like to bond?"

"Of course I do, but this isn't my hearing," she said flatly.

"Then you must know how special it should be!" Ava-Marie said passionately. "But I was *robbed* of the experience by none other than Charlie Wahkin!"

I leaned over to whisper to Professor Baine. "She's pointing at me, isn't she?"

He chuckled lightly. "Yes."

"Charlie Wahkin *stole* my Familiar, Your Honors," Ava claimed. "He bonded with her first and yanked the most precious experience of my life right out from under me. And that's not the only thing he's taken from me! Your Honors, he *stole my wallet!*"

"Oh my god," I mumbled. Could this girl get any more infuriating?

"Charlie Wahkin is a thief," Ava accused. "If anyone should be sentenced today, it is the man sitting in that chair."

"Still pointing at me, huh?" I asked Professor Baine. I *so* wasn't amused.

"Mr. Wahkin, is that true?" Chieftess Vanessa asked. "Did you really steal Miss Mitoh's wallet?"

I could've strangled this girl. "Your Honor, I found it after she bumped into me. I intended to return it."

It wasn't a total lie. I *had* found it— on her. And I'd gladly give the *wallet* back, but I was keeping the money.

"Then why haven't you?" Ava-Marie demanded. "Stealing my wallet wasn't enough, was it?

You had to go steal my Familiar, too. Are you starting a collection of all things *Ava* now? Are you obsessed?"

"God, no," I snapped. "I'd rather I never met you."

A gavel pounded, and Chieftess Vanessa called out, "Order! Miss Mitoh, please take your seat. If the defendants have nothing else to add to their statements, we can proceed to sentencing."

I couldn't exactly add what I was thinking. *Ava-Marie is a psycho bitch who needs to stay the hell away from me.*

"That's all, Your Honor," Ava said, before taking her seat. "I rest my case."

Chieftess Vanessa shifted in her chair. "Very well. The council will take a brief intermission to consult on this hearing."

The gavel banged again, and the Elders shuffled out of the courtroom to speak quietly. Before they left, I heard one of the male Elders whisper to the other. "Ava-Marie *can't* keep showing up here. We let it slide every time. We can't keep giving any more favors to her parents."

"Agreed," the other replied. "Something's got to happen this time."

That was all I heard before the doors shut behind them. Meanwhile, the courtroom got loud again as people started whispering.

A bit of rage burned in my guts. Ava-Marie was a spoiled little rich girl who had powerful parents and too many friends. I'd never had such favoritism in the court system. The government had never failed to throw the book at me. Why not her, too?

"Oberi," Ava called. "Oberi, come get a treat."

A bag rustled open, and the smell of dog treats wafted over to me. Oberi perked up and padded over to Ava across the aisle.

"Ugh, you have to be kidding me," I groaned. "Oberi doesn't like dog treats, pidge."

"How would *you* know?" she snarled.

"Because I tried feeding him some the other day," I told her.

Oberi's teeth clicked together as he chewed on the treats.

"Well, he likes *my* treats," Ava said proudly. "They're homemade."

I scoffed. "With what? The blood of your enemies?"

Ava laughed, but it wasn't cute or sexy. It sounded evil. "Not a bad idea, Charlie. I'll use your blood next time."

"Ava!" her mother scolded.

I crossed my arms and turned away from Ava-Marie. I'd quickly learned the best way to get her to shut up was to stop talking myself. The girl always had to get the last word in. It wasn't worth it with her.

It wasn't long before the Elder Council returned. They called the court to order again, and everything went quiet.

Chieftess Vanessa cleared her throat. "In the case of the Hawkei Tribe versus Ava-Marie Mitoh and Charlie Wahkin, the defendants have been charged with three misdemeanors and are hereby sentenced to eighty hours of community service and six months of probation."

My shoulders immediately relaxed. I could live with this. It was basically a slap on the wrist.

Ava-Marie, on the other hand, was furious. She slammed her hands down on the table as she shot to her feet. "Community service! *Probation*? I can't have a misdemeanor on my record, let alone three!"

Chieftess Vanessa didn't sound amused. "It's not as bad as it sounds, Miss Mitoh. Be glad we're not sending you to the Darke Institute, because the next time we find you in court, rest assured, you *will* be going there. This is your last warning. If you mess up again, you will leave us no choice."

A shiver ran down my spine at the name. The Darke Institute. Hell yeah, I was glad I wasn't going there. It sounded ominous as hell.

"But I'm the daughter of a chief! You can't do this to me!" Ava burst.

"Ava, peanut," her father said softly as he approached her. "It's only community service. As long as you're on your best behavior, you won't even notice the probation."

"That's not the point, Daddy!" Ava cried. Like literally *cried*. "Charlie stole my Familiar. Now he's stolen the next six months of my life. It's not fair!"

My stomach twisted. Could she really blame me for this?

"Ava…" I stood and reached out for her. I didn't know why— I just felt like I had to comfort her. Maybe I could talk some sense into her. I'd seen so much shit go down in the legal system. This was nothing.

"Get away from me!" Ava-Marie snapped. "I don't want anything to do with you. Thanks for ruining my life!"

Ava-Marie took off running out of the courtroom. I couldn't *stand* this girl, and yet a part of me couldn't help but feel sorry for her. It had to be the whole soul-connection thing, because I sure as hell didn't feel bad about her sentencing. Maybe a little community service would do her some good.

Oberi whined at my side. I sighed. "Yeah, boy. You might as well go after her. She needs you."

Oberi nudged his head into my hand, then ran off behind Ava. I could still hear Ava-Marie's cries echo down the hall.

Dear God. What had I gotten myself into?

ava-marie
FOUR

Fuck Charlie Wahkin. He could go straight to hell.

I had to get up early to attend community service. Oberi wasn't with me— my Familiar spent most of the time with Charlie.

I *hated* him. He'd had more time with Oberi, and as a result, she was closer to him than me. The one thing I'd been looking forward to was having a Familiar, and he'd messed that up. I felt incredibly alone, and it was all his fault.

I made sure to wear something cute— because maybe my probation officer was hot— before I went downstairs. When I got there, Daddy, Mama, and Grandpa Elliot— or as Charlie called him, *Professor Baine*— were all sitting around the table near the kitchen. They weren't eating anything, and like hawks, their eyes fixated on me once I walked into the room.

Oh, great. Another intervention, *again*.

"Guys, can we please save the guilt trip for later? I'm so not in the mood."

"Honey, we need to talk about this," Mama started. "Sit down."

I groaned and made a show of dragging myself into a chair and collapsing into it. Daddy rolled his eyes.

Mama folded her hands and sat forward. "Ava, we're all concerned. I think it's obvious that if your father wasn't who he was, you'd be in hot water right now."

I scoffed. "Please. The Elders won't touch me."

"And that's the problem! You believe you don't need any consequences." Daddy was already irritated. I noticed he had more bags than usual under his eyes. He was exhausted. Had I done that?

"Your father's right," Grandpa Elliot broke in. "This has been going on for too long."

Grandpa pulled out a list. "As of right now, Ava's current list of infractions include arson—"

"That was an accident. I'd just gotten my Fire. I didn't know how to use it," I argued.

"Minor shoplifting—"

"It was just a dare." I hadn't meant to steal the shoes *and* the sweater, just the shoes. It was a harmless freaking game. I was going to bring them back.

"Property Damage—"

"That was a good one."

"Possession of Supernatural Contraband—"

"Like love potions should be illegal."

"Grand theft auto—"

"*Grand theft auto?!*" both of my parents screamed at once.

"Grandpa, you weren't supposed to tell them about that one," I growled. They knew about all the others.

"You stole a *car?*" Daddy yelled. Holy ancestors, he was mad.

"It was just a little joyride. Nothing serious," I said. If looks could kill, I'd be a puddle on the ground right now.

"It took some convincing to get her out of that one, along with a large bribe," Grandpa Elliot said. "Though the record still stands."

"I can't believe you bought her out of a car theft charge and didn't inform us," Mama snapped. "This is out of line."

"Well… look at her. She's so sweet." Grandpa Elliot gave me a warm smile, and I flashed one back.

"That's because she's so innocent looking! She wouldn't have gotten away with half of this crap if she wasn't so damn cute! People give her whatever she wants," Daddy bellowed.

"Like you can talk, Liam." Mama was fuming. My charm wouldn't work on her, and unlike Daddy, she looked *scary*. I was surprised her hair hadn't caught fire.

"None of this stuff should be illegal, anyway. No one's getting hurt. It's all in good fun," I argued.

"You can't think that way," Grandpa Elliot insisted. "You're on probation. That means no trouble of any kind. If you miss community service or reporting to your officer, it's immediate jail time."

I huffed. Like that would ever happen.

"Ava, you've got an addiction for causing trouble. You're always pushing to see how far you can go. It's like you need the adrenaline rush," Daddy said.

"Oh, gee, I wonder where she gets *that* from," Mama said sarcastically.

Daddy narrowed his eyes, and Grandpa Elliot stepped in.

"Look, the bottom line is, Ava's record is far from clean," Grandpa Elliot said firmly. "We can go on about this all day, but even if she wiggles out of this one and attends Orenda Academy, employment will be difficult for her to obtain after graduation. No one will want to hire her with a track record like this."

He sighed. "But there is another option— the Darke Institute. If she attends the Institute, she'll be given a clean slate. Opportunities will be better for her."

Fear wasn't a common emotion for me. I wasn't scared of much. But the Darke Institute was one of those things I *was* afraid of. I didn't know much about it, but I did know it was where the magical world shipped all their bad kids— and that it had been brought up as an option for me several times in court.

"You guys can't be serious about sending me to a prison for supernatural delinquents," I stated flatly.

"It's a reform school!" Grandpa Elliot protested.

"It's a *prison*," I clarified.

Just then, the doors blew open with all the fury of hell. Grandmother Eleanor strode in with her head held high, her dress billowing around her. I always admired how good my grandmother could look while scaring the living daylights out of people. I wanted to have nice hair when I was mowing people over.

Mama's gaze hardened when she looked at her mother. I sensed there was going to be an argument.

"My dear, we weren't expecting you." Grandpa Elliot shrank under her harsh gaze. He lost a foot in height.

Grandmother Eleanor's eyebrows pinched as she raged, and she placed a manicured hand on her elegant hip before jutting it out sharply. "I will bring hell down upon *anyone* who forces my granddaughter to attend an institution for low-life thugs. There won't be a school left standing when I'm done!"

"Grandmother, you were the one who sent me to court in the first place," I mumbled.

"I *am* Head Dean. I have to keep up appearances, and I can't let others see my granddaughter getting special privilege," Grandmother Eleanor argued. "Even if you *do* get it behind closed doors."

Grandpa Elliot always cowered to Grandmother. He said nothing in protest, but Mama stood up. "No. I'm sorry, but this has gone on long enough."

"Sophia, don't be delusional," Grandmother snapped. "Ava-Marie doesn't belong in a prison academy."

"Maybe she does." Mama turned to Daddy. "Liam, we've tried everything to help Ava, and it hasn't worked. The Institute might not be such a bad idea. Maybe this is the help she needs."

"Can you stop talking about me like I'm not even here?" I asked, but Mama didn't even acknowledge me. I hated her saying that I needed *help*. I didn't need *help*. I was fine.

Daddy's look was cold. "Have you forgotten what Maddie told us about the Institute years ago?"

"I am aware," Mama replied. "But we can look into it. Maybe things have changed."

My ears perked up at that. Aunt Maddie was my dad's sister. She wasn't just an elemental—she was a *naderei*, a prophet. She could foresee the future. Had my aunt seen something about the Institute that was a threat?

"What did Aunt Maddie say?" I leaned forward, keen on finding out.

"Never you mind," Daddy said. "The bottom line is, you're not going anywhere near the Darke Institute. That's the end of it."

Mama let out an angry breath, but didn't add anything more. I should've been relieved— I really didn't want to be sentenced to the Institute.

But he *told me no*. And that was always the first way to catch my interest. Why didn't he want me going there?

I decided I needed to find out.

"You're going to be late, Ava," Daddy said with a look at the clock. "Run along."

He still talked to me like I was a little girl. I couldn't decide if I loved it or hated it. I grabbed my purse and left. I was sure the four of them weren't done with this conversation, and were having a talk on what to do with me.

It was ridiculous. Didn't anybody care to ask what I wanted?

My probation officer *was not* hot. He led me to a local park. Charlie and Oberi were already there. My heart started when I saw Oberi, though my mood totally soured when I saw Charlie. He was scanning the ground for garbage using a trash picker and putting it into a bag.

Oberi was in his husky form. He barked, then changed when he saw me, transforming into the unicorn mare.

I rubbed Oberi's head as she came to me. "Hey, girl. How are you?"

Oberi nickered. The probation officer handed me a bag and a trash pick. "You'll be cleaning up the park today. Once this place is spotless, you can go."

Red cups were everywhere. A bunch of kids had a party here last night. I wrinkled my nose, but I knew complaining wasn't going to do me any good, so I got to work.

Oberi stabbed cups with her horn and put them into my bag as we walked. Charlie kept silent. The probation officer watched us carefully as we cleaned up the area. I was already bored. It didn't take long for me to lose interest, and I was thinking of ways to get myself out of this.

"You think if I run he'll catch me?" I asked Charlie under my breath. I didn't like him, but I needed someone to talk to out here. The silence was deafening.

Charlie's look was incredulous. "Picking up trash too much work for you, princess?"

"No," I shot back. "I just have better things to do."

"Fuck that." His tone was pissed. "I'm not letting you run off and get us into more trouble."

"You wouldn't be able to stop me."

Charlie's features blazed. "Try me."

"Believe me, I'd love to." Running off would be a stupid idea, but at least it'd bring some excitement. This job was *so dull.*

"You're such a brat." Charlie steamed. "Someone should teach you some manners."

"Like you?" I stood in front of Charlie and got so close I could feel his breath on my cheek. His body stiffened. I didn't know if the guy was going to yell at me… or kiss me.

Either would be interesting. Both made my heart race. And if he kissed me, I'd get the excuse to punch him across the mouth… which I *really* wanted to do. Win-win.

"Hey, you two, break it up," the officer called. His voice held a warning.

I stepped away. Charlie smoldered in my direction before he turned his back and went the other way.

Charlie didn't get it. Boredom was always the best way to bring on more psychosis. And I'd do *anything* to stop that from happening— including cause a fight.

I could hear the voices bordering on the edge of my mind, fighting a way to get in. I picked up the pace and cleaned up that park like it was my life's work. Charlie's expression grew confused as he heard me rush from this place to that. My probation officer was obviously impressed when I handed him a full bag in less than an hour.

"You two can go," he said, giving me side-eye. "Just don't get into any more trouble."

I sighed. Finally. As the probation officer left, I turned to Oberi. "Come on, girl. Let's go."

Oberi trotted forward, until Charlie let out a note of protest. "I'm not letting you run off with Oberi."

"You've had her for a full day!" I complained. "It's my turn."

Charlie's jaw tightened. "I don't care. I need Oberi more than you do."

He had no idea. I went to say something back, but Oberi tossed her head, her horn glinting in the sun. She stomped her hoof a few times, pounding it into the dirt.

"Oberi, what's wrong?" I asked. I went to touch her, but she backed away. The Fire unicorn let out a whinny before she whirled around and took off, racing into the woods.

"Oberi!" I called. I took off running after her. What had gotten into my Familiar?

Twigs snapped beneath my feet as I followed Oberi into the woods. I caught sight of her flaming tail, leading me onward.

I hoped I'd left Charlie behind, but no. I could feel gusts of Air move around me as Charlie used his magic to navigate his way through the woods. I felt the bond between us tug, and I realized he was using it as a guide, to feel his way after me.

I couldn't get rid of this guy. He was fighting for Oberi, but he didn't understand. If I had my Familiar, maybe I could make the voices go away. I *had* to have her near.

The forest sloped downward, into a hill. Oberi continued down it, still several paces ahead. Eventually, my feet met sand, and the trees broke as Oberi and I stepped onto the beach.

But this wasn't any ordinary beach. My mouth dropped open as I surveyed the incredible sight around me. Washed up on the beach near an alcove of rock were all kinds of sailing ships.

They were wooden, with white sails and tall masts. Strange carvings, in runes I didn't understand, decorated the sides of the ships, while ropes twisted in the wind.

Figureheads spanned the front of the ships. They were carvings of beautiful people— people with pointed ears that had their arms thrown backwards against the wind.

Many of the ships were broken or had holes in them. They looked like they'd been left here for ages— a hundred years or more.

I found myself transfixed by one of the male figureheads, staring into its wooden eyes. For some reason, the figurehead seemed... so familiar.

Charlie took deep breaths as he reached the shore. "What's going on?" He'd noticed I wasn't speaking.

"Ships. Dozens of ships," I said in a mystified voice.

Charlie cocked his head. He put his hand out and felt the ship closest to him. His expression became awed as he moved along the ship's edge, feeling how massive it was.

"Why are these here? Did the Hawkei leave them?" Charlie asked.

"These aren't Elementai ships," I said. "Toaqua are the only Hawkei who sailed, and they used canoes, not schooners or brigs."

"So who brought them here?"

"I don't know. They must've come from another supernatural race— that's what I can tell from the carvings. But whoever left them here, they're long gone now. These ships have been abandoned for at least a few decades."

"Do you think anyone on the reservation knows about them?" he asked.

"I don't think so." I peered into a hole in the belly of one of the ships— it was empty. "My grandpa's an explorer, and if he knew about this place, he definitely would've told me about it. It's been abandoned for years. The alcove must've hid it from everyone."

The explorer in me wanted to look around, document what I found here in my guidebook. But my gut told me I needed to get the hell out of here. Something about this place was off. It was more than eerie— it was haunted, like the spirits of the sailors who'd been shipwrecked here wanted me to leave them alone. I got a sick feeling in my gut just being here— as if the spirits around me were pressing in, suffocating me.

Charlie must've felt it too, because he said, "Let's go."

For once, I didn't argue with him. Oberi walked between us as we trekked uphill through the woods. I didn't speak again until we'd almost gotten back into town.

"Oberi led us there. Why do you think she wanted us to find it?" I asked.

"I'm not sure. But we probably shouldn't go back," Charlie said. "I don't know a lot about magic yet, but I know well enough not to go messing with stuff you shouldn't."

At least we could agree on *something*. As the grass turned to cobblestone beneath our feet, the voices in my head got louder and louder. They hadn't left, but their tones had been a dull buzz when we'd been at the ships. Now, they were roaring in my head.

I clenched my teeth. I put a hand on Oberi's coat, and the voices grew quiet for a few moments. I let out a sigh of relief. Oberi's presence *did* have an effect on the voices, and that was all the information I needed to know she had to stay with me today.

Charlie's head turned in my direction. I couldn't explain how, but Charlie must've felt what I was experiencing through our connection. His face twisted, like he was going to be sick.

I didn't want to share that with him. That kind of information was private. He didn't know I was seeing things, but he could feel my emotions about it... and I didn't like that.

Why couldn't I feel his emotions? If we were connected through Oberi, I should've been able to... but Charlie was a brick wall that I couldn't break through. It wasn't fair he could feel what I went through and it didn't work the other way around. It made our connection unbalanced.

Once we entered into Kinpago, Charlie came to a stop. "You can have Oberi," he said abruptly. "Just bring her back later."

I was so shocked it was hard for me to get any words out. "Uh… thanks?"

"Sure. Whatever."

Charlie turned on his heel and walked away. I watched him as he carefully navigated the streets back to Orenda Academy. I caught myself counting the steps he took.

I had been assigned a dorm, but I was still spending most of my time at home, as classes hadn't started yet and I hadn't moved all my stuff. I went back to my house on the island. Oberi changed into a male husky once I walked into the house, so he could fit better.

My brother was carrying boxes around the living room. Ezekiel had a dorm, too, but he hadn't moved anything. He did everything last-minute.

"How was community service?" he asked.

I threw my bag on the couch. "It sucked. I can't believe the Elders sentenced me like that."

"I mean, can you blame them? The Hawkei court system basically has to pencil you in every month. It's like a recurring thing," Ezekiel said.

"Chieftess Vanessa is practically our aunt! Her son is the same age as us. We grew up together. She should let me off easy," I grumbled.

"She has— a million times," Ez protested. "She can't keep letting it slide. I think she's serious this time, Ava. If you mess up again and violate your probation, the Elders are going to send you to the Institute. You don't have any option but to behave."

"No woman who ever did something great *behaved*."

Ezekiel shook his head. "I'm just saying, you're on thin ice."

"And I've been coasting along just fine. Lay off it." I got a water bottle from the fridge before I flung myself on the couch. As I did so, Oberi lay across my legs.

A thought came to me as I stared up at the ceiling fan. "Do you think Mama and Daddy are hiding something from us?"

Ezekiel put a box down. "Why do you say that?"

"Daddy mentioned something about Aunt Maddie this morning, something she told them about the Institute. He wouldn't tell me what it was. And they've been pretty shady about their council meetings lately," I said. "Usually they're so open. They're acting off."

Ezekiel's face was concerned. "If it was serious, they'd tell us, right?"

"I'm not sure." I reached down to scratch Oberi's tail, and his tongue lolled out. "Where would they keep something they wouldn't want us to find?"

"Probably in the safe." Ezekiel's face fell as he watched a smile spread across my face. "Ava, no. That's private. We shouldn't be poking around in there."

"Why not?" I sat up, and Oberi jumped off my legs. "If we find nothing, I promise I'll drop it."

"We don't even have a combination," Ezekiel whined.

"I don't need a combination. I have Water powers." I began running up the stairs. Ezekiel followed, letting out protests, while Oberi barked in excitement.

Mama and Daddy weren't home, but they would be soon. This was the perfect time to look.

I snuck into my parents' bedroom while my brother trailed behind. In the walk-in closet was a large metal safe. I'd never been inside it— hadn't felt the need to look until now.

But for some reason, it was calling to me. I was undyingly curious. It'd got me into bad situations one too many times before, but this didn't feel like a bad thing— it felt like something good.

I knelt by the safe and uncapped the water bottle. I moved my hand in a circular motion over the bottle, and water rose in a steady stream. I sent droplets into the small crack that lined the safe's door. I could feel the water as it moved into the safe's locking mechanisms, through the pores of the metal. Briskly, I froze it, and I heard the lock audibly break as the water shattered it.

"They're gonna see the lock's broken, you know," Ez said sourly.

"Better to ask forgiveness than permission." I opened the door of the safe. It was heavy. Oberi put his shoulder against it and moved it aside for me.

At first, I was disappointed. There wasn't much— some money, important papers like birth certificates, and a couple family valuables. Nothing stood out.

Then I saw it. A small leather journal, sitting on the topmost shelf. Ezekiel went pale as he saw it.

"Ava, what if it's a diary?" he asked as my hand reached out to grab it. "This is wrong."

"I'll only read the first page. I won't intrude." It was like my fingers were magnetized to the journal. I couldn't describe why... only that the feeling in my gut told me this journal was meant for *me*. Oberi's eager eyes were on me as I took the journal and opened it to the first page. From what I could tell, it'd been written by my Aunt Maddie— and in a hurry. A poem, scribbled tightly across the page.

The balance between the light and the dark
Will be brought together by the light of the new dawn

A discovery of the ancient ones on the island of shadow
Will change the course of our universe

A second war breaches the horizon
Mountains will fall and villains will stand

The heavens will crumble and hell will open wide
Unleashing the demons that fester within

The path she will walk determines our fate
She dances the line both dead and alive

A new world formed from gods of old,
One from ashes or one from light
The choice is hers alone.

As I ended the script, a sickening feeling settled into my organs. This wasn't a poem.

It was a prophecy.

"What the fuck?" Ezekiel whispered as his eyes moved over the words. I shared his exact reaction. As I turned the page, a note fell onto my lap. I turned it over. The note was in Mama's handwriting; *For when Ava turns eighteen.*

Fire burned in my chest so brightly, it felt like it was going to explode out the top of my head.

I'd turned eighteen over a year and a half ago. I'd be twenty in four damn months. And they'd *kept* this from me this long?

Reality set in. This prophecy was about *me*. Aunt Maddie had foreseen my future and written it down for me years ago. I'd always been different, but now I knew just how much. I was a chosen one— just like my mother was.

And my choices were going to determine the future... determine the fate of *everyone*.

I heard the front door close, and a dragon's roar as Julian took off from the beach outside.

Ezekiel went to grab me, but I jumped up before he could stop me and ran downstairs. I kept the journal tucked tightly to my side as I flew down the stairs so fast, I nearly got dizzy. Oberi was hot on my heels, nails clicking against the hardwood.

Mama and Daddy were placing groceries on the counter after taking a trip into town. Buttercup was eagerly ruffling through the bags to see what they'd bought. For once, I was glad Alana and Maverick weren't around— they didn't need to hear this.

"You're back early," Mama said as she turned to face me. "Was community service okay?"

I didn't answer. I wasn't about to fuck with that shit when something serious like this was on the line. "What the hell is this?" I shouted. I took the journal out from under my arm and tossed it on the table in front of them.

At the same time, both of their faces went completely white. My suspicions were confirmed. They didn't want me to find this.

Mama was the first to speak. "How did you—?"

"It doesn't matter." I was aware of Ezekiel shifting awkwardly behind me. "Why would you keep something like this from me? A prophecy, really?"

Daddy cleared his throat as he shuffled forward slowly. "We didn't want to hurt you."

I gave a laugh. "Whatever's in this book couldn't be worse than you lying to me."

"It is, Ava." Mama sat at the table. Her hand trembled as she lifted it to her head. "You don't understand what you're getting into."

"Have you read it?" I asked.

"No!" Mama slapped her hand on the table. "It was meant only for you. Maddie made that clear."

"When? Why wouldn't she tell me?" I felt like I was being betrayed by my entire family. My parents, my aunt... who else knew?

"Maddie made the prophecy a few months after you were born," Daddy said. "She told us to give it to you when you came of age."

"I need to talk to Aunt Maddie. I have to understand what this means," I said firmly.

"Maddie is in the Himalayas right now, doing research. You won't be able to get ahold of her for at least another week," Daddy said.

I huffed impatiently. Aunt Maddie was a teacher at a school for seers, but she often took research trips with her husband for her alchemy projects. This was the worst possible time for her to be out of reach.

"I deserved to know. That you kept this from me is unforgivable," I shot at them.

"You have to understand. The prophecy about your mother— it nearly ruined our lives," Daddy said weakly. He put a hand on the counter to steady himself. "We didn't want that for you."

"It wasn't your choice!" I protested.

Mama had gone through horrible things in the Hawkei Civil War— I knew that. But if I had known about my own prophecy years ago, it would've given me more time to prepare. Who knew when my aunt's words would start coming true?

"Ava..." Daddy's tone was strained.

"I can't believe you!" I took a few steps closer. I could feel my Fire burning up and down my skin, dying to get out. "I'm not a little kid anymore. I'm almost twenty! You have to start trusting me to do the right thing!"

It happened in an instant. While I was still shouting at him, Daddy's eyes rolled back in his head, and he collapsed. Ezekiel gasped, and Mama shot up from her chair. Oberi began barking in alarm.

The stupid prophecy was gone from my mind in an instant. I rushed forward to catch Daddy before he hit his head on the counter. He was heavy, and my arms couldn't support him.

We crashed to the floor, and I rolled under him so I took most of the blow. My shoulder smacked against the counter, but I refused to let out a cry of pain. I needed to protect him.

"Liam!" Mama fell beside me, while Ezekiel helped pull Daddy off me. He was already coming to, but his eyes were bleary. He looked dazed, like he didn't know where he was. His hands shook, and he appeared so pale.

Tears instantly welled in my eyes, and my lip trembled. This was all *my fault*. I knew Daddy had a medical condition, and I'd pushed him. I shouldn't have questioned what he did. I just wanted him to be okay.

"Help me get him to bed," Mama told Ez. She dragged Daddy to his feet, and my brother helped her. I worried as they carried him up the stairs. Daddy fainting wasn't exactly an unusual occurrence, but I always felt terrible whenever it happened.

Once Daddy was put in bed, Mama fussed around like a mother hen. She fired up the oxygen machine and slipped the nasal tubes over his face before looking for a fresh bag of IV fluid to attach to the surgical pole.

Julian was nosing at the bedroom window. He knew something was wrong. Ezekiel opened it up for him, and the dragon poked his large snout in, sniffing in concern— it was the only part of him that would fit.

"I'm fine, Jules." Daddy raised a weak hand to pat Julian on the nose, and the dragon snorted.

"I *knew* you weren't feeling well this morning." Mama poured water into a mug from the sink, then warmed it up with her Fire magic and slipped in a tea bag before giving it to Daddy. Daddy made a face as she pushed it at him, but he drank it without his usual complaint that it tasted like shit.

I sat on the side of the bed. Guilt bubbled within me so bad, it made me feel like I was drowning. "Daddy, I'm so sorry."

"It's all right, peanut. You didn't mean it," he offered in a weak voice.

Daddy always said that no matter what came out of my mouth. I felt really guilty this time.

I swallowed. "About the prophecy…"

"We'll talk about it later, Ava." Mama's voice had become gentle again. She swept back Daddy's hair, and I took that as an indication he needed to rest. Ezekiel shut the door behind me slowly. By that time, Daddy was already asleep.

Ezekiel gave me a sad look. "It's not your fault, sis. It's bullshit they kept this from you when you had a right to know."

"It *is* my fault. He barely survived the last trip to the hospital." Two tears leaked out and ran down my cheeks before I dashed them away. I wasn't a girl who cried, but for Daddy? I cried buckets.

"He hasn't been admitted in three years. He's doing really well," Ezekiel said. "We just caught him on a bad day."

Ezekiel jerked his head toward the stairs. "You think we should take another look at that?"

The journal came back to mind. I realized that Oberi had gone downstairs and retrieved it for me— it was in his mouth. He nudged me with it, and I took the journal from his jaws.

Mama wouldn't leave Daddy for hours now, which meant Ez and I had time to look at that prophecy alone. I slipped into my room, and the others followed. I lay on my bed with Oberi while my brother sat in the computer chair and twirled in circles. I recited the prophecy aloud three times, but it still didn't make sense.

"Is there anything else in that journal?" Ezekiel asked. "What about a clue?"

I shuffled through the pages. There were drawings and riddles, but they were just as cryptic as the prophecy was. The pages were only half-filled. In the middle of the journal, the writing grew more and more frantic, until the words abruptly stopped altogether. What had my Aunt Maddie been thinking?

This wasn't helping. I read the prophecy again. One line stuck out above all the others.

"*A discovery of the ancient ones on the island of shadow…*" I read aloud. Oberi's ears perked up at the line.

Ezekiel sat forward. "That sure sounds like Darke Island to me."

"It damn well does." Darke Island was where the Institute was— the last place I wanted to go.

Ezekiel caught the look on my face before I could speak. "Ah, no. You're not going to suggest what I *know* you're thinking."

"Excuse me? Have you *heard* this prophecy?" I waved the book around.

Ezekiel frowned. "Only the first five times you read it."

"Yeah, and it's pretty fucking obvious it means business. We don't know what's going to happen, but we do know what's to come *isn't good*." I flipped the journal shut.

"So what do you want to do about it?" Ezekiel raised an eyebrow.

I took a deep breath. "What else is there *to* do? I have to go to Darke Island."

Ezekiel groaned and rolled his eyes. "That's not what I had in mind."

"Information is critical when you're dealing with prophecies. If I know what the future is before it happens, I have a better chance of changing it," I argued.

"Why don't you just wait until you can call Aunt Maddie? That's the logical choice." Ezekiel crossed his arms.

"That's a whole week! It can't wait that long. We're talking about the fate of all supernatural kind, here. One day could be the difference between life and death for a whole race of people."

It sounded dramatic, but I wasn't over exaggerating. Whenever my mother had talked about her own prophecy— and that was very rare— she always made it clear that the fate of the elementals had been determined by her choices as chosen one, and hers alone. Her decisions had saved… and killed… countless numbers of people in the Hawkei Civil War.

If I was a chosen one, too, I had the same responsibility. Waiting around could cost the people I loved. I wouldn't take that chance; not if it meant being decisive now could save lives.

Ezekiel scowled. "You're being impulsive, Ava."

My temper spiked. "This isn't my bipolar."

"Sure acting like it."

"Do I have a choice? Look, I'll go to Darke Island, investigate the prophecy, and figure out what it means. I'll be back in a few days, before classes at Orenda get too far ahead for me to catch up."

Ez looked pretty damn skeptical, but he knew there was no stopping me, so he sighed in defeat. "So when are you leaving?"

I knew the answer the second I looked into Oberi's eyes. "Tonight."

It was around midnight when I crept out of bed, fully dressed. By moonlight, I walked over to my backpack. It was packed with my exploring gear, my guidebook, the journal, my wallet, and clothes that would be suitable for crawling around in ancestors knew where.

I really wanted to take my designer dresses, but I knew I wouldn't need them. I slipped my phone into my pocket and grabbed a picture off the nightstand. It was one of my entire family, at a big summer party last year. It never left my bedside, and no matter what, I was taking it with me.

As a second thought, I took the unicorn nightlight I had since I was a baby and tossed it in.

So I was afraid of the dark. Big fucking deal.

Oberi watched me as I sat on my bed and laced up my boots. There was nothing left to pack. "It's just a few days, right?" I asked weakly. "I won't be long."

Just a few days.

Or weeks.

Or... months...

Oberi placed a paw on my knee. By the look in his eyes, I felt deep in my gut that I wasn't coming back home for a very, very long time.

Who knew how long this prophecy would take to figure out? I had to be prepared to not see my family for a while.

That really freaking sucked. It wasn't like I wanted to get away. I was really close with all of them.

Especially Daddy.

I couldn't think about Daddy; otherwise, I wouldn't go. I crept downstairs and left a letter on his desk, just for him, written in Hawkei.

I didn't leave myself any more time to hesitate. I walked out of my house with my head held high, into the cool night.

Ezekiel was waiting outside to say goodbye, as he was the only one who knew about my plan. But he wasn't the only one. Mama was also by the shoreline, watching as the waves came in and out.

Dammit all. Had Ez told her my plan? What a freaking snitch. I sighed and prepared myself to march right back in the house. Everything was ruined now.

When my mother turned around, her eyebrows pinched at the sight of the backpack on my back. Oberi transformed into a unicorn beside me and tilted her head, horn glowing in the moonlight as her embers fizzled into the air.

In Mama's arms was something small and folded. She held it out and pressed it into me. "Here. My sister gave me these jeans, the day I left for Orenda Academy with your father. They're good luck. You'll need them."

Shock ran through my body as I tucked the jeans into my bag. "You're letting me go?"

"I can't stop this, Ava-Marie. I knew from the moment you were born you were destined for great things, and anything I did to prevent you from walking your path would only separate us," Mama said. "You're a chosen one. You're part of a prophecy. Whatever you do from this moment on is your choice alone. I trust that I've raised you well enough to make the right decisions."

Tears welled in my eyes. My parents *never* trusted me. It wasn't like they didn't want to. I'd just messed up so many times that to do so would be foolish. But Mama was trusting me now to make the right call, and that meant everything to me. "What about Daddy?"

"Your father doesn't know. I'll explain to him when you're gone." Mama rubbed her hands up and down my arms. "Liam isn't going to understand, but he will. I know what you're going through. And I want to make it as easy as I can, because trust me, the road ahead won't be. But I know you have the strength to carry on through it."

A shiver raced up and down my spine at her words, and I suppressed a shudder. Mama dropped her hands from my shoulders. After a moment's thought, she reached behind herself and unfastened the clip of a gold chain, taking it off her neck before looping it around mine, fastening the chain at the base of my neck.

"Mama, no. Not your necklace. Daddy gave it to you on your wedding day." I touched the pendant. It was a copper key, aged with green patina. There was a crown sitting at the center of the key's handle, which was formed into a heart. She never took it off.

"You need it more than I do," Mama said. "When you wear this necklace, you carry my heart with you wherever you go."

I flung my arms around her. Mama held me tight. I thought I heard a sniff from her before she pulled away. "May the ancestors be my eyes, watch where you go and guide your path. May the Great Spirit help you achieve wisdom, which you can use when you lose your way. May your spirit guides always keep you safe, until they lead you to a place where we can meet again."

Mama touched my head and ran her fingers through my hair, completing the blessing. When her fingertips left the tendrils of my hair, it felt like my entire body was glowing. It was as if the ancestors themselves had enlightened me for the road ahead.

Ezekiel came forward to give me a hug. "I wish I could come with you."

My heart ached. I didn't want to leave my brother. We hadn't been apart more than a few days before. He was my protector, and I didn't know what I was going to face out there.

"I wish you could, too." I squeezed him tightly and pulled away. Letting him go was like prying what I loved most out of my arms, but I had to do this. To save everyone.

Before I could lose my nerve, I climbed onto Oberi's back. She reared on her hind legs before she started forward. As her hooves reached the ocean, I used my Water powers to support our weight, so she ran over the ocean, ice hardening beneath her at my command as we galloped full speed away from the only home I'd ever known.

I knew it had to be killing Mama to let me go. She lived for her kids. But she knew I could do this. I couldn't let her down.

When Oberi and I got to the mainland, I saw the spires of Orenda Academy shine in the distance, and I thought of Charlie. I'd promised to bring back Oberi to Charlie later... but I was going on a quest. A *dangerous* quest, one where I'd be in terrible peril, and fight monsters, probably, and all that adventurous bullshit.

I needed a Familiar to protect me. Charlie could get by until I came back.

My mind worked on a plan. Darke Island was in the middle of the Pacific Ocean. I needed a boat to get there— a big one.

The strange marooned ships I'd seen earlier came to mind. I could use my Toaqua powers to sail one out to sea. I just had to find one that didn't have any holes in it.

Oberi galloped through the forest, weaving in and out of trees. I held on tightly to her mane and flattened myself against her neck as I heard a wolf howl against the night.

I thought this was only temporary, but as I raced away from Kinpago, I was certain this was the first night of the rest of my life.

We came to the shipwrecks. I slid off Oberi's back, and she nickered as I began looking through the wreckage for a boat that would sail. I found an old schooner that was more intact than the others sitting on the far shore. I climbed onto it, and Oberi transformed back into a husky, padding up to the mast and taking a seat.

I looked out at the ocean. At my command, the waves began churning up the beach, flooding the sands. The ship slowly began to rise. I ordered the water to cradle the ship, and I held on to a banister as the ocean righted the ship in the proper direction. We sailed out to sea. Once we were in deep water, I urged the ocean to rush us forward, and the waves started pushing the ship at top speed, racing along the edges like we were on a speedboat.

Oberi fiddled with the sails, trying to yank one free with his teeth while I took a map out of my backpack. Darke Island was six hundred miles off the coast of California, to the west. Though I was pushing the ship, it would take me a day or two to get there.

I went to the front of the ship and looked out at the wide, open ocean. The shoreline of California was already long behind me. My heart raced as I looked ahead. I *loved* the horizon line. It called to me like nothing else. I always wanted to know what else was out there. Today, I'd finally get the chance to know.

Oberi let out a couple loud barks behind me that sounded excited. I turned around. Rage welled up in my chest as I saw a man crawl out from behind a few crates. Seriously? This guy ruined everything!

"You think you can get away with abducting *my* Familiar?" Charlie's voice had taken on a hard edge. "Nice try, pidge. I'm not that gullible."

My hands clenched into fists. This was ridiculous. Charlie Wahkin had stowed away on *my* ship.

He had seriously picked the wrong day to fuck with me— and I was going to let him know it.

The sound of Fire crackled, and heat waves rolled out of Ava-Marie's palm. "Jump ship now, or you're getting a fireball to the face," she growled.

 I wasn't scared of her. I took a casual step her way and sat down on a nearby crate. "You wouldn't do that, pidge."

"Try me," she hissed.

I shrugged. "It's your choice. But then you risk this whole ship going up in flames."

Ava-Marie's fireball faltered, and I heard the last of the sparks fizzle away to nothing. But her rage had gone nowhere. "Get off this boat, Charlie, or so help me, I will make you."

"You threatening to drown me, pidge?" I questioned. I didn't think she could do it, even if she wanted to.

"We're not that far from shore. You can swim back."

No, I couldn't. But I wasn't about to admit to her that I couldn't swim.

"We have to be miles off by now!" I cried. "No way am I swimming back. Turn the boat around."

"I'm leaving, and nothing you say will stop me."

I crossed my arms. "You're free to leave, but you're not taking Oberi with you."

"Well, I'm not leaving without him," she snapped. "How'd you know where to find me anyway?"

"Oberi and I have a connection," I reminded her. "He was worried for you— practically begged me to come talk you out of it. I followed the bond to where you were."

"Th-that's not possible," she stammered.

Did I detect a hint of jealousy in her tone? Ava's connection with Oberi must've been weaker than mine.

"You can hear Oberi speak?" she asked, sounding irritated.

I tilted my chin up proudly. "Yes."

It was true, but it wasn't quite what she was asking. Oberi had spoken to me once— to tell me his name. This time, it'd been more or less a feeling, a notion that I had to come stop Ava at whatever cost.

Ava-Marie huffed. "So help me, Charlie Wahkin. You get off this boat *now*, or I'll—"

"You'll what?" I was in front of her in a second. We were so close, I could feel the heat of her skin on mine.

Ava-Marie breathed heavily, but she didn't answer.

"You forget I'm the one with Air magic, pidge." I lifted my hands. At my command, a gust of wind caught the sail, and the boat lurched. Ava stumbled into a stack of crates, and they crashed to the deck. Much to my disappointment, she hadn't fallen on her ass.

"Stop it, Charlie!" Ava-Marie cried, stomping toward me. "How are you doing that? You have no training. You shouldn't be this good."

I spoke coolly as we started turning toward shore. "I've been navigating the world by magic for a long time. I'm a natural."

"Cut it out!" Ava-Marie screamed. She reached for my arms and tried to yank them down at my sides, but I was stronger than she was. I kept them raised. Oberi didn't like to see us fighting. He barked, and it echoed over the ocean toward shore.

"Shh, Oberi," Ava hissed. "We're going to get caught."

"What are you running away for anyway?" I asked. "Did someone hurt your poor little feelings?"

"None of your business." Ava shoved her way past me and headed toward the stern of the ship. The boat rocked, and something fought against my Air power to turn the boat around.

"What are you doing?" I demanded.

"I'm making sure *you* don't mess this up," she shot back.

"You're Fire. You can't control the boat," I claimed. "How are you doing that?"

I could hear the smirk in her tone. "I have something better to help me sail the seas."

"What's that? An oar?" I cracked.

"Water power!" she shot back.

The boat went dead silent. I'd never heard Ava-Marie go so quiet. I might've thought she'd fallen overboard, but I'd never heard a splash. She must've realized she said something she hadn't meant to say.

"How's that possible?" I asked. "Professor Baine said Elementai inherit the powers of their same-sex parent. You can't be Fire *and* Water."

"Well, I'm not going to explain it to *you*," Ava sneered.

My mind raced. If this was possible, maybe I could control more than Air. Professor Baine said my mother was Nivita— an Earth Elementai— which meant that her power traveled through my veins. Could I be two elements— Air and Earth?

I unfortunately didn't have the luxury of pondering it. I had to get this boat turned back toward shore, but Ava-Marie's powers were *strong*. It was impossible to fight against the water currents themselves.

"You can't take me with you," I growled.

"You're right, I can't," she practically sang.

"Finally," I huffed. "We agree on something."

Oberi didn't seem to think so, because he barked in protest again.

"Which is why you need to leave while you still can!" Ava-Marie insisted.

"I told you, I'm not going anywhere without Oberi. So what are you going to do, pidge? Kidnap me?"

"You're the one who got on this boat in the first place," she shot back. "I didn't force you to come."

"No, but you—"

"*Attention!*" a voice boomed over the water, as if projected through a megaphone. The boat rocked beneath us, and the air no longer shifted to my command. It was as if someone had ripped the controls right out of my hand.

"Fuck! How did they find us?" Ava-Marie muttered. She started rushing around the boat, pulling on ropes and who knows what the hell else.

"What's going on?" I tilted my head toward the sound of the voice, but I couldn't hear anything over the churning water beneath us.

"The Toaqua Coast Guard," Ava-Marie growled. "*You* brought them, didn't you!?"

"No, I didn't—"

"We have you surrounded!" the voice called. "You are in violation of coastal code forty-three. You will now be escorted back to shore."

"What the hell does that mean?" I asked her.

She spoke between clenched teeth as she tugged hard on various ropes. "It means we're in possession of an illegal sea craft."

I raked my fingers through my hair. "Hell, you say that like you've violated code forty-three a million times."

Ava-Marie didn't seem bothered. "Once or twice."

The boat continued rocking, and I had to grab the mast to steady myself. "What are you doing, pidge?"

"I'm trying to get this thing moving," she snapped. "The Coast Guard is using Water magic to turn us around. We have to overpower them."

"Overpower them?" I balked. "No way. Not if they're taking us back to shore."

"Charlie, you don't understand," Ava pleaded. "I *have* to leave. The fate of all supernatural societies depends on it."

"Ah, why didn't you say so?" I asked sarcastically. I didn't believe her for a second.

"I don't care what you think," she snapped. "It doesn't matter— ah!"

The boat lurched forward— harder than before. Crates crashed to the deck as Ava-Marie fell into them. I couldn't stay upright, either, and I went spiraling downward. Oberi caught me before I face-planted onto the deck. I must've distracted Ava, because the Coast Guard had overpowered her. The ship sailed full-speed toward shore, and cool wind rushed through my hair. I had to hold on tight to Oberi to steady myself on my knees. Ava made a ruckus trying to stand upright, but she toppled over every time she got to her feet. I chuckled lightly under my breath.

It didn't matter how much Ava tried. She couldn't regain control of the ship. The boat slowed and came to an abrupt halt as it bottomed out at shore.

"Ancestors!" Ava cried, sounding in pain.

"You okay, pidge?" I asked breathlessly. I was glad to be back on shore, but the shakiness of her tone alarmed me.

"No, Charlie, I am not okay," Ava wailed. "I *broke a nail!*"

"Oh my god," I groaned.

"*Ancestors,*" she corrected me with a sneer.

Footsteps pounded across the beach and through the sand. "Ava-Marie Mitoh and Charlie Wahkin," a man said. "You are under arrest for the theft of this seacraft."

I opened my mouth to object, but Ava beat me to it. She started wailing— literally *wailing*. The sound pierced my ears and made me flinch.

"Thank the ancestors you're here!" she cried. "Ch-Charlie abducted my Familiar and t-tried to take her away. I had to stop him!"

"Ancestors," I sighed, for her sake. "You're a compulsive liar."

Several men climbed onto the boat, and their footsteps pounded across the deck.

"*I* was the one trying to stop her," I said. "I didn't steal anything."

Someone grabbed my arm and yanked it behind my back. Metal cuffs clinked and tightened around my wrists. "Your record suggests otherwise," the man stated.

"You can't touch me!" Ava-Marie cried as someone cuffed her. "I'm the daughter of a chief!"

Oberi growled at the men, and Ava screeched, "Get that muzzle off my Familiar!"

Ancestors, I could strangle this girl. We wouldn't be in this mess if it wasn't for her.

"I didn't do anything wrong!" Ava cried as the men started leading us off the boat. "Ask my mother!"

"Ava, I'm just doing my job," the man in charge told her. "You can speak to your mother when you get to the Elders' Quarters."

"That won't be necessary, Jack," a female voice cut across the beach.

My feet sank into the sand, and Oberi's paws padded beside me. Two pairs of footsteps shuffled across the beach toward us. One was quicker and more heavy-footed than the other.

"Let them go," a man boomed. He used a tone of ultimate authority.

"Yes, Chief," the Coast Guard captain stammered. The cuffs on my wrist loosened, and I breathed a sigh of relief.

"Daddy!" Ava-Marie cried. She ran forward, and a *thud* sounded as their bodies collided. "Thank the ancestors."

"Ava," her father said, but she didn't seem to listen. He spoke more firmly. "Ava!"

I sensed Air rush between the two of them as she drew away from the hug. "What is it, Daddy?"

The chief cleared his throat, though his words came out sounding strained. "I'm not here to save you. I'm here to sentence you."

"Sentence me?" Ava balked. "What do you mean, Daddy?"

Ava's mother spoke softly. "He means you're going to the Institute— properly."

Ava went silent for several beats. Her voice came out smaller than I'd ever heard it. "Really?"

The feeling of Ava-Marie's hair in the wind settled as her father smoothed it down. "Your mother told me what you were planning. You stole a boat, peanut. You violated your probation. As your chief, I have no choice but to sentence you to four years at the Darke Institute for Supernatural Offenders."

I expected Ava-Marie to protest, but she didn't say a damn thing. The silence was too weird, and her father's tone too soft. It was like he spoke of her probation to justify the sentencing to everyone else.

But Ava? She almost seemed *glad*.

I wasn't buying the charade. Something was up. I could feel it in my connection to Ava. This didn't make a damn bit of sense. A couple of days ago she was willing to do anything to get out of going to the Institute. Now she was going there willingly?

This girl was up to something. And I needed to find out what it was. Her father was *helping* to get her there somehow. But why?

"Well, if I have no choice..." Ava-Marie said, in a tone that sounded totally fake. Then her voice changed, and became genuine. "I love you, Daddy."

"I love you, too, sweetheart," he replied. "The bus is already en route to the Institute. It will be passing through Kinpago in the morning. The two of you will leave at sunrise."

"*The two of us!*" Ava and I shouted at the same time.

"Of course," her father answered, like it was obvious. "You both violated your probation. You will *both* be attending the Institute."

"I wasn't the one who stole this boat!" I protested.

At the same time, Ava-Marie said, "Charlie's *not* coming with me!"

Her father's tone hardened. "As Toaqua Chief, I have the authority to make this call. Charlie *will* be accompanying you, Ava, and that is final."

I crossed my arms as rage built up inside of me. "Shouldn't the Yapluma Chief be the one to sentence me? I *am* from the Air House."

"Oh, believe me," he snarled, "the Yapluma Chief will agree with me. You're going whether you like it or not."

"But Daddy—" Ava started.

"No buts," he insisted. "Mister Wahkin, may I have a word?"

Not a chance, I thought. But I didn't have a choice. The man was a chief.

My hands curled into fists as he led me down the beach away from Ava-Marie, her mother, and the Toaqua Coast Guard. I feared what he might have to say to me. Probably wanted to wring my neck for getting his daughter into this mess. I suppose he wouldn't believe me if I told him it was all her fault.

"Sir—" I began to say, but he cut me off.

"Look. I'd rather not send you to the Institute if I can help it." His tone was rough. This guy meant business.

Oh? I perked up and listened closer.

"Whether you believe it or not, I'm doing you a favor," he told me.

My eyebrows shot up. "A favor?"

"Yes. I know what it's like to lose a Familiar, and it is not something I wish upon any Elementai— not even my worst enemy. Ava-Marie *must* go to the Institute, and she will need Oberi there with her."

Ava must go? What did that mean? Is that where she'd been trying to run away to? Why in the hell would she do that… run away to a literal prison?

The chief placed a firm hand on my shoulder. I tried shrugging him off, but he didn't move. "I'm sending you with her so you can stay close to your Familiar. In exchange, I'm going to need you to do something for me?"

Oh, sure. Being sentenced to prison is such *a favor. I'd do anything to repay you.*

"I'm not doing anything for you," I snapped. "You're sending me to a prison. This is a death sentence."

"It's only a death sentence if you can't handle it," he growled.

"I can handle anything," I said in a clipped tone.

"Then you'll do this for me," he stated, no question.

"Oh, and what's that?" I asked, with no intention of providing *any* favors. His daughter kept dragging me into her crimes. I didn't deserve this.

He took a deep breath. "I need you to keep an eye on Ava."

I almost snorted. "I'm not sure I could do that, even if I *could* see. Ava's one strong-headed bi — girl."

"I don't like it any more than you do," he assured me. "But if anyone can do it, it's you. I wouldn't be sending her to the Institute if you weren't going with her."

I furrowed my brow. "Why me?"

"Because you two share a connection," he reminded me. "She is part of your soul, and just as you would with your Familiar, you will protect Ava as well."

He wasn't threatening me. He was more or less stating the facts. Whether I wanted to protect her or not, self-preservation would kick in, and I'd do whatever it took to keep her alive — if just to protect my own soul.

All three of us— Oberi, Ava and I— had to stay alive for the rest to keep living. So I was obligated to protect her… if only to save my own ass.

Ava's voice carried across the beach, though I couldn't hear what she was saying. Warmth settled into my bones before I could tell it to fuck off. Damn it. The chief was right. I *had* to go with Ava— not because I wanted to, but because I was being pulled by some unknown force.

Damn magic.

"You *have* to do this, Charlie." The chief wasn't begging me. This time, it *was* a threat. It was obvious he hated my guts and wouldn't hesitate to blame me if anything happened to Ava. "You don't want to know what I'm capable of if Ava-Marie gets hurt."

A lump formed in my throat. "I won't let anything happen to her."

He clapped me on the back. "That's exactly what I like to hear. Now, go get cleaned up. You have a bus to catch."

"What is *that*?" Ava-Marie sneered as I approached the bus stop the next morning.

Oberi was in husky form at my side. He'd spent the night with Ava, but came to help me at sunrise. I didn't think I'd have found the bus stop without his help.

"This?" I asked, gesturing to myself. "Some people call it a walking chick magnet."

"Not you!" Ava smacked my shoulder. "The garbage bag?"

I shrugged the bag on my shoulder. "It's my luggage."

"Luggage?" Ava balked. She turned away from me, flipping her hair so that it smacked in my face. "Nobody told me I was going with a guy who carries his clothes in a garbage bag."

That really pissed me off. As a foster kid my whole life, I didn't have any other choice. Garbage bags were all we had when we moved. The only other bag I had was a ratty old backpack I'd found in a dumpster a few years ago.

"Sorry I'm not *rich* enough for your taste," I snapped.

"I'm not rich," she protested. "These designer bags were on sale!"

Ancestors, she was bringing designer bags to *prison*? How did she not realize how well-off she'd been her whole life? Her pretty little ass wasn't going to last a day.

"Ava, please," our probation officer said, sounding more than a little irritated. I hadn't even realized he'd been there. I suppose it made sense. Someone had to make sure we made it on the bus.

"What? I was just—" She cut off as the sound of a diesel engine approached. "Oh, look. Our ride is here."

My guts knotted. Oberi must've sensed my unease, because he leaned into me. I stroked the top of his head for comfort.

The brakes squealed as the bus came to a stop in front of us. Ava was quick to rush in front of me, even before the doors squeaked open. She climbed onto the bus, and I followed, using Oberi as my guide. Several footsteps followed behind me, and I realized we weren't the only Elementai being sentenced to the Institute. Our probation officer stopped to talk to the bus driver, but I was already so distracted that I didn't hear what they said.

The second I stepped onto the bus, my senses went into overdrive, trying to pick up every little thing. It was so much that I found it overwhelming. To start with, there was a strange buzz in the air that seemed to suck the energy right out of me. I gripped tight to the railing as I climbed the stairs.

Ava leaned back and whispered. "It's noxite. The bus must be reinforced with it."

"What's noxite?" I asked.

"It's a magical metal," she explained. "It affects your powers. They don't want us to escape."

I swallowed, feeling a heaviness settle in my gut. Without my powers, I'd have one hell of a time navigating the Institute. I'd come to rely on them more than I realized.

"Don't worry," Ava assured me. "I did my research. Most of the Institute is noxite-free. Part of their reform program is teaching us how to use and control our powers. You'll feel better once we get there. Just watch for the noxite tranquilizer guns. Those things will knock your powers out for hours."

"Good to know."

We started down the aisle, and various overwhelming scents assaulted me. It was as if someone had shoved an old leather seat up my nose. I wanted to gag. Underneath that was the scent of sweaty socks and something coppery— like blood.

Then there was the noise. Judging by the voices, there were nearly a dozen kids on the bus with us. They bitched at each other so loudly I couldn't make sense of one conversation over the other.

"You think you're so great because you're a fucking fae? Eat a whale cock."

Whale cock? Where the hell did that expression come from?

"You're mermaid scum," someone shot back. "You're an *animal!*"

"Oh, and your angel friend there isn't? I've never seen a *human* with wings before."

"Would you all shut the fuck up?" a guy groaned. "I'll drain you, I swear it."

"Come at me, vamp," a girl challenged.

Ava-Marie passed by everyone and stopped toward the back of the bus. I sensed a man a few seats back. I could tell by the way the air moved around him he had a strong build. No air moved through his hair, so I assumed he was bald. He kept quiet.

"Is baldy back there dangerous?" I whispered to Ava as she sat in an empty seat. I took the seat across the aisle, since there was plenty of room for us all. Oberi opted to sit by Ava, and my frustration swelled.

Ava chuckled. "It's a guard, Charlie. Considering he's not stopping these degenerates, I think it's safe to say he's harmless."

"Who the fuck are you calling a degenerate?" a girl snapped. She was two seats ahead of Ava. I could practically hear the murderous intent in her tone.

Ava tossed her hair over her shoulder, sending the smell of her perfume in my direction. "Oh, I suppose *you're* innocent. That's why you're on a prison bus."

The girl cracked her knuckles. "Hell no. I killed a warlock with my bare hands. Sucked him dry."

"Oh, so you're a vampire?" Ava sounded less than impressed. "I'm so scared."

"I'm no vampire, kitten," she snapped as the bus began to move. "I'm a succubus. I'm far worse than any vampire."

Ava chuckled. "A succubus, huh? So you're a vampire who fucked a demon."

"Hell yeah," she snarled. "Best lay of my life. I've got powers you couldn't even dream of."

She sounded serious about fucking a demon, but I'd bet anything she was lying about killing a man with her bare hands. If she was a murderer, she'd be cuffed, and certainly wouldn't be on the bus with a couple of minor thieves.

Ava chuckled. The soft sound of her fingers running over Oberi's fur met my ears. "I don't have to dream of power. I've got enough of my own. Don't underestimate an Elementai, or you just might find yourself burned alive."

"You threatening me, bitch?" the succubus snapped. "What are you going to do? Set your little dog on me?"

Oberi growled.

Ava's laughter turned maniacal. "Oberi's not a *little dog,* and he doesn't appreciate being called one, either."

The succubus scoffed. "Doesn't change that you brought your *pet* with you. Poor Elementai needs her emotional support animal?"

"Oberi's my Familiar," Ava snapped. "Elementai are permitted to bring their Familiars with them to the Institute. Say one more thing about him, and I'll pound your face in—"

"Stop!" I shot to my feet and put my hand on the seat in front of Ava, positioning myself in front of Oberi. I lowered my voice and hissed, "You're provoking her, Ava. Quit."

"You Elementai act like you're so—" the succubus started, but I cut her off.

"Leave us alone, or you'll regret it," I snarled.

"What are you going to do?" she challenged. "Sprinkle me with a little water?"

I kept my temper in check. "You underestimate the Elementai."

"They're not worth it, Naya," a girl cut in. "The Institute will eat them alive."

Naya paused a few moments, then laughed. "You're right, Danielle. Might as well let the Institute deal with them. No use getting in trouble on my first day over Elementai scum."

I breathed a sigh of relief when Naya tossed her hair and turned back to the front of the bus. My powers may have been weak right now, but I could still feel the air currents around me. I slumped into the bench next to Ava, squeezing in beside Oberi.

"Why'd you stop me?" Ava demanded. "I could fry that bitch."

I lowered my voice so the others wouldn't hear. "I promised your dad I wouldn't let you get into trouble. Starting fights isn't going to cut it in prison."

The fabric of Ava's shirt rustled as she crossed her arms. "You spoke to Daddy about me?"

"Pidge, you're missing the point. The Elders won't be there to protect you. Your father won't be either. Prison is nothing like Kinpago. You have to be careful."

She scoffed. "You say that like you know."

"I've never been convicted, if that's what you're implying," I snarled. "But I've known plenty of people who have."

Ava considered this for a moment, but it didn't seem to bother her. "Please, Charlie. I can take care of myself."

"Not if you're willingly putting targets on your back!" I hissed. "You don't want attention in prison. We have to keep a low profile and stay out of trouble."

Ava snorted. "Ever met me, Charlie? My brother says *trouble* is my middle name."

"Well, get rid of it," I growled. "Unless you want to end up in actual prison and not just a reform school."

"Big deal. Same thing."

"Not the same thing. These people are criminals, pidge," I reminded her in a low whisper. "You don't know what they've done or what they're *willing* to do. Push the wrong button, and you'll end up raped or beaten to death."

Ava stilled, and Oberi let out a soft whine. My hand was on his back, but he drew away from me to lay his head on Ava's lap.

After a beat of silence, Ava spoke. "You really think something like that could happen?"

I cocked an eyebrow. "In prison? Hell yeah."

Ava got really quiet, so much that I could hear her swallow. "Fine, Charlie. You win. We'll stick close together. But I can't make any promises."

I huffed. "Just try to stay out of trouble, will you?"

"Try," she scoffed, like the idea was ludicrous. "I'll *try*."

The bus began to speed up, and my fingers tightened on the seat in front of us. All around, gasps came from the other passengers. I felt the bus rattle underneath me, like we were driving off-road on rocks and gravel instead of pavement.

"What's going on?" I asked.

"Ancestors," Ava breathed. Her weight lifted from the seat as she stood to get a better look. "We're headed toward a cliff!" There was no fear in her voice. Rather, she sounded thrilled.

"No, we're not," I stated flatly.

"No, seriously. We are!" Ava cried.

I didn't believe her, until the other passengers began crying the same thing.

"What's this moron doing?"

"There's nothing but ocean ahead!"

"We'll drown!"

"Ancestors," I gasped, clutching the seat so tight my knuckles started to hurt. With my other hand, I grabbed Oberi's fur. He was on high alert now, padding his feet on the bench seat. My heart pulsed in my ears. The thought crossed my mind that there was no Institute at all. Officials just loaded up the bad kids and sent them to their deaths by driving off a cliff. "They're going to kill us!"

Ava-Marie didn't seem bothered by the notion at all. She started laughing— a crazy, maniacal laugh that made my skin crawl. Ava was officially a mad woman.

"We're getting closer," she told me, eagerness in her tone.

"Thanks, but I don't need my death narrated!" I cried.

"Closer… closer… aaand… gone!" Ava said gleefully.

My stomach dropped out of my abdomen as the bus went hurdling off the edge of the cliff. Passengers screamed in unison— all but Ava-Marie. The psycho spread her arms wide like she was flying and smacked her wrist into my face, letting out a happy scream like she was on a rollercoaster.

I couldn't stop screaming. My stomach somersaulted, and my heart rattled around in my chest like a rabid dog trying to escape. I'd never felt such terror in my life.

Thwack!

The bus abruptly slowed, and my head snapped forward into the seat in front of me. My head swam, and I rubbed the bruise forming between my eyes.

"We're alive!" Ava cried triumphantly.

"No shit," I growled. "What the hell is going on?"

Ava drew a sharp breath. "Ancestors, it's beautiful."

Oberi shifted between us and climbed halfway onto Ava's lap— like he was looking out the window.

"What is *it*?" I snapped. I was really starting to get pissed. Someone better explain what the hell that was.

"The bus is a submarine!" Ava cried.

I stilled. Though the other passengers were loud and distracting, I managed to focus on the vibrations of the bus. The bus was moving, but it was incredibly smooth— like it was gliding through the ocean. All around me, I heard voices crying out to look at the fish, gasping in amazement at the sea life that was all around us.

"We're underwater?" I asked Ava.

"Yes, and the ocean is so pretty! There are schools of fish everywhere. Ancestors, a kelpie just swam by! Charlie, did you see—?"

She cut off before she could finish her sentence.

"Don't worry about it," I said flatly. "I've seen kelpies a million times before."

"Really?" she asked.

I blew a breath. "No, pidge. I'm blind!"

"You can't expect me to know everything," she huffed. "Were you *born* blind?"

"What kind of a question is that?" I snapped. "Were you born with that stick up your ass?"

"Nah, that showed up when I met you," she shot back.

"Unlikely," I stated flatly.

Ava pushed at me. "Go sit over there. You're ruining the view."

"Only if I get Oberi," I insisted.

"No way."

I shrugged and settled deeper into the seat. "Fine by me, pidge."

I closed my eyes and pretended to sleep. Ava groaned under her breath, but she didn't say anything else. I felt her shift in the chair and turn to look out the window again.

I hated her. Not just because she was… well, Ava. But when everything was going to shit, she still found beauty in something extraordinary.

I wondered what that was like. I'd entered into a magical world, but most of the magic in my life was already gone due to the way I'd grown up.

After a few moments, Ava started talking under her breath. "Aw, the sea turtles are so cute. So many different colors— blue, purple, green. Which one is your favorite, Oberi? Oh, look! The eels are *dancing*. Oberi, wave to Thalassa! That's my grandpa's Familiar. She looks so majestic in the ocean— her blue scales twinkling in the sunlight. She's such a pretty sea serpent, isn't she? She must be close to a hundred feet long, I bet."

The more I listened to her, the more I realized how oddly detailed she was getting for Oberi. Unless she wasn't narrating for Oberi's benefit at all, but for *mine*.

Normally, I'd tell her to piss off. I didn't *ask* her to do that. But as much as I wanted to be mad at Ava, the gesture soothed me. For a brief moment, it felt like she actually cared.

At some point, I must've drifted off, because I felt Ava shaking me awake a few hours later.

I startled. "What is it, pidge?"

"Wake up, Charlie," she whispered. "The bus has surfaced. We're here."

ava-marie

SIX

The prison submarine drenched water onto the shore as we rolled upon it. I pressed my nose to the window, watching as the fins retracted into the main hub. There was a loud sound from above, like the starboard fin and periscope were retracting. I felt wheels form beneath us as the submarine transformed completely into a bus, rolling onto the rocky landscape with a jostling motion.

"It must be some kind of enchantment that makes the bus change," I said to Charlie. "Not sure which supernatural race made it, though."

He let out a *humph,* which told me he wasn't interested in finding out. I rolled my eyes. Ancestors, did this guy give a shit about *anything*?

The bus rolled up the rocky beach shore and onto a road that was in poor disrepair. The bus hit a pothole, and Oberi yelped as he was tossed into Charlie's lap. Several people loudly complained.

I continued to observe my surroundings. Darke Island was nothing to write home about. The entire island was covered in a thin layer of fog. Grey clouds above blocked out the sun, and for miles all that could be seen were scraggly dead trees and mossy grass. I didn't see an inkling of life. It was like the plants didn't even want to grow here. We drove past a few swamps and entered into the creepiest looking forest as we went further inland.

Seriously. It was like the trees had eyes here. I couldn't shake the feeling of being watched.

Charlie felt it, too. I noticed he shifted uncomfortably as goosebumps rose over his skin.

Conversation died down completely. Nobody spoke. Everyone had seemingly become very afraid. I wasn't one to admit when I was freaked out, but this forest had something about it that was beyond supernatural. I never wanted to step foot in it again.

When we emerged from the forest, a few buildings caught my attention. They were shabby and in disrepair. I caught names of bars, restaurants, a couple offices. Some buildings were abandoned completely and boarded up, while others had broken windows.

I would've thought the place was a ghost town if it weren't for a few people walking along the streets. One a vampire, the other a witch, maybe. They kept their heads down and their hoods up as they walked against the drizzling rain. I noticed they stayed to opposite sides of the sidewalk as they passed by, like they were wary the other was some sort of killer.

"Now entering Shade Hills," a voice over the bus's intercom announced. This must be the town that surrounded the prison. As the bus took a roundabout, I read off some of the names on the shops. There were stores for necromancy, demonology, and conjuring evil spirits. I bet all those places had loads of magical contraband.

Damn place screamed dark magic. Something that intrigued me, but only for research purposes. As an elemental, I could only wield weather magic. You'd never see these kinds of shops in any other supernatural community. Most of this shit was forbidden.

A shiver crawled across my spine as I realized I was going to a place where plenty of prisoners would have no problem putting a hex or curse on me. Charlie was right when he said I needed to watch my big mouth. There were dangerous people in Shade Hills, and they wouldn't hesitate to kill me.

The bus left Shade Hills, and that's when I saw the fence. Dread crawled up my stomach as I saw miles and miles of iron fencing, the tops edged with curled barbed wire. Four tall guard towers were posed at the corners of the fence line, adorned with spotlights and armed guards.

This was it. We were at the Institute.

We drove down a long, winding road, which led to a large metal gate. Brawny guards in blue uniforms opened the gate, using their magic to pull the two sides open. The bus drove inside, and the last thing I saw of the free world was the sign outside the gate. It read; *Darke Institute for Supernatural Offenders.*

"You okay, pidge?" Charlie asked as I sank lower in my seat. Oberi let out a whine.

"I don't like being put in a cage." My heart was already beating out of my chest. What had I gotten myself into?

"Well, you put us here on purpose, so I hope whatever you're here for is worth it," Charlie grumbled resentfully.

He was right. Somewhere, the answers to the prophecy were on Darke Island, and I needed to find them.

The bus stopped in front of a large stone building, big enough to fit hundreds of people. It was Gothic, with tall, twisting spires and large glass windows— that were fitted with bars. Guards with noxite guns prowled at the doors, preventing any prisoners from getting out.

An insane asylum. They *literally* put us in an abandoned insane asylum.

Beside it, a crumbling cathedral stood tall against the rain, dirty stained glass windows appearing gloomy in the murky atmosphere. The campus… or rather, prison yard… was large and vast, with paths for students to walk on. In the distance was a dark lake. Ancestors only knew what lurked within it.

This place was Halloween all year long— and not the fun kind. This was more of the *serial-killer, get-me-out-of-here* vibe.

The voice came on over the intercom again. "You have arrived at the Institute. Leave your belongings on the bus. They will be delivered to your assigned dormitory."

I *really* didn't want to leave my designer bags, but as Charlie yanked on my wrist, I begrudgingly left them behind. People shoved each other trying to get off. That bitchy succubus girl, Naya, knocked a girl over while swaggering to the front. The girl fell over into the other seat and smacked her head on the window. I flinched as she struggled to sit up.

I stopped and reached over in the seat where the girl had been tossed, holding out a hand. "You okay?"

The girl had blue hair in beachy waves and green eyes that swam like the ocean. She flinched at my extended hand, like she thought I might hit her with it.

She smelled like sea water. She was probably a mermaid. After a moment, the girl cautiously took my hand and got to her feet. "I'm fine," she replied. "I'm Opal."

"Ava-Marie." I gave her a kind smile. Opal seemed very innocent. What the hell was she doing in a place like this?

"Hey, you're holding up the line!" I heard someone shout from the back— a shifter. "Move your ass, prissy bitch!"

"Fuck off, asshole!" I snapped at him. The shifter guy shoved someone aside to get to me, but Charlie blocked his way.

"You might want to back off," Charlie warned. "Don't want to piss off the guards on your first day."

The shifter hesitated as Oberi growled. I moved before the shifter could make up his mind and left the bus. Opal followed me, flanked closely by Charlie and Oberi. As our feet hit gravel, the wind howled, and an eerie chill permeated the air. Loud screeching sounds met my ears. At first, I thought it was someone being tortured, until I realized that the sound was coming from the lake.

"What's that noise?" Charlie asked, cocking his head.

"Sirens," I said in a mystified voice. "They're singing in the lake."

Charlie's mouth opened in wonder as he listened to them. Waiting for us at the gate were six people. A guard shouted at us as we milled about, wondering what to do.

"New arrivals, please go with your student guide, designated by your supernatural race," the guard instructed. "You will be assigned your number and your uniform before you are taken to the Warden for your introductory welcome."

We had to wear *uniforms*? Gross! I totally wasn't here for that.

A crawling feeling crept up my skin as Opal leaned over and asked, "Who's the Warden?"

"I don't know," I whispered. Whoever he was, he didn't sound pleasant.

"Elementals, with me!" a Latina girl shouted. A Mexican gray wolf prowled at her side. It must've been her Familiar. The wolf had red and black mottled fur and keen eyes. The girl herself was curvy, with curly black hair and a scar across her eye that told me not to fuck with her.

I gave a sad wave to Opal as she separated with her guide. It would've been nice to stick with somebody other than *Mister Sensitive-and-Serious* all day. Charlie and I were among the few Elementai. There was one other boy and girl here, neither of whom had bonded with Familiars yet. I didn't know them.

The guide put her hands on her hips. She had to be in her Third Year, and was a bit older than me. "I'm Guadalupe Lopez, but you can call me Lupe for short. My Familiar's name is Rosita. We'll be introducing you to the Institute. Keep up, or we'll leave you behind, and trust me when I say you won't like it when the guards beat your ass for wandering off."

She was a *sweetheart*. Lupe turned on her heel, and the guards opened the big wooden doors that led into the Institute. She gestured us through, while the other groups entered through different entrances.

Above the great doors to the Institute was an insignia, a stone symbol etched into a large coat of arms. A winged snake wrapped in an infinity symbol around a key, which was standing upright. That had to be the Institute's sigil.

When we entered the building, I looked around in astonishment as I took in our surroundings.

"What's it look like?" Charlie asked under his breath. We were at the back of the group, and pressed so close together we could be holding hands.

I nearly wanted to. This place was nuts.

"The outside is an old asylum, with a cathedral attached. It's all fancy inside. There's red rug for the carpet, and the walls have pretty wallpaper. There are statues everywhere of supernatural creatures, and the furniture here is new and well-taken care of. There are portraits everywhere, and the ceiling is so high. It's nearly like a palace," I replied.

"Doesn't sound much like a prison," Charlie said.

"Yet." I wasn't fooled. This might be a pretty cage, but it was still a prison nonetheless. We were trapped here, and there was no way of escape.

My mood flipped instantaneously. I went from good to bad in seconds, and once that spiral started, I couldn't crawl out of it.

"Fuck this place, fuck this place…" I sang under my breath as we walked. The further I got into the school, the more I wanted to run. The absolute finery of the mansion was such a contrast to the barbed wire fencing outside. No matter how much they dressed this asylum up, I had a bad feeling they'd done horrible things to people here. I was going to jump out of my skin with an anxiety attack any second. Oberi put his head under my hand and pressed into me for comfort.

Lupe overheard my words and whirled on me. "Look, you're here, so that means you're guilty. We all are. Just keep your head down and don't get into any trouble, and you might just get out of here in one piece."

Charlie nodded, like he completely agreed with her. I swallowed and didn't argue back. My hands were shaking so badly that it caused my arms to quiver, too. I didn't like this. I didn't like this at all.

Lupe took us down another hallway, one that was sparser and devoid of decoration. She was speaking, but I couldn't decipher her words against the screaming in my head. The voices were getting bad again.

This isn't safe, Ava.

You have to escape, Ava.

The prophecy, Ava!

I let out a whimper. Charlie's head tilted slightly as he noticed. Before I knew it, he'd slipped his fingers between mine and held tight.

Holding his hand should've disgusted me, but it didn't. I squeezed back and pressed into his arm as I tried to ignore the sensation of the walls closing in around me, colors distorting as they suffocated me. Charlie winced as I grasped his hand so hard it hurt, but he didn't let go. Oberi let out a sigh of relief.

I was able to focus on the sensation of Charlie's hand in mine and come back down to reality. As my mind stopped floating and I was firmly back on the ground again, Lupe's voice came back into focus, and overpowered the ones in my head. "Decades ago, the humans attempted to settle Darke Island. They were eventually chased off as they realized the island was a place of heavy supernatural activity. Here, people disappeared without a trace, never to come back. Monsters ran rampant and devoured souls, while ghosts who refused to cross over to the afterlife haunted the woods. Strange things happened here, and while it frightened the humans, the supernatural community saw an opportunity to change the island into a prison."

Lupe tossed her hair as she continued. "The worst of the worst were sent to the cathedral here, which was fashioned into a makeshift prison. The baddest criminals were housed in the cathedral itself, while the rest were sent to building Shade Hills. When the cathedral got too crowded, an asylum was built next to it, to house the most deranged inmates."

One of the other Elementai raised their hand. "Didn't they use to… perform experiments on the inmates here?"

My gut churned as Lupe nodded. "That story's true. They *did* perform terrible experiments on people, years ago. But that's over now. The United Supernatural Union found out about it and shut it down. They changed the asylum into a reform school for supernatural delinquents, which is why all of you are here today."

"Is there any way out?" the other Elementai asked. I could hear an edge of hope in her voice.

Lupe made a *pshing* sound. "Good luck. There's a magical ward around Darke Island. Even if you escape the Institute, the ward will prevent you from leaving the island without permission. There's truly no escape once you end up here. Your only option is to graduate."

I had to spend *four years* here? This was ridiculous. I was starting to think my brother had been right, and this was another one of my impulsive decisions that had screwed me over. Damn my brain.

"Your classes will mostly be centered around reformation," Lupe said. "You'll have one course teaching you the basics of your supernatural race and their magic. The rest of your classes will focus on behavior, substance abuse, and anger management. You'll be expected to attend group therapy every week to chart your progress."

I'd been in and out of therapy all my life and wasn't looking forward to going back. I hated the idea of sharing my deepest thoughts with a bunch of weirdos, who'd probably stab me before they cried with me.

But it would all be worth it, if I could stop the prophecy and save the people I loved. I just had to keep my goal in mind.

Lupe led us down a dark corridor, which stretched into a series of doors. "This is the Elementai section of the prison, where your dormitories are; Cellblock 5. You'll find your name on the door of your cell. Most of the cell blocks are separated by boys and girls, but the Elementai one is not, as it was built in the smallest corridor of the prison."

That was typical, giving the native person the shaft. Lupe stopped at the head of the cellblock. "Change into your uniforms so you can be ready for the Warden's speech."

I searched for Charlie's name before I searched for mine. I caught his last name on the first door in the hallway, before I read my own on the door beside it.

We were right next to each other. I didn't know if I was relieved or annoyed. I pulled him over to his dormitory, then dropped his hand. I didn't want to hold it anymore— touching him felt way too real.

"This is it." I left Charlie at his door before I went to my own. When I opened it, I nearly let out a shriek. *This* was what they were giving us? A metal bed frame was pushed against the wall. On top of the lumpy and stained mattress was a folded, scratchy blanket, with a pillow that looked hard as a rock. The room contained nothing else but a small desk and chair, with a small window that had bars across it.

On the desk was a uniform that made me shudder. These uniforms were a major fashion *faux pas*. There was a long-sleeved white button-up with the Institute sigil on it, along with a black and green tie and a plaid wool skirt that went to the knees. Long white socks and Mary Jane shoes completed the disgusting array.

I put the outfit on with a groan. As I turned the shirt around, I noticed opposite the sigil near the left shoulder was a number: 721.

My prisoner number. My mouth instantly soured. So much for feeling like a student. I was a convict; nothing more, nothing less.

"Do we really have to wear these?" I complained to Lupe when I emerged from my cell.

"During all classes," Lupe said. "You can wear what you like in your free time, as long as it isn't inappropriate."

I bet that meant half my wardrobe. I blew a wayward strand of hair out of my eyes. "Where are the bathrooms?"

"They're down the hall. Communal showers," she replied. "Boys and girls are separate."

I gave another groan. "Do they *really* expect us to live like this?"

"Hey, be lucky that you got your own room," Lupe said. "Most people have to share."

Yuck. Couldn't imagine sharing that closet.

Charlie came out of his dorm with a slight smile on his face. "Seems pretty dry, and it has a nice bed."

This guy must've grown up sleeping on benches if he thought that bed was nice. My back was going to be so sore.

Charlie had put on his uniform, and I had to admit, he looked really cute in a tie. Guy wasn't such a tramp when he cleaned up a little. Oberi barked twice and wagged his tail.

"Yours is better than mine," I complained. His uniform was simple black pants, a black striped tie and a green sweater... which clung tightly to his biceps, by the way. His prisoner number read 137.

"Hey, at least it's not a prison jumpsuit," Charlie said with a shrug.

"Don't joke about that," Lupe snapped. Her wolf let out a growl.

"Um, okay," Charlie started. "Why?"

"The only people who get orange jumpsuits are in Cellblock 9, in the basement of the prison," Lupe said flatly. "Trust me, you don't want to end up down there."

Lupe turned her back on us and walked away. By this point, the other Elementai were dressed and ready to go. Nobody asked about Cellblock 9 as she led us onward.

"Do you think she's trying to scare us?" I whispered to Charlie.

"She seemed pretty serious." Charlie looked concerned. "I wouldn't mess with her, pidge. Asking questions seems like a good way to get hurt around here."

I thought so, too. Still... what was Cellblock 9? And why was it such a bad place to be?

Oberi changed into the Fire unicorn mare as the halls widened. She pressed against me, and I placed a hand against her side, feeling her fiery warmth. I didn't have to worry about getting hurt here. Oberi would protect me, I was sure.

There was a line outside of a classroom near our dorms. Lupe grabbed a box from a desk and began distributing signs. "Everyone at the Institute has to take a booking photograph for identification purposes. You will receive a school ID in a week that you must carry with you at all times."

We were taking *mugshots*? This place couldn't get any more cliché. Lupe handed me my sign, and I looked down.

AVA-MARIE MITOH

RACE: ELEMENTAL - DUAL CASTER (FIRE / WATER)

ID #: 721

Charlie played with his sign. The line moved steadily, until I was in front of a guard with a camera. I smiled sinisterly as he took my photo, making it my every intention that my grin told the Institute to fuck off.

After our mugshots, Lupe led us to what I figured had to be the center of the school, into a hall hundreds of feet long. The ceiling was made of glass, and the floors were marble. A balcony stretched above the main floor, capped by two winding staircases on either side. From the balcony hung black and green flags, the Institute's sigil blazing on it like a warning. The walls were covered in floor-to-ceiling mirrors.

It looked like some kind of ballroom. The people who'd been on the bus with us earlier were here, all dressed in their new uniforms.

"This is the Room of Mirrors. It is where most school events are held, and where the Warden will give his welcome speech," Lupe said. "I've done all I can to get you used to this place. The rest is up to you. Good luck."

816

Lupe left the Room of Mirrors with Rosita as if her ass was on fire. She certainly didn't want to be stuck with us for longer than she had to. I surveyed the students, looking them over. There was a blonde-haired girl talking to Naya. The girl was muscular and had a stocky build like an athlete. She sneered when I caught her eye.

"Would you mind staring somewhere else?" she snapped. "I'm trying to have a conversation."

As she turned to face me, I caught a glimpse of sparkling butterfly wings. They were dark blue and had glimmering diamonds within them that made the wings appear to be galaxies. They disappeared before I could inspect them further.

Ugh. A fae. They were *so* stuck up.

"I wasn't looking at *you*," I snapped.

"Sure seemed like it." The blonde drew herself up. "You better watch it. I'm Kalina, and I'm going to run this school."

"Says who?" I squared up with her immediately. Naya watched the two of us, an amused expression on her face. She was *loving* this.

"You obviously didn't get the memo. I'm a fae sorceress. We don't associate with those of a *lower class*," Kalina hissed. "Go bother your own kind."

This girl was a bitch. I raised my hand to jam a fireball into her face, but Charlie caught my wrist. "Knock it off," he growled. "You're already looking for trouble."

Naya let out a cruel laugh. "Aw, how cute. She's got a little boyfriend. Come on, Kalina. We have better things to do than fight with a couple of savages."

My. Blood. Boiled. Kalina frowned. Charlie froze, and I added, "You're about to see how much of a *savage* I can be when I choke your ass out."

"I'd like to see you try," Naya threatened.

I was about to jump her and start pulling hair, until all sound in the Room of Mirrors immediately drained out. The lights dimmed as a dark voice from above spoke. "Greetings, new arrivals."

Kalina and I broke off our argument and turned to the balcony above. My heart skipped a beat as I took in the sight of the person above me. The man had deep-set, hooded eyes, and a face that was so taut it looked like a skeleton, skin stretched over high cheekbones. He had a strong build and wide shoulders, and his head was thrown high and proud. His dark hair was cut short in a military style, and his lips pressed tight and thin. He was both beautiful and ugly at the same time. He had great white feathery wings behind him, several feet long in length— an angel.

I knew who he was without having to be told. The Warden.

The Warden beat his wings a few times, and they vanished behind him before he clasped his hands together. "Welcome to the Darke Institute for Supernatural Offenders. I am the Warden of this school, Doctor Ophio Taurus. I'd like to begin by saying you are all very welcome here."

What a lie. This man had a voice that hissed like a snake. He wasn't welcoming at all.

The Warden continued. As he spoke, the sinister smile on his face spread... like he was enjoying the attention. "This will be easier for all of you if we lay down a few simple ground rules. First, forget about your old life. Forget about your family, your friends. You are now the property of the United Supernatural Union, in care of me, your Warden. I have full authority to use whatever means I deem necessary to reform you into a proper member of magical society."

I nearly shook in rage. Forget about my *family*? No fucking way. This dude could go to hell. Charlie put a hand on my shoulder, to tell me to stay put.

"At the Institute, our goal is to succeed by making you succeed," the Warden continued. "The program is simple. You will receive four years of education. If the board considers you reformed, you will graduate, and your criminal record will be wiped clean. You will be allowed to return to your homes as free members of society. We have many employers in Shade Hills who would love to have you."

Yeah, right. Like I'd stick around and get a job on Creepy Island.

The Warden smiled even bigger. "However, if the board determines that you have *not* been reformed, you will be transferred to an adult prison somewhere else on the island. After this, your chances of returning to your homes are lost, and you will be given a life sentence. That is, if you make it that far."

What did he mean by that? There were a couple of uneasy glances, but no one dared to speak.

The Warden spread his arms wide, like he was a benevolent god welcoming us into a heaven that felt more like hell. "Do well in your classes, and you will go far here. Good grades and good behavior will be rewarded with Commissary points and privileges to take trips into Shade Hills. Unruly behavior will result in consequences. If infractions go too far, you will be punished with solitary confinement in Cellblock 9. You have been warned."

So that's what was in Cellblock 9. The worst of the worst were sent down there, and by the sound of it, nobody came out.

"Let's go over a few ground rules. No cell phones are permitted on campus," the Warden boomed. "Students are allowed one phone call a week through the school phones, and as many letters as they can afford to send out. There is a curfew from ten p.m. until six a.m., where you are required to stay in your dorms. All students are expected to contribute to the well-being of the prison by doing chores, which includes cleaning and laundry. There are no cameras, as I assume you all know, technology does not work well with an abundance of magic… however, be very aware that there are enchantments to keep you in. Certain items, such as bobby pins and other items that can be used as weapons, are not permitted. The guards are searching your belongings now, to be sure nothing contraband is on campus."

Great. I wondered what was missing from my stuff. Like I was going to take a bobby pin and stab someone's eye out… though I was sure there were people here that would.

The Warden straightened his tie. "You are allowed to use magic on school grounds. However, if a student has been found to break several severe rules, they will be forced to wear a noxite cuff that will inhibit the power of their magic."

I definitely didn't want one of those cuffs. I resolved that if I broke any rules, I couldn't get caught.

"You will receive your class list and related textbooks in the morning." The Warden tilted his head. "For now, get to know your surroundings. Trust that we are here for you. We care about you. And we are devoted to your future as a contributing member of magical society."

This guy was pure fucking evil. I could feel it coming off him in waves. His words sounded noble, but make no mistake, he was at this job because he loved torturing kids— not because he wanted to help them get better.

I vowed not to let him get to me. No matter what he did.

As the Warden walked through a set of double doors behind the balcony, I turned so I could sink my claws into Kalina. Charlie pulled me away before I could. Oberi began shepherding us back in the direction of the dorms with her horn, throwing nervous glances behind her.

"What are you doing?" I snapped. I yanked my hand out of Charlie's the moment we got in front of our dormitory. "We can't let her talk to us like that!"

"That's the least of our problems," Charlie growled. "For fuck's sake, pidge, can you *try* not to get thrown in Cellblock 9 your first day here?"

"We can't let people walk all over us. They'll take advantage," I protested.

Charlie gave a humorless laugh. "Trust me, pidge, there are times to fight back and times to shut your mouth. You really need to learn the difference."

"At least I'm not going to avoid conflict, like you," I snapped.

Charlie shook his head in disgust. "I'm not going to keep sticking up for you. You need to watch your back."

He fished in his pocket for something. "By the way, tell your old man he can't scare me."

Charlie tossed something, and I caught it last minute. My mouth fell open when I saw it. Daddy's wallet.

I rifled through it quickly. It didn't look like Charlie had taken anything. Everything was still there, including the money. He just wanted to prove a point.

"You're unbelievable," I sneered. "Was that really necessary?"

Charlie shrugged. "You need to learn there are other ways to show people you won't be pushed around."

He turned his back on me and entered his dorm. Oberi let out a soft nicker.

I facepalmed. This guy was really too much. I went inside my dorm. Oberi tried to squeeze in, but she was too big to fit through the door, and she cried out impatiently.

"Hold on," I told her as I pushed her back out. "I'll be there in a sec."

My suitcases had been delivered to my dorm. When I looked at them, sadness flooded my veins.

Did Charlie *really* not have anything to put his clothes in but trash bags? That was so sad.

I sat at the desk. When I opened the drawers, I found paper and a singular pencil. I took them out and began to write.

Dear Daddy,

Everything is fine here at the Institute. I got here safe and well. My dorm is nice, and my uniform is great. I am already making new friends!

I scowled, thinking of Kalina. The letter sounded so fake. Truth was, I was miserable here.

But I didn't want Daddy to worry, so I put as much false cheer into the letter as I could muster, hoping he wouldn't catch on to it.

It looks like Charlie took your wallet. He says he's sorry. Nothing's missing. It's like a game to him, so I hope you'll forgive him. I'll try to mail it back with the letter.

Can you please send along a new suitcase, dark purple in color? I'd like to pay for it— the money's in my account. You know where the card is.

Give Mama, Ez, Alana and Maverick all my love. I'll write as much as I can, and I look forward to your letters.

P.S. Some chocolate would be nice, too. I'm dying for it.

Love, Ava-Marie.

A couple of teardrops fell from my eyes, but I wiped them away before they could fall on the letter. I wanted my parents to think I was happy here, so I'd pretend to be happy. Maybe if I pretended long enough, it would become real.

I wasn't sure where to take the letter, but I'd walk around the school and find a way. I personally didn't feel safe enough to go anywhere alone, but I didn't want to drag Charlie with me, so I left with just Oberi.

I relaxed when I saw Opal standing near a gargoyle, a letter in her hands and looking worried. Her face softened in relief when she saw me. "Hey. Where are you off to?"

"I have to mail a letter to my parents," I said. "Do you want to come with me?"

"Sure." Opal's face beamed. "We can find the mailroom together."

Opal linked her arm in mine. We stayed close as we roamed through the halls. A couple of guys catcalled us, but when Oberi lowered her horn at them, they shut the fuck up.

"Hey, Ava…" Opal said, her voice thoughtful. "What the Warden said. About the people who don't make it far enough to leave the Institute and transfer to the adult prison. Where do you think they go?"

I honestly had no idea. And I wasn't so sure I wanted to find out.

charlie
SEVEN

The Darke Institute was nothing like Orenda Academy, but it wasn't the prison I'd been envisioning. Curfew sucked, but at least the food was good. I'd worried we'd be living on stale bread and broth water for the next four years. I was surprised when we were served chicken Alfredo and chocolate pie on our first night there.

"You look like you're enjoying this," Ava-Marie noted in disgust. She clearly thought it was disgusting.

I shrugged. "It's delicious."

Ava leaned across the table to whisper, "Don't let the food fool you. They only serve comfort food so we don't run. It's all an illusion."

"Or they want to feed us… because you know, this is a school," I pointed out.

"A *prison*," Ava snarled.

"A *reform school*," I corrected her.

"Then why is there a fence around the property, locks on our dorm room doors, and bars on our windows?" Ava challenged.

Oberi barked in agreement.

"For people like you who think the rules don't apply to them," I snapped.

"Is that why the kids call this place the *Villain Institute?*" she huffed. Before I could answer, she continued. "I've heard the whispers in the halls. The Warden thinks we're all criminals—villains."

I snorted. "Well, you're not innocent."

"Neither are you," she shot back.

I blew a breath of annoyance. "I don't even know what I'm doing here. I'm too old for some juvenile reform school."

"Not in the supernatural world," Ava pointed out. "In supernatural societies, we don't get our magic until around age eighteen, which is when we go to college or university to learn how to use it. It isn't until we graduate that we come of age. The Institute is a facility aged between juvenile detention and prison, for people ages eighteen to twenty-two. Some inmates are older, I guess, but only because they were sentenced earlier and have to serve their four years. If we were sentenced to an adult prison before learning our magic, we'd be killed by the other inmates."

A shiver traveled down my spine. I'd be twenty-six before I got out of here. I wasn't sure if me being older than most of the other students was an advantage or a hindrance at this place.

That was the last thing she said to me all night.

In the morning, I woke to the sound of a paper being slid under my door. It must've been six a.m. because the lock used to enforce curfew disengaged with a *click*.

I crawled out of bed and picked up the paper, but it was useless to me. I couldn't read it. Outside my door, I heard the sound of claws scratching. I opened it and bent to pet Oberi.

"Hey, boy," I said, scratching him behind the ears. "I hope things weren't too bad on your first night with Ava. Wish you could've stayed with me, though."

Oberi licked my hand, then nuzzled his head into my arms like he'd missed me. I returned to my room and gathered my things. Oberi helped me find the bathroom, and I showered and dressed.

I returned to my room— and promptly toppled over something that wasn't there before. It'd been sitting right inside my door. Oberi barked as I went tumbling to the ground, then hurried over to help me up.

"What the hell?" I mumbled under my breath.

I reached out and ran my hands over the thing I'd tripped over. It was taller than my knee and about half as wide, shaped like a box and covered in thick canvas. As my fingers ran over the zipper, I realized what it was— a suitcase. Who the hell left their suitcase in my room?

Unless it wasn't a mistake…

Damn it, Ava. I noticed how apprehensive she seemed about my garbage bag. Didn't she realize I didn't want— didn't *need*— handouts? This could only mean she expected something in return.

I wanted to stomp over to her room immediately and return the luggage, but Oberi stepped in my way when I stood. I hesitated, and the thought crossed my mind to keep it. I'd never had anything this nice to hold my things before… and I really wanted it.

Oberi pressed his nose to the luggage, pushing it into my leg. He must've been able to sense Ava's intentions better than I could, because apparently, he really wanted me to have it.

"Fine," I caved. "I'll keep it. But I'm not taking anything else from *her*."

I set the luggage on the bed. Heels clicked in a confident rhythm outside the door.

"Ava, is that you?" I asked.

My door creaked open wider.

"It's me," she said. "Did you get your schedule yet? I thought we could compare."

I gestured to the paper I'd set on the desk. "Is that my schedule?"

The paper rustled as she picked it up. "Sure is. Looks like we have Elementai Magic together."

"Figures." I waited for Ava to say something about the luggage, but she didn't acknowledge it. Instead, I asked, "What are my other classes?"

"Your first is Introduction to Work-Study this morning," she told me. "You've also been enrolled in Juvenile Justice and Substance Abuse."

"Just the classes I wanted," I deadpanned. "I hope they count toward my major."

Ava laughed, but she sounded more uncomfortable than anything. "What are you majoring in? Pissing off the inmates?"

"Just *one* inmate in particular," I teased.

Ava got quiet for a second, before asking, "What *would* you major in, if you could? I wanted to get my degree in Anthropology… before the Institute happened."

She sounded really sad. I quickly answered her question to distract her. "I never really thought about it. I didn't think I'd ever make it to college, considering I never graduated from high school."

"You never *what*?" Ava balked.

I realized I'd said too much, and I snatched my schedule out of her hands. "It's a long story. Anyway, I'm going to need Oberi today to help me get to my classes."

"I need his support, too," she argued.

"You can find your classes on your own," I pointed out. "Until I learn the layout of this school, I need a little guidance."

Ava went silent. "Fine, but I want Oberi to sleep by *me* tonight."

"You had him last night!"

"And?" she challenged. "If you get him all day, I get him at night. We have to play fair."

I snorted. There was no playing fair with Ava-Marie. But at least she agreed to let me take Oberi for the day. That was better than I'd hoped for.

Oberi wasn't a trained guide dog, but he wasn't really a *dog*, either. He was far more intelligent and knew how to navigate the school by instinct. We stopped by the cafeteria for breakfast, then started toward my first class.

As we made our way down the hall, I took note of any major landmarks we passed. Voices bounced off a high ceiling as we walked through the main entrance. Not far from there, I heard the sound of an air hockey table whirring and a puck clicking back and forth.

"Six to nothing," a young voice said.

I realized I was passing a recreation room. Must've been the Villain's Den— it was the nickname for the place where everybody hung out between classes. I made a mental note so I'd remember where it was located.

I counted my steps, and we took twenty more before Oberi turned left down a hall. We slowed and entered a classroom. Voices filled the room as students flooded in. Oberi led me to the back row, and I took a seat at the desk in the corner. He sat dutifully beside me, panting in glee.

At least someone's happy.

"Aww, a *puppy*," a female voice cooed as she took the seat beside me.

Oberi let out a low growl.

"Don't pet him." I tried not to sound rude, but it was instinctual. No one touched my Familiar but me... and Ava. "He's on duty."

"Duty...? Dear Goddess, I'm so sorry!" the girl cried. I could hear it in her voice the moment she realized I was blind. "I didn't mean... I'm Alice, by the way. Alice Tucker."

"Charlie," I said. "I've never heard the phrase *Dear Goddess* before. Is that a colloquialism?"

"I'm a witch," she explained. "From the Miriamic Coven."

"Oh," I said like it made sense, but it didn't really. I didn't know that much about other societies yet. I'd only just learned of the Elementai.

"You look confused," she pointed out.

"I'm new," I admitted. "Haven't gotten the whole supernatural run-down yet."

"It's simple," she said, sounding happy to help. "There are six main supernaturals at the Institute. First is the Celestials, like the Warden. They call themselves angels, but they're actually Nephilim, or half-angels. Then you have the Arcanea— fae sorceresses and their shifter mates. Try to stay away from the Midnighters, which are the vampires and succubi. They're forbidden from feeding on any students, but accidents have happened here more than once."

Sure... accidents.

"Then there are witches and warlocks like me, and I'm assuming Elementai like you?"

I nodded.

She sounded pleased as she continued. "And the final race is the Atlanteans, or the mermaids and sirens. We occasionally get Astromancers, but they have their own prison system and don't tend to send people to the Institute."

"Astromancers?" I questioned.

"Wow, you weren't lying. You *are* new." Alice wasn't mean about it. In fact, she sounded really bubbly and nice. "Astromancers are enchanters who get their magic from the stars. Anyway, most supernatural societies are split into their own factions. Elementai, as you know, have a House for every element. In the Miriamic Coven, we're split into Casts. They're—"

"Whoa," I stopped her. "Slow down. I already have five Houses to remember and seven other societies you just mentioned. Give a guy some time to process it."

Alice snickered. "You don't seem like you belong here. You're too nice. What are you in for?"

I groaned. "It's a long story."

Alice lowered her voice and leaned toward me. "Are you innocent, too?"

"I wouldn't exactly say *innocent*," I replied with a coy smirk. "Wait... what do you mean, *too*?"

Alice hesitated a moment. "I shouldn't be here," she admitted. "I was accused of hexing a fae on my trip to Europe, but I would *never*. That's what I get for taking a gap year and traveling. Don't *ever* visit Europe, by the way. Not unless you want to run into the fae. They're horrible."

"Noted," I said.

Alice shifted in her chair and went quiet. She'd been really helpful and nice, but I wasn't sure I believed she was innocent. Like Lupe said when we arrived, no one here was innocent. Even though my crimes in Kinpago weren't exactly worthy of a prison sentence, I was far from innocent. I'd done some seriously shady stuff. I deserved to be here.

The class quieted, and a pair of footsteps marched across the front of the room. "Welcome, students. I'm Professor Cusak, and this is your introduction to your work-study program."

Alice leaned over and whispered, "He's an angel. You'd think you could trust them, but you'd be wrong. I hear this guy is tough on his students."

"Then I guess we better not attract his attention," I replied.

"Your work-study program will begin next semester," Professor Cusak explained. "It is an apprenticeship program to teach you the skills needed to pursue careers outside of the Institute. This semester will prepare you for entering the mines."

"The mines?" I asked Alice in a low whisper.

"There are noxite and crystal mines that run under the island," Alice explained quietly. "Students are expected to work in the mines as part of the rehabilitation program. They believe hard work is good for us."

My guts twisted at the idea. Something about it didn't sit right with me. "Do we get paid?"

"A couple dollars a day, I think," Alice answered. "We can cash in at the campus store for clothes, soap, stamps, and things like that."

"What happens to the stuff we mine?"

"I don't know," Alice whispered. "I guess the Institute collects and sells it."

A shiver ran down my spine. I was starting to think maybe Ava was right— this place *was* a prison, and a *for-profit* prison nonetheless.

"That's just—" I started to say.

"Excuse me," Professor Cusak snapped. "You two in the back. Do you have something to share with the class?"

"No," I said the same time Alice answered.

"I w-was only explaining the p-program to Charlie," Alice stammered.

"If you have questions, you may ask me directly," Professor Cusak snapped. "No talking during class, or I'll have you thrown in Cellblock 9."

That seemed a little extreme, based on what I'd heard of Cellblock 9, but I wasn't about to risk it. Alice and I both went quiet.

Professor Cusak continued, ignoring the two of us. "We will start the semester learning the art of transference, as some of you will be assigned to transference for your work-study program."

Professor Cusak began walking around the room. A *clink* came, one after another. I couldn't tell what it was, until he reached my desk and placed something on top of it. I reached out to feel the object. It was cold and smooth in my hand— a rock of some sort.

"As you all know, transference is a very advanced form of magic," Professor Cusak continued. "It involves transferring your magic into crystals so that someone else of your race may draw from it. You are expected to learn transference by the end of your first term at the Darke Institute. You may begin."

My brow furrowed as I tested the weight of the crystal in my hand. I'd had zero magical instruction before, and I was already expected to perform advanced magic? What kind of a shit school was this?

Apparently, I wasn't the only one who felt totally out of my element, because someone at the front of the room spoke. "Sir, how exactly does transference work? I mean, how do we do it?"

"We will get to that in a later lesson," he replied, sounding less than pleased at the question. "For now, I would like to see if anyone is able to accomplish the task without instruction. Begin."

Nobody spoke, but I could hear the shared frustrations around the room. Someone in front of me hummed in concentration, and a girl across the room kept huffing. Teeth gritted from the row ahead of me, and Alice couldn't stop clicking her tongue.

I had no hope of getting this on my first try, so I didn't even put in the effort. It didn't seem like anyone else knew what they were doing anyway, so why try?

By the end of class, not a single person had managed to transfer their magic into the crystals. Oberi led me out of the room behind everyone else.

"That was a horrible lesson," a boy sneered.

"Agreed," a girl said. "How can he expect us to just *know* these things?"

"He's obviously trying to separate the good students from the great," another boy added. "If anyone got it today, they'd be put into the transference work-study right away."

The girl huffed. "Well, no one did, so the joke's on him."

The voices faded down the hall, until eventually, I couldn't hear the conversation anymore.

"Well, Oberi," I said to my Familiar. "We have some time before our next class. What should we do?"

Oberi barked, and his wagging tail hit my leg repeatedly. He started leading me back the way we came, then stopped at the rec room.

"What is it, boy?" I asked. "You want to go inside?"

Oberi barked and ran away from me, but he came back a few moments later.

I furrowed my brow. "I don't understa—"

Oberi shoved his nose into my hand. I felt something furry and round and grabbed on to it. It fit easily inside my palm. "A tennis ball? You want to play fetch?"

Oberi barked happily.

"Where are we going to play?"

Oberi didn't hesitate. He rounded on me and pressed his head into my leg, pushing me forward. As soon as I started walking, he came back to my side and led me through the rec room. We stopped at a wall, and I reached my hands out to feel my surroundings. My fingers curled around a door handle, and I twisted.

Hot, humid air met my skin, and Oberi and I stepped outside. I could feel the expansiveness of the open air, but my magic seemed to hit a block hundreds of yards away. It felt a lot like when I'd stepped on the bus, though not as strong, since we weren't in confined quarters. I noted the feeling as noxite and assumed that was the fence Ava had mentioned that surrounded the property. Though it was hot out, I couldn't feel the sun on my skin, as if thick clouds covered the sky.

Voices filled the yard— so many that I couldn't make them out. A *twang* sounded each time a basketball connected with the pavement, then came the clink of chains as the ball sank into the basket.

In the distance, someone yelled, "Hut!" Bodies collided together with hard *thuds*.

Ouch. Football sounded like a good way to get beaten inside the prison. I couldn't believe the guards allowed it, to be honest.

"So you've taken me to the prison yard, Oberi?" I asked, stroking his head. I lowered my voice and muttered, "I am *not* looking forward to this."

Oberi whimpered, and I knew I couldn't tell him no. Even magical huskies couldn't be expected to be cooped up inside all day.

"Fine." I sighed. "But only because I care."

I avoided the basketball players and headed to the other end of the prison yard, where the voices were far off. I tossed the ball toward the fence, and Oberi took off running. He yipped happily, then returned a few moments later and dropped the ball into my hand. It was coated in saliva and smelled of dog breath.

"Ew, Oberi," I complained. He barked again and panted. "Hell, why do you have to be such a good boy?"

I drew my arm back and threw the ball farther this time. Oberi went tearing across the yard so fast that dirt flew up from where his paws dug into the grass. Chunks hit me in the leg.

Oberi returned less than a minute later, and I threw the ball again. I heard the football players too late. Someone came sprinting toward us just as I tossed the ball. Cheers followed behind him.

Thwack. The tennis ball hit somebody square on.

"Touchdown!" someone yelled, but it was too far off to be the guy I'd hit.

"What the *fuck*?" a deep voice roared. That was definitely the guy who just took the blow from my tennis ball. *Shit.*

The man stepped toward me. Oberi threw himself in front of me and growled, the tennis ball totally forgotten.

"Who the fuck do you think you are?" he snapped.

I opened my mouth to respond, but I never got a word out. A heavy fist cracked into my jaw, and I was thrown sideways.

"What the hell!?" I growled as I steadied myself. My head spun. I pressed my fingers to my lip, and they came away covered in a warm liquid. "It was an accident."

"Bullshit," the guy growled. "You did that on purpose."

Oberi barked as the man reached out to grab me. His hands landed on my shoulders, and I noticed they were *huge*. "You want to pick a fight with a vamp?" he snarled. His chilling breath crossed the top of my head. The guy must've been a whole head taller than me. "Be my guest, but your sorry ass is going to lose."

Air rushed toward my face, and I ducked his fist. A chorus of *oohs* rang out from behind him. He moved faster than I could react, though, and I didn't have time to dodge the next blow. He swung an uppercut at my jaw, and my feet left the ground as I went flying backward. I slammed to the ground hard, and breath whipped out of my lungs. I gasped. Oberi rushed over and licked my face. I used my magic to force air into my lungs, but it only helped a little. My ears rang, and my sense of balance was shot.

"Go Mad Dog!" someone shouted.

Mad Dog must've been encouraging them, because several others joined in on the cheers, and they only grew louder.

"Get up!" a boy hissed from above me— someone different than the others. His voice was smoother, not quite as rough and angry as the vampire gang. He placed his hands on my shoulders, but they were smaller and softer than Mad Dog's. Whoever it was wasn't gentle, though. He yanked me to my feet. A cat mewed lightly beside him. "You have to fight back!"

"Fight back?" I balked. I was still trying to figure out which way was up and which way was down. That punch had nearly knocked me out. "Who are you?"

"I'm Marcus. I'm the guy who's gonna make sure you don't get killed," he said in a rush.

"I can't fight back," I argued. "He's huge! And a vampire, no less. This isn't a fair fight."

"So he's faster and stronger than you," Marcus said, like it wasn't a big deal. "Use your magic against him."

"What for?" I demanded. Something lurched in my guts. I doubled over, feeling like I might hurl.

Marcus caught me. "You're new here, aren't you? If you want to survive in this prison, you can't let anyone walk over you. You win this fight, you win every fight afterward. This is the only chance you've got. Now get back in there and finish this."

Marcus clapped me on the back, and I stumbled forward toward Mad Dog. I didn't know who my new ally was, but he was right. This wasn't a street fight I could just walk away from afterward. I was locked in here with Mad Dog, and losing this fight meant I'd be marked as an easy target. If I walked away, I was inviting him to come after me again. And not just him, but anyone who was hungry for blood. Winning was the only way to show everyone they couldn't mess with me. I had to do this— not just for myself, but for Oberi. I wouldn't let him become a target, too.

"You throw a good punch," I said, wiping the blood from my lip.

The chorus of cheers died down, and Mad Dog let out a low chuckle. "You must have a death wish."

I shrugged. "Something like that. So, is that all you've got?"

"There's a lot more where that came from," Mad Dog snarled.

I quickly realized Mad Dog liked to fight with his fists, because a punch came rushing toward my face again. I felt it by the change in the air. I ducked out of the way and reacted before he could get another punch in. I thrust my arms outward, and the Air followed my command. I felt the resistance as it slammed into him. The *thud* I expected from his body hitting the ground never came. He barely even stumbled.

Use my magic… not as effective as it sounds.

How the hell was I supposed to fight a vampire? It's not like I could suck the air out of his lungs. He was undead, and didn't need to breathe. It wouldn't affect him… right?

Hell if I knew.

Mad Dog approached me again, but before he reached me, Oberi darted in front of me. He growled and snapped his jaw, but the vampire was faster than he was. Air swirled by me as Mad Dog swung out a foot. Oberi whimpered as it connected with his gut. I heard the *thud* as my Familiar landed in the grass a few feet away.

Pure, unadulterated anger rushed to the surface. I didn't think. I just reacted.

I flung my hands out, and Air magic blasted through them. I felt it streaming around Mad Dog's body, and though he resisted, he couldn't fight the wind gusts enough to get close to me.

"Nobody hurts my Familiar!" I screamed.

My rage came bursting through, and Air magic unlike anything I'd ever used began to circle around Mad Dog. My magic felt like a rope, tightening around the low life and pinning his arms to his sides. I might as well have been summoning a tornado, because that's how strong the winds felt. Dirt swirled through the air, sending particles bouncing off my skin and into my eyes. Trash and other debris could be heard tumbling across the pavement near the basketball courts, and the hoops rattled. Screams filled the prison yard. The guards began yelling to get things under control, but it was nearly inaudible over the winds.

"I'll make you sorry you ever touched my Familiar," I sneered.

I threw my arms upward, and the air followed. The mini cyclone I'd created blasted upward, taking Mad Dog with it. His screams could be heard echoing in the distance as he fell from a great height. I heard a *splash*, but I could barely process it. I just stood there, shaking.

"Holy shit, man," Marcus said as he returned to my side. "Right in the lake! A classic."

I furrowed my brow. "There's a lake?"

"Hell yeah." He sounded pleased. "Mad Dog is siren food. He won't be messing with you again."

"Holy shit. Did I kill him?" My stomach hollowed at the thought. I hadn't meant to take things that far.

"No, he'll be— get down!"

Marcus grabbed me by the neck and shoved me to the ground. We landed side-by-side in the grass as something small whizzed above our heads. I nearly crushed Marcus' cat, but the creature wiggled out from under my arm.

"What the hell—?"

"Noxite darts," he breathed. "The guards will shoot at anyone! Let's get out of here."

I grabbed Oberi's scruff and scurried to my feet. I kicked up another whirlwind around us to throw any noxite tranquilizers off their course. I followed Marcus and Oberi around the side of the building, and we ducked into the school. The entrance was narrow, like a long hallway. I heaved heavy breaths, but it hardly felt like there was enough air in here.

"Holy shit," I gasped as I leaned against the wall.

"Holy shit is right," Marcus agreed. "You beat Mad Dog! Good job, man."

"I'm not talking about Mad Dog!" I cried. "I'm talking about the guards. Did they see us?"

I hoped not. The last thing I needed was to head to Cellblock 9 my first day of class.

"With that whirlwind you created?" Marcus panted. "I couldn't see anything through that. I think you're safe. You've got some crazy skills, though. I've never seen elemental magic like that."

"Mad Dog's gonna want revenge," I stated.

"Nah, you did good," Marcus said. "I got in a fight with one of his buddies my first day here. Won it like a champ, and they haven't bothered me since. Anyway, good luck at the Institute."

"Wait!" I stopped him before he could walk away. "Why'd you help me? Are you an Elementai like me?"

Marcus chuckled. "What, because of my cat? Nah, Rishi's not a Familiar. My tattoo marks me as a warlock. I'm surprised you didn't notice."

I didn't say anything. Marcus hadn't caught on that I was blind, which was a good thing. I didn't want anyone in this prison thinking they could take advantage of me.

I shrugged. "I'm new."

"Well, it was a good thing I was out in the yard when I was," Marcus said. "You have to be careful here, new guy."

I scoffed. "Believe me, I know. Thanks for the help."

Marcus chuckled. "Seeing you kick Mad Dog's ass was worth it."

"This might sound dumb, but…" I wondered how to word the question. "I thought vampires couldn't be outside during the day. Shouldn't Mad Dog and his crew… I don't know, burn up in the prison yard or something? Or is that just a myth?"

"Nah, it's true," Marcus said. "But the cloud cover on Darke Island is so thick vamps don't have to worry about the sun."

Damn. I had so much to learn about this world.

"See you around," Marcus said.

"Yeah," I replied. "See ya."

After Marcus and his cat walked away, I realized that he never told me why he helped me. It was like he'd avoided the question all together— like he was hiding something.

Prison wasn't the place to go poking into people's secrets, but I'd be damned if I didn't want to know what Marcus was hiding.

ava-marie

EIGHT

My brain buzzed with static.

I hated that they woke us up at six a.m. by turning all the lights on and unlocking the doors. I was *not* a morning person.

Today, I doubted if I was even a person.

I hadn't slept but an hour. Since the beginning of the week, I'd been totally wired, and today was worse than ever. My thoughts raced so fast I couldn't comprehend one thought before it surged into another. I was riding so high right now I didn't think I could ever come down.

Oberi whimpered and nosed my feet. He was lying at the edge of the bed in his husky form, and he hadn't been apart from me all night.

I had to do something to get all this energy out of my body. My body was so jittery, it nearly felt like I was on drugs, and I hadn't taken anything.

Maybe a jog around the prison yard would help me calm down. I got dressed in my workout gear and tied my hair back while Oberi let out a whine.

"Go on. Go back to Charlie," I told him as I opened the door. "He needs your help to get around the prison. I'll be fine."

Oberi gave me a look that told me not to go getting into any trouble. No promises.

When Oberi was gone, I walked to the prison yard. I took in the sight of the immense property. There was a basketball court and a small area for lifting weights. In the distance were the sparse woods and the lake that held the sirens. A big track circled the entire yard, which people walked on daily during breaks.

That horrible fence was the worst part. It made me feel boxed in. The yard was still pretty isolated. Two people kicked a soccer ball back and forth on the grass a ways down, but besides that, the place was deserted.

I set a timer on my watch at six fifteen and started running down the track. Within the first few laps, my lungs had already developed a sharp, stabbing feeling, but I didn't allow myself to slow down. Instead, I pushed harder.

It was eight o'clock when my body forced me to stop. I skidded to a halt in front of the double doors that led to the yard and vomited into a trash can. All that came up was stomach acid. A couple people looked at me and edged away, like I was carrying a disease.

I was exhausted, but my mind still whirled like a merry-go-round. I dragged my ass back to the Elementai dorms and washed up in the gross community showers. I turned the water as hot as it could go, to try to drown out the thousands of voices that were already ringing in my ears. No one was in here, thank the ancestors, but I'd seen more ass and boobs in the past seven days than I ever wanted to in my life. Privacy was nonexistent at the Institute… but at least in the girls' showers, I felt safe.

There were locker rooms here for people to get dressed in. I scowled when I opened my locker and saw the same boring uniform I had to wear, day in and day out. It was Friday, so at least I'd get a break from wearing it tomorrow.

Even so. If I had to put on that crime against fashion one more time, I would lose my shit.

I tapped my chin and gave a small smile. This uniform needed a *major* upgrade.

Do it, Ava.

Start something.

Cause trouble.

We weren't allowed to have scissors, for obvious reasons. I took the skirt out of the locker and sawed it on the edge of a bench, until it created a small tear. I ripped the edge of the skirt and threw away the large piece, before I took the white shirt and tore the sleeves off that, too.

I slipped the clothes on. I unbuttoned the bottom of the shirt so it exposed my midriff, then tied it just underneath my boobs. I loosened the top two buttons of my shirt, too, to show off some cleavage. The newly-ripped skirt just ended at my ass.

I looked *so hot*. Very sexy schoolgirl vibe. This would break a million dress codes— and was risky as hell to wear in a place where people were looking for prey.

But right now, I didn't care about the risk. The adrenaline pumping through my blood was so strong, I couldn't avoid the temptation. I walked out of that locker room with my head held high and a big smile on my face.

Students who took medications had to line up to get them from the nurse's station every morning. I had to report; otherwise, they'd come looking for me.

Opal was standing in the medication line outside the infirmary. The mermaid's green eyes widened like saucers when she saw my outfit. "Ava-Marie, what are you *wearing*?"

"I'm still in uniform," I pointed out. All the guys in the hallway were looking at me— some of the girls, too. Nobody made a move, though.

"You're going to get an infraction," she whispered.

"What more can they do to me? I'm already behind bars," I said.

Opal shook her head, but didn't say anything more. When I got to the front of the line, the nurse wrinkled her nose at my outfit, but she said nothing. The nurse handed me lithium and an antipsychotic in a small paper cup. She watched as I took them and made me lift my tongue to show her I wasn't hiding them, to spit them out later.

Ancestors, she reminded me of Mama and Daddy. They'd eventually caught on I was dumping my pills down the drain a few years ago. They'd started watching as I took them. Apparently, this place had the same policy. Nothing got past the staff around this joint.

I wish the pills were helping. Usually, they did.

Not this week.

"You heading to class?" Opal asked as we left the line.

I shook my head. "No. I haven't gotten breakfast yet."

"Better do that. Don't want another violation on your record other than the one you're going to get for your uniform." Opal giggled.

"Sure." We had to report for meals, too. We had to report for *everything* around here. Our lives were so structured I felt like I was in kindergarten.

The walk from the infirmary to the cafeteria seemed to take mere moments. I was aware of eyes on me, though any voices that cried out were muddled in the background. If anyone tried to bother me, I didn't notice them. I was too far into my fog.

The cafeteria had to be the most boring place in the school. Long metal benches were placed in big lines everywhere around the room. At the head of the room was the counter, where you could pick up whatever gross thing the other inmates were serving that day. The area was sparsely decorated, with gray paint, gray carpet, and gray, mushy goo for dinner nearly every night.

My mind started to clear as I walked through the cafeteria line. I didn't feel hungry at all. I was required to take *something*, so I grabbed a breakfast smoothie and an apple. As I turned around to find a place to sit, I smacked into a large, broad chest.

A sharp grin immediately made my insides curl. "Hey, baby. Just where do you think you're going?"

I knew who he was— Mad Dog. He had a reputation around here for being the worst of the worst. He had an ugly pug face, skin so pale it was nearly white. His eyes burned red, and the uniform he wore stretched around his massive frame. For ancestors' sake, he had fangs so large, I didn't know how they fit in his mouth.

"Away from you." I tried to maneuver around him, but Mad Dog blocked my way. His eyes roamed me in a way I didn't like.

"You wouldn't dress like that if you didn't want attention," Mad Dog said. He leaned in closer, and a shiver crawled up my skin. "You smell pretty good. Let's go around back for a quick bite."

A couple of people looked our way, but nobody intervened. No one was brave enough to stand up to Mad Dog.

But I was. He needed to learn he didn't run this school. "Eat shit, dickhead." I walked around him. Mad Dog grabbed my wrist, and that was a mistake. I took the smoothie in my hand and smashed it over his head.

It went everywhere. Mad Dog let me go, and I staggered backward. His grip had been like iron. People weren't kidding when they said vampires were strong.

Mad Dog was still wiping the smoothie out of his eyes. I had to suppress a laugh of glee. The lust in his eyes was gone, though. It'd been replaced with rage.

"You're gonna pay for that, slut," he seethed. "Dress like a whore, you'll get treated like one."

I felt my Fire ignite in my belly. No matter how much time passed or how society changed, there was always some bigot telling a woman what she could and couldn't do with her vagina.

But I *needed* this. I longed to beat the crap out of the first guy who dared to try to hurt me— to get some fucking revenge. I wanted to teach some sick, twisted pervert he couldn't do whatever he wanted to women.

I had magic now, when I didn't before. I had power. All I wanted to do was shove a fireball down this creep's throat, and laugh while imagining it was John. If I couldn't get back at *him*, this was the next best thing. I'd make sure this bastard never did anything to another girl.

But before I could toss a fireball into his face, I heard a growl behind me. Oberi was there, the hair on his back standing upright as he faced off with Mad Dog.

Charlie was right beside him. He swung an arm around my shoulders and said, "Your little swim in the lake didn't teach you much, did it, *Mad Dog*?"

His words were clearly a taunt. Mad Dog paused. His eyes clouded as he looked over Charlie. He was afraid of him.

Mad Dog quickly disguised the fear in his voice. "You know what? You can have her. I'm not interested in used goods."

I felt my face flush. I went to kick Mad Dog in the fucking throat, but Charlie's arms locked around my waist and held me there, hands crossed over my bare stomach.

It didn't bother me when Charlie touched me. Any other guy, it would. But I could sense through our bond that he had good intentions. And right now, his intention was to prevent me from doing something really fucking stupid.

Even I could admit it. Trying to provoke Mad Dog was asking to get my ass beat.

But maybe if it happened, the noise in my brain would stop. The voices were so loud they were nearly shouting now. I could hardly stand it.

Mad Dog left the cafeteria, thank the ancestors. People's eyes turned back to their food, but I could hear the whispers that had started buzzing around us.

"Get off me." I wriggled out of Charlie's grip. "Can't you see I'm trying to fight my own battles?"

"Fight your own— what the hell!" Charlie threw his hands up. "I can't win with you, can I? And what the fuck are you wearing? You barely have any clothes on!"

"Oh, so *you're* feeling me up, too?" I challenged.

He gave an angry noise. "Well, when I've gotta pin you down to stop you from punching a vampire in the face, I'm gonna notice a few things."

"It doesn't matter what a woman's wearing. She shouldn't be attacked, not even if she's walking naked down the street!" I burst.

"I know that, but most men here aren't going to think that way. They're predators," Charlie said. "You have to be careful. Even if guys harassing you isn't your fault."

It felt good to hear someone say it. That it wasn't my fault.

Though Charlie had no idea what he was referencing.

"Well, thanks for the help, but I can handle myself," I told him shortly.

"Can you? Because you act like you have something to prove." He crossed his arms. "Is it really that upsetting I want you to be safe?"

It was the first time he admitted he cared. Warmth spread throughout my core and covered me like a soft, welcoming blanket. It felt so nice.

But his concern was far too close. Intimacy was uncomfortable. So I drove a knife through it by saying, "Just watch your own back, Wahkin, and I'll watch mine."

"Fucking hell. Can you try not to start shit for *one day*?" Charlie hissed. "You are seriously pushing your luck here."

I rolled my eyes. "Look, Charlie, if you're gonna ride my ass, at least pull my hair."

He snorted. "You wish. Come on, let's go."

Charlie grabbed my arm and started hauling me alongside him. Oberi changed into a Fire unicorn and trotted behind us, her head held high. I reached out to her and fed her the apple. She munched on it happily.

"I did what I did because people have to know who's boss around here," I said. "I won't be intimidated."

"I think you did this on purpose, because you wanted to start a fight," Charlie snapped. "Look, you obviously have a bone to pick with someone, and you're looking to take it out on everyone else. I don't know why, but you have to let it go. If you don't, you'll get killed in here."

Rage flared inside me. I could *never* let it go.

"I have you. You'll protect me," I said with a shrug.

"I'm not your personal bodyguard," he grumbled.

"No, but Daddy put you up to making sure I get out of here alive," I said. "Plus, as the other half of your soul, you are obligated to make sure I don't cork off, because if I do, you will, too."

Charlie paused. "You think our bond goes that far?"

"I mean… probably?" I lifted my hands. "Look, if your Familiar dies, so do you. Since we're bonded, I figure if one of us dies, we *all* die. So it's in your benefit to keep me alive."

"Don't you think it'd go the other way around, and you want to keep me out of trouble as well?" he growled.

"Yeah, but I'm not worried about you. I heard what you did to Mad Dog the other day. You can protect yourself," I said with a wave of the hand.

Charlie sighed. "You're unbelievable."

Oberi led us to a corner of the cafeteria, toward a deserted bench. There was a guy sitting there I didn't know. He had wavy dark hair that fell around his shoulders, and five o'clock shadow around his chin. He was muscular and tall, but not so much as Charlie. The sleeves of his sweater were pushed up, exposing the intricate tattoo of a cat on his left arm, winding around symbols like a cauldron and an eye. The tattoo was colorful, done in a graffiti style. There were a few tattoos on his right arm, too, but the sleeve he had on the left was the one that had caught my attention, because it was so beautiful. The guy had a cat sitting on his lap, which was mostly black with brown splotches around the eyes. Dude must be a warlock.

"Marcus, meet Ava-Marie," Charlie said as we slid onto the bench.

Marcus smirked. "The pain-in-the-ass?"

"Excuse me?" I raised an eyebrow.

"Hey, that's just what Charlie calls you," Marcus said. "I'm not involved."

Charlie ate his scrambled eggs and didn't comment. Charlie didn't talk much when there was food around. He inhaled whatever was placed in front of him in seconds.

"Rishi and I saw you provoking the Mad Dog," Marcus teased, and the feline beside him purred. "You have a death wish or something?"

"No. I just like putting jerks in their place." I stroked Oberi's cheek, and she nickered. "What's he in for?"

"Murder," Marcus said, and Rishi meowed. "He killed a couple humans a few years back. Nearly exposed the supernatural world. He's already blown his chances to get out of here. Once he graduates, he's getting transferred to the adult penitentiary."

"Which means he has nothing to lose," Charlie said. He'd paused long enough to lecture me. "Don't mess with him again."

I scoffed, but didn't object. "If Mad Dog is so horrible, why isn't he in Cellblock 9?"

"Because he's not even *that* bad," Marcus countered. "You can't imagine the type of people they drag down there. And once you're in, you don't come back out."

He shrugged. "Not to mention Mad Dog's got guard friends who look the other way…"

Marcus started drawing on his arm with a black marker. He made little designs on the bare parts that weren't covered in tattoos. I noticed he had paint on his hands and uniform. He had to be an artist.

"Did you hear about one of the new arrivals?" Marcus asked as he drew. "There was one shifter that came on the bus with you guys, and he's already dead."

My jaw dropped open. Was he talking about the kid who yelled at me? "He's dead?"

"Yeah," Marcus said. "Got a hex to the face yesterday. Guards couldn't save him."

"Don't shifters heal really fast?" I asked.

"I guess the person who cursed him got him good." Marcus took a bite of his eggs, like this was an everyday conversation here at the Institute.

A chill ran over my skin. Charlie poked me. "See what I mean? People die in here. You need to keep your head down."

I didn't say another word, just messed around with my plate. I guess Charlie was right and I should listen to him.

Wouldn't give him the satisfaction of admitting it, though.

"By the way," Charlie said, "Our first group therapy session is in a half-hour. It's four people, two girls and two boys. Marcus is with us."

Marcus didn't seem too terrible. But I didn't know who the other girl would be, and I was worried about it. I didn't like opening up to strangers. It gave them too much ammunition to use against you later.

"We might as well go together," Marcus suggested. "I haven't been to one yet, so I don't know what to expect."

Neither did I. As we were walking to our group therapy session, I heard a sharp voice cry out, "Miss Mitoh!"

I groaned and turned around. Professor Hemlock stood straight by the entrance to her classroom. Her hair was in a tight bun, and square glasses sat on her pointed nose. Not an inch of her green robe was out of place. She was an elderly fae who taught my Alchemy class. She wasn't *bad*, but damn, she was strict. The woman must've run a convent before she came here.

Her pinched look as she observed my uniform was nearly funny. "I do not think that is an appropriate outfit."

"I mean, I get what you're saying, but if I agreed we'd both be wrong," I said.

Her eyes narrowed. "I am giving you an infraction, for the dress code violation and for your impertinence toward a teacher." Her eyes went to the boys. "And just what do you think you're doing, gawking about? Hurry along!"

Charlie and Marcus rushed off. Professor Hemlock personally escorted me back to the Elementai dorms, where she made me change into a plain uniform and confiscated the one I'd modified. It made me late for my group therapy session.

Just as well. I didn't want to go anyway.

I followed the map I'd gotten from my student packet to the counseling room. It wasn't what I expected. I had to follow a long, winding tower upward. When I opened the door, I saw that the ceiling was a glass dome that let the sunlight in. The room itself was swathed in tones of blue and gold. Star charts and zodiac posters hung all over the walls, and there was a big mahogany desk before a picture window that showed the entire prison grounds. A red-crested crane stood on a perch behind the desk, observing me with intelligence. When it flapped its white wings, bits of starlight fluttered off its feathers and onto the floor.

Charlie and Marcus were sitting in wooden chairs, which had been placed in a circle. Oberi lay beside Charlie as a unicorn and nickered when I entered. In another chair sat an old man. He had a weathered face, with short black hair and glasses that made him appear very studious. His dark eyes were friendly and welcoming. By his appearance, I figured him to be Japanese. He inclined his head to me, and my shoulders loosened. I actually thought this wasn't going to be that bad, until I caught sight of the blonde sitting in the chair across from Marcus.

You had to be kidding me. *Kalina* was in this group? No way was I opening up in front of her. She gave me a scathing look that told me she felt the same.

The old man cleared his throat. He reached out to a side table next to him, where he'd placed a clipboard and a cup of tea. "I'm happy you're joining us, Ava-Marie. I am Professor Takahashi," he said kindly. "I am the head social worker here at the Institute. I will be your counselor for all your group therapy sessions."

"Are you an Elementai?" I asked, gesturing to the beautiful bird.

Takahashi laughed. "No. I am an Astromancer. Aiko is my animal companion, not my Familiar."

That was interesting. As far as I knew, there weren't many Astromancers at this prison. Why had he chosen to leave his own society in order to teach here?

"We were going around the circle, speaking about why we're here," Takahashi said as I took a seat next to Charlie. "Kalina was going first."

"What's there to go over?" Kalina challenged. "I tried to kill the fae king, I got caught, now I'm here."

So she was an assassin. That fit her venomous personality.

Marcus' mouth dropped open. "You tried to kill the *king*? Like, the king of all Malovia."

"Yeah. You wanna be next?" Kalina raised a fist, and Marcus shrunk back.

"Are you comfortable speaking on why you attempted to take the king's life?" Takahashi asked.

"I'm just trying to do my time so I can get out of here," Kalina said. "There's nothing else to it."

Yeah, right. I bet she had a history. We all did.

"Charlie, would you like to go next?" Takahashi began. His tone was so soothing. He was probably the nicest person I'd met at this prison. I warmed up to him immediately.

Didn't mean I wanted to sit here and talk about my feelings, though.

We all waited. Charlie didn't say anything. It was like he was scared to talk. I spoke for him. "We got in an argument," I said. "It got out of hand, and we nearly burnt down a building."

"*You* nearly burnt down a building," Charlie growled.

I ignored him. "We were on probation, until we stole a ship."

Kalina laughed. "A *boat*? That's it?"

"I have a bigger criminal record than that, if you want to sit here all day," I mumbled.

"I think that's enough, Ava," Takahashi said. "Marcus, how about you?"

Marcus puffed out his chest. "I... uh... I killed twelve people. In *cold blood*."

Kalina rolled her eyes, but my own widened. Marcus had done that? I didn't believe it.

"Yeah. That's right." Marcus drew himself up. "I *forced* my Goddess to give me my magic early, because she was scared of me. One time, I got bit by a vampire, and I slaughtered it on my own. With one hand tied behind my back!"

"Oh, *really*," Takahashi said, writing something down on his clipboard. "What else?"

Marcus blabbed on forever. It was like he was trying to fill the silence. Most of the session was taken up by his ridiculous claims. Marcus said he'd beaten up a mermaid, choked out an angel and wrestled with a wolf shifter all in one day, but when Takahashi asked for details, he failed to clarify.

By the end of his speech, I didn't know what was true and what wasn't. What I did know, though, was nobody in this room was fooled by his tales.

Takahashi seemed amused at the conclusion of the rant. "That is a very interesting story, Marcus."

"Bull! He's so full of shit his eyes are brown," Kalina said, pointing at Marcus. "Do you really expect any of us to believe him?"

Marcus cringed, and Takahashi held up a hand. "We don't judge in this room, Kalina. What is spoken here remains within the safety of our circle. I expect all of you to be vulnerable, but more than that, I expect all of you to be confidants of each other. You will be in this group for four years, until you graduate. I hope that by the end of that time, the four of you will regard each other to be friends, if not at least trusted companions."

Kalina scowled. She wasn't looking forward to being my therapy buddy for four years any more than I was.

"Ava-Marie, I understand you've been in therapy before," Takahashi said, turning the room's attention to me. "Would you like to talk about it?"

I swallowed as Charlie sat up, and Oberi's ears perked forward. Talk about my disorder? No, I really didn't want to. But these people were going to find out anyway, so I really didn't have a choice.

"I have bipolar disorder," I said. "I was diagnosed when I was a little girl."

"Bipolar I or II?" Takahashi asked.

"It's unspecified."

"And what do you think is the greatest challenge of being bipolar?" Professor Takahashi asked.

I took a moment to think over the question. "I hate… that people hear my diagnosis and expect me to act a certain way. Mental illness affects everyone differently. We all have different triggers, different symptoms. And people think I'm a bad person when I'm reacting to my illness in a way that's different than what they expect."

Takahashi nodded. "You don't want to be perceived in a way that's inauthentic to who you are."

"Yeah. People think I'm just acting out because I want to. I don't know how many times I've told someone I see something, or hear things, or feel a certain way, and they just throw it out as invalid. *Oh, bipolar disorder doesn't affect people in that way.* My bipolar does. And I need people to support my experience, instead of just telling me what I'm going through is wrong."

Marcus nodded introspectively. Charlie's expression was passive. I couldn't read what he was thinking, or feeling.

Kalina sniffed. "Well *I* don't like people who use being sick as an excuse to be assholes."

"And what's that supposed to mean?" I jumped up so fast my chair fell over. Kalina got to her feet, too. Marcus looked nervously between us, while Charlie tensed.

"It means feeling like crap isn't an excuse to treat people like shit," Kalina growled.

"So says the girl who tried to murder her king!" I shouted back. "Didn't put much thought into how he'd *feel* about dying, did you?"

"Girls, this is a safe environment," Takahashi reminded us.

Neither of us heard him. Kalina struck first. She lashed out with a powerful fae illusion. Her purple magic ricocheted across the room in a thin bolt. I dodged it, and it slammed into the wall, knocking a painting askew. I immediately conjured a fireball and flung it at her, but Kalina spun her arm in a circle, and it manifested a purple shield that immediately caused my fireball to fizzle out when it hit. She sent spells back at me while I tossed fireballs at her. Charlie and Marcus both dove to the floor. Takahashi sat calmly in his chair, observing the situation as magic flew around him. Oberi flattened herself to the rug, while Rishi yowled, hair standing up on his back.

"You think your little fireballs can hurt me? Bring it!" Kalina screamed.

This girl had major anger issues, and ancestors, I was *bringing it.* We abandoned magic and just started swinging hands. Kalina's fist collided with my right eye just as I grabbed on to her hair. I yanked on it as my free hand smashed into her lip, making it bleed. I barely felt Kalina's punches when she hit me, because honestly, it felt good just to have someone who could take it — and she'd give it right back.

"I think that is enough." Kalina and I were pulled to opposite sides of the room as an invisible force yanked us apart. Takahashi remained in his chair, while Marcus and Charlie scrambled back to their seats.

I wasn't sure how astromancy magic worked, but it was enough to get Kalina and I to separate. Takahashi drank his tea in peaceful tranquility while the crane looked on.

How could he be so calm while Kalina and I were wailing on each other? It was eerie. Takahashi gave me a bottle of water from under the table, which I froze with my Water magic to use as an ice pack. I put it against my swollen eye as Takahashi handed Kalina a handkerchief to clean up the blood.

"As we were saying," Takahashi began. "Marcus, would you like to give your thoughts on the situation?"

Marcus gulped, then launched into a story about his mom that was totally unrelated. I shot dagger eyes at Kalina, but she didn't send them back. She held the handkerchief to her mouth, appearing to be deep in thought.

We were dismissed shortly after that. I took off as soon as possible down the staircase, but once I was on the main floor, I felt a hand on my shoulder. "Hey."

It was Kalina. Ugh. What did she want now, to give me another black eye? Marcus and Charlie stood at my sides, expecting another brawl. Oberi tapped her hooves and waited.

"Did you come back for round two?" I asked. "Because I'll fight all day."

"I'm sorry," she started, and I nearly fell over backwards in shock. "I've been mean to you."

"Just a little." I shrugged her hand off my shoulder. Why was she apologizing? This had to be a trap.

"I just wanted to see what you were made of," Kalina said. "I can respect a girl who can take a punch. There aren't a lot of supernaturals who can keep up with me. And around here, you have to command respect, or you don't get any."

I frowned. "That might be true, but it's not the best way to make friends. Maybe try being kind."

Kalina looked down. "I'm uh… not very good at that."

"Then work on it."

"Ava," Charlie warned. He was telling me to get along.

Marcus was dying of embarrassment as Rishi curled around Kalina's legs. She tried to shake him off, but Rishi rubbed his head on her calf, and eventually, she gave up.

I struggled to hold my tongue as Kalina took a deep breath. "I've heard about you. You're the only Elementai who can use both Fire and Water. You feel like an outcast here. So do I," she admitted. "I haven't told anyone this, but… I'm the only sorceress amongst my kind who's a shifter as well. The males of our race are the only ones who can change into animals… except me. I'm the only female fae who has the power to become a wolf, and no one knows why. So you aren't the only one who's different."

That got my attention. Though I didn't like it, a connection immediately formed between Kalina and me. I was a freak, but she was, too.

"It doesn't help you're racist. We know what you think about Elementai," I said scathingly.

"It's not like that." Kalina frowned. "I'm sorry Naya called you guys savages. It wasn't okay. I didn't agree with it. I should've spoken up."

"Then why didn't you?"

Kalina's shoulders dropped. "Look. We might've gotten off on the wrong foot. I'm not so sure I want friends, but I *need* allies. Everyone at the Institute does. And since we're in the same counseling group, the four of us should try to get along. The shifter that was murdered yesterday was a loner. And loners don't last long here."

Marcus scowled. "I've been a loner for a bit. People have left *me* alone."

"It won't work for long. You have to stay in a group if you want to survive," Kalina spat at him, and Marcus recoiled before she turned back to me. "So what do you say? You want to be in mine?"

I wasn't fooled by the nice act. Kalina wanted me around her because I had power, and she sensed that. She wanted to use my magic as a shield, to protect her when shit went down.

I almost wanted to tell her no. But Oberi nuzzled my shoulder, and I said, "Yeah. I guess that's okay."

Charlie relaxed behind me.

Kalina gave a phantom of a smile. "Thanks. I think this will work out for the both of us. A hell of a lot better than trusting Naya, anyway."

"If you don't like Naya, why do you talk to her?" I asked.

"I felt obligated," Kalina said. "Vampires are high on the supernatural hierarchy. As a fae, I'm *supposed* to hang out with them. We're in a similar social class."

"You don't have to hang with anyone you don't want to." Marcus spoke up. His cheeks turned pink as Kalina turned back to him.

Kalina stared at him for a moment before she said, "Yeah, well. Pickings are slim around here."

"Let's just agree to work together," Charlie said. "We might not like each other, but getting along is going to benefit all of us."

"Should we make a blood pact?" Marcus asked nervously. "Something to seal the deal?"

Kalina rolled her eyes. "Matching prison tattoos would be better. Gods, Marcus, you're so lame."

"A verbal pact is fine for now," Charlie cut in, to avoid starting another argument. "So we're all in agreement? I've got your back, you've got mine. For now, at least."

Kalina and Marcus nodded, and realization struck me at the bargain we'd made. None of us *wanted* to stick together, we just didn't have any other choice.

Oh, great. I was in a prison gang. A very *lame* gang at that, with the weirdest people in the school.

But it was a hell of a lot better than going at it alone. And if we stuck together, we just might make it out of here.

Saturday was my designated day to get my one free phone call a week. I was standing by the phones before anyone else was that morning. No shit, the school literally had *rotary telephones* you had to spin the numbers to dial. It took forever.

These things were like a hundred years old. But they were my only connection to the outside world, and so, I treasured them. Everyone else had handed their cell phone over when we got here, but I'd hid mine under my mattress in my dorm. It didn't get service here in Shade Hills, but I kept it just in case I needed it for something later... whatever it might be.

I really wanted to use my one phone call to contact my parents. I missed them like crazy. But I had to talk to my Aunt Maddie, and I couldn't wait for it to be in person. This prophecy was more important than anything else. I dialed her number on the rotary phone and waited for her to pick up. Each ring sounded like an eternity.

"Ava," Maddie said in a bright way. "I'm glad to finally hear from you. How's the Institute?"

"Why didn't you tell me about the prophecy?"

There was a long, drawn-out silence. "That was your parents' responsibility."

"But you made it." My back hit the wall as I pressed the phone to my ear. "You must've had visions of me. Can you tell me what they mean, so I can fulfill what the prophecy says and avoid all the bad stuff?"

"Everything I have is in that journal," Maddie said firmly. "I haven't had a vision of you in nearly twenty years. What I do remember, I don't understand."

"You *forgot* what you saw?" My voice was incredulous.

"Yes. I'm sorry. I did the best I could, but no matter what I tried, I couldn't comprehend what my visions foretold. I sought help from other seers, but they couldn't decipher it, either. You're the biggest mystery the prophets have, Ava."

Of course I was. It couldn't be easy. "Whatever you could give me at this point would be helpful. Even if it's the tiniest thing," I pleaded.

"After I created the prophecy, the ancestors wiped my memory of anything that might be useful to you," Maddie said. "Every note and clue is in that journal. While I was attempting to translate it, it became clear that you have to be the one to decipher my visions, because the message was meant for *only you*. I was merely the messenger."

"But why would the ancestors do that?" I smacked the wall in frustration. "Why would they take away the only help I have in figuring this thing out?"

Silence infiltrated the space between us, until Maddie said, "I'm going to speak of this only once, and you're never to ask about it again."

"I'm listening."

Maddie took a deep breath. "You will be the cornerstone. The deciding factor in a war between gods."

"Gods?" I squeaked. I began sliding down the wall. When I hit the floor, the line on the phone tugged.

"You know there's another war coming. You'll have the power to shape the outcome," Maddie explained. "The Elementai worship the Great Spirit, but he's at risk, Ava. All the gods of the magical world are. You're the person that will decide what will happen to them, depending on the path you follow— the darkness or the light. You will choose what the fate of the supernatural world will be, if magic will continue to exist or if it will die out. That is all I know."

My mouth went extremely dry. I was so nauseous the room spun. "Do I have to do this? Is there no other way?"

"Prophecies cannot be avoided; they can only be shaped by the chosen one's choices. Which is why it is imperative you make the right decisions," Maddie pleaded. "As your prophet, I am here to support you in any way you need me to. But I can't take the path for you. That journey is yours alone."

I heard my uncle's voice in the background, and Maddie said, "I have to go. But I love you, Ava. Trust that wherever the ancestors are leading you, the destination will end where you're meant to be."

The phone clicked. I let the phone hang there as I stared off into space, comprehending the vastness of what she'd just told me.

This prophecy was no joke. My aunt was telling me that the god my people followed was in danger— as were all the others. How could I possibly wield such power? What was so special about me that I would determine the fate of all supernatural kind?

One thing I did know— if the world was relying on me to make the right choices, we were totally screwed.

charlie

NINE

Any confidence I had in the Institute when I arrived slowly began to unravel over the following week. The facilities were fine, and though Ava gagged at every meal, I liked the food. It was the people who fucking sucked.

"Leave me alone," a male voice spat.

I was on my way to Juvenile Justice when I heard it. The hall was quiet, apart from soft footsteps padding on the carpet.

A female let out a chilling laugh. "You think you can resist me, Carson? I'm a succubus. I'll have you in bed before noon."

"My mother was a siren," Carson growled. "Your powers won't work on me."

She chuckled. "Oh, you think I need powers to seduce you? By the time I'm done with you, you'll be begging for it."

Carson's voice came through gritted teeth. "Naya, I swear to the gods, if you come one step closer, I'll—"

"You'll what?" she asked, amused. "Scream?"

He scoffed. "You'd be surprised at what an Atlantean's scream can do."

"Then show me. I like it when my bedmates scream." She paused for a moment, then added, "I admit, I don't usually go for Atlanteans, but what kind of girl would I be if I resisted *you*."

I heard a snap, then something flew through the air and hit me in the face as I was passing by. I bent down to pick it up and realized it was the button from our uniform slacks. I just kind of stood there, dumbstruck. Oberi growled under his breath.

"Naya, what the fuck?" Carson cried. He sounded truly scared this time.

"Ooh," Naya sang. "We're starting on the dirty talk early. Say it again, Carson."

"Nay—AAA!" Carson's voice got really high-pitched. It was the cry of a guy who'd just been groped.

Aw, hell. I'd hoped I could sneak by the argument without making a scene. But I'd quickly learned that keeping to yourself was a sure-fire way to become a target at this school. Kalina had been right. We had to stick together around here.

I was done standing around. I reached for Naya's shoulder and yanked her away from Carson. His underwear snapped as her hand came out of them.

"I believe he told you to *back off*," I growled.

"*You* can back the fuck off," Naya shot back. "What are you, an Elementai? I'm a succubus. I can kick your ass any day."

"Oh, really?" I challenged. "With what powers?"

I didn't actually know what a succubus could do. I knew they were some sort of vampire, but I'd already beaten Mad Dog in a fight. I could handle her.

Naya got up in my face, her breath passing over my jaw. She whispered, like she was trying to seduce me. "I can compel you to do whatever I want."

Carson zipped his pants. "How's that working with that noxite bracelet?"

Naya drew away from me and huffed. "So they don't want the succubi compelling the guards. Big deal. I'll find a way to destroy it."

My lips tightened. "Well, until then, you can find another way to get off, because he isn't sleeping with you."

Naya hesitated a moment, then said, "Whatever. He's an Atlantean. Probably tastes like seaweed and saltwater anyway. I don't know why I wasted my time."

Air whipped past me as Naya turned and tossed her hair over her shoulder. Her heels clicked on the thin carpet as she walked away.

Oberi yipped happily. I handed the torn button back to Carson.

He breathed a sigh of relief. "Thanks for sticking up for me, man. The chicks in this place will really eat a guy alive."

I shrugged. "It's no problem."

"Hey, I saw you in my Juvenile Justice class earlier this week, right?" he asked.

"I guess so."

"You headed there now? We can walk together." Carson seemed strangely nice for an inmate. Though maybe he just didn't want to run into Naya again.

A few moments of silence passed.

"So, you're a merman…" I stated awkwardly as we headed to class. "What kind of crimes gets an Atlantean thrown in here?"

"Same as everyone else," Carson said. "Theft. Assault. Arson."

"Arson?" I cocked an eyebrow. "I thought you lived in the ocean. How's that possible?"

"We come onto land," he pointed out. "Don't be surprised if you meet some Atlanteans in for grand theft auto. Living under the surface most of your life gives some of these guys a real fascination with cars. Very expensive sports cars, to be exact."

"So is that what you're in for?" I asked.

"If you read my record, it would be," he admitted. "But it was my buddy who stole the car and crashed it. Well, he *was* my buddy. Not since he pinned it on me, though."

"Wow. One car crash and they toss you in here. How many people got hurt?"

"None," Carson said. "The car belonged to an Atlantean Senator. It was worth over half a million."

My jaw dropped at the number. I couldn't imagine that kind of money. It could feed me and Oberi for life.

"That's… wild." I didn't know what else to say.

Carson scoffed. "Tell me about it."

Oberi turned, and I followed him into the classroom. Carson and I must've been the last ones there, because the room buzzed with chatter.

"Ah, look," he said. "Two spots up front just for us."

This kid was mental if he thought the front row was a coveted seating area. No one wanted to sit in the front at this school.

My eyes didn't follow his, because I had no idea where to look. He must've noticed, because he lowered his voice. "You can't see them, can you?"

I shrugged. "Nope. Kinda totally blind."

"You are a *master* at hiding it," he said. "You could've totally fooled me. I won't tell anyone."

"Thanks," I mumbled.

Oberi led me to the seat in the front row and curled up beneath me. The class quieted soon after.

Heels clicked across the floor in a quick staccato. "What are you all doing just sitting there?" our professor snapped. "Get out your notebooks and a pencil."

Oh, joy. I'd almost forgotten how *lovely* Professor Mazur was. I hadn't picked up on her supernatural race in our first class, but today, I felt the air breeze off feathery wings. She was an angel for sure. It explained the same snippy tone and *above-you-all* attitude. I could tell by the way the air moved around her that Professor Mazur was tall and lean, and she moved with the energy of a younger woman.

"As we learned earlier this week, the function of this class is to teach you the roles of the supernatural justice system, so that you may uphold the laws set forth by the United Supernatural Union upon your rehabilitation," she started. "You are all here because you broke the law. For some of you—"

Professor Mazur stopped her lecture dead. "Excuse me, Mr…"

Carson cleared his throat from beside me, and Oberi pawed at my foot. It occurred to me she must be looking at me.

"Me?" I asked. "Wahkin, Professor. Charlie Wahkin."

"Mr. Wahkin, why are you not taking notes?" she demanded.

I hesitated. "I'm, um, an auditory learner."

"I don't care," she snapped. "I asked you to take notes. You are to do so, or you will fail this class. Do you understand?"

I swore I could feel every eye in the room on me. "I can't," I admitted.

"You can't what?" she pressed.

"Take notes. Miss, I can't read. I'm blind."

She let out a sinister laugh. "That's a new one."

Her voice quickly became serious again. "But I don't take excuses in my class, Mr. Wahkin."

This bitch was *harsh*. I wanted to sink into my seat and disappear.

"It's hardly an excuse when it's true," I said. "There must be something else I can do for credit."

"And how's a blind man supposed to take notes?" she mocked. "What alternative do you suggest?"

My blood began to boil. "If I was provided a laptop, I could take notes, with a text-to-speech program installed to read them back to me. Or you could give me a recording device, so I could play back the lecture later."

"How would such technology be *fair* to your classmates?" she asked, like I'd just requested the moon.

She walked away, then came to stand in front of my desk moments later. Something slapped down onto the desk, and she tossed a long, skinny object into my lap. I reached out to feel both and realized they were a notebook and pencil.

She leaned so close to me, I could feel her angry breath on my cheek. "You will take notes like everyone else in the class. If you interrupt my class again, I'll send you straight to the Warden. Do you understand?"

A lump so large I couldn't breathe grew in my throat. I suddenly had flashbacks of high school. There was a reason I'd never graduated. No one wanted to help a blind guy learn. The school wrote me off as stupid and wanted me to repeat all the classes I'd failed. But it was *their* failure for denying me accommodations.

I knew at that moment the Institute would be worse. I'd never make it through the reform program if my grades were shot. I'd be lucky if I ever made it out of here at *all*.

Professor Mazur turned from me and returned to the front of the room.

"That was bullshit, man," Carson whispered under his breath.

Bullshit didn't even cut it. I was fuming. I squeezed the pencil so tight that it cracked. I wanted nothing more than to storm out of the room, but I knew it wouldn't do me any good. It'd only get me sent to the Warden or thrown in Cellblock 9. I had no power here, and the professors really knew how to rub that shit in.

Professor Mazur continued her lesson like nothing had happened. I opened the notebook and pressed the pencil to the paper, but I more or less just doodled nonsense to make it look like I was taking notes. This class was useless already.

"As you all know, each supernatural society has their own justice system," Professor Mazur said. "It is up to them what to do with their own citizens. Sometimes, the crimes are punished in-house. Other times, they are handled by the United Supernatural Union. This often occurs in situations where rehabilitation is an option— hence, why you were all sent here. Other times, the Union steps in on more serious crimes in which a society does not have the resources to prosecute the accused. Most notably, the Union *always* has authority over intersociety crimes. For example, if a witch attacks a fae, neither the Miriamic Imperium Council nor the Arcanea Alliance reserve jurisdiction to prosecute. That responsibility lies solely with the United Supernatural Union."

Professor Mazur began scribbling something on the board. "I say this to warn you. Any crime committed against someone outside your own race will result in far harsher consequences than what punishments your own government may impose. The United Supernatural Union is unforgiving of intersociety crimes, as even the smallest infractions may lead to war."

There was something dark in her tone. She was trying to scare us— to get us to comply in the Institute. She wanted us to know that if we started fights in here, we'd be answering to a much higher power than the ones who sent us here.

"The United Supernatural Union is very good at their jobs," Professor Mazur continued. "If you think you can hide from them, you'd be wrong. No one gets away from a supernatural bounty hunter."

I'd only been half listening up to this point, but when she said *supernatural bounty hunter*, my curiosity piqued. I stopped doodling and raised my hand.

"Yes, Mr. Wahkin," she called on me, sounding annoyed.

"How does someone become a supernatural bounty hunter?"

"Well, they need a clean record, for starters." She sounded amused, like she never saw me getting out of here and getting a real job. "And they must show incredible supernatural powers. You know, like the power of *sight*."

She accented the last word, and laughter traveled around the room. Oberi stood, but I placed a hand on his back to calm him.

"I don't need my eyesight, Professor." I smirked. "My magic works just fine without it."

She laughed. I didn't need my eyesight or my magic to spot a raging bitch.

"I'd advise you from getting too confident, Mr. Wahkin," she said. "The United Supernatural Union doesn't take well to people who abuse their power. Tread carefully, or you just might end up with the death penalty."

That was a threat if I'd ever heard one. I was so angry, I couldn't hold my words back. "I'm sure the electric chair would be better than this class."

I was horrified with myself for a second, until she began to laugh in a condescending way.

"Oh, child. You think the Union would sentence you to the electric chair?" she asked. "No, your death would be *far* worse. The death penalty is only given when one has committed a crime against all supernatural races, and as such, every race partakes in the sentence. The death penalty starts with the bite of a siren, followed by elemental torture from the Elementai. They'll burn your skin off, starting at your toes. The witches will curse you with nightmares, and the vampires will suck you dry. Angels will draw out your life force, making you age in a matter of minutes. And finally, the fae will open a portal to the afterlife, where any type of monster can escape to eat you whole— or drag you straight into the fiery inferno."

My bones chilled when she started, but by the time she finished, I was unamused. I didn't believe a word she said. She was speaking in half-truths, at best.

"Sounds awful," I said dryly.

"It is," she snapped. "And that's why you *all* best take your rehabilitation seriously."

She returned to the lesson, but I was so pissed at her I barely heard a word she said. I had a teacher who hated me, and what was worse, she wasn't allowing me to learn in the only way I could. This place did everything it could to make sure you failed.

After class, I started back toward the dorms, but Oberi went in the other direction.

"Oberi," I growled. "Where are you going?"

He barked, and I had no choice but to follow.

"I'm not in the mood," I grumbled. "I just want to go back to my dorm and—"

"There you are, Oberi!" Ava-Marie cried cheerfully.

Oh, fun. I got to deal with *her* now.

Oberi's energy changed, and I sensed him shift into a Fire unicorn. She took up a lot more room now, and her heat rolled off her in waves. I placed my hand on Oberi's side, because I was lost and agitated. I had a hard time reading my surroundings.

"Where are we?" I asked Ava.

"Study area," she said. Her voice came from below me, like she was sitting on a chair. She shuffled a few papers, then zipped up her bag.

"What are you working on?" I questioned as Oberi took a few steps forward. I reached out and felt an empty chair, then sat beside Ava.

She sighed, like she was exhausted. "Just studying a formula for my Alchemy class. You?"

I curled my hands around the arms of the chair, and my nostrils flared. "Raging. Professor Mazur's a bitch."

Ava drew a sharp breath. "The tall angel professor? Yeah, I've heard the worst. I don't have her, but if she's bothering you, I'd love to give her a piece of my—"

"Don't bother." I sank deeper into my chair. "It's not like it's going to help. Kicking her ass won't teach me how to take notes."

"Notes?" Ava's voice rose a few pitches.

I tossed her the notebook I'd been doodling on all class period. Ava began flipping through the pages.

"She says they're graded," I growled. "Even for a blind guy."

Ava shot to her feet. "Charlie, this is unfair!"

I scoffed. "You think I don't know that? I have enough problems with inmates already. I don't need to get on a professor's hit list."

"We have to go to the Warden," she insisted. "He *has* to provide you with accommodations."

I cocked an eyebrow. "Does he? I don't think the ADA applies here, Ava. We're under supernatural jurisdiction."

"Those are some big words for a guy who's only taken *one* Juvenile Justice class," she said pointedly.

"Well, I'm not wrong, am I?" I challenged. "Do I have to remind you this is a prison? Inmates don't get a voice. And if you try, they threaten you with the death penalty."

Ava gasped. "She did *not*."

I crossed my arms. "They don't *really* burn you to death and steal your life force, do they?"

Ava sighed and sat back down. "Depends on the society. The Elementai did away with the death penalty years ago, but back then, you were tortured with your opposite element. Toaqua were burned to death, and Koigni were drowned. Yapluma were crushed with rocks, and Nivita were suffocated."

My stomach twisted into all sorts of knots. "That's horrible."

"Which is exactly why they stopped," she said. "But if the crime's bad enough, the United Supernatural Union will still go through with the death penalty. They mostly use monsters— grotesque animal-like creatures created by demons. They want to make an example out of you, so other people are deterred from committing crimes."

"That sounds like bullshit," I said. "The system needs fixing."

Ava scoffed. "Don't get me started on *the system*."

After a few beats, I asked, "What are the monsters like?"

"Anything and everything," she replied. "You never know what you're going to get. It could be an evil spirit possessing the skeleton of a dragon, or a fifty-foot serpent with wings. There are so many. You want a list?"

I knew she was being facetious, but I answered anyway. "No, thanks. It's not like I'll be around long enough to see one."

"What do you mean?" Ava asked.

I shrugged. "Isn't it obvious? We're never getting out of here. This program isn't going to work for me. I'm going to die in here."

"Charlie," Ava sighed. "Don't say that."

"Why not?" I seethed. "It's true."

Ava got really quiet, but Oberi gave a nicker, like I was making her uncomfortable.

"You can't die," she finally said. "Because that would mean Oberi and I—"

"It's not like I have a choice, Ava!" I burst. "*Something's* going to get me in here, whether it's a monster, a professor, or another inmate. And if it's not in here, it'll be wherever I'm transferred to. The system doesn't work for people like me. At some point, you're going to have to accept that."

Ava gave an obnoxious noise. "It's too early to give up, Charlie."

I shot to my feet. "No! I was a goner the second I stepped through those gates."

"Stop being ridiculous," Ava demanded. "We're going to get through this program, and we're going to get out of here together!"

"You think I can last in here for four years?" I scoffed. "Then you're kidding yourself."

"At least promise me you'll try!" she cried.

I gritted my teeth. "I can't make any promises, Ava. The best I can do is survive as long as possible."

But I had to survive— because Ava and Oberi were counting on me.

I wasn't looking forward to the day I let them down.

ava-marie

TEN

"Miss Mitoh, may I remind you that this is the *third* dress code violation you've had this week?" Professor Hemlock tapped her heeled boot against the floor as she stared at my shoes.

I was wearing all the parts of the Institute uniform, unmodified— but for ancestors' sakes, I couldn't go another damn day in those deplorable Mary Janes. They hurt my feet. I was wearing moccasins that had been made by my Aunt Imogen. They were white leather, and had blue beads sewn on to them, and had fringes on the top, and were *so* comfy, and—

"Miss Mitoh, are you listening?" Professor Hemlock snapped her fingers, and I straightened in my seat. "We're all waiting to hear your explanation."

Everyone in the Alchemy lab stared at me. No one dared to speak when Professor Hemlock was lecturing someone.

I cleared my throat and slowly rose from my seat. "If you'll pardon me, madame, but when you interrupt a young woman's school day by forcing her to change her attire, society is saying that it's more important for her to hide her body than to receive an education. By dictating what a female student can and cannot wear, the institution of learning of where she is at, by default, is admitting a boy's education is more valuable than hers. Therefore, for the sake of my own instruction, I implore you to allow me to wear these moccasins— which are extremely cute, by the way. I rest my case!"

Opal squirmed in her seat next to me. She would've jumped out of her seat and applauded, if Hemlock wasn't running the show.

"That is all very well and good, and you've made the debate convincing enough I agree with you." Hemlock scowled. "*However*, this is a reform school, and boys *as well as girls* have to adhere to the standards the Warden sets, for their safety and comfort as much as the school's. I cannot be shown playing favorites. Do I have to send another personal letter to your family about your misbehavior?"

Ugh, no fucking thanks. Daddy had nearly reached through the phone and strangled me when he'd learned about that stunt I'd pulled with the skirt a few weeks ago. I didn't feel like getting chewed out again.

I started to whine. "Come *on*. They're moccasins. I'm a Hawkei. Can't you look the other way just this once?"

Her eye twitched. She gave a long, drawn out sigh. "I will not take away your class time and disrupt your learning for some shoes. But once you are dismissed, I expect you to return to your dormitory and change into proper footwear *immediately*. And sit down, please. For the gods' sakes, this isn't a courtroom."

Score. I loved winning arguments with teachers. Hemlock tapped the blackboard, where she'd written down a potion recipe. "Today we'll be brewing a potion with ingredients that can commonly be found on Darke Island. If made correctly, this potion is an excellent combatant against negative energy. No dark spirits or entities can withstand the effects of this potion— save for some demonic forces, which can be exceptionally powerful and negate the effects of the potion. However, this combination of ingredients is incredibly strong, and is able to banish all but the strongest of negative forces. You will find the necessary ingredients on your desk— get to work."

There was the scraping of chairs as people stood over their cauldrons. Opal and I shared a desk and a small cast-iron cauldron. The mermaid girl chewed her lip nervously as she looked down at the ingredients on the table. There were cloves, thyme, a magical plant called star weed, and a special kind of sage that only grew here.

I narrowed my eyes as I read the chalkboard. "That's wrong."

"What?" Opal tied her blue hair back. "How?"

"Hemlock wants us to add thyme, but that's going to weaken the effects of the cloves," I said. "We need to add bay leaves instead."

"But she said—"

"Don't listen to Hemlock," I said as I started combining ingredients. "Just trust me."

Opal made a face. "Okay. I'm shit at potions, so I'll follow you."

I fell into a stupor as the bustle of the classroom buzzed around me. The Alchemy classroom was cozy and dark, formed by stone walls and stone floors. Candles lit the area, providing light that the tiny windows failed to. Hemlock always kept a hearthfire going at the front of the room, breaking the early October chill. There was a slight drizzle hitting the glass panes, and the smell of sage burning throughout the room immediately put me at ease. Opal filled the cauldron with water and lit a flame underneath it while I began chopping up the star weed. Hemlock wanted us to cut up the other ingredients, but I put them in whole. Opal's nervous expression grew even more worrisome.

"So how's Atlantis?" I asked Opal, to get her to stop fretting. "I've heard it's amazing down there under the ocean. As a Toaqua, I'd love to see it."

"I'm not really from Atlantis," Opal confessed. "Mermaids have colonies stationed all over the world, in places like Sydney, Venice and the Bahamas. I'm from a colony in Honolulu. My mermaid pod mated with the native tribe there many years ago and decided to stay."

"So you've never been to Atlantis?"

"No. But I hope to go, someday."

I stirred the cauldron counter-clockwise, instead of clockwise like Hemlock asked. The potion began bubbling. Our conversation fell flat as Hemlock stomped over, probably to lecture me. "Miss Mitoh, what exactly are you doing? The instructions were clear."

"I understand, but this is the correct way," I insisted. "Taste it and see."

A couple of people laughed under their breath, expecting me to get another lecture from Hemlock. She pursed out her lip and picked up a ladle, pouring my potion into a wooden cup and lifting it to her mouth.

When Hemlock tasted the potion, her expression became amazed. She quickly disguised it. "Yes. I wouldn't have thought to add bay leaves. Very good, Miss Mitoh. You and your partner shall receive full credit for the day."

Opal brightened, but several people around me cursed under their breath. Hemlock re-wrote the recipe on the board. I got a lot of dirty looks from people who'd already added their thyme.

Someone tapped me on the shoulder, and I turned around. A girl I didn't know stood there. She twisted her hands nervously, and was comparable to a lost sheep. She had to be a vampire. Her eyes were red.

"I'm Despona. You seem to know what you're doing, and I'm totally lost," she confessed. "Will you help me?"

She didn't have a partner. "Sure." I walked over to her table. Her ingredients were a hope-less, chopped mess. I began separating them out and slowly added them to the cauldron as Despona watched.

"You had the right idea, but next time, don't mix them all together," I said. "It weakens the potency. Add them one by one next time."

"Thanks," Despona said. "I'm new to all this. I just arrived at the Institute a week ago. I'm one of the few succubi here."

"You… slept with a demon?" It was an awkward thing to ask, but that was the only way a vampire could increase their powers.

"Yeah." She sighed. "First love. I was young and stupid, and thought he cared about me. Big mistake, by the way. Never sleep with a demon— all they care about is themselves."

"So what are you in for?" It was always the first question you asked someone at the Insti-tute, because it was the quickest way to know if who you were dealing with was dangerous. I knew a lot of people's stories by now— except Opal's, because she seemed too upset to tell, and I didn't want to pry.

"I killed someone who was trying to kidnap me," she said offhandedly. "He hired me for a job at his company, but it turned out to be fake in the end. It was just a ploy to get me there, so he could do what he wanted with me. I tried to use my mind control on him, but he was too powerful and it didn't work. I did what I had to, in order to escape. But the judge who sentenced me didn't see it that way."

I felt goosebumps rise on my skin. She'd been defending herself, and the legal system had branded her a murderer. It was so wrong. "I'm sorry. That's awful."

"He deserved it." Despona sighed. "I just wish I hadn't ended up here."

"There are worse places," I offered. "Though not very many."

"Thanks. Better here than in the clutches of that guy, anyway." She shivered.

I said nothing, just handed Despona the spoon. As she stirred, I noticed some jerk inching toward Opal from behind. He had a slimy worm in his hand from the alchemy cupboard. In one quick move, he slipped the worm down the back of her sweater.

Opal jumped into the air and screamed— but it wasn't a normal scream. It was high-pitched and eerie, a sound only magic could create. People covered their ears, and my eardrums throbbed as Opal's yell continued to pulse around the room. I could visibly see the shockwaves as they emitted from her mouth. The glass vials around the room shattered, and the cauldrons tipped over, spilling liquid onto the floor. I ducked under the desk to try to shield myself from the scream, which was nearly strong enough to knock me over.

Once Opal's scream ended, the worm dropped out the bottom of her sweater and inched along the stone floor. Glass was everywhere. Nobody had gotten hurt, but the floor was slick with the remnants of our potions.

Damn. I knew mermaids had powerful voices, but I'd never imagined anything like that.

"I'm sorry. I didn't mean to!" Opal apologized as Hemlock stepped amongst the broken glass. A couple people rubbed their ears. The guy who'd put the worm down her dress— Digger, I think his name was— had blood coming from his own ears, and he winced in pain.

Hemlock sighed. She waved her hands, and her illusion magic dissolved the shattered vials into sand, which sucked up the spilled puddles of potion around the room. "Since Miss Kealoha has shattered our available vials, we will have to pivot and take this week's exam early."

Everyone groaned. Opal reddened. I was busy flipping off the asshole who'd put the worm in her clothes. Digger gave me a look that said he'd love to fight later, but I'd like to see him try.

I returned to my desk. Hemlock flicked her wrist, and a stack of paper that had been lying on her desk began distributing itself around the room. I looked at the sheet in front of me and got out my pencil.

"I expect this test will take all of you the rest of the hour to complete," Hemlock spoke. "You have forty minutes remaining. Begin."

Several others had already begun the test in order to get a head start. Noises of frustration and upset mingled in the room, along with the scratching of paper. Opal had obviously gotten stuck on the first question, and stared at the paper in sheer horror.

I glanced down at the test and nearly rolled my eyes. This was easy. My pencil flew across the paper as I answered every question like it was child's play. Opal took a glance at me in surprise, clearly shocked I was moving through it, but I didn't understand what the big deal was. This test was a piece of cake.

The end of the exam required written formulas. Alchemy was pretty straightforward in most cases, but the most advanced potions needed a lot of math. The last few questions required trigonometry. I used the entire paper to write out my formula, putting numbers down as quickly as I thought of them. I didn't use my calculator. I didn't need it.

I completed the test in ten minutes. Students glanced up in astonishment as I walked to the front of the classroom and placed my exam on Hemlock's desk. "I'm finished."

Hemlock gave me a cold stare. "Miss Mitoh, I will not permit you to fail this exam merely so you can get out of class early."

"I double-checked my answers. Promise."

Hemlock took the paper as she shook her head. As her red pen scanned my answers, her eyes narrowed. She breezed through my answers, looking for a mistake and finding none.

When she'd gotten to the end of the test, she laid down her red pen and took off her glasses. "Very well. You may go, Miss Mitoh."

I got my bag and left. Opal stared open-mouthed after me, while several others clearly desired my demise.

I headed to the cafeteria for an early lunch. I hadn't been eating much of anything this week, but my appetite, little as it was, had finally returned, so I planned to binge as much as I possibly could before another manic period hit and I refused to eat for another three days.

What followed me was an elevated sense of relief. Things were good today. No psychosis. No voices. Didn't know how long it would last, but I wanted to take advantage of it.

I recognized a slender figure shuffling a deck of cards by the cafeteria entrance. He was thin and tall, with feathery wings that were peppered with gray. He smiled as I came near. "Got an offer for you, Mitoh."

"Not interested, Chancey," I said, but it was kind of a lie. There was mischief in his gaze I just couldn't turn away from.

Chancey was an angel who'd gotten sentenced for running an illegal gambling ring. I didn't know his real name, but it hardly mattered. Practically everyone had a nickname here at the Institute. Apparently, he hadn't learned his lesson, because he still bet on anything and everything. There was a rumor going around that he ran the wagers at an underground fight club here at the prison, but so far, I hadn't seen anything to back that up.

"A pretty lady like you should know when the odds are in your favor," he teased, giving me a wink.

I tried not to scoff. Chancey *also* had a major crush on me. He was harmless, so I let him have his fun, but I totally wasn't interested. Angels, even the bad ones, were far too attached to their rules for my taste.

Chancey shuffled the deck in his hands. I watched, pretending to be bored. Chancey always had a deck on him. It's how he got money out of people. He knew how to count cards.

"What are you betting on today?" I asked. He wouldn't be talking to me if he wasn't trying to hustle— and out of everyone at this prison, he knew I was one of the few people who came from money.

"You know Ghost? He tried to break out of the Institute," Chancey said, eyes sparking with excitement. "He actually got past the fence. They're still chasing him around out there."

"What?" My eyes widened. That was unheard of.

"Yeah. Chances are fifty-fifty he'll escape the guards now that he's outside the fence. You wanna take that bet?" Chancey gave a sly smile.

"Aren't angels supposed to be virtuous?" I asked with a sigh.

"I ain't from no heaven, sweetheart." Chancey put the deck in his pocket. "So are you in, or what?"

"Put me down for twenty." I slipped him a note. Gambling was another violation on your personal record if you got caught, but I participated out of boredom. It was practically the only entertainment we got here at the Institute.

I followed Chancey out to the prison yard. Hundreds of students milled about out here at the fence line. I made a beeline for Charlie, Kalina and Marcus, who were standing at the edge by the gate. All of them were pressed against the fence line. Oberi was in his husky form, wagging his tail as I stooped down to give him a pet. Rishi was on Oberi's back, his paws on the fence as he tried to get a closer look.

Less than a quarter mile beyond the fence line, we saw a warlock high-tailing it for the trees. He was followed by a mess of guards. Even from here, I could see the panic on Ghost's face. There was a shifter guard who'd changed into his animal form that was running as fast as he could to catch up. Ghost gave a cry, but he couldn't outrun the wolf.

Everyone moaned in disappointment when the wolf tackled Ghost to the ground. A bunch of other guards piled on top of him, shouting and cursing. They put Ghost in cuffs, then started hauling him back this way. The crowd began to disperse.

"Dammit." Another twenty to Chancey, lost. I had a weakness for betting on the underdog.

Kalina shrugged. "That's on him for being stupid enough to try to break out in broad daylight. If he'd escaped at night, he would've made it."

"Nuh-uh," Marcus said. "*We* tried to break out last night, and it didn't work."

"You tried to break out?" My jaw dropped open, while Kalina gave Marcus the nastiest look she could. He instantly shut up.

"Okay, I've got to hear about this," Charlie said. "What did you guys do?"

Kalina gave an eyeroll, then leaned in. "*I* tried to break out. Marcus decided to tag along."

"Yeah, and you *left me* to be eaten by sirens!" Marcus yelped.

"You're fine." Kalina played with the edges of her ponytail. "Anyway, long story short, Marcus and I tried to escape by swimming through the siren lake and getting close enough to the woods to climb the fence, but we got caught long before we were even close."

"How'd you guys get out of your rooms? We're locked in during the night," Charlie whispered.

"I know how to pick locks, and apparently, the guard who locks Marcus' dorm is a total idiot, and never does it right," Kalina said. "I could teach you how if you wanted to."

Learning how to pick locks would be a useful skill here at the Institute. But I was more interested in breaking out. "Do you think we could all try again, and succeed this time?"

If I could get out of the Institute, I could start surveying Darke Island for what I was really here for— learning about the prophecy.

But Kalina shook her head. "No one has ever broken out of the Institute. I thought I could, but after last night, I'm convinced it's impossible. I was able to get past fae security when I committed my crime against the crown, but these guards are even tougher than that. They're professionals at keeping us stuck here."

My heart fell. So there really was no way out. Even if I tried to break out, I'd probably be unsuccessful. The only way to leave would be to serve my time.

Marcus' voice was gloating. "It wasn't a complete loss. Now you owe me a favor."

Kalina's face reddened, and Charlie asked, "Favor?"

"I owe Marcus a life debt. He saved me from being eaten by a siren." Kalina frowned. "Fae take life debts *very seriously*, so unfortunately, I'm bound to him until I fulfill it somehow."

"And how sweet it is," Marcus sang.

"I'm sure it won't take more than a week," Kalina shot back at him.

"This little debate is cute, but it's not going to help us get out of here," Charlie said. "Let's just stop talking about it. It's pointless to get our hopes up. We're never leaving."

My emotions curdled like sour milk, and they tasted just as bitter to digest.

Kalina shook out her ponytail. "Whatever. I'm hungry. See you guys in an hour."

Kalina hurried off. We had another one of our group therapy sessions soon, but it was clear she didn't want to be seen eating with us.

She was so stuck-up. But my instincts twisted in my gut, telling me something about her seemed... I don't know, off. Like she was pretending to be tougher than she was.

"I already ate," Marcus said flatly. "I just need to be alone."

Marcus turned and left us. He sat on one of the benches in the yard with his sketchbook and started drawing. Rishi perched on his shoulder and observed.

A spark of annoyance crossed through my gut. We had agreed to come together to protect each other, but our little "group" was anything but united. Kalina didn't wish to be bothered with the riff-raff, and Marcus was still too much of a loner to be comfortable in a group.

Which left me with Charlie. Woo-hoo.

I sensed the tension as Charlie and I walked to the cafeteria. Oberi changed into a unicorn and walked between us to give us some distance, but it hardly helped. For some reason, I felt closer to him now than ever before... and I hated it. I could feel the two parts of our bond colliding, and it was uncomfortable. It wasn't like the seamless connection I had with Oberi, that flowed like water and felt comforting. I didn't know how to relate to this guy, or how to incorporate him in my life, and it really showed.

I didn't think he knew what to do with me, either. It felt like a rejection, which only made the resentment grow.

Charlie coughed, and I gave an irritated huff.

His eyebrows immediately furrowed. "I'm sorry, am I annoying you?"

"Only when you're breathing."

"You're acting pissed. Something I said must've bothered you." Charlie's face soured. "What did I do this time?"

"What you said back there, about it being pointless to get our hopes up," I snapped. "Last week you were going on about how we're destined to die in here, and now you're insistent we'll never leave the grounds. I'm sorry if I don't want to be buried on this property like you."

"I'm not saying that, but look at the facts," Charlie snarled. "Kalina and Marcus tried to get out, and they failed. Our chances of surviving four long years at the Institute are slim."

"Look, buddy, I know you think *you're* going to have an early demise, but I'm not putting up with that crap," I shot at him. "I would very much like to live, so it'd be nice if you could be a little positive every once in a while."

Charlie scowled. "I've been around and I've seen things. People I know who ended up in prison rarely got out."

"That's too bad, but we're not them. We have a chance."

"I'm just trying to be realistic. Having faith is setting us up for disappointment."

I didn't like that. I didn't like that at all. I couldn't give up, because if I did, I'd fall to pieces. Charlie *had* to believe we'd get out of here. I couldn't do this all alone.

And I didn't want Charlie to die. He hadn't done anything to deserve it. Was it so bad to admit that I cared about him, even if I really couldn't stand the guy?

So what came out of my mouth next was more out of discouragement than anything else. "You know, I could try to see things from your perspective, but it'd be too difficult to get my head that far up my own ass."

Charlie rubbed his face. "Hell, you are the *most frustrating* person. I'd tell you to take today off from being a jerk, since you're putting in so much overtime."

"And I'd tell *you* to go fuck yourself, but that'd be cruel and unusual punishment."

"You are such a—" Charlie took a deep breath. "I'm not going to sit here and banter with you. You wanna be delusional, fine. But don't try to drag me along on your little road of sunshine and rainbows, because there's no such thing as happy endings, *princess*. Not here."

Charlie pivoted and went the other way. Oberi stuck with me. We'd been here a month, and Charlie had mapped out the school well enough he knew where he was going without her. Apparently I'd ruined his appetite.

I scratched Oberi's chin. "I just keep putting my foot in my mouth, huh, girl?"

She nickered.

I ate lunch alone. I had a salad, but I fed most of it to Oberi. I couldn't stomach more than a few bites.

I had to take a different route to Professor Takahashi's office than I typically did, because there'd been a stabbing in the hallway with a sharpened toothbrush and the guards were trying to clean it up. An unfortunate result of a gang fight, I assumed. Chills ran up and down my spine as I heard the whispered bits of gossip that permeated the hallways, how the student who'd been stabbed might not make it.

Maybe Charlie was right. Scary shit happened at the Institute every day. I might not get a chance to fulfill the prophecy and save the world. Some deranged inmate might kill me first.

But I couldn't think that way. I'd go down a dark path devoid of any hope, and hope was the only thing that would get me out of here.

As was usual, I was the last one to show up to our group therapy session. Charlie's arms were crossed when I sat beside him. He was still pissed at me.

The last few sessions hadn't been very helpful. Most of the time was taken up by Professor Takahashi's speeches on emotional management. None of us had confessed anything personal while we were here. It still felt too raw.

Professor Takahashi observed us with a bright smile. "I'm so happy to see you all have made it. I have a special opportunity I'd like to introduce to you today."

"What is it?" Kalina asked.

Professor Takahashi crossed his legs. "Every year, the Warden offers a scholarship program exclusively for students at the Institute. A competition, if you will, made up of teams of students that compete for the grand prize."

Charlie huffed skeptically. "What, do the guards throw us all into an arena and see who comes out alive?"

"You don't understand, Mister Wahkin. This is no average competition," Takahashi explained. "These are the Darke Games, and the winners receive the chance of a lifetime— the opportunity to have your sentence erased, and release from the Institute as free members of magical society."

A lump grew in my throat. Marcus' face paled, and Kalina gave a strangled gasp.

Charlie had gone so still it was almost unnatural to see. "There's a catch," Charlie objected. "There always is."

Takahashi's smile fell, but only slightly. "It is a… dangerous competition. One that not all survive."

"Of course it is," Charlie said, but Kalina cut him off.

"I don't care," she said quickly. "I didn't know a sentence could be erased."

Takahashi inclined his head. "It can be, but only by participation in the Darke Games— and only by winning the competition with your team. Teams of volunteers are sent out on Darke Island to win points. The team with the most points at the end of the competition wins. However, accumulation of these points can be a bit… deadly."

The question of how teams gathered points was barely a factor to me. My heart pounded so harshly against my ribcage that I longed to rip it out. There *was* a way out of the Institute— it just depended on me putting my life on the line.

If I won these Darke Games, I would be free to pursue the prophecy on my own… and be that much closer to stopping the chaos it was bound to bring.

I had to get a team, and win these games at whatever cost. The supernatural world depended on it.

I leaned forward. "Tell us more."

charlie
ELEVEN

I was skeptical as hell. The Warden wouldn't sanction the Darke Games without a reason. It was more than just a scholarship program— that much was obvious.

An edge to Ava-Marie's tone confirmed she knew it as well, but that didn't matter to her. She'd do whatever she had to in order to get out of here. Which was saying something, considering it was her fault we were here in the first place.

I slumped in my chair. "Yes, Professor Takahashi," I stated flatly. "*Do* tell us more. What's the purpose of these *games*?"

"As you all know, Darke Island is a hub for supernatural activity, due to its location along a dark magic ley line," Professor Takahashi explained. "Once a year, this magical ley line causes a collection of portals to open, unleashing evil spirits and hellish monsters onto the island from the evil afterlife— the Underworld, hell, whatever you wish to call it. The Darke Games were developed to protect the island from these monsters— to eliminate them before they can hurt the residents of Shade Hills."

There it was. They were *using* us, like they did with the noxite mines.

"So the pardon is a bribe," I accused. Only someone who'd lost everything— like the kids at the Institute— would be stupid enough to go up against monsters from hell.

Professor Takahashi sounded offended by the accusation. "The Darke Games are a chance to prove yourself. It's an opportunity to show that you are willing to put your life on the line for your community and for others— to prove that you've truly been reformed, as is the goal within the Institute."

"So shouldn't all volunteers get pardoned, then?" Marcus asked hesitantly.

"Not all have what it takes to make it through to the end," Takahashi explained. "Only those who are mentally stable enough to leave the Institute make it through."

I snorted. Mentally stable, my ass. This wasn't a competition of mental stability. It was all about who was most desperate for freedom.

"I fail to see what you find funny about this, Mister Wahkin," Takahashi said calmly. "Don't you want a chance to win your freedom?"

When I didn't answer, he continued. "The winners don't just get their record wiped clean. They are promised jobs and many other opportunities when they are released. Their futures are set for life."

It sounded like the opportunity of a lifetime. So why did my stomach twist into such ugly knots when I thought of the Games?

"The winners are chosen based on the team that makes the most points," Takahashi explained. "The judges will evaluate your progress as you're filmed fighting the monsters that free roam around the island. Points are earned each time a monster or dark spirit is killed. Make more points than any other team, and you will be released from the Institute."

"Why don't the fae just shut down the portals?" Kalina cracked her knuckles. She sounded willing to go in single-handedly to shut the portals down herself.

"The portals cannot be controlled, I'm afraid," Professor Takahashi said. "It is the way with the island. Since Shade Hills is on a ley line, if you close one portal, another one opens up. They can, however, be predicted, which gives you all time to prepare for the Darke Games."

"When?" Ava asked desperately, like the fate of the world hung on these deadly games.

"The end of December," Takahashi announced. "Each team is made up of four students. I suggest those who would like to compete begin forming their team now, so you have time to train. Sign-up sheets are located outside the Warden's office."

Takahashi excused us, and my classmates shuffled quickly toward the door. Kalina hurried down the stairs in a rush, though her footsteps were light— as was the way with the fae. She seemed to dance down the staircase, though it was less like ballet and more like tap-dancing. Her movements were hurried. Oberi's hoofsteps were light as we wound downward.

"We have to enter, Charlie," Ava whispered lowly from beside me.

"Enter a deadly tournament?" I asked skeptically. "We're better off waiting to serve our time. At least then we have a chance of survival. The Darke Games are a death sentence."

Ava stopped at the bottom of the stairs and grabbed my arm. Her grip was freaking strong. I tried to shrug her off, but she kept a tight hold on me. Kalina and Marcus continued on ahead.

"One second you're sure you're going to die in here. Now it's your only chance of survival?" she snapped. "You make no sense. Charlie, we *have* to do this. The Darke Games are my one chance at getting out early, and I can't go in without Oberi. And Oberi's not going without you."

I finally managed to yank my arm out of her grasp. "You're right— Oberi's not going anywhere. I'm not letting her get in the way of danger like that!"

I reached out to stroke Oberi's velvety nose. "Tell her, girl."

Oberi huffed a breath, though I wasn't sure what she meant by it.

"See? She wants to," Ava objected.

"The answer is no, pidge," I said through gritted teeth. "We're not entering the Darke Games."

"Yes we are."

It wasn't Ava's stern voice that answered, but Kalina's. I hadn't heard her turn around to approach us. I must've been too wrapped up in arguing with Ava, because now I could easily make out Marcus' loud footsteps as the two of them returned.

"You want to be on our team?" Ava asked Kalina, sounding surprised.

"We agreed to stick together, didn't we?" Kalina pressed.

"Yeah, so we didn't get pummeled by some prison gang," I pointed out. "Not so we could attend each other's funerals."

"Look," Kalina said. "I'm not staying in here a second longer than I have to. If there's a chance to get out, I'm taking it."

"At what cost?" I demanded. No one seemed to resonate with the word *deadly* like I did. "This place isn't bad enough to risk your life for."

"If you have plans once you get out of here, it is," Kalina rebutted.

That struck a chord with me, and I quieted. I'd never really had plans for the future. I didn't know what it felt like to risk your life for them. It sounded stupid to me. Wouldn't you rather survive at any cost?

"I'm entering the Darke Games, no question," Kalina said. "But if I'm going to win this thing, I need a damn good team."

"And you want us?" Ava asked skeptically.

"The only way I'm winning this is if I diversify," Kalina pointed out. "I can't team up with fae. They all have the same powers as me, and I'm better than all of them anyway." She didn't sound smug about it. She was simply stating what she believed to be fact. "I need Elementai on my team— someone who can kill monsters with Fire and whip up a storm with Air. And since the two of you seem to be attached at the hip—"

"We are *not* attached at the hip," I protested.

"—Then I'm going to have to take you both," she concluded without missing a beat. "Plus, Charlie beat Mad Dog's ass. I could use a guy like him on my team."

Ava's shoulder brushed up against mine as she shifted, crossing her arms. "And what is it you can offer us?"

Kalina lowered her voice. "You know my secret— that I'm a sorceress *and* a shifter. My illusion magic is strong, so strong I can turn illusions into reality. Try finding another fae in this hellhole who can do that with ease. You need me."

Ava paused for a few moments, like she was actually considering this. "Who do you have in mind for a fourth member?"

"I'm not sure yet," Kalina admitted. "I say we get an angel or vampire on board. We'll need their strength."

"Hey!" Marcus protested. "What about me?"

Kalina's skirt rustled the air around her as she whirled toward him. "First of all, I didn't realize you were standing there."

How could she not? He was the loudest mouth-breather in this place.

"And second, you're just a warlock," Kalina said.

"Just a warlock!" Marcus sputtered. "I'll have you know, the Miriamic Coven is strong."

"Together," Kalina emphasized. "Individually, none of you can pull off anything impressive. What are you going to do? Read a crystal ball for us?"

Marcus huffed. "And why wouldn't that be helpful? I could keep you out of danger. Besides, I'm not just *any ordinary* warlock."

"Oh yeah?" Kalina asked skeptically. "What's your specialty?"

"See this?" A thread on Marcus' uniform popped as he yanked up his sleeve. "Every witch or warlock receives a tattoo from our goddess, marking us for our powers. Everyone gets a single symbol— either a cauldron, a tree, an eye, a skull, or a crescent moon. I'm the first to receive *all five*. I have magic from every Cast. My powers are unlimited."

Kalina didn't sound like she was buying it. "Tattoos can be faked."

"Not mine," Marcus promised. "The Goddess wanted me to have my powers so badly, she granted them to me early. I can see the future and raise the dead. I can brew potions and read minds."

"Why haven't I seen you do any of this then?" Kalina challenged.

"I don't like to show off," Marcus admitted. "It's a good way to get my ass kicked around here, being different."

"Prove it to me," Kalina stated. "What am I thinking right now?"

Amusement entered Marcus' voice. "There are other things you'd like to do to my pretty little ass."

Kalina huffed, while Ava and I both tried to stifle giggles. Wow. I guess Marcus really could read minds.

"I-I didn't mean it," she stammered. "It was only a test."

"A test I passed," Marcus said proudly.

"Fine," Kalina caved. "You can be on our team. I guess it will help if we have someone who can predict what's coming."

"Perfect," Marcus said brightly. "Shall we sign up?"

"No!" I protested. "Is anyone listening to me? Takahashi said this thing was voluntary. Well, I'm not volunteering."

"What if Oberi volunteers to go?" Ava challenged.

My teeth ground together. "That's out of the question. I won't let her."

"Oh yeah?" Ava turned to the Fire unicorn. "Familiars are meant to run, to be *free*. You want to leave here as much as I do, don't you, Oberi?"

I reached out to stroke my Familiar. "Ava's wrong. You wouldn't let either of us run into danger."

Oberi ducked her head, and my stomach sank. She drew away from me, and her hooves padded on the carpet as she rounded Ava.

My jaw dropped at the betrayal. "Oberi! How could you?"

Oberi's fur bristled as Ava stroked it. "Because Oberi knows how crucial it is that we win this thing and get out of here. She's with me no matter what. The question is… are you?"

My hands curled into fists, and my nostrils flared. How *dare* Ava use my Familiar against me. Her father did the same thing to get me to this island, and now she was using Oberi to get me to risk my life for… for what?

The problem was, it didn't matter if the outcome was worth it. The risks of leaving Oberi alone were far greater. I wouldn't let Oberi go into that tournament without me, and I knew Ava. One way or another, she'd get Oberi to go with her, like she had the night she tried to run away on the boat. If something bad happened to them in the tournament, I would perish along with them. It was how the bond worked. And so I had to go to protect Oberi… to protect Ava.

"Damn you, Ava-Marie," I growled.

She laughed evilly. She knew she had me.

I stomped down the hall, only to realize I had no idea where I was going. "Where's the damned Warden's office?"

Ava snickered. "Glad to see you so… enthusiastic."

I frowned. "Don't mistake this pretty face for enthusiasm, sweetheart. I'm royally pissed."

"Ooh, *royally*," Kalina teased.

Ava took my arm. "Come on, *pretty face*. It's this way."

"You realize the school is just using us because we're expendable," I pointed out on our way to the Warden's office. "They don't want to deal with these monsters themselves."

"Of course they are," Kalina said. "But why wouldn't we take advantage of it?"

I shrugged Ava off me, because I was mad. Instead, I placed a hand on Oberi's back to lead me through the halls. I spoke to take my mind off how pissed I was. "So, what *are* your plans if we win?"

Kalina spoke from in front of me without turning back. "For one, to get *my* throne back, of course."

"Your throne?" Marcus questioned.

Kalina stammered. "Yeah. Every twenty years or so, the King's Contest in Malovia is held.

It's a competition among the fae to choose the next monarch. I lost the crown to the current king's jackass son."

"I'm guessing he's the one you tried to kill?" Ava questioned.

Kalina scoffed. "Yeah. He's lucky my blade missed. He won the Contest by manipulation, not by any talent. He's going to make a shit king. I've been working my entire life to take over as queen. I'm not going to give up due to a little attempted murder charge."

I gave a sarcastic noise. She was nearly as bad as Ava.

Kalina continued. "And the other reason I want to get out... well, let's save that for the therapy session. What are *you* going to do, Charlie?"

Ava was quick to answer for me. "Mope around, probably."

"Yeah, because you'll all be dead," I growled.

Ava skipped on ahead toward Kalina, and they continued talking about what they'd do if they made it out of here early. Ava apparently had plans to start her own designer fashion brand. Typical.

Marcus' footsteps slowed. Rishi walked with light steps beside him. I didn't care to speed up, because I didn't want to catch up with the girls.

"So, what would you *really* do?" he asked me. "If we won."

I shrugged. "Take that job offer, I guess. Save up some money to get myself a decent place. Go back to school in Kinpago to learn my magic."

Marcus considered my words for a few moments. "Is that really all you'd do? Don't you have any dreams?"

I shrugged. "You're the one who can read minds. You tell me."

Marcus lowered his voice and leaned closer to me. "It's only the dirty thoughts I can read. Shh... don't tell Kalina."

I laughed lightly, which was a miracle considering we were marching to sign our own death certificates. "That doesn't sound that useful in the Darke Games."

"No," Marcus admitted, "but I had to say *something* to get on your team. If anyone has a chance of winning, it's you guys."

I furrowed my brow. "Why do you say that? Have you seen the Games in action?"

"Well, uh." Marcus scratched the side of his face. "My premonitions don't work quite like that, but you could say I have a feeling about it."

"Well, that's... encouraging," I mumbled.

We'd turned down so many halls by now I couldn't tell where we were. It was a part of the school I'd never been before. Ava and Kalina's footsteps slowed ahead of us, and we stopped when we reached them.

"Well, are you guys ready for this?" Kalina asked.

"Hell yeah," Ava said, taking a step forward. Though the hall was quiet, the scratch of the pen on paper sounded like painful wails to my ears. It was less like she was signing up for a competition and more like she was signing away her soul— in blood. Too damn bad she was signing mine along with it.

Ava took a step back. "That wasn't scary at all. The Darke Games will be easy."

"Will they, now?" a male voice said from behind us.

I didn't recognize the voice, until Marcus sputtered. "D-Doctor Taurus."

The Warden.

"I like your confidence," he said as he came toward us. "You must believe you'll win."

"That's the idea," Ava replied, though she sounded bitter when she spoke to the Warden.

I didn't think she liked him much, and I couldn't blame her. He'd said all the right things during his welcome speech, but they'd felt ingenuine. I didn't believe he cared about the students here, and the Darke Games were proof of that.

"I can't wait to see what you four have to offer during the Darke Games," the Warden said. He meant to come off as encouraging, I was sure, but there were dark undertones to his words.

"I'll bet," Ava said.

The Warden sounded confused. "Whatever do you mean by that?"

"I'm entering this thing for one reason, and one reason only— to get out of here," Ava stated. "Don't think for a second it means any of us care about what you're doing here. Your for-profit prison system is unethical, for one, and the Darke Games are simply—"

"Pidge," I warned, but she ignored me.

"— An excuse to throw unskilled laborers to the lions so that you can continue mining—"

"Ava!" I cried. She was launching into one of her courtroom arguments. Normally, I'd let her finish, but this was the freaking *Warden*. He could throw her in Cellblock 9 for sneezing in his direction. I hated to see what would happen to Ava if she seriously pissed him off.

Ava paused for a moment, long enough for the Warden to cut in. "You misunderstand, Miss…"

"Mitoh," Ava stated confidently. "Ava-Marie Mitoh, and don't you forget it."

"No," the Warden said with a smirk in his tone. "I don't think I will. I'm not sure where you got your idea of a for-profit prison, but this is a reform school. The Darke Games offer you an opportunity to prove your reformation and leave the school early. You seem very passionate. If your magic measures up to your temper, perhaps I may award the prize to you."

"There's no question about it," Ava said. "We're going to win this thing."

"Very good," the Warden said, though it sounded more like he was praising a puppy than congratulating her. "I'll be sure to keep my eye on you, Miss Mitoh."

That was all he said before he continued down the hall and his footsteps faded up a flight of stairs to his office.

"Pidge," I complained. "Insulting people around here is a good way to make enemies."

"On the contrary, I think I impressed him," she said proudly. "I did us a favor. The closer he and the other judges watch us during the Darke Games, the better chance we have of racking up points."

I gritted my teeth again. It was starting to hurt my jaw. "I wouldn't be so sure about that."

"It doesn't matter," Kalina cut in. "Just stay out of trouble until the Games, and we'll win."

Kalina approached the sign-up sheet next. The pen moved over the paper smoothly. "Your turn, Marcus."

He hesitated.

"Make up your mind! I can't have a pussy on my team," Kalina snapped.

Rishi hissed at her, like he didn't care for her choice of words.

"Just take the pen," she pressed. "I thought you wanted to win this thing."

"I do," he replied. The pen clinked to the ground as Marcus dropped it. He scribbled down his name, then turned and handed the pen to me.

"I, um," I stammered.

Ava was at my side in a moment. "I already wrote down your name. They just need your signature."

She led me forward and guided my hand to the line where I was supposed to sign my name. My stomach became hollow, and my throat felt like sandpaper.

"Are you sure about this, pidge?" I asked. "Once we sign up for this thing, there's no turning back."

"I'm sure," she stated confidently.

"It's not just your life you're messing with," I growled under my breath. "Every choice you make affects me and Oberi."

"Every choice I make affects *everyone*," she hissed, though she didn't explain what she meant. "Don't treat me like I haven't thought this through, Charlie. I *have* to do this."

"Why?" I demanded. Kalina and Marcus were bickering amongst themselves, but I kept my voice low for only Ava to hear. "Your designer brand isn't going to change the world. I know you think it is, but—"

"This isn't about that," Ava snapped.

"Then why do you want out early?" I asked harshly. "Your own father sent you here. You *wanted* to come, didn't you? That's why you stole that boat."

Ava's breath brushed across my skin. "I wouldn't expect you to understand."

"Then help me," I insisted. "If I'm going to sign my name on this thing, I need to know why."

Ava's head swiveled, and her long hair brushed against my arm. She shot several glances toward Marcus and Kalina before speaking. "I can't tell you here. I just need you to trust me."

I had no reason to trust her. She'd turned her back on me more than once already. But there was something in her voice— a desperation I'd never heard her use before. It wasn't fake, like the act she put on for other people. It was genuine, and that frightened me far more than entering the Darke Games.

I couldn't explain what possessed me to scribble my signature on that line. Maybe it was the bond between the two of us. Maybe it was because I actually *did* want to win this thing— to have a future like Professor Takahashi promised. Whatever the reason, I found myself signing up for the Darke Games.

I just hoped I hadn't made a terrible mistake.

ava-marie

TWELVE

"That was beautiful, Opal. Do it again."

I sat at the edge of the student pool in my bikini as Opal leapt out of the water. She jumped and twisted in the air like a dolphin, her mermaid tail sparkling in the fluorescent light. I cheered, and she twisted to perform a beautiful dive as she fell back into the deep end of the pool.

Each magical race at the Institute had their own personal room with which to experiment. The sirens and the mermaids had an Atlantean bathhouse in the basement. Greek marble pillars lined the bathhouse, and statues of mermaids twisted beside stone archways and fountains. There was an Olympic-size pool in the middle of the room, surrounded by smaller pools of varying temperatures, and even a few jacuzzi tubs. There were even pools for mud baths, and pools that had seaweed in them that connected to the lake outside the Institute. Long reclining chairs and large hot stones that mermaids could lie on lined the room. I could hear the eerie croons of the sirens beneath the murky lighting that set the relaxing tone of the bathhouse, like a song known only to sailors lost to the sea. A mirror covered the entire length of the ceiling, so you could watch yourself swim as you looked up.

I continued to nibble on the chocolate my parents had sent me and watched Opal do laps. She swam around the pool at lightning speed. I was Toaqua, but even with my Water powers, I couldn't catch up with her when we'd raced in the water.

Opal's mermaid tail was beautiful. Her scales were a mottled turquoise and sapphire that glistened like gems in the water, her fin feathery and long like that of a betta fish. She wore a bikini top that was the same color as her green eyes.

Opal came up beside me. "Don't you think it's a little weird this room is so nice? I mean, there are hot tubs in here."

"It's just an excuse the staff can use to pretend they care about us," I said. "They have to keep us happy somehow, and we can't say they're treating us cruelly if we have *some* nice things."

"Guess so." Opal dove and took off like a rocket. She swam around a vampire in the shallow end, who sent her a dirty look. The pool was mostly meant for mermaids and sirens to use, but other students swam here as well.

I was practicing my Water magic. My right hand held the chocolate bar as my left hand twisted above the pool. I made a tiny humpback whale out of the ripples in the pool, and swam it around before transforming it into a salmon, and then a sea serpent.

Toaqua magic was as easy for me as casting a flame. I didn't even have to think about it. I was lucky to be talented in elemental magic, because the class they had here for Elementai was a fucking joke.

The doors to the pool opened. Charlie and Marcus walked in. Marcus was only wearing swim trunks, but Charlie had on a shirt over his thin shorts. Oberi followed Charlie as a husky, his tongue lolling out of his mouth.

I'd talked to Daddy last night. He'd finally gotten his wallet back, and lectured me to be careful around Charlie because, *"That boy is up to no good."*

My nose wrinkled in distaste as I watched Charlie walk around the pool. Daddy was right. Charlie Wahkin was low-life trash, and Ava-Marie Mitoh wasn't known for getting her nails dirty. He might be bonded to me, and we might be competing in the Darke Games together, but that didn't mean I trusted him.

Marcus jumped into the pool with a *whoop*. It was then Charlie pulled off his shirt. My eyes widened as I took in his washboard abs and chiseled shoulders. Damn, the guy was toned. And tan. And built.

Charlie's swim trunks were almost too big for him. They sagged on his hips and showed off the V that dipped below his stomach. My eyes couldn't help but navigate down his happy trail to the bulge in his shorts. He looked pretty gifted.

Strike that. If Charlie Wahkin was trash, I was a raccoon, and I *loved* garbage.

Charlie slid into the pool. Marcus splashed him, and the two started goofing off. Oberi barked and jumped into the pool. He swam around, his head bobbing as his tail wagged in the water. Charlie grabbed him and spun him around. Oberi let out a few more loud barks that echoed around the pool.

I finished my chocolate and tossed the wrapper away into a bin nearby. Opal pulled herself out of the water and sat beside me. As she did, her mermaid tail transformed back into two legs. "You know, Charlie's single. He's on the market."

I gave a laugh. "Please. There are plenty of hot dickheads around here. Charlie being one of them. I can look and not touch."

"But you *want* to touch," she teased. I summoned a wave to rise up, and Opal yelped as it grabbed her and dragged her back into the pool.

Opal waved her tail fin at me while I continued to watch Charlie wrestle with Marcus. There were perks to Charlie being blind. He couldn't catch me checking him out.

Charlie won and flung Marcus off of him. Oberi saw me and came swimming over. I reached down to pet his head. "Hey, good boy. How are you doing today?"

Oberi barked. Charlie must've heard me speak, because he waded near. It wasn't very graceful... could Charlie not swim? Opal coyly paddled off with a gloating look.

"This is my second time running into you today," Charlie said as he came close.

"Second?" I hadn't seen him all day.

"Yeah. The first was in your dreams."

"Ugh!" I pushed his face away. He sank under the water for a moment, before he reached up and yanked me into the water by my ankle. I screamed before I went under.

What. An. Ass. Charlie smirked. I sent out a jet of water from my left hand. My Toaqua magic socked his stomach and carried him all the way to the other side of the pool.

I dragged myself out of the pool and dried off using my powers. Charlie came up for air, rubbing his gut. "Was that really necessary?"

"Yes. You ruined my hair, jackass." I smoothed down my newly-dried hair and tied it back into a fishtail braid. I helped Oberi onto the concrete as he scrambled out of the pool.

Charlie ducked to avoid being hit by water droplets. "Yeah, your perfect hair. How are you going to manage playing the Darke Games without your precious straightener? You'll probably use a hair dryer to finish off a monster."

"I can be *very* violent with a hair dryer. It's heavy."

Charlie huffed. "Sure."

"You need to stop worrying about me and focus on yourself," I snapped. "Maybe practice a little, so we don't get killed out there, and you can do whatever you want once we're set free. Steal a few more wallets, maybe."

"In my opinion, we either win or we don't." He shrugged. "I'll figure out my plans after it's a sure thing we're getting out of here."

I sighed. "Charlie, you *have* to have some reason for escaping other than just wanting to survive the Institute," I insisted. "Being passive isn't going to help us win the Games."

"Sorry if I don't have anything as grand as a clothing company," he replied scathingly.

I scowled. I'd made up some bullshit about starting a designer label to the others, because I didn't want them to know why I really needed to get out of here. Once I won the Darke Games, I'd be free to explore Darke Island at will, and figure out the prophecy, as well as how to stop it.

Unfortunately, I needed Oberi to help me, and Charlie wasn't going anywhere without her. But I'd figure out how to get rid of him once I won the Games. I'd promised to tell him later the true motives for my escape, but how could I make him understand if he didn't have his own reasons for getting out of here?

"Why don't you ask your spirit guides for help?" I suggested. "They might have some tips."

"What are spirit guides?" Charlie raised his eyebrows.

I gave a noise of frustration. "Ancestors, you're so ignorant. How could you not know this? It's like, the basics of Hawkei lore."

Charlie's tone grew rough. "I don't get what's so hard for you to understand, but I'm an orphan. The tribe threw me out because I was a mixed-House baby, and I was raised outside Hawkei culture. I literally don't know anything about where I came from, so don't blame me."

Sorrow welled within me, making shame creep over my skin. I'd spoken too harshly and too soon, again. As much as I despised Charlie, I didn't want to hurt him. He'd been through enough without my bossy ass telling him off.

"I'm sorry," I offered. "You're right, I'm being a bitch."

Charlie pulled back in surprise. "I'm shocked you admit it."

"I'm wrong about a lot of things." I stroked Oberi's ears. "But you have to know your heritage before we go into the Games. You can't know what you want out of the future if you don't know your past, right?"

"I guess… what are you saying?"

I stood up. "Meet me by the cafeteria after dinner. We need to go somewhere private."

"There aren't a lot of places without guards in the prison," Charlie said skeptically.

"There are more than you think. You just have to be smart enough to notice them."

I walked off then. Oberi watched me, his eyes appreciative and warm.

Charlie had to know where he came from. Survival wasn't enough at the Institute. You had to have something to fight for, something waiting for you at the end. Hope was what would sustain the reward, and if Charlie wasn't willing to put himself on the line for a dream he'd die for, he'd run off once it got tough during the Games. Perhaps learning about who he was as a Hawkei would inspire him.

I also needed to do this before I physically *couldn't*. I was experiencing a rare time when I wasn't in an extremely low or extremely high period of my mood. This was important; I didn't want to get it wrong. Charlie needed to know this stuff, and I didn't want my bipolar getting in the way.

Here's to hoping I could hold myself together during the Darke Games.

Charlie met me outside the cafeteria around seven, as promised. I had a purse around my shoulder, which held some of the things we'd need. It was already dark outside. Oberi sat by him dutifully and wagged his tail. "So where are we going?"

"You'll see." I walked ahead. Oberi changed into a unicorn. Charlie put his hand on her back, to guide him along as we left the doors of the Institute.

I led Charlie into the forest that was still securely locked inside the fence line. We wandered through a collection of pine trees, and Charlie said, "You sure we won't get in trouble out here?"

"We're still inside the prison yard. As long as we make it back before curfew, they won't bother us."

I lit a flame in my hand, to give myself some light. We walked for five more minutes, until Charlie asked, "Where are you going, exactly?"

"I was just going to find an open spot in the trees."

Oberi nudged him, and Charlie shook his head. "I have a feeling. Follow me."

Charlie walked on. Oberi went ahead of him, and I threw my arms up. Charlie took us through a particularly dense part of the woods. Oberi used her horn to clear the way for Charlie, but she forgot all about me as I snagged my uniform on branches and thorns, being careful not to light the woods on fire with my magic.

"Ow. Charlie, do you know where the hell you're going?"

He didn't answer. We finally stepped out of the brush, and my mouth fell open as I looked up.

There was a gigantic stone in the middle of the woods. It was massive. It looked like someone had carved out a cliff side and just dropped it in the forest. If I had to guess, the rock was over a hundred feet tall, and nearly as long.

There were carvings in the rock that looked like doorways, wide enough for large animals to fit through. Oberi walked forward. My firelight shone off the walls of the stone as we looked inside. Charlie entered and trailed his hand over the stone, as if he could feel what the structure was thinking.

We wound through a twisted hallway until we came to a large room in the center of the rock. It was big enough to hold a hundred people. I expanded the flame in my hand as I looked toward the ceiling.

"Whoa. Charlie, how did you find this?" I marveled.

"I don't know," he mused. "Oberi sort of… gave me the idea. I can't explain it, but I've always had ease whenever I needed to navigate rocks and earth, or plants. It's like I can feel where they are, or sense them, energetically."

"Well, you are half-Nivita." It wasn't that odd. Charlie's father might have been an Air elemental, but his mother had been Earth, and he'd clearly inherited some of her talents.

"A Nivita must've carved it," Charlie said. "I don't know who else could make a room out of rock like this."

"Probably a prisoner at the Institute." Whoever they were, they were long gone now. This place had been abandoned for ages. There were no footprints in the dirt beneath our feet, and massive cobwebs were growing in some corners.

There was a crack as I stepped on something. A wooden bow lay beside my feet, but it didn't look Hawkei. I picked it up, and my brow furrowed.

"What is it?" Charlie asked, noticing my silence.

"A bow, but it's not from our tribe," I said. "The symbols on it… they're the same runes that were on the abandoned boats we found in the shipyard weeks ago."

"That's freaky."

"Just a bit." Why did we keep running into these runes, and what did they mean?

I tossed the bow to the other side of the room and tried not to shiver. "This is perfect. We won't be disturbed."

I sat on the ground in the middle of the room and began rifling through my purse. Charlie sat across from me, while Oberi lay down between us, her flaming mane giving off a warm glow.

"So what are we here for?" Charlie asked.

"You know the basics of Hawkei lore, but you don't know the important things. Since no one else will teach you, I will," I began. I set a bundle of sage and a leather pouch full of incense before me. I slipped bells onto my wrist and set a leather drum into my lap.

I didn't have my smudging wand, but this would have to do. It'd been a pain in the ass to sneak in the few Hawkei things I had. I placed the fireball on the ground, and it burned by itself of its own accord, sustained by my magic.

"What you have to know about the Hawkei is we're survivors," I began. "You already know that Native Americans got the short end of the stick."

"I don't know much, but I have heard that millions of natives died while Europeans were colonizing the United States," Charlie said.

"Yes. The Hawkei were a part of that genocide. That's why we call them colonizers, not settlers. The land was already settled by indigenous people before Europeans ever arrived in America. We had no need to be ruled by their governments until we were forced to do so. What the Hawkei went through was horrible. Our people nearly starved to death. We were driven to the brink of extinction by disease and war with the colonizers. The only reason we survived was because the ancestors bestowed upon us our elemental powers, and gave us the ability to bond with our Familiars. Without that, our people would've been wiped out."

Charlie gave a thoughtful look. "Kinpago seemed very diverse, from what I gathered while I was there."

"The Hawkei didn't remain within their own borders. The people in our tribe went all over the world, to befriend others and to even start families with them. That's why there's so much variation within Hawkei culture, because we've integrated our lives and had children with many other societies while keeping our traditions alive."

I frowned. "Even with our magic, it still wasn't easy. The United States government did whatever they could to stomp us out. We were the only people in the country who could only be considered native if we had enough of a *blood quotient* to qualify— like some kind of animal. Natives weren't even allowed to vote in every state until 1962. My great-great-grandmother was taken from her home as a child and sent to a rehabilitation boarding school, to try to force her to assimilate. They cut her hair, beat her, and forbid her to practice her religion. When she finally escaped, she didn't come back the same."

"That's horrible." Charlie frowned. "Except… I can't help but feel bitter that the Elementai did the same thing to me, by sending me into the foster care system and executing my parents before I could even remember them. Why should I want to be part of a tribe that would do that to me?"

"I know you were sent away because you were a mixed-House child. You weren't lucky enough to stay secret until the laws changed," I said in sympathy. "Your parents didn't deserve to die because they loved each other. It was wrong."

I drew myself up. "But I'm mixed-House, too. My parents are from different Houses, and eventually, the tribe accepted their relationship. I think our people have changed for the better."

Charlie scowled. "I wish I could believe that."

"I understand your skepticism, but you have to give your tribe a chance. The Hawkei have to stick together. It's the only way we've survived this long."

"Have there been other threats to our tribe?" he asked.

I nodded. "Yes. A hundred years ago, during the 1940s, there was a conflict called the Great Supernatural War. It was the biggest war of our time. Nobody had ever seen anything like it before. The fae, the angels, and the vampires joined together against the witches, the mermaids, and the Astromancers."

"What did the fae want to do?" Charlie asked.

"They wanted to expose magic to the humans, and enslave them, along with any other supernatural races they deemed inferior," I said. "It was a huge deal."

"What side did the Hawkei take?" Charlie asked.

"The Elementai tried to stay out of it, but eventually, we had no choice. We had to side with the witches, and stop the other side from destroying the supernatural world. We won, but millions of supernaturals died to keep magic a secret. The Elves went extinct as a result of it."

"The Elves?" Charlie asked.

"Yes. There was a genocide committed against them. There's none left now, because the Great Supernatural War took place. The Elven Union was wiped out. The fae, the vampires and the angels made it a point to exterminate them, and unfortunately, they succeeded before we could stop them."

I shifted uneasily. "Even now, the peace between supernatural races is very uneasy. The wrong thing could tip the balance and send the world back into chaos. Some people even say the Great Supernatural War could happen again, during our time."

Charlie frowned. "Let's hope it never does."

"Maybe." I was worried. If the students at the Institute were any indication of cooperation between magical races, we were bound to go to war again any day.

Charlie took a breath. "Okay. Tell me more about the Hawkei religion— what we worship."

"The Hawkei believe that everything on our planet has a spirit, from the smallest rock to the tallest tree, to the fastest fish to the stillest deer. Everything has an energy they can use to influence the world around them, and a name they can call their own."

Charlie nodded. "I can understand that. I can feel the spirits of the earth when I use my magic to navigate the world. I can even feel the spirit of the rock we're sitting in."

"Exactly. This is why the Elementai respect our earth. We give thanks whenever we plant a seed to grow, or take the life of a creature so we can feed our families. Everything is alive and deserves to be treated with reverence. This is how the Great Spirit intended us to live."

"Who's the Great Spirit?"

"Many indigenous tribes worship their own variation of the Great Spirit. To the Hawkei, he — or she, as I view her— is the Creator of the entire world," I spread my arms wide, and the shadows the fire cast flickered off the wall. "The Great Spirit breathed life into all, and takes life away. He has no end or beginning, merely always was. At the beginning of the world, the Great Spirit separated into hundreds, even thousands of gods. Some pieces became the moon, and the sun. Others became gods like Coyote Spirit, the deity of the Koigni tribe, or Whale Spirit, the deity of Toaqua. The Great Spirit is beyond understanding and manifests in all things. There is a part of him living in all beings, including you and me."

Charlie's look was introspective as Oberi nuzzled his hair. "I always felt like there was *something* out there. Didn't know what, though."

"Most magical races are in agreement there's a divine force at work in the world, though many can't agree which philosophy is right. Hawkei are accepting and inclusive in all religions. We don't dispute that the Goddess of the Miriamic Coven, or the Seven Gods the fae worship, or any other gods in the magical world, are wrong, because in our eyes, they're all just different pieces and variations of the same deity. All gods are the Great Spirit to us."

"That makes sense." Charlie leaned forward, his head in his hand. "What about the afterlife?"

"Our hell is *Aiya Nocshun*— the Mighty Darkness. You don't go there unless the ancestors banish you," I explained. "Most Hawkei go to the Ancestral Lands. You merge with your Familiar and your element, and your soul is united in harmony with the ancestors for eternity afterward."

Charlie's lip curled in disgust. "So… when I get to the Ancestral Lands, I have to share Oberi's body with you for the rest of my freaking existence?"

"Trust me, I'm not thrilled about it either," I shot back at him.

"Why do the ancestors get to decide everything?" Charlie asked. "It seems like they have a lot of power."

"Because that's what the Great Spirit has called upon them to do. We ask them for guidance, and for help on our journey. Some ancestors volunteer to become our spirit guides. They are chosen when we are born, and guide us along our life path."

I picked up the drum. "Firstborns of chieftains can summon the ancestors on any given day. Firstborns inherit the tribe they originate from, and keep our traditions alive and safe," I explained. "I'm going to summon your ancestors and your spirit guides for you, so you can meet them."

"Meet them?" Charlie lunged back.

"Yes. Sit back and shut up."

Charlie scowled. "Just what should I be expecting, here?"

I bit my lip as I began to concentrate. "When my dad summons the ancestors, it's always a big show, you know. Lots of colors, a huge tunnel full of Hawkei spirits that have passed on. My magic's a little quieter. You'll see."

I played the drum and began to sing in Hawkei. When my voice rang out, Charlie stiffened. His expression became complicated as my voice lifted and fell on the different notes, blending with the sounds of the bells and the drum.

Other voices began to join in… that of our ancestors. It created a heavenly harmony of thousands of songs, forging together to create a unanimous chorus. The anthem blended with the sound of a flute upon the air. I stopped playing the drum and removed the wristlet, but the sound of the drum kept pounding, and the bells continued to quiver and shake. Charlie didn't question where the music came from. He relaxed into the song, enjoying the beautiful melody the ancestors were creating.

I lit the sage, then threw dirt into the bowl and called water up from the ground beneath me. Droplets hovered through the air and splattered into the bowl moments before my Fire magic ignited the incense, burning it and the leather bag to smoldering embers.

Once the incense had burned to ash, I grabbed the embers and scattered them throughout the air. The embers hovered there for a moment before the cave exploded with colors.

Beams of blue, green, purple and orange flickered around the cave, like the Aurora Borealis lighting up the skies. The lights danced off the walls of the stone room, and from within them, shadows emerged. Like cave paintings our ancestors had created so long ago, images of animals began forming against the stone. There were dragons, winged deer, serpents and hippogriffs. A whale swam upon the air, while a tiger roared beside it. There were kelpies, krakens, and every other kind of animal imaginable twirling around us in the cave. Some were even extinct, long forgotten by the Hawkei but never by the ancestors.

The creatures ran along the stone wall, until they pulled themselves free and began taking on wispy spiritual forms. The cave became packed with dozens of ancestors. A group of salmon swam by, twirling around me and lifting my hair. I laughed as a thunderbird flew overhead, dancing with an eagle and a flaming firebird while a black wolf kept up beneath them.

Charlie couldn't see the spectacular show around him, but he could feel it. He stood slowly and put out a shaking hand. The ancestors began passing through his fingers. He shivered when he felt the cold skin of the whale, and the feathery torso of the thunderbird as they passed by. Charlie gasped as an enfield— a fox-bird hybrid— passed straight through his chest, as if taking his spirit with him. I could feel the chilly connection the ancestor made through our bond, and shivers ran across my skin.

Oberi whinnied in joy, dancing her hooves upon the stone floor as a Pegasus reared beside her. The creatures came down to the ground of the cave, and as they did so, transformed into people. So many faces appeared in the cave, all of them Hawkei, all of them gone on. They began to dance in time with the music, turning around us as their feet stomped into the earth.

Charlie could feel the vibrations the ancestors made as they danced, hear their song and experience the electrical currents of magical energy they emitted. He turned in place, as if his magic was going haywire trying to keep up with it all.

Five ancestors landed beside me. I waved as I recognized their familiar faces, as I'd summoned them and met them before. A snow leopard transformed into a gorgeous woman with long black hair that trailed upon the ground. A jackalope hopped by my feet and changed into a tall man with a smirking gaze. A three-headed dragon, covered in white feathers, became a tiny girl who'd died young. Beside her danced a hippocampus, a horse with a mermaid tail, who changed into a strong man with clear eyes.

Their clothing was from different time periods, Hawkei that had lived and died while scattered amongst history. The only spirit guide I could name was the grizzly bear beside me, which transformed into a tall, broad-shouldered man who looked so much like my father. He was my Grandpa Liwanu, and he'd died in the Hawkei Civil War. He was one of my spirit guides, and I'd seen him many times. My ancestors bowed to me, and I bowed back before they retreated to join the dance.

Charlie's ancestors came down before him, too. A lynx with horns became a Hawkei brave, his head shaved and arms decorated with indigenous tattoos. A manticore roared, twitching its scorpion tail before he transformed into a pixie-like woman who was thin and mischievous. A tiny deer with wings on its ankles jumped from this place to that, before taking shape into an old woman with a wizened face and a wise grin. A snowy owl became a woman with white hair. She had strange markings on her face that looked like warrior tattoos, but I couldn't place from what tribe. Lastly, the enfield changed into a man with blonde hair, standing before Charlie with a kind and welcoming smile.

Charlie's ancestors looked strong. Instead of bowing to him, they reached out to brush against his hand. Charlie nearly lunged backward, as if in shock, but I was proud to say he kept his feet in place. His mouth dropped open in awe as he observed his spirit guides in his own special way.

Eventually, the ancestors' song grew too loud for us to bear, and their dancing made the stone walls shake so violently, I was afraid the stone room would collapse with their power. I called water from the air, and as a puddle formed in my hand, I knelt to pour the droplets over the last remaining bits of incense that was still burning, bringing the ceremony to an end.

The dance ceased, and the ancestors vanished, taking the music with them and causing the room to go absolutely silent. The lights went with them, casting us into darkness again. Our presence was lit only by the small flame of my fireball, which was still burning on the floor.

There was nothing between Charlie and me but silence, and the sound of Oberi's huffing as she blew wind through her nose. "Well?" I asked. "Was that cool, or what?"

"That was way better than cool. It was *amazing*." Charlie's voice was mystified. "I can't believe I really met my ancestors."

"Yeah." I frowned. "I'm sorry you couldn't see them."

"It's hard to explain, but... I *can* see them, in my head," Charlie said. "When they connect with me, I know what they look like. I saw them once they touched me."

"That's awesome." I'd never heard of that happening before. "Now that you've met them, maybe you can try connecting with them on your own."

"How can I do that?" Charlie asked.

"You can meditate. Sometimes they'll send messages. Other times, if you ask for help, they'll send signs," I explained. "But the only way you can see them in person is to have a firstborn or a chieftain summon them, or contact them on Ancestors' Day. It's a special Hawkei holiday in May."

Oberi grew impatient. She tossed her head and tapped one of her hooves on the stone, letting out a couple of snorts.

"I think she's trying to say it's getting late," I said. "We've been here a while. We should get back, before the guards start creeping around."

"Yeah. Let's go."

I gathered my things, and we left the stone room. The sight of the broken bow in the corner was still on my mind, even long after we'd abandoned it for the darkness of the forest.

Charlie's tone was cautious. "So... since you're firstborn, and firstborns inherit the tribe, are you going to become the Toaqua chieftess someday?"

My soul filled with dread. "I don't think I'm my father's first choice to lead the Toaqua tribe anymore."

"Why not? If you're firstborn, isn't it your obligation?"

"I've got a lot of criminal charges on my record," I pointed out.

"Which will be wiped away if we win the Darke Games, or if you graduate from the Institute," Charlie objected. "Your past won't get in the way of you leading the Water tribe."

I sighed. "I know that Daddy *wants* me to be chieftess. But that's not me. I want to explore the world. I don't desire to stay in any place long enough to get comfortable. Traveling is my passion. I always have to be in a new location. Being a leader would bore me. I have no interest in becoming a chieftess."

I tucked a strand of hair behind my ear. "Besides... there's never *been* a Toaqua chieftess before. The leaders of the Water tribe have all been male. I don't want to be the first. There's too much expectation on me to be perfect, so I can leave the door open for other female leaders in the future. If I screw it up, who's to say they'll let another woman have power in the Toaqua tribe again?"

"What about your brother?"

I nearly laughed. "Ezekiel would make an awful chief. He can't make tough decisions, and he's a follower, not a leader. He does whatever I tell him to... not to mention he's too easily influenced."

"Well, someone has to lead the Water tribe."

"I know." My voice was very disheartened. "I don't want it to be me, but I'll probably have no choice, in the end."

"At least you have a future," Charlie replied dully. "I know where I come from now, but I still don't know who I am, or what I want."

"You'll figure it out, Charlie." I really wanted him to. He deserved to have a future.

But I wanted him to be able to choose his *own* future, for himself. It was the one luxury he was afforded that I was not. No matter what I did, I could never escape my birthright, the prophecy… or my fate as the chosen one.

My future was already chosen for me. I had no choice but to follow it.

charlie

THIRTEEN

I never pictured anything incredible would take place at the Institute, but meeting my ancestors was one of the most amazing things that had ever happened to me.

I'd never been very religious. I'd tried to learn Christianity in one of my foster homes— but that ended quickly when my foster dad claimed I was blind because I was a sinner. At twelve years old, I was more or less looking for answers no god could give me.

I never really connected with anything until that moment in the cave. Everything Ava said— about our ancestors, about the Great Spirit— it all made sense. And there was no denying the ancestors now, not after I'd witnessed them for myself. For the first time in a long time, I felt like I actually had answers.

I was still riding the high a week later on my way to my Substance Abuse class. I'd taken the class seriously the first couple of weeks, until I overheard two of my classmates making a drug deal in the middle of class— literally. I didn't know how anyone managed to sneak drugs into the school, but I wouldn't be surprised if there was enough magic in this place to brew it yourself. As soon as I realized how many drugs were being passed around inside the Institute, I gave up on the class. The staff was too clueless to notice. I didn't trust them to properly teach the subject.

Besides, I didn't need to be told to stay away from drugs. I'd had enough bad experiences to run at the first sight of them.

Oberi led me into the classroom, though I'd become accustomed to my normal route now. I didn't need to hang on to him anymore. We didn't have assigned seats in here, and every couple of classes, Mad Dog and his jerk friends would sit in a new spot, just to get a rise out of someone. The rest of the class had quickly picked up on their tactics and stopped falling for it. I could hear them across the room, blabbing loudly like they owned the place. It was obvious they craved attention.

Oberi guided me to an empty chair, and I sat. I listened in as the guy in front of me twisted around.

"Five bucks says Mad Dog initiates a fist-fight before the end of class," he offered.

For a second, I wasn't sure he was talking to me. "Oh, uh. I don't have the cash."

"Right." He sounded disappointed. "Then how about a bar of soap?"

Everything was hard to come by at the Institute, even simple toiletries. People fought over them all the time. "That sounds fair," I agreed. "Though I'm not sure I'd want to bet against that. He's got one hell of a temper."

The guy in front of me snorted. "You could say that again."

"*But*," I added, "I suppose I could use another bar of soap. I'll take my chances."

I held out my hand, and he shook it. His hand was warm, so I figured I wasn't dealing with a vampire.

"Wesley," he introduced. "You're Charlie, right?"

I furrowed my brow. "How'd you know?"

"There's only one blind kid in this school with a guide dog," he said sheepishly.

"Ah, so I'm a hot piece of gossip? I thought that would've died down by now."

"Don't worry about it," he promised. "It's only people like Mad Dog who give you shit. Everyone else figures you must be innocent."

I reared back a little in my chair. "They do?"

"Sure," he said nonchalantly. "What kind of trouble could a blind kid get into?"

I frowned. "Well, that's stereotypical, but you're half right. I *did* get roped into coming here. What are you in for?"

He paused a moment before answering. "Battery."

My eyebrows shot up. "Oh, wow. It must've been bad to end up here."

"It was pretty bad," Wesley admitted. "Almost killed the guy."

"Wow, what'd he do to deserve that?" It wasn't an unusual question to ask at the Institute. Most people were pretty open about why they were here— either to claim innocence or to show how tough they were.

"Some low-life vamp passing through Malovia tried to drag my sister off the street," he said.

Malovia. Wesley must've been a shifter of some sort— a male Arcanea descended from the fae.

"I'm sorry," I said honestly. "I hope she's okay."

"Oh, she made it out just fine," he said proudly. "Can't say the same for the other guy. Sent him straight to the ICU."

"Good for you," I said. It sounded like the asshole had deserved it. Wesley on the other hand, didn't deserve to be here. He was only protecting his sister.

"And impressive," I added. I didn't know much about Arcanean shifters, but if they could kick a vampire's ass, they were a lot stronger than I initially thought.

"Thanks," he said proudly. He inhaled another breath to say something, but a scuffle on the other side of the room cut him off.

"You want a piece of this!?" a man shouted. I couldn't pick most voices out of the crowd— not unless I knew the person well, like Ava— but Mad Dog's deep voice was hard to miss. "Come at me!"

A *thud* sounded, and gasps traveled around the room.

"What was that about?" I asked Wesley.

"Looks like Jeffrey Johnson tried to challenge Mad Dog to his seat. He lost, obviously."

My shoulders slumped. "Guess I owe you that bar of soap, huh?"

"Nah," Wesley said. "Keep it. I have enough already."

Wesley's offer only confirmed for me he didn't belong here. Other students in the Institute would never pass up resources of any kind.

"What is the meaning of this!?" our professor boomed as he came through the door. He walked in so swiftly I felt the air brush off his feathery wings. Obviously he'd just witnessed the aftermath of the fist fight. It was hard to tell what was going on across the room, but judging by how quickly things had quieted, I'd have to guess Jeffrey had been knocked out in a single punch.

"Guy fell asleep," Mad Dog said nonchalantly. "Must have narcolepsy or something."

"Guards!" our professor shouted down the hall. The shuffle of three pairs of footsteps arrived within moments. "Handle this, will you? I have a class to teach."

The guards dragged Jeffrey, Mad Dog, and a few of his friends out of the room, and the class quieted.

Professor Gael began his lecture immediately. This kind of thing happened so frequently at the Institute, no one batted an eye. It was always the newbies who were most sensitive to it.

"Substance abuse comes in many forms," Professor Gael began. "We have talked about many drugs and their side effects in this class. What we haven't talked about is how to recognize the symptoms of substance abuse in others. Should you notice any of the following symptoms in your fellow classmates, you should report it immediately— so that your friends may be cared for properly."

It sounded like he'd tacked on that ending as an afterthought, to placate us. I got the sense that the Institute was more interested in punishing drug addicts than helping them.

"An individual suffering from substance abuse may show less interest in school or hobbies," Professor Gael continued. "They might refuse to sit with you in the dining hall, or stop hanging out with you in the recreation room. You may notice they stop eating and start losing weight. Their physical appearance might change, such as showering less, or neglecting to wear a clean uniform."

He went on and on with this, but I already knew it all. I'd been around drug use first-hand one too many times. And to be honest, he was hard to take seriously. Professor Gael spoke like he was a saint. He was an angel, so there was no surprise there, but I'd bet he never touched a drug in his life. This guy didn't seem to know shit what it was *actually* like to take drugs— only what he'd read out of a textbook.

I was relieved when class got out. The first thing I noticed when I left the classroom was Oberi stiffening at my side. Then I heard the sound of Ava-Marie's voice down the hall.

"I will not!" she shouted. "Who do you think you are?"

"Uh, oh," Wesley muttered under his breath. My stomach sank.

"I'm campus security," a man sneered. "And you'll do as you're told, or you'll answer to the Warden. Empty your pockets."

Oberi took off running, and I followed quickly behind. My Familiar stopped next to Ava, growling lowly at the guard.

"This is a violation of my privacy," Ava argued.

"Pidge, what's going on?" I asked.

The guard ignored me. "You want to know what noxite cuffs feel like?" he threatened Ava. "Because I can slap them on *real* fast."

I reached out for her hand to find that they were clenched into fists. Her whole body shook. "We don't want any trouble—"

"Step back, or you'll be next!" the guard thundered.

I was suddenly aware of how quiet the hall had become. I sensed a crowd forming, but they barely moved.

"What's going on?" a girl hissed to someone.

Wesley was close by and answered her in a low whisper. "Hey, Alice. Looks like a drug bust or something."

The guard waited another moment, but Ava didn't move. The sound of clinking chains met my ears, and I knew he'd pulled out his noxite cuffs.

Oberi's growl intensified, and I grabbed Ava by the shoulders. "Pidge, you have to do as you're told."

"I'm not doing anything I don't want to do," she snapped. Heat flashed through her arms, and I yanked my hands away like I'd touched a hot stove. The guard must've reached for her, because he yelled, too. The cuffs clinked to the ground.

"Filthy savage!" the guard yelled.

He was on her in flash— so fast it wasn't humanly possible. I could only guess he was a vampire. His elbow shoved me aside with the strength of a boulder, and the wind knocked out of my chest. I gasped for breath, and I heard Ava do the same.

"You want to know what Cellblock 9 looks like?" the guard threatened. "Because you've just earned yourself a one-way ticket for attacking a guard."

"Ah— ow!" Ava cried. "I didn't attack you! I was defending myself. Let me go!"

It took me a few moments to catch my breath and understand what was going on. By the strained sound in Ava's voice, I'd say the guard had pinned her up against the wall. His cuffs clinked again as he retrieved them from the ground. Oberi shifted into a Fire unicorn, and I could feel the anger— the intense urge to protect— rolling off her in waves. She was about to attack.

I wanted to, too. An intense fury bubbled up in my gut. Had he not been a vampire, I could suck the air right out of his lungs, but it wouldn't even faze him, I was sure. They didn't need air to breathe.

You can't attack a guard, Charlie, my rational mind reminded me. I barely heard it, but it was enough to make me switch tactics a split-second before I was about to whip up a wind storm. I had to make this better, not worse.

"Stop!" I threw myself in front of Oberi, next to the guard. "This is absurd. Sir, she's not even worth the paperwork."

"Charlie," Ava gaped. "How could you—?"

"She didn't mean to attack you," I drawled smoothly. "She's only just come into her powers, and doesn't know how to use them well. Pidge, please, just do as he asked."

"Her skill level means nothing," the guard sneered. "She's got drugs on her. I can smell it."

"I don't— ow!" Ava cried. She was in pain, as if the guard had yanked on her arm to shut her up. Oberi reared on her hind legs, but I lifted a hand to calm her.

"Ava's not doing drugs," I assured the guard.

"Oh, you want to bet on that?" he snapped.

I crossed my arms. "Actually, yeah, I do. If you search her and find anything, you can take us *both* to Cellblock 9. If you find nothing, you let her go."

The guard hesitated, obviously intrigued by my offer. We weren't supposed to make deals with the guards, but the opportunity to punish us both must've been tempting enough. I would bet he got some sort of commission off booking us both. And he seemed pretty certain Ava was hiding something.

"I suppose if she's not carrying anything, there's no reason to book her," the guard said, but I heard the darkness in his tone. He was saying it for the benefit of the onlookers— to make it look like he wasn't participating in any sort of off-limits bet. But there was enough edge to his tone that I heard the truth. He was taking me on, and he sounded certain he would win.

The guard stepped away from Ava, and she took a deep breath. "Fucking finally," she gasped.

"Pidge," I encouraged.

"Charlie—" she started to protest.

I leaned in and whispered lowly, cutting her off. "I'm trying to protect you. It's this or Cellblock 9. Just do as you're told, and we can get out of here."

Ava sucked in ragged breaths. Something about her was different today. She was more irritable than normal. I mean, the girl was *always* irritated about something, but this was different. There was no snark, no pep. Just pure fury.

"Charlie Wahkin, you owe me for this," she growled under her breath. Then she turned to the guard. "You want to see my pockets? Fine."

Fabric rustled as she turned her pockets inside out, though I didn't hear anything fall out of them.

"And for good measure, why don't you check my shoes?" she asked as she started taking them off. "And inside my socks."

She yanked her socks off and tossed them at me. I just barely caught them.

"What else do you want?" Ava demanded. "Want to check the folds of my tie?"

She tugged that off next and shoved it in my arms. "Or maybe you want to check my panties?"

Hell, she'd taken this too far. I knew she'd strip those off too under her skirt if anyone let her get that far. I grabbed her hand to stop her. "Pidge, I think that's enough."

Her arm was hot, and her voice cracked. "I *told* him I didn't have anything, and he wanted to invade my personal space anyway! And you of all people, Charlie, encouraged it. So what the hell else do you want me to do? Check my bra? I could be hiding drugs in there, couldn't I? Well, *couldn't I?*"

Ava was raging now. It wasn't in her social-justice speech kind of way, either. She was angry and hurt. I hated to think I had anything to do with that.

"That won't be necessary," the guard said, sounding slightly disgusted. He must've realized Ava wasn't kidding around, and I was sure his job would be on the line if he was caught strip-searching a student in the middle of the hall. He obviously didn't want to deal with Ava, because he let it drop. "You're clearly not hiding anything. Put your clothes back on, and get out of here."

"Oh, joy," Ava said flatly, snatching her socks and tie from my arms. "You're *so* generous."

She blew a breath and began marching away, her shoes clicking together as they dangled from her fingers.

I rushed to keep up with her, and Oberi followed behind. The hall broke into chatter then, and Ava and I disappeared into the sea of students.

"Pidge, what the hell was that?" I demanded.

She didn't slow, just kept on walking like she was determined to get somewhere— anywhere but here. "I don't fucking know, Charlie. I wasn't the one who started it."

"Then tell me your side of the story," I insisted.

"Why?" she growled. "You'll just blame me, anyway."

"No, I won't," I promised. "Please, tell me what's going on."

"It's not like it affects you."

I didn't think Ava knew where she was going, other than wherever her feet took her. She stomped into a large room. Even the quiet pad of her footsteps seemed to echo off the massive ceiling. I only knew one room in the whole Institute that was this large— the chapel. It was left over from the old cathedral, and no one used it anymore.

"But it *does* affect me," I argued. I stepped around her and planted myself in front of her. She stopped in her tracks. "Like it or not, we share the same soul, and when you get pissed off, so do I. So I deserve a damn good reason why I want to rip that guard's head off."

Ava bent over, and her shoulder brushed my leg. Her socks snapped against her skin as she yanked them back on. She grabbed my shoulder for support and slipped on her shoes. She didn't say anything the whole time, as if stalling.

Finally, she said, "I don't want to talk about this here."

"Then we'll go someplace private," I insisted. "I want answers."

Ava huffed, then grabbed me by the tie. "Fine. Follow me."

She dragged me behind herself down the chapel aisle— nearly choking me— until we exited the room into a narrow hallway. She hesitated a moment, then twisted a doorknob. The door creaked open, and she pushed me inside. "In here."

It was hard to tell where we were, until I stumbled forward and caught myself on a flight of stairs. The sound of Oberi's fiery hair wisping with flames died as she shifted into husky form to fit in the narrow stairwell. I rubbed my neck and scowled.

"Well, go on," Ava said. "Up the stairs we go."

"Where does this lead?" I asked curiously.

"Don't know. But it's as good of place as any, isn't it?"

The stairwell smelled musty, like no one had been up here in a long time. The stairs twisted in a circular pattern, like we were climbing a tower. My hand ran along the wall to guide me as we went up.

Finally, the air expanded, and we entered a larger room— I could only guess it was a balcony of sorts. It was completely silent, and I knew we were alone.

Ava whirled toward me, her hair nearly brushing my face. "You want to know what happened? I don't like being told what to do, especially when it comes to my clothes and body. You should know that by now."

I knew Ava was a rebel. It was what landed her here in the first place. But there was something else she wasn't saying. I wasn't sure if it was something I sensed in her tone, or something that came through our bond, but there was real pain there— pain beyond anything I could imagine. I could only make assumptions about what it meant, and it wasn't fair of me to ask.

My anger immediately washed away, replaced by a gaping hole in my stomach. I thought it belonged to me, but then I sensed our bond, and I realized that hole inside was within *Ava*, carving her from the inside out.

"Pidge, I'm sorry," I whispered. It was all I could say.

Without thinking about it, I reached for her and drew her into a hug. It should've felt weird, but it was as natural as crawling into bed at night. Ava was warm and soft. She was wearing a perfume that smelled like pears, raspberries and sandalwood. The scent drove me completely nuts, and I couldn't explain why.

But something was different about her, too. She felt incredibly tiny in my arms... hard like stone but intensely fragile. Instinctively, I knew she was too thin.

Ava didn't shove me away like I expected. Instead, her shoulders slumped, and she melted into me. Oberi leaned into the hug, wrapping his body around us. Ava sniffled, though I could tell she was trying to hide it.

"Don't cry, pidge," I said. I didn't know how to deal with crying girls. "You'll smudge your makeup."

Ava chuckled lightly, but it was only to break the tense mood. It sounded forced. "I'm not wearing any today."

That was odd. Usually, Ava was all fashion, hair, and makeup. I didn't care, since I wouldn't know the difference either way, but I knew it mattered to her. Something was obviously really bothering her, and it set me on edge.

"Ava..." I started cautiously. "You *aren't* doing drugs, are you?"

Hell, that was the wrong thing to say, and I knew it the second it came out of my mouth.

"What? *No!*" She instantly pushed me away. "How could you say that, Charlie? And all those other things you said— that I'm not even worth the paperwork, and I'm not talented. Do you really hate me that much?"

"Absolutely not," I promised. "I lied so he'd go easy on you."

She quieted. "Oh," she said. "You lied?"

"Of course. You didn't actually think I thought those things, did you?" I raked my fingers through my hair. "Pidge, that guard would be *damn* lucky to run your paperwork. And you're the most talented Elementai I know."

It didn't mean much, since I barely knew any Elementai, but Ava seemed to soften at the compliment.

"How did you know I didn't have any drugs on me?" she asked in an even tone.

"I didn't," I admitted. "I only had to trust that I knew you, and apparently, I do. Why'd the guard suspect you, anyway?"

"I don't know. I was just coming from taking my meds when he started accusing me of stuff and threatening to search me. He's a vamp, so I guess he smelled my medication and jumped to conclusions. I refused to be searched, and you saw the rest."

"Pidge…" I blew a breath. I wanted to tell her that she had to follow the rules around here, but how could I say that when I agreed with her? No one had a right to touch her without her consent. And yet pushing back would get you in trouble. It wasn't fair.

I didn't know how to put it all into words, so instead, I asked, "Where are we?"

Ava turned, and her heels clicked across the room. "Some sort of music room above the chapel."

Something screeched across the wooden floor, and Ava mumbled something about *so much dust*. Then came the sound of a music note filling the room— middle C, I realized immediately, from an organ. I half expected the sound of the organ to fill the whole chapel outside our private sanctuary, but it was quiet... meant only for us.

I walked over to join her. "Mind if I sit?"

The fabric of her skirt rustled as she slid down the bench to make room for me. "Go ahead."

There was enough room on the bench for both of us, though we were close enough that our elbows touched. Something strange happened in my chest when her skin brushed mine. It was so foreign, like my heart had turned to light, airy clouds.

Ava had gone really quiet. I didn't know what else to do but reach out and begin moving my fingers over the keys. I tinkered the tune to *Fur Elise* with one hand.

"I didn't know you played," Ava said lightly.

I shrugged. "I know a song or two."

A few beats passed, then Ava started snickering.

"What?" I asked, hovering my hand above the keys.

"Don't stop," she said. "Oberi was dancing. Well, more or less swaying. I think he likes it."

"Oh, well, I've got you covered, boy." I ran my fingers over the keys and found middle C again. My fingers moved on what felt like their own accord as I transitioned to an upbeat tune. I hadn't played in years, but my memory didn't fail me. It was like riding a bike.

Oberi's paws padded on the hardwood, and he yipped in excitement.

"Ancestors, he's adorable," Ava snickered. I was just glad to be cheering her up. "What song is that? *Piano Man*?"

"Yeah. An oldie, but a goodie."

"So, are you like, a child prodigy?" she asked, sounding serious.

I frowned. "Way to go stereotyping the blind guy."

"I thought being blind made your other senses better," she said, obviously meaning no offense. "Aren't blind people supposed to be good at music?"

"As good or bad as anyone else," I replied, never missing a beat. "I can only play because of all the practice I had as a kid."

"Oh," she said flatly, like she didn't know what else to say. Another totally non-Ava mood. Usually she had more than enough to say. "Charlie, can I ask you something?"

"Sure."

"Why did you run away from the guard?"

I stopped playing. Oberi whined lightly, and the organ echoed a few moments before the room fell completely silent.

"I wasn't *running*, pidge. I was…"

"You were running," she finished before I could find a better phrase for it.

"There are certain things you have to do in here to survive," I told her. "Like *not* getting thrown in Cellblock 9."

"You keep talking like that, and it's driving me nuts," she complained.

"Talking like what?"

"You use that word all the time. *Survive.* Ugh, I hate it."

I was starting to get a little irritated with her again. "Doesn't everyone want to survive?"

"Not like you," she said matter-of-factly.

I furrowed my brow. "What's that supposed to mean?"

"You want to *survive*, not *live*."

"What's the difference?"

She blew a breath, obviously exasperated with me. "You don't get the difference, do you? You'd rather dig your own grave and take your time doing it than anything else. I'd rather die young than live a life that's not worth living."

"That's the problem, pidge," I practically growled. "I don't want you to die in here."

"Don't you get it, Charlie!?" Her voice rose several pitches. "I wouldn't have cared if that guard took me down to Cellblock 9 for sucker-punching his ass. I'd die there, but at least I'd go out punching a vampire. That's more than you can say. What have you ever done?"

My nostrils flared. I thought Ava and I at least had a clue about each other by now. Turns out, she didn't know a damn thing about me. "I'm not the one who doesn't get it, pidge. *You* obviously haven't been pushed hard enough into survival mode that it's your only option left."

"Oh, I've been pushed," she argued.

"Yeah, and you're still pushing back," I growled. "I've reached the point where I can't push back anymore. Because I know what happens to people who do."

The thought of Ava pushing to her limits terrified me, because I knew it was a real possibility. I couldn't lose her.

You know… because she was part of my soul or whatever.

I winced as the possibilities flipped through my mind. She'd piss a guard off and be sentenced for life, or get in a fight with a siren and be eaten alive. There were a million ways for her to die in here, each one more gruesome than the last.

I did the only thing I knew to get rid of the thoughts. I started playing the organ. It was a soft, slow melody in a minor key, one I knew she wouldn't recognize. I was half surprised I remembered it after all these years. Then again, how could I forget? I was the one who wrote it.

"I didn't always think like this," I explained as I continued playing the tune. "I guess that's what happens when life beats you down."

Ava didn't say anything. Usually, she couldn't seem to control her big mouth. Today, I was grateful for the silence. I wasn't sure I could tell her the truth if she interrupted me.

"Until Professor Baine found me, I didn't know what happened to my parents," I continued. "All I knew was I was put into the foster care system long before I could remember anything else. I spent my entire life hopping from home to home— if I can even call it that. I've never really had a *home*."

I wasn't sure if it was conscious or not, but Ava leaned closer to me. Her arm brushed against mine, sending tingles across my skin.

The confessions continued to pour out of me. "As I aged out of the foster care system, I moved to Detroit and went on the search for a job— a real job so I could take care of myself. At this point, it was easy to convince everyone else I wasn't blind, but I couldn't convince employers. No way could I work construction without being able to see the blueprints, or work a cash register without knowing which dollar bills a customer handed me."

I paused for a moment, wondering how far I would take the confessions. Ava hadn't said a word, though, and her warm arm was comforting on mine. I actually felt like I could talk to her — *trust* her, even— which was something I hadn't found in a long time.

I continued. "One day, I was down on my luck and just had another job rejection in a long string of denials. I had a single dollar in my pocket and was starving, so I bought the largest thing I could get at the convenience store for a dollar— a slushie. When I finished it, I slumped to the ground on the edge of the sidewalk and placed my cup beside me. I thought I'd abandon it. To my surprise, I heard the sound of a coin clink into the cup. Then another, and another. That was the first time I realized that I didn't need a *job* to make money. Hell, I was *blind!* People would just hand it to me if they felt sorry enough."

I reached the end of the song and started playing it from the beginning again. "The first day, I made enough to get myself off the streets and into a hostel for the night. It was there I met Marty. He soon became my closest friend. He assured me panhandling would only get me so far, and that the only way to make real money was by running cons and a hell of a lot of other illegal shit— drug dealing and illegal gambling, to name a few. If it was criminal and made us money, we probably did it."

I started to choke up at the thought of Marty. My hands slowed over the keys, until I was playing long notes that didn't seem to suit any melody. But I couldn't take the silence, so I let the organ play.

"Marty was shot three years later," I choked out. "He couldn't pay his debt to his drug dealer, and they got to him. The man taught me everything I know— including to stay the hell away from drugs. Never touched any after that. But hell, I survived."

But Marty hadn't, and that shook me to my core.

"We were just walking down the street…" I shuddered as I worked up the courage to revisit that night. "A car drove by, and six shots rang out. I didn't even realize what had happened before the car drove away. Marty collapsed and… never got back up."

Ava reached out and placed her hand over mine. I stopped playing, and the room fell eerily silent. But there was warmth in the air, too. It wasn't so unbearable when she was next to me.

"My best friend died, too," she whispered.

My spine straightened. How was it that we had that in common? It didn't seem fair to either of us. "Really? How?"

"It's hard to talk about," she said, before redirecting the conversation. "That's why you focus on just surviving. Because you don't want to get hurt like your friend did."

I ducked my head. Hell if she saw me cry. I didn't do shit like that. "I'm one hell of a con man, pidge, but I can't outtalk a bullet. That's why I try not to stay in one place too long, because I don't want to draw attention to myself."

"I think I get it now, Charlie," she said softly.

"What do you mean?"

"I get why you don't want to go through with the Darke Games, and why you're so passive with the guards," she said. "You *have* to focus on survival, because you've never known anything else. I never had to worry about where my next meal was coming from, or if I'd be sleeping in a warm bed at night."

"Yeah," I scoffed, feeling kind of jealous of her. "If I can make it to the night with food in my belly and a roof over my head, I'm golden."

"So you almost *want* to stay, don't you?" Ava asked.

I shrugged. I'd never thought of it *that* way, but she had a point. At least in here I knew I wasn't going to starve.

"I'm sorry, Charlie," Ava whispered.

"For what? None of it is your fault."

"I'm sorry you've never had the chance to live."

That struck a chord with me, and the room went really quiet. Oberi padded over to me and rested his head on my knee. I wondered what it was like to live by Ava's definition. She seemed carefree at times, like she actually had something to stand up for besides herself. Her social justice speeches weren't just for her benefit, I realized. She wanted things to change for everyone, for life to give us all an equal shot at greatness.

I hadn't noticed before now how vastly differently we approached things. I always knew I had it rough, but I assumed people like Ava didn't have anything to worry about. I'd thought her behavior was over-the-top and irrational, because she didn't know what it was like to truly struggle. Now that she pointed out we were experiencing things from a different perspective, I realized she worried as much as I did— just about different things.

I didn't want to have to keep worrying about myself. It was damn exhausting. I wished I could be like Ava. She didn't seem to care what happened to her... only what happened to other people.

Ava took her hand off mine, and I began tinkering on the organ again. "So, how did you learn the piano?" she asked.

I sighed as the memories came back to me. "I was forced to learn by one of my foster moms. She thought it'd be good for me because I was blind. She wanted to give me something to do. Turns out, she was using the piano to babysit me and keep me out of the way of her in-house brothel."

"Ew," Ava said. "I can't believe you lived in places like that."

I shrugged. "It was normal. I can't believe you grew up next door to a castle. To be honest, it wasn't the worst place I've been."

"What do you mean by that?" she asked curiously.

I swallowed the lump in my throat. "I lived on the streets. I had to do what I could to survive, and winters can be harsh in Detroit. There were times I had to go home with someone just to stay warm."

Ava stiffened beside me. "Wait. You mean... people took advantage of you?"

"Yes... and no," I hesitated. "We both took advantage of each other. The woman would use my body, and I would sleep in a warm bed and get something to eat. Sometimes, I'd take things before I left, then sell them off on the streets. It'd hold me over for a while."

"That doesn't make what those women did right," Ava said in disgust.

"It was necessary," I replied. It was all consensual— even if I didn't care for the physical part. But it was better than freezing to death on a park bench.

"I'm sorry you had to do that," Ava whispered. After a few beats, she spoke again. "Charlie, can I ask you something?"

"Sure," I said. I'd already made it through the hard stuff. I had nothing to hide from her. If I didn't tell her now, she'd figure it out eventually. She was part of my own soul, for the ancestors' sake.

"How did you go blind?" she asked in a small voice.

I stiffened at first, but I relaxed a little the more I played. "I went blind when I was three, and don't remember much before that. I don't remember how it happened, and nobody ever told me. It was a medical fluke, they said. It's actually unusual to be totally blind, to see absolutely nothing like I do. Most blind people can see *something*— shadows or colors, maybe even just blurry images. It's not like that for me, which made it extra strange."

"You hide it so well," she remarked. "Is that because of your magic?"

I shrugged. "Partially, maybe. I don't have cataracts, so people can't tell at first-glance. Honestly, I just try not to bring attention to it."

"Why not?" She sounded confused. "It's part of who you are. Shouldn't you embrace that?"

She almost spoke like there was beauty to my blindness.

"I didn't want to be treated differently," I admitted, though I rushed to clarify. "I wasn't always treated differently for my blindness. But when I was, people would go to one extreme or the other. Like, foster moms would coddle me extra hard, or kids would bully me. It wasn't uncommon for other foster children to steal my belongings or take food off my plate— straight from under my nose."

I took a deep breath. "When I was fourteen, a group of boys from school cornered me and beat me up before stealing my cane. I was forced to navigate the urban streets without it and find my way back to my foster home alone. My foster parents agreed to buy me a new one, but I was moved to another home shortly afterward, before I ever received a new cane. I was shocked at how well people treated me when I didn't have it. At first, I thought they just felt sorry for me. But the more I began to navigate the world without my cane, the more I realized that without it, people couldn't tell I was blind. Finally, no one stole my food when they thought I had my eyes on my plate. My belongings were safe. Of course, I had multiple run-ins with bullies after that, but it was always for something else— never because I was blind. I learned from then on to act as if I could see. If I did, no one took advantage of me."

"How did you manage without a cane?" Ava leaned closer, sounding intrigued.

"I used my other senses and learned tricks to navigate my world," I told her. "I'd fold bills in certain ways so I knew which ones I was grabbing to pay for things. I had my own way of navigating the world without sight. If I focused hard enough, I could create images in my mind of the world around me just by concentrating on the air pressure. I learned to hone the skill, until I had perfected it by the age of eighteen."

"So, you're like *Daredevil?*" Ava asked. "You're not *really* blind because your magic helps you."

Ava didn't sound like she meant anything by it, but the question rubbed me the wrong way. I'd been compared to the comic book character one too many times. I hated it.

"It's not the same thing," I assured her, trying to keep an even tone. "My powers don't negate my blindness. I'm the same as I was before I got them. I'm just better at hiding it. My powers simply *became* my cane, a tool to help me navigate my environment. I still experience the world as a blind person. Yeah, maybe my magic gives me an advantage, but there's still a lot I miss out on and times I need to ask for help."

"I didn't mean to offend you," she said softly, and I realized how harsh my tone had grown. "I just meant sometimes it seems like you *can* see things."

"I don't, though. I just experience the world in a different way," I explained. "Like I know when someone is walking toward me, because I can hear their footsteps, or I can hear when they turn away from me by the sound of their voice."

Ava's elbow bumped against mine as she knotted her hands in her lap. "I guess I rely too much on sight."

"You use the tools at your disposal," I said, like it was nothing. And it wasn't. "You shouldn't feel guilty about that."

Ava processed my words for a few moments, then spoke again. "How else are things different for you? Do you have to read braille to do school assignments or something?"

"No. I can't read braille," I said. "It's not something every blind person knows. I learned enough to read public signage, like numbers on the elevator. But it's a complicated language and takes years to learn. I'd like to learn, but I never had anyone to teach me. As far as school assignments go, I need accommodations, which unfortunately in my experience many teachers aren't willing to provide."

"What kind of accommodations?"

"I can't read textbooks, but I can learn through audiobooks or videos," I explained. "I can't write with a pen and paper, but I can use dictation software."

"Oh," Ava said, like the thought made her sad. "Has the Institute given you any of that?"

"No," I replied sourly. "There's the whole thing with technology working shitty around magic, right?"

"Sometimes," she said. "Depends on how much magic is being used. At the Institute, I doubt something like that would work— except maybe the ancient computers in the library. There's so much noxite here, and that's a type of magic itself. I'm sorry the school can't do better for you."

I snorted. "Don't worry about it. I'm used to it. It's why I never graduated from high school. The school wouldn't provide adequate accommodations, so they thought I was just dumb and wanted to hold me back. Couldn't keep going to school without a foster home, though, because I needed money just to live. I left as soon as I turned eighteen."

Ava seemed magnetized toward me, because her body brushed up against mine. Warm tingles spread through me, though I didn't think she meant anything by it. This bench just wasn't big enough to keep our distance.

Ava quickly dove into her next question. "What about color? Does it make any sense to you?"

"I get the concept," I told her. "And I sort of remember color from before I was blind, but it's been so long, I could be remembering it wrong. I make associations differently than you."

"What do you mean?" Ava asked. "Blue is blue. Red is red. How can you associate that with anything else?"

I smirked playfully. "They taste different."

Ava chuckled under her breath. It was good to hear her laugh, because she hadn't sounded like herself all day. "Colors don't have a *taste*, Charlie."

"Sure they do," I said. "Red tastes like strawberry candy. Blue feels like water running over your hands, or blueberries. Green is the smell of grass, and yellow is warm, like sunlight on your face."

Ava laughed and shoved me. I faltered on the notes I was playing. "You can't just make up rules."

"Sure I can." I stopped playing and shoved her back. "Rule number one: stop invading my personal space."

I poked her, and she giggled. I couldn't say it with a straight face, because the truth was, I didn't *want* Ava to respect my personal space. I wanted her next to me— to touch me.

I tossed the thought out of my mind the second I thought it. What the hell was I thinking? I *hated* Ava-Marie. And yet when she was next to me, I felt… I don't know. The closest to home I'd ever felt before.

"What was that?" she teased. "Keep invading your personal space?"

She pushed her hips and shoulder into mine on the bench. Oberi jumped back, shaking his fur and barking. I lost my balance and wrapped my arms around Ava to stay upright, but gravity had other plans. I went tumbling off the bench, dragging Ava with me. The organ keys let out noise as we smashed into them on the way down.

Ava crashed on top of me, her hips pressed into mine. She breathed rapidly, the sweet scent of her breath rushing across my cheeks. For a moment, neither of us moved. We simply lay there, my hands on her waist and her breasts heaving with each breath against my chest.

Something stirred deep within my belly. I couldn't explain it, but it must've had something to do with our bond, because I'd never felt it with anyone else before. Or maybe I was just nervous about what she thought of me now— now that I'd let myself become vulnerable with her.

My uniform slacks suddenly began to tighten. Oberi licked my face, and I came back to reality. I was suddenly aware of the very sexual position Ava and I were in. I practically shoved her off of me, and she started laughing again.

"It's not a good rule if you're not going to enforce it," she joked as she reached down to take my hand and help me up.

"It'd be a fine rule, if you didn't insist on breaking it," I shot back playfully. "But that is the Ava-Marie way. If a rule is made, she's bound to break it."

And hell, I *wanted* her to break this one.

"Damn straight," she said proudly. She still didn't quite sound like her normal self, but she seemed better than before— more relaxed, perhaps.

I cleared my throat in the following silence. "Uh, thanks, Ava."

"For what?" she asked, like she hadn't done anything.

"For listening," I said simply.

She didn't know how much I meant it. The way she sat quietly to hear my story meant a lot to me. She cared, and she was one of the first people in my life to do so.

"Oh, well, don't mention it," she said, but there was something in her tone that didn't match her words. It was soft and delicate— like the conversation had meant something to her, too.

"We should probably get back downstairs," she suggested quickly. "Someone might start wondering where we went."

"Yeah." I cleared my throat. "Probably best."

Except I didn't want to leave here. As Ava turned and Oberi followed dutifully down the stairs, I couldn't help but stand there and simply take in the room— the smell of the dust that seemed sweet now, and the sound of Ava's footsteps echoing up the twisted staircase.

This was our little hidden corner of the Institute. I'd shared things with her here that I'd never spoken about to anyone before. The confessions seemed to permeate the walls, to sink into the keys on the organ, and would remain there permanently in this place.

Our place.

ava-marie

FOURTEEN

"Ancestors' cock," I cursed under my breath as the sunlight illuminated the pages of the journal. I wiped the sleep from my eyes and read the prophecy over again, but like the million times I had before, it didn't make any sense.

I slammed my head into my pillow. I'd been up all night, deciphering the journal, and it was just as confusing as it had been the first day I got it. This was getting me nowhere. I tossed the journal against the other side of my dorm, where it slid against the wall and propped open against the ground.

I'd been studying the journal every day for weeks, and I hadn't made any progress with the prophecy. It was the only thing I could do, seeing as how I was still trapped within these walls. I figured there had to be *something* in the journal that would give me a clue on where to start investigating the prophecy once I got the hell out of here.

There was nothing. I'd read the journal a million times, and though I'd memorized countless wordings, drawings, and hints, none of it made any sense. I'd spoken to Mama about it, but she insisted the prophecy would unfold itself when I was ready, and not before.

I didn't have time. I wanted to stop this *now*, before people got hurt. I was tired of being an instrument of fate.

Your destiny is uncontrollable.

Everyone's after you.

Hide, Ava!

I had to get up. I had class in fifteen minutes. I forced myself out of bed and picked the same uniform I'd worn yesterday off the floor. It was wrinkled and dirty, but I didn't give a shit. I couldn't be bothered to care what I looked like. I slipped it on and tied back my hair without brushing out the tangles that had formed within. I was breaking out along my nose, and yet, I didn't reach for any concealer. On a different day, a single blemish was enough to send me spiraling into a breakdown.

Today? Fuck it all.

My reflection was haunted and gaunt. I looked like a freaking mess. The depression had pulled me so low, I had bags under my eyes. But I'd rolled out of bed, so that was a plus for me. On days like today, breathing felt like a curse.

I was in a low period. A very low period. I missed my family. I'd give anything to talk face-to-face with Daddy, or have a plate of some of my mother's famous Italian. I really wanted to write a song with Ez, go shopping with Alana, or work on the bike with Maverick in the garage. I'd never been away from them this long before, and it was eating me up from the inside out.

The only thing that seemed to help was having Oberi around... and Charlie. There was something different between us— I sensed it now. The way he'd opened up to me the other night felt raw and special. I didn't think he'd ever told someone his story before.

I couldn't imagine what Charlie had been through. To be forced to prostitute yourself for a safe place to stay the night...

I shivered. Our lives were so different, but even though I couldn't understand what he went through, I could still empathize. The only reason I'd had everything I wanted growing up was because I was privileged enough to have rich parents with a lot of power and influence. As a mixed-House child, if the Hawkei Civil War had been lost, I could've easily ended up like Char-lie... shuffled from foster home to foster home and desperate to survive.

If Charlie kept fighting, I had to, too. I opened the door and found Oberi outside, waiting for me in the hallway in her unicorn form. She stomped up to me and pushed me over. I went falling back into the wall.

"Ow, Oberi, what the hell?" I complained.

She huffed and shook her head, three times in a row. Her fiery mane went everywhere, and she bumped me again, tossing her head in a circle.

She wanted her mane braided today. I laughed and grabbed a couple of hair ties from my pocket before I started in on her mane. I felt tingles go up and down my fingers as they touched the flames, braiding the tendrils of fire together so they made a beautiful array. My Koigni magic made it so I didn't feel the heat or experience any burns. As I worked, Oberi's eyes closed in relaxation.

"You like being pampered, huh, girl?" I asked.

She nickered as I finished my work. When we passed a mirror in the hallway, Oberi stopped and admired her reflection before pursing out her lips, exposing her teeth and waving her mouth in the air.

Ancestors, she was an attention hog. I giggled and patted her shoulder. "You're gorgeous, Oberi. The prettiest unicorn there ever was."

Smoke emitted from her nostrils as she snorted, as if to say, *I better be.*

Supernatural Behavioral Science was a class about intermagical cooperation. It was held in a dark classroom at the end of the Institute that was damp and musty. When I walked in, I felt a chill wash over me. It was always freezing in here. I heard strange moans, like that ghosts made, and it caused the hair to stand up on the back of my neck. The classroom was decorated with skeletons of supernatural creatures, as well as a skull I was sure was from a vampire, due to the fangs. Fairy wings were held up by pins in glass cases on the walls, and the fin of a mermaid was placed in a case on the teacher's desk in front of the room.

A dragon skeleton hung suspended from the ceiling. I was certain our teacher had killed it herself. Professor McCauley was an Air Elementai who seriously took no shit. She appeared like a corpse, taunt yellow skin and beady eyes, held together by minuscule pieces of flesh and bone. She had to be half-vampire, because she'd taught my dad at Orenda Academy, and she'd been ancient back then. Immortality was the only explanation for why she was still creeping around. I don't know why she'd transferred to teach at the Institute, but it was always good to have another Elementai around, I supposed.

Her Familiar, Bram, remained in a corner of the room and watched us with beady eyes. He was a wendigo, an animal you didn't want to cross. Bram's body was the skeleton of a horse, with a long dragon's tail and paws like that of a wolf's for feet. A deer's skull with violent antlers served as Bram's head, and within it, there were no eyes— only sockets. The taunt black skin that stretched over his form only made him more terrifying.

Wendigos were dangerous creatures. You didn't fuck with them unless you wanted to die.

Kalina was in this class with me. She looked up as I took my spot at a desk, but didn't say anything, just kept her eyes forward.

McCauley counted the number of students in her classroom, making sure all were here before she launched into a lecture.

"Magical cooperation is very important for the survival of our world," McCauley said. "Humans are a threat to us all. They outnumber us, and for the first time, their technology poses a risk. Which is why it is critical all supernatural races work together in order to ensure the continuation of magic."

Bram began moving around the room, his skeletal form clicking together as he patrolled, making sure we all paid attention. McCauley's was the one class in the entire school where no one dared to pull anything. We were all too afraid of Bram to try back talking her.

"There is a type of magic that allows different magical races to combine their powers into one fluent method of power," McCauley said. "This magic is called *simultension.* Simultension allows a mermaid to combine their voice magic with a shifter's telepathy, for example, or an angel's light magic with a witch's necromancy. The possibilities are endless. Only together can certain types of magic be created, through the efforts of two or more supernatural species. Miss Lopez, Miss Demauley. A demonstration, if you please."

Lupe headed to the front of the room. I hadn't seen her much since she'd been our tour guide at the start of the semester, but she worked in this class as a teacher's aide. Despona also rose from her seat. The Elementai and the succubi faced each other, waiting for McCauley's instruction.

"Miss Lopez, use your Koigni magic and merge it with Miss Demauley's mind control," McCauley said. "Focus your powers on working together, instead of against each other."

Despona appeared a little worried, but Lupe's face was calm. She emitted a stream of fire from her hands, which wrapped slowly around Despona like a ribbon. It didn't burn the vampire, or hurt her.

Despona took a deep breath. As she exhaled, the Fire magic dispersed around her, and Lupe directed it toward Bram. The Fire created shackles around the wendigo's feet. Despona's eyes flashed red, and she lifted her hand, moving it like a puppeteer. Bram began to dance, but clearly not of his own accord— the Fire shackles around his feet appeared to work like strings, moving Bram's feet from one spot to another.

"Excellent work," McCauley said, and the Fire shackles faded as Bram was set free. "As you can see, creativity is the hallmark of using simultension. Everyone, partner up with someone that is not of your own magical race, and get to work. If you create a spell I haven't seen before, you will get an A for the day."

That had to be impossible. McCauley was so old, she must've seen everything. I looked around for a partner, but most people had already been taken.

McCauley assigned one for me. "Ava-Marie, you'll work with Kalina," McCauley said. "Get to it. No use in lazing about."

I frowned. I didn't want to be with Kalina, but she was already moving her things to my desk.

She sat across from me and fiddled with her pencil. "So, what should we make?"

"I don't know. Isn't fae magic limitless?" I asked.

"In a way. Fae have illusion magic. We can create and manifest any illusion we like into reality, as long as we believe it's real. That's the hard part," Kalina said. "If I don't believe I can do it, it won't happen."

"So let's do something easy," I suggested. "What's the simplest illusion for you to create?"

"Weapons," Kalina responded instantly. "I can make a blade appear out of thin air without breaking a sweat."

"What if you try to make a weapon out of my elemental magic?" I suggested. "An Elementai's magic is pretty powerful, but it doesn't last very long. In most cases, weather magic fades pretty quickly once it's been cast. Maybe we should try making it stick."

"Sounds good to me. Give me what you've got," Kalina suggested.

I nodded. I raised my right hand, and a fireball appeared before us, floating in mid-air. I lifted my left hand and uncapped the water bottle next to me. The water began rising out of the bottle, until it became a ball right next to the glaring fire, rippling with tiny waves as the fire-light reflected off of it harshly.

"You might want to move fast," I suggested. "It won't last long."

Kalina stared at the fireball so intensely, I thought it might fizzle out at her gaze. But that wasn't what happened. Metal began to take shape around the fireball. My jaw dropped as I watched a sword forge right before my eyes and become solid out of thin air. Within the blade of the sword, fire danced, as if there was a window within the weapon that displayed the flames raging inside.

Kalina created a second sword around the water ball, and it flowed outwardly within the middle of the blade just as the fire did. I froze the water inside the sword, and it became a weapon of ice, the still water gleaming inside the blade.

I could feel Kalina's magic as it merged with mine. It felt a lot like the bond between Charlie and me, but it was farther away. I surveyed the feeling of illusion magic with interest. It felt whimsical, and unbound.

"Badass," Kalina said in approval as she observed the floating swords. "Want to try these out?"

"Sure," I said. We moved the desk aside to make room. I grabbed the Water sword, and Kalina took the Fire one. We squared off. Kalina struck first, and as she swung the blade toward me, I brought up my own to block her. Sparks flew everywhere, and I felt my elemental magic quiver when the blades touched.

To my surprise, the swords held. I thought for certain that they'd fall apart once we struck them together, but as long as my magic was intertwined with Kalina's, the swords remained intact. Kalina struck again. I blocked her a second time, and we sparred lightly, testing the strength of our weapons. Sparks continued to fly, along with water droplets, as the swords clashed again and again.

Kalina swung her sword upward in an arc, and I batted it away. The Fire sword left small remnants of flame trailing through the air. As an experiment, I pointed my sword at her, and an icicle emitted from the tip and flew outward. Kalina ducked to avoid it. When the icicle hit a desk nearby, it immediately froze it.

People stopped what they were doing to watch us spar. Kalina and I put all our might into it and really hammered on each other's weapons, but no matter how hard we struck, our magic didn't break.

"Well done, both of you," McCauley said approvingly. "Full points for the day."

Kalina drew back, panting. I was out of breath, too. I could feel Kalina's illusion magic ebbing away as she attempted to take back the power that was hers. I pulled my magic back from Kalina's. The swords instantly dissolved, as if they were never there at all. The fire faded into smoke, and the water became vapor upon the air.

"It looks like we both have to sustain the spell in order to keep it going," Kalina said. She plopped into her seat to take a break.

"Yeah. I guess simultension doesn't work without cooperation." I took a chair beside her. I wish I hadn't used all the water from my bottle, because I was thirsty now.

Kalina gave a roguish smile. "Have you ever sparred before? You're really good."

"No. That was my first time," I admitted.

"You must be a natural." She leaned back in her seat. "My dad taught me. He's the best swordsman that ever was."

"I guess if I can keep up with you, I'm not that bad, Kalina," I joked.

Kalina's smile faltered, and I felt like I struck a nerve. "Did I say something wrong?"

"It's just… I don't really want to be called that anymore," Kalina said. "*Kalina* is a high-born fae name, and I want to separate myself from that life as much as possible."

"Why?" I loved my name, and couldn't imagine being called anything else, but maybe she had a good reason.

"I was exiled. My people and my country abandoned me. I want to get my throne back, but at the same time, I don't know if I ever can go back to that life," Kalina said. "My name is just a reminder of what I lost. I need to become someone different if I'm going to be happy."

"So… what do you want me to call you?" I asked.

She gave an introspective look toward the ceiling. "I was thinking… Kallie."

"Okay, Kallie," I said. "If that's what you want to be called, then that's who you are to me."

"Thanks. I really appreciate it," she said in relief. "I just need to reinvent myself. Start over, once we win the Darke Games."

I got it. So many people at the Institute wanted to forget their pasts. It was the only way to move on once you'd been thrown in jail.

I giggled. "You know, I'm all for reinventing yourself, but if you want to change your sense of fashion, you'll probably have to wait until we get out of the Institute."

Kallie moaned. "I know, right? The uniforms at Arcanea University are *so* much better. The fae have better taste. I feel so matronly in this skirt."

"Same," I agreed. "I'd do anything to go to the mall."

Kallie cocked her head. "Aren't you the girl who got in trouble for modifying the uniform and making it sexy?"

"That's me," I said proudly.

"I like rebels who don't follow the rules," Kallie said in approval. "If you can't tell, I have a problem with authority."

I snickered. "Girl, I feel you. What good are rules if they're not meant to be broken?"

Kallie nodded. "You're a badass bitch. I could get used to hanging around a girl like you."

"You're not so bad yourself," I said.

Kallie was actually kind of cool. Maybe I hadn't given her a chance. Trusting people was never my strong suit… but even if I didn't trust Kallie, perhaps she could still be a friend, and that was good enough for me.

When I peeked out my door on Wednesday morning, my eyes widened. I saw an array of students walk by, dressed in various costumes like scarecrows, ringmasters, pirates and movie characters. It was so different from the dull uniforms we were forced to wear every day.

Crap. It was freaking Halloween. And I'd totally forgotten.

Oberi wasn't around. She had gone back to Charlie yesterday, and the man got up so damn early ancestors only knew where the hell he was.

My eyes scanned the hall until I saw Opal. She was dressed as a ladybug, waiting for me so we could walk together to the nurse's station to take our pills. I ran over and grabbed her shoulder. "We're allowed to dress up?" I didn't think the Institute approved anything *fun*.

"It's Halloween," Opal said. "It's the one day of the year we don't have to wear those stupid uniforms. They actually let us wear whatever we want, as long as it isn't violent. Most people get their parents to send something, or order costumes from the shop in Shade Hills to be delivered to the Institute."

Fuck. I loved Halloween, but I'd been so wrapped up in my own thoughts lately, I hadn't even paid attention. I didn't have a costume, but I was sure I could find *something*. "Wait here."

I ran back into my dorm and began throwing clothes around. I didn't want to be the only loser without a costume.

I found a pink knee-length wool skirt with the design of a white poodle on the edge. It was a poodle skirt I'd bought a few years ago, but I'd never found the right opportunity to wear it. I'd packed it in a hurry when I was throwing things into my suitcase for the Institute. I put it on, then pulled my hair back into a ponytail and slipped on a plain white button-up. They matched my white tights and black shoes from my uniform. I wrapped a polka-dotted scarf around my hair to use as a headband, and called it a day.

Opal's smile widened as she saw me. "You're a 1950s sock hop girl," she gushed. "Very cute."

"You think so?" I smoothed down my shirt. "I'm really into vintage stuff."

"It totally fits your personality," Opal said. "I couldn't put something together like that last-minute."

As we waited in line to take our pills, I observed all the different costumes people had on. It looked like Mad Dog had decided to fuck the rules, because he'd chosen to dress up as a serial killer, bloody shirt and all. I wasn't so sure the blood was fake, either. He walked around school with a hockey mask, following kids around until they started running out of fear.

Halloween wasn't fun for people like Mad Dog. It was an excuse to terrify people. I rolled my eyes and turned away. I wouldn't let that loser ruin my holiday.

After we took our pills, Opal and I began on our walk to the cafeteria. In the hallway, I saw Naya heckling with a couple of her cronies. Naya had on a really revealing devil costume that looked more like lingerie than an actual outfit. The horns and pitchfork fit her black heart *perfectly*.

"What the fuck are you wearing?" Naya asked a girl who passed by. The girl had on a very large gown, with a big lace collar around her neck. It was a beautiful, intricate costume that had obviously taken a lot of work to make.

The girl skidded to a halt. Her face went pale. "It's… a renaissance period costume," she whispered. "I worked all month on making it in Arts and Crafts."

"Well, it's freaking stupid," Naya snapped. "Try a sexier costume next year, and maybe guys will stop thinking you're such a prude."

The girl blushed and blinked tears away before she sniffed and ran off. I went to give Naya a good piece of my mind— meaning, my fist in her face— but Opal put an arm out to stop me.

"Leave her be," Opal whispered. "You don't want to be next."

The guards were stationed around the area, looking for people who wanted to start a fight. Opal was right. I'd already gotten into one altercation with a guard last week. I was pushing my luck as it was.

My temper steamed as Opal forced me to walk away. I didn't really care that Naya was wearing a skimpy costume. Monica and I had been Playboy bunnies one year, *without* Daddy knowing about it, of course. But Naya was using her outfit to act like she was hotter than everyone else, and shame other girls. It was gross.

Opal had class, so she grabbed something quick from the take-out line and ran off. I stood in line alone to pick up food. I was planning to get the sludge-like oatmeal, so I could use its grossness as an excuse to throw it out without taking a bite.

I yelped as I felt a pair of arms wrap around me from behind. It was Charlie. I knew immediately by the way he smelled— like leather, bergamot, and warm spices that were woodsy and earthy. He picked me up a few feet off the ground and let me hang there. Oberi wagged his tail and barked, running circles around us as Charlie swung me around.

"Charlie, what are you doing?" I asked with a laugh.

"Trying to scare you. Happy Halloween." He didn't make a move to let me down. I didn't mind it like I thought I would.

"You don't have to try because it's a holiday. You scare me every day of the year," I countered.

"Stop." Charlie paused. "You've lost weight, pidge."

He let me go. I slid out of his arms and took a step away. He felt too close. "I've been working out."

Charlie was still in his uniform. I didn't think he had a costume, which made me sad. I went to open my mouth to say something about it, before Charlie cut me off. "So, what are you having for breakfast?"

"What does it matter?" I asked. "I'll just grab something."

His face was slightly puzzled. Or perhaps concerned. "We can share a plate."

Was he trying to outsmart me? It might be working. I said nothing as Charlie loaded eggs and bacon onto a large plate. Oberi was drooling so badly that he made a puddle on the floor.

We sat down on a bench. Oberi shoved his head between us and set it there, staring at the bacon with huge eyes.

Charlie started in, but I didn't touch anything. He couldn't see me. It's not like he could notice if I wasn't—

"You're not eating, pidge."

How could he tell? It was wholly aggravating. "I'm just not hungry today."

"It's more than that. You never eat."

Charlie refused to fill the silence. I sighed. This guy wouldn't take anything less than the truth for an explanation. "When I get in really high manic periods, or really low, I don't eat. I can't explain it, but food makes me anxious. I try to make up for it when I come back down to a somewhat normal state. I'll binge eat until I puke it back up."

"Ava, that's really bad for you," Charlie scolded. "When was the last time you had an actual meal?"

My voice was small. "Yesterday morning."

Charlie frowned. "That's not okay."

"Why do you care? It's not your stomach," I snapped.

Charlie's voice was flustered. "You need to keep your strength up for the Darke Games. You know, so we can win and get out of here."

I let out a *pshing* sound.

"If you're not eating, I'm not eating," Charlie said. He put his fork down and set his elbows on the table.

Ancestors damn him. Nobody had ever managed to get me to eat when I really didn't want to— not even my parents. But I couldn't let Charlie and Oberi starve, and Charlie could hold on to his hunger strike. He had experience with going hungry.

So I had to eat something. Just to keep him happy. He'd notice how much food was left as he ate. I might as well start in.

I ate a few bites of egg and nibbled on a piece of bacon. It felt like a feast, but as I continued to eat, the aching in my middle ebbed, and energy rushed back into my body.

"So… where's your costume?" I asked. I gave an extra egg to Oberi, and he swallowed it greedily, licking the yolk off his large nose with loud laps.

"It's not like I could afford to buy one," Charlie said. "It's not a big deal. Just let it be."

I didn't want Charlie to be left out. When we finished our meal, I jumped up and tugged on his arm. "Come on. Let's go back to your dorm."

Charlie raised an eyebrow. "I didn't realize we had that kind of relationship."

"Ew! Not that, you idiot. You need a costume."

I dragged on his arm and wouldn't take no for an answer. Charlie hemmed and hawed all the way back to the Elementai cellblock while Oberi jumped from spot to spot on the hallway ahead of us, playing his own game of *The Floor is Lava*.

"You aren't going to find anything. I have nothing," Charlie complained as we entered his room.

"You aren't being creative enough." I shuffled through the dresser, but he wasn't kidding— beside his uniforms, Charlie only had a handful of clothes, barely enough to fit in a grocery bag.

But I was Ava-Marie Mitoh, and I'd never been backed into a corner when it came to fashion.

I grabbed a pair of ripped jeans, a white t-shirt, and his leather jacket out of the closet. I threw them at Charlie, and he caught them clumsily.

"Put these on. We'll match," I offered. "We can be Sandy and Danny from *Grease*."

"That movie is so ancient," Charlie complained.

"But still a good one. Stay here." I went to my dorm and came back with a small bottle of hair gel. Amazingly, he'd done as I asked and changed into the clothes I'd picked out for him.

I forced Charlie to sit down in the desk chair and began styling. I coated all of Charlie's hair before I combed the gel through and parted it back, so his hair looked slick and wavy. In minutes, he was a total shoe-in for Danny Zuko.

"You look really cute," I gushed. Nothing was more fun than making Charlie my personal dress-up doll.

"You think so?" He couldn't see it, but he tilted his head from side to side, and reached up a hand to run his fingers through his gelled hair. He seemed… hesitant, but also a little excited. Geez, when was the last time this kid had dressed up for Halloween?

Probably never. His foster mom had been too busy running a brothel to buy him a costume, I bet.

Oberi was barking loudly, spinning in circles. He wanted a costume, too. I reached into my dress shirt pocket and yanked out a pink handkerchief. I tied it around Oberi's neck, and he panted in glee.

"We all match. We've totally won Halloween," I said.

"If you say so." Charlie stood up. "We've got some time before Elementai Magic. Let's go hang out in the Villain's Den. You can tell me what everyone's wearing."

People called the rec room the Villain's Den. Teachers didn't approve of the name, which is what had made it stick. Students hung out there whenever they didn't have class, as it was one of the few places on campus you couldn't be yelled at by the guards for loitering.

The Villain's Den was dark, decorated with purple Gothic wallpaper and dark carpet. Inside were a couple of tables and chairs, along with a rickety foosball table. There was a cart with basketballs and other sports items you could take into the prison yard— save for baseball bats, and anything else that you could bludgeon people with. Old school arcade games, like *Pac-Man* and *Space Invader*, sat in the corner. In the middle of the room was a fireplace surrounded by ratty, holey couches. Above the fireplace was a TV that had a crack in the screen. Usually, the local news was playing, but you could watch an Institute-approved movie as well. None of the other channels worked. There were no computers— the only laptops you could access were in the library, and you had to get permission for those.

It was nothing elaborate, but at least you wouldn't be harassed. The Villain's Den had been decorated for Halloween. Black and orange streamers hung from the ceiling, and decorations had been taped to the walls. A tray of doughnuts and apple cider had been set out for people to grab on their way to class.

It was busier than usual, and creepy music played from the old stereo near the foosball table. Marcus was in here, drawing in his sketchbook at a table by a barred window.

Marcus had painted himself to look like Van Gogh. Colors ran across his skin in thin lines, like oil paint spread carefully across a canvas. He wore a tan suit, though he'd painted over that as well, blending colors together so he appeared to be a moving painting.

At his side, Rishi meowed loudly. Rishi was dressed as a pumpkin. The outfit was hilarious. It made Rishi look like a giant orange ball, a tiny green hat fitted to the cat's head.

Marcus' costume was very creative, but I don't think the idiots around here got it. A guy playing one of the arcade games stopped to look at Marcus in confusion. "Dude, what are you supposed to be?"

Marcus' mouth dropped open in indignation. "I'm a depiction of the self-portrait of Van Gogh that currently resides at the *Musée d'Orsay* in Paris, *obviously*."

"Uh, cool," the guy said, still looking totally lost. Charlie and I slid into the seats next to Marcus.

"Everyone here is so uncultured," Marcus bitched. "Is it really that hard to know the name of a famous—"

Marcus stopped speaking as someone got his attention. Kallie waltzed into the room wearing a superhero costume. A long cape draped behind her, and the pleather skirt she'd chosen to wear rose up on her thighs.

Marcus blushed and put his eyes back on his work. His pencil moved quicker, but the lines were sloppy. Kallie took a seat next to me.

"You teased me for wearing a short skirt. That outfit definitely toes the line," I said.

"This is the first time I've worn a Halloween costume," she explained. "I wanted to go all-out."

"Really?" My eyebrows shot up.

"In Malovia we celebrate a different holiday," she said. "But I'm here now, so when in Rome."

Kallie looked between Charlie and me. "Are you two going steady?" she teased.

"Stop it. This isn't 1954." I laughed, but Charlie scowled.

"You sure act like it," Kallie said as she wiggled her eyebrows.

Oberi had decided to torment Rishi. He picked Rishi up in his mouth by the fluffy pumpkin part of his costume, and tossed him in the air over and over. Rishi yowled in displeasure each time he went up and down.

Eventually, Rishi landed far enough away he could crawl off. Oberi chased after him, but Rishi scampered up the couch and launched himself on top of the fireplace to get away from Oberi. Oberi paced and whined, wondering how to get to Rishi from here. Rishi began knocking things off the fireplace, aiming them at Oberi. My Familiar jumped to the side, but he hadn't been fast enough, and a tissue box had hit him on the head. He growled in annoyance. They were only playing around, but it was funny. I laughed.

Kallie leaned forward. "So guess what I found out. I was passing by Contraband when I went to pick up my costume, and I heard one of the teachers say that it would be unguarded from ten to eleven o'clock."

I checked my watch. "That's fifteen minutes from now."

"Exactly! Let's bust in. I bet there's some good shit in there," she exclaimed.

"How do we know this isn't a trap?" Charlie asked skeptically. "It sounds weird to leave a room like that unguarded."

"The Institute's understaffed at the moment. All that's blocking us from getting in is a lock enchantment, and I know I can break it," Kallie whispered.

"Where are we gonna put it? The guards are gonna notice us walking around with an armful of stuff," Charlie protested.

"Witches and warlocks can subconjure and conjure items," Marcus whispered. "It's like a file on a computer. We can save something and then bring it up again later. It's personal storage for our kind."

"Aren't those searched?" I asked.

"Every week by the warlock guards, but mine won't be searched again until tomorrow," Marcus said. "If we break in now, I can get the stuff and hide it somewhere else, before they look."

"Then let's go," Kallie urged. "Maybe there's something in there that'll help us win the Darke Games."

Marcus gave a wary look to me, but fuck that. This sounded cool. "I'm in."

"Ava, we need to be careful. We shouldn't do this," Charlie said, an edge of warning to his tone.

"Charlie, *please*," I begged. "It'll be fun. I really need to let loose for a change."

His face twisted. "Well… all right. An empty room sounds like child's play. Let's do it."

Oberi and Rishi followed as the four of us took the winding halls down to Contraband. It was near the mailroom, so students were allowed down here, but as we came closer, the halls got sparser and sparser. As we faced the big metal doors to Contraband, a chill came over my body. I don't know why, but something about this didn't feel right— and not in a moral way. Like, a *this-is-going-to-come-back-to-fuck-us* way.

That didn't stop Kallie. She walked up to the doors and placed her hands on the metal. She closed her eyes to concentrate. As she did so, the doors began glowing with a deep purple magic.

I heard a heavy tumbler *click*, and the door unlocked. Kallie pushed it open. I ignited fire in my hand for light, and we went inside.

Contraband was a plain room, filled with metal shelves that were piled with all kinds of different items. Most of it was drugs, but there were other curious things— illegal potions, magical knives, and books that were banned from the library.

"Be careful when touching things. Some of this stuff might be cursed," Marcus said.

Kallie didn't bother. She started throwing things around carelessly, like this was her room. So much for not leaving any traces behind.

Marcus glared at her. She shrugged. "What? They're going to notice stuff is missing, anyway. Doesn't mean they have to know it's us."

At first glance, it didn't look like there was anything here that would help us win the Darke Games. The majority of this stuff was petty weaponry. We avoided the drugs and started looking through the rest of the junk.

"Wow," Marcus said as he lifted a black quill off a counter. "This is amazing."

"What is it?" I asked.

"A tattoo quill. It can give you permanent magical tattoos. They're pretty rare."

Marcus waved his hand, and the quill vanished as he subconjured it into his magical storage space.

Kallie immediately went for the booze lining the shelves. "Score! We can have a party!"

She began handing bottles off to Marcus, who subconjured them as quickly as they came into his grasp.

"Anything good, pidge?" Charlie asked me. He was standing by the door to alert us if anyone walked by. Weird to put a blind guy on watch, but his Air magic would sense if anyone was coming.

"Ooh, diamonds," I said as I spotted a giant ring. "I love diamonds."

I gave it to Marcus, then grabbed a few more things— a supernatural makeup kit, and a pair of earphones I wanted to give to Charlie. If he could get to one of the school computers, he could use them.

Oberi was stubbornly pushing a dog toy against Marcus' leg. Marcus subconjured it. Rishi found a bag of catnip. He placed it on Marcus' shoe and basically screamed.

"No way. You have an addiction," Marcus snapped.

Rishi hissed and swiped at Marcus' shoe. He sighed and subconjured the catnip.

"By the gods, look at all this *porn*!" Kallie cried, holding up a box of magazines. Marcus facepalmed. I laughed.

"If I get searched, I'm not going down because the guards think I'm a pervert," Marcus snapped. "Put it back."

Kallie laughed. "Well, I thought it was funny."

I didn't find anything else of worth, until I came to the end of the aisleway. There was a shimmering green stone sitting on the edge of a shelf, the outside decorated with tiny blue crystals.

I picked it up. On closer inspection, I realized the stone had to be an egg, though I couldn't identify what kind of creature it had come from. I tapped on it. The egg was as hard as stone.

The egg was probably fossilized. Whatever was inside was long since dead, but it looked really cool. I gave it to Marcus. "I want this back later."

"Guys, let's go," Charlie hissed. "We've been in here for ten minutes."

"Relax. We have an hour," Kallie said lazily.

"I never take my time on a job," Charlie said. "We go, and we go now."

Fine by me. There was nothing else in here I wanted. Marcus subconjured the last of the contraband, and we hurried out of the room. Kallie locked it again before we left the area.

"I can't believe we got away with that," Kallie nearly sang. "We made off with so much stuff!"

"Don't brag about it," Charlie said. "Unless you want to get caught."

We heard noise up ahead. It sounded like a fight— typical for the Institute— except the shouts coming didn't sound like that of a student.

Marcus froze. "That sounds like Professor Warbright. He's my teacher for my warlock classes."

Noises of pain rang down the hallway, the sounds of a grown man in trouble. Someone was definitely beating him up.

"He's a teacher. Can't he defend himself?" Kallie asked.

"He's shit at magic. Even I know more than he does." Marcus' face paled with every yell that emitted from Professor Warbright.

"Should we help?" Charlie asked. His voice was nervous.

"We can't. Marcus has contraband," Kallie protested, but her face twisted as she said the words.

"We owe him, Kallie," Marcus insisted. "He got us off when we tried to break out."

Kallie paused, then said, "Okay. Let's go."

We darted down the hallway. At the end, we saw two prisoners— a fae and a vampire— cornering Professor Warbright against the wall. Professor Warbright was on his hands and knees. Blood ran down his face, and his arms shook as he struggled to get up. He was a short, stumpy man in his mid-fifties, and looked about as inept at magic as Marcus said. He went to cast a spell, but the fae raised a magical shield, and the spell bounced back uselessly.

"Hey, dickheads," Marcus called, and the two looked up. "Why don't you pick on someone who can actually fight back?"

The fae laughed. "Quit ruining our fun." He kicked Professor Warbright in the stomach. He groaned, curling into a ball on the floor.

Marcus' tone was deadly. "You better back off."

"Or what?" the vampire spat, and he made a disgusted sound.

"Or I'll make you wish you'd never been born." Marcus looked ready to make good on his threat. He took a wide stance, and Rishi yowled.

The vampire snorted. "You sure act like a peacock, strutting around here like you know it all. Do you really think anyone believes your tough guy bullshit? It's all an act."

"Yeah. Peacock's the perfect name for you. All show," the fae added.

The bullies laughed. Marcus' face flushed, but he didn't speak up.

Kallie did it for him. "Leave Marcus alone," she snapped. "At least he's got a reputation, unlike you losers. Nobody even knows your name."

The fae's eyes flashed. "No one asked for your opinion, *traitor*. You've really sunk low, if you're hanging out with a filthy witch and a couple of savages."

Kallie conjured a purple orb and flung it at the fae's face. The fae took a step aside and snarled. Immediately, he shifted into an alicorn— a unicorn with wings. The shifter charged at Kallie with his horn down, but in seconds, she had changed into a large, silver wolf. She launched herself at the alicorn, and the two began dueling fiercely.

Oberi gave a growl and went to help Kallie. He ran toward the alicorn and jumped onto his back, dealing sharp bites to his wings. The alicorn screamed and went to buck Oberi off, though my Familiar held on tight.

Marcus faced off with the vampire. The vampire charged, his form becoming a blur as he launched himself at Marcus. Then Marcus flung his hands out, and the vampire sank to the floor, screaming out in pain as Marcus assaulted him with battle magic.

Shit. Maybe Marcus wasn't all kidding when he bragged about what he could do.

Charlie and I ran to Professor Warbright. We knelt by his side. "Are you okay?" I asked.

Professor Warbright wavered, then touched the blood on his face. He immediately slumped to the floor.

Great. He'd fainted. I shook him, to wake him back up. "Professor? Professor!"

He didn't rise. I jumped to my feet. The fae had changed back into a man and was flinging out shields to keep Kallie and Oberi back. I summoned a fireball and stomped toward him, ready to shove it down his throat.

"What is the meaning of this?" the Warden's deep voice boomed down the hall, and my stomach fell as I saw him approach, flanked by a whole group of guards.

The fight immediately ended as everyone pulled back their magic, Professor Warbright still on the floor.

The fae pointed at Marcus. "This guy was trying to hurt Professor Warbright!"

"He's lying!" Kallie shouted back. "We found *them* beating him up!"

The Warden raised his eyebrows. "If no one is willing to tell the truth, we'll have to perform an investigation to see who's the most honest. I hope none of you are carrying anything that would be incriminating."

Marcus couldn't get searched. If he was, we were in deep shit.

So I did the only thing I could think of to cause a distraction. I kicked the fae right in the balls.

He went down. The fae gave a groan and curled into a ball on the floor. The guards went to grab me, but the Warden held up an arm and shook his head no.

It gave us enough time for Professor Warbright to come around. He groaned as he ventured back into consciousness, sitting up slowly and holding his head.

The Warden didn't bother to see if his staff member was all right. He got right to business. "Professor Warbright, can you tell me who *exactly* did this to you?"

Professor Warbright trembled at the Warden's appearance. His eyes flickered to the fae and the vampire.

It was enough for the Warden. "Guards, take these two into custody," the Warden said, nodding to the fae and the vampire. "The rest of you may take Professor Warbright to the infirmary. I am going to have a private conversation with Miss Mitoh."

"What?" Charlie snarled. "She didn't do anything!"

"We were all in that fight together. We should all be punished," Kallie snapped.

"Be that as it may, Miss Mitoh was the instigator after I arrived," the Warden said coolly. "I advise that she come with me."

The rest of them went to say more, but I waved them off. "It's fine, guys," I said. "Just take care of Professor Warbright."

"You aren't the one giving the orders around here," the Warden reminded me. "Come."

The Warden turned his back on me, and I had no choice but to follow. Oberi gave a whimper as I left him behind. Charlie's expression was desperate, but I knew when I was walking on thin ice, so I forced myself to walk away.

Out of everyone at the Institute, the Warden was the one person who scared me the most. He was an angel I didn't want to cross. I really hoped he didn't throw me in Cellblock 9 for my actions.

I followed the Warden throughout the school. Everyone's eyes looked at me in fear as they realized I was going to the Warden's office, but I refused to be afraid. *Fear is a useless emotion*, I reminded myself. It wouldn't help me here.

We wound up a tower until we came to a large iron door. The Warden opened the door for me, and I stepped inside.

The Warden's office was huge. The ceiling was a huge glass dome, revealing the cloudy weather outside. It was certainly the most glamorous room in the prison. Supernatural artifacts were placed in glass cases around the room, beside cabinets full of expensive potions. Books lined the shelves next to globes and maps of supernatural cities. In several places around the room, there were gold cages, like those for birds... but they were empty. The largest cage, big enough for a person, was suspended overhead on thick chains. That one was empty, too.

A giant mahogany desk sat in the center of the office, in front of a large, imposing chair. I took a seat on the other side of the desk and tried not to squirm.

"You have an interesting record, Miss Mitoh," the Warden said. He began rifling through a large filing cabinet next to his desk. "Your teachers have reported your behavior to me these past few weeks, and I can say I am... concerned."

"I'm nothing special," I countered. Why had I been singled out? This guy was wasting my time.

The Warden kept thumbing through files. "You can fool your teachers, but you certainly can't fool me. You are not my average criminal."

The Warden slapped a file on the desk and sat across from me in that big, overbearing chair. "You speak four languages. You became an exceptional pianist at a very young age, and a talented vocalist. The laurels hardly end there. You were a championship ballroom dancer, the Captain of your high school cheerleading team, and even earned a Cosmetology certificate through a trade program before you finished your Junior year of high school. Unlike most of your peers at the Institute, you seem to be a prodigy at whatever you do."

"So I pick things up quickly, big fucking deal," I muttered under my breath. Was this a lecture, or an interrogation?

The Warden continued. "You have an outstanding IQ score, and you passed all your standardized tests with flying colors. In fact, you were set to become the valedictorian of your graduating class... until your unusual choice to withdraw from school, and finish your studies at home in your senior year, where you earned an unimpressive C average."

The Warden learned forward, eyes narrowed. "Now why would such a talented student throw all that away?"

Fuck. How did this guy get his hands on my records? He was a dirty bastard. That he'd investigated me so thoroughly was downright concerning. It was like he'd waited for the moment I'd mess up, so he could get me in here for a private conversation.

I crossed my arms. "Seems like you know all the answers. Why don't you conjure up a solution to your last question?"

The Warden smiled, and by the ancestors, it made goosebumps trail over my skin. "I think you're hiding something. People don't end up here by accident. Make no mistake, your attendance here is for a reason. I just haven't figured it out yet."

I gave a skeptical sound. "You act like this was my first-choice college. I hardly figure employers are going to be interested in hiring someone with a degree from the Darke Institute of Supernatural Offenders."

"Of course they will. Employers know that any graduate of the Institute is a reliable, upstanding member of society."

I huffed and crossed my ankles. "Whatever label you slap on me, I'm never going to be a changed woman."

"I don't think we're clear, Miss Mitoh. Rehabilitation is not optional here at the Institute. It's a requirement. If you want your degree, you'll come to learn how things work around here. If we have to, we'll take whatever measures necessary to make sure you become a non-violent individual. If it proves to be an impossible feat to ensure your compliance, well... no one has ever graduated from the Institute without becoming an obedient individual of magical society. It's simply not done. And I will not put the Institute's perfect record for reforming supernatural delinquents at risk for anyone."

A shiver ran up my spine at his words, and I realized his meaning. People were forcibly rehabilitated by the Institute. You either got in line, or got taken care of.

If I wasn't a brainwashed indoctrinate of the Institute by the time I walked out of here... I wasn't walking out of here at all.

Ever.

No wonder the graduation rate was so low. Kids really did die in here. It hit me how crucial it was to play along with the Warden's games. His reputation for reforming magical criminals was on the line, and he would kill people to keep that reputation untarnished.

"I am very good at my job," the Warden went on. "The magical world hangs in a delicate balance. One false move, and it could be destroyed forever. I am here to either reform— or destroy— those that threaten to upset that balance. It is my duty to keep the supernatural world safe from the next criminal mastermind."

I let out a harsh laugh. "And you think that's me."

"I have absolutely no doubt it could be you, Miss Mitoh. You are too smart to have landed yourself in here by accident, and if I'm not mistaken, I believe you *wanted* to be here. Deep down, you know this is the only place where the world can be safe from you."

"Bull," I spat, but a tiny bit of guilt festered within me at his words. He thought I was a criminal genius, just biding my time for the right opportunity.

I couldn't say he was wrong.

The Warden smiled again. He knew he caught me in a lie. "Regardless, your bad attitude will not continue to be tolerated. Consider this a warning. You might want to work harder in your group therapy sessions. Before I have to consider more *permanent* options for you."

The Warden bent over his paperwork, as if the conversation didn't happen at all. It was clear our discussion was done. I rose slowly from my seat. Paranoia crept over my skin like spiders as I turned my back on him to leave. The Warden was someone you should never turn your back on, ever. He'd put a knife in it the first chance he got. The feeling of being watched followed me even as I left the Warden's office far behind.

I had to win the Darke Games. I wouldn't survive four years of schooling. Not here.

The pressure was on, and the Warden would make good on his threats. He wasn't kidding around.

But neither was I. If the Warden thought his will was strong, he hadn't met mine yet.

charlie

FIFTEEN

va-Marie was avoiding me.

Not in a physical sense, but she hardly spoke a word to me over the following week. It was driving me crazy, because the sound of her voice was the only thing keeping me sane at the Institute. I'd tried to ask what the Warden had said to her, but she refused to spill the beans. She had a million reasons to keep quiet— she didn't want to talk about the Warden, didn't want to hear me lecture her on healthy eating, and was all around going through a low episode.

It was really starting to worry me. Oberi wouldn't stop nudging my hand during mealtimes, trying to get me to talk to her, but I finally resolved to let her come at her own pace.

I wanted to ask her to take me back to the rock formation we'd found in the woods, to summon the ancestors for me again. When we'd gone there, it was like I could forget we were at the Institute at all. I wanted to go back. Whether it was for my own spiritual journey, or to feel close to her again, I didn't know. But Ava didn't seem ready, so I didn't ask her.

I was roaming the border of the prison yard after class one day when I decided to hell with it. Ava or not, I was going back.

Oberi wasn't with me. It was Ava's turn. But surely I could navigate the forest on my own… right?

I couldn't remember where we'd entered last time, so I didn't really know where to go. But this forest was enclosed by a fence. It couldn't be *that* big.

I was wrong.

I figured the forest couldn't be more than ten acres or so, but it turned out ten acres was freaking easy to get lost in when you didn't know where to go. Loose brush tangled around my ankles, and low-hanging tree branches grabbed at my face and shoulders. Surely I'd feel that pull I had before— that ethereal nudge guiding me to our hidden cave. I *had* to find it.

An hour must've passed, then two. I'd fallen down a few times and could feel the grains of dirt embedded in my fingernails. Blood trickled down my cheek from where a tree branch had bit me. The top few buttons of my shirt were undone to let in the gradually cooling air. Though it was the beginning of November, the air was warm. The Island didn't experience the harsh temperature swings I was used to in Michigan. I was sweating buckets.

It must've been twilight by now. I thought about turning around and heading back so I wouldn't miss curfew— it'd take me that long to get out of here— but I'd gotten so turned around I didn't know which way *out* was. I was determined to find that hidden cave again. It was my one sanctuary outside of the Institute.

I pushed through another clump of trees and stumbled into a clearing. My throat felt like sandpaper, as I hadn't thought to bring water. I didn't plan on being out here this long. My mind raced with thoughts of Ava and regrets on coming here alone. I was so unfocused I almost didn't notice the rock.

My Air magic resisted up ahead, bouncing off a large natural formation in the middle of the woods. I breathed a sigh of relief, and the life of the forest seemed to seep into my bones as I relaxed. The rock was easy to feel now, and I honestly didn't know how I'd missed it.

"I made it," I gasped to the empty forest.

I stumbled forward and caught myself on the edge of the giant rock. Though I had Air magic, I couldn't seem to suck in enough for comfort. I leaned my head against the cool stone and gave myself a few moments to catch my breath. When I finally felt like I could breathe, I inched my way along the stone, until my Air magic sensed the opening in the rock up ahead. I slipped through the narrow slit and walked until I felt the small space open to a large cavern.

The magic Ava had conjured the last time we were here was gone, but there was something that lingered. It wasn't magic, but it was close— a sense of peace nestled deep into a recent memory.

I dropped to my knees. "Ancestors," I breathed.

Though my voice was soft, it echoed through the chamber. My ragged breaths filled the silence. It wasn't until several minutes later, when my breathing finally returned to normal, that I realized how eerily quiet it was in here. There were no sounds of flutes floating through the air, no drum beats pounding to the beat of my heart, no fire crackling in the corner. It was empty… lonely.

The loneliness did something to me. I was used to being alone, but it'd been months since I'd experienced true solitude. I thought prison was supposed to isolate you, but it'd done anything but. Even in the privacy of my dorm room, I could hear the other students through the walls. Out here in the woods, in this cavern, I was completely alone. It didn't feel right without Ava or Oberi.

"Ancestors," I spoke again. I didn't know why. Surely, they couldn't hear me if I didn't summon them. And I couldn't— not without Ava. But I had to try. "Ancestors… why? Why am I here? What is any of this for? Ava says I'm just surviving, and she's right. But what is life without purpose? What am I surviving *for*?"

Tears pricked at my eyes, but I choked them back. "There has to be a reason! Why did you send me away from the tribe? What kind of lessons were you trying to teach me? Why did you take away my sight!?"

My voice echoed off the walls of the cave, and a shiver traveled down my spine. I was met with nothing but silence.

I didn't know why I'd brought up my blindness. It wasn't something I was bitter about… just curious. It was a question no one had ever been able to give me an answer to. The ancestors must be able to tell me what happened.

And yet they couldn't… because they wouldn't speak to me.

"Answer me!" I yelled, slamming my fist into the dirt.

My hands shook. I was tired, thirsty, and freaking frustrated. If my ancestors were here to guide me, why weren't they answering? Why had they left me without guidance my whole life?

Why? Why? Why?

The word echoed through my mind. I wasn't even looking for a solution. All I wanted was an explanation.

All I got was silence.

Damn it!

I pounded my fists into the dirt again, until my knuckles felt raw. Sinking to the ground, defeat overcame me. I buried my face into my dry, aching hands.

I wasn't the kind of guy who did this. I didn't get vulnerable, not even in solitude. Vulnerability is what got you killed on the streets. But ever since I'd opened up to Ava, something had broken within me. I felt different.

I *felt*… felt things I'd never felt before, things I couldn't explain or come close to understanding.

It hurt. Everything hurt.

I didn't want to feel this way— down, broken, hopeless. And yet I never wanted to go back to feeling nothing at all. I hadn't realized how detached I'd let myself become, how numb I'd been for so long.

I didn't even know who I was anymore. I wasn't sure I ever knew. And my damn ancestors weren't here to guide me.

Lucky bastards.

I bet it was nice in the Ancestral Lands. I bet they had all the food they could ever want and slept on beds made from clouds. I bet they were surrounded by loved ones and didn't have to question every feeling that tugged at something in their guts.

I wanted that. For me. For Ava. For Oberi. But the ancestors wouldn't take me until I was ready.

I had to make sure that when the time came, I was ready for them. Yet for the life of me, I couldn't understand why I was still here.

Getting out of the forest was easier than getting in, since I'd finally found my bearings at the cave. I'd snuck past my dorm room and to the showers before Ava could spot me. She hadn't seen what a mess I'd looked like, and yet she seemed to sense something in our Elementai Magic class the following day.

"Is something bothering you, Charlie?" Ava asked while Professor Summers lectured at the front of the class.

"Why would you think that?" I whispered back, avoiding her question.

"You look distant today, like you're thinking about something."

I was deep in thought, but I wasn't about to tell her that— not when my train of thought had revolved solely around her. And it wasn't in a desperate, sexual way, either. I was trying to decipher what the ancestors wanted from me, and everything seemed to come back to Ava. After all, she *was* a part of my soul. Of course my purpose in life intertwined with hers in some way. But… how?

"Don't go worrying your pretty little mind, pidge," I told her. "I'll be fine."

"Mister Wahkin," Professor Summers called from the front of the class. "Something you'd like to share with the class?"

Professor Summers was an elderly woman who could go from *caring grandmother* to *ultimate authority* in point-five seconds. Ava had told me that was the way with Koigni women. They were made of fire— of passion— and that tender fire could shift into an inferno at any moment. It didn't quite help my confidence around Ava knowing that, but Professor Summers was different. I didn't appreciate her inferno the way I did Ava's.

I cleared my throat. "No, Professor Summers."

Her Familiar snorted at me. It was a pig of some sort, though I'd never gotten close enough to really inspect its uniqueness. All I'd felt was its miniature stature when it roamed up and down the rows on occasion. Ava-Marie had described the creature as a red river hog, a type of swine with long red fur and tufts growing off its black ears.

"Well, then," Professor Summers said. "Shall we take this lesson outside?"

Chairs squeaked across the floor as the other Elementai in the class stood to follow her. Almost everyone in here had a Familiar, except for the few unlucky souls who hadn't bonded yet. They probably wouldn't until they got out of this place and back to Kinpago. There were at least two Toaqua students who were bonded but couldn't take their Familiars to class, on account of them being completely water-bound creatures who lived in the pools below the school.

Hoofbeats of equestrian Familiars sounded on the floor, along with the scratch of talons from various birds. I knew at least one guy in the class was bonded to a griffin. The flap of feathery wings sounded above me, and heat traveled over the top of my head— a phoenix. Ahead of us, a young basilisk hissed and slithered on ahead.

Oberi strutted in unicorn form between Ava and me. I leaned into her so Ava could hear me better. "I totally zoned out. What's the lesson on today?"

Ava blew an exasperated breath. "I *knew* something was bothering you. We're supposed to team up today and try to sense the power of another Elementai."

"You think we can do that? Sense an element that isn't ours?"

"I don't know," Ava admitted. "But I'm sure as hell going to try. I need to be able to sense if there's an enemy nearby."

I furrowed my brow. "How could another Elementai be your enemy?"

Ava practically snorted. "I grew up making enemies in Kinpago. It was practically a hobby. If one of them wants to drive a rock through my skull, I need to know they're coming. Besides, every society has their disputes. My parents fought in the Hawkei Civil War, remember?"

"Yeah," I muttered. "I remember."

I just didn't know how anyone could turn against their own people. If I found a place I belonged, people to call my own, I'd never turn on them. Did loyalty mean nothing to anyone?

It was quiet in the prison yard, which felt strange. Everyone was in class, so the sound of basketballs pounding on the pavement and football players slamming into each other was nonexistent. Instead, the noises of Familiars squawking and nickering filled the yard. I could almost imagine I was at Orenda Academy.

"Everyone, pair up with someone who is not of your element," Professor Summers announced. "I will come around with blindfolds. One team member will wear the blindfold, while the other manipulates their element. You must be able to correctly guess *when* the element is conjured *and* the approximate spell cast. You may begin."

The yard filled with chatter as Nivita teamed up with Anichi and Yapluma partnered with Koigni. There were so many different combinations between the five elements.

"I guess that means we're partners, huh?" Ava asked.

When she said the word *partners*, my heart gave a jolt.

I cleared my throat. "Uh, yeah. Partners."

Professor Summers approached us. "A blindfold for you, Miss Mitoh. I'm assuming you don't need one, Mister Wahkin."

I chuckled lightly. "I think I'm good."

She breathed a sigh of relief, like she was worried to ask, then hurried on to the next student.

"What does she think?" Ava snapped. "That this is a joke?"

"Relax, pidge," I said. "I'm used to it."

Before she could say anything else, I grabbed her by the shoulders and spun her around. "Go stand over there and conjure some Fire."

She shrugged me off. "You don't have to tell me what to do, Charlie. I'm a big girl."

"Okay, then I'll give you a choice. Do you want to go first, or me?"

She hesitated a moment, as if surprised I was letting her choose. "I'll conjure first," she decided.

Ava walked off, far enough away that I wouldn't feel the heat of her Fire coming off her. Oberi followed at her side.

I waited, concentrating on the sound of her footsteps through the grass, and feeling the subtle wave of her hair in the cool breeze. The air seemed to dance around her when she moved, in a way it didn't with everyone else. It didn't obey her like it did me. It *honored* her.

I was so concentrated on Ava that my Air sensed every one of her movements. She turned to face me. Several beats passed and nothing happened. Then, something ignited in my chest. It was subtle at first, but it brought warmth to the yard.

"You've conjured a fireball," I announced confidently.

"What?" Ava sounded surprised. "How can you tell?"

I shrugged. "I can feel the heat."

"Oh," she said in realization. "Through your Air power."

"Yeah, sure. Let's go with that."

Truth was, it went deeper than that, but it wasn't something I could put into words. I felt it in my chest, blooming through me. It didn't come from *within* me, but rather felt like whispers of flames brushing over my skin.

Ava didn't say anything, but her magic shifted. Her power grew so large I could sense it in the air. Her Fire ate at the surrounding oxygen, creating a chemical reaction that immediately alerted my magical senses.

"Your spell is stronger," I said, "but I can't distinguish the specifics. It's complicated for sure, like you're creating an image within the Fire."

Ava drew back on her magic, and it fizzled out. "I created a Fire unicorn," she admitted. "How did you know?"

"I used my Air," I explained. "All elements are interconnected, right? When you conjure Fire, you borrow oxygen from the air. The larger the spell, the more oxygen you need to sustain it."

Ava sounded skeptical. "Okay, Charlie Wahkin. Let's try this again. No cheating."

She strolled across the grass toward me, and I felt fabric on my face.

"What are you doing?" I demanded.

"I'm blindfolding you," she said simply. "It's only fair."

I gaped. "You don't believe I'm blind, pidge?"

"Just covering my bases," she said.

I stilled as her fingers brushed over my face to smooth out the blindfold. I couldn't even protest, as I'd turned to a statue. Ava's fingers moved through my hair as she tied the blindfold back.

"Oh, I see," I teased to hide the tension. "This was just an excuse to get close to me."

Ava finished tying the blindfold, and she smacked my chest. "You wish. Let's try this again."

Ava returned to Oberi's side. The seconds ticked by, and nothing happened. She was testing me, waiting for me to guess her spell when she hadn't cast anything at all. A full minute must've passed, and then I felt it.

It was like ice crawling over my skin, but it wasn't unpleasant. I sensed the air around Ava becoming dry, and I knew instantly what she'd done.

"You're conjuring a water ball from the air," I said.

"How are you doing this?" She didn't sound frustrated, but more or less intrigued.

"Please, pidge," I scoffed. "You're making this easy. You want to make this hard on me? Stop drawing from my own element to create yours."

"But I *need* air," she argued. "I need—"

Ava-Marie cut off so abruptly I knew she'd come up with an idea. But she wasn't as clever as she thought she was. I heard the wave coming and the water sloshing above her head as she showed off her powers.

"You're manipulating water from the lake," I told her simply. "The spell is huge, at least ten feet across."

Ava huffed, and the giant water ball she'd created went splashing back into the lake. She was obviously frustrated I was picking up on this so fast. "Let me try."

Ava stomped toward me and pulled the blindfold off my eyes. She tied it around herself so fast a few threads snapped. She clapped her hands, sounding ready for anything. "Okay, Charlie. Show me what you've got."

I took several steps away so she wouldn't feel my Air power. When I was confident I was far enough away, I summoned a stream of Air above me, twisting it toward the ground and back up again. The air blew my hair back, but it didn't touch Ava.

"Oh," she said in surprise. "*Oh.*"

"What is it?" I asked.

Ava paused a few beats, as if she wasn't sure how to describe it. "I feel something, but it's different from Fire or Water. It's like your magic gives off this frequency that touches the surface of my skin— whereas Fire comes from my chest and I summon Water from my stomach. But Air… it's like… like…"

The blindfold fabric rustled as Ava pulled it off. Only when she'd gone quiet did I realize that the students around us had quieted, too.

"What's going on, pidge?" I asked.

"Um… everyone's staring at us."

It couldn't have been *everyone* in class, because I could still hear voices throughout the yard and feel the air moving in unnatural currents from other Yapluma. But as Ava said it, there must've been at least a dozen footsteps shuffling through the grass, closing in on us.

"What do you want?" Ava practically snapped at our classmates.

A timid girl spoke up first. "Can you teach us how to do that?"

"Sure," I offered, before Ava could tell them to go to hell.

Ava approached me. "What are you doing, Charlie?" she hissed.

I shrugged. "What does it hurt to help out? Besides, these people look up to you. I thought you loved being the center of attention."

"Well… when you put it that way…" Ava turned toward the other students. "Everyone, listen up, because this is going to be on the test."

Ava was being sarcastic, milking every second of it. I laughed under my breath. Oberi shook her mane, like she couldn't bear to watch.

"You all know how to sense your own element," Ava began. "When I cast Fire, every Koigni in this clearing will feel it, because their magic is attuned to the element."

A fireball crackled in her hand as she demonstrated.

"Same with Water," she continued. "Every Toaqua should feel me pulling the water molecules from the air, or sense the shift in currents of the lake. You'd know if I were about to make it rain. Easy, right?"

A few students mumbled in agreement.

"Sensing another element is the same, but in a much more subtle way," she said. "You'll feel it in different ways. The first is in how it affects your own element. As Charlie mentioned earlier, when I conjure Fire, I'm borrowing oxygen from the air, and he can sense that through his own powers. Same with drawing water molecules out of the air. But what if Charlie wasn't Yapluma? What if he were, say, Nivita?"

A male student responded. "You'd have to touch his element for him to feel it— like burning the grass."

"Wrong," she stated bluntly. "You *feel* the magic vibrations, like you feel your Familiar, or the magic coming from someone else's Familiar. You tap into it like intrafusion."

"What's intrafusion?" someone asked.

"You've never heard of intrafusion?" Ava sounded a little annoyed, but she explained anyway. "It's an advanced technique of pulling magic from sources that aren't your own Familiar— usually another magical creature. You see, we're all interconnected. Every element affects the others. And so even though we can't *manipulate* all the elements, we can *sense* them, like Toaqua can sense the moon, and Koigni can sense the sun. You have to get outside of your own element and realize there's more out there than just you and your own Familiar."

Ava was really getting into it now, obviously at ease with being the class know-it-all. I didn't mind. It was good that she knew her stuff.

"All it takes is focus," Ava said. "If you're focused enough, you'll be able to feel another element from a hundred yards away..."

I could sense the disturbance in the air with ease now. Ava summoned water from the lake, forming it into a giant ball bigger than the last one, before letting it fall back down into the water and splash ashore.

"Or if you're a mere inch away..." Ava finished.

She came to my side, so close I felt heat radiating off of her. Then something shifted. Ava held her hand above my arm, sending drops of water hovering just inches above my skin. I sensed their coolness, even though they never touched me. The hairs on my arm stood up, and I shivered under her contactless caress.

The chill continued up my arm, over my shoulder, and across my face. I didn't move an inch, afraid that if I allowed the water to touch me, this would be over. There was something serene about it... something oddly intimate about having her magic so close, and yet so far away. It was as if the water droplets held a promise— a promise I wasn't sure they would keep.

Ava was so close to me, her hand hovering just inches from my face as she controlled the water droplets between us. I could reach out and touch her, wrap my arms around her waist and pull her close. My heart began pitter-pattering against my chest.

Ava continued her lesson, but her voice came out soft, almost a whisper. "And when you can sense that kind of magic, anything is possible."

There was something in her tone I couldn't quite place. She wasn't talking to the rest of the class, and I didn't think she was talking about elemental magic, either. Something else was happening between us— like our magic was intertwining together, and that was why I could sense her water droplets like they were my own.

I could lean over and kiss her right now, I caught myself thinking.

For the first time, I moved, and I began leaning toward Ava.

Almost instantly, she drew back. "Charlie, the bond!" she cried.

I snapped out of my daze. "W-what?"

"What if we feel each other's magic this way because of the bond?" she asked.

"Oh," I said flatly. I'd thought for a second perhaps it was something else— a *different* type of bond. I pushed the thought from my mind as soon as I realized what I was thinking. "You might be right. Why don't we try other partners?"

Ava cleared her throat. "Yeah… probably best."

She jumped straight into leader mode and shoved some poor helpless Nivita kid in my direction. He seemed younger than most students at the institute, judging by the youthfulness of his voice.

"Charlie Wahkin," I introduced, shaking his hand.

"Thaddeus Blake," he said, sounding a little intimidated. A creature squawked from his shoulder, some sort of bird— probably a hawk.

"Ready whenever you are," I told him.

A few moments passed as Thaddeus got in position. Then I felt it. The spell was simple, but it was easier to feel than Ava's magic. It was almost as if I was casting the spell myself. Several yards off, Thaddeus was making the grass grow around him. Long blades of grass grew up from the ground, and a couple of clovers sprouted flowers.

"How many buds is that, Thaddeus?" I asked, showing off just a little. "Four? Five?"

"I-it's…" Thaddeus sputtered.

"*Charlieee!*" Ava cried, drawing out my name.

"What?" I asked innocently.

"How are you doing that?" she demanded. "I'm paired with a Nivita, too, and I don't feel a damn thing. And she lifted three rocks the size of my fist! No offense, Thaddeus, but your spell is child's play."

I shrugged. "Nivita magic is easy. It travels through the ground and up through your feet. You have to ground yourself and focus on the magic buzzing through the plants and the dirt."

Ava took a few seconds to mull it over, then spoke slowly. "Charlie, do you think you could recreate Thaddeus' spell?"

"What?" I was taken aback. "Of course not. I'm not Nivita."

"You have Nivita ancestry," she pointed out. "You *have* to be more connected to Nivita magic than we know. Otherwise, how did you guess the clovers?"

"I don't know," I admitted. "It's like walking over the terrain. You can always tell where the grass ends and the sand begins, or when you're about to step on a pile of rocks."

"Yeah, I can," Ava said. "*Because I can see it.* I don't *feel* it like you can, Charlie. This is different."

I furrowed my brow. I *had* always been particularly sensitive to the earth, but I couldn't *control* it like I could with air.

"Try the spell, Charlie," Ava encouraged.

"It's not going to work, pidge."

"Then prove me wrong," she challenged.

I sighed and aimed my hands at the ground. Sure, I could probably sense earth because my mother was Nivita, but Ava was crazy if she thought—

"Charlie!" Ava belted out. Oberi nickered proudly.

The entire yard must've quieted then. The hair on the back of my neck tingled, and I sensed dozens of eyes on me.

"Charlie, you did it!" Ava cried.

I nearly reeled over in shock. At first, I thought Ava must've been lying or pulling some sort of prank. But when I reached my hands out, my fingers brushed over long blades of grass that went up to my waist.

"Another Nivita must've done this," I whispered. Even *I* knew dual-powers were unusual. Ava's case was special, because *she* was special. Things like this didn't happen to me.

I wasn't special… was I?

"That was all you, Charlie," Ava said softly.

As if to reaffirm what she said, Oberi nuzzled her nose into my hair. I shrugged her off, because she was getting snot everywhere.

"I really did that?" I asked in disbelief.

Ava reached out to take my hand, and my heart swelled. She ran her fingers over my palm, as if it might've left traces of magic behind. "You did," she replied in wonder.

"Okay, that's enough for today!" Professor Summers announced. "Class dismissed."

I didn't know why she'd dismissed the class early, until people began dispersing and Professor Summers approached Ava and me.

"Miss Mitoh, Mister Wahkin," she said in her gentle, grandmotherly tone. "What you two have is very special."

Ava was still holding my hand, which I found comforting. Even more so when Professor Summers called us special.

"Dual-casters are very unique in Hawkei society," she continued. "Most mixed children only inherit one power from their parents. Add that to your... *unique* bond. I suspect the two of you may be capable of extraordinary things together."

For how *extraordinary* Professor Summers seemed to think Ava and I were together, she didn't sound afraid. She sounded intrigued.

"Your prospects for employment once you graduate will be great," Professor Summers said. "I am very interested to see where your powers might take you as you continue through my class."

At that, Professor Summers turned and headed back toward the school, her hog Familiar grunting as it hurried to catch up with her.

Once Professor Summers was gone, Ava flung her arms around my neck. I was so shocked, I didn't know what to do at first. Her floral scent filled my nose, and my hands settled on her back as I relaxed into the embrace.

"Charlie, this is wonderful!" she exclaimed.

"What do you mean?" I drew away from her.

"You're a dual-caster, like me! I'm *so* relieved I'm not the only one."

"But it made you special," I argued. I hadn't realized I was running my hands down her arms until they stopped at her hands. Instinctually, I entwined my fingers with hers, but she didn't pull away.

"I don't *want* to be *special.*" Ava practically spat the word. "I want to be normal."

Just then, a gust of wind breezed past us, and Ava's hair tickled my face. I reached up to push the strands behind her ear. "Ava-Marie Mitoh, you will never be *normal.* You're too exceptional for that."

Ava froze under my touch, and I realized what I'd said. "You think I'm extraordinary?" she whispered.

I hesitated. Truth was, the girl drew me in for reasons I couldn't explain. I thought it was the bond at first, but as I held her hand in mine, I felt magnetized to her by some other force. It was a force that wanted her outside of the bond. Something had changed all those weeks ago when she'd summoned my ancestors. It was only amplified in the room above the chapel when I'd opened up to her. Ava was different than I expected, and softer than she let anyone else know. She had so much life inside of her, an energy that put most people off, but drew me in. An energy I wanted to learn from and share with her. I'd never met anyone quite like her.

"You're intriguing for sure," I told her.

"Well, I can live with intriguing, I guess," she teased.

Ava took a deep breath. We were so close now that the rise of her chest caused her breasts to touch me, though only slightly. My fingers were still frozen against her hair. All I had to do was shift my hand slightly to wrap it around the back of her neck… to draw her in and press my lips to hers. It would be effortless. It could be perfect…

Or it could ruin everything.

I drew away from her before I caved to the temptation.

I had one rule about sex— apart from always using protection. Rule number one: *You don't fuck your friends.*

Friends were hard to find in this world, but easy as hell to lose. One white lie, one hurt feeling, one night of bliss…

It could all end in disaster.

And so I could only get so close to Ava. If I let myself fall for her and ruined it, it would level my whole fucking heart. Ava wasn't just a friend. This bond we shared connected us for life, and I knew if something bad happened, I would never recover.

I had to protect us both from that.

And yet there was only so far I could stay away. Ava called to me like a beacon in the middle of a raging storm. She might be annoying as all hell, but she'd become my sanctuary.

Ava had said I was forced into survival mode because I'd never known anything else. And she was right. But I wanted to know something else. I wanted to know *Ava*. She was worth it.

I made a decision I never had before. In the Darke Games and beyond, I wanted to fight for *her*.

ava-marie

SIXTEEN

My dorm room door opened. I scurried to hide what I'd been looking at. The journal was open in front of me. I snapped it shut and shoved it under my pillow, hurriedly gathering the notes I'd been writing.

"Just a sec!" Who'd be so fucking rude as to not knock before entering? This was *my* room, after all.

It was only Charlie. I sighed in relief and gathered the papers more slowly. He couldn't see what I was reading, so I didn't have to rush to hide. Oberi walked forward and began throwing the papers off the bed with his paw. They scattered to the floor. "Oberi, you asshole."

He wagged his tail. Charlie heard the rustling of papers and asked, "Homework?"

"Yeah," I lied as I picked the mess off the floor. "What's that you got?"

"Food." He held up two takeout boxes and placed one in front of me. "I signed for you so you won't get caught skipping dinner. Here. Brought you something."

I flipped open the lid. It was a burger. They were seriously one of the few good things the Institute served. "This is perfect. I'm actually kind of hungry."

I shoved the journal and the notes into my desk drawer, then rummaged through a box by my bed that my parents had sent, and took out a couple of jars. "Do you need anything?"

"I'm good." Charlie had gotten a load of onions, tomatoes and cheese on his burger, smothered in mustard. There was a second burger in his takeout box, with only ketchup. Oberi drooled as he watched him take a bite.

We were only allowed utensils in the lunchroom, save for an ugly brown spoon that was made of a weird material that couldn't be melted down or sharpened. I took the spoon and dipped it into one of the jars my parents had sent. I dumped a huge glob of crunchy peanut butter and strawberry jelly all over the bun, then smashed it together on top of the burger. I took a bite and chewed happily.

"Do I smell… peanut butter and jelly?" Charlie asked.

"Yes," I gushed. "It's amazing on burgers. It's the only way I'll eat it."

"Let me try it," he said curiously. I tore off a piece and handed it to him. Charlie chewed thoughtfully. "It's not the *best*, but I'd still eat it if I was hungry."

"Really? Everyone else thinks it's gross," I said.

"I'll literally eat almost anything," he said. "But even I have limits."

"I used to put all kinds of weird stuff on my food," I said. "My mom came up with the idea. It was the only way she could get me to eat. She'd put mayonnaise on barbeque chicken pizza, or dip my grilled cheese in applesauce. It nearly made my dad puke. He's a really picky eater."

"If you put mayonnaise on pizza, our bond is over," Charlie teased. He took the second burger and tossed it to Oberi. He snatched it out of the air and gobbled it down, smearing ketchup all over his jowls.

There was another knock, then Kallie poked her head in. She slipped inside my room and closed the door behind her. "Are you guys ready for this?" she whispered. "Tonight's the night!"

"For what?" Charlie asked.

"Marcus and I are throwing that party we talked about when we stole the booze from Contraband," Kallie whispered. "We've asked a handful of people. I paid off a couple guards, so they'll look the other way."

"Where?" I asked.

"The chapel." Kallie's eyes gleamed in excitement. "No one will hear us in there."

"What about curfew?" We were locked in at ten o'clock at night, every night.

"Apparently there's a big fight tonight in the illegal brawling ring the guards run. The dorms are left open. It's the perfect time," Kallie insisted. "We don't even have to worry about bed check."

Charlie appeared hesitant.

"We should go," I said. "Let loose a little before the Darke Games."

"I don't know…" he said, and Oberi huffed. "If we get caught, we'll be in big trouble."

I rolled my eyes. "Come *on*, Charlie. You need to start living."

A smile twisted his expression. "Well… I always did like parties."

"That's the Yapluma in you," I said. "The Air House is always the party House, and since you're half-Yapluma, I'm expecting you to have a good time."

"Perfect," Kallie said. "I'll get everything ready. Be there at nine."

We entered the chapel late— because I was never on time. As the doors to the chapel opened, I was overtaken with awe once again. This was the most gorgeous place in the entire Institute, even though it'd been abandoned. The dusty broken pews and the dirty marble floors held a particular beauty against the colorful stained-glass windows. Some of them were shattered, but that didn't interrupt the intricacy of the pictures they portrayed— a person from every supernatural race.

The Elementai window was my favorite. It was near the back of the chapel and portrayed a beautiful Hawkei woman, dressed in regalia with an eagle on her shoulder, feathers woven into her dark hair. A bare-chested Hawkei man stood behind her, his hand around her waist. The other windows were just as glorious in their depictions of mermaids, vampires, angels and others. I felt sad that no one had bothered to repair them in so many years.

But their loss was our gain. About fifteen people had shown up for the party. Most were gathered around a couple of speakers by the wall, which were totally blown and playing pop music. I spotted a few familiar faces in the crowd. Chancey was gambling, as usual, playing a poker game with a couple of shifters. Opal had shown up, to my surprise, and was sipping on a wine cooler while she chatted with Despona in a nearby pew. Opal laughed as Despona shook up a beer can, then sprayed it all over her.

Marcus was sitting at a table in the corner with his tattoo quill, giving people new tattoos.

He was currently working on a full spread of roses on an angel's back, eyes knitted as he worked on the intricacies of the petals. Rishi played with a shot glass at his feet. Kallie was beside a pew that was loaded with all the booze we stole, making deals with other prisoners.

"So we're in agreement. One fifth of vodka for a week's worth of cleaning," Kallie asked.

"Agreed," the vampire said, taking the bottle. "I'll clean your room for a week."

Kallie smiled widely, and I gave a laugh under my breath. These poor souls had no idea what they were getting into, making a deal with a fae. They'd live to regret it. Kallie was roping them into more than just cleaning her room, I was sure.

I went to walk forward, but Charlie grabbed my arm. "Hold on." He turned toward the potted trees that were on either side of the doors and waved his hands. Charlie grew the trees, until their branches wound through the handles, bolting them shut.

"There. If the guards come by, it'll give us time to run," he said.

"You've been working on your Nivita magic," I said, impressed.

"Every day," Charlie replied. "Earth is even easier than Air. I can just think about it, and plants and rocks do whatever I tell them to. I can't believe I hadn't noticed before."

"You are a dual-caster, which means you're already a talented supernatural," I said. "It's not surprising you're good."

We approached the bar Kallie was running. She faced us with a smile as she put out a punch bowl on a nearby table, a cocktail brew freshly made. "You guys want a drink? My current offer is one full bottle for one week's worth of homework."

"I don't think so. I'm not going to make a shady deal with a fae just to get wasted," I told her. "You can lay off the tricks."

Kallie waggled her eyebrows. "Should've known you'd catch on."

"You didn't get thrown in here for being a good girl," I pointed out. "What did you make that vampire agree to?"

Kallie leaned in. "He didn't listen to my wording. I said a week's worth of *cleaning*. He doesn't know I just got detention, and was told to clean out the Alchemy classroom all next week by Professor Hemlock. The magic will make him do it for me."

"Tricky fae," I teased. "What'd you get detention for?"

Kallie cackled. "I cut Naya a deal. Two days' worth of Commissary points to use at the school store for an answer key on her exam. Sorry to say, I don't know shit about Vampire Theory and she failed. Once she figured out she'd been fooled, she ran and told a teacher."

"Ooh." Charlie winced. "You don't snitch at the Institute, no matter how bad."

You didn't. We might be prisoners, but we had a code around here, and telling on people was a good way to get a black eye, or worse. It was always better to get revenge on your own.

"I'll get her back eventually." Kallie grabbed a bottle of swirling pink liquid. "This is the strongest stuff I've got, and since you're too smart to fall for my tricks, it's on the house. Enjoy, guys."

Kallie handed me the bottle. Charlie and I walked off near the speakers. I uncapped it and took a swig.

Okay, this drink had to be *magical*. Once I took a sip, a glow settled over my body, and pink butterflies manifested in my vision, kissing my cheeks and nesting in my hair. I giggled and put my hand out to touch them. Oberi could see them, too. He barked and ran in circles, attempting to chase the butterflies around the chapel.

This was some fae illusion shit. Maybe Kallie had enchanted it before the party began. It was strong, too. A few more sips, and I could already feel myself getting intoxicated. I handed the bottle to Charlie. When he touched it, the drink turned purple, and violet butterflies appeared when he started drinking.

He handed me back the bottle with a grimace. "That's some girly shit."

"It's sweet! It tastes like mangoes." I tilted back the bottle and began to chug. More butterflies appeared, bursting around me in a swirling vortex.

I *loved* getting drunk. You couldn't feel anything, and the voices inside my head were muddled with the effects of the alcohol.

The party went on. I danced with Opal in front of the speakers, and Chancey and I played a game of poker. I won, and he challenged me to a drinking game. I won that, too. Chancey scowled as he placed a hundred dollar bill in my hand, and I walked off swooning.

Charlie stood behind me like a shadow as I continued to take drink after drink. I threw back so many shots from the fae vodka, I lost count of how many I'd taken.

When a song came on he didn't like, Oberi climbed on a speaker and knocked it down. Charlie stood it back up, but even then, didn't go too far.

"What's the matter with you?" I complained. "It's a college party. Loosen up. Get wasted."

Charlie was tailing me like a puppy. And I already had one. He was drinking out of the punch bowl.

"I *am* drunk," he said. Charlie took a couple of sips here and there, working himself up to a buzz. He whistled for Oberi, who drew away from the punch bowl and staggered our way.

Was Charlie's voice slurred, or were my ears ringing? Couldn't tell.

The party had been fun in the beginning, but I was starting to get bored. I wanted to do something reckless. My eyes fell on Marcus in the corner, who was tattooing the shoulder of a mermaid nearby.

I got an idea. An awful idea, but one that sounded incredible nonetheless. "Charlie!" I laughed and stumbled toward him. "Charlie, let's get matching tattoos!"

His reaction was curious. "Uh, okay. What should we get?"

"Each other's names," I suggested. "Yours on my wrist, mine on yours."

Charlie's eyes sparked. "That sounds like an *amazing* idea."

Oberi barked in cheerful agreement. We laughed as we staggered toward Marcus, arm in arm. The mermaid walked off, the fresh tattoo of a seashell on her shoulder.

"Marcus!" I cried. "Charlie and I want to get each other's names. Can you do it?"

"Name tattoos?" Marcus raised an eyebrow. "Those are always terrible. Are you sure—?"

"Lighten *up!*" I smacked him on the arm. "Charlie and I are just *friends.*"

"You two are drunk." Marcus scowled. "It's against my policy to tattoo people who—"

"Do you have to be such a limp dick?" Charlie complained. "Just do it, man."

Marcus narrowed his eyes. "Fine. Sit the fuck down."

Charlie sat across from Marcus. He laid his right arm down on the table. Marcus bent over Charlie's wrist and began writing *Ava-Marie* in a pretty script font. I watched as the ink spanned over Charlie's skin, like it would across paper. Marcus took his time, detailing the tattoo and making sure each line was perfect. I bounced impatiently as I waited. The design took a flowing shape, and Marcus finished the *e* in an infinity symbol.

"There. Your turn," Marcus said.

I shoved Charlie out of his seat. He went sprawling out of it, and I plopped down.

I put my left arm on the table— because, like, when we held hands the tattoos would touch, and that would be *so cute.*

"Are you *sure* about this?" Marcus asked again.

I waved a hand in the air. "You really are a limp dick, Marcus. Just go with the flow."

He shook his head and put the quill to my skin. A cool sensation spread across my arm as the ink in the quill began forming letters. It didn't hurt, like a tattoo machine would. It felt more like a massage as the quill's point made Charlie's name take shape. Like the other tattoo, Marcus put an infinity symbol on the *e* at the end of Charlie's name.

"There," Marcus said as he finished. "You won't need to let it heal— the quill took care of that. It's as ready to go as it would be six months from now."

Marcus eyeballed us. "And just as permanent."

Oh. My. Gosh. They looked *so good.* I jumped up, squealed and yanked on Charlie's arm. I already had another idea. "Charlie, play me a song on the organ!" I pleaded.

"I can't play when I'm wasted," he protested.

"Yes you can, come *on.*" I dragged on his arm and pulled him up the stairs to the chapel's loft. We tripped and fell several times while going up.

Finally, we emerged onto the loft above the chapel. There was a large balcony that looked down upon the pews below. We were so high up, we could barely hear the music playing from the speakers below. The organ was huge. The pipes reached all the way up to the ceiling. In the loft were a collection of old instruments that hadn't been used in what looked like decades. Violins, drums and clarinets lay discarded everywhere, coated in a thick layer of dust. It was like the Institute had abandoned the chapel long ago and just didn't care to renovate it.

The loft was just beneath the chapel's vast ceiling. A circular stained-glass window with dozens of colors gleamed behind the giant organ. The Institute's sigil— a winged snake wrapped around a key— was depicted in the window's glass. I grabbed the key around my neck Mama had given me the night I left. I held it as I took in the sight of the magnificent window once again, completely awed by it while I was up close.

The chapel was my favorite place in the entire school. It was so peaceful and beautiful up here.

Or at least, it was. Oberi scampered to the old drums in the corner and began banging on them with his tail, being as loud as possible.

"Oberi," I scolded. "Play nice, or you'll break them."

Oberi looked at me, then changed into a unicorn and kicked one of the drums over the balcony. It fell to the first floor with a giant *crash*, smashed to pieces.

"Ugh. You're a jerk."

Oberi whinnied in response. She went to kick another drum over the side, but I pointed at her sharply. She ducked her head, acting like she hadn't seen me and looking in the other direction.

Charlie sat down on the organ's bench and began playing a song. The notes were beautiful and bright. It was a song I wasn't familiar with.

I sat beside him on the bench. "What are you playing?"

"I made it up," Charlie said.

"On the spot?" I was surprised. That was the mark of a spectacular musician.

"Yeah, just now," he said.

"Keep playing, Charlie." I leaned closer to watch his hands, memorizing the placement of the keys and creating a score in my head. The song seemed to hold everything Charlie couldn't manage to say.

"Is it a love song?" I asked. I didn't understand what he was trying to tell me.

"I don't know what love feels like," Charlie said. "No one's ever given a shit about me."

My head fell on his shoulder, and Charlie increased the tempo. "It's for you," he said.

For me? Couldn't be. This song must be for someone else.

The notes swelled around me, and my eyes began to drift closed as the lullaby lulled me into a stupor. Charlie was lying. He thought nobody cared.

But I did.

I woke up on the floor of the pitch-black chapel loft, resting against Oberi's side. She was still asleep, her fiery mane providing the only light, save for the full moon gleaming through the windows.

It had to be around three in the morning. Charlie was sleeping next to me, on the other side of Oberi. I looked over Oberi's back and glanced through the bars of the balcony, but no one was down there. I didn't know where Marcus and Kallie had run off to, or where the rest of the party had gone.

My buzz had worn off, so I could see clearly now. Fae vodka, for as strong as it was, didn't last very long. The effects were powerful but short-lived.

Charlie's chest rose and fell softly. I studied him carefully. The feeling that came over me was protective and warm. He might be a huge pain in my ass, but Charlie was sweet. Instead of the tight anxiety that usually plagued his features, his face was relaxed, and he shifted closer to Oberi as if he needed her.

It was the first time I'd ever seen him look at peace.

The next thing I saw was Charlie's name on my wrist. I observed the cursive letters across my skin and felt hollow.

Oh, *shit*. What did we *do*? Getting Charlie's name inked permanently onto my skin had *definitely* been a spur-of-the-moment bipolar decision.

Charlie stirred, and his eyes fluttered open. He didn't make a sound as he slowly sat up.

"I don't remember how we got down here on the floor," he said.

I didn't either. We'd been messing with the organ for a few hours, from what I could recall. "I think we just laid down. A nap sounded good."

"Sure. What are we going to do about these?" Charlie waved his wrist in the air, and I caught a glimpse of my name in the moonlight.

I shrugged. "It shouldn't bother you. You can't see it."

"But I *know* it's there," Charlie objected. "And soon, everyone else will, too."

"Psh. Who cares. Everyone's got a tattoo at the Institute."

"People are going to think we're a thing."

"Would you relax? It was just a drunk tattoo. Not like it means anything."

Charlie frowned.

I laid my arm against Oberi. "So how are we getting out of here?"

"We can't go back now," Charlie whispered. "We walk the halls this late, we'll for sure get caught. Let's hope they think they locked us in our dorms and didn't check."

"So, what? We just stay in here until sunrise?"

"Probably our only option."

I groaned and looked at the ceiling. "Three hours seems like forever."

"It's not that long. At least we can be alone."

I think we both blushed then. He was talking about the guards being up our asses twenty-four-seven, but it came out like we actually wanted to be alone together. Like we needed privacy to just be… ourselves? Certainly not a couple.

Yet Charlie and I were a unit. We'd only known each other for a few months, but we were both bonded to Oberi. We shared the same soul. We came as a package deal now, and it had only taken a few weeks to make it confusing to me where he ended and I began. Every day that passed melded us closer together. Would there come a day when we'd be a singular person, one mind and one dream instead of just one spirit?

I couldn't handle that. I loved my independence. I wouldn't get lost in someone else. It was the quickest way to get hurt.

"You seem better than you were last week," Charlie confessed. "I was worried about you. You weren't acting like… Ava."

His concern was sweet, but I wished he wouldn't. Too many people worried about me. "I am, for now. But it's not going to last long."

"Why not?"

Oberi continued sleeping beside us, but Charlie's attention was only on me. Everything was vulnerable at this time, on this night. It was like the things I whispered wouldn't leave this chapel.

"You know I have bipolar. The way my personal condition works, my mood varies week after week," I explained. "I could be up at the start of the month and be down by the end. My medicine stabilizes me, so sometimes I'm just flatline, and that's really nice. But if I have a lot of triggers, the medicine might as well be candy, for all the good it does."

"What kind of triggers?" He actually seemed interested.

"Stress. The past. I really miss my family," I confessed. "Being apart from them this long is really getting to me."

"You have me and Oberi," Charlie offered. "That's got to count for something."

I put my arms around my knees. "I know. But maybe it's a good thing I'm far away from home. I can't hurt anybody."

"You would never hurt anyone you loved on purpose," he said.

"But I do it by accident," I pointed out. "It's a productive day for me if I don't hurt someone's feelings. My emotions are like a live wire. They're destructive. Some days I can't even minimize the damage. I try to remain in control, but it's like taming a wild animal. I only have so much power to restrain this… monster within me."

"You're not a monster. You just have problems. We've all got 'em."

"These are more than problems," I insisted. "This constant rollercoaster of up and down makes me sick. And as much as I hate to admit it, I'd rather ride the high than endure the lows."

I sat back against Oberi. "Depression gets so *boring*, Charlie. The worst part about being sad is that it's incredibly uninteresting. I pick up on things so easily that I get tired of them just as quickly. And I will do absolutely anything on earth to prevent myself from being bored. Even if there's consequences."

I began playing with my hair. "That's why I like things like fashion. It's always changing, and it's so open to interpretation you can't nail it down to perfection. It keeps my attention."

"You were down for a while, but you're not now," Charlie pointed out. "From what I could tell, it lasted a few weeks, but at least you're better today."

"Yeah, well, it's getting worse. I have such a short tolerance when I get in a low period now, because I know it's not going to last. Just a few weeks, or maybe a month, and I can stop feeling like I want to die again. So I get impatient. I just want it to hurry up so the joy can come back. Because that's where I excel. At least if I'm in a manic period I'm out there doing things, not wasting away in some room watching the hours tick by."

"All that can land you in hot water."

"Maybe I tempt the fire because I like the way it burns."

"Is that supposed to be a metaphor for something?" Charlie's voice was on edge.

"No. A lot of people with bipolar self-harm, but I never did. I didn't see the point in destroying myself when I could destroy something else. I liked breaking things— particularly the law. I got a high off the trouble. I guess that makes me fucked up."

"Everyone's fucked up at the Institute. I'm not innocent either," Charlie said. "I've stolen and scammed thousands of dollars out of people."

"You did it to survive. I committed crimes because… you know… why not?" I turned toward him. "Sometimes it was my illness. And sometimes I just wanted the thrill. There were days I was so depressed that I got into trouble because I was worried about being alone."

I scoffed. "And I hardly ever was. I felt so guilty growing up. I had a great family. I had awesome parents. And I put them through absolute hell. The way I act, you'd think I grew up in an abusive home or something, but it was never like that. I was just crazy for no reason."

Charlie shook his head. "People are never crazy for no reason. I'm sure you had your own. People just didn't understand."

His words were so reassuring. It was nearly like he understood. Charlie went on. "I did a lot of fucked up shit in high school. People didn't think I had a reason to be that way. But I was blind with no resources. I was just acting out in my environment. I'm sure you had to do the same."

"Ancestors. High school was absolute hell." I rolled my eyes. "I'd be at the Institute any day before I'd go back to those years. It was just crisis after crisis."

"It couldn't have been that bad," Charlie argued.

"It was," I insisted. "I'm not even being dramatic. I'd just turned sixteen when my dad got sick… I mean really, really sick."

"He has a chronic illness, doesn't he?"

"Yeah. Combined Magical Suppression Syndrome, it's called. Basically, his magic drains energy from his organs and body. My mom heals him with her Anichi magic, but it can't cure him completely. He's been sick long before I was born."

"That must've been rough."

"Honestly? It wasn't *too* awful." I tilted my head as I thought. "He was always tired. He couldn't always play with me as much as I wanted. But no matter how bad he was feeling, he always made time for me. I don't feel like I missed out on anything because he was sick. He was a really great dad, and the best chieftain that ever was."

I made a disgusted noise. "People gave him shit for it, though. Said he shouldn't be chief if he couldn't handle the job. He's done more for the Toaqua tribe than any chieftain in existence. But since he has to take more days off than others, some don't see it that way."

"What happened when you were sixteen?" Charlie asked.

"Daddy had been in and out of the hospital my entire life. The nurses knew our family by our first names up there. Me and my siblings grew up playing in the hallways. It wasn't unusual for him to stay a few days here and there, but this was different. A couple days after Christmas… his lungs collapsed."

Charlie's eyebrows knitted together. Tears burned at the corners of my eyes, but I pushed them back and said, "He was in the hospital for over a month. It was a bad respiratory illness. He'd had a million before, but this one was worse than the others. A bad bout of pneumonia when he was in his twenties had already scarred the tissue in his lungs, so we knew he didn't have a great shot. A couple weeks passed and he slipped into a coma. They had to put a breathing tube in… nothing they tried worked. We had the best Anichi try to heal him, but Spirit magic only goes so far, and their powers couldn't make his lungs work again. There was no chance of recovery."

I dashed tears away with the heel of my hand. "Mama was falling apart. She couldn't function. I had to be the strong one. I had to make sure my siblings ate and rested. I kept everyone together when no one else was fit to stand. I did it because I knew Daddy needed me to."

I played with a strand of hair as I recalled the memories. "I just remember standing outside the hospital room… I'd gone to get Mama some coffee, because she'd been up all night. I heard her crying. She kept saying, *you're not leaving me alone to raise these kids.* She begged Daddy to get up, but by now, he was already half gone."

I let out a sigh. "I knew it was over when Mama told Daddy it was okay to let go. He really deteriorated after that… we had medicine men come in, to give him final rites and prepare his spirit for the Ancestral Lands."

"But your dad's still here, so he had to have made a turnaround," Charlie objected.

"He did. It was a miracle." I scooted closer. "I was with him that last night. The doctors figured he'd be dead in the morning. Mama and the rest of them had gone home to get some sleep, because there was nothing more we could do, but I insisted I had to stay. I sat by his bedside and slept through the night with my head beside his chest. I could hear his breathing… it was really rattled."

My voice cleared. "Then something happened. I remember a bright white light, hovering above the bed. I saw a pair of large blue eyes, like those of a creature, shining in the light, though I couldn't make out the rest of the animal's features. The eyes blinked at me, and— I really can't explain this— I felt the urge to lay my hands on Daddy's chest. The light got bigger, until it was so blinding I had to look away. When I opened my eyes again, the light and the creature were gone. But Daddy's vitals were strong again. They removed the breathing tube the next morning, and shortly after, he woke up. His lungs were absolutely clear. All the scarred tissue was gone. It was like they'd been completely replaced."

I couldn't help the victory that rang out in my voice. "And ever since, his disease has still been there, but it's not as bad as it was before. I didn't tell anyone what happened… didn't think they'd believe me. I knew that creature had to have *some* part in that healing, though I don't know where it came from, or how it showed up."

"Do you think you healed your dad?" Charlie asked.

I bit my lip. "I don't know what happened. I don't have Anichi powers… I think," I said slowly. "And if I do, why haven't they shown up again?"

"Maybe they only come out when you need them the most," Charlie suggested. "Your dad just didn't heal on his own."

I shrugged. "I don't know. Maybe the ancestors did it. Whatever happened, he's alive, and I thank the ancestors for it every day. I couldn't live without Daddy."

"But what about you?" Charlie's voice was anxious. "Did you inherit his illness?"

"I'm already clear. Symptoms would've shown up in me by now, and I have a clean bill of health, save for my bipolar diagnosis. I got lucky. The condition passed me over."

"Do you think your other siblings might've inherited it?"

My voice was guarded. "Maverick and Alana are pretty healthy."

"What about Ezekiel?"

I swallowed a lump in my throat. "When I was five or so, I walked into Ezekiel's room. He was still in his crib. He'd gone pale white and cold. He wouldn't move. I called for Mama. When she saw him, she just screamed and tried to heal him over and over. It worked and brought him around, but he still had to go to the hospital. Ez needed a blood transplant, and I was the only match. The doctor took my blood, and I asked him how long it would be before I died."

I laughed out loud. "It's funny now, but back then, it wasn't. I thought I had to give up myself to save him, and I was totally okay with it. He's better than me. I wanted him to live."

Charlie mused that over. "Do you think your brother has your father's disease?"

My heart twisted and grew black, like a dying old tree. "If he does, he's not going to admit it. Not until he has no other choice."

Ez had been sick on and off for a long time. Nothing quite severe, and he'd never gone to the hospital again after that one time, but there were enough clues to make me wonder. I'd fought with Ez a million times about getting tested, or getting a genetic workup so we had the proof.

Or tried, anyway. He ran away every time I brought it up. After a lifetime of seeing our dad in and out of the hospital, he didn't want to accept what could be his own reality.

"Your mother might have an idea, if she can heal," Charlie suggested.

"I don't know if she does. If my brother's illness feels different from my dad's, or if it's still dormant, my mom might not be able to pick up on it."

"That's rough." Charlie frowned.

"Yeah, I know. And it's not fair that it has to be him. He's the best person. He doesn't deserve it."

"You don't deserve your bipolar, either," Charlie said softly.

I scoffed. "I deserve what I get. Probably why I'm serving my penance."

"Hey, you're here because I pissed you off, nothing more." Charlie laughed.

"I'm not talking about the Institute." He was going to think I was totally nuts. "I hear voices."

"Huh?" Charlie slid back in surprise.

"It's called psychosis. It's a part of my condition. There are voices in my head, telling me to do things. I've always heard them, ever since I was a little girl."

"And… do you listen?" He hoped everything bad I'd done was a result of me obeying the voices inside my mind.

Too bad for him. It was all me, and my own decisions.

I laughed darkly. "I'm kinda shit at doing what I'm told, even if it's my own brain. I mostly ignore them… though sometimes, the voices get out of control."

"Has that happened lately?"

"Not in a long time. They're always talking to me. Even right now."

Charlie leaned forward. "Do they have anything to say about me?"

"The voices get… quiet when they're around you," I said. "I don't know why. Maybe it's our bond. Magic is the only solution I can think of."

Charlie's expression sorrowed. "I wish I'd been around sooner, then."

"I wish you had too. Maybe things would've turned out different." My voice was despondent and aching.

Charlie moved closer. "Like?"

"You know my best friend died," I said. "I feel responsible for that."

Charlie said nothing, and I took a breath. "Monica and I met at a pageant when we were really little. You know, one of those competitions for little kids, with the big dresses and songs and whatnot. I begged my mom to let me compete. I drove her so nuts she finally let me sign up. I practiced for weeks and weeks, because I wanted to win. My Aunt Imogen made me a really sparkly dress, and my Uncle Jonah choreographed this awesome dance for me.

"Then the day of the pageant came. There was a girl there with a homemade costume. Her mom was yelling at her in the dressing room. I could tell she really wanted that trophy. At the end of the competition, they announced my name. I was so shocked. I couldn't believe I'd won! But then I saw the look on Monica's face, and I just couldn't take the crown. I whispered to the announcer I wanted to give my win to her, and they put the crown on her head instead of mine."

A huge grin spread across my face. I couldn't suppress it… didn't want to. "That was the best moment ever. She just lit up. Ever since, we became best friends. She wanted to be a Film Studies major. We made all kinds of videos of me doing makeup tutorials, and wrote songs together. They're still up on my old vlogging channel. We made so many, she hardly ever left my house. She didn't want to."

Charlie gave a thoughtful sound. "I take it her home life wasn't the best."

"Her parents were just garbage," I snarled. "There was a reason she practically lived at my place. When we were seventeen, she got tired of it. She wanted to run away. I agreed, because it sounded like an adventure, and I wanted Monica to be happy. She was never happy when she was around them."

I continued on, voice moving quickly… like I was a murderer attempting to explain my sentence away. "I didn't think we'd *really* run away for good. I figured Monica would have her fill after a few days, and go back home. I thought I'd get grounded for making everyone worry, and she'd hear it from her parents, and that would be the end of it. And it was fun, for a while. We found an old car and drove it all around California. We were free."

My head fell against Oberi, and I stroked her coat for comfort. Her nostrils blew warm air on my shoelaces as she slumbered. "After a couple of days of stealing food from the gas station and washing our hair in bathroom sinks, I'd had enough. I wanted to go home, and told Monica so. But she didn't. She insisted living like this was better than dealing with her parents. We had a big argument. But she won, in the end. She wasn't going back home, and I refused to leave without her."

"That's honorable," Charlie said quietly. "I was homeless for a while. That you stuck with her through it shows you're loyal. I don't think I could live that way again. Not for anyone."

"I don't know how you survived it." My voice wavered on the edge of freefall. "But then, some people don't. Monica was one of them. We were walking out of a rest stop one night when these two guys started following us. I was scared. Neither of us had our magic yet, so we couldn't defend ourselves. They cornered us. One of them grabbed me and tried to shove me into a van. Monica freaked out. She went to protect me, but the other guy pulled a knife…"

I was so choked up, I could hardly speak. I couldn't verbalize what I'd seen. The images replayed so quickly in my mind all I saw was red. I still recalled the shocked look in Monica's eyes, like it'd been only yesterday.

I squeezed the next words out of my throat. "I heard my Grandmother Eleanor. She and my mom had been looking for me for days, and ancestors know there's no rock on earth I could hide under that my grandmother won't turn over to find me. When Mama saw those guys trying to stuff me in the van— fuck, she lost it. She didn't even have to move. Her Fire magic turned both of those guys to dust in an instant. They didn't even burn. There were no flames. They just combusted into a pile of ashes. I'd never seen that kind of power from her before. And then I knew exactly why she was a chosen one, and why she'd brought the Hawkei Civil War to an end. She was, and still is, the most terrifying person I know."

Charlie didn't speak, but his expression was shocked. But the worst part of the story was still to come, so I went on.

"Mama tried to use her healing powers to save Monica, but by then, it was already too late. Her Anichi magic couldn't bring back the dead, and Monica had almost bled out by the time they'd shown up. I fell to the ground and held Monica just before she passed. Her last words were my name. She died in my arms."

My voice was quivering so badly, and I hated myself for it. "Her parents didn't even let me come to the funeral. They said it was *my* fault she died. And every shitty lie they'd ever told me didn't matter, because what they said then was the truth. I should've brought her home… should've forced her. And because I didn't, she's gone."

Charlie remained silent, and I forged a way through my memories, because the only way through them was out. "I just remember them turning me away at the door… there was so much hate. I looked up at Mama, and these tears were just pouring out of my eyes. I couldn't stop them. We rushed home and had our own private ceremony on the beach for Monica. It was the only way I could say goodbye."

I sniffed and wiped my face with my sleeve. "So now you now. Monica's dead because of me."

"She's not," Charlie insisted, softness in his voice. "You went with her because you wanted to protect her. You couldn't have saved Monica any more than I could've saved Marty. They both made bad decisions. We had no choice but to stand there and watch."

I didn't acknowledge whether he was right or wrong. It wouldn't make any difference anyway. Either resulted in Monica being gone.

I cleared my voice and began to speak normally again… finally… achingly. "After Monica died, I just deteriorated. I spiraled into the worst manic period of my life. I couldn't make videos or music again— that was our thing, and to do it without her felt like a betrayal. One day, my psychosis got out of control. I thought I was in the circus… like I was some kind of acrobat. I climbed from the stairs onto the chandelier we have in the living room."

My mouth went dry. "I started swinging from it upside down by my legs. I tried to do a backflip off of it. I would've broken my neck if Ezekiel hadn't caught me. The chandelier fell, and Alana had to jump out of the way. She cut up her hands and knees on the glass, but it could've been worse. The chandelier almost crushed her. She had to be rushed to the hospital so she didn't bleed out. When I finally came down, I couldn't remember anything. The only way I recalled what I did was when my brother told me what I'd been mumbling while I was up there."

Charlie's silence filled the aching space. He didn't rush to explanations or comfort like most people did. He just let me say what I had to say.

"Alana didn't blame me for what happened. Ez didn't, either. Or anyone else. But that my siblings had seen me fall apart and be vulnerable like that gave me so much guilt, I felt bad for merely existing. I almost killed myself and my sister in one go. Just like I killed Monica."

"What happened to Monica wasn't your doing," Charlie said. "And it wasn't her fault that she got killed. Monica didn't want to die. This falls on the person who wanted to end her life."

"She was my friend. People who get close to me get hurt. I destroy everything in my path, and she was collateral damage. And that's what you'll be, if you continue to hang around me."

"I'm pretty good about shielding myself from destructive people. I've done it all my life. And no matter what you think, what happened to Monica wasn't your fault." Charlie grabbed my arm and gave a squeeze, as if he wanted me to believe him.

"There are a lot of things that were my fault." I dropped my voice, terrified someone would overhear us even though we were alone up here. My biggest secret felt so dark, I was afraid of even the ancestors finding out.

Charlie came so close, our bodies were touching. Instinctively, he opened his arms and wrapped them around me. I didn't resist. Instead, I fell into his arms and against his chest. I held his forearms as he squeezed me, and he put his chin on top of my head. I could hear his heartbeat as it thudded on steadily behind me, like the sound of a Hawkei drum.

Cuddling. We were fucking *cuddling*. It'd be freaking adorable if I wasn't spilling my guts right now. Oberi sighed, as if she could sense our barriers falling away and was finally resting in that peace.

As he held me close, Charlie asked, "What happened?"

He implied that he knew there was more, or maybe had guessed. It was useless trying to hide something this vital from someone you had a soul bond with. He could feel my pain. And he knew how broken I was.

I could use the alcohol as an excuse tomorrow morning, but I didn't think either one of us would buy it. We weren't drunk anymore.

But Charlie would go along with the lie, for my sake. Because what I was about to tell him next, I'd never told anyone.

"A couple weeks after Monica died, some people in my class invited me to a party," I said. "Monica and I were never really close with anyone, just relied on each other, but these girls felt sorry for me. I figured I had to get out and try to distract myself, so I went."

My voice was emotionless this time. There weren't any tears, or feelings. I just couldn't muster up any for this situation. I'd put it away, compartmentalized it deep within myself in a place not even my spirit could reach. "There was a guy there. John. He was in mine and Monica's friend group, though she never liked him. I thought he was cool. We talked a lot and I'd known him since I was a freshman. He wanted to go for a walk in the woods, talk about Monica. Nobody ever mentioned her anymore, so off I went."

Charlie's body went rigid as I spoke. "He got me far enough into the woods that nobody heard me scream. I tried to fight him off, but he was stronger. He pushed me face down and climbed on top of me. You can guess what happened after that."

I could still remember what the leaves smelled like, and what the dirt felt like all over my face. I remembered it was so cold that night that I could see John's breath. Didn't remember much else except how badly I wanted to escape.

Charlie pressed his lips to my hair and rocked me. He wasn't much of a talker. But he always said what he needed to. The movement gave me strength to go on.

"John finished inside of me and just let me lay there… like some kind of object. I was still in the woods long after the party was over. Eventually, I got up off the ground and forced myself to walk into town… because I knew I couldn't go missing again. It would worry my family."

I was rattling off random facts now, snippets of what I remembered. "There's a woman's shelter in Kinpago. The lady at the front counter— her name was Mia— she patched me up, gave me a morning-after pill… asked me to do a rape kit. I did it, because she said it was a good idea, but it never went farther than that. I begged her not to tell anyone, and she said she wouldn't. Then I washed my face and went back home, and haven't talked about it since. Nobody knows but you."

Charlie stiffened a little in shock, but he quickly relaxed. "I never told anyone about Marty, either. I'm glad we can trust each other like that."

Trust. It was such a strange word to me. I couldn't comprehend what it was like to trust again. Outside of my family, I'd never trusted anyone but Monica.

So I launched into another explanation, to avoid the vulnerability. "My mania got worse afterward. I was out of control. I went on a spree and just blew all my savings. Thousands of dollars, gone in a few hours. That's why my parents have access to all my credit cards, and my bank account. I want them to monitor me in case it happens again. So I don't lose everything twice."

"Do you think there's a risk for that?" Charlie murmured.

"I don't know. I can't imagine being in a worse place emotionally than I was at that moment. I took everything out on Daddy. I treated him so terribly after the whole thing, but I knew that I could say or do anything to him, and he'd never hold it against me. I just used him like a punching bag for everything I was feeling, and he just… took it. It was so wrong, and I feel so bad about it. I want to say I'm sorry, but it's not like I can tell him the reason why. It'd break his heart."

I leaned my head into Charlie's shirt. Leather and bergamot… the scent I loved. "Things got so awful between me and Daddy that I told Mama I wanted to move out for a while. I stayed with my Uncle Jonah and Uncle Jake. They're both big guys, you know? I figured no one would be able to hurt me again, not with them around. Josee and I shared a room. I think she suspected something, but she never asked."

I finally relaxed against Charlie's hold and sighed, because the hard part was over, and at last, I felt like my wings had grown back after being clipped— like the chains holding me down for years no longer had any bearing on me. "There isn't much more to tell. I went back home, eventually. I told Mama I couldn't go back to high school— because I couldn't bear sitting in class with my rapist— and made up some excuse. I studied at home and barely got by. Once I graduated, I committed crime after crime… until I ended up here."

I cleared my throat. "The day I got my magic was *the best*. I never felt more powerful than when I conjured a fireball for the first time. I knew if John tried anything again… if anyone did… I'd burn them to ash, like my mother did. And I'd never have to be helpless. I could rescue myself."

Charlie's voice was astonished. "You kept silent about it for almost three years."

"I thought about telling people. But I'm the daughter of the Toaqua chief and the chosen one. It can't get out that I was raped," I told Charlie. "So many people already scrutinize Daddy because he has a disease. They'd say he wasn't capable of protecting his own daughter. They might even ask him to step down."

"Your dad can handle the scrutiny," Charlie said. "Your family's not going to be ashamed of you."

"But I'm ashamed of myself," I insisted. "I was too scared to fight back, so I just took it. After that night, I promised myself I'd *always* fight back, no matter what. I vowed I'd never let anyone violate me like that again. I'd die first."

Charlie's grip tightened around me. "Ava, I want you to listen to me. You could've done *nothing* to stop him. If you had fought back at all, he might've killed you. Keeping yourself alive is nothing to be ashamed of."

His words grew firmer, with a greater conviction. "I didn't *want* those women to use my body. I hated every moment of it. But I let them do it, because staying alive to see the next morning was more important. And no matter how you feel about yourself, you should be damn glad you're still here. I know for certain I am. I would've been missing a piece of my soul forever if you were gone. No matter what's happened to me so far, I think it was worth it just to get to you. You're a fighter. And I'm proud of you for that."

He was proud of me? But how could he be? Wasn't I a monster?

"I'm really tired," I whispered. Telling Charlie all that had worn me out.

"We still have a few hours until sunrise. Might as well catch up on some sleep," he suggested.

"I've barely slept in days, Charlie."

"I know, pidge."

My head fell back against his chest, which was soft and warm. I was closer this time. His heartbeat was louder, and I came to a scary realization.

Charlie made me feel something. The first something in a long time.

I wasn't used to feeling. I didn't like it. I wanted to be numb.

But I needed to feel in order to be free.

"Sleep softly, princess," he said quietly. "I'll ward off your nightmares."

I liked that. I liked that a lot. I let my eyes close and allowed myself to slip back into oblivion, finally safe.

Once the sun rose, we'd go back to hating each other. It was the only way we knew how.

But in the darkness, we didn't have to pretend.

charlie

SEVENTEEN

I hadn't been to a party in ages. I'd gotten drunk enough as a teenager to know that alcohol only got you into trouble. But with Ava-Marie, it was different. She was carefree and reckless, and as much as that scared me, I also wanted to be a part of it.

Ava didn't seem to remember much after the fae wine, but while she was downing shots like they were candy, I was drinking in *her*. Someone had to protect her if things got out of hand, after all. I didn't get the tattoo because I was drunk. I got it because... well, I *wanted* it— though I could barely admit the fact to myself. Ava and I were bonded. Whether anything else happened between us, that was never going to change. I only had to pretend it wasn't a big deal, because I knew Ava didn't feel the same way.

But the party, the tattoos, the fun... it couldn't compare to that morning in the loft when Ava opened her heart to me and entrusted me with her deepest secrets. I held her close, inhaling her scent and tearing up when she told me about what happened to her. I didn't think she saw me cry, and I didn't want her to. She'd make a speech about how everyone had been trying to protect her her whole life, and how she could take care of herself. She didn't want me to feel sorry for her.

But I did. Ancestors, I felt the pain sink into every pore of my body, eating at me until my stomach became hollow and my limbs lost all feeling. Ava-Marie didn't deserve what happened to her. I didn't blame her for the way she acted after the fact. Ava may not have realized what she was doing, but I recognized a cry for help when I saw one.

And I wanted with every fiber of my being to be the one to answer that call.

I burned to drive a knife through the men who had killed her best friend. I craved the chance to pummel the face of the rapist who hurt her. I prayed for everyone who had ever left a mere scratch on my poor pidge's heart to suffer the consequences.

Forget the fiery inferno she could rain down upon them. I'd steal the air from their lungs and force dirt down their throats, then crush them with boulders over and over, never giving them a moment to beg for mercy, but not giving them the freedom of death, either.

Those assholes deserved a lifetime of torture for hurting Ava. I'd savor every moment of it.

I would never hurt her, not in this life or the next. I would always be at her side to support her, and to protect her when she couldn't manage on her own.

But Ava would never know. She was a strong, dual-casting Elementai with incredible power. It would be an insult if she knew I was lurking… watching and waiting for anyone who dare touch my pidge.

Ava was back to her normal self in the morning, as if she'd forgotten our conversation altogether. But I knew it was an act. Her tone was hesitant, and I could feel the emotions coming off of Oberi, like she too smelled a hint of Ava's bullshit.

I didn't blame her, though. She didn't want to talk about it, so I wouldn't bring it up. But damn it all if it didn't keep me up at night. I barely slept over the following week, like this was some type of problem I was meant to solve and had no answer to. Not here at the Institute, at least.

I tried telling myself it had happened a long time ago— that I couldn't bring Monica back from the dead any more than I could revive Marty. I couldn't go back in time and change what John had done.

And yet I felt there was something more I could do— something I *had* to do. It hit me one morning. I'd been having a dream… a really good dream, though the details began to drift from my mind as soon as I woke. I struggled to hang on to the memory. I'd been sitting in a crowd somewhere, stroking Oberi's fur. A beautiful voice had filled the room, warming my heart…

It had been Ava's voice.

Not the Ava I knew, but the girl she was before she met me— before all that crap had turned her life upside down.

I wanted to know who Ava used to be, and I wanted to help her find that girl again.

I didn't know how to do it, but an idea struck after I got out of the shower. Oberi was waiting for me in my dorm. He was in husky form, and he shoved something into my hands. I ran my fingers over it and felt soft bristles.

"You telling me I need to groom myself or something?" I teased.

Oberi barked.

"Ah, you want to be brushed," I said with a sigh. "Roll over."

Oberi followed my command, and I started brushing his fur while I tickled his belly. He rubbed his head across the floor in pleasure.

"Five more minutes," I warned. "I've got stuff to do today."

Oberi wasn't satisfied after five minutes of grooming, but I set the brush aside anyway. I really *did* have stuff to do before class. I leaned down and felt behind my dresser, where I'd stashed the few things Marcus had snuck out of Contraband for me. My fingers curled around the headphones, and I tucked them into my jacket.

"You coming?" I asked Oberi, and he yipped happily.

Oberi and I stopped by the dining hall and ate quickly before making our way to the library. The computers here were kind of shit, and not just because they didn't work well around magic. Tons of websites were blocked, and they didn't have any software installed to help navigate while blind. Luckily, Oberi had learned how to help me find the icons I needed, as I'd started coming in here to work on schoolwork.

"Fire up the Internet, bud," I told him.

Oberi pressed his nose against the touchscreen, while I fumbled around looking for the headphone jack. I finally found it on the side of the computer and plugged it in. I wasn't supposed to have these headphones, but it was early enough in the day that the library was pretty secluded. I didn't think anyone would notice me, as long as I didn't take too long.

It took forever for the page to load. Oberi nudged me once it did. I typed in what I was looking for. Oberi got so excited his tongue lolled out of his mouth and he slobbered all over my arm.

I turned my nose up and wiped the slobber off. "Ew, Oberi. I guess that means we found it."

Oberi leaned forward to press his nose to the screen, and his wagging tail smacked me in the arm.

I was about to complain, until the sound of a beautiful voice filled the speakers. I went as still as a statue.

"Hello, magical creatures," the girl in the video said. "It's Ava-Marie and Monica back with another video. This song was written at two a.m. while we were high on gummy bears and caffeine, so we hope you like it. It's called *Until the Sun Rises*."

It was Ava's old vlog... the one where she and Monica wrote songs and did makeup tutorials.

The sound of a soft piano filled my ears, followed shortly by an acoustic guitar accompanying the slow melody. Ava began to sing, and I swore I nearly fell out of my chair. It was so much more beautiful than anything I could've ever dreamt. The sound of her voice sent a shiver down my spine. I'd heard her sing once— when she'd summoned the ancestors in the cave— but she was more incredible than I remembered.

The stars above won't leave me alone
But they're all just dim disguises.
I won't escape from the dark of night
Until the sun rises.

The whole song was a metaphor that talked about a girl who was being chased by so many guys, but none of them could satisfy her. She was holding out for the one who could pull her from the darkness and brighten up her days. She was waiting for her *sun*.

Could I be the one Ava had been waiting for?

I pushed the thought away quickly. Ava and I were bonded, and that was it. It wasn't like we were dating, or like we ever would. That was a sure-fire way to damn our bond to hell and ruin every good thing we might possibly ever have.

Oberi clicked on another video, and Ava's voice filled my headphones once again. It was really nice to hear her sing at first, but the more I listened, the sadder I got. She was *so* incredible, and she'd let it all go. She didn't think it was fair to Monica to continue without her, but Ava was throwing her talent away. She could use her music for so much good— to reconnect with Monica's memory and help make sense of what happened. Eventually, she could use her music to inspire others to overcome similar turmoil. Instead, she'd turned to raising hell and getting herself into trouble.

It was sad, really. I wished she would play again.

"Hey, man."

Someone placed a heavy hand on my shoulder, and I jumped. I quickly pulled the headphones off and hid them in my lap, but I'd already been caught.

"What?" I asked.

"It's me, Marcus," he announced.

Marcus was nice like that. Most people expected me to know who they were by the sound of their voice or their scent— like I was a dog or something— but it wasn't that easy. Ava's was really the only voice I could pick out of a crowd.

"Since when do you come to the library in the morning?" he asked as he slid into the chair next to me. The computer in front of him made a slight *whirring* noise as it turned on. "I never see you here."

I pressed the power button on the computer so he wouldn't see what I was up to. "I, uh, just had some stuff to catch up on."

"Don't you have class right now?"

Shit. I hadn't realized how long I'd been sitting there listening to Ava's vlog. How many videos had I listened to? A dozen?

"What time is it?" I asked.

"Almost ten."

"Crap." I shoved my headphones in my bag and stood. "I gotta get to class."

"Oh, Charlie?" Marcus stopped me. "Kallie's trying to get everyone together after class to do some training for the Darke Games. You in?"

"Training?" I asked skeptically. I barely knew what we'd be up against during the Darke Games, let alone how to train for it.

"Yeah, we want to win, don't we?" Marcus asked. "We're meeting at the Villain's Den after dinner. You in?"

"Yeah, sure," I mumbled, though my heart swelled. As long as the rest of us were there, Ava would be, too. "I'll catch you later."

I didn't see Ava the rest of the day, which was strange because we usually ate together during meals. I was starting to worry when I arrived at the Villain's Den after dinner.

All I had to do was follow the sound of arguing.

"Come on, Kalina. What's in the box?"

"That's Kallie to you, *Marcus*," she said sternly. "And I told you— it's a surprise."

"Can't you give me a *hint*?" he begged.

"Sure," she said brightly. "If you volunteer to be the one who opens it."

Marcus hesitated. "Okay…"

Kalina sounded proud. "Your hint is you'll be sorry you volunteered."

Marcus groaned. "Not fair."

Oberi padded along at my side, but he didn't get excited, which told me Ava hadn't arrived yet.

"Where's Ava?" I asked as I sat down beside them.

"She should be here any minute," Kalina— sorry, *Kallie*— said. She'd insisted she was trying to make a turnaround with her life, so I needed to respect that by calling her by her chosen name.

It was mere moments later when Ava walked in the room. I didn't know how I sensed her, because I was sitting a good ten feet from the door. But her scent hit me immediately, and the whole room warmed when she entered.

"Late, as usual," Kallie teased.

"I'm not late," Ava argued as she approached us. "You're all early… ancestors, Oberi. Did someone skimp on your grooming this morning? Your fur is a mess!"

Something like glass clinked as Ava set it on the table. She plopped down beside me and started running her fingers through Oberi's fur. The husky barked in pleasure. I swear he'd be purring if he could.

"Where have you been?" I asked. "You missed lunch and dinner."

"Did I?" Ava asked, like she hadn't realized what time it was. "I got held up in the Alchemy room. We're working on a healing potion, but it's hardly effective. There *has* to be a more potent mixture than the recipe in the book. I simply *must* figure it out… hey, Marcus. Maybe you can help. The recipe originated from the Miriamic Coven."

Ava's voice grew strained as she spoke, then a *pop* like a cork sounded. "Here, smell it."

Marcus snorted. "Don't ask *me* about healing salves."

"I thought you could perform *any* warlock magic," she pointed out. "Isn't that what your tattoos mean?"

"I *can*," Marcus emphasized. "I just… haven't taken the class yet."

"Here, Charlie." Ava shoved something into my hands, and I took it. It was a small glass vial and heavy enough to be filled to the brim. "Doesn't this smell off?"

I lifted the potion to my nose and sniffed it. It smelled of citrus, but more on the *tart* side than the *sweet*. "It doesn't smell *bad*, but I haven't taken Alchemy. I don't know what it *should* smell like."

"No matter," Kallie said, taking charge. "We're not here to talk about classes. We're here to train for the Darke Games."

"Where are we training?" I asked as I handed the potion back to Ava.

Kalina stood. "Follow me."

The three of us, along with Rishi and Oberi, followed behind Kallie.

"Does anyone know what exactly we're training for?" I asked. "I mean, we know monsters are going to be coming through the portals, but what kind?"

"It could be anything," Kallie answered.

A thought struck. "Just how many possibilities are there?"

"You're wondering how many monsters there are in hell?" Kallie asked, sounding slightly amused. "Thousands of species… millions, maybe. Which is why we have to be prepared for *anything*. Ah, yes. This will do."

I didn't realize where we were going until we stepped into the room. The air was warmer and humid. My Air magic expanded, but it met resistance high above our heads against the ceiling. The room was almost as big as the chapel, but not as tall. The smell of dirt and flowers hit my nose, and my Earth magic immediately sensed plant species of all kinds filling the room. Oberi's footsteps beside mine turned from soft padding on the carpet to scratches, like he was walking over stone. Birds chirped from the rafters, and a small waterfall trickled off in the distance.

"Where are we?" I asked.

"This is the school's greenhouse, sometimes called the Arboretum," Kallie explained. "I'm surprised you haven't been in here before. This room was specifically designed for Elementai."

Ava had been silent, like she was taking it all in, but when Kallie explained the nature of the room, Ava huffed. "Well, no one mentioned it to *us*. Jerks."

Kallie didn't seem to hear her. "Anyway, I thought this would be a good place to train. There's plenty of room, but unlike the prison yard, it's not crawling with people."

Oberi seemed thrilled. Oberi shifted into a Fire unicorn and took off running down the stone path, hooves beating against the ground. Rishi meowed and ran after her.

"Don't go too far," I called.

"Relax," Ava said, like we were parenting a child together. "Let her have fun. She doesn't get many chances to be free."

For a moment, it didn't sound like she was talking about Oberi.

"First things first," Kallie said. "Marcus, hold this."

"Can I open it yet?" he asked.

"Not yet," Kallie instructed. "I think we should start with some sparring. I want to see what you guys are capable of."

Ava cracked her knuckles. "Are you doubting me?"

Kallie scoffed. "You? No. But I need to know what your limits are. Ava, you'll be on Marcus' team. Charlie, you're with me."

Ava huffed. "Who says *you're* in charge? I want to be on Charlie's team."

"I didn't see *you* stepping up to be team Captain," Kallie shot back. "I *am* the one who planned this training session."

"I say we vote on team captain," Ava insisted. "I'd like to nominate myself."

"You can't nominate yourself!" Kallie cried.

I sighed. Ancestors, we hadn't even started training yet and already we were fighting. "Maybe we should draw straws," I suggested.

"No way!" Ava protested. "With our luck, *Marcus* will be named team captain."

"Hey!" Marcus objected.

"Well, this is just a great way to start off our *team training session*," I groaned. "Why can't you two be co-captains?"

"Co-captains?" they balked in unison.

"Excuse me," Ava said. "There were no *co*-captains on my cheerleading squad—"

"And there are no co-captains to the crown," Kallie added before Ava could finish.

"Our team needs one leader," Ava insisted.

"And a cool name," Marcus added.

"How about *you all shut up and listen*," I growled. "You guys want me on your team for the Darke Games? Then you're going to have to get your shit together. There's no way we're fighting monsters if we can't get through *one* training session without arguing over team Captain. So either come to a mutual agreement, or there *will* be no team to captain."

Marcus piped up immediately. "I vote for Charlie."

"Yeah," Ava agreed quickly. "Charlie can be captain."

I groaned. That was *so* not what I meant.

"Fine," Kalina conceded. It was obvious she wasn't going to get what she wanted. "Tell me, Captain, where shall we start?"

I hesitated. I longed to tell them I wasn't Captain material, but that was a good way to stir up another fight. If I had to be Captain to keep the peace, then so be it. "Let's start with some sparring, like you suggested. Ava and me against Kallie and Marcus."

"Okay," Kallie agreed. "Let's find somewhere with more space— ah!"

Kallie's shriek echoed off the windows of the greenhouse. Ava and Marcus both started laughing so hard that neither of them could hardly breathe.

I was about to ask what just happened when Kallie shouted, "I'm soaked! What the hell, Ava?"

Ava must've summoned water from the greenhouse fountain and splashed it all over Kalina.

"I thought we were sparring," Ava defended between laughs. "You have to be ready for anything, right?"

"Yeah, like my battle orb up your ass," Kalina shot back, though she laughed like she was only joking.

Except the battle orb was no joke. Magic crackled through the air, and Ava gasped. Immediately, I heard the *whoosh* of a fireball and felt the heat cross my skin as Ava threw it past me. The two must've collided, because an explosion sounded between us. Kallie immediately threw another orb, and Ava grabbed me by the shirt to drag me down another path.

"Hell, you two turned this place into a battle zone in less than two seconds," I hissed as we ducked down behind foliage.

Ava chuckled, like she was having fun. Was this normal in the magical community, like laser tag or paintball back in Detroit?

"That's kind of the point, isn't it?" Ava said. Her clothes brushed against me as she stood quickly to throw another fireball. She ducked down just as fast.

"Shit," she muttered under her breath.

"What? Is someone hurt?" I asked in alarm.

"No," she said, like that was the least of her worries. "Kallie's got shield magic."

"Isn't that good news?"

"We'll lose!" Ava cried.

"But she's on our side in the Darke Games," I pointed out.

Ava scoffed. "Yeah, but she's about to murder us in the meantime. Come on."

Ava grabbed me again, and we went sprinting down another trail. Ava stopped in her tracks, and I came to a halt beside her. Something had changed, though I couldn't describe what. The scent of flowers around me vanished, though I could still sense their presence through my Earth magic. The ground below me squished, though I knew I was still on the path. A horrid smell like a rotting carcass filled my nose.

"What's going on?" I demanded.

Ava's voice turned sour. "It's Kallie. Some sort of an illusion. All I see ahead is a dark swamp. I don't know where the path went."

"How do we break the illusion? There has to be a way!"

Ava sounded calm and collected, but I was freaking out. I couldn't navigate my world if I was being tricked by my own senses.

"Kallie's strong, but it's only an illusion," Ava explained. "My Aunt Imogen taught me about fae magic as a kid. It's all in your head, so all you have to do is override the illusion and convince yourself what you're seeing isn't real."

"But it *feels* so real," I argued. My feet sank deeper into the mud, and the stench grew stronger.

"Focus on what you *know* to be true," Ava encouraged.

"I know we're in the greenhouse," I said, my voice calming. "I can feel the plants around us. And the air meets resistance at the ceiling. It's not wide-open like a swamp."

"Exactly," Ava said, though it sounded like she was still trying to fight the illusion herself.

"The rock beneath me speaks to me," I observed. "The mud isn't real."

As I said it, the sinking sensation vanished, and I found myself standing on solid ground again. The illusion wasn't totally over, though. I still smelled the stench of death permeating through the air.

"I know the greenhouse shouldn't smell like this," I continued. "It should smell green and like flowers. There was the scent of dirt when we walked in, too, and some sort of cleaner in the water."

Slowly, the horrid scent faded, and the smells and sounds of the greenhouse returned.

"We're back!" Ava cried, before taking my hand. "Come on. Kallie's illusion slowed us down. Let's get out of here before she finds us."

We took off running again. Oberi's hooves sounded ahead, but she stopped dead when she saw us coming.

"Up you go." I grabbed Ava around the waist and shoved her onto Oberi's back, then climbed on myself. I wrapped my arms around Ava and held her close. She either didn't notice or didn't seem bothered by it. "Let's get to the fountain. You'll need a source of water."

"It's not a fountain," Ava said. "It's a pool. I can feel it."

Oberi took off running, and we made it to the other side of the greenhouse. Marcus was nearby, which was obvious in his heavy footsteps, but Kalina either wasn't moving or was sneaking along soundlessly. We slid off Oberi, and Ava planted herself in front of me.

"Come and get me," she called. "I dare you!"

A growl erupted from behind a large tree, and the brush rustled as a creature lunged from behind it. Instinct took over, and I thrust my Air magic outward. A gust of wind rushed by, snatching the creature from the air. It was large— almost as big as Oberi. It tumbled through the air and landed hard on one of the pathways. A whimper came, but it morphed into the sound of Kalina's groans.

I realized then that the creature *had* been Kalina, though she'd been in her wolf form when she attacked.

"Ow!" she breathed. "That was one hell of a blow, Charlie."

"I'm sorry," I said quickly. "I didn't know it was you."

"Sorry?" she balked. "We can totally use magic like that in the Darke Games. Don't hold back on my account."

"She's right," Ava agreed. "Give it all you've got. Kallie can take it."

And now they were back on the same page. I'd never understand girls.

"Dear Goddess!" Marcus cried as he finally wound his way through the path over to us. "Kallie, are you okay— whoa!"

Marcus must've tripped, because the next thing I knew, the box in his hands had clattered to the ground. Rishi let out a high-pitched shriek, and Marcus grunted a few times before a huge *splash* sounded and water soaked the front of my pants.

Ava cackled from beside me, and Oberi whinnied. Marcus sputtered water and continued splashing it everywhere.

"Do we need to go in and save him?" I asked.

"Relax," Ava laughed. "It's less than three feet deep. Marcus, stop flailing! Your ass is touching the bottom."

"Gods," Kalina sighed. "Marcus, stop fooling around. I could use your help out here."

Marcus must've found his bearings, because he stopped sputtering and splashing. Water dripped onto the path as he dragged himself out of the water. "I-I'm fine," he gasped.

"You better be," Kalina said. "If you drowned in a koi pond, we're going to have problems during the Games."

"You know I don't swim well," Marcus growled.

"Learn," Kallie snapped.

"Hey," I cut in before another fight broke out. I quickly changed the subject. "I think we've all proved to each other we can handle ourselves in combat. But that illusion magic was something else, Kallie. Any chance we'll be up against something like that in the Games?"

"It's possible," she replied. "Honestly, I'm surprised you managed to break through it so fast."

"Your illusion was strong," Ava admitted, "but you put all the details in the scenery. Charlie could break through the rest with ease."

"Mm..." Kallie mused. "I'll have to work on that."

To be honest, Kallie's illusion was enough to convince me. The dead tell was how quickly the scene had shifted. Had she knocked me out beforehand, I never would've known.

"Let's try something else," I suggested. "What's the box for?"

"Oh, this is a good one," Kallie said brightly. She walked over to retrieve the box from where Marcus had dropped it. "Marcus, if you'd do the honors."

Marcus stepped forward, his clothes making *dripping* sounds on the ground.

"Hold up," Ava sighed. "Marcus, let me dry you off."

Ava used her Toaqua magic to draw the water out of Marcus' clothes. It must've been a lot, because it made a *splash* when she dropped it back into the pond.

"Thanks," Marcus said sheepishly, before addressing Kalina. "Are you going to tell me what's in the box?"

"Just open it," she said impatiently.

Marcus hesitated, then a hinge squeaked.

"Ancestors!" Ava cried in a high-pitched voice, as if she was looking down at a newborn baby. "It's adorable. What is it?"

"Ugh, it's ugly!" Marcus sounded repulsed. "What's with all the glitter?"

"Glitter is *fabulous*," Ava argued.

Meanwhile, Kalina just laughed without explaining. It was like she was waiting for something.

"What is it?" I asked.

Ava turned to me, gushing. "It's the most beautiful glowing fairy! She's sitting at the bottom of the box, staring up at us with the most gorgeous ruby eyes. I just want to take her home and—"

Whiz!

It sounded like wings flapping a thousand beats per minute, but it was gone as soon as it came. Marcus coughed, choking on something, and the box clattered to the ground again.

"Ancestors!" Ava cried.

She grabbed for Marcus, but he fell backward into both of us. I helped stand him upright, but he seemed to have lost control of his limbs.

"That thing flew up his nose!" Ava cried. Her awe had vanished. "What is it, Kallie?"

Kallie's laugh was muffled. "It's a minor demon known as an *allure*. It possesses you and makes you want to have sex all the time."

"Kallie!" I roared, still trying to hold Marcus upright. "How could you!?"

"He volunteered!" she defended.

"He didn't know what he was volunteering for!" I shot back.

Suddenly, Marcus went silent. Rishi must've noticed something was off about him, because he hissed.

"Well, hellooo there," Marcus drawled in a seductive tone toward Ava. It was pretty obvious he was possessed, because the real Marcus had the charm of a limp dick. "What's your name, beautiful?"

He went to drape an arm around Ava's shoulder and nearly punched me in the nose in the process. I reeled back a step, but Ava knew how to handle her own.

"Not happening," Ava snapped. She must've had Marcus' hand in a painful hold, because he sucked air between his teeth.

"Feisty," Marcus— or rather, the allure— said in amusement. "You and I could have lots of fun."

"Hell no." Ava shoved him away. "Even if you're possessed, I'm not falling for that. Try it on someone else."

"My, my." Marcus' voice came directly in front of me, so I could only guess he was speaking to me. He drew in a deep, hungry breath. "Aren't you a tall glass of water? And let me tell you, boy. I. Am. Thirsty."

Marcus ran a finger down my chest, and my guts twisted. I grabbed him by the wrists to stop him.

"Kallie, what exactly is the point of this exercise?" I demanded.

"Demon possession," she said like it was obvious. "Do I have to remind you we'll be up against demons from hell? There's a chance we'll have to exorcise one."

I blew a breath. "Are you freaking kidding me?"

Ava burst at the same time. "And you decided to possess our *warlock*— the one race that can actually perform exorcisms correctly?"

"We needed a challenge!" Kallie insisted. "Besides, this demon is harmless. It's just horny."

"Harmless my ass," I scoffed. She was standing there looking pretty while I was trying to keep Marcus at a distance. My hand was shoved into his face, getting slobber all over while he tried to make out with me.

"You think *I'm* sexy?" I challenged the demon. "Check out Kallie!"

I grabbed Marcus by the shoulders and spun him around. He stopped dead.

"Oh," he said breathlessly. "Yes… how could I not have seen you before? You glow like a radiant goddess. I must have you, my queen!"

"Hey!" Kallie protested. "I didn't ask for this."

"It was your idea," I said with a shrug.

Marcus stepped away from me, thank the ancestors. Meanwhile, Ava turned my way, sounding irritated. "You think *Kallie's* sexy?"

I scoffed. "I haven't even seen the girl— literally. I just said that to get him off our back while we come up with a solution."

"Oh." Ava sounded pleased. "Well, I don't know much about exorcisms. I know the Miriamic Coven has rituals to cast out demons, but we're SOL there."

"No, Marcus!" Kallie shouted. "I will *not* sleep with you! Go away!"

I cocked an eyebrow at Ava. "You think he's really possessed?"

"Hard to tell," Ava chuckled. "But if you saw the look in his eyes, then the answer is yes. He looks weirdly starstruck."

"Okay, so a ritual is out of the question," I said thoughtfully. "How do demons survive in a host?"

"I don't know," Ava mused. "Most demon possessions are spiritual, but this one… it was like her body entered his. She's grabbed the controls to his brain and is turning it into a mush of hormones."

"So the allure is like a parasite. What happens if we make the host body uninhabitable?" I asked.

"Uninhabitable how?"

"I don't know," I admitted. "Could we give him some sort of antidote, or maybe something that'll make him sick? If his immune system isn't up to snuff, it could flush the demon out."

"So we want him to run a fever?" Ava asked thoughtfully.

"It's just a theory—" I started, but she cut me off.

"No, it's a good one," Ava said. "I think I know how to do it. Marcus! Come here. I'll have sex with you!"

"Pidge!" I cried. Oberi shook her head like she hadn't heard her right.

"Relax," Ava whispered under her breath. "I just wanted to get the demon's attention."

Marcus strolled up to Ava. "I knew it. My charm works every time."

"Yeah, yeah," Ava said flatly. "Just kiss me, will you?"

My blood ran cold.

"Gladly." Marcus sounded a little too enthused if you asked me, but I had to remind myself it was the demon, and not him.

Marcus slurped on Ava's lips like she was a slushie. I couldn't stand to listen. I had to steady myself against Oberi, because I thought I might puke. Had she *really* just asked Marcus to kiss her? It felt like a knife had embedded itself in my guts. I knew it was a ploy, but still, it felt like a betrayal.

"It's not working!" Ava said.

"What are you doing?" Kallie demanded.

"I'm using my Fire to heat Marcus' internal organs," she explained. "He's got to have a fever of a hundred-and-four already. If I go any further, I might kill him."

"You've *got* to be kidding me," Kallie sighed. "This is a sex demon, remember? Heat is kind of their thing."

I wanted to get in on the conversation, to throw out solutions so I didn't have to keep listening to the two of them suck face, but I couldn't find my bearings. The whole thing made me sick.

"I've got it!" Ava cried, but Marcus silenced her with another gross kiss.

Kallie gasped. "Gods, Ava, what are you doing?"

Ava drew away from Marcus to speak. "Toaqua can create ice. I'm using my powers to *lower* his body temperature. That should draw the demon—"

Marcus sputtered before Ava could finish her sentence.

"It's working!" Kallie exclaimed. "Keep going, Ava."

Marcus continued coughing, and his hands slapped to the pavement.

Oh, shit. Now we were killing him. That was just great.

"Pidge, no!" I cried. "We'll find another way. We'll get a professor to help."

Kallie scoffed. "So I can get locked in Cellblock 9 for sneaking this demon out of class? No, thank you."

"He's obviously in pain," I pointed out.

"Trust me, Charlie," Ava insisted. "This is working."

Damn it, I wanted to trust her, but I couldn't stand here listening to Marcus cough like that. He was going to lose a lung.

"Pidge," I pressed.

"It's almost out," she promised. "I can feel it. Just a little more…"

Marcus hacked so loud it echoed off the windows of the greenhouse. The demon let out a scream as it tumbled out of his body. Relief flooded through me.

"You did it!" Kallie cried. She shuffled forward, presumably to capture the demon and place it back in the box.

I finally found my legs and rushed over to Marcus. He lay on the ground, wheezing. Rishi raced under my feet. I nearly tripped over him as I knelt beside Marcus.

"You okay?" I asked, slapping him a little to get him to wake. "Marcus!"

"Fuuuck…" he breathed, his teeth clattering together. "It's cold in here. What the hell happened?"

I frowned. "The girls happened."

"Hey, it was a good training exercise!" Kallie protested. "And we did it— without your help, mind you."

"Actually, it was Charlie's idea," Ava said. "Marcus, I'm going to use my Fire to warm you up, okay?"

"O…kay," he whispered, shivering.

I placed my hands on Marcus to calm him. He was ice cold. It was pretty obvious when Ava started funneling heat into his body, because his skin returned to a normal temperature.

"Are you okay?" Ava asked.

"I kind of feel like I'm going to puke," he admitted.

"Here, take this," Ava said.

"What's that?" I asked as I heard a cork pop off a bottle.

"It's the healing potion I made in Alchemy," Ava said. "It should help with the nausea— or not…"

Kallie snapped the top of the box closed, then inhaled a sharp breath when she turned to us. "Gods, Marcus! You're turning blue!"

Marcus had already taken a big gulp of potion, and it apparently wasn't working the way it was supposed to.

"I thought you knew how to brew a potion, pidge!" I growled.

"I do!" Ava cried. "This was an experiment."

Marcus groaned. "You could've warned me. I look like a fucking Smurf!"

"How do you feel?" Ava asked breathlessly.

"How does he *feel*?" I balked. "He's blue!"

His temperature had stabilized, though, so that was a good thing.

"I feel fine, actually," Marcus said. "But, um… am I going to be blue forever?"

"Um…" Ava hesitated. "No, no. That should wear off."

"Pidge," I warned.

"He says he feels fine!"

I sighed and helped Marcus to his feet. "Okay, that's it. As team Captain, I am banning everyone from putting our teammates in any further danger. I think Marcus has been picked on enough for the day. Marcus, why don't you sit out?"

"I actually feel okay—" He cut off abruptly. "Actually, you know what? You're probably right. I should take it easy. I *am* blue, after all."

"And you'll tell me the second any other symptoms arise," I stated sternly. I wasn't giving him a choice.

"Sure thing, Captain." Marcus walked away to go sit by Oberi, and Rishi followed.

"So, what?" Kallie sounded annoyed. "Our training session is over?"

"No," I snapped. "Clearly, we need to go over a few things— like how *not* to put your teammate in danger."

"I don't know why you're so mad," Kallie sighed. "The exercise worked. We learned something new."

"You went about it in the wrong way," I argued, running my hand over my face. "Let's just forget about it. It's over, and we're not going to try it again."

"Yes, sir," Kallie said sarcastically.

I began pacing. "Look, if we're going to make it through the Darke Games, we have to work together. So let's play up our strengths. What kind of things are we all best at?"

"You've already seen my illusions," Kallie said.

"And she can create weapons out of thin air," Ava added. "I saw it in class."

I furrowed my brow. "You can do that?"

"If I believe in the illusion enough, I can make it real," Kallie explained. "What's your strength, Air boy?"

I hesitated. I had Air and Earth power, but I was still learning what I could do with it. I didn't know exactly how it would help us against monsters.

Marcus piped up from several feet away. "He tossed Mad Dog nearly a hundred yards into the lake. He's gotta be able to levitate."

"Levitation…?" I was skeptical.

"Marcus is right," Ava said. "Yapluma back home can use Air magic to make things fly through the air, including themselves. It could help us escape a bad situation during the games."

"You're telling me I can *fly*?" I gaped.

"Well, yeah," Ava said, like it was obvious. "I mean, probably not over the prison gates, because as soon as you get close enough the noxite will screw with your magic. But outside the Institute? For sure."

"And in here?" I asked.

"Well, this *is* the Elementai room," Ava mused. "These rooms are meant for us to explore our magic. I hardly feel any noxite. I think you should give it a try."

"Any chance you could offer me a theory lesson?" I asked.

Ava didn't sound amused. "I'm not Yapluma. You just… I don't know… manipulate the air currents around you."

"Let's start with something small," Kallie suggested. "Here, try this."

"Hey!" Marcus protested.

Rishi let out a high-pitched shriek, and Kallie swore under her breath. "Jerk," she growled at the cat.

"Yeah, frighten the cat to death," I deadpanned. "That's the way to do it."

"What about this leaf?" Ava asked as she snapped something off a nearby plant.

I cocked an eyebrow at her. "Is that a joke? Of course I can make a leaf fly!"

I swiped my hand through the air, and my magic swept up the leaf and took off with it.

"Perfect," Ava said. "If you can do that, you can levitate yourself."

I gestured to myself. "I'm not exactly a weightless leaf, pidge."

She sighed in frustration. "Just try it, Charlie. It should come naturally."

"Fine," I conceded through gritted teeth.

I walked to a part of the path that was more open, so I wouldn't hurt anybody. I took a few moments to take in my surroundings— the sound of the waterfall trickling into the pool, the birds chirping high above me, and the air buzzing at its magical frequency. I focused on the air and drew it closer to me, pressing the air particles together and creating a small whirlwind around myself. Air swept under my shoes, and my feet became unstable for a moment, though I didn't fall. I settled the air currents to maintain my balance, then tried again.

Air swirled beneath my feet, lifting my shoes from the pavement. I gasped as I went floating several inches into the air. I started to wobble, but I pulled more air particles toward me to keep me from tipping one way or the other.

I stabilized and let out a shocked laugh. "Ancestors, I'm doing it."

Ava clapped, and Oberi nickered. "Keep going, Charlie."

I willed myself to move higher, then shifted the air in another direction. I hovered forward at least three feet off the ground. It was amazing how free and weightless I felt. I figured I had what it took to push further, so I levitated myself higher.

Kallie's teasing voice came from far below me. "Don't hurt yourself up there!"

I teetered for show and plastered a look of terror on my face. Let's see how *she* liked being messed with. "Uh oh!"

I fell forward, tumbling quickly toward the ground. I sensed the plants and dirt approaching, and knew I had plenty of time to save myself.

Kallie and Ava screamed in unison, their voices echoing throughout the room. Just as I was about to plummet into the shallow pool, I caught myself with another air current. I shot back into the air, laughing.

"Charlie, you ass!" Kallie screamed from below.

"Get back down here," Ava insisted. "You're grounded until you learn to behave yourself!"

"Can't," I called back. I looped several times, always trusting my magic to catch me. Then I shot straight upward, arms held straight out at my sides. "I'm off to Neverland!"

I went zooming around the room, feeling totally and completely free. Ironic, considering I was locked in a prison, but for the first time in years, I felt like a kid again. It was like a dream.

Finally, after Ava and Kallie had their fill of yelling at me, I flew to the ground and landed.

"I'm impressed," Ava said.

I tilted my head at her. "I thought you said it was natural for Air elementals."

"Yeah, sure," she admitted. "But the flips and shit usually take some practice. I wonder if you have enough power to levitate one of us."

I shrugged. I was feeling pretty confident. "Might as well try."

"I volunteer!" Kallie offered immediately. "That looked mega fun."

"Don't you have wings?" Marcus asked her.

"In fae form," she admitted, though she sounded irritated.

"Shouldn't you have them in wolven form, too?" Marcus' question was innocent, but it set Kallie off.

"Yes, *asshole*," she growled. "I don't know why I got my fae wings and not my shifter wings. Maybe it's the fact that I'm a *girl* and I'm not supposed to be able to shift at all. It's whatever. If you know what's best for you, you don't ask a fae if they've earned their wings. It's insulting."

"Sorry," Marcus dragged out the word. "I didn't know."

"Anyway, this is different," Kallie said. "I want to see how Charlie's magic feels."

"I can't make any promises," I told her.

"Well, let's see what you *can* do."

Kallie stood ready, and my Air swirled around her. I could feel her stance by the way my magic resisted against her form. I repeated what I'd done with myself and sent air particles swirling beneath her feet. A small space formed between her shoes and the floor.

"Whoa!" she cried. Kallie wobbled, and I tried to stabilize her with my magic, but I couldn't anticipate her movements. I overcorrected, and she went flying straight into a tree. I winced as I heard her smash into it.

"Fuck the gods!" she screamed as she slumped to the ground.

"Kallie, hell…" I rushed over to her, but she shrugged me off. "I'm sorry."

"Ugh, forget about it," she said. "I'll fly myself around."

A *whoosh* sounded, then came the fluttering of her insect-like wings. Kallie jumped and took off, flying so close to me the air blew my hair back.

I turned to Ava, gaping. "Should I say something to her?"

Ava sighed. "Nah. Let her cool down. I think you hurt her pride more than anything. You can try me next."

"No," I declined immediately. I hated the thought of possibly hurting her. "I don't think I can do it. With myself, it's easy, but I couldn't track Kallie's movements. I don't want anyone getting hurt."

"Let's move on, then," Ava suggested. "We already know I'm a badass with Fire and Water. Marcus, what can you do?"

Marcus groaned from where he sat by Oberi. "I'm, uh… not feeling so great right now."

"Do you need a medic?" I asked.

"No," Marcus insisted. "I think it'll pass. Why don't you give Oberi a shot?"

At the sound of her name, Oberi perked up and shook out her mane. The sound of fire crackled.

I stroked her velvety nose as she came up to me. "Okay, Oberi. Show us what you've got."

Oberi blew a breath through her mouth, making her lips buzz together. Her hooves clicked on the path as she readied herself.

"Anytime now," I pressed.

Oberi swung her hips out so her giant ass slammed into my side. I fell on my face away from her, and I swore I heard her *laugh*— as much as a unicorn could, at least.

"She gets offended easily," Ava reminded me, amusement in her tone.

I rubbed my arm. "Yeah, I see that. Is she doing anything yet?"

"She's taking aim at a tree," Ava narrated. "And— ancestors!"

I felt it the moment Ava cursed. Heat exploded through the air, as if Oberi had turned into a fireball herself. A hot ball of fire whizzed through the air and made impact with the tree up ahead. My Earth magic sensed it go up in flame, but I didn't need magic to feel it. The tree blazed so hot I could feel the heat on my skin. My ears rang. I slapped my hands over them, but it didn't dull the ache pulsing through my head. It was excruciating.

"Put it out!" I cried to Ava. "The tree is in pain! Put it out!"

Ava quickly complied, and the room returned to a normal temperature. She stepped toward me and placed a gentle hand on my arm. "Charlie, are you okay?"

My hands shook as I dropped them from my ears. "The tree was screaming," I said breathlessly.

"That's the Nivita in you," Ava said. "I should've realized. But Charlie, you should've seen it! Flames covered Oberi's whole body, and the fireball came out of her horn. It was beautiful."

"Yeah, well, it would've been prettier if she hadn't destroyed that tree," I argued.

Oberi heard me and sighed, almost like she agreed. The heat coming off her mane disappeared, and I felt a shift in her energy as she shrank to husky form.

"What's he doing?" I asked Ava.

Oberi's paws padded on the stone as he made his way over to the tree.

"He's placing his paws on the tree like he..." Ava trailed off.

I felt it through my magic. The twisting sensation in my gut eased, and I smelled the green scent of fresh leaves. Oberi was using *Earth magic* to heal the wounds on the tree. In the process, new leaves sprouted, and the tree must've grown another three feet.

I gaped as the magic consumed me. "I-I thought Oberi was Air, like me."

Ava seemed equally surprised. "You're a dual-caster, so I guess he has your Nivita side. We know he's a *mutabeecha* and can shift between genders and bodies. My aunt theorized he has a different form for each of the five Houses. I guess his husky form is Earth."

I barely had a moment to process this incredible information before Kallie landed and strolled up to us.

"Well, it looks like your Familiar has earned a spot on the team for the Darke Games." Kallie turned away from us and spoke to Marcus. "What can Rishi do?"

"What?" Marcus sounded clueless. "Nothing. He's just a cat."

Kallie blew a breath. "Lame. So, when do we get to practice simultension?"

"Simultension?" I repeated.

"Ava and I learned about it in class," Kallie explained.

"Yes, we should definitely try with everyone," Ava agreed. "Kallie and I melded our powers together and created elemental weapons. For a while, at least, as long as the illusion lasted."

Marcus finally got to his feet, apparently feeling better. "How's that possible?"

Ava was the one to answer. "Professor McCauley said it's a type of magic where different races can combine their powers."

"Sounds useful," I said thoughtfully. "What can our powers do together?"

"I don't know," Ava admitted. "Anything, I guess. McCauley said the possibilities were endless. We just have to get creative."

I shrugged. "Let's try it."

Ava tapped her foot and mumbled under her breath. "Mm... what can we do? Oh, I have an idea! Marcus can read minds, and Kallie can cast illusions. What if we combined those and cast whatever the person *wanted* to see!"

"That might help mask the illusion," Kallie said thoughtfully. "So they can't break it. Ava, you're a test subject."

"What? Me?" Ava balked.

"Yeah, it was your idea."

I remembered what Marcus had told me about his mind reading. I wasn't so sure this was a good plan.

"Maybe we should start with something else," Marcus suggested.

"You're well enough to read minds, aren't you?" Ava asked.

Kallie quickly added, "We haven't seen you do anything all day. Your turn to shine, Marcus."

Marcus sighed. "How does this simultension work, exactly?"

Kallie was the one to explain. "We'll intertwine our magic, so that it works as a unit. We should probably hold hands."

Marcus hesitated.

"Godsdammit, it's not like I have cooties," Kallie snapped.

"Okay." He sighed in defeat. "I'll *try* it."

"Ready whenever you are," Ava announced.

We stood there in silence for at least a whole minute, but nothing happened.

"You're resisting me, Marcus," Kallie told him. "Stop trying to project your magic on Ava, and focus on melding it with *mine*. This should be easy."

"It's not like I've ever done it," Marcus snapped.

Kallie huffed. "Just work with me here, okay?"

Another several beats passed. Oberi stood at my side dutifully, waiting patiently. I was starting to think this wasn't going to work.

"Something's happening," Ava said. "My vision is changing and— oh, for the love of all the ancestors, *turn it off!*"

"What'd you see?" Kallie asked in interest.

Ava sounded less than pleased. "Like you don't know. That is *not* what I pictured!"

"Actually, I *don't* know," Kallie insisted. "Marcus was the one pulling it from your mind. All I did was project what you wanted to see."

Ava cleared her throat. "Well, it wasn't... I, um... how about I spare you the details? I wouldn't want to corrupt your innocent minds."

Kallie legit cackled. "Oh, princess. You think I'm *innocent*? How sweet."

"Whatever," Ava snapped. "Let's move on."

Marcus came up beside me and elbowed me in the side. "She had eyes on you the whole time, bro."

My jaw dropped. "So she saw..."

I could only imagine what she'd seen, since Marcus could only read *dirty* thoughts— which Ava and Kallie didn't know about yet. My pulse picked up double time, but I quickly told it to calm down.

Ava had been right. That wasn't something she wanted to see.

"I'm sure it was a mistake," I muttered to Marcus. My stomach twisted, and I wanted nothing more than to move on. I raised my voice so the girls could hear. "What can we try next?"

"Charlie hasn't had a chance to try simultension," Ava said thoughtfully. "But what can we fuse with Air or Earth?"

"Your Fire?" I suggested.

Kallie sounded thoughtful. "I don't think simultension works with people of the same magical race."

"It has to," Ava argued. "Maybe you just have to be strong enough to do it."

"And you think we are?" I asked.

"Charlie," she sighed. "You just flew around the room no problem on your first try. I think we can handle it."

I shrugged. "I guess it's worth a shot. What's the objective?"

Ava thought about it a moment. "We can't exactly light the air on fire, so we'll have to work with Earth."

I groaned. "Another tree?"

"It won't hurt it if we do it right," Ava promised. "That's how simultension works. We combine our powers to become one."

I felt like I could do it, with Ava at least, but I didn't know where to start. Ava took the lead for me. She approached and took my hand, then led me forward.

"We'll try it on this tree," she offered. She guided my hand to the trunk of the tree, and I ran my fingers up and down the bark. It was smooth, unlike any tree I'd felt before. I might not have realized it was a plant if I didn't feel the life of it pulsing against my Earth magic.

"What kind of tree is this?" I asked.

"It's a magical tree that grows only on Darke Island," she told me. "We learned about it in my Alchemy class. The buds are used for different potions."

"What should I do?" I asked.

"Focus on strengthening the tree," Ava suggested. "I'll work my Fire power on it, but we have to make sure it's strong enough to take it. Are you ready?"

I nodded. "I think so."

Ava and I locked hands again, and her fingers began to warm in mine. I kept my other hand pressed to the tree. I worked my magic into it, feeding it with nourishment from the ground. I could feel it growing beneath my touch.

Ava's hand heated even more, but it wasn't so hot that I couldn't take it. Her magic swelled and seemed to move through me until—

I jumped back as flames ignited across the tree bark. It had singed the hair on my arm, but I was apparently the only one who couldn't handle it. This tree didn't scream like the other one had. It seemed perfectly content with the fire consuming its base and crackling off its leaves.

Ava and I had done it. We'd made our magic become one.

"Wow, Charlie," she breathed beside me. "The tree is on fire, but it's not burning. It's like it created a Fire shield around it and is protecting it. It's— look out!"

Ava grabbed my shoulder and yanked me downward. We barely had time to flatten ourselves to the ground before something *whooshed* by over our heads. A wave of heat traveled over us.

"Was that—?" I started to say, but Marcus cut me off.

"The tree is alive!" he cried.

"Fuck!" Ava screamed, scrambling to her feet. "That's *not* supposed to happen."

"Your magic must've done something to it," Kalina said through heavy breaths.

"Done what?" Ava asked. "Made it grow a conscience?"

"I don't know but— oh, gods!"

Kallie's cry alerted me to another incoming attack. Only this time, the tree didn't aim its branches at us. The ground beneath us began to shake, and the surrounding trees seemed to groan in pain as the sentient one tugged at their roots.

Snap!

Dirt flew everywhere, splattering into my face. The tree was uprooting itself!

"Charlie, get back!" Ava cried.

She shoved me backward, but like hell was I letting her put herself in the line of fire.

"I'm Earth," I argued. "I'll handle this."

"I have to put the fire out," she insisted. "Charlie, if you don't run—"

"Ahhh!" Marcus' scream of terror tore through the greenhouse.

"The tree's got Marcus!" Kallie screamed.

His scream traveled through the air as the tree launched Marcus forward. I caught him with my Air power, but heat seared my magic. Marcus' clothes were on fire! I quickly set him down into the pool, and the fire hissed out. Meanwhile, Kalina threw battle orbs at the tree, but all they did was explode against its trunk with minor *bangs*.

"What are we going to do?" Kallie shouted.

"Hang on!" Ava called back. "I just have to— ancestors!"

Roots slapped against the path, and twigs snapped as the tree took off running through the greenhouse. Oberi barked loudly, but it did nothing to slow it down.

"We have to do something before it escapes!" I yelled. I took off running after it, but for a tree, it was pretty dang fast. You know, since they weren't supposed to move *at all*. We couldn't have picked a worse tree in the whole greenhouse. I should've protested the second Ava said it was magical. Of course this was going to blow up in our faces.

I summoned Air and drew it away from the area surrounding the tree. If I could suffocate the fire, maybe the tree would stop.

Ava's footsteps sounded from a distant path, then rounded back in my direction. "Keep going, Charlie! We've got it cornered."

I willed the tree to stop moving, but I only slowed it down. I couldn't concentrate on Earth magic while trying to use my Air magic to suffocate the fire.

The heat in the air seemed to cool, and I knew Ava and I were making progress. I twisted my hands, pushing my magic harder, until we finally broke through. The temperature returned to normal.

"Charlie, the tree!" Ava cried.

Branches cracked, and the trunk groaned. We'd put the fire out and stopped the tree, but it was uprooted. It had no leg to stand on.

"Timber!" Marcus shouted.

"It's going down!" Kallie yelled at the same time.

I tried to work quickly, to force its roots back into the ground, but it wasn't fast enough. The tree toppled. I heard the glass shatter first, then came the *boom* of the tree slamming into the ground. The greenhouse floor shook beneath my feet, and cool air rushed in through the broken window.

"Fuck!" Ava cried. "Vandalism will get us all thrown in Cellblock 9!"

"Shit," Marcus muttered. "I can't be searched right now. I've still got Contraband in my stash."

"You idiot," Kallie growled. "You were supposed to get rid of that!"

"I did… for a while."

"We can use magic to repair it, right?" I asked desperately. The last thing I wanted was for us to get into trouble. "Kallie can turn illusions into reality, so we just have to clean this up and fix the window—"

"Hey!" a deep voice boomed from the opposite side of the greenhouse. "Who's in here!?"

"Too late," Ava breathed. "The guards already found us."

"Calm down, everyone," Marcus insisted. "I know what to do."

"What?" I growled. He sure was taking his sweet time to explain.

"Run!" Marcus screamed.

Nobody questioned it. We all rushed toward the broken window in unison, because coming back the way we came was obviously not an option. We'd run into guards on the way there for sure.

"Quickly," I hissed.

Judging from the huge breeze coming in, the hole in the window had to be huge, since the entire side of the greenhouse was made of glass. I helped Ava through first, and then Kallie. Marcus, Rishi, and Oberi quickly followed. I ducked out behind them and raced across the prison yard.

"Into the trees," Ava huffed.

"I'm casting a cloaking illusion!" Kallie said. "So they won't see us run."

"Good idea," I said through labored breaths. "Let's get to cover as quickly as we can, just in case."

The team closed in on me on all sides. We ran faster, and I felt the trees up ahead. *Almost there…*

My Air magic felt everything that happened next. Rishi must've not been looking where he was going, because as soon as we reached the trees, he shifted course and darted in front of Marcus. Marcus screamed, and Rishi let out a howl. He tumbled to the ground, and Kallie quickly followed. Ava yelped as she tripped over the two of them, and I was only a split-second behind. I nearly crushed Ava as I fell, but I barely had a chance to process it before Oberi was on top of me.

He shook his head, getting slobber everywhere. After a moment, he started jumping on us, like this was some sort of a game.

"Oberi!" I gasped as his paw sank into my groin. "Oberi, get off!"

The husky jumped off of me, but I could hardly move after the blow I'd just taken to the crotch. I rolled off Ava so I wouldn't hurt her, and lay on the forest floor, panting.

Nobody else moved, either. We lay there in silence, as if waiting for the sound of guards to follow. But it was quiet, all except for the wind rustling the trees above us.

Finally, Kallie broke the silence. "That cat is going to kill us, Marcus."

"Rishi's harmless," he argued.

I waited for Ava to say something, but instead, she broke into a fit of laughter. It was quiet at first, but it soon became too much that she clutched her stomach and rolled over so she was pressed into my side. "Ancestors!" she laughed. "That was…"

She trailed off, unable to finish her sentence. After a few moments, Oberi started laughing, too, though he more or less sounded like a hyena. Marcus couldn't help but giggle, and Kallie's laughter soon followed.

It was infectious. Soon, even I was laughing at the absurdity of it all.

"We're failures," Ava laughed. I wasn't sure if she actually found it funny, or if it was just so sad you either had to laugh or cry. "We're utter failures."

"But we had fun," I said, unable to believe the words were actually coming from my mouth. "That's what counts, right?"

Ava's laughter settled. "Yeah, Charlie. That's what counts."

"Okay, I agree, watching Marcus roll into the pool and possessing him with a sex demon was hilarious," Kallie agreed. "But none of this is going to help us win the Games."

"Hey, we were doing perfectly fine before the sex demon," Marcus teased.

"Ugh," I groaned. "What are we doing, guys?"

"I believe it's called *training*," Marcus joked.

The laughter continued for another few moments, but it quickly died. Ava curled up beside me, and I instinctually ran my fingers through her hair. I stopped the moment I realized what I was doing.

The atmosphere between the group suddenly changed, like we all realized at once how serious this was. The Darke Games were a death sentence if we didn't know what we were doing.

I just hoped we got our shit together in time.

ava-marie

EIGHTEEN

"Ava-Marie, if your mother and I get another notice of a dress-code violation, I'm going to lose it."

"It's *fine*, Daddy."

I twirled the phone cord around my finger, on the receiving end of another lecture. I looked out the window to see the lightest snowfall. It'd be gone in a few hours, as Darke Island didn't really get that cold, but it was nice to have snow on December first.

Daddy impatiently sighed at the other end of the line. "Why in the world would you think that socks that said *fuck you* are an appropriate addition to your uniform?"

"Well, I thought that everyone should know."

Daddy groaned. "The Hawkei Civil War was a warm-up for raising you."

I couldn't help but let out a mischievous smile. "Just wait until everyone sees me kick butt in the Darke Games."

Daddy let out a couple swear words. "Ava, I don't agree with this."

"You don't have to agree! Just support me." I rubbed my eyes. Daddy and I had been going back and forth about the Games ever since he found out that I signed up, and so far, his attempts to talk me out of it were nothing short of annoying.

"It's dangerous. One of the reasons your mother and I fought in the war is so you and your siblings wouldn't have to partake in deadly competitions. The Darke Games sound like an even worse version of the Elemental Cup."

"I have to do this, Daddy. You don't understand."

"Peanut, I sentenced you to the Institute because I wanted you to *stay there*," Daddy said sternly. "When your mother was looking for answers to her own prophecy, all the clues we needed were right there at Orenda Academy. The Institute could provide the same answers to your own prophecy. The school might be hiding secrets. What sense does it make to end your own sentence, then stay on Darke Island looking for clues that might be in the wrong place?"

"Daddy, I get your motives, but we don't have any proof that my own prophecy is connected to the Institute in any way," I insisted. "The Institute is a distraction. I'm not backing out of the Darke Games now."

"Just think about what I said, all right?" Daddy paused. "Your mother wants to talk to you. I have to go. I'm late for a meeting. Love you, peanut."

Mama came on the line. "Hi, sweetheart. How are things?"

"They're okay," I said, thinking of our disastrous practice for the Games the other day. It'd been fun, but my team had totally bombed. No matter what I said to Daddy, I was worried about how this whole thing was going to go.

"Just okay? Hm."

I rolled my eyes. "Don't be like that. I'm competing in the Games, and that's final."

"And if that's what you want to do, I'll back you up," Mama said. "I'm always here for whatever you need."

I gave a skeptical noise. "Yeah, well, Daddy could do the same, but he's not."

"Never mind your father. You know he complains, but he's behind you all the way."

I kept quiet, and Mama filled the silence. "Ezekiel got his powers. A little late, but now he's casting Water like a natural."

"That's so great!" I'd been worried about him— a semester at Orenda Academy without any magic had to be uncomfortable.

"And we received the school paper," Mama went on. "You and Charlie look adorable."

The Institute sent out a monthly review to all the parents who still gave a damn. Mine and Charlie's Halloween costumes had made the front page.

Mama brought up Charlie all the time. It was so different from Daddy, who liked to pretend he didn't exist.

I chewed on my lip as I pondered what to say. I wanted to talk to Mama about how I felt, but how would she react? Nobody wanted their daughter with a convict— even if she was one herself.

I decided to let it fly. "Mama, I think I'm in love with a criminal."

"Hmm. Are you now?"

Her answer was so cryptic, I couldn't tell what she thought. "Maybe. It's hard to sort out my feelings."

"It wouldn't happen to be Charlie, would it?"

Ancestors, Mama was good with shit like this. It was like she had a fucking radar. "How did you know?"

"You talk about him quite a bit. He seems like a nice young man."

Yeah, and I'm sure everyone else back home talked about Charlie and me a lot, too. I bet Auntie Imogen and Uncle Jonah gossiped constantly about it. "He's really sweet, Mama. But I don't know if he feels the same. Also, I kind of hate him at the same time I like him. Is that weird?"

"I don't think it's odd," Mama mused. "If he likes you, you'll know."

"You don't know Charlie." Guy was secretive as all hell. Reading his feelings was like trying to read a brick wall.

"But I know you two share a bond, and he's probably just as lonely as you are," Mama said. "Give it some time."

The old phone crackled. "Sweetheart, are you *sure* that the Darke Games are what you want to do?"

"Yes, Mama. I'm not backing out."

"Okay. That's all I wanted to know." I heard Maverick yell from inside the garage, and Mama said, "Oh, damn. Your brother set the bike on fire again. I have to go. See you soon, Ava."

The line went dead, and I sighed as I hung the phone back up. At least I knew Mama liked Charlie, but what would Daddy say if he knew about my true feelings? He made it clear he hated Charlie with a passion.

It was hard to think that what Daddy felt didn't matter. I really— *really*— liked Charlie, but I don't know if I could be with someone my father didn't approve of. His blessing meant everything to me.

I started back to my dorm, feeling grumpy as fuck. None of this mattered anyway. Charlie didn't like me. If he did, he would've shown some interest by now, and nothing had happened. I wasn't the kind of girl who chased after guys. Guys chased me, and I didn't want to embarrass myself falling all over someone who clearly hated my guts.

Speak of the devil. I was hanging up Christmas decorations in my room when Charlie came walking in. I couldn't hang any of my decorations that I'd used at home— they were *dangerous weapons* or something stupid the Institute had decided— so I'd made a bunch of my own. Paper snowflakes and red and green paper garlands hung from the ceiling and on every open patch of wall.

Charlie was so tall he walked right into a garland. It wrapped around his neck and nearly knocked him backward. He made a choking sound as he wrenched it off.

"Ancestors, would you get a hold of yourself?" I asked. "How do you expect to win the Darke Games if you get taken out by a fucking Christmas decoration?"

Charlie reached up and felt all the snowflakes I had hanging from the ceiling. "Holy hell, it's like Christmas Town in here!"

"I'm Christmas crazy," I said. "My birthday is on December twenty-fifth, which means all of December is about *me*, and also, Jesus."

"Uh, my birthday's on the twenty-first, so your logic's way off on that one," Charlie replied.

We shared the same birthday month, too? Charlie practically mirrored me in every way.

Oberi strolled behind Charlie in his husky form. He had a big red bow around his neck that I'd tied on earlier, and was parading it around like he was a king with a new crown. He wasn't looking where he was going and bumped into my desk. He growled, rubbing his head with his paw.

"How'd your talk with your parents go?" Charlie knew I always spoke with my family on Saturdays.

"Daddy wanted to nag at me, *again*," I told him. "He went on and on about how the Darke Games were just like the Elemental Cup, and he didn't want me to compete."

"What's the Elemental Cup?" Charlie asked.

"It's a coming-of-age competition that seals the bond between you and your Familiar. Every Elementai has to participate," I explained. "Back when my parents were kids, it used to be a deadly competition. You'd go out into the wilderness, and the Elders would pit magic against you. A lot of people died. My parents barely made it out alive. They fought in the war so no more kids had to die."

I shrugged. "The Elemental Cup still happens, and it's hard, but nobody dies anymore. I thought I'd get my chance to compete this year with Oberi, but since we're at the Institute, guess not."

"Well, maybe the Darke Games can be our way to seal the bond with Oberi," Charlie suggested.

Maybe... but when he said that, I immediately recoiled. Sealing the bond with Oberi would only bring me closer to Charlie, and if he didn't feel the same way about me, it would only hurt. I kinda wanted to keep my distance.

Charlie leaned against the wall. "Marcus and I are going down to the Villain's Den to people watch. We take bets on what they're gonna do. Wanna come?"

"That's okay. I'm just gonna chill out here," I said.

"Oh." Did he sound disappointed? No. Had to be just my imagination.

Charlie turned toward the door. "Well, I'll leave Oberi with you. It's your day to have him."

"Thanks." I felt relief when Charlie finally left my presence. Oberi whined and put his paw on my thigh, and I stroked his ears back. "Guess it's just you and me, huh puppy?"

Oberi sneezed snot all over my hand. *Gross.*

I was still decorating my room that afternoon when Kallie ran inside. "Girl, I've been looking for you all day. Why are you in here being socially awkward?"

"Uh, I just had stuff to do," I lied. "What's up?"

"I thought we could go get dresses! You know, for the Darke Ball?" Kallie asked. "Everyone around here calls it the Villain's Ball. It's a dance the school hosts after the Darke Games are over."

That got my attention. I *loved* dressing up, and there was nothing better than a big, poofy gown. Prom had practically been the highlight of my life— and I'd only gotten one, seeing as how I'd been homeschooled my senior year. A ball sounded fucking amazing— and a Villain's Ball, with an evil, creepy theme, sounded even better.

"How are we supposed to get dresses? Students can't leave campus unless it's on supervised field trips," I said.

"The school has a temporary consignment shop set up in one of the classrooms. People in Shade Hills donate their old dresses and suits for students to use for free," Kallie said. "I figure we should go through them before all the good ones are taken."

"Ooh, let's go."

When we got to the classroom, I saw that it was filled with racks upon racks of beautiful, dresses just waiting to be tried on in the makeshift dressing rooms the school had set up. There was a rack of suits for guys, too, but there were a lot more girls in here than boys. Gushing sounds of women rang throughout the shop as everyone found their perfect dress.

Opal was working the front counter. She waved us over. "Hey, guys," she said. "Here to find a dress?"

"Yeah. What are you wearing to the ball?" I asked.

Opal blushed. "Um... I don't think I'm going. No one's asked me."

"Come with us! You don't need a date," Kallie insisted.

"I really don't think so," Opal said. "It's probably best if I sit out."

I frowned. I really wanted Opal to be there, but I couldn't make her attend the ball if she didn't want to.

"What kind of dress are you looking for?" Kallie asked as we rummaged through the options available. Oberi stuck his head out between a bunch of tulle skirts, and I laughed.

"Um, well, I like pastels, pink especially," I said. "And florals. Lots of rhinestones and glitter. And it's gotta be a big skirt. Like, five feet across minimum."

"Don't know if you're gonna find that here." Kallie tilted her head. "I've literally been to a million royal balls in my life. I'm tired of wearing big, fancy dresses. I want to wear something naughty."

"Like this?" I held up a slinky red dress with a plunging neckline that went all the way down to the waist.

Kallie's eyes sparked. "Exactly." She ran into the dressing room to try it on. When she came out, my eyes widened in appreciation.

"Damn, girl. You've got some nice boobs," I said.

"You think so?" Kallie turned as she looked in the mirror. "Do you think Marcus will like it?"

Why did that matter? "Your goods are on full display, so I'd say so." I giggled.

Out of the corner of my eye, I noticed Naya eyeing the dress with jealousy. She hated how good Kallie looked.

"Then I'm totally getting it." Kallie looked at the bundle of dresses in my arms. "Think you've got enough to try on?"

"Not nearly." I headed into a dressing room. I tried on a white dress with a black bow, and a purple dress with a flared skirt, but neither of them fit right. I slipped on dress after dress, and yet nothing felt good.

I came out in a silver dress that totally washed me out. Kallie shook her head no. There was a rustling sound in the corner as Oberi went through a bunch of cardboard boxes full of fancy hats. He clenched his teeth and waved a wide-brimmed sun hat in the air, making a whining sound at Kallie.

"Apparently he loves hats." I laughed. Kallie went to help Oberi, switching the hats out for him. He made faces in the mirror as Kallie switched from a fascinator to a fedora, fluttering his eyelashes like a model.

Oberi kept changing back and forth between his unicorn form and husky form, trying on the hats and seeing which ones looked best in which form. Finally, Oberi changed into a unicorn. Kallie put a long black veil on her head, decorated with fake black roses that congregated around her horn. She gave a nicker and stomped her hoof. Apparently, that was her Villain Ball look.

"You're too cute, Oberi." I headed back inside the dressing room and continued my endless dress raid. I found I was too skinny for most of the dresses. They fell right off me. I guess Charlie was right and I had lost a lot of weight this semester. I'd barely noticed.

When I came out wearing a neon green dress, Kallie scrunched her nose. "It's pretty, but it's not you."

"I know." I sighed. This was impossible. I really wanted the perfect look for the ball, but none of these even came close to what I had in my head.

Kallie had her dress hanging on one arm. Just at that moment, Naya walked by. She saw the dress on Kallie's arm, then reached out and snatched it for herself.

"Hey!" Kallie shouted. "That was mine!"

"I saw it first," Naya sneered as she bundled the dress in her arms. "I tried it on earlier, and was thinking about getting it before *you* took it from me."

"It was hanging on the rack. No one wanted it," Kallie snapped back.

"Well, I do, so keep your filthy hands off of it," Naya threatened. "That is, if you know what's good for you."

I could see an illusion spell sparking at Kallie's fingers. I stepped in, before she could hurt Naya and get us both into trouble. "It's okay, Kallie. We'll find you a *better* dress," I said, with a nasty look at Naya.

Naya wore this disgusting sneer of victory. She walked away to join Danielle.

Kallie raged, "Why does she get away with everything? I really wanted that dress."

"It had a snag in it. I noticed when you tried it on," I said. "We can do better."

Kallie scowled. "But I'm helping *you* find a dress. You can't go to the ball without one."

"It's fine. I don't think I'm going to find anything I like here, anyway." I changed again, and Kallie and I began looking through the racks once more. We'd searched through the whole shop, and my heart had nearly fallen as I realized there was nothing else Kallie could wear that fit her dream look.

"What about this?" Kallie pulled out a black dress, and my interest piqued as I looked at it. It had all kinds of geometrical shapes cut out of the bodice and a slit going up the skirt.

"Daring," I commented. "Try it on."

When Kallie came out of the dressing room again, my jaw *dropped*. The black dress was way more revealing than the red one. The geometrical slits all over the bodice exposed her midriff and back, covering only her breasts. The slit in the skirt barely stopped just before her panties. I wasn't sure if that dress was actually a dress or just lingerie, but she looked *amazing* in it.

"Do I look okay?" Kallie turned nervously as she looked in the mirror.

"Okay? It's phenomenal!" I exclaimed. "If Marcus was going to be drooling when he saw you in the first dress, he's going to pass out at the sight of you in this one, because it is totally *hawt.*"

That seemed to make up her mind. "I think this is perfect. Let's go, before Naya steals this one off me, too."

Kallie carried out her new dress in a paper bag, while I left empty-handed— save for Oberi's veil. I wasn't sure what I was going to wear to the ball. I could have Mama send me a dress I had at home... but at the same time, I didn't want to wear something I'd already worn. I wanted something new.

"Do you want to get coffee down at Commissary?" Kallie asked. "I seriously need a boost."

"Sure." Oberi whinnied at my response. She *loved* coffee.

Commissary was set up like a student shop near the lunch room. It was almost like a mini-grocery store. There was a small coffee shop inside, along with a couple of coolers for drinks and a few rows of snacks. Commissary was bought with points. You either earned them as a reward in class, or your parents put money on your ID card. Everything you bought in Commissary was purchased with your ID. Students weren't allowed to carry cash money at the Institute, but most of us hid a few dollars under our mattresses and such in spite of the rules.

Despona was behind the coffee counter, grinding coffee beans. I scanned the menu. There were blood drinks for vampires, specialty drinks for angels, and other magical concoctions in every flavor you could think of. I mostly stuck to the basics— magical properties added to my drinks fucked pretty bad with my bipolar meds.

"I think I'll take a white chocolate latte," I told Despona. "Extra whipped cream. And an iced caramel macchiato for Oberi."

"I'll have a vanilla hazelnut frappe," Kallie added.

"Coming right up." Despona made our coffees, then handed them to us with a fanged smile. "So, you guys ready for the Darke Games? My team and I have been working non-stop to win."

"You're participating in the Darke Games too?" I asked in surprise.

"Yeah. I've made a team with Alice, Carson, and Wesley," Despona said.

"Well, good luck," I said. If we didn't win, I hoped Despona and her team did. They deserved to get out of here.

Though, if I was honest, they were kind of the underdog team. No one on that team was particularly powerful. I worried they didn't stand a chance of staying alive, let alone winning the competition.

We swiped our ID cards for our coffees, then sat down at a table inside Commissary. "Aren't the four of them all innocent?" Kallie asked me.

"Yeah," I said. "None of them deserve to be here."

"Isn't it a little weird that most of their stories involve an attempted abduction of some sort?" Kallie asked. "It's like there's something going on."

My stomach tumbled, thinking of the time those two guys had nearly pulled Monica and I into that van. "There might be, but it's not exactly uncommon to get kidnapped. I mean, not with the people around here, right?"

"I guess so."

Oberi lapped at his mug, getting whipped cream all over his face.

"I thought dogs couldn't have coffee," Kallie commented as she watched Oberi.

"Familiars are a bit different," I said. "And Oberi is a *mutabeecha*, a changeling creature. I haven't seen him eat anything that makes him sick yet."

"Fae have changelings in our culture, too, though they're not as cute as Oberi." Kallie patted Oberi, and he burped. "It's crazy that you have such a rare Familiar. I've never heard of *mutabeecha* before."

I shrugged. "I don't think it's odd I got a unique Familiar. Weird stuff happens around me."

"Like what?" Kallie raised her eyebrows.

"Like…" I took a breath. "I haven't really thought about this since I was a kid. But… when I was five or so, I remember this strange voice, calling out to me in the woods. I live on an island, but once I heard the voice, I blinked, and I was on the mainland. I didn't recall how I got there, either."

"Wow." Kallie's expression widened. "That's insane."

"I know, right?" I paused as I mused on that night. The voice I'd heard hadn't been part of my psychosis— at least, I didn't think it was. It didn't explain how I'd gotten from my island to the mainland, or why I couldn't remember.

"What happened after that?" Kallie asked.

"I'm… not sure." I scratched my head. "The memory is fuzzy, but I remember walking through the woods in my pajamas. I wasn't sure where I was going. Then this… *thing* came out of the trees."

I shuddered. "I don't recall exactly what it looked like, but it was literally so scary. It was big, and dark… gnashing teeth and red eyes. I pissed myself, I remember that. I was so terrified, I cried and screamed. I thought for sure it was going to eat me alive. Then…"

I glanced at Oberi. He looked up with a wagging tail. "Something came from behind to protect me. It growled, and tackled the black shape. Some sort of brown blur. I didn't stick around to see what it was. I ran for it. By this time, my parents had half of Kinpago looking for me. I was so terrified I didn't speak for three days. My mom couldn't convince me to go outside for a month. Everyone thought that I must've run into a dragon or something, though they couldn't figure out how I got to the mainland on my own."

"Do you think it *was* a dragon?" Kallie asked.

I shook my head. "No. I was never afraid of dragons, or any other magical creature. This thing was sinister. Like it was straight out of hell."

The strange pair of blue eyes I saw when my dad was healed… the monster I saw in the woods, and the big creature that had fought it off… why had I seen such strange creatures as a child, and why did they seem attracted to me?

"You know… this is gonna sound crazy, but weird stuff happens around me, too," Kallie confessed. "When I was really little, I was playing with my brother in the parlor room. It was early morning, just after breakfast."

Kallie blinked. "Then all of a sudden… it was nighttime. We're talking pitch black midnight. I was completely alone. Then this sorceress appeared. She was beautiful— silver hair with blue wings. I'd never seen her before. She smiled at me, and once she did, it went back to daytime again. My brother was there and everything… as if nothing had happened at all."

"Damn," I said. "That's really intense."

"Isn't it?" Kallie blushed. "My mom's a really powerful sorceress, so I know I must've inherited some of her talent. But some of the stuff that happens around me is just plain odd. I've never told anyone about it, because I'm worried people will think I'm crazy."

"Do you think you had a vision?" I asked.

Kallie made a skeptical sound. "I don't know. It seemed so real… but I couldn't explain it."

"At least we can be weird together," I offered. "It's better than going at it alone."

"I'll drink to that." Kallie clinked her coffee cup against mine. The doors to Commissary opened. Marcus and Charlie walked in, Rishi balancing on Marcus' shoulder. Marcus tugged on Charlie's arm, and they wandered our way.

"Hey girls," Marcus said. "You know, Kallie, there's this dance thing, and—"

"Marcus, you're my date to the ball," Kallie said, without any sort of greeting.

Marcus' eyes popped out. "What?"

"I don't have a date, and I'm not going alone," Kallie said. "You're a slightly less embarrassing option than everyone else, so make sure you wear something suitable. You have to make me look good."

Marcus blushed, but he didn't object further. I resisted rolling my eyes. Kallie made it sound like Marcus was her last option as a date, but I wasn't fooled. He was for sure her first choice.

"Charlie, are you going to the Villain's Ball?" I asked.

He shrugged. "I don't have anything to wear."

"Go to the consignment shop. Suits are free," I suggested.

He paused, as if considering it. "I don't have anyone to go with."

"Well, neither do I," I said, a twinge of irritation working into my tone.

"Maybe you'll find someone," he said.

Ugh. This guy couldn't take a hint. This was a huge signal that he *for sure* didn't like me. Otherwise, why wouldn't he ask to be my date?

"You know, we shouldn't split Oberi up," I suggested. "He has an outfit for the ball and everything. It wouldn't be fair to make him go back and forth between us all night."

Charlie's jaw worked. "Do you... want to go together?"

Fucking finally. "Yeah. I guess that's cool."

"Don't act too excited," Charlie mumbled under his breath.

"Geez, I said it was cool! Don't take it that way."

Charlie blew out a breath. "Come on, Marcus. I need to get a suit."

"Something tailored, please!" I called out. Charlie flipped me off as he left, Marcus scuttling behind.

Kallie sipped at her coffee and eyed me. "You hoping for something to happen on ball night?"

"Psh. Please," I scoffed. Charlie wasn't interested. He was going with me out of obligation.

But then... if that was true, why had he been smiling on his way out?

Charlie was in a bad mood the next day. I thought it was because of me, but as we were studying together in my dorm that afternoon, I realized the stress of our upcoming exams was getting to him. I was reading some keywords from his textbook out to him, so he memorized it before his big test. Oberi sat at our feet and chewed on the dog toy we'd stolen from Contraband.

"This is useless. I'm not going to pass," Charlie said. "The exam is a written one, and my teacher's not letting me use a computer to type up an essay. She wants them *handwritten*."

"What if you can convince her to make an exception?" I asked.

He scoffed. "Yeah, right. I'm failing Juvenile Justice. My teacher's such a dick. She doesn't provide me with any accommodation."

I frowned. "Don't give up. You'll pass."

"Sure." Charlie sighed. "Or I'll just flunk out of the Institute like I flunked out of high school."

"I'm not going to let that happen. We're walking across that graduation stage together."

Charlie didn't say anything. I reached under my mattress and pulled out my phone. I scrolled through it, then pressed *play* on one of my playlists. The first one that came on was one of Charlie's favorites. I jumped up from my bed and began dancing around the room. Oberi barked and followed me, rising on his hind paws to hop behind.

"What the hell are you doing?" Charlie asked as I gave another hip thrust.

"I have to take short dance breaks while studying," I said. "You wouldn't get it."

I grabbed his hand and tugged. "Come on! Join me!"

"I… don't dance," Charlie said with a shaky laugh. "I can't exactly see what I'm doing. I'm afraid I'll look stupid."

"You *have* to dance at the ball," I begged. "I'll teach you."

Charlie hesitated. "Maybe later."

My heart fell. Charlie was so concerned with what others thought of him. It stopped him from having fun.

Charlie stood up. "We should get something to eat. It's almost dinnertime, anyway."

"Yeah, I suppose." I turned my phone off and hid it again. I wasn't giving up on this dancing thing. Charlie was going to learn how to shake his ass, or my name wasn't Ava-Marie Mitoh.

We walked to the cafeteria. "So, do you know what you're wearing to the ball?" Charlie asked.

I huffed. "No. I looked, but I couldn't find a dress I liked. I'm not sure what I'm going to wear."

"I suppose it's a good thing we showed up."

I knew that voice. I could hardly believe my ears. Tears came to my eyes as I realized that Mama and Daddy were standing right there, in the flesh. They wore lanyards with tags, certifying they'd gone through security and had a visitors' pass. Mama was carrying a big duffel bag, which she had slung over her shoulder.

"Ancestors!" I screamed and jumped on both of them. I hugged them so tightly I thought my arms would break. I missed them *so much*. After all this time, I could finally see them again.

Daddy laughed. "Hello, peanut."

All the bad stuff that happened over the last semester didn't matter. I was in Daddy's arms, and that made everything okay. Oberi barked and ran around us in a circle, going nuts.

As I pulled away, Mama brushed back my hair. "We thought we'd surprise you."

"Hello, Mister and Mrs. Mitoh," Charlie said in a dull tone. He wasn't exactly thrilled they'd arrived.

"Hello, Charlie," Mama said kindly. "I hope you've had a nice semester."

Charlie shrugged and mirrored my dad by not saying anything. The two of them acted so cold toward one another it was awkward.

"What are you doing here?" I asked. I couldn't believe they were right before my eyes. This had to be some kind of dream.

"We're staying in town. We came to watch you in the Darke Games," Mama said. "Your siblings couldn't come, per Institute rules, but they wish you luck."

"*And* we came to supervise the dance, as the school asked for chaperones," Daddy added, with a side glance at Charlie. Good thing he couldn't see it, because Daddy's stare was absolutely glowering.

Ancestors, Daddy, I'm not going to sex Charlie up on the dance floor, I thought. He was sure acting like it.

I grabbed both of their hands and pulled them along. "Come on! I need to show you *everything* about my school!"

I walked along the hallways, pointing at everything and anything that I could. "That's the Alchemy classroom. Professor Hemlock is my *favorite* teacher. She's okay if I brew poisons so long as I dump them out later. And there's the Villain's De— I mean— the *rec room*. It's really nice in there if you don't mind the spiders and rats. Oh, and don't go down that way. The astronomy hallway is really isolated, so it's the best place to get stabbed. Like, three people have died down there this semester."

"Uh… sounds wonderful, peanut," Daddy said. He gave a look to Mama, who shook her head.

As we rounded back to the cafeteria, Charlie asked, "Are either of you hungry? We could have dinner together."

He was just trying to be polite, but Mama said, "I think that'd be nice."

Tonight's dinner was spaghetti and meatballs. Daddy looked grossed out by the soggy noodles. Charlie piled a plate high for the both of us. As we sat down and both Charlie and I began eating, Daddy asked, "You two… share a plate?"

"Oh, it's just this thing we do," I explained. I didn't want to tell them that we'd fallen into this habit because it was the only way Charlie could make sure I was eating. That felt too personal— some things were just for Charlie and me.

Daddy huffed. "Sounds like a good way to share germs."

"It's fine, Liam," Mama scolded. Mama hardly cared that I was sharing a plate with Charlie. She was just happy I was eating.

Oberi had his own plate of spaghetti and meatballs. He wolfed it down, then set his saucy mouth on Daddy's leg, staining his pants with marinara. Daddy sighed but didn't object.

After we were finished with dinner, Mama leaned in. "Sweetheart, can we talk to you privately? There are some things we should discuss as a family."

My insides flip-flopped. Was something wrong? "Sure. See you later, Charlie."

"See you." Charlie walked off with Oberi, clearly happy to be excused.

I got up from the table and led my parents to the prison yard. There were a lot of people out here, but I found a bench by an isolated spot and sat down. Mama sat across from me, while Daddy stood with crossed arms, like he was going to beat up anyone who got within a few feet of my presence.

I rolled my eyes. "Daddy, you're not my bodyguard. I've been here for months and nothing has happened."

"These are dangerous prisoners," he rebutted. "I'm just keeping watch."

"*I'm* a dangerous prisoner! I'm here, aren't I?" I asked. He was being ridiculous.

Daddy huffed. Mama rushed to say something before we could argue. "Ava, the truth is, the Games aren't the only reason we came," she confessed. "We thought we'd spend the next few weeks searching Darke Island for clues on your prophecy."

My eyes widened. "Really?"

"Yes. We thought our experience with my own prophecy might help you unveil your own. That is, if we have your permission to research it," Mama said.

"Of course you do," I replied. "I need all the help I can get."

"If we find anything, we'll tell you straight away," Daddy said. "Your mother and I are planning to turn this island upside down."

He was hoping they'd find something in time to talk me out of the Darke Games. Not gonna happen.

I looked at the big bag Mama carried. "What's that you got there?"

Mama smiled and unzipped the bag. "I heard there was a ball after the Games. I thought you needed something to wear."

Mama pulled a ballgown out of the bag, and I gasped. An A-line dress with a big tulle skirt flooded my vision. It was sky-blue, and had the cutest cap sleeves, with lace petals above the waistline. It was so timeless.

"I wore this to the Elemental Ball my freshman year. Your father was my date." Fond memories flickered across my mother's eyes as she looked at the dress, and Daddy smiled. "I thought I'd pass it on to you."

"Mama, it's so beautiful." My hand ran over the fabric in awe. I'd never seen this dress before. It was gorgeous.

Mama tilted her head. "I know that look. You have an idea."

I bit my lip. "It's… *almost* perfect," I said. "But it needs some updates. Could you go into town and get me some fabric? There are sewing machines in the Arts and Crafts room."

"I'm surprised they let the students around needles." Mama's eyebrows shot up.

"Only with supervision. The Arts and Crafts room is monitored at all times. Can you help me?" I asked.

"I'm not as good at sewing as your grandmother or Aunt Imogen, but I know enough," Mama said with a gleam in her eye. "Let's make your perfect dress."

charlie
NINETEEN

Exams were a two-week ordeal at the Institute, and I was *freaking out*. Each exam stretched hours, and classes were split into blocks. We'd take half our exams this week, and half next week, right up until the Darke Games began. So much for training for the Darke Games when studying for exams took up every hour of the day.

These weren't the pesky little exams I remembered from high school. They were *college* exams, complete with written portions and physical assessments. I wasn't worried about the physical part. I could conjure Air and Earth like it was nothing, and I was certain to pass Elementai Magic. It was the written exams I was sure to fail.

I should've been worried about the Darke Games, but exams seemed to be a death sentence just the same. If we *did* survive the Games and didn't win, we'd be right back at the Institute next semester. And if I didn't pass, I'd be repeating classes until my sentence was up. If the Warden saw my grades and thought I hadn't learned enough by graduation to be "rehabilitated," I was going to a *real* supernatural prison, full of convicts with powers I couldn't even imagine.

All for what…? Stowing away on a boat I didn't even steal? No way was I being transferred.

And so I had to pass my exams.

My first exam was Juvenile Justice. Might as well get the hell over to begin with. I'd be back here next semester anyway— assuming a monster didn't rip my head off during the Games. At this point, it might be preferable if I never had to listen to Professor Mazur speak again.

My heart hammered, and my palms began to sweat as I took my seat at the back of the room. Oberi panted and rested his chin on my leg, but even that didn't help soothe me. I was screwed.

"Half the exam will be multiple choice, and the other half will consist of essay questions," Professor Mazur announced. She marched down the rows with a quick staccato to her step. Papers rustled as she handed them out. "Professor Gael will be assisting me in proctoring the exam, so don't even *think* about cheating. If you so much as move your eyes from your own paper, you will be caught, and you will be punished accordingly."

954

Professor Mazur strolled by my desk, but she completely ignored me, as if I were invisible. I was given no exam, no pencil… not so much as an explanation.

My pulse quickened. Hell, I hated taking tests. Worst part of prison, for sure.

I cleared my throat. "Um, Professor? I didn't receive an exam."

Her heels clicked against the floor as she turned toward me. "Mister Wahkin, what are you doing here?"

I furrowed my brow. "Um… I've been enrolled in this class all semester."

"No, I mean what are you doing *here*? Didn't I tell you Professor Takahashi was proctoring your exam?"

Her tone was harsh, and I wasn't sure how to respond. No, she hadn't told me a damn thing.

"Well…?" she pressed. "What are you waiting for? You're late! Professor Takahashi is surely waiting for you in his office. Hurry along."

I barely had a moment to process the sudden change in schedule, but I hurried out of the classroom as fast as I could. Oberi followed at my side.

I was skeptical as I made my way to Professor Takahashi's office. Professor Mazur hadn't provided me with one accommodation all semester. What had made her change her mind now?

By the time I arrived at Takahashi's office, my pulse had slowed to normal anxiety levels. I knocked on the door, and his voice came from behind it.

"Come in," he called. "Ah, Charlie. I've been waiting for you. Are you ready for your exam?"

Oberi led me to a chair opposite Takahashi, and I sighed as I plopped into it. "Ready as I'll ever be."

Honestly, even if I aced the exam, I wasn't sure I'd pass the class.

"How will this work?" I asked.

"I'll read the questions aloud and record your answer on the exam sheet. Essay questions will be given verbally and graded immediately," he explained. "I am unable to say anything during the exam, apart from reading the questions. Do you understand?"

My hands weren't shaking quite as much anymore, so that was good news. "Ready whenever you are."

Professor Takahashi began reading the multiple-choice questions. I was surprised when I knew the answer to the first three. A couple of the questions stumped me, but overall I was pretty confident in the multiple-choice questions. Takahashi didn't say anything when I gave him my essay answers. All I heard was a slight scribble on the page, though I didn't know if it was good or bad.

I was relieved by the time the exam was over. It felt like I'd been sitting there for hours. A huge weight had just been lifted from my shoulders. Whether I passed the class or not, at least I didn't have to worry about it again for the next few weeks.

Paper slid over paper, like Takahashi was putting my test into an envelope. "You should be proud of yourself, Charlie."

"Does that mean I passed?" I asked hopefully.

He laughed lightly. "I unfortunately can't give you details of your grade yet. I have to return this to Professor Mazur personally. You should stick around, though, seeing as your counseling session begins in…"

He paused, like he was checking the time. "Less than twenty minutes."

"Professor," I stopped him before he could get to the door.

"Yes, Charlie?"

"Thanks for proctoring my exam."

"My pleasure," he said, before leaving the room.

Oberi nudged me, forcing me to pet his head. "One exam down." I sighed. "Maybe I'll survive."

The sound of footsteps came just outside the door. At first, I thought Takahashi had returned, like he forgot something, but the footsteps were lighter. Oberi perked up and started barking. That's when I knew it was Ava.

"You're early," I remarked.

"Hardly," she said. "I came by an hour ago, but the door was closed. It sounded like he was in a meeting."

"Takahashi was proctoring my Juvenile Justice exam," I explained.

Ava didn't sit, but rather paced around the room. "Oh. Mazur let you take it?"

"Yeah, I'm as surprised as you are."

"Well, money talks," Ava muttered. I wasn't sure if I heard her right.

I stiffened. "What's that supposed to mean?"

I think I already knew. It was a miracle Mazur gave me a proctor, to be honest. I should've known something was up.

"Oh, it's just a phrase," Ava said as innocently as a convict.

"Pidge, I didn't need your help," I snapped. I knew Ava's family had money, but using it to bribe the professors sounded like a good way to get in trouble around here.

"I don't know what you're talking about," Ava replied, but I could hear it in her tone. She knew *exactly* what I meant.

I crossed my arms. "If I'm caught cheating—"

"It's not *cheating* to receive accommodations, Charlie," she said harshly. "Just be grateful you got the test out of the way, and let's not talk about it again, all right?"

I hesitated. I really was going to fail the class without taking that exam. It was worth a huge part of my grade. I guess I owed Ava for whatever she'd said to Mazur— or bribed her with— to secure my accommodations. No one had ever cared enough to do something like that for me. I stood to make my way over to Ava, a *thank you* present on my tongue.

But then I realized what I was doing, and I sank back into my chair.

"I don't owe you anything," I finally said.

"Of course not," she replied, still playing stupid. "Because I didn't do anything."

Ava's footsteps continued around the room, like she couldn't just sit still.

"Something on your mind, pidge?" I asked.

She sighed heavily, as if half glad and half annoyed I'd asked. "I think I bombed my Supernatural Behavioral Science exam."

"But you studied so hard!"

"I know, but I rushed it. That's why I was here so early."

"Why rush? You had all that time."

Ava didn't speak for a few beats, just continued pacing around the room. My hand rested on Oberi's head, and he bobbed it back and forth, watching her.

"I can't stop thinking about my parents," she admitted.

"What about them?" I asked. "They're okay, right? I mean, the island is safe… until the Games, at least."

"Yeah, but they're not really here for the Games. They're here for—" She cut off abruptly.

It felt like she was trying to tell me something, but I didn't know what it was. "They're here for what?"

Ava's breath wavered. "I can't sit still. Can we go for a walk?"

I shrugged. We still had twenty minutes until our counseling session. "Sure."

Ava and I strolled down the hall side-by-side, with Oberi beside her. We were so close our hands kept brushing one another. It brought me comfort, though Ava didn't seem to notice. I waited for her to say something, but she didn't speak until we'd climbed a flight of stairs and she opened a door. Cool air rushed through, and we stepped out in the open. Oberi immediately left our side, sniffing around for whatever he could find.

"I didn't know students were allowed on the roof," I remarked. I tried to read the area with my Air power, but it was hard when it was all so open. I couldn't quite tell where the edge was, and I didn't want to get too close.

"This isn't the roof," Ava said. "That's up another level. It's a balcony. I found this place over the weekend. It's a good place to come and relax. I don't think many students know about it, because no one's interrupted me yet."

Ava noticed my hesitation and took my hand. "Don't be afraid. You won't fall off."

She led me forward and placed my hand on a thick stone railing that lined the balcony. I felt around to see that it was made of stone pillars, each one carved into an intricate arch.

"The view is really nice from up here," Ava said as she leaned against the banister. "You can see over the fence— almost all the way to Shade Hills."

"Well, *you* can." I chuckled.

She barely responded, and I could tell something was bothering her.

"What is it, pidge? You said your parents weren't here for the Games."

"No. They want to help me."

"With what?" They weren't going to help her escape, were they? Not after her father had sentenced her here in the first place, right? Unless he was suffering some kind of guilt for it now.

Ava took a few breaths. "Charlie… do you remember that I promised you I'd tell you why I was entering the Darke Games?"

"Yeah," I said, a little bitterly. "You never did."

"Well, I meant to. I just didn't know how to tell you. It's all so confusing. And honestly, I didn't know if I could trust you with the truth at the time."

It took a moment before her words hit me. She *didn't know at the time…*

Did that mean she trusted me now?

"It would help a lot to know," I told her gently. "But if you need more time…"

"No," she said quickly. "I need you to know before we go into the Darke Games, because if anything happens… well, then you know why I have to do *anything* to win."

She was starting to scare me. I knew Ava was intense and competitive, but this seemed to go far beyond that. It almost sounded like it was something she didn't *want* to do, but *had* to do— like she was bound by duty.

I reached out and took her hand, rubbing the back of it with my fingers. "You can tell me anything, pidge."

Ava took a long time to respond, like she was mulling it over in her mind. She didn't pull away from me, but she didn't engage, either. I had no idea what she was thinking, and Oberi wasn't being any help. He was over in a corner sniffing all the new smells.

Finally, Ava spoke. "The truth is, I came here because I've been chosen."

"Chosen…?" I prodded. I wasn't sure I understood what she meant.

"Chosen by the ancestors," she said, sounding completely serious. As soon as the confession came, she couldn't seem to stop herself. "My aunt Maddie is a *naderei*, or a prophet. When I was born, she made a prophecy about how I was to save the supernatural world from some gigantic catastrophe. I can't really explain it, because I don't know what it means yet, and my aunt's visions were never very specific. She wrote it down in a journal, but it's difficult to make sense of. What I *do* know is that the answers to the prophecy lie somewhere on Darke Island. Daddy sentenced me here so I could investigate. But the Institute has been a bust. The answers have to be out *there*, on the rest of the island."

Hell, this was a lot to take in. I would've accused her of bluffing if she didn't sound so scared. My heart broke for her.

"Now that I'm here, my sentence is in the hands of the Warden. Daddy can't get me out of it anymore," she continued. "So you see why I have to win the Games and earn that pardon. I have to explore the rest of the Island for answers— or the entire supernatural world may be in jeopardy."

A shiver ran down my spine. I could hardly wrap my head around what she was saying. Her words felt so heavy. How could my pidge be caught in the middle of this?

"Say something, Charlie," she pleaded.

"It all sounds... unreal," I breathed.

"Well, it *is* real," she said bitterly, finally pulling her hand away from me. She turned to the balcony to look out over the landscape. Her voice turned to a whisper. "It's not something I would choose for myself, but Mama was a chosen one, too. She had to do it during the Hawkei Civil War, and now it's my turn. My parents are here looking for clues, but I'm worried about them. They aren't as young as they once were, and I don't want them anywhere near the island when those portals open and monsters come flooding into our world."

"I bet they don't want you anywhere near those monsters, either," I said reassuringly. "Your parents care about you just as much as you care about them."

"Yeah, but *I* signed up to fight the monsters, to protect the people of Darke Island," she said. "I shouldn't have to protect my parents, too. But Daddy insists, and you don't argue with the chief."

She sighed. "Those monsters are only half the battle, Charlie. I have to find out what this island can tell me about the prophecy."

I could hear the fear in her tone. I didn't mean to do it, but I found myself reaching out for her. I wrapped her in my arms. She stiffened for a moment, before melting into me and embracing me back. A breeze passed by us, rustling her hair. Her scent was intoxicating. I couldn't help it when I leaned in to press my lips to her forehead.

"We'll find the answers, pidge," I assured her.

"We?" she asked in a whisper.

"Yeah," I confirmed, the promise already searing itself into my heart. "We'll win the Darke Games, leave the Institute, and figure out what the ancestors want from you. I'll be by your side every step of the way."

She leaned her head against my chest. "But it could be dangerous, Charlie."

"Which is exactly why you can't do it alone," I reminded her. "I can't exactly let you run off with Oberi, now can I?"

She seemed to understand that and relaxed into me deeper. "No, I guess not. I just hope the answers are actually here. I would hate for this all to be for nothing."

I smoothed down her hair. "It won't be, pidge."

What I didn't say was that it *wasn't*— present tense. Coming to Darke Island, being sentenced to the Institute... it wasn't all for nothing. Because it brought us together. Prophecy or not, wherever she went, I'd follow.

"Can we just stay up here all night?" Ava asked. "It'd be nice to forget about everything."

"Not if you don't want to disappoint Kallie and Marcus," I reminded her. "Or get another strike on your record. We've got a mandatory counseling session scheduled. We don't want to be late."

She sighed in disappointment and drew away from me. "I guess that means I *have* to go."

I frowned. I didn't want to leave, either. This balcony was quiet and felt safe, though it might have been the company I kept.

"I guess so," I replied reluctantly.

Ava turned toward the door and took my hand to lead me behind her. She patted her leg to get Oberi's attention. "Come on, boy! It's time to go back inside."

Oberi whined. He loved the outdoors, especially when he could feel the air through his fur. After a few more tries, he followed us inside.

We made our way back to Professor Takahashi's office. We could hear Marcus and Kallie talking to him inside the room.

"Ah, there you are," Takahashi said brightly. "I was going to give you two a few more minutes before launching a search party."

"Are we late?" I asked.

"Nothing to worry about," Professor Takahashi said. "Ava, would you close the door, so we can get started?"

The chairs were lined in a circle like normal. I took my usual chair between Marcus and Ava.

"We've reached the end of the semester, and I'm sure emotions are running high over exams," Takahashi began. "However, I'm concerned that we've missed some important points in our counseling sessions. Usually by this point, most groups I work with are a little more... open with each other."

I didn't know what he was getting at. I'd opened up to Ava more than I had with anyone before.

"Today, I suggest we start with an exercise in which we tell our fellow classmates one thing no one else in the room knows about us," Takahashi suggested.

I knew what he was doing. He was trying to make us each vulnerable— like we might spill our deepest, darkest secrets right in front of him. But there were things you didn't tell your counselor— only your closest friends.

"Marcus, would you like to start?" Takahashi asked.

Marcus cleared his throat, but he didn't speak right away. It was like this every counseling session. None of us ever really said much, just mostly listened to Takahashi fill the time with life lessons he thought would help, but rarely applied to us. If he wanted us to get vulnerable and speak to each other, it'd be down in the Villain's Den or out in the prison yard— not in this circle that reeked of obligation.

"When I was, uh, twelve," Marcus began, "I got a really bad sliver in my hand. Hurt too much to pull out, so I let it fester for a week. I nearly went into septic shock."

Kallie snickered.

"What's so funny?" Marcus asked, sounding confused.

Kallie's tone was sarcastic. "Your war story is a *sliver*? In Malovia, you can be impaled by a lance, and fae are expected to yank that sucker right out and keep on fighting."

Marcus blew a breath and mumbled, "It was a bad sliver."

Kallie started to say something else, but Takahashi cut her off. "Let's not argue over who had it worse. This is a judgement-free zone. Marcus, while that story was... interesting... I was hoping you might start with talking about your *feelings*."

Oh, great. Here we go.

"I guess there is one thing," Marcus admitted.

"Whenever you're ready," Takahashi encouraged.

Marcus paused a few beats, and Rishi purred in his lap. Finally, he spoke. "I left someone behind when I came to the Institute. Kellen... he was like a younger brother to me. He was the kind of kid who got suspended a lot. The teachers thought he was trouble, but I knew he was just misunderstood. I took him under my wing and taught him how to draw and paint. Things started getting better, and then... well, then I was sentenced to the Institute, and I never got a chance to explain. That's why I'm entering the Games— so I can get out and make amends."

Everyone was totally silent during Marcus' confession, even Oberi. It was the first time Marcus had ever spoken about his life before the Institute. Kind of broke my heart, to be honest.

After a few moments, Kallie scoffed. "You call that a sob story?"

"Yeah," Marcus snapped. "I do."

"Please," Takahashi pressed. "Let's not go comparing our suffering."

Marcus barely let him finish before challenging Kallie. "Let's hear yours, then."

"You want to hear a *real* sob story?" Kallie asked, obviously up for the challenge. "How about the one where I lost the *fae crown*? I deserved it, too! I won the King's Contest."

"What's the King's Contest again?" I asked. She'd mentioned it before, but hadn't fully explained it.

"It's a competition in Malovia designed to seek out those most worthy of the crown. Winner becomes king— or queen, in my case," Kallie explained. "Before entering, you have to choose a mate, because a king or queen is stronger with their mate at their side."

She didn't quite sound like she believed it, but rather wrote it off as tradition.

"I declared a mate, but I didn't really love him, and I didn't bond with him, either," she continued, her voice intense. "He was obsessed with me. I knew he'd agree to compete if I asked, so that's why I chose him. Anyway, that's a story for another day. But in the Contest, I fought my brother for the crown in the final duel."

"Your own brother?" Marcus asked.

"*Twin* brother," Kallie clarified. "I had to. We were both competing. One of us had to win."

"So he won and sent you here?" Ava guessed.

Kallie blew a breath. "I wish it were that simple. No. I defeated my brother and won the King's Contest. But the Circle— that's like our parliament back home, those sexist pigs— voted that a woman couldn't inherit the country— a woman who could *unnaturally shift*, as they put it. I'm of high fae blood, for the gods' sake! But that wasn't good enough for them, nor was my chosen mate."

She said the words as if they weren't her own.

"So what does the Circle do?" she continued rhetorically. "They give the crown to my brother, the runner up, all because he was born with a set of balls! The king tried to stop the vote, but the Circle forced it."

"What did you do?" Ava asked, sounding invested in the story.

"The only thing I could!" Kallie's voice grew harsher. "I had to get my crown back, so I made an assassination attempt on the future king."

"But that was your own brother!" Marcus balked.

I'd gone totally speechless. I knew Kallie was in here for a good reason, but I didn't know what she was truly capable of.

"A brother who stole my crown!" Kallie shot back. "I was wronged. I worked my ass off and earned my right to the throne, and it was taken away because I'm a *woman*— an outcast considered a freak because I can shift."

Kallie took heavy breaths. "I didn't even get the job done, thanks to the queen. I was caught and almost executed. If my mom hadn't fought for my banishment over execution, I'd be dead right now— executed for treason. My one consolation prize is that going to the Institute gave me a chance to publicly reject my creepy stalker, and I didn't have to mate with him."

Kallie's breaths turned into sobs. It caught me completely off guard, because I'd never seen her cry before. "I *earned* that crown! I worked toward it my entire life! And without it I... I don't even know who I am."

Her voice cracked, and she sniffled. "It feels like I have to find the pieces of myself that shattered after losing the throne, but that I'll never be able to put myself back together. This was all I ever wanted, and now I have to learn who I am without it. Now, I'm nothing but a fake! So forgive me if you got a sliver and lost your friend, but it's *nothing* compared to what I lost. My family, the crown… even myself."

The room went dead silent, apart from Kallie's intermittent sniffling. I was so shocked, I couldn't offer any comforting words even if I wanted to.

Professor Takahashi finally spoke. "Thank you very much for sharing your story, Kalina. I hope you feel better now that you've gotten it off your chest."

"Right now I feel like shit." Kallie hiccupped. "It's someone else's turn."

"I'll go," Ava offered. The atmosphere in the room seemed to shift instantly as attention turned to her. I thought it was kind of her to offer to go next. It gave Kallie an opportunity to compose herself.

"I'm not sure what I can say that no one else in the room already knows," Ava started slowly.

I understood her meaning immediately. All the hard stuff— the kind of stuff Kallie had just admitted to, and the horrors Ava had gone through a few years ago— she'd already told to me. It was a loophole to Professor Takahashi's request, a way to get out of telling Marcus and Kallie the worst of it.

"But there is one thing I've never admitted to anyone," Ava continued. "Everyone says I'm good at arguing and that I should've become a lawyer, and I used to want to be one. I thought about defending people who couldn't defend themselves. Abused kids, maybe rape victims."

A shiver traveled down my spine. To think of what Ava had been through made my whole body turn to stone. I didn't move— didn't breathe.

"My mom talked me out of it. She didn't think I could handle losing cases, and she was right. I'd fall to pieces if a child had to go back to their abusive family, or if a rapist walked free. Besides, my heart was in exploring. I like studying people more like I like fighting over them."

Ava paused for a long breath. "This is going to sound weird, but… I never quite felt like I was part of a group of people. I always felt like I was… different— a freak. That's why I love anthropology and wanted to major in it. I can study people instead of pretending to be a part of them. It's the only way I understand how to communicate with others."

Ava quieted, then reached over to stroke Oberi's head. Her fingers grazed against mine, and I wasn't sure if it was intentional or not.

"You're not a freak," I blurted. It was instinctual. I had to comfort her, even if everyone else watched.

"But I *am* different," Ava argued. "I have to try harder than everyone else to control myself. It's… exhausting sometimes."

She was quick to clarify. "I mean, I know bipolar isn't an excuse for the way I act. It's not like everyone else with bipolar is sentenced to a reform school. I chose the life I did for myself, but that has to make me different, because who else would choose this?"

An uncomfortable silence settled over the room, and I reached out to squeeze Ava's hand. I swallowed the lump in my throat. "We all did, pidge. I chose a life of crime, too."

Ava scoffed. "You did what you had to do to survive."

Oh, pidge, I thought. *We have so much more in common than you think.*

I shook my head. "You don't get it. Want to know *my* secret? I *like* the trouble."

"You what?" Ava asked breathlessly. She seemed so shocked. It was in that moment that I realized how deep I had buried this confession. I hadn't even admitted it to myself.

"Do you think I'd still be stealing and conning if it was merely a survival tactic?" I asked Ava. "If I really didn't like it, or had severe moral objections, don't you think I would've given up by now? I do it because it feels *good* to be in control. There's a high that comes with the scam, and doing bad things is the only way I can get that. It's all I know. Things have been falling apart my whole life. Even if there were better options, how could I stop when those options would fall away from me, too?"

Ava didn't say anything. I wished I could read her expression right now, because it was killing me to not know what she was thinking. Hell, I could barely make sense of it myself.

I crossed my arms and slumped in my chair. "I always had a reason for what I'd done before, but here in the Institute, where I have a warm meal three times a day and a bed to sleep in at night, the cravings haven't gone away. I'm sick of sitting around just waiting to pass my classes. I want to fight somebody or steal something and get away with it. And I can't, because I'll get caught here. I guess that's the true test of a villain, huh? What do they do when they don't have a reason… when they're no longer desperate?"

The question was rhetorical, but I knew the answer. I was a bad guy— a villain. And I didn't even know it until just now. I committed crimes because they *felt good*, and just used survival as a reason to cover it up.

I kept speaking, because I feared someone might interrupt and accuse me of what I'd just realized myself. "When I came to the Institute, there were two choices. I could either keep up the cons, or survive. I thought I'd been conning people for survival all along, but that was only one piece of it. I'm good at conning and thieving. But not here… without it, it's like I'm just going through the motions. But I don't know how long I can keep up this act, because I don't know how to be anything but bad."

I wanted to say more, just to kill time so I would never have to hear their reactions. But there was nothing more to say. I was bad— it was that simple. And it wasn't because I didn't have any other choice. It was because I didn't *want* another choice.

"Charlie," Ava whispered, like something about my speech had touched her. Screw that. I wasn't here to *inspire* anyone.

Professor Takahashi cleared his throat. "Thank you for sharing, Charlie, but you're not a bad person. Each and every one of you have made mistakes, yes, but you are here at the Institute to correct them."

Ah, here came another lecture. A useless one, I was sure. Takahashi meant well, but I didn't think he understood a damn thing I'd said.

But everyone else had. I felt the tension in the air and the understanding in their silence. They knew exactly what it felt like to crave trouble.

Takahashi spoke the rest of the counseling session. I didn't think he'd expected us to reveal so much, and I bet he felt like he had to fill the silence for our benefit. He let us out early.

Kallie clapped me on the back on our way down the stairs. "I appreciate what you said in there, Charlie."

"Why?" I grumbled. "You should just forget about it. It was dumb."

"It was the *truth*," Ava argued. "I know if I'm not causing trouble, I get bored. It's fun to take risks."

"Exactly," Kallie agreed. "I was expected to be perfect my whole life, and look how far that got me. My own country rejected me. If I'm not good enough to be their queen, I'm damn well good enough to be their villain."

I chuckled lightly, my mood lifting.

"You're good enough to be anything you want, Kallie," Marcus praised. "I was always a disappointment back home. No one took notice of me until I was sentenced to the Institute. The straight and narrow is dull. It's better to be a felon than to be nothing at all."

Their words should've bothered me. I mean, what kind of psycho group of kids preferred this kind of shit to a normal life?

Instead, it only brought me comfort, because I was part of a team that shared in this strange, twisted way of thinking.

The monsters unleashed during the Darke Games wouldn't know what was coming—because they'd never seen a group of villains like us before.

ava-marie

TWENTY

The Darke Games had arrived, and I had never been more ready to kick some ass.

I stood in the prison yard on December nineteenth, before the large gates that led to the outside world with the other competitors. I jogged in place and did a couple of air-punches to warm up, burning off some nervous energy. Above us, drones hovered, recording our every move. It was just before noon, the time when the Games were scheduled to begin.

The Darke Games were televised. The judges would watch our performance and award us points from inside the safety of the Institute while we fought monsters. The students were gathered in the stands in front of a big jumbo screen in the prison yard, where the broadcast of the Games would go on all day and into the night. The school had made this into a big deal. There were booths outside selling popcorn and drinks, and for one night only, the cells would remain completely unlocked so students could go in and out in order to watch the Games.

My parents were in the stands. They'd failed to find anything on Darke Island regarding the prophecy. It made my mission even more crucial. My gut instinct was right. I was the only one who was able to find the true meaning of the prophecy, and to do it, I had to get out there.

My teammates stood around me. Marcus was pale. He kept pacing and muttering things under his breath I couldn't hear. Kallie cracked her knuckles and stretched like this was a sports game. She'd been through similar things in the King's Contest, and to her, this was like any other event.

Charlie was… calm. I thought he'd be freaking out, but he waited patiently for the Games to start like it was the first chance he'd finally be let out of his cage. Beside him, Oberi stood in her unicorn form, staring out at the beyond.

"Why aren't our school uniforms this badass?" Kallie asked. She observed her clothes with pride, and I had to agree. The school had given everyone the same outfit for the Games; a black bodysuit, with elements of leather and breathable mesh, and sleek black boots. The suits were tailored and fitted to our bodies to give us ample room to move. Purple and green piping was sewn on to the legs and arms.

"We look like we're secret agents," Marcus complained. Rishi had already scratched Marcus' uniform.

"Or supervillains," Charlie added, feeling the arms of the outfit.

Supervillains was right. I felt like I was gonna fight Batman in this getup.

"I can't believe they're going to make us fight monsters right after exams. Hell week was hard enough," Marcus complained.

"It wasn't that bad," Charlie said, and I had to smile.

Charlie had passed all his exams. I'd asked Daddy for help, and though he didn't like Charlie, he had a disability himself, and knew what it was like not to receive accommodation. He'd paid off all of Charlie's teachers, who promised they'd give Charlie whatever accommodations he needed in the future to pass.

But we wouldn't need them, because we were getting out of here today. Professors had confirmed that multiple portals to hell had opened up on Darke Island, and monsters were flooding out of them at this very moment.

Even from here, I could hear the moans of monsters and demons as they lurked in the woods beyond. There were some big fuckers out there. Their roars shook the ground, and I watched as tiny pebbles moved over the gravel beneath our feet.

Marcus quivered in his boots. "Tell me again why I can't subconjure weapons and supplies. I'd be a lot happier out there with a sword."

Kallie laughed. "If you could handle one."

Marcus blushed. I doubted he'd ever touched a sword in his life. Marcus' magical stash had been searched this morning, to make sure he wasn't sneaking anything into the Games.

"It's unfair to the other teams," I reminded him. "It'd give us too much of an advantage."

"But why do the judges *care*?" Marcus argued. "Shouldn't they give us every opportunity to kill those monsters? Isn't that the point of the Games?"

"Not to the inmates," Kallie pointed out. "Everyone here is trying to win that pardon. I bet the angels and vampires bitched about witch magic long enough to ban your conjuring abilities."

"Well, it's unfair," Marcus complained. "Might as well ban angel wings and vampire strength. I don't have that!"

"It doesn't matter," Charlie said. "If we want to win, we have to play by the rules— no matter how twisted."

"Agreed," I added. "We'll kick ass no matter what comes our way."

Mama waved to me from her seat in the stands. I gave a huge smile and waved back. Mama's look was confident, but beside her, Daddy looked ready to pass out. He *did not* want me going out there, and had spent up until the last minute trying to convince me to withdraw.

But Mama had taken me by the shoulders and said, "We're Koigni women. We don't back down. Go out there and show them that Fire runs in your veins."

And Water, too, I thought excitedly. Oberi bucked beside me, as if she could hear my thoughts.

"Are anyone else's parents here?" Charlie asked.

"I didn't tell my family I was doing this. I didn't want them to freak out," Marcus said.

Kallie scoffed. "Pretty sure I was disowned when I tried to kill my brother. I haven't talked to my parents since I was banished."

Ouch. So I was the only one here with any outside support. That sucked.

I didn't think that many parents had shown up for the other teams, either. It looked like there were about forty-eight contestants in total, about twelve teams. I thought the number would be higher, but apparently, not even prisoners at the Institute were brave enough to risk death for a chance at a clean record.

Despona, Alice, Carson, and Wesley were strategizing only a few feet away. If we didn't win, I hoped they did. Unlike the rest of us, they were all innocent and deserved to get out of here.

Across the way, Mad Dog barked orders at his team. He'd picked Naya and a couple of his other vampire goons. Naya fawned over him while Mad Dog pushed his teammates around, trying to get them hyped up.

I hoped to the ancestors they didn't win. Mad Dog and Naya were the kind of people who needed to be in jail. Society wasn't safe with those assholes on the streets— and that was coming from me.

The Warden's face came on the jumbotron, and the prison yard went silent. A chill ran up and down my spine as his cold face looked out blankly at the world. "Good afternoon, and welcome to the Darke Games!"

There were a couple of claps, but it was mostly quiet. People were even afraid to cheer when the Warden was amping them up.

The Warden gave a grim smile. "I speak directly to the participants of these games. Outside the fence, monsters lurk. Each monster is given a set of points, which you will gain if you destroy it. You have from now until the end of the Games to gather points. The Games do not end until each monster is vanquished. Once all monsters are killed, the Games are over and the winners will be announced."

My heart stuttered nervously as the Warden straightened his shoulders. "From the moment you step outside these gates, the doors to the Institute are closed. You will not be let back in until the portals to the other world have been shut and all monsters are slain. The portals will remain open for the next twenty-four hours. From this point on, you will receive no outside help— even if you are in dire need, no one will come to your aid. You are on your own. Stay vigilant. Stay alive."

The Institute gates opened. Even as I stepped into danger, the first gust of fresh wind gave me a breath of freedom. I never wanted to set foot inside the Institute again. I'd risk my neck if it meant never going back.

The gates closed behind us, and an alarm sounded as they locked shut. The crowd cheered. I was very aware that the people I loved were behind that fence, and I was now outside it, quite literally walking into the jaws of hell.

We followed the rest of the participants. All the competitors walked down the long road leading to the Institute and into the forest, the drones above us capturing the footage.

When we entered those eerie woods again, I immediately felt something was off. My teammates felt it, too. Charlie bristled beside me, and Oberi let out a nervous breath. People around us began to mutter as we came across trees that had been ripped out of the ground or shattered to splinters. Something big was out here.

A tree toppled. Charlie reached out to drag me out of the way. He pulled me aside just before the tree could smack me in the head, using his Air magic to push it in the other direction. It fell, and I looked up. Several people screamed as our gaze fell upon the first official monster of the Games.

The best way I could describe it was a giant eyeball with tentacles. The monster hovered ten feet above ground, its piercing eye searching as its nasty, slimy tentacles reached out for victims, ripping out trees by their roots. I had no idea what culture it was from, or what kind of magical society could've created it. I'd never heard of something like it before. All I knew is that it was definitely a creature from hell, and that I didn't want to end up smushed.

"What the hell is it?" Charlie asked. He couldn't see it, but knew we'd run into something bad.

"Uh, imagine a giant floating octopus, except that octopus is an eyeball and it literally wants to kill us," I told him. Fear quaked through my guts as the eyeball's red gaze landed on me and narrowed, pinning me to the spot.

Kallie and Marcus dove out of the way of another falling tree. Meanwhile, other competitors launched themselves at the eyeball, trying to attack it. Spells whizzed through the air, but they bounced off the eyeball like they couldn't affect it. One battle spell ricocheted off the eyeball and hit a shifter in the chest. He went down, expression shocked as he felt the giant hole that was in his torso. He slumped to the ground, and I knew immediately... he was dead.

I stared in shock at the shifter's body. To witness his death in such a violent way... it brought back memories of Monica. Her death replayed in my mind as the carnage continued around me. It felt like my feet were stuck to the ground. I was so frozen I couldn't move.

"Pidge, come on!" Charlie grabbed me again and threw me on Oberi's back.

He hauled himself onto her behind me and called for Kallie and Marcus. They were backing off as the multitudes of people tried to fight off the giant eyeball. Mad Dog ran at it with his vampire speed and launched himself into the air, clinging to the eyeball and punching it over and over. The monster screeched and began flinging its tentacles around, trying to get Mad Dog off. One of the tentacles wrapped around a teammate of Mad Dog's. He screamed in pain, then his head slumped lifelessly as the monster crushed his insides and tore his body in two. It wasn't easy to kill a vampire, and this monster had done it no problem.

My jaw dropped open. Two people were gone already. This couldn't be real.

Oberi left us no time to watch. She galloped away, dodging trees as she ran through the forest. Behind us, Kallie changed into a wolf. Marcus climbed onto her back, and he hung on to Rishi, who screeched as Kallie ran to keep up with Oberi.

Oberi didn't stop until we were at least a mile into the woods. Kallie skidded to a halt beside her. Marcus slid off and smoothed down Rishi's fur. It was stuck up every which way, and the cat yowled in displeasure. Rishi was merely a cat— not a Familiar like Oberi— but Marcus had insisted on bringing him along. He never left his side.

Charlie slid off of Oberi, and I copied him, turning around to face him. "Charlie, what are you doing? We could've killed it!"

"We need to play this smart," Charlie said. "Everyone is going to go after that thing. It makes more sense for us to look for our own target, so we can get the points."

I paused. Charlie was right. There was no use trying to kill a monster that almost fifty people were after. We had to find our own.

"Maybe this was a mistake," Marcus said nervously. "The Games have only been going on for five minutes, and two people are already dead."

Kallie shifted back to human form. "It's too late to back out now. Gates are closed. We need to make the most of it and hunt some monsters."

I put my arms around myself and shivered. Charlie laid a hand on my shoulder. "Pidge, you okay?"

The deaths of the shifter and the vampire were mingling before my eyes, along with Monica. I couldn't separate them. The scenes replayed in my mind as the voices in my head grew louder.

Look, they're dead.

So dead.

Dead just like Monica.

You'll be dead, too.

Death will come for you all.

I'd made a massive miscalculation. I wanted this to be an adventure, but I hadn't taken it seriously when I was told people died during this competition. They were called the Darke Games, but there was nothing fun about them.

"I'm fine," I said. "I just... wasn't expecting that."

Charlie frowned. "You have to be ready for anything out here. If you don't put that mask on and separate yourself from the chaos, you'll be dragged right into it. Steel yourself, pidge. It's gonna get a whole lot worse from this point out."

Charlie had become someone totally different. I didn't recognize this part of him. I now saw that this was the piece of him he dragged out when he had to. He had experience fighting to survive. Even with monsters and magic, this was what he was used to— what he'd fought so hard to get out of.

And I'd dragged him right back into it, because I didn't know what I was dealing with. I felt like an ass.

One drone had followed us to capture our participation. I tried to ignore it and said, "Where do you think the next monster is?"

Kallie's head turned. "I can smell it," she said. "My shifter senses are telling me it's not far off."

Marcus looked at the ground, then tilted his head. He knelt by a strange patch in the mud, which might've been a footprint, but I couldn't really tell.

After a moment of observation, Marcus stood. "It went this way." He pointed to the south.

"How can you tell?" I asked.

"My mom's a detective. She taught me how to read tracks and things like that." Marcus shrugged.

"Your mom's a fucking *cop*?" Kallie asked scathingly.

"Yeah. Doesn't make sense for her to have a felon for a son, does it?" Marcus said.

"Lead the way," Charlie said, and Marcus went ahead. Charlie kept his hand on Oberi's back, and she guided him through the trees.

As Kallie and Marcus went on ahead, I whispered to Charlie, "How do you deal with it so well?"

"I have a lot of experience with people dying in front of me," Charlie said. "Marty wasn't the only one."

"What happened?"

"Bad drug deals. Cons gone wrong. People getting shot when you're trying to rob them." Charlie shrugged. "You just learn to deal with it."

I don't ever think I could learn to deal with people dying in front of me. But maybe I could. Kallie and Marcus seemed largely unaffected as well— or at least, they were trying not to show it. Kallie had seen people die in the King's Contest. She'd told me. But Marcus? When that shifter died, he'd barely even flinched. What the hell had happened to him to make him so used to death?

We walked until we came to a wide river. Here, the mud sloped off into the water, like some massive creature had slid from the bank into the river's depths.

"It's here," Marcus said. "Tracks are fresh."

I knelt by the water. I reached my left hand into the stream and used my Toaqua magic to feel around. My magic came to a halt at the bottom of the river, where I felt a giant creature lurking in the depths.

The moment my magic touched it, the creature moved. It swam up to the surface and broke free, screeching its rage to the world. It was some sort of reptile, a cross between a sea-serpent and a dragon. It had black scales peppered with an emerald sheen, webbed feet with long claws, and a spiky tail that would crush you if you were unlucky enough to get smacked by it.

The most terrifying thing about it was it had three heads. Each of the heads had a long snout that reminded me of a crocodile's. Sharp teeth poked out of the mouths. Each head was big enough to swallow Oberi whole.

"Ava, what are we looking at?" Charlie screamed as the creature continued to roar.

"Uh— big water monster, twenty feet long, three heads," I blurted.

"It's a *balur*! Move!" Kallie cried.

She changed into a wolf and shoved Marcus out of the way before one of the giant heads could bite him in two. The balur reached out and snapped its jaws on thin air. Oberi darted out of the way before she turned, pawing at the ground. She lowered her horn and charged, but the balur lunged out of the way before she could stab it in the eye. Oberi fought with the balur, the fire on her mane raging to become an inferno. The balur stayed away, fearful it would burn itself on Oberi, though its eyes raged in anger.

I was an Elementai. I could deal with a magical creature, right? It's what we were born to do.

But apparently not, because when I raised a hand back to throw a fireball, one of the balur's massive webbed paws reached out and smacked me to the side. I flew six feet before I slammed against a tree. I cried out in pain.

"Pidge, you okay?" Charlie shouted.

"Get down!" The balur had noticed Charlie was blind and had taken him for a target. The three heads lunged forward, but Charlie flattened himself against the ground at the last second. The heads collided against each other, smacking together. The balur groaned and retreated a few feet, shaking its head.

Kallie growled and launched herself at the balur. She attempted to rip one of the throats out, but the balur shook her off. Though she'd gotten a chunk of scales in her mouth, the monster was unharmed.

Kallie changed back and shook her head. "I can't bite through its skin. It's too thick!"

Marcus threw balls of battle magic at the creature, but they sizzled against its scales uselessly. It was like the creature's skin was its armor. The balur snapped at Marcus, and he fell backward with a yell. He kicked the creature's middle head to get away, scrambling for cover. Rishi ran up a tree and cowered in the branches.

I summoned the water from the river. I wrapped it around the balur's legs and froze it to ice, to keep the creature contained. But the balur ripped free of my ice like it was nothing. Charlie commanded roots to spring up from underneath the balur. He had the same idea I did, and wrapped them around the balur's legs. Yet the balur reached down and tore the branches in half with his teeth, tossing the roots aside like mere twigs.

Great. All that, and we'd just made it mad. The balur drew a breath, and from all three heads he shot out red-hot flames. I jumped in front of the group and threw out my hands at the last second. The fire misdirected at my command, shooting toward the sky. Even so, it was hot. Sweat ran down my forehead as I kept the balur's breath at bay. I turned it around, so that the balur's own flames enveloped him.

It didn't do anything. His scales heated to a molten-like color and stayed that way. The balur's entire form glowed, sizzling hot. Oberi backed away, tossing her horn and snorting out smoke as she observed the balur's brand-new flaming coat.

"That's cool, just make it more dangerous than it already is!" Marcus called out.

"I'm trying, okay!" I backed away and called up more water from the riverbed to cool off the balur's scales. It landed on the balur's back and instantly evaporated into hot steam. It was so intense it made the area grow unbearably hot.

Charlie yanked me behind a nearby boulder, where the rest of us were taking shelter. Oberi panted, trying to regain her stamina from chasing the balur around. Marcus clenched at his hair anxiously, while Kallie shook.

Nothing we were trying was working. It wasn't that surprising. This creature had spent time in literal hell, for crying out loud. At most, we were annoying it.

"We're gonna be dinner if we don't figure out something in the next five seconds!" Marcus replied. The balur was taking another breath, to blow fire once again.

"Charlie, you're Captain! What do we do?" Kallie shouted.

I could see Charlie's mind work. "We have to combine our magic," he said.

It clicked. "Yes! Kallie, like we did in class!"

Her eyes brightened. "I need whatever you can give me."

Charlie, Marcus and I focused on merging our powers with Kallie's. Three swords appeared in mid-air; one infused with my Fire magic, one mixed with Charlie's Air magic, and one with Marcus' battle magic. We each took our own weapons. I grasped mine tightly, feeling a bit more confident now that I had something to use.

"How is this supposed to help?" Marcus asked as he held up his sword.

"A regular sword won't cut through its skin, but a sword infused with magic might," Kallie said. "They'll break on impact with a monster like that, so you only get one shot. My suggestion is to aim for the neck."

"Okay, so we have to get close enough to cut its heads off," Marcus said warily. "How are we going to do that without being killed?"

"Kallie, can you put an illusion on it?" Charlie asked. He held up his sword, and I had to admit it was pretty cool. There was a little tornado swirling inside the blade that looked badass.

"I can try, but with something that strong, it won't hold for long. You guys are gonna need to move fast," she said quickly.

We didn't have time to come up with another plan, because the balur unleashed his flames once again. Our whole group launched ourselves out of the way as the flames enveloped the boulder. The flames melted the entire stone to molten lava, making a hot puddle on the ground.

Oberi guided Charlie to the left, while Marcus dodged to the right. I remained in the middle and charged. Kallie threw her arms out, and the balur's flames stopped. Its eyes glazed over, and it looked around in confusion as Kallie's illusion spell overtook its mind. The balur took his giant webbed claws and batted at its faces, attempting to end the illusion that had claimed its vision. The monster spun in a circle, and all three of us had to jump over its tail, so we wouldn't get hit. I cried out, to let Charlie know it was time to jump, and the three of us leapt together.

Well, Charlie and I jumped. Marcus more or less tripped. He fell forward and almost smashed his dick on one of the balur's spikes before he twisted to the side and just avoided being shish-kabobbed. He crawled back upward sloppily. As the balur turned back around, I raised my sword, so ready to cut this bitch's head off.

Kallie gave a scream behind me. I glanced back, and I saw that she'd fallen to her knees in pain. Tears ran down her cheeks as she dug her fingers into the earth.

"Run!" she cried. "It broke my spell!"

And apparently the effort had weakened her, because Kallie struggled to get up. The balur saw an opportunity and ran forward with jaws extended to swallow Kallie whole.

"Kallie!" Marcus abandoned the plan and ran back to save her. He planted himself in front of her and swung back the sword. When the balur lunged forward, Marcus swung the sword like a baseball bat. The tip of it almost hit the balur, but the monster jumped back, hissing.

Of course, Marcus let the sword go after he swung. It went flying backward and embedded itself right into a tree. Kallie groaned just as Marcus started to panic.

Rishi launched himself from a tree branch with a yell. He landed on the balur's middle head and began clawing at its eyes. The balur reared up on his hind legs and threw its head back. Rishi went soaring backward and crashed in the river. His yowls could be heard over the battle as the water carried him downstream.

"Rishi!" Marcus screamed as he helped Kallie to her feet, but the cat was already out of sight. Tears dotted Marcus' eyes, yet he stayed by Kallie's side.

I thought we were dead for sure. Then a great wind came in from the west, and the balur was picked up off its feet. The wind smashed the balur back into the ground again. The gust was gone as quickly as it came.

Charlie had pointed his sword at the creature, and his Air magic had come spiraling out of it. He gasped. It took a lot of energy for him to use the sword to knock the monster over. Charlie fell to one knee, and Oberi ran over to him. She put her neck underneath him and lifted him upward. I felt her energy flow from her body into Charlie's as she helped him stand, sustaining him through our bond.

The balur hissed in displeasure as he rolled, stubby legs flailing. Charlie's magic had knocked it down, but it wouldn't stay that way for long.

Kallie hobbled over to the tree that had Marcus' sword embedded in it. She ripped it out with one arm and growled, "Trust a warlock to be shit with a sword. Just get me near the damn thing."

"How?" Marcus yelped.

The balur's flames unleashed once again. I flung out my right hand, redirecting the flames back toward the clouds. As I did so, I tried to stop the flames from coming out of the balur's throats. The flames halted at my command, and although they didn't cause the balur to explode like I hoped, the monster choked and coughed, like it was trying and failing to breathe.

Holding back the balur's flames was really hard. My arm shook, and I felt my knees begin to buckle. I gripped the sword in my left hand for an anchor, until I felt the hilt cut into my palm. I was holding back the strength of dynamite with nothing more than sheer will, and ancestors, it hurt.

I couldn't hold it any longer. I let go, and the flames lunged out of the balur's mouth— directly toward me.

I screamed, but Oberi charged in front of me. The three streams of fire combined into one huge plume, enveloping Oberi like a powerful explosion. Her form vanished completely as the flames consumed her whole.

"Oberi, *no!*" I shouted. My heart broke, and time ceased to move. Terror ran through me as I realized that my Familiar had sacrificed herself for *me*. I would never see her again… she was gone.

But when the flames stopped, I saw with amazement Oberi was still standing, not a scratch on her. Oberi hadn't been killed by the balur's flames. She had *powered up*. The energy of the flames had gone directly to her horn. The horn blazed powerfully, and Oberi reared up. From the tip of her horn burst a huge column of flame, socking the balur right in the chest.

The creature screamed and backed up. Oberi's flames were able to hurt it— little by little, the flame column ate away at the monster's scales, injuring it and leaving us an opening.

Charlie, Kallie and I all ran forward at once. Kallie swung first. She gave a wild yell as she sliced through the neck of the right head, severing it completely. As the head dropped, Kallie's sword disappeared. The balur's other heads gave a scream, but the left head was silenced when Charlie cut through its neck, the Air sword dissolving into vapor.

The only head left was the middle one, and I was coming for it. The balur rose up, ready to attack me with its claws. But I felt a gust of wind rush me upward, and I swung back, not giving myself time to think as I severed the middle head completely off. Blood splattered my outfit, and the sword in my hands vanished. The head came down with a *thud*, and the air carrying me stopped. I fell to the side and landed on my hip next to the balur's nasty skull.

The balur's body fell to the side. It twitched a few times before going still. The monster's body dissolved into ash, floating away on the wind. I watched as the particles dissolved on the breeze, and the three severed heads collapsed into dust on the ground.

I took a few quick breaths, hardly able to believe it. We'd done it. We'd beaten our first monster!

Only a million more to go.

"You okay, pidge?" Charlie was at my side. He reached out a hand, and I took it to get to my feet.

"I'm good. See, you picked me up there," I told Charlie. "Maybe you *can* fly other people around."

"I also dropped you," Charlie pointed out. "We can't try that again. You could've gotten hurt."

I rolled my eyes. He was being overdramatic. Everything was fine.

"Good girl," I told Oberi as I stroked her forehead. She nickered and pushed her nose against me. "I wasn't expecting that from you."

"She's more powerful than I realized," Charlie said.

"That's an understatement. She saved our asses," Kallie said. She wiped off blood on her pants, like it was no big deal.

"What else are you hiding, girl?" I asked. Oberi bobbed her head and stuck out her tongue. I giggled.

"Rishi!" Marcus ran downriver. He hurtled by as fast as he could. The rest of us hurried to keep up with him, and anxiety made my insides whirl. Was Rishi okay? I didn't think Marcus could handle it if his cat was dead.

There was a yowl from nearby, and I sighed in relief. Rishi was clinging to a branch that was hanging into the river for dear life, calling out for Marcus.

Marcus went barreling into the water. He fell down— again— getting soaked. He grabbed Rishi and slipped on the river bank. Kallie sighed and reached out to pull him up.

Rishi shivered in Marcus' arms. I reached out with my left hand. "Here, let me dry you off."

The water seeped out of Marcus' clothes and Rishi's fur as I commanded it to go back into the river. They were fully dry, but Rishi was obviously displeased. The grumpy cat gave a very pissed-off look as the rest of us drew near.

"Good plan, guys," Kallie praised. "We got our first few points."

"Oh yeah, great plan," Marcus bitched. "Typical fae solution. Something bothering you? Just cut its head off!"

"It worked, didn't it?" Kallie asked.

"Guys, that's enough." Charlie crossed his arms. "We need to get along out here. We don't get points if we kill each other."

"If only," Marcus grumbled. Kallie gave him the finger.

The drone that was following us came out of the sky. It hovered at eye-level. From the top of the drone emerged a small screen. One of the judges for the Institute came on— it was Professor Warbright.

"Congratulations on claiming your first kill," Warbright said. "Each monster has a different score value, based on the difficulty of the kill. For slaying the balur, your team has gained four points, putting you in third place."

The screen flashed a quick review of the scoreboard. I ran through the numbers. Three teams had been eliminated already— all of their teammates were dead. The rest of the teams under us had either zero or two points. The second-place team had five points, killing a monster that was only slightly above the difficulty of the balur.

I noticed with spite that Mad Dog and Naya's team was at the top of the leaderboard with seven points. Looked like they'd claimed the kill of the first monster we'd met, and had already found another one.

Warbright came back on screen. "There are still more monsters out there, and plenty of time to claim the prize. Stay vigilant. Stay alive."

The screen went blank and folded back inside the drone. The drone hovered above us again, ready to follow.

"We've gotta move," I said in near despair. "We can't let Naya and Mad Dog win."

"We don't need to be worried about them. We should think about ourselves," Charlie said firmly. "Comparison only leads to distraction."

I knew he was right. And yet, I couldn't help but feel doubt. There was more at stake than just the competition. The world was depending on me to get free, so I could figure out the prophecy.

But if the rest of these monsters were just as bad as the balur, I might not have a chance to fulfill it, because the Darke Games would kill me anyway.

Fuck. What had I gotten us into?

tay vigilant. Stay alive.

That would be a hell of a lot easier if we'd just stayed at the Institute. I never thought I was safe behind those gates, but hell, that was the place to be right now.

But Ava needed me. She had to win, to get out of the Institute and learn about the prophecy. I was done sticking my tail between my legs. I was done playing it safe. Ava was right—survival was fucking boring without adventure.

I'd never felt so alive as when I was fighting that balur. I was hungry for another fight, yearning to slay another monster. At least out here in the Games, I was doing something worthwhile. I was protecting Shade Hills from monsters, not hiding under my bed waiting for them to go away like I'd done when I was a kid. Maybe dying out here wouldn't be so bad, as long as I died with honor.

We forged ahead, staying alert for another fight that would earn us points. The air seemed to expand as we made it out of the trees. My feet met solid earth, and Oberi's hooves clacked loudly. The sound echoed off the nearby buildings, but the street was otherwise eerily silent.

"Where are we?" I whispered.

"Outskirts of Shade Hills," Ava-Marie whispered back. She took slow, calculated footsteps, and her voice came from several directions as she swiveled her head back and forth. "We've reached a residential neighborhood."

Kallie cracked her knuckles. "There has to be a monster nearby. Most of them feed off super-naturals— either literally or energetically. They're attracted to us."

"How do you know so much about monsters?" I asked.

"It's kind of a thing in Malovia," she explained. "We should keep moving."

Ava quickened her footsteps, until she was practically running.

"What is it, pidge?" I demanded.

"I see a checkpoint up ahead," she called back. "Let's get to it before someone else does."

Checkpoints were part of the Games, but the Warden had warned us they were limited.

They were boxes filled with supplies like food, first-aid kits, and weapons. If the monsters didn't kill you out here, another team might— just to get their hands on those supplies.

Ava came to a screeching halt and cursed under her breath. "Dammit. Someone else got to it first. Everything is gone."

"We'll find another one," I assured her. It'd taken a lot of our energy to fight the balur, but we were good to go for another fight or two. If we didn't find another checkpoint, there were other ways to get food.

"I hope to the ancestors we do," Ava said. "In the meantime, everyone needs a drink of water."

Ava drew water out of the air and trickled it into our mouths to keep us all hydrated. I wiped my chin clean with the back of my hand.

"Um… guys," Marcus said nervously. "I think we have an audience."

"What do you mean?" I asked.

"I just saw those curtains move," he replied. "People are watching us."

Ava chuckled lightly. "They've been watching over the drones the whole time. I say we give them a good show."

"If we can find a monster," I stated. "The street sounds pretty quiet—"

Meow.

A small mew came from several paces up ahead. At first, I thought it was Rishi, then I heard him hiss from Marcus' shoulders.

"Aww," Ava swooned.

The cat hissed at her, and she jumped back against me.

"Everybody get back!" Marcus shouted. He flung his arm out, catching me in the chest. My heart leapt at his urgency, and I grabbed Ava to drag her away. Oberi stomped several times.

"What's the big deal?" Ava asked. "It's just a cat."

"It has like, a million teeth! And they're *bloody*!" Kallie shouted.

"But it's *sooo* cute!" Ava crooned.

"It's not a regular cat!" Marcus insisted. "It's a *malumuto*— or an evil shifter. It's a creature of Miriamic lore. They can shapeshift into different animals. First, it gains your trust in one form. As soon as you're close enough, it changes and rips your heart out."

"I've never heard of it," Ava said, as if Marcus had no idea what he was talking about.

"I'm serious!" Marcus shouted, pushing us further back on the street. "Those two markings above its eyes are where its horns go in its real form. It can hide them when it shifts, but the markings never go away."

Kallie took another step back, as if she wasn't willing to risk it. The cat meowed.

"This should be easy, then," I stated, swirling my arms around to create a gust of air.

Marcus grabbed my hand. "It's not that easy. Malumuto are creatures of spirit. They can't be killed by traditional means."

Ava had already conjured a fireball next to me, and it crackled loudly. "Then it hasn't felt one of my fireballs yet."

"Pidge," I warned. "While I appreciate your confidence, it's a recipe for trouble. Listen to Marcus. How do we get rid of this thing?"

Marcus didn't answer right away. The cat's footsteps approached, and Rishi hissed again. The four of us, along with Oberi, took another step back, careful not to trigger the cat to shift.

"Marcus!" Kallie cried. "What do we do?"

"I'm thinking!" he shot back. "Just give me a second… there's a spell to vanquish it to the Abyss— or hell. An incantation."

"So say it," I pressed.

Marcus hesitated.

"It's coming closer!" Kallie cried. "Now would be a good time to remember that incantation."

"Yeah, Marcus. Do your thing!" Ava encouraged.

Marcus' arm finally left my chest, and he held his hands out toward the malumuto. *"By candle flame and moonlight's kiss—"*

Marcus was cut off by the sound of the creature screeching. The cat's cry came closer, flying through the air and poised for attack. The thing moved faster than a normal animal, and I barely had a second to respond.

Before I could counterattack, the creature landed on Marcus' chest. He reeled backward, cursing as the monster clawed at him. Rishi yowled and fought back, knocking the monster off of Marcus. Rishi's paws hit the pavement, and he chased the creature around in circles.

Ava, Kallie, and I attacked immediately. Ava's Fire crackled as it whizzed through the air, and Kallie's battle orb exploded like a bomb on the pavement. I thrust my Air upward, carrying the creature high into the sky. Its high-pitched shriek echoed through Shade Hills as it fell from an incredible distance. I heard the *thud* as it landed, but there was no crunch of bones. I wasn't sure that the fall had slowed it down. The three of us kept attacking, while Marcus sucked in deep breaths. A stream of Fire erupted from Oberi's horn, just passing by my face.

"Marcus!" Ava shouted. "Our powers aren't doing shit. This creature is immortal or something!"

"I-I..." Marcus stammered.

"Yeah, you're bleeding," Kallie snapped. "Big whoop. We'll clean you up in a minute. Say the incantation!"

Marcus' breath grew ragged. *"By candle flame and moonlight's kiss, I vanquish you to the Abyss!"*

I expected something fantastic to happen, like for the air pressure to shift. But nothing changed. The cats continued to yowl at one another, and the girls and I kept throwing magic to slow the damn thing down.

"It didn't work!" Kallie cried, stating the obvious.

"Try again," I insisted.

"I-I can't!" Marcus wailed.

"Well, we need to do something," Ava snapped.

I switched from using Air magic and turned to my Earth magic. Roots snaked out from trees next to the road. If I could trap the monster, then perhaps we had a chance. But every time I came close, the creature slipped out from my grasp.

Oberi pulled back on her Fire and lowered her head, poking my arm with her horn. I stepped aside to give her room. She scuffed her hooves on the pavement and blew a breath out her nose.

I grabbed Ava and dragged her back. "I think Oberi has a plan."

Ava stopped shooting fireballs to watch. Oberi charged, and Rishi shrieked as he jumped out of the way. The malumuto's yowls turned into roars as it shifted into another form.

"Ancestors, Charlie!" Ava struggled beneath my hold, but I tightened my arms around her. Ancestors knew she'd get herself killed if she intervened. "It's shifted into a lion with horns. Oberi's going to get hurt!"

No sooner did Ava say it did I hear the sound of Oberi's hoof smack the lion's head. It growled, then took off running. Oberi followed, chasing it out of range. Sticks snapped, and garbage cans were knocked over as the creature made its escape. Ava struggled to go after it, but I wouldn't let her.

"I think Oberi has it covered," I said, impressed.

Oberi came trotting back, her footsteps sounding proud and happier than ever. The sound of the lion's claws on the pavement faded, but I heard another collection of footsteps approaching.

They weren't monsters, though. They sounded familiar, like sneakers on the street. Something jingled as they moved.

I leaned over to Ava. "What's that tinkling sound?"

Her tone was harsh. "Carabiners on their backpacks. I guess we know who got to the checkpoint first."

"Where did it go!?" Mad Dog's deep voice thundered. He stomped up to me and grabbed me by the shoulders, shaking me. I didn't even flinch. "Tell me where it went!"

"Where did *what* go?" Kallie demanded.

"The monster!" Mad Dog sneered. "Don't play stupid with me, because we heard it."

"And *we're* going to get the points for killing it," Naya snapped.

"Be our guest," I said casually.

"Charlie, no!" Ava objected. "You can't let them get our points."

I turned to her, my voice raging. "That thing attacked Marcus! I'm not going to put my team in mortal danger for a half dozen points. We'll find another monster to kill."

"A half dozen?" Mad Dog sounded impressed. I could practically hear him panting in thirst for the fight.

"Seriously," I said. "Be careful. This one is worse than anything we've seen so far."

Mad Dog's breathing rate increased, obviously growing more intrigued as I spoke.

"It went that way." I pointed to our right.

"Come on," Mad Dog called to his team. "We're in the lead. Let's make sure we stay there."

His team took off running.

It wasn't until they were long gone that Ava turned to me. "The monster didn't go that way."

I shrugged. "So I lied to mislead them. We need a chance to get more points and get ahead."

"Good thinking," Ava replied.

Kallie had nothing to say about that. Instead, she whirled on Marcus. "What *was* that!?" she shouted. "I thought you were a strong warlock! Incantations should be simple for you."

Rishi purred in Marcus' arms while he got to his feet. "I'm sorry to disappoint, but they're not."

Marcus started to walk away, but Kallie kept up with him. "What about all the stories? I thought you were some badass warlock. You must be good at *something*!"

Marcus snapped. "The only thing I'm good at is lying!"

I stifled a laugh. Marcus talked a big talk, but he was the furthest thing from a good liar, and Kallie knew it. She'd been trying to get him to crack.

I wasn't expecting what came next. Marcus broke out in *sobs*— full on hiccupping and everything. "I'm a fraud!" he wailed. "The stories were all fake. I can't do anything."

We all just stood there for a second, stunned. Marcus had never crumbled like this before, or ever admitted he couldn't do magic well.

Finally, Ava spoke. "Then why did you enter the Games?"

"I don't know," Marcus sobbed. "I thought I'd figure it out by now. I-I…"

He trailed off, obviously distracted.

"It's just blood," Kallie said gently— it was odd to hear her speak that way. Marcus' breakdown must've had an effect on her. "Come here."

Kallie led Marcus across the street and to a bench that squeaked when they sat down. The tear of fabric met my ears, and I realized Kallie was ripping up her uniform to tie around Marcus' wounds.

"Have you ever done *anything* with your powers?" Ava asked.

Marcus sniffled. "Once."

"Oh, so you *do* have magic?" Ava snapped, obviously irritated by this fight.

"Lighten up," I snapped at her. I knew what it was like to feel like you couldn't do things everyone else could. Marcus needed someone on his side right now— even if we were in the middle of a deadly tournament.

"My tattoo is real," Marcus said. "I *do* have powers from all five witch Casts. It's just... limited."

"Limited how?" Kallie asked curiously.

"Like, I *can* read minds, but only dirty thoughts." Marcus spoke so quietly I barely heard him.

"Gods, ew!" Kallie cried. "You've been reading my dirty thoughts this whole time!?"

"No," Marcus said quickly. "I-I try not to. It can get disturbing sometimes, and I don't want to invade people's privacy. As for my other powers... I don't want to hurt anyone."

"You wouldn't do that," I assured him.

"Wouldn't I?" he challenged. "You don't know why I was sentenced to the Institute."

The street went quiet as we all considered what he said. It was Ava who spoke up, though she chose her words carefully. "Why *were* you sentenced to the Institute?"

"The real story this time," Kallie clarified. "I don't want some bogus lie about a mass murder."

Marcus' breath wavered. "That's just the thing. That one wasn't a lie."

"What?" I nearly choked. I couldn't imagine Marcus hurting anyone— let alone being a serial killer.

"It happened right when my powers awakened," Marcus admitted. "My girlfriend and I got in an argument in the middle of town. She thought I should hide my powers, and I wanted to use them. She figured people would be afraid of me... and I guess she was right. *She* should've been afraid of me. I lost my temper, and I couldn't control my magic. It exploded out of me, and..."

Marcus' voice wavered. "She died... along with ten other innocent people standing nearby."

The three of us drew a breath in unison. Marcus seemed like the kind of guy sentenced to the Institute for stealing a loaf of bread, not killing nearly a dozen people. What he'd gone through horrified me.

"The coven wanted to hang me," Marcus admitted solemnly. "But my mom must've persuaded the Imperium Council, because the priestesses sentenced me to the Institute instead."

Marcus' face came out muffled as he said, "My girlfriend... I blew her to pieces. It was an accident, but it didn't matter. I saw it all."

"Marcus," Kallie breathed. "I had no idea."

I heard the brush of fabric and Marcus' stifled breathing as she pulled him into a tight hug.

"So you can see why magic is difficult for me," Marcus continued when she drew away. "I don't want to lose control. I killed my girlfriend, and so many others. I destroyed so many families, so many lives. I don't want to hurt anyone like that again."

"You won't," I promised, though I had no way to be sure. "You'll learn how to control it."

"Charlie's right," Ava said gently. For a moment, we all seemed to forget we were in the middle of the Games as Marcus' pain permeated deep into each of us, opening our own wounds.

"I just... I..." Marcus didn't seem to know what to say. He seemed like he wanted to say more, but didn't know how to talk in front of all of us.

"Could you guys give us a moment?" I asked.

"Sure," Kallie said, rising from the bench. She and Ava walked off, though close enough that

I could still hear their hushed whispers. Oberi followed Ava. I took a seat beside Marcus. He shivered, and Rishi continued purring.

I swallowed the lump in my throat. "I can't say I know what it was like for you, but I was there when my best friend died, too."

"You were?" Marcus sounded surprised.

I wanted to tell him Ava had a similar experience, so he would know he was far from alone, but her story wasn't my secret to tell.

"His name was Marty," I said, because I could tell he needed the distraction from his own confession. "He was my mentor. I still remember the sound of the gunshots, the way his blood felt on my hands when I went to his side. He died in my arms."

"I'm sorry you had to go through that," Marcus said.

"Same," I told him. "But it's not your fault, Marcus. What happened with your magic was an accident. You can't blame yourself."

"I don't blame myself," he countered, but I heard the lie in his tone.

"I know what it's like to be afraid," I told him. "I know what it feels like to replay the scenario over and over, telling yourself you could've done something to prevent it."

Marcus paused for a few beats, absorbing my words. "I might know what that feels like. I'm scared to love another girl, because what if I hurt her like I hurt Anya? And if I get close to anyone, I'll disappoint them, like I did when I left her little brother behind. That's the kid I told you about, who I was teaching art to."

The confession shocked me, because I swore I was getting major love-sick vibes between him and Kallie. "Isn't there *anyone* you're interested in at the Institute?" I asked, hoping to draw an explanation out of him.

"Sure, I guess," he admitted. "But it's not like I've gotten over Anya. To be honest, I'm not sure I ever will. I thought the way to survive in prison was to keep everyone at a distance. That way, I couldn't hurt anyone. But when you guys took me in, I thought maybe things would be different. I wanted to start new, to try to overcome all that baggage. And I knew I couldn't just walk away from you guys because..." He trailed off.

"Because of what?" I asked.

He sighed. "Because the day I met you, I had my first real vision."

I sat up straighter. "What do you mean?"

"One of my powers is the power of a Seer, which can involve things like seeing the past, present or future, depending on your specialty," Marcus explained. "For me, my visions always came through taste, which I gotta tell you is fucking hard to interpret. I never know what they mean. But the day I met you, I *foresaw* Mad Dog beating your ass. I knew I had to step in to prevent it."

I didn't know what to say. "Thanks again for that."

"I didn't know why I did it at the time," Marcus said. "I like to think that maybe stepping in gave you a chance to enter the Darke Games. You, Kallie, and Ava can win this thing for sure. You can get out of here."

"What are you talking about?" I demanded. "You're part of this team, too. If we win this thing, we *all* go free."

Marcus turned away from me. "Come on, man. Don't say that. I've made it through fighting one monster. I'm not going to last another. I couldn't even get through a simple incantation."

Okay, clearly trying to connect with him wasn't working. It was time for some tough love.

I placed a heavy hand on his shoulder and smacked Marcus in the chest. "Listen to me, Marcus," I said firmly. "You possess the mark of every Cast within your coven. You're a strong warlock, and your council knows it. That's why they sent you here. Not because you committed a crime. That was an accident. It's because they were scared of you, because they know how powerful you'll become."

"How can I be comfortable with a power that scares everyone else?" he asked. "Shouldn't I be just as afraid, if not more?"

I shook my head. "You can't be afraid of yourself, because you get to *choose* how to use that power. Good and evil isn't about who has more power— it's about how they use it. And right now, Marcus, you have the chance to do some real good, by protecting Shade Hills from these monsters."

"I never thought of it that way," he admitted. "I just thought my powers were destructive."

"They don't have to be," I said. "Take my Air magic, for instance. Air gives us life— it's literally what we breathe. Without oxygen, there would be no fire, which means no heat in the winter. But tornadoes can level entire cities. I get to choose how I'm going to use that power— by giving life, or taking it away. Warlock magic can't be any different."

I actually didn't know for sure. I hadn't taken any classes on the topic and only knew what I'd picked up from the Institute. But something I said must've resonated with Marcus, because his voice seemed brighter when he spoke.

"You're right," he said. "I've been hiding from it for too long. I'll never figure out the good I can do if I'm not willing to face the bad. I have to do my part and defeat these monsters with the rest of the team."

I clapped him on the back. "That's more like it!"

Marcus cleared his throat and stood. "I think I've wasted enough time. We're losing points as we speak. Let's go find a monster to kill."

"Finally," Ava sighed, her footsteps approaching. "I'm ready for another slaying."

"Agreed," I said. "But before we go… anyone want to explain to me what this is?"

I drew out what I could only describe as a *stick* from where I'd tucked it in my uniform. At first, I'd thought it was a knife or some type of weapon, but it was thinner and smooth on all sides.

Kallie gasped, but her voice turned sour. "Where did you get that?"

I shrugged. "Swiped it off Mad Dog when he came through. Is it useful?"

Marcus yanked it out of my hands and spoke breathlessly. "Are you kidding me? This is a *wand!*"

"Oh." I hadn't realized wands were even *real*, but the answer seemed obvious now. "So it *is* useful."

"If you want to practice dark magic," Kallie sneered.

"This isn't dark magic," Marcus protested.

She scoffed. "Depends on your definition."

"Well, in my coven, wands are perfectly fine," Marcus shot back.

"It's cheating!" Kallie cried. "Your magic should come straight from you, and your power should be measured on your own merit."

Marcus sounded offended. "Even if that were true, which it's not, I'm surprised you of all people would object to dark magic."

"If you're suggesting I used dark magic to win the King's Contest—"

"Not at all," Marcus insisted. "I just meant we want to win this thing, don't we? And wands aren't against the rules in the Darke Games."

Kallie hesitated. "I guess not."

"I say we let Marcus use it," Ava voted.

"If it helps, I agree," I added. "How does it work?"

"Well, it doesn't contain magic of its own," Marcus explained. "Though this one seems to have some magical influence. It was maybe made with… unicorn hair?"

Oberi sniffed the wand and blew a breath, like she agreed.

"How can you tell?" I asked.

"I'm part Curse Breaker," Marcus reminded me. "It's one of the classifications of the Miriamic Coven. A Curse Breaker's magic is a lot more complex than the name suggests, though. They can sense magic and move it from one place to another, even change its intention."

"You can *move* magic?" Kallie balked. "So we could siphon it out of one of the monsters?"

"In theory…" Marcus said thoughtfully. "But I've never done it. The best I can do is sense how powerful they are."

"That's still useful," I encouraged. "Who should get the wand?"

"Marcus, of course," Ava said. "Wands are kind of a witch thing."

"Oh," I said lamely. I didn't know. "Have you ever used one?"

"No," Marcus admitted. "But it might help. Wands are meant to focus your powers."

Which was exactly what Marcus needed. I was glad I'd swiped the wand when I could've gone for the water bottle on the outside of Mad Dog's pack. Marcus needed to focus so we didn't all end up splattered on the pavement.

"Okay, the wand is Marcus'," I said. "Let's head further into town. Kallie said monsters like to hunt supernaturals, so that's our best bet to gather points."

"Agreed—" Ava started to say, but the sound of screams cut her off.

Several pairs of footsteps pounded on the pavement, though as I listened closely, it sounded like the team was several people short.

Ava grabbed my arm. "It's Mad Dog and Naya. They're covered in blood. They must've found the malumuto. It looks like they lost another teammate."

Mad Dog and Naya never even noticed us. They crossed the street and kept on running, the sound of their screams echoing off the houses.

"It was their mistake for not diversifying their team," I pointed out. "I say we find that malumuto and finish it off. You can do it, can't you, Marcus?"

He hesitated.

"Marcus, we don't have time," I pressed. "Are you in or out?"

Marcus' voice became firm. "I'm in."

I smirked. "Then let's go slay a demon."

It didn't take long to find the creature. All we had to do was follow the sounds of destruction. We turned down two streets before coming to a long road. The sound of wood planks— like fences being destroyed— clattered across the pavement. Trash cans clanked, and aluminum cans tumbled down the road.

I reached my Air magic out to get a sense of how far the monster was from us. This was no cat, though. This creature was much bigger, at least my size, but my Air touched something else — wings, perhaps?

Ava breathed raggedly from beside me. Her footsteps stopped, as if she needed a moment to take in the monster.

"A quick description would be helpful," I told her. "Is it the malumuto?"

Marcus was the one to answer. "It's the malumuto all right— in its true demon form."

Ava spoke quickly as she described the creature to me. "It's humanoid, but barely a man. He's shirtless, and his skin is dry and crusty, like rock. His eyes are red. Black, curved horns grow out of his forehead, and his wings are massive and leathery— like a bat's. His hands are… not even hands. He has long, black claws for fingers."

"I'm glad you can't see this, Charlie," Kallie whispered. "It's terrifying."

"What's the plan?" Marcus asked.

"I'm assuming it hasn't seen us yet?" I questioned. Judging by the ongoing sounds of destruction, it was my best guess.

"No," Marcus confirmed.

"Then Marcus is going to swing around the block and come up from behind," I decided. The best way was to make sure the demon never knew he was there. "Ava, Kallie, and I will distract it the best we can, giving Marcus the chance to speak the incantation."

"That's not going to work," Ava protested. "We should go at it from all different angles. It's our best chance to disorient it and take it out. If we all go at it head-on, we create a single target."

"That's what we want," I told her. "We want it focused on us so it never notices Marcus."

"Charlie, we have to overwhelm it," Ava insisted. "It's the only way to weaken it."

"It's not our job to kill it," I reminded her. "We're here to back up Marcus, and that's it."

"Charlie!" Ava stomped her foot.

Not a good idea. I knew the second the malumuto noticed us, because the sound of approaching destruction stopped instantly. I could practically feel its eyes narrowed on us, and dark energy seemed to roll off it in waves.

"Go, Marcus!" I cried, shoving him.

The monster's leathery wings flapped as it charged toward us. Instinctively, I thrust out a blast of Air magic, and it slammed into the demon with enough force to knock him onto the pavement. He must've not felt a thing, because his footsteps began approaching again moments later.

"*Who unleashed me*?" he growled in a voice that sounded anything but human. It was deep and distorted, sending a shiver down my spine. I always knew monsters were real, but I believed they lurked among us. This was a whole new meaning of the word *monster*.

"*Answer me!*" the demon cried in his horrifying voice. "*Who unleashed—?*"

He was cut off by the sound of gurgling, as if he was choking on water.

"Nice shot!" Kallie cried.

"What'd you do?" I demanded of Ava.

She laughed maniacally. "Just funneled some water down his throat and into his lungs."

I fumed. The dirtier we played, the more blood this demon would seek. "We want to distract it, not piss it off!"

"Too late," Ava said innocently.

My whole body shook. You know what, fuck it. This was a demon who freaking ate hearts. It was going to suffer before we sent it back where it belonged.

I blasted my Air magic outward in thin sheets. I expected the Air to slice through the demon's torso, but Ava had been right when she said his skin was like rock. My Air bounced off of it, and no amount could penetrate its shell.

Ava and Kallie weren't having any luck, either. Even Kallie's battle orbs didn't explode upon impact, but went shooting off in different directions. I heard them explode like bombs on either side of us. Ava threw a few fireballs, but abandoned those when she realized they were no use. She continued attacking with water, though the demon seemed to get over the initial shock and couldn't care less, because his footsteps were approaching. Oberi shot Fire out of her horn, and huffed in frustration beside me when that didn't work.

Something flew through the air, though I barely sensed it with my magic before the object made impact. Something sharp tore through my uniform and into the flesh on my leg. I sucked a sharp breath and cursed. Kallie cried out, and Ava grunted like she was trying to hide how much it fucking hurt. I'd been in enough knife fights to know what one felt like, and this was not it. This was something different— perhaps even magical.

"What the fuck?" I growled. Warm blood trickled down my leg.

I hadn't expected an answer, but Ava offered one anyway. "They're like... thorns!"

There came a sickening sound, like Ava ripping one of the thorns from her shoulder.

"Not thorns," Kallie gasped. "*Claws.* He's shooting his claws at us— and they're growing back!"

"Damn it, we have to slow him down!" I said to no one in particular. I hoped Marcus was close by now.

"We are," Kallie replied. "But we have to do better!"

"I'm telling you we go at all angles," Ava insisted. "He won't know who to target."

"Or he'll target one of us and that person will be SOL," I snapped. "Stick to the plan, Ava."

Another set of claws whipped through the air, but this time, I was prepared for them. I sent a gust of wind whipping sideways, and the claws went flying away from us. I tried to do the same to the demon, but he remained rooted in place. My Air magic had slowed the demon down to begin with, but something must've happened to his wings— like he'd shifted them away or something— because my Air moved around him now with ease. I couldn't get to him.

I turned to using Earth magic. Trees on the side of the road fell at my command. I aimed for him, hoping to pin him down, but he sensed them coming. The best it did was slow him down a few paces as we backed away. His rocky skin scraped the tree bark as he climbed over the fallen trees and advanced.

"Oberi, if we use the tree branches, we can hold him down—" I cut off when I realized Oberi was no longer at my side. "Oberi!?"

The unicorn nickered from at least fifteen yards away. Her hooves slapped against the pavement as she trotted in place. What was she—? *Ava!*

I heard her running now. She must've taken off when I was falling trees, so I hadn't heard her. Oberi had followed and now didn't know whose side to take.

Damn her! I gritted my teeth.

The demon moved quicker, so much that Kallie and I started running to stay away— all while throwing magic over our shoulder to slow him down.

"Pidge!" I screamed. I was too fucking angry to say anything else. She was going to get an earful later— if we made it out of this.

I heard the sound of Ava's Fire crackling, but it was more than just a mere fireball. She was whipping up a whole freaking firestorm!

"Hey!" Ava shouted to the demon. "How do you like *this*?"

I sensed the heat of the fire moving through the air, blasting toward the demon long enough to stop him in his tracks. Ava's move had pissed me off, but I couldn't stand here trying to change it. My only choice was to work with it now.

"Kallie," I snapped. "Simultension."

Kallie understood immediately. I summoned Air and quickly felt her illusion magic entangling with it. A huge weapon that hadn't been there moments ago materialized.

"It's an Air cannon," Kallie said quickly. "Use it!"

Before I could, another claw shot through the air and sliced across my shoulder. I screamed out as pain pulsed up and down my arm.

"Oh, no you don't," Ava growled loud enough for me to hear her down the street. I didn't know what she'd done, because I was dealing with my own shit over here, but it was enough to distract the demon. He turned on her, and Ava screamed.

I fucking lost it. I'd never used a weapon like Kallie's before, but I was in no position to stop and learn. I let my intuition guide me and funneled more magic into the cannon. Pressure built up until— *boom!*

An explosion went off, and Air magic so strong it could knock over a building blasted out of the cannon. I felt my magic slam into the demon before he could get to Ava. He tumbled over and over again, but like everything else we tried, he didn't seem fazed.

"*I'll have your heart for that,*" he snarled.

"You won't touch him!" Ava screamed.

Her Fire magic cut through the air like water coming out of a fire hose. Air spun around the demon as he whirled on her.

"Fuck," Kallie muttered. "Marcus is so close. Your girlfriend's going to get him— *Marcus!*"

Her words came out as a petrifying screech. Though Ava's magic continued to blast down the street, I swear my heart stopped as I heard Marcus' body hit pavement. He groaned out in pain.

Kallie took off running. My stomach hollowed out, and I raced alongside her, hoping that it wasn't as I suspected. I could only picture one of those thorn-like claws embedded in Marcus' chest.

Kallie skidded to halt at his side and bent next to him. "Marcus," she cried. "I thought he…"

Marcus sucked a breath. "It's just my arm. But we can finish this. We can—"

The demon's claws sliced through the air like paper as he swiped his arm over us. Something that felt like a bag of bricks slammed into my chest, launching me yards away from Marcus. It was the demon's rock-hard arm. I gasped for breath that didn't come as I lay there immobile. Even my magic wouldn't help me suck air into my lungs.

I'd made a horrible mistake. The thought of Marcus lying on the ground and bleeding out had distracted me more than I realized. The demon had abandoned Ava and Oberi and had come for us. I'd never seen his attack coming.

A loud *thud* came, and Kallie gasped as she too was launched in the opposite direction. Her body slammed into the grass nearby. The demon's wings flapped as it followed her, landing in front of her so her breath seemed muffled from where I lay.

"You *have unleashed me*," the demon growled in that unearthly voice. "*I will carve your hearts out one by one.*"

"Charlie!" Ava cried as she raced over to me. She knelt at my side and helped me sit up.

I shoved her off. "Forget about me. Help Kallie."

The sound of Kallie's uniform tearing sent my whole body quaking. I barely had a moment to take it all in. He was ripping through her clothes. Next, it would be her chest! Kallie screamed as she fought against the demon that was trying to take her heart.

"Leave her alone!" Marcus shouted. Something whizzed out of his palm, but it did nothing except explode against the demon's skin like all of Kallie's battle orbs had. That's when I realized it was the same thing— a battle orb, though not nearly as powerful as Kallie's.

Before Ava or I could react, Marcus ran up to us. He dropped his wand next to me. "I need your magic!" he cried.

Marcus grabbed both Ava and I by the shoulder, and an odd sensation came over me. My whole body chilled, and I felt weak as Marcus drew my magic out of me with his Curse Breaker powers. I went still as a statue, unable to control it.

Kallie screamed again, and I knew we'd reached the point of no return. The demon would take her heart, and soon, we would all die.

"Not today, motherfucker," Marcus mumbled under his breath as he shot to his feet.

This time when he created a battle orb, it was unlike anything I'd ever experienced before. It crackled above my head like electricity. It hurt my ears, and the energy tingled across my whole body. Whatever he'd created was a hell of a lot bigger than the little balls Kallie had conjured. This must've been bigger than Marcus himself.

The battle orb set free and shot through the air, tumbling over and over. It made impact with the demon, thrusting him off of Kalina. He must've flown nearly fifty yards down the street before finally landing. The battle orb exploded so loud my ears rang. Dirt and debris rained down on us.

I barely had a chance to take a breath. Marcus ducked beside me and snatched up the wand he'd dropped. His voice came out stronger than I'd ever heard it before. *"By candle flame and moonlight's kiss, I vanquish you to the Abyss!"*

Magic sizzled over my head as it shot out of the wand. The magic struck the demon, and he shrieked as it overwhelmed him. The cry grew in intensity, piercing my ears and rocking the earth—

Then, silence. Nothing but silence that seemed to weigh a thousand pounds.

"Is… is it over?" I gasped.

Marcus didn't answer me. He raced to Kallie, and I heard him swear as he stumbled over the curb to reach her.

"It's over. He's gone." Ava heaved heavy breaths, matching Oberi's beside her. "The wand, too. I guess it was a one-time use."

"Marcus did it," I remarked, partially surprised but mostly relieved.

"I wasn't sure he could," Ava admitted.

"He has the power," I said, more to myself than to her. "All the wand did was give him the confidence to use it."

The drone buzzed as it came down from the sky. "Congratulations on your second kill," a male voice came. "For slaying the malumuto, your team has gained six points, putting you in second place."

"Damn it," Kallie muttered. "Another team already got a second kill, too. We have to keep up."

"Monsters continue to roam the streets," the announcer said. "Do not underestimate their power. Stay vigilant. Stay alive."

The drone flew away, and Ava turned to me. "Look, Charlie. I'm sorry I—"

"I don't want to hear it," I snapped, cutting her off. "Kallie almost had her heart ripped out. Let's deal with that first."

To be honest, I was so pissed, I couldn't deal with Ava's apology right now. If it hadn't been for her, the demon wouldn't have noticed Marcus. It never would've gotten that close to Kallie.

We all almost died because Ava went off-script. If she pulled that again, we'd be dead by the end of the night.

I'd had enough of Ava's disobedience. I was going to make sure she didn't get us all killed.

ava-marie

TWENTY-TWO

We had to get these wounds patched up. We couldn't continue to fight monsters like this. Kallie was bleeding heavily from her chest. The demon's large claws had ripped her skin to shreds, and Marcus was sporting several cuts and bruises all over his body.

Charlie, Oberi and I were mostly fine. We'd taken hits from the claws and were bleeding, but they weren't bad injuries like Kallie and Marcus' were.

I felt guilty. Their wounds were my fault. I hadn't listened… I'd only been trying to help.

"There has to be another checkpoint somewhere," Charlie said. His voice had a tone of authority— like he wouldn't tolerate anyone defying him this time. "Let's search the area."

Kallie slowly started forward, clutching her tattered jacket to her chest. Marcus helped her walk as Charlie and I went on ahead.

Charlie was smoldering. I could feel his anger radiating at me as it pulsed through our bond. Ancestors, he was pissed. I decided it was best not to say anything and just kept my eyes ahead.

Night was falling by this time. Twilight settled over the horizon, and the sun vanished behind the thick clouds to give way to stars quicker than I anticipated. Rishi let out a yowl from up ahead. I saw with relief we'd discovered a checkpoint that no one had found yet. A small first aid kit was all that was inside.

Marcus strode forward and grabbed the first aid-kit, turning to Kallie. "Don't worry, I'll help you," he said.

Kallie winced as she shrugged off her jacket. Underneath she wore a thin white camisole that was stained with blood. Marcus began putting antibiotic cream on her wounds, and wrapped her chest slowly. Kallie's eyes were wet with pain, but she didn't even so much as hiss in discomfort.

Charlie grabbed my arm roughly and pulled me aside, far enough away so Kallie and

Marcus wouldn't hear. Oberi followed us cautiously, keeping her ears up for whatever may be hiding in the woods.

"What are you doing?" I tried to wrench my arm out of his grip, but he held tight.

"Asking you what the hell you're doing out here," Charlie snarled. "That stunt you pulled was completely uncalled-for. It nearly got Kallie killed!"

My cheeks burned. "I'm sorry! I didn't want anyone to get hurt. I just thought it'd be better if—"

"Who's the Captain here, me or you?"

The drone hovered nearby, filming our performance. No doubt the screen back at the Institute was showing every moment of Charlie scolding me. I felt like a little kid who was being punished.

I scuffed my toe against the ground. "You."

"Then *listen to me*," Charlie growled. "I don't understand why it's so hard for you to do as you're told."

"I'm just trying to prove myself!" I flung my arms out wide. "I know my parents are watching. *Everyone's* watching! I want the world to see I'm not just a massive screw-up, that I can actually do something right!"

"You don't have an obligation to your parents out there. You have a responsibility to your team," Charlie said forcefully. "Fuck everyone else. If you want to stay alive, we need to be a unit. That means you need to do as I say, and not whatever you fucking feel like. We won't get through the Games if we're not together out here."

Tears beaded the corners of my eyes, and my throat got tight. He was right. I was so busy trying to impress people by doing my own thing that I put the group in danger. If Kallie, or any of the others, got killed out here because of me, I'd never forgive myself.

Oberi let out a breath that ruffled Charlie's hair, telling him to be gentler. Charlie's body went rigid as he let out a sigh. "Please, just trust me," he pleaded. "You can't keep relying on only yourself. It hurts you, Ava. Let us in and let us help you."

My throat burned even hotter, because that was the hardest thing of all. I trusted Charlie— to a point. Then my walls went up and it was hard to let him in. To be honest, I hadn't just run off because I wanted to display my powers. I was worried his plan wouldn't work, and after a lifetime of disappointments, I couldn't take one more person letting me down… especially not Charlie.

Anyone but Charlie.

But my feelings didn't matter out here. If Charlie was supposed to be my leader, I had to follow him, if only for Kallie and Marcus' sake. "Okay."

Charlie took my hand, tenderly this time. He led me back to the group, where Marcus was finishing bandaging his arm. "You guys good?"

"We'll be fine," Kallie said as she stood. She seemed a little better already. "My shifter powers will heal me quickly, and Marcus was just banged up."

"Here." Marcus handed Charlie and me a few bandages for our wounds.

"Thanks," I said as I peeled off the wrapper and helped Charlie with his leg. He did the same for my shoulder. Soon, we were all patched up.

"We should keep this kit on us," Marcus said as he clutched it to his chest. "We might need it later."

No sooner had he said that than I heard a crackle in the bushes. All four of us whipped around. Four people staggered out of the trees. One of them was clutching his stomach and wincing. The others stood tall. The rival Captain had his eyes on the first aid kit in Marcus' hands.

I didn't know his name, but I knew he was one of the leaders of one of the biggest gangs at the school. The leader sneered and said, "If you know what's good for you, you'll hand that over."

Marcus clutched the kit tighter, and Charlie said, "You can have some supplies to heal your teammate, but you can't have all of it. We'll give you what you need and go."

"Fuck that," the leader snarled. "Attack!"

Everything erupted in seconds. The gang leader had to be a warlock, because he sent a stunning spell straight at Marcus. Marcus jumped out of the way, and Kallie transformed into a wolf. She snarled and charged at the warlock. They danced around each other, Kallie lashing out with her fangs and the warlock shooting off more spells.

Charlie and Oberi took on the other guy, who had to be a shifter. Charlie shot off air funnels at the fae, who dodged him to respond with battle orbs of his own.

I summoned a fireball and flung it at the nearest enemy, which was a merman only a few feet away. He dodged my fireballs and screamed. His sonic voice knocked me off my feet, and I cried out as I went slamming into a tree.

I threw another fireball from my place on the ground, but the merman was super fast. He lunged out and dragged me upward by my hair. I yelled in terror as the merman latched his arms around me. I tried to summon a spell, but it fizzled out at my fingers as he squeezed tight.

I didn't realize how strong merpeople were. This guy was going to turn my insides to fucking jelly. I knew merpeople had water running through their veins, more so than most supernaturals. Maybe if I could summon it, and rush it to his heart, I could kill him.

But the merman was squeezing so tightly, I couldn't breathe. There was no way to command my magic when I felt this lightheaded. He was literally crushing me.

"Charlie," I whimpered helplessly, using my last breath to call out his name.

When Charlie heard me cry out for him, he immediately abandoned the fight with the shifter. Oberi charged at the shifter and chased him off with her horn, leaving Charlie able to come to my aid. He ran to me as quickly as possible. He flung out his hand, and I blacked out for a second as the merman dropped me. I collapsed on the ground, gasping for precious air.

But I wasn't the only one. The merman clutched at his own throat, face turning purple as Charlie used his Air magic to suffocate him. Blood vessels burst in his eyes, and a horrible noise emitted from his throat as he pleaded for mercy.

The fight stopped. Kallie and Marcus observed in horror, and the teammates of the merman began backing away in fear.

Charlie was going to kill him. I knew he was. I could feel his murderous intent as it rushed through our bond. And as much as the merman might've deserved it for trying to kill me... I wouldn't allow Charlie to have blood on his hands.

I dragged myself up Charlie's body, forcing myself to my feet. "Charlie, stop! This isn't who you are!"

Charlie didn't listen. The deadliness in his face made my body turn cold. The merman slumped to the side, giving a few pathetic gasps.

"Charlie!" I put both hands on the side of his face and forced his forehead to connect with mine. "Just breathe."

Charlie seemed to realize what he was doing. He dropped the spell, and the merman took in a huge gulp of air as he fell to the side. Bruises had accumulated all over his neck.

I stared at the merman, hardly able to believe it. *Charlie* had done that. *For me.*

The gang leader had taken the momentary shock to grab the first aid kit out of Marcus' hands. He wrenched it away and began running. The other teammates followed— even the merman, though he had to stagger to get away.

"Hey!" Marcus cried out.

"Marcus, let them have it," Charlie said roughly. I watched as the other team fled into the woods, until they disappeared entirely.

Kallie scowled. "Great. Now we gave away our only supplies."

"We'll find more. It's not worth dying over." Charlie grasped my arms tightly. "You okay, pidge?"

There were still stars dancing in front of my eyes. "Yeah. I'm okay."

There was a bit of silence. Then Marcus spoke. "Dude, what did you *do* to that guy?"

"Almost crushed his windpipe," Charlie answered casually.

"Gods, Charlie!" Kallie cried.

"He'll live. For now," Charlie said darkly. He moved to put his arm around me and drew me close. I felt my shoulders relax, and Oberi let out a nicker.

Charlie was a totally different person out here. That side of him that ruled on the streets had come out during the Darke Games. I was scared of him.

But I respected him, too. And even more, I was proud to be bonded to him, because it made me feel safe. No one would fuck with me… not when Charlie was around.

I rubbed my temple. I had a headache.

"We should move on," Charlie suggested. "If there are other teams around the area, it puts us at risk."

Fine by me. We started walking deeper into the forest. Charlie's grip remained on my shoulders as we continued onward. Eventually, I got my breath back, and there was only an aching in my body to remind me of what I'd just endured.

We walked in silence for ten minutes before Charlie whispered, "You gonna be okay to get through the rest of the Games?"

"I don't have a choice, do I?" I asked. "The prophecy has to come first."

Charlie opened his mouth to say something more, but didn't. A weird feeling came over me as we stepped into this part of the woods. It was near the same road that led to the Institute, that creepy area where it felt like the very trees had eyes. I had a very bad notion we'd gone the wrong way.

Then I smelled it— a sulfur-like scent. Black pits of pitch black water spanned all around us. They weren't very big— five feet or so across— but they seemed bottomless. They weren't tar… I wasn't quite sure what kind of substance they were. I tried summoning the black water within the pits, but it didn't move to my command.

That scared me. Water had always listened to me before. That these waters didn't was simply unnatural.

Marcus knelt by one of the pools. He put his hand out to touch the water, but Kallie stopped him. "Don't," she whispered.

Marcus stood. We began weaving around the pools, taking care not to touch the water. I pressed closer to Charlie. I felt these frightening pools were one of the most evil things about Darke Island.

Kallie froze. She halted so abruptly that Marcus ran into her. He went to say something, but she waved her hand to shut him up. All of us paused, waiting for her assessment.

Kallie sniffed the air. Then her eyes contracted, and her face paled of all color just as a wicked laugh echoed through the woods.

That laugh made a shiver creep into my bones. It was the most menacing thing I'd ever heard… some sort of sound straight out of hell. Instinct told me whatever happened, we needed to get as far away from that sound as possible.

The laugh echoed again, closer this time. That's when Kallie sprang into action. "Run!" she screamed. She changed into a wolf. Marcus jumped onto her back before she started running away at top speed. He barely had time to grab Rishi.

We didn't ask any questions. Charlie and I clambered onto Oberi's back and held on tight as she galloped after Kallie. The laugh echoed behind us. My heart sped up and beat on in fear as we ran away from a faceless terror.

Kallie ran so fast, she outpaced us. We were losing her. Not even Oberi could keep up, and she let out a whinny, telling Kallie to wait for us. Oberi had to dart between all the black pools lying before us, jumping over some and nearly spinning out in her race to avoid the others.

"Kallie, slow down!" Charlie cried out. She was so terrified trying to get away from whatever was chasing us, she didn't hear, and only increased her strides.

Oberi tripped. Charlie's hands entangled in her mane, and he stayed on, but I lost my balance and fell off. I went tumbling downward, straight into one of the black pits we'd been so desperately trying to avoid.

I sank into the water. Immediately, everything went dark as my head and the rest of my body went under. The black water was slimy. I cast a spell so my Water magic would push me up, but like before, nothing happened. I attempted to swim, but the water was so thick, every movement of my arms and legs was like moving in concrete. I only sank deeper into the pool as the voices inside my mind began screaming louder than ever before.

You killed your best friend.

You didn't mean enough to her to make her stay.

If you were a better person she wouldn't have died.

My heart clenched and began to wither. It *was* my fault Monica was dead. I deserved this.

Your family is glad you're gone.

They love you out of obligation.

How could anyone want a daughter, a sister, like you?

I was such a terrible person that my parents were ashamed of me, too. My whole family was.

Charlie will get tired of you.

You're too much to handle.

It won't take long for him to abandon you.

If I could cry underwater, I'd be sobbing buckets. Charlie couldn't love me. No one could.

It's useless, Ava.

Let go.

Nothing lasts forever.

The voices were right. Eventually, everyone would leave, and I'd be alone in the world.

The darkness vanished as I returned to the day Monica died. Her death replayed in front of my eyes, over and over. The scene switched to John, and that forsaken night he'd forced himself on me. I kept reliving both, unable to escape this awful, cruel fate. My lungs tightened as I began to drown. I welcomed the end, just to make the flashbacks stop.

I wanted to give up. Dying was better than feeling this pain.

"Pidge!" I heard Charlie scream. "*Pigeon!*"

I hated that nickname, but ancestors, I wanted to hear it now. I needed to hear Charlie's voice. It was the only thing keeping me alive.

I struggled not to go under, but it was a useless endeavor. The voices were pulling me to the abyss.

I knew then. I was going to die down here.

Then I felt a hand around my arm. Someone pulled me up. I knew by the feeling of his body against mine that it had to be Charlie. He'd jumped in after me.

Despair grew in my heart. I'd condemned us both. If I was to die, so be it, but I didn't want Charlie to die along with me.

I loved him too much.

Charlie held me tightly to his form. A root wrapped around our middle and began to pull us up. Another root latched around our legs, and our arms. Charlie used the roots to pull us up, and the voices shattered my eardrums. Our heads broke the surface, and my eyes opened as I took a giant gulp of air.

Oberi had changed into his husky form. He grabbed my jacket with his teeth and pulled me out as Charlie used the roots to burst himself out of the pit. We both crawled to a nearby tree, covered in the black muck that was the pit's residue. Charlie opened his arms to me, and I fell into them.

I couldn't help but stutter. "Wh-what… w-was… t-hat?"

Charlie's voice was even, but still held an edge of fright. "Professor Cusak talked about them in class… they're called the Pits of Despair. They're living entities that feed off supernaturals. They make you relive the worst parts of your life, until you give up, and the pit consumes you whole."

My stomach bottomed out, and my voice steadied. "You knew what they were, and you still jumped in after me?"

Charlie nodded. My body gave a shudder as I asked, "What did you hear?"

"Marty. Over and over. He kept telling me to turn back and leave you," Charlie responded, haunted.

"You didn't."

"I couldn't."

Charlie and I held each other for long moments as the wind whipped through the trees. Oberi laid across our legs, to keep us warm.

The padding of paws made me look up. Kallie and Marcus had come back for us. Marcus slid off of Kallie's back with Rishi in his arms.

Kallie changed back. "I'm so sorry. I didn't mean to leave you guys like that— I panicked. I didn't turn around until Marcus said you two had fallen in."

"You came back. That's what matters," Charlie responded. We listened again for the wicked laugh, but it was nowhere to be heard. What was chasing us must've gotten bored and run off.

Marcus turned toward Kallie. "What exactly were we running from?" he asked.

Kallie's face was still pale. "Don't ask. Just know it's something we can't fight. But I don't smell it anymore. We got away."

As Charlie and I stood, I wavered. I nearly passed out, but he caught me before I fell against the ground.

The black pit had drained me. I'd been inside longer than Charlie had, and as a result, it'd sapped all my strength.

"Guys, we're tired," Charlie said. "We need a break."

"We can't stop," Kallie insisted. "The more downtime we have, the more chances it gives the other team to earn points. We can keep going."

I wasn't sure. All of us were dead on our feet after everything that had gone on earlier. We needed some time to recover.

"A few hours' sleep is better than nothing. We'll be in a better position to fight if we rest now, rather than the teams who've been at it all night," Charlie said. "We should preserve our strength."

Kallie's eyes flickered to me, and my shaking appearance must've made her change her mind. "All right. Hold on. I'll whip something up."

We walked until we were out of the pits. I wanted nothing to do with them, and I was sure Charlie felt the same.

We came to a small clearing, and Kallie stopped. She waved her hands, and before our very eyes, a small cabin appeared. It wasn't huge— four-hundred square feet or less— but it was something. As we stepped inside, I saw that there was only a fireplace, a pot, a couch, and an armchair, along with a room that had a small double bed in the back. Her illusion magic was strong enough to make the cabin real. I pressed a hand against the wall and found it was solid.

Marcus eyed Kallie at the sight of the bare house, and she said, "Look, I'm not very good at big illusions yet. This is the best you're gonna get."

Marcus rubbed his stomach. "Man, I'm so hungry. I wish we had something to eat."

Kallie conjured up a sandwich on a plate and gave it to Marcus. He inhaled it in seconds, frowning as he finished. "I still feel hungry."

"Yeah, because food conjured by a fae illusion doesn't do anything to actually nourish you. It's basically for enjoyment only," Kallie said. "If you're hungry, we need to find something out here."

Oberi trotted out the door, wagging his tail. Rishi followed him in interest.

"Where are they going?" I asked.

"Oberi wants to investigate the area, just to be safe," Charlie said. "They'll come back in a bit. Let's get a fire started."

I was a bit jealous Oberi was communicating with Charlie over me, but I was too tired to argue. I was freezing. Charlie and Marcus went out to grab firewood, and I sat on the floor by the fireplace. I was too exhausted to move much further.

Kallie sat beside me. "Are you okay? Those pits look like they did a number on you."

"I'm fine," I lied. "I just need a nap."

"Same. It's probably for the best we stopped," she said.

She bounced nervously next to me, and I asked, "What's wrong? You seem really tense."

"Well… um, I'm a bit paranoid," Kallie confessed. "It's really awkward now with Marcus."

"Why?"

"He admitted he can only read *dirty thoughts*," Kallie hushed. "And, well… I've been having a lot of them. About… him."

"*Kallie!*" I playfully smacked her shoulder. "Are you telling me you're having daydreams about Marcus sexing you up?"

Her cheeks turned red. "No! Yes. Maybe."

She sat back. "To tell you the truth, we might've kissed when we were trying to break out forever ago. He was giving me CPR after we fought the sirens in the lake, but it turned into… more."

"No shit." I beamed, a smile spreading across my face. "You totally have the hots for Marcus!"

Kallie let out a breath. "It doesn't matter. He's a warlock. I'm a fae. Our races are constantly at war. They hate each other. We can't be together."

"Fuck that. You guys already broke the law. You're both in prison. What's stopping you?" I asked.

Kallie looked down. "I don't know. I've already disgraced my family by messing up so badly. If I mated with a warlock… I'm not sure if I could ever go back home again. Even though I'm banished, I have some hope that maybe one day, they'll take me back. And I don't want to screw that up."

"If your family doesn't approve of who you love, they're not worth it anyway," I insisted. "If you want to be with Marcus, be with him. I'm sure he likes you, too."

Kallie scowled. "If he does, he doesn't act like it. After all, I'm pretty sure he's already seen my thoughts of him screwing me over a table in the Alchemy classroom, and he hasn't acted on any of it."

"Damn, girl, that's so naughty!" I giggled. "Don't get too worried. Marcus is just shy. I'm sure he's got a hard-on for you."

Kallie didn't answer, because just then, Marcus and Charlie came back with a bundle of sticks and fallen branches. Marcus' face was red, like he knew what we'd been talking about. I guess he really *did* only see the dirty thoughts.

Charlie gave me the branches. I arranged them in the fireplace and lit them aflame. Just as I got the fire started, Oberi and Rishi returned. They were carrying small packages in their mouths. When I gave a closer look, I saw that they were bags of freeze-dried food.

"They must've found another checkpoint," I said. "Good boy, Oberi."

He panted and licked my hand. I summoned water from the air to put into the pot. We boiled the food, then ate what was inside quickly— chicken and rice. It wasn't very good, but it made the hunger pangs in my stomach fade, and some of my energy returned.

"You guys have Oberi, so you can take the bed. I'll sleep on the armchair. Marcus and Rishi can sleep on the couch," Kallie suggested.

Charlie took my hand. "Come on, pidge."

I dragged my feet to the bedroom. Charlie closed the door behind us as I drew the shades.

At least the damn drone hadn't followed us inside the cottage. We could get some privacy. We took off our boots, which were caked with mud, and threw them to the side.

Oberi hopped onto the bed just as Charlie and I lay down on it. The husky spread across our feet to warm them, and sighed as he slipped off to sleep. The dirt from the black pit spread over the sheets from our clothes, but I didn't care. It'd all disappear anyway when we left in a few hours.

"Pidge," Charlie whispered, and my eyes fluttered open. I could barely see his face by the moonlight peeking around the curtains.

"Yeah?" He'd better make this quick, because I was two seconds away from passing out.

He moved closer to me. "I'm sorry if I was too harsh on you earlier. I freaked out."

"No, Charlie. Don't apologize. You did the right thing," I said. "I needed a wake-up call."

His voice broke as he said, "You nearly died twice."

"But I didn't. You saved me. That's what counts."

I entwined my fingers with his. "What you said earlier… about listening to you. I think I'm ready to do that now. I can do it right this time. I can be obedient."

His eyebrows crinkled. "I don't want you to obey me because you think I want control."

"It's not like that. You proved you're willing to kill to protect me. I think that kind of devotion warrants my respect."

Charlie rubbed his thumbs on the backs of my hands. "I just want you to make it through this. If something happened…"

"I will make it, because I have you. I respect you so much for what you did out there. I can let you take the lead, because I know you'll make the right call."

He cleared his throat. "I, uh… appreciate all that, pidge."

My opinion from earlier had changed drastically. I thought I couldn't trust Charlie with everything, and then he'd shown me just how far he was willing to go to make sure I got through this competition safe and well. That had earned my submission.

I wanted to prove to Charlie how much I trusted him. I didn't know how, but by the end of the competition, I'd prove how much he meant to me.

"Let's get some sleep," he said. "We've still got plenty to face tonight."

Yeah, we did. I moved closer to him, just because he was warm, and it felt good to have his body conform around mine. I flipped onto my side and pressed my back against his front. He put his arm around me, and the cottage fell silent.

Damn, this was paradise. Charlie molded to me like we were two pieces of a puzzle that'd been glued together. A warm sensation grew in my chest when I felt his heartbeat against my back again… my favorite feeling. His tense muscles loosened as he held me, and I scooted back, just to be that much closer to him.

My ass hit something. *Holy ancestors almighty*, he had a hard-on. Like, the legendary kind girls gossip about, but I wasn't actually sure was real. Proof of the rare perfect dick's existence was pressed up against me, and it was still in his pants, for crying out loud. I think I was obsessed.

Charlie's breaths rose and fell evenly behind me. I think he was already asleep. Did he not notice?

The feel of him against me should've made me freak out, but… I was totally okay with it. It felt natural. I didn't feel the need to do anything with it, either. It just felt good to have him there.

My eyes closed. I counted his breaths, and it didn't take me but a few moments afterward to completely pass into peaceful oblivion.

Charlie and I awoke at the sound of a shrill scream in the night.

We bolted upright, breathing raggedly. It was still dark. We couldn't have slept for more than a few hours.

The door to our bedroom was open, and Oberi was gone. Without a word, we both clambered out of bed, put our boots back on and crept to the living room.

The cabin had gone so deathly cold there was frost on the windows. I could see my breath. Marcus sat on the edge of the couch, hands shaking. Oberi, Rishi, and Kallie were all facing the door, Kallie in her wolf form. The hair on their backs stood up, and their ears pricked. Kallie was still as a statue. Oberi let out a low growl, and Rishi followed it up with a hiss.

"Something's moving out there," Kallie said. She used her magic to project her thoughts outward, so she could speak in her wolf form. She put a paw forward, waiting to attack.

There was a sound on the side of the cottage like nails on a chalkboard. Something was dragging their claws over the wood. Goosebumps quivered over my skin, and my eyes grew wide as I realized thick ice was spreading all over the wall. I lashed out a hand to stop it, but as I stopped the growth of one ice patch, another took its place.

"We need to leave. Now." Kallie nudged the door open with her head and began hurrying as silently as she could into the woods. The rest of us followed. Oberi guided Charlie so he could keep up. As I looked behind, the cottage vanished as the illusion faded.

Except there was nothing waiting in its stead to hunt us down. That had to be the scariest thing of all.

There was a crackle in the bushes. Kallie froze. She changed back, clinging to Marcus' arm. Oberi began to whine.

"Shit." Kallie started freaking out. "Shit, shit, shit! He found us."

"I'm guessing you're talking about the monster we fled from earlier?" Marcus asked hoarsely.

"Yes. I thought he'd abandoned the hunt, but apparently…" Kallie swallowed and shook her head, like she was spooked.

"How close is he?" I remained at the ready to light a fireball.

"Close. Maybe we can lose him again." Kallie hurried on ahead.

The forest was so dark I could barely see a thing, even with the moonlight. Then Marcus let out a yell, and my shoe met something soft and squishy at the same time.

I couldn't help it. Instinctually, I lit a fireball for light. I wished I hadn't. My firelight illuminated the forest, showing four bodies… one of the other teams. They'd been ripped open. There was so much blood that the area was coated red. Organs were spewed all over the place. I'd stepped on an intestine while walking onto the scene.

Marcus threw up. I barely held it in myself. I told myself those weren't people. Just animals, deer, like I'd hunted with my dad. I forced myself to look into the trees instead of at the bodies.

I was grateful Charlie couldn't see this, but he could still smell it. He covered his nose to muffle the metallic smell of blood and rotting corpses.

Kallie's voice was hollow. "He made them fight each other, then when he got bored, he eviscerated them. It's how these kind of monsters hunt."

"What is it?" Charlie's tone steeled, preparing himself.

"It's a lichen," Kallie said breathlessly. "It's a sorcerer that's sold his soul to dark forces to literally become demonic."

"He did that to them?" Marcus asked weakly as he wiped his mouth.

"Yes. And that's what we'll be if we don't get out of—"

Kallie didn't finish her sentence, because she was blasted off her feet by a ray of red light. All of us called for her. She sailed through the air and landed on her hip, crying out in pain as she looked at what attacked her.

A sorcerer made of bone stood across from us. A bloody red robe hung around his skeletal form, skull still dripping with rotted flesh. The lichen held a twisted staff forged from dark wood, a red ruby on top that looked like an eye. His bones clicked together as he raised a hand to point at us, and from his rotting fingertips erupted yet another spell. The red ray shot out of his hand and collided with a tree. It began falling over, and Marcus leapt out of the way with a scream.

Rishi didn't stick around. He ran into the trees with a yowl, vanishing into the night as he fled to ancestors only knew where.

"Fuck! We're dead, we're dead!" Kallie screamed.

Kallie's reaction told me everything I needed to know. We'd found the wrong monster, and now, the lichen was going to make us his bitch.

We began an all-out attack just to survive. Every single one of us lashed out with a spell. Charlie flung out his Air magic, I created two tunnels of both Fire and Water, Kallie flung her battle orbs, and Marcus conjured the biggest stunning spell he could muster. Oberi changed into a unicorn and blasted fire out of her horn.

Magic came at the lichen from all sides, but he merely threw a hand up, and a red shield expanded in front of him. Our magic immediately died once it hit the shield.

My mouth dropped open. If I had thought the balur was out of our league, the lichen was practically a god. Nothing we had in our arsenal could handle this.

The lichen pointed his staff at each of the bodies littering the area. Like twitching spiders, they began to rise. More organs slopped out of their bodies as they walked forward, controlled by the lichen's necromancy magic, blankness in their eyes. Kallie screamed as one of the zombies grabbed her. She kicked it away, though they continued to stalk toward us at the lichen's command.

A surge of protectiveness came over me, and I blasted the biggest Fire column I could possibly muster. I screamed as the Fire column enveloped the zombies, turning them to ash. They flailed against my flames, as if trying to put them out, before they fell to the ground again and dissolved into ash.

The lichen was unbothered. The black holes in his skull glittered… like he thought this was a game.

"Use simultension!" Charlie cried out.

Kallie conjured the swords for us again. I infused my weapon with my Fire, and yelled as I charged at the lichen. He reached out and grabbed the blade, then squeezed. It melted away at his touch, and my chest grew cold. The lichen pounded his staff into the ground, and the swords that the others held melted away, too. Charlie gasped as the molten liquid burned his hand, though he dropped the hilt before any real damage could be done.

The lichen let out that deceptive, mocking laugh, and ancestors, it nearly made me want to vomit. He waved his staff, and before my very eyes, the lichen began to duplicate. He became three different bone sorcerers, facing Kallie, Marcus, and Charlie in turn.

I didn't have time to react. The sorcerers changed into balls of light, and went zooming into my friends' bodies. Each of them cried out as the light settled into their bodies... then went utterly still as their eyes glowed red.

Kallie, Marcus, and Charlie all turned at the exact same time. Oberi gave a nervous noise, and I realized... the lichen had possessed them. I was the only one left still in control of my body.

Charlie raised a hand, and I had to duck as an Air column cut a tree in half behind me. Kallie and Marcus both began firing off battle orbs. They exploded all around me, and I screamed once again. *This* is what the lichen had done to the other team— made them fight each other until they were all dead.

I flung Water magic out at them. Maybe I could freeze the demon out, like I tried in practice. But as Kallie, Marcus, and Charlie halted in place, ice creeping across their skin, I realized my efforts were all but pointless. Their skin was turning blue, and I was certain I was hurting them more than the lichen. I drew away the freezing spell, acknowledging that it had no effect.

If I wanted to survive, I only had one option— I had to *kill my friends.*

I couldn't think, but Oberi had more sense than I did. She used her neck to swing me onto her back, and she turned to gallop away.

"Oberi, we can't leave them!" I protested.

She didn't listen. Oberi fled the area, mane flying backward as her hooves pounded into the earth. I glanced behind. I didn't see the lichen, but his terrible laughter crawled across my skin as he chased me through the dark forest, looming closer and closer.

Ancestors, Great Spirit, anyone! I pleaded in my head. *Save us!*

The lichen's laugh was growing so loud, it rang in my ears. Then all of a sudden... it stopped. I could feel the lichen's presence leave me abruptly, like it turned back somehow. I don't know why it would, but I was so grateful to be free of him that I cried tears of relief.

Then tears of sorrow, because the team I loved was still back there in his grasp.

Oberi slowed to a standstill in a clearing in the middle of the woods. Here, the trees were less thick, and a strong ray of moonlight illuminated the area.

I slid off of Oberi's back and faced her. "How could you do that?" I yelled. "Charlie is still back there!"

Oberi nickered. She bobbed her head, like she wanted me to turn around.

"Why did you even bring me here?" I threw my hands up as I spun on my heel. My frustration with my Familiar fell flat as I saw there was someone else with me in the clearing.

It wasn't a monster. I knew that much. This was something different. The creature in front of me was a coyote, but it wasn't like any animal I'd ever seen before. The coyote's fur was orange, with red lines running through his fur and over his amber eyes. Hawkei runes, like the ones chieftains used to write their edicts, were written over the red lines in a soft blue. The entire coyote gleamed like a candle against the night. His tail was nothing but a flame that fanned out behind him.

The animal gave a toothy grin. *Well, this is nice,* the coyote spoke in my mind. *Usually when I meet supernaturals, they bow before me, professing how great I am. You are a divergence from the typical.*

I tilted my head. I couldn't believe who was standing in front of me... but from all the

Hawkei tales I'd heard from my father, I knew this could only be but one deity. "You're Coyote Spirit. The Fire god. You're one of the pieces of the Great Spirit."

I am the Koigni god, yes, Coyote replied. *How coy of you to notice.*

His voice dripped with sarcasm. My heartbeat picked up speed. "Wh— why are you here?"

You called me, remember? Coyote replied. *You asked for help, and here I am.*

I had asked for help… but I'd never had a god show up before me when I prayed before. I threw a nervous glance over my shoulder, and Coyote said, *You need not fear. The lichen will not follow you if I am around. It is afraid of me.*

By all respects, I should've been afraid of Coyote, too. I mean, I was talking to a god, here. And not just any god— a trickster god, one of the most famous to play pranks on supernaturals for his own entertainment.

But I didn't feel any fear when I looked at Coyote. Merely reassurance.

"You want to help me? I didn't think I was that special."

I have been following you for a long time, Coyote said, and he gave a delighted cackle. *I tricked your father to fall in love with your mother, and you are the fantastic result… one of my greatest creations.*

"You made me?" I asked.

Coyote gave a casual shrug. *With the help of others. Many years ago.*

I scowled when I thought of how Coyote said he'd tricked my father. He might've thought bringing a Koigni and a Toaqua together was funny, but my parents truly loved one another. They weren't pawns for him to play with.

But what if he saw me in the same way… as a toy? "How do I know you haven't tricked me, and this isn't a trap?"

Coyote gave a scathing sound. *As if I need to trick you to get you to make the wrong decision.*

Coyote cast his head around, like he was indicating my participation in the Darke Games. Then he paused and said, *Or is it the right one?*

This god was a major douchebag. And part of the Great Spirit or not, I really didn't feel like putting up with his sass.

"Are you here to torment me, or are you actually going to give me a message?" I crossed my arms. "Because I seriously don't have time to be dicking around."

Coyote blinked. Then he shifted, transforming into a man. His skin still had that orange hue, red lines and blue runes running over his form. His clothes were made of animal bones, leather, and furs. His eyes remained animalistic. *"Do you want my guidance, or not? There are other supernaturals who'd be more grateful for my help."*

I tapped my chin. "Well… can you like, go back there and kick that lichen's butt for me? Because that would be really awesome."

Coyote shook his head. *"I cannot do that. Your participation in these Games is a test by the gods, and you must pass this test to move on to the next one. There will be many more."*

"Excuse me?"

"Your prophecy speaks of a war of gods. Here I am, one of the first to appear. There will be others, if you survive."

"One of the first?"

"Different gods have come to you before."

Memories popped out at me. Ending up alone in the forest as a child, facing that mysterious creature in the forest. The blue eyes I'd seen the night my father was healed.

"You might want to get a move on," Coyote purred. *"The public is waiting."*

Coyote pointed upward. The drone hovered above. I hadn't realized it was still following me.

I raised an eyebrow. "Um… aren't you afraid of being caught on film?"

"You're the only one who can see me. Right now, the audience thinks you've gone insane and are talking to yourself."

"That's perfect," I grumbled.

"It's not like you have a spotless reputation," Coyote said.

"So what do I do? My friends are possessed, and aside from my Familiar, I'm all alone," I said in despair.

"You have everything you need to save your friends. Look all around you. The Great Spirit does not lead one into a situation without providing a way to get out," Coyote replied.

"How? The lichen is so powerful!" I objected.

"I didn't say it'd be pleasant or easy," Coyote drawled. *"You've received the lessons you need. All you must do is apply them."*

Coyote began to fade away. His maniacal snickers rang in my ears as he vanished before my eyes. Oberi snorted, and we were once again alone in the clearing... though I felt like Coyote's eyes were on me, watching me.

I wasn't sure if that was one of my psychotic visions or if I'd actually seen a god, but it didn't matter, did it? Coyote was right. I couldn't just give up. There had to be *something* I could do to save my team.

Professor Hemlock's lecture came back to me. The potion we'd brewed in class. She said it was effective for exorcising evil spirits— and all the ingredients were on Darke Island. I was good at potions. I knew I could handle this.

I immediately began scouring the forest. Oberi followed, changing into a husky and putting his nose to the ground to sniff out what we needed.

I remembered the ingredients of the potion exactly. *Bay leaves, cloves, star weed, and sage.* Oberi and I looked everywhere. Dawn began rising over the horizon, igniting the forest in color. As I found the star weed— the last ingredient— I felt a bit of victory, though the next step made me pause.

I had the ingredients, but I didn't have a way to brew them. I needed a cauldron, and a vial. Kallie could generate them if she was here... but she wasn't. I had to find them on my own.

I was just about to give up when I smelled something on the air. Soup... someone was cooking something. It might be one of the other teams.

I could steal their pot away... it might give me a shot. I followed the smell. Oberi pressed close to me as I peered out from the trees.

It was Alice and her team of innocents. They were gathered around a fire, eating some kind of stew from the pot I needed. The pot had been pulled off the fire and looked cool. Beside it sat a few empty food jars that would be perfect for containing my potion.

They must've gotten those items from another checkpoint. I paused. Could I really take from Alice and the others?

If it was to save my friends? Yes. I moved forward, preparing to attack from behind.

My shoe broke a twig, and I cursed. Alice, Despona, Carson and Wesley all jumped. Their eyes met mine, and I gave up. I came out of the bushes, giving a sigh.

"Ava," Despona said. "What are you doing here? Where's the rest of your team?"

"They've been possessed," I admitted. "I'm the only one left."

I raised a hand to show them the ingredients in my hand. "I can brew a potion to save them, but I need a pot, and..."

My head dropped. "You know what, you guys can just kill me. I know you want to win, and my team's pretty much done for, anyway. It would help your rankings if you got rid of us. So, go on. Just make it quick."

Despona stared at me. Then she reached out and grabbed the pot and a vial from the ground. She held them out to me. "Here. Take them."

I blinked. "Huh?"

"We're done eating. You can have them," she said.

"But… you guys might need them to brew your own potion later," I said.

"It doesn't matter. You need them more now." Despona pushed.

I felt so honored by her offer. They didn't need to help me. It'd be in their benefit if they didn't. Yet they didn't just care about themselves out here.

I took the pot and the jar. "Thank you so much. You're literally saving my ass."

"Hey, we all gotta look out for each other out here," Carson said. "Don't mention it."

I gave them a nod, then ran off before they could change their minds. I stopped by a stream that I found in the forest, then washed out the pot and the jar before I filled the pot with water. I lit a fire, then began adding ingredients, using stones as knives to cut up what I needed. I felt a beading of sweat along my brow as I worked faster than ever before. I hoped to the ancestors my friends were still alive, and that the lichen hadn't killed them.

Finally, I poured the finished mixture into the jar. I was certain I had it right, but there'd be only one way to tell.

I had the potion. If I got it down my teammate's throats, I could make it so they were no longer possessed. But that would only go so far. We still didn't have a way to kill the lichen.

A bout of inspiration struck me. I was two Houses— Toaqua and Koigni. What if I could use simultension on *myself*?

Fusing my Fire and Water together seemed impossible. They were total opposites. But it was worth a shot, right? I didn't have any other ideas.

I conjured Fire in my right hand and Water in my left. I began bringing the two sides together slowly, focusing my intention on melding the two.

I thought it would be hard. But it was as easy as breathing. The water ball and the fire combined, and they swirled in my palm until the result was a burning blue flame, suspended at the tips of my fingers. In awe, I felt the edge of the blue fire. It was cool to the touch, like ice. But when I pushed my hand in further to the fire's core, my skin was met with a blazing inferno. I pulled back, marveling at the magic in my hands.

Clever girl, Coyote purred. I looked around, but didn't see him.

I wasn't sure if my blue fire would kill the lichen, but it was the best chance I had. I stood with the potion in one hand and my blue fire in the other.

Marcus seemed like the easiest target. I'd go after him first. "Find Marcus, boy," I told Oberi. He barked and put his nose against the ground, searching out for Marcus' scent.

We walked for half a mile before I saw him. He was walking around, looking for me. His eyes still burned red as the lichen used his body to navigate.

Oberi pressed to the ground as I snuck up on Marcus from behind. When I was close enough, I jumped. But the lichen must've sensed me coming, because Marcus spun around, malice on his face.

I immediately felt a telekinetic burst that erupted out of Marcus' mind. It grabbed me and threw me backward, knocking the wind out of me.

Okay, Marcus apparently wouldn't be as easy as I thought. Shit.

I clenched at my gut and rolled out of the way as Marcus began levitating logs using his mind, tossing them at me at high speed. I'd only just managed to jump to my feet before Marcus used his telekinesis powers to wrench a huge tree out of the ground. He tossed it my way, and Oberi yelped. I dodged the massive trunk of the uprooted tree as it slammed into the ground.

Okay, Marcus was either holding back on his powers, or he didn't believe in himself, because the lichen was using his body like a fucking master warlock. Marcus went to levitate the tree again, to use as a hammer to smack me into the earth. Before he could, Oberi growled and launched himself on Marcus. He pinned Marcus to the ground, and as the tree dropped to the forest floor again, I scrambled for the potion. I unscrewed the cap and forced Marcus' jaw open. I poured it down his throat, and Marcus wretched for a moment, giving a gasp as a red blur shot out of his throat.

One of the manifestations of the lichen appeared. The skeleton clacked its teeth and moved in, stretching his arms toward me. Marcus screamed, but I reached my hand back and flung my blue fireball.

The lichen put up a shield, but the blue fireball sailed right through it. It connected with the skeleton's head and made it explode in a flash of blue light.

I didn't realize I'd been holding my breath until my lungs began to ache. The rest of the lichen's body dissolved into dust upon the wind. Marcus' eyes bulged out of his head.

My blue Fire could kill the lichen. We still had a chance!

"Di-did you kill it?" he asked.

"There are still two parts of the lichen in Kallie and Charlie," I said as I helped him to his feet. "If we can kill both, we'll be safe."

Rishi came out of the woods. He hadn't gone far from Marcus, and was only hiding. Oberi licked his ears as Rishi greeted him.

"Where do you think Kallie is?" Marcus whispered.

"She can't be far from here. Oberi will show the way," I said.

Oberi wagged his tail, then trotted forward. Marcus and I stayed close as he led us to a part of the forest that was far less dense, with fewer trees to hide behind.

I saw a flash of silver fur. Kallie was in her wolf form, eyes shining bright red. She snarled and growled, though there was no enemy in her sight. We were upwind, so she couldn't smell us… not until the wind changed, at least, and I didn't know how long that would be.

Kallie had killed a deer. Her fur was stained red as she tore at it, eating the heart whole. My nose wrinkled. The lichen had to be hungry.

I really didn't want to fight Kallie, especially not in her wolf form. She was a brutal fighter, and she'd rip us to shreds.

"How do you plan on getting that potion past her massive jaws without being bitten in half?" Marcus hissed.

"We can't fight her, that's for sure. We need to trick her," I whispered.

Marcus nodded. "I have an idea. Follow my lead."

He slipped off with Rishi. I waited for a few moments, until suddenly, the dead deer shot upright, blank eyes shooting wide open.

Kallie leapt backward, giving a yelp of surprise. The dead deer bounded off, and I realized Marcus was using his necromancy powers to make it run. The deer's insides and blood slicked out of its body as it ran to get away from Kallie.

Kallie growled and chased after her prey, the lichen's magic driving her on. I remained behind a tree and prayed this would work.

The dead deer ran past. Kallie zoomed by a second later. By then, Oberi and I were waiting for her. Oberi tackled Kallie to the ground with a snarl. Though he was only a third the size of her, he was strong, and he held her down. Kallie's jaws snapped and snarled, but Oberi didn't let her up.

My hand almost slipped on the jar as I danced around Kallie's violent fangs, attempting to spill the potion inside. A few drops fell past her lips. Her eyes widened, and a red blaze erupted from her mouth.

The lichen materialized a few feet away. He flew forward like some cursed ghost, pointing his staff at me, but I had a blue fireball waiting. I smashed it into his face, and the lichen howled before that part of him burst into ash.

Kallie changed back into a woman. There was still blood on her face from her recent kill. The dead deer slumped to the side as Marcus let go of the necromancy spell.

"How the fuck did you kill that thing?" Kallie asked.

"I've been experimenting," I told her, showing her the blue fireball. "And I'm not done yet. We still have to save Charlie."

"Kallie!" Marcus lunged forward and hugged her so tightly, he lifted her feet off the ground. Kallie closed her eyes and hugged Marcus back, body slumping in relief.

"How'd you do that, Marcus?" I asked. "I've never seen you pull off magic like you've been doing in the Games."

"Honestly, I didn't really know I *could* do all that stuff," he admitted. "I just… realized I had to, in the moment."

Oberi barked, insistent we get a move on. Anxiety bloomed in my stomach. Charlie was the last person we had to save, but he was also the most powerful. If we got into a fight, I might have to hurt him to save the others.

I didn't know if I could do that. Hurting Charlie would be like hurting myself. Worse, even.

Though I might have to make a choice to save my friends.

Charlie wasn't far from where the others had been. He waited in the trees, being ever still as he listened for any sound of life. The warmness in his brown eyes was gone, replaced with red.

We had a slight advantage. Charlie was blind, and the lichen controlling his body didn't know how to navigate without sight. He wouldn't see us coming, but he would hear us. We had to be quiet.

All of us remained silent. Kallie brought out her fae wings. She began fluttering in a circle around Charlie, planning to creep up on him from behind. Marcus conjured a stunning spell and went in from the side.

I faced Charlie head-on, a blue fireball in my hands. Oberi was beside me. Marcus drew back his spell. I nodded, and Kallie flew forward.

Charlie must've heard the beat of her wings, because he turned on his heel and waved his arm. A tree limb shot out and punched her backward. Kallie gave a sound of pain as she was slapped against a tree trunk. She slumped against it, unconscious.

Marcus let out a cry when he saw Kallie pass out. He flung out his stunning spell, but Charlie emitted such a powerful gust of wind that it caught Marcus' ball of electricity and sent it spiraling back at him. Marcus' own spell smacked him in the chest, and his eyes rolled backward as he knocked himself out.

Fucking great. Both my allies were down. A wave of terror ran through me, and that's when Charlie turned back around in my direction.

I hadn't made any noise, and he couldn't see me… how could he realize I was right there?

Then I felt a nauseating expression of bloodthirst radiate from Charlie, and I realized… our bond. Charlie had felt my fear. He knew I was right in front of him.

Charlie cut through the air with his palm, and I flattened myself against the ground. A shockwave of Air so powerful blasted over my head, knocking over the trees behind me. Charlie used his Earth power to make the uprooted trees move, their spindly branches reaching for me like fingers.

If those trees got their branches around me, they'd rip me to shreds. I swung my arm outward. Blue fire ignited the branches, and the trees withdrew as their wood burned to ash. I forced myself to my feet before Charlie could make another move.

"I'm just as bullheaded as you, you stubborn bastard," I growled. "And I am *not* letting this monster use you like this."

Charlie sent out another gust of wind, but I rolled out of the way. Oberi came in from the other side and knocked him down. Just as Charlie lost his balance and fell onto his back, I opened the jar and forced the rest of the potion into his mouth.

Charlie coughed and sputtered. The red beam flung past his lips like a beacon, and the last piece of the lichen materialized in front of me. The lichen raised his staff, and red magic pulsed through the air, a crackling noise resonating that threatened to do to us what had been done to the other team.

"Oh, no you don't," I snapped. I shoved my palm outward, and a column of blue fire smashed into the lichen's chest. The lichen dropped his staff, throwing his head back and emitting an inhumane screech.

Sweat ran down my skin as I infused my blue Fire into the lichen's bones, making it spread all throughout his body. The demon's entire form began to glow blue, until the lichen gave one final infernal scream, and I forced my magic outward.

The lichen blew up. Pieces of bone scattered everywhere, pinging off trees, until all that was in the lichen's stead was a dismembered skeleton.

I gave a couple of gasps to recover my breath. Charlie sat up slowly, like he wasn't sure what had just happened.

"Pidge," he said, as if worried the lichen was still here.

"It's over. I got him." I sat back against a tree trunk and allowed myself a five-second break. Damn, that fucker had been hard to beat. But at least we were still alive.

Kallie and Marcus crawled over to us. They'd come around, but moved slowly, as if they were still recovering.

"That was some powerful magic, girl," Kallie said as she leaned on Marcus.

"Don't thank me. Thank Alice and her team," I said. "They gave me the cauldron to brew that potion. Without them, we'd probably all be dead."

"Pidge," Charlie said again. It was like that was all he could say. He leaned forward, and I put my head against his. He was still trembling.

Ancestors, I was so fucking glad he was alive. We'd gotten lucky this time.

Oberi gave a whine, and Charlie reached out a hand to pet him. Rishi sat at our feet and lashed his tail, playing with one of the pieces of the lichen's bones.

I heard the sound of the drone again, coming down from the sky. Marcus, Kallie and I looked up as the screen emerged from the drone, and Professor Hemlock's visage appeared before us.

"Well done," she praised. "For defeating the lichen, your team has earned ten points, tying you up with two other rivals."

The rankings flashed on screen, and my blood ran cold. There were only four teams left—ours, Mad Dog's, the gang leader's, and Alice's group of innocents.

The rest hadn't made it through the night.

With another glance at the points, I realized we were tied up with Mad Dog and Alice. The gang leader's team had fallen so far behind, there was no way for him to catch up.

Professor Hemlock's face appeared on screen again. "There is but one monster left to defeat. Stay vigilant. Stay alive."

The screen shut off, and the drone hovered away. A chill wracked my body as I realized our only option.

We were tied with two other teams. There was only one monster left... one way to gain more points. If we wanted to earn our pardon, and win the Games, we had to find the final monster, and kill it before anyone else.

It was our last shot at getting out of here.

charlie
TWENTY-THREE

My shoulders sagged. Only one monster left. That was good news. But it also meant one more battle with my teammates, and I didn't know how much more we could handle. We'd barely slept, and our meal last night was hardly a meal. Each of my teammates had been in mortal danger more than once. I couldn't handle losing even one of them. I just couldn't.

Get it together, Charlie. The voice in my head was my own, but the feeling had come from Oberi. She was in unicorn form, ready to take on the final monster. She nudged me with her velvet nose, nuzzling into my shoulder. The energy she emitted was calming and sure.

I stroked her nose. She was right. I had to get it together and lead my team through our final battle. All we had to do was kill one more monster, and we'd be free of the Institute. Ava-Marie and I would be free to pursue information about the prophecy. Marcus could go home and resume teaching his mentee. Kallie would have a chance to see her family again and make amends. It didn't seem to matter what shape we were in. The rewards were far too great. We'd do anything to win those points.

"Which way, Captain?" Marcus asked as Ava and I got to our feet.

I sighed and titled my head to the side, listening to the sounds of Shade Hills. The morning sun touched my skin, but it felt dull and cold, like there was a thick layer of clouds in front of it. The island was eerily quiet. I was so used to the bustle of the city. Even in the Institute, mornings were filled with slamming doors and the thump of footsteps as students hurried to class. Out here at the edge of the forest, there was nothing... not even the chirp of birds. It was as if the wildlife was terrified of what hid in the woods.

"I don't know," I admitted. "The monster could be anywhere on the island."

"I told you before," Kallie said, "monsters seek out prey. We have to go back to Shade Hills."

"Are you sure that's *all* monsters?" Ava asked. "If it's terrorizing the town, where are the screams? Where's the sound of destruction?"

Kallie thought about it for a moment. "Maybe it's waiting for its victims, so it can catch them off-guard."

"Either way, that means we have to head back toward town," I decided.

"I agree with the Captain," Marcus said. "We only have one chance to get to this thing first and win those points. We have to give it our best shot."

"Then let's move." I placed my hand on Oberi's back, and she navigated us toward the main road. The air expanded, and the drone above hummed. I paid close attention to the sounds around us, focused solely on spotting any signs of the monster.

"It would've been helpful if they told us what type of monster we were up against—" Marcus said, but I held up a hand to cut him off.

"Shh… I heard something," I hissed.

We all froze and listened intently, but we were only met with silence.

"What did you hear?" Ava breathed.

"Something like a stick breaking," I answered. "It's at least twenty yards off, but close—"

A figure leapt from out of the trees. I could tell by the way it moved through the air that it was about my size— a little bigger. It growled like a human. If I was supposed to be scared, I wasn't.

Marcus yelped, and Rishi hissed.

"Don't move!" a deep voice warned. That's when I realized this wasn't the monster at all. It was Mad Dog.

Another figure stepped out of the trees, though her footsteps were lighter. "Take another step, and you're dead," Naya threatened. "That monster is ours."

Ava took a confident step forward. "Oh, yeah? And you two are going to stop the four of us?"

Naya's teeth ground together. "Turn around, and go back to the Institute."

To my surprise, Marcus followed her instructions. His boots clunked loudly on the road as he walked away from us. I was quick to grab him. "We're not going anywhere! Marcus, don't quit on me now."

"He's not quitting on you," Kallie seethed. "Naya's compelling him!"

The blood drained from my face. Within the Institute, succubi wore low-powered noxite bracelets so they couldn't compel the guards. Out here, they had no such restrictions.

"It should be working on all *four* of you!" Naya yelled. "Turn back! You're not taking that monster from us."

Ava just laughed. "You have to be *powerful* to compel another supernatural. You can't brainwash all four of us at once."

"Do as she says," Mad Dog sneered, but nobody listened. He was only a vampire and didn't have the extra powers of an incubus or succubus. I'd learned from the other inmates that succubi like Naya were basically vampires on steroids. They were superior to vampires because of their power of compulsion.

But Naya's compulsion wasn't strong enough. It wasn't something the Institute taught or allowed her to practice.

I slapped Marcus a few times to get him to come back to us. After a third slap, he shook his head.

Mad Dog let out a heavy sigh, though there was satisfaction in his tone. "It looks like we're going to have to do this the hard way."

Kallie shrieked and jumped backward, almost toppling over Marcus and me. "He's got a knife!"

He must've found one at a checkpoint. Mad Dog moved at an inhuman speed, so fast that the air billowed behind him. He aimed for the girls first. I threw out my hands, and a gust of wind blasted him backward onto his ass. Satisfying as hell.

I stalked forward, planting myself in front of the girls so he couldn't get to them. "You really want to have this fight again?"

Mad Dog laughed as he got to his feet. "Gladly. Because this time, I'll win."

"Like hell!" I conjured up another blast of air, but Mad Dog moved so fast that it never reached him. He dodged around it and tackled me to the ground. The blade he held sliced through the air. I caught his wrist before the dagger could cut my face, though I felt the point of the knife against my cheek.

Hell, he was strong. I had to use my Air powers to press against him. Sweat broke out on my brow. Oberi whined, and I was sure Ava called out my name, but I couldn't make sense of the scuffle going on nearby. Naya was attacking my friends. I was sure of it. But all I could focus on was the blade hovering a mere inch from my nose.

"I won't get points for killing you," Mad Dog sneered. "But it will be worth it, you filthy Elementai."

"In your fucking dreams," I snapped. I gathered enough energy to create another blast of wind. Mad Dog went flying off of me, flipping several times as he flew through the air.

I scrambled to my feet just in time to hear the unfolding of wings. At first, I thought it was Kallie, but these wings weren't the small, delicate ones Kallie had. They were heavy and leathery, like a bat's.

The succubus. She had freaking *wings*!

Kallie laughed, and then came the buzz of her insect-like wings. "You think flying makes you stronger, Naya? I'll kick your ass in the air and be proud of it."

"Be my guest." Naya chuckled.

The two took off to the skies. I was ready to knock Naya out of the air with my magic, but Mad Dog was on the move again. Marcus screeched as he dove for him, and Ava conjured a fireball. It hit Mad Dog, but didn't slow him down. The buzz of a battle orb sounded as it erupted from Marcus' hands. Mad Dog tripped, but he was on his feet again in moments.

How the hell did you fight a vampire? We could match his strength and speed with our magic, but he was freaking immortal.

I wasn't here to kill the other teams, though. Our only goal was to kill that monster— and kill it first.

I conjured roots from the ground. If I couldn't kill Mad Dog, slowing him down was the next best thing. He tripped as my roots wrapped around his legs. His heavy body shook the earth as he landed, and the dagger skidded across the ground. Mad Dog let out a pained cry as the roots tugged on his legs.

"We have to get out of here!" I cried.

Ava already had another fireball blazing in her hand. "It's not going to do anything, pidge," I told her as I hoisted her onto Oberi's back. "Let's go!"

I reached up to knock Naya out of the sky with my Air, but Oberi grabbed my collar in her teeth and threw me onto her back. She took off running. I was only half on, and had to dig my fingers into her coat to keep from falling off.

"Oberi!" I yelled, heart pounding. We couldn't leave the others behind! The trees rustled around us as we raced through the woods. I couldn't tell how far we'd gone.

"*Oberi!*" I repeated.

Ava must've tugged on Oberi's mane, because the unicorn slowed to a trot. I groaned as I pulled myself onto her fully and sat behind Ava.

Ava's tone was hollow. "We lost Marcus and Kallie."

My head swiveled from side to side as I listened for his clumsy footsteps or the sound of Kallie's paws, but they never came. Even the sound of the drone was gone.

"They shouldn't be far behind," I said, more to myself than to Ava. I was sure Marcus and Kallie could handle the vampire and succubus themselves, but they shouldn't have to.

"We have to go back," I ordered Oberi.

Oberi spun, and she stomped in place.

"What is it, girl?" I demanded. "Let's go!"

Oberi didn't move.

"Shit, we're lost," I realized. "Why'd you take off, girl?"

"I think she got spooked," Ava said, stroking Oberi's fur softly. "We'll find them. Marcus and Kallie can handle those pricks."

"I know that," I stated, though my confidence wavered. Marcus had proven himself in the Games, and Kallie had long before that. But there were more to the Games than the other teams. They might not make it if they ran into the monster alone. We had to find them— and fast.

"Any idea where we came from?" I asked Ava. I hadn't been paying close enough attention.

"It all looks the same to me," she admitted.

"Oberi, come on," I pleaded. "Your sense of direction has been infallible until now."

Oberi nickered and shook her head, like she wasn't quite sure she deserved the compliment. She'd spun in so many circles, I couldn't find my bearings.

"Let's continue straight ahead," Ava suggested.

I'd been thinking the same thing, but it was unusual for Ava and I to have the same idea. Usually, we disagreed on everything. "Why that way?" I asked.

"I don't know…" she said slowly. "It just feels right."

I nodded. "That way it is, then."

I couldn't explain it, but something about it felt right to me, too.

Oberi didn't run this time. She took slow, deliberate steps. I listened carefully to the forest. Like earlier, the wildlife was quiet, but there was something that seemed to hum out in the distance. A waterfall, perhaps?

No, that wasn't right. This was less like a sound in my ears and more like an energy buzzing through me— like the high-pitched hum of a television.

Oberi walked farther, and the hum grew. Ava gasped. She reeled backward so fast I had to catch her to keep her from falling off Oberi's back.

"What is it?" I asked.

"I-I don't know how to explain it," Ava said breathlessly.

"Is it bad?" I questioned. Her tone was one of shock, but otherwise difficult to read.

"No," she replied. "It's… beautiful. There's a clearing ahead, but it's small enough that the canopy covers the whole thing— all except a small opening in the center. The sun is shining down onto this… Charlie, I can't explain it. Come see for yourself."

Oberi stopped, and Ava slid off her back. I was too curious to stay away. Whatever it was Ava saw, I *felt*. There was beauty and wonder here, permeating deep into my bones.

"Is this an illusion?" I asked. I couldn't imagine feeling this way on Darke Island. This wasn't the place for wonders. And yet it felt so real.

"This is real," Ava assured me.

She took my hand and led me forward. My Air magic met a block in the center of the forest, but I couldn't make sense of what it was. Ava guided my hand forward and placed it upon a rock. The rock was cool to the touch, but there was warmth to it, too— as if some sort of life force flowed straight through it. I was accustomed to the energy of the earth through my powers, but this was stronger. I didn't know what it meant.

I ran my hands over the rock. It was a wall, each stone placed expertly to fit together. As I began walking down the wall, it grew taller, until I couldn't reach the top. I moved my hands over the face of the wall, and the texture became smooth. It wasn't a rock at all. I would've guessed it was wood, but it seemed to emit a different energy signature than the trees.

"What is it?" I asked Ava.

"It's some sort of stone gate," Ava said in wonder. "There's a round wooden door right in the center. It's *sooo* pretty."

I could feel what she was talking about. As my hands moved over the door, I noticed it was intricately carved, obviously the work of a skilled craftsman. My fingers met cool metal, which outlined a hole in the door. I continued feeling and counted seven holes.

"What are these?" I asked. "Key holes?"

"That's what they look like," Ava said, leaning closer to the door.

"Why would a door need *seven* locks?" I wondered. "And in the middle of the forest, no less. What's on the other side?"

"Let's see…" Ava's footsteps shuffled through the underbrush as she rounded the stone gate. "There's nothing over here."

"So this door leads nowhere," I said.

"You're thinking with your human brain," Ava accused. "Think from a supernatural perspective."

"Oh," I realized. "You think it's a portal?"

"A door that leads to nowhere? You bet." Ava returned to my side and brushed her hands over the carvings. "What I want to know is what these runes mean."

"Runes?" I asked. "It's not just art?"

"No," Ava said. "They're letters of some sort, but I can't tell which language. It's old for sure. Maybe Arcanean, but something about this doesn't quite look fae."

Her voice mingled with surprise. "You know what? These are the same runes that we saw on the abandoned ships, and on the bow in the cave we found. I didn't realize this before, but I think these are Elvish."

My eyebrows shot up. "Elvish? I thought the Elves died out."

"Only a hundred years ago," Ava pointed out. "Who knows how long this door has been here?"

"So, what does this mean?" I asked. I sensed it had to be significant, but I didn't know how.

"I have no idea," Ava admitted. "I could be wrong about the portal. It could just be part of an old building that collapsed."

"Well, whatever it was, it seemed pretty important to need *seven* keys," I emphasized.

"You're right…" Ava said thoughtfully. "Too bad we don't have those keys."

Her curiosity was getting to her bad. I could hear it in her tone.

"We're not going to figure it out in the middle of the Games," I pointed out. "I'm sure it's nothing."

"I disagree. This is important." Ava stomped her foot and crossed her arms. She got so close to me, I could feel the heat of her skin. She thought she was exercising her dominance. *How cute.*

I frowned. "It doesn't matter right now, because we're supposed to be looking for Kallie and Marcus. We can investigate this weird ass door once we win the games."

Ava inched closer to me. "Who are you to say it doesn't matter?"

"I'm team Captain," I stated, closing the distance between us. I liked how close we were— like last night in the cabin. It made me want to reach out and grab her… make her mine.

I shouldn't have been thinking about that right now. I should've had my mind on one thing — finding my teammates. But Ava was right… there was something weird about this door. And finding it with her felt like we had one more secret to share. I *liked* sharing secrets with Ava.

"And I suppose the team *Captain* always gets his way," Ava challenged.

I smirked. "Now you understand."

Ancestors, this girl infuriated me sometimes. She drove me crazy when she'd gone against my orders and nearly gotten Kallie killed. She could be a real pain in the ass.

And yet... all I wanted was to save her. I was so torn. I barely understood what I was doing in the Games to begin with. Was it all for Ava? Or is that just what I'd told myself?

Ava must've been staring me down, because she didn't say anything for several long seconds. "So, what is the team Captain's plan?"

"I'm gonna kiss you." I heard the words come out of my mouth, but I hadn't planned on saying them. I wanted to take them back, but more than anything, I wanted to hear her response.

Ava's breath wavered. "Is that so?"

I nodded firmly. "It is."

"Then do it."

It was a challenge— that much was clear. Ava didn't think I would. *I* didn't think I would.

And yet my body betrayed me.

Before I could make sense of what was happening, I pressed my lips to hers. When her mouth touched mine, my whole world flipped on end. It was as if we weren't fighting in the Games anymore. There wasn't a deadly monster roaming the forest, nor a battle waiting for us as a ticket to our freedom. Right here beside Ava-Marie, I'd already found freedom a hundred times over. Air magic might as well have swept under my feet and carried me into the clouds, because I was flying. Beneath me, the earth was totally still and tranquil, like it'd been waiting a thousand years just for us to make this kiss.

Ava drew away far too soon, breathless. "I didn't expect you to—"

I couldn't think. I swooped down and kissed her again, cutting her off. All I wanted was to kiss her again, because when her lips were pressed against mine, all felt right in the world. Earth, Water, Fire and Air were all within balance and in perfect harmony.

Magic surged through me as my heart raced, and air swirled around us, rustling leaves all the way up into the canopy. The forest spun around me, and my knees grew weak. Oberi had to be watching nearby, but she totally fell from my mind, because nothing else existed but Ava.

Ava's lips were soft and sweet— intoxicating. I wrapped my arms around her body, pulling her small frame close to me. My pants tightened, and I was sure she could feel me against her. But I didn't care. She should know how I felt about her— like how she'd felt it last night.

All that mattered were her lips. She parted them, and my tongue slid into her mouth. The tip of my tongue rolled over something hard that tasted metallic.

A tongue ring.

I'd never given much thought to piercings, but on Ava, it was fucking hot. I couldn't control it when my hands went into her hair and cradled the back of her neck. She let out a breath, and her whole body sagged in my arms. Her hands moved over me, sending tingles over every inch of my body.

We pulled away only to catch our breath. It should've felt unnatural to kiss Ava, but it hadn't. It felt *right*.

And still, Ava stepped away from me, crushing my balls and my heart all in one swift move.

"We shouldn't have done that," Ava said quickly. "It's the excitement of the tournament... right?"

Ava was looking for my answer. She wanted me to say the same, that it was all in the heat of the moment. And I almost did, just to placate her.

But I couldn't lie.

"Pidge," I sighed. "If that's not what you wanted, I'm sorry. But I needed to know."

"Know what?" she asked hesitantly.

I stepped closer to her and reached out my fingers to run across her skin. "I needed to know if I was doing this for the right reasons."

She gulped. "Doing what? For what reasons?"

"Everything," I told her. "This tournament. Helping you with the prophecy once we win."

"And?" Ava asked, sounding hopeful.

"And I am," I said, though my voice wavered when I admitted it out loud. "I don't want to keep worrying about if I'm going to die young. If I do, it'll be worth it, because it will be for *you*."

Ava jerked away from me. She sounded horrified. "I don't want you dying for me! If you think you have to, I don't want your help with the prophecy!"

My stomach sank. "That's not what I meant, pidge. We're part of the same soul. I *have* to fight for you. And if we don't win the Games, so what? The fight was worth it."

"You *have* to?" she asked, sounding slightly offended.

Hell, what had I said?

"I'm not *obligated*," I quickly clarified. "I *choose* to. You're not just some fashion-centric Cali-girl like the persona you give off. You're so much more than that. You care about others, even when you act like you don't."

Ava opened her mouth to protest, but I cut her off.

"You can stop pretending around me," I told her. "I know you like to act like some badass chick who doesn't give a damn about the rules, but your heart is big, pidge. If you didn't care, would you have told me about Monica? Would you have fought so hard for my life— and Marcus and Kalina— while we were possessed by the lichen? Would you have entered this tournament at all? No, you wouldn't, because you're doing this for the prophecy. You're here to save the freaking *world*. I know what selfishness looks like, what it feels like to live day in and day out for only yourself. And you're not it, pidge. You're compassionate and adventurous and strong. You got all the good parts of our soul, and I'm *proud* to say I share a soul with you. And that's why I'm here, why I'm going to help you decode the prophecy. Because you care so much about everyone else. It's time that someone cares about you, too, Ava-Marie."

Ava had been silent the whole time I spoke. Though she stood right next to me, I couldn't read her at all. She'd gone as still as a statue.

It made me nervous. *I should take it all back.* But damn, it felt so good to say out loud. Ava had to know all this. She was worthy of knowing someone cared.

"Damn it, pidge, will you say something?" I demanded.

"You... you called me Ava-Marie," she said breathlessly.

"Yeah, that's your na—"

I was cut off by the warmth of her lips on mine once again, as she kissed me this time. I inhaled a deep breath, drinking in her sweet taste. Ancestors, I could kiss her forever and it wouldn't be enough. My lips parted—

Boom!

A huge explosion went off in the distance, and the earth trembled beneath us. Ava probably hadn't felt it, but my Earth magic buzzed. Ava and I jumped apart, the moment broken.

"Marcus and Kallie!" she cried breathlessly, as if she'd just remembered them.

My heart raced, and I spun around. "Where's Oberi?"

Oberi's hooves crunched sticks beneath her as she trotted over to us.

"Come on, girl. Time to go," Ava said as she swung herself onto Oberi's back. I jumped on behind her, and we took off through the forest in the direction of the explosion.

Voices came from up ahead, but they seemed closer than the explosion had been. Oberi slowed briefly as we passed by. The voices quieted.

"What's going on?" I asked lowly.

"It's one of the other teams," Ava said. "The gang who's in last place. They're just sitting in the middle of the forest, like they've given up."

"They have no chance of winning," I remarked. "It's better for them to keep their team alive. Let's keep moving."

Oberi sped up again, and we broke out of the trees and back onto the main road.

"How close are we to town?" I asked.

"Close," Ava replied. "I can see it from here."

"Any signs of the explosion?"

Ava was pressed so close to me I felt her moving her head around. "I don't see— ancestors!"

I heard the sounds of footsteps the same time Ava cursed. They were fast, like a few people were sprinting, along with a small animal. Ancestors, this better be my team.

Ava jumped off Oberi's back. "Marcus! Kallie! What happened?"

They slowed beside us, and Marcus heaved to catch his breath. "We knocked out Mad Dog and Naya. Our fight must've attracted the monster, because it came after us."

"And the explosion?" I questioned. "Did you kill it?"

Kallie laughed maniacally. "I tried. Biggest damn battle orb I ever conjured. But it didn't hardly touch it."

"What are we up against?" Ava asked in a rush.

"I'm not sure," Kallie admitted. "Nothing I've ever seen before. It's huge and ugly, like a troll, but it doesn't have any eyes. I think it hunts by smell and sound."

The ground began to shake, though the others didn't seem to notice. Each tremble came in even intervals… like footsteps.

"The monster's coming," I realized. I quickly jumped into Captain mode. "Kallie's battle orb didn't hurt it, which means we'll have to get creative. Blunt force isn't going to win us this fight. Kallie, can you create a trap with your illusion magic? Something to hold the monster down long enough for us to find its weakness and target it?"

"I can," she said confidently.

"And it'll be strong enough to become reality?"

Kallie cracked her fingers. "Now's not the time to underestimate me, Captain."

"Get to work, then," I ordered. "Anyone want to volunteer as bait?"

Marcus sighed. "That sounds like a job for a warlock."

I clapped him on the shoulder. "Don't worry. We'll be right here to back you up."

"Just don't let me get crushed by this thing," he said. "Or I'll haunt you from the afterlife."

I laughed, which felt a little unnatural in the middle of the Games, but it felt good, too. "If you don't haunt me, this was never a true friendship."

The ground trembled again, so hard this time that Ava stumbled into me. I grabbed her hand. "Let's go."

Ava and I ducked into the trees, along with Oberi and Rishi. Kallie was further down the road, creating an illusion to trap our troll friend. The ground shook, and a mighty roar erupted from the monster's mouth as he came around the bend in the road. As my Air magic reached out, I couldn't get a sense of what the creature looked like, only that it was huge— at least two stories tall.

"Hey, you ugly troll!" Marcus called. Rocks clinked against the monster's tough skin as Marcus threw them to get the monster's attention. "Over here!"

The creature grunted, and his heavy footsteps followed Marcus as he took off sprinting down the road.

"Ancestors," Ava breathed.

"What is it, pidge?"

"*Troll* was an apt description," she said. "But trolls aren't real. This is different. It's like a giant ogre, with skin that looks like rock. It doesn't have any eyes, just slits for its nose and ears. I swear I learned about them somewhere, but I can't remember. Come on, we're up."

Ava tugged on my arm, and we took off running. Marcus was already a ways down the road, still yelling at the monster and luring him toward Kallie's trap.

"Kallie's made a pit in the ground," Ava said as we ran. "Get ready with your magic. It's almost there."

I sensed the lightweight beat of Kallie's wings in the air as she swooped down to grab Marcus out of the way of the trap. "Now!" she screamed.

Ava and I reacted at once. I thrust out a blast of Air, and Ava shot a huge fireball at the monster. I felt the monster teeter beneath my magic, then came the sound of a loud *crash* as it fell into the pit.

"It's in!" Ava cried. "Kallie's creating ropes to hold it down."

Ava and I skidded to a halt near the edge of the pit. The sound of snapping ropes met my ears.

"That's not going to be enough!" I immediately used my Air to press the monster back into the pit, but he was strong and resisted me. I turned to Earth magic and made roots grow over top of the pit, but I couldn't create them fast enough. The monster snapped them as fast as I could create them.

"It's too strong for our magic," Ava breathed. "Oh, Great Spirit."

"What?" I demanded. The sheer horror in her tone was impossible to miss.

"Kallie's ropes are turning against her!" she screamed.

All the blood drained from my face. "How's that possible?"

"Fuck," Ava growled. "I remember where I learned about this monster. We used the hair of a deceptem demon in alchemy to brew illusion potions. It's more dangerous than we realized!"

"Kallie," I called to the other side of the pit. "Drop the illusion!"

"I can't!" she screamed, which quickly turned into sounds of pain. Marcus cried out from beside her, and I knew the ropes had them both. The monster had manipulated the illusion, so the magic worked for him instead.

"We have to give it all we've got!" I insisted.

"I thought you said brute force wouldn't work," Ava replied.

Hell, I didn't know what I was doing anymore. I didn't even know what a deceptem demon was. How the hell was I supposed to know how to fight it? "We have to try!"

Ava conjured fireballs, but they were cool in temperature beside me. Oberi shifted into husky form, and together we used our Earth magic to lift large boulders and throw them into the pit on top of the monster.

But neither of our magic was any use. The pavement cracked beneath our feet, and the deceptem groaned as it pulled itself out of the pit.

"How do you kill one of these things?" I asked, heart racing.

"I don't know!" Ava cried. "We didn't learn that."

I thrust another blast of Air at the creature, but the air swirled around it instead of impacting like I'd planned. The deceptem drew a heavy arm back, interrupting the air flow. I knew what was coming and didn't have time to get out of the way. I acted on instinct and shoved Ava to the ground. Instead of hitting her, the demon's arm swung out to meet my chest. I was thrown off my feet and soared through the air. I quickly gathered air around me to slow my fall, but I still landed on my ass with a hard *thud*. Fuck, that hurt.

The wind had been knocked out of me, but I knew I had to move. I scrambled to my feet, but before I could get upright, the most sickening sound met my ears. It was a rough, harsh *snap* that stopped the world from spinning—

And it'd come from right where Ava had been.

Something hit the ground... a sound I could only guess was a body.

I heard nothing. No screams. No cries of pain. Just my own pulse pumping in my ears.

"*Ava!*" I wailed. My voice echoed across the landscape.

Slowly, sound came back into focus. Marcus and Kallie screamed as the deceptem took heavy steps toward them. Magic whizzed through the air, but I couldn't focus enough to join in on the fight.

I raced over to where I thought Ava was. Oberi's hooves clicked on the pavement, and she blew a distressed breath. I knew she had to be standing over Ava.

I fell to my knees as my heart dropped out of my chest. Tremors went up my legs as I landed hard on the road. I barely felt them. All the pain was in my chest, tearing me apart from the inside out. I felt around, and my fingers met Ava's body. She was still, and her skin was cold to the touch.

"Pidge," I sobbed as tears began running down my face. I hoisted her into my lap, cradling her lifeless body. Her neck hung over my arm at an odd angle, and a warm, sticky liquid stuck to me all over.

Blood.

My whole body shook as I pushed the hair back from her face. I was acutely aware of each contour of her features. She was so beautiful. How had this happened so fast? Why hadn't I saved her?

I pulled her closer to my chest, trembling as I held my very soul in my arms. I wished that she would move... but she didn't. The troll had broken her neck... ended her life in one blow.

"I'm so sorry, pidge," I sobbed into her hair.

Oberi leaned down to nudge me. I expected her to show some goddamn emotion, but she bit my collar and tried to drag me upright. Rishi dug his claws into my leg.

I shrugged Oberi off. "Forget it. It's not worth it anymore. Not without my pidge."

Oberi stomped, pacing back and forth. She whinnied loudly, as if trying to get me to listen.

But I didn't care what she had to say. Ava-Marie was gone— her life force severed.

So why did it feel like she was waiting for something?

I felt it through the bond, frustration like I'd never felt from Ava before. Was it possible we were still connected, even if she was in the afterlife? And what was she so *mad* about?

Hold on. Ava and I shared a soul, along with Oberi. Which meant that if one of us died, we all did.

The tears halted in their tracks as realization hit. Slowly, I lifted my head. Ava had said they'd used deceptem hair for illusion potions, and the monster had managed to take control of Kallie's illusion. That's what Ava meant when she said it was more dangerous than we realized. This monster was fucking with our heads!

Oberi nudged me again and bit my ear.

"Ow! Fuck!" I cried, slapping a hand over my ear. After a moment for the shock to slip away, I turned to Oberi. "It's an illusion, isn't it? That's what you're trying to tell me?"

As soon as I said it, Ava's voice broke through. Her dead body was still wrapped in my arms, but her voice came from several paces away.

"No shit it's an illusion!" Ava-Marie snapped. "That's what makes deceptem demons dangerous! Now get up and help me! This deceptem is not going down easy."

My heart swelled, and the body vanished from my lap. I jumped to my feet and ran over to Ava— the *real* Ava. I threw my arms around her and drew her in close. "You're alive!"

Ava shrugged me off. "Of course I am. You don't think I'm going down without a fight, do you? What'd this bastard make you see?"

I swallowed the lump in my throat and answered quickly. "Nothing."

Ava threw another fireball. "Then help me!"

It took me a moment to take in the scene. The deceptem was smashing his heavy hands into the ground away from us— probably aimed at Kallie and Marcus. Its back was to us, so Ava and I had the advantage.

My nostrils flared. "Give it everything you've got."

"On it, Captain."

The air began to dry out around me as Ava drew water out of it. The water formed into a huge ball above our heads, sloshing like a swimming pool suspended in mid-air. I uprooted trees and used my Air magic to levitate them, shooting them at the monster at high speed. They cracked and splintered against his hard skin, but he roared like they hurt. Finally, I was getting somewhere.

"It's no use!" Marcus wailed. "Ava's gone. We're going to die, too!"

I realized they'd seen the same thing I had, and they hadn't broken through the illusion yet.

"Listen to me!" I yelled over the sound of magic whizzing through the air. Ancestors, I hoped they could hear me, because they were pretty far away. "Ava's not dead! It's an illusion demon!"

I could hear Kallie's sobs from here. My teammates kept fighting, but only to hang on to dear life. They sounded about ready to give up.

"Kallie!" I screamed. "It's not real!"

"Are you sure?" she cried.

"Yes, Ava's standing right next to me!" I told her. "We have a chance. We can still win this thing. But he's playing with our heads. We have to take away his greatest weapon. Can you do that?"

"I can try!" she responded, before yelping as another one of the monster's attacks came.

I threw another heavy tree branch at it, and this time, I felt it continue past his strong exterior, sinking into soft flesh. The creature roared.

"Right in the ear!" Ava said proudly.

The deceptem whirled on us.

"Get down!" Ava called.

I followed her instructions immediately and flattened myself to the ground. Oberi and Ava did the same on either side of me, and Rishi hissed. The demon's arm swept over top of us, and heavy winds billowed my hair.

"I've broken the illusion!" Kallie screamed at us. "Its mind games are over!"

That meant brute force was our last option. Maybe if I could get another branch in its ear, it'd do some real damage.

I didn't have time to come up with a plan. The ground shook as the deceptem took another step toward us.

"Charlie, what do we do!?" Ava screamed.

I ripped another tree from the ground, but it was bigger than the others. It took all I had to thrust it up into the air. But I had no point of reference for aiming. The log clunked off the top of the deceptem's head, and I knew that I'd missed.

"Run!" I didn't want to run from a fight, but staying here was a good way to get killed. We had to stay alive long enough to fight this thing.

Ava and I grabbed hands. We ducked into the trees, and she guided me as we started running toward Shade Hills. The monster followed, along with the sound of falling trees as he barreled his way through the forest. He was getting closer…

I was starting to formulate a plan, a way to lose the monster, but I never got the chance to share it with Ava. She yelped and was dragged upward, her hand slipping from mine. Oberi cried out in horror.

"*Charlie!*" Ava screamed, and I knew the deceptem had gotten her.

I whipped out blasts of air so narrow and fast it should've chopped the deceptem's arm off, but then held them back at the last second. I didn't want to hurt Ava. I had to keep on running, because the demon was still barreling toward me, and if I stopped I'd be crushed.

I sent another blast of air outward and thought I'd hit one of the deceptem's legs, then— *thwack!*

I hadn't been paying attention to where I was going. My whole body slammed into something hard, so much that I bounced backward and landed on my ass. My head spun, and I couldn't make sense of which way was up and which way was down. My ribs ached from whatever I'd run into, and my pulse thumped in my ears.

Oberi yanked me to my feet, but I was still coming to. As the world came back into focus, I realized something was off. I didn't know what it was at first.

Then I noticed the vibrations of the deceptem's footsteps were farther away, and getting even farther. It was leaving with Ava!

I stumbled forward and caught myself on a wall— the one I'd run into. It was a building, probably a house judging by the feel of the siding. We'd reached the outskirts of Shade Hills.

I gasped shallow breaths as I tried to find my bearings. *Ava's still alive*, I told myself. I could feel it in our bond.

Oberi made a loud noise in my ear, and I snapped back to attention. I quickly jumped onto her back and kicked her sides. "Follow that monster!"

Oberi found the main road quickly. I could hear Marcus and Kallie shouting in the distance, along with the hum of the drone overhead.

"Gods, Ava!" Kallie screamed as Oberi and I rushed to them. We came to a skidding halt beside Marcus and Kallie.

"What's happening!?" I demanded.

"Ava burned it to get away. The monster's chasing Ava up an apartment building. She's using the fire escape," Marcus said breathlessly. Rishi yowled loudly in worry.

Part of me feared for her. The other felt immensely proud. She'd escaped the demon's hold on her own. *That's my pidge.*

"How are we going to defeat it?" Marcus asked. "This monster is impenetrable."

"It has to have a weakness," Kallie insisted. "They always do."

"Its ears," I said. "One of my branches stuck in, but not far enough. If we can stab it with something else, there's no way it can survive."

"How do we get something in there?" Kallie asked.

I didn't have the luxury of thinking it through too long. "We need another trap— a bigger one this time," I decided. "Let's get to Ava first."

No sooner had we started forward did I hear the sound of crushing rock. Kallie screamed, and the first of the pebbles rained down on me. I threw my hands up on instinct and caught several large rocks with my Earth magic before they crushed us.

"What was that?" I asked in a clipped tone.

"Piece of building," Marcus answered. "The monster's trying to climb to get to Ava. Bricks are everywhere!"

My guts twisted. "And the people inside?"

"Looks like a new development," Kallie quickly explained. "It's not finished yet. I bet there's no one inside."

That was a relief, but it didn't do anything for rescuing Ava. Another crushing sound came, but this time, I couldn't control all the bricks coming at us. There were too many, and the bricks were too large.

"Ah!" Kallie screamed as one of the larger chunks smashed her into the ground. "My wings! Gods, my wings!"

Marcus rushed to her side and groaned as he tried moving the heavy piece of building. I jumped in with my Earth magic and moved it out of the way. It wasn't entirely made of earth, but there was enough rock inside the brick that I could control it.

"Goddess, Kallie," Marcus breathed as he knelt beside her.

Kallie whimpered in pain, and I hesitated. I didn't ask, but I knew Kallie's wings had to be crushed.

"I've got this," Marcus told me. "Make sure Ava's okay."

He didn't have to tell me twice. I whirled back around toward the building the demon was trying to scale. I could tell by the sound of crumbling brick that he was struggling to climb. I searched for Ava with my magic and found hot pockets of air. Those would be her fireballs.

"Ava!" I called up to her.

"I'm fine!" she called back— she had to be a hundred feet up. "Charlie, you have to level the building!"

"What!?" I screamed. "Not with you up there."

"You'll catch me with your Air," she insisted. Fireballs continued to whiz out of her hands.

I summoned an air stream to try knocking the monster off the side of the building, but he held on tight. I'd barely summoned half the power I'd intended. I swayed on my feet and grabbed Oberi to steady myself.

"I can't!" I yelled up at her. "My magic's wearing thin."

"You can do it, Charlie," she promised. "I *know* you can!"

Leveling the building was the smart thing to do. It would crush the demon and pin it down, if it didn't kill it. We could get our points and win this thing. We would be free of the Institute.

But I couldn't do it at the risk of Ava-Marie's life. I hadn't been able to fly anyone else around during practice. How could I catch her while she was falling through the sky?

"I trust you, Charlie!" Ava called down to me. "Hurry up and do it!"

The decision was impossible to make, until I realized that the only alternative was the monster catching her. It was obviously the kind to play with its prey, but Ava had already escaped its grasp once. It was done playing around. If it got Ava in its grasp again, she'd be dead— no illusion this time.

Fuck, what was I about to do?

I inhaled a deep breath and placed a hand on Oberi's back. "I'm going to need your help."

Oberi instantly shrank to the size of a husky and barked. I blew out the breath I'd been holding and shoved all doubt aside. I couldn't question my magic right now. I had to do this right.

"Here goes nothing…"

My heart hammered as I lifted my hands. At my command, the ground began to shake beneath our feet. It was nothing but tremors at first, but as Ava-Marie's screams grew from above me, power built inside my chest. The tremors grew to earthquake proportions. I forced a hole to open in the ground below the deceptem. It took everything I had, but I pushed myself even further, and my magic broke open the ground. The building began to creak and groan, and I could feel the structural integrity waning with each sway of the earth.

This was unlike any magic I'd ever done before. I'd never cast a spell on anything bigger than a tree. This was a fucking apartment complex. I wasn't sure I could do it.

And still, I pushed my magic as hard as I could, because it was my only choice. I had one chance to get Ava out of the deceptem's grasp. I had one chance to finish it off and win the Games. One chance…

Air began to swirl around the apartment complex, and the ground shook so much that it cracked nearby.

"Keep going, Charlie!" Marcus encouraged. "You're almost there!"

I would've told him to shut up and let me concentrate, but I couldn't focus on that right now. All I could do was hone in on my magic.

And I let it snap.

The Air spell I'd conjured blasted forward with tornado-grade speed. I commanded the earth to thrust upward on one end of the building, breaking all structural integrity left. The far wall crumbled, taking the others down like dominoes. The deceptem let out a deep roar as it realized it was going down. The sound of the falling building was deafening— but it wasn't the only one. All along the street, buildings groaned and fell over.

I let gravity do the rest of the work, because I had one goal, and one goal only. *Save pidge.*

Finding her was easy, as if she was tethered to me by a string. She'd jumped off the top of the building just as it began to crumble, and her legs flailed in the air.

Catching her? Not so easy.

I gritted my teeth and prayed to the ancestors that my power would be enough to hold her. Air swirled around her, but she was falling too fast. Fuck, no! I couldn't let this happen!

The urge to protect her swelled within me, and my Air magic burst. A strong gust of wind I didn't even realize I was capable of swept by, swooping my pidge out of the air as she fell.

I sighed in relief when she didn't smash into the ground. Instead, I manipulated the current to carry her toward me, setting her gently on her feet in front of me. All I could do was sweep her up into my arms and hold her tight. I buried my face into her hair, inhaling her sweet scent.

She hugged me back. "I told you that you could do it."

I chuckled in relief as I drew away from her, but all I wanted to do was weep. "You got lucky."

"You were good," she countered. "You trapped the deceptem."

Ava turned to admire my handiwork. The ground was still, and the town seemed eerily quiet.

"We won?" I asked breathlessly.

"Not yet," she replied solemnly. "The monster's under a pile of rubble, but he doesn't look dead yet."

I squared my shoulders. "Then let's kill it."

I walked forward toward the cavern I'd created. Oberi panted at my side, and the two of us worked together to uproot a large tree nearby. We twisted its branches until we formed a point — a massive weapon that would impale the monster straight through.

I lifted my hands—

Then came the sound of approaching footsteps. They were running, but they didn't seem like something to be afraid of. Rather, it sounded as if someone was rushing to our aid.

"Marcus! Kallie!" a girl with a high-pitched voice cried. "Are you okay?"

"We will be, cousin," Marcus replied. "Once we get to the infirmary. This thing is almost over."

Cousin? He could only be talking about one person— the last witch left in the Games.

Voices overlaid one another, and I counted two males and two females. I realized it was the last team. There was Alice, the witch who'd been falsely accused of crimes on her trip to Malovia; Despona, the vampire who'd killed a man trying to kidnap her; Carson, the merman who was framed for stealing an expensive car; and Wesley, the fae shifter who'd attempted to murder the vamp who touched his sister.

Ava grabbed my wrist before I could take the kill shot.

"What is it?" I asked.

"Just wait..." Ava trailed off thoughtfully.

"Pidge, I can't wait for the monster to come to. We have to finish it off and end this."

"I know, but…" Ava hesitated. "Alice's team saved us. They gave me the pot I needed to brew the potion against the lichen. Without them, we'd all be dead. They deserve to win."

I gaped. I'd known how much Ava wanted to win the Games— how much she wanted freedom. To hand the win over was awfully kind…

But it was also why I felt about her the way I did. She may have a criminal record, but she believed in doing the right thing.

And I believed in her.

"What about the prophecy?" I whispered.

"We'll find another way," Ava said. "If we win, I'm still staying here on Darke Island. It doesn't seem fair when the rest of them can get out of here. They *deserve* to go home, Charlie."

Everything I'd ever learned about survival told me to kill that demon and go free. We were so close.

But I hadn't entered the Games hoping to survive. I'd entered them for Ava, and if this was what she wanted, then I would back her up.

"As long as Marcus and Kallie agree," I said. "I won't give up their chance at freedom."

"All right," Ava agreed.

We walked to the other team, who were talking to Marcus and Kallie.

"Are your wings going to heal?" Despona asked, sounding worried.

"They damn well better," Kallie said. She was still on the ground, and Marcus was knelt beside her.

I turned to the other team. "Do you guys mind if we have a moment with our teammates?"

"Not at all," Carson said, and the four of them walked off.

"What's going on?" Kallie asked. "I thought you were going to take care of that thing!"

Ava was the one to answer. "I think we should give the win to the other team."

"What!?" Marcus and Kallie yelped at the same time.

"They're innocent," Ava reminded them.

Marcus sounded skeptical. "Didn't Despona kill a guy?"

"I heard Wesley tried, too," Kallie added.

"They were both in self-defense," Ava argued. "I know how hard we've fought for this, but we're all in the Institute for *real crimes*. We deserve to be here. The other team doesn't. If I took their ticket to freedom… well, I'm just not sure how I could live with that."

Marcus and Kallie were silent, as if contemplating it.

"They helped Ava with the potion that saved our asses," I added. At this point, I didn't even care about what was *fair*. This felt *right*. If Ava and I were going to decode a prophecy to save the world, it started here— with saving the ones we could. "These guys are the good guys. And let's be honest, guys— we're not."

Marcus made a sound of agreement. "Look, if it were any other team, I'd be killing that monster right now to win us points," Marcus said. "But Alice is my cousin— distant, but she's family. Our coven will be better off with her in it than me. I say we give it to them."

Kallie groaned. "You know I hate it when you're right. The Institute is probably the best place for me right now anyway, seeing as I was banished. I try to go back home now, I'll get my head cut off."

"So we're in agreement?" Ava asked.

"Yes," the three of us answered in unison.

Ava breathed a sigh. "Then let's tell them."

She took my hand and called the other team back over.

"What's up?" Despona asked.

"We want you to take the win," Ava told them.

"No way," Alice protested. "You guys found the monster first. This was your fight, and you're the ones who knocked it out. You deserve the points. It's your kill."

"I don't care about the points," Ava said. "This is about who gets to leave the Institute. You guys deserve that."

They stood there in shock, nobody saying anything.

Finally, Alice spoke. "Is your team sure about this?"

I squeezed Ava's hand. "We're sure. The monster has a weak spot near its ears. Pierce it there, and it should be enough to kill it."

Alice sniffled, like she was crying. "You guys have no idea what this means to us. Thank you so much. If there's anything we can do—"

"You can kill the monster before it wakes," Ava interrupted. "Go get those points. It's time for you to win the Games."

Alice squealed and threw her arms around Ava, nearly slapping me in the face as she did. Wesley and Carson both approached me in turn and shook my hand.

"How will we ever repay you?" Despona asked as she hugged Ava.

"Go live good lives once you're out of the Institute," Ava said. "That's all we can ask."

"Thank you," Alice repeated. "You truly don't know what you've done for us."

Ava turned, and we walked back toward Kallie and Marcus. We knelt beside Kallie and began helping her to her feet. I couldn't tell what the other team was doing to kill the monster. All I heard was a commotion that I couldn't make sense of. But it didn't really matter. I was done with the show. All I wanted was to go back home and sleep.

Home.

I chuckled lightly.

"What?" Ava asked.

"I just had the thought that I wanted to go home." I laughed as I draped Kallie's arm over my shoulder. "To the *Institute.*"

"It is our home now," Ava said softly.

"It's a shithole," Kallie teased, but she winced as she moved.

"Yeah," Marcus agreed from the other side of her. "But it's *our* shithole."

Ava snickered. "Our shithole for sure."

Marcus and I hoisted Kallie onto Oberi's back. Everyone stilled as the monster roared loudly from behind us, but the sound was quickly silenced as death overtook him. A single breath blew out of his monstrous nose, and then… nothing.

It didn't matter if I wanted to take back the offer. It was done. The other team had won.

The drone above us whirred as it flew down from the sky. I heard the gates of the Institute creak from beyond as they were opened, and the Warden's delighted voice rang out with the announcement. "Well done to all our teams. We have found our winners of this year's Darke Games. All other competitors must return to the Institute within the hour, or will be escorted back by guards. The winning team may remain in Shade Hills, where they will soon receive their just reward. Congratulations to all our participants, and remember— stay vigilant, stay alive."

As the broadcast ended, I thought the Warden's final farewell was odd. The Darke Games were over. What need was there to continue warning us about survival?

Whatever. It was probably some marketing thing for the Games. It wasn't worth my attention.

I should've been disappointed. We'd put all that effort into the Games, only to lose. But it didn't feel like we'd lost at all. I was walking home with all three of my teammates alive.

Even better… I had Ava.

I called that a win.

ava-marie

TWENTY-FOUR

"Do you think we fucked up, giving up our only shot at getting out?" Kallie asked.

"No. It was the right thing to do."

Kallie and I hurried to get ready for the Villain's Ball inside my dorm room. There was a heavy snowfall outside, coating the grounds and making everything seem magical.

Oberi sat on the bed and panted, wagging his tail as he watched me put the finishing touches on my hair. I set it in a low bun with curls framing my face.

"Since when have we ever been worried about doing the *right thing*?" Kallie sat beside Oberi as she glided on some red lipstick. She was wearing the very revealing dress she'd chosen, and I'd done a blowout on her hair earlier. She looked so hot. Marcus was going to flip.

"We're at the Institute for a reason," I said. "Maybe it's starting to change our bad behavior."

Kallie scoffed. "As if."

I pulled my mother's dress out of the closet. As I slipped it on, Kallie's face softened. "Oh, Ava, it suits you perfectly! Fire and ice."

"It turned out just like I planned it." I smoothed down the skirt and did a twirl. Over the blue dress I'd added layers of red and orange tulle that twisted around the skirt, as well as ruby rhinestones that mingled with the sapphire glitter. It gave the dress the appearance of a plume of fire wrapping around a column of ice, the different fabrics melding together as if I'd cast a spell over them. I really wanted something that symbolized both parts of my magic, and this dress pulled it off.

"No one else is going to have a dress like that at the party. Naya will be so jealous." Kallie snorted.

"She won't be looking at me when she's too busy worrying about you," I said. "You're hotter than she is for sure."

Kallie frowned. "At least all of Naya's parts work correctly. I can't say the same for my wings."

"Are your wings going to heal?" I asked.

"They're on the mend. Should be back to normal in a few weeks. I got very lucky," Kallie said. "But I already miss being able to fly."

"Don't bother with Naya. She's not our problem."

I finished my outfit by fastening the key Mama had given me around my neck. No matter what outfit I was wearing, the key always seemed to compliment it.

I put Oberi's veil on his head, over his ears. He jumped off the bed and threw back his head, parading around like he was a bride on the way to his reception.

"Oberi, you're so obnoxious." I laughed as he struck a pose, sticking out his butt.

There was a knock on the door, and Daddy poked his head inside. He and Mama were here to chaperone for the dance. His face softened when he saw me. "Oh, peanut, you look so beautiful."

"Don't get sentimental on me now," I teased. If Daddy teared up, so would I.

"Your mother and I want a quick word," he said. "It won't take long."

"I'm almost ready," Kallie said. "I'll meet you at the ball."

I nodded, then followed my dad out. Oberi pranced behind me, swinging his head to make the veil swish.

Mama was wearing a red gown that accentuated her figure. She looked so pretty. She never got dressed up anymore. It was nice they were going to the ball, even if they were only chaperoning. She beamed and took my hands as her eyes roamed the dress. "Ava, you are a *vision*. I knew that dress would suit you."

"It's so perfect. Thanks, Mama."

Mama's gaze shone with affection as she gave me a huge hug. "Honey, I'm *so* proud of you. You did the right thing during the Darke Games, giving your win to the other team."

"I figured they deserved it more than we did," I said. "And I think you were right all along. My place is here, at the Institute. Maybe if I stick around, I can get some answers from the school on what the prophecy means."

I stepped away from her. There was a curl dangling in my eyes, so I took my left hand to part it back. Daddy's eyes went upward, to my wrist.

Shit. I realized my mistake a second too late. I tried to hide it away, but Daddy grabbed my wrist and upturned it, exposing the sight of Charlie's name written all over my skin.

Daddy made a tiny noise of horror that would've been very funny in any other situation. Mama appeared smugger than I'd ever seen her.

"Ava, what did you do?" Daddy whimpered. His voice was high-pitched.

I went to unbury myself before this hole could get bigger. "Ancestors, it's no big deal. Charlie has my name on his wrist, too," I said.

"They're *matching*?" Daddy yelped. Mama covered her mouth, trying not to laugh.

"It's like, just a friend tattoo. It means nothing." I yanked my wrist away and hid it behind my skirt. Daddy went pale. Mama smiled.

"You're getting that removed as soon as possible," Daddy insisted.

My mouth dropped open. "Excuse me? No I'm not!"

"Don't backsass me! I'm not letting you walk around with a— a *tattoo* of a criminal's name on your wrist!"

"Oh my ancestors, you never let me do *anything* I want!" I whined.

Mama shook her head. "You two."

Daddy took a breath. "I suppose I can't force you to change your mind—"

"Yep."

Daddy's expression hardened, and I shut up. He went on to say, "But I do think we should have a quick talk."

"Oh, Liam, not this *again*," Mama complained.

Daddy's tone was impatient. "I just need a moment with my daughter, *please.*"

Mama made an annoyed sound and walked off, like she'd been trying to talk Daddy out of this all night and was giving up.

Once Mama was out of sight, Daddy dug in his pocket. "Ava, sweetheart, I want you to have these."

"A present? Really?" My mood brightened. I thought he'd give me something sweet— you know, jewelry, or an equally cute father-daughter gift, to mark the night of my first-ever college dance.

My mouth fell open when I looked down at the packet he'd placed in my hands. "Are you kidding me? Fucking *condoms!?*"

"It's a college dance. Things happen," Daddy retorted.

"What the hell am I supposed to use these for?" I shouted.

"I… assume you know how to put them on. At least, I would hope."

Ancestors, save me. Apparently he thought now was a great time for the sex talk. I bet anything this was Uncle Jonah's doing. There was no other explanation. I could hear him right now. *Liam, I know you want to keep pretending Ava's your sweet little girl, but let's face the cold, hard facts. Remember what all of us were like as kids? Trust me, I teach college students, and they're feistier than rabbits.*

Oberi's tongue lolled, like he thought this was hilarious. I was still gaping. "What, do you think I'm gonna… go on some wild sexcapade or something?"

"I… don't know." Daddy's tone was firm. "But whatever you do, I want you to be safe."

"Ancestors!" I smacked my face. "Isn't this Mama's job?"

"Well, your mother insisted you didn't need them, but I thought it would be best if—"

"Mama was right! How do you expect me to use these? It's not like I'm dating anyone."

Daddy's face cleared. "You're… not?"

"Um, no." I scrunched up my nose. "Did you think I was with somebody?"

Daddy looked very confused. "I guess it doesn't matter."

"Yeah, it doesn't! And I'm not the type for one-night stands, just in case you're that paranoid."

"I don't need to know what you're up to," Daddy said quickly. "Trust me, that's none of my business."

"Apparently you're funding my supply!" I shouted, waving the foil packets in the air.

"I'm not saying I *approve*. I just know better," he grumbled. "I was your age once, you know."

I blew a curl out of my eyes. "Daddy, I know you're worried, but I promise I'm not going to have an accident like you and Mama."

Daddy's face contorted. "You were not an *accident*. You were one of the best things that's ever happened to me."

"Awesome, so are we done with this conversation?" I asked.

Daddy said, "Well—"

"Great, bye!"

I stomped away and shoved the condoms into my handbag before I hauled ass to the Room of Mirrors, where the dance was being held. It was the same room where we'd first met the Warden and heard his welcome speech.

Kallie was waiting for me outside the entrance. "Gods, you took long enough," she complained.

"Don't ask." I fixed my hair before we walked through the double doors.

I gasped in amazement as I took in the surrounding scene. From the ballroom's ceiling hung beautiful fabric canopies in black, purple, and green. The room was dark, only lit by the various pulsing lights around the room, which shone people's faces in emerald or amethyst. Tables swathed in black cloth were decorated with gold-colored plates, and a DJ at the front of the room played creepy, haunting music. Thunder clapped for ambiance, and lights flickered against the ceiling, giving the appearance lightning was flashing. Green fire crept up the walls and danced off the mirrors, an illusion sustained by one of the fae teachers, and black candles hovered over the dance floor. There was a table full of food, adorned with things like bubbling green punch, chocolate in the shape of bat wings, and apples that were dipped in purple caramel, giving the decorative appearance they were poisoned. There was a kissing booth in the corner that a few of the sirens were running, with a sign that said *Kisses of Death.* Professor Warbright used his necromancy magic to make a few skeletons dance. The skeletons twirled and turned with each other, dressed in elaborate ball gowns and suit tails as they waltzed around the room.

It definitely looked like a party for villains. I was loving this.

We waited in line to get in. Kallie and I stood by a twisted black arch, and Lupe took a few pictures of us with the school's professional camera. I was shocked it functioned at all, considering the finicky way electronics worked at the school. My eyes scanned the room, but I didn't see him… yet.

"You guys look amazing," Lupe said as she snapped the camera. "Hope you don't tear your gowns!"

"What do you mean?" I asked.

"There's always a huge brawl at the end, during the last dance. It's the best part. Everyone just goes at it before the guards can break it up," Lupe gushed.

"I get to punch people for fun and get away with it? That sounds *incredible,*" Kallie cried.

"And dangerous. Is it like a riot?" I asked.

"Nah. It's just for shits and giggles. Nobody gets hurt… bad." Lupe gave a sinister grin. "Anyway, enjoy the party!"

Kallie and I walked along the edge of the dance floor. Her face brightened as she waved. "Marcus! Hi!"

Marcus stood across from us, wearing a suit that was half open. His tie hung loose, and the top few buttons of his shirt were undone, exposing his chest.

Kallie was clearly enjoying the show. Her eyes roved Marcus' chest, but the warlock himself was speechless. His eyes nearly exploded out of his skull as he looked from Kallie's giant boobs to the slit in her dress revealing her thigh, and everything else.

Kallie batted her eyelashes. "So? How do I look?"

Marcus gulped. He was trying *so hard* not to rock a boner right now. Rishi was at his feet, meowing and wearing a tiny top hat.

My heart fell as I realized Marcus was alone. Charlie wasn't with him. Maybe he'd decided not to come.

But… he'd agreed to be my date to the ball, right? He wouldn't stand me up.

I hoped.

Marcus and Kallie moved to the food table and started taking appetizers. Kallie did most of the talking, while Marcus mostly tried not to gape. I wasn't very hungry. My gaze kept roaming the ball, and I didn't see a hint of Charlie anywhere. My parents had showed back up. They remained along the wall, supervising the dance with a few other guardians who'd volunteered. Daddy's expression was sullen. I was certain Mama was laughing at him.

As we sat down at a table, Kallie poked me. "So what did your dad want?"

"Huh?" I came out of my reverie. "Oh, um, it was stupid, really. He tried to give me the sex talk."

Not like I needed it. Charlie wasn't going to show, anyway.

"What?" Marcus broke his silence for the first time and laughed. "That's crazy."

"Isn't it? And he gave me these." I took the condoms out of my bag and threw them on the table. "I feel like I'm sixteen all over again."

"Um, I don't know who your dad thinks you're sleeping with, but these are extra-large," Kallie said, picking up a condom and waving it around.

"Oh my fucking—" I sighed and put my head in my hand. "We're a pretty open family, but this goes too far."

"Did he give you a play-by-play of where it's supposed to go? Because my dad would *not* shut up about it when he gave me the sex talk. I swear, I never needed to know that much about their wedding night," Marcus complained.

"He probably thought you'd put it in the wrong place," I suggested. Marcus sent me the finger.

"My parents *never* talk about their sex life in front of me, thank the gods," Kallie said. "I have no idea of how I came into this world, and I like it that way. I think they expected me to figure it out on my own."

"I was conceived out of wedlock!" I burst.

I was too loud. Daddy heard me from across the room and scowled. I quieted down.

Kallie dropped her voice and leaned in. "Speaking of… where's tall, dark and handsome? Isn't he supposed to be your date?"

"I'm not sure…" I mused. "Marcus, have you spoken to Charlie?"

Marcus shook his head as he bit into an apple. "Haven't seen him all day."

Dammit. He really had stood me up. Tears rose to my eyes, but I fought them back. No need to ruin good eyeliner.

"It's fine," I said. "I can have plenty of fun on my own."

"Miss Mitoh. May I interest you in a dance?"

A chilling voice made a crawling sensation creep up my spine. The Warden stood beside us, extending a hand. His large, feathery wings were out and draping on the floor. Every stitch of his designer suit was in place. It only made him that more intimidating.

Oberi gave a low growl, but I knew better than to refuse. "Certainly." I took the Warden's hand, and he led me to the dance floor.

The Warden put a hand on my waist and grabbed my hand just as the DJ put on a sharp and eerie tango. I felt like a rat trapped in a cage as he forced me to move with him. Ancestors, this was nearly as bad as being held down by John. The Warden's hollow stare penetrated right through me, making my knees quake and my stomach scramble.

I knew I was safe— relatively. Mama and Daddy were watching from afar, just in case they needed to step in, and Oberi would never let the Warden hurt me.

I wanted them to stay back. I knew they were powerful, but the Warden was dangerous, too. I didn't know what he might do.

As the tempo increased, the Warden said, "You and your team were very exceptional during the Darke Games. Color me impressed."

I swallowed down my nervousness. "Thank you, Doctor Taurus. It was a team effort."

"Please don't play coy with me, Miss Mitoh. The magic you and your friends performed during the Games is far beyond the power of any first-year college student, and even surpasses the abilities of the most talented supernaturals alive today. None of you should've been able to pull off the kind of power that you displayed in the Games. There is something very interesting about all of you."

I forced my voice to remain steady. "Perhaps you overestimate us. We didn't win."

"You didn't win because you chose to lose. You threw your chance at salvation away."

"I don't know what you're talking about. My team hesitated. The other team took advantage. It was a careless mistake."

"Clearly." The Warden smiled. His hand tightened on mine until I was in pain. I didn't wince, or give him the satisfaction of pulling away. I could take it.

The Warden drew away, then. My hand was white by the time he let go. "You are a curious thing, Miss Mitoh. I will be keeping an eye on you and those you associate with. Don't forget, you are living in *my* world. And in the world I have created, the lord sees all."

This guy had such a god complex. I didn't breathe until the Warden had turned his back and walked away. It was an effort not to shake in my heels.

Yes, the Warden scared me. And I wasn't afraid of much in this world. But he frightened me worse than any monster I'd fought in the Games. He wanted to use me.

For what, I wasn't sure.

I returned to Kallie and Marcus, who both wore knitted expressions. "You okay? The Warden looked intense," Marcus said.

"I just need some air." My eyes flickered to look for my parents. They were dealing with separating a couple who were shouting at each other near the food table.

Good. I couldn't take them suffocating me right now. I had to get some space. I picked up my skirts and ran out of the Room of Mirrors. Oberi followed me, nails clicking on the floor.

There was an abandoned cell block not too far away. People went there to smoke or get away from teachers. I just needed a second to stop my thoughts from racing.

My lungs stung when I finally stopped to get some air. I paused underneath a small barred window in a deserted hallway that was dark and damp.

I wasn't sure if I was strong enough to fight the Warden when he ordered me to do his bidding. I was just starting to get better. I couldn't become a pawn for someone else's evil plans. I wouldn't.

The snow smacked against the window outside. As I stared upward, the voices in my mind began to ramble and race.

You need to get out of here, Ava.

The Warden will kill you.

He'll use you to hurt the people you love.

Don't let him. Run.

Most of the guards were at the party, containing all the students within one place. I had a better chance. I could use my blue fire to melt the bars, break the window. Maybe get off the grounds before I was hunted down.

What if... what if I tried to break out, and never looked back? The Warden couldn't use me then. It seemed foolish, to try to run again when I'd thrown my only opportunity away during the Darke Games...

But I hadn't known the Warden's intentions then. I lit a blue fireball in my hand and drew back, taking aim.

"Trying to sneak out?"

A knot formed in my throat. I turned and saw two rivals— the gang leader that we'd defeated in the Games, and the merman Charlie had almost suffocated. There was malice in the leader's eyes... like he'd been looking for me. I bet he'd followed me out after he'd watched me leave the dance.

Stupid. I was unprotected.

The fireball in my hand grew larger. "You'll stay back if you know what's good for you."

"Deuce, maybe we should let her be," the merman said. His voice was raspy now. He'd probably lost most of it after Charlie had nearly killed him.

"Fuck that," Deuce spat. "Her and the dog are getting it."

Oberi's growls were so vicious and cruel. The gang member's friend appeared wary, but the leader himself didn't want to hold back.

"You took away our only chance of getting out of here," Deuce growled. "We're going to make you pay for it."

Deuce advanced, but before he could, a broad figure stepped in front of me. The merman paled and took a few steps back. The gang leader remained in place, but his confidence faltered as he faced off with none other than Charlie… who'd totally planted himself between them and me.

"Turn around if you don't want me to kill you," Charlie said coolly. "You know I won't hesitate."

Deuce's face flushed in rage. "I couldn't give a shit if she's your girl. She cost me my freedom. She's going to pay!"

I remained behind Charlie and berated myself for getting into another stupid situation. I was stuck here for good now, so I might as well get with the program. There were three rules to the Institute. One, don't try to break out, because they *will* catch you. Two, keep your head down and you just might stay alive.

And three: if you ever want to get out of here, don't fall for an inmate.

Those three rules? I just broke them all.

Charlie's knuckles cracked as he faced the thug. I could hear the deadly intent in his tone. "You dare to lay a hand on her, you won't be able to walk."

Was he serious? The Darke Games were over… and yet he was still being overprotective, defensive of me. Charlie, the guy I literally couldn't stand, the guy who swore up and down he wanted nothing to do with me just a few weeks ago, was defending me from a gang leader?

And I had completely fallen for him.

I was totally screwed.

"I'm outta here, man." The other guy scampered. He didn't want Charlie to suffocate him again.

The gang member looked between Charlie, Oberi and me. He knew he couldn't take us on alone. He spat at our feet. "Better watch your back. I don't forget."

Charlie didn't turn around until he no longer heard their footsteps. When he faced me, my heart stuttered. Now that we weren't in danger, I could appreciate what Charlie had to offer. He was wearing a tailored black suit that he must've gotten from the consignment shop, with a black shirt and matching tie. His hair was styled with gel and combed perfectly. He looked like some dark prince straight out of hell, and I was here for it.

"Are you all right?" Charlie asked. He grasped my elbows, and I drooled. What were my most secret fantasies? Sleeping with a mob boss? A gangster, maybe? Because he fit the description.

"Ava?" Charlie shook my arms.

Oberi barked, and I said, "Uh, sure. Just got cornered by those goons."

"What are you doing out here? I showed up at the ball just for Marcus to tell me you left a second before."

I couldn't lie to him. "I got scared," I confessed. "Before you arrived, the Warden spoke with me. It wasn't good… he knows we blew the Darke Games on purpose, and told me he's watching us. I have a bad feeling he wants to use me for something."

"So… you decide trying to run away again is a good idea?"

"It was a spur of the moment freak-out. I wasn't thinking."

"Ava, if the Warden wants you, you're safer here than anywhere else," Charlie insisted. "If you leave, he'll hunt you down. At least if you're in his grasp, it gives you a chance to outsmart him before he can make a move."

I relaxed then. "I know you're right."

Charlie's voice was scolding. "You shouldn't run off on your own. Why didn't you wait for me? It wasn't like I was going to stand you up."

The comment stung. "That's news to me. It sure felt like it when I showed up by myself," I bit back.

"If I tell you I'm going to show up, I'll be there. You should know better."

"Are you going to lecture me like a little girl?"

"So long as you keep acting like one."

My temper rose then, and I had to react. "I can't *stand* you." I shoved Charlie away from me, though once I touched him, heat spread throughout my body, making it tremble.

Oh, I had it bad. As much as I hated to admit it, something big was going on between us.

Charlie smirked. "The feeling's mutual, sweetheart."

I wasn't sure if he was pointing out how much he despised me… or the passion he'd shown in the dark moments we'd secretly had before, in front of the stone gate merely days ago.

I didn't care if the man made my panties melt off and run for cover. I had to stay away from him. For his own sake as much as mine. People couldn't know you were in love at the Institute. It made you a target— vulnerable and weak. "We can't do this again. We'll get caught."

Charlie leaned against the wall. "We've already been sent to a prison, princess. Might as well make it a life sentence."

He moved in front of me, so that both of his arms were on either side of my body. The action made my muscles turn to gelatin. When he boxed me in, it didn't feel like a prison, but a safe place. His broad shoulders left me nowhere to run but into him.

"I can't do this," I said.

"Can't, or don't want to?"

It wasn't the second one. "It doesn't matter what I want. Feeling this way… it's the worst thing I could do."

"Sometimes it's good to be bad," Charlie said. "If you need one more reason to sin, just use me."

"Kiss me, then," I told him. "And make sure it's worth the price I have to pay."

He did. And fuck, it felt *so good*. I'd kissed dozens of guys before, but Charlie made me forget about each of them in one fell swoop. Kissing him was like uniting two pieces of one soul. I was addicted to this madness he made me feel. I thought I'd been crazy before, but I hadn't been insane before this moment. Every movement of his mouth against my own made me grow weak. His tongue rolled against mine, and his heartbeats were pounding against my breasts. The effort made me so lightheaded I couldn't breathe.

I sagged toward the floor, and couldn't help it. Charlie's kisses made me go boneless. I'd thought I'd collapse with the bliss they made me experience, but Charlie didn't let me fall. He held me up and pressed closer against me, inviting me to lean into him so he could support us both.

I hadn't thought about our first kiss since we'd shared it. I'd forced myself not to, scared of what it might mean, but I had to confront it now. Charlie scared me because his passion made me let go, and I came undone at what he did to me. I didn't like feeling out of control.

That's why this couldn't happen. He made me so fragile. In his arms, I forgot everything and became vulnerable. I was falling all over him like an obsessed schoolgirl.

It'd be embarrassing if my desire wasn't so bad. His masculine energy poured out of him and collided with my feminine nature, not overpowering it, but melding together in a seamless symphony.

I ran my hands through his hair and pulled as he kissed me, doing everything in my power to hold back the moans. He was practically making love to me with his mouth alone. Sex couldn't feel this good. The emotions I'd refused my body the pleasure of indulging in welled to the surface, and I realized that running away from Charlie was like running from myself. I could try to cover up all the bad parts, but it wouldn't do any good. I was constantly naked around him, and I knew that it showed.

I didn't want to keep hurting. I didn't want to keep closing the door on us over and over. I couldn't change for Charlie… but I didn't have to. He accepted the person I was, and no matter how little, or how much, he had to offer me, it was enough. All I wanted was him. Despite trying to conceal that from him, he saw straight through my walls, and was breaking them down brick by brick just to be able to touch me. We were two shattered people, but sometimes you could fit the broken pieces back together and make something new. His broken pieces fit with mine, and I swore now that the picture looked better than ever before.

If Charlie was my drug, this was one hell of a good high.

Charlie pressed me into the wall, and our bodies collided. I felt his hard dick press against my stomach, straining through his pants. I felt a roll of greed, a thirsting lust that craved and begged for his attention.

Oh, shit. Maybe I *did* need those condoms after all.

Charlie ended the kiss long before I was ready for it to be over. I was the one who had pulled back the first time, but now, that seemed like such a cruel gesture. Charlie ran his thumb over my warm cheeks. "You're blushing, pidge."

Yeah, something else is warm, too, I thought. I seriously needed to go to the bathroom and ditch the panties. Flash flood alert.

"I like your dress," Charlie said. He ran his hand over the fabric, then gently through a few of my curls. I didn't even care if he messed up my hair. I just wanted him to touch me again.

"You look amazing. The suit… defines you," I said as my fingers graced his sleeves.

"I prefer nicer things. Didn't always have access to them, but I enjoy looking good."

He was as vain as I was. He didn't have the money to buy designer labels, but I'm sure if he did, they'd be in his closet.

Charlie took a breath. "Pidge, I—"

"Don't ruin it." I put a finger to his mouth. "Give me this night. Just one night."

Charlie hesitated, but didn't press. It wasn't like I didn't want to tell him how I felt. I felt more for Charlie than I could ever imagine feeling for anyone else in this universe.

But if I said all that, I'd break down. And I wanted this to be a happy night. We deserved to celebrate, after everything we'd been through.

I dug in my handbag. "I have something for you."

"For me?"

"Yes. It's your birthday, isn't it? December twenty-first."

Charlie's face softened, like he was shocked I remembered. I slipped something soft over his right wrist.

"It's an armband," I explained as he ran his fingers over the threads curiously. "Every Hawkei child gets one. Someone close to them usually weaves it. Mine is red and green, for me and Monica. Your armband is red and purple… for us."

Charlie reached out and grasped my forearm. "Ava-Marie… I don't know what to say."

I loved it when he said my name. It felt like he truly knew me. "Don't say anything. Keep it perfect."

Oberi wound between us and wagged his tail. Charlie patted his head, while I stared at him. He was twenty-three years old today. And he'd been through more in two decades than most people suffered through in several lifetimes.

But he had me, and I wasn't going to let anyone make him suffer again. I was coming for all those who had hurt him. Everyone that had caused him pain, everyone that was the source of his sorrow. They'd touched his dreams and twisted them into dark realities he couldn't escape.

I remembered Charlie's ruthless actions during the Games, his desperate efforts to keep me alive. The greatest monsters we had to fight weren't out there; they were inside of us.

They turned Charlie into a monster. Now I was going to be their reckoning.

A guard peeked down the hall. "Hey, what are you kids doing down there?" he barked. "Get back to the dance immediately, before I escort you personally!"

Charlie ducked his head, and we ran off. When we came back to the dance, I saw Marcus had found a way to use the condoms. He blew them up and tied them off into balloon animals. Kallie used her magic to levitate them into the air. They flew over the crowd, and people bonked them back and forth, like volleyballs.

As he was making the balloon animals, a crowd had formed around him. Marcus was bragging loudly about his efforts during the Darke Games, which I found to be exaggerated.

"Yeah, all those monsters were totally running from me," he boasted. "Ripping up trees, using necromancy, casting battle magic, it was a total snoozefest. The Warden made it too easy. I think I'm gonna enter again next year, you know? I could win all by myself. My team just slowed me up."

He'd nearly pissed himself every moment of the Games, but I let him have his fun. Kallie sat up when she saw us approaching. "There you two are. I was beginning to think you'd left the Institute for the holidays."

"We can't leave," Charlie said. "We don't get to leave the Institute for summer break or holidays. We're stuck here until we graduate."

"*Most* people are. All the rich kids get to go home for Christmas. The ones that pay off the Warden, anyway," Marcus said.

"Yeah. They let a certain wealthy percentage of the prison population go home for the holidays. They don't have to call it a *real* prison if some kids can visit home during break." Kallie gave a skeptical sound. "We figured you two must've been getting ready to leave with Ava's parents."

"Don't think so," Charlie said. "Ava's dad doesn't really like me."

But he leaned into me as a question, and I said, "Um... my dad bribed the Warden to get me home for a few weeks, but I have to check in with an Institute officer every day, so they're certain I don't go running off. I'm leaving tonight and won't be back until the first."

"Oh." Charlie's voice was disappointed. "I hoped you'd be spending Christmas here."

I kinda hoped so, too. I really missed my family, but... Charlie.

"Hey, at least you'll have us," Kallie subbed. "I'm not leaving."

"Me, neither," Marcus added.

Kallie jumped up. "Let's stop talking about sad shit. We're here tonight! We need to celebrate!"

Both she and I let out screams, and Rishi batted a balloon animal away. Oberi began chasing it around, and nearly yelped as a girl came out of Marcus' crowd and staggered up to us. I didn't know her, but she looked half-drunk. Someone had probably snuck some booze in. She completely fawned over us as she said, "Oh my gosh! You guys did *amazing* in the Games! I watched every second. I couldn't take my eyes away!"

"Thanks," I told her. "It was hard, but I'm sure all the teams did pretty good."

The girl shook her head. "No, you don't get it. Everyone has *massive* respect for you now, for the magic you pulled off. You guys are like, the prison's premier villain's club!"

The girl stumbled away, giggling. Marcus, Kallie and I looked between each other, while Charlie leaned in.

"The Villain's Club..." I mused. "That sounds like a pretty good gang name, right?"

"Only the best," Marcus said.

"People will know not to fuck with us," Kallie added.

"At the Institute, reputation is everything." Charlie put an arm around my shoulders. "I think it's time the Villain's Club earned a bad one for itself."

Kallie and Marcus both agreed at once, and excitement coursed through me. The Villain's Club was going down in infamy, and from this moment on, I knew whatever I was going through, I could depend on my fellow villains to be there.

Out of the corner of my eye, I saw someone prowling along the edge of the room. I recognized Coyote's heckling smile at an instant. He switched from his animal form to his human one, beckoning me to him with his playful eyes. Though he passed near students and teachers alike, none of them noticed him or looked his way. No one else could see him.

I touched Charlie's arm lightly. "I'll be right back. I need to talk to someone."

Oberi trotted after me. He looked up at Coyote and wagged his tail, like he was greeting an old friend. Not wanting to look crazy, I leaned against the wall near Coyote and stared out ahead. Though the music of the dance was loud, I still dropped my voice. "You're back."

"*I'll be around,*" Coyote said. "*You did well during the Games. The Great Spirit is pleased.*"

"Are you going to tell me what the gods want with me now?" I asked.

Coyote hissed with laughter. "*That would ruin the fun.*"

"I hope someone more helpful is being sent my way, or I'm doomed." Coyote wasn't very much help in terms of a guide.

Coyote played with the strands of my hair. I ignored him. He tugged on my curls as he said, "*Do you know about demigods?*"

He had my attention. "Not extensively," I admitted.

"*Your grandfather has studied them. They aren't children of the gods, but rather, supernaturals of astonishing power. Claims they no longer exist, but walked the earth in centuries before. They were harnessers of exceptional magic. Stronger than talented supernaturals, but not as great as the gods that came before them.*"

"What's that got to do with me?"

"*Have you ever considered you could be one of them?*"

"Me?"

"*You, and your friends.*"

My veins froze over as my heart skipped. The Warden's accusations that my team was too powerful came rushing back at me. The monsters had been difficult to beat, yes, but our abilities during the Darke Games had been unmatched. The fights themselves were difficult, but the magic? Easy. Me and my teammates were pulling off spells that would kill most other supernaturals our age, flinging them around like they were child's play.

And the scariest thing was, I knew I hadn't hit my limits yet. Not even close.

I swallowed. "What does this mean for the prophecy?"

"*What do you think it means?*"

"Dammit, can you just answer me plainly?" I snapped.

"Ava?" Charlie's voice broke our conversation. He stood beside me and took my hand. His mouth turned down as Coyote continued to snicker. "Are you okay? Is this guy bothering you?"

My eyes widened as I realized Charlie could hear him, too. And I was pretty sure if he had his eyesight, he'd be able to see Coyote just as well as I could.

"He's just a friend," I said. "Let's go, Charlie."

Coyote's laughter grew more intense as I took Charlie's arm and led him away. Oberi went on ahead, and I looked back. By the time I did, Coyote had vanished.

"Is that guy deranged?" Charlie asked me. "He seemed a little… off."

"More than you know," I said. I was still reeling with the fact Charlie could hear him. What did it all mean? I wanted to tell him about Coyote, but… I felt like now wasn't the time. I still needed to come up with an explanation of how and why this was all possible, and dropping a bombshell on Charlie like that would only be cruel on a night when we were supposed to be celebrating.

I was more confused than ever. I had no answers to the prophecy. If anything, I only had more questions.

But I was certain this changed everything. I was no longer a defenseless little girl. I was a full-on demigoddess. And I was going to imprison every single liar who'd dared to lay a finger on me. After that, I'd tear apart anyone else who tried again. There were too many innocent victims on this earth who went without justice. Too many evil-doers who walked free.

If I had the power to change that, I would. The magic I'd been given… it was a gift. I had people to fight for and friends who'd fight with me. If Coyote was right and I was a demigod, there were no boundaries to what my magic could do. I would reshape this world into a better one, and if it fought back, I'd force it to succumb to my will. I'd push myself every moment until this world bowed at my feet. If it refused to succumb, I'd level it to the ground.

The Warden, the gods… they could all come for me. Or at least, they could try.

I'd be waiting to save the world— if there was still a chance it could be saved. And if not, so be it.

At least I'd enjoy watching it burn.

charlie
TWENTY-FIVE

I twirled Ava-Marie around as we headed back to our table. Her dress flared, and the fabric brushed against my legs. Ava giggled as I caught her around the waist. I didn't know why I did it. It just felt right in the moment.

"Pidge, I've been meaning to ask you something," I admitted.

Ava stopped, and we stood near the edge of the dance floor to talk in low whispers. "Ask me what?"

I cocked my head toward Oberi, who I could feel through our bond. He radiated glee, and was obviously having the time of his life at the Villain's Ball. I could only guess how many cupcakes Marcus had slipped him already.

"I thought things would feel different with Oberi after the Games," I said. "I thought... maybe I'd be able to hear him talk to me now, but I haven't. It was only the one time when we bonded. What does it mean to secure your bond with your Familiar?"

Ava paused. "I don't know what it's supposed to feel like, to be honest," she said sheepishly. "It happens when you and your Familiar go through trauma together. The trauma brings you closer, and the stronger bond intensifies your magic."

"That's what I mean," I said. "I don't feel any closer to Oberi than I did before."

Ava drew a deep breath. Her tone was hollow. "I'm not sure we secured the bond, Charlie."

My stomach sank. "Oh. That's... um..."

"Unexpected? Not ideal?" Ava listed off options. "I agree. I thought for sure the Games would change us."

They did, I thought, but I didn't say it out loud.

Ava continued. "And maybe it would've worked, if Oberi wasn't bonded to us both. He was torn between us the whole time."

I remembered how Oberi had hesitated when Ava went running off to fight the malumuto. Somehow, the Games had brought Ava and I together, but it'd only driven a wedge between us and Oberi. It didn't feel right.

I fingered the beads around Ava's hips. "What if we *never* secure the bond, pidge? I don't want you going through any more trauma than you've been through."

Ava scoffed. "I'm part of a prophecy. There's plenty more to come."

"I wish you wouldn't think that way." Just the thought of Ava going through more pain felt like a knife to the gut.

"It's not about the trauma," Ava explained. "It's about what brings you and your Familiar together. We'll secure the bond, Charlie. I know it."

I relaxed a little and smirked. "And to think how powerful you were during the Games. You'll be *amazing* once the bond is secure."

Ava groaned. "Can we not talk about our powers, or the prophecy, or any of it right now? I just want to have fun at the dance."

"Okay, pidge." I took her hand. "Let's have fun."

Ava started dragging me back toward our table. I knew the dance was nothing more than an illusion— a way to keep the students in their place— but I didn't care about that right now. Ava's hand in mine was all that seemed to matter.

We returned to our table, where Marcus and Kallie were gossiping about the other students.

"Ew, look at Naya and Mad Dog," Kallie complained. "This isn't a fucking porno."

Marcus laughed. "The way she's grinding on him? It could be."

"Naya's giving Mad Dog a lap dance?" I balked as I sat.

"Believe me, you don't want to see it," Ava replied. "Mad Dog just reached up Naya's skirt, and I'm pretty sure I just saw vadge."

I almost gagged.

Ava went to grab the chair next to me, but I accidentally stepped on the hem of her dress. She tripped, and I caught her in my lap.

"Whoa," Ava laughed, before leaning in to whisper. "Is that some kind of a move or something?"

I smirked as my hands curled around her waist. "Do you want it to be?"

She hesitated a moment. "Charlie Wahkin, you are a mystery to me."

That was all she said before she turned and leaned forward to grab something off the table. She didn't get off my lap, and I wasn't sure what it meant. I didn't ask, though, because I didn't want her to leave.

"Here, try this," Ava said with a full mouth.

I didn't trust people with that kind of offer, but I trusted Ava. I opened my mouth, and she popped something sweet into it. I crunched into a hard outer shell, and sweet, fruity flavors burst inside my mouth.

"Mm..." I said. "Chocolate-covered strawberries."

"They're the best, aren't they?" Ava replied.

"Oh, get a room," Kallie said sarcastically.

Marcus whispered something to Kallie, and she burst out in laughter.

"Hey!" Ava scolded. "You better not be reading minds again."

"I didn't mean to!" Marcus defended.

I sank a little in my chair. What thoughts exactly had he heard? Mine, or Ava's? I couldn't deny there were some pretty dirty thoughts going through my head right now. Bro or not, Marcus did *not* need to know what I was thinking.

"I'm really trying to block it out," Marcus promised. "But it's like Junior prom in here. Everyone's hormones are all over the place. There aren't enough guards at the Institute to deal with all the fucking that's going to happen tonight."

I shivered at the thought of Ava and me running off together after the dance. But we wouldn't, because no matter how Ava kissed me, I didn't think she'd let me get that close.

I was okay with it. She could have all the time she needed. No matter what, I'd always be here.

"Rishi!" Marcus cried, the same time Ava yelled, "Oberi!"

"Bad kitty," Marcus scolded.

"What happened?" I questioned.

Ava blew a breath. "They're getting themselves into trouble. Oberi, stop drinking from the punch bowl!"

Ava jumped off my lap to deal with Oberi, and Marcus hurried after her.

"Gods," Kallie sighed.

"What?" I asked.

"Ava's straightening Oberi's veil. She's more worried about the veil getting in the punch bowl than about Oberi's slobber."

I crossed my arms as Ava returned. "Is that how we're going to deal with him?"

"What?" Ava asked innocently as she sat beside me. I was a little disappointed she hadn't taken my lap again, but I wasn't being exactly welcoming.

"You can't coddle him!" I cried. "He needs to learn how to behave himself."

"I was not coddling— how did you even know?" Ava gasped. "Kallie!"

"Hey," she replied. "I just say it like it is. I didn't interject any opinions."

Marcus returned, but Rishi was screeching. "Um… a little help?"

"Ancestors, did Rishi fall *in*?" Ava sighed.

"Only a little," Marcus said sheepishly. He set Rishi on the table, but the cat immediately took off running. He jumped onto my lap, before racing across the dance floor. I was soaked.

"Ew, Marcus," I complained. "That's what you call *a little*? Now I've got punch in places I don't care to admit."

"Here, let me help," Ava offered. Immediately, the punch began to draw out of my clothing as Ava used her Water magic to gather it up.

"Thanks," I said.

"Hey, can you do that on Rishi?" Marcus asked.

"If you can catch him," Ava replied.

Marcus sighed. "I'll try."

Kallie's chair squeaked as she stood. "Well, I'm going to gorge myself on fae cheesecake. All the flavor with none of the calories."

Kallie abandoned us, leaving Ava and I alone with Oberi. Silence stretched between us, and I waited for her to stay something. Oberi nudged my leg with his nose, and it clicked. Ava was waiting for me.

Ugh. I had to *ask her* to dance? It felt so awkward. Just the thought of it made my heart speed up. I didn't get the chance to ask, though. Ava caved first.

"Everyone's dancing." She made it sound like she was making small-talk, but I heard the suggestion in her tone.

"I'm no good at dancing," I told her.

"It's not that hard," she insisted.

"For a guy who's never been to a dance, it is."

"You've never been to a dance!?" Ava balked. She grabbed my hand before I could protest. "Now you *have* to dance."

I drew back as she yanked on my arm. "I don't know how."

"Then let me teach you. You can't spend your first dance sitting here the whole time."

"I won't be," I objected. "I'll visit the snack table eventually."

"Come on, Charlie," Ava begged. "*Please.* Just one dance."

Hell, when Ava said *please*, I couldn't resist. She might as well have been begging for all of me— and I would've given it to her, too.

I grumbled as Ava dragged me to my feet, because I couldn't let her know I was kind of eager to get on the dance floor. At least there, I could hold her in my arms.

"Oberi, stay," I commanded as I stood. Oberi whined, because he knew he was in trouble for drinking from the punch bowl.

We started toward the dance floor. I didn't miss the pad of Oberi's feet as he escaped.

"He's gone already, isn't he?" I asked.

Ava sighed. "I think he's off to find some of the fae cheesecake Kallie mentioned."

"As long as he doesn't get into the real stuff. He could get sick," I pointed out.

"He'll be fine," Ava promised. "He can eat anything."

The song changed to a slow melody I recognized— an old Motown song from the 1960s. Ava faced me. "Your hands go here," she told me as she planted them around her waist.

Holy shit, they were close to her ass. I wondered if she meant to do that.

Ava draped her arms around my shoulders and began gently swaying from side to side. The tempo was slow enough to sway in circles with her, but with an upbeat edge that had her moving her hips.

Ancestors, her hips must've been carved by the Great Spirit himself. She was so freaking hot. I began singing the words to the song under my breath.

"You like this song?" she asked.

I shrugged. "The classics are the best. I come from Detroit— it's practically gospel to know Motown music."

"Agreed," she said, before we both went silent again.

I didn't know how long we danced without saying anything. It could've been a lifetime, or only seconds. Time didn't seem to have any meaning when I held Ava. All I could do was drink in every second with her.

"See?" She finally broke the silence. "Dancing isn't hard at all."

I melted into her, daring to draw her closer to me until our bodies were pressed against each other. Based on the description I got from my friends earlier, I assumed this was one of the more chaste positions on the dance floor. Ava leaned her head against my shoulder, and all the tension in my body left me.

"Yeah." I sighed. "Not hard at all."

And it wasn't. When I held Ava in my arms, everything seemed easy. The Games were over, and I could breathe again. Even the prophecy seemed a distant worry. The Warden was nowhere nearby. There was nothing here that could touch us.

"Marcus!" Ava gasped.

"Hey, now," I teased. "I thought I was your date for the night."

"No, not that!" Ava drew away from me, and I heard a foot connect with someone's gut, followed by an *oof*. "Marcus, what the fuck are you doing under my dress?"

My hands curled into fists.

"Rishi slid under your skirt to hide!" Marcus defended. "I had to sneak up on him, or he'd run away."

"Ask next time, you douche!" Ava slapped Marcus' shoulder, but it didn't sound like it hurt.

The song changed to a more upbeat tempo. Kallie's heels clicked on the dance floor as she came running over to us. She slammed into Ava, body-checking her.

"Hey, bit—" Ava started, but Kallie quickly cut in.

"Partner change!" Kallie started dancing on me, grinding her ass against my dick. I wish I could say it turned me on, but she wasn't the girl I was interested in tonight. I had to assume this was some sort of move to make Marcus jealous.

"What the hell is this?" I asked.

"It's the Monster Mash!" Kallie cried. "A classic. I requested it. It seemed perfect for the Villain's Ball."

"Ancestors," Ava said. "I've never seen the Monster Mash like *this* before. Everyone is being so filthy."

"Exactly," Kallie laughed. "Except for you. Partner change!"

Kallie grabbed Ava and shoved her in my direction. I had to catch her so she wouldn't trip over her dress.

"Now that's what I'm talking about!" Marcus cried in glee. I could only assume that meant Kallie was grinding against him now. "Woohoo!"

Ava hesitated. "Well, everyone else is doing it."

My heart sped up. I couldn't *admit* I wanted her on me, but I'd be damned if I weren't thinking about it. "We can't disappoint Kallie."

I was glad to say I didn't have to do anything but stand there as Ava danced around me. She spun around me a few times, before ending in front, her ass pressed against me. Holy shit, Ava could twerk. I had to resist the urge to reach out and grab it while she shimmied.

"Hell, pidge," I teased. "Where'd you learn to do that?"

Ava laughed. "You wouldn't believe me if I told you."

"Well, I'm already thinking strip club."

"I learned from my Aunt Imogen," she admitted, before sheepishly adding, "who learned from my Uncle Jonah."

I grimaced. "I think I'm going to have to have a talk with your Uncle Jonah. He sounds like a creep."

"He's harmless!" Ava defended. "And the sweetest guy you'll ever meet."

"Partner change!" Kallie announced again. She shoved herself between Ava and me, then dragged Ava away.

"Ooh, work it, girl!" Ava yelled over the dance floor.

I felt someone come up to me, their ass shaking in my direction as awkward as could be. "What the hell, Marcus!?" I shoved him away.

"Kallie said partner change," he explained nonchalantly.

"It works for girls. Not so much for us bros."

"Don't be homophobic," Marcus insisted.

"I am not! I don't even want *Kallie* on me."

"Ooh," Marcus sang. "So you only have a boner for one lady."

"Shut up." I shoved him again. "It's not like you haven't already read my mind."

"Hey, I don't eavesdrop and tell." Marcus made a zipping noise, like he was locking his lips.

"Wait… you won't even tell me what you hear from Ava?" I asked. "I thought we were friends."

"Psychic confidentiality," he stated. "But let's just say whatever you're thinking, you can bet your ass Ava's version is ten times worse."

My jaw dropped, and Marcus made a whipping sound. I frowned at him. "Stop it. Ava is *not* into whips and chains."

Though as I said it, I realized it wouldn't surprise me. I'd bet anything if she managed to get cuffs off one of the guards, she'd sure as hell use them.

What was I thinking? Ava wasn't going to be using fucking *handcuffs* at the Institute! I mean, I knew people fooled around in here, but never in the dorms where the guards could catch them. We'd have to go—

Marcus started snickering, and I realized he was reading my thoughts.

"Would you stop!?" I snapped.

"I told you I don't mean it!" he defended. "There are just too many thoughts to block out. Though that time—"

I shoved my hand into his face. "Partner change."

"Hey," Kallie objected. "You're not the one who gets to announce partner change."

Ava whispered something to Kallie, but I couldn't hear it over the music. The two of them came over without a word and started grinding on me from both sides. A huge grin spread across my face.

"Hey, where's the love for your favorite warlock?" Marcus asked.

"I'll dance with you!" a girl nearby offered.

"Ooh, looking hot tonight, Lupe," Marcus said in a tease.

Kallie immediately jumped away from me. "Oh, *hell no.*"

Ava laughed loudly as Kallie rushed off to claim Marcus. "Well, that was— oh, no."

Ava's tone immediately shifted as the song changed.

I groaned. "Someone requested a heavy metal song?"

"I don't think this is a request," Ava pointed out. "I think it's the last song of the night, which means—"

"Mosh pit!" someone screamed.

I barely had a chance to process it before bodies were pressing in on me from all angles. Someone threw a punch, and my head snapped to the side at the impact.

For a moment, I was totally clueless. I thought it might be some sort of terrorist attack or something. Then I heard the sound of Ava's maniacal laughter.

"Come on, Charlie!" She dragged me deeper into the crowd of people. "It's the final send-off for the night. Enjoy the brawl!"

"Enjoy the—?"

Another fist cracked into my jaw, and I heard Oberi yowl from the edge of the dance floor. Ava whirled around, her dress billowing near my ankles. "Hey!" she screamed. "Don't fucking touch my date."

Ava's fist cracked into someone's face. I didn't know who it was, but all I heard in response was laughter.

"This is nuts!" I cried.

Ava laughed with glee. "It's *amazing!* Now punch someone before the guards can stop you!"

"Grr… gaaah!" Marcus made noises like he was the freaking Hulk. "I just knocked out a vampire!"

"I punched Naya in the back of the head!" Kallie cried happily. "She didn't even see me. It felt great!"

Oberi finally pushed his way through the crowd. He growled and snapped his jaws at anyone who dared come close to Ava and me. But Ava didn't give a shit about being protected. She dove into the crowd, stirring up trouble in her wake. And she sounded like she was having one hell of a great time doing it.

My hands curled into fists, and pent-up energy rocked my body. What the hell?

I spun around and flung my fists into any flesh I could find— first a face, then a gut. I knew I had one hell of a punch, but no one seemed to care how much it hurt. We just shoved and kicked and punched… and laughed. It was total insanity.

It was villainy.

By the time the guards broke up the brawl, I was sweating buckets. I'd stripped off my suit coat at one point and couldn't find it, but I didn't really care. It wasn't like I was going to be wearing a suit anytime soon again. I yanked off my bow tie and unbuttoned the first few buttons of my shirt, using my Air power to blow cool air across my skin.

Marcus nudged me as we headed out of the Room of Mirrors. "Ava's digging the look."

My heart fluttered, and my voice came out a pitch higher than normal. "Really?"

"Oh, yeah," Marcus sang. "Somebody's getting some tonight."

I elbowed him in the side. "Shut up. It's not like that between us."

Or was it?

I didn't know what we were. We'd never really talked about it. And I didn't want to ask either, because I was afraid it would only drive Ava away. The last thing I wanted to do was scare her off.

"*Sure* it isn't," Marcus said sarcastically. "Have fun with your hand tonight."

"I'm sure you and Kallie have all sorts of plans."

Marcus lowered his voice. "I don't kiss and tell."

"Liar," I accused. He hadn't made a move, and I knew it, because he'd tell me the second it happened. And if he didn't, Kallie would tell Ava, who would tell me.

"Shh…" Marcus hissed. "The girls are coming."

Ava and Kallie came over, giggling. Oberi nudged his wet nose into my hand, and I stroked his back.

"What's so funny?" I asked.

"Nothing." Kallie dragged out the word, and the girls laughed again. It had to be sexual.

"We should probably get back to our dorms before the guards catch us," I suggested.

"Charlie's right," Kallie agreed. "We'll see you two later."

Marcus and Kallie headed off toward their respective dorms, while Ava and I walked back to ours. Other students were shuffling back to their rooms, so we weren't totally alone.

Too bad. I really liked what happened when we were alone.

"I hope you enjoyed yourself," I told her.

"I had the *best* time," Ava said. "I wish the school held more dances."

"Same." I let the confession slip. Despite my protests against dancing, I really had enjoyed myself.

"Charlie Wahkin had a good time?" Ava gasped playfully. "Is the world on fire?"

I laughed. "No, I just… finally gave myself permission."

Ava stopped outside our dorm rooms and turned to me. "I'm glad. That makes this night totally worth it."

We stood there a few seconds, as if waiting for the other to say something. I didn't think we really knew how to say goodbye.

"I have to grab my stuff," Ava said. "My parents want to get back to the mainland tonight. They've been away from my siblings too long."

My shoulders fell. "Well, um… thanks again for the gift."

I was blabbing. This was new. What the hell was wrong with me?

"Don't mention it," Ava said.

Doors throughout the hall closed as students returned to their rooms. Ava and I were the last ones in the hall. Oberi came up behind me and shoved his head into my legs. I stumbled forward and caught myself on Ava.

She laughed. "I think Oberi might be trying to tell you something."

I couldn't help but smile. "Oberi gets what Oberi wants."

I leaned down until my lips were a mere inch from hers. My heart lifted in my chest, giving me a high that could rival any hard drug. Ava closed the distance between us, pressing her soft mouth against mine. I melted all over again, dragging her close. She inhaled a deep breath.

She drew away far too soon. "You make me…" she started breathlessly, before trailing off.

I pressed my forehead against hers. "I make you…?"

Ava drew a deep breath and whispered, "I hate the way you make me feel, Charlie Wahkin."

Her tone didn't reflect her words. She loved every second of it, though she wouldn't admit it.

"I hate you, too, pidge," I whispered.

Ava's hands roamed over my chest, before curling around my collar and dragging me closer. "You should hate me more."

She pressed her lips to mine again. I couldn't help it when my tongue slid inside her mouth.

"I hate you so much," I gasped. My hands dropped to grab her ass, and she bit my lower lip. I moaned as my dick jerked inside my pants.

Hell, where were those handcuffs right about now? Ava could chain me up and do whatever she wanted to me.

"I hate you more," Ava claimed, but the way she kissed me and the way her hands moved over my body said otherwise. Prison had taught her nothing— she was still a bad liar.

Passion surged between us as we made out, intensified by our bond. I feared my heart may beat straight out of my chest and I might come at the first stroke of my dick. Just the thought of her touching me there made me shiver.

A door opened, and Ava and I leapt apart. I heard heavy footsteps coming down the hall, and suddenly my heart was pounding for different reasons. Had we been caught?

"We should get going," Ava said quickly. "The guards are coming for bed check, and I'm supposed to be leaving already."

I squeezed her hand one final time. "Sweet dreams, pidge."

"You too, Charlie," she whispered, before turning to her door and slipping inside. Oberi licked my hand as a goodbye before following Ava into her room.

I was still riding the high of her kiss, and I stumbled into the wall when I turned. Hell, I was two feet off from my door! I grabbed the handle and hurried inside before the guards could catch me.

The moment I stepped inside, I knew I wasn't alone. I could feel a person's presence in the air, then came the squeak of the bed springs as someone stood.

"Charlie," a female voice said.

My palms shot upward instinctively, warning the intruder of my magic. "Who the hell are you?"

"Don't attack!" she exclaimed in a hushed whisper. "Please. I'm only here to help."

"Then answer the question," I demanded.

"My name is Maddie Mitoh," she introduced.

"Mitoh," I repeated flatly. "You're one of Ava's aunts— the one who wrote her prophecy."

"Yes," she answered. "I've come tonight because it was the only time I could get into the school unnoticed."

"You could've called, or wrote," I suggested, lowering my hands. "Ava's room is the next door down."

"You misunderstand, Charlie," she said in a low voice, as if she was afraid someone might overhear. "I didn't come to talk to Ava. I came to speak to *you*. What I have to say must be heard in person."

I furrowed my brow. I wasn't entirely sure if I could trust her— or if she was even who she said she was. "Talk fast, or I'm calling Ava in here."

"No, please," Maddie begged. "She can't know I've come. There are parts of the prophecy that I did not write down for her— pieces meant only for *you*."

I took a step back and caught myself on the door. "What do you mean?"

"You're a part of it, Charlie," she said ominously, sending a shiver down my spine. "You and Ava share a soul, which means you are just as involved in this prophecy as she is."

I held my chin up. "Whatever you have to say to me, you can say in front of Ava. I'll tell her myself either way."

"You *can't*," Maddie insisted. "Doing so could compromise the future of supernatural society as a whole. Ava's choices cannot be influenced by what I'm about to tell you. You must keep what I say a secret, even from her."

The air seemed as cold as ice— or maybe it was just that all the blood had drained to my toes. What could Maddie possibly have to say to me? And how could I keep it from Ava?

I didn't have answers, but I had to know what she came here to tell me. It could help Ava unravel the mysteries around the prophecy.

My breath wavered. "What is it?"

Maddie sounded worried, which chilled me to the bone. "There will come a time when you need to make a choice. There will be no other options. You will need to destroy Ava— or the world will be destroyed *by her*."

I sagged against the wall. It was worse than I could possibly fear. Somehow, I managed to find my voice. "Hell no. I'm not killing Ava."

"You won't kill her," Maddie stated firmly. "You don't understand. What you will do... this is a fate far worse than death."

What could possibly be worse than dying? Nothing I wanted to do to Ava, I was certain.

My tongue turned to ash. "Then I won't do it," I snarled. "Nothing can make me harm her."

"You don't have any other option." Maddie's tone was firm and clear. "You have a choice, Charlie Wahkin. The decision is in your hands. If you want to save the world, you must bring Ava to her end— or doom us all. Which will you choose?"

END OF BOOK ONE

Continue Ava-Marie and Charlie's story in The Criminal Lair (Hidden Legends: Prison for Supernatural Offenders, Book Two).

About the Authors

Megan Linski (left) and Alicia Rades (right) are best friends and the authors of the Hidden Legends universe. Both are USA Today bestselling authors of young adult and new adult fiction. Megan Linski is a coffee connoisseur who enjoys ice skating, horseback riding, and shopping. Her stories feature themes of community and friendship while advocating for the rights of the disabled. Alicia Rades is a mother who loves baking cookies, reading tarot, and binge-watching Netflix. She has a passion for personal development and strives to incorporate emotional-empowerment themes into her books. Both girls love nature, animals, sexy romances, and eating cheese.